EVERYMAN'S LIBRARY

EVERYMAN,
I WILL GO WITH THEE,
AND BE THY GUIDE,
IN THY MOST NEED
TO GO BY THY SIDE

JOHN UPDIKE

Rabbit Angstrom

A Tetralogy

Rabbit Run Rabbit Redux
Rabbit Is Rich Rabbit at Rest

with an Introduction by
the Author

EVERYMAN'S LIBRARY

Alfred A. Knopf New York Toronto

214

THIS IS A BORZOI BOOK

PUBLISHED BY ALFRED A. KNOPF

Rabbit Angstrom, comprising the four novels *Rabbit, Run*,
Rabbit Redux, *Rabbit Is Rich*, and *Rabbit at Rest*, published for the
first time as a single volume by Everyman's Library, 1995.
Individual volumes originally published by Alfred A. Knopf, Inc.
Fifth printing

Rabbit, Run Copyright © 1960 by John Updike
Rabbit Redux Copyright © 1971 by John Updike
Rabbit Is Rich Copyright © 1981 by John Updike
Rabbit at Rest Copyright © 1990 by John Updike

Introduction Copyright © 1995 by John Updike
Bibliography and Chronology Copyright © 1995 by David
Campbell Publishers Ltd.
Typography by Peter B. Willberg

The acknowledgments at the back of this volume constitute an
extension of the copyright page.

www.randomhouse.com/everymans

ISBN 0-679-44459-9

Book Design by Barbara de Wilde and Carol Devine Carson

Printed and bound in Germany
by GGP Media, Pössneck

CONTENTS

———

INTRODUCTION

The United States, democratic and various though it is, is not an easy country for a fiction-writer to enter: the slot between the fantastic and the drab seems too narrow. An outsiderish literary stance is traditional; such masterpieces as *Moby-Dick* and *Huckleberry Finn* deal with marginal situations and eccentric, rootless characters; many American writers have gone into exile to find subjects of a congenial color and dignity. The puritanism and practicality of the early settlers imposed a certain enigmatic dullness, it may be, upon the nation's affective life and social texture. The minimization of class distinctions suppressed one of the articulating elements of European fiction, and a close, delighted grasp of the psychology of sexual relations – so important in French and English novels – came slowly amid the New World's austerities. Insofar as a writer can take an external view of his own work, my impression is that the character of Harry 'Rabbit' Angstrom was for me a way in – a ticket to the America all around me. What I saw through Rabbit's eyes was more worth telling than what I saw through my own, though the difference was often slight; his life, less defended and logocentric than my own, went places mine could not. As a phantom of my imagination, he was always, as the contemporary expression has it, *there* for me, willing to generate imagery and motion. He kept alive my native sense of wonder and hazard.

A writer aspires not to describe his work but to call it into being. Of these four related novels, I know principally – and that by the fallible light of recollection – what went into them, what stimuli and ambitions and months of labor. Each was composed at the end of a decade and published at the beginning of the next one; they became a kind of running report on the state of my hero and his nation, and their ideal reader became a fellow-American who had read and remembered the previous novels about Rabbit Angstrom. At some point between the second and third of the series, I began to visualize four completed novels that might together make a single coherent volume, a mega-novel. Now, thanks to Everyman's Library, this volume exists, titled, as I had long hoped, with the name of the protagonist, an everyman who, like all men, was unique and mortal.

Rabbit, Run was begun, early in 1959, with no thought of a sequel. Indeed, it was not yet clear to me, though I had one short novel to my credit, that I was a novelist at all. At the age of twenty-seven I was a short-story writer by trade, a poet and light-versifier on the side, and an ex-reporter for *The New Yorker*. I had come, two years before, to New England to try my luck at freelancing. *Rabbit, Run* at first was modestly conceived as a novella, to form with another, *The Centaur*, a biune study of complementary moral types: the rabbit and the horse, the zigzagging creature of impulse and the plodding beast of stoic duty. *Rabbit* took off; as I sat at a little upright desk in a small corner room of the first house I owned, in Ipswich, Massachusetts, writing in soft pencil, the present-tense sentences accumulated and acquired momentum. It was a seventeenth-century house with a soft pine floor, and my kicking feet, during those excited months of composition, wore two bare spots in the varnish. The handwritten draft was completed, I noted at the end, on 11 September 1959. I typed it up briskly and sent it off to my publisher just as the decade ended and headed, with my family, to the then-remote Caribbean island of Anguilla.

There, after some weeks of tropical isolation, I received a basically heartening letter from my publisher, Alfred A. Knopf himself, indicating acceptance with reservations. The reservations turned out to be (he could tell me this only face to face, so legally touchy was the matter) sexually explicit passages that might land us – this was suggested with only a glint of irony – in jail. Books were still banned in Boston in those days; no less distinguished an author than Edmund Wilson had been successfully prosecuted, in New York State in 1946, for *Memoirs of Hecate County*. My models in sexual realism had been Wilson and D. H. Lawrence and Erskine Caldwell and James M. Cain and of course James Joyce, whose influence resounds, perhaps all too audibly, in the book's several female soliloquies. Not wishing, upon reflection, to lose the publisher who made the handsomest books in America, and doubting that I could get a more liberal deal elsewhere, I did, while sitting at the elbow of a young lawyer evidently expert in this delicate area, consent to a number of excisions – not always the ones I would have expected. It was, I thought, a tactful and non-fatal operation. The American edition appeared toward the end of 1960 without legal incident; in England, Victor Gollancz asked for still more cuts and declined to publish the Knopf text as it was, but the youthful firm of André Deutsch did. The dirty-word situation was changing rapidly, with the legally vindicated publication of Lawrence's *Lady Chatterley's Lover* and Henry Miller's *Tropic of Cancer*. Censorship went from retreat to rout, and when I asked Penguin Books, late in 1962, if I could make some emendations and restorations for their edition, they permissively consented. For ten pages a day that winter, sitting in a rented house in Antibes, France, I went through *Rabbit, Run*, restoring the cuts and trying to improve the prose throughout. This text was the one that appeared in the Modern Library and eventually in Knopf hardcover; I have made a few further corrections and improvements for this printing. *Rabbit, Run*, in keeping with its jittery, indecisive protagonist, exists in more forms than any other novel of mine.

Yet my intent was simple enough: to show a high-school athletic hero in the wake of his glory days. My father had been a high-school teacher, and one of his extra-curricular duties was to oversee the ticket receipts for our basketball games. Accompanying him, then, at home and away, I saw a great deal of high-school basketball, and a decade later was still well imbued with its heroics, as they are thumpingly, sweatily enacted in the hotly lit intimacy of jam-packed high-school gymnasiums. Our Pennsylvania town of Shillington was littered, furthermore, with the wrecks of former basketball stars, and a thematically kindred short story, 'Ace in the Hole', and poem, 'Ex-Basketball Player', had preceded Rabbit into print:

> Once Flick played for the high-school team, the Wizards.
> He was good: in fact, the best. In '46
> He bucketed three hundred ninety points,

RABBIT ANGSTROM

A county record still. The ball loved Flick.
I saw him rack up thirty-eight or forty
In one home game. His hands were like wild birds.

To this adolescent impression of splendor my adult years had
added sensations of domestic interdependence and claustrophobia. Jack Kerouac's *On the Road* came out in 1957 and,
without reading it, I resented its apparent instruction to cut
loose; *Rabbit, Run* was meant to be a realistic demonstration
of what happens when a young American family man goes on
the road – the people left behind get hurt. There was no
painless dropping out of the Fifties' fraying but still tight social
weave. Arriving at so prim a moral was surely not my only
intention: the book ends on an ecstatic, open note that was
meant to stay open, as testimony to our heart's stubborn
amoral quest for something once called grace. The title can
be read as a piece of advice. (My echo of a British music
show tune from 1939, by Noel Gay and Ralph Butler, was
unintentional; just recently I was given the sheet music of
'Run, Rabbit, – Run!' and read the lyrics' injunction 'Don't
give the farmer his fun, fun, fun. / He'll get by without his
rabbit pie.')

The present tense was a happy discovery for me. It has
fitfully appeared in English-language fiction – Damon Runyon
used it in his tough tall tales, and Dawn Powell in the mid-
Thirties has a character observe, 'It was an age of the present
tense, the stevedore style.' But I had encountered it only in
Joyce Cary's remarkable *Mister Johnson*, fifteen or so years after
its publication in 1939. In a later edition of that ground-
breaking portrait of a West African entrapped by colonialism,
Cary wrote of the present tense that it 'can give to a reader
that sudden feeling of insecurity (as if the very ground were
made only of a deeper kind of darkness) which comes to a
traveller who is bushed in unmapped country, when he feels
all at once that not only has he utterly lost his way, but also
his own identity.' At one point Rabbit is literally lost, and
tears up a map he cannot read; but the present tense, to me
as I began to write in it, felt not so much ominous as
exhilaratingly speedy and free – free of the grammatical bonds
of the traditional past tense and of the subtly dead, muffling

x

hand it lays upon every action. To write 'he says' instead of 'he said' was rebellious and liberating in 1959. In the present tense, thought and act exist on one shimmering plane; the writer and reader move in a purged space, on the travelling edge of the future, without vantage for reflection or regret or a seeking of proportion. It is the way motion pictures occur before us, immersingly; my novella was originally to bear the sub-title 'A Movie', and I envisioned the credits unrolling over the shuffling legs of the boys in the opening scuffle around the backboard, as the reader hurried down the darkened aisle with his box of popcorn.

A non-judgmental immersion was my aesthetic and moral aim, when I was fresh enough in the artistic enterprise to believe that I could, in the Poundian imperative, 'make it new'. *The Centaur*'s fifteen-year-old narrator, Peter Caldwell, awakes with a fever after three trying days with his plodding, prancing father, and looks out the window. He is a would-be painter:

The stone bare wall was a scumble of umber; my father's footsteps thumbs of white in white. I knew what this scene was – a patch of Pennsylvania in 1947 – and yet I did not know, was in my softly fevered state mindlessly soaked in a rectangle of colored light. I burned to paint it, just like that, in its puzzle of glory; it came upon me that I must go to Nature disarmed of perspective and stretch myself like a large transparent canvas upon her in the hope that, my submission being perfect, the imprint of a beautiful and useful truth would be taken.

The religious faith that a useful truth will be imprinted by a perfect artistic submission underlies these Rabbit novels. The first one, especially, strives to convey the quality of existence itself that hovers beneath the quotidian details, what the scholastic philosophers called the *ens*. Rather than arrive at a verdict and a directive, I sought to present sides of an unresolvable tension intrinsic to being human. Readers who expect novelists to reward and punish and satirize their characters from a superior standpoint will be disappointed.

Unlike such estimable elders as Vonnegut, Vidal, and Mailer, I have little reformist tendency and instinct for social criticism. Perhaps the Lutheran creed of my boyhood imbued

me with some of Luther's conservatism; perhaps growing up
Democrat under Franklin Roosevelt inclined me to be unduly
patriotic. In any case the rhetoric of social protest and revolt
which roiled the Sixties alarmed and, even, disoriented me.
The calls for civil rights, racial equality, sexual equality, freer
sex, and peace in Vietnam were in themselves commendable
and non-threatening; it was the savagery, between 1965 and
1973, of the domestic attack upon the good faith and common
sense of our government, especially of that would-be Roosevelt
Lyndon B. Johnson, that astonished me. The attack came,
much of it, from the intellectual elite and their draft-vulnerable
children. Civil disobedience was antithetical to my Fifties
education, which had inculcated, on the professional level, an
impassioned but cool aestheticism and implied, on the private,
salvation through sensibility, which included an ironical
detachment from the social issues fashionable in the Thirties.
But the radicalizing Thirties had come round again, in psychedelic colors.

I coped by moving, with my family, to England for a year,
and reading in the British Museum about James Buchanan.
Buchanan (1791–1868) was the only Pennsylvanian ever elected
to the White House; the main triumph of his turbulent term
(1857–61) was that, though elderly, he survived it, and left it
to his successor, Abraham Lincoln, to start the Civil War. A
pro-Southern Democrat who yet denied any Constitutional
states' right to secede, he embodied for me the drowned-out
voice of careful, fussy reasonableness. For over a year, I
read American history and tried unsuccessfully to shape this
historical figure's dilemmas into a work of fiction. But my
attempted pages showed me too earthbound a realist or too
tame a visionary for the vigorous fakery of a historical novel.

By the first month of 1970, back in the United States, I gave
up the attempt. But then, what to do? I owed my publisher a
novel, and had not come up with one. From the start of our
relationship, I had thought it a right and mutually profitable
rhythm to offer Knopf a novel every other book. In the ten
years since *Rabbit, Run* had ended on its ambiguous note, a
number of people asked me what happened to him. It came
to me that he would have run around the block, returned to

Mt. Judge and Janice, faced what music there was, and be now an all-too-settled working man – a Linotyper. For three summers I had worked as a copy boy in a small-city newspaper and had admired the men in green eyeshades as they perched at their square-keyed keyboards and called down a rain of brass matrices to become hot lead slugs, to become columns of type. It was the blue-collar equivalent of my sedentary, word-productive profession. He would be, my thirty-six-year-old Rabbit, one of those middle Americans feeling overwhelmed and put upon by all the revolutions in the air; he would serve as a receptacle for my disquiet and resentments, which would sit more becomingly on him than on me. Rabbit to the rescue, and as before his creator was in a hurry. An examination of the manuscript reveals what I had forgotten, that I typed the first draft – the only novel of the four of which this is true. I began on 7 February 1970, finished that first draft on 11 December, and had it typed up by Palm Sunday 1971 – which means that my publisher worked fast to get it out before the end of that year. If the novel achieved nothing else, it revived the word *redux*, which I had encountered in titles by Dryden and Trollope. From the Latin *reducere*, 'to bring back', it is defined by Webster's as 'led back; specif., *Med.*, indicating return to health after disease'. People wanted to pronounce it 'raydoo', as if it were French, but now I often see it in print, as a staple of journalese.

Rabbit became too much a receptacle, perhaps, for every item in the headlines. A number of reviewers invited me to think so. But though I have had several occasions to reread the novel, few excisions suggested themselves to me. As a reader I am carried along the curve that I described in my flap copy: 'Rabbit is abandoned and mocked, his home is invaded, the world of his childhood decays into a mere sublunar void; still he clings to semblances of patriotism and paternity.' The novel is itself a moon shot: Janice's affair launches her husband, as he and his father witness the takeoff of Apollo 11 in the Phoenix bar, into the extraterrestrial world of Jill and Skeeter. The eventual reunion of the married couple in the Safe Haven Motel is managed with the care and gingerly vocabulary of a spacecraft docking. It is the most violent and bizarre of these four novels, but then the Sixties were the most violent and bizarre of these decades. The possibly inordinate emphasis on sexual congress – an enthusiastic mixture of instruction manual and de Sadeian ballet – also partakes of the times.

In *Rabbit, Run*, there is very little direct cultural and political reference, apart from the burst of news items that comes over his car radio during his night of fleeing home. Of these, only the disappearance of the Dalai Lama from Tibet engages the fictional themes. In *Rabbit Redux*, the trip to the moon is the central metaphor. 'Trip' in Sixties parlance meant an inner journey of some strangeness; the little apple-green house in Penn Villas plays host to space invaders – a middle-class runaway and a black rhetorician. The long third chapter – longer still in the first draft – is a Sixties invention, a 'teach-in'. Rabbit tries to learn. Reading aloud the words of Frederick Douglass, he becomes black, and in a fashion seeks solidarity with Skeeter. African Americans, Old-World readers should be reminded, have an immigrant pedigree almost as long as that of Anglo-Americans; 'the Negro problem' is old in the New World. The United States is more than a tenth black; black music, black sorrow, black jubilation, black English, black style permeate the culture and have contributed much of what makes American music, especially, so globally potent. Yet the society continues racially divided, in the main, and Rabbit's reluctant crossing of the color line represents a tortured form of progress.

The novel was meant to be symmetric with *Rabbit, Run*: this time, Janice leaves home and a young female dies on Harry's watch. Expatiation of the baby's death is the couple's joint quest throughout the series; Harry keeps looking for a daughter, and Janice strives for competence, for a redeemed opinion of herself. Nelson remains the wounded, helplessly indignant witness. He is ever shocked by 'the hardness of heart' that enables his father to live so egocentrically, as if enjoying divine favor. *Rabbit, Run*'s epigraph is an uncompleted thought by Pascal: 'The motions of Grace, the hardness of the heart; external circumstances.' In *Rabbit Redux*, external circumstances bear nightmarishly upon my skittish pilgrim; he

achieves a measure of recognition that the rage and destruct-
iveness boiling out of the television set belong to him. Many
of the lessons of the Sixties became part of the *status quo*.
Veterans became doves; bankers put on love beads. Among
Harry's virtues, self-centered though he is, are the national
curiosity, tolerance, and adaptability. America survives its
chronic apocalypses. I did not know, though, when I abandoned to motel sleep the couple with a burnt-out house and
a traumatized child, that they would wake to such prosperity.

Rabbit is rich, of course, in 1979, only by the standards of
his modest working-class background. It was a lucky casual
stroke of mine to give the used-car dealer Fred Springer a
Toyota franchise in *Rabbit Redux*, for in ten years' time the
Japanese-auto invasion had become one of the earmarks of an
inflated and teetering American economy, and the Chief Sales
Representative of a Toyota agency was well situated to reap
advantage from American decline. As these novels had
developed, each needed a clear background of news, a 'hook'
uniting the personal and national realms. In late June, visiting
in Pennsylvania for a few days, I found the hook in the OPEC-
induced gasoline shortage and the panicky lines that cars were
forming at the local pumps; our host in the Philadelphia
suburbs rose early and got our car tank filled so we could get
back to New England. A nuclear near-disaster had occurred at
Three-Mile Island in Harrisburg that spring; Carter's approval
rating was down to thirty per cent; our man in Nicaragua was
being ousted by rebels; our man in Iran was deposed and
dying; John Wayne was dead; Sky-Lab was falling; and Rabbit,
at forty-six, with a wife who drinks too much and a son dropping out of college, could well believe that he and the U.S.
were both running out of gas. Except that he doesn't really
believe it; *Rabbit Is Rich*, for all its shadows, is the happiest
novel of the four, the most buoyant, with happy endings for
everybody in it, even the hapless Buddy Inglefinger. The novel
contains a number of scenes distinctly broad in their comedy:
amid the inflationary abundance of money, Harry and Janice
copulate on a blanket of gold coins and stagger beneath the
weight of 888 silver dollars as they lug their speculative loot
up the eerily deserted main drag of Brewer. A Shakespearian

swap and shuffle of couples takes place in the glimmering Arcadia of a Caribbean island, and a wedding rings out at the novel's midpoint. 'Life is sweet, that's what they say,' Rabbit reflects in the last pages. Details poured fast and furious out of my by now thoroughly mapped and populated Diamond County. The novel is fat, in keeping with its theme of inflation, and Pru is fat with her impending child, whose growth is the book's secret action, its innermost happiness.

My own circumstances had changed since the writing of *Rabbit Redux*. I was married to another wife, which may help account for Janice's lusty rejuvenation, and living in another town, called Georgetown, twenty minutes inland from Ipswich. Each of the Rabbit novels was written in a different setting – *Redux* belonged to my second house in Ipswich, on the winding, winsomely named Labor-in-Vain Road, and to my rented office downtown, above a restaurant whose noontime aromas of lunch rose through the floor each day to urge my writing to its daily conclusion. Whereas Ipswich had a distinguished Puritan history and some grand seaside scenery, Georgetown was an unassuming population knot on the way to other places. It reminded me of Shillington, and the wooden house that we occupied for six years was, like the brick house I had spent my first thirteen years in, long and narrow, with a big back yard and a front view of a well-trafficked street. The town was littered with details I only needed to stoop over and pick up and drop into Mt. Judge's scenery; my evening jogs through Georgetown could slip almost unaltered into Rabbit's panting peregrinations three hundred miles away. In two respects his fortunes had the advantage of mine: I was not a member of any country club, nor yet a grandfather. Within five years, I would achieve both privileged states, but for the time being they had to be, like the procedures of a Toyota agency, dreamed up. A dreamy mood pervades the book; Rabbit almost has to keep pinching himself to make sure that his bourgeois bliss is real – that he is, if not as utterly a master of householdry and husbandry as the ineffable Webb Murkett, in the same exalted league.

Once in an interview I had rashly predicted the title of this third installment to be *Rural Rabbit*; some of the words Harry and Janice exchange in the Safe Haven Motel leave the plot open for a country move. But in the event he remained a small-city boy, a creature of sidewalks, gritty alleys, roaring highways, and fast-food franchises. One of *Rabbit, Run*'s adventures in my mind had been its location in Brewer, whose model, the city of Reading, had loomed for a Shillington child as an immense, remote, menacing, and glamorous metropolis. Rabbit, like every stimulating alter ago, was many things the author was not: a natural athlete, a blue-eyed Swede, sexually magnetic, taller than six feet, impulsive, and urban. The rural Rabbit turns out to be Ruth, from the first novel, whom he flushes from her cover in his continued search for a daughter. Farms I knew first-hand, at least in their sensory details, from the years of rural residence my mother had imposed on her family after 1945. Rabbit spying on Ruth from behind the scratchy hedgerow is both Peter Rabbit peeking from behind the cabbages at the menacing Mr. McGregor and I, the self-exiled son, guiltily spying on my mother as, in plucky and self-reliant widowhood, she continued to occupy her sandstone farmhouse and eighty acres all by herself. She did not, in fairness, keep the shell of a school bus in her yard; rather, the town fleet of yellow school buses was visible from the window of my drafty study in Georgetown.

Though 1979 was running out, I seem to have worked at a leisurely speed: the end of the first draft is dated 19 April 1980, and seven more months went by before my typing of the manuscript was completed on 23 November. Happily, and quite to my surprise, *Rabbit Is Rich* won all three of 1981's major American literary prizes for fiction (as well as a place in the Washington critic Jonathan Yardley's list of the Ten Worst Books of the Year). An invigorating change of mates, a move to a town that made negligible communal demands, a sense of confronting the world in a fresh relation cleared my head, it may be. The Rabbit novels, coming every ten years, were far from all that I wrote; the novel that precedes *Rabbit Is Rich*, *The Coup*, and the semi-novel that followed it, *Bech Is Back*, in retrospect also seem the replete but airy products of a phase when such powers as I can claim were exuberantly ripe.

Ripeness was the inevitable theme of my fourth and concluding entry in this saga. By 1989 my wife and I had moved to Beverly Farms, a bucolic enclave of old summer homes. Most of our neighbors and new acquaintances were elderly; many spent part of their year in Florida. My children were all adult, and three stepsons nearly so; as it happened, my wife and I each had a widowed mother living in solitude. My mother, well into her eighties, was my principal living link with Rabbit's terrain; countless visits over the years had refreshed my boyhood impressions and reassured me that southeastern Pennsylvania was changing in tune with the rest of the nation. Thirty years before, a reader had asked me if Harry didn't die at the end of *Rabbit, Run*, and it did seem possible that death might come early to him, as it often does to ex-athletes, especially those who are overweight and not usefully employed. All men are mortal; my character was a man. But I, too, was a man, and by no means sure how much of me would be functioning in 1999. The more research I did to flesh out my hero's cardio-vascular problems, the more ominous pains afflicted my own chest. As a child, just beginning to relate my birth year to the actuarial realities, I had wondered if I would live to the year 2000. I still wondered. I wanted Harry to go out with all the style a healthy author could give him, and had a vision of a four-book set, a squared-off tetralogy, a boxed life. I began *Rabbit at Rest* early in 1989, on 12 January, as if anxious to get started, and finished the first draft on the last day of September, and the typed draft on 20 January 1990. Like *Rabbit, Run*, it was published in a zero year.

And like *Rabbit, Run*, it is in three parts. The hero of both novels flees south from domestic predicaments. In March of 1959 'his goal is the white sun of the south like a great big pillow in the sky'. He fails to get there and, lost and exasperated on the dark roads of West Virginia, turns back; but his fifty-six-year-old self knows the way. Harry has acquired the expertise and the money and he gets there, and lays his tired head upon that great big pillow. No distinctly American development, no moon shot or gas crunch, offered itself as a dominant metaphor, at this end of Reagan's decade; instead, the mid-air explosion of Pan Am Flight 103 over Lockerbie, which occurred before Christmas of 1988, haunts Rabbit acrophobically. And he senses the coming collapse of the Soviet Union and its empire, whose opposition to the free world has shadowed and shaped his entire adult life. Freedom has had its hazards for him, and capitalist enterprise its surfeit, but he was ever the loyal citizen. God he can doubt, but not America. He is the New World's new man, armored against eventualities in little but his selfhood.

The novel's two locales have an exceptional geographical density. For the Florida city of Deleon, I did several days of legwork in the vicinity of Fort Myers. To give substance to Harry's final, solitary drive south, I drove the route myself, beginning at my mother's farm and scribbling sights, rivers, and radio emissions in a notebook on the seat beside me, just as, more than three decades previous, I turned on my New England radio on the very night, the last night of winter, 1959, and made note of what came. Accident rules these novels more than most, in their attempt to take a useful imprint of the world that secretes in newspapers clues to its puzzle of glory. The fictional name Deleon, along with the murals Rabbit notices in the hospital lobby, constitutes homage to my mother, whose cherished project it had long been to write and publish a novel about the Spanish governor of Puerto Rico and discoverer of Florida, Juan Ponce de León. She enriched, too, the city of Brewer, for a grim interplay developed between my novel, in the year of its writing, and her physical decline. Her several hospitalizations generated medical details that I shamelessly fed into Rabbit's ordeal; my frequent filial visits exposed me more intensely to Reading and its environs than at any time since the Fifties, and so Rabbit's home turf, especially as evoked at the beginning of Chapter II, acquired substance and the poignance of something slipping away. I became, as I have written elsewhere, 'conscious of how powerfully, inexhaustibly rich real places are, compared with the paper cities we make of them in fiction. Even after a tetralogy, almost everything is still left to say. As I walked and drove the familiar roads and streets, I saw them as if for the first time with more than a child's eyes and felt myself beginning, at last, to understand the place. But by then it was time to say goodbye.'

RABBIT ANGSTROM

My mother died two weeks after I had completed the first draft of *Rabbit at Rest*. If she pervades its landscape and overall mortal mood, my father, who died in 1972, figures strongly also. Rabbit, in his near-elderly, grandpaternal condition, more and more talked, I could not but notice, like George Caldwell in *The Centaur*. My two projected novellas had merged: the dodgy rabbit had become the suffering horse; the man of impulse and appetite had aged into humorous stoicism. In trying to picture a grandfather (my own enactment of that role had just barely begun) I fell back upon memories of my father, whose patient bemusement and air of infinite toleration had enchanted my own children. A number of readers told me how much more lovable Harry had become. My intention was never to make him – or any character – lovable. He was imagined, at a time when I was much taken with Kierkegaard, as a creature of fear and trembling; but perhaps my college exposure to Dostoevsky was more central. Rabbit is, like the Underground Man, *incorrigible*; from first to last he bridles at good advice, taking direction only from his personal, also incorrigible God.

His adventure on the Sunfish with Judy rehearses once more the primal trauma of *Rabbit, Run*, this time successfully, with the baby saved by a self-sacrificing parent. Ripeness brings to fruition many of the tendencies of Rabbit's earthly transit. His relations with the opposite sex appear to have two main aspects, the paternal and erotic; they come to a momentarily triumphant climax in his contact with his daughter-in-law. His lifelong involvement with Ronnie Harrison – that repugnant locker-room exhibitionist whose very name seems a broken mirroring of Rabbit's – reaches its terminus in a tied golf match. Harry's shy but determined advance into the bodies of women slowly brings him to a kind of forgiveness of the flesh. Whatever his parental sins, their wages are generously paid him by his son in an act of corporate destruction. Harry's wary fascination with his black fellow-Americans leads him to explore the black section of Deleon, in its stagnation comfortingly similar to the Depression world of his childhood. So many themes convene in *Rabbit at Rest* that the hero could be said to sink under the burden of the accumulated past, and to find relief in that 'wide tan emptiness under the sun', the recreation fields next to the abandoned Florida high school.

A problem for the author of sequels is how much of the previous books to carry along. The nuclear family – Harry, Janice, Nelson – and Ronnie Harrison figure in all four installments of *Rabbit Angstrom*. The older generation, potently present in the first two novels, has dwindled to the spunky figure of Bessie Springer in *Rabbit Is Rich*; I was charmed to find her so spirited and voluble as she manipulated the purse strings of her little dynasty. Characters dominant in one novel fall away in the next. Ruth vanishes from *Rabbit Redux* but returns in the next decade. I have restored to *Redux* an omitted brief reappearance by Jack Eccles, who almost became the co-protagonist of Rabbit's first outing, and whose own 'outing' seemed to deserve a place in the full report. Skeeter, who takes over *Redux*, dwindles to a news item and a troubling memory; what later novel could hold him? Perhaps he returns in the form of Tiger. That the neo-Babbitt of the third volume contains the witness to the apocalyptic events of the second would strain plausibility did not so many peaceable citizens contain lethal soldiers, so many criminals contain choirboys, so many monogamous women contain promiscuous young things. An adult human being consists of sedimentary layers. We shed more skins than we can count, and are born each day to a merciful forgetfulness. We forget most of our past but embody all of it.

For this fresh printing, apt to be the last I shall oversee, I have tried to smooth away such inconsistencies as have come to my attention. Various automotive glitches – a front engine assigned to a rear-engine make of car, a convertible model that never existed in all of Detroit's manufacture – have been repaired. The flora and fauna of commercial products and popular culture posed many small spelling problems that should be now resolved. Birthdays: real people have them, but fictional characters usually do without, unless an extended chronicle insists. To my best knowledge Harold C. (a mystery initial) Angstrom was born in February 1933, and Janice Springer sometime in 1936. They were married in March of

1956, and their son Nelson was born the following October, seven months later – on the 22nd, by my calculations. Nelson's daughter, Judith, was born in January of 1980 and his son, Roy, in November of 1984. *Rabbit, Run* takes place from 20 March 1959 to 24 June of that year; *Rabbit Redux* from 16 July 1969 to late October; *Rabbit Is Rich* from 23 June 1979 to 20 January 1980; and *Rabbit at Rest* from 28 December 1988 to 22 September 1989. Spring, fall, summer, winter: a life as well as a year has its seasons.

John Updike

SELECT BIBLIOGRAPHY

CLARKE TAYLOR, C., *John Updike: A Bibliography*, Kent State University Press, Kent, Ohio, 1968.

DE BELLIS, JACK, *John Updike: A Bibliography, 1968–1993*, Greenwood Publishing Group, Westport, Connecticut, 1994.

INTERVIEWS WITH JOHN UPDIKE
Life (4 November 1968); *Paris Review* (Winter 1968); *New York Times Book Review* (10 April 1977); *Salmagundi* 57 (1982).

PLATH, JAMES, ed., *Conversations with John Updike*, University Press of Mississippi, Jackson, Mississippi, 1994.

CRITICISM
BAKER, NICHOLAS, *U & I: A True Story*, Random House, New York, 1991.

BLOOM, HAROLD, ed., *Modern Critical Views of John Updike*, Chelsea House, New York, 1987.

DETWEILER, ROBERT, *John Updike*, Twayne, Boston, 1984.

GREINER, DONALD, *John Updike's Novels*, Ohio University Press, Athens, Ohio, 1984.

HAMILTON, ALICE and KENNETH, *The Elements of John Updike*, William B. Eerdmans, Grand Rapids, Michigan, 1970.

HUNT, GEORGE, *John Updike and the Three Great Secret Things: Sex, Religion, and Art*, William B. Eerdmans, Grand Rapids, Michigan, 1980.

MACNAUGHTON, WILLIAM R., ed., *Critical Essays on John Updike*, G. K. Hall, Boston, 1982.

MARKLE, JOYCE B., *Fighters and Lovers: Theme in the Novels of John Updike*, New York University Press, New York, 1973.

NEWMAN, JUDIE, *John Updike*, Macmillan, London, 1988.

SEARLES, GEORGE J., *The Fiction of Philip Roth and John Updike*, Southern Illinois University Press, Carbondale, Illinois, 1984.

TALLENT, ELIZABETH, *Married Men and Magic Tricks: John Updike's Erotic Heroes*, Creative Arts Book Company, Berkeley, California, 1982.

TANNER, TONY, *City of Words: American Fiction, 1950–1970*, Jonathan Cape, London, 1971.

THORBURN, DAVID, and EILAND, HOWARD (eds), *John Updike: A Collection of Critical Essays*, Prentice Hall, Englewood Cliffs, New Jersey, 1979.

UPHAUS, SUZANNE H., *John Updike*, Ungar, New York, 1980.

CHRONOLOGY

DATE	AUTHOR'S LIFE	LITERARY CONTEXT
1932	Birth of John Hoyer Updike at Shillington, Pennsylvania (18 March).	1932 Huxley: *Brave New World*. Faulkner: *Light in August*.
		1934 Fitzgerald: *Tender is the Night*. Miller: *Tropic of Cancer*. Waugh: *A Handful of Dust*. 1935 Lewis: *It Can't Happen Here*. 1936 Faulkner: *Absalom, Absalom!* Eliot: *Collected Poems*.
		1937 Steinbeck: *Of Mice and Men*. Hemingway: *To Have and Have Not*. 1938 Sartre: *Nausea*. 1939 Steinbeck: *The Grapes of Wrath*. Joyce: *Finnegans Wake*. 1940 Hemingway: *For Whom the Bell Tolls*. Greene: *The Power and the Glory*. 1941 Fitzgerald: *The Last Tycoon*. 1942 Eliot: *Four Quartets*. Camus: *The Stranger*.
1945	Moves with family to old Hoyer farm, eleven miles away.	1945 Orwell: *Animal Farm*. Waugh: *Brideshead Revisited*. Borges: *Fictions*. 1948 Greene: *The Heart of the Matter*. 1949 Orwell: *Nineteen Eighty-Four*. de Beauvoir: *The Second Sex*.
1950	Graduates as co-valedictorian from Shillington High School.	
		1951 Frost: *Complete Poems*. Salinger: *The Catcher in the Rye*. 1952 Beckett: *Waiting for Godot*.
1953	Marries Mary Pennington.	1953 Bellow: *The Adventures of Augie March*.

HISTORICAL EVENTS

1932 Election of Roosevelt in US. Nazis become largest party in German Reichstag.

1933 Roosevelt announces 'New Deal.' Hitler becomes German Chancellor.

1936 Outbreak of Spanish Civil War. Hitler and Mussolini form Rome–Berlin Axis. Edward VIII abdicates; George VI crowned in UK. Stalin's 'Great Purge' of the Communist Party (to 1938).
1937 Japanese invasion of China.

1938 Germany annexes Austria; Munich crisis.
1939 Nazi–Soviet Pact; Hitler invades Poland. World War II beings.

1940 Fall of France; Battle of Britain.

1941 Japan attacks Pearl Harbor; US enters war. Hitler invades the Soviet Union.

1944 Allied landings in Normandy.
1945 Unconditional surrender of Germany. Roosevelt dies; Truman becomes President. US drops atomic bombs on Hiroshima and Nagasaki. End of World War II. United Nations founded.
1948 Jewish state of Israel comes into existence. Russian blockade of West Berlin.
1949 Communists win Chinese civil war. North Atlantic Treaty signed.

1950 Korean War begins.

1952 Eisenhower elected US President. Accession of Elizabeth II in UK.
1953 Korean War ends. Death of Stalin.

DATE	AUTHOR'S LIFE	LITERARY CONTEXT
1954–5	Harvard College *summa cum laude* (1954). Attends Ruskin School of Drawing and Fine Art, Oxford, on Knox Fellowship.	1954 Amis: *Lucky Jim*.
		1955 Nabokov: *Lolita*.
1955–7	Staff reporter for *The New Yorker*. Birth of daughter, Elizabeth (1955) and son, David (1957). Moves to Ipswich, Massachusetts (1957).	
		1956 Osborne: *Look Back in Anger*.
		1957 Kerouac: *On the Road*.
1958	*The Carpentered Hen* (in UK as *Hoping for a Hoopoe*) (poetry).	1958 Pasternak: *Doctor Zhivago*.
		Achebe: *Things Fall Apart*.
1959	*The Poorhouse Fair* (wins Rosenthal Award in 1960). *The Same Door* (stories). Birth of second son, Michael.	1959 Burroughs: *Naked Lunch*. Bellow: *Henderson the Rain King*.
1960	*Rabbit, Run*. Birth of second daughter, Miranda.	
		1961 Heller: *Catch-22*. Naipaul: *A House for Mr Biswas*.
1962	*Pigeon Feathers* (stories).	1962 Nabokov: *Pale Fire*. Solzhenitsyn: *One Day in the Life of Ivan Denisovich*.
1963	*The Centaur* (wins National Book Award). *Telephone Poles* (poetry).	
1964	*Olinger Stories*. Elected to National Institute of Arts and Letters. 'The Bulgarian Poetess' (first Bech story).	1964 Bellow: *Herzog*.
1965	*Of the Farm. Assorted Prose*.	1965 Calvino: *Cosmicomics*.
1966	*The Music School* (stories).	
		1967 Márquez: *One Hundred Years of Solitude*.
1968–9	Lives with family in London. *Couples* (1968). *Midpoint* (poetry, 1969).	1968 Solzhenitsyn: *Cancer Ward*.
1970	*Bech: A Book*.	
1971	*Rabbit Redux*.	
1972	Father dies. *Museums and Women* (stories).	

CHRONOLOGY

1954 Vietnam War begins.

1956 Soviets invade Hungary. Suez crisis.

1957 Civil Rights Commission established in US to safeguard voting rights.

1959 Castro seizes power in Cuba.

1960 Kennedy elected US President.

1961 Erection of Berlin Wall.

1962 Cuban missile crisis.

1963 Assassination of Kennedy. Johnson becomes US President.

1964 Civil Rights Act prohibits discrimination in US. Brezhnev becomes Communist Party General Secretary in USSR.

1968 Student unrest in US and throughout Europe. Assassination of Martin Luther King, Jr. Soviet invasion of Czechoslovakia. Nixon elected US President.
1970 Death of de Gaulle.

DATE	AUTHOR'S LIFE	LITERARY CONTEXT
		1973 Pynchon: *Gravity's Rainbow*. Solzhenitsyn: *The Gulag Archipelago* (to 1975).
1974	Lives alone in Boston. *Buchanan Dying* (play).	
1975	*A Month of Sundays*. *Picked-Up Pieces* (essays).	1975 Levi: *The Periodic Table*.
1976	Divorced. Moves to Georgetown, Massachusetts. *Marry Me*. Elected to Academy of Arts and Letters.	
1977	Marries Martha Bernhard. *Tossing and Turning* (poetry).	1977 Morrison: *Song of Solomon*.
1978	*The Coup*.	
1979	*Too Far to Go* and *Problems* (stories).	1979 Calvino: *If on a Winter's Night a Traveler*.
1981	*Rabbit Is Rich* (wins American Book Award for Fiction, Pulitzer Prize, and National Book Critics Circle Award in 1982).	1981 Rushdie: *Midnight's Children*.
1982	Moves to Beverly Farms, Massachusetts. *Bech Is Back*.	1982 Levi: *If Not Now, When?* Márquez: *Chronicle of a Death Foretold*.
1983	*Hugging the Shore* (wins National Book Critics Circle Award for Criticism in 1984).	
1984	*The Witches of Eastwick*.	
1985	*Facing Nature* (poetry).	1985 Márquez: *Love in the Time of Cholera*.
1986	*Roger's Version*.	1986 Levi: *The Drowned and the Saved*.
1987	*Trust Me* (stories).	1987 Morrison: *Beloved*.
1988	*S.*	1988 Rushdie: *The Satanic Verses*.
1989	Mother dies. *Self-Consciousness* (memoirs). *Just Looking* (art criticism). Awarded the National Medal of Arts.	1989 DeLillo: *Libra*. M. Amis: *London Fields*. Márquez: *The General in His Labyrinth*.
1990	*Rabbit at Rest* (wins Pulitzer Prize and National Book Critics Circle Award in 1991).	1990 Walcott: *Omerus*.
1991	*Odd Jobs* (essays).	1991 M. Amis: *Time's Arrow*.
1992	*Memories of the Ford Administration*.	
1993	*Collected Poems*.	1993 Roth: *Operation Shylock*.

CHRONOLOGY

1974 Nixon resigns in wake of Watergate scandal; Ford becomes US President.
1975 Vietnam War ends.

1976 Death of Mao Tse-Tung. Carter elected US President.

1978 P. W. Botha comes to power in South Africa.
1979 Margaret Thatcher first woman Prime Minister in UK. Carter and Brezhnev sign SALT-2 arms limitation treaty. Soviets occupy Afghanistan.
1980 Lech Walesa leads strikes in Gdansk, Poland. Reagan US President.
1981 Mitterand elected President of France.

1984 Famine in Ethiopia. Indira Gandhi assassinated.
1985 Gorbachev becomes General Secretary in USSR.

1986 Gorbachev–Reagan summit.

1988 Gorbachev announces big troop reductions, suggesting end of Cold War.
1989 Collapse of Communism in Eastern Europe. Fall of the Berlin Wall. First democratic elections in USSR. Tiananmen Square massacre in China.

1990 End of Communist monopoly in USSR. Yeltsin elected first leader of Russian Federation. Nelson Mandela released from jail after 27 years' imprisonment. John Major becomes Prime Minister in UK.
1991 Gulf War. Central government in USSR suspended. War begins in former Yugoslavia.
1992 Clinton elected US President.
1993 Palestinian leader Arafat and Israeli Prime Minister Rabin sign peace agreement in US. Maastricht Treaty (creating European Union) ratified.

DATE	AUTHOR'S LIFE	LITERARY CONTEXT
1994	*Brazil. The Afterlife and Other Stories.*	1994 Heller: *Closing Time.*
1995	Awarded Howells Medal from American Academy of Arts and Letters for *Rabbit at Rest.* Four Rabbit novels published in one volume, *Rabbit Angstrom.*	1995 M. Amis: *The Information.* Rushdie: *The Moor's Last Sigh.*
1996	*In the Beauty of the Lilies. Golf Dreams.*	
1997	*Toward the End of Time.*	1997 Roth: *American Pastoral.* McEwan: *Enduring Love.* Bellow: *The Actual.*
1998	*Bech at Bay.* *A Century of Arts and Letters* (editor). Awarded the National Book Foundation Lifetime Achievement Award.	1998 Morrison: *Paradise.* DeLillo: *Underworld.* Heller: *Now and Then.* McEwan: *Amsterdam.*
1999	*More Matter* (essays). *The Best American Short Stories of the Century* (editor).	1999 Rushdie: *The Ground Beneath Her Feet.*
2000	*Gertrude and Claudius. Licks of Love.*	2000 Bellow: *Ravelstein.* Roth: *The Human Stain.*

CHRONOLOGY

1994 Mandela and ANC sweep to victory in South African elections. Civil war in Rwanda. Russian military action against Chechen republic. IRA ceasefire announced.

1995 Rabin assassinated.

1996 President Clinton re-elected.

1997 Tony Blair elected Prime Minister (first Labour government in the UK since 1979).

1998 President Clinton impeached in December (acquitted February 1999). Referendum in Northern Ireland accepts Good Friday agreement; an assembly elected.

1999 Serbs attack ethnic Albanians in Kosovo; US leads NATO in bombing of Belgrade.

2000 Putin succeeds Yeltsin as Russian President. Further violence in Chechen republic. Milosevic's regime in the former Yugoslavia collapses; Vojislav Kostunica elected President.

RABBIT
ANGSTROM

A TETRALOGY

RABBIT, RUN

*The motions of Grace, the hardness of the heart;
external circumstances.*

—Pascal, Pensée 507

BOYS are playing basketball around a telephone pole with a backboard bolted to it. Legs, shouts. The scrape and snap of Keds on loose alley pebbles seems to catapult their voices high into the moist March air blue above the wires. Rabbit Angstrom, coming up the alley in a business suit, stops and watches, though he's twenty-six and six three. So tall, he seems an unlikely rabbit, but the breadth of white face, the pallor of his blue irises, and a nervous flutter under his brief nose as he stabs a cigarette into his mouth partially explain the nickname, which was given to him when he too was a boy. He stands there thinking, the kids keep coming, they keep crowding you up.

His standing there makes the real boys feel strange. Eyeballs slide. They're doing this for themselves, not as a show for some adult walking around town in a double-breasted cocoa suit. It seems funny to them, an adult walking up the alley at all. Where's his car? The cigarette makes it more sinister still. Is this one of those going to offer them cigarettes or money to go out in back of the ice plant with him? They've heard of such things but are not too frightened; there are six of them and one of him.

The ball, rocketing off the crotch of the rim, leaps over the heads of the six and lands at the feet of the one. He catches it on the short bounce with a quickness that startles them. As they stare hushed he sights squinting through blue clouds of weed smoke, a suddenly dark silhouette like a smokestack against the afternoon spring sky, setting his feet with care, wiggling the ball with nervousness in front of his chest, one widespread white hand on top of the ball and the other underneath, jiggling it patiently to get some adjustment in air itself. The cuticle moons on his fingernails are big. Then the ball seems to ride up the right lapel of his coat and comes off his shoulder as his knees dip down, and it appears the ball will miss because though he shot from an angle the ball is not

going toward the backboard. It was not aimed there. It drops into
the circle of the rim, whipping the net with a ladylike whisper.
"Hey!" he shouts in pride.

"Luck," one of the kids says.

"Skill," he answers, and asks, "Hey. O.K. if I play?"

There is no response, just puzzled silly looks swapped. Rabbit
takes off his coat, folds it nicely, and rests it on a clean ashcan lid.
Behind him the dungarees begin to scuffle again. He goes into the
scrimmaging thick of them for the ball, flips it from two weak
grubby-knuckled child's hands, has it in his own. That old
stretched-leather feeling makes his whole body go taut, gives his
arms wings. It feels like he's reaching down through years to touch
this tautness. His arms lift of their own and the rubber ball floats
toward the basket from the top of his head. It feels so right he
blinks when the ball drops short, and for a second wonders if it
went through the hoop without riffling the net. He asks, "Hey
whose side am I on?"

In a wordless shuffle two boys are delegated to be his. They
stand the other four. Though from the start Rabbit handicaps
himself by staying ten feet out from the basket, it is still unfair.
Nobody bothers to keep score. The surly silence bothers him. The
kids call monosyllables to each other but to him they don't dare a
word. As the game goes on he can feel them at his legs, getting
hot and mad, trying to trip him, but their tongues are still held.
He doesn't want this respect, he wants to tell them there's nothing to getting old, it takes nothing. In ten minutes another boy
goes to the other side, so it's just Rabbit Angstrom and one kid
standing five. This boy, still midget but already diffident with a
kind of rangy ease, is the best of the six; he wears a knitted cap
with a green pompon well down over his ears and level with his
eyebrows, giving his head a cretinous look. He's a natural. The
way he moves sideways without taking any steps, gliding on a
blessing: you can tell. The way he waits before he moves. With
luck he'll become in time a crack athlete in the high school;
Rabbit knows the way. You climb up through the little grades and
then get to the top and everybody cheers; with the sweat in your
eyebrows you can't see very well and the noise swirls around you
and lifts you up, and then you're out, not forgotten at first, just

out, and it feels good and cool and free. You're out, and sort of melt, and keep lifting, until you become like to these kids just one more piece of the sky of adults that hangs over them in the town, a piece that for some queer reason has clouded and visited them. They've not forgotten him: worse, they never heard of him. Yet in his time Rabbit was famous through the county; in basketball in his junior year he set a B-league scoring record that in his senior year he broke with a record that was not broken until four years later, that is, four years ago.

He sinks shots one-handed, two-handed, underhanded, flat-footed, and out of the pivot, jump, and set. Flat and soft the ball lifts. That his touch still lives in his hands elates him. He feels liberated from long gloom. But his body is weighty and his breath grows short. It annoys him, that he gets winded. When the five kids not on his side begin to groan and act lazy, and a kid he accidentally knocks down gets up with a blurred face and walks away, Rabbit quits readily. "O.K.," he says. "The old man's going. Three cheers."

To the boy on his side, the pompon, he adds, "So long, ace." He feels grateful to the boy, who continued to watch him with disinterested admiration after the others grew sullen. Naturals know. It's all in how it feels.

Rabbit picks up his folded coat and carries it in one hand like a letter as he runs. Up the alley. Past the deserted ice plant with its rotting wooden skids on the fallen loading porch. Ashcans, garage doors, fences of chicken-wire caging crisscrossing stalks of dead flowers. The month is March. Love makes the air light. Things start anew; Rabbit tastes through sour aftersmoke the fresh chance in the air, plucks the pack of cigarettes from his bobbling shirt pocket, and without breaking stride cans it in somebody's open barrel. His upper lip nibbles back from his teeth in self-pleasure. His big suede shoes skim in thumps above the skittering litter of alley gravel.

Running. At the end of this block of the alley he turns up a street, Wilbur Street in the town of Mt. Judge, suburb of the city of Brewer, fifth largest city in Pennsylvania. Running uphill. Past a block of big homes, small fortresses of cement and brick inset with doorways of stained and beveled glass and windows of potted plants; and then half the way up another block, which holds a development built all at once in the Thirties. The frame homes climb the hill like a single staircase. The space of six feet or so that each double house rises above its neighbor contains two wan windows, wide-spaced like the eyes of an animal, and is covered with composition shingling varying in color from bruise to dung. The fronts are scabby clapboards, once white. There are a dozen three-story homes, and each has two doors. The seventh door is his. The wood steps up to it are worn; under them there is a cubbyhole of dirt where a lost toy molders. A plastic clown. He's seen it there all winter but he always thought some kid would be coming back for it.

Rabbit pauses in the sunless vestibule, panting. Overhead, a daytime bulb burns dustily. Three tin mailboxes hang empty above a brown radiator. His downstairs neighbor's door across the hall is shut like a hurt face. There is that smell which is always the same but that he can never identify; sometimes it seems cabbage cooking, sometimes the furnace's rusty breath, sometimes something soft decaying in the walls. He climbs the stairs to his home, the top floor.

The door is locked. In fitting the little key into the lock his hand trembles, pulsing with unusual exertion, and the metal scratches. But when he opens the door he sees his wife sitting in an armchair with an Old-fashioned, watching television turned down low.

"You're *here*," he says. "What's the door locked for?"

She looks to one side of him with vague dark eyes reddened by the friction of watching. "It just locked itself."

"Just locked itself," he repeats, but bends down to kiss her glossy forehead nevertheless. She is a small woman whose skin tends toward olive and looks tight, as if something swelling inside is straining against her littleness. Just yesterday, it seems to him, she stopped being pretty. With the addition of two short wrinkles at the corners, her mouth has become greedy; and her hair has thinned, so he keeps thinking of her skull under it. These tiny advances into age have occurred imperceptibly, so it seems just possible that tomorrow they'll be gone and she'll be his girl again. He makes a stab at kidding her into it. "Whaddeya afraid of ?

Whodeya think's gonna come in that door? Errol Flynn?"

She doesn't answer. Carefully he unfolds his coat and goes to the closet with it and takes out a wire hanger. The closet is in the living room and the door only opens halfway, since the television set is in front of it. He is careful not to kick the wire, which is plugged into a socket on the other side of the door. One time Janice, who is especially clumsy when pregnant or drunk, got the wire wrapped around her foot and nearly pulled the set, a hundred and forty-nine dollars, down *smash* on the floor. Luckily he got to it while it was still rocking in the metal cradle and before Janice began kicking out in one of her panics. What made her get that way? What was she afraid of? An order-loving man, he deftly inserts the corners of the hanger into the armholes of the coat and with his long reach hangs it on the painted pipe with his other clothes. He wonders if he should remove the Demonstrator badge from the lapel but decides he will wear the same suit tomorrow. He has only two, not counting a dark blue that is too hot for this time of year. He presses the door shut and it clicks but then swings open again an inch or two. Locked doors. It rankles: his hand trembling in the lock like some old wreck and her sitting in here listening to the scratching.

He turns and asks her, "If you're home where's the car? It's not out front."

"It's in front of my mother's. You're in my way."

"In front of your mother's? That's terrific. That's just the frigging place for it."

"What's brought this on?"

"Brought what on?" He moves out of her line of vision and stands to one side.

She is watching a group of children called Mouseketeers perform a musical number in which Darlene is a flower girl in Paris and Cubby is a cop and that smirky squeaky tall kid is a romantic artist. He and Darlene and Cubby and Karen (dressed as an old French lady whom Cubby as a cop helps across the street) dance. Then the commercial shows the seven segments of a Tootsie Roll coming out of the wrapper and turning into the seven letters of "Tootsie." They, too, sing and dance. Still singing, they climb back into the wrapper. It echoes like an echo chamber. Son of a bitch: cute. He's seen it fifty times and this time it turns his stomach. His heart is still throbbing; his throat feels narrow.

Janice asks, "Harry, do you have a cigarette? I'm out."

"Huh? On the way home I threw my pack into a garbage can. I'm giving it up." He wonders how anybody could think of smoking, with his stomach on edge the way it is.

Janice looks at him at last. "You threw it into a garbage can! Holy Mo. You don't drink, now you don't smoke. What are you doing, becoming a saint?"

"Shh."

The big Mouseketeer has appeared, Jimmie, a grown man who wears circular black ears. Rabbit watches him attentively; he respects him. He expects to learn something from him helpful in his own line of work, which is demonstrating a kitchen gadget in several five-and-dime stores around Brewer. He's had the job for four weeks. "Proverbs, proverbs, they're so true," Jimmie sings, strumming his Mouseguitar, "proverbs tell us what to do; proverbs help us all to *bee* – better – Mouse-ke-teers."

Jimmie sets aside his smile and guitar and says straight out through the glass, "Know Thyself, a wise old Greek once said. Know Thyself. Now what does this mean, boys and girls? It means, be what you are. Don't try to be Sally or Johnny or Fred next door; be yourself. God doesn't want a tree to be a waterfall, or a flower to be a stone. God gives to each one of us a special talent." Janice and Rabbit become unnaturally still; both are Christians. God's name makes them feel guilty. "God wants some of us to become scientists, some of us to become artists, some of us to become firemen and doctors and trapeze artists. And He gives to each of us the special talents to become these things, *provided we work to develop them*. We must *work*, boys and girls. So: Know Thyself. Learn to understand your talents, and then work to develop them. That's the way to be happy." He pinches his mouth together and winks.

That was good. Rabbit tries it, pinching the mouth together and then the wink, getting the audience out front with you against some enemy behind, Walt Disney or the MagiPeel Peeler Company, admitting it's all a fraud but, what the hell, making it likable. We're all in it together. Fraud makes the world go round.

The base of our economy. Vitaconomy, the modern housewife's password, the one-word expression for economizing vitamins by the MagiPeel Method.

Janice gets up and turns off the set when the six-o'clock news tries to come on. The little hard star left by the current slowly dies.

Rabbit asks, "Where's the kid?"

"At your mother's."

"At *my* mother's? The car's at your mother's and the kid's at my mother's. Jesus. You're a mess."

She stands up and her pregnancy infuriates him with its look of stubborn lumpiness. She wears one of those maternity skirts with a U cut in the belly. A white crescent of slip shines under the hem of her blouse. "I was tired."

"No wonder," he says. "How many of those have you had?" He gestures at the Old-fashioned glass. Sugar has stained the side she drank from.

She tries to explain. "I left Nelson at your mother's on my way to my mother's to go into town with her. We went in in her car and walked around looking at the spring clothes in the windows and she bought a nice Liberty scarf at Kroll's at a sale. Purply Paisley." She falters; her little narrow tongue pokes between her parted lips.

He feels frightened. When confused, Janice is a frightening person. Her eyes dwindle in their frowning sockets and her little mouth hangs open in a dumb slot. Since her hair has begun to thin back from her shiny forehead, he keeps getting the feeling of her being brittle, and immovable, of her only going one way, toward deeper wrinkles and skimpier hair. He married relatively late, when he was twenty-three and she was two years out of high school, still scarcely adult, with shy small breasts that when she lay down flattened against her chest so that they were only there as a tipped softness. Nelson was born seven months after the Episcopal service, in prolonged labor: Rabbit's fright then mixes with his fright now and turns it tender. "What did you buy?"

"A bathing suit."

"A bathing suit! Chh. In March?"

She closes her eyes for a moment; he can feel the undertow of liquor sweep over her and is disgusted. "It made it seem closer to when I could fit into it."

"What the hell ails you? Other women *like* being pregnant. What's so damn fancy about you? Just tell me. What *is* so frigging fancy?"

She opens her brown eyes and tears fill them and break over the lower lids and drop down her cheeks, pink with injury, while she looks at him and says "You bastard" very thoughtfully.

Rabbit goes to his wife and, putting his arms around her, has a vivid experience of her – her tear-hot breath, the blood-tinged white of her eyes. In an affectionate reflex he dips his knees to bring his loins against her, but her solid belly prevents him. He straightens to his full height above her and says, "O.K. You bought a bathing suit."

Sheltered by his chest and arms she blurts with an earnestness he didn't know she still could hold, "Don't run from me, Harry. I love you."

"I love *you*. Now come on, you bought a bathing suit."

"Red," she says, rocking sadly against him. But her body when tipsy has a brittleness, an unconnectedness, that feels disagreeable in his arms. "With a strap that ties behind your neck and a pleated skirt you can take off for the water. Then my varicose veins hurt so much Mother and I went into the basement of Kroll's and had chocolate sodas. They've redone the whole luncheonette section, the counter isn't there any more. But my legs still hurt so Mother brought me home and said you could pick up the car and Nelson. I thought a drink might help the pain."

"Hnuh."

"I thought you'd be home before now. Where were you?"

"Oh, clowning around. I played ball with some kids down the alley." The couple has parted.

"I tried to take a nap but I couldn't. Mother said I looked tired."

"You're supposed to look tired. You're a modern housewife."

"And meanwhile you're off in the alley playing like a twelve-year-old?"

It gripes him that she didn't see his crack about being a house-wife, based on the "image" the MagiPeel people tried to have their salesmen sell to, as ironical and at bottom pitying and fond. There seems no escaping it: she is dumb. He says, "Well what's the difference if you're sitting here watching a program for kids under two?"

"Who was *shushing* a while ago?"

"Ah, Janice." He sighs. "Screw you. Just screw you."

She looks at him clearly a long moment. "I'll get supper," she at last decides.

He is all repentance. "I'll run over and get the car and bring the kid back. The poor kid must think he has no home. What the hell makes your mother think my mother has nothing better to do than take care of other people's kids?" Indignation rises in him again at her missing the point of why he wanted to watch Jimmie, for professional reasons – to earn a living to buy sugar for her to put into her rotten old Old-fashioneds.

She moves into the kitchen, angry but not angry enough. She should be really sore, or not sore at all, since all he had said was what he has done a couple hundred times. Say, on the average once every three days for three years. What's that? Three hundred. That often? Then why is it always a struggle? She used to make it easier before they got married. She could be sudden then. Just a girl. Nerves like new thread. Skin smelled like fresh cotton. Her girlfriend at work had an apartment in Brewer they used. Pipe-frame bed, silver medallions in the wallpaper; a view westward of the great blue gas tanks by the edge of the river. After work, working both at Kroll's then, she selling candy and cashews in a white smock with "Jan" stitched on her pocket and he lugging easy chairs and maple end tables around on the floor above, hammering apart packing crates from nine to five, the itch of the packing excelsior getting into his nose and eyes and making them burn. That filthy black crescent of bins behind the elevators, the floor covered with bent nails, his palms black and Chandler the fairy mincing in every hour on the hour telling him to wash his hands so he wouldn't foul the furniture. Lava soap. Its lather was gray. His hands grew yellow calluses from using the crowbar. After 5:30, the dirty day done, they would meet by the doors, chained to keep customers out, a green-glass-paved chamber of silence between the two sets of doors, in the shallow side windows the bodiless mannequin heads in their feathered hats and necklaces of pink pearls eavesdropping on the echoing farewell gossip. Every employee hated Kroll's, yet they left it slow as swimming. Janice and Rabbit would meet in this chamber, with the dim light and green floor like something underwater, and push at the one unchained door, push up into the light, and walk, never admitting they were going there, toward the silver medallions, hand in hand tired walking gently against the current of home-going traffic, and make love with the late daylight coming level in the window. She was shy about him seeing her. She made him keep his eyes shut. And then with a shiver come as soon as he was in, her inside softly grainy, like a silk slipper. Lying side by side on this other girl's bed, feeling lost, having done the final thing; the wall's silver and the fading day's gold.

The kitchen is a small room off the living room, a tight aisle between machines that were modern five years ago. She drops something metal, a pan or cup. "Think you can make it without burning yourself?" he calls in.

"Are you still here?" is the answer.

He goes to the closet and takes out the coat he hung up so neatly. It seems to him he's the only person around here who cares about neatness. The clutter behind him in the room – the Old-fashioned glass with its corrupt dregs, the chock-full ashtray balanced on the easy-chair arm, the rumpled rug, the floppy stacks of slippery newspapers, the kid's toys here and there broken and stuck and jammed, a leg off a doll and a piece of bent cardboard that went with some breakfast-box cutout, the rolls of fuzz under the radiators, the continual crisscrossing mess – clings to his back like a tightening net. He tries to sort out picking up his car and then his kid. Or should he pick up the kid first? He wants more to see the kid. It would be quicker to walk over to Mrs. Springer's, she lived closer. But suppose she was watching out the window for him to come so she could pop out and tell him how tired Janice looked? *Who wouldn't be tired after tramping around trying to buy something with you you miserable nickel-hugger? You fat hag. You old gypsy.* If he had the kid along this might not happen. Rabbit likes the idea of walking up from his mother's place with his boy. Two-and-a-half, Nelson walks like a trooper, with choppy stubborn steps. They'd walk along under the trees and then like magic there would be Daddy's car at a curb. But it will take longer this way, what with his own mother talking slyly and roundabout about how incompetent Janice is. He hated it when his mother went on like that; maybe she did it just to kid him, but he couldn't take her lightly, she was somehow too powerful, at least with him. He had better go for the car first and pick the kid up with it. But he doesn't want to do it this way. He just doesn't. The problem knits in front of him and he feels sickened by the intricacy.

Janice calls from the kitchen, "And honey pick up a pack of cigarettes, could you?" in a normal voice that says everything is forgiven, everything is the same.

Rabbit freezes, standing looking at his faint yellow shadow on the white door that leads to the hall, and senses he is in a trap. It seems certain. He goes out.

Outdoors it is growing dark and cool. The Norway maples exhale the smell of their sticky new buds and the broad living-room windows along Wilbur Street show beyond the silver patch of a television set the warm bulbs burning in kitchens, like fires at the backs of caves. He walks downhill. The day is gathering itself in. He now and then touches with his hand the rough bark of a tree or the dry twigs of a hedge, to give himself the small answer of a texture. At the corner, where Wilbur Street meets Potter Avenue, a mailbox stands leaning in twilight on its concrete post. Tall two-petaled street sign, the cleat-gouged trunk of the telephone pole holding its insulators against the sky, fire hydrant like a golden bush: a grove. He used to love to climb the poles. To shinny up from a friend's shoulders until the ladder of spikes came to your hands, to get up to where you could hear the wires sing. Their song was a terrifying motionless whisper. It always tempted you to fall, to let the hard spikes in your palms go and feel the space on your back, feel it take your feet and ride up your spine as you fell. He remembers how hot your hands felt at the top, rubbed full of splinters from getting up to where the spikes began. Listening to the wires as if you could hear what people were saying, what all that secret adult world was about. The insulators giant blue eggs in a windy nest.

As he walks along Potter Avenue the wires at their silent height strike into and through the crowns of the breathing maples. At the next corner, where the water from the ice plant used to come down, sob into a drain, and reappear on the other side of the street, Rabbit crosses over and walks beside the gutter where the water used to run, coating the shallow side of its course with ribbons of green slime waving and waiting to slip under your feet and dunk you if you dared walk on them. He can remember falling in but not why he was walking along this slippery edge in the first place. Then he remembers. To impress the girls – Lotty Bingaman, Margaret Schoelkopf, sometimes Barbara Cobb and Mary Hoyer – he walked home from grade school with. Margaret's nose would often start bleeding, for no reason. She had had so much life. Her father was a drunk and her parents had made her wear high-laced shoes long after everybody else had stopped.

He turns down Kegerise Street, a narrow gravel alley curving past the blank back side of a small box factory where mostly middle-aged women work, the cement-block face of a wholesale beer outlet, and a truly old stone farmhouse, now boarded up, one of the oldest buildings in town, thick crude masonry of Indianskin sandstone. This farmhouse, which once commanded half of the acreage the town is now built on, still retains, behind a shattered and vandalized fence, its yard, a junkheap of brown stalks and eroded timber that will in the summer bloom with an unwanted wealth of weeds, waxy green wands and milky pods of silk seeds and airy yellow heads almost liquid with pollen.

So there is some space between the old stone house and the Sunshine Athletic Association, a tall thin brick building like a city tenement misplaced in this disordered alley of back sides and left-overs. The entrance is made ominous by a strange shed, the size of an outhouse, erected each winter across the door, to protect the bar from the weather. Rabbit has several times entered the club. There was no sunshine in it. The first floor was a bar and the second was full of card tables where the old bucks of the town sat muttering strategically. Alcohol and cards Rabbit both associates with a depressing kind of sin, sin with bad breath, and he was further depressed by the political air of the place. His old basketball coach, Marty Tothero, who before scandal had ousted him from the high school had a certain grip on local affairs, lived in this building supposedly and still, they said, manipulated. Rabbit dislikes manipulation but he had liked Tothero. Next to his mother Tothero had had the most *force*.

The thought of his old coach crouching in there frightens him. He walks on, past a body shop and an unused chicken house. His progress is always down, for the town of Mt. Judge is built on the east side of the mountain Mt. Judge, whose west face overlooks the city of Brewer. Though the town and the city meet along the highway that skirts the mountain on the south on the way to Philadelphia fifty miles away, they will never merge, for between them the mountain lifts a broad green spine, two miles long north to south, assaulted by gravel pits and cemeteries and new developments but above a line preserved, hundreds of acres of forest Mt. Judge boys can never wholly explore. Much of it is penetrated by the sound of cars climbing the scenic drives in second gear. But in long patches of forgotten pine plantation the needle-hushed floor of land glides up and up, on and on, under endless tunnels of dead green and you seem to have passed through silence into something worse. And then, coming upon a patch of sunlight the branches neglect to keep out or upon a softened stone-filled cellar pit dug by some brave and monstrous settler centuries ago, you become vividly frightened, as if this other sign of life will call attention to yourself, and the menace of the trees will become active. Your fear trills like an alarm bell you cannot shut off, the louder the faster you run, hunchbacked, until distinctly, with a gasp of the clutch, a near car shifts gears, and the stumpy white posts of the guard fence dawn behind the pine trunks. Then, safe on the firm blacktop, you can decide whether to walk back down home or to hike up to the Pinnacle Hotel for a candy bar and a view of Brewer spread out below like a carpet, a red city, where they paint wood, tin, even red bricks red, an orange rose flowerpot red that is unlike the color of any other city in the world yet to the children of the county is the only color of cities, the color all cities are.

The mountain brings dusk early to the town. Now, just a few minutes after six a day before the vernal equinox, all the houses and gravel-roofed factories and diagonal hillside streets are in the shadow that washes deep into the valley of farmland east of the mountain. Huts on the shadow's shore, twin rows of ranch-houses blare from their picture windows the reflection of the setting sun. One by one, as suddenly as lamps, these windows dim as the sunlight ebbs, drawing across the development and across the tan fenced land waiting for planting and a golf course that at the distance could be a long pasture except for the yellow beans of sand, which are traps. Rabbit pauses at the end of the alley, where he has an open view. He used to caddy over there.

Pricked by an indefinite urgency, he turns away, going left on Jackson Road, where he lived for twenty years. His parents' home is in a two-family brick house on the corner; but it is their neighbors, the Bolgers, who had the corner half, with a narrow side yard Mrs. Angstrom had always envied. *The Bolgers' windows getting all that light and here we sit wedged in.*

Rabbit stealthily approaches his old home on the grass, hopping the little barberry hedge and the wire meant to keep kids on the pavement. He sneaks down the strip of grass between the two cement walks that go with the two brick walls; he used to live behind the one and the Zims behind the other. All day long Mrs. Zim, who was plain, with big thyroid eyes and bluish, slack skin, screamed at her daughter Carolyn, who was prettier than a five-year-old girl had a right to be. Mr. Zim was a thick-lipped red-head, and in Carolyn thick and thin, red and blue, health and high-strungness had blended just right; her precocious beauty was like something that had happened elsewhere, in France or Persia or Heaven. Even Harry, six years older and blind to girls, could see this. All day long Mrs. Zim screamed at her and when Mr. Zim came home from work the two of them would shout together for hours. It would begin with Mr. defending the little girl, and then as the neighbors listened old wounds opened like complicated flowers in the night. Sometimes Mom said that Mr. would murder Mrs., sometimes she said that the little girl would murder them both, as they lay asleep. It was true there was something cold-blooded about Carolyn; when she reached school age, she never left the house without a smile on her smart little face, swinging herself along like she owned the world, though the

Angstroms had just heard her mother throw hysterics at her all through breakfast, the kitchen windows not six feet apart. *How does that poor man endure? If Carolyn and her mother don't settle their differences they're going to wake up some fair morning without a protector.* But Mom was never proved right in any of her predictions. When the Zims left, it was together, Mr. and Mrs. and Carolyn, vanishing in a station wagon while half their furniture still stood on the sidewalk beside the mover's truck. He had a new job in Cleveland, Ohio. Poor souls, they won't be missed. But they were. They had sold their half-house to an old couple, strict Methodists, and the old man refused to cut the strip of grass between his house and the Angstroms'. Mr. Zim, who worked outdoors rain or shine on weekends, *as if it's his only pleasure in life and I don't wonder*, had always cut it. The old Methodist cut exactly his half, one swath of a lawnmower, and then pushed his lawnmower back inverted on his own walk, when it would have been just as easy to push it back along the other half of the strip and not leave such a ridiculous job. *When I hear that old fool's wheels rattle along his walk so self-righteously, my blood pressure goes up so I hear my ears pop.* Mother refused to let him or his father mow their half for one whole summer, and the grass grew knee-high in that little sunless space and stalks of like wheat came up and one or two goldenrod until a man from the town came around in August and said they must cut it on account of an ordinance; he was sorry. Harry had gone to the door and was saying, Sure, O.K., when Mother came up behind him saying, What did he mean? That was her flowerbed. She had no intention of letting it be destroyed. As her son, Rabbit felt terribly embarrassed. The man just looked at her and got a little thumbed book out of his hip pocket and showed her the ordinance. She still said it was her flowerbed. The man read to her what the fine was and went off the porch. That Saturday when she was in Brewer shopping, Pop got the sickle out of the garage and chopped all the weeds down and Harry pushed the lawnmower back and forth across the stubble until it looked as trim as the Methodist's half, though browner. He felt guilty doing it, and was frightened of the fight his parents would have when Mother came back. He dreaded their quarrels: when their faces went angry and flat and words flew, it was as if a pane of glass were put in front

of him, cutting off air; his strength drained away and he had to
go to a far corner of the house. This time there was no fight.
His father shocked him by simply lying, and doubled the shock
by winking as he did it. He told her the Methodist had at last
broken down and cut the strip of grass himself. Mother believed it
but wasn't pleased; she talked all the rest of the day and off and
on all week about suing the old holy-roller. In a way she had
come to think it *was* her flowerbed. From cement to cement
the strip is not much more than eighteen inches across. Walking
along it feels slightly precarious to Harry, like treading the top of
a wall.

He walks back as far as the lit kitchen window and steps onto
the cement without the sole of his shoe scraping and on tiptoe
looks in one bright corner. He sees himself sitting in a high chair,
and a quick odd jealousy comes and passes. It is his son. The boy's
little neck gleams like one more clean object in the kitchen among
the cups and plates and chromium knobs and aluminum cake-
making receptacles on shelves scalloped with glossy oilcloth. His
mother's glasses glitter as she leans in from her place at the table
with a spoon of smoking beans at the end of her fat curved arm.
Her face shows none of the worry she must be feeling about
why nobody comes for the boy and instead is focused, her nose a
faceted beak, into one wish: that the boy eat. Her mouth is tensed
into white crinkles. They smooth in a smile; Nelson's lips, hidden
from Rabbit's angle, must have taken the beans. The
others around the table express praise, blurred syllables from his
father, piercing from his sister, something thin about both voices.
Rabbit, with the intervening glass and the rustle of blood in his
head, can't hear what they say. His father, fresh from work, is in
an ink-smeared blue shirt and, when his face lapses from applaud-
ing his grandson, looks old: tired and grizzled. His throat a loose
bundle of cords. The new teeth he got a year ago have changed
his face, collapsed it a fraction of an inch. Miriam, dolled up in
gold and jet for Friday night, picks at her food indifferently and
offers a spoonful to the kid; the reach of her slender white
braceleted arm across the steaming table rings a barbaric chord into
the scene. She makes up too much; at nineteen she would be good
enough without green eyelids. Because she has slightly buck teeth

she tries not to smile. Nelson's big whorly head dips on its bright neck and his foreshortened hand, dots of pink, dabbles toward the spoon, wants to take it from her. Pop's face lurches into laughter above his plate, and Mim's lips leap in a grin that cracks her cautious wised-up squint and breaks through to the little girl Rabbit used to ride on his handlebars, her streaming hair tickling his eyes as they coasted down the steep Mt. Judge streets. She lets Nelson take her spoon and he drops it. The kid cries "Peel! Peel!": this Rabbit can hear, and understand. It means "spill." Pop and Mim smile and make remarks but Mom, mouth set, comes in grimly with her spoon. Harry's boy is being fed, this home is happier than his, he glides a pace backward over the cement and rewalks the silent strip of grass.

His acts take on decisive haste. In darkness he goes down another block of Jackson. He cuts up Joseph Street, runs a block, strides another, and comes within sight of his car, its grid grinning at him, parked the wrong way on this side of the street. He taps his pocket and fear hits him. He doesn't have the key. Everything depends, the whole pure idea, on which way Janice was sloppy. Either she forgot to give him the key when he went out or she never bothered to take it out of the ignition. He tries to imagine which is more likely and can't. He doesn't know her that well. He never knows what the hell she'll do. She doesn't know herself. Dumb.

The back but not the front of the big Springer house is lit up. He moves cautiously in the sweet-smelling shadows under the trees in case the old lady is waiting inside the darkened living room to tell him what she thinks. He crosses around in front of the car, the '55 Ford that old man Springer with his little sandy Hitler mustache sold him for an even thousand in 1957 because the scared bastard was ashamed, cars being his business he was ashamed of his daughter marrying somebody who had nothing but a '39 Nash he bought for $125 in the Army in Texas in 1953. Made him cough up a thousand he didn't have when the Nash had just had eighty dollars' worth of work. That was the kind of thing. The Springers like to push you around. He opens the car from the passenger side, wincing at the *pung* of the brittle door spring and quickly ducking his head into the car. Praise be. Beneath the knobs for lights and wipers the octagon of the ignition key tells in silhouette. Bless that dope. Rabbit slithers in, closing the side door until metal touches metal but not slamming it. The front of the stucco Springer house is still unlit. It reminds him for some reason of an abandoned ice-cream stand. He turns the key through On into Start and the motor churns and catches. In his anxiety to be secret he is delicate on the accelerator and the motor, idle for hours in the air of winter's last day, is cold, sticks, and stalls. Rabbit's heart rises and a taste of straw comes into his throat. But of course what the hell if old lady Springer *does* come out? The only thing suspicious is that he doesn't have the kid and he can say he's on his way to pick him up. That would have been the logical way to do it anyway. Nevertheless he doesn't want to be put to the inconvenience of lying, however plausibly. He pulls the hand choke out a fraction, just enough to pinch his fingertips, and starts the motor again. He pumps once, and glances aside to see the Springers' living-room light flash on, and lets the clutch out, and the Ford bucks away from the curb.

He drives too fast down Joseph Street, and turns left, ignoring the sign saying STOP. He heads down Jackson to where it runs obliquely into Central, which is also 422 to Philadelphia. STOP. He doesn't want to go to Philadelphia but the road broadens on the edge of town beyond the electric-power station and the only other choice is to go back through Mt. Judge around the mountain into the thick of Brewer and the supper-time traffic. He doesn't intend ever to see Brewer again, that flowerpot city. The highway turns from three-lane to four-lane and there is no danger of hitting another car; they all run along together like sticks on a stream. Rabbit turns on the radio. After a hum a beautiful Negress sings, "Without a song, the dahay would nehever end, without a song." Rabbit wishes for a cigarette to go with his cleaned-out feeling inside and remembers he gave up smoking and feels cleaner still. He slumps down and puts one arm up on the back of the seat and glides on down the twilight pike left-handed. "A field of corn" the Negress's voice bending dark and warm like the inside of a cello "the grasses grow" the countryside dipping around the road like a continuous dark bird "it makes no mind no how" his scalp contracts ecstatically "wihithout a." The smell of parched rubber says the heater has come on and he turns the little lever to MOD.

"Secret Love," "Autumn Leaves," and something whose title he missed. Supper music. Music to cook by. His mind nervously shifts away from the involuntary vision of Janice's meal sizzling in the pan, chops probably, the grease-tinted water bubbling disconsolately, the unfrozen peas steaming away their vitamins. He tries to think of something pleasant. He imagines himself about to shoot a long one-hander; but he feels he's on a cliff, there is an abyss he will fall into when the ball leaves his hands. He tries to repicture his mother and sister feeding his son, but the boy is crying in backward vision, his forehead red and his mouth stretched wide and his helpless breath hot. There must be something: the water from the ice plant running in the gutter, yellowish, the way it curled on pebbles and ran in diagonal wrinkles, waving the fragile threads of slime attached to its edges. Suddenly Janice shivers in memory on the other girl's bed in declining daylight. He tries to blot out the sensation with Miriam, Mim on his handlebars, Mim on a sled in dark snowfall being pulled up Jackson Street by him, the little kid laughing in her hood, himself the big brother, the red lights in snowfall marking the trestles the town crew have used to block off the street for sledding, down, down, the runners whistling on the dark packed slick, *Hold me Harry*, the sparks as the runners hit the cinders spread at the bottom for safety, the scraping stop like the thump of a great heart in the dark. *Once more Harry, then we'll go home, I promise Harry, please, oh I love you*, little Mim only seven or so, in her dark hood, the street waxy with snow still falling. Poor Janice would probably have the wind up now, on the phone to her mother or his mother, somebody, wondering why her supper was getting cold. So dumb. Forgive me.

He accelerates. The growing complexity of lights threatens him. He is being drawn into Philadelphia. He hates Philadelphia. Dirtiest city in the world, they live on poisoned water, you can taste the chemicals. He wants to go south, down, down the map into orange groves and smoking rivers and barefoot women. It seems simple enough, drive all night through the dawn through the morning through the noon park on a beach take off your shoes and fall asleep by the Gulf of Mexico. Wake up with the stars above perfectly spaced in perfect health. But he is going east, the worst direction, into unhealth, soot, and stink, a smothering hole where you can't move without killing somebody. Yet the highway sucks him on, and a sign says POTTSTOWN 2. He almost brakes. But then he thinks.

If he is heading east, south is on his right. And then, as if the world were just standing around waiting to serve his thoughts, a broad road to the right is advertised, ROUTE 100 WEST CHESTER WILMINGTON. Route 100 has a fine ultimate sound. He doesn't want to go to Wilmington but it's the right direction. He's never been to Wilmington. The du Ponts own it. He wonders what it's like to make it to a du Pont.

He doesn't drive five miles before this road begins to feel like a part of the same trap. The first road offered him he turns right on. A keystone marker in the headlights says 23. A good number. The first varsity game he played in he made 23 points. A sophomore and a virgin. Trees overshadow this narrower road.

A barefoot du Pont. Brown legs probably, bitty birdy breasts. Beside a swimming pool in France. Something like money in a naked woman, deep, millions. You think of millions as being white. Sink all the way in softly still lots left. Rich girls frigid? Nymphomaniacs? Must vary. Just women after all, descended from some old Indian-cheater luckier than the rest, inherit the same stuff if they lived in a slum. Glow all the whiter there, on drab mattresses. That wonderful way they have of coming forward around you when they want it. Otherwise just fat weight. Funny how the passionate ones are often tight and dry and the slow ones wet. They want you up and hard on their little ledge. The thing is play them until just a touch. You can tell: their skin under the fur gets all loose like a puppy's neck.

Route 23 works west through little tame country towns, Coventryville, Elverson, Morgantown. Rabbit likes these. Square high farmhouses nuzzle the road. Soft chalk sides. In one town a tavern blazes and he stops at a hardware store opposite with two gasoline pumps outside. He knows from the radio it's about seven-thirty, but the hardware store is still open, shovels and seeders and post-hole diggers and axes blue and orange and yellow in the window, along with some fishing rods and a string of fielder's gloves.

A middle-aged man comes out in boots, baggy suntans, and two flannel shirts. "Yes *sir*," he says, coming down on the second word with forced weight, like a lame man stepping.

"Couldya fill it up with regular?"

The man starts to pump it in and Rabbit gets out of the car and goes around to the back and asks, "How far am I from Brewer?"

The farmer looks up with a look of curt distrust from listening to the gas gurgle. He lifts a finger. "Back up and take that road and it's sixteen miles to the bridge."

Sixteen. He has driven forty miles to get sixteen miles away.

But it was far enough, this was another world. It smells differently, smells older, of nooks and pockets in the ground that nobody's poked into yet. "Suppose I go straight?"

"That'll take you to Churchtown."

"What's after Churchtown?"

"New Holland. Lancaster."

"Do you have any maps?"

"Son, where do you want to go?"

"Huh? I don't know exactly."

"Where are you headed?" The man is patient. His face at the same time seems fatherly and crafty and stupid.

For the first time, Harry realizes he is a criminal. He hears the gasoline rise in the neck of the tank and notices with what care the farmer squeezes every drop he can into the tank without letting it slosh over the lip insolently the way a city garageman would. Out here a drop of gas isn't supposed to escape and he's in the middle of it at night. Laws aren't ghosts in this country, they walk around with the smell of earth on them. Senseless fear cakes over Rabbit's body.

"Check the oil?" the man asks after hanging up the hose on the side of the rusty pump, one of the old style, with the painted bubble head.

"No. Wait. Yeah. You better had. Thanks." Simmer down. All he'd done was ask for a map. Damn dirtdigger – what was so suspicious about that? Somebody was always going somewhere. He better get the oil checked because he wasn't going to stop again until he was halfway to Georgia. "Hey, how far is Lancaster south of here?"

"Due south? Don't know. It's about twenty-five miles on the road. Your oil's all right. You think you're going to Lancaster now?"

"Yeah, I might."

"Check your water?"

"No. It's O.K."

"Battery?"

"It's great. Let's go."

The man lets the hood slam down and smiles over at Harry. "That's three-ninety on the gas, young fella": the words are pronounced in that same heavy cautious crippled way.

Rabbit puts four ones in his hand, which is stiff and crusted and has fingernails that remind you of those old shovels you see worn into weird shapes. The farmer disappears into the hardware store; maybe he's phoning the state cops. He acts like he knows something, but how could he? Rabbit itches to duck into the car and drive off. To steady himself he counts the money left in his wallet. Seventy-three; today was payday. Fingering so much lettuce strengthens his nerves. Switching off the lights in the hardware store as he comes, the farmer comes back with the dime and no map. Harry cups his hand for the dime and the man pushes it in with his broad thumb and says, "Looked around inside and the only road map is New York State. You don't want to go that way, do you now?"

"No," Rabbit answers, and walks to his car door. He feels through the hairs on the back of his neck the man following him. He gets into the car and slams the door and the farmer is right there, the meat of his face hung in the open door window. He bends down and nearly sticks his face in. His cracked thin lips with a scar tilting toward his nose move thoughtfully. He's wearing glasses, a scholar. "The only way to get somewhere, you know, is to figure out where you're going before you go there."

Rabbit catches a whiff of whisky. He says in a level way, "I don't think so." The lips and spectacles and black hairs poking out of the man's tear-shaped nostrils show no surprise. Rabbit pulls out, going straight. Everybody who tells you how to act has whisky on their breath.

He drives to Lancaster and all the way his good airy feeling inside is spoiled. That that guy didn't know a thing but was just half-crocked makes the whole region seem sinister. Outside of Churchtown he passes an Amish buggy in the dark and catches a glimpse of a bearded man and a woman in black in this horsedrawn shadow glaring like devils. The beard inside the buggy like hairs in a nostril. He tries to think of the good life these people lead, of the way they keep clear of all this phony business, this twentieth-century vitamin racket, but in his head they stay devils, risking getting killed trotting along with one dim pink reflector behind, hating Rabbit and his kind, with their big furry tail lights. Who they think they were? He can't shake them, mentally. They never appeared in his rear-view mirror. He passed them and there was nothing. It was just that one sideways glance; the woman's face a hatchet of smoke in the square shadow. Tall coffin lined with hair clopping along to the tune of a dying horse. Amish overworked their animals, he knew. Fanatics. Hump their women standing up, out in the fields, wearing clothes, just hoist black skirts and there it was, nothing underneath. No underpants. Fanatics. Worship manure.

The rich earth seems to cast its darkness upward into the air. The farm country is somber at night. He is grateful when the lights of Lancaster merge with his dim beams. He stops at a diner whose clock says 8:04. He hadn't intended to eat until he got out of the state. He takes a map from the rack by the door and while eating two hamburgers at the counter studies his position. He is in Lancaster, surrounded by funny names, Bird in Hand, Paradise, Intercourse, Mt. Airy, Mascot. They probably didn't seem funny if you lived in them. Like Mt. Judge. You get used. A town has to be called something.

Bird in Hand, Paradise: his eyes keep going back to this dainty lettering on the map. He has an impulse, amid the oil-filmed shimmer of this synthetic and desultory diner, to drive there. Little plump women, toy dogs in the street, candy houses in lemon sunshine.

But no, his goal is the white sun of the south like a great big pillow in the sky. And from the map he's been travelling more west than south; if the dirtdigger back there had had a map he could have gone due south on 10. Now the only thing to do is go

into the heart of Lancaster and take 222 out and take it all the way
down into Maryland and then catch 1. He remembers reading in
the *Saturday Evening Post* how 1 goes from Florida to Maine
through the most beautiful scenery in the world. He asks for a glass
of milk and to go with it a piece of apple pie; the crust is crisp and
bubbled and they've had the sense to use cinnamon. His mother's
pies always had cinnamon. He pays by cracking a ten and goes out
into the parking lot feeling pleased. The hamburgers had been
fatter and warmer than the ones you get in Brewer, and the buns
had seemed steamed. Things are better already.

It takes him a half-hour to pick his way through Lancaster. On
222 he drives south through Refton, Hessdale, New Providence,
and Quarryville, through Mechanics Grove and Unicorn and then
a long stretch so dull and unmarked he doesn't know he's entered
Maryland until he hits Oakwood. On the radio he hears "No
Other Arms, No Other Lips," "Stagger Lee," a commercial for
Rayco Clear Plastic Seat Covers, "If I Didn't Care" by Connie
Francis, a commercial for Radio-Controlled Garage Door
Operators, "I Ran All the Way Home Just to Say I'm Sorry,"
"That Old Feeling" by Mel Torme, a commercial for Big Screen
Westinghouse TV Set with One-finger Automatic Tuning,
"needle-sharp pictures a nose away from the screen," "The Italian
Cowboy Song," "Yep" by Duane Eddy, a commercial for
Papermate Pens, "Almost Grown," a commercial for Tame
Cream Rinse, "Let's Stroll," news (President Eisenhower and
Prime Minister Harold Macmillan begin a series of talks in
Gettysburg, Tibetans battle Chinese Communists in Lhasa, the
whereabouts of the Dalai Lama, spiritual ruler of this remote and
backward land, are unknown, a $250,000 trust fund has been left
to a Park Avenue maid, Spring scheduled to arrive tomorrow),
sports news (Yanks over Braves in Miami, somebody tied with
somebody in St. Petersburg Open, scores in a local basketball
tournament), weather (fair and seasonably warm), "The Happy
Organ," "Turn Me Loose," a commercial for Schuylkill Life
Insurance, "Rocksville, P-A" (Rabbit loves it), "A Picture No
Artist Could Paint," a commercial for New Formula Barbasol
Presto-Lather, whose daily cleansing action tends to prevent skin
blemishes and emulsifies something, "Pink Shoe Laces" by Dody

Stevens, a word about a little boy called Billy Tessman who was hit by a car and would appreciate cards or letters, "Petit Fleur," "Fungo" (great), a commercial for Wool-Tex All-Wool Suits, "Fall Out" by Henry Mancini, "Everybody Like to Do the Cha Cha Cha," a commercial for Lord's Grace Table Napkins and the gorgeous Last Supper Tablecloth, "The Beat of My Heart," a commercial for Speed-Shine Wax and Lanolin Clay, "Venus," and then the same news again. Where is the Dalai Lama?

Shortly after Oakwood he comes to Route 1, which with its hot-dog stands and Calso signs and roadside taverns aping log cabins is unexpectedly discouraging. The farther he drives the more he feels some great confused system, Baltimore now instead of Philadelphia, reaching for him. He stops at a gas station for two dollars' worth of regular. What he really wants is another map. He unfolds it standing by a Coke machine and reads it in the light coming through a window stained green by stacked cans of liquid wax.

His problem is to get west and free of Baltimore-Washington, which like a two-headed dog guards the coastal route to the south. He doesn't want to go down along the water anyway; his image is of himself going right down the middle, right into the broad soft belly of the land, surprising the dawn cottonfields with his northern plates.

Now he is somewhere here. Further on, then, a road numbered 23 will go off to his left – no, his right. That goes up and over and back into Pennsylvania but at this place, Shawsville, he can take a little narrow blue road without a number. Then go down a little and over again on 137. There is a ragged curve then that this road makes with 482 and then 31. Rabbit can feel himself swinging up and through that curve into the red line numbered 26 and down that into another numbered 340. Red, too; he is really gliding and suddenly sees where he wants to go. Over on the left three red roads stream parallel northeast to southwest; Rabbit can just feel them sliding down through the valleys of the Appalachians. Get on one of them it would be a chute dumping you into sweet low cottonland in the morning. Yes. Once he gets on that he can shake all thoughts of the mess behind him.

He gives two dollars for gas to the attendant, a young but tall colored boy whose limber lazy body slumping inside his baggy Amoco coveralls Rabbit has a weird impulse to hug. This far south the air already feels warmed. Warmth vibrates in brown and purple arcs between the lights of the service station and the moon. The clock in the window above the green cans of liquid wax says 9:10. The thin red second hand sweeps the numbers calmly and makes Rabbit's way seem smooth. He ducks into the Ford and in that fusty hot interior starts to murmur, "Ev, reebody loves the, cha cha cha."

He drives bravely at first. Over blacktop and whitetop, through towns and fields, past false intersections with siren voices, keeping the map on the seat beside him, keeping the numbers straight and resisting the impulse to turn blindly south. Something animal in him knows he is going west.

The land grows wilder. The road evades great lakes and tunnels through pines. In the top of the windshield the telephone wires continually whip the stars. The music on the radio slowly freezes; the rock and roll for kids cools into old standards and show tunes and comforting songs from the Forties. Rabbit pictures married couples driving home to babysitters after a meal out and a movie. Then these melodies turn to ice as real night music takes over, pianos and vibes erecting clusters in the high brittle octaves and a clarinet wandering across like a crack on a pond. Saxes doing the same figure eight over and over again. He drives through Westminster. It takes forever to reach Frederick. He picks up 340 and crosses the Potomac.

Growing sleepy, Rabbit stops before midnight at a roadside café for coffee. Somehow, though he can't put his finger on the difference, he is unlike the other customers. They sense it too, and look at him with hard eyes, eyes like little metal studs pinned into the white faces of young men sitting in zippered jackets in booths three to a girl, the girls with orange hair hanging like wiggly seaweed or loosely bound with gold barrettes like pirate treasure. At the counter middle-aged couples in overcoats bunch their faces forward into the straws of gray ice-cream sodas. In the hush his entrance creates, the excessive courtesy the weary woman behind the counter shows him amplifies his strangeness. He orders coffee quietly and studies the rim of the cup to steady the sliding in his stomach. He had thought, he had read, that from shore to shore all America was the same. He wonders, Is it just these people I'm outside or is it all America?

Outside in the sharp air, he flinches when footsteps pound behind him. But it is just two lovers, holding hands and in a hurry to reach their car, their locked hands a starfish leaping through the dark. Their license plate says West Virginia. All the plates do except his. On the other side of the road the wooded land dips down so he can look over the tops of trees at the side of a mountain like a cutout of stiff paper mounted on a slightly faded blue sheet. He climbs into his Ford distastefully, but its stale air is his only haven.

He drives through a thickening night. The road unravels with infuriating slowness, its black wall wearilessly rising in front of his headlights no matter how they twist. The tar sucks his tires. He realizes that the heat on his cheeks is anger; he has been angry ever since he left that diner full of mermaids. So angry his cheeks feel parched inside his mouth and his nostrils water. He grinds his foot down as if to squash this snake of a road, and nearly loses the car on a curve, as the two right wheels fall captive to the dirt shoulder. He brings them back but keeps the speedometer needle leaning to the right of the legal limit.

He turns off the radio; its music no longer seems a river he is riding down but instead speaks with the voice of the cities and brushes his head with slippery hands. Yet into the silence that results he refuses to let thoughts come. He doesn't want to think, he wants to fall asleep and wake up pillowed by sand. How stupid, how frigging, fucking stupid he was, not to be farther than this. At midnight, the night half gone.

The land refuses to change. The more he drives the more the region resembles the country around Mt. Judge. The same scruff on the embankments, the same weathered billboards for the same products you wondered anybody would ever want to buy. At the upper edge of his headlight beams the naked tree-twigs make the same net. Indeed the net seems thicker now.

The animal in him swells its protest that he is going west. His mind stubbornly resists. His plan calls for him to bear left twenty-eight miles after Frederick and that twenty-eight miles is used up now and, though his instincts cry out against it, when a broad road leads off to the left, though it's unmarked, he takes it. It is unlikely that the road *would* be marked, from its thickness on the map. But it is a short cut, he knows. He remembers that when Marty Tothero began to coach him he didn't want to shoot fouls underhand but that it turned out in the end to be the way. There is this quality, in things, of the right way seeming wrong at first.

The road is broad and confident for miles, but there is a sudden patched stretch, and after that it climbs and narrows. Narrows not so much by plan as naturally, the edges crumbling in and the woods on either side crowding down. The road twists more and more wildly in its struggle to gain height and then without warning sheds its skin of asphalt and worms on in dirt. By now Rabbit knows this is not the road but he is afraid to stop the car to turn it around. He has left the last light of a house miles behind. When he strays from straddling the mane of weeds, brambles rake his painted sides. Tree trunks and low limbs are all his headlights pick up; the scrabbling shadows spider backward through the web of wilderness into a black core where he fears his probe of light will stir some beast or ghost. He prays that the road not stop, remembering how on Mt. Judge even the shaggiest most forgotten logging lane eventually sloped to the valley. His ears itch; his height presses on them.

The prayer's answer is blinding. The trees at a far bend leap like flame and a car comes around and flies at him with its beams tilted high. Rabbit slithers over close to the ditch and, faceless as death, the bright car rips by at a speed twice his own. For more than a minute Rabbit drives through this bastard's insulting dust. Yet the good news makes him meek, the news that this road goes two ways. And shortly he seems to be in a park. His lights pick up green little barrels stenciled PLEASE and the trees are thinned on both sides and in among them picnic tables and pavilions and outhouses show their straight edges. The curves of cars show too, and a few are parked close to the road, their passengers down out of sight. So this road of dread is a lovers' lane. In a hundred yards it ends.

It meets at right angles a smooth broad highway overhung by the dark cloud of a mountain ridge. One car zips north. Another zips south. There are no signs. Rabbit puts the shift in neutral and pulls out the emergency brake and turns on the roof light and studies his map. His hands and shins are trembling. His brain flutters with fatigue behind sandy eyelids; the time must be 12:30 or later. The highway in front of him is empty. He has forgotten the numbers of the routes he has taken and the names of the towns he has passed through. He remembers Frederick but can't find it and in time realizes he is searching in a section due west of Washington where he has never been. There are so many red lines and blue lines, long names, little towns, squares and circles and stars. He moves his eyes north but the only line he recognizes is the straight dotted line of the Pennsylvania-Maryland border. The Mason-Dixon Line. The schoolroom in which he learned this recurs to him, the rooted desk rows, the scarred varnish, the milky black of the blackboard, the pieces of tight girlish ass packed all up and down the aisles in alphabetical order. His eyes blankly founder. Rabbit hears a clock in his head beat, monstrously slow, the soft ticks as far apart as the sound of waves on the shore he had wanted to reach. He burns his attention through the film fogging his eyes down into the map again. At once "Frederick" pops into sight, but in trying to steady its position he loses it, and fury makes the bridge of his nose ache. The names melt away and he sees the map whole, a net, all those red lines and blue lines and stars, a net he is somewhere caught in. He claws at it and tears it; with a gasp of exasperation he rips away a great triangular piece and tears the large remnant in half and, more calmly, lays these three pieces on top of each other and tears them in half, and then those six pieces and so on until he has a wad he can squeeze in his hand like a ball. He rolls down the window and throws the ball out; it explodes, and the bent scraps like disembodied wings flicker back over the top of the car. He cranks up the window. He blames everything on that farmer with glasses and two shirts. Funny how the man sticks in his throat. He can't think past him, his smugness, his *solidity*, somehow. He stumbled over him back there and is stumbling still, can't get him away from his feet, like shoelaces too long or a stick between his feet. The man mocked, whether out of his mouth or in the paced motions of his work-worn hands or through his hairy ears, somewhere out of his body he mocked the furtive wordless hopes that at moments give Harry a sensation of arrival. *Figure out where you're going before you go there:* it misses the whole point and yet there is always the chance that, little as it says, it says it. At any rate if he'd trusted to instinct he'd be in South Carolina now. He wishes he had a cigarette, to help him decide what his instinct is. He decides to go to sleep in the car for a few hours.

But a car starts up in the petting grove behind him and the headlights wheel around and press on Rabbit's neck. He stopped his car right in the middle of the road to look at the map. Now he must move. He feels unreasoning fear of being overtaken; the other headlights swell in the rear-view mirror and fill it like a burning cup. He stamps the clutch, puts the shift in first, and releases the handbrake. Hopping onto the highway, he turns instinctively right, north.

The trip home is easier. Though he has no map and hardly any gas, an all-night Mobilgas appears near Hagerstown as if a wizard waved a wand and green signs begin to point to the Pennsylvania Turnpike. The music on the radio is soothing now, lyrical and unadvertised, and, coming first from Harrisburg and then from Philadelphia, makes a beam he infallibly flies in on. He has broken through the barrier of fatigue and come into a calm flat world where nothing matters much. The last quarter of a basketball game used to carry him into this world; you ran not as the crowd thought for the sake of the score but for yourself, in a kind of idleness. There was you and sometimes the ball and then the hole, the high perfect hole with its pretty skirt of net. It was you, just you and that fringed ring, and sometimes it came down right to your lips it seemed and sometimes it stayed away, hard and remote and small. It seemed silly for the crowd to applaud or groan over what you had already felt in your fingers or even in your arms as you braced to shoot or for that matter in your eyes: when he was hot he could see the separate threads wound into the strings looping the hoop. Yet at the start of the game when you came out for warm-up and could see all the town clunkers sitting in the back of the bleachers elbowing each other and the cheerleaders wisecracking with the racier male teachers, the crowd then seemed right inside you, your liver and lungs and stomach. There was one fat guy used to come who'd get on the floor of Rabbit's stomach and really make it shake. *Hey, Gunner! Hey, Showboat, shoot! Shoot!* Rabbit remembers him fondly now; to that guy he had been a hero of sorts.

Throughout the early morning, those little hours that are so black, the music keeps coming and the signs keep pointing. His brain feels like a frail but alert invalid with messengers bringing down long corridors all this music and geographical news. At the same time he feels abnormally sensitive on the surface, as if his skin is thinking. The steering wheel is thin as a whip in his hands. As he turns it lightly he can feel the shaft stiffly pivot, and the differential gears part, and the bearings rotate in their sealed tunnels of grease. The phosphorescent winkers at the side of the road beguile him into thinking of young du Pont women: strings of them winding through huge glassy parties, potentially naked in their sequinned sheath gowns. Are rich girls frigid? He'll never know.

He wonders why there are so many signs coming back and so few going down. Of course he didn't know what he was going toward going down. He takes the Brewer turnoff off the Pike and the road takes him through the town where he first bought gas. As he takes the road marked BREWER 16 he can see cattycornered across the main street the dirtdigger's pumps and his dark window full of glinting shovels and fishing rods. The window looks pleased. There is just a lavender touch of light in the air. The radio's long floe of music is breaking up in warm-weather reports and farm prices.

He comes into Brewer from the south, seeing it in the smoky shadow before dawn as a gradual multiplication of houses among the trees beside the road and then as a treeless waste of industry, shoe factories and bottling plants and company parking lots and knitting mills converted to electronics parts and elephantine gas tanks lifting above trash-filled swampland yet lower than the blue edge of the mountain from whose crest Brewer was a warm carpet woven around a single shade of brick. Above the mountain, stars fade.

He crosses the Running Horse Bridge and is among streets he knows. He takes Warren Avenue through the south side of town and comes out on 422 near City Park. He drives around the mountain in company with a few hissing trailer trucks. Sunrise, an orange strip crushed against a far hill, flares between their wheels. As he turns left from Central into Jackson he nearly sideswipes a milk truck idling yards out from the curb. He continues up Jackson, past his parents' house, and turns into Kegerise Alley. Suddenly cool pink pallor tinges the buildings. He glides past the old chicken house, past the silent body shop, and parks the car in front of the Sunshine Athletic Association, a few steps from the boxed-in entrance, where anyone coming out would have to notice. Rabbit glances up hopefully at the third-story windows but no light shows. Tothero, if he is in there, is still asleep.

Rabbit settles himself to sleep. He takes off his suit coat and lays it over his chest like a blanket. But the daylight is growing, and the front seat is far too short, and the steering wheel crowds his shoulders. He doesn't move to the back seat because that would make him vulnerable; he wants to be able to drive away in a second if he must. Further, he doesn't want to sleep so heavily he will miss Tothero when he comes out.

So there he lies, his long legs doubled and no place for his feet, gazing up with crusty vision across the steering wheel and through the windshield into the sky's renewed flat fresh blue. Today is Saturday, and the sky has that broad bright blunt Saturday quality Rabbit remembers from boyhood, when the sky of a Saturday morning was the blank scoreboard of a long game about to begin. Roofball, box hockey, tether ball, darts . . .

His eyes have closed. A car purrs by, up the alley. The darkness behind his lids vibrates with the incessant automobile noises of the night past. He sees again the woods, the narrow road, the dark grove full of cars each containing a silent couple. He thinks again of his goal, lying down at dawn in sand by the Gulf of Mexico, and it seems in a way that the gritty seat of his car is that sand, and the rustling of the waking town the rustling of the sea.

He must not miss Tothero. He opens his eyes and tries to rise from his stiff shroud. He wonders if he has missed any time. The sky is the same.

He becomes anxious about the car windows. He hoists his chest up on one elbow and checks them all. The window above his head is open a crack and he cranks it tight and pushes down all the lock buttons. This security relaxes him hopelessly. He turns his face into the crack between seat and back. This twisting pushes his knees into the tense upright cushion, an annoyance that for the moment makes him more wakeful. He wonders where his son slept, what Janice has done, where his parents and her parents hunted. Whether the police know. The thought of police for a second paints his mind blue. He feels the faded night he left behind in this place as a net of telephone calls and hasty trips, trails of tears and strings of words, white worried threads shuttled through the night and now faded but still existent, an invisible net overlaying the steep streets and in whose center he lies secure in his locked hollow hutch.

Cotton and gulls in half-light and the way she'd come on the other girl's bed, never as good on their own. But there were good things: Janice so shy about showing her body even in the first weeks of wedding yet one night coming into the bathroom expecting nothing he found the mirror clouded with steam and Janice just out of the shower standing there doped and pleased with a little blue towel lazily and unashamed her bottom bright pink with hot water the way a woman was of two halves bending over and turning and laughing at his expression whatever it was and putting her arms up to kiss him, a blush of steam on her body and the back of her soft neck slippery. Rabbit adjusts his position and returns his mind to its dark socket: the back of her neck slippery, the small of her back pliant, both on their knees together, contortions that never were. His shin knocks the door handle, the pain becoming oddly mixed with the knocks of metal on metal down in the body shop. Work had begun. Eight o'clock? He recognizes elapsed time in the parched puffiness on his lips. He writhes and sits up, the covering coat falling to the car floor, and indeed through the splotched windshield there *is* Tothero, walking away down the alley, up beyond the very old farmhouse. Rabbit jumps from the car, puts on his coat, and runs after him. "Mr. Tothero! Hey Mr. Tothero!" His voice sounds flaked and rusty after hours of disuse.

The man turns, looking stranger than Rabbit had expected. He looks like a big tired dwarf. He seems foreshortened: a balding big head and a massively checkered sports coat and then stubby legs in blue trousers that are too long, so the crease buckles and zig-zags above the shoes. As he brakes his run, and walks the last strides, Rabbit fears he's made a mistake.

But Tothero says the perfect thing. "Harry," he says, "wonderful Harry Angstrom." He puts out his hand for Harry to seize and with the other squeezes the boy's arm in a clasp of rigor. It comes back to Rabbit how he always had his hands on you. Tothero just stands there holding on and looking at him, smiling crookedly, the nose bent, one eye wide open and the other heavy-lidded. His face has grown more lopsided with the years. He is not going bald evenly; brushed strands of gray and pale brown streak the top of his skull.

"I need your advice," Rabbit says, and corrects himself. "What I really need right now is a place to sleep."

Tothero is silent before replying. His great strength is in these silences; he has the disciplinarian's trick of waiting a long moment while his words gather weight. At last he asks, "What's happened to your home?"

"Well, it kind of went."

"How do you mean?"

"It was no good. I've run out. I really have."

Another pause. Rabbit narrows his eyes against the sunlight that rebounds off the asphalt. His left ear aches. His teeth on that side feel as if they might start hurting.

"That doesn't sound like very mature behavior," Tothero says.

"It was a mess as it was."

"What sort of mess?"

"I don't know. My wife's an alcoholic."

"And have you tried to help her?"

"Sure. How?"

"Did you drink with her?"

"No sir, never. I can't stand the stuff, I just don't like the taste." He says this readily, proud to be able to report to his old coach that he has not abused his body.

"Perhaps you should have," Tothero offers after a moment. "Perhaps if you had shared this pleasure with her, she could have controlled it."

Rabbit, dazed by the sun, numb through weariness, can't follow this thought.

"It's Janice Springer, isn't it?" Tothero asks.

"Yeah. God she's dumb. She really is."

"Harry, that's a harsh thing to say. Of any human soul."

Rabbit nods because Tothero himself seems certain of this. He is beginning to feel weak under the weight of the man's pauses. These pauses seem longer than he remembered them, as if Tothero too feels their weight. Fear touches Rabbit again; he suspects his old coach is addled, and begins all over. "I thought maybe I could sleep a couple hours somewhere in the Sunshine. Otherwise I might as well go home. I've had it."

To his relief Tothero becomes all bustling action, taking his elbow, steering him back along the alley, saying, "Yes of course, Harry, you look terrible, Harry. Terrible." His hand holds Rabbit's arm with metallic inflexibility and as he pushes him along Rabbit's bones jolt, pinned at this point. Something frantic in so tight a grip diminishes the comfort of its firmness. Tothero's voice, too, having turned rapid and precise, cuts into Rabbit's woolly state too sharply. "You asked me for two things," he says. "Two things. A place to sleep, and advice. Now, Harry, I'll give you the place to sleep provided, provided, Harry, that when you wake up the two of us have a serious, a long and serious talk about this crisis in your marriage. I'll tell you this now, it's not so much you I'm worried about, I know you well enough to know you always land on your feet, Harry; it's not so much you as Janice. She doesn't have your coördination. Do you promise?"

"Sure. Promise what?"

"Promise, Harry, we'll thrash out a way between us to help her."

"Yeah, but I don't think I can. I mean I'm not that interested in her. I was, but I'm not."

They reach the cement steps and the wooden storm shed at the entrance. Tothero opens the door with a key he has. The place is empty, the silent bar shadowy and the small round tables looking rickety and weak without men sitting at them. The electrical advertisements behind the bar, tubing and tinsel, are unplugged and dead. Tothero says, in a voice too loud, "I don't believe it.

I don't believe that my greatest boy would grow so hard-hearted."

Hard-hearted: the word seems to clatter after them as they climb the stairs to the second floor. Rabbit apologizes: "I'll try to think when I get some sleep."

"Good boy. That's all we want. Try is all we can ask." What does he mean, we? All these tables are empty. Sunlight strikes blond squares into the drawn tan shades above a low radiator dyed black with dust. Men's steps have worn paths in the narrow bare floorboards.

Tothero leads him to a door painted to blend with the wall; they go up a steep flight of attic stairs, a kind of nailed-down ladder between whose steps he sees sections of insulated wire and ragged gaps of carpentry. They climb into light. "Here's my mansion," Tothero says, and fidgets with his coat pocket flaps.

The tiny room faces east. A slash in a window shade throws a long knife of sun on a side wall, above an unmade Army cot. The other shade is up. Between the windows stands a bureau cleverly made of six beer cases wired together, three high and two wide. In the six boxes are arranged shirts in their laundry cellophane, folded undershirts and shorts, socks balled in pairs, handkerchiefs, shined shoes, and a leatherbacked brush with a comb stuck in the bristles. From two thick nails some sport coats, jarringly gay in pattern, are hung on hangers. Tothero's housekeeping stops at caring for his clothes. The floor is dotted with rolls of fluff. Newspapers and all kinds of magazines, from the *National Geographic* to teen-age crime confessions and comic books, are stacked around. The space where Tothero lives merges easily with the rest of the attic, which is storage space, containing old pinochle tournament charts and pool tables and some lumber and metal barrels and broken chairs with cane bottoms and a roll of chicken wire and a rack of softball uniforms, hung on a pipe fixed between two slanting beams and blocking out the light from the window at the far end.

"Is there a men's?" Rabbit asks.

"Downstairs, Harry." Tothero's enthusiasm has died; he seems embarrassed. While Rabbit uses the toilet he can hear the old man fussing around upstairs, but when he returns he can see nothing changed. The bed is still unmade.

Tothero waits and Rabbit waits and then realizes Tothero wants to see him undress and undresses, sliding into the rumpled lukewarm bed in his T-shirt and Jockey shorts. Though the idea is distasteful, getting into the old man's hollow, the sensations are good, being able to stretch out at last and feeling the solid cool wall close to him and hearing cars moving maybe hunting him far below. He twists his neck to say something to Tothero and is surprised by solitude. The door at the foot of the attic steps closes and footsteps diminish down a second flight of stairs, and an outside door closes and a bird cries by the window and the clangor of the body shop comes up softly. The old man's standing there was disturbing but Rabbit is sure that's not his problem. Tothero was always known as a lech but never a queer. Why watch? Suddenly Rabbit knows. It takes Tothero back in time. Because of all the times he had stood in locker rooms watching his boys change clothes. Solving this problem relaxes Rabbit's muscles. He remembers the couple with linked hands running on the parking lot outside the diner in West Virginia and it seems a great loss that it hadn't been him about to nail her, her seaweed hair sprawling. Red hair? There? He imagines West Virginia girls as coarse hard-bodied laughers, like the young whores in Texas. Their sugar drawls always seemed to be poking fun but then he was only nineteen. Coming down the street with Hañley and Jarzylo and Shamberger the tight khaki making him feel nervous and the plains breaking away on all sides the horizon no higher than his knees it seemed and the houses showing families sitting on sofas inside like chickens at roost facing TV's. Jarzylo a maniac, cackling. Rabbit couldn't believe this house was right. It had flowers in the window, actual living flowers innocent in the window and he was tempted to turn and run. Sure enough, the woman who came to the door could have been on television selling cake mix. But she said, "Come on in boys, don't be shaeh, come on in and heyiv a good taam," said it so motherly, and there they were, the hooers, not as many as he had pictured, in the parlor, on old-fashioned-looking furniture with scrolls and knobs. That they were pretty homely made him less timid: just ordinary factory-looking women, you wouldn't even call them girls, with a glaze on their faces like under fluorescent lights. They pelted the soldiers with remarks like pellets of dust and the men sneezed into laughter and huddled together surprised and numb. The one he took, but she took him, came up and touched him, hadn't buttoned her blouse more than one button from the last one and upstairs asked him in her gritty sugar voice if he wanted the light on or off and, when out of a choked throat he answered "Off," laughed, and then now and then smiled under him, working around to get him right, and even speaking kindly: "You're all right, honey. You're gone along all right. Oh yeaas. You've had lessons." So that when it was over he was hurt to learn, from the creases of completion at the sides of her lips and the hard way she wouldn't keep lying beside him but got up and sat on the edge of the metal-frame bed looking out the dark window at the green night sky of Texas, that she had faked her half. Her mute back showing in yellow-white the bar of a swimming-suit bra angered him; he took the ball of her shoulder in his hand and turned her roughly. The weighted shadows of her front hung so careless and undefended he looked away. She said down into his ear, "Honey, you didn't pay to be no two-timer." Sweet woman, *she* was money. The clangor of the body shop comes up softly. Its noise comforts him, tells him he is hidden and safe. While he hides, men are busy nailing the world down, and toward the disembodied sounds his heart makes in darkness a motion of love.

His dreams are shallow, furtive things. His legs switch. His lips move a little against the pillow. The skin of his eyelids shudders as his eyeballs turn, surveying the inner wall of vision. Otherwise he is as dead, beyond harm. The slash of sun on the wall above him slowly knifes down, cuts across his chest, becomes a coin on the floor, and vanishes. In shadow he suddenly awakes, his ghostly blue irises searching the unfamiliar planes for the source of men's voices. These voices are downstairs, and a rumble suggests that they are moving the furniture, tramping in circles, hunting him. But a familiar bulbous basso rings out, it is Tothero, and around this firm center the noises downstairs crystallize as the sounds of card-playing, drinking, horseplay, companionship. Rabbit rolls in his hot hollow and turns his face to his cool companion, the wall, and through a red cone of consciousness falls asleep again.

"Harry! Harry!" The voice is plucking at his shoulder, rumpling his hair. He rolls away from the wall, squinting upward into vanished sunshine. Tothero sits in the shadows, a hulk of darkness dense with some anxiousness. His dirty-milk face leans forward, scarred by a lopsided smile. There is a smell of whisky. "Harry, I've got a girl for you!"

"Great. Bring her in."

The old man laughs, uneasily? What does he mean?

"You mean Janice?"

"It's after six o'clock. Get up, get up, Harry; you've slept like a beautiful baby. We're going out."

"Why?" Rabbit meant to ask "Where?"

"To eat, Harry, to dine. D, I, N, E. Rise, my boy. Aren't you hungry? Hunger. Hunger." He's a madman. "Oh Harry, you can't understand an old man's hunger, you eat and eat and it's never the right food. You can't understand that." He walks to the window and looks down into the alley, his lumpy profile leaden in the dull light.

Rabbit slides back the covers, angles his naked legs over the edge, and holds himself in a sitting position. The sight of his thighs, parallel, pure, aligns his groggy brain. The hair on his legs, once a thin blond fur, is getting dark and whiskery. The odor of his sleep-soaked body rises to him. "Whatsis girl business?" he asks.

"What is it, yes, what is it? Cunt," Tothero exclaims in a stream, and in the gray light by the window his face falls; he seems amazed to hear himself say such an abrupt ugly thing. Yet he's also watching, as if this was some sort of test. The result determined, he corrects himself, "No. I have an acquaintance, an acquaintance in Brewer, a lady-love perhaps, whom I stand to a meal once in a blue moon. But it's nothing more than that, little more than that. Harry, you're so innocent."

Rabbit begins to be afraid of Tothero; these phrases don't follow. He stands up in his underclothes. "I think I just better run along." The floor-fluff sticks to the soles of his bare feet.

"Oh Harry, Harry," Tothero cries in a rich voice mixed of pain and affection, and comes forward and hugs him with one arm.

"You and I are two of a kind." The big lopsided face looks up into his with eager confidence, but Rabbit doesn't understand. Yet his memory of the man as his coach still disposes him to listen. "You and I know what the score is, we know –" And right here, arriving at the kernel of his lesson, Tothero is balked, and becomes befuddled. He repeats, "We know," and removes his arm.

Rabbit says, "I thought we were going to talk about Janice when I woke up." He retrieves his trousers from the floor and puts them on. Their being rumpled disturbs him, reminds him that he has taken a giant step, and makes nervous wrinkles in his stomach and throat.

"We will, we will," Tothero says, "the moment our social obligations are satisfied." A pause. "Do you want to go back now? You must tell me if you do."

Rabbit remembers the dumb slot of her mouth, the way the closet door bumps against the television set. "No. God."

Tothero is overjoyed; it is happiness making him talk so much. "Well then, well then; get dressed. We can't go to Brewer undressed. Do you need a fresh shirt?"

"Yours wouldn't fit me, would it?"

"No, Harry, no? What's your size?"

"Fifteen three."

"Mine! Mine exactly. You have short arms for your height. Oh, this is wonderful, Harry. I can't tell you how much it means to me that you came to me when you needed help. All those years," he says, taking a shirt from the bureau made of beer cases and stripping off the cellophane, "all those years, all those boys, they pass through your hands and into the blue. And never come back, Harry; they never come back."

Rabbit is startled to feel and to see in Tothero's wavy mirror that the shirt fits. Their difference must be all in their legs. With the rattling tongue of a proud mother Tothero watches him dress. His talk makes more sense, now that the embarrassment of explaining what they're going to do is past. "It does my heart good," he says. "Youth before the mirror. How long has it been, Harry, now tell me truly, since you had a good time? A long time?"

"I had a good time last night," Rabbit says. "I drove to West Virginia and back."

"You'll like my lady, I know you will, a city petunia," Tothero goes on. "The girl she's bringing I've never met. She says she's fat. All the world looks fat to my lady – how she eats, Harry: the appetite of the young. That's a fascinating knot, you young people have so many tricks I never learned."

"It's just a Windsor." Dressed, Rabbit feels a return of calm. Waking up had in a way returned him to the world he deserted. He had missed Janice's crowding presence, the kid and his shrill needs, his own walls. He had wondered what he was doing. But now these reflexes, shallowly scratched, are spent, and deeper instincts flood forward, telling him he is right. He feels freedom like oxygen everywhere around him; Tothero is an eddy of air, and the building he is in, the streets of the town, are mere stairways and alleyways in space. He adjusts his necktie with infinite attention, as if the little lines of this juncture of the Windsor knot, the collar of Tothero's shirt, and the base of his own throat were the arms of a star that will, when he is finished, extend outward to the rim of the universe. *He* is the Dalai Lama. Like a cloud breaking in the corner of his vision Tothero drifts to the window. "Is my car still there?" Rabbit asks.

"Your car is blue. Yes. Put on your shoes."

"I wonder if anybody saw it there. While I was asleep, did you hear anything around town?" For in the vast blank of his freedom there remain a few imperfections: his wife, their apartment, their child – clots of concern. It seems impossible that the passage of time should have so soon dissolved them, but Tothero's answer implies it.

"No," he says. He adds, "But then of course I didn't go where there would have been talk of you."

It annoys Rabbit that Tothero shows no interest in him except as a partner on a joyride. "I should have gone to work today," he says in a pointed voice, as if blaming the old man. "Saturday's my big day."

"What do you do?"

"I demonstrate a kitchen gadget called the MagiPeel Peeler in five and dime stores."

"A noble calling," Tothero says, and turns from the window. "Splendid, Harry. You're dressed at last."

"Is there a comb anywhere, Mr. Tothero? I ought to use the can."

Under their feet the men in the Sunshine Athletic Association laugh and catcall at some foolishness. Rabbit pictures passing among them and asks, "Say, should everybody see me?"

Tothero becomes indignant, as he used to now and then at practice, when everybody was just fooling around the basket and not going into the drills. "What are you afraid of, Harry? That poor little Janice Springer? You overestimate people. Nobody cares about her. Now we'll just go down there and don't be too long in the toilet. And I haven't heard any thanks from you for all I've done for you, and all I *am* doing." He takes the comb stuck in the brush bristles and gives it to Harry.

A dread of marring his freedom blocks the easy gesture of expressing gratitude. Thin-lipped, Rabbit pronounces, "Thanks."

They go downstairs. Contrary to what Tothero had promised, all of the men – old men, mostly, but not very old, so their mis-shapen bodies have a nasty vigor – look up with interest at him. Insanely, Tothero introduces him repeatedly: "Fred, this is my finest boy, a wonderful basketball player, Harry Angstrom, you probably remember his name from the papers, he twice set a county record, in 1950 and then he broke it in 1951, a wonderful accomplishment."

"Is that right, Marty?"

"Harry, an honor to meet you."

Their alert colorless eyes, little dark smears like their mouths, feed on the strange sight of him and send acid impressions down to be digested in their disgusting big beer-tough stomachs. Rabbit sees that Tothero is a fool to them, and is ashamed of his friend and of himself. He hides in the lavatory. The paint is worn off the toilet seat and the wash-basin is stained by the hot-water faucet's rusty tears; the walls are oily and the towel-rack empty. There is something terrible in the height of the tiny ceiling: a square yard of a dainty metal pattern covered with cobwebs in which a few white husks of insects are suspended. His depression deepens, becomes a kind of paralysis; he walks out and rejoins Tothero limping and stiffly grimacing, and they leave the place in a dream. He feels affronted, vaguely invaded, when Tothero gets into his

car. But, just as in a dream he never stops to question, Rabbit slides
in behind the wheel. In the renewed relation of his arms and legs
to the switches and pedals, he finds power. His wet-combed hair
feels chilly on his head.

He says sharply, "So you think I should've drunk with Janice."

"Do what the heart commands," Tothero says. "The heart is
our only guide." He sounds weary and far away.

"Into Brewer?"

There is no answer.

Rabbit drives up the alley, coming to Potter Avenue, where
the water from the ice plant used to run down. He goes right,
away from Wilbur Street, where his apartment is, and two more
turns bring him into Central Street heading around the mountain
to Brewer. On the left, land drops away into a chasm floored by
the slick still width of the Running Horse River; on the right,
gasoline stations glow, twirlers flicker on strings, spotlights protest.

As the town thins, Tothero's tongue loosens. "The ladies we're
going to meet, now Harry, I have no conception of what the other
one will be like, but I know you'll be a gentleman. And I guarantee you'll like my friend. She is a remarkable girl, Harry, with
seven strikes against her from birth, but she's done a remarkable
thing."

"What?"

"She's come to grips. Isn't that the whole secret, Harry; to
come to grips? It makes me happy, happy and humble, to have, as
I do, this very tenuous association with her. Harry?"

"Yeah?"

"Do you realize, Harry, that a young woman has hair on every
part of her body?"

"I hadn't thought about it." Distaste stains his throat.

"Do," Tothero says. "Do think about it. They are monkeys,
Harry. Women are monkeys."

He says it so solemn, Rabbit has to laugh.

Tothero laughs too, and comes closer on the seat. "Yet we love
them, Harry, don't we? Harry, why do we love them? Answer
that, and you'll answer the riddle of life." He is squirming around,
crossing and uncrossing his legs, leaning over and tapping Rabbit's
shoulder and then jerking back and glancing out the side window

and turning and tapping again. "I am a hideous person, Harry. A person to be abhorred. Harry, let me tell you something." As a coach he was always telling you something. "My wife calls me a person to be abhorred. But do you know when it began? It began with her skin. One day in the spring, in nineteen forty-three or four, it was during the war, without warning it was hideous. It was like the hides of a thousand lizards stitched together. Stitched together *clumsily*. Can you picture that? That sense of it being *in pieces* horrified me, Harry. Are you listening? You're not listening. You're wondering why you came to me."

"What you said about Janice this morning kind of worries me."

"Janice! Let's not talk about little mutts like Janice Springer, Harry boy. This is the night. This is no time for pity. The real women are dropping down out of the trees." With his hands he imitates things falling out of trees. "Plip, plip, plippity!"

Even discounting the man as a maniac, Rabbit becomes expectant. They park the car off Weiser Avenue and meet the girls in front of a Chinese restaurant.

The girls waiting under crimson neon have a floral delicacy; like a touch of wilt the red light rims their fluffy hair. Rabbit's heart thumps ahead of him down the pavement. They all come together and Tothero introduces Margaret: "Margaret Kosko, Harry Angstrom, my finest athlete, it's a pleasure for me to be able to introduce two such wonderful young people to one another." The old man's manner is queerly shy; his voice has a cough waiting in it.

After Tothero's build-up Rabbit is amazed that Margaret is just another Janice – the same sallow density, that stubborn smallness. Scarcely moving her lips, she says, "This is Ruth Leonard. Marty Tothero, and you, whatever your name is."

"Harry," Rabbit says. "Or Rabbit."

"That's right!" Tothero cries. "The other boys used to call you Rabbit. I had forgotten." He coughs.

"Well you're a big bunny," Ruth remarks. She is fat alongside Margaret, but not *that* fat. Chunky, more. But tall, five eight or nine. She has flat blue eyes in square-cut sockets. Her thighs fill the front of her pseudo-silk pale-green dress so that even standing up she has a lap. Her hair, kind of a dirty ginger color, is bundled in a roll at the back of her head. Beyond her the parking meters with their red tongues recede along the curb, and at her feet, pinched in lavender straps, four sidewalk squares meet in an X.

"Just big outside," he said.

"That's me too," she says.

"God I'm hungry," Rabbit tells them all, just to say something. From somewhere he's got the jitters.

"Hunger, hunger," Tothero says, as if grateful for the cue. "Where shall my little ones go?"

"Here?" Harry asks. He sees from the way the two girls look at him that he is expected to take charge. Tothero is moving back and forth like a crab sideways and bumps into a middle-aged couple strolling along. His face shows such surprise at the collision, and he is so elaborately apologetic, that Ruth laughs; her laugh rings on the street like a handful of change thrown down. At the sound Rabbit begins to loosen up; the space between the muscles of his chest feels padded with warm air. Tothero pushes into the glass door first, Margaret follows, and Ruth takes his arm and says, "I know you. I went to West Brewer High and got out in fifty-one."

"That's *my* class." Like the touch of her hand on his arm, her being his age pleases him, as if, even in high schools on opposite sides of the city, they have learned the same things and gained the same view of life. The Class of '51 view.

"You beat us," she says.

"You had a lousy team."

"No we didn't. I went with three of the players."

"Three at once?"

"In a way."

"Well. They looked tired."

She laughs again, the coins thrown down, though he feels ashamed of what he has said, she is so good-natured and maybe was pretty then. Her complexion isn't good now. But her hair is thick, and that's the sign.

A young Chinaman in a drab linen coat blocks their way past the glass counter where an American girl in a kimono sits counting threadbare bills. "Please, how many?"

"Four," Rabbit says, when Tothero is silent.

In an unexpected trusting gesture Ruth slips off her short white coat and gives it to Rabbit; soft, bunched cloth. The motion stirs up a smell of perfume on her.

"Four, yes please, this way," and the waiter leads them to a red booth. The place has just recently reopened as Chinese; pink paintings of Paris are still on the wall. Ruth staggers a little; Rabbit sees from behind that her heels, yellow with strain, tend to slip sideways in the net of lavender straps that pin her feet to the spikes of her shoes. But under the silky stretch of her mint-green dress her broad bottom packs the cloth with a certain composure. Her waist tucks in trimly, squarely, like the lines of her face. The cut of the dress bares a big V-shaped piece of fat fair back. In arriving at the booth, he bumps against her; the top of her head comes to his nose. The prickly smell of her hair stitches the store-bought scent stirred up on her. They bump because Tothero is ushering Margaret into her seat too ceremoniously, a gnome at the mouth of his cave. Standing there waiting, Rabbit is elated to think that a stranger passing outside the restaurant window, like himself last night outside that West Virginia diner, would see him with a woman. He seems to be that stranger, staring in, envying himself his body and his woman's body. Ruth bends down and slides over. The skin of her shoulders gleams and then dims in the shadow of the booth. Rabbit sits down too and feels her rustle beside him, settling in, the way women do, fussily, as if making a nest.

He discovers he has held on to her coat. Pale limp pelt, it sleeps in his lap. Without rising he reaches up and hangs it on the coat-pole hook above him.

"Nice to have a long arm," she says, and looks in her purse and takes out a pack of Newports.

"Tothero says I have short arms."

"Where'd you meet that old bum?" This so Tothero can hear if he cares.

"He's not a bum, he's my old coach."

"Want one?" A cigarette.

He wavers. "I've stopped."

"So that old bum was your coach," she sighs. She draws a cigarette from the turquoise pack of Newports and hangs it between her orange lips and frowns at the sulphur tip as she strikes a match, with curious feminine clumsiness, away from her, holding the paper match sideways and thus bending it. It flares on the third scratch.

Margaret says, "*Ruth.*"

"Bum?" Tothero says, and his heavy face looks unwell and lopsided in cagey mirth, as if he's started to melt. "I am, I am. A vile old bum fallen among princesses."

Margaret sees nothing against her in this and puts her hand on top of his on the table and in a solemn dead voice insists, "You're nothing like a bum."

"Where is our young Confucian?" Tothero asks and looks around with his free arm uplifted. When the boy comes he asks, "Can we be served alcoholic beverages here?"

"We bring in from next door," the boy says. Funny the way the eyebrows of Chinese people look embedded in the skin instead of sticking out from it.

"Double Scotch whisky," Tothero says. "My dear?"

"Daiquiri," Margaret says; it sounds like a wisecrack.

"Children?"

Rabbit looks at Ruth. Her face is caked with orange dust. Her hair, her hair which seemed at first glance dirty blonde or faded brown, is in fact many colors, red and yellow and brown and black, each hair passing in the light through a series of tints, like the hair of a dog. "Hell," she says. "I guess a Daiquiri."

"Three," Rabbit tells the boy, thinking a Daiquiri will be like a limeade.

The waiter recites, "Three Daiquiri, one double whisky Scotch on the rock," and goes.

Rabbit asks Ruth, "When's your birthday?"

"August. Why?"

"Mine's February," he says. "I win."

"You win." She agrees as if she knows how he feels: that you can't be master, quite, of a woman who's older.

"If you recognized me," he asks, "why didn't you recognize Mr. Tothero? He was coach of that team."

"Who looks at coaches? They don't do any good, do they?"

"Don't do any good? A high-school team is all coach; isn't it?"

Tothero answers, "It's all boy, Harry. You can't make gold out of lead. You can't make gold out of lead."

"Sure you can," Rabbit says. "When I came out in my freshman year I didn't know my head from my" – he stops himself;
after all these are ladies of a sort – "elbow."

"Yes you did, Harry, yes you did. I had nothing to teach you;
I just let you run." He keeps looking around. "You were a young
deer," he continues, "with big feet."

Ruth asks, "How big?"

Rabbit tells her, "Twelve D. How big are yours?"

"They're tiny," she says. "Teeny weeny little."

"It looked to me like they were falling out of your shoes." He
pulls his head back and slumps slightly, to look down past the table
edge, into the submarine twilight where her foreshortened calves
hang like tan fish. They dart back under the seat.

"Don't look too hard, you'll fall out of the booth," she says,
ruffled, which is good. Women like being mussed. They never say
they do, but they do.

The waiter comes with the drinks and begins laying their places
with paper placemats and lusterless silver. He does Margaret and
is halfway done on Tothero when Tothero takes the whisky glass
away from his lips and says in a freshened, tougher voice,
"Cutlery? For Oriental dishes? Don't you have chopsticks?"

"Chopsticks, yes."

"Chopsticks all around," Tothero says positively. "When in
Rome."

"Don't take mine!" Margaret cries, slapping her hand with a
clatter across her spoon and fork when the waiter reaches. "I don't
want any sticks."

"Harry and Ruth?" Tothero asks. "Your preference?"

The Daiquiri does have the taste of limeade, riding like oil on
the top of a raw transparent taste. "Sticks," Rabbit says in a deep
voice, delighted to annoy Margaret. "In Texas we never touched
metal to chicken hoo phooey."

"Ruth?" Tothero's facial attitude toward her is timid and forced.

"Oh I guess. If this dope can I can." She grinds out her cigarette and fishes for another.

The waiter goes away like a bridesmaid with his bouquet of
unwanted silver. Margaret is alone in her choice, and this preys on
her. Rabbit is glad; she is a shadow on his happiness.

"You ate Chinese food in Texas?" Ruth asks.

"All the time. Give me a cigarette."

"You've stopped."

"I've started. Give me a dime."

"A dime! The hell I will."

The needless urgency of her refusal offends him, it sounds as if she wants a profit. Why does she think he'd steal from her? What would he steal? He dips into his coat pocket and comes up with coins and takes a dime and puts it into the little ivory jukebox that burns mildly on the wall by their table. Leaning over, close to her face, he turns the leaves listing titles and finally punches the buttons, B and 7, for "Rocksville, P-A." "Chinese food in Texas is the best Chinese food in the United States except Boston," he says.

"Listen to the big traveller," Ruth says. She gives him a cigarette. He forgives her about the dime.

"So you think," Tothero says steadily, "that coaches don't do anything."

"They're worthless," Ruth says.

"Hey come on," Rabbit says.

The waiter comes back with their chopsticks and two menus. Rabbit is disappointed in the chopsticks; they feel like plastic instead of wood. The cigarette tastes rough, a noseful of straw. He puts it out. Never again.

"We'll each order a dish and then share it," Tothero tells them. "Now who has favorites?"

"Sweet and sour pork," Margaret says. One thing about her, she is very definite.

"Harry?"

"I don't know."

"Where's the big Chinese-food specialist?" Ruth asks.

"This is in English. I'm used to ordering from a Chinese menu."

"Come on, come on, tell me what's good."

"Hey cut it out; you're getting me rattled."

"You were never in Texas," she says.

He remembers the house on that strange treeless residential street, the green night growing up from the prairie, the flowers in the window, and says, "Absolutely I was."

"Doing what?"

"Serving Uncle."

"Oh, in the Army; well that doesn't count. Everybody's been to Texas with the Army."

"You order whatever you think is good," Rabbit tells Tothero. He is irritated by all these Army veterans Ruth seems to know, and strains to hear the final bars of the song he spent a dime to play. In this Chinese place he can just make out a hint, coming it seems from the kitchen, of the jangling melody that lifted his spirits last night in the car.

Tothero gives the waiter the order and when he goes away tries to give Ruth the word. The old man's thin lips are wet with whisky. "The coach," he says, "the coach is concerned with developing the three tools we are given in life: the head, the body, and the heart."

"And the crotch," Ruth says. Margaret, of all people, laughs. She really gives Rabbit the creeps.

"Young woman, you've challenged me, and I deserve the respect of your attention." He speaks with grave weight.

"Shit," she says softly, and looks down. "Don't bleed on *me*." He has hurt her. The wings of her nostrils whiten; her coarse make-up darkens.

"One. The head. Strategy. Most boys come to a basketball coach from alley games and have no conception of the, of the *elegance* of the game played on a court with two baskets. Won't you bear me out, Harry?"

"Yeah, sure. Just yesterday –"

"Second – let me finish, Harry, and then you can talk – second, the body. Work the boys into condition. Make their legs hard." He clenches his fist on the slick table. "Hard. Run, run, run. Run every minute their feet are on the floor. You can't run enough. Thirdly" – he puts the index finger and thumb of one hand to the corners of his mouth and flicks away the moisture – "the heart. And here the good coach, which I, young lady, certainly tried to be and some say *was*, has his most solemn opportunity. Give the boys the will to achieve. I've always liked that better than the will to win, for there can be achievement even in defeat. Make them feel the – yes, I think the word is good –

the *sacredness* of achievement, in the form of giving our best."
He dares a pause now, and wins through it, glancing at each
of them in turn to freeze their tongues. "A boy who has had
his heart enlarged by an inspiring coach," he concludes, "can
never become, in the deepest sense, a failure in the greater game
of life." He lifts his plump hand. "And now may the peace of God,
et cetera . . ." He draws on his glass, which is mostly ice cubes. As
he tilts it up they ride forward and rattle against his lips.

Ruth turns to Rabbit and asks quietly, as if to change the
subject, "What do you do?"

He laughs. "Well I'm not sure I do anything any more. I should
have gone to work this morning. I, uh, it's kind of hard to describe,
I demonstrate something called the MagiPeel Kitchen Peeler."

"And I'm sure he does it well," Tothero says. "I'm sure that
when the MagiPeel Corporation board sits down at their annual
meeting and ask themselves, 'Now who has done the most to
further our cause with the American public?' the name of Harry
Rabbit Angstrom leads the list."

"What do you do?" Rabbit asks her in turn.

"Nothing," Ruth answers. "Nothing." And her eyelids make
a greasy blue curtain as she sips her Daiquiri. Her chin takes something of the liquid's green light.

The Chinese food arrives. Eager saliva fills his mouth. He
really hasn't had any since Texas. He loves this food that contains
no disgusting proofs of slain animals, no bloody slab of cow
haunch or hen's sinewy skeleton; these ghosts have been minced
and destroyed and painlessly merged with the shapes of mute
vegetables, plump green bodies that invite his appetite's innocent
gusto. Candy. Heaped on a smoking breast of rice. Each is given
such a tidy hot breast, and Margaret is in a special hurry to muddle hers with glazed chunks; all eat well. Their faces take color and
strength from the oval plates of dark pork, sugar peas, chicken, stiff
sweet sauce, shrimp, water chestnuts, who knows what else. Their
talk grows hearty.

"He was terrific," Rabbit says of Tothero. "He was the greatest coach in the county. I would've been nothing without him."

"No, Harry, no. You did more for me than I did for you. Girls,
the first game he played he scored twenty points."

"Twenty-three," Harry says.

"Twenty-three points! Think of it." The women eat on. "Remember, Harry, the state tournaments in Harrisburg; Dennistown and their little set-shot artist?"

"He was tiny," Harry tells Ruth. "About five two and ugly as a monkey. Really a dirty player too."

"Ah, but he knew his trade," Tothero says, "he knew his trade. Harry had met his match."

"Then he tripped me, remember?"

"So he did," Tothero says. "I'd forgotten."

"This runt trips me, and over I go, bonk, against the mat. If the walls hadn't been padded I'd'a been killed."

"Then what happened, Harry? Did you cream him? I've forgotten this whole incident." Tothero's mouth is full of food and his hunger for revenge is ugly.

"Why, no," Rabbit says slowly. "I never fouled. The ref saw it and it was his fifth foul and he was out. Then we smothered 'em."

Something fades in Tothero's expression; his face goes slack. "That's right, you never fouled. He never did. Harry was always the idealist."

Rabbit shrugs. "I didn't have to."

"The other strange thing about Harry," Tothero tells the two women. "He was never hurt."

"No, I once sprained my wrist," Rabbit corrects. "The thing you said that really helped me –"

"What happened next in the tournaments? I'm frightened at how I've forgotten this."

"Next? Pennoak, I think. Nothing happened. They beat us."

"They won? Didn't we beat them?"

"Oh hell no. They were good. They had five good players. What'd we have? Just me, really. We had Harrison, who was O.K., but after that football injury he never had the touch, really."

"*Ronnie* Harrison?" Ruth asks.

Rabbit is startled. "You *know* him?" Harrison had been a notorious bedbug.

"I'm not sure," she says, complacently enough.

"Shortish guy with kinky hair. A little bitty limp."

"No, I don't know," she says. "I don't think so." She is pleasingly dexterous with the chopsticks, and keeps one hand lying palm up on her lap. He loves when she ducks her head, that thick simple neck moving forward making the broad tendons on her shoulder jump up, to get her lips around a piece of something. Pinched with just the right pressure between the sticks; funny how plump women have that delicate touch. Margaret shovels it in with her dull bent silver.

"We didn't win," Tothero repeats, and calls, "Waiter." When the boy comes Tothero asks for another round of the same drinks.

"No, not for me, thanks," Rabbit says. "I'm high enough on this as it is."

"You're just a big clean-living kid, aren't you, you," Margaret says. She doesn't even know his name yet. God, he hates her.

"The thing, I started to say, the thing you said that really helped me," Rabbit says to Tothero, "is that business about almost touching your thumbs on the two-handers. That's the whole secret, really, getting the ball in front of your hands, where you get that nice lifty feeling. Just zwoops off." His hands show how.

"Oh, Harry," Tothero says sadly, "you could shoot when you came to me. All I gave you was the will to win. The will to achievement."

"You know my best night," Rabbit says, "my best night wasn't that forty-pointer that time against Allenville, it was in my junior year, we went down to end of the county real early in the season to play, a funny little hick school, about a hundred in all six grades; what was its name? Bird's Nest? Something like that. You'll remember."

"Bird's Nest," Tothero says. "No."

"It was the only time I think we ever scheduled them. Funny little square gymnasium where the crowd sat up on the stage. Some name that meant something."

"Bird's Nest," Tothero says. He is bothered. He keeps touching his ear.

"Oriole!" Rabbit exclaims, perfect in joy. "Oriole High. This little kind of spread-out town, and it was early in the season, so it was kind of warm still, and going down in the bus you could see the things of corn like wigwams out in the fields. And the school itself kind of smelled of cider; I remember you made some joke about it. You told me to take it easy, we were down there for practice, and we weren't supposed to try, you know, to *smother* 'em."

"Your memory is better than mine," Tothero says. The waiter comes back and Tothero takes his drink right off the tray, before the boy has a chance to give it to him.

"So," Rabbit says. "We go out there and there are these five farmers clumping up and down, and we get about fifteen points up right away and I just take it easy. And there are just a couple dozen people sitting up on the stage and the game isn't a league game so nothing matters much, and I get this funny feeling I can do anything, just drifting around, passing the ball, and all of a sudden I know, you see, I *know* I can do anything. The second half I take maybe just ten shots, and every one goes right in, not just bounces in, but doesn't touch the rim, like I'm dropping stones down a well. And these farmers running up and down getting up a sweat, they didn't have more than two substitutes, but we're not in their league either, so it doesn't matter much to them, and the one ref just leans over against the edge of the stage talking to their coach. Oriole High. Yeah, and then afterwards their coach comes down into the locker room where both teams are changing and gets a jug of cider out of a locker and we all passed it around. Don't you remember?" It puzzles him, yet makes him want to laugh, that he can't make the others feel what was so special. He resumes eating. The others are done and on their second drinks.

"Yes, sir, Whosie, you're a real sweet kid," Margaret tells him.

"Pay no attention, Harry," Tothero says, "that's the way tramps talk."

Margaret hits him: her hand flies up from the table and across her body into his mouth, flat, but without a slapping noise.

"Touché," Ruth says. Her voice is indifferent. The whole thing is so quiet that the Chinaman, clearing their dishes away, doesn't look up, and seems to hear nothing.

"We're going, by jingo," Tothero announces, and tries to stand up, but the edge of the table hits his thighs, and he can stand no higher than a hunchback. The slap has left a little twist in his mouth that Rabbit can't bear to look at, it's so ambiguous and blurred, such a sickly mixture of bravado and shame and, worst, pride or less than pride, conceit. This deathly smirk emits the words, "Are you coming, my dear?"

"Son of a bitch," Margaret says, yet her little hard nut of a body slides over, and she glances behind her to see if she is leaving anything, cigarettes or a purse. "Son of a bitch," she repeats, and there is something friendly in the level way she says it. Both she and Tothero seem calmer now, on the move.

Rabbit starts to push up from the table, but Tothero sets a rigid urgent hand on his shoulder, the coach's touch, that Rabbit had so often felt on the bench, just before the pat on the bottom that sent him into the game. "No, no, Harry. You stay. One apiece. Don't let our vulgarity distract you. I couldn't borrow your car, could I?"

"Huh? How would I get anywhere?"

"Quite right, you're quite right. Forgive my asking."

"No, I mean, you can if you want —" In fact he feels deeply reluctant to part with a car that is only half his.

Tothero sees this. "No no. It was an insane thought. Good night."

"You bloated old bastard," Margaret says to him. He glances toward her, then down fuzzily. She is right, Harry realizes, he is bloated; his face is lopsided like a tired balloon. Yet this balloon peers down at him as if there was some message bulging it, heavy and vague like water.

"Where will you go?" Tothero asks.

"I'll be fine. I have money. I'll get a hotel," Rabbit tells him. He wishes, now that he has refused him a favor, that Tothero would go.

"The door of my mansion is open," Tothero says. "There's the one cot only, but we can make a mattress —"

"No, look," Rabbit says severely. "You've saved my life, but I don't want to saddle you. I'll be fine. I can't thank you enough anyway."

"We'll talk sometime," Tothero promises. His hand twitches, and accidentally taps Margaret's thigh.

"I could kill you," Margaret says at his side, and they go off, looking from the back like father and daughter, past the counter where the waiter whispers with the American girl, and out the glass door, Margaret first. The whole thing seems so *settled:* like little wooden figures going in and out of a barometer.

"God, he's in sad shape."

"Who isn't?" Ruth asks.

"You don't seem to be."

"I eat, is what you mean."

"No, listen, you have some kind of complex about being big. You're not fat. You're right in proportion."

She laughs, catches herself, looks at him, laughs again and squeezes his arm and says, "Rabbit, you're a Christian gentleman." Her using his own name enters his ears with unsettling warmth.

"What she hit him for?" he asks, giggling in fear that her hands, resting on his forearm, will playfully poke his side. He feels in her grip the tension of this possibility.

"She likes to hit people. She once hit me."

"Yeah, but you probably asked for it."

She replaces her hands on the table. "So did he. He likes being hit."

He asks, "You know him?"

"I've heard her talk about him."

"Well, that's not knowing him. That girl is dumb."

"Isn't she. She's dumber than you can know."

"Look, I know. I'm married to her twin."

"Ohhh. Married."

"Hey, what's this about Ronnie Harrison? Do you know him?"

"What's this about you being married?"

"Well, I was. Still am." He regrets that they have started talking about it. A big bubble, the enormity of it, crowds his heart. It's like when he was a kid and suddenly thought, coming back from somewhere at the end of a Saturday afternoon, that this – these trees, this pavement – was life, the real and only thing.

"Where is she?"

This makes it worse, picturing Janice; where would she go? "Probably with her parents. I just left her last night."

"Oh. Then this is just a holiday. You haven't left her."

"Don't be too sure about that."

The waiter brings them a plate of sesame cakes. Rabbit takes one tentatively, thinking they will be hard, and is delighted to have it become in his mouth mild elastic jelly, through the shell of bland seeds. The waiter asks, "Gone for good, your friends?"

"It's O.K., I'll pay," Rabbit says.

The Chinaman lifts his sunken eyebrows and puckers into a smile and retreats.

"You're rich?" Ruth asks.

"No, poor."

"Are you really going to a hotel?" They both take several sesame cakes. There are perhaps twenty on the plate.

"I guess. I'll tell you about Janice. I never thought of leaving her until the minute I did; all of a sudden it seemed obvious. She's about five six, sort of dark-complected —"

"I don't want to hear about it." Her voice is positive; her many-colored hair, as she tilts back her head and squints at a ceiling light, settles into one grave shade. The light flatters her hair more than her face; on this side of her nose there are some spots in her skin, blemishes that make bumps through her powder.

"You don't," he says. The bubble rolls off his chest. If it doesn't worry anybody else why should it worry him? "O.K. What shall we talk about? What's your weight?"

"One forty-seven."

"Ruth, you're tiny. You're just a welterweight. No kidding. Nobody wants you to be all bones. Every pound you have on is priceless."

He's talking just for happiness, but something he says makes her tense up. "You're pretty wise, aren't you?" she asks, tilting her empty glass toward her eyes. The glass is a shallow cup on a short stem, like an ice-cream dish at a fancy birthday party. It sends pale arcs of reflection skidding across her thoughtful face.

"You don't want to talk about your weight, either. Huh." He pops another sesame cake into his mouth, and waits until the first pang, the first taste of jelly, subsides. "Let's try this. What you need, typical American homemaker, is the MagiPeel Kitchen Peeler. Preserve those vitamins. Shave off fatty excess. A simple adjustment of the plastic turn screw, and you can grate carrots *and* sharpen your husband's pencils. A host of uses."

"Don't. Don't be so funny."

"O.K."

"Let's be nice."

"O.K. You start."

She plops a cake in and looks at him with a funny full-mouth smile, the corners turned down tight, and a frantic look of agreeableness strains her features while she chews. She swallows, her blue eyes widened round, and gives a little gasp before launching into what he thinks will be a remark but turns out to be a laugh, right in his face. "Wait," she begs. "I'm trying." And returns to looking into the shell of her glass, thinking, and the best she can do, after all that, is to say, "Don't live in a hotel."

"I got to. Tell me a good one." He instinctively thinks she knows about hotels. At the side of her neck where it shades into her shoulder there is a shallow white hollow where his attention curls and rests.

"They're all expensive," she said. "Everything is. Just my little apartment is expensive."

"Where do you have an apartment?"

"Oh a few blocks from here. On Summer Street. It's one flight up, above a doctor."

"It's yours alone?"

"Yeah. My girlfriend got married."

"So you're stuck with all the rent and you don't do anything."

"Which means what?"

"Nothing. You just said you did nothing. How expensive is it?"

She looks at him curiously, with that alertness he had noticed right off, out by the parking meters.

"The apartment," he says.

"A hundred-ten a month. Then they make you pay for light and gas."

"And you don't do anything."

She gazes into her glass, making reflected light run around the rim with a rocking motion of her hands.

"Whaddeya thinking?" he asks.

"Just wondering."

"Wondering what?"

"How wise you are."

Right here, without moving his head, he feels the wind blow. So this is the drift; he hadn't been sure. He says, "Well I'll tell ya. Why don't you let me give you something toward your rent?"

"Why should you do that?"

"Big heart," he says. "Ten?"

"I need fifteen."

"For the light and gas. O.K. O.K." He is uncertain what to do now. They sit looking at the empty plate that had held a pyramid of sesame cakes. They have eaten them all. The waiter, when he comes, is surprised to see this; his eyes go from the plate to Rabbit to Ruth, all in a second. The check amounts to $9.60. Rabbit puts a ten and a one on top of it, and beside these bills he puts a ten and a five. He counts what's left in his wallet; three tens and four ones. When he looks up, Ruth's money has vanished from the slick table. He stands up and takes her little soft coat and holds it for her, and like a great green fish, his prize, she heaves across and up out of the booth and coldly lets herself be fitted into it. He calculates, A dime a pound.

And that's not counting the restaurant bill. He takes the bill to the counter and gives the girl the ten. She makes change with a studious frown. The purple simplicity of her kimono does not go with her complicated permed hair and rouged, sweet-and-sour American face. When she puts his coins on the pink cleats of the change pad, he flicks his hand in the air above the silver, adds the dollar to it, and nods at the young Chinese waiter, who is perched attentively beside her. "Tank you vewy much, sir. We tank you vewy much," the boy says to him. But his gratitude does not even last until they are out of sight. As they move toward the glass door he turns to the cashier and in a reedy, perfectly inflected voice completes his story: "– and then this other cat says, 'But man, mine was *he*lium!' "

*   *   *

With this Ruth, Rabbit enters the street. On his right, away
from the mountain, the heart of the city shines: a shuffle of lights,
a neon outline of a boot, of a peanut, of a top hat, of an enormous
sunflower erected, the stem of neon six stories high, along the
edge of one building to symbolize Sunflower Beer. The yellow
flower center is a second moon. One block down, a monotone
bell tolls hurriedly, and the red-tipped railroad-crossing gates
descend through the soft mass of neon, and the traffic slows, halts.

Ruth turns left, toward the shadow of Mt. Judge, and Rabbit
follows; they walk uphill on the rasping pavement. The slope of
cement is a buried assertion, an unexpected echo, of the terrain
that had been here before the city. For Rabbit the pavement
is a shadow of the Daiquiri's luminous transparence; he is lighthearted, and skips once, to get in step with this girl he adores. Her
eyes are turned up, toward where the Pinnacle Hotel adds its
coarse constellation to the stars above Mt. Judge. They walk
together in silence while behind them a freight train chuffs and
screaks through the crossing.

He recognizes his problem; she dislikes him now, like that
whore in Texas. "Hey," he says. "Have you ever been up to the
top there?"

"Sure. In a car."

"When I was a kid," he says, "we used to walk up from the
other side. There's a sort of gloomy forest, and I remember once
I came across an old house, just a hole in the ground with some
stones, where I guess a pioneer had had a farm."

"The only time I ever got up there was in a car with some eager
beaver."

"Well, congratulations," he says, annoyed by the self-pity
hiding in her toughness.

She bites at being uncovered. "What do you think I care about
your pioneer?" she asks.

"I don't know. Why shouldn't you? You're an American."

"How? I could just as easy be a Mexican."

"You never could be, you're not little enough."

"You know, you're a pig really."

"Oh now baby," he says, and puts his arm around the substance
of her waist, "I think I'm sort of neat."

"Don't tell me."

She turns left, off Weiser, out of his arm. This street is Summer. Faces of brick run together to make a single block-long face. The house numbers are set in fanlights of stained glass above the doors. The apple-and-orange-colored light of a small grocery store shows the silhouettes of some kids hanging around the corner. The supermarkets are driving these little stores out of business, make them stay open all night.

He puts his arm around her and begs, "Come on now, be a pleasant cunt." He wants to prove to her that her talking tough won't keep him off. She wants him to be content with just her heavy body, but he wants whole women, light as feathers. To his surprise her arm mirrors his, comes around his waist. Thus locked, they find it awkward to walk, and part at the traffic light.

"Didn't you kind of like me in the restaurant?" he asks. "The way I tried to make old Tothero feel good? Telling him how great he was?"

"All I heard was you telling how great *you* were."

"I *was* great. It's the fact. I mean, I'm not much good for anything now, but I really was good at that."

"You know what I was good at?"

"What?"

"Cooking."

"That's more than my wife is. Poor kid."

"Remember how in Sunday school they'd tell you everybody God made was good at something? Well, that was my thing, cooking. I thought, Jesus, now I'll really be a great cook."

"Well aren't you?"

"I don't know. All I do is eat out."

"Well, stop it."

"It's how you meet guys," she says, and this really stops him. It frightens him to think of her this way. It makes her seem, in terms of love, so vast.

"Here I am," she says. Her building is brick like all the others on the west side of the street. Across the way a big limestone church hangs like a gray curtain behind the streetlamp. They go in her doorway, passing beneath stained glass. The vestibule has a row of brass mailboxes and a varnished umbrella rack and a rubber mat on the marble floor and two doors, one to the right with frosted glass and another in front of them of wire-reinforced glass through which he sees rubber-treaded stairs. While Ruth fits a key in this door he reads the gold lettering on the other: F. X. PELLIGRINI, M.D. "Old fox," Ruth says, and leads Rabbit up the stairs.

She lives one flight up. Her door is the one at the far end of a linoleum hall, nearest the street. He stands behind her as she scratches her key at the lock. Abruptly, in the yellow light of the streetlamp which comes through the four flawed panes of the window by his side, tall panes so thin-seeming the touch of one finger might crack them, he begins to tremble, first his legs, and then the skin of his sides. The key fits and her door opens.

Once inside, as she reaches for the light switch, he knocks her arm down, pulls her around, and kisses her. It's insanity, he wants to crush her, a little gauge inside his ribs doubles and redoubles his need for pressure, just pure pressure, there is no love in it, love that glances and glides along the skin, he is unconscious of their skins, it is her heart he wants to grind into his own, to comfort her completely. By nature in such an embrace she fights back. The small moist cushion of slack willingness with which her lips had greeted his dries up and turns hard, and when she can get her head back and her hand free she fits her palm against his jaw and pushes as if she wanted to throw his skull back into the hall. Her fingers curl and a long nail scrapes the tender skin below one eye. He lets her go. The nearly scratched eye squints and a tendon in his neck aches.

"Get out," she says, her chunky mussed face ugly in the light from the hall.

He kicks the door shut with a backward flip of his leg. "Don't," he says. "I had to hug you." He sees in the dark she is frightened; her big black shape has a pocket in it which his instinct feels like a tongue probing a pulled tooth. The air tells him he must be motionless; for no reason he wants to laugh. Her fear and his inner knowledge are so incongruous: he knows there is no harm in him.

"Hug," she says. "Kill felt more like it."

"I've been loving you so much all night," he says. "I had to get it out of my system."

"I know all about your systems. One squirt and done."

"It won't be," he promises.

"It better be. I want you out of here."

"No you don't."

"You all think you're such lovers."

"I am," he assures her. "I am a lover." And on a wave of alcohol and stirred semen he steps forward, in a kind of swoon. Though she backs away, it is not so quickly that he cannot feel her socket of fear healing. The room they are in, he sees by streetlight, is small, and two armchairs and a sofa-bed and a table furnish it. She walks to the next room, a little larger, holding a double bed. The shade is half drawn, and low light gives each nubbin of the bedspread a shadow.

"All right," she says. "You can get into that."

"Where are you going?" Her hand is on a doorknob.

"In here."

"You're going to undress in there?"

"Yeah."

"Don't. Let me undress you. Please." In his concern he has come to stand beside her, and touches her arm now.

She moves her arm from under his touch. "You're pretty bossy."

"Please. Please."

Her voice grates with exasperation: "I have to go to the *john*."

"But come out dressed."

"I have to do something else, too."

"Don't do it. I know what it is. I hate them."

"You don't even feel it."

"But I know it's there. Like a rubber kidney or something."

Ruth laughs. "Well aren't you choice? Do you have the answer then?"

"No. I hate them even worse."

"Look. I don't know what you think your fifteen dollars entitles you to, but I got to protect myself."

"If you're going to put a lot of gadgets in this, give me the fifteen back."

She tries to twist away, but now he holds the arm he touched. She says, "Say, do you think we're married or something the way you boss me around?"

The transparent wave moves over him again and he calls to her in a voice that is almost inaudible, "Yes; let's be." So quickly her arms don't move from hanging at her sides, he kneels at her feet and kisses the place on her fingers where a ring would have been. Now that he is down there, he begins to undo the straps of her shoes. "Why do you women wear heels?" he asks, and yanks her one foot up, so she has to grab the hair on his head for support. "Don't they hurt you?" He heaves the shoe, sticky web, through the doorway into the next room, and does the same to the other. Her feet being flat on the floor gives her legs firmness all the way up. He puts his hands around her ankles and pumps them up and down briskly, between the boxy ankle bones and the circular solid fat of her calves. He should be an athletic trainer.

"Come on," Ruth says, in a voice slightly tense with the fear of falling, his weight pinning her legs. "Get into bed."

He senses the trap. "No," he says, and stands up. "You'll put on a flying saucer."

"No, I won't. Listen, you won't know if I do or don't."

"Sure I will. I'm very sensitive."

"Oh Lord. Well anyway I got to take a leak."

"Go ahead, I don't care," he says, and won't let her close the bathroom door. She sits, like women do, primly, her back straight and her chin tucked in. Her knees linked by stretched underpants, Ruth waits above a whispering gush. At home he and Janice had been trying to toilet-train Nelson, so leaning in the doorway tall as a parent he feels a ridiculous impulse to praise her. She is so tidy, reaching under her dress with a piece of lemon-colored paper; she tugs herself together and for a sweet split second the whole intimate vulnerable patchwork of stocking tops and straps and silk and fur and soft flesh is exposed.

"Good girl," he says, and leads her into the bedroom. Behind them, the plumbing vibrates and murmurs. She moves with shy stiffness, puzzled by his will. Trembling again, shy himself, he brings her to a stop by the foot of the bed and searches for the catch of her dress. He finds buttons on the back and can't undo them easily; his hands come at them reversed.

"Let me do it."

"Don't be in such a hurry; I'll do it. You're supposed to enjoy this. This is our wedding night."

"Say, I think you're sick."

He turns her roughly and falls again into a deep wish to give comfort. He touches her caked cheeks; she seems small as he looks down into the frowning planes of her set, shadowed face. He moves his lips into one eye socket, gently, trying to say this night has no urgency in it, trying to listen through his lips to the timid pulse beating in the bulge of her lid. With a careful impartiality he fears she will find comic, he kisses also her other eye; then, excited by the thought of his own tenderness, his urgency spills; his mouth races across her face, nibbling, licking, so that she does laugh, tickled, and pushes away. He locks her against him, crouches, and presses his parted teeth into the fat hot hollow at the side of her throat. Ruth tenses at his threat to bite, and her hands shove at his shoulders, but he clings there, his teeth bared in a silent exclamation, crying out against her smothering throat that it is not her body he wants, not the flesh and bones, but her, her.

Though there are no words she hears this, and says, "Don't try to prove you're a lover on me. Just come and go."

"You're *so* smart," he says, and starts to hit her, checks his arm, and offers instead, "Hit me. Come on. You want to, don't you? Really pound me."

"My Lord," she says, "this'll take all night." He plucks her limp arm from her side and swings it up toward him, but she manages her hand so that five bent fingers bump against his cheek painlessly. "That's what poor Maggie has to do for your old bastard friend."

He begs, "Don't talk about them."

"Damn men," she continues, "either want to hurt somebody or be hurt."

"I don't, honest. Either one."

"Well then undress me and stop farting around."

He sighs through his nose. "You have a sweet tongue," he says.

"I'm sorry if I shock you." Yet in her voice is a small metallic withdrawal, as if she really is.

"You don't," he says and, business-like, stoops and takes the hem of her dress in his hands. His eyes are enough accustomed to the dark now to see the silky cloth as green. He peels it up her body, and she lifts her arms, and her head gets caught for a moment in the neck-hole. She shakes her head crossly, like a dog with a scrap, and the dress comes free, skims off her arms into his hands floppy and faintly warm. He sails it into a chair hulking in a corner. "God," he says, "you're pretty." She is a ghost in her silver slip. Dragging the dress over her head has loosened her hair. Her solemn face tilts as she quickly lifts out the pins. Her hair falls out of heavy loops. Women look like brides in their slips.

"Yeah," she says. "Pretty plump."

"No," he says, "you are," and in the space of a breath goes to her and picks her up, great glistening sugar in her sifty-grained slip, and carries her to the bed, and lays her on it. "So pretty."

"You lifted me, wow. That'll put you out of action."

Harsh direct light falls on her face: the caked makeup, the creases on her neck. He asks, "Shall I pull the shade?"

"Please. It's a depressing view."

He goes to the window and bends to see what she means. There is only the church across the way, gray, grave, and mute. Lights behind its rose window are left burning, and this circle of red and purple and gold seems in the city night a hole punched in reality to show the abstract brilliance burning underneath. He lowers the shade on it guiltily. He turns, and Ruth's eyes watch him out of shadows that also seem gaps in a surface. The curve of her hip supports a crescent of silver; his sense of her weight seems to make an aroma.

"What's next?" He takes off his coat and throws it; he loves this throwing things, the way the flying cloth puts him at the center of a gathering nakedness. "Stockings?"

"They're tricky," she says. "I don't want a run."

"You do it then."

In a sitting position, with a soft-pawed irritable deftness, she extricates herself from a web of elastic and silk and cotton. When she has peeled off the stockings and tucked them, tidily rolled, into the crevice by the footboard of the bed, she lies flat and arches her back to push off the garter belt and pants. As swiftly, he bends his face into a small forest smelling of spice, where he is out of all dimension, and where a tender entire woman seems an inch away, around a kind of corner. When he straightens up on his knees, kneeling as he is by the bed, Ruth under his eyes is an incredible continent, the pushed-up slip a north of snow.

"So much," he says.

"Too much."

"No, listen. You're good." Cupping a hand behind her hot sheltered neck, he pulls her up, and slides her slip over her head. It comes off with liquid ease. Clothes just fall from a woman who wants to be stripped. The cool hollow his hand finds in the small of her back mixes in his mind with the shallow shadows of the stretch of skin that slopes from the bones of her shoulders. He kisses this expanse. Where her skin is whiter it is cooler. The hardness of his chin hits the hardness of her bra. He whispers "Hey let me" when Ruth's one arm crooks back to unfasten it. He gets behind her. She sits upright with her fat legs jackknifed sideways and her back symmetrical as a great vase. The tiny dingy catches are hard to undo; she draws her shoulder blades together. With a pang the tough strap parts. Her back broadens and turns convex as she shrugs the straps down off her shoulders. As one arm tosses her brassière over the edge of the bed the other, on his side, presses against her breast, so he won't see. But he does see: a quick glimmer of tipped weight. He moves away and sits on the corner of the bed and drinks in the pure sight of her. She keeps her arm tight against the one breast and brings up her hand to cover the other; a ring glints. Her modesty praises him by showing she is feeling something. The straight arm props her weight. Her belly is a pond of shadow deepening to a black eclipsed by the inner swell of her thighs. Light seizes her right side as her body turns in its stillness, rigidity her one defense against the hunger of his eyes. She holds the pose until his eyes smart with echoes of white. When her voice breaks from her stilled form, he is startled: "What about you?"

He is still dressed, even to his necktie. While he is draping his trousers over a chair, arranging them to keep the crease, she slips beneath the covers. He stands over her in his underclothes and asks, "Now you really don't have anything on?"

"You wouldn't let me."

He remembers the glint. "Give me your ring."

She brings her right hand out from under the covers and he carefully works a thick brass ring, like a class ring, past her bunching knuckle. In letting her hand drop she grazes the distorted front of his Jockey shorts.

He looks down at her, thinking. The covers come up to her throat and the pale arm lying on top of the bedspread has a slight serpent's twist. "There's nothing else?"

"I'm all skin," she says. "Come on. Get in."

"You want me?"

"Don't flatter yourself. I want it over with."

"You have all that crust on your face."

"God, you're insulting!"

"I just love you too much. Where's a washrag?"

"I don't want my Goddamned face washed!"

He goes into the bathroom and turns on the light and finds a facecloth and holds it under the hot faucet. He wrings it out and turns off the light. As he comes back across the room Ruth laughs from the bed. He asks, "What's the joke?"

"In those damn underclothes you *do* look kind of like a rabbit. I thought only kids wore those elastic kind of pants."

He looks down at his T-shirt and snug underpants, pleased and further stirred. His name in her mouth feels like a physical touch. She sees him as special. When he puts the rough cloth to her face, it goes tense and writhes with a resistance like Nelson's, and he counters it with a father's practiced method. He sweeps her forehead, pinches her nostrils, abrades her cheeks and, finally, while her whole body is squirming in protest, scrubs her lips, her words shattered and smothered. When at last he lets her hands win, and lifts the washrag, she stares at him, says nothing, and closes her eyes.

When he knelt by the bed to grip her face he pressed the sensitive core of his love against the edge of the mattress and now without his will a little spills, like cream forced over the neck of the bottle by the milk's freezing. He backs away from contact; the shy series of hops, puzzled, throbs to a slow halt. He stands and presses the cloth against his own face, like a man sobbing. He goes to the foot of the bed, throws the rag toward the bathroom, peels out of his underclothes, bobs, and hurries to hide in the bed, in the long dark space between the sheets.

He makes love to her as he would to his wife. After their marriage, and her nerves lost that fineness, Janice needed coaxing; he would begin by rubbing her back. Ruth submits warily when he tells her to lie on her stomach. To lend his hands strength he sits up on her cushiony buttocks and leans his weight down through stiff arms into his thumbs and palms as they work the broad muscles and insistent bones. She sighs and shifts her head on the pillow. "You should be in the Turkish-bath business," she says. He goes for her neck, and advances his fingers around to her throat, where the columns of blood give like reeds, and massages her shoulders with the balls of his thumbs, and his fingertips just find the glazed upper edges of her pillowing breasts. He returns to her back, until his wrists ache, and flops from astride his mermaid truly weary, as if under a sea-spell to sleep. He pulls the covers up over them, to the middle of their faces.

Janice was shy of his eyes so Ruth heats in his darkness. His lids flutter shut though she arches anxiously against him. Her hand seeks him, and angles him earnestly for a touch his sealed lids feel as red. He sees blue when with one deliberate hand she pries open his jaw and bows his head to her burdened chest. Lovely wobbly bubbles, heavy: perfume between. Taste, salt and sour, swirls back with his own saliva. She rolls away, onto her back, the precious red touch breaking, twists, giving him cool new skin. Rough with herself, she forces the dry other breast into his face, coated with a pollen that dissolves. He opens his eyes, seeking her, and sees her face a soft mask gazing downward calmly, caring for him, and closes his eyes on the food of her again; his hand abandoned on the breadth of her body finds at arm's length a split pod, an open fold, shapeless and simple. She rolls further, turning her back, cradling her bottom in his stomach and thighs. They enter a lazy space. He wants the time to stretch long, to great length and thinness. Between her legs she strokes him with her fingertips. She brings back her foot and he holds her heel. As they deepen together he feels impatience that through all their twists they remain separate flesh; he cannot dare enough, now that she is so much his friend in this search; everywhere they meet a wall. The body lacks voice to sing its own song. She floats through his blood as under his eyelids a salt smell, damp pressure, the sense of her smallness as her body hurries everywhere into his hands, her breathing, bedsprings' creak, accidental slaps, and the ache at the parched root of his tongue each register their colors.

"Now?" Ruth asks, her voice croaky. He kneels in a kind of sickness between her spread legs. With her help their blind loins fit. Something sad in the capture. The capture grows. He braces himself on his arms above her, afraid, for it is here he most often failed Janice, by coming too soon. Yet, what with the alcohol drifting in his system, or his coming a little before, his love is slow to burst in her warmth. He hides his face beside her throat, in the mint of her hair. With thin, thin arms she hugs him and presses him down and rises above him. From her high smooth shoulders down she is one long underbelly erect in light above him; he says in praise softly, "Hey."

She answers, "Hey."

"You're pretty."

"Come on. Work."

Galled, he shoves up through her and in addition sets his hand under her jaw and shoves her face so his fingers slip into her mouth and her slippery throat strains. As if unstrung by this anger, she tumbles and carries him over and he lies on top of her again, the skin of their chests sticking together; she reaches her hand down and touches their mixed fur and her breathing snags on something sharp. Her thighs throw open wide and clamp his sides and throw open again so wide it frightens him; she wants, impossible, to turn inside out; the muscles and lips of her expanded underside press against him as a new anatomy, of another animal. She feels transparent; he sees her heart. So she is first, and waits for him while at a trembling extremity of tenderness he traces again and again the arc of her eyebrow with his thumb. His sea of seed buckles, and sobs into a still channel. At each shudder her mouth smiles in his and her legs, locked at his back, bear down.

She asks in time, "O.K.?"

"You're pretty."

Ruth takes her legs from around him and spills him off her body like a pile of sand. He looks in her face and seems to read in its shadows an expression of forgiveness, as if she knows that at the moment of release, the root of love, he betrayed her by feeling despair. Nature leads you up like a mother and as soon as she gets her little contribution leaves you with nothing. The sweat on his skin is cold in the air; he brings the blankets up from her feet.

"You were a beautiful piece," he says from the pillow listlessly, and touches her soft side. Her flesh still soaks in the act; it ebbs slower in her.

"I had forgotten," she says.

"Forgot what?"

"That I could have it too."

"What's it like?"

"Oh. It's like falling through."

"Where do you fall to?"

"Nowhere. I can't talk about it."

He kisses her lips; she's not to blame. She lazily accepts, then in an afterflurry of affection flutters her tongue against his chin.

He loops his arm around her waist and composes himself against her body for sleep.

"Hey. I got to get up."

"Stay."

"I got to go into the bathroom."

"No." He tightens his hold.

"Boy, you better let me up."

He murmurs, "Don't scare me," and snuggles more securely against her side. His thigh slides over hers, weight on warmth. Wonderful, women, from such hungry wombs to such amiable fat. Best bedfriend, fucked woman. Bowl bellies. Oh, how! when she got up on him like the bell of a big blue lily slipped down on his slow head. He could have hurt her shoving her jaw. He reawakens enough to feel his dry breath drag through sagged lips as she rolls from under his leg and arm. "Hey get me a glass of water," he says.

She stands by the edge of the bed, baggy in nakedness, and goes off into the bathroom to do her duty. There's that in women repels him: handle themselves like an old envelope. Tubes into tubes, wash away men's dirt – insulting, really. Faucets cry. The more awake he gets the more depressed he is. From deep in the pillow he stares at the horizontal strip of stained-glass church window that shows beneath the window shade. Its childish brightness comes from years away.

Light from behind the closed bathroom door tints the air in the bedroom. The splashing sounds are like the sounds his parents would make when as a child Rabbit would waken to realize that they had come upstairs, the whole house would soon be dark, and the sight of morning would be his next sensation. He is asleep when like a faun in moonlight Ruth, washed, creeps back to his side, holding a glass of water.

During this sleep he has an intense dream. He and his mother and father and some others are sitting around their kitchen table. It's the old kitchen. A girl at the table reaches with a very long arm weighted with a bracelet and turns a handle of the wood icebox and cold air sweeps over Rabbit. She has opened the door of the square cave where the cake of ice sits; and there it is, inches from Harry's eyes, lopsided from melting but still big, holding within its semi-opaque bulk the white partition that the cakes have when they come bumping down the chute at the ice plant. He leans closer into the cold breath of the ice, a tin-smelling coldness he associates with the metal that makes up the walls of the cave and the ribs of its floor, delicate rhinoceros gray, mottled with the same disease the linoleum has. Having leaned closer he sees that under the watery skin are hundreds of clear white veins like the capillaries on a leaf, as if ice too were built up of living cells. And further inside, so ghostly it comes to him last, hangs a jagged cloud, the star of an explosion, whose center is uncertain in refraction but whose arms fly from the core of pallor as straight as long erasermarks diagonally into all planes of the cube. The rusted ribs the cake rests on wobble through to his eyes like the teeth of a grin. Fear probes him; the cold lump is alive.

His mother speaks to him. "Close the door."

"I didn't open it."

"I know."

"She did."

"I know. My good boy wouldn't hurt anyone." The girl at the table fumbles a piece of food and with terrible weight Mother turns and scolds her. The scolding keeps on and on, senselessly, the same thing over and over again, a continuous pumping of words like a deep inner bleeding. It is himself bleeding; his grief for the girl distends his face until it feels like a huge white dish. "Tart can't eat decently as a baby," Mother says.

"Hey, hey, hey," Rabbit cries, and stands up to defend his sister. Mother rears away, scoffing. They are in the narrow place between the two houses; only himself and the girl; it is Janice Springer. He tries to explain about his mother. Janice's head meekly stares at his shoulder; when he puts his arms around her he is conscious of her eyes being bloodshot. Though their faces are not close he feels her breath, hot with tears. They are out behind the Mt. Judge Recreation Hall, out in back with the weeds and tramped-down bare ground and embedded broken bottles; through the wall they hear music on loudspeakers. Janice has a pink dance dress on, and is crying. He repeats, sick at heart, about his mother, that she was just getting at *him* but the girl keeps crying, and to his horror her face begins to slide, the skin to slip slowly from the bone, but there is no bone, just more melting stuff underneath; he cups his hands with the idea of catching it and patting it back; as it drips in loops into his palms the air turns white with what is his own scream.

The white is light; the pillow glows against his eyes and sunlight projects the bubble flaws of the window panes onto the drawn shade. This woman is curled up under the blankets between him and the window. Her hair in sunlight sprays red, brown, gold, white, and black across her pillow. Smiling with relief, he gets up on an elbow and kisses her solid slack cheek, admires its tough texture of pores. He sees by faint rose streaks how imperfectly he scrubbed her face in the dark. He returns to the position in which he slept, but he has slept too much in recent hours. As if to seek the entrance to another dream he reaches for her naked body across the little distance and wanders up and down broad slopes, warm like freshly baked cake. Her back is toward him; he cannot see her eyes. Not until she sighs heavily and stretches and turns toward him does he know she is awake.

Again, then, they make love, in morning light with cloudy mouths, her breasts floating shallow on her ridged rib cage. Her nipples are sunken brown buds, her bush a brass froth. It is almost too naked; his climax seems petty in relation to the wealth of brilliant skin, and he wonders if she pretends. She says not; no, it was different but all right. Really all right. He goes back under the covers while she pads around on bare feet getting dressed. Funny how she puts on her bra before her underpants. Her putting on her underpants makes him conscious of her legs as separate things: thick pink liquid twists diminishing downward into her ankles. They take a rosy light from the reflection of each other as she walks around. Her accepting his watching her flatters him, shelters him. They have become domestic.

Church bells ring loudly. He moves to her side of the bed to watch the crisply dressed people go into the limestone church across the street, whose lit window had lulled him to sleep. He reaches and pulls up the shade a few feet. The rose window is dark now, and above the church, above Mt. Judge, the sun glares in a façade of blue. It strikes a shadow down from the church steeple, a cool stumpy negative in which a few men with flowers in their lapels stand and gossip while the common sheep of the flock stream in, heads down. The thought of these people having the bold idea of leaving their homes to come here and pray pleases and reassures Rabbit, and moves him to close his own eyes and bow his head with a movement so tiny that Ruth won't notice. *Help me, Christ. Forgive me. Take me down the way. Bless Ruth, Janice, Nelson, my mother and father, Mr. and Mrs. Springer, and the unborn baby. Forgive Tothero and all the others. Amen.*

He opens his eyes to the day and says, "That's a pretty big congregation."

"Sunday morning," she says. "I could throw up every Sunday morning."

"Why?"

She just says, "Fuh," as if he knows the answer. After thinking a bit, and seeing him lie there looking out the window seriously, she says, "I once had a guy in here who woke me up at eight o'clock because he had to teach Sunday school at nine-thirty."

"You don't believe anything?"

"No. You mean you do?"

"Well, yeah. I think so." Her rasp, her sureness, makes him wince; he wonders if he's lying. If he is, he is hung in the middle of nowhere, and the thought hollows him. Across the street a few people in their best clothes walk on the pavement past the row of worn brick homes; are they walking on air? Their clothes, they put on their best clothes: he clings to the thought giddily; it seems a visual proof of the unseen world.

"Well, if you do what are you doing here?" she asks.

"Why not? You think you're Satan or somebody?"

This stops her a moment, standing there with her comb, before she laughs. "Well you go right ahead if it makes you happy."

He presses her. "Why don't you believe anything?"

"You're kidding."

"No. Doesn't it ever, at least for a second, seem obvious to you?"

"God, you mean? No. It seems obvious just the other way. All the time."

"Well now if God doesn't exist, why does anything?"

"Why? There's no why to it. Things just are." She stands before the mirror, and her comb pulling back on her hair pulls her upper lip up; women are always looking that way in the movies.

"That's not the way I feel about you," he says, "that you just are."

"Hey, why don't you get some clothes on instead of just lying there giving me the Word?"

This, and her turning, hair swirling, to say it, stir him. "Come here," he asks. The idea of making it while the churches are full excites him.

"No," Ruth says. She is really a little sore. His believing in God grates against her.

"You don't like me now?"

"What does it matter to you?"

"You know it does."

"Get out of my bed."

"I guess I owe you fifteen more dollars."

"All you owe me is getting the hell out."

"What! Leave you all alone?" He says this as with comical speed, while she stands there startled, he jumps from bed and gathers up some of his clothes and ducks into the bathroom and closes the door. When he comes out, in underclothes, he says, still clowning, "You don't like me any more," and moves pouting to where his trousers are neatly laid on the chair. While he was out of the room she made the bed.

"I like you enough," she says in a preoccupied voice, tugging the bedspread smooth.

"Enough for what?"

"Enough."

"Why do you like me?"

"'Cause you're bigger than I am." She moves to the next corner and tugs. "Boy that used to gripe hell out of me, the way these little women everybody thinks are so cute grab all the big men."

"They have something," he tells her. "They seem easier to nail down."

She laughs and says, "To nail down or screw?"

He pulls up his trousers and buckles the belt. "Why else do you like me?"

She looks at him. "Shall I tell you?"

"Tell me."

"'Cause you haven't given up. In your stupid way you're still fighting."

He loves hearing this; pleasure spins along his nerves, making him feel immense. But American modesty has been drilled into him, and "the will to achievement" glides out of his mouth, which he tries to make look lopsided. She gets it.

"That poor old bastard," she says. "He really is a bastard too."

"Hey, I'll tell you what," Rabbit says. "I'll run out and get some stuff at that grocery store you can cook for our lunch."

"Say, you settle right in, don't you?"

"Why? Were you going to meet somebody?"

"No, I don't have anybody today."

"Well, then. You said last night you liked to cook."

"I said I used to."

"Well, if you used to you still do. What shall I get?"

"How do you know the store's open?"

"Isn't it? Sure it is. Those little stores make all their money on Sundays, what with the supermarkets." He goes to the window and looks up at the corner. Sure, the door of the store opens and a man comes out with a newspaper.

"Your shirt's filthy," she says behind him.

"I know." He moves away from the window light. "It's Tothero's shirt. I got to get my own clothes. But let me get us food now. What shall I get?"

"What do you like?" she asks.

He leaves pleased. The thing about her is, she's good-natured. He knew it the second he saw her standing by the parking meters. He could just tell from the way her thighs made a lap. With women, you keep bumping against them, because they want different things; they're a different race. The good ones develop give. In all the green world nothing feels as good as a woman's good nature. The pavement kicks under his feet as he runs to the grocery store in his dirty shirt. *What do you like?* He has her. He knows he has her.

He brings back eight hot dogs in cellophane, a package of frozen lima beans, a package of frozen French fries, a quart of milk, a jar of relish, a loaf of raisin bread, a ball of cheese wrapped in red cellophane, and, on top of the bag, a Ma Sweitzer's shoo-fly pie. It all costs $2.43. As she brings the things out of the bag in her tiny stained kitchen, Ruth says, "You're not a very healthy eater."

"I wanted lamb chops but he only had hot dogs and salami and hash in cans."

While she cooks he wanders around her living room and finds a row of pocketbook mysteries on a shelf under a table beside a chair. The Jewish guy in the bunk beside his at Fort Larson used to read those all the time. Ben Shamberger. A smart mouth but mournful inky eyes. Hated the Army. Broke his arm from riding a steer one weekend on a dare from that maniac Jarzylo. Ruth has opened the windows, and the cool March air is sharpened by this memory of baking Texas. Ruth's curtains of dingy dotted Swiss blow; their gauze skin gently fills and they lean in toward him as he stands paralyzed by another memory: his home, when he was a child, the Sunday papers rattling on the floor, stirred by the afternoon draft, and his mother rattling the dishes in the kitchen. When she is done, she will organize them all, Pop and him and baby Miriam, to go for a walk. Because of the baby, they will not go far, just a few blocks maybe to the old gravel quarry, where the ice pond of winter, melted into a lake a few inches deep, doubles the height of the quarry cliff by throwing its rocks upside down into a pit of reflection. But it is only water; they take a few steps farther along the edge and from this new angle the pond mirrors the sun, the illusion of inverted cliffs is wiped out, and the water is as solid as ice with light. Rabbit holds little Mim hard by the hand. "Hey," he calls to Ruth. "I got a terrific idea. Let's go for a walk this afternoon."

"Walk! I walk all the time."

"Let's walk up to the top of Mt. Judge from here." He can't remember having ever gone up the mountain from the Brewer side. Gusts of anticipation sweep over him, and as he turns, exalted, away from the curtains stiff and leaning with the breeze, huge church bells ring. "Yeah let's," he calls into the kitchen. "How about it?" Out on the street people leave church carrying wands of green absentmindedly at their sides.

When Ruth serves lunch he sees she is a better cook than Janice; she has boiled the hot dogs somehow without splitting them. With Janice, they always arrived at the table torn and twisted and tortured-looking. He and Ruth eat at a small por- celain table in the kitchen. As he touches his fork to his plate he remembers the cold feel in his dream of Janice's face dropping into his hands, and the memory spoils his first bite, makes it itself a kind of horror. Nevertheless he says "Terrific" and gamely goes ahead and eats and does regain his appetite.

Ruth's face across from him takes some of the pale glare of the table-top; the skin of her broad forehead shines and the two blemishes beside her nose are like spots something spilled has left. She seems to sense that she has become unattractive, and eats with quick little self-effacing bites.

"Hey," he says.

"What?"

"You know I still have that car parked over on Cherry Street."

"You're O.K. The meters don't matter on Sunday."

"Yeah, but they will tomorrow."

"Sell it."

"Huh?"

"Sell the car. Simplify your life. Get rich quick."

"No, I mean – oh. You mean for you. Look, I still have thirty dollars, why dontcha let me give it to you now?" He reaches toward his hip pocket.

"No, no, I did *not* mean that. I didn't mean anything. It just popped into my fat head." She is embarrassed; her neck goes splotchy and his pity is roused, to think how beautiful she appeared last night.

He explains. "You see, my wife's old man is a used-car dealer and when we got married he sold us this car at a pretty big discount. So in a way it's really my wife's car and anyway since she has the kid I think she ought to have it. And then as you say my shirt's dirty and I ought to get my clothes if I can. So what I thought was, after lunch why don't I sneak over to my place and leave the car and pick up my clothes?"

"Suppose she's there?"

"She won't be. She'll be at her mother's."

"I think you'd like it if she was there," Ruth says.

He wonders; he imagines opening the door and finding Janice sitting there in the armchair with an empty glass watching television and feels, like a piece of food stuck in his throat at last going down, his relief at finding her face still firm, still its old dumb tense self of a face. "No, I wouldn't," he tells Ruth. "I'm scared of her."

"Obviously," Ruth says.

"There's something about her," he insists. "She's a menace."

"This poor wife you left? *You're* the menace, I'd say."

"Me?"

"Oh that's right. You think you're a rabbit." Her tone in saying this is faintly jeering and irritable, he doesn't know why.

She asks, "What do you think you're going to do with these clothes?"

He admits, "Bring them here."

She takes in the breath but comes out with nothing.

"Just for tonight," he pleads. "You're not doing anything are you?

"Maybe. I don't know. Probably not."

"Well then, great. Hey. I love you."

She rises to clear away the plates and stands there, thumb on china, staring at the center of the white table. She shakes her head heavily and says, "You're bad news."

Across from him her broad pelvis, snug in a nubbly brown skirt, is solid and symmetrical as the base of a powerful column. His heart rises through that strong column and, enraptured to feel his love for her founded anew yet not daring to lift his eyes to the test of her face, he says, "I can't help it. You're such good news."

He eats three pieces of shoo-fly pie and a crumb in the corner of his lips comes off on her sweater when he kisses her breasts goodbye in the kitchen. He leaves her with the dishes. His car is waiting for him on Cherry Street in the cool spring noon mysteriously; it is as if a room of a house he owned had been detached and scuttled by this curb and now that the tide of night was out stood up glistening in the sand, slightly tilting but unharmed, ready to sail at the turn of a key. Under his rumpled dirty clothes his body feels clean, narrow, hollow. He has scored. The car smells of rubber and dust and painted metal hot in the sun: a sheath for the knife of himself. He cuts through the Sunday-stunned town, the soft rows of domestic brick, the banistered porches of wood. He drives around the southern flank of Mt. Judge; its slope by the highway is dusted the yellow-green of new leaves; higher up, the evergreens make a black horizon with the sky. The view has changed since the last time he came this way. Yesterday morning the sky was ribbed with thin-stretched dawn clouds, and he was exhausted, heading into the center of the net, where alone there seemed a chance of rest. Now the noon of another day has burned away the clouds, and the sky in the windshield is blank and cold, and he feels nothing ahead of him, Ruth's blue-eyed nothing, the nothing she told him she did, the nothing she believes in. Your heart lifts forever through that blank sky.

His mood of poise crumbles as he descends into the familiar houses of Mt. Judge. He becomes cautious, nervous. He turns up Jackson, up Potter, up Wilbur, and tries to make out from some external sign if there is anyone in his apartment. No telltale light would show; it is the height of day. No car is out front. He circles the block twice, straining his neck to see a face at the window. The panes are high and opaque. Ruth was wrong; he does not want to see Janice.

The bare possibility makes him so faint that when he gets out of the car the bright sun almost knocks him down. As he climbs the stairs, the steps seem to calibrate, to restrain by notches, a helpless tendency in his fear-puffed body to rise. He raps on the door, braced to run. Nothing answers on the other side. He taps again, listens, and takes the key out of his pocket.

Though the apartment is empty, it is yet so full of Janice he begins to tremble; the sight of that easy chair turned to face the television attacks his knees. Nelson's broken toys on the floor derange his head; all the things inside his skull, the gray matter, the bones of his ears, the apparatus of his eyes, seem clutter clogging the tube of his self; his sinuses choke, with a sneeze or tears he doesn't know. The living room smells of desertion. The shades are still drawn. Janice drew them in the afternoons to keep glare off the television screen. Someone has made gestures of cleaning up; her ashtray and her empty glass have been taken away. Rabbit puts the door key and the car keys on top of the television case, metal painted brown in imitation of wood grain. As he opens the closet door the knob bumps against the edge of the set. Some of her clothes are gone.

He means to reach for his clothes but instead turns and wanders toward the kitchen, trying to gather up the essence of what he has done. Their bed sags in the filtered sunlight. Never a good bed. Her parents had given it to them. On the bureau there is a square glass ashtray and a pair of fingernail scissors and a spool of white thread and a needle and some hairpins and a telephone book and a Baby Ben with luminous numbers and a recipe she never used torn from a magazine and a necklace made of sandalwood beads carved in Java he got her for Christmas. Insecurely tilted against the wall is the big oval mirror they took away when her parents had a new bathroom put in; he always meant to attach it to the plaster above her bureau for her but never got around to buying molly bolts. A glass on the windowsill, half full of stale, bubbled water, throws a curved patch of diluted sun onto the bare place where the mirror should have been fixed. Three long nicks, here, scratched in the wall, parallel; what ever made them, when? Beyond the edge of the bed a triangle of linoleum bathroom floor shows; the time after her shower, her bottom blushing with steam, lifting her arms gladly to kiss him, soaked licks of hair in her armpits. What gladness had seized her, and then him, unasked?

In the kitchen he discovers an odd oversight: the pork chops never taken from the pan, cold as death, riding congealed grease. He dumps them out in the paper bag under the sink and with a spatula scrapes crumbs of the stiff speckled fat after them. The bag, stained dark brown at the bottom, smells of something sweetly rotting. He puzzles. The garbage can is downstairs out back, he doesn't want to make two trips. He decides to forget it. He draws scalding water into the sink and puts the pan in to soak. The breath of steam is a whisper in a tomb.

In frightened haste he takes clean Jockey pants, T-shirts, and socks from a drawer, three shirts in cellophane and blue cardboard from another, a pair of laundered suntans from a third, draws his two suits and a sports shirt from the closet, and wraps the smaller clothing in the suits to form a bundle he can carry. The job makes him sweat. Clutching his clothes between two arms and a lifted thigh, he surveys the apartment once more, and the furniture, carpeting, wallpaper all seem darkly glazed with the murk filming his own face; the rooms are filled with the flavor of an awkward job, and he is glad to get out. The door snaps shut behind him irrevocably. His key is inside.

Toothbrush. Razor. Cufflinks. Shoes. At each step down he remembers something he forgot. He hurries, his feet patter. He jumps. His head almost hits the naked bulb burning at the end of a black cord in the vestibule. His name on the mailbox seems to call at him as he sweeps past; its letters of blue ink crowd the air like a cry. He feels ridiculous, ducking into the sunlight like one of those weird thieves you read about in the back pages of newspapers who instead of stealing money and silver carry away a porcelain washbasin, twenty rolls of wallpaper, or a bundle of old clothes.

"Good afternoon, Mr. Angstrom."

A neighbor is passing, Miss Arndt, in a lavender church hat, carrying a palm frond in clutched hands. "Oh. Hello. How are you?" She lives three houses up; they think she has cancer.

"I am just splendid," she says. "Just splendid." And stands there in sunshine, bewildered by splendor, flatfooted, leaning unconsciously against the slope of the pavement. A gray car goes by too slowly. Miss Arndt sticks in Rabbit's way, amiably confused, grateful for something, her simple adherence to the pavement it seems, like a fly who stops walking on the ceiling to marvel at itself.

"How do you like the weather?" he asks.

"I love it, I love it; Palm Sunday is always blue. It makes the sap rise in my legs." She laughs and he follows; she stands rooted to the hot cement between the feathery shade of two young maples. She knows nothing, he becomes certain.

"Yes," he says, for her eyes have fixed on his arms. "I seem to be doing spring cleaning." He shrugs the bundle to clarify.

"Good," she says, with a surprising sarcastic snarl. "You young husbands, you certainly take the bit in your teeth." Then she twists, and exclaims, "Why, there's a clergyman in there!"

The gray car has come back, even more slowly, down the center of the street. With a dismay that makes the bundle of clothes double its weight in his arms, Rabbit realizes he is pinned. He lurches from the porch and strides past Miss Arndt saying, "I got to run," right on top of her considered remark, "It's not Reverend Kruppenbach."

No, of course not Kruppenbach; Rabbit knows who it is, though he doesn't know his name. The Episcopalian. The Springers were Episcopalians, more of the old phony's social climbing, they were originally Reformeds. Rabbit doesn't quite run. The downhill pavement jars his heels at every stride. He can't see the cement under the bundle he carries. If he can just make the alley. His one hope is the minister can't be sure it's him. He feels the gray car crawling behind him; he thinks of throwing the clothes away and really running. If he could get into the old ice plant. But it's a block away. He feels Ruth, the dishes done, waiting on the other side of the mountain.

As a shark nudges silent creases of water ahead of it, the gray

fender makes ripples of air that break against the back of Rabbit's
knees. The faster he walks the harder these ripples break. Behind
his ear a childishly twanging voice pipes, "I beg your pardon. Are
you Harry Angstrom?"

With a falling sensation of telling a lie Rabbit turns and half-
whispers, "Yes."

The fair young man with his throat manacled in white lets his
car glide diagonally against the curb, yanks on the handbrake, and
shuts off the motor, thus parking on the wrong side of the street,
cockeyed. Funny how ministers ignore small laws. Rabbit
remembers how Kruppenbach's son used to tear around town on
a motorcycle. It seemed somehow blasphemous. "Well, I'm Jack
Eccles," this minister says, and inconsequently laughs a syllable.
The white stripe of an unlit cigarette hanging from his lips makes
with the echoing collar a comic picture in the car window. He
gets out of his car, a '58 Buick four-door Special, with those
canted fins and that rocket-arc of chrome on the side, and offers
his hand. To accept it Rabbit has to put his big ball of clothes
down in the strip of grass between the pavement and curb.

Eccles' handshake, eager and practiced and hard, seems to symbolize for him an embrace. For an instant Rabbit fears he will
never let go. He feels caught, foresees explanations, embarrass-
ments, prayers, reconciliations rising up like dank walls; his skin
prickles in desperation. He senses tenacity in his captor.

The minister is about his age or a little older and a good bit
shorter. But not small; a sort of needless muscularity runs under
his black coat. He stands edgily, with his chest faintly cupped. He
has long reddish eyebrows that push a worried wrinkle around
above the bridge of his nose, and a little pale pointed knob of a
chin tucked under his mouth. Despite his looking vexed there is
something friendly and silly about him.

"Where are you going?" he asks.

"Huh? Nowhere." Rabbit is distracted by the man's suit; it
only feigns black. It is really blue, a sober but elegant, lightweight,
midnight blue. While his little vest or bib or whatever is black as
a stove. The effort of keeping the cigarette between his lips twists
Eccles' laugh into a snort. He slaps the breasts of his coat. "Do you
have a match by any chance?"

"Gee I'm sorry, no. I quit smoking."

"You're a better man than I am." He pauses and thinks, then looks at Harry with startled, arched eyebrows. The distention makes his gray eyes seem round and as pale as glass. "Can I give you a lift?"

"No. Hell. Don't bother."

"I'd like to talk to you."

"No; you don't really want to, do you?"

"I do, yes. Very much."

"Yeah. O.K." Rabbit picks up his clothes and walks around the front of the Buick and gets in. The interior has that sweet tangy plastic new-car smell; he takes a deep breath of it and it cools his fear. "This is about Janice?"

Eccles nods, staring out the rear window as he backs away from the curb. His upper lip overhangs his lower; there are scoops of weary violet below his eyes. Sunday would be his heavy day.

"How is she? What did she do?"

"She seems much saner today. She and her father came to church this morning." They drive down the street. Eccles adds nothing, just gazes through the windshield, blinking. He pokes the lighter in on the dashboard.

"I *thought* she'd be with them," Rabbit says. He is getting slightly annoyed at the way the minister isn't bawling him out or something; he doesn't seem to know his job.

The lighter pops. Eccles puts it to his cigarette, inhales, and seems to come back into focus. "Evidently," he says, "when you didn't come back in half an hour she called your parents and had your father bring your boy over to your apartment. Your father, I gather, was very reassuring and told her you had probably been sidetracked somewhere. She remembered you had been late getting home because of some street game and thought you might have gone back to it. I believe your father even walked around town looking for the game."

"Where was old man Springer?"

"She didn't call them. She didn't call them until two o'clock that morning, when I suppose the poor thing had given up all hope." "Poor thing" is one word on his lips, worn smooth.

Harry asks, "Not until two?" Pity grips him; his hands tighten on the bundle, as if comforting Janice.

"Around then. By then she was in such a state, alcoholic and otherwise, that her mother called me."

"Why you?"

"I don't know. People do." Eccles laughs. "They're supposed to; it's comforting. To me at least. I always thought Mrs. Springer hated me. She hadn't been to church in months." As he turns to face Rabbit, to follow up this joke, a little quizzical pang lifts his eyebrows and forces his broad mouth open.

"This was around two in the morning?"

"Between two and three."

"Gee, I'm sorry. I didn't mean to get you out of bed."

The minister shakes his head irritably. "That's not a consideration"

"Well I feel terrible about this."

"Do you? That's hopeful. Uh, what, exactly, is your plan?"

"I don't really have a plan. I'm sort of playing it by ear."

Eccles' laughter surprises him; it occurs to Rabbit that the minister is an expert on affairs like this – broken homes, fleeing husbands – and that "playing it by ear" has struck a fresh note. He feels flattered. Eccles has this knack.

"Your mother has an interesting viewpoint," the minister says. "She thinks it's all an illusion your wife and I have, that you've deserted. She says you're much too good a boy to do anything of the sort."

"You've been busy on this, haven't you?"

"This, and a death yesterday."

"Gee, I'm sorry."

They have been driving idly, at low speed, through the familiar streets; once they passed the ice plant, and at another point rounded a corner from which you can see across the valley to the next ridge of hills. "Say, if you really want to give me a lift," Rabbit says, "you could drive over into Brewer."

"You don't want me to take you to your wife?"

"No. Good grief. I mean I don't think it would do any good, do you?"

For a long time it seems that the other man didn't hear him; his tidy, tired profile stares through the windshield as the big car hums forward steadily. Harry has taken the breath to repeat himself when Eccles says, "Not if you don't want good to come of it."

The matter seems ended this simply. They drive down Potter Avenue toward the highway. The sunny streets have just children on them, some of them still in their Sunday-school clothes. Little girls wear pastel organdy dresses that stick straight out from their waists. Their ribbons match their socks.

Eccles asks, "What did she do that made you leave?"

"She asked me to buy her a pack of cigarettes."

Eccles doesn't laugh as he had hoped; he seems to dismiss the remark as impudence, a little over the line. But it was the truth. "It's the truth. It just felt like the whole business was fetching and hauling, all the time trying to hold this mess together she was making all the time. I don't know, it seemed like I was glued in with a lot of busted toys and empty glasses and the television going and meals late or never and no way of getting out. Then all of a sudden it hit me how easy it was to get out, just walk out, and by damn it *was* easy."

"For less than two days, it's been."

"It's been not *only* easy. It's been strange, too." Rather than try to describe the strangeness, he asks, "What's Janice going to do, do you think?"

"She doesn't know. Your wife seems almost paralyzed; she doesn't want anyone to do anything."

"Poor kid. She's such a mutt."

"Why are you here?"

" 'Cause you caught me."

"I mean why were you in front of your home?"

"I came back to get clean clothes."

"Do clean clothes mean so much to you? Why cling to that decency if trampling on the others is so easy?"

Rabbit feels now the danger of talking; his words are coming back to him, little hooks and snares are being fashioned. "Also I was leaving her the car."

"Why? Don't you need it, to explore your freedom in?"

"I just thought she should have it. Her father sold it to us cheap. Anyway it didn't do me any good."

"No?" Eccles stubs his cigarette out in the car ashtray and goes to his coat pocket for another. They are rounding the mountain, at the highest stretch of road, where the hill rises too steeply on one side and falls too steeply on the other to give space to a house or gasoline station. The river darkly shines down below. "Now if *I* were to leave *my* wife," he says, "I'd get into a car and drive a thousand miles." It almost seems like advice, coming calmly from above the white collar.

"That's what I did!" Rabbit cries, delighted by how much they have in common. "I drove as far as West Virginia. Then I thought the hell with it and came back." He must try to stop swearing; he wonders why he's doing it. To keep them apart, maybe; he feels a dangerous tug drawing him toward this man.

"Should I ask why?"

"Oh I don't know. A combination of things. It seemed safer to be in a place I know."

"You didn't come back to protect your wife?"

Rabbit is wordless at the idea.

Eccles continues, "You speak of this feeling of muddle. What do you think it's like for other young couples? In what way do you think you're exceptional?"

"You don't think there's any answer to that but there is. I once did something right. I played first-rate basketball. I really did. And after you're first-rate at something, no matter what, it kind of takes the kick out of being second-rate. And that little thing Janice and I had going, boy, it was really second-rate."

The dashboard lighter pops. Eccles uses it and quickly returns his eyes to his driving. They've come down into the outskirts of Brewer. He asks, "Do you believe in God?"

Having rehearsed that this morning, Rabbit answers without hesitation, "Yes."

Eccles blinks in surprise. The furry lid in his one-eyed profile shutters, but his face does not turn. "Do you think, then, that God wants you to make your wife suffer?"

"Let me ask you. Do you think God wants a waterfall to be a tree?" This question of Jimmie's sounds, Rabbit realizes, ridiculous; he is annoyed that Eccles simply takes it in, with a sad drag of smoke. He realizes that no matter what he says, Eccles will take it in with the same weary smoke; he is a listener by trade. His big fair head must be stuffed with a gray mash of everybody's precious secrets and passionate questions, a mash that nothing, young as he is, can color. For the first time, Rabbit dislikes him.

"No," Eccles says after thought. "But I think He wants a little tree to become a big tree."

"If you're telling me I'm not mature, that's one thing I don't cry over since as far as I can make out it's the same thing as being dead."

"I'm immature myself," Eccles offers.

It's not enough of an offering. Rabbit tells him off. "Well, I'm not going back to that little soppy dope no matter how sorry you feel for her. I don't know what she feels. I haven't known for years. All I know is what's inside *me*. That's all I have. Do you know what I was doing to support that bunch? I was demonstrating a penny's worth of tin called a frigging MagiPeeler in McCrory's five and dime!"

Eccles looks at him wide-eyed. "Well that explains your oratorical gifts," he says.

This aristocratic sneer rings true; puts them both in place. Rabbit feels less at sea. "Hey, I wish you'd let me out," he says. They're on Weiser Street, heading toward the great sunflower, dead in day.

"Won't you let me take you to where you're staying?"

"I'm not staying anywhere."

"All right." With a trace of boyish bad temper Eccles pulls over and stops in front of a fire hydrant. As he brakes racily, something clatters in the trunk.

"You're coming apart," Rabbit tells him.

"Just my golf clubs."

"You play?"

"Badly. Do you?" He seems animated; the cigarette burns forgotten in his fingers.

"I used to caddy."

"Could I invite you for a game?" Ah. Here's the hook.

Rabbit gets out hugging his great ball of clothes and stands on the curb and sidesteps, clowning in his freedom. "I don't have clubs."

"They're easy to rent. Please. I mean it." Eccles leans far over, to speak through the door. "It's hard for me to find partners. Everybody works except me." He laughs.

Rabbit knows he should run, but the thought of a game, and an idea that it's safest to see the hunter, make resistance.

Eccles presses. "I'm afraid you'll go back to demonstrating peelers if I don't catch you soon. Tuesday? Tuesday at two? Shall I pick you up?"

"No; I'll come to your house."

"Promise?"

"Yeah. But don't trust a promise from me."

"I have to." Eccles names an address in Mt. Judge and they call goodbye at the curb. An old cop walks with a wise squint along the pavement beside the shut, stunned Sunday storefronts. To him it must look like a priest parting from the president of his Youth Group, who is carrying a bundle of clothes for the poor. Harry grins at this cop, and walks along the sparkling pavement with his stomach singing. Funny, the world just can't touch you once you follow your instincts.

Ruth lets him in, a pocket mystery in one hand. Her eyes look sleepy from reading. She has changed into another sweater. Her hair is loose and seems darker. He dumps the clothes on her bed. "Do you have hangers?"

"Say. You really think you have it made."

"I made you," he says. "I made you and the sun and the stars." Squeezing her in his arms it seems that he did. She is tepid and solid in his embrace, not friendly, not not. The filmy smell of soap lifts into his nostrils while dampness touches his jaw. She has washed her hair. Clean, she is clean, a big clean woman; he puts his nose against her skull to drink in the demure sharp scent. He thinks of her naked in the shower, her hair hanging oozy with lather, her neck bowed to the whipping water. "I made you bloom," he says.

"Oh you're a wonder," she answers, and pushes away from his chest. As he hangs up his suits tidily, Ruth asks, "You give your wife the car?"

"There was nobody there. I snuck in and out. I left the key inside."

"And nobody caught you?"

"As a matter of fact somebody did. The Episcopal minister gave me a ride back into Brewer."

"Say; you *are* religious, aren't you?"

"*I* didn't ask him."

"What did he say?"

"Nothing much."

"What was he like?"

"Kind of creepy. Giggled a lot."

"Maybe just *you* make him giggle."

"I'm supposed to play golf with him on Tuesday."

"You're kidding."

"No, really. I told him I don't know how."

She laughs, on and on, in that prolonged way women use when they're excited by you and ashamed of it. "Oh my Rabbit," she exclaims in a fond final breath. "You just grab what comes, don't you?"

"He got hold of *me*," he insists, knowing his attempts to explain will amuse her, for shapeless reasons. "I didn't do anything."

"You poor soul," she says. "You're just irresistible."

With keen secret relief, he at last takes off his dirty clothes and changes into clean underwear, fresh socks, and suntans. He left his razor at home but Ruth has a little curved female one for armpits that he uses. He chooses a wool sports shirt, for these afternoons in spring cool off sharply, and puts his suede shoes back on. He forgot to steal any other shoes. "Let's go for that walk," he announces, dressed.

"I'm reading," Ruth says from a chair. The book is open to near the end. She reads books nicely, without cracking their backs, though they cost only 35¢. She has combed her hair and put it back in a roll at the nape of her neck.

"Come on. Get out in the weather." He goes over and tries to tug the mystery from her hand. The title is *The Deaths at Oxford*. Now what should she care about deaths at Oxford? When she has him here, wonderful Harry Angstrom.

"Wait," she pleads, and turns a page, and reads some sentences as the book is pulled slowly up, her eyes shuttling, and then suddenly lets him take it. "God, you're a bully."

He marks her place with a burnt match and looks at her bare feet. "Do you have sneakers or anything? You can't wear heels."

"No. Hey I'm sleepy."

"We'll go to bed early."

Her eyeballs turn on him at this, her lips pursed a little. There is this vulgarity in her, that just couldn't let that just go by.

"Come on," he says. "Put on flat shoes and we'll get your hair dry."

"I'll have to wear heels, they're all I have." As she bows her head to pinch them on, the white line of her parting makes him smile, it's so straight. Like a little birthday girl's parting.

They approach the mountain through the city park. The trash baskets and movable metal benches have not been set out yet. On the concrete-and-plank benches fluffy old men sun like greater pigeons, dressed in patches of gray multiple as feathers. The trees in small leaf dust the half-bare ground with shadow. Sticks and strings protect the newly seeded margins of the unraked gravel walks. The breeze, flowing steadily down the slope from the empty bandshell, is cool out of the sun. The wool shirt was right. Pigeons with mechanical heads waddle away from their shoetips and resettle, chuffling, behind them. A derelict stretches an arm along the back of a bench to dry, and out of a gouged face daintily sneezes like a cat. A few toughs, fourteen or younger, smoke and jab near the locked equipment shed of a play pavilion on whose yellow boards someone has painted in red TEX & JOSIE, RITA & JAY. Where would they get red paint? He takes Ruth's hand. The ornamental pool in front of the bandshell is drained and scum-stained; they move along a path parallel to the curve of its cold lip, which echoes back the bandshell's silence. A World War II tank, made a monument, points its empty guns at far-off clay tennis courts. The nets are not up, the lines unlimed.

Trees darken; pavilions slide downhill. They walk through the upper region of the park, which delinquents haunt at night, scattering condoms and candy-bar wrappers. The beginning of the steps is almost hidden in an overgrowth of great bushes tinted dull amber with the first buds. Long ago, when hiking was customary entertainment, the city built stairs up the Brewer side of the mountain. They are made of six-foot tarred logs with dirt filled in flat behind them. Iron pipes have since been driven, to hold these tough round risers in place, and fine blue gravel scattered over the packed dirt they dam. The footing is difficult for Ruth; Rabbit watches her body struggle to propel her weight on the digging points of her heels. They catch and buckle. Her backside lurches, her arms swim for balance.

He tells her, "Take off your shoes."

"And kill my feet? You're a thoughtful bastard."

"Well then, let's go back down."

"No, no," she says. "We must be halfway."

"We're nowhere near half up. Take off your shoes. These blue stones are stopping; it'll just be mashed-down dirt."

"With chunks of glass in it."

But further on she does take off her shoes. Bare of stockings, her white feet lift lightly under his eyes; the yellow skin of her heels flickers. Under the swell of calf her ankles are thin. In a fond gesture he takes off his shoes and socks, to share whatever pain there is. The dirt is trod smooth, but embedded pebbles stab his skin with the force of his weight. Also the ground is cold. "Ouch," he says. "*Owitch*."

"Come on, soldier," she says, "be brave."

They learn to walk on the grass at the ends of the logs. Tree branches overhang part of the way, making it an upward tunnel. At other spots the air is clear behind them, and they can look over the rooftops of Brewer into the twentieth story of the courthouse, the city's one skyscraper. Concrete eagles stand in relief, wings flared, between its top windows. Two middle-aged couples in plaid scarves, bird-watchers, pass them on the way down; as soon as this couple has descended out of sight behind the gnarled arm of an oak, Rabbit hops up to Ruth's step and kisses her, hugs her hot bulk, tastes the salt in the sweat on her face, which is unresponsive. She thinks this is a silly time; her one-eyed woman's mind is intent on getting up the hill. But the thought of her city girl's paper-pale feet bare on the stones for his sake makes his heart, pumping with exertion, swell, and he clings to her broad body. An airplane goes over, rapidly rattling the air.

"My queen," he says, "my good horse."

"Your what?"

"Horse."

Near the top, the mountain rises sheer in a cliff, and here modern men have built concrete stairs with an iron railing that in a Z of three flights reach the macadam parking lot of the Pinnacle Hotel. Ruth and Rabbit put their shoes back on and, climbing the stairs, watch the city slowly flatten under them.

Rails guard the cliff edge. He grips one white beam, warmed by the sun that now is sinking away from the zenith, and looks straight down, into the exploding heads of trees. A frightening view, remembered from boyhood, when he used to wonder if you jumped would you die or be cushioned on those green heads as on the clouds of a dream? In the lower part of his vision the stone-walled cliff rises to his feet foreshortened to the narrowness of a knife; in the upper part the hillside slopes down, faint paths revealed and random clearings and the steps they have climbed.

Ruth's gaze, her lids half-closed as if she were reading a book, rests on the city.

O.K. He brought them up here. To see what? The city stretches from dollhouse rows at the base of the park through a broad blurred belly of flowerpot red patched with tar roofs and twinkling cars and ends as a rose tint in the mist that hangs above the distant river. Gas tanks glimmer in this smoke. Suburbs lie like scarves in it. But the city is huge in the middle view, and he opens his lips as if to force the lips of his soul to receive the taste of the truth about it, as if truth were a secret in such low solution that only immensity can give us a sensible taste. Air dries his mouth.

His day has been bothered by God: Ruth mocking, Eccles blinking – why did they teach you such things if no one believed them? It seems plain, standing here, that if there is this floor there is a ceiling, that the true space in which we live is upward space. Someone is dying. In this great stretch of brick someone is dying. The thought comes from nowhere: simple percentages. Someone in some house along these streets, if not this minute then the next, dies; and in that suddenly stone chest the heart of this flat prostrate rose seems to him to be. He moves his eyes to find the spot; perhaps he can see the cancer-blackened soul of an old man mount through the blue like a monkey on a string. He strains his ears to hear the pang of release as this ruddy illusion at his feet gives up this reality. Silence blasts him. Chains of cars creep without noise; a dot comes out of a door. What is he doing here, standing on air?

Why isn't he home? He becomes frightened and begs Ruth, "Put your arm around me."

She carelessly obliges, taking a step and swinging her haunch against his. He clasps her tighter and feels better. Brewer at their feet seems to warm in the sloping sunlight: its vast red cloth seems to lift from the valley in which it is sunk concavely, to fill like a breast with a breath, Brewer the mother of a hundred thousand, shelter of love, ingenious and luminous artifact. So it is in a return of security that he asks, voicing like a loved child a teasing doubt, "Were you really a hooer?"

To his surprise she turns hard under his arm and twists away and stands beside the railing menacingly. Her eyes narrow; her chin changes shape. In his nervousness he notices three Boy Scouts staring at them across the asphalt. She asks, "Are you really a rat?"

He feels the need of care in his answer. "In a way."

"All right then."

They take a bus down.

Tuesday afternoon, overcast, he takes a bus to Mt. Judge. Eccles' address is at the north end of town; he rides past his own neighborhood in safety, gets off at Spruce, and walks along singing in a high voice to himself the phrase, "Oh *I'm* just *wild* about Harry" – not the beginning of the song, but the place at the end where the girl, repeating, goes way up on "I'm."

He feels on even keel. For two days he and Ruth have lived on his money and he still has fourteen dollars left. Furthermore he has discovered, poking through her bureau this morning while she was out shopping, that she has an enormous checking account, with over five hundred dollars in it at the end of February. They have gone bowling once and have seen four movies – *Gigi; Bell, Book and Candle; The Inn of the Sixth Happiness;* and *The Shaggy Dog.* He saw so many snippets from *The Shaggy Dog* on the Mickey Mouse Club that he was curious to see the whole thing. It was like looking through a photograph album with about half familiar faces. The scene where the rocket goes through the roof and Fred

MacMurray runs out with the coffee pot he knew as well as his own face.

Ruth was funny. Her bowling was awful; she just sort of paddled up to the line and dropped the ball. *Plok.* Every time, in *Gigi*, the stereophonic-sound loudspeaker behind them in the theater would blare out she turned around and said "Shh" as if it were somebody in the theater talking too loud. In *The Inn of the Sixth Happiness* every time Ingrid Bergman's face appeared on the screen she leaned over to Rabbit and asked him in a whisper, "Is she really a hooer?" He was upset by Robert Donat; he looked awful. He knew he was dying. Imagine knowing you're dying and going ahead pretending you're a mandarin. Ruth's comment about *Bell, Book and Candle* last night was, "Why don't you ever see any bongo drums around here?" He vowed secretly to get her some. A half-hour ago, waiting for the bus on Weiser Street, he priced a set in the window of the Chords 'n' Records music store. $19.95. All the way out on the bus he was beating bongo patterns on his knees.

"For *I'm* just *wild* about Harrr-ree—"

Number 61 is a big brick place with white wood trim, a little porch imitating a Greek temple, and a slate roof that shines like the scales of a big fish. Out back a wire fence encloses a yellow swing frame and a sandbox. A puppy yaps in this pen as Harry goes up the walk. The grass wears that intense greasy green that promises rain, the color of grass in color snapshots. The place looks too cheerful to be right; Rabbit thinks of ministers as living in gloomy Lutheran houses. But a small plate above the fish-shaped door-knocker says in engraved script *The Rectory*. He bangs the fish twice and, after waiting, twice again.

A crisp little number with speckled green eyes opens the door. "What is it?" Her voice as good as says, "How dare you?" As she adjusts her face to his height her eyes enlarge, displaying more of the vividly clear whites to which her bright irises are buttoned.

At once, absurdly, he feels in control of her, feels she likes him. Freckles dot her little bumpy nose, kind of a pinched nose, narrow and pale under the dots of tan. Her skin is fair, and fine-grained as a child's. She is wearing orange shorts. With a pleasantness that amounts to arrogance he says, "Hi."

"Hello."

"Say, is Reverend Eccles in?"

"He's asleep."

"In the middle of the day?"

"He was up much of the night."

"Oh gosh. The poor guy."

"Do you want to come in?"

"Well gee, I don't know. He told me to be here. He really did."

"He might well have. Please come in."

She leads him past a hall and staircase into a cool room with a high ceiling and silver wallpaper, a piano, watercolors of scenery, a lot of sets of books in a recessed bookcase, a fireplace whose mantel supports one of those clocks with a pendulum of four gold balls that are supposed to run practically for ever. Photographs in frames all around. Furniture heavy brown and red except for a long sofa with a scrolling back and arms whose cushions are cream white. The room smells coldly kept. From far off comes the warmer odor of cake baking. She stops in the center of the rug and says, "Listen."

He stops. The faint bump that he also heard is not repeated. She explains, "I thought that brat was asleep."

"Are you the babysitter?"

"I'm the wife," she says, and sits down in the center of the white sofa, to prove it.

He takes a padded wing chair opposite. The plum fabric feels softly gritty against his naked forearms. He is wearing a checked sports shirt, with the sleeves turned back to his elbows. "Oh, I'm sorry." Of course. Her bare legs, crossed, show the blue dabs of varicose veins. Her face, when she sits, is not as young as at the door. Double chin when she relaxes, head tucked back. Smug little cookie. Firm little knockers. He asks, "How old is your child?"

"Two children. Two girls, one and three."

"I have a boy who's two."

"I'd like a boy," she says. "The girls and I have personality problems; we're too much alike. We know exactly what the other's thinking."

Dislikes her own children! Rabbit is shocked, this from a minister's wife. "Does your husband notice this?"

"Oh, it's wonderful for Jack. He loves to have women fighting over him. It's his little harem. I think a boy would threaten him. Do you feel threatened?"

"Not by the kid, no. He's only two."

"It starts earlier than two, believe me. Sexual antagonism begins practically at birth."

"I hadn't noticed."

"Good for you. I expect you're a primitive father. I think Freud is like God; you make it true."

Rabbit smiles, supposing that Freud has some connection with the silver wallpaper and the watercolor of a palace and a canal above her head. Class. She brings her fingertips to her temples, pushes her head back, shuts her lids, and through plump open lips sighs. He is struck; she seems at this moment a fine-grained Ruth. There is a world of women beyond Janice.

Eccles' thin voice, oddly amplified in his home, cries down the stairs, "Lucy! Joyce is getting into bed with me!"

Lucy opens her eyes and says to Rabbit proudly, "See?"

"She says you told her it's all right," the voice whines on, piercing banisters, walls, and layers of wallpaper.

Mrs. Eccles gets up and goes to the archway. The seat of her orange shorts is wrinkled from sitting; the hitched-up legs expose most of the oval backs of her thighs. Whiter than the sofa. The blush of pink from the pressure of sitting fades from her skin. "I told her no such thing!" she calls upward while an aware hand tugs the shorts down and smooths the cloth around her mussed rump. A pocket is stitched with black thread to the right half. "Jack," she goes on, "you have a visitor! A very tall young man who says you invited him!"

At the mention of himself Rabbit has risen, and right behind her he says, "To play golf."

"To play golf!" she echoes in a yell.

"Oh, dear," the voice upstairs says to itself, then shouts, "Hello, Harry! I'll be right down."

A child up there is crying, "Mommy did too! Mommy did too!"

Rabbit shouts in answer, "Hello!"

Mrs. Eccles turns her head with an inviting twist. "Harry —?"

"Angstrom."

"What do you do, Mr. Angstrom?"

"Well. I'm kind of out of work."

"Angstrom. Of course. Aren't you the one who disappeared? The Springers' son-in-law?"

"Right," he replies smartly and, in a mindless follow-through, an overflow of coördination, she having on the drop of his answer turned with prim dismissal away from him again, slaps! her sassy ass. Not hard: a cupping hit, rebuke and fond pat both, well-placed on the pocket.

She swiftly pivots, swinging her backside to safety behind her. Her freckles dart sharp as pinpricks from her shocked face. Her leaping blood bleaches her skin, and her rigidly cold stare is so incongruous with the lazy condescending warmth he feels toward her, that he pushes his upper lip over his lower in a burlesque expression of penitence.

A chaotic tumble on the stairs shakes the wall. Eccles jolts to a stop in front of them, off-balance, tucking a dirty white shirt into rumpled suntans. His shadowed eyes weep between his furry lids. "I'm sorry," he says. "I hadn't really forgotten."

"It's kind of cloudy anyway," Rabbit says, and smiles involuntarily. Her backside had felt so good, just right, dense yet springy: kind of smacked back. He supposes she'll tell, which will finish him here. Just as well. He doesn't know why he's here anyway.

Maybe she would have told, but her husband starts annoying her immediately. "Oh, I'm sure we can get in nine before it rains," he tells Rabbit.

"Jack, you aren't *really* going to play golf again. You said you had all those calls to make this afternoon."

"I made calls this morning."

"Two. You made two. On Freddy Davis and Mrs. Landis. The same old safe ones. What about the Ferrys? You've been talking about the Ferrys for six months."

"What's so sacred about the Ferrys? They never do anything for the church. She came on Christmas Sunday and went out by the choir door so she wouldn't have to speak to me."

"Of course they don't do anything for the church and that's why you should call as you know perfectly well. I don't think anything's sacred about the Ferrys except that you've been brooding about her going out the side door and making everybody's life miserable for months. Now if she comes on Easter it'll be the same thing. To tell you my honest opinion you and Mrs. Ferry would hit it off splendidly, you're both equally childish."

"Lucy, just because Mr. Ferry owns a shoe factory doesn't make them more important Christians than somebody who works in a shoe factory."

"Oh Jack, you're too tiresome. You're just afraid of being snubbed and don't quote Scripture to justify yourself. I don't care if the Ferrys come to church or stay away or become Jehovah's Witnesses."

"At least the Jehovah's Witnesses put into practice what they say they believe." When Eccles turns to Harry to guffaw conspiratorially after this dig, bitterness cripples his laugh, turns his lips in tightly, so his small-jawed head shows its teeth like a skull.

"I don't know what that's supposed to mean," Lucy says, "but when you asked me to marry you I told you what I felt and you said all right fine."

"I said as long as your heart remained open for *Grace*." Eccles pours these words on her in a high strained blast that burns his broad forehead, soils it with a blush.

"Mommy I had a *rest*." The little voice, shyly penetrating, surprises them from above. At the head of the carpeted stairs a small tan girl in underpants hangs in suspense. She seems to Rabbit too dark for her parents, braced on silhouetted legs of baby fat knotted on longer stalks. Her hands rub and pluck her naked chest in exasperation. She hears her mother's answer before it comes.

"Joyce. You go right back into your own bed and have a *nap*."

"I can't. There's too many noises."

"We've been screaming right under her head," Eccles tells his wife.

"*You've* been screaming. About Grace."

"I had a scary dream," Joyce says, and thumpingly descends two steps.

"You did not. You were never asleep." Mrs. Eccles walks to

the foot of the stairs, holding her throat as if to keep some emotion down.

"What was the dream about?" Eccles asks his child.

"A lion ate a boy."

"That's not a dream at all," the woman snaps, and turns on her
husband: "It's those hateful Belloc poems you insist on reading
her."

"She asks for them."

"They're hateful. They give her traumas."

"Joyce and I think they're funny."

"Well you *both* have perverted senses of humor. Every night
she asks me about that damn pony Tom and what does 'die'
mean?"

"Tell her what it means. If you had Belloc's and my faith in
the afterlife these perfectly natural questions wouldn't upset you."

"Don't harp, Jack. You're awful when you harp."

"I'm awful when I take myself seriously, you mean."

"Hey. I smell cake burning," Rabbit says.

She looks at him and recognition frosts her eyes. That there is
some kind of cold call in her glance, a faint shout from the midst
of her enemies, he feels but ignores, letting his gaze go limp on
the top of her head, showing her the sensitive nostrils that sniffed
the cake.

"If only you *would* take yourself seriously," she says to her
husband, and on glimpsey bare legs flies down the sullen hall of
the rectory.

Eccles calls, "Joyce, go back to your room and put on a shirt
and you can come down."

The child instead thumps down three more steps.

"Joyce, did you hear me?"

"You get it, Dayud–dee."

"Why should I get it? Daddy's all the way downstairs."

"I don't know where it is."

"You do too. Right on your bureau."

"I don't know where my bruro is."

"In your room, sweet. Of course you know where it is. You
get your shirt and I'll let you downstairs."

But she is already halfway down.

"I'm frightened of the li–un," she sighs with a little smile that
betrays consciousness of her own impudence. Her voice has a
spaced, testing quality; Rabbit heard this note of care in her
mother's voice too, when she was teasing the same man.

"There's no lion up there. There's nobody up there but
Bonnie sleeping. Bonnie's not afraid."

"Please, Daddy. Please please please please *please*." She has
reached the foot of the stairs and seizes and squeezes her father's
knees.

Eccles laughs, bracing his unbalanced weight on the child's
head, which is rather broad and flat-topped, like his own. "All
right," he says. "You wait here and talk to this funny man." And
bounds up the stairs with that unexpected athleticism.

Called into action, Rabbit says, "Joyce, are you a good girl?"

She waggles her stomach and pulls her head into her shoulders.
The motion forces a little guttural noise, "*cukk*," out of her throat.
She shakes her head; he has the impression she is trying to hide
behind a screen of dimples. But then she says with unexpectedly
firm enunciation, "Yes."

"And is your mommy good?"

"Yes."

"What makes her so good?" He hopes Mrs. Eccles hears this in
the kitchen. The hurried oven sounds have stopped.

Joyce looks up at him and like a sheet being rippled fear tugs a
corner of the surface of her face. Really tears seem close. She
scampers from him down the hall, the way her mother went.
Fled from, Rabbit wanders uneasily in the hall, trying to attach his
excited heart to the pictures hanging there. Surfaces of foreign
capitals, a woman in white beneath a tree whose every leaf is
rimmed in gold, a laborious pen rendering, brick by brick, of the
St. John's Episcopal Church, dated 1927 and signed large by
Mildred L. Kramer. Above a small table halfway down the hall hangs
a studio photograph of some old rock with white hair above his ears
and a clerical collar staring over your shoulder as if square into the
heart of things; stuck into the frame is a yellowed photo clipped from
a newspaper showing in coarse dots the same old gent gripping a
cigar and laughing like a madman with three others in robes. He
looks a little like Jack but fatter and stronger. He holds the cigar in

a fist. Further on is a colored print of a painted scene in a workshop where the carpenter works in the light given off by his Helper's head: the glass this print is protected by gives back to Rabbit the shadow of his own head. There is a tangy scent in the hallway of, spot cleaner? new varnish? mothballs? old wallpaper? He hovers among these possibilities, "the one who disappeared." *Sexual antagonism begins practically at birth* – what a bitch, really. Yet with a nice low flame in her, lighting up her legs. Those bright white legs. She'd have an anxious little edge and want her own. A cookie. A sharp little vanilla cookie. In spite of herself he loves her.

There must be a back stairs, because he next hears Eccles' voice in the kitchen, arguing Joyce into her sweater, asking Lucy if the cake was ruined, explaining, not knowing Rabbit's ears were around the corner, "Don't think this is pleasure for me. It's work."

"There's no other way to talk to him?"

"He's frightened."

"Sweetie, everybody's frightened to you."

"But he's even frightened *of* me."

"Well he came through that door cocky enough."

This was the place for, *And he slapped my sweet ass, that's yours to defend.*

What! Your sweet ass! I'll murder the rogue. I'll call the police.

In reality Lucy's voice stopped at "enough," and Eccles is talking about if so-and-so telephoned, where are those new golf balls?, Joyce you *had* a cookie ten minutes ago, and at last calling, in a voice that has healed too smooth over the scratches of their quarrel, "Goodbye, my dears." Rabbit pads up the hall and is leaning on the front radiator when Eccles, looking like a young owl – awkward, cross – pops out of the kitchen.

They go to his car. Under the threat of rain the skin of the Buick has a greasy waxiness. Eccles lights a cigarette and they go down, across Route 422, into the valley toward the golf course. Eccles says, after getting several deep drags settled in his chest, "So your trouble isn't really lack of religion."

"Huh?"

"I was remembering our other conversation. About the waterfall and the tree."

"Yeah well: I stole that from Mickey Mouse."

Eccles laughs, puzzled; Rabbit notices how his mouth stays open after he laughs, the little inturned rows of teeth waiting a moment while his eyebrows go up and down expectantly. "It stopped me short," he admits, closing this flirtatious cave. "Then you said you know what's inside you. I've been wondering all weekend what that was. Can you tell me?"

Rabbit doesn't want to tell him anything. The more he tells, the more he loses. He's safe inside his own skin, he doesn't want to come out. This guy's whole game is to get him out into the open where he can be manipulated. But the fierce convention of courtesy pries open Rabbit's lips. "Hell, it's nothing much," he says. "It's just that, well, it's all there is. Don't you think?"

Eccles nods and blinks and drives without saying a word. In his way he's very sure of himself.

"How's Janice now?" Rabbit asks.

Eccles is startled to feel him veer off. "I dropped by Monday morning to tell them you were in the county. Your wife was in the back yard with your boy and what I took to be an old girl friend, a Mrs. – Foster? Fogleman?"

"What did she look like?"

"I don't really know. I was distracted by her sunglasses. They were the mirror kind, with very wide sidepieces."

"Oh, Peggy Gring. She's walleyed. She was in Janice's high-school class and married that jerk Ollie Fosnacht."

"Fosnacht. That's right. Like the doughnut. I knew there was something local about the name."

"You'd never heard of Fosnacht Day before you came here?"

"Never. Not in Norwalk."

"The thing I remember about it, when I was, oh I must have been six or seven, because he died in 1940, my grandfather would wait upstairs until I came down so I wouldn't be the Fosnacht. He lived with us then." Rabbit hasn't thought or spoken of his grandfather in years, it seems; a mild dry taste comes into his mouth.

"What was the penalty for being a Fosnacht?"

"I forget. It was just something you didn't want to be. Wait. I remember, one year I was the last downstairs and my parents or somebody teased me and I didn't like it and I guess I cried, I don't know. Anyway that's why the old man stayed up."

"He was your father's father?"

"My mother's. He lived with us."

"I remember my father's father," Eccles says. "He used to come to Connecticut and have dreadful arguments with my father. My grandfather was the Bishop of Providence, and had kept his church from going under to the Unitarians by becoming almost Unitarian himself. He used to call himself a Darwinian Deist. My father, in reaction I suppose, became very orthodox; almost Anglo-Catholic. He loved Belloc and Chesterton. In fact he used to read to us those poems you heard my wife objecting to."

"About the lion?"

"Yes. Belloc has this bitter mocking streak my wife can't appreciate. He mocks children, which she can't forgive. It's her psychology. Children are very sacred in psychology. Where was I? Yes; along with his watered-down theology my grandfather had kept in his religious *practice* a certain color and a, a *rigor* that my father had lost. Grandpa felt Daddy was *extremely* remiss in not having a family worship service every night. My father would say he didn't want to bore his children the way he had been bored with God and anyway what was the good of worshipping a jungle god in the living room? 'You don't think God is in the forest?' my grandfather would say. 'Just behind stained glass?' And so on. My brothers and I used to tremble, because it put Daddy into a terrible depression, ultimately, to argue with him. You know how it is with fathers, you never escape the idea that maybe after all they're *right*. A little dried-up old man with a Yankee accent who was really awfully dear. I remember he used to grab us by the knee at mealtimes with this brown bony hand and croak, 'Has he made you believe in Hell?' "

Harry laughs; Eccles' imitation is good; being an old man fits him. "Did he? Do you?"

"Yes, I think so. Hell as Jesus described it. As separation from God."

"Well then we're all more or less in it."

"I don't think so. I don't think so at all. I don't think even the blackest atheist has an idea of what real separation will be. Outer darkness. What we live in you might call" – he looks at Harry and laughs – "inner darkness."

Eccles' volunteering all this melts Rabbit's caution. He wants to bring something of himself into the space between them. The excitement of friendship, a competitive excitement that makes him lift his hands and jiggle them as if thoughts were basketballs, presses him to say, "Well I don't know all this about theology, but I'll tell you, I *do* feel, I guess, that somewhere behind all this" – he gestures outward at the scenery; they are passing the housing development this side of the golf course, half-wood half-brick one-and-a-half-stories in little flat bulldozed yards containing tricycles and spindly three-year-old trees, the un-grandest landscape in the world – "there's something that wants me to find it."

Eccles tamps out his cigarette carefully in the tiny cross-notched cup in the car ashtray. "Of course, all vagrants think they're on a quest. At least at first."

Rabbit doesn't see, after trying to *give* the man something, that he deserved this slap. He supposes this is what ministers need, to cut everybody down to the same miserable size. He says, "Well I guess that makes your friend Jesus look pretty foolish."

Mention of the holy name incites pink spots high on Eccles' cheeks. "He *did* say," the minister says, "that saints shouldn't marry."

They turn off the road and go up the winding drive to the clubhouse, a big cinder-block building fronted with a long sign that has CHESTNUT GROVE GOLF COURSE lettered between two Coca-Cola insignia. When Harry caddied here it was just a clapboard shack holding a wood-burning stove and charts of old tournaments and two armchairs and a counter for candy bars and golf balls you fished out of the swamp and that Mrs. Wenrich resold. He supposes Mrs. Wenrich is dead. She was a delicate old rouged widow like a doll with white hair and it always seemed funny to hear talk about greens and divots and tourneys and par come out of her mouth. Eccles parks the long Buick on the asphalt lot and says, "Before I forget."

Rabbit's hand is on the door handle. "What?"

"Do you want a job?"

"What kind?"

"A parishioner of mine, a Mrs. Horace Smith, has about eight acres of garden around her home, toward Appleboro. Her husband was an incredible rhododendron enthusiast. I shouldn't say incredible; he was a terribly dear old man."

"I don't know beans about gardening."

"Nobody does, that's what Mrs. Smith says. There are no gardeners left. For forty dollars a week, I believe her."

"A buck an hour. That's pretty poor."

"It wouldn't be forty hours. Flexible time. That's what you want, isn't it? Flexibility? So you can be free to preach to the multitudes."

Eccles really does have a mean streak. Him and Belloc. Without the collar around his throat, he kind of lets go. Rabbit gets out of the car. Eccles does the same, and his head across the top of the car looks like a head on a platter. The wide mouth moves. "Please consider it."

"I can't. I may not even stay in the county."

"Is the girl going to kick you out?"

"What girl?"

"What is her name? Leonard. Ruth Leonard."

"Well. Aren't you smart?" Who could have told him? Peggy Gring? By way of Tothero? More likely Tothero's girl Whatsername. She looked like Janice. It doesn't matter; the world's such a web anyway, things just tremble through. "I never heard of her," Rabbit says.

The head on the platter grins weirdly in the sunglare off the grease-gray metal.

They walk side by side to the cement-block clubhouse. On the way Eccles remarks, "It's the strange thing about you mystics, how often your little ecstasies wear a skirt."

"Say. I didn't have to show up today, you know."

"I know. Forgive me. I'm in a very depressed mood."

There's nothing exactly wrong with his saying this, but it rubs Harry's inner hair the wrong way. It kind of clings. It says, *Pity me. Love me.* The prickly sensation makes his lips sticky; he is unable to open them to respond. When Eccles pays his way, he can scarcely negotiate thanking him. When they pick out a set of clubs for him to rent, he is so indifferent and silent the freckled kid in charge stares at him as if he's a moron. The thought flits through his brain that Eccles is known as a fag and he has become the new pet. As he and Eccles walk together toward the first tee he feels dragged down, lame.

And the ball feels it too, the ball he hits after a little advice from Eccles. It sputters away to one side, crippled by a perverse topspin that makes it fall from flight as dumpily as a blob of clay.

Eccles laughs. "That's the best first drive I ever saw."

"It's not a first drive. I used to hit the ball around when I was a caddie. I should do better than that."

"You expect too much of yourself. Watch me, that'll make you feel better."

Rabbit stands back and is surprised to see Eccles, who has a certain spring in his unconscious movements, swing with a quaint fifty-year-old stiffness. As if he has a pot to keep out of the way. He punches the ball with a cramped backswing. It goes straight, though high and weak, and he seems delighted with it. He fairly prances into the fairway. Harry trails after him heavily. The soggy turf, raw and wet from recently thawing, sinks beneath his big suede shoes. They're on a seesaw; Eccles goes up, he comes down.

Down in the pagan groves and green alleys of the course Eccles is transformed. A brainless gaiety animates him. He laughs and swings and clucks and calls. Harry stops hating him, he himself is so awful. Ineptitude seems to coat him like a scabrous disease; he is grateful to Eccles for not fleeing from him. Often Eccles, fifty yards further on – he has an excited gleeful habit of running ahead – comes all the way back to find a ball Harry has lost. Somehow Rabbit can't tear his attention from where the ball *should* have gone, the little ideal napkin of clipped green pinked with a pretty flag. His eyes can't keep with where it *did* go. "Here it is," Eccles says. "Behind a root. You're having terrible luck."

"This must be a nightmare for you."

"Not at all. You're extremely promising. You never play and yet you haven't once missed the ball completely."

This does it; Harry sets himself and in the murderous strength of his desire to knock it out in spite of the root he misses the ball completely.

"Your only mistake is trying too hard," Eccles says. "You have a beautiful natural swing." Rabbit whacks again and the ball flops out and wobbles a few yards.

"Bend to the ball," Eccles says. "Imagine you're about to sit down."

"I'm about to lie down," Harry says. He feels sick, giddily sick, sucked deeper into a vortex whose upper rim is marked by the tranquil tips of the leafing trees. He seems to remember having been up there once. He skids into puddles, is swallowed by trees, infallibly sinks into the mangy scruff at the sides of the fairways.

Nightmare is the word. In waking life only animate things slither and jerk for him this way. His unreal hacking dazes his brain; half-hypnotized, it plays tricks whose strangeness dawns on him slowly. In his head he is talking to the clubs as if they're women. The irons, light and thin yet somehow treacherous in his hands, are Janice. *Come on, you dope, be calm; here we go, easy.* When the slotted clubface gouges the dirt behind the ball and the shock jolts up his arms to his shoulders, his thought is that Janice has struck him. *So dumb, really dumb. Screw her. Just screw her.* Anger turns his skin rotten, so the outside seeps through; his insides go jagged with the tiny dry forks of bitter scratching brambles, where words hang like caterpillar nests that can't be burned away. *She stubs stubs fat she stubs the dirt* torn open in a rough brown mouth *dirt stubs fat:* with the woods the "she" is Ruth. Holding a three wood, absorbed in its heavy reddish head and grass-stained face and white stripe prettily along the edge, he thinks *O.K. if you're so smart* and clenches and swirls. *Ahg:* when she tumbled so easily, to balk at this! The mouth of torn grass and the ball runs, hops and hops, hides in a bush. And when he walks there, the bush is damn somebody, his mother; he lifts the huffy branches like skirts, in a fury of shame but with care not to break any, and these branches bother his legs while he tries to pour his will down into the hard irreducible pellet that is not really himself yet in a way is; just the way it sits there white and Number 1 in the center of everything. As the seven iron chops down *please Janice just once* awkwardness spiders at his elbows and the ball as he stares bending one way bends the other way into more sad scruff further on, the khaki color of Texas. *Oh you moron go home.* Home is the hole, and above, in the scheme of the unhappy vision that frets his conscious attention with an almost optical overlay of presences, the mild gray rain sky is his grandfather waiting upstairs so that young Harry will not be a Fosnacht.

And, now at the corners, now at the center of this striving golf dream, Eccles flits in his grubby shirt like a white flag of forgiveness, crying encouragement, fluttering from the green to guide him home.

The greens, still dead from the winter, are salted with a dry dirt: fertilizer? The ball slips along making bits of grit jump. "Don't stab your putts," Eccles says. "A little easy swing, arms stiff. Distance is more important than aim on the first putt. Try again." He kicks the ball back. It took Harry about twelve to get up here on the fourth green, but this arrogant assumption that his strokes are past counting irritates him. *Come on, sweet*, he pleads as if with his wife, *there's the hole, big as a bucket. Everything will be all right.*

But no, she has to stab in a feeble, panicked way; what was she afraid of? The ball is maybe six feet short. Walking toward Eccles, he says, "You never did tell me how Janice is."

"Janice?" Eccles with an effort drags his attention up from the game. He is absolutely in love with winning; *he is eating me up*, Harry thinks. "She seemed in good spirits on Monday. She was out in the back yard with this other woman, and they were both giggling when I came. You must realize that for a little while, now that she's adjusted somewhat, she'll probably enjoy being back with her parents. It's her own version of your irresponsibility."

"Actually," Harry says gratingly, squatting to line up the putt, the way they do it on television, "she can't stand her parents any more than I can. She probably wouldn't've married me if she hadn't been in such a hurry to get away from 'em." His putt slides past on the down side and goes two or three fucking feet too far. Four feet. Fuck.

Eccles sinks his. The ball wobbles up and with a glottal rattle bobbles in. The minister looks up with the light of triumph in his eyes. "Harry," he asks, sweetly yet boldly, "why have you left her? You're obviously deeply involved with her."

"I *told* ja. There was this thing that wasn't there."

"What thing? Have you ever seen it? Are you sure it exists?"

Harry's four-foot putt dribbles short and he picks up the ball with furious fingers. "Well if you're not sure it exists don't ask me. It's right up your alley. If you don't know nobody does."

"No," Eccles cries in the same strained voice in which he told his wife to keep her heart open for Grace. "Christianity isn't looking for a rainbow. If it were what you think it is we'd pass out opium at services. We're trying to *serve* God, not *be* God."

They pick up their bags and walk the way a wooden arrow tells them.

Eccles goes on, explanatorily, "This was all settled centuries ago, in the heresies of the early Church."

"I tell you, I know what it is."

"What is it? What *is* it? Is it hard or soft? Harry. Is it blue? Is it red? Does it have polka dots?"

It hits Rabbit depressingly that he really wants to be told. Underneath all this I-know-more-about-it-than-you heresies-of-the-early-Church business he really wants to be told about it, wants to be told that it is there, that he's not lying to all those people every Sunday. As if it's not enough to be trying to get some sense out of this crazy game you have to carry around this madman trying to swallow your soul. The hot strap of the bag gnaws at his shoulder.

"The truth is," Eccles tells him with womanish excitement, in a voice embarrassed but determined, "you're monstrously selfish. You're a coward. You don't care about right or wrong; you worship nothing except your own worst instincts."

They reach the tee, a platform of turf beside a hunchbacked fruit tree offering fists of taut ivory-colored buds. "Let me go first," Rabbit says. " 'Til you calm down." His heart is hushed, held in mid-beat, by anger. He doesn't care about anything except getting out of this tangle. He wants it to rain. In avoiding looking at Eccles he looks at the ball, which sits high on the tee and already seems free of the ground. Very simply he brings the clubhead around his shoulder into it. The sound has a hollowness, a singleness he hasn't heard before. His arms force his head up and his ball is hung way out, lunarly pale against the beautiful black blue of storm clouds, his grandfather's color stretched dense across the north. It recedes along a line straight as a ruler-edge. Stricken; sphere, star, speck. It hesitates, and Rabbit thinks it will die, but he's fooled, for the ball makes its hesitation the ground of a final leap: with a kind of visible sob takes a last bite of space before vanishing in falling. "That's *it!*" he cries and, turning to Eccles with a grin of aggrandizement, repeats, "That's it."

SUN AND MOON, sun and moon, time goes. In Mrs. Smith's acres, crocuses break the crust. Daffodils and narcissi unpack their trumpets. The reviving grass harbors violets, and the lawn is suddenly coarse with dandelions and broad-leaved weeds. Invisible rivulets running brokenly make the low land of the estate sing. The flowerbeds, bordered with bricks buried diagonally, are pierced by dull red spikes that will be peonies, and the earth itself, scumbled, stone-flecked, horny, raggedly patched with damp and dry, looks like the oldest and smells like the newest thing under Heaven. The shaggy golden suds of blooming forsythia glow through the smoke that fogs the garden while Rabbit burns rakings of crumpled stalks, perished grass, oak leaves shed in the dark privacy of winter, and rosebush prunings that cling together in infuriating ankle-clawing clumps. These brush piles, ignited soon after he arrives, crusty-eyed and tasting coffee, in the midst of the webs of dew, are still damply smoldering when he leaves, making ghosts in the night behind him as his footsteps crunch on the spalls of the Smith driveway. All the way back to Brewer in the bus he smells the warm ashes.

Funny, for these two months he never has to cut his fingernails. He lops, lifts, digs. He plants annuals, packets the old lady gives him — nasturtiums, poppies, sweet peas, petunias. He loves folding the hoed ridge of crumbs of soil over the seeds. Sealed, they cease to be his. The simplicity. Getting rid of something by giving it to itself. God Himself folded into the tiny adamant structure, Self-destined to a succession of explosions, the great slow gathering out of water and air and silicon: this is felt without words in the turn of the round hoe-handle in his palms.

Now, after the magnolias have lost their grip but before any but the leaves of the maple have the breadth to cast much shade, the cherry trees and crabapples and, in a remote corner of the grounds, a solitary plum tree ball with bloom, a whiteness the black limbs seem to gather from the blowing clouds and after a moment hurl away, so the reviving grass is bleached by an astonishing storm of confetti. Fragrant of gasoline, the power mower chews the petals; the lawn digests them. The lilac bushes bloom by the fallen tennis-court fences. Birds come to the birdbath. Busy one morning with a crescent-shaped edger, Harry is caught in a tide of perfume, for behind him the breeze has turned and washes down through a thick sloping bank of acrid lily-of-the-valley leaves in which on that warm night a thousand bells have ripened, the high ones on the stem still the faint sherbet green of cantaloupe rind. Apple trees and pear trees. Tulips. Those ugly purple tatters the iris. And at last, prefaced by azaleas, the rhododendrons themselves, with a profusion increasing through the last week of May. Rabbit has waited all spring for this crowning. The bushes puzzled him, they were so big, almost trees, some twice his height, and there seemed so many. They were planted all along the edges of the towering droop-limbed hemlocks that sheltered the place, and in the acres sheltered there were dozens of great rectangular clumps like loaves of porous green bread. The bushes were evergreen. With their zigzag branches and long oval leaves fingering in every direction they seemed to belong to a different climate, to a different land, whose gravity pulled softer than this one. When the first blooms came they were like the single big flower Oriental temptresses wear on the sides of their heads on the covers of the paperback spy stories Ruth reads. But when the hemispheres of blossom appear in crowds they remind him of nothing so much as the hats worn by cheap girls to church on Easter. Harry has often wanted and never had a girl like that, a little Catholic from a shabby house, dressed in flashy bargain clothes. In the swarthy leaves under the pert soft cap of five-petaled flowers he can fancy her face; he can almost smell her perfume. He draws within an inch of the massed petals. Odorless, but each individual flower wears on the roof of its mouth two fans of freckles where the anthers tap.

At this climax of her late husband's garden, Mrs. Smith comes out of the house and on Rabbit's arm walks deep into the rhododendron plantation. A woman once of some height, she is bent small, and the lingering strands of black look dirty in her white hair. She carries a cane, but in forgetfulness, perhaps, hangs it over her forearm and totters along with it dangling loose like an outlandish bracelet. Her method of gripping her gardener is this: he crooks his right arm, pointing his elbow toward her shoulder, and she shakily brings her left forearm up within his and bears down heavily on his wrist with her lumpish and freckled fingers. Her hold is like that of a vine to a wall; one good pull will destroy it, but otherwise it will survive all weathers. He feels her body jolt with every step, and every word twitches her head. Not that the effort of speaking is so great; it is the need for emphasis that seizes her, wrinkling the arch of her nose fiercely, making her lips snarl above her snaggle-teeth with a comic over-expressiveness that is self-conscious, like the funny faces made by a thirteen-year-old girl in constant confession of the fact that she is not beautiful. She sharply tips her head to look up at Harry, and in tiny brown sockets afflicted by creases like so many drawstrings, her cracked blue eyes bulge frantically with captive life as she speaks: "Oh, I *don't* like Mrs. R. S. Holford; she always looks so washed-out and flossy to me. Horace loved those salmon colors so; I'd say to him, 'If I want red, give me red; a fat red rose. And if I want white, give me white, a tall white lily; and don't bother me with all these inbetweens and would-be-pinks and almost-purples that don't know what their mind is. Rhody's a mealymouthed plant,' I'd say to Horace, 'she does have a brain, so she gives you some of everything,' just to tease him. But in truth I meant it." The thought seems to strike her. She stops dead on the path of grass and her eyes, the irises a kind of broken-glass white within rings of persisting blue, roll nervously, looking from one side of him to the other. "In truth I meant every word of it. I'm a farmer's daughter, Mr. Angstrom, and I would have rather seen this land gone under to alfalfa. I'd say to him, 'Why don't you plant buckwheat if you must fuss in the ground? Now there's a real crop. You raise the wheat, I'll bake the bread.' I would have, too. 'What do we want with all these corsages that after they're gone we have to look at their homely leaves all the year round?' I'd say to him, 'What pretty girl are you growing these for?' He was younger than I, that's why I took advantage of my right to tease him. I won't say by how much. What are we standing here for? Old body like mine, stand still in one place you'll stick fast." She jabs the cane into the grass, the signal for him to extend his arm. They move on down the alley of bloom. "Never thought I'd outlive him. That was his weakness. Come in out of the garden, he'd be forever sitting. A farmer's daughter never learns the meaning of sit."

Her unsteady touch on his wrist bobs like the swaying tops of the tall hemlocks. He associates these trees with forbidden estates; it gives him pleasure to be within their protection. "Ah. Now here is a *plant*." They stop at a corner and she lifts her dangling cane toward a small rhododendron clothed in a pink of penetrating purity. "Horace's Bianchi," Mrs. Smith says. "The only rhody except some of the whites, I forget their names, silly names anyway, that says what it means. It's the only true pink there is. When Horace first got it, he set it among the other so-called pinks and it showed them up as just so muddy he tore them right out and backed the Bianchi with all crimsons. The crimsons are by, aren't they? Is today June?" Her wild eyes fix him crazily and her grip tightens.

"Not quite. Memorial Day's next Saturday."

"Oh, I remember so well the day we got that silly plant. Hot! We drove to New York City to take it off the boat and put it in the back seat of the Packard like a favorite aunt or some such thing. It came in a big blue wooden tub of earth. There was only one nursery in England that carried the stock and it cost two hundred dollars to ship. A man came down to the hold to water it every day. Hot, and all that vile traffic through Jersey City and Trenton and this scrawny bush sitting in its blue tub in the back seat like a prince of the realm! There weren't any of these turnpikes then so it was a good six-hour trip to New York. The middle of the Depression and it looked like everybody in the world owned an automobile. You came over the Delaware at Burlington. This was before the war. I don't suppose when I say 'the war' you know which one I mean. You probably think of that Korean thing as the war."

"No, I think of the war as World War Two."

"So do I! So do I! Do you really remember it?"

"Sure. I mean I was pretty old. I flattened tin cans and bought War Stamps and we got awards at grade school."

"Our son was killed."

"Gee. I'm sorry."

"Oh he was old, he was old. He was almost forty. They made him an officer right off."

"Still –"

"I know. You think of only young men being killed."

"Yeah, you do."

"It was a good war. It wasn't like the first. It was ours to win, and we won it. All wars are hateful things, but that one was satisfying to win." She gestures with her cane again at the pink plant. "The day we came over from the boat docks it of course wasn't in flower that late in the summer so it looked just like foolishness to me, to have it riding in the back seat like a" – she realizes she is repeating herself, falters, but goes on – "like a prince of the realm." In her almost transparent blue eyes there is pinned this little sharpness watching his face to see if he smiles at her addlement. Seeing nothing, she snaps roughly, "It's the only one."

"The only Bianchi?"

"Yes! Right! There's not another in the United States. There's not another good pink from the Golden Gate to – wherever. The Brooklyn Bridge, I suppose they say. All the truly *good* pink in the nation is right here under our eyes. A florist from Lancaster took some cuttings but they died. Probably smothered them in lime. Stupid man. A Greek."

She claws at his arm and moves on more heavily and rapidly. The sun is high and she probably feels a need for the house. Bees swim in the foliage; hidden birds scold. The tide of leaf has overtaken the tide of blossom, and a furtively bitter odor breathes from the fresh walls of green. Maples, poplars, oaks, elms, and horse-chestnut trees compose a thin forest that runs, at a varying depth, along the far property-line. In the damp shaded fringe between the lawn and this copse, the rhododendrons are still putting forth, but the unsheltered clumps in the center of the lawn have already dropped petals, in pale neat lines, along the edge of the grass paths. "I don't like it, I don't like it," Mrs. Smith says, hobbling with Rabbit down past the overblown blooms. "I appreciate the beauty but I'd rather see alfalfa. A woman – I don't know why it should vex me so – Horace used to encourage the neighbors to come in

and see the place in blooming time, he was like a child in many
ways. This woman, Mrs. Foster, from down the hill in a little brick
shack with a metal cat climbing up the shutters, used to in*var*iably
say, turn to me with lipstick halfway up to her nose and say" – she
mimics a too-sweet voice with a spirited spite that shakes her
frame – " 'My, Mrs. Smith, this must be what Heaven is like!' One
year I said to her, I couldn't hold my tongue any longer, I said,
'Well if I'm driving six miles back and forth to St. John's Episcopal
Church every Sunday just to get into another splash of rhodies, I
might as well save the mileage because I don't want to *go*.' Now
wasn't that a dreadful thing for an old sinner to say?"

"Oh, I don't know –"

"To this poor woman who was only trying to be civil? Hadn't
a bean of a brain in her head, of course; painting her face like a
young fool. She's passed on now, poor soul; Alma Foster passed
on two or three winters back. Now she knows the truth and I
don't."

"Well, maybe what looks like rhododendrons to her will look
like alfalfa to you."

"*Heh!* Eh-HA! Exactly! Exactly! You know, Mr. Angstrom,
it's *such* a pleasure –" She stops them in the walk and caresses his
forearm awkwardly; in the sunshine the tiny tan landscape of her
face tips up toward his, and in her gaze, beneath the fumbling girlish flirtatiousness and the watery wander, there glitters an old
acuteness, so that Rabbit uneasily standing there feels a stab of the
penetrating force that drove Mr. Smith out to the brainless
flowers. "You and I, we think alike. Don't we? Now *don't we?*"

"You have it pretty good, don't you?" Ruth asks him. They
have gone on the afternoon of this Memorial Day to the public
swimming pool in West Brewer. She was self-conscious about
getting into a bathing suit but in fact when she came out of the
bath-house she looked great, her head made small by the bathing
cap and her shoulders round and wide. Standing in the water she
was cut off at the thighs like a broken statue. She swam easily, her
big legs kicking slowly and her clean arms lifting and her back and

bottom shimmering black under the jiggled green. Once she stopped and floated, putting her face down in the water in a motion that quickened his heart with its slight danger. Her bottom of its own buoyance floated up and broke the surface, a round black island glistening there, a clear image suddenly in the water wavering like a blooey television set: the solid sight swelled his heart with pride, made him harden all over with a chill clench of ownership. His, she was his, he knew her as well as the water, like the water has been everywhere on her body. When she did the backstroke the water bubbled and broke and poured down her front into her breastcups, flooding her breasts with touch; the arch of her submerged body tightened; she closed her eyes and moved blindly. Two skinny boys dabbling at the shallow end of the pool splashed away from her headfirst approach. She brushed one with a backsweep of her arm, awoke, and squatted smiling in the water; her arms waved bonelessly to keep her balance in the nervous tides of the crowded pool. The air sparkled with the scent of chlorine. Clean, clean: it came to him what clean was. It was nothing touching you that is not your element. Ruth in water, him in grass and air. He is not a water animal. Wet is cold to him. Having dunked, he prefers to sit on the tile edge dipping his feet and imagining that high-school girls behind him are admiring the muscle-play of his broad back; he revolves his shoulders and feels the blades stretch his skin in the sun. Ruth wades to the end, through water so shallow the checked pattern of the pool floor is refracted to its surface. She climbs the little ladder, shedding water in great pale-green grape-bunches. He scrambles back to their blanket and lies down so that when she comes over he sees her standing above him straddling the sky, the black hair high on the insides of her thighs pasted into swirls by the water. She tears off her cap and shakes out her hair and bends over for the towel. Water on her back drips over her shoulders. As he watches her rub her arms the smell of grass rises through the blanket and shouts shake the crystalline air. She lies down beside him and closes her eyes and submits to the sun. Her face, seen so close, is built of great flats of skin pressed clean of color except for a burnish of yellow that adds to their size mineral weight, the weight of some pure porous stone carted straight from quarries to temples. Words come from this monumental Ruth in the same scale, as massive wheels rolling to the porches of his ears, as mute coins spinning in the light. "You have it pretty good."

"How so?"

"Oh" – her words seem slightly delayed in passage from her lips; he sees them move, and then hears – "look at all you've got. You've got Eccles to play golf with every week and to keep your wife from doing anything to you. You've got your flowers, and you've got Mrs. Smith in love with you. You've got me."

"You think she really is in love with me? Mrs. Smith."

"All I know is what I get from you. You say she is."

"No, I never actually said that. Did I?"

She doesn't bother to answer him out of her huge face, magnified by his drowsy contentment.

He repeats, "Did I?" and pinches her arm, hard. He hadn't meant to do it so hard; something angered him at the touch of her skin. The sullen way it yielded.

"Ow. You son of a bitch."

Still she lies there, paying more attention to the sun than him. He gets up on an elbow and looks across her dead body to the lighter figures of two sixteen-year-olds standing sipping orange crush from cardboard cones. The one in a white strapless peeks up at him from sucking her straw with a brown glance, her skinny legs dark as a Negro's. Her hipbones make gaunt peaks on either side of her flat belly.

"Oh all the *world* loves you," Ruth says suddenly. "What I wonder is why?"

"I'm lovable," he says.

"I mean why the hell *you*. What's so special about *you?*"

"I'm a saint," he says. "I give people faith." Eccles has told him this. Once, with a laugh, probably meaning it sarcastically. You never knew what Eccles was really meaning; you had to take what you wanted to. Rabbit took this to heart. He never would have thought of it himself. He doesn't think that much about what he gives other people.

"You give *me* a pain," she says.

"Well I'll be damned." The injustice: after he was so proud of her in the pool, loved her so much.

"What in hell makes you think you don't have to pull your own weight?"

"What's your kick? I support you."

"The hell you do. I have a job." It's true. A little after he went to work for Mrs. Smith she got a job as a stenographer with an insurance company that has a branch in Brewer. He wanted her to; he was nervous about how she'd spend her afternoons with him away. She said she never enjoyed turning tricks; he wasn't so sure. She wasn't exactly suffering when he met her.

"Quit it," he says. "I don't care. Sit around all day reading mysteries. I'll support ja."

"You'll support me. If you're so big why don't you support your wife?"

"Why should I? Her father's rolling in it."

"You're so *smug*, is what gets me. Don't you ever think you're going to have to pay a price?" She looks at him now, squarely with eyes bloodshot from being in the water. She shades them with her hand. These aren't the eyes he met that night by the parking meters, flat pale discs like a doll might have. The blue of her irises has deepened inward and darkened with a richness that, singing the truth to his instincts, disturbs him.

These eyes sting her and she turns her head away to keep down the tears, thinking, That's one of the signs, crying easily. God, at work she has to get up from the typewriter and rush into the john like she had the runs and sob, sob, sob. Standing there in a booth looking down at a toilet laughing at herself and sobbing till her chest hurts. And sleepy. God, after coming back from lunch it's all she can do to keep from stretching out in the aisle right there on the linoleum floor between Lilly Orff and Rita Fiorvante where slimy-eyed old Honig would have to step over her. And hungry. For lunch an ice-cream soda with the sandwich and then a doughnut with the coffee and still she has to buy a candy bar at the cash register. After she's been trying to slim down for him and *had* lost six pounds, at least one scale said. For him, that was what was rich, changing herself in one direction for him when in his stupidity he was changing her in just the other. He was a menace, for all his mildness. Still he did have the mildness and was the first man she ever met who did. You felt at least you were *there* for him instead of being something pasted on the inside of their dirty heads. God she used to hate them with their wet mouths and little laughs but when she had it with Harry she kind of forgave them all, it was only half their fault, they were a kind of wall she kept battering against because she knew there was something there and all of a sudden with Harry there it was and it made everything that had gone before seem pretty unreal. After all nobody had ever really hurt her, left her scarred or anything, and when she tries to re-member it it sometimes seems it happened to somebody else. They seemed sort of vague, as if she had kept her eyes shut, vague and pathetic and eager, wanting some business their wives wouldn't give, a few dirty words or a whimper or that business with the mouth. That. What do they see in it? It can't be as deep, she doesn't know. After all it's no worse than them at your bees and why not be generous, the first time it was Harrison and she was drunk as a monkey anyway but when she woke up the next morn-ing wondered what the taste in her mouth *was*. But that was just being a superstitious kid there isn't much taste to it a little like sea-water, just harder work than they probably think, women are always working harder than they think. The thing was, they wan-ted to be admired there. They really did want that. They weren't that ugly but they thought they were. That was the thing that surprised her in high school how ashamed they were really, how grateful they were if you just touched them there and how quick word got around that you would. What did they think, they were monsters? If they'd just thought, they might have known you were curious too, that you could like that strangeness there like they liked yours, no worse than women in their way, all red wrinkles, my God, what was it in the end? No mystery. That was the great thing she discovered, that it was no mystery, just a stuck-on-looking bit that made them king and if you went along with it could be good or not so good and anyway put you with them against those others, those little snips running around her at hockey in gym like a cow in that blue uniform like a baby suit, she wouldn't wear it in the twelfth grade and took the demerits. God she hated some of those girls with their contractors and druggists for fathers. But she got it back at night, taking what they didn't know existed like a queen. Boy, there wasn't any fancy business then, you didn't even need to take off your clothes, just a little rubbing through the cloth, your mouths tasting of the onion on the hamburgers you'd just had at the diner and the car heater ticking as it cooled, through all the cloth, everything, off they'd go. They couldn't have felt much it must have been just the *idea* of you. All their ideas. Sometimes just French kissing not that she ever really got with that, sloppy tongues and nobody can breathe, but all of a sudden you knew from the way their lips went hard and opened and then eased shut and away that it was over. That there was no more push for you and you better back off if you wanted to keep your dress dry. They wrote her name on the lavatory walls; she became a song in the school. Allie told her about that, kindly. But she had some sweet things with Allie; once after school with the sun still up they drove along a country road and up an old lane and stopped in a leafy place where they could see Mt. Judge, the town against the mountain, both dim in the distance, and he put his head in her lap, her sweater rolled up and her bra undone, and it was like a baby gently, her bees (who called them her bees? not Allie) firmer and rounder then, more sensitive; his waiting wet mouth so happy and blind and the birds making their warm noises overhead in the sunshine. Allie blabbed. He had to blab. She forgave him but it made her wiser. She began the older ones; the mistake if there was one but why not? Why not? was the question and still held; wondering if there was a mistake makes her tired just thinking, lying wet from swimming and seeing red through her eyelids, trying to move back through all that red wondering if she was wrong. She was wise. With them, being young did for being pretty, and them being older it wasn't such a rush. Boy some bastards you think *never*, like their little contribution's the greatest thing the world's ever going to see if it ever gets here.

But *this* one. What a nut. She wonders what he has. He's beautiful for a man, soft and uncircumcised lying sideways in his fleece and then like an angel's horn, he fits her tight but it must be more than that, and it isn't just him being so boyish and bringing her bongo drums and saying sweet grateful things because he has a funny power over her too; when they're good together she feels like next to nothing with him and that must be it, that must be what she was looking for. To feel like next to nothing with a man. Boy

that first night when he said that so sort of proudly "Hey" she
didn't mind so much going under in fact it felt like she should. She
forgave them all then, his face all their faces gathered into a scared
blur and it felt like she was falling under to something better than
she was. But then after all it turns out he's not so different, hanging
on you all depressed and lovey and then when he's had it turning
his back to think of something else. Men don't live by it the way a
woman must. It's getting quicker and quicker more like a habit, he
really hurries now when he senses or she tells him she's lost it. Then
she can just lie there and in a way listen and it's soothing; but then
she can't go to sleep afterwards. Some nights he tries to bring her
up but she's just so sleepy and so heavy down there it's nothing;
sometimes she just wants to push him off and shake him and shout,
I *can't*, you dope, don't you know you're a *father!* But no. She
mustn't tell him. Saying a word would make it final; it's just been
one period and the next is coming up in a day maybe she'll have it
and then she won't have anything. As much of a mess as it is she
doesn't know how happy that would make her really. At least this
way she's *doing* something, sending those candy bars down. God she
isn't even sure she doesn't want it because *he* wants it from the way
he acts, with his damn no stripper just a nice clean piece. She isn't
even sure she didn't just deliberately bring it on by falling asleep
under his arm just to show the smug bastard. For the thing about
him he didn't mind her getting up when he was asleep and crawling into the cold bathroom just so long as he didn't have to watch
anything or do anything. That was the thing about him, he just
lived in his skin and didn't give a thought to the consequences of
anything. Tell him about the candy bars and feeling sleepy he'll
probably get scared and off he'll go, him and his good clean piece
and his cute little God and his cute little minister playing golf every
Tuesday. For the damnedest thing about that minister was that,
before, Rabbit at least had the idea he was acting wrong but now
he's got the idea he's Jesus Christ out to save the world just by doing
whatever comes into his head. I'd like to get hold of the bishop or
whoever and tell him that minister of his is a menace. Filling poor
Rabbit full of something nobody can get at and even now, filling
her ear, his soft cocksure voice answers her question with an idle
remote smugness that infuriates her so the tears *do* come.

"I'll tell you," he says. "When I ran from Janice I made an interesting discovery." The tears bubble over her lids and the salty taste of the pool-water is sealed into her mouth. "If you have the guts to be yourself," he says, "other people'll pay your price."

Making awkward calls is agony for Eccles; at least anticipation of them is. Usually, the dream is worse than the reality: God rules reality. The actual presences of people are always bearable. Mrs. Springer is a plump, dark, small-boned woman with a gypsy look about her. Both the mother and the daughter have a sinister aura, but in the mother this ability to create uneasiness is a settled gift, thoroughly meshed into the strategies of middle-class life. With the daughter it is a floating thing, useless and as dangerous to herself as to others. Eccles is relieved that Janice is out of the house; he feels guiltiest in her presence. She and Mrs. Fosnacht have gone into Brewer to a matinee of *Some Like It Hot.* Their two sons are in the Springers' back yard. Mrs. Springer takes him through the house to the screened-in porch, where she can keep an eye on the children. Her house is expensively but confusedly furnished; each room seems to contain one more easy chair than necessary. To get from the front door to the back they take a crooked path in the packed rooms. She leads him slowly; both of her ankles are bound in elastic bandages. The pained littleness of her steps reinforces his illusion that her hips are encased in a plaster cast. She gently lowers herself onto the cushions of the porch glider and startles Eccles by kicking up her legs as, with a squeak and sharp sway, the glider takes her weight. The action seems to express pleasure; her bald pale calves stick out stiff and her saddle shoes are for a moment lifted from the floor. These shoes are cracked and rounded, as if they've been revolved in a damp tub for years. He sits down in a trickily hinged aluminum-and-plastic lawn chair. Through the porch screen at his side, he can see Nelson Angstrom and the slightly older Fosnacht boy play in the sun around a swing-slide-and-sandbox set. Eccles once bought one of those and when it came, all in pieces in a long cardboard box, was humiliated to find himself unable to put it together; Angus, the old deaf sexton, finally had to do it for him.

"It's nice to see you," Mrs. Springer says. "It's been so long since you came last."

"Just three weeks, isn't it?" he says. The chair presses against his back and he hooks his heels around the pipe at the bottom to keep it from folding. "It's been a busy time, with the confirmation classes and the Youth Group deciding to have a softball team this year and a number of deaths in the parish." His previous contacts with this woman have not disposed him to be apologetic. Her having so large a home offends his aristocratic sense of caste; he would like her better, and she would be more comfortable, if her place were smaller.

"Yes I wouldn't want your job for the world."

"I enjoy it most of the time."

"They say you do. They say you're becoming quite an expert golf player."

Oh dear. And he thought she was relaxing. He thought for the moment they were on the porch of a shabby peeling house and she was a long-suffering fat factory wife who had learned to take life as it came. That is what she looked like; that is easily what she might have been. Fred Springer when he married her was probably less likely-looking than Harry Angstrom when her daughter married him. He tries to imagine Harry four years ago, and gets a presentable picture: tall, fair, famous in his school days, clever enough – a son of the morning. His air of confidence must have especially appealed to Janice. David and Michal. *Defraud ye not one the other.* . . . He scratches his forehead and says, "Playing golf with someone is a good way to get to know him. That's what I try to do, you understand – get to know people. I don't think you can lead someone to Christ unless you know him."

"Well now what do you know about my son-in-law that I don't?"

"That he's a good man, for one thing."

"Good for what?"

"Must you be good *for* something?" He tries to think. "Yes, I suppose you must."

"Nelson! Stop that this minute!" She turns rigid in the glider but does not rise to see what is making the boy cry. Eccles, sitting by the screen, can see. The Fosnacht boy stands by the swing, holding two red plastic trucks. Angstrom's son, some inches shorter, is batting with an open hand toward the bigger boy's chest, but does not quite dare to move forward a step and actually strike him. Young Fosnacht stands fast, with the maddening invulnerability of the stupid, looking down at the flailing hand and contorted face of the smaller boy without even a smile of satisfaction, a true scientist, observing without passion the effect of his experiment. Mrs. Springer's voice leaps to a frantic hardness and cuts through the screen: "*Did you hear me I said stop that bawling!*"

Nelson's face turns up toward the porch and he tries to explain, "Pilly have – Pilly –" But just trying to describe the injustice gives it unbearable force, and as if struck from behind he totters forward and slaps the thief's chest and receives a mild shove that makes him sit on the ground. He rolls on his stomach and spins in the grass, revolved by his own incoherent kicking. Eccles' heart seems to twist with the child's body; he knows so well the propulsive power of a wrong, the way the mind batters against it and each futile blow sucks the air emptier until it seems the whole frame of blood and bone must burst in a universe that can be such a vacuum.

"The boy's taken his truck," he tells Mrs. Springer.

"Well let him get it himself," she says. "He must learn. I can't be getting up on these legs and running outside every minute; they've been at it like that all afternoon."

"*Billy.*" The boy looks up in surprise toward Eccles' male voice. "Give it back." Billy considers this new evidence and hesitates indeterminately. "*Now*, please." Convinced, Billy walks over and pedantically drops the toy on his sobbing playmate's head.

The new pain starts fresh grief in Nelson's throat, but seeing the truck on the grass beside his face chokes him. It takes him a moment to realize that the cause of his misery is removed and another moment to rein the emotion in his body. His great dry gasps as he rounds these corners seem to heave the sheet of trimmed grass and the sunshine itself. A wasp bumping persistently against the screen dips and the aluminum chair under Eccles threatens to buckle; as if the wide world is participating in Nelson's readjustment.

"I don't know why the boy is such a sissy," Mrs. Springer says. "Or maybe I do."

Her sly adding this irks Eccles. "Why?"

The liverish skin under her eyes lifts and the corners of her mouth pull down in an appraising scowl. "Well, he's like his dad: spoiled. He's been made too much of and thinks the world owes him what he wants."

"It was the other boy; Nelson only wanted what was his."

"Yes and I suppose you think with his dad it was all Janice's fault." The way she pronounces "Janice" makes the girl seem more substantial, precious, and important than the pathetic shadow in Eccles' mind. He wonders if she's not, after all, right: if he hasn't gone over to the other side.

"No I don't," he says. "I think his behavior has no justification. This isn't to say, though, that his behavior doesn't have reasons, reasons that in part your daughter could have controlled. With my Church, I believe that we are all responsible beings, responsible for ourselves and for each other." The words, so well turned-out, taste chalky in his mouth. He wishes she'd offer him something to drink. Spring is turning warm.

The old gypsy sees his uncertainty. "Well that's easy to say," she says. "It's not so easy maybe to take such a view if you're nine months expecting and from a respectable home and your husband's running around a few miles away with some bat and everybody thinks it's the funniest thing since I don't know what." The word "bat" darts into the air like one, quick and black.

"Nobody thinks it's funny, Mrs. Springer."

"You don't hear the talk I do. You don't see the smiles. Why, one woman as good as said to me the other day if she can't keep him she has no right to him. She had the gall to grin right in my face. I could have strangled her. I said to her, 'A man has duty too. It isn't all one way.' It's women like her give men the ideas they have, that the world's just here for their pleasure. From the way you act you half-believe it too. Well if the world is going to be full of Harry Angstroms how much longer do you think they'll need your church?"

She has sat up and her dark eyes are lacquered by tears that do not fall. Her voice has risen in pitch and abrades Eccles' face like a file; he feels covered with cuts. Her talk of the smiling gossip encircling this affair has surrounded him with a dreadful reality, like the reality of those hundred faces when on Sunday mornings at 11:30 he mounts the pulpit and the text flies from his mind and his notes dissolve into nonsense. He fumbles through his memory and manages to bring out, "I feel Harry is in some respects a special case."

"The only thing special about him is he doesn't care who he hurts or how much. Now I mean no offense, Reverend Eccles, and I'm sure you've done your best considering how busy you are, but to be honest I wish that first night I had called the police like I wanted to."

He seems to hear that she is going to call the police to arrest *him*. Why not? With his white collar he forges God's name on every word he speaks. He steals belief from the children he is supposed to be teaching. He murders faith in the minds of any who really listen to his babble. He commits fraud with every schooled cadence of the service, mouthing Our Father when his heart knows the real father he is trying to please, has been trying to please all his life, the God who smokes cigars. He asks her, "What can the police do?"

"Well I don't know but more than play golf I expect."

"I'm quite sure he will come back."

"You've been saying that for two months."

"I still believe it." But he doesn't, he doesn't believe anything. There is silence while Mrs. Springer seems to read this fact in his face.

"Could you" – her voice is changed; it beseeches – "bring me over that stool there in the corner? I have to get my legs up."

When he blinks, his eyelids scratch. He rouses from his daze and gets the stool and takes it to her. Her broad shins in their green childlike socks lift meekly, and as he places the stool under the heels, his bending, with its echo of religious-pamphlet paintings of Christ washing the feet of beggars, fits his body to receive a new flow of force. He straightens up and towers above her. She plucks at her skirt at the knees, tugging it down.

"Thank you," she says. "That's a real relief for me."

"I'm afraid it's the only sort of relief I've given you," he confesses with a simplicity that he finds, and mocks himself for finding, admirable.

"Ah," she sighs. "There's not much anybody can do I guess."

"No, there are things to do. Perhaps you're right about the police. Or at least a lawyer."

"Fred's against it."

"Mr. Springer has good reasons. I don't mean merely business reasons. All the law can extract from Harry is financial support; and I don't think, in this case, that money is really the point. In fact I'm not sure money is *ever* really the point."

"That's easy to say if you've always had enough." He doesn't mind. It seems to slip from her automatically, with less malice than lassitude; he is certain she wants to listen.

"That may be. I don't know. But at any rate my concern – everyone's concern for that matter, I'm sure – is with the general health of the situation. And if there's to be a true healing, it must be Harry and Janice who act. Really, no matter how much we want to help, no matter how much we try to do on the fringes, we're *outside*." In imitation of his father he has clasped his hands behind him and turned his back on his auditor; through the screen he watches the one other who, perhaps, is not outside, Nelson, lead the Fosnacht boy across the lawn in pursuit of a neighbor's dog. Nelson's laughter spills from his head as his clumsy tottering steps jar his body. The dog is old, reddish, small, and slow; the Fosnacht boy is puzzled yet pleased by his friend's cry of "Lion! Lion!" It interests Eccles to see that under conditions of peace Angstrom's boy leads the other. The green air seen through the muzzy screen seems to vibrate with Nelson's noise. Eccles feels the situation: this constant translucent outpour of selfless excitement must naturally now and then dam in the duller boy's narrower passages and produce a sullen backflow, a stubborn bullying act. He pities Nelson, who will be stranded in innocent surprise many times before he locates in himself the source of this strange reverse tide. It seems to Eccles that he himself was this way as a boy, always giving and giving and always being suddenly swamped. The old dog's tail wags as the boys approach. It stops wagging and droops in an uncertain wary arc when they surround it like hunters, crowing. Nelson reaches out and beats the dog's back with both hands. Eccles wants to shout; the dog might bite; he can't bear to watch.

"Yes but he drifts further *away*," Mrs. Springer is whining. "He's well off. He has no reason to come back if we don't give him one."

Eccles sits down in the aluminum chair again. "No. He'll come back for the same reason he left. He's fastidious. He has to loop the loop. The world he's in now, the world of this girl in Brewer, won't continue to satisfy his fantasies. Just in seeing him from week to week, I've noticed a change."

"Well not to hear Peggy Fosnacht tell it. She says *she* hears he's leading the life of Riley. I don't know how many women he has."

"Just one, I'm sure. The strange thing about Angstrom, he's by nature a domestic creature. Oh *dear*."

There is a flurry in the remote group; the boys run one way and the dog the other. Young Fosnacht halts but Nelson keeps coming, his face stretched by fright.

Mrs. Springer hears his sobbing and says angrily, "Did they get Elsie to snap again? That dog must be sick in the head the way she keeps coming over here for more."

Eccles jumps up – his chair collapses behind him – and opens the screen door and runs down to meet Nelson in the sunshine. The boy shies from him. He grabs him. "Did the dog bite?"

The boy's sobbing is paralyzed by this new fright, the man in black grabbing him.

"Did Elsie bite you?"

The Fosnacht boy hangs back at a safe distance.

Nelson, unexpectedly solid and damp in Eccles' arms, releases great rippling gasps and begins to find his voice.

Eccles shakes him to choke this threat of wailing and, wild to make himself understood, with a quick lunge clicks his teeth at the child's cheek. "Like that? Did the dog do that?"

The boy's face goes rapt at the pantomime. "Like dis," he says, and his fine little lip lifts from his teeth and his nose wrinkles and he jerks his head an inch to one side.

"No bite?" Eccles insists, relaxing the grip of his arms.

The little lip lifts again with that miniature fierceness. Eccles feels mocked by a petite facial alertness that recalls, in tilt and cast,

Harry's. Sobbing sweeps over Nelson again and he breaks away and runs up the porch steps to his grandmother. Eccles stands up; in just that little time of squatting the sun has started sweat on his black back.

As he climbs the steps he is troubled by something pathetic, something penetratingly touching, in the memory of those tiny square teeth bared in that play snarl. The harmlessness yet the reality of the instinct: the kitten's instinct to kill the spool with its cotton paws.

He comes onto the porch to find the boy between his grandmother's legs, his face buried in her belly. In worming against her warmth he has pulled her dress up from her knees, and their repulsive breadth and pallor, laid bare defenselessly, superimposed upon the tiny, gamely gritted teeth the boy exposed for him, this old whiteness strained through this fine mesh, make a milk that feels to Eccles like his own blood. Strong – as if pity is, as he has been taught, not a helpless outcry but a powerful tide that could redeem the world – he steps forward and promises to the two bowed heads, "If he doesn't come back when she has the baby, then you should get the law after him. There *are* laws, of course; quite a few."

"Elsie snaps," Mrs. Springer says, "because you and Billy tease her."

"Naughty Elsie," Nelson says.

"Naughty Nelson," Mrs. Springer corrects. She lifts her face to Eccles and continues in the same correcting voice, "Yes well she's a week due now and I don't see him running in."

His moment of sympathy for her has passed; he leaves her on the porch. *Love never ends*, he tells himself, using the Revised Standard Version. The King James has it that it never fails. Mrs. Springer's voice carries after him into the house, "Now the next time I catch you teasing Elsie you're going to get a whipping from your grandmom."

"No, Mom-mom," the child begs coyly, fright gone.

Eccles thought he would find the kitchen and take a drink of water from the tap but the kitchen slips by him in the jumble of rooms. He makes a mouth that works up saliva and swallows it as he leaves the stucco house. He gets into his Buick and drives down

Joseph Street and then a block along Jackson Road to the Angstroms' number, 303.

Mrs. Angstrom has four-cornered nostrils. Lozenge-shape, they are set in a nose that is not so much large as extra-defined; the little pieces of muscle and cartilage and bone are individually emphatic and divide the skin into many facets in the sharp light. Their interview takes place in her kitchen amid several burning light bulbs. Burning in the middle of day: their home is the dark side of a two-family brick house. She came to the door wearing suds on her red forearms and returns with him to a sink full of bloated shirts and underwear. She plunges at these things vigorously while they talk. She is a vigorous woman. Mrs. Springer's fat – soft, aching excess – had puffed out from little bones, the bones once of a slip of a woman like Janice; Mrs. Angstrom's is packed on a great harsh frame. Harry's size must come from her side. Eccles is continually conscious of the long faucets, heraldic of cool water, shielded by her formidable body; but the opportunity never arises for a request so small as a glass of water.

"I don't know why you come to me," she says. "Harold's one and twenty. I have no control over him."

"He hasn't been to see you?"

"No sir." She displays her profile above her left shoulder. "You've made him so ashamed I suppose he's embarrassed to."

"He *should* be ashamed, don't you think?"

"I wouldn't know why. I never wanted him to go with the girl in the first place. Just to look at her you know she's two-thirds crazy."

"Oh now, that's not true, is it?"

"Not true! Why the first thing that girl said to me was, Why don't I get a washing machine? Comes into my kitchen, takes one look around, and starts telling me how to manage my life."

"Surely you don't think she meant anything."

"No, she didn't mean anything. All she meant was, What was I doing living in such a run-down half-house when she came from a great big stucco barn on Joseph Street with the kitchen full of gadgets, and, Wasn't I lucky to be fobbing off my boy on such a well-equipped little trick? I never liked that girl's eyes. They never met your face full-on." She turns her face on Eccles and, warned, he returns her stare. Beneath her misted spectacles – an old-fashioned type, circles of steel-rimmed glass in which the bifocal crescents catch a pinker tint of light – her arrogantly tilted nose displays its meaty, intricate underside. Her broad mouth is stretched slightly by a vague expectation. Eccles realizes that this woman is a humorist. The difficulty with humorists is that they will mix what they believe with what they don't – whichever seems likelier to win an effect. The strange thing is how much he likes her, though in a way she is plunging at him as roughly as she plunges the dirty clothes. But that's it, it's the same to her. Unlike Mrs. Springer, she doesn't really see him at all. Her confrontation is with everybody, and secure under the breadth of her satire he can say what he pleases.

He bluntly defends Janice. "The girl is shy."

"Shy! She wasn't too shy to get herself pregnant so poor Hassy has to marry her when he could scarcely tuck his shirt-tail in."

"He was one and twenty, as you say."

"Yes, well, years. Some die young; some are born old."

Epigrams, everything. My, she is funny. Eccles laughs out loud. She doesn't acknowledge hearing him, and turns to her wash with furious seriousness. "About as shy as a snake," she says, "that girl. These little women are poison. Mincing around with their sneaky eyes getting everybody's sympathy. Well she doesn't get mine; let the men weep. To hear her father-in-law talk she's the worst martyr since Joan of Arc."

He laughs again; but isn't she? "Well, uh, what does Mr. Angstrom think Harry should do?"

"Crawl back. What else? He will, too, poor boy. He's just like his father underneath. All soft heart. I suppose that's why men rule the world. They're all heart."

"That's an unusual view."

"Is it? It's what they keep telling you in church. Men are all heart and women are all body. I don't know who's supposed to have the brains. God, I suppose."

Eccles smiles, wondering if the Lutheran church gives everyone such ideas. Luther himself was a little like this, perhaps – overstating half-truths in a kind of comic wrath. The whole black

Protestant paradox-thumping maybe begins there. Helpless, predestined Man, the king of Creation. Utterly fallen: a *hubris* in shoving the particular aside. Maybe: he's forgotten most of the theology they made him absorb. It occurs to him that he should see the Angstroms' pastor.

Mrs. Angstrom picks up a dropped thread. "Now my daughter Miriam is as old as the hills and always was; I've never worried about her. I remember, on Sundays long ago when we'd walk out by the quarry Harold was so afraid – he wasn't more than twelve then – he was so afraid she'd fall over the edge. I knew she wouldn't. You watch her. She won't marry out of pity like poor Hassy and then have all the world jump on him for trying to get out."

"I'm not so sure the world *has* jumped on him. The girl's mother and I were just discussing that it seemed quite the contrary."

"Don't you think it. That girl gets no sympathy from me. She has everybody on her side from Eisenhower down. They'll talk him around. *You'll* talk him around. And there's another."

The front door has opened with a softness she alone hears. Her husband comes into the kitchen wearing a white shirt and a tie but with his fingernails outlined in black; he is a printer. He is as tall as his wife but seems shorter. His mouth works self-deprecatorily over badly fitted false teeth. His nose is Harry's, a neat smooth button. "How do you do, Father," he says; either he was raised as a Catholic or among Catholics.

"Mr. Angstrom, it's very nice to meet you." The man's hand has tough ridges but a soft, dry palm. "We've been discussing your son."

"I feel terrible about that." Eccles believes him. Earl Angstrom has a gray, ragged look. This business has blighted him. He thins his lips across his slipping teeth like a man with stomach trouble biting back gas. He is being nibbled from within. Color has washed from his hair and eyes like cheap ink. A straight man, who has measured his life with the pica-stick and locked the forms tight, he has returned in the morning and found the type scrambled.

"He goes on and on about the girl as if she was the mother of Christ," Mrs. Angstrom says.

"That's not true," Angstrom says mildly, and sits down in his white shirt at the porcelain kitchen table. Four settings, year after year, have worn black blurs through the enamel. "I just don't see how Harry could make such a mess. He wasn't like other boys, sloppy. He was a tidy worker."

With raw sudsy hands Mrs. Angstrom has set about heating coffee for her husband. This small act of service seems to bring her into harmony with him; they begin, in the sudden way of old couples apparently at odds, to speak as one. "It was the Army," she says. "When he came back from Texas he was a different boy."

"He didn't want to come into the shop," Angstrom says. "He didn't want to go into a dirty trade."

"Reverend Eccles, would you like some coffee?" Mrs. Angstrom asks.

At last, his chance. "No, thank you. What I would *love*, though, is a glass of water."

"Just water? With ice?"

"Any way. Any way would be lovely."

"Yes, Earl is right," she says. "People now say how lazy Hassy is, but he's not. He never was. When you'd be proud of his basketball in high school you know, people would say, 'Yes well but he's so tall, it's easy for him.' But they didn't know how he had worked at that. Out back every evening banging the ball way past dark; you wondered how he could see."

"From about twelve years old on," Angstrom says, "he was at that night and day. I put a pole up for him out back; the garage wasn't high enough."

"When he set his mind to something," Mrs. Angstrom says, "there was no stopping him." She yanks powerfully at the lever of the ice-cube tray and with a brilliant multiple crunch that sends chips sparkling the cubes come loose. "He wanted to be best at that and I honestly believe he was."

"I know what you mean," Eccles says. "I play a little golf with him and already he's become better than I am."

She puts the cubes in a glass and holds the glass under a spigot and brings it to him. He tilts it at his lips and Earl Angstrom's palely vehement voice wavers through the liquid. "Then he comes back from the Army and all he cares about is chasing ass."

"Your language, Earl," his wife says, setting coffee in a flowered cup on the table between his hands.

He looks down into the steam and says, "Excuse me. When I think of what that boy's doing my stomach does somersaults. He's become the worst kind of Brewer bum. If I could get my loving hands on him, Father, I'd try to thrash him if he killed me in the process." His ashen face bunches defiantly at the mouth; his colorless eyes swarm with glitter.

Eccles says "No" into his tilted glass like a megaphone and then drinks until no more water can be sucked from under the ice cubes that bump his upper lip. He wipes the moisture from his mouth and says, "There's a great deal of goodness in your son. When I'm with him – it's rather unfortunate, really – I feel so cheerful I quite forget what the point of my seeing him is." He laughs, first at Mr., and, failing here to rouse a smile, at Mrs.

"This golf you play," Angstrom says. "What is the point? In my opinion a good swift kick is what he needs. The girl's parents should call in the Brewer police, him living in sin with a tart like that."

Eccles glances toward Mrs. Angstrom and feels the arch of his eyebrows like drying paste on his forehead. He didn't expect, a minute ago, to be looking toward her as an ally and toward this worn-out good man as a rather vulgar and disappointing foe.

"Don't talk nonsense, Earl," Mrs. Angstrom says. "What does Springer want with his name in the papers? The way you talk you'd think poor Harry was your enemy."

"He is my enemy," Angstrom says. He touches the saucer from both sides with his stained fingertips. "That night I spent walking the streets looking for him he became my enemy. You can't talk. You didn't see the girl's face."

"What do I care about her face? You talk about tarts: they don't become ivory-white saints in my book just by having a marriage license. That girl wanted Harry and got him with the only trick she knew and now she's run out of tricks."

"Don't *talk* that way, Mary. It's just words with you. Suppose I had acted the way Harry has."

"Ah," she says, and turns, and Eccles flinches, seeing her face taut to release a missile. "I didn't want *you*; you wanted *me*. Or wasn't it that way?"

"Yes of course it was that way," Angstrom mutters.

"Well then: where's the comparison?"

Angstrom has hunched his shoulders over the coffee, drawn himself in very small, as if she has boxed him into a tiny corner. "Oh Mary," he sighs, not daring move with words.

Eccles tries to defend him; he goes to the weaker side of a fight almost automatically. "I don't think you can say," he tells Mrs. Angstrom, "that Janice didn't imagine that her marriage was built on mutual attraction. If the girl was such a clever schemer she wouldn't have let Harry slip away so easily."

Mrs. Angstrom's interest in this discussion, now that she knows she pressed her husband too hard, has waned; she maintains a position – that Janice is in control – so obviously false that it amounts to a concession. "She hasn't let him slip away," she says. "She'll have him back, you watch."

Eccles asks the man, "Do you think too that Harry will come around?"

"No," Angstrom says, looking down, "never. He's too far gone. He'll just slide deeper and deeper now until we might as well forget him. If he was twenty, or twenty-two; but at his age . . . In the shop sometimes you see these young Brewer bums. They can't stick it. They're like cripples only they don't limp. Human garbage, they call them. And I sit there at the machine for two months wondering how the hell it could be my Harry, that used to hate a mess so much."

Eccles looks over at Harry's mother and is jarred to see her leaning against the sink with soaked cheeks gleaming under the glasses. He gets up in shock. Is she crying because she thinks her husband is speaking the truth, or because she thinks he is saying this just to hurt her, in revenge for making him admit that he had wanted her? "I hope you're wrong," Eccles says. "I must go now; I thank you both for discussing this with me. I realize it's painful."

Angstrom takes him back through the house and in the dark of the dining room touches his arm. "He liked things just so," he says. "I never saw a boy like him. Any rumpus in the family he'd take hard out of all reason – when Mary and I, you know, would have our fun." Eccles nods, but doubts that "fun" quite describes what he's seen.

In the living-room shadows a slender girl stands in a bare-armed summer dress. "Mim! Did you just get in?"

"Yeah."

"This is Father – I mean Reverend –"

"Eccles."

"Eccles, he came to talk about Harry. My daughter Miriam."

"Hello, Miriam. I've heard Harry speak very fondly of you."

"Hi."

With that word the big window behind her takes on the intimate glaze of the big window in a luncheonette. Flip greetings seem to trail behind her with wisps of cigarette smoke and drug-store perfume. Mrs. Angstrom's nose has delicacy on the girl's face, a sharpness Saracen or even more ancient, barbaric. Taken with the prominent nose her height at first glance seems her mother's, but when her father stands beside her, Eccles sees that it is his height; their bodies, the beautiful girl's and the weary man's, are the same. They have the same narrowness, and a serviceable vulgarity that offends him. They'll get through. They know what they're doing. It's a weakness of his, to prefer people who don't know what they're doing. The helpless: these, and the people on top, beyond help. The ones who maneuver more or less well in the middle seem to his aristocratic prejudices to be thieving from both ends. When they bunch at the door, Angstrom puts his arm around his daughter's waist and Eccles thinks of Mrs. Angstrom silent in the kitchen with her wet cheeks and red arms, a mad captive. Yet, turning on the pavement to wave at the two of them in the doorway, he has to smile at their incongruous sym-metry, the earringed Arab boy with her innocent contempt for his eunuch's collar, and the limp-faced old woman of a printer, paired in slenderness, interlocked.

He gets into the Buick thirsty and vexed. There was something pleasant said in the last half-hour but he can't remember what it was. He feels scratched, hot, confused, and dry; he's spent an afternoon in a bramble patch. He's seen half a dozen people and a dog and nowhere did an opinion tally with his own, that Harry

Angstrom was worth saving and could be saved. Instead down there between the brambles there seemed to be no Harry at all: nothing but stale air and last year's dead stalks. The day is declining through the white afternoon to the long blue spring evening. He drives past a corner where someone is practicing on a trumpet behind an open upstairs window. *Du du do do da da dee. Dee dee da da do do du.* Cars are whispering home from work. He drives across the town, tacking on the diagonal streets along a course parallel to the distant ridge of the mountain. Fritz Kruppenbach, Mt. Judge's Lutheran minister for twenty-seven years, lives in a high brick house not far from the cemetery. The motorcycle belonging to his college-age son is on its side in the driveway, partly dismantled. The sloping lawn, graded in fussy terraces, has the unnatural chartreuse evenness that comes with much fertilizing, much weed-killing, and much mowing. Mrs. Kruppenbach – will Lucy ever achieve that dimpled, obedient look? – comes to the door in a dark wool dress that makes no compromise with the season. Her gray hair girdles her head with braids of great compactness. When she lets all that hair down, she must be a witch. "He's mowing out back," she says.

"I'd like to talk to him for just a few minutes. It's a problem that involves our two congregations."

"Go up to his room, why do-an tcha? I'll fetch him."

The house – foyer, halls, staircase, even the minister's leathery den upstairs – is flooded with the smell of beef roasting. Eccles sits by the window of Kruppenbach's den on an oak-backed choir pew left over from some renovation. Seated on the bench he feels an adolescent compulsion to pray but instead peers across the valley at the green fragments of the golf course where he would like to be, with Harry. Eccles has found other partners either better or worse than he; only Harry is both, and only Harry gives the game a desperate gaiety, as if they are together engaged in an impossible quest set by a benevolent but absurd lord, a quest whose humiliations sting them almost to tears but one that is renewed at each tee, in a fresh flood of green. And for Eccles there is an additional hope, a secret determination to trounce Harry. He feels that the thing that makes Harry unsteady, that makes him unable to repeat his beautiful effortless swing every time, is the thing at the root of all the problems that he has created; and that by beating him decisively he, Eccles, will get on top of this weakness, this flaw, and hence solve the problems. In the meantime there is the pleasure of hearing Harry now and then cry, "Hey, hey," or "I love it, *love* it!" Their rapport at moments attains for Eccles a pitch of pleasure, a harmless ecstasy, that makes the world with its vicious circumstantiality seem remote and spherical and green.

The house shudders to the master's step. Kruppenbach comes up the stairs into his den, angry at being taken from his lawn-mowing. He wears old black pants and an undershirt soaked with sweat. His shoulders are coated with wiry gray wool.

"Hello, Chack," he says at pulpit volume, with no intonation of greeting. His German accent makes his words seem stones, set angrily one on top of another. "What is it?"

Eccles, not daring "Fritz" with the older man, laughs and blurts, "Hello!"

Kruppenbach grimaces. He has a massive square head, crew-cut. He is a man of brick: as if he was born as a baby literally of clay and decades of exposure have baked him to the color and hardness of brick. He repeats, "What?"

"You have a family called Angstrom."

"Yes."

"The father's a printer."

"Yes."

"Their son, Harry, deserted his wife over two months ago; her people, the Springers, are in my church."

"Yes, well. The boy. The boy's a *Schussel*."

Eccles isn't certain what that means. He supposes that Kruppenbach doesn't sit down because he doesn't want to stain his furniture with his own sweat. His continuing to stand puts Eccles in a petitionary position, sitting on the bench like a choir-boy. The odor of meat cooking grows more insistent as he explains what he thinks happened: how Harry has been in a sense spoiled by his athletic successes; how the wife, to be fair, had perhaps showed little imagination in their marriage; how he himself, as minister, had tried to keep the boy's conscience in touch with his wife without pressing him into a premature reunion, for the boy's problem wasn't so much a lack of feeling as an uncontrolled excess of it; how the four parents, for various reasons, were of little help; how he had witnessed, just minutes ago, a quarrel between the Angstroms that perhaps offered a clue as to why their son –

"Do you think," Kruppenbach at last interrupts, "do you think this is your job, to meddle in these people's lives? I know what they teach you at seminary now: this psychology and that. But I don't agree with it. You think now your job is to be an unpaid doctor, to run around and plug up the holes and make everything smooth. I don't think that. I don't think that's your job."

"I only –"

"No now let me finish. I've been in Mt. Judge twenty-seven years and you've been here two. I've listened to your story but I wasn't listening to what it said about the people, I was listening to what it said about you. What I heard was this: the story of a minister of God selling his message for a few scraps of gossip and a few games of golf. What do you think now it looks like to God, one childish husband leaving one childish wife? Do you ever think any more what God sees? Or have you grown beyond that?"

"No, of course not. But it seems to me our role in a situation like this –"

"It seems to you our role is to be cops, cops without handcuffs, without guns, without anything but our human good nature. Isn't it right? Don't answer, just think if I'm not right. Well, I say that's a Devil's idea. I say, let the cops be cops and look after their laws that have nothing to do with us."

"I agree, up to a point –"

"There *iss* no up to a point! There is no reason or measure in what we must do." His thick forefinger, woolly between the knuckles, has begun to tap emphasis on the back of a leather chair. "If Gott wants to end misery He'll declare the Kingdom now." Jack feels a blush begin to burn his face. "How big do you think your little friends look among the billions that God sees? In Bombay now they die in the streets every minute. You say role. I say you don't know what your role is or you'd be home locked in prayer. *There* is your role: to make yourself an exemplar of faith. *There* is where comfort comes from: faith, not what little finagling a body can do here and there, stirring the bucket. In running back and forth you run from the duty given you by God, to make your faith powerful, so when the call comes you can go out and tell them, 'Yes, he is dead, but you will see him again in Heaven. Yes, you suffer, but you must *love* your pain, because it is *Christ's* pain.' When on Sunday morning then, when we go before their faces, we must walk up not worn out with misery but full of Christ, *hot*" – he clenches his hairy fists – "with Christ, on *fire: burn* them with the force of our belief. That is why they come; why else would they pay us? Anything else we can do or say anyone can do and say. They have doctors and lawyers for that. It's all in the Book – a thief with faith is worth all the Pharisees. Make no mistake. Now I'm serious. Make no mistake. There is nothing but Christ for us. All the rest, all this decency and busyness, is nothing. It is Devil's work."

"Fritz," Mrs. Kruppenbach's voice calls carefully up the stairs. "Supper."

The red man in his undershirt looks down at Eccles and asks, "Will you kneel a moment with me and pray for Christ to come into this room?"

"No. No I won't. I'm too angry. It would be hypocritical."

The refusal, unthinkable from a layman, makes Kruppenbach, not softer, but stiller. "Hypocrisy," he says mildly. "You have no seriousness. Don't you believe in damnation? Didn't you know when you put that collar on, what you risked?" In the brick skin of his face his eyes seem small imperfections, pink and glazed with water as if smarting in intense heat.

He turns without waiting for Jack to answer and goes downstairs for supper. Jack descends behind him and continues out the door. His heart is beating like a scolded child's and his knees are weak with fury. He had come for an exchange of information and been flagellated with an insane spiel. Unctuous old thundering Hun, no conception of the ministry as a legacy of light, probably himself scrambled into it out of a butcher's shop. Jack realizes that these are spiteful and unworthy thoughts but he can't stop them. His depression is so deep that he tries to gouge it deeper by telling himself *He's right, he's right* as he sits behind the pearl-gray steering wheel. He bows his head so his forehead touches an arc of its perfect plastic circle, but he can't cry; he's parched. His shame and failure hang downward in him heavy but fruitless.

Though he knows that Lucy wants him home – if dinner is not quite ready he will be in time to give the children their baths – he instead drives to the drugstore in the center of town. The poodle-cut girl behind the counter is in his Youth Group and two parish-ioners buying medicine or contraceptives or Kleenex hail him gaily. It is here that in truth they come to find the antidotes to their lives. He feels at home; Eccles feels most at home in Godless public places. He rests his wrists on the cold clean marble and orders a vanilla ice-cream soda with a scoop of maple-walnut ice cream, and drinks two Coca-Cola glasses full of miraculous clear water before it comes.

Club Castanet was named during the war when the South American craze was on and occupies a triangular building where Warren Avenue crosses Running Horse Street at an acute angle. It's in the south side of Brewer, the Italian-Negro-Polish side, and Rabbit distrusts it. With its glass-brick windows grinning back from the ridge of its face it looks like a fortress of death; the interior is furnished in the glossy low-lit style of an up-to-date funeral parlor, potted green plants here and there, music piped soothingly, and the same smell of strip rugs and fluorescent tubes and Venetian-blind slats and, the most inner secretive smell, of alcohol. You drink it and then you're embalmed in it. Ever since a man down from them on Jackson Road lost his job as an under-taker's assistant and became a bartender, Rabbit thinks of the two professions as related; men in both talk softly and are always seen standing up. He and Ruth sit at a booth near the front, where they get through the window a faint fluctuation of red light as the neon castanet on the sign outside flickers back and forth between its two positions, that imitate clicking.

This pink tremor takes the weight off Ruth's face. She sits across from him. He tries to picture the kind of life she was lead-ing; a creepy place like this probably seems as friendly to her as a locker room would to him. But just the thought of it that way makes him nervous; her sloppy life, like his having a family, is something he's tried to keep behind them. He was happy just

hanging around her place at night, her reading mysteries and him
running down to the delicatessen for ginger ale and some nights
going to a movie but nothing like this. That first night he really
used that Daiquiri but since then he didn't care if he ever had
another and hoped she was the same way. For a while she was but
lately something's been eating her; she's heavy in bed and once in
a while looks at him as if he's some sort of pig. He doesn't know
what he's doing different but knows that somehow the ease has
gone out of it. Tonight her so-called friend Margaret called up. It
scared him out of his skin when the phone rang. He has the idea
lately it's going to be the cops or his mother or somebody; he has
the feeling of something growing on the other side of the mountain. A couple times after he first moved in, the phone rang and it
was some thick-voiced man saying "Ruthie?" or just hanging up
at Rabbit's voice answering. When they hung on, Ruth just said
a lot of "No's" into the receiver and that seemed to settle it. She
knew how to handle them, and anyway there were only about five
that ever called; the past was a vine hanging on by just these
five tendrils and it tore away easily, leaving her clean and blue and
blank. But tonight it was Margaret out of this past and she wanted
them to come down to the Castanet and Ruth wanted to and
Rabbit went along. Anything for a little change. He's bored.

He asks her, "What do you want?"

"A Daiquiri."

"You're sure? You're sure now it won't make you sick?" He's
noticed that, that she seems a little sick sometimes, and won't eat,
and sometimes eats the house down.

"No, I'm not sure but why the hell shouldn't I be sick?"

"Well I don't know why you shouldn't. Why shouldn't anybody?"

"Look, let's not be a philosopher for once. Just get me the
drink."

A colored girl in an orange uniform that he guesses from the
frills is supposed to look South American comes and he tells her
two Daiquiris. She flips shut her pad and walks off and he sees her
back is open halfway down her spine, so a bit of black bra shows.
Compared with this her skin isn't black at all. Soft purple shadows
flitter on the flats of her back where the light hits. She has a

pigeon-toed way of sauntering, swinging those orange frills. She doesn't care about him; he likes that, that she doesn't care. The thing about Ruth is lately she's been trying to make him feel guilty about something.

She asks him, "What are *you* looking at?"

"I'm not looking at anything."

"You can't have it, Rabbit. You're too white."

"Say you really are in a sweet mood."

She smiles defiantly. "I'm just myself."

"God I hope not."

The Negress returns and sets the Daiquiris between them as they sit there silently. The door behind them opens and Margaret comes in with the chill. On top of everything, the guy with her is, he isn't very happy to see, Ronnie Harrison. Margaret says to Rabbit, "Hello, you. You still hanging on?"

"Hell," Harrison says, "it's the great Angstrom," as if he's trying to take Tothero's place in every way. "I've been hearing about you," he adds slimily.

"Hearing what?"

"Oh. The word."

Harrison was never one of Rabbit's favorites and has not improved. In the locker room he was always talking about making out and playing with himself under his little hairy pot of a belly and that pot has really grown. Harrison is fat. Fat and half bald. His kinky brass-colored hair has thinned and the skin of his scalp shows, depending on how he tilts his head. This pink showing through disgusts Rabbit, like the one bald idea that is always showing through Harrison's talk. Still, he remembers one night when Harrison came back into the game after losing two teeth to somebody's elbow and tries to be glad to see him. There were just five of you out there at a time and the other four for that time were unique in the world.

But it seems long ago, and every second Harrison stands there smirking it seems longer. He is wearing a narrow-shouldered seersucker suit and its cool air of business success annoys Rabbit. He feels hemmed in. The problem is, who shall sit where? He and Ruth have gotten on opposite sides of the table, which was the mistake. Harrison decides, and ducks down to sit beside Ruth, with a little catch in the movement that betrays the old limp from his football injury. Rabbit becomes obsessed by Harrison's imperfections. He's ruined the effect of his Ivy League suit by wearing a white tie like a wop. When he opens his mouth the two false teeth don't quite match the others.

"Well, how's life treating the old Master?" he says. "The word is you got it made." His eyes make his meaning by flicking sideways to Ruth, who sits there like a lump, her hands folded around the Daiquiri. Her knuckles are red from washing dishes for him. When she lifts the glass to drink, her chin shows through distorted.

"He made me," she says, setting it down.

"He and who else?" asks Harrison.

Margaret wriggles at Rabbit's side. She feels somehow like Janice: jumpy. Her presence in the left corner of his vision feels like a dark damp cloth approaching that side of his face.

"Where's Tothero?" he asks her.

"Totherwho?"

Ruth giggles, damn her. Harrison bends his head toward Ruth's, pink showing, and whispers a remark. Her lips tuck up in a smile; it's just like that night in the Chinese place, anything he says will please her, except that tonight he is Harrison and Rabbit sits across from them married to this girl he hates. He's sure what Harrison whispers is about him, "the old Master." From the second there were four of them it was clear he was going to be the goat. Like Tothero that night.

"You know damn well who," he tells Margaret. "Marty Tothero."

"Our old coach, Harry!" Harrison cries, and reaches across the table to touch Rabbit's fingertips. "The man who made us immortal!"

Rabbit curls his fingers an inch beyond Harrison's reach and Harrison, with a satisfied smirk, draws back, pulling his palms along the slick table-top so they make a slippery screech of friction.

"Me, you mean," Rabbit says. "You were nothing."

"Nothing. That seems a little stern. That seems a little stern, Harry old bunny. Let's cast our minds back. When Tothero wanted a guy roughed up, who did he send in to do it? When he wanted a hot shot like you guarded nice and close, who was his boy?" He pats his own chest. "You were too much of a star to dirty your hands. No, you never fouled anybody, did you? You didn't play football either, and get your knee scrambled, either, did you? No sir, not Harry the bird; he was on wings. Feed him the ball and watch it go in."

"It went in, you noticed."

"Sometimes. Sometimes it did. Harry now don't wrinkle your nose. Don't think we all don't appreciate your ability." From the way he's using his hands, chopping and lifting in a practiced way, Rabbit thinks he must do a lot of talking around a table. Yet there's a tremor; and in seeing that Harrison is afraid of him, Rabbit loses interest. The waitress comes – Harrison orders vodka-and-tonics for himself and Margaret and another Daiquiri for Ruth – and Rabbit watches her back recede as if it is the one real thing in the world: the little triangle of black bra under the two blue-brown pillows of muscle. He wants Ruth to see him looking.

Harrison is losing his salesman's composure. "Did I ever tell you what Tothero once said to me about you? Ace, are you listening?"

"What did Tothero say?" God, this guy is a middle-aged bore and he's not even thirty.

"He said to me, 'This is in confidence, Ronnie, but I depend on you to spark the team. Harry is not a team player.'"

Rabbit looks down at Margaret and over at Ruth. "Now I'll tell ya what really happened," he says to them. "Old Harrison here went in to Tothero and he said, 'Hey, I'm a real spark plug, ain't I, coach? A real play-maker, huh? Not like that lousy showboat Angstrom, huh?' And Tothero was probably asleep and didn't answer, so Harrison goes through the rest of his life thinking, 'Gee, I'm a real hero. A real play-maker.' On a basketball team, you see, whenever you have a little runty clumsy guy that can't do any-thing he's called the play-maker. I don't know where he's sup-posed to be making all these plays. In his bedroom I guess." Ruth laughs; he's not sure he wanted her to.

"That's not true." Harrison's practiced palms flicker more hastily. "He volunteered it to me. Not that it was anything I didn't know; the whole school knew it."

Did it? Nobody ever told him.

Ruth says, "God, let's not talk *bas*ketball. Every time I go out with this bastard we talk nothing but."

He wonders, Did doubt show on his face and she say that to reassure him? Does she in any part of her feel sorry for him?

Harrison perhaps thinks he's been uglier than befits his sales-conference suavity. He takes out a cigarette and a lizard-skin Ronson. They can't help but watch him while he snaps a shapely flame into being.

Rabbit turns to Margaret. Something in the way this arranges the nerves in his neck rings a bell, makes him think he turned to her exactly like this a million years ago. He says, "You never answered me."

"Nuts, I don't know where he is. I guess he went home. He was sick."

"Just sick, or" – Harrison's mouth does a funny thing, smiling and pursing both, as if he is introducing, with deference, this bit of Manhattan cleverness to his rural friends for the first time, tapping his head to make sure they will "get it" – "sick, sick, sick?"

"All ways," Margaret says. A serious shadow crosses her face that seems to remove her and Harry, who sees it, from the others. Ruth and Harrison across from them, touched by staccato red light, seem to smile from the furnace of damnation.

"Dear Ruth," Harrison says, "how have you been? I often worry about you."

"Don't worry about *me*," she says, yet seems pleased.

"I just wonder," he goes on, "about the ability of our mutual friend to support you in the style to which you are accustomed."

The Negress brings their drinks and Harrison, as if flashing a badge, shows her the lizard-skin Ronson in his hand. "Real skin," he says.

"Mmm," the waitress says, with lots of throat. "Your own?"

Rabbit laughs. He loves that black chick.

When she goes, Harrison leans forward with the sweet smile you use on children. "Did you know," he asks Harry, "that Ruth and I once went to Atlantic City together?"

"There was another couple," she hastily tells Harry.

"A disgusting pair," Harrison says, "who preferred the shabby privacy of their own bungalow to the golden sunshine outdoors. The male of this twosome later confided to me, with ill-concealed pride, that he had enjoyed the orgasmatic climax eleven times in the all-too-short period of thirty-six hours."

Margaret laughs. "Honestly, Ronnie, to hear you talk sometimes you'd think you went to Harvard."

"Princeton," he corrects. "Princeton is the effect I want to give. Harvard is suspect around here."

Rabbit looks toward Ruth and sees that the second Daiquiri is on its way and the first has been delivered. She titters. "The awful thing about them," she says, "was that they did it in the car. Here was poor Ronnie, trying to drive through all this Sunday-night traffic, and I looked back at a stoplight and Betsy's dress was up around her neck."

"I didn't drive all the way," Harrison tells her. "Remember we *fin*ally got him to drive." His head tips toward her for confirmation and his pink scalp glints.

"Yeah." Ruth looks into her glass and titters again, maybe at the image of Betsy naked.

Harrison watches narrowly the effect of this on Rabbit. "This guy," he says, in the pushy-quiet voice of offering a deal, "had an interesting theory. He thought" – Harrison's hands grip air – "that right at the crucial, how shall I say? – development, you should *slap* your partner, as hard as you can, right in the face. If you're in a position to. Otherwise slap what you can."

Rabbit blinks; he really doesn't know what to do about this awful guy. And just there, in the space of blinking, with the alcohol vaporizing under his ribs, he feels himself pass over. He laughs, really laughs. They can all go to Hell. "Well what did he think about biting?"

Harrison's I've-got-your-number-buddy grin grows fixed; his reflexes aren't quick enough to take this sudden turn. "Biting? I don't know."

"Well he couldn't have given it much thought. A good big bloody bite: nothing better. Of course I can see how you're handicapped, with those two false teeth."

"Do you have false teeth, Ronnie?" Margaret cries. "How exciting! You've never told."

"Of course he does," Rabbit tells her. "You didn't think those two piano keys were his, did you? They don't even come close to matching."

Harrison presses his lips together but he can't afford to give up that forced grin and it sharply strains his face. His talking is hampered too.

"Now there was this place we used to go to in Texas," Rabbit says, "where there was this girl whose backside had been bitten so often it looked like a piece of old cardboard. You know, after it's been out in the rain. It's all she did. She was a virgin otherwise." He looks around at his audience and Ruth shakes her head minutely, one brief shake, as if to say, *No, Rabbit*, and it seems extremely sad, so sad a film of grit descends on his spirit and muffles him.

Harrison says, "It's like that story about this whore that had the biggest − ah − you don't want to hear it, do you?"

"Sure. Go ahead," Ruth says. "I might learn something."

"Well, this guy, see, was making out and he loses his, ahem, device." Harrison's face bobbles in the unsteady light. His hands start explaining. Rabbit thinks the poor guy must have to make a pitch five times a day or so. He wonders what he sells; some sort of deal it must be, nothing as definite as the MagiPeel Peeler. ". . . up to his elbow, up to his shoulder, then he gets his whole head in, and his chest, and starts crawling along this tunnel . . ." Good old MagiPeel, Rabbit thinks: he can almost feel one in his hand. Its handle came in three colors, which the company called turquoise, scarlet, and gold. The funny thing about it, it really did what they said, really took the skin off turnips, carrots, potatoes, radishes, neat, quick; it had a long sort of slot with razor-sharp edges. ". . . sees this *other* guy and says, 'Hey, have you seen . . .'" Ruth sits there resigned and with horror he believes it's all the same to her in her mind, there's no difference between Harrison and him, and for that matter *is* there a difference? The whole interior of the place muddles and runs together red like the inside of a stomach in which they're all being digested. ". . . and the other guy says, 'Stripper, hell. I've been in here three weeks looking for my *motorcycle!*'"

Harrison, waiting to join the laughter, looks up in silence. He's failed to sell it. "That's too fantastic," Margaret says.

Rabbit's skin is clammy under his clothes; this makes the draft from the door opening behind him sharp. Harrison says, "Hey, isn't that your sister?"

Ruth looks up from her drink. "Is it?" He makes no sign and she says, "They have the same horsy look."

One glance told Rabbit. Miriam and her escort luckily walk a little into the place, past their table, and wait there to spot an empty booth. The place is shaped like a wedge and widens out from the entrance. The bar is in the center, and on either side there is an aisle of booths. The young couple heads for the opposite aisle. Mim wears bright white shoes with very high heels. The boy with her has woolly blond hair cut just long enough to comb and one of those smooth caramel tans people who play but don't work out-doors in summer get.

"Is that your sister?" Margaret says. "She's attractive. You and her must take after different parents."

"How do *you* know her?" Rabbit asks Harrison.

"Oh —" His hand flicks diffidently, as if his fingertips slide across a streak of grease in the air. "You see her around."

Rabbit's instinct was to freeze at first but this suggestion of Harrison's that she's a tramp makes him get up and walk across the orange tile floor and around the bar.

"Mim."

"Well, *hi*."

"What are you doing here?"

She tells the boy with her, "This is my brother. He's back from the dead."

"Hi, big brother." Rabbit doesn't like the boy's saying this and he doesn't like the way the kid is sitting on the inside of the booth with Mim on the outside in the man's place. He doesn't like the whole feel of the thing, that Mim is showing him around. The kid is wearing a blue blazer and a narrow tie and looks, in a smirched prep-school way, too young and too old. His lips are too thick. Mim doesn't give his name.

"Harry, Pop and Mom fight all the time about you."

"Well if they knew you were in a dump like this they'd have something else to talk about."

"It's not so bad, for this section of town."

"It stinks. Why don't you and Junior get out?"

"Say. Who's in charge here?" the kid asks, drawing his shoulders up and making his lips thicker.

Harry reaches over, hooks his finger around the kid's striped necktie, and snaps it out. It flies up and hits his thick mouth and makes his manicured face go slightly fuzzy. He starts to rise and Rabbit puts his hand on top of his tidy haircut and pushes him down again and walks away, with the hardness of the kid's brush-cut head still tingling in his fingertips. At his back his sister half-calls, "Harry!"

His ears are so good he hears, as he rounds the bar, Junior explain to her, in a voice husky with cowardice, "He's in love with you."

To his own table he says, "Come on, Ruth. Get on your motorcycle."

She protests, "I'm happy."

"Come *on*."

She moves to collect her things and Harrison, after looking around in doubt, gets out of the booth to let her up. He stands there beside Rabbit and Rabbit on an impulse puts his hand on Ronnie's unpadded would-be-Princeton shoulder. In comparison with Mim's kid he likes him. "You're right, Ronnie," he tells him, "you were a real play-maker." It comes out nasty but he meant it well, for the sake of the old team.

Harrison, too slow to feel that he means it, knocks his hand away and says, "When are you gonna grow up?" It's telling that lousy story that has rattled him.

Outside on the red-painted steps of the place Rabbit starts laughing. "Looking for my *moto*rcycle," he says, and lets go, "Hwah hwah *hyaaa*," under the castanet neon light.

Ruth is in no humor to see it. "Well you *are* a nut," she says.

It annoys him that she is too dumb to see that he is really sore. The way she shook her head "No" at him when he was gagging it up annoys him; his mind goes back over the minute again and again and every time snags on it. He is angry about so many things he doesn't know where to begin; the only thing clear is he's going to give her hell.

"So you and that bastard went to Atlantic City together."

"Why is he a bastard?"

"Oh. He's not and I am."

"I didn't say you were."

"You did too. Right back in there you did."

"It was just an expression. A *fond* expression, though I don't know why."

"You don't."

"No I don't. You see your sister come in with some boyfriend and practically pee in your pants."

"Did you see the punk she was with?"

"What was the matter with him?" Ruth asks. "He looked all right."

"Just about everybody looks all right to you, don't they?"

"Well I don't see what you're doing going around like some almighty judge."

"Yes sir, just about anything with a pecker looks all right to you."

They are walking up Warren Avenue. Their place is seven blocks away. People are sitting out on their steps in the late spring air; their conversation is in this sense public and they fight to keep their voices low.

"Boy, if this is what seeing your sister does to you I'm glad we're not married."

"What brought that up?"

"What brought what up?"

"Marriage."

"You did, don't you remember, the first night, you kept talking about it, and kissed my ring finger."

"That was a nice night."

"All right then."

"All right then nothing." Rabbit feels he's been worked into a corner where he can't give her hell without giving her up entirely, without obliterating the sweet things. But then she did that by taking him to that stinking place. "You've laid for Harrison, haven't you?"

"I guess. Sure."

"You guess. You don't know?"

"I said sure."

"And how many others?"

"I don't know."

"A hundred?"

"It's a pointless question."

"Why is it pointless?"

"It's like asking how many times you've taken a crap. O.K. I've taken a crap."

"They're about the same to you, is that it?"

"No they're not the same but I don't see what the count matters. You knew what I was."

"I'm not sure I did. You were a real hooer?"

"I took some money. I've told you. There were boyfriends when I was working as a stenographer and they had friends and I lost my job because of the talk maybe I don't know and some older men got my number I guess through Margaret, I don't know. Look. It's by. If it's a question of being dirty or something a lot of married women have had to take it more often than I have."

"Did you pose for pictures?"

"You mean like for dirty books? No."

"Did you blow guys?"

"Look, maybe we should say bye-bye." At the thought of that her chin softens and eyes burn and she hates him too much to think of sharing her secret with him. Her secret inside her seems to have no relation to him, this big body loping along with her under the streetlamps, hungry as a ghost, wanting to hear the words to whip himself up. That was the thing about men, the importance they put on the mouth. Rabbit seems like another man to her, with this difference: in ignorance he has welded her to him and she can't let go.

With degrading gratitude she hears him say, "No I don't *want* to say bye-bye. I just want an answer to my question."

"The answer to your question is yes."

"Harrison?"

"Why does Harrison mean so much to you?"

"Because he stinks. And if Harrison is the same to you as me then I stink."

They are, for that moment, the same to her – in fact she would prefer Harrison, just for the change, just because he doesn't insist on being the greatest thing that ever was – but she lies. "You're not at all the same. You're not in the same league."

"Well I got a pretty funny feeling sitting across from you two in that restaurant. What all did you do with him?"

"Oh, I don't know, what *do* you do? You make love, you try to get close to somebody."

"Well, would you do everything to me that you did to him?"

This stuns her skin in a curious way, makes it contract so that her body feels squeezed and sickened inside it. " Sure. If you want me to." After being a wife a whore's skin feels tight.

His relief is boyish; his front teeth flash happily. "Just once," he promises, "honest. I'll never ask you again." He tries to put his arm around her but she pulls away.

Up in the apartment he asks plaintively, "Are you going to?" She is struck by the helplessness in his posture; in the interior darkness, to which her eyes have not adjusted, he seems a suit of clothes hung from the broad white knob of his face.

She asks, "Are you sure we're talking about the same thing?"

"What do you think we're talking about?" He's too fastidious to mouth the words.

She says, "Sucking you off."

"Right," he says.

"In cold blood. You just want it."

"Uh-huh. Is it so awful for you?"

This glimmer of her gentle rabbit emboldens her. "It's not so bad. May I ask what I've done?"

"I didn't like the way you acted tonight."

"How did I act?"

"Like what you were."

"I didn't mean to."

"Even so. I saw you that way tonight and it put a wall between us and this is the one way through it."

"That's pretty cute. You just want it, really." She yearns to hit out at him, to tell him to go. But that time is past.

He repeats, "Is it so awful for you?"

"Well it is because you think it is."

"Maybe I don't. Maybe I think it'd be nice."

"Look, I've loved you."

"Well I've loved *you*."

"And now?"

"I don't know. I want to still."

Now those damn tears again. She tries to hurry the words out before her voice crumbles. "That's good of you. That's heroic."

"Don't be smart. Listen. Tonight you turned against me. I need to see you on your knees. I need you to" – he still can't say it – "do it."

The two tall drinks have been a poor experiment; she wants to go to sleep and her tongue tastes sour. She feels in her queasy stomach her need to keep him and wonders, Will this frighten him? Will this kill her in him?

"If I did it what would it prove?"

"It'd prove you're mine."

"Shall I take my clothes off?"

"Sure." He takes his off quickly and neatly and stands by the dull wall in his brilliant body. He leans awkwardly and brings one hand up and hangs it on his shoulder not knowing what to do with it. His whole shy pose has these wings of tension, like he's an angel waiting for a word. Sliding her last clothes off, her arms feel cold touching her sides. This last month she's felt cold all the time; her temperature being divided or something. In the growing light he shifts slightly. She closes her eyes and tells herself, they're not ugly. Not.

Mrs. Springer called the rectory a little after eight. Mrs. Eccles told her Jack had taken the young people's softball team to a game fifteen miles away and she didn't know when he'd be home. Mrs. Springer's panic carried over the wire and Lucy spent nearly two hours calling numbers in an attempt to reach him. It grew dark. She finally reached the minister of the church whose softball team they were playing and he told her the game had been over for an hour. The darkness thickened outside; the window whose sill held the phone became a waxy streaked mirror in which she could see

herself, hair unpinning, slump back and forth between the address
book and the phone. Joyce, hearing the constant ticking of the
dial, came downstairs and leaned on her mother. Three times Lucy
took her up to the bed and twice the child came down again and
leaned her damp weight against her mother's legs in frightened
silence. The whole house, room beyond room surrounding with
darkness the little island of light around the telephone, filled with
menace and when, the third time, Joyce failed to come down from
her bed, Lucy felt guilty and forsaken both, as if she had sold her
only ally to the shadows. She dialed the number of every problem
case in the parish she could think of, tried the vestrymen, the
church secretary, the three co-chairmen of the fund-raising
drive, Angus the old deaf sexton, and even the organist, a piano-
teaching professional who lived in Brewer.

The hour hand has moved past ten; it's getting embarrassing.
It's sounding as if she's been deserted. And in fact it frightens her,
that her husband seems to be nowhere in the world. She makes
coffee and weeps weakly, in her own kitchen. How did she get
into this? What drew her in? His gaiety, he was always so gay. To
know him back in seminary you would never think he would take
all this so seriously; he and his friends sitting in their bare old rooms
lined with handsome blue exegetical works made it all seem an
elegant joke. She remembers playing with them in a softball game
that was the Athanasians against the Arians. And now she never
saw his gaiety, it was all spent on other people, on this grim in-
tangible parish, her enemy. She hates them, all those clinging quaint
quavering widows and Young People for Christ – the one good
thing if the Russians take over is they'll make religion go extinct.
It should have gone extinct a hundred years ago. Maybe it shouldn't
have, maybe our weakness needs it, but let somebody else carry it
on. On Jack it was so dreary. Sometimes she feels sorry for him
and, abruptly, this is one of the times.

When he does come in, at quarter of eleven, it turns out he's
been sitting in a drugstore gossiping with some of his teenagers;
the idiotic kids tell him everything, all smoking like chimneys, so
he comes home titillated silly with "how far" you can "go" on
dates and still love Jesus.

Eccles sees at once she is furious. He had been having far too happy a time in the drugstore. He loves kids; their belief is so real to them and sits so light.

Lucy delivers her message as sufficient rebuke, but it fails as that; for, with hardly a backward glance at the horrid evening she has, implicitly, spent, he rushes to the phone.

He takes his wallet out and between his driver's license and his public-library card finds the telephone number he has been saving, the key that could be turned in the lock just once. He wonders, dialing it, if it will fit, if he was a fool to lean the entire weight of the case on the word of young Mrs. Fosnacht, with her mirroring, brittle, vacant sunglasses. The distant phone rings often: it is as if electricity, that amazingly trained mouse, has scurried through miles of wire only to gnaw at the end of its errand on an impenetrable plate of metal. He prays, but it is a bad prayer, a doubting prayer; he fails to superimpose God upon the complexities of electricity. He concedes them their inviolable laws. Hope has vanished, he is hanging on out of despair, when the gnawing ringing stops, the metal is lifted, and openness, an impression of light and air, washes back through the wires to Eccles' ear.

"Hello." A man's voice, but not Harry's. It is more sluggish and brutal than that of his friend.

"Is Harry Angstrom there?" Sunglasses mock his sunk heart; this is not the number.

"Who's this?"

"My name is Jack Eccles."

"Oh. Hi."

"Is that you, Harry? It didn't sound like you. Were you asleep?"

"In a way."

"Harry, your wife has started to have the baby. Her mother called here around eight and I just got in." Eccles closes his eyes; in the dark tipping silence he feels his ministry, sum and substance, being judged.

"Yeah," the other breathes in the far corner of the darkness. "I guess I ought to go to her."

"I wish you would."

"I guess I should. It's mine I mean too."

"Exactly. I'll meet you there. It's St. Joseph's in Brewer. You know where that is?"

"Yeah, sure. I can walk it in ten minutes."

"You want me to pick you up in the car?"

"No, I'll walk it."

"All right. If you prefer. Harry?"

"Huh?"

"I'm very proud of you."

"Yeah. O.K. I'll see you."

Eccles had reached for him, it felt like, out of the ground. The minister's voice had sounded tinny and buried. Ruth's bedroom is dim; the streetlamp like a low moon burns shadows into the inner planes of the armchair, the burdened bed, the twisted sheet he tossed back finally when he realized the phone would never stop. The bright rose window of the church opposite is still lit: purple red blue gold like the notes of different bells struck. His body, his whole frame of nerves and bone, tingles, as if with the shaking of small bells hung up and down his silver skin. His spent groin tingles. He wonders if he had been asleep, and how long, ten minutes or five hours. He finds his underclothes and trousers draped on a chair and fumbles with them; his white shirt seems to crawl, like a cluster of glowworms in grass. He hesitates a second before poking his fingers into its illusion, that turns under his touch to safe cloth, dead. He carries it in his hand to the bed with its silent burden.

"Hey. Baby."

The long lump under the covers doesn't answer. Just the top of Ruth's hair peeks out. He doesn't feel she is asleep. When she is asleep her breathing is noisier.

"Hey. I got to go out."

No answer. If she wasn't asleep she heard everything he said on the phone, but what did he say? He remembers nothing except this sense of being reached. Ruth lies heavy and sullen and her body hidden. The night is hot enough for just a sheet but she put a blanket on the bed saying she felt cold. It was just about the only thing she did say. He shouldn't have made her do it. He doesn't know why he did except it felt right at the time. He thought it might be a breakthrough. She had done it for others, what was wrong with him? If she didn't want to, if it would spoil him for her, why didn't she say No? He kept touching her cheeks with his fingertips. He kept wanting to lift her up and hug her in simple thanks and say *Enough you're mine again* but somehow couldn't bring himself to have it stop and kept thinking the *next* moment, until it was too late, done. Right down her sweet red gullet. With it went instantly that strange floating feeling of high pride. Shame plunged in.

"My wife's having her baby. I got to go see her through it. I'll be back in a couple hours. I love you."

Still the body under the covers and the frizzy crescent of hair peeking over the top edge of the blanket don't move. He is so sure she is not asleep he thinks, *I've killed her.* It's ridiculous, such a thing wouldn't kill her, it has nothing to do with death; but the thought paralyzes him from going forward to touch her and make her listen.

"Ruth. I got to go this once, it's my baby she's having and she's such a mutt I don't think she can do it by herself. Our first one came awfully hard. It's the least I owe her."

Perhaps this wasn't the best way to say it but he's trying to explain and her stillness frightens him and is beginning to make him sore.

"Ruth. Hey. If you don't say anything I'm not coming back. Ruth."

She lies there like some dead animal or somebody after a car accident when they put a tarpaulin over. He feels if he went over and lifted her she would come to life but he doesn't like being manipulated and grows angry. He puts on his shirt and doesn't bother with a coat and necktie but it seems to take forever putting on his socks; the soles of his feet are tacky.

When the door closes the taste of seawater in her mouth is swallowed by the thick grief that mounts in her throat so fully she has to sit up to breathe. Tears slide from her blind eyes and salt the corners of her mouth as the empty walls of the room become real and then dense. It's like when she was fourteen and the whole world trees sun and stars would have swung into place if she could lose twenty pounds just twenty pounds what difference would it make to God Who guided every flower in the fields into shape? Only now it's not that she's asking she knows now that's supersti- tious all she wants is what she had a minute ago *him* in the room who when he was good could make her into a flower who could undress her of her flesh and turn her into sweet air Sweet Ruth he called her and if he had just said "sweet" talking to her she might have answered and he'd still be between these walls. No. She had known from the first night the wife would win they have the hooks and anyway she feels really lousy: a wave of wanting to throw up comes over her and washes away caring much about anything. She goes into the john and kneels on the tiles and watches the still oval of water in the toilet as if *it's* going to do something. She doesn't think after all she has it in her to throw up but stays there anyway because it pleases her, her bare arm resting on the icy porcelain lip; she grows used to the threat in her stomach, which doesn't dissolve, which stays with her, so in her faint state it comes to seem that this thing that's making her sick is some kind of friend.

He runs most of the way to the hospital. Up Summer one block, then down Youngquist, a street parallel to Weiser on the north, a street of brick tenements and leftover business places, shoe-repair nooks smelling secretively of leather, darkened candy stores, insurance agencies with photographs of tornado damage in the windows, real-estate offices lettered in gold, a bookshop. On an old-fashioned wooden bridge Youngquist Street crosses the railroad tracks, which slide between walls of blackened stone soft with soot like moss through the center of the city, threads of metal deep below in a darkness like a river, taking narrow sunset tints of pink from the neon lights of the dives along Railway Street. Music rises to him. The heavy boards of the old bridge, waxed black with locomotive smoke, rumble under his feet. Being a small-town boy, he always has a fear of being knifed in a city slum. He runs harder; the pavement widens, parking meters begin, and a new drive-in bank faces the antique Y.M.C.A. He cuts up the alley between the Y and a limestone church whose leaded windows show the reverse sides of Biblical scenes to the street. He can't make out what the figures are doing. From a high window in the Y.M.C.A. fall the clicks of a billiard game; otherwise the building's broad side is lifeless. Through the glass side door he sees an old Negro sweeping up in green aquarium light. Now the pulpy seeds of some tree are under his feet. Its tropically narrow leaves are black spikes against the dark yellow sky. Imported from China or Brazil or somewhere because it can live in soot and fumes. The St. Joseph's parking lot is a striped asphalt square whose sides are lined with such city trees; and above their tops, in this hard open space, he sees the moon, and for a second stops and communes with its mournful face, stops stark on his small scrabbled shadow on the asphalt to look up toward the heavenly stone that mirrors with metallic brightness the stone that has risen inside his hot skin. *Make it be all right*, he prays to it, and goes in the rear entrance.

The hospital light is bright and blue and shadowless. He walks down a linoleum hall perfumed with ether to the front desk. "Angstrom," he tells the nun behind the typewriter. "I think my wife is here."

Her plump washerwoman's face is rimmed like a cupcake with scalloped linen. She surveys her cards and says "Yes" and smiles. Her little wire spectacles perch way out from her eyes on the pads of fat at the top of her cheeks. "You may wait over there." She points with a pink ballpoint pen. Her other hand rests, beside the typewriter, on a string of black beads the size of the necklace of beads carved in Java he once got Janice for Christmas. He stands there staring, expecting to hear her say, *She's been here hours, where were you?* He can't believe she'll just accept him as another about-to-be father. As he stares, her nerveless white hand, that has never seen the sun, slides the black necklace off the desktop into her lap.

Two other men are already established in the waiting end of the room. This is the front entrance hall; people drift in and out. Rabbit sits down on an imitation leather chair with chrome arms and from this touch of metal and the furtive clicking quiet gets the idea he's in a police station and these other two men are the cops who made the arrest. It seems they ignore him pointedly. In his nervousness he plucks a magazine from the table. It's a Catholic magazine the size of the *Reader's Digest*. He tries to read a story about a lawyer in England who becomes so interested in how legally un*fair* it was for Henry VIII to confiscate the property of the monasteries that he becomes a Roman Catholic convert and eventually a monk. The two men whisper together; one maybe is the other's father. The younger one keeps kneading his hands together and nodding to what the older man whispers.

Eccles comes in, blinking and looking scrawny in his collar. He greets the sister behind the desk by name, Sister Bernard. Rabbit stands up on ankles of air and Eccles comes over with that familiar frown in his eyebrows. By the harsh hospital light his forehead is etched in purple. He's had a haircut that day; as he turns his skull, the shaved planes above his ears shine like the blue throat feathers of a pigeon.

Rabbit asks, "Does she know I'm here?" He wouldn't have predicted that he would whisper too. He hates the panicked choke in his voice.

"I'll see that she's told if she's still conscious," Eccles says in a loud voice that makes the whispering men look up. He goes over to Sister Bernard. The nun seems happy to chat, and both laugh, Eccles in the startled guffaw Rabbit knows well and Sister Bernard with a pure and girlish fat woman's fluting that springs from her throat slightly retracted, curbed by the frame of stiff frills around her face. When Eccles moves away she lifts the phone beside her skirted elbow.

Eccles comes back and looks him in the face, sighs, and offers him a cigarette. The effect is somehow of a wafer of repentance and Rabbit accepts. The first drag, after so many clean months, unhinges his muscles and he has to sit down. Eccles takes a hard chair nearby and makes no attempt at conversation. Rabbit can't think of much to say to him off the golf course and, shifting the smoking cigarette awkwardly to his left hand, pulls another magazine off the table, making sure it's unreligious, the *Saturday Evening Post*. It opens to an article in which the author, who from the photograph looks Italian, tells how he took his wife and four children *and* mother-in-law on a three-week camping trip to the Canadian Rockies that only cost them $120 not counting the initial investment of a Piper Cub. His mind can't keep with the words but keeps skidding up and branching away and flowering into little visions of Janice screaming, of the baby's head blooming out of blood, of the wicked ridged blue light Janice must be looking into if she's conscious, *if she's conscious* Eccles said, of the surgeon's red rubber hands and gauze face and Janice's babyish black nostrils widening to take in the antiseptic smell he smells, the smell running everywhere along the white walls of their having been washed, of blood being washed and shit washed and retching washed until every surface smells like the inside of a bucket but it will never come clean because we will always fill it up again with our filth. A damp warm cloth seems wrapped around his heart. He is certain that as a consequence of his sin Janice or the baby will die. His sin a conglomerate of flight, cruelty, obscenity, and conceit; a black clot embodied in the entrails of the birth. Though his bowels twist with the will to dismiss this clot, to retract, to turn back and undo, he does not turn to the priest beside him but instead reads the same sentence about delicious fried trout again and again.

On the extreme edge of his tree of fear Eccles perches, black bird, flipping the pages of magazines and making frowning faces to himself. He seems unreal to Rabbit, everything seems unreal that is outside of his sensations. His palms tingle; a strange impression of pressure darts over his body, seizing now his legs, now the base of his neck. His armpits itch the way they used to when he was little and late for school, running up Jackson Road.

"Where's her parents?" he asks Eccles.

Eccles looks surprised. "I don't know. I'll ask the sister." He moves to get up.

"No no, sit still for Chrissake." Eccles' acting like he half-owns the place annoys him. Harry wants to be unnoticed; Eccles makes noise. He rattles the magazines so it sounds like he's tearing orange crates apart, and flips cigarettes around like a juggler.

A woman in white, not a nun, comes into the waiting-room and asks Sister Bernard, "Did I leave a can of furniture polish in here? I can't find it anywhere. A green can, with one of those pushy things on top that makes it spritz."

"No, dear."

She looks for it and goes out and after a minute comes back and announces, "Well that's the mystery of the world."

To the distant music of pans, wagons, and doors, one day turns through midnight into another. Sister Bernard is relieved by another nun, a very old one, dressed in sky blue. As if in her climb toward holiness she got stalled in the sky. The two whispering men go to the desk, talk, and leave, their crisis unresolved. Eccles and he are left alone. Rabbit strains his ears to catch the cry of his child somewhere deep in the hushed hospital maze. Often he thinks he hears it; the scrape of a shoe, a dog in the street, a nurse giggling – any of these are enough to fool him. He does not expect the fruit of Janice's pain to make a very human noise. His idea grows, that it will be a monster, a monster of his making. The thrust whereby it was conceived becomes confused in his mind with the perverted entry he forced, a few hours ago, into Ruth. Momentarily drained of lust, he stares at the remembered contortions to which it has driven him. His life seems a sequence of grotesque poses assumed to no purpose, a magic dance empty of belief. *There is no God; Janice can die:* the two thoughts come at once, in one slow wave. He feels underwater, caught in chains of transparent slime, ghosts of the urgent ejaculations he has spat into the mild bodies of women. His fingers on his knees pick at persistent threads.

Mary Ann. Tired and stiff and lazily tough after a game he would find her hanging on the front steps under the school motto and they would walk across mulching wet leaves through white November fog to his father's new blue Plymouth and drive to get the heater warmed and park. Her body a branched tree of warm nests yet always this touch of timidity. As if she wasn't sure but he was much bigger, a winner. He came to her as a winner and that's the feeling he's missed since. In the same way she was the best of them all because she was the one he brought most to, so tired. Sometimes the shouting glare of the gym would darken behind his sweat-burned eyes into a shadowed anticipation of the careful touchings that would come under the padded gray car roof and once there the bright triumph of the past game flashed across her quiet skin streaked with the shadows of rain on the windshield. So that the two kinds of triumph were united in his mind. She married when he was in the Army; a P.S. in a letter from his mother shoved him out from shore. That day he was launched.

But he feels joy now; cramped from sitting on the eroded chrome-armed chair sick with cigarettes he feels joy in remembering his first girl; the water of his heart has been poured into a thin vase of joy that Eccles' voice jars and breaks.

"Well I've read this article by Jackie Jensen all the way to the end and I don't know what he said," Eccles says.

"Huh?"

"This piece by Jackie Jensen on why he wants to quit baseball. As far as I can tell the problems of being a baseball player are the same as those of the ministry."

"Say, don't you want to go home? What time is it?"

"Around two. I'd like to stay, if I may."

"I won't run off if that's what you're afraid of."

Eccles laughs and keeps sitting there. Harry's first impression of him had been tenacity and now all the intervening companionship has been erased and it's gone back to that.

Harry tells him, "When she had Nelson the poor kid was at it for twelve hours."

Eccles says, "The second child is usually easier," and looks at his watch. "It hasn't quite been six hours."

Events create events. Mrs. Springer passes through from the privileged room where she has been waiting and stiffly nods at Eccles; seeing Harry in the corner of her eye makes her stumble on her sore legs and tumbledown saddle shoes. Eccles gets up and goes with her through the door to the outside. After a while the two of them come back in along with Mr. Springer, who wears a tiny-knotted necktie and a laundry-fresh shirt. His little sandy mustache has been trimmed so often his upper lip has kind of shrivelled under it. He says, "Hello, Harry."

This acknowledgment from her husband, despite some talking-to they've probably had from Eccles, goads the fat hag into turning on Harry and telling him, "If you're sitting there like a buzzard young man hoping she's going to die, you might as well go back

to where you've been living because she's doing fine without you
and has been all along."

The two men hustle her away while the old nun peers with a
quaint smile across her desk, deaf? Mrs. Springer's attack, though
it ached to hurt him, is the first thing anybody has said to Harry
since this began that seems to fit the enormity of the event going
on somewhere behind the screen of hospital soap-smell. Until her
words he felt alone on a dead planet encircling the great gaseous
sun of Janice's labor; her cry, though a cry of hate, pierced his
solitude. The thought of Janice's death: hearing it voiced aloud
has halved its terror. That strange scent of death Janice breathed:
Mrs. Springer also smelled it, and this sharing seems the most
precious connection he has with anybody in the world.

Mr. Springer returns and passes through to the outside, bestow-
ing upon his son-in-law a painfully complex smile, compounded
of a wish to apologize for his wife (we're both men; I know), a
wish to keep distant (nevertheless you've behaved unforgivably;
don't touch me), and the car salesman's mechanical reflex of
politeness. Harry thinks, *You crumb;* hurls the thought at the
slammed door. *You slave.* Where is everybody going? Where are
they coming from? Why can't anybody rest? Eccles comes back
and feeds him another cigarette and goes away again. Smoking it
makes the floor of his stomach tremble. His throat feels like it does
when you wake up after sleeping all night with your mouth open.
His own bad breath brushes his nostrils. A doctor with a barrel
chest and skinned-looking hands held curled in front of the pouch
of his smock comes into the anteroom uncertainly. He asks Harry,
"Mr. Angstrom? I'm Dr. Crowe." Harry has never met him;
Janice used another obstetrician for the first baby and after her hard
time her father made her switch to this one. Janice used to visit
him once a month and bring home tales of how gentle he was,
how wonderfully soft his hands were, how he seemed to know
exactly what it was like to be a pregnant woman.

"How –?"

"Congratulations. You have a beautiful little daughter."

He offers his hand so hastily Harry has only time partly to rise,
and thus absorbs the news in a crouching position. The scrubbed
pink of the doctor's face – his sterile mask is unknotted and hangs

from one ear, exposing pallid beefy lips – becomes involved in Rabbit's process of trying to give shape and tint to the unexpected word "daughter."

"I do? It's O.K.?"

"Six pounds ten ounces. Your wife was conscious throughout and held the baby for a minute after delivery."

"Really? She held it? Was it – did she have a hard time?"

"No-o. It was normal. In the beginning she seemed tense, but it was a normal delivery."

"That's wonderful. Thank you. Good grief, thank you."

Crowe stands there smiling uneasily. Coming up from the pit of creation, he stammers in the open air. In these last hours he has been closer to Janice than Harry ever was, has been grubbing with his hands in her roots, riding her body in its earthquake, yet he has brought back nothing to confide: no curse, no blessing. Harry dreads that the doctor's eyes will release with thunder the mystery they have absorbed; but Crowe's gaze contains no wrath. Not even a reprimand. He seems to see Harry as just another in the parade of more or less dutiful husbands whose brainlessly sown seed he spends his life trying to harvest.

Harry asks, "Can I see her?"

"Who?"

Who? That "her" is a forked word now startles him. The world is thickening. "My, my wife."

"Of course, surely." Crowe seems in his mild way puzzled that Harry asks for permission. He must know the facts, yet seems unaware of the gap of guilt between Harry and humanity. "I thought you might mean the baby. I'd rather you waited until visiting hours tomorrow for that; there's not a nurse to show her right now. But your wife is conscious, as I say. We've given her some Equanil. That's just a tranquillizer. Meprobamate. Tell me" – he moves closer gently, pink skin and clean cloth – "is it all right if her mother sees her for a moment? She's been on our necks all night." He's asking *him*, him, the runner, the fornicator, the monster. He must be blind. Or maybe just being a father makes everyone forgive you, because after all it's the only sure thing we're here for.

"Sure. She can go in."

"Before or after you?"

Harry hesitates, and remembers the way Mrs. Springer came and visited him on his empty planet. "She can go in before."

"Thank you. Good. Then she can go home. We'll get her out in a minute. It'll be about ten minutes all told. Your wife is being prepared by the nurses."

"Swell." He sits down to show how docile he is and rises again. "Say, thanks by the way. Thank you very much. I don't see how you doctors do it."

Crowe shrugs. "She was a good girl."

"When we had the other kid I was scared silly. It took ages."

"Where did she have it?"

"At the other hospital. Homeopathic."

"Nn-*huh*." And the doctor, who had gone into the pit and brought back no thunder, emits a spark of spite at the thought of the rival hospital and, wagging his scrubbed head sharply, walks away.

Eccles comes into the room grinning like a schoolboy and Rabbit can't keep his attention on his silly face. He suggests thanksgiving and Rabbit bows his head blankly into his friend's silence. Each heartbeat seems to flatten against a wide white wall. When he looks up, objects seem infinitely solid and somehow tip, seem so full they are about to leap. His real happiness is a ladder from whose top rung he keeps trying to jump still higher, because he knows he should.

Crowe's phrase about nurses "preparing" Janice has a weird May Queen sound. When they lead him to her room he expects to find her with ribbons in her hair and paper flowers twined in the bedposts. But it's just old Janice, lying between two smooth sheets on a high metal bed. She turns her face and says, "Well look who it isn't."

"Hey," he says, and goes over to kiss her, intending it so gently. He bends as you would bend to a glass flower. Her mouth swims in the sweet stink of ether. To his surprise her arms come out from the sheets and she puts them around his head and presses his face down into her soft happy swimming mouth. "Hey take it easy," he says.

"I have no legs," she says, "it's the funniest feeling." Her hair is drawn tight against her skull in a sanitary knot and she has no makeup on. Her small skull is dark against the pillow.

"No legs?" He looks down and there they are under the sheets, stretched out flat in a motionless V.

"They gave me a spinal or whatever at the end and I didn't feel anything. I was lying there hearing them say push and the next thing here's this teeny flubbly *baby* with this big moon face looking cross at me. I told Mother it looks like you and she didn't want to hear it."

"She gave me hell out there."

"I wish they hadn't let her in. I didn't want to see her. I wanted to see *you*."

"Did you, God. Why, baby? After I've been so crummy."

"No you haven't. They told me you were here and all the while I was thinking then it was your baby and it was like I was having *you*. I'm so full of ether it's just like I'm floating; without any legs. I could just talk and talk." She puts her hands on her stomach and closes her eyes and smiles. "I'm really quite drunk. See, I'm flat."

"Now you can wear your bathing suit," he says, smiling and entering the drift of her ether-talk, feeling himself as if he has no legs and is floating on his back on a great sea of cleanness, light as a bubble amid the starched sheets and germless surfaces before dawn. Fear and regret are dissolved, and gratitude is blown so large it has no cutting edge. "The doctor said you were a good girl."

"Well isn't that silly; I wasn't. I was horrible. I cried and screamed and told him to keep his hands to himself. Though the thing I minded worst was when this horrible old nun shaved me with a dry razor."

"Poor Janice."

"No it was wonderful. I tried to count her toes but I was so dizzy I couldn't so I counted her eyes. Two. Did we want a girl? Say we did."

"*I* did." He discovers this is true, though the words discover the desire.

"Now I'll have somebody to side with me against you and Nelson."

"How is Nelson?"

"Oh. Every day, 'Daddy home day?' until I could belt him, the poor saint. Don't make me talk about it, it's too depressing."

"Oh, damn," he says, and his own tears, that it seemed didn't exist, sting the bridge of his nose. "I can't believe it was me. I don't know why I left."

"Vnnn." She sinks deeper into the pillow as a lush grin spreads her cheeks apart. "I had a little baby."

"It's terrific."

"You're lovely. You look so tall." She says this with her eyes shut, and when she opens them, they brim with an inebriated idea; he has never seen them sparkle so. She whispers, "Harry. The girl in the other bed in here went home today so why don't you sneak around when you go and come in the window and we can lie awake all night and tell each other stories? Just like you've come back from the Army or somewhere. Did you make love to lots of other women?"

"Hey, I think you ought to go to sleep now."

"It's all right, now you'll make better love to me." She giggles and tries to move in the bed. "No I didn't mean that, you're a good lover you've given me a baby."

"It seems to me you're pretty sexy for somebody in your shape."

"That's how you feel," she says. "I'd invite you into bed with me but the bed's so narrow. Ooh."

"What?"

"I just got this terrible thirst for orangeade."

"Aren't you funny?"

"*You're* funny. Oh that baby looked so *cross.*"

A nun fills the doorway with her wings. "Mr. Angstrom. Time."

"Come kiss," Janice says. She touches his face as he bends to inhale her ether again; her mouth is a warm cloud that suddenly splits and her teeth pinch his lower lip. "Don't leave," she says.

"Just for now. I'll be back tomorrow."

"Love you."

"Listen. I love *you.*"

Waiting for him in the anteroom, Eccles asks, "How was she?"

"Terrific."

"Are you going to go back now, to uh, where you were?"

"No," Rabbit answers, horrified, "for Heaven's sake. I can't."

"Well, then, would you like to come home with me?"

"Look, you've done more than enough. I can go to my parents' place."

"It's late to get them up."

"No, really, I couldn't put you to the trouble." He has already made up his mind to accept. Every bone in his body feels slack.

"It's no trouble; I'm not asking you to *live* with us," Eccles says. The long night is baring his nerves. "We have *scads* of room."

"O.K. O.K. Good. Thanks."

They drive back to Mt. Judge along the familiar highway. At this hour it is empty even of trucks. Though this is the pit of the night the sky is a strangely relenting black, really a gray. Harry sits wordless staring through the windshield, rigid in body, rigid in spirit. The curving highway seems a wide straight road that has opened up in front of him. There is nothing he wants to do but go down it.

The rectory is asleep. The front hall smells like a closet. Eccles takes him upstairs to a room that has tassels on the bedspread. He uses the bathroom stealthily and in underclothes curls up between the rustling clean sheets, making the smallest possible volume of himself. Thus curled near one edge, he draws backward into sleep like a turtle drawing into his shell. Sleep this night is not a dark haunted domain the mind must consciously set itself to invade, but a cave inside himself, into which he shrinks while the claws of the bear rattle like rain outside.

Sunshine, the old clown, rims the room. Two pink chairs flank the gauze-filled window buttered with light that smears a writing desk furry with envelope-ends. Above the desk is a picture of a lady in pink stepping toward you. A woman's voice is tapping the door. "Mr. Angstrom. Mr. Angstrom."

"Yeah. Hi," he calls, hoarse.

"It's twelve-twenty. Jack told me to tell you the visiting hours at the hospital are one to three." He recognizes Eccles' wife's crisp little twitty tone, like she was adding, *And what the hell are you doing in my house anyway?*

"Yeah. O.K. I'll be right out." He puts on the cocoa-colored trousers he wore last night and, displeased by the sense of these things being dirty, he carries his shoes and socks and shirt into the bathroom with him, postponing putting them against his skin, giving them another minute to air. Still foggy despite splashing water all around, he carries them out of the bathroom and goes downstairs in bare feet and a T-shirt.

Eccles' little wife is in her big kitchen, wearing khaki shorts this time and sandals and painted toenails. "How did you sleep?" she asks from behind the refrigerator door.

"Like death. Not a dream or anything."

"It's the effect of a clear conscience," she says, and puts a glass of orange juice on the table with a smart click. He imagines that seeing how he's dressed, with just the T-shirt over his chest, makes her look away quickly.

"Hey don't go to any bother. I'll get something in Brewer."

"I won't give you eggs or anything. Do you like Cheerios?"

"Love 'em."

"All right."

The orange juice burns away some of the fuzz in his mouth. He watches the backs of her legs; the white tendons behind her knees jump as she assembles things at the counter. "How's Freud?" he asks her. He knows this could be bad, because if he brings back that afternoon he'll bring back how he nicked her fanny; but he has this ridiculous feeling with Mrs. Eccles, that he's in charge and can't make mistakes.

She turns with her tongue against her side teeth, making her mouth lopsided and thoughtful, and looks at him levelly. He smiles; her expression is that of a high-school tootsie who wants to seem to know more than she's telling. "He's the same. Do you want milk or cream on the Cheerios?"

"Milk. Cream is too sticky. Where is everybody?"

"Jack's at the church, probably playing ping-pong with one of his delinquent boys. Joyce and Bonnie are asleep, Heaven knows why. They kept wanting to look at the naughty man in the guest room all morning. It took real love to keep them out."

"Who told them I was a naughty man?"

"Jack did. He said to them at breakfast, 'I brought home a naughty man last night who's going to stop being naughty.' The children have names for all of Jack's problems – you're the Naughty Man; Mr. Carson, an alcoholic, is the Silly Man; Mrs. MacMillan is the Woman Who Calls Up in the Night. Then there's the Droopsy Lady, Mr. Hearing-Aid, Mrs. Side-Door, and Happy Beans. Happy Beans is just about the least happy man you ever wanted to see, but once he brought the children some of those celluloid capsules with a weight in them, so they jiggle around. Ever since that he's Happy Beans."

Rabbit laughs, and Lucy, having delivered the Cheerios – too much milk; he is used to living with Ruth, who let him pour his own milk; he likes just enough to take away the dryness, so that the milk and cereal come out even – chats on confidingly. "The worst thing that happened, in connection with some committee or other Jack was talking with one of the vestrymen over the phone and had the idea that it would buck this poor soul up to be given a church job so he said, 'Why not make Happy Beans the chairman of something or other?' Well, the man on the other end of the line said 'Happy Who?' and Jack realized what he'd said but instead of just sluffing it off like anybody else would have, Jack told the whole story about the children calling him Happy Beans and of course this stuffy old vestryman didn't think it was at all that funny. He was a friend, you see, of Happy Beans; they weren't exactly business associates but often had lunch together over in Brewer. That's the thing about Jack; he always tells people too much. Now this vestryman is probably telling everybody how the rector pokes fun of this poor miserable Happy Beans."

He laughs again. His coffee comes, in a thin shallow cup monogrammed in gold, and Lucy sits down opposite him at the table with a cup of her own. "He said I'm going to stop being naughty," Rabbit says.

"Yes. He's overjoyed. He went out of here virtually singing. It's the first constructive thing he thinks he's done since he came to Mt. Judge."

Rabbit yawns. "Well I don't know what he did."

"I don't either," she says, "but to hear him talk the whole thing was on his shoulders."

This suggestion that he's been managed rubs Rabbit the wrong way. He feels his smile creak. "Really? Did he talk about it?"

"Oh, all the time. He's very fond of you. I don't know why."

"I'm just lovable."

"That's what I keep hearing. You have poor old Mrs. Smith wrapped around your little finger. She thinks you're marvellous."

"And you don't see it?"

"Maybe I'm not old enough. Maybe if I were seventy-three." She lifts the cup to her face and tilts it and the freckles on her narrow white nose sharpen in proximity to the steaming brown coffee. She is a naughty girl. Yes, it's plain as day, a naughty-girl type. She sets the cup down and looks at him with mocking round eyes. "Well tell me. How does it feel? To be a new man. Jack's always hoping I'll reform and I want to know what to expect. Are you 'born anew'?"

"Oh, I feel about the same."

"You don't act the same."

He grunts "Well" and shifts in his chair. Why does he feel so awkward? She is trying to make him feel foolish and sissy, just because he's going to go back to his wife. It's quite true, he doesn't act the same; he doesn't feel the same with her, either; he's lost the nimbleness that led him so lightly into tapping her backside that day. He tells her, "Last night driving home I got this feeling of a straight road ahead of me; before that I was sort of in the bushes and it didn't matter which way I went."

Her small face above the coffee cup held in two hands like a soup bowl is perfectly tense with delight; he expects her to laugh and instead she smiles silently. He thinks, *She wants me.*

Then he remembers Janice with her legs paralyzed talking about toes and love and orangeade and this perhaps seals shut something in his face, for Lucy Eccles turns her head impatiently and says, "Well you better get going down that nice straight road. It's twenty of one."

He begins to put on his shoes and socks. "How long does it take to walk to the bus stop?"

"Not long. I'd drive you to the hospital if it weren't for the children." She listens to the stairs. "Speak of the devil: here comes one."

The older girl sneaks into the kitchen, dressed just in underpants.

"Joyce." Her mother halts halfway to the sink with the empty cups. "You get right back up to bed."

"Hello, Joyce," Rabbit says. "Did you come down to see the naughty man?"

Joyce stares and hugs the wall with her shoulder blades. Her long golden stomach protrudes thoughtfully.

"Joyce," Lucy says. "Didn't you hear me?"

"Why doesn't he have his shirt on?" the child asks distinctly.

"I don't know," her mother says. "I suppose he thinks he has a nice chest."

"I have a T-shirt on," he protests. It's as if neither of them see it.

"Is that his boo–zim?" Joyce asks.

"No, darling: only ladies have bosoms. We've been through that."

"Hell, if it makes everybody nervous," Rabbit says, and puts on his shirt. It's rumpled and the inside of the collar is gray; he put it on clean to go to the Club Castanet. He has no coat, he left Ruth too hastily. "O.K.," he says, tucking in the tail. "Thank you very much."

"You're very welcome," Lucy says. "Be good now." The two females walk with him down the hall. Lucy's white legs mix in pallor with the child's naked chest. Little Joyce keeps staring up at him. He wonders what she's puzzling about. Children and dogs sense the invisible. He tries to calculate how much sarcasm was in that "Be good now" and what it meant, if anything. He wishes she could drive him; he wants, he really wants, to get into a car with her. His reluctance to leave pulls the air between them taut.

They stand at the door, he and Eccles' baby-skinned wife and between them Joyce's face looking up with her father's wide lips and arched eyebrows and under them all Lucy's painted toenails, tiny scarlet shells in a row on the carpet. He strums the air with a vague disclaimer and puts his hand on the hard doorknob. The thought that only ladies have bosoms haunts him foolishly. He looks up from the toenails to Joyce's watching face and from there to her mother's bosom, two pointed bumps under a buttoned blouse that shows through its summer weave the white shadow of the bra. When his eyes reach Lucy's an amazing thing enters the silence. The woman winks. Quick as light: maybe he imagined it. He turns the knob and retreats down the sunny walk with a murmur in his chest as if a string in there had snapped.

At the hospital they say Janice has the baby with her for a moment and would he please wait? He is sitting in the chair with chrome arms leafing through a *Woman's Day* backwards when a tall woman with backswept gray hair and somehow silver, finely wrinkled skin comes in and looks so familiar he stares. She sees this and has to speak; he feels she would have preferred to ignore him. Who is she? Her familiarity has touched him across a great distance. She looks into his face reluctantly and tells him, "You're an old student of Marty's. I'm Harriet Tothero. We had you to dinner once. I can almost think of your name."

Yes, of course, but it wasn't from that dinner he remembers her, it was from noticing her on the streets. The students at Mt. Judge High knew, most of them, that Tothero played around, and his wife appeared to their innocent eyes wreathed in dark flame, a walking martyr, a breathing shadow of sin. It was less pity than morbid fascination that singled her out; Tothero was himself such a windbag, such a speechifier, that the stain of his own actions slid from him, oil off a duck. It was the tall, silver, serious figure of his wife that accumulated the charge of his wrong-doing, and released it to their young minds with an electrical shock that snapped their eyes away from the sight of her, in fear as much as embarrassment. Harry stands up, surprised to feel that the world she walks in is his world now. "I'm Harry Angstrom," he says.

"Yes, that's your name. He was so proud of you. He often talked to me about you. Even recently."

Recently. What did he tell her? Does she know about him? Does she blame him? Her long schoolmarmish face, as always, keeps its secrets in. "I've heard that he was sick."

"Yes, he is, Harry. Quite sick. He's had two strokes, one since he came into the hospital."

"He's here?"

"Yes. Would you like to visit him? I know it would make him very happy. For just a moment. He's had very few visitors; I suppose that's the tragedy of teaching school. You remember so many and so few remember you."

"I'd like to see him, sure."

"Come with me, then." As they walk down the halls she says, "I'm afraid you'll find him much changed." He doesn't take this in fully; he is concentrating on her skin, trying to see if it *does* look like a lot of little lizard skins sewed together. Just her hands and neck show.

Tothero is in a room alone. Like waiting presences white curtains hang expectantly around the head of his bed. Green plants on the windowsills exhale oxygen. Canted panes of glass lift the smells of summer into the room. Footsteps crunch on the gravel below.

"Dear, I've brought you someone. He was waiting outside in the most miraculous way."

"Hello, Mr. Tothero. My wife's had her baby." He speaks these words and goes toward the bed with blank momentum; the sight of the old man lying there shrunken, his tongue sliding in his lopsided mouth, has stunned him. Tothero's face, spotted with white stubble, is yellow in the pillows, and his thin wrists stick out from candy-striped pajama sleeves beside the shallow lump of his body. Rabbit offers his hand.

"He can't lift his arms, Harry," Mrs. Tothero says. "He is helpless. But talk to him. He can see and hear." Her sweet patient enunciation has a singing quality that is sinister, as if she is humming to herself.

Since he has extended his hand, Harry presses it down on the back of one of Tothero's. For all its dryness, the hand, under a faint scratchy fleece, is warm, and to Harry's horror moves, revolves stubbornly, so the palm is presented upward to Harry's touch. Harry takes his fingers back and sinks into the bedside chair. His old coach's eyeballs shift with scattered quickness as he turns his head an inch toward the visitor. The flesh under them has been so scooped that they are weakly protrusive. *Talk*, he must talk. "It's a little girl. I want to thank you" – he speaks loudly – "for the help you gave in getting me and Janice back together again. You were very kind."

Tothero retracts his tongue and shifts his face to look at his wife. A muscle under his jaw jumps, his lips pucker, and his chin crinkles repeatedly, like a pulse, as he tries to say something. A few dragged vowels come out; Harry turns to see if Mrs. Tothero can decipher them, but to his surprise she is looking elsewhere. She is looking out the window, toward an empty green courtyard. Her face is like a photograph.

Is it that she doesn't care? If so, should he tell Tothero about Margaret? But there was nothing to say about Margaret that might make Tothero happy. "I'm straightened out now, Mr. Tothero, and I hope you're up and out of this bed soon."

Tothero's head turns back with an annoyed quickness, the mouth closed, the eyes in a half-squint, and for this moment he looks so coherent Harry thinks he will speak, that the pause is just his old disciplinarian's trick of holding silent until your attention is complete. But the pause stretches, inflates, as if, used for sixty years to space out words, it at last has taken on a cancerous life of its own and swallowed the words. Yet in the first moments of the silence a certain force flows forth, a human soul emits its invisible and scentless rays with urgency. Then the point in the eyes fades, the drooping lids close, the lips part, the tip of the tongue appears.

"I better go down and visit my wife," Harry shouts. "She just had the baby last night. It's a girl." He feels claustrophobic, as if he's inside Tothero's skull; when he stands up, he has the fear he will bump his head, though the white ceiling is yards away.

"Thank you very much, Harry. I know he's enjoyed seeing you," Mrs. Tothero says. Nevertheless from her tone he feels he's flunked a recitation. He walks down the hall springingly, dismissed. His health, his reformed life, make space, even the anti-septic space in the hospital corridors, delicious. Yet his visit with Janice is disappointing. Perhaps he is still choked by seeing poor Tothero stretched out as good as dead; perhaps out of ether Janice is choked by thinking of how he's treated her. She complains a lot about how much her stitches hurt, and when he tries to express his repentance again she seems to find it boring. The difficulty of pleasing someone begins to hem him in. She asks how he spent the night and, sure enough, she asks him to describe Mrs. Eccles.

"About your height," he answers carefully. "A few freckles."

"Her husband's been wonderful," she says. "He seems to love everybody."

"He's O.K.," Rabbit says. "He makes me nervous."

"Oh, everybody makes you nervous."

"No now that's not true. Marty Tothero never made me nervous. I just saw the poor old bastard, stretched out in a bed up the hall. He can't say a word or move his head more than an inch."

"He doesn't make you nervous but I do, is that right?"

"I didn't say that."

"Oh no. Ow. These damn stitches they feel like barbed wire. I just make you so nervous you desert me for two months. Over two months."

"Well Jesus Janice. All you did was watch television and drink all the time. I mean I'm not saying I wasn't wrong, but it felt like I had to. You get the feeling you're in your coffin before they've taken your blood out. On that first night, when I got in the car in front of your parents' place, even then I might just as easy have gone down to get Nelson and driven it home. But when I let the brake out —" Her face goes into that bored look again. Her head switches from side to side, as if to keep flies from settling. He says, "Shit."

This gets her. She says, "I see your language hasn't been improved by living with that prostitute."

"She wasn't a prostitute, exactly. She just kind of slept around. I think there are a lot of girls like her around. I mean if you're going to call everybody who isn't married a prostitute —"

"Where are you going to stay now? Until I get out of the hospital."

"I thought Nelson and me would move into our apartment."

"I'm not sure you can. We didn't pay any rent on it for two months."

"Huh? You didn't?"

"Well my *good*ness, Harry. You expect a lot. You expect Daddy to keep paying rent? *I* didn't have any money."

"Well did the landlord call? What happened to our furniture? Did he put it out on the street?"

"I don't know."

"You don't *know?* Well what *do* you know? What have you been doing all this time? Sleeping?"

"I was carrying your baby."

"Well hell, I didn't know you have to keep your whole mind on *that* all the time. The trouble with you, kid, is you just don't give a damn. Really."

"Well listen to you."

He does listen to what he's been sounding like, remembers how he felt last night, and after a pause tries to begin all over again. "Hey," he says, "I love you."

"I love you," she says. "Do you have a quarter?"

"I guess. I'll look. What do you want it for?"

"If you put a quarter in that" – she points toward a small television set on a high stand, so patients can see it over the foot of their beds – "it'll play for an hour. There's a silly program on at two that Mother and I got to watching when I was home."

So for thirty minutes he sits by her bed watching some crew-cut M.C. tease a lot of elderly women from Akron, Ohio, and Oakland, California. The idea is all these women have tragedies they tell about and then get money according to how much applause there is, but by the time the M.C. gets done delivering commercials and kidding them about their grandchildren and their girlish hairdos there isn't much room for tragedy left. Rabbit keeps thinking that the M.C., who has that way of a Jew of pronouncing very distinctly, no matter how fast the words, is going to start plugging the MagiPeel Peeler but the product doesn't seem to have hit the big time yet. It isn't too bad a show; a pair of peroxide twins with twitchy tails push the women around to various microphones and booths and applause areas. It even makes for a kind of peace; he and Janice hold hands. The bed is almost as high as his shoulders when he sits down, and he enjoys being in this strange relation to a woman – as if he's carrying her on his shoulder but without the weight. He cranks her bed up and pours her a drink of water and these small services suit some need he has. The program isn't over when a nurse comes and says, "Mr.

Angstrom, if you want to see your baby the nurse is holding them to the window now."

He goes down the hall after her; her square hips swing under the starched white. From just the thickness of her neck he figures her for a good solid piece: haunchy. Big above the knee. He does like women big above the knee. Also he's worrying about what a woman from Springfield, Illinois, was going to say happened after her son's dreadful automobile accident, in which he lost an arm. So he's quite unprepared when the nurse in the baby room, where little bundles with heads like oranges lie in rows of supermarket baskets, some tilted, brings his girl to the viewing window, and it's like a damper being slid back in his chest. A sudden stiff draft freezes his breath. People are always saying how ugly new babies are, maybe this is the reason for the amazement. The baby is held by the nurse so her profile is sharp red against the buttoned white bosom of the uniform. The folds around the nostril, worked out on such a small scale, seem miraculously precise; the tiny stitchless seam of the closed eyelid runs diagonally a great length, as if the eye, when it is opened, will be huge. In the suggestion of pressure behind the tranquil lid and in the tilt of the protruding upper lip he reads a delightful hint of disdain. She knows she's good. What he never expected, he can feel she's feminine, feels something both delicate and enduring in the arc of the long pink cranium, furred in bands with black licked swatches. Nelson's head had been full of lumps and frightening blue veins and bald except at the base of the neck. Rabbit looks down through the glass with a timidity in the very act of seeing, as if rough looking will smash the fine machinery of this sudden life.

The smile of the nurse, foreshortened and flickering cutely between his eyes and the baby's nose, reassures him that he is the father. Her painted lips wrinkle a question through the glass, and he calls, "O.K., yeah," and gestures, throwing his hands, fingers splayed, to the height of his ears. "She's great," he adds, in a forced voice meant to carry through glass, but the nurse is already returning his daughter to her supermarket basket. Rabbit turns the wrong way, into the sleepless face of the father next in line, and laughs outright. He goes back to Janice with the wind swirling through him and fire the red of the baby's skin blazing. In the soap-scented hall he gets the idea: they should call the girl June. This is June, she was born in June. He's never known a June. It will please Janice because of the J. But Janice has been thinking about names too and wants to call her after her mother. Harry never thinks of Mrs. Springer as having a first name. It is Rebecca. His warm gust of pride in his child mollifies Janice, and he in turn is touched by her daughterly wish; it worries him at times that she does not seem to love her mother. They compromise: Rebecca June Angstrom.

The straight path is made smooth. Mr. Springer had been paying rent on the apartment all along, it turns out; he is a personal friend of the landlord and had arranged it without troubling his daughter. He always had a hunch Harry would come back but didn't want to advertise it in case he was wrong. Harry and Nelson move in and start housekeeping. Rabbit has a gift for housekeeping; the sensation of dust sucking into the vacuum cleaner, down the cloth hose, into a paper bag that when it is full of compact gray fluff will pop the cover of the Electrolux like a gentleman tipping his hat, pleases him. He was not entirely miscast as a barker for the MagiPeel Peeler; he has an instinctive taste for the small appliances of civilization, the little grinders and slicers and holders. Perhaps the oldest child should always be a girl; Mim, coming after him to the Angstrom household, was never exposed direct to the bright heart of the kitchen, but was always in his shadow with the housework, and sullen about assuming her share, which eventually became the greater share, because he was, after all, a boy. He supposes it will be the same with Nelson and Rebecca.

Nelson is a help. Closer to three now than two, the child can carry out orders that do not take him out of the room, understands that his toys belong in the bushel basket, and feels the happiness in cleanness, order, and light. The June breeze sighs at the screens of the long-closed windows. The sun dots the mesh with hundreds of sparkling T's and L's. Beyond the windows Wilbur Street falls away. The flat tin-and-tar roofs of their neighbors, weathered into gentle corrugations, glitter with mysterious pockets of rubble, candy-bar wrappers and a pool of glass flakes, litter that must have fallen from the clouds or been brought by birds to this street in the sky, planted with television aerials and hooded chimneys the size of fire hydrants. There are three of these roofs on the down side, tipped like terraces for drainage, three broad dirty steps leading to a brink below which the better homes begin, the stucco and brick forts, rugged with porches and dormer windows and lightning rods, guarded by conifers, protected by treaties with banks and firms of lawyers. It was strange that a row of tenements had been set above them; they had been tricked by growth. But in a town built against a mountain, height was too common to be precious; above them all there was the primitive ridge, the dark slum of forest, separated from the decent part of town by a band of unpaved lanes, derelict farmhouses, a cemetery, and a few raw young developments. Wilbur Street was paved for a block past Rabbit's door, and then became a street of mud and gravel between two short rows of ranch-houses of alternating color erected in 1953 on scraped red earth that even now is unsteadily pinned by the blades of grass that speckle it, so that after a good rain the gutter-water flows orange down Wilbur Street. The land grows steeper still, and the woods begin.

Straight out from the windows Rabbit can look in the opposite direction across the town into the wide farm valley, with its golf course. He thinks, *My valley. My home.* The blemished green-papered walls, the scatter rugs whose corners keep turning under, the closet whose door bumps the television set, unknown to his senses for months, have returned with unexpected force. Every corner locks against a remembered corner in his mind; every crevice, every irregularity in the paint clicks against a nick already in his brain.

Under the sofa and chairs and behind doors and in the foot-space under the kitchen cabinets he finds old fragments of toys that delight Nelson. The child has a perfect memory for his own possessions. "Mom-mom gay me dis." Holding up a plastic duck that had lost its wheels.

"She did?"

"Yop. Mom-mom did."

"Wasn't that nice of Mom-mom?"

"Yop."

"You know what?"

"What?"

"Mom-mom is Mommy's mommy!"

"Yop. Where Mommy?"

"At the hospital."

"At hop-pital? Come back Fi-day?"

"That's right. She'll come back Friday. Won't she be happy to see how clean we make everything?"

"Yop. Daddy at hop-pital?"

"No. Daddy wasn't at the hospital. Daddy was away."

"Daddy away" – the boy's eyes widen and his mouth drops open as he stares into the familiar concept of "away"; his voice deepens with the seriousness of it – "*long*." His arms go out to measure the length, so far his fingers bend backward. It is as long as he can measure.

"But Daddy's not away now, is he?"

"Nope."

He takes Nelson with him in the car the day he goes to tell Mrs. Smith he has to quit working in her garden. Old man Springer has offered him a job in one of his lots. The rhododendron trees by the crunching driveway look dusty and barren with a few brown corsages still hanging to their branches. Mrs. Smith herself comes to the door. "Yes, yes," she croons, her brown face beaming.

"Mrs. Smith, this is my son Nelson."

"Yes, yes, how do you do, Nelson? You have your father's head." She pats the small head with a hand withered like a tobacco leaf. "Now let me think. Where did I put that jar of old candy? He can eat candy, can't he?"

"I guess a little but don't go looking for it."

"I will too, if I want to. The trouble with you, young man, you never gave me credit for any competence whatsoever." She totters off, plucking with one hand at the front of her dress and poking the other into the air before her, as if she's brushing away cobwebs.

While she's out of the room he and Nelson stand looking at the high ceiling of this parlor, at the tall windows with mullions as thin as chalk-lines, through whose panes, some of which are tinted lavender, they can see the elms and hemlocks that guard the far rim of the estate. Paintings hang on the shining walls. One shows, in dark colors, a woman wrapped in a whipping strip of silk apparently having an argument, from the way her arms are flailing, with a big swan that just stands there pushing. On another wall there is a portrait of a young woman in a black gown sitting in a padded chair impatiently. Her face, though squarish, is fine-looking, with a triangular forehead caused by her hairdo. Round white arms curve into her lap. Rabbit moves a few steps closer to get a less oblique view. She has that short puffy little upper lip that is so good in a girl: the way it lifts to let a dab of dark come between her lips. There is this readiness about her all over. He feels that she's about to get out of the chair and step forward toward him with a frown on her triangular forehead. Mrs. Smith, returning with a crimson glass ball on a stem like a wineglass, sees where he's looking and says, "What I always minded was, Why did he have to make me look so irritable? I didn't like him a whit and he knew it. A slick little Italian. Thought he knew about women. Here." She has crossed to Nelson with the candy glass. "You try one of these. They're old but good like a lot of old things in this world." She takes off the lid, a knobbed hemisphere of translucent red glass, and holds it waggling in her hand. Nelson looks over and Rabbit nods at him to go ahead and he chooses a piece wrapped in colored tinfoil.

"You won't like it," Rabbit tells him. "That's gonna have a cherry inside."

"Shoosh," Mrs. Smith says. "Let the boy have the one he wants." So the poor kid goes ahead and takes it, bewitched by the tinfoil.

"Mrs. Smith," Rabbit begins, "I don't know if Reverend Eccles has told you, but my situation has kind of changed and I have to take another job. I won't be able to help around here any more. I'm sorry."

"Yes, yes," she says, alertly watching Nelson fumble at the tinfoil.

"I've really enjoyed it," he goes on. "It was sort of like Heaven, like that woman said."

"Oh that foolish woman Alma Foster," Mrs. Smith says. "With

her lipstick halfway up to her nose. I'll never forget her, the dear soul. Not a brain in her body. Here, child. Give it to Mrs. Smith." She sets the dish down on a round marble table holding only an oriental vase full of peonies and takes the piece of candy from Nelson and with a frantic needling motion of her fingers works the paper off. The kid stands there staring up with an open mouth; she thrusts her hand down jerkily and pops the ball of chocolate between his lips. With a crease of satisfaction in one cheek she turns, drops the tinfoil on the table, and says to Rabbit, "Well, Harry. At least we brought the rhodies in."

"That's right. We did."

"It pleased Horace, I know, wherever he is."

Nelson bites through to the startling syrup of the cherry and his mouth curls open in dismay; a dribble of brown creeps out one corner and his eyes dart around the immaculate palace room. Rabbit cups a hand at his side and the boy comes over and silently spits the mess into it, bits of chocolate shell and stringy warm syrup and the broken cherry.

Mrs. Smith sees none of this. Her eyes with their transparent irises of crazed crystal burn into Harry's as she says, "It's been a religious duty to me, to keep Horace's garden up."

"I'm sure you can find somebody else. Vacation's started; it'd be a perfect job for some high-school kid."

"No," she says, "no. I won't think about it. I won't be here next year to see Harry's rhodies come in again. You kept me alive, Harry; it's the truth; you did. All winter I was fighting the grave and then in April I looked out the window and here was this tall young man burning my old stalks and I knew life hadn't left me. That's what you have, Harry: life. It's a strange gift and I don't know how we're supposed to use it but I know it's the only gift we get and it's a good one." Her crystal eyes have filmed with a liquid thicker than tears and she grabs his arms above his elbows with hard brown claws. "Fine strong young man," she murmurs, and her eyes come back into focus as she adds, "You have a proud son; take care."

She must mean he should be proud of his son and take care of him. He is moved by her embrace; he wants to respond and did moan "No" at her prediction of death. But his right hand is full of melting mashed candy, and he stands helpless and rigid hearing her quaver, "Goodbye. I wish you well. I wish you well."

In the week that follows this blessing, he and Nelson are often happy. They go for walks around the town. One day they watch a softball game played on the high-school lot by men with dark creased faces like millworkers, dressed in gaudy felt-and-flannel uniforms, one team bearing the name of a fire hall in Brewer and the other the name of the Sunshine Athletic Association, the same uniforms, he guesses, that he saw hanging in the attic the time he slept in Tothero's bedroom. The number of spectators sitting on the dismantleable bleachers is no greater than the number of players. All around, behind the bleachers and the chicken-wire-and-pipe backstop, kids in sneakers scuffle and run and argue. He and Nelson watch a few innings, while the sun lowers into the trees. It floods Rabbit with an ancient, papery warmth, the oblique sun on his cheeks, the sparse inattentive crowd, the snarled pepper chatter, the spurts of dust on the yellow infield, the girls in shorts strolling past with chocolate popsicles. Brown adolescent legs thick at the ankle and smooth at the thigh. They know so much, at least their skins do. Boys their age scrawny sticks in dungarees and Keds arguing frantically if Williams was washed up or not. Mantle ten thousand times better. Williams ten million times better. Harry and Nelson share an orange soda bought from a man in a Boosters' Club apron who has established a bin in the shade. The smoke of dry ice leaking from the ice-cream section, the *ffp* of the cap being pulled from the orange. The artificial sweetness fills his heart. Nelson spills some on himself trying to get it to his lips.

Another day they go to the playground. Nelson acts frightened of the swings. Rabbit tells him to hold on and pushes very gently, from the front so the kid can see. Laughs, pleads, "Me out," begins to cry, "me out, me out, Da-dee." Dabbling in the sandbox gives Rabbit a small headache. Over at the pavilion the rubber thump of roof ball and the click of checkers call to his memory, and the forgotten smell of that narrow plastic ribbon you braid bracelets and whistle-chains out of and of glue and of the sweat on the handles on athletic equipment is blown down by a breeze laced with children's murmuring. He feels the truth: the thing that has left his life has left irrevocably; no search would recover it. No flight would reach it. It was here, beneath the town, in these smells and these voices, forever behind him. The fullness ends when we give Nature her ransom, when we make children for her. Then she is through with us, and we become, first inside, and then outside, junk. Flower stalks.

They visit Mom–mom Springer. The child is delighted; Nelson loves her, and this makes Rabbit like her. Though she tries to pick a fight with him he refuses to fight back, just admits everything; he was a crumb, a dope, he behaved terribly, he's lucky not to be in jail. Actually there's no real bite in her attack. Nelson is there for one thing, and for another she is relieved he has come back and is afraid of scaring him off. For a third, your wife's parents can't get at you the way your own can. They remain on the outside, no matter how hard they knock, and there's something relaxing and even comic about them. He and the old lady sit on the screened sunporch with iced tea; her bandaged legs are up on a stool and her little groans as she shifts her weight make him smile. It feels like one of those silly girls in high school you kind of liked without there ever being a question of love. Nelson and Billy Fosnacht are inside the house playing quietly. They're too quiet. Mrs. Springer wants to see what's happening but doesn't want to move her legs; in her torment she starts to complain about what a crude child little Billy Fosnacht is, and from this shifts over to the kid's mother. Mrs. Springer doesn't much like her, doesn't trust her around the corner; it isn't just the sunglasses, though she thinks that's a ridiculous affectation; it's the girl's whole manner, the way she came cozying around to Janice just because it looked like juicy gossip. "Why, she came around here so much that I had more charge of Nelson than Janice did, with those two off to the movies every day like high-school girls that don't have the responsibility of being mothers." Now Rabbit knows from school that Peggy Fosnacht, then Peggy Gring, wears sunglasses because she is freakishly, humiliatingly walleyed. And Eccles has told him that her company was a great comfort to Janice during the trying period now past. But he does not make either of these objections; he listens contentedly, pleased to be united with Ma Springer, the two of them against the world. The cubes in the iced tea melt, making the beverage doubly bland; his mother-in-law's talk laves his

ears like the swirling mutter of a brook. Lulled, he lets his lids
lower and a smile creeps into his face; he sleeps badly at nights,
alone, and drowses now on the grassy breadth of day, idly blissful,
snug on the right side at last.

It is quite different at his own parents' home. He and Nelson
go there once. His mother is angry about something; her anger
hits his nostrils as soon as he's in the door, like the smell of age on
everything. This house looks shabby and small after the Springers'.
What ails her? He assumes she's always been on his side and tells
her in a quick gust of confiding how terrific the Springers have
been, how Mrs. Springer is really quite warmhearted and seems to
have forgiven him everything, how Mr. Springer kept up the rent
on their apartment and now has promised him a job selling cars in
one of his lots. He owns four lots in Brewer and vicinity; Rabbit
had no idea he was that much of an operator. He's really kind of
a jerk but a successful jerk at least; at any rate he thinks he, Harry
Angstrom, has got off pretty easily. His mother's hard arched nose
and steamed spectacles glitter bitterly. Her disapproval nicks him
whenever she turns from the sink. At first he thinks it's that he
never got in touch with her but if that's so she should be getting
less sore instead of more because he's in touch with her now. Then
he thinks it's that she's disgusted he slept with Ruth, and committed adultery, but out of a clear sky she explodes that by asking
him abruptly, "And what's going to happen to this poor girl you
lived with in Brewer?"

"Her? Oh, she can take care of herself. She didn't expect
anything." But as he says this he tastes the lie in it. Nobody expects
nothing. It makes his life seem cramped, that Ruth can be mentioned out of his mother's mouth.

Her mouth goes thin and she answers with a smug flirt of her
head, "I'm not saying anything, Harry. I'm not saying one word."

But of course she is saying a great deal only he doesn't know
what it is. There's some kind of clue in the way she treats Nelson.
She as good as ignores him, doesn't offer him toys or hug him, just
says, "Hello, Nelson," with a little nod, her glasses snapping into
white circles. After Mrs. Springer's warmth this coolness seems
brutal. Nelson feels it and acts hushed and frightened and leans
against his father's legs. Now Rabbit doesn't know what's eating

his mother but she certainly shouldn't take it out on a two-year-old kid. He never heard of a grandmother acting this way. It's true, just the poor kid's being there keeps them from having the kind of conversation they used to have, where his mother tells him something pretty funny that happened in the neighborhood and they go on to talk about him, the way he used to be as a kid, how he dribbled the basketball all afternoon until after dark and was always looking after Mim. Nelson's being half Springer seems to kill all that. For the moment he stops liking his mother; it takes a hard heart to snub a tiny kid that just learned to talk. He wants to say to her, *What is this, anyway? You act like I've gone over to the other side. Don't you know it's the right side and why don't you praise me?*

But he doesn't say this; he has a stubbornness to match hers. He doesn't say much at all to her, after telling her what good sports the Springers are falls flat. He just hangs around, him and Nelson rolling a lemon back and forth in the kitchen. Whenever the lemon wobbles over toward his mother's feet he has to get it; Nelson won't. The silence makes Rabbit blush, for himself or for his mother he doesn't know. When his father comes home it isn't much better. The old man isn't angry but he looks at Harry like there isn't anything there. His weary hunch and filthy fingernails annoy his son; it's as if he's willfully aging them all. Why doesn't he get false teeth that fit? His mouth works like an old woman's. But one thing at least, his father pays some attention to Nelson, who hopefully rolls the lemon toward him. He rolls it back. "You going to be a ballplayer like your Dad?"

"He can't, Earl," Mom interrupts, and Rabbit is happy to hear her voice, believing the ice has broken, until he hears what she says. "He has those little Springer hands."

"For Chrissake, Mom, lay off," he says, and regrets it, being trapped. It shouldn't matter what size hands Nelson has. Now he discovers it does matter; he doesn't want the boy to have Springer hands, and, if he does – and if Mom noticed it he probably does – he likes the kid a little less. He likes the kid a little less, but he hates his mother for making him do it. It's as if she wants to pull down everything, even if it falls on her. And he admires this, her willingness to have him hate her, so long as he gets her message. But he rejects her message: he feels it poking at his mind and rejects it. He doesn't want to hear it. He doesn't want to hear her say another word. He just wants to get out with a little piece of his love of her left.

At the door he asks his father, "Where's Mim?"

"We don't see much of Mim any more," the old man says. His blurred eyes sink and he touches the pocket of his shirt, which holds two ballpoint pens and a little soiled packet of cards and papers. Just in these last few years his father has been making little bundles of things, cards and lists and receipts and tiny calendars that he wraps rubber bands around and tucks into different pockets with an elderly fussiness. Rabbit leaves his old home depressed, with a feeling of his heart having slumped off center.

The days go all right as long as Nelson is awake. But when the boy falls asleep, when his face sags asleep and his breath drags in and out of helpless lips that deposit spots of spit on the crib sheet and his hair fans in fine tufts and the perfect skin of his fat slack cheeks, drained of animation, lies sealed under a heavy flush, then a dead place opens in Harry, and he feels fear. The child's sleep is so heavy he fears it might break the membrane of life and fall through to oblivion. Sometimes he reaches into the crib and lifts the boy's body out, just to reassure himself with its warmth and the responsive fumbling protest of the tumbled limp limbs.

He rattles around in the apartment, turning on all the lights and television, drinking ginger ale and leafing through old *Life*s, grabbing anything to stuff into the emptiness. Before going to bed himself he stands Nelson in front of the toilet, running the faucet and stroking the taut bare bottom until wee-wee springs from the child's irritated sleep and jerkily prinkles into the bowl. Then he wraps a diaper around Nelson's middle and returns him to the crib and braces himself to leap the deep gulf between here and the moment when in the furry slant of morning sun the boy will appear, resurrected, in sopping diapers, beside the big bed, patting his father's face experimentally. Sometimes he gets into the bed, and then the clammy cold cloth shocking Rabbit's skin is like retouching a wet solid shore. The time in between is of no use to Harry. But the urgency of his wish to glide over it balks him. He lies in bed, diagonally, so his feet do not hang over, and fights the tipping sensation inside him. Like an unsteered boat, he keeps

scraping against the same rocks: his mother's ugly behavior, his
father's gaze of desertion, Ruth's silence the last time he saw her,
his mother's oppressive not saying a word, what ails her? He rolls
over on his stomach and seems to look down into a bottomless
sea, down and down, to where crusty crags gesture amid blind
depths. Good old Ruth in the swimming pool. That poor jerk
Harrison sweating it out Ivy-League style the ass-crazy son of a
bitch. Margaret's weak little dirty hand flipping over into
Tothero's mouth and Tothero lying there with his tongue floating around under twittering jellied eyes: No. He doesn't want to
think about that. He rolls over on his back in the hot dry bed and
the tipping sensation returns severely. Think of something pleasant. Basketball and cider at that little school down at the end of
the county Oriole High but it's too far back he can't remember
more than the cider and the way the crowd sat up on the stage.
Ruth at the swimming pool; the way she lay in the water without
weight, rounded by the water, slipping backwards through it, eyes
shut and then out of the water with the towel, him looking up her
legs at the secret hair and then her face lying beside him huge and
burnished and mute. No. He must blot Tothero and Ruth out of
his mind both remind him of death. They make on one side this
vacuum of death and on the other side the threat of Janice coming home grows: that's what makes him feel tipped, lopsided.
Though he's lying there alone he feels crowded, all these people
troubling about him not so much their faces or words as their mute
dense presences, pushing in the dark like crags under water and
under everything like a faint high hum Eccles' wife's wink. That
wink. What was it? Just a little joke in the tangle at the door, the
kid coming down in her underpants and maybe she conscious of
him looking at her toenails, a little click of the eye saying *On your
way Good luck* or was it a chink of light in a dark hall saying *Come
in?* Funny wise freckled piece he ought to have nailed her, that wink
bothering him ever since, she wanted him to really nail her. The
shadow of her bra. Tipped bumps, in a room full of light slips
down the shorts over the child-skin thighs sassy butt two globes
hanging of white in the light Freud in the white-painted parlor
hung with watercolors of canals; come here you primitive father
what a nice chest you have and here and here and here. He rolls

over and the dry sheet is the touch of her anxious hands, himself tapering tall up from his fur, ridges through which the thick vein strains, and he does what he must with a tight knowing hand to stop the high hum and make himself slack for sleep. A woman's sweet froth. Nails her. Passes through the diamond standing on his head and comes out on the other side wet. How silly. He feels sorry. Queer where the wet is, nowhere near where you'd think, on the top sheet instead of the bottom. He puts his cheek on a fresh patch of pillow. He tips less, Lucy undone. Her white lines drift off like unraveled string. He must sleep; the thought of the far shore approaching makes a stubborn lump in his glide. Think of things pleasant. Out of all his remembered life the one place that comes forward where he can stand without the ground turning into faces he is treading on is that lot outside the diner in West Virginia after he went in and had a cup of coffee the night he drove down there. He remembers the mountains around him like a ring of cutouts against the moon-bleached blue of the night sky. He remembers the diner, with its golden windows like the windows of the trolley cars that used to run from Mt. Judge into Brewer when he was a kid, and the air, cold but alive with the beginnings of spring. He hears the footsteps tapping behind him on the asphalt, and sees the couple running toward their car, hands linked. One of the red-haired girls that sat inside with her hair hanging down like wiggly seaweed. And it seems right here that he made the mistaken turning, that he should have followed, that they meant to lead him and he should have followed, and it seems to him in his disintegrating state that he did follow, that he *is* following, like a musical note that all the while it is being held seems to travel though it stays in the same place. On this note he carries into sleep.

But awakes before dawn being tipped again, frightened on the empty bed, with the fear that Nelson has died. He tries to sneak back into the dream he was having but his nightmare fear dilates and he at last gets up and goes to hear the boy breathe and then urinates with slight pain from having come and returns to a bed whose wrinkles the first stirrings of light are etching into black lines. On this net he lies down and steals the hour left before the boy comes to him, hungry and cold.

On Friday Janice comes home. For the first days the presence
of the baby fills the apartment as a little casket of incense fills a
chapel. Rebecca June lies in a bassinet of plaited rushes painted
white and mounted on a trundle. When Rabbit goes over to look
at her, to reassure himself that she is there, he sees her somehow
dimly, as if the baby has not gathered to herself the force that
makes a silhouette. Her averted cheek, drained of the bright red
he glimpsed at the hospital, is mottled gray, yellow, and blue,
marbled like the palms of his hands when he is queasy; when Janice
suckles Rebecca, yellow spots well up on her breast as if in answer
to the fainter shadows of this color in the baby's skin. The union
of breast and baby's face makes a globular symmetry to which both
he and Nelson want to attach themselves. When Rebecca nurses,
Nelson becomes agitated, climbs against them, pokes his fingers
into the seam between the baby's lips and his mother's udder and,
scolded and pushed away, wanders around the bed intoning, a
promise he has heard on television, "Mighty Mouse is on the
way." Rabbit himself loves to lie beside them watching Janice
manipulate her swollen breasts, the white skin shiny from fullness.
She thrusts the thick nipples like a weapon into the blind blistered
mouth, that opens and grips with birdy quickness. "Ow!" Janice
winces, and then the nerves within the baby's lips begin to work in
tune with her milk-making glands; the symmetry is established;
her face relaxes into a downward smile. She holds a diaper against
the other breast, mopping the waste milk it exudes in sympathy.
Those first days, full of rest and hospital health, she has more milk
than the baby takes. Between feedings she leaks, the bodices of all
her nighties bear two stiff stains. When he sees her naked, naked
all but for the elastic belt that holds her Modess pad in place, her
belly shaved and puffed and marked with the vertical brown line
only mothers have, his whole stomach stirs at the fierce sight of
her breasts, braced high by the tension of their milk, jutting from
her slim body like glossy green-veined fruit with coarse purple
tips. Top-heavy, bandaged, Janice moves gingerly, as if she might
spill, jarred. Though with the baby her breasts are used without
shame, tools like her hands, before his eyes she is still shy, and
quick to cover herself if he watches too openly. But he feels a
difference between now and when they first loved, lying side by

side on the borrowed bed, his eyes closed, together making the filmy sideways descent into one another. Now, she is intermittently careless, walks out of the bathroom naked, lets her straps hang down while she burps the baby, seems to accept herself with casual gratitude as a machine, a white, pliant machine for fucking, hatching, feeding. He, too, leaks; thick sweet love burdens his chest, and he wants her – just a touch, he knows she's a bleeding wound, but just a touch, just enough to get rid of his milk, to give it to her. Though in her ether trance she spoke of making love, she turns away from him in bed, and sleeps with a forbidding heaviness. He is too grateful, too proud of her, to disobey. He in a way, this week, worships her.

Eccles comes calling and says he hopes to see them in church. Their debt to him is such that they agree it would be nice of them, at least one of them, to go. The one must be Harry. Janice can't; she has been, by this Sunday, out of the hospital nine days and, with Harry off at his new job since Monday, is beginning to feel worn-out, weak, and abused. Harry is happy to go to Eccles' church. Not merely out of uneasy affection for Eccles, though there's that; but because he considers himself happy, lucky, blessed, forgiven, and wants to give thanks. His feeling that there is an unseen world is instinctive, and more of his actions than anyone suspects constitute transactions with it. He dresses in his new pale-gray suit to sell cars in and steps out at quarter of eleven into a broad blue Sunday morning a day before the summer solstice. He always enjoyed those people parading into church across from Ruth's place and now he is one of them. Ahead of him is the first hour in over a week when he won't be with a Springer, either Janice at home or her father at work. The job at the lot is easy enough, if it isn't any work for you to bend the truth. He feels exhausted by midafternoon. You see these clunkers come in with 80,000 miles on them and the pistons so loose the oil just pours through and they get a washing and the speedometer tweaked back and you hear yourself saying this represents a real bargain. He'll ask forgiveness.

He hates all the people on the street in dirty everyday clothes, advertising their belief that the world arches over a pit, that death is final, that the wandering thread of his feelings leads nowhere.

Correspondingly he loves the ones dressed for church: the pressed business suits of portly men give substance and respectability to his furtive sensations of the invisible, the flowers in the hats of their wives seem to begin to make it visible; and their daughters are themselves whole flowers, their bodies each a single flower, petaled in gauze and frills, a bloom of faith, so that even the plainest walk in Rabbit's eyes glowing with beauty, the beauty of belief. He could kiss their feet in gratitude, they release him from fear. By the time he enters the church he is too elevated with happiness to ask forgiveness. As he kneels in the pew on a red stool that is padded but not enough to keep his weight from pinching his knees painfully, his head buzzes with joy, his blood leaps in his skull, and the few words he frames, *God, Rebecca, thank you* bob inconsecutively among senseless eddies of gladness. People who know God rustle and stir about him, upholding him in the dark. When he sinks back into sitting position the head in front of him takes his eye. A woman in a wide straw hat. She is smaller than average with narrow freckled shoulders, probably young, though women tend to look young from the back. The wide hat graciously broadcasts the gentlest tilt of her head and turns the twist of blond hair at the nape of her neck into a kind of peeping secret he alone knows. Her neck and shoulders are given a faint, shifting lambency by their coat of fine white hairs, invisible except where the grain lies with the light. He smiles, remembering Tothero talking about women being covered all over with hair. He wonders if Tothero is dead now and quickly prays not. He becomes impatient for the woman to turn so he can see her profile under the rim of the hat, a great woven sun-wheel, garnished with an arc of paper violets. She turns to look down at something beside her; his breath catches; the thinnest crescent of cheek gleams, and is eclipsed again. Something in a pink ribbon pops up beside her shoulder. He stares into the inquisitive tan face of little Joyce Eccles. His fingers fumble for the hymnal as the organ heaves into the service; it is Eccles' wife rising within reach of his arm.

Eccles comes down the aisle shuffling behind a flood of acolytes and choristers. Up behind the altar rail he looks absentminded and grouchy, remote and insubstantial and stiff, like a Japanese doll in his vestments. The affected voice, nasal-pious, in which he intones prayers affects Rabbit disagreeably; there is something disagreeable about the whole Episcopal service, with its strenuous ups and downs, its canned petitions, its cursory little chants. He has trouble with the kneeling pad; the small of his back aches; he hooks his elbows over the back of the pew in front of him to keep from falling backward. He misses the familiar Lutheran liturgy, scratched into his heart like a weathered inscription. In this service he blunders absurdly, balked by what seem willful dislocations of worship. He feels too much is made of collecting the money. He scarcely listens to the sermon at all.

It concerns the forty days in the Wilderness and Christ's conversation with the Devil. Does this story have any relevance to *us*, here, now? In the twentieth century, in the United States of America? Yes. There exists a sense in which *all* Christians must have conversations with the Devil, must learn his ways, must hear his voice. The tradition behind this legend is very ancient, was passed from mouth to mouth among the early Christians. Its larger significance, its greater meaning, Eccles takes to be this: suffering, deprivation, barrenness, hardship, lack are all an indispensable part of the education, the initiation, as it were, of any of those who would follow Jesus Christ. Eccles wrestles in the pulpit with the squeak in his voice. His eyebrows jiggle as if on fishhooks. It is an unpleasant and strained performance, contorted, somehow; he drives his car with an easier piety. In his robes he seems a sinister man-woman. Harry has no taste for the dark, tangled, visceral aspect of Christianity, the *going through* quality of it, the passage *into* death and suffering that redeems and inverts these things, like an umbrella blowing inside out. He lacks the mindful will to walk the straight line of a paradox. His eyes turn toward the light however it catches his retinas.

Lucy Eccles' bright cheek ducks in and out of view under its shield of straw. The child, hidden – all but her ribbon – behind the back of the pew, whispers to her, presumably that the naughty man is behind them. Yet the woman never turns her head directly to see. This needless snub excites him. The most he gets is her profile; the soft tuck of doubleness in her chin deepens as she frowns down at the child beside her. She wears a dress whose narrow blue stripes meet at the seams at sharp angles. There is something sexed in her stillness in the church, in her obedience to its man-centered, rigid procedure. Rabbit flatters himself that her true attention radiates backward at him. Against the dour patch-work of subdued heads, stained glass, yellowing memorial plaques on the wall, and laboriously knobbed and beaded woodwork, her hair and skin and hat glow singly, their differences in tint like the shades of brilliance within one flame.

So that when the sermon yields to a hymn, and her bright nape bows to receive the benediction, and the nervous moment of silence passes, and she stands and faces him, it is anticlimactic to see her face, with its pointed collection of dots – eyes and nostrils and freckles and the tight faint dimples that bring a sarcastic tension to the corners of her mouth. That she wears a facial expression at all shocks him slightly; the luminous view he had enjoyed for an hour did not seem capable of being so swiftly narrowed into one small person.

"Hey. Hi," he says.

"Hello," she says. "You're the last person I ever expected to see here."

"Why?" He is pleased that she thinks of him as an ultimate.

"I don't know. You just don't seem the institutional type."

He watches her eyes for another wink. He has lost belief in that first one, weeks ago. She returns his gaze until his eyes drop. "Hello, Joyce," he says. "How are you?"

The little girl halts and hides behind her mother, who con-tinues to maneuver down the aisle, walking with small smooth steps while distributing smiles to the faces of the sheep. He has to admire her social coördination.

At the door Eccles clasps Harry's hand with his broad grip, a warm grip that tightens at the moment it should loosen. "It's exhilarating to see you here," he says, hanging on. Rabbit feels the whole line behind him bunch and push.

"Nice to be here," he says. "Nifty sermon."

Eccles, who has been peering at him with a feverish smile and a blush that seems apologetic, laughs; the roof of his mouth glim-mers a second and he lets go.

Harry hears him tell Lucy, "In about an hour."

"The roast's in now. Do you want it cold or overdone?"

"Overdone," he says. He solemnly takes Joyce's tiny hand and says, "How do you do, Mrs. Pettigrew? How splendid you look this morning!"

Startled, Rabbit turns and sees that the fat lady next in line is startled also. His wife is right, Eccles is indiscreet. Lucy, Joyce behind her, walks up beside him. Her straw hat comes up to his shoulder. "Do you have a car?"

"No. Do you?"

"No. Walk along with us."

"O.K." Her proposition is so bold there must be nothing in it; nevertheless the harpstring in his chest tuned to her starts trembling. Sunshine quivers through the trees; in the streets and along unshaded sections of the pavement it leans down with a broad dry weight. It has lost the grainy milkiness of morning sun. Mica fragments in the pavement glitter; the hoods and windows of hurrying cars smear the air with white reflections. Lucy pulls off her hat and shakes her hair. The church crowd thins behind them. The waxy leaves, freshly thick, of the maples planted between the pavement and curb embower them rhythmically; in the broad gaps of sun her face, his shirt, feel white, white; the rush of motors, the squeak of a tricycle, the touch of a cup and saucer inside a house are sounds conveyed to him as if along a bright steel bar. As they walk along he trembles in light that seems her light.

"How are your wife and baby?" she asks.

"Fine. They're just fine."

"Good. Do you like your new job?"

"Not much."

"Oh. That's a bad sign, isn't it?"

"I don't know. I don't suppose you're supposed to like your job. If you did, then it wouldn't be a job."

"Jack likes his job."

"Then it's not a job."

"That's what he says. He says it's not a job, which is the way I'd treat it. But I'm sure you know his line as well as I do."

He knows she's needling him, but he doesn't feel it, tingling all over anyway. "He and I in some ways I guess are alike," he says.

"I know. I know." Her odd quickness in saying this sets his heart ticking quicker. She adds, "But naturally it's the differences that I notice." Her voice curls dryly into the end of this sentence; her lower lip goes sideways.

What is this? He has a sensation of touching glass. He doesn't know if they are talking about nothing or making code for the deepest meanings. He doesn't know if she's a conscious or unconscious flirt. He always thinks when they meet again he will speak firmly, and tell her he loves her, or something as blunt, and lay the truth bare; but in her presence he is numb; his breath fogs the glass and he has trouble thinking of anything to say and what he does say is stupid. He knows only this: underneath everything, under their minds and their situations, he possesses, like an inherited lien on a distant piece of land, a dominance over her, and that in her grain, in the lie of her hair and nerves and fine veins, she is prepared for this dominance. But between that preparedness and him everything reasonable intervenes. He asks, "Like what?"

"Oh – like the fact that you're not afraid of women."

"Who is?"

"Jack."

"You think?"

"Of course. The old ones, and the teenagers, he's fine with; the ones who see him in his collar. But the others he's very leery of; he doesn't like them. He doesn't really think they even ought to come to church. They bring a smell of babies and bed into it. That's not just in Jack; that's in Christianity. It's really a very neurotic religion."

Somehow, when she fetches out her psychology, it seems so foolish to Harry that his own feeling of foolishness leaves him. Stepping down off a high curb, he takes her arm. Mt. Judge, built on its hillside, is full of high curbs difficult for little women to negotiate gracefully. Her bare arm remains cool in his fingers.

"Don't tell that to the parishioners," he says.

"See? You sound just like Jack."

"Is that good or bad?" There. This seems to him to test her bluff. She must say either good or bad, and that will be the fork in the road.

But she says nothing. He feels the effort of self-control this takes; she is accustomed to making replies. They mount the opposite curb and he lets go of her arm awkwardly. Though he is awkward, there is still this sense of being nestled against a receptive grain, of fitting.

"Mommy?" Joyce asks.

"What?"

"What's rottic?"

"Rottic. Oh. *Neu*rotic. It's when you're a little bit sick in the head."

"Like a cold in the head?"

"Well yes, in a way. It's about that serious. Don't worry about it, sweetie. It's something most everybody is. Except our friend Mr. Angstrom."

The little girl looks up at him across her mother's thighs with a spreading smile of self-conscious impudence. "He's naughty," she says.

"Not extraordinarily," her mother says.

At the end of the rectory's brick wall a blue tricycle has been abandoned and Joyce runs ahead and mounts it and rides away in her aqua Sunday coat and pink hair ribbon, metal squeaking, spinning ventriloquistic threads of noise into the air. Together they watch the child a moment. Then Lucy asks, "Do you want to come in?" In waiting for his reply, she contemplates his shoulder; her eyelashes from his angle hide her eyes. Her lips are parted and her tongue, a movement in her jaw tells him, touches the roof of her mouth. In the noon sun her features show sharp and her lipstick looks cracked. He can see the inner lining of her lower lip wet against her teeth. A delayed gust of the sermon, a whining exhortation like a dusty breeze off the desert, sweeps through him, accompanied grotesquely by a vision of Janice's breasts – green-veined, tender. This wicked snip wants to pluck him from them.

"No thanks, really. I can't."

"Oh come on. You've been to church, have a reward. Have some coffee."

"No, look." His words come out soft but somehow big. "You're a doll, but I got this wife now." And his hands, rising from his sides in vague explanation, cause her to take a quick step backward.

"I beg your pardon."

He is conscious of nothing but the little speckled section of her green irises like torn tissue paper around her black pupil-dots; then he is watching her tight round butt jounce up the walk. "But thanks, anyway," he calls in a hollowed, gutless voice. He hates being disliked. She slams the door behind her so hard the fish-shaped knocker clacks by itself on the empty porch.

He walks home blind to the sunlight. Was she mad because he had turned down a proposition, or because he had shown that he thought she had made one? Or was it a mixture of these opposites, that had somehow exposed her to herself? His mother, suddenly caught in some confusion of her own, would turn on the heat that way. In either case, he feels tall and elegant and potent striding along under the trees in his Sunday suit. Whether spurned or mis-understood, Eccles' wife has jazzed him up, and he reaches his apartment clever and cold with lust.

His wish to make love to Janice is like a small angel to which all afternoon tiny lead weights are attached. The baby scrawks tire-lessly. It lies in its crib all afternoon and makes an infuriating noise of strain, *Hnnnnnah ah ah nnnnh*, a persistent feeble scratching at some interior door. What does it want? Why won't it sleep? He has come home from church carrying something precious for Janice and keeps being screened from giving it to her. The noise spreads fear through the apartment. It makes his stomach ache; when he picks up the baby to burp her he burps himself; the pressure in his stomach keeps breaking and re-forming into a stretched bubble as the bubble in the baby doesn't break. The tiny soft marbled body, weightless as paper, goes stiff against his chest and then floppy, its hot head rolling as if it will unjoint from its neck. "Becky, Becky, Becky," he says, "go to sleep. Sleep, sleep, sleep."

The noise makes Nelson fretful and whiny. As if, being closest to the dark gate from which the baby has recently emerged, he is most sensitive to the threat the infant is trying to warn them of. Some shadow invisible to their better-formed senses seems to grab Rebecca as soon as she is left alone. Rabbit puts her down, tiptoes into the living room; they hold their breath. Then, with a bitter scratch, the membrane of silence breaks, and the wobbly moan begins again, *Nnnh, a-nnnnnih!*

"Oh my God," Rabbit says. "Son of a bitch. Son of a bitch."

Around five in the afternoon, Janice begins to cry. Tears burble down her dark pinched face. "I'm dry," she says. "I'm dry. I just don't have anything to feed her." The baby has been at her breasts repeatedly.

"Forget it," he says. "She'll conk out. Have a drink. There's some old whisky in the kitchen."

"Say; what is this Have a drink routine of yours? I've been trying not to drink. I thought you didn't like me to drink. All afternoon you've been smoking one cigarette after another and saying, 'Have a drink. Have a drink.' "

"I thought it might loosen you up. You're tense as hell."

"I'm no tenser than you are. What's eating you? What's on your mind?"

"What's happened to your milk? Why can't you give the kid enough milk?"

"I've fed her three times in four hours. There's nothing there any more." In a plain, impoverished gesture, she presses her breasts through her dress.

"Well have a drink of something."

"Say, what did they tell you at church? 'Go on home and get your wife soused'? *You* have a drink if that's on your mind."

"I don't need a drink."

"Well you need something. You're the one's upsetting Becky. She was fine all morning until you came home."

"Forget it. Just forget it. Just forget the whole frigging thing."

"Baby *cry!*"

Janice puts her arm around Nelson. "I know it honey. She's hot. She'll stop in a minute."

"Baby hot?"

They listen for a minute and it does not stop; the wild feeble warning, broken by tantalizing gaps of silence, goes on and on. Warned, but not knowing of what, they blunder about restlessly through the wreckage of the Sunday paper, inside the apartment, whose walls sweat like the walls of a prison. Outside, the wide sky hosts a high sun, blue through the hours, and Rabbit is further panicked by the thought that on such a day his parents used to take him and Mim on walks to the quarry – they are wasting a beautiful Sunday. But they can't get organized enough to get out. He and Nelson could go but Nelson's strange fright makes him reluctant to leave his mother, and Rabbit, hoping to possess her eventually, hovers near her like a miser near treasure. His lust glues them together.

She feels this and is oppressed by it. "Why don't you go out? You're making the baby nervous. You're making *me* nervous."

"Don't you want a drink?"

"No. *No.* I just wish you'd sit down or stop smoking or rock the baby or something. And stop touching me. It's too hot. I think I should be back at the hospital."

"Do you hurt? I mean down there."

"Well I wouldn't if the baby would stop. I've *fed* her three times. Now I must feed you supper. Ohh. Sundays make me sick. What did you *do* in church that makes you so busy?"

"I'm not busy. I'm trying to be helpful."

"I know. That's what's so unnatural. Your skin smells funny."

"How?"

"Oh I don't know. Stop bothering me."

"I love you."

"Stop it. You can't. I'm not lovable right now."

"You just lie down on the sofa and I'll make some soup."

"No no no. You give Nelson his bath. I'll try to nurse the baby again. Poor thing there's nothing there."

They eat supper late but in broad light; the day is one of the longest of the year. They sip soup by the flickering light of Rebecca's urgent cries; her feeble voice is a thin filament burning with erratic injections of power. But as, amid the stacked dishes on the sink, under the worn and humid furniture, and in the coffin-like hollow of the plaited crib, the shadows begin to strengthen, the grip of the one with which Becky has been struggling all afternoon relaxes, and suddenly she is quiet, leaving behind a solemn guilty peace. They had failed her. A foreigner speaking no English but pregnant with a great painful worry had been placed among them and they had failed her. At last, night itself had swept in and washed her away like a broken piece of rubbish.

"It couldn't have been colic, she's too young for colic," Janice says. "Maybe she was just hungry, maybe I'm out of milk."

"How could that be, you've been like footballs."

She looks at him squinting, sensing what's up. "Well don't think you're going to play." But he thinks he spies a smile there.

Nelson goes to bed as he does when he's sick, willingly, whimpering. His sister was a drain on him today. Sunk in the pillow, Nelson's brown head looks demure and compact. As the child hungrily roots the bottle in his mouth, Rabbit hovers, seeking what you never find, the expression with which to communicate, to transfer, those fleeting burdens, ominous and affectionate, that are placed upon us and as quickly lifted, like the touch of a brush. Obscure repentance clouds his mouth, a repentance out of time and action, a mourning simply that he exists in a world where the tan heads of little boys sink gratefully into narrow beds sucking bottles of rubber and glass. He cups his hand over the bulge of Nelson's forehead. The boy drowsily tries to brush it off, waggles his head with irritation, and Harry takes it away and goes into the other room.

He persuades Janice to have a drink. He makes it – he doesn't know much about alcoholic things – of half whisky and half water. She says it tastes hateful. But after a while consumes it.

In bed he imagines that he can feel its difference in her flesh. There is that feeling of her body coming into his hand, of fitting his palm, that makes a sexy texture. All under her nightie up to the pit of her throat her body is quiet for him. They lie sideways, facing each other. He rubs her back, first lightly, then toughly, pushing her chest against his, and gathers such a feel of strength from her pliancy that he gets up on an elbow to be above her. He kisses her dark, hard face scented with alcohol. She does not turn her head, but he reads no rejection in this small refusal of motion, that lets him peck away awkwardly at a profile. He stifles his tide of resentment, reschooling himself in her slowness. Proud of his patience, he resumes rubbing her back. Her skin keeps its secret, as does her tongue; is she feeling it? After Ruth, she is mysterious, an opaque and virginal wife. Is he kindling the spark? His wrist aches. He dares undo the two buttons of her nightie front and lifts the leaf of cloth so a long arc is exposed in the rich gloom of the bed, and her warm breast flattens against the bare skin of his chest. She submits to this maneuver and he is filled with the joyful thought that he has brought her to this fullness. He is a good lover. He relaxes into the warmth of the bed and pulls the bow on his pajama waist. She has been shaved and scratches; he settles lower, on the cotton patch. This unnaturalness, this reminder of her wound, makes his confidence delicate, so he is totally destroyed when her voice – her thin, rasping, dumb-girl's voice – says by his ear, "Harry. Don't you know I want to go to sleep?"

"Well, why didn't you tell me before?"

"I don't know. I didn't know."

"Didn't know what?"

"I didn't know what you were doing. I thought you were just being nice."

"So this isn't nice."

"Well it's not nice when I can't *do* anything."

"You can do *some*thing."

"No I can't. Even if I wasn't all tired and confused from Rebecca's crying all day I can't. Not for six weeks. You know that."

"Yeah, I know, but I thought –" He's terribly embarrassed.

"*What* did you think?"

"I thought you might love me anyway."

After a pause she says, "I *do* love you."

"Just a touch, Jan. Just let me touch you."

"Can't you go to sleep?"

"No I can't. I can't. I love you too much. Just hold still."

It would have been easy a minute ago to get it over with but all this talk has taken the fine point off. It's a bad contact and her stubborn limpness makes it worse; she's killing it by making him feel sorry for her and ashamed and foolish. The whole sweet thing is just sweat and work and his ridiculous inability to finish it against the dead hot wall of her belly. She pushes him back. "You're just using me," she says. "It feels horrible."

"Please, baby. I'm almost there."

"It feels so cheap."

Her daring to say this infuriates him; he realizes she hasn't had it for three months and in all that time has got an unreal idea of what sex is. She has imagined it into something rare and precious she's entitled to half of when all he wants is to get rid of it so he can move on, on into sleep, down the straight path, for her sake. It's for her sake.

"Roll over," he says.

"I love you," she says with relief, misunderstanding, thinking he's dismissing her. She touches his face in farewell and turns her back.

He scrunches down and fits himself lengthwise between her buttocks, just so they kind of grip. It's beginning to work, steady, warm, when she twists her head and says over her shoulder, "Is this a trick your whore taught you?"

He thumps her shoulder with his fist and gets out of bed and his pajama bottoms fall down. The night breeze filters in through the window screen. She turns over on her back into the center of the bed and explains stupidly out of her dark face, "I'm not your whore, Harry."

"Damn it," he says, "that was the first thing I've asked from you since you came home."

"You've been wonderful," she says.

"Thanks."

"Where are you going?"

He is putting on his clothes. "I'm going out. I've been cooped up in this damn hole all day."

"You went out this morning."

He finds his suntans and puts them on. She asks, "Why can't you try to imagine how I *feel*? I've just had a baby."

"I can. I can but I don't want to, it's not the thing, the thing is how *I* feel. And I feel like getting out."

"Don't. Harry. Don't."

"You can just lie there with your precious ass. Kiss it for me."

"Oh for God's sake," she cries, and flounces under the covers, and smashes her face down into her pillow.

Even this late he might have stayed if she hadn't accepted defeat by doing this. His need to love her is by, so there's no reason to go. He's stopped loving her at last so he might as well lie down beside her and go to sleep. But she asks for it, lying there in a muddle sobbing, and outside, down in the town, a motor guns and he thinks of the air and the trees and streets stretching bare under the streetlamps and goes out the door.

The strange thing is she falls asleep soon after he goes; she's been used to sleeping alone lately and it's a physical relief not having him in bed kicking his hot legs and twisting the sheets into ropes. That business of his with her bottom made her stitches ache and she sinks down over the small pain all feathers. Around four in the morning Becky cries her awake and Janice gets up; her nightie taps her body lightly. Her skin feels unnaturally sensitive as she walks about. She changes the baby and lies down on the bed to nurse her. As Becky takes the milk it's as if she's sucking a hollow place into her mother's body; Harry hasn't come back.

The baby keeps slipping off the nipple because she can't keep her mind on her; she keeps listening for Harry's key to scratch at the door.

Mother's neighbors will laugh their heads off if she loses him again, she doesn't know why she should think of Mother's neighbors except that all the time she was home Mother kept reminding her of how they sneered and there was always that with Mother the feeling she was dull and plain and a disappointment, and she thought when she got a husband it would be all over, all that. She would be a woman with a house on her own. And she thought when she gave this baby her name it would settle her mother but instead it brings her mother against her breast with her blind mouth poor thing and she feels she's lying on top of a pillar where everyone in the town can see she is alone. She feels cold. The baby won't stay on the nipple nothing will hold to her.

She gets up and walks around the room with the baby on her shoulder patting to get the air up and the baby poor thing so floppy and limp keeps sliding and trying to dig its little boneless legs into her to hold tight and the nightie blown by the breeze keeps touching her calves the backs of her legs her ass as he called it. Makes you feel filthy they don't even have decent names for parts of you.

If there would be a scratch at the lock and he would come in the door he could do whatever he wanted with her have any part of her if he wanted what did she care that was marriage. But when he tried tonight it just seemed so unfair, she still aching and him sleeping with that prostitute all those weeks and him just saying Roll over in that impatient voice like it was just something he wanted to have done with and who was she not to let him after she had let him run off what right had she to any pride? Any self-respect. That was just why she had to have some because he didn't think she dared have any after she let him run off that was the funny thing it was his bad deed yet she was supposed not to have any pride afterwards to just be a pot for his dirt. When he did that to her backside it was so practiced and reminded her of all those weeks he was off doing what he pleased and she was just helpless Mother and Peggy feeling sorry for her and everybody else laughing she couldn't bear it.

And then his going off to church and coming back full of juice. What right did he have to go to church? What did he and God talk about behind the backs of all these women exchanging winks that was the thing she minded if they'd just think about love when they make it instead of thinking about whatever they do think about – whatever they're going to do whenever they've got rid of this little hot clot that's bothering them. You can feel in men's fingers if they're thinking about you and tonight Harry was at first and that's why she let him go on it was like lying there in a bath of yourself his hands going around you but then he began to be rough and determined and it made her mad to feel him thinking about himself what a good job he was doing sucking her along and not at all any more about how she felt, exhausted and aching, poking his thing at her belly like some elbow elbowing her aside. It was so *rude*.

Just plain rude. Here he called her dumb when he was too dumb to have any idea of how she felt any idea of how his going off had changed her and how he must nurse her back not just wade in through her skin without having any idea of what was there. That was what made her panicky ever since she was little this thing of nobody knowing how you felt and whether nobody *could* know or nobody cared she had no idea. She didn't like her skin, never had, it was too dark made her look like an Italian even if she never did get pimples like some of the other girls and then in those days both working at Kroll's she on the salted nuts when Harry would lie down beside her on Linda Hannacher's bed the silver wallpaper he liked so much and close his eyes and let just the nearness of her make it happen down there it got her hot too she thought it was all over she was with somebody. But then they were married (she felt awful about being pregnant before but Harry had been talking about marriage for a while and anyway laughed when she told him in early February about missing her period and said Great she was terribly frightened and he said Great and lifted her put his arms around under her bottom and lifted her like you would a child he could be so wonderful when you didn't expect it in a way it seemed important that you *didn't* expect it there was so much nice in him she couldn't explain to anybody she had been so frightened about being pregnant and he made her be proud) they were married after her missing her second period in March and she was still little clumsy dark-complected Janice Springer and her husband was a conceited lunk who wasn't good for anything in the world Daddy said and the feeling of being alone would melt a little with a little drink. It wasn't so much that it dissolved the lump as made the edges nice and rainbowy.

She's been walking around patting the baby until her wrists and ankles hurt and poor tiny Rebecca is asleep with her legs around the breast that still has all its milk in it. She wonders if she should try to make her take some and thinks no if she can sleep let her sleep. She lifts the poor tiny thing weighing nothing off the sweaty place on her shoulder and lays her down in the cool shadows of the crib. Already the night is dimming, dawn comes early to the town facing east on its mountainside. Janice lies down on the bed but the sense of light growing beside her on the white sheets keeps her awake. Pleasantly awake at first; the coming of morning is so gentle and makes her feel like she did through the second month Harry was hiding, Mother's great Japanese cherry tree blooming below her window and the grass coming up and the ground smelling wet and ashy and warm. She had thought things out and was resigned to her marriage being finished. She would have her baby and get a divorce and never get married again. She would be like a kind of nun she had just seen that beautiful picture with Audrey Hepburn. And if he came back it would be equally simple; she would forgive him everything and stop her drinking which annoyed him so though she didn't see why and they would be very nice and simple and clean together because he would have gotten everything out of his system and love her so because she had forgiven him and she would know now how to be a good wife. She had talked with Peggy and Reverend Eccles and prayed and had come to understand that marriage wasn't a refuge it was a sharing and she and Harry would start to share everything. And then, it was a miracle, these last two weeks had been that way.

And then Harry had suddenly put his whore's filthiness into it and asked her to love it and the unfairness makes her cry aloud softly, as if startled by something in the empty bed with her.

The last hours are like some narrow turn in a pipe that she can't force her thought through. Again and again she comes up to the sound of him saying *Roll over* and can't squeeze through it, can't not feel panicked and choked. She gets out of bed and wanders around with her one tight breast the nipple stinging and goes into the kitchen in her bare feet and sniffs the empty glass Harry made her drink whisky out of. The smell is dark and raw and cozy and deep, and she thinks maybe a sip will cure her insomnia. Make her sleep until the scratch at the door awakens her and she sees his big, white body ramble in sheepishly and she can say *Come to bed, Harry, it's all right, do me, I want to share it, I really want it, really.*

She puts just an inch of whisky in, and not much water because it would take too long to drink, and no ice cubes because the noise of the tray might wake up the children. She takes this dose to the window and stands looking down past the three tar roofs at the sleeping town. Already a few kitchen and bedroom lights show pale here and there. A car, its headlights dull discs that do not throw beams into the thinning darkness, eases down Wilbur Street toward the center of town. The highway, half-hidden by the silhouettes of houses like a river between banks of trees, this early swishes with traffic. She feels the workday approaching like an army of light, feels the dark ridged houses beneath her on the verge of stirring, waking, opening like castles to send forth their men, and regrets that her own husband is unable to settle into the rhythm of which one more beat is about to sound. Why him? What was so precious about him? Anger at Harry begins to bloom, and to stifle it she drains the glass and turns in the dawn to look where she lives: everything in the apartment is a shade of brown. The pressure in the unused breast pulls her to one side.

She goes into the kitchen and makes another drink, stronger than the first, thinking that after all it's about time she had a little fun. She hasn't had a moment to herself since she came back from the hospital. The thought of fun makes her movements quick and airy; she fairly runs in her bare feet across the gritty carpet back to the window, as if to a show arranged just for her. Mounted in her white gown above everything she can see, she touches her fingers to her tight breast so that the milk starts to leak, stains the white cloth with slow warmth.

The wetness slides down her front and turns cold in the air by the window. Her varicose veins ache from standing. She goes and sits in the moldy brown armchair and is sickened by just the angle at which the mottled wall meets the pasty ceiling. The angle tips her, muddles up and down. The pattern on the wallpaper swarms; the flowers are brown spots that swim in the murk and chase each other and merge hungrily. It's hateful. She turns her face away and studies the calm green globe of the dead television set. The front of her nightie is drying; the crusty stiffness scratches her. The baby book said *Keep nipples clean, Soap gently*: germs enter scratches. She sets the drink on the round chair arm and stands up and pulls her nightgown over her head and sits down again. It gives her nakedness a mossy hug. She puts the bunched nightgown in her lap on top of her Modess pad and belt and pulls the footstool over cleverly with her toes and rests her ankles on it and admires her legs. She always thought she had good legs. Straight small nice even thighs. She does have good legs. Their tapering wavering silhouettes are white against the deep shadow of the rug. The dim light erases the blue veins left from carrying Becky. She wonders if her legs are going to go as bad as Mother's. She tries to imagine the ankles as thick as the knees and they do seem to swell. She reaches down to reassure herself by feeling the ankles' hard narrow bones and her shoulder knocks the whisky glass off the chair arm. She jumps up, startled to feel the air embrace her bare skin, cool space sweep around her wobbly, knobbed body. She giggles. If Harry could see her now. Luckily there wasn't much in the glass. She tries to walk boldly into the kitchen with no clothes on like a whore but the sense of somebody watching her, which began when she stood at the window and made her milk flow, is too strong; she ducks into the bedroom and wraps the blue bathrobe around her and then mixes the drink. There is still a third of the bottle left. Tiredness makes the rims of her lids dry but she has no desire to go back to bed. She has a horror of it because Harry should be there. This absence is a hole that widens and she pours a little whisky into it but it's not enough and when she goes to the window for the third time it is now light enough to see how drab everything is. Someone has smashed a bottle on one of the tar roofs. The gutters of Wilbur Street are full of mud that washes down from the new development. While she looks, the street-lights, great pale strings of them, go off in patches. She pictures the man at the power plant pulling the switches, little and gray and hunchbacked and very sleepy. She goes to the television set and the band of light that suddenly flares in the green rectangle sparks joy in her brain but it's still too early, the light is just a speckling senseless brightness and the sound is nothing but static. As she sits there watching the blank radiance a feeling of some other person standing behind her makes her snap her head around several times. She is very quick about it but there is always a space she can't see, which the other person could dodge into if he's there. It's the tele-vision has called him into the room but when she turns off the set she starts to cry immediately. She sits there with her face in her hands, her tears crawling out between her fingers and her sobs shaking through the apartment. She doesn't stifle them because she *wants* to wake somebody; she is sick of being alone. In the bleaching light the walls and furniture are clear and regain their colors and the merging brown spots have gone into herself.

She goes and looks at the baby, the poor thing lying there snuffling the crib sheet, its little hands twitching up by its ears, and reaches down and strokes its hot membranous head with its piti-ful bits of black hair and lifts it out its legs all wet and takes it to nurse in the armchair that looks toward the window. The sky beyond it is a pale smooth blue that looks painted on the panes. There is nothing to see but sky from this chair, they might be a hundred miles up, in the basket of a great balloon. A door on the other side of the partition slams and her heart leaps but then of course it's just another tenant maybe old Mr. Cappello who never says a civil word to anybody going off to work, the stairs rumbling reluctantly. This wakes Nelson and for a time her hands are full. In making breakfast for them she breaks an orange-juice glass, it just drifts away from her thumb into the brittle sink. When she bends over Nelson to serve him his Rice Krispies he looks up at her and wrinkles his nose; he smells sadness and its familiar odor makes him timid with her. "Daddy go way?" He's such a good boy saying this to make it easy on her, all she has to do is answer "Yes."

"No," she says. "Daddy went out to work early this morning before you got up. He'll be home for supper like he always is."

The child frowns at her and then parrots with sharp hope, "Like always is?"

Worry has stretched his head high, so his neck seems a stem too thin to support the ball of his skull with its broad whorl of pillow-mussed hair. "Daddy will be home," she repeats. Having taken on herself the burden of lying, she needs a bit more whisky for support. There is a murk inside her which she must tint brighter or collapse. She takes the dishes out to the kitchen but they slide so in her hands she doesn't try to wash them. She thinks she must change out of her bathrobe into a dress but in taking the steps into the bedroom forgets her purpose and begins making the bed. But something whose presence she feels on the wrinkled bed frightens her so that she draws back and goes into the other room to be with the children. It's as if in telling them Harry would be back as normal she's put a ghost in the apartment. But the other person does not feel like Harry, it feels like a burglar, a teasing burglar dancing from room to room ahead of her.

When she picks up the baby again she feels its wet legs and thinks of changing it but cleverly realizes she is drunk and might stab it with the pins. She is very proud of thinking this through and tells herself to stay away from the bottle so she can change the baby in an hour. She puts good Becky in her crib and, wonderfully, doesn't once hear her cry. Then she and Nelson sit and watch the tail end of Dave Garroway and then a program about Elizabeth and her husband entertaining a friend of his who is always going away on camping trips being a bachelor and turns out to be a better cook than Elizabeth. For some reason watching this makes her so nervous that just out of television-watching habit she goes to the kitchen and makes herself a little drink, mostly ice cubes, just to keep sealed shut the great hole that is threatening to pull open inside of her again. She takes just a sip and it's like a swallow of a light that makes everything clear. She must just arch over this one little gap and at the end of the day after work Harry will be back and no one will ever know, no one will laugh at Mother. She feels like a rainbow arching protectively over Harry, who seems infinitely small under her, like some children's toy. She thinks how good it would be to play with Nelson; it is bad for him to watch television all morning. She turns it off and finds his coloring book and crayons and they sit on the rug and color opposite pages.

Janice repeatedly hugs him and talks to make him laugh and is very happy doing the actual coloring. In high school, art was the one subject she wasn't afraid of and she always got a B. She smiles in the delight of coloring her page, a barnyard, so well, of feeling the little rods of color in her fingers make such neat parallel strokes and her son's small body intent and hard beside hers. Her bathrobe fans out on the floor around her and her body seems beautiful and broad. She moves to get her shadow off the page and sees that she has colored one chicken partly green and not stayed within the lines at all well and her page is ugly; she starts to cry; it is so un*fair*, as if someone standing behind her without understanding a thing has told her her coloring is ugly. Nelson looks up and his quick face slides wide and he cries, "Don't! Don't, Mommy!" She prepares to have him pitch forward into her lap but instead he jumps up and runs with a lopsided almost crippled set of steps into the bedroom and falls on the floor kicking.

She pushes herself up from the floor with a calm smile and goes into the kitchen, where she thinks she left her drink. The important thing is to complete the arch to the end of the day, to be a protection for Harry, and it's silly not to have the one more sip that will make her capable. She comes out of the kitchen and tells Nelson, "Mommy's stopped crying, sweet. It was a joke. Mommy's not crying. Mommy's very happy. She loves you very much." His rubbed stained face watches her. Then like a stab from behind the phone rings. Still carrying that calmness she answers it. "Hello?"

"Darling? It's Daddy."

"Oh, Daddy!" Joy just streams through her lips.

He pauses. "Baby, is Harry sick? It's after eleven and he hasn't shown up at the lot yet."

"No, he's fine. We're all fine."

There is another pause. Her love for her father flows toward him through the silent wire. She wishes the conversation would go on forever. Daddy is just so capable, and Mother never thanks him. He asks, "Well where is he? Is he there? Let me speak to him, Janice."

"Daddy, he's not here. He went out early this morning."

"Where did he go? He's not at the lot." She's heard him say the word "lot" a million times it seems; he says it like no other man; it's dense and rich from his lips, as if all the world is concentrated in it. All the good things of her growing-up, her clothes, her toys, their house, came from the "lot."

She is inspired; car-sale talk is one thing she knows. "He went out early, Daddy, to show a station wagon to a prospect who had to go to work or something. Wait. Let me think. He said the man had to go to Allentown early this morning. He had to go to Allentown and Harry had to show him a station wagon. Everything's all right, Daddy. Harry loves his job."

The third pause is the longest. "Darling. Are you sure he's not there?"

"Daddy, aren't you funny? He's not here. See?" As if it has eyes she thrusts the receiver into the air of the empty room. It's meant as a daughter's impudent joke but unexpectedly just holding her arm straight out makes her step sideways. When she brings the receiver back to her ear he is saying in a remote ticky voice, "– darling. All right. Don't worry about anything. Are the children there with you?"

Feeling dizzy, she hangs up. This is a mistake, but she thinks on the whole she's been clever enough. She thinks she deserves a drink. The brown liquid spills down over the smoking ice cubes and doesn't stop when she tells it to; she snaps the bottle angrily and blot-shaped drops topple into the sink. She goes into the bath-room with the glass and comes out with her hands empty and a taste of toothpaste in her mouth. She remembers looking into the mirror and patting her hair and from that she went to brushing her teeth. With Harry's toothbrush.

She discovers herself making lunch, like looking down into a food advertisement in a magazine, bacon strips sizzling in a pan at the end of a huge blue arm. She sees the BB's of fat flying in the air like the pretty spatter of a fountain in a park and wonders at how quick their arcs are. They prick her hand on the handle and she turns the purple gas down. She pours a glass of milk for Nelson and pulls some leaves off of a head of lettuce and sets them on a yellow plastic plate and eats a handful herself. She thinks she won't set a place for herself and then thinks she will because maybe this trembling in her stomach is hunger and gets another plate and stands there holding it with two hands in front of her chest won-dering why Daddy was so sure Harry was here. There *is* another person in the apartment she knows but it's not Harry and the per-son has no business here anyway and she determines to ignore him and continues setting lunch with a slight stiffness operating in her body. She holds onto everything until it is well on the table.

Nelson says the bacon is greasy and asks again if Daddy go away and his complaining about the bacon that she was so clever and brave to make at all annoys her so that after his twentieth refusal to eat even a bit of lettuce she reaches over and slaps his rude face. The stupid child can't even cry he just sits there and stares and sucks in his breath again and again and finally does burst forth. But luckily she is equal to the situation, very calm, she sees the unreason of his whole attempt and refuses to be bullied. With the smoothness of a single great wave she makes his bottle, takes him by the hand, oversees his urinating, and settles him in bed. Still shaking with the aftermath of sobs, he roots the bottle in his mouth and she is certain from the glaze on his watchful eyes that he is locked into the channel to sleep. She stands by the bed, surprised by her stern strength.

The telephone rings again, angrier than the first time, and as she runs to it, running because she does not want Nelson disturbed, she feels her strength ebb and a brown staleness washes up the back of her throat. "Hello."

"Janice." Her mother's voice, even and harsh. "I just got back from shopping in Brewer and your father's been trying to reach me all morning. He thinks Harry's gone again. Is he?"

Janice closes her eyes and says, "He went to Allentown."

"What would he do there?"

"He's going to sell a car."

"Don't be silly. Janice. Are you all right?"

"What do you mean?"

"Have you been drinking?"

"Drinking what?"

"Now don't worry, I'm coming right over."

"Mother, don't. Everything is fine. I just put Nelson into his nap."

"I'll have a bite to eat out of the icebox and come right over. You lie down."

"Mother, *please* don't come over."

"Janice, now don't talk back. When did he go?"

"Stay away, Mother. He'll be back tonight." She listens and adds, "And stop crying."

Her mother says, "Yes you say stop when you keep bringing us all into disgrace. The first time I thought it was all his fault but I'm not so sure any more. Do you hear? I'm not so sure."

Hearing this speech has made the sliding sickness in her so steep that Janice wonders if she can keep her grip on the phone. "Don't come over, Mother," she begs. "Please."

"I'll have a bite of lunch and be over in twenty minutes. You go to bed."

Janice replaces the receiver and looks around her with horror. The apartment is horrible. Coloring books on the floor, glasses, the bed unmade, dirty dishes everywhere. She runs to where she and Nelson crayoned, and tests bending over. She drops to her knees, and the baby begins to cry. Panicked with the double idea of not disturbing Nelson and of concealing Harry's absence, she runs to the crib and nightmarishly finds it smeared with orange mess. "Damn you, damn you," she moans to Rebecca, and lifts the little filthy thing out and wonders where to carry her. She takes her to the armchair and biting her lips unpins the diaper. "Oh you little shit," she murmurs, feeling that the sound of her voice is holding off the other person who is gathering in the room. She takes the soaked daubed diaper to the bathroom and drops it in the toilet and dropping to her knees fumbles the bathtub plug into its hole. She pulls on both handles as wide as they will go, knowing from experiment that both opened wide make the right tepid mixture. The water bangs out of the faucet like a fist. She notices the glass of watery whisky she left on the top of the toilet and takes a long stale swallow and then puzzles how to get it off her hands. All the while Rebecca screams as if she has mind enough to know she's filthy. Janice takes the glass with her and spills it on the rug with her knee while she strips the baby of its nightie and sweater. She carries the sopping clothes to the television set and puts them on top while she drops to her knees and tries to stuff the crayons back into their box. Her head aches with all this jarring up and down. She takes the crayons to the kitchen table and dumps the uneaten bacon and lettuce into the paper bag under the sink but the mouth of the bag leans partly closed and the lettuce falls behind into the darkness in back of the can and she crouches down with her head pounding to try to see it or get it with her fingers and is unable. Her knees sting from so much kneeling. She gives up and to her surprise sits flatly on a kitchen chair and looks at the gaudy soft noses of the crayons poking out of the Crayola box. Hide the whisky. Her body doesn't move for a second but when it does she sees her hands with the little lines of dirt on her fingernails put the whisky bottle into a lower cabinet with some old shirts of Harry's she was saving for rags he would never wear a mended shirt not that she was any good at mending them. She shuts the door, it bangs but doesn't catch, and on the edge of linoleum beside the sink the cork cap of the whisky bottle stares at her like a little top hat. She puts it in the garbage bag. Now the kitchen is clean enough. In the living-room Rebecca is lying naked in the fuzzy armchair with her belly puffing out sideways to yell and her lumpy curved legs clenched and red. Janice's other baby was a boy and it still seems unnatural to her, between the girl's legs, those two little buns of fat instead of a boy's plump stub. When the doctor had Nelson circumcised Harry hadn't wanted him to he hadn't been and thought it was unnatural, she had laughed at him he was so mad. The baby's face goes red with each squall and Janice closes her eyes and thinks how really horrible it is of Mother to come and ruin her day just to make sure she's lost Harry again. She can't wait a minute to find out and this awful baby can't wait a minute and there are the clothes on top of the television set. She takes them into the bathroom and drops them into the toilet on top of the diaper and turns off the faucets. The wavery gray line of the water is almost up to the lip of the tub. On the skin quick wrinkles wander and under it a deep mass waits colorless. She wishes she could have the bath. Brimful of composure she returns to the living room. She tips too much trying to dig the tiny rubbery thing out of the chair so drops to her knees and scoops Rebecca into her arms and carries her into the bathroom held sideways against her breasts. She is proud to be carrying this to completion; at least the baby will be clean when Mother comes. She drops gently to her knees by the big calm tub and does not expect her sleeves to be soaked. The water wraps around her forearms like two large hands; under her eyes the pink baby sinks down like a gray stone.

With a sob of protest she grapples for the child but the water pushes up at her hands, her bathrobe tends to float, and the slippery thing squirms in the sudden opacity. She has a hold, feels a heartbeat on her thumb, and then loses it, and the skin of the water leaps with pale refracted oblongs that she can't seize the solid of; it is only a moment, but a moment dragged out in a thicker time. Then she has Becky squeezed in her hands and it is all right.

She lifts the living thing into air and hugs it against her sopping chest. Water pours off them onto the bathroom tiles. The little weightless body flops against her neck and a quick look of relief at the baby's face gives a fantastic clotted impression. A contorted memory of how they give artificial respiration pumps Janice's cold wet arms in frantic rhythmic hugs; under her clenched lids great scarlet prayers arise, wordless, monotonous, and she seems to be clasping the knees of a vast third person whose name, Father, Father, beats against her head like physical blows. Though her wild heart bathes the universe in red, no spark kindles in the space between her arms; for all of her pouring prayers she doesn't feel the faintest tremor of an answer in the darkness against her. Her sense of the third person with them widens enormously, and she knows, knows, while knocks sound at the door, that the worst thing that has ever happened to any woman in the world has happened to her.

JACK comes back from the telephone a shocking color. "Janice Angstrom has accidentally drowned their baby."

Lucy asks, "How *could* she?"

"I don't know. I'm afraid she was drunk. She's unconscious now."

"Where was *he?*"

"Nobody knows. I'm supposed to find out. That was Mrs. Springer."

He sits down in the great walnut-armed chair that had been his father's and Lucy realizes with resentment that her husband is middle-aged. His hair is thinning, his skin is dry, he looks exhausted. She cries, "Why must you spend your life chasing after that worthless heel?"

"He's not worthless. I love him."

"You love him. That's sickening. Oh I think that's sickening, Jack. Why don't you try loving me, or your children?"

"I do."

"You *don't*, Jack. Let's face it, you don't. You couldn't bear to love anybody who might return it. You're afraid of that, aren't you? Aren't you afraid?"

They had been drinking tea in the library when the phone rang and he picks his empty cup off the floor between his feet and looks into the center. "Don't be clever, Lucy," he says. "I feel too sick."

"You feel sick, yes, and I feel sick. I've felt sick ever since you got involved with that animal. He's not even in your church."

"Any Christian is in my church."

"Christian! If he's a Christian thank God I'm not one. Christian. Kills his baby and that's what you call him."

"He didn't kill the baby. He wasn't there, it was an accident."

"Well he as good as did. Runs off and sends his idiot wife on a bender. You never should have brought them back together.

The woman had adjusted and something like this never would have happened."

Eccles blinks; shock has put a great analytic distance between him and things. He's rather impressed by the way she has reconstructed what must have happened. He wonders a little why her speech is so vengeful. "Heel" was a strange word for her to have used. "So you're saying I really killed the baby," he says.

"Of course not. I didn't mean to say that at all."

"No. I think you're probably right," he says, and lifts himself out of the chair. He goes into the hall to the telephone and again draws out of his wallet the number written in pencil below the faint name, Ruth Leonard. The number worked once but this time the mouse of electricity gnaws at the remote membrane of metal in vain. He lets it ring twelve times, hangs up, dials the number again, and hangs up after seven rings. When he returns to the study Lucy is ready for him.

"Jack, I'm sorry. I didn't mean to suggest you were responsible at all. Of course you're not. Don't be silly."

"It's all right, Lucy. The truth shouldn't be able to hurt us." These words are a shadow of his idea that if faith is true, then nothing that is true is in conflict with faith.

"Oh mercy, the martyr. Well I can see it's an idea you have that it's your fault and nothing I can say will change your mind. I'll save my breath."

He keeps silent to help her save her breath but after a moment she asks in a softer voice, "Jack?"

"What?"

"Why *were* you so anxious to get them back together?"

He picks the slice of lemon up from the saucer of his teacup and tries to squint through it into the room. "Marriage is a sacrament," he says.

He half-expects her to laugh but instead she asks earnestly, "Even a bad marriage?"

"Yes."

"But that's ridiculous. That's not common sense."

"I don't believe in common sense," he says. "If it'll make you happy, I don't believe in anything."

"That doesn't make me happy," she says. "You're being very

neurotic. But I'm sorry this has happened. I'm truly sorry." She takes away their cups and swishes into the kitchen and leaves him alone. Afternoon shadows gather like cobwebs on the walls of books, most of them belonging not to him but to his predecessor in the rectory, the much-admired bachelor Randolph Langhorne. He sits waiting numbly but not too long. The phone rings. He hurries to answer it before Lucy can; through the window above the sill where the phone rests he can see his neighbor unpinning her wash from the line.

"Hello?"

"Hey, Jack? This is Harry Angstrom. I hope I'm not interrupting anything."

"No, you're not."

"You don't have any old ladies sitting around sewing or anything, do you?"

"No."

"Why, I've been trying to call my apartment and nobody answers and I'm kind of nervous about it. I didn't spend last night there and I'm getting sort of a prickly feeling. I want to go home but I want to know if Janice has done anything like call the cops or anything. Do you know?"

"Harry, where are you?"

"Oh, at some drugstore in Brewer."

The neighbor has bundled the last sheet into her arms and Jack's sight leans on the bare white line. One of the uses society seems to have for him is to break tragic news and the cave of his mouth goes dry as he braces for the familiar duty. *No man, having put his hand to the plough* . . . He keeps his eyes wide open so he will not seem too close to the presence by his ear. "I guess to save time I'd better tell you over the phone," he begins. "Harry. A terrible thing has happened to us."

When you twist a rope and keep twisting, it begins to lose its straight shape and suddenly a kink, a loop leaps up in it. Harry has such a hard loop in himself after he hears Eccles out. He doesn't know what he says to Eccles; all he is conscious of is the stacks of merchandise in jangling packages he can see through the windows of the phone-booth door. On the drugstore wall there is a banner bearing in red the one word PARADICHLOROBENZENE. All the while he is trying to understand Eccles he is rereading this word, trying to see where it breaks, wondering if it can be pronounced. Right when he finally understands, right at the pit of his life, a fat woman comes up to the counter and pays for two bottles of vitamins. He steps into the sunshine outside the drugstore swallowing, to keep the loop from rising in his body and choking him. It's a hot day, the first of summer; the heat comes up off the glittering pavement into the faces of pedestrians, strikes them sideways off the store windows and hot stone façades. In the white light faces wear the American expression, eyes squinting and mouths sagging open in a scowl, that makes them look as if they are about to say something menacing and cruel. In the street under glaring hardtops drivers bake in stalled traffic. Above, milk hangs in a sky that seems too exhausted to clear. Harry waits at a corner with some sweating footsore shoppers for a Mt. Judge bus, number 16A; when it hisses to a stop it is already packed. He hangs from a steel bar in the rear, fighting to keep from doubling up with the kink inside. Curved posters advertise filtered cigarettes and suntan lotion and C.A.R.E.

He had ridden one of these buses last night into Brewer and gone to Ruth's apartment but there was no light on and nobody answered his ring, though there was a dim light behind the frosted glass lettered F. X. PELLIGRINI. He sat around on the steps, looking down at the delicatessen until the lights went out and then looking at the bright church window. When the lights went out behind that he felt alone and hopeless and thought of going home. He wandered up to Weiser Street and looked down at all the lights and the great sunflower and couldn't see a bus and kept walking, down to the south side, and became afraid by himself and went into a low-looking hotel and bought a room. He didn't sleep very well; a neon tube with a taped connection fizzled outside the window and some woman kept laughing in another room. He woke up early enough to go back to Mt. Judge and get a suit and go to work but something held him back. Something held him back all day. He tries to think of what it was because whatever it was murdered his daughter. Wanting to see Ruth again was some of it but it was clear after he went around to her address in the morning that she wasn't there probably off to Atlantic City with some prick and still he wandered around Brewer, going in and out of department stores with music piping from the walls and eating a hot dog at the five and dime and hesitating outside a movie house but not going in and keeping an eye out for Ruth. He kept expecting to see the fat shoulders he used to kiss jostle out of a crowd and the ginger hair he used to beg to unpin shining on the other side of a rack of birthday cards. But it was a city of over a hundred thousand and the odds were totally against him and anyway there was tons of time, he could find her another day. No, what kept him in the city despite the increasing twisting inside that told him something was wrong back home, what kept him walking through the cold air breathed from the doors of movie houses and up and down between counters of perfumed lingerie and tinny jewelry and salted nuts (poor old Jan) and up into the park along paths he walked once with Ruth to watch from under a horsechestnut tree five mangy kids play cat with a tennis ball and a broomstick and then finally back down Weiser to the drugstore he called from, what kept him walking was the idea that somewhere he'd find an opening. For what made him mad at Janice wasn't so much that she was in the right for once and he was wrong and stupid but the closed feeling of it, the feeling of being closed in. He had gone to church and brought back this little flame and had nowhere to put it on the dark damp walls of the apartment, so it had flickered and gone out. And he realized that he wouldn't always be able to produce this flame. What held him back all day was the feeling that somewhere there was something better for him than listening to babies cry and cheating people in used-car lots and it's this feeling he tries to kill, right there on the bus; he grips the chrome bar and leans far over two women with white pleated blouses and laps of packages and closes his eyes and tries to kill it. The kink in his stomach starts to take the form of nausea and he clings to the icy bar bitterly as the bus swings around the mountain.

He gets off, in a sweat, blocks too soon. Here in Mt. Judge the shadows have begun to grow deep, the sun baking Brewer rides the crest of the mountain, and his sweat congeals, shortening his breath. He runs to keep his body occupied, to joggle his mind blank. Past a dry-cleaning plant with a little pipe hissing steam at the side. Through the oil and rubber smells riding above the asphalt pond around the red pumps of an Esso station. Past the Mt. Judge town-hall lawn and the World War II honor roll with the name plaques crumbled and blistered behind glass. His chest begins to hurt and he slows to a walk.

When he gets to the Springers' house Mrs. comes to the door and shuts it in his face. But he knows from the gray Buick parked outside big as a battleship that Eccles is in there and in a little while Jack comes to the door and lets him in. He says conspiratorially in the dim hall, "Your wife has been given a sedative and is asleep."

"The baby . . ."

"The undertaker has her."

Rabbit wants to cry out, it seems indecent, for the undertaker to be taking such a tiny body, that they ought to bury it in its own simplicity, like the body of a bird, in a small hole dug in the grass. But he nods. He feels he will never resist anything again.

Eccles goes upstairs and Harry sits in a chair and watches the light from the window play across an iron table of ferns and African violets and baby cacti. Where it hits the leaves they are bright yellow-green; the leaves in shadow in front of them look like black-green holes cut in this golden color. Somebody comes down the stairs with an erratic step. He doesn't turn his head to see who it is; he doesn't want to risk looking anybody in the face. A furry touch on his forearm and he meets Nelson's eyes. The child's face is stretched shiny with curiosity. "Mommy sleep," he says in a deep voice imitating the tragedy-struck voices he has been hearing.

Rabbit pulls him up into his lap. He's heavier and longer than he used to be. His body acts as a covering; he pulls the boy's head down against his neck. Nelson asks, "Baby sick?"

"Baby sick."

"Big, big water in tub," Nelson says, and struggles to sit up so he can explain with his arms, which go wide. "Mom-mom came and took Mommy away." What all did the poor kid see? He wants to get off his father's lap but Harry holds him fast with a kind of terror; the house is thick with a grief that seems to threaten the boy. Also the boy's body wriggles with an energy that threatens the grief, might tip it and bring the whole house crashing down on them. It is himself he is protecting by imprisoning the child.

Eccles comes downstairs and stands there studying them. "Why don't you take him outside?" he asks. "He's had a nightmare of a day."

They all three go outdoors. Eccles takes Harry's hand in a long quiet grip and says, "Stay here. You're needed, even if they don't tell you." After Eccles pulls away in his car, he and Nelson sit in the grass by the driveway and throw bits of gravel down toward the pavement. The boy laughs and talks in excitement but out here the sound is not so loud. Harry feels thinly protected by the fact that this is what Eccles told him to do. Men are walking home from work along the pavement; Nelson tosses a pebble too near the feet of one and the man looks up. This unknown face seems to stare at Harry from deep in another world, the world of the blameless, the world outside the bubble of Becky's death. He and Nelson change their target to a green lawn-seeder leaning against the wall of the garage. Harry hits it four times running. Though the air is still light the sunshine has shrunk to a few scraps in the tops of trees. The grass is growing damp and he wonders if he should sneak Nelson in the door and go.

Mr. Springer comes to the door and calls, "Harry." They go over. "Becky's made a few sandwiches in place of supper," he says. "You and the boy come in." They go into the kitchen and Nelson eats. Harry refuses everything except a glass of water. Mrs. Springer is not in the kitchen and Harry is grateful for her absence. "Harry," Mr. Springer says, and stands up, patting his mustache with two fingers, like he's about to make a financial concession, "Reverend Eccles and Becky and I have had a talk. I won't say I don't blame you because of course I do. But you're not the only one to blame. Her mother and I somehow never made her feel secure, never perhaps you might say made her welcome, I don't know" – his little pink crafty eyes are not crafty now, blurred and chafed – "we gave her all we had, I'd like to think. At any rate" – this comes out harsh and crackly; he pauses to regain quietness in his voice – "life must go on. Am I making any sense to you?"

"Yes sir."

"Life must go on. We must go ahead with what we have left. Though Becky's too upset to see you now, she agrees. We had a talk and agree that it's the only way. I mean, what I mean to say, I can see you're puzzled, is that we consider you in our family, Harry, despite" – he lifts an arm vaguely toward the stairs – "this." His arm slumps back and he adds the word "accident."

Harry shields his eyes with his hand. They feel hot and vulnerable to light. "Thank you," he says, and almost moans in his gratitude to this man, whom he has always despised, for making a speech so generous. He tries to frame, in accordance with an etiquette that continues to operate in the thick of grief as if underwater, a counter-speech. "I promise I'll keep my end of the bargain," he brings out, and stops, stifled by the abject sound of his voice. What made him say bargain?

"I know you will," Springer says. "Reverend Eccles assures us you will."

"Dessert," Nelson says distinctly.

"Nelly, why don't you take a cookie to bed?" Springer speaks with a familiar jollity that, though strained, reminds Rabbit that the kid lived here for months. "Isn't it your bedtime? Shall Mommom take you up?"

"Daddy," Nelson says, and slides off his chair and comes to his father.

Both men are embarrassed. "O.K.," Rabbit says. "You show me your room."

Springer gets two Oreo cookies out of the pantry and unexpectedly Nelson runs forward to hug him. He stoops to accept the hug and his withered dandy's face goes blank against the boy's cheek; big black square cufflinks, thinly rimmed and initialed S in gold, creep out of his coat sleeves as his arms tighten the hug.

As Nelson leads his father to the stairs they pass the room where Mrs. Springer is sitting. Rabbit has a glimpse of a puffed face slippery with tears, like an interior organ surgically exposed, and averts his eyes. He whispers to Nelson to go in and kiss her good night. When the boy returns to him they go upstairs and down a smooth corridor papered with a design of old-style cars into a little room whose white curtains are tinted green by a tree outside. On either side of the window symmetrical pictures, one of kittens and one of puppies, are hung. He wonders if this was the room where Janice was little. It has a musty innocence, and a suspense, as if it stood empty for years. An old teddy bear, the fur worn down to cloth and one eye void, sits in a broken child's rocker. Has it been Janice's? Who pulled the eye out? Nelson becomes queerly passive in this room. Harry undresses the sleepy body, tanned brown all but the narrow bottom, puts it into pajamas and into bed and arranges the covers over it. He tells him, "You're a good boy."

"Yop."

"I'm going to go now. Don't be scared."

"Daddy go way?"

"So you can sleep. I'll be back."

"O.K. Good."

"Good."

"Daddy?"

"What?"

"Is baby Becky dead?"

"Yes."

"Was she scared?"

"Oh no. No. She wasn't scared."

"Is she happy?"

"Yeah, she's very happy now."

"Good."

"Don't you worry about it."

"O.K."

"You snuggle up."

"Yop."

"Think about throwing stones."

"When I grow up, I'll throw them very *far*."

"That's right. You can throw them pretty far now."

"I know it."

"O.K. Go to sleep."

Downstairs he asks Springer, who is washing dishes in the kitchen, "You don't want me to stay here tonight, do you?"

"Not tonight, Harry. I'm sorry. I think it would be better not tonight."

"O.K., sure. I'll go back to the apartment. Shall I come over in the morning?"

"Yes, please. We'll give you breakfast."

"No, I don't want any. I mean, to see Janice when she wakes up."

"Yes of course."

"You think she'll sleep the night through."

"I think so."

"Uh – I'm sorry I wasn't at the lot today."

"Oh, that's nothing. That's negligible."

"You don't want me to work tomorrow, do you?"

"Of course not."

"I still have the job, don't I?"

"Of course." His talk is gingerly; his eyes fidget; he feels his wife is listening.

"You're being awfully good to me."

Springer doesn't answer; Harry goes out through the sunporch, so he won't have to glimpse Mrs. Springer's face again, and around the house and walks home in the soupy summer dark, which tinkles with the sounds of dishes being washed. He climbs Wilbur Street and goes in his old door and up the stairs. There is still that faint smell of something like cabbage cooking. He lets himself into the apartment with his key and turns on all the lights as rapidly as he can. He goes into the bathroom and the water is still in the tub. Some of it has seeped away so the top of the water is an inch below a faint gray line on the porcelain but the tub is still more than half full. A heavy, calm volume, odorless, tasteless, colorless, the water shocks him like the presence of a silent person in the bathroom. Stillness makes a dead skin on its unstirred surface. There's even a kind of dust on it. He rolls back his sleeve and reaches down and pulls the plug; the water swings and the drain gasps. He watches the line of water slide slowly and evenly down the wall of the tub, and then with a crazed vortical cry the last of it is sucked away. He thinks how easy it was, yet in all His strength God did nothing. Just that little rubber stopper to lift.

In bed he discovers that his legs ache from all the walking he did in Brewer today. His shins feel splintered; no matter how he twists, the pain, after a moment of relief gained by the movement, sneaks back. He tries praying to relax him but it doesn't do it. There's no connection. He opens his eyes to look at the ceiling and the darkness is mottled with an unsteady network of veins like the net of yellow and blue that mottled the skin of his baby. He remembers seeing her neat red profile through the window at the hospital and a great draft of grief sweeps through him, brings him struggling out of bed to turn on the lights. The electric glare seems thin. His groin aches to weep. He is afraid to stick even his hand into the bathroom; he fears if he turns on the light he will see a tiny wrinkled blue corpse lying face up on the floor of the drained tub. The pressure in his bladder grows until he is at last forced to dare; the dark bottom of the tub leaps up blank and white.

He expects never to go to sleep and, awaking with the slant of sunshine and the noise of doors slamming downstairs, feels his body has betrayed his soul. He dresses in haste, more panicked now than at any time yesterday. The event is realer. Invisible cushions press against his throat and slow his legs and arms; the kink in his chest has grown thick and crusty. *Forgive me, forgive me*, he keeps saying silently to no one.

He goes over to the Springers' and the tone of the house has changed; he feels everything has been rearranged slightly to make a space into which he can fit by making himself small. Mrs. Springer serves him orange juice and coffee and even speaks, cautiously.

"Do you want cream?"

"No. No. I'll drink it black."

"We have cream if you want it."

"No, really. It's fine."

Janice is awake. He goes upstairs and lies down beside her on the bed; she clings to him and sobs into the cup between his neck and jaw and the sheet. Her face has been shrunk; her body seems small as a child's, and hot and hard. She tells him, "I can't stand to look at anyone except you. I can't bear to look at the others."

"It wasn't your fault," he tells her. "It was mine."

"I've got my milk back," Janice says, "and every time my breasts sting I think she must be in the next room."

They cling together in a common darkness; he feels the walls between them dissolve in a flood of black; but the heavy knot of apprehension remains in his chest, his own.

He stays in the house all that day. Visitors come, and tiptoe about. Their manner suggests that Janice upstairs is very sick. They sit, these women, over coffee in the kitchen with Mrs. Springer, whose petite rounded voice, oddly girlish divorced from the sight of her body, sighs on and on like an indistinct, rising and falling song. Peggy Fosnacht comes, her sunglasses off, her walleyes wide to the world, and goes upstairs. Her son Billy plays with Nelson, and no one moves to halt their squeals of anger and pain in the back yard, which, neglected, in time die away. Even Harry has a visitor. The doorbell rings and Mrs. Springer goes and comes into the dim room where Harry is sitting looking at magazines and says, in a surprised and injured voice, "A man for you."

She leaves the doorway and he gets up and walks a few steps forward to greet the man coming into the room, Tothero, leaning on a cane and his face half-paralyzed; but talking, walking, alive. And the baby dead. "Hi! Gee, how are you?"

"Harry." With the hand that is not on the cane he grips Harry's arm. He brings a long look to bear on Harry's face; his mouth is tweaked downward on one side and the skin over his eye on this side is dragged down diagonally so it nearly curtains the glitter. The gouging grip of his fingers trembles.

"Let's sit down," Rabbit says, and helps him into an easy chair. Tothero knocks off a doily in arranging his arms. Rabbit brings over a straight chair and sits close so he won't have to raise his voice. "Should you be running around?" he asks when Tothero says nothing.

"My wife brought me. In the car. Outside, Harry. We heard your terrible news. Didn't I warn you?" Already his eyes are bulging with water.

"When?"

"When?" The stricken side of his face is turned away, perhaps consciously, into shadow, so his smile seems wholly alive, wise, and sure. "That first night. I said go back. I begged you."

"I guess you did. I've forgotten."

"No you haven't. No you haven't, Harry." His breath chuffs on the "Ha" of "Harry." "Let me tell you something. Will you listen?"

"Sure."

"Right and wrong," he says, and stops; his big head shifts, and
the stiff downward lines of his mouth and bad eye show. "Right
and wrong aren't dropped from the sky. We. We make them.
Against misery. Invariably, Harry, invariably" – he grows confident of his ability to negotiate long words – "misery follows their
disobedience. Not our own, often at first not our own. Now
you've had an example of that in your own life." Rabbit wonders
when the tear-trails appeared on Tothero's cheeks; there they are,
like snail-tracks. "Do you believe me?"

"Sure. Sure. Look, I know this has been my fault. I've felt like
a, like an insect ever since it happened."

Tothero's tranquil smile deepens; a faint rasping purr comes out
of his face. "I warned you," he says, "I warned you, Harry, but
youth is deaf. Youth is careless."

Harry blurts, "But what can I do?"

Tothero doesn't seem to hear. "Don't you remember? My
begging you to go back?"

"I don't know, I guess so."

"Good. Ah. You're still a fine man, Harry. You have a healthy
body. When I'm dead and gone, remember how your old coach
told you to avoid suffering. Remember." The last word is intoned
coyly, with a little wag of the head; on the thrust of this incongruous vivacity he rises from his chair, and prevents himself from
pitching forward by quick use of his cane. Harry jumps up in
alarm, and the two of them stand for the moment very close.
The old man's big head breathes a distressing scent, not so much
medicine as a vegetable staleness. "You young people," he says
with a rising intonation, a schoolteacher's tone, scolding yet sly,
"tend to forget. Don't you? Now don't you?"

He wants this admission mysteriously much. "Sure," Rabbit
says, praying he'll go.

Harry helps him to his car, a '57 blue-and-cream Dodge waiting in front of the orange fire hydrant. Mrs. Tothero offers, rather
coolly, her regrets at the death of his infant daughter. She looks
harried and noble. Gray hair straggles down across her finely
wrinkled silver temple. She wants to get away from here, away
with her prize. Beside her on the front seat Tothero looks like a

smirking gnome, brainlessly stroking the curve of his cane. Rabbit returns to the house feeling depressed and dirtied by the visit. Tothero's revelation chilled him. He wants to believe in the sky as the source of all dictates.

Eccles comes later in the afternoon, to complete the arrangements for the funeral: it will be held tomorrow afternoon, Wednesday. As he leaves Rabbit catches his attention and they talk in the front hall a moment. "What do you think?" Rabbit asks.

"About what?"

"What shall I do?"

Eccles glances up nervously. His face has that pale babyish look of someone who has not slept enough. "Do what you are doing," he says. "Be a good husband. A good father. Love what you have left."

"And that's enough?"

"You mean to earn forgiveness? I'm sure it is, carried out through a lifetime."

"I mean" – he's never before felt *pleading* with Eccles – "remember that thing we used to talk about? The thing behind everything?"

"Harry, you know I don't think that thing exists in the way you think it does."

"O.K." He realizes that Eccles wants to get away too, that the sight of himself is painful, disgusting.

Eccles must see that he senses this, for he curtly summons up mercy and makes an attempt. "Harry, it's not for me to forgive you. You've done nothing to me *to* forgive. I'm equal with you in guilt. We must work for forgiveness; we must *earn* the right to see that thing behind everything. Harry, I *know* that people are brought to Christ. I've seen it with my eyes and tasted it with my mouth. And I do think this. I think marriage is a sacrament, and that this tragedy, terrible as it is, has at last united you and Janice in a sacred way."

Through the next hours Rabbit clings to this belief, though it seems bear no relation to the colors and sounds of the big sorrowing house, the dabs and arcs of late sunshine in the little jungle of plants on the glass table, or the almost wordless supper he and Janice share in her bedroom.

* * *

He spends that night in the Springers' house, sleeping with Janice. Her sleep is so solid. A thin snore out of her black mouth sharpens the moonlight and keeps him awake. He gets up on an elbow and studies her face; it is frightening in the moonlight, small and so vague in the dark it could be anybody. He resents her sleep. When, in first light, he feels her weight stir and slide off the bed, he turns his face deeper into the pillow, retracts his head half under the covers, and goes back to sleep stubbornly. The thought that today is the day of the funeral somehow drugs him.

During this stolen doze he has a vivid dream. He is alone on a large sporting field, or vacant lot, littered with small pebbles. In the sky two perfect discs, identical in size but the one a dense white and the other slightly transparent, move toward each other slowly; the pale one is directly above the dense one. At the moment they touch he feels frightened and a voice like over a loudspeaker at a track meet announces, "*The cowslip swallows up the elder.*" The downward gliding of the top one continues steadily until the other, though the stronger, is totally eclipsed, and just one circle is before his eyes, pale and pure. He understands: "the cowslip" is the moon, and "the elder" the sun, and that what he has witnessed is the explanation of death: lovely life eclipsed by lovely death. Intensely relieved and excited, he realizes he must go forth from this field and found a new religion. There is a feeling of the discs, and the echo of the voice, bending over him importunately, and he opens his eyes. Janice stands by the bed in a brown skirt and a pink sleeveless blouse. There is a drab thickness of fat under her chin he has never noticed before. He is surprised to be on his back; he almost always sleeps on his stomach. He realizes it was a dream, that he has nothing to tell the world. The knot regathers in his chest. In getting out of bed he kisses the back of her hand, which is hanging by her side helpless and raw.

She makes him breakfast, the cereal drowned in milk, the coffee scalded in her style. With Nelson they walk over to the apartment to get clothes for the funeral. Rabbit resents her being able to walk; he liked her best when she was unconscious. What kind of second-rate grief is it that permits them to walk? The sense of their thick bodies just going on, wrapping their hearts in numbness and small needs, angers him. They walk with their child through streets they walked as children. The gutter along Potter Avenue where the slime-rimmed ice-plant water used to run is dry. The houses, many of them no longer lived in by the people whose faces he all knew, are like the houses in a town you see from the train, their brick faces stern in posing the riddle, Why does anyone live here? Why was he set down here; why is this particular ordinary town for him the center and index of a universe that contains great prairies, mountains, deserts, forests, cities, seas? This childish mystery – the mystery of "any place," prelude to the ultimate, "Why am I me?" – re-ignites panic in his heart. Coldness spreads through his body. The details of the street – the ragged margin where the pavement and grass struggle, the tarry scarred trunks of the telephone poles – no longer speak to him. He is no one; it is as if he stepped outside of his body and brain a moment to watch the engine run and stepped into nothingness, for this "he" had been merely a refraction, a vibration within the engine, and now can't get back in. He feels he is behind the windows of the houses they walk by, watching this three-cornered family stroll along solidly with no sign that their universe has convulsed other than the woman's quiet tears. Janice's tears have come as gently as dew comes; the sight of the morning-fresh streets seems to have sprung them.

When they get inside the apartment she gives a sharp sigh and collapses against him. Perhaps she didn't expect the place to be full of sunshine; buttresses of dust drifting in milky light slant from the middle of the floor to the tops of the windows. The door to his closet is near the entry door so they needn't go very deep into the apartment at first. He opens the closet door as far as he can without bumping the television set and reaches far in and unzips a plastic zippered storage bag and takes out his blue suit, a winter suit made of wool, but the only dark one he owns. His gray car-salesman's suit is too pale. Nelson, happy to be here, ranges through the apartment, going into the bathroom, finding an old rubber panda in his bedroom that he wants to take along. His exploring drains enough of the menace from the rooms for them

to go into their bedroom, where Janice's clothes hang. On the way
she indicates a chair. "Here I sat," she tells him, "Monday morning, watching the sun come up." Her voice is lifeless; he doesn't
know what she wants him to say and says nothing. He is holding
his breath.

Yet in the bedroom there is a pretty moment. She takes off her
skirt and blouse to try on an old black suit she has, and as she moves
about in her slip, barefoot on the carpet, she reminds him of the
girl he knew, with her narrow ankles and wrists and small
shy head. The black suit, bought when she was in high school,
doesn't fit; her stomach is still too big from having the baby. And
maybe her mother's plumpness is beginning. Standing there trying to get the waist of the suit skirt to link at her side, the tops of
her breasts, swollen with untaken milk, pushing above her bra, she
does have a plumpness, a fullness that call to him. He thinks *Mine,
my woman*, but then she turns and her smeared frantic face blots
out his pride of possession. She becomes a liability that painfully
weights the knot below his chest. This is the wild woman he must
steer with care down a lifelong path, away from Monday morning. "It won't *do* it!" she screams, and jerks her legs out of the skirt
and flings it, great twirling bat, across the room.

"You have nothing else?"

"What am I going to *do?*"

"Come on. Let's get out of here and go back to your place.
This place is making you nervous."

"But we're going to have to *live* here!"

"Yeah, but not today. Come on."

"We *can't* live here," she says.

"I know we can't."

"But where *can* we live?"

"We'll figure it out. Come on."

She stumbles into her skirt and puts her blouse over her arms
and turns away from him meekly and asks, "Button my back."
Buttoning the pink cloth down her quiet spine makes him cry; the
hotness in his eyes works up to a sting and he sees the little babyish buttons through a cluster of discs of watery light like petals of
apple blossoms. Water hesitates on his lids and then runs down his
cheeks; the wetness is delicious. He wishes he could cry for hours,

for just this tiny spill relieves him. But a man's tears are grudging and his stop before they are out of the apartment. As he closes the door he feels he has spent his whole life opening and closing this door.

Nelson takes the rubber panda along and every time he makes it squeak Rabbit's stomach aches. The town now is bleached by a sun nearing the height of noon.

The hours that follow are so long they seem to contain the same incidents over and over. Back in the house, Janice and her mother merge and re-merge in soft little conversations that take them from room to room. They seem to be worrying what Janice will wear. The two of them go upstairs and in half an hour Janice comes down in a pinned-in black dress of her mother's that makes her look like her mother. "Harry. Does it look all right?"

"What in hell do you think this is going to be? A fashion show?" He adds regretfully, "You look fine," but the damage is done. Janice emits a long startled whimper and goes upstairs and collapses into her mother. Mrs. Springer revokes the small measure of pardon she had extended him. The house again fills with the unspoken thought that he is a murderer. He accepts the thought gratefully; it's true, he is, he is, and hate suits him better than forgiveness. Immersed in hate he doesn't have to do anything; he can be paralyzed, and the rigidity of hatred makes a kind of shelter for him.

It becomes one o'clock. Mrs. Springer comes into the room where he is sitting and asks, "Do you want a sandwich?"

"Thanks, I can't eat anything."

"You better have something." He finds this insistence so strange he goes into the kitchen to see what is there. Nelson is having soup and raw carrots and a Lebanon baloney sandwich by himself at the table. He seems uncertain if he should smile at his father or not. Mrs. Springer keeps her back turned.

Harry asks, "Has the kid had a nap?"

"You might take him up," she says, without turning. Upstairs in the room with the one-eyed teddy bear Harry reads the boy a

Little Golden Book about a little choo-choo who was afraid of
tunnels. By the time the choo-choo has proved he is no longer
afraid Nelson has fallen asleep under his father's arm. Harry
goes downstairs again. Janice is having a rest in her room and the
sound of Mrs. Springer's sewing machine, as it adjusts the dress for
Janice to wear, spins out into the birdsong and murmur of the early
afternoon.

The front door slams and Springer comes into the living room.
None of the shades has been pulled up and he starts at seeing Harry
in a chair. "Harry! Hello!"

"Hello."

"Harry, I've been down at Town Hall talking to Al Horst. He's
the coroner. Al looked the little body over and he's satisfied. No
marks. Accidental drowning. He promised there won't be a man-
slaughter charge. He's been talking to just about everybody and
wants to talk to you sometime. Unofficially."

"O.K." Springer hangs there, expecting some kind of congratulation. "Why don't they just lock me up?" Harry adds.

"Harry, that's a very negative way to think. The question I
always ask myself in a bad situation is, How do we cut the losses
from here on in?"

"You're right. I'm sorry." It disgusts him to feel the net of law
slither from him. They just won't do it for you, they just won't
take you off the hook.

Springer trots upstairs to his women. Footfalls pad above.
Fancy dishes in the glass-fronted cupboard behind Harry vibrate.
It's not yet two o'clock, he sees by the little silver-faced clock on
the mantel of the fake fireplace.

He wonders if the pain in his stomach comes from eating so
little in the last two days and goes out to the kitchen and eats two
crackers. He can feel each bite hit a scraped floor inside. The pain
increases. The bright porcelain fixtures and metal surfaces seem
charged with a negative magnetism that pushes against him and
makes him extremely thin. He goes into the shadowy living room
and pulls the shade and at the front window watches two teenage
girls in snug shorts shuffle by on the sunny sidewalk. Their
bodies are already there but their faces are still this side of being
good. Funny about girls about fourteen, their faces have this kind

of eager bunchy business. Too much candy, sours their skin. They walk as slowly as time to the funeral passes, as if if they go slow enough some magic transformation will meet them at the corner. Daughters, these are daughters, would June —? He chokes the thought. The two girls passing, with their perky butts and two-pointed T-shirts, seem distasteful morsels. He himself, watching them behind the window, seems a smudge on the glass. He wonders why the universe doesn't just erase a thing so dirty and small. He looks at his hands and they seem ugly, worse than claws.

He goes upstairs and with intense care washes his hands and face and neck. He doesn't dare use one of their fancy towels. Coming out with wet hands he meets Springer in the muted hallway and says, "I don't have a clean shirt." Springer whispers "Wait" and brings him a shirt and black cufflinks. Harry dresses in the room where Nelson sleeps. Sunlight creeps under the drawn shades, which flap softly back and forth almost in time to the boy's heavy breathing. Though he spaces the stages of dressing carefully, and fumbles for minutes with the unaccustomed cufflinks, it takes less time to dress than he hoped it would. The wool suit is uncomfortably hot, and doesn't fit as well as he remembered. But he refuses to take off the coat, refuses to give somebody, he doesn't know who, the satisfaction. He tiptoes downstairs and sits, immaculately dressed, the shirt too tight, in the living room looking at the tropical plants on the glass table, moving his head so that now this leaf eclipses that, now that this, and wondering if he is going to throw up. His insides are a clenched mass of dread, a tough bubble that can't be pricked. The clock says only 2:25.

Of the things he dreads, seeing his parents is foremost. He hasn't had the courage to call them or see them since it happened; Mrs. Springer called Mom Monday night and asked her to the funeral. The silence from his home since then has frightened him. It's one thing to get hell from other people and another from your own parents. Ever since he came back from the Army Pop had been nibbling at a grudge because he wouldn't go to work in the print shop and in a way had nibbled himself right into nothing in Harry's heart. All the mildness and kindness the old man had ever shown him had faded into nothing. But his mother was something else; she was still alive and still attached to his life by some cord. If she comes in and gives him hell he thinks he'll die rather than take it. And of course what else is there to give him? Whatever Mrs. Springer says he can slip away from because in the end she has to stick with him and anyway he feels somehow she wants to like him but with his mother there's no question of liking him they're not even in a way separate people he began in her stomach and if she gave him life she can take it away and if he feels that withdrawal it will be the grave itself. Of all the people in the world he wants to see her least. Sitting there by himself he comes to the conclusion that either he or his mother must die. It is a weird conclusion, but he keeps coming to it, again and again, until the sounds of stirring above him, of the Springers getting dressed, lift his mind out of himself a little.

He wonders if he should go up but he doesn't want to surprise anyone undressed and one by one they come down, dressed, Mr. Springer in a spiffy graphite-gray drip-and-dry and Nelson in a corduroy sissy suit with straps and Mrs. in a black felt hat with a veil and a stiff stem of artificial berries and Janice looking lost and shapeless in the pinned and tucked dress of her mother's. "You look fine," he tells her again.

"Whez big black cah?" Nelson asks in a loud voice.

There is something undignified about waiting and as they mill around in the living room watching the minutes ebb in the silver-faced clock they become uncomfortably costumed children nervous for the party to begin. They all press around the window when the undertaker's Cadillac stops out front, though by the time the man has come up the walk and rings the doorbell they have scattered to the corners of the room as if a bomb of contagion has been dropped among them.

The funeral parlor was once a home but now is furnished the way no home ever was. Unworn carpets of a very pale green deaden their footsteps. Little silver half-tubes on the walls shield a weak glow. The colors of the curtains and walls are atonal half-colors, colors no one would live with, salmon and aqua and a violet like the violet that kills germs on toilet seats in gas stations.

They are ushered into a little pink side room. Harry can see into the main room; on a few rows of auditorium chairs about six people sit, five of them women. The only one he knows is Peggy Gring. Her little boy wriggling beside her makes seven. It was meant to be at first nobody but the families, but the Springers then asked a few close friends. His parents are not here. Invisible hands bonelessly trail up and down the keys of an electric organ. The unnatural coloring of the interior comes to a violent head in the hothouse flowers arranged around a little white coffin. The coffin, with handles of painted gold, rests on a platform draped with a deep purple curtain; he thinks the curtain might draw apart and reveal, like a magician's trick, the living baby underneath. Janice looks in and yields a whimper and an undertaker's man, blond and young with an unnaturally red face, conjures a bottle of spirits of ammonia out of his side pocket. Her mother holds it under her nose and Janice suppresses a face of disgust; her eyebrows stretch up, showing the bumps her eyeballs make under the thin membrane. Harry takes her arm and turns her so she can't see into the next room.

The side room has a window through which they can look at the street, where children and cars are running. "Hope the minister hasn't forgotten," the young red-faced man says, and to his own embarrassment chuckles. He can't help being at his ease here. His face seems lightly rouged.

"Does that happen often?" Mr. Springer asks. He is standing behind his wife, and his face tips forward with curiosity, his mouth a birdy black gash beneath his sandy mustache. Mrs. Springer has sat down on a chair and is pressing her palms against her face through the veil. The purple berries quiver on their stem of wire.

"About twice a year," is the answer.

A familiar old blue Plymouth slows against the curb outside. Rabbit's mother gets out and looks up and down the sidewalk angrily. His heart leaps and trips his tongue: "Here come my parents." They all come to attention. Mrs. Springer gets up and Harry places himself between her and Janice. Standing in formation with the Springers like this, he can at least show his mother that he's reformed, that he's accepted and been accepted. The undertaker's man goes out to bring them in; Harry can see them standing on the bright sidewalk, arguing which door to go into, Mim a little to one side. Dressed in a church sort of dress and with no makeup, she reminds him of the little sister he once had. The sight of his parents makes him wonder why he was afraid of them.

His mother comes through the door first; her eyes sweep the line of them and she steps toward him with reaching curved arms. "Hassy, what have they done to you?" She asks this out loud and wraps him in a hug as if she would carry him back to the sky from which they have fallen.

This quick it opens, and seals shut again. In a boyish reflex of embarrassment he pushes her away and stands to his full height. As if unaware of what she has said, his mother turns and embraces Janice. Pop, murmuring, shakes Springer's hand. Mim comes and touches Harry on the shoulder and then squats and whispers to Nelson, these two the youngest. All under him Harry feels these humans knit together. His wife and mother cling together. His mother began the embrace automatically but has breathed a great life of grief into it. Her face creases in pain; Janice, rumpled and smothered, yet responds; her weak black arms try to encircle the big-boned frame yearning against her. Mary Angstrom yields up two words to her. The others are puzzled; only Harry from his tall cool height understands. His mother had been propelled by the instinct that makes us embrace those we wound, and then she had felt this girl in her arms as a woman like her and then had sensed that she too, having restored her son to himself, must be deserted.

He had felt in himself these stages of grief unfold in her as her arms tightened. Now she releases Janice, and speaks, sadly and properly, to the Springers. They have let her first outcry pass as madness. They of course have done nothing to Harry, what has been done he has done to them. His liberation is unseen by them. They become remote beside him. The words his mother spoke to Janice, "My daughter," recede. Mim rises from squatting; his father takes Nelson into his arms. Their motions softly jostle him.

And meanwhile his heart completes its turn and turns again, a wider turn in a thinning medium to which the outer world bears a decreasing relevance.

Eccles has arrived by some other entrance and from a far doorway beckons them. The seven of them file with Nelson into the room where the flowers wait, and take their seats on the front row. Black Eccles reads before the white casket. It annoys Rabbit that Eccles should stand between him and his daughter. It occurs to him, what no one has mentioned, the child was never baptized. Eccles reads. "I am the resurrection and the life, saith the Lord: he that believeth in me, though he were dead, yet shall he live: and whosoever liveth and believeth in me, shall never die."

The angular words walk in Harry's head like clumsy blackbirds; he feels their possibility. Eccles doesn't; his face is humorless and tired. His voice is false. All these people are false: except his dead daughter, the white box with gold trim.

"He shall feed his flock like a shepherd: he shall gather the lambs with his arms, and carry them in his bosom."

Shepherd, lamb, arms: Harry's eyes fill with tears. It is as if at first the tears are everywhere about him, a sea, and that at last the saltwater gets into his eyes. His daughter is dead: June gone from him; his heart swims in loss, that had skimmed over it before, dives deeper and deeper into the limitless volume of loss. Never hear her cry again, never see her marbled skin again, never cup her faint weight in his arms again and watch the blue of her eyes wander in search of the source of his voice. Never, the word never stops, there is never a gap in its thickness.

They go to the cemetery. He and his father and Janice's father and the undertaker's man carry the white box to the hearse. There is weight to it but the weight is all wood. They get into their cars and drive through the streets uphill. The town hushes around them; a woman comes out on her porch with a basket of wash and waits there, a small boy stops himself in the middle of throwing a ball to watch them pass. They pass between two granite pillars linked by an arch of wrought iron. The cemetery is beautiful at four o'clock. Its nurtured green nap slopes down somewhat parallel to the rays of the sun. Tombstones cast long slate shadows. Up a crunching blue gravel lane the procession moves in second gear, its destination a meek green canopy smelling of earth and ferns. The cars stop; they get out. Beyond them at a distance stands a crescent sweep of black woods; the cemetery is high on the

mountains, between the town and the forest. Below their feet
chimneys smoke. A man on a power lawnmower rides between
the worn teeth of tombstones near the far hedge. Swallows in a wide
ball dip and toss themselves above a stone cottage, a crypt. The
white coffin is artfully rolled on casters from the hearse's resonant
body onto crimson straps that hold it above the small nearly square
but deep-dug grave. The small creaks and breaths of effort scratch
on a pane of silence. Silence. A cough. The flowers have followed
them; here they are, densely banked within the tent. Behind
Harry's feet a neat mound of dirt topped with squares of sod waits
to be replaced and meanwhile breathes a deep word of earth. The
undertaking men look pleased, their job near done, and fold their
gloved hands in front of their flies. Silence.

"The Lord is my shepherd: therefore can I lack nothing."

Eccles' voice is fragile outdoors. The distant buzz of the power
mower halts respectfully. Rabbit's chest vibrates with excitement
and strength; he is sure his girl has ascended to Heaven. This feeling
fills Eccles' recited words like a living body a skin. "O God, whose
most dear Son did take little children into his arms and bless them;
Give us Grace, we beseech thee, to entrust the soul of this child to
thy never-failing care and love, and bring us all to the heavenly kingdom; through the same thy Son, Jesus Christ, our Lord. Amen."

"Amen," Mrs. Springer whispers.

Yes. That is how it is. He feels them all, the heads as still around
him as tombstones, he feels them all one, all one with the grass,
with the hothouse flowers, all, the undertaker's men, the unseen
caretaker who has halted his mower, all gathered into one here to
give his unbaptized baby force to leap to Heaven.

An electric switch is turned, the straps begin to lower the
casket into the grave and stop. Eccles makes a cross of sand on the
lid. Stray grains roll one by one down the curved lid into the hole.
An ungloved hand throws crumpled petals. "Deal graciously, we
pray thee, with all those who mourn, that, casting every care on
thee . . ." The straps whine again. Janice at his side staggers. He
holds her arm and even through the cloth it feels hot. A small
breath of wind makes the canopy fill and luff. The smell of
flowers rises toward them. ". . . and the Holy Ghost, bless you and
keep you, now and for evermore. Amen."

Eccles closes his book. Harry's father and Janice's, standing side by side, look up and blink. The undertaker's men begin to be busy with their equipment, retrieving the straps from the hole. Mourners move into the sunshine. *Casting every care on thee . . .* The sky greets him. A strange strength sinks down into him. It is as if he has been crawling in a cave and now at last beyond the dark recession of crowding rocks he has seen a patch of light; he turns, and Janice's face, dumb with grief, blocks the light. "Don't look at *me*," he says. "I didn't kill her."

This comes out of his mouth clearly, in tune with the simplicity he feels now in everything. Heads talking softly snap around at a voice so sudden and cruel.

They misunderstand. He just wants this straight. He explains to the heads, "You all keep acting as if *I* did it. I wasn't anywhere near. *She's* the one." He turns to her, and her face, slack as if slapped, seems hopelessly removed from him. "Hey it's O.K.," he tells her. "You didn't mean to." He tries to take her hand but she snatches it back like from a trap and looks toward her parents, who step toward her.

His face burns. His embarrassment is savage. Forgiveness had been big in his heart and now it's hate. He hates his wife's face. She doesn't *see*. She had a chance to join him in truth, just the simplest factual truth, and she turned away. He sees that among the heads even his own mother's is horrified, blank with shock, a wall against him; she asks him what have they done to him and then she does it too. A suffocating sense of injustice blinds him. He turns and runs.

Uphill exultantly. He dodges among gravestones. Dandelions grow bright as butter among the graves. Behind him his name is called in Eccles' voice: "Harry! Harry!" He feels Eccles chasing him but does not turn to look. He cuts diagonally through the stones across the grass toward the woods. The distance to the dark crescent of trees is greater than it seemed from beside the grave. The romping of his body turns heavy; the slope of land grows steeper. Yet there is a resilience in the burial ground that sustains his flight, a gentle settled bumpiness that buoys him up with its memory of the dodging spurting runs down a crowded court. He arrives between the arms of the woods and aims for the center of the crescent. Once inside, he is less sheltered than he expected; turning, he can see through the leaves back down the graveyard to where, beside the small green tent, the human beings he had left cluster. Eccles is halfway between them and him. He has stopped running. His black chest heaves. His wide-set eyes concentrate into the woods. The others, thick stalks in dark clothes, jiggle: maneuvering, planning, testing each other's strengths, holding each other up. Their pale faces flash mute signals toward the woods and turn away, in disgust or despair, and then flash again full in the declining sun, fascinated. Only Eccles' gaze is steady. He may be gathering energy to renew the chase.

Rabbit crouches and runs raggedly. His hands and face are scratched from plowing through the bushes and saplings that rim the woods. Deeper inside there is more space. The pine trees smother all other growth. Their brown needles muffle the rough earth with a slippery blanket; sunshine falls in narrow slots on this dead floor. It is dim but hot in here, like an attic; the unseen afternoon sun bakes the dark shingles of green above his head. Dead lower branches thrust at the level of his eyes. His hands and face feel hot where they were scratched. He turns to see if he has left the people behind. No one is following. Far off, down at the end of the aisle of pines he is in, a green glows which is perhaps the green of the cemetery; but it seems as far off as the patches of sky that flicker through the treetops. In turning he loses some sense of direction. But the tree-trunks are at first in neat rows that carry him along between them, and he walks always against the slope of the land. If he walks far enough uphill he will in time reach the scenic drive that runs along the ridge. Only by going downhill can he be returned to the others.

The trees cease to march in rows and grow together more thickly. These are older trees. The darkness under them is denser and the ground is steeper. Rocks jut up through the blanket of needles, scabby with lichen; collapsed trunks hold intricate claws across the path. At places where a hole has been opened up in a roof of evergreen, prickly bushes and yellow grasses grow in a hasty sweet-smelling tumble, and midges swarm. These patches, some of them broad enough to catch a bit of the sun slanting down the mountainside, make the surrounding darkness darker, and in pausing in them Rabbit becomes conscious, by its cessation, of a whisper that fills the brown tunnels all around him. The surrounding trees are too tall for him to see any sign, even a remote cleared landscape, of civilization. Islanded in light, he becomes frightened. He is conspicuous; the bears and nameless menaces that whisper through the forest can see him clearly. Rather than hang vulnerable in these wells of visibility he rushes toward the menace, across the rocks and rotting trunks and slithering needles. Insects follow him out of the sun; his sweat is a strong perfume. His chest binds and his shins hurt from jarring uphill into pits and flat rocks that the needles conceal. He takes off his binding hot blue coat and carries it in a twisted bundle. He struggles against his impulse to keep turning his head, to see what is behind him; there is never anything, just the hushed, deathly life of the woods, but his fear fills the winding space between the tree-trunks with agile threats that just dodge out of the corner of his eye each time he whips his head around. He must hold his head rigid. He's terrorizing himself. As a kid he often went up through the woods. But maybe as a kid he walked under a protection that has now been lifted; he can't believe the woods were this dark then. They too have grown. Such an unnatural darkness, clogged with spider-fine twigs that finger his face incessantly, a darkness in defiance of the broad daylight whose sky leaps in jagged patches from treetop to treetop above him like a silent monkey.

The small of his back aches from crouching. He begins to doubt his method. As a kid he never entered from the cemetery. Perhaps walking against the steepest slope is stupid, carrying him along below the ridge of the mountain when a few yards to his left the road is running. He bears to his left, trying to keep himself in a straight path; the whisper of woods seems to swell louder and his heart lifts with hope: he was right, he is near a road. He hurries on, scrambling wildly, expecting the road to appear with every step, its white posts and speeding metal to gleam. The slope of the ground dies unnoticed under his feet. He stops, stunned, on the edge of a precipitate hollow whose near bank is strewn with the hairy bodies of dead trees locked against trunks that have managed to cling erect to the steep soil and that cast into the hollow a shadow as deep as the last stage of twilight. Something rectangular troubles this gloom; it dawns on him that on the floor of the hollow lie the cellarhole and the crumbled sandstone walls of a forgotten house. To his shrill annoyance at having lost his way and headed himself downhill again is added a clangorous fear, as if this ruined evidence of a human intrusion into a world of blind life tolls bells that ring to the edges of the universe. The thought that this place was once self-conscious, that its land was tramped and cleared and known, blackens the air with ghosts that climb the ferny bank toward him like children clambering up from a grave. Perhaps there were children, fat girls in calico fetching water from a spring, boys scarring the trees with marks of play, growing old on boards stretched above the cellarhole, dying with a last look out the window at the bank where Rabbit stands. He feels more conspicuous and vulnerable than in the little clearings of sunshine; he obscurely feels lit by a great spark, the spark whereby the blind tumble of matter recognized itself, a spark struck in an encounter a terrible God willed. His stomach slides; his ears seem suddenly open to the sound of a voice. He scrambles back uphill, thrashing noisily in the deepening darkness to drown out the voice that wants to cry out to him from a source that flits from tree to tree in the shadows. In the treacherous light the slope of land is like some fleeing, dodging creature.

The light widens enough for him to spy off to his right a nest of old tin cans and bottles sunken into the needles. He is safe. He strikes the road. He jacks his long legs over the guard fence and straightens up. Gold spots are switching on and off in the corners of his eyes. The asphalt scrapes under his shoes and he seems entered, panting, on a new life. Chilly air strokes his shoulder blades; somewhere in there he split old man Springer's shirt right down the back. He has come out of the woods about a half-mile below the Pinnacle Hotel. As he swings along, jauntily hanging his blue coat over his shoulder on the hook of one finger, Janice and Eccles and his mother and his sins seem a thousand miles behind. He decides to call Eccles, like you'd send somebody a postcard. Eccles had liked him and put a lot of trust in him and deserves at least a phone call. Rabbit rehearses what he'll say. *It's O.K.*, he'll tell him, *I'm on the way. I mean, I think there are several ways; don't worry. Thanks for everything.* What he wants to get across is that Eccles shouldn't be discouraged.

On the top of the mountain it is still broad day. Up in the sea of sky a lake of fragmented mackerel clouds drifts in one piece like a school of fish. There are only a couple cars parked around the hotel, jalopies, '52 Pontiacs and '51 Mercs like Springer Motors sells to these blotchy kids that come in with a stripper in their wallets and a hundred dollars in the bank. Inside the cafeteria a few of them are playing a pinball machine called BOUNCING BETSY. They look at him and make wise faces and one of the boys even calls, "Did she rip your shirt?" But, it's strange, they don't really know anything about him except he looks mussed. You do things and do things and nobody really has a clue. The clock says twenty of six. He goes to the pay-phone on the mustard-colored wall and looks up Eccles' number in the book.

His wife answers dryly, "Hello?" Rabbit shuts his eyes and her freckles dance in the red of his lids.

"Hi. Could I speak to Reverend Eccles please?"

"Who is this?" Her voice has gotten up on a hard little high horse; she knows who.

"Hey, this is Harry Angstrom. Is Jack there?"

The receiver at the other end of the line is replaced. That bitch. Poor Eccles probably sitting there his heart bleeding to hear the word from me and she going back and telling him wrong number, that poor bastard being married to that bitch. He hangs up himself, hears the dime rattle down, and feels simplified by this failure. He goes out across the parking lot.

He seems to leave behind him in the cafeteria all the poison she must be dripping into the poor tired guy's ears. He imagines her telling Eccles about how he slapped her fanny and thinks he hears Eccles laughing and himself smiles. He'll remember Eccles as laughing; there was that in him that held you off, that you couldn't reach, the nasal official business, but through the laughter you could get to him. Sort of sneaking in behind him, past the depressing damp clinging front. What made it depressing was that he wasn't sure, but couldn't tell you, and worried his eyebrows instead, and spoke every word in a different voice. All in all, a relief to be free of him.

From the edge of the parking lot, Brewer is spread out like a carpet, its flowerpot red going dusty. Some lights are already turned on. The great neon sunflower at the center of the city looks small as a daisy. Now the low clouds are pink but up above, high in the dome, tails of cirrus still hang pale and pure. As he starts down the steps he wonders, *Would she have?* Lucy. Are ministers' wives frigid? Like du Ponts.

He goes down the mountainside on the flight of log stairs and through the park, where some people are still playing tennis, and down Weiser Street. He puts his coat back on and walks up Summer. His heart is murmuring in suspense but it is in the center of his chest. That lopsided kink about Becky is gone, he has put her in Heaven, he felt her go. If Janice had felt it he would have stayed. Or would he? The outer door is open and an old lady in a Polish sort of kerchief is coming mumbling out of F. X. Pellegrini's door. He rings Ruth's bell.

The buzzer answers and he quickly snaps open the inner door and starts up the steps. Ruth comes to the banister and looks down and says, "Go away."

"Huh? How'd you know it was me?"

"Go back to your wife."

"I can't. I just left her."

He has climbed to the step next to the top one, and their faces are on a level. "You're always leaving her," she says.

"No, this time it's different. It's really bad."

"You're bad all around. You're bad with me, too."

"Why?" He has come up the last step and stands there a yard away from her, excited and helpless. He thought when he saw her, instinct would tell him what to do but in a way it's all new, though it's only been a few weeks. She is changed, graver in her motions and thicker in the waist. The blue of her eyes is no longer blank.

She looks at him with a contempt that is totally new. "*Why?*" she repeats in an incredulous hard voice.

"Let me guess," he says. "You're pregnant."

Surprise softens the hardness a moment.

"That's great," he says, and takes advantage of her softness to push her ahead of him into the room. Just from the touches of pushing he remembers what Ruth feels like in his arms. "Great," he repeats, closing the door. He tries to embrace her and she fights him successfully and backs away behind a chair. She had meant that fight; his neck is scraped.

"Go away," she says. "Go *away*."

"Don't you need me?"

"*Need* you," she cries, and he squints in pain at the straining note of hysteria; he feels she has imagined this encounter so often she is determined to say everything, which will be too much. He sits down in an easy chair. His legs ache. She says, "I needed you that night you walked out. Remember how much I needed you? Remember what you made me do?"

"She was in the hospital," he says. "I had to go."

"God, you're cute. God, you're so holy. You had to go. You had to stay, too, didn't you? You know, I was stupid enough to think you'd at least call."

"I wanted to but I was trying to start clean. I didn't know you were pregnant."

"You didn't, why not? Anybody else would have. I was sick enough."

"When, with me?"

"God, yes. Why don't you look outside your own pretty skin once in a while?"

"Well why didn't you tell me?"

"Why should I? What would that have done? You're no help. You're nothing. You know why I didn't? You'll laugh, but I didn't because I thought you'd leave me if you knew. You wouldn't ever let me do anything to prevent it but I figured once it happened you'd leave me. You left me anyway so there you are. Why don't you get out? Please get out. I begged you to get out the first time. The damn first time I begged you. Why are you *here?*"

"I want to be here. It's right. Look. I'm happy you're pregnant."

"It's too fucking late to be happy."

"Why? Why is it too late?" He's frightened, remembering how she wasn't here when he came before. She's here now, she had been away then. Women went away to have it done, he knew. There was a place in Philadelphia even the kids in high school had known about.

"How can you sit there?" she asks him. "I can't understand it, how you can sit there; you just killed your baby and there you sit."

"Who told you that?"

"Your ministerial friend. Your fellow saint. He called about a half-hour ago."

"God. He's still trying."

"I said you weren't here. I said you'd never be here."

"I didn't kill the poor kid. Janice did. I got mad at her one night and came looking for you and she got drunk and drowned the poor kid in the bathtub. Don't make me talk about it. Where *were* you, anyway?"

She looks at him with dull wonder and says softly, "Boy, you really have the touch of death, don't you?"

"Hey; have you done something?"

"Hold still. Just sit there. I see you very clear all of a sudden. You're Mr. Death himself. You're not just nothing, you're worse than nothing. You're not a rat, you don't stink, you're not enough to stink."

"Look, I didn't do anything. I was coming to see you when it happened."

"No, you don't do anything. You just wander around with the kiss of death. Get out. Honest to God, Rabbit, just looking at you makes me sick." Her sincerity in saying this leaves her so limp that for support she grips the top slat of the back of a straight chair – one of the chairs they used to sit in to eat – and leans forward over it, open-mouthed and staring.

He, who always took a pride in dressing neatly, who had always been led to think he was all right to look at, blushes to feel this sincerity. The sensation he had counted on, of being by nature her mate, of getting on top of her, hasn't come. He looks at his fingernails, with their big cuticle moons. His hands and legs are suffused with a paralyzing sensation of reality; his child is really dead, his day is really done, this woman is really sickened by him. Realizing this much makes him anxious to have all of it, to go as far in this direction as he can. He asks her flat, "Did you get an abortion?"

She smirks and says hoarsely, "What do *you* think?"

He closes his eyes and while the gritty grained fur of the chair arms rushes up against his fingertips he prays, *God, dear God, no, not another, you have one, let this one go.* A dirty knife turns in his intricate inner darkness. When he opens his eyes he sees, from the tentative hovering way she is standing there, trying to bring off a hard swagger in her stance, that she means to torment him. His voice goes sharp with hope: "Have you?"

A crumbling film comes over her face. "No," she says, "*no*. I should but I keep not doing it. I don't want to do it."

Up he gets and his arms go around her, without squeezing, like a magic ring, and though she stiffens at his touch and twists her head sideways on her muscled white throat, he has regained that feeling, of being on top. "Oh," he says, "good. That's so good."

"It was too ugly," she says. "Margaret had it all rigged up but I kept – thinking about –"

"Yes," he says. "Yes. You're so good. I'm so glad," and tries to nuzzle the side of her face. His nose touches wet. "You have it," he coaxes. "Have it." She is still a moment, staring at her thoughts, and then jerks out of his arms and says, "Don't touch me!" Her face flares; her body is bent forward like a threatened animal's. As if his touch *is* death.

"I love you," he says.

"That means nothing from you. Have it, have it, you say: how? Will you marry me?"

"I'd love to."

"You'd love to. You'd love to be the man in the moon, too. What about your wife? What about the boy you already have?"

"I don't know."

"Will you divorce her? No. You love being married to her too. You love being married to everybody. Why can't you make up your mind what you want to *do?*"

"Can't I? I don't know."

"How would you support me? How many wives can you support? Your jobs are a joke. You aren't worth hiring. Maybe once you could play basketball but you can't do *any*thing now. What the hell do you think the world is?"

"Please have the baby," he says. "You got to have it."

"Why? Why do you *care?*"

"I don't know. I don't know any of these answers. All I know is what feels right. You feel right to me. Sometimes Janice used to. Sometimes nothing does."

"Who cares? That's the thing. Who cares *what* you feel?"

"I don't know," he says again.

She groans – from her face he feared she would spit – and turns and looks at the wall that is all in bumps from being painted over peeling previous coats so often.

He says, "I'm hungry. Why don't I go out to the delicatessen and get us something. Then we can think."

She turns, steadier. "I've *been* thinking," she says. "You know where I was when you came here the other day? I was with my parents. You know I have parents. They're pretty poor parents but that's what they are. They live in West Brewer. They know. I mean they know some things. They know I'm pregnant. Pregnant's a nice word, it happens to everybody, you don't have to think too much what you must do to get that way. Now I'd like to marry you. I would. I mean whatever I said but if we're married it'll be all right. Now you work it out. You divorce that wife you feel so sorry for about once a month, you divorce her or forget me. If you can't work it out, I'm dead to you; I'm dead to you and this baby of yours is dead too. Now: get out if you want to." Saying all this unsteadies her and makes her cry, but she pretends she's not. She grips the back of the chair, the sides of her nose shining, and looks at him to say something. The way she is fighting for control of herself repels him; he doesn't like people who manage things. He likes things to happen of themselves.

He has nervously felt her watching him for some sign of resolution inspired by her speech. In fact he has hardly listened; it is too complicated and, compared to the vision of a sandwich, unreal. He stands up, he hopes with soldierly effect, and says, "That's fair. I'll work it out. What do you want at the store?" A sandwich and a glass of milk, and then undressing her, getting her out of that cotton dress harried into wrinkles and seeing that thickened waist calm in its pale cool skin. He loves women when they're first pregnant; a kind of dawn comes over their bodies. If he can just once more bury himself in her he knows he'll come up with his nerves all combed.

"I don't want anything," she says.

"Oh you got to eat," he says.

"I've eaten," she says.

He tries to kiss her but she says "No" and does not look inviting, fat and flushed and her many-colored hair straggled and damp.

"I'll be right back," he says.

As he goes down the stairs worries come as quick as the click of his footsteps. Janice, money, Eccles' phone call, the look on his mother's face all clatter together in sharp dark waves; guilt and responsibility slide together like two substantial shadows inside his chest. The mere engineering of it – the conversations, the phone calls, the lawyers, the finances – seems to complicate, physically, in front of his mouth, so he is conscious of the effort of breathing, and every action, just reaching for the doorknob, feels like a precarious extension of a long mechanical sequence insecurely linked to his heart. The doorknob's solidity answers his touch, and turns with a silky click.

Outside in the air his fears condense. Globes of ether, pure nervousness, slide down his legs. The sense of outside space scoops at his chest. Standing on the step he tries to sort out his worries. Two thoughts comfort him, let a little light through the dense pack of impossible alternatives. Ruth has parents, and she will let his baby live; two thoughts that are perhaps the same thought, the vertical order of parenthood, a kind of thin tube upright in time in which our solitude is somewhat diluted. Ruth and Janice both have parents: on this excuse he dissolves them both. Nelson remains: here is a hardness he must carry with him. On this small fulcrum he tries to balance the rest, weighing opposites against each other: Janice and Ruth, Eccles and his mother, the right way and the good way, the way to the delicatessen – gaudy with stacked fruit lit by a naked bulb – and the other way, down Summer Street to where the city ends. He tries to picture how it will end, with an empty baseball field, a dark factory, and then over a brook into a dirt road, he doesn't know. He pictures a huge vacant field of cinders and his heart goes hollow.

Afraid, really afraid, he remembers what once consoled him by seeming to make a hole where he looked through into underlying brightness, and lifts his eyes to the church window. It is, because of church poverty or the late summer nights or just carelessness, unlit, a dark circle in a limestone façade.

There is light, though, in the streetlights; muffled by trees their mingling cones retreat to the unseen end of Summer Street. Nearby, to his left, directly under one, the rough asphalt looks like dimpled snow. He decides to walk around the block, to clear his head and pick his path. Funny, how what makes you move is so simple and the field you must move in is so crowded. His legs take strength from the distinction, scissor along evenly. Goodness lies inside, there is nothing outside, those things he was trying to balance have no weight. He feels his inside as very real suddenly, a pure blank space in the middle of a dense net. *I don't know*, he kept telling Ruth; he doesn't know, what to do, where to go, what will happen, the thought that he doesn't know seems to make him infinitely small and impossible to capture. Its smallness fills him like a vastness. It's like when they heard you were great and put two men on you and no matter which way you turned you bumped into one of them and the only thing to do was pass. So you passed and the ball belonged to the others and your hands were empty and the men on you looked foolish because in effect there was nobody there.

Rabbit comes to the curb but instead of going to his right and around the block he steps down, with as big a feeling as if this little sidestreet is a wide river, and crosses. He wants to travel to the next patch of snow. Although this block of brick three-stories is just like the one he left, something in it makes him happy; the steps and windowsills seem to twitch and shift in the corner of his eye, alive. This illusion trips him. His hands lift of their own and he feels the wind on his ears even before, his heels hitting heavily on the pavement at first but with an effortless gathering out of a kind of sweet panic growing lighter and quicker and quieter, he runs. Ah: runs. Runs.

RABBIT REDUX

CHAPTERS

LIEUT. COL. VLADIMIR A. SHATALOV:
I am heading straight for the socket.

LIEUT. COL. BORIS V. VOLYNOV, SOYUZ 5 COMMANDER:
Easy, not so rough.

COLONEL SHATALOV:
It took me quite a while to find you, but now I've got you.

I. POP/MOM/MOON

MEN emerge pale from the little printing plant at four sharp, ghosts for an instant, blinking, until the outdoor light overcomes the look of constant indoor light clinging to them. In winter, Pine Street at this hour is dark, darkness presses down early from the mountain that hangs above the stagnant city of Brewer; but now in summer the granite curbs starred with mica and the row houses differentiated by speckled bastard sidings and the hopeful small porches with their jigsaw brackets and gray milk-bottle boxes and the sooty ginkgo trees and the baking curbside cars wince beneath a brilliance like a frozen explosion. The city, attempting to revive its dying downtown, has torn away blocks of buildings to create parking lots, so that a desolate openness, weedy and rubbled, spills through the once-packed streets, exposing church façades never seen from a distance and generating new perspectives of rear entryways and half-alleys and intensifying the cruel breadth of the light. The sky is cloudless yet colorless, hovering blanched humidity, in the way of these Pennsylvania summers, good for nothing but to make green things grow. Men don't even tan; filmed by sweat, they turn yellow.

A man and his son, Earl Angstrom and Harry, are among the printers released from work. The father is near retirement, a thin man with no excess left to him, his face washed empty by grievances and caved in above the protruding slippage of bad false teeth. The son is five inches taller and fatter; his prime is soft, somehow pale and sour. The small nose and slightly lifted upper lip that once made the nickname Rabbit fit now seem, along with the thick waist and cautious stoop bred into him by a decade of the Linotyper's trade, clues to weakness, a weakness verging on anonymity. Though his height, his bulk, and a remnant alertness in the way he moves his head continue to distinguish him on the street, years have passed since anyone has called him Rabbit.

"Harry, how about a quick one?" his father asks. At the corner where their side street meets Weiser there is a bus stop and a bar, the Phoenix, with a girl nude but for cowboy boots in neon outside and cactuses painted on the dim walls inside. Their buses when they take them go in opposite directions: the old man takes number 16A around the mountain to the town of Mt. Judge, where he has lived his life, and Harry takes number 12 in the opposite direction to Penn Villas, a new development west of the city, ranch houses and quarter-acre lawns contoured as the bull-dozer left them and maple saplings tethered to the earth as if otherwise they might fly away. He moved there with Janice and Nelson three years ago. His father still feels the move out of Mt. Judge as a rejection, and so most afternoons they have a drink together to soften the day's parting. Working together ten years, they have grown into the love they would have had in Harry's childhood, had not his mother loomed so large between them.

"Make it a Schlitz," Earl tells the bartender.

"Daiquiri," Harry says. The air-conditioning is turned so far up he unrolls his shirt cuffs and buttons them for warmth. He always wears a white shirt to work and after, as a way of cancelling the ink. Ritually, he asks his father how his mother is.

But his father declines to make a ritual answer. Usually he says, "As good as can be hoped." Today he sidles a conspiratorial inch closer at the bar and says, "Not as good as could be hoped, Harry."

She has had Parkinson's Disease for years now. Harry's mind slides away from picturing her, the way she has become, the loosely fluttering knobbed hands, the shuffling sheepish walk, the eyes that study him with vacant amazement though the doctor says her mind is as good as ever in there, and the mouth that wanders open and forgets to close until saliva reminds it. "At nights, you mean?" The very question offers to hide her in darkness.

Again the old man blocks Rabbit's desire to slide by. "No, the nights are better now. They have her on a new pill and she says she sleeps better now. It's in her mind, more."

"What is, Pop?"

"We don't talk about it, Harry, it isn't in her nature, it isn't the type of thing she and I have ever talked about. Your mother and I have just let a certain type of thing go unsaid, it was the way we were brought up, maybe it would have been better if we hadn't, I don't know. I mean things now they've *put* into her mind."

"Who's this they?" Harry sighs into the Daiquiri foam and thinks, He's going too, they're both going. Neither makes enough sense. As his father pushes closer against him to explain, he becomes one of the hundreds of skinny whining codgers in and around this city, men who have sucked this same brick tit for sixty years and have dried up with it.

"Why, the ones who come to visit her now she spends half the day in bed. Mamie Kellog, for one. Julia Arndt's another. I hate like the Jesus to bother you with it, Harry, but her talk is getting wild and with Mim on the West Coast you're the only one to help me straighten out my own mind. I hate to bother you but her talk is getting so wild she even talks of telephoning Janice."

"Janice! Why would she call Janice?"

"Well." A pull on the Schlitz. A wiping of the wet upper lip with the bony back of the hand, fingers half-clenched in an old man's clutching way. A loose-toothed grimacing getting set to dive in. "Well the talk is *about* Janice."

"*My* Janice?"

"Now Harry, don't blow your lid. Don't blame the bearer of bad tidings. I'm trying to tell you what they say, not what I believe."

"I'm just surprised there's anything to say. I hardly see her any more, now that she's over at Springer's lot all the time."

"Well, that's it. That may be your mistake, Harry. You've taken Janice for granted ever since – the time." The time he left her. The time the baby died. The time she took him back. "Ten years ago," his father needlessly adds. Harry is beginning, here in this cold bar with cactuses in plastic pots on the shelves beneath the mirrors and the little Schlitz spinner doing its polychrome parabola over and over, to feel the world turn. A hopeful coldness inside him grows, grips his wrists inside his cuffs. The news isn't all in, a new combination might break it open, this stale peace.

"Harry, the malice of people surpasses human understanding in my book, and the poor soul has no defenses against it, there she lies and has to listen. Ten years ago, wouldn't she have laid them out? Wouldn't her tongue have cut them down? They've told her that Janice is running around. With one certain man, Harry. Nobody claims she's playing the field."

The coldness spreads up Rabbit's arms to his shoulders, and down the tree of veins toward his stomach. "Do they name the man?"

"Not to my knowledge, Harry. How could they now, when in all likelihood there is no man?"

"Well, if they can make up the idea, they can make up a name."

The bar television is running, with the sound turned off. For the twentieth time that day the rocket blasts off, the numbers pouring backwards in tenths of seconds faster than the eye until zero is reached: then the white boiling beneath the tall kettle, the lifting so slow it seems certain to tip, the swift diminishment into a retreating speck, a jiggling star. The men dark along the bar murmur among themselves. They have not been lifted, they are left here. Harry's father mutters at him, prying. "Has she seemed any different to you lately, Harry? Listen, I know in all probability it's what they call a crock of shit, but – has she seemed any, you know, different lately?"

It offends Rabbit to hear his father swear; he lifts his head fastidiously, as if to watch the television, which has returned to a program where people are trying to guess what sort of prize is hidden behind a curtain and jump and squeal and kiss each other when it turns out to be an eight-foot frozen-food locker. He might be wrong but for a second he could swear this young housewife opens her mouth in mid-kiss and gives the m.c. a taste of her tongue. Anyway, she won't stop kissing. The m.c.'s eyes roll out to the camera for mercy and they cut to a commercial. In silence images of spaghetti and some opera singer riffle past. "I don't know," Rabbit says. "She hits the bottle pretty well sometimes but then so do I."

"Not you," the old man tells him, "you're no drinker, Harry. I've seen drinkers all my life, somebody like Boonie over in engraving, there's a drinker, killing himself with it, and he knows it, he couldn't stop if they told him he'd die tomorrow. You may have a whisky or two in the evening, you're no spring chicken anymore, but you're no drinker." He hides his loose mouth in his beer and Harry taps the bar for another Daiquiri. The old man nuzzles closer. "Now Harry, forgive me for asking if you don't want to talk about it, but how about in bed? That goes along pretty well, does it?"

"No," he answers slowly, disdainful of this prying, "I wouldn't exactly say well. Tell me about Mom. Has she had any of those breathing fits lately?"

"Not a one that I've been woken up for. She sleeps like a baby with those new green pills. This new medicine is a miracle, I must admit – ten more years the only way to kill us'll be to gas us to death, Hitler had the right idea. Already, you know, there aren't any more crazy people: just give 'em a pill morning and evening and they're sensible as Einstein. You wouldn't exactly say it does, go along O.K., is that what I understood you said?"

"Well we've never been that great, Pop, frankly. Does she fall down ever? Mom."

"She may take a tumble or two in the day and not tell me about it. I tell her, I *tell* her, stay in bed and watch the box. She has this theory the longer she can do things the longer she'll stay out of bed for good. I figure she should take care of herself, put herself in deep freeze, and in a year or two in all likelihood they'll develop a pill that'll clear this up simple as a common cold. Already, you know, some of these cortisones; but the doctor tells us they don't know but what the side effects may be worse. You know: the big C. My figuring is, take the chance, they're just about ready to lick cancer anyway and with these transplants pretty soon they can replace your whole insides." The old man hears himself talking too much and slumps to stare into his empty beer, the suds sliding down, but can't help adding, to give it all point, "It's a terrible thing." And when Harry fails to respond: "God she hates not being active."

The rum is beginning to work. Rabbit has ceased to feel cold, his heart is beginning to lift off. The air in here seems thinner, his eyes adjusting to the dark. He asks, "How's her mind? You aren't saying they should start giving her crazy pills."

"In honest truth, I won't lie to you Harry, it's as clear as a bell, when her tongue can find the words. And as I say she's gotten hipped lately on this Janice idea. It would help a lot, Jesus I hate to bother you but it's the truth, it would help a lot if you and Janice could spare the time to come over tonight. Not seeing you too often her imagination's free to wander. Now I know you've promised Sunday for her birthday, but think of it this way: if you're stuck in bed with nobody but the idiot box and a lot of malicious biddies for company a week can seem a year. If you could make it up there some evening before the weekend, bring Janice along so Mary could look at her – "

"I'd like to, Pop. You know I would."

"I know, Jesus I know. I know more than you think. You're at just the age to realize your old man's not the dope you always thought he was."

"The trouble is, Janice works in the lot office until ten, eleven all the time and I don't like to leave the kid alone in the house. In fact I better be getting back there now just in case." In case it's burned down. In case a madman has moved in. These things happen all the time in the papers. He can read in his father's face – a fishy pinching-in at the corners of the mouth, a tightened veiling of the washed-out eyes – the old man's suspicions confirmed. Rabbit sees red. Meddling old crock. Janice: who'd have that mutt? In love with her father and there she stuck. Happy as a Girl Scout since she began to fill in at the lot, half these summer nights out way past supper, TV dinners, tuck Nelson in alone and wait up for her to breeze in blooming and talkative; he's never known her to be so full of herself, in a way it does his heart good. He resents his father trying to get at him with Janice and hits back with the handiest weapon, Mom. "This doctor you have, does he ever mention a nursing home?"

The old man's mind is slow making the switch back to his own wife. Harry has a thought, a spark like where train wheels run over a track switch. Did Mom ever do it to Pop? Play him false. All this poking around about life in bed hints at some experience. Hard to imagine, not only who with but when, she was always in the house as long as he could remember, nobody ever came to visit but the brush man and the Jehovah's Witnesses, yet the thought excites him, like Pop's rumor chills him, opens up possibilities. Pop is saying, "... at the beginning. We want to hold off at least until she's bedridden. If we reach the point where she can't take care of herself before I'm on retirement and there all day, it's an option we might be forced into. I'd hate to see it, though. Jesus I'd hate to see it."

"Hey Pop – ?"

"Here's my forty cents. Plus a dime for the tip." The way the old man's hand clings curlingly to the quarters in offering them betrays that they are real silver to him instead of just cut-copper sandwich-coins that ring flat on the bar top. Old values. The Depression when money was money. Never be sacred again, not even dimes are silver now. Kennedy's face killed half-dollars, took them out of circulation and they've never come back. The metal got sent to the moon. The niggling business of settling their bill delays his question about Mom until they are outdoors and then he sees he can't ask it, he doesn't know his father that well. Out here in the hot light his father has lost all sidling intimacy and looks merely old – liverish scoops below his eyes, broken veins along the sides of his nose, his hair the no-color of cardboard. "What'd you want to ask me?"

"I forget," Harry says, and sneezes. Coming into this heat from that air-conditioning sets off an explosion between his eyes that turns heads around halfway down the block and leaves his nostrils weeping. "No, I remember. The nursing home. How can we afford it? – fifty bucks a day or whatever. It'll suck us right down the drain."

His father laughs, with a sudden snap to retrieve his slipping teeth, and does a little shuffling dance-step, right here on the baking sidewalk, beneath the white-on-red BUS STOP sign that people have scratched and lipsticked to read PUS DROP. "Harry, God in His way hasn't been all bad to your mother and me. Believe it or not there's some advantages to living so long in this day and age. This Sunday she's going to be sixty-five and come under Medicare. I've been paying in since '66, it's like a ton of anxiety rolled off my chest. There's no medical expense can break us now. They called LBJ every name in the book but believe me he did a lot of good for the little man. Wherever he went wrong, it was his big heart betrayed him. These pretty boys in the sky right now, Nixon'll hog the credit but it was the Democrats put 'em there, it's been the same story ever since I can remember, ever since Wilson – the Republicans don't do a thing for the little man."

"Right," Harry says blankly. His bus is coming. "Tell her we'll be over Sunday." He pushes to a clear space at the back where, looking out while hanging onto the bar, he sees his father as one of the "little men." Pop stands whittled by the great American glare, squinting in the manna of blessings that come down from the government, shuffling from side to side in nervous happiness that his day's work is done, that a beer is inside him, that Armstrong is above him, that the U.S. is the crown and stupefaction of human history. Like a piece of grit in the launching pad, he has done his part. Still, he has been the one to keep his health; who would have thought Mom would fail first? Rabbit's mind, as the bus dips into its bag of gears and surges and shudders, noses closer into the image of her he keeps like a dreaded relic: the black hair gone gray, the mannish mouth too clever for her life, the lozenge-shaped nostrils that to him as a child suggested a kind of soreness within, the eyes whose color he had never dared to learn closed bulge-lidded in her failing, the whole long face, slightly shining as if with sweat, lying numbed on the pillow. He can't bear to see her like this is the secret of his seldom visiting, not Janice. The source of his life staring wasted there while she gropes for the words to greet him. And that gentle tawny smell of sickness that doesn't even stay in her room but comes downstairs to meet them in the front hall among the umbrellas and follows them into the kitchen where poor Pop warms their meals. A smell like gas escaping, that used to worry her so when he and Mim were little. He bows his head and curtly prays, *Forgive me, forgive us, make it easy for her. Amen.* He only ever prays on buses. Now this bus has that smell.

The bus has too many Negroes. Rabbit notices them more and more. They've been here all along, as a tiny kid he remembers streets in Brewer you held your breath walking through, though they never hurt you, just looked; but now they're noisier. Instead of bald-looking heads they're bushy. That's O.K., it's more Nature, Nature is what we're running out of. Two of the men in the shop are Negroes, Farnsworth and Buchanan, and after a while you didn't even notice; at least they remember how to laugh. Sad business, being a Negro man, always underpaid, their eyes don't look like our eyes, bloodshot, brown, liquid in them about to quiver out. Read somewhere some anthropologist thinks Negroes instead of being more primitive are the latest thing to evolve, the newest men. In some ways tougher, in some ways more delicate. Certainly dumber but then being smart hasn't amounted to so much, the atom bomb and the one-piece aluminum beer can. And you can't say Bill Cosby's stupid.

But against these educated tolerant thoughts leans a certain fear; he doesn't see why they have to be so noisy. The four seated right under him, jabbing and letting their noise come out in big silvery hoops; they know damn well they're bugging the fat Dutchy wives pulling their shopping bags home. Well, that's kids of any color: but strange. They are a strange race. Not only their skins but the way they're put together, loose-jointed like lions, strange about the head, as if their thoughts are a different shape and come out twisted even when they mean no menace. It's as if, all these Afro hair bushes and gold earrings and hoopy noise on buses, seeds of some tropical plant sneaked in by the birds were taking over the garden. His garden. Rabbit knows it's his garden and that's why he's put a flag decal on the back window of the Falcon even though Janice says it's corny and fascist. In the papers you read about these houses in Connecticut where the parents are away in the Bahamas and the kids come in and smash it up for a party. More and more this country is getting like that. As if it just grew here instead of people laying down their lives to build it.

The bus works its way down Weiser and crosses the Running Horse River and begins to drop people instead of taking them on. The city with its tired five and dimes (that used to be a wonderland, the counters as high as his nose and the Big Little Books smelling like Christmas) and its Kroll's Department Store (where he once worked knocking apart crates behind the furniture department) and its flowerpotted traffic circle where the trolley tracks used to make a clanging star of intersection and then the empty dusty windows where stores have been starved by the suburban shopping malls and the sad narrow places that come and go called Go-Go or Boutique and the funeral parlors with imitation

granite faces and the surplus outlets and a shoeshine parlor that sells
hot roasted peanuts and Afro newspapers printed in Philly crying
MBOYA MARTYRED and a flower shop where they sell numbers and
protection and a variety store next to a pipe-rack clothing retailer
next to a corner dive called JIMBO'S *Friendly* LOUNGE, cigarette
ends of the city snuffed by the bridge – the city gives way, after
the flash of open water that in his youth was choked with coal silt
(a man once tried to commit suicide from this bridge but stuck
there up to his hips until the police pulled him out) but that now
has been dredged and supports a flecking of moored pleasure
boats, to West Brewer, a gappy imitation of the city, the same
domino-thin houses of brick painted red, but spaced here and
there by the twirlers of a car lot, the pumps and blazoned overhang of a gas station, the lakelike depth of a supermarket parking
lot crammed with shimmering fins. Surging and spitting, the bus,
growing lighter, the Negroes vanishing, moves toward a dream of
spaciousness, past residential fortresses with sprinkled lawn around
all four sides and clipped hydrangeas above newly pointed retaining walls, past a glimpse of the museum whose gardens were
always in blossom and where the swans ate the breadcrusts school-
children threw them, then a glimpse of the sunstruck windows,
pumpkin orange blazing in reflection, of the tall new wing of the
County Hospital for the Insane. Closer at hand, the West Brewer
Dry Cleaners, a toy store calling itself Hobby Heaven, a Rialto
movie house with a stubby marquee: 2001 SPACE OD'SEY. Weiser
Street curves, becomes a highway, dips into green suburbs where
in the Twenties little knights of industry built half-timbered
dream-houses, pebbled mortar and clinker brick, stucco flaky as
pie crust, witch's houses of candy and hardened cookie dough
with two-car garages and curved driveways. In Brewer County,
but for a few baronial estates ringed by iron fences and moated by
miles of lawn, there is nowhere higher to go than these houses;
the most successful dentists may get to buy one, the pushiest insurance salesmen, the slickest ophthalmologists. This section even has
another name, distinguishing itself from West Brewer: Penn Park.
Penn Villas echoes the name hopefully, though it is not incorpo-
rated into this borough but sits on the border of Furnace Township,
looking in. The township, where once charcoal-fed furnaces had

smelted the iron for Revolutionary muskets, is now still mostly
farmland, and its few snowplows and single sheriff can hardly cope
with this ranch-house village of muddy lawns and potholed
macadam and sub-code sewers the developers suddenly left in its
care.

Rabbit gets off at a stop in Penn Park and walks down a street
of mock Tudor, Emberly Avenue, to where the road surface
changes at the township line, and becomes Emberly Drive in Penn
Villas. He lives on Vista Crescent, third house from the end. Once
there may have been here a vista, a softly sloped valley of red barns
and fieldstone farmhouses, but more Penn Villas has been added
and now the view from any window is as into a fragmented
mirror, of houses like this, telephone wires and television aerials
showing where the glass cracked. His house is faced with apple-
green aluminum clapboards and is numbered 26. Rabbit steps
onto his flagstone porchlet and opens his door with its three baby
windows arranged like three steps, echoing the door-chime of
three stepped tones.

"Hey Dad," his son calls from the living room, a room on his
right the size of what used to be called a parlor, with a fireplace
they never use. "They've left earth's orbit! They're forty-three
thousand miles away."

"Lucky them," he says. "Your mother here?"

"No. At school they let us all into assembly to see the launch."

"She call at all?"

"Not since I've been here. I just got in a while ago." Nelson,
at twelve, is under average height, with his mother's dark complexion, and something finely cut and wary about his face that may
come from the Angstroms. His long eyelashes come from
nowhere, and his shoulder-length hair is his own idea. Somehow,
Rabbit feels, if he were taller it would be all right, to have hair so
long. As is, the resemblance to a girl is frightening.

"Whadja do all day?"

The same television program, of people guessing and getting
and squealing and kissing the m.c., is still going on.

"Nothing much."

"Go to the playground?"

"For a while."

"Then where?"

"Oh, over to West Brewer, just to hang around Billy's apartment. Hey, Dad?"

"Yeah?"

"*His* father got him a mini-bike for his birthday. It's real cool. With that real long front part so you have to reach up for the handles."

"You rode it?"

"He only let me once. It's all shiny, there isn't a speck of paint on it, it's just metal, with a white banana seat."

"He's older than you, isn't he?"

"By four months. That's all. Just four months, Dad. I'm going to be thirteen in three months."

"Where does he ride it? It's not legal on the street, is it?"

"Their building has a big parking lot he rides it all around. Nobody says anything. It only cost a hundred-eighty dollars, Dad."

"Keep talking, I'm getting a beer."

The house is small enough so that the boy can be heard by his father in the kitchen, his voice mixed with gleeful greedy spurts from the television and the chunky suck of the refrigerator door opening and shutting. "Hey Dad, something I don't understand."

"Shoot."

"I thought the Fosnachts were divorced."

"Separated."

"Then how come his father keeps getting him all this neat junk? You ought to see the hi-fi set he has, that's all his, for his room, not even to share. Four speakers, Dad, and earphones. The earphones are fantastic. It's like you're way in*side* Tiny Tim."

"That's the place to be," Rabbit says, coming into the living room. "Want a sip?"

The boy takes a sip from the can, putting a keyhole width of foam on the fuzz of his upper lip, and makes a bitter face.

Harry explains, "When people get divorced the father doesn't stop liking the kids, he just can't live with them any more. The reason Fosnacht keeps getting Billy all this expensive crap is probably he feels guilty for leaving him."

"Why did they get separated, Dad, do you know?"

"Beats me. The bigger riddle is, why did they ever get married?" Rabbit knew Peggy Fosnacht when she was Peggy Gring, a big-assed walleyed girl in the middle row always waving her hand in the air because she thought she had the answer. Fosnacht he knows less well: a weedy little guy always shrugging his shoulders, used to play the saxophone in prom bands, now a partner in a music store on the upper end of Weiser Street, used to be called Chords 'n' Records, now Fidelity Audio. At the discount Fosnacht got, Billy's hi-fi set must have cost next to nothing. Like these prizes they keep socking into these young shriekers. The one that French-kissed the m.c. is off now and a colored couple is guessing. Pale, but definitely colored. That's O.K., let 'em guess, win, and shriek with the rest of us. Better that than sniping from rooftops. Still, he wonders how that black bride would be. Big lips, suck you right off, the men are slow as Jesus, long as whips, takes everything to get them up, in there forever, that's why white women need them, white men too quick about it, have to get on with the job, making America great. Rabbit loves, on *Laugh-In*, when Teresa does the go-go bit, the way they paint the words in white on her skin. When they watch, Janice and Nelson are always asking him what the words are; since he took up the printer's trade he can read like a flash, upside down, mirror-wise too: he always had good quick eyes, Tothero used to tell him he could see the ball through the holes of his ears, to praise him. A great secret sly praiser, Tothero. Dead now. The game different now, everything the jump shot, big looping hungry blacks lifting and floating there a second while a pink palm long as your forearm launched the ball. He asks Nelson, "Why don't you stay at the playground anymore? When I was your age I'd be playing Horse and Twenty-one all day long."

"Yeah, but you were good. You were tall." Nelson used to be crazy for sports. Little League, intramural. But lately he isn't. Rabbit blames it on a scrapbook his own mother kept, of his basketball days in the late Forties, when he set some county records: last winter every time they would go visit Mt. Judge Nelson would ask to get it out and lie on the floor with it, those old dry-yellow games, the glue dried so the pages crackle being turned, MT. JUDGE TOPPLES ORIOLE, ANGSTROM HITS FOR 37, just happening for the kid, that happened twenty years ago, light from a star.

"I *got* tall," Rabbit tells him. "At your age I wasn't much taller than you are." A lie, but not really. A few inches. In a world where inches matter. Putts. Fucks. Orbits. Squaring up a form. He feels bad about Nelson's height. His own never did him much good, if he could take five inches off himself and give them to Nelson he would. If it didn't hurt.

"Anyway, Dad, sports are square now. Nobody does it."

"Well, what isn't square now? Besides pill-popping and draft-dodging. And letting your hair grow down into your eyes. Where the hell is your mother? I'm going to call her. Turn the frigging TV down for once in your life."

David Frost has replaced *The Match Game* so Nelson turns it off entirely. Harry regrets the scared look that glimmered across the kid's face: like the look on his father's face when he sneezed on the street. Christ they're even scared to let him sneeze. His son and father seem alike fragile and sad to him. That's the trouble with caring about anybody, you begin to feel overprotective. Then you begin to feel crowded.

The telephone is on the lower of a set of see-through shelves that in theory divides the living room from a kind of alcove they call a breakfast nook. A few cookbooks sit on them but Janice has never to his knowledge looked into them, just dishes up the same fried chicken and tasteless steak and peas and French fries she's always dished up. Harry dials the familiar number and a familiar voice answers. "Springer Motors. Mr. Stavros speaking."

"Charlie, hi. Hey, is Janice around?"

"Sure is, Harry. How's tricks?" Stavros is a salesman and always has to say something.

"Tricky," Rabbit answers.

"Hold on, friend. The good woman's right here." Off-phone, his voice calls, "Pick it up. It's your old man."

Another receiver is lifted. Through the knothole of moment-ary silence Rabbit sees the office: the gleaming display cars on the showroom floor, old man Springer's frosted-glass door shut, the green-topped counter with the three steel desks behind: Stavros at one, Janice at another, and Mildred Kroust the bookkeeper

Springer has had for thirty years at the one in between, except she's usually out sick with some sort of female problem she's developed late in life, so her desk top is empty and bare but for wire baskets and a spindle and a blotter. Rabbit can also see last year's puppy-dog calendar on the wall and the cardboard cutout of the Toyota station wagon on the old coffee-colored safe, behind the Christmas tree. The last time he was at Springer's lot was for their Christmas party. Springer is so tickled to get the Toyota franchise after years of dealing in second-hand he has told Harry he feels "like a kid at Christmas all year round." He tried ten years ago to turn Rabbit into a car salesman but in the end Harry opted to follow his own father into honest work. "Harry sweet," Janice says, and he does hear something new in her voice, a breathy lilt of faint hurry, of a song he has interrupted her singing. "You're going to scold me, aren't you?"

"No, the kid and I were just wondering if and if so when the hell we're going to get a home-cooked meal around here."

"Oh I know," she sings, "I hate it too, it's just that with Mildred out so much we've had to go into her books, and her system is really zilch." Zilch: he hears another voice in hers. "Honestly," she sings on, "if it turns out she's been swindling Daddy of millions none of us will be surprised."

"Yeah. Look, Janice. It sounds like you're having a lot of fun over there –"

"*Fun?* I'm *work*ing, sweetie."

"Sure. Now what the fuck is really going on?"

"What do you mean, *going on?* Nothing is going on except your wife is trying to bring home a little extra bread." Bread? "'Going on' – really. You may think your seven or whatever dollars an hour you get for sitting in the dark diddling that machine is wonderful money, Harry, but the fact is a hundred dollars doesn't buy anything anymore, it just *goes*."

"Jesus, why am I getting this lecture on inflation? All I want to know is why my wife is never home to cook the fucking supper for me and the fucking kid."

"Harry, has somebody been bugging you about me?"

"Bugging? How would they do that? Janice. Just tell me, shall I put two TV dinners in the oven or what?"

A pause, during which he has a vision: sees her wings fold up, her song suspended: imagines himself soaring, rootless, free. An old premonition, dim. Janice says, with measured words, so he feels as when a child watching his mother levelling tablespoons of sugar into a bowl of batter, "Could you, sweet? Just for tonight? We're in the middle of a little crisis here, frankly. It's too complicated to explain, but we have to get some figures firm or we can't do the paychecks tomorrow."

"Who's this we? Your father there?"

"Oh sure."

"Could I talk to him a second?"

"Why? He's out on the lot."

"I want to know if he got those tickets for the Blasts game. The kid's dying to go."

"Well, actually, I don't see him, I guess he's gone home for supper."

"So it's just you and Charlie there."

"Other people are in and out. We're *des*perately trying to untangle this mess Mildred made. This is the last night, Harry, I promise. I'll be home between eight and nine, and then tomorrow night let's all go to a movie together. That space thing is still in West Brewer, I noticed this morning driving in."

Rabbit is suddenly tired, of this conversation, of everything. Confusing energy surrounds him. A man's appetites diminish, but the world's never. "O.K. Be home when you can. But we got to talk."

"I'd love to talk, Harry." From her tone she assumes "talk" means fuck, when he did mean talk. She hangs up: a satisfied impatient sound.

He opens another beer. The pull-tab breaks, so he has to find the rusty old church key underneath everything in the knife drawer. He heats up two Salisbury steak dinners; while waiting for the oven to preheat to 400°, he reads the ingredients listed on the package: water, beef, peas, dehydrated potato flakes, bread crumbs, mushrooms, flour, butter, margarine, salt, maltodextrin, tomato paste, corn starch, Worcestershire sauce, hydrolyzed vegetable protein, monosodium glutamate, nonfat dry milk, dehydrated onions, flavoring, sugar, caramel color, spice, cysteine and thiamine hydrochloride, gum arabic. There is no clue from the picture on the tinfoil where all this stuff fits in. He always thought gum arabic was something you erased with. Thirty-six years old and he knows less than when he started. With the difference that now he knows how little he'll always know. He'll never know how to talk Chinese or how screwing an African princess feels. The six o'clock news is all about space, all about emptiness: some bald man plays with little toys to show the docking and undocking maneuvers, and then a panel talks about the significance of this for the next five hundred years. They keep mentioning Columbus but as far as Rabbit can see it's the exact opposite: Columbus flew blind and hit something, these guys see exactly where they're aiming and it's a big round nothing. The Salisbury steak tastes of preservative and Nelson eats only a few bites. Rabbit tries to joke him into it: "Can't watch TV without a TV dinner." They channel-hop, trying to find something to hold them, but there is nothing, it all slides past until, after nine, on Carol Burnett, she and Gomer Pyle do an actually pretty funny skit about the Lone Ranger. It takes Rabbit back to when he used to sit in the radio-listening armchair back on Jackson Road, its arms darkened with greasespots from the peanut-butter cracker-sandwiches he used to stack there to listen with. Mom used to have a fit. Every Monday, Wednesday, and Friday night *The Lone Ranger* came on at seven-thirty, and if it was summer you'd come in from kick-the-can or three-stops-or-a-catch and the neighborhood would grow quiet all across the back yards and then at eight the doors would slam and the games begin again, those generous summer days, just enough dark to fit sleep into, a war being fought across oceans so he could spin out his days in such happiness, in such quiet growing. Eating Wheaties, along with Jack Armstrong, and Jell—O, which brought you Jack Benny.

In this skit the Lone Ranger has a wife. She stamps around a cabin saying how she hates housework, hates her lonely life. "You're never home," she says, "you keep disappearing in a cloud of dust with a hearty 'Heigh-ho, Silver.' " The unseen audience laughs, Rabbit laughs. Nelson doesn't see what's so funny. Rabbit tells him, "That's how they always used to introduce the program."

The kid says crossly, "I *know*, Dad," and Rabbit loses the thread of the skit a little, there has been a joke he didn't hear, whose laughter is dying.

Now the Lone Ranger's wife is complaining that Daniel Boone brings his wife beautiful furs, but "What do I ever get from you? A silver bullet." She opens a door and a bushel of silver bullets comes crashing out and floods the floor. For the rest of the skit Carol Burnett and Gomer Pyle and the man who plays Tonto (not Sammy Davis Jr. but another TV Negro) keep slipping and crunching on these bullets, by accident. Rabbit thinks of the millions who are watching, the millions the sponsors are paying, and still nobody took time to realize that this would happen, a mess of silver bullets on the floor.

Tonto tells the Lone Ranger, "Better next time, put-um bullet in gun first."

The wife turns to complaining about Tonto. "*Him*. Why must we always keep having him to dinner? He *never* has *us* back."

Tonto tells her that if she comes to his teepee, she would be kidnapped by seven or eight braves. Instead of being frightened, she is interested. She rolls those big Burnett eyes and says, "Let's go, *que más sabe*."

Nelson asks, "Dad, what's *que más sabe?*"

Rabbit is surprised to have to say, "I don't know. Something like 'good friend' or 'boss,' I suppose." Indeed come to think of it he understands nothing about Tonto. The Lone Ranger is a white man, so law and order on the range will work to his benefit, but what about Tonto? A Judas to his race, the more disinterested and lonely and heroic figure of virtue. When did he get his pay-off? Why was he faithful to the masked stranger? In the days of the war one never asked. Tonto was simply on "the side of right." It seemed a correct dream then, red and white together, red loving white as naturally as stripes in the flag. Where has "the side of right" gone? He has missed several jokes while trying to answer Nelson. The skit is approaching its climax. The wife is telling the Lone Ranger, "You must choose between him or me." Arms folded, she stands fierce.

The Lone Ranger's pause for decision is not long. "Saddle up, Tonto," he says. He puts on the phonograph a record of the

William Tell Overture and both men leave. The wife tiptoes over, a bullet crunching underfoot, and changes the record to "Indian Love Call." Tonto enters from the other side of the screen. He and she kiss and hug. "I've always been interested," Carol Burnett confides out to the audience, her face getting huge, "in Indian affairs."

There is a laugh from the invisible audience there, and even Rabbit sitting at home in his easy chair laughs, but underneath the laugh this final gag falls flat, maybe because everybody still thinks of Tonto as incorruptible, as above it all, like Jesus and Armstrong. "Bedtime, huh?" Rabbit says. He turns off the show as it unravels into a string of credits. The sudden little star flares, then fades.

Nelson says, "The kids at school say Mr. Fosnacht was having an affair, that's why they got divorced."

"Or maybe he just got tired of not knowing which of his wife's eyes was looking at him."

"Dad, what is an affair exactly?"

"Oh, it's two people going out together when they're married to somebody else."

"Did that ever happen to you and Mom?"

"I wouldn't say so. I took a vacation once, that didn't last very long. You wouldn't remember."

"I do, though. I remember Mom crying a lot, and everybody chasing you at the baby's funeral, and I remember standing in the place on Wilbur Street, with just you in the room beside me, and looking down at the town through the window screen, and knowing Mom was in the hospital."

"Yeah. Those were sad days. This Saturday, if Grandpa Springer has got the tickets he said he would, we'll go to the Blasts game."

"I know," the boy says, unenthusiastic, and drifts toward the stairs. It unsettles Harry, how in the corner of his eye, once or twice a day, he seems to see another woman in the house, a woman who is not Janice; when it is only his long-haired son.

One more beer. He scrapes Nelson's uneaten dinner into the Disposall, which sometimes sweetly stinks because the Penn Villas sewers flow sluggishly, carelessly engineered. He moves through the downstairs collecting glasses for the dishwasher; one of Janice's stunts is to wander around leaving dreggy cups with saucers used as ashtrays and wineglasses coated with vermouth around on whatever ledges occurred to her – the TV top, a windowsill. How can she be helping untangle Mildred's mess? Maybe out of the house she's a whirlwind of efficiency. And a heigh-ho Silver. Indian affairs. Poor Pop and his rumor. Poor Mom lying there prey to poison tongues and nightmares. The two of them, their minds gone dry as haystacks rats slither through. His mind shies away. He looks out the window and sees in dusk the black lines of a TV aerial, an aluminum clothes tree, a basketball hoop on a far garage. How can he get the kid interested in sports? If he's too short for basketball, then baseball. Anything, just to put something there, some bliss, to live on later for a while. If he goes empty now he won't last at all, because we get emptier. Rabbit turns from the window and everywhere in his own house sees a slippery disposable gloss. It glints back at him from the synthetic fabric of the living-room sofa and chair, the synthetic artiness of a lamp Janice bought that has a piece of driftwood weighted and wired as its base, the unnatural-looking natural wood of the shelves empty but for a few ashtrays with the sheen of fairgrounds souvenirs; it glints back at him from the steel sink, the kitchen linoleum with its whorls as of madness, oil in water, things don't mix. The window above the sink is black and as opaque as the orange that paints the asylum windows. He sees mirrored in it his own wet hands. Underwater. He crumples the aluminum beer can he has absentmindedly drained. Its contents feel metallic inside him: corrosive, fattening. Things don't mix. His inability to fasten onto any thought and make something of it must be fatigue. Rabbit lifts himself up the stairs, pushes himself through the underwater motions of undressing and dental care, sinks into bed without bothering to turn out the lights downstairs and in the bathroom. He hears from a mournful smothered radio noise that Nelson is still awake. He thinks he should get up and say good night, give the kid a blessing, but a weight crushes him while light persists into his bedroom, along with the boy's soft knocking noises, opening and shutting doors, looking for something to do. Since infancy Rabbit sleeps best when others are up, upright like nails holding down the world, like lamp-posts, street-signs, dandelion stems, cobwebs ...

Something big slithers into the bed: Janice. The fluorescent dial on the bureau is saying five of eleven, its two hands merged into one finger. She is warm in her nightie. Skin is warmer than cotton. He was dreaming about a parabolic curve, trying to steer on it, though the thing he was trying to steer was fighting him, like a broken sled.

"Get it untangled?" he asks her.

"Just about. I'm so sorry, Harry. Daddy came back and he just wouldn't let us go."

"Catch a nigger by the toe," he mumbles.

"What sort of evening did you and Nelson have?"

"A kind of nothing sort of evening."

"Anybody call?"

"Nobody."

He senses she is, late as it is, alive, jazzed up, and wants to talk, apologetic, wanting to make it up. Her being in the bed changes its quality, from a resisting raft he is seeking to hold to a curving course to a nest, a laden hollow, itself curved. Her hand seeks him out and he brushes her away with an athlete's old instinct to protect that spot. She turns then her back on him. He accepts this rejection. He nestles against her. Her waist where no bones are nips in like a bird dipping. He had been afraid marrying her she would get fat like her mother but as she ages more and more her skinny little stringy go-getter of a father comes out in her. His hand leaves the dip to stray around in front to her belly, faintly lovably loose from having had two babies. Puppy's neck. Should he have let her have had another to replace the one that died? Maybe that was the mistake. It had all seemed like a pit to him then, her womb and the grave, sex and death, he had fled her cunt like a tiger's mouth. His fingers search lower, touch tendrils, go lower, discover a moistness already there. He thinks of feathering the Linotype keys, of work tomorrow, and is already there.

The Verity Press lives on order forms, tickets to fund-raising dances, political posters in the fall, high-school yearbooks in the spring, throwaway fliers for the supermarkets, junk-mail sales announcements. On its rotary press it prints a weekly, *The Brewer*

Vat, which specializes in city scandal since the two dailies handle all the hard local and syndicated national news. Once it also published a German-language journal, *Der Schockelschtuhl*, founded 1830. In Rabbit's time here they had let it die, its circulation thinned down to a few thousand farmers in odd corners of the county and counties around. Rabbit remembers it because it meant the departure from the shop of old Kurt Schrack, one of those dark scowling Germans with whiskers that look tattooed into the skin rather than growing out of it to be shaved. His hair was iron but his jaw was lead as he sat scowling in the corner that belonged only to him; he was paid just to proofread the Pennsylvania Dutch copy and hand-set it in the black-letter fonts no one else was allowed to touch. The borders, and the big ornamental letters used on the inside pages, had been carved of wood, blackened by a century of inky handling. Schrack would concentrate down into his work so hard he would look up at lunchtime and talk in German to Pajasek the Polish foreman, or to one of the two shop Negroes, or to one of the Angstroms. Schrack had been likable in that he had done something scrupulously that others could not do at all. Then one Monday he was let go and his corner was soon walled in for the engravers.

Der Schockelschtuhl has gone and the *Vat* itself keeps threatening to take its custom to one of the big offset plants in Philadelphia. You simply paste it up, ads and photos and type, and send it off. Over Verity hangs a future that belongs to cool processes, to photo-offset and beyond that to photo-composition, computerized television that throws thousands of letters a second onto film with never the kiss of metal, beamed by computers programmed even for hyphenation and runarounds; but just an offset press is upwards of thirty thousand dollars and flatbed letterpress remains the easiest way to do tickets and posters. And the *Vat* might fold up any week. It is certainly a superfluous newspaper.

BREWER FACTORY TOOLS COMPONENT HEADED TOWARD MOON, is this week's front-page story. Rabbit sets, two-column measure, his white fingers feathering, the used matrices dropping back into their channels above his head like rain onto tin.

When Brewerites this Sunday gaze up at the moon, it may look a little bit different to them.

Why?
Because there's going to be a little bit of Brewer on

No. Widow. He tries to take it back but the line is too tight to close so he settles for the widow.

it.
    Zigzag Electronic Products Inc., of Seventh and Locust Streets, City,

Oops.

Locust Streets, city, revealed to VAT reporters this week that a crucial electronic switching sequence in the on-board guidance and nabifiation computer was the on-board guidance and navigation computer was manufactured by them here, in the plain brick building, once the cite if Gossamer Ho؛irey Co, that thouing, once the site of Gossamer Hosiery Co., that thousands of Brewer citizens walk unknowingly by each day.
    If the printed circuits of their switches—half the size of a postage stamp and weighing less than a sunflower seed—fail to function, astronauts Armstrong, Aldrin and Collin will drift past the moon and perish in the infinite vacuum of so-called ''deep space.''
    But there is no danger of that, Zigzag Electronics general manager Leroy ''Spin'' Lengel assured the

Jump after twenty lines. Switch to single-column lines.

VAT reporter in his highly modern, light-green office.
    ''It was just another job to us,'' he said. ''We do a hundred like it every week.
    ''Naturally all of us at Zigzag are proud as punch,'' Lengel added. ''We're sailinggeatoin added. ''We're sailing on a new sea.''

The machine stands tall and warm above him, mothering, muttering, a temperamental thousand-parted survival from the golden age of machinery. The sorts tray is on his right hand; the Star Quadder and the mold disc and slug tray on his left; a green-shaded light bulb at the level of his eyes. Above this sun the machine shoulders into shadow like a thunderhead, its matrix return rod spiralling idly, all these rustling sighing tons of

intricately keyed mass waiting for the feather-touch of his intelligence. Behind the mold disc the molten lead waits; sometimes
when there is a jam the lead squirts out hot: Harry has been
burned. But the machine is a baby; its demands, though inflexible, are few, and once these demands are met obedience automatically follows. There is no problem of fidelity. Do for it, it does
for you. And Harry loves the light here. It is cream to his eyes, this
even bluish light that nowhere casts a shadow, light so calm and
fine you can read glinting letters backwards at a glance. It contrasts
to the light in his home, where standing at the kitchen sink he casts
a shadow that looks like dirt over the dishes, and sitting in the living room he must squint against the bridge lamp Janice uses to read
magazines by, and bulbs keep burning out on the stair landing, and
the kid complains except when it's totally dark about the reflections on the television screen. In the big room of Verity Press,
ceilinged with fluorescent tubes, men move around as spirits,
without shadows.

At the ten-thirty coffee break Pop comes over and asks, "Think
you can make it over this evening?"

"I don't know. Janice said something last night about taking
the kid to a movie. How's Mom?"

"As good as can be hoped."

"She mention Janice again?"

"Not last night, Harry. Not more than in passing at least."

The old man sidles closer, clutching his paper cup of coffee
tightly as if it held jewels. "Did you say anything to Janice?" he
asks. "Did you search her out any?"

"Search her out, what is she, on trial? I hardly saw her. She was
over at Springer's until late." Rabbit winces, in the perfect
light seeing his father's lips pinch in, his eyes slide fishily. Harry
elaborates: "Old man Springer kept her trying to untangle his
books until eleven, ever since he started selling Jap cars he's a
slavedriver."

Pop's pupils widen a hairline; his eyebrows lift a pica's width.
"I thought he and his missus were in the Poconos."

"The Springers? Who told you that?"

"I guess your mother, I forget who told her, Julia Arndt maybe.
Maybe it was last week. Mrs. Springer's legs they say can't take the

heat, they swell up. I don't know what to tell you about growing old, Harry; it isn't all it's cracked up to be."

"The Poconos."

"It must have been last week they said. Your mother will be disappointed if you can't come over tonight, what shall I tell her?"

The bell rings, ending the break; Buchanan slouches by, wiping his morning shot of whisky from his lips, and winks. "Daddy knows best," he calls playfully. He is a sleek black seal.

Harry says, "Tell her we'll try after supper but we've promised the kid a movie and probably can't. Maybe Friday." His father's face, disappointed and unaccusing, angers him so he explodes: "Goddammit Pop I have a family of my own to run! I can't do everything." He returns to his machine gratefully. And it fits right around him, purrs while he brushes a word from his mind ("Poconos"), makes loud rain when he touches the keys, is pleased he is back.

Janice is home when he comes back from work. The Falcon is in the garage. The little house is hazed by her cigarette smoke; a half-empty glass of vermouth sits on top of the television set and another on one of the shelves between the living room and the breakfast nook. Rabbit calls, "Janice!" Though the house is small and echoing, so that the click of the television knob, the unstoppering of a bottle, the creaking of Nelson's bedsprings can be heard anywhere, there is no answer. He hears steady tumbling water, climbs the stairs. The upstairs bathroom is packed with steam. Amazing, how hot women can stand water.

"Harry, you've just let a lot of cold air in."

She is shaving her legs in the tub and several small cuts are brightly bleeding. Though Janice was never a knockout, with something sullen and stunted and tight about her face, and a short woman in the decade of the big female balloons Hollywood sent up before it died, she always had nice legs and still does. Taut perky legs with a bony kneecap that Rabbit has always liked; he likes to see the bones in people. His wife is holding one soaped leg up as if for display and he sees through the steam the gray soap-curdled water slopping in and out and around her pussy and belly and bottom as she reaches to shave the ankle, and he is standing at the top of a stairway of the uncountable other baths he has heard her take or seen her have in the thirteen years of their marriage. He can keep count of these years because their marriage is seven months older than their child. He asks, "Where's Nelson?"

"He's gone with Billy Fosnacht to Brewer to look at mini-bikes."

"I don't want him looking at mini-bikes. He'll get killed." The other child his daughter was killed. The world is quicksand. Find the straight path and stick to it.

"Oh Harry, it won't do any harm to look. Billy has one he rides all the time."

"I can't afford it."

"He's promised to earn half the money himself. I'll give him our half out of *my* money, if you're so uptight." Her money: her father gave her stocks years ago. And she earns money now. Does she need him at all? She asks, "Are you sure you closed the door? There's a terrible draft suddenly. There's not much privacy in this house, is there?"

"Well Jesus how much privacy do you think I owe you?"

"Well you don't have to stand there staring, you've seen me take a bath before."

"Well I haven't seen you with your clothes off since I don't know when. You're O.K."

"I'm just a cunt, Harry. There are billions of us now."

A few years ago she would never have said "cunt." It excites him, touches him like a breath on his cock. The ankle she is reaching to shave starts to bleed, suddenly, brightly, shockingly. "God," he tells her, "you are clumsy."

"Your standing there staring makes me nervous."

"Why're you taking a bath right now anyway?"

"We're going out to supper, remember? If we're going to make the movie at eight o'clock we ought to leave here at six. You should wash off your ink. Want to use my water?"

"It's all full of blood and little hairs."

"Harry, really. You've gotten so uptight in your old age."

Again, "uptight." Not her voice, another voice, another voice in hers.

Janice goes on, "The tank hasn't had time to heat enough for a fresh tub."

"O.K. I'll use yours."

His wife gets out, water spilling on the bathmat, her feet and buttocks steamed rosy. Her breasts sympathetically lift as she lifts her hair from the nape of her neck. "Want to dry my back?"

He can't remember the last time she asked him to do this. As he rubs, her smallness mixes with the absolute bigness naked women have. The curve that sways out from her waist to be swelled by the fat of her flank. Rabbit squats to dry her bottom, goosebumpy red. The backs of her thighs, the stray black hairs, the moss moist between. "O.K.," she says, and steps off. He stands to pat dry the down beneath the sweep of her upheld hair: Nature is full of nests. She asks, "Where do you want to eat?"

"Oh, anywhere. The kid likes the Burger Bliss over on West Weiser."

"I was wondering, there's a new Greek restaurant just across the bridge I'd love to try. Charlie Stavros was talking about it the other day."

"Yeah. Speaking of the other day —"

"He says they have marvellous grape leaf things and shish kebab Nelson would like. If we don't make him do something new he'll be eating at Burger Bliss the rest of his life."

"The movie starts at seven-thirty, you know."

"I *know*," she says, "that's why I took a bath *now*," and, a new Janice, still standing with her back to him, nestles her bottom against his fly, lifting herself on tiptoe and arching her back to make a delicate double damp spreading contact. His mind softens; his prick hardens. "Besides," Janice is going on, edging herself on tiptoes up and down like a child gently chanting to Banbury Cross, "the movie isn't just for Nelson, it's for *me*, for working so hard all week."

There was a question he was about to ask, but her caress erased it. She straightens, saying, "Hurry, Harry. The water will get cold." Two damp spots are left on the front of his suntans. The muggy bathroom has drugged him; when she opens the door to their bedroom, the contrast of cold air cakes him; he sneezes. Yet he leaves the door open while he undresses so he can watch her dress. She is practiced, quick; rapidly as a snake shrugs forward over the sand she has tugged her black pantyhose up over her legs. She nips to the closet for her skirt, to the bureau for her blouse, the frilly silvery one, that he thought was reserved for parties. Testing the tub with his foot (too hot) he remembers.

"Hey Janice. Somebody said today your parents were in the Poconos. Last night you said your father was at the lot."

She halts in the center of their bedroom, staring into the bathroom. Her dark eyes darken the more; she sees his big white body, his spreading slack gut, his uncircumcised member hanging boneless as a rooster comb from its blond roots. She sees her flying athlete grounded, cuckolded. She sees a large white man a knife would slice like lard. The angelic cold strength of his leaving her, the anticlimax of his coming back and clinging: there is something in the combination that she cannot forgive, that justifies her. Her eyes must burn on him, for he turns his back and begins to step into her water: his buttocks merge with her lover's, she thinks how all men look innocent and vulnerable here, reverting to the baby they were. She says firmly, "They were in the Poconos but came back early. Mom always thinks at these resorts she's being snubbed," and without waiting for an answer to her lie runs downstairs.

While soaking in the pool tinged by her hair and blood Rabbit hears Nelson come into the house. Voices rise muffled through the ceiling. "What a crummy mini-bike," the child announces. "It's busted already."

Janice says, "Then aren't you glad it isn't yours?"

"Yeah, but there's a more expensive kind, really neat, a Gioconda, that Grandpa could get at discount for us so it wouldn't cost any more than the cheap one."

"Your father and I agree, two hundred dollars is too much for a toy."

"It's *not* a toy, Mom, it's something I could really learn about engines on. And you can get a license and Daddy could drive it to work some days instead of taking a bus all the time."

"Daddy likes taking the bus."

"I hate it!" Rabbit yells, "it stinks of *Neg*roes," but no voice below in the kitchen acknowledges hearing him.

* * *

Throughout the evening he has this sensation of nobody hearing him, of his spirit muffled in pulpy insulation, so he talks all the louder and more insistently. Driving the car (even with his flag decal the Falcon feels more like Janice's car than his, she drives it so much more) back down Emberly to Weiser, past the movie house and across the bridge, he says, "Goddammit I don't see why we have to go back into Brewer to eat, I spend all frigging day in Brewer."

"Nelson agrees with me," Janice says. "It will be an interesting experiment. I've promised him there are lots of things that aren't gooey, it's not like Chinese food."

"We're going to be late for the movie, I'm sure of it."

"Peggy Fosnacht says —" Janice begins.

"That dope," Rabbit says.

"Peggy Fosnacht says the beginning is the most boring part. A lot of stars, and some symphony. Anyway there must be short subjects or at least those things that want you to go out into the lobby and buy more candy."

Nelson says, "I heard the beginning is real neat. There's a lot of cave men eating meat that's really raw, he nearly threw up a guy at school said, and then you see one of them get really zapped with a bone. And they throw the bone up and it turns into a spaceship."

"Thank you, Mr. Spoil-It-All," Janice says. "I feel I've seen it now. Maybe you two should go to the movie and I'll go home to bed."

"The hell," Rabbit says. "You stick right with us and suffer for once."

Janice says, conceding, "Women don't dig science."

Harry likes the sensation, of frightening her, of offering to confront outright this faceless unknown he feels now in their lives, among them like a fourth member of the family. The baby that died? But though Janice's grief was worse at first, though she bent under it like a reed he was afraid might break, in the long years since, he has become sole heir to the grief. Since he refused to get her pregnant again the murder and guilt have become all his. At first he tried to explain how it was, that sex with her had become too dark, too *serious*, too kindred to death, to trust anything that might come out of it. Then he stopped explaining and she seemed to forget: like a cat who sniffs around in corners mewing for the drowned kittens a day or two and then back to lapping milk and napping in the wash basket. Women and Nature forget. Just thinking of the baby, remembering how he had been told of her death over a pay phone in a drugstore, puts a kink in his chest, a kink he still associates, dimly, with God.

At Janice's directions he turns right off the bridge, at JIMBO's *Friendly* LOUNGE, and after a few blocks parks on Quince Street. He locks the car behind them. "This is pretty slummy territory," he complains to Janice. "A lot of rapes lately down here."

"Oh," she says, "the *Vat* prints nothing but rapes. You know what a rape usually is? It's a woman who changed her mind afterward."

"Watch how you talk in front of the kid."

"He knows more now than you ever will. That's nothing personal, Harry, it's just a fact. People are more sophisticated now than when you were a boy."

"How about when you were a girl?"

"I was very dumb and innocent, I admit it."

"But?"

"But nothing."

"I thought you were going to tell us how wise you are now."

"I'm not wise, but at least I've tried to keep my mind open."

Nelson, walking a little ahead of them but hearing too much anyway, points to the great Sunflower Beer clock on Weiser Square, which they can see across slate rooftops and a block of rubble on its way to being yet another parking lot. "It's twenty after six," he says. He adds, not certain his point was made, "At Burger Bliss they serve you right away, it's neat, they keep them warm in a big oven that glows purple."

"No Burger Bliss for you, baby," Harry says. "Try Pizza Paradise."

"Don't be ignorant," Janice says, "pizza is purely Italian." To Nelson she says, "We have plenty of time, there won't be anybody there this early."

"Where *is* it?" he asks.

"Right here," she says; she has led them without error.

The place is a brick row house, its red bricks painted ox-blood red in the Brewer manner. A small un-neon sign advertises it, The Taverna. They walk up sandstone steps to the doorway, and a motherly mustached woman greets them, shows them into what once was a front parlor, now broken through to the room beyond, the kitchen behind swinging doors beyond that. A few center tables. Booths along the two walls. White walls bare but for some picture of an oval-faced yellow woman and baby with a candle flickering in front of it. Janice slides into one side of a booth and Nelson into the other and Harry, forced to choose, slides in beside Nelson, to help him with the menu, to find something on it enough like a hamburger. The tablecloth is a red checked cloth and the daisies in a blue glass vase are real flowers, soft, Harry notices, touching them. Janice was right. The place is nice. The only music is a radio playing in the kitchen; the only other customers are a couple talking so earnestly they now and then touch hands, immersed in some element where they cannot trust their eyes, the man red in the face as if choking, the woman stricken pale. They are Penn Park types, cool in their clothes, beige and pencil-gray, the right clothes insofar as any clothes can be right in this muggy river-bottom in the middle of July. Their faces have an edgy money look: their brows have that frontal clarity the shambling blurred poor can never duplicate. Though he can never now be one of them Harry likes their being here, in this restaurant so chaste it is *chic*. Maybe Brewer isn't as dead on its feet as it seems.

The menus are in hectographed handwriting. Nelson's face tightens, studying it. "They don't have any sandwiches," he says.

"Nelson," Janice says, "if you make a fuss out of this I'll never take you out anywhere again. Be a big boy."

"It's all in gobbledy-gook."

She explains, "Everything is more or less lamb. *Kebab* is when it's on a skewer. *Moussaka*, it's mixed with eggplant."

"I *hate* eggplant."

Rabbit asks her, "How do you know all this?"

"Everybody knows that much; Harry, you are so pro*vin*cial. The two of you, sitting there side by side, determined to be miserable. Ugly Americans."

"You don't look all that Chinese yourself," Harry says, "even in your little Lord Fauntleroy blouse." He glances down at his fingertips and sees there an ochre smudge of pollen, from having touched the daisies.

Nelson asks, "What's *kalamaria?*"

"I don't know," Janice says.

"I want that."

"You don't know what you want. Have the *souvlakia*, it's the simplest. It's pieces of meat on a skewer, very well done, with peppers and onions between."

"I *hate* pepper."

Rabbit tells him, "Not the stuff that makes you sneeze, the green things like hollow tomatoes."

"I know," Nelson says. "I hate them. I know what a *pep*per is, Daddy; my *God*."

"Don't swear like that. When did you ever have them?"

"In a Pepperburger."

"Maybe you should take him to Burger Bliss and leave me here," Janice says.

Rabbit asks, "What are *you* going to have, if you're so fucking smart?"

"Daddy swore."

"Ssh," Janice says, "both of you. There's a nice kind of chicken pie, but I forget what it's called."

"You've been here before," Rabbit tells her.

"I want *melopeta*," Nelson says.

Rabbit sees where the kid's stubby finger (Mom always used to point out, he has those little Springer hands) is stalled on the menu and tells him, "Dope, that's a dessert."

Shouts of greeting announce in the doorway a large family all black hair and smiles, initiates; the waiter greets them as a son and rams a table against a booth to make space for them all. They cackle their language, they giggle, they coo, they swell with the joy of arrival. Their chairs scrape, their children stare demure and big-eyed from under the umbrella of adult noise. Rabbit feels naked in his own threadbare little family. The Penn Park couple very slowly turn around, underwater, at the commotion, and then resume, she now blushing, he pale – contact, touching hands on the tablecloth, groping through the stems of wineglasses. The Greek flock settles to roost but there is one man left over, who must have entered with them but hesitates in the doorway. Rabbit knows him. Janice refuses to turn her head; she keeps her eyes on the menu, frozen so they don't seem to read. Rabbit murmurs to her, "There's Charlie Stavros."

"Oh, really?" she says, yet she still is reluctant to turn her head.

But Nelson turns his and loudly calls out, "Hi, Charlie!" Summers, the kid spends a lot of time over at the lot.

Stavros, who has such bad and sensitive eyes his glasses are tinted lilac, focuses. His face breaks into the smile he must use at the close of a sale, a sly tuck in one corner of his lips making a dimple. He is a squarely marked-off man, Stavros, some inches shorter than Harry, some years younger, but with a natural reserve of potent gravity that gives him the presence and poise of an older person. His hairline is receding. His eyebrows go straight across. He moves deliberately, as if carrying something fragile within him; in his Madras checks and his rectangular thick hornrims and his deep squared sideburns he moves through the world with an air of having chosen it. His not having married, though he is in his thirties, adds to his quality of deliberation. Rabbit, when he sees him, always likes him more than he had intended to. He reminds him of the guys, close-set, slow, and never rattled, who were play-makers on the team. When Stavros, taking thought, moves around the obstacle of momentary indecision toward their booth, it is Harry who says, "Join us," though Janice, face downcast, has already slid over.

Charlie speaks to Janice. "The whole caboodle. Beautiful."

She says, "These two are being horrible."

Rabbit says, "We can't read the menu."

Nelson says, "Charlie, what's *kalamaria?* I want some."

"No you don't. It's little like octopuses cooked in their own ink."

"Ick," Nelson says.

"Nelson," Janice says sharply.

Rabbit says, "Sit yourself down, Charlie."

"I don't want to butt in."

"It'd be a favor. Hell."

"Dad's being grumpy," Nelson confides.

Janice impatiently pats the place beside her; Charlie sits down and asks her, "What *does* the kid like?"

"Hamburgers," Janice moans, theatrically. She's become an actress suddenly, every gesture and intonation charged to carry across an implied distance.

Charlie's squarish intent head is bowed above the menu.

"Let's get him some *keftedes*. O.K., Nelson? Meatballs."

"Not with tomatoey goo on them."

"No goo, just the meat. A little mint. Mint's what's in Life Savers. O.K.?"

"O.K."

"You'll love 'em."

But Rabbit feels the boy has been sold a slushy car. And he feels, with Stavros's broad shoulders next to Janice's, and the man's hands each sporting a chunky gold ring, that the table has taken a turn down a road Rabbit didn't choose. He and Nelson are in the back seat.

Janice says to Stavros, "Charlie, why don't you order for all of us? We don't know what we're doing."

Rabbit says, "*I* know what *I'm* doing. I'll order for myself. I want the" – he picks something off the menu at random – "the *païdakia*."

"*Païdakia*," Stavros says. "I don't think so. It's marinated lamb, you need to order it the day before, for at least six."

Nelson says, "Dad, the movie starts in forty minutes."

Janice explains, "We're trying to get to see this silly space movie."

Stavros nods as if he knows. There is a funny echo Rabbit's ears pick up. Things said between Janice and Stavros sound dead, duplicated. Of course they work together all day. Stavros tells them, "It's lousy."

"Why is it lousy?" Nelson asks anxiously. There is a look his face gets, bloating his lips and slightly sucking his eyes back into their sockets, that hasn't changed since his infancy, when his bottle would go dry.

Stavros relents. "Nellie, for you it'll be great. It's all toys. For me, it just wasn't sexy. I guess I don't find technology that sexy."

"Does everything *have* to be sexy?" Janice asks.

"It doesn't have to be, it tends to be," Stavros tells her. To Rabbit he says, "Have some *souvlakia*. You'll love it, and it's quick." And in an admirable potent little gesture, he moves his hand, palm outward as if his fingers had been snapped, without lifting his elbow from the table, and the motherly woman comes running to them.

"*Yasou.*"

"*Kale spera*," she answers.

While Stavros orders in Greek, Harry studies Janice, her peculiar glow. Time has been gentle to her. As if it felt sorry for her. The something pinched and mean about her mouth, that she had even in her teens, has been relaxed by the appearance of other small wrinkles in her face, and her hair, whose sparseness once annoyed him, as another emblem of his poverty, she now brings down over her ears from a central parting in two smooth wings. She wears no lipstick and in certain lights her face possesses a gypsy severity and the dignity present in newspaper photographs of female guerrilla fighters. The gypsy look she got from her mother, the dignity from the Sixties, which freed her from the need to look fluffy. Plain is beautiful enough. And now she is all circles in happiness, squirming on her round bottom and dancing her hands through arcs of exaggeration quick white in the candlelight. She tells Stavros, "If you hadn't shown up we would have starved."

"No," he says, a reassuring factual man. "They would have taken care of you. These are nice people."

"*These* two," she says, "are so American, they're helpless."

"Yeah," Stavros says to Rabbit, "I see the decal you put on your old Falcon."

"I told Charlie," Janice tells Rabbit, "*I* certainly didn't put it there."

"What's wrong with it?" he asks them both. "It's our flag, isn't it?"

"It's somebody's flag," Stavros says, not liking this trend and softly bouncing his fingertips together under his sheltered bad eyes.

"But not yours, huh?"

"Harry gets fanatical about this," Janice warns.

"I don't get fanatical, I just get a little sad about people who come over here to make a fat buck —"

"I was born here," Stavros quickly says. "So was my father."

"— and then knock the fucking flag," Rabbit continues, "like it's some piece of toilet paper."

"A flag is a flag. It's just a piece of cloth."

"It's more than just a piece of cloth to me."

"What is it to you?"

"It's —"

"The mighty Mississippi."

"It's people not finishing my sentences all the time."

"Just half the time."

"That's better than all the time like they have in China."

"Look. The Mississippi is very broad. The Rocky Mountains really swing. I just can't get too turned-on about cops bopping hippies on the head and the Pentagon playing cowboys and Indians all over the globe. That's what your little sticker means to me. It means screw the blacks and send the CIA into Greece."

"If we don't send somebody in the other side sure as hell will, the Greeks can't seem to manage the show by themselves."

"Harry, don't make yourself ridiculous, they invented civilization," Janice says. To Stavros she says, "See how little and tight his mouth gets when he thinks about politics."

"I don't *think* about politics," Rabbit says. "That's one of my Goddam precious American rights, not to think about politics. I just don't see why we're supposed to walk down the street with our hands tied behind our back and let ourselves be blackjacked by every thug who says he has a revolution going. And it really burns me up to listen to hotshot crap-car salesmen dripping with Vitalis sitting on their plumped-up asses bitching about a country that's been stuffing goodies into their mouth ever since they were born."

Charlie makes to rise. "I better go. This is getting too rich."

"Don't go," Janice begs. "He doesn't know what he's saying. He's sick on the subject."

"Yeah, don't go, Charlie, stick around and humor the madman."

Charlie lowers himself again and states in measured fashion, "I want to follow your reasoning. Tell me about the goodies we've been stuffing into Vietnam."

"Christ, exactly. We'd turn it into another Japan if they'd let us. That's all we want to do, make a happy rich country full of highways and gas stations. Poor old LBJ, Jesus, with tears in his eyes on television, you must have heard him, he just about offered to make North Vietnam the fifty-first fucking state of the damn Union if they'd just stop throwing bombs. We're begging them to rig some elections, any elections, and they'd rather throw bombs. What more can we do? We're trying to give ourselves away, that's all our foreign policy is, is trying to give ourselves away to make little yellow people happy, and guys like you sit around in restaurants moaning, 'Jesus, we're rotten.' "

"I thought it was us and not them throwing the bombs."

"We've stopped; we stopped like all you liberals were marching for and what did it get us?" He leans forward to pronounce the answer clearly. "Not shit."

The whispering couple across the room look over in surprise; the family two booths away have hushed their noise to listen. Nelson is desperately blushing, his eyes sunk hot and hurt in his sockets. "Not shit," Harry repeats more softly. He leans over the tablecloth, beside the trembling daisies. "Now I suppose you're going to say 'napalm.' That frigging magic word. They've been burying village chiefs alive and tossing mortars into hospitals for twenty years, and because of napalm they're candidates for the Albert F. Schweitzer peace prize. S, H, it." He has gotten loud again; it makes him frantic, the thoughts of the treachery and ingratitude befouling the flag, befouling him.

"Harry, you'll get us kicked out," Janice says; but he notices she is still happy, all in circles, a cookie in the oven.

"I'm beginning to dig him," Stavros tells her. "If I get your meaning," he says to Rabbit, "we're the big mama trying to make this unruly kid take some medicine that'll be good for him."

"That's right. You got it. We are. And most of 'em *want* to take the medicine, they're dying for it, and a few madmen in black pajamas would rather bury 'em alive. What's your theory? That we're in it for the rice? The Uncle Ben theory." Rabbit laughs and adds, "Bad old Uncle Ben."

"No," Stavros says, squaring his hands on the checked table-cloth and staring level-browed at the base of Harry's throat – gingerly with him, Harry notices: Why? – "my theory is it's a mistaken power play. It isn't that we want the rice, we don't want *them* to have it. Or the magnesium. Or the coastline. We've been playing chess with the Russians so long we didn't know we were off the board. White faces don't work in yellow countries any-more. Kennedy's advisers who thought they could run the world from the dean's office pushed the button and nothing happened. Then Oswald voted Johnson in who was such a bonehead he thought all it took was a bigger thumb on the button. So the machine overheated, you got inflation and a falling market at one end and college riots at the other and in the middle forty thousand sons of American mothers killed by shit-smeared bamboo. People don't like having Sonny killed in the jungle anymore. Maybe they never liked it, but they used to think it was necessary."

"And it isn't?"

Stavros blinks. "I see. You say war has to be."

"Yeah, and better there than here. Better little wars than big ones."

Stavros says, his hands on edge, ready to chop, "But you *like* it." His hands chop. "Burning up gook babies is right where you're at, friend." The "friend" is weak.

Rabbit asks him, "How did you do your Army bit?"

Stavros shrugs, squares his shoulders. "I was 4-F. Tricky ticker. I hear you sat out the Korean thing in Texas."

"I went where they told me. I'd still go where they told me."

"Bully for you. You're what made America great. A real gun-slinger."

"He's silent majority," Janice says, "but he keeps making noise," looking at Stavros hopefully, for a return on her quip. God, she is dumb, even if her ass has shaped up in middle age.

"He's a normal product," Stavros says. "He's a typical good-hearted imperialist racist." Rabbit knows, from the careful level way this is pronounced, with that little tuck of a sold-car smile, that he is being flirted with, asked – his dim feeling is – for an alliance. But Rabbit is locked into his intuition that to describe any of America's actions as a "power play" is to miss the point.

America is beyond power, it acts as in a dream, as a face of God. Wherever America is, there is freedom, and wherever America is not, madness rules with chains and darkness strangles millions. Beneath her patient bombers, paradise is possible. He fights back, "I don't follow this racist rap. You can't turn on television now without some black face spitting at you. Everybody from Nixon down is sitting up nights trying to figure out how to make 'em all rich without putting 'em to the trouble of doing any work." His tongue is reckless; but he is defending something infinitely tender, the low flame of loyalty lit with his birth. "They talk about genocide when *they're* the ones planning it, they're the ones, the Negroes plus the rich kids, who want to pull it all down; not that they can't run squealing for a lawyer whenever some poor cop squints funny at 'em. The Vietnam war in my opinion – anybody want my opinion? –"

"Harry," Janice says, "you're making Nelson miserable."

"My opinion is, you have to fight a war now and then to show you're willing, and it doesn't much matter where it is. The trouble isn't this war, it's this country. We wouldn't fight in Korea now. Christ, we wouldn't fight Hitler now. This country is so zonked out on its own acid, sunk so deep in its own fat and babble and laziness, it would take H-bombs on every city from Detroit to Atlanta to wake us up and even then, we'd probably think we'd just been kissed."

"Harry," Janice asks, "do you want Nelson to die in Vietnam? Go ahead, tell him you do."

Harry turns to their child and says, "Kid, I don't want you to die anyplace. Your mother's the girl that's good at death."

Even he knows how cruel this is; he is grateful to her for not collapsing, for blazing up instead. "*Oh*," she says. "Oh. Tell him why he has no brothers or sisters, Harry. Tell him who refused to have another child."

"This is getting too rich," Stavros says.

"I'm glad you're seeing it," Janice tells him, her eyes sunk deep; Nelson gets that from her.

Mercifully, the food arrives. Nelson balks, discovering the meatballs drenched in gravy. He looks at Rabbit's tidily skewered lamb and says, "That's what I wanted."

"Let's swap then. Shut up and eat," Rabbit says. He looks across to see that Janice and Stavros are having the same thing, a kind of white pie. They are sitting, to his printer's sense, too close, leaving awkward space on either side. To poke them into adjustment he says, "I think it's a swell country."

Janice takes it up, Stavros chewing in silence. "Harry, you've never *been* to any other country."

He addresses himself to Stavros. "Never had the desire to. I see these other countries on TV, they're all running like hell to be like us, and burning our Embassies because they can't make it fast enough. What other countries do *you* get to?"

Stavros interrupts his eating grudgingly to utter, "Jamaica."

"Wow," Rabbit says. "A real explorer. Three hours by jet to the lobby of some Hilton."

"They hate us down there."

"You mean they hate *you*. They never see *me*, I never go. Why do they hate us?"

"Same reason as everywhere. Exploitation. We steal their bauxite."

"Let 'em trade it to the Russkis for potatoes then. Potatoes and missile sites."

"We have missile sites in Turkey," Stavros says, his heart no longer in this.

Janice tries to help. "We've dropped two atom bombs, the Russians haven't dropped any."

"They didn't have any then or they would have. Here the Japanese were all set to commit hari-kari and we saved them from it; now look at 'em, happy as clams and twice as sassy, screwing us right and left. We fight their wars for them while you peaceniks sell their tinny cars."

Stavros pats his mouth with a napkin folded squarely and regains his appetite for discussion. "Her point is, we wouldn't be in this Vietnam mess if it was a white country. We wouldn't have gone in. We thought we just had to shout Boo and flash a few jazzy anti-personnel weapons. We thought it was one more Cherokee uprising. The trouble is, the Cherokees outnumber us now."

"Oh those fucking poor Indians," Harry says. "What were we

supposed to do, let 'em have the whole continent for a campfire site?" Sorry, Tonto.

"If we had, it'd be in better shape than it is now."

"And we'd be nowhere. They were in the way."

"Fair enough," Stavros says. "Now you're in their way." He adds, "Paleface."

"Let 'em come," Rabbit says, and really is, at this moment, a defiant bastion. The tender blue flame has become cold fire in his eyes. He stares them down. He stares at Janice and she is dark and tense: an Indian squaw. He'd like to massacre her.

Then his son says, his voice strained upward through choked-down tears, "*Dad*, we're going to be *late* for the *mo*vie!"

Rabbit looks at his watch and sees they have four minutes to get there. The kid is right.

Stavros tries to help, fatherly like men who aren't fathers, who think kids can be fooled about essentials. "The opening part's the dullest, Nellie, you won't miss any of the space parts. You got to try some *baklava* for dessert."

"I'll miss the cave men," Nelson says, the choking almost complete, the tears almost risen.

"I guess we should go," Rabbit tells the two other adults.

"That's rude to Charlie," Janice says. "Really rude. Anyway I won't be able to stay awake during this *inter*minable movie without coffee." To Nelson: "*Baklava* is really yummy. It's honey and flakes of thin dough, just the kind of dry thing you love. Try to be considerate, Nelson, your parents so rarely get to eat in a restaurant."

Torn, Rabbit suggests, "Or you could try that other stuff you wanted for the main deal, mellow patties or whatever."

The tears do come; the kid's tense face breaks. "You *prom*ised," he sobs, unanswerably, and hides his face against the white bare wall.

"Nelson, I am disappointed in you," Janice tells him.

Stavros says to Rabbit, tucking that pencil behind his ear again, "If you want to run now, she could get her coffee and I'll drop her off at the movie house in ten minutes."

"That's a possibility," Janice says slowly, her face opening cautiously, a dull flower.

Rabbit tells Stavros, "O.K., great. Thanks. You're nice to do that. You're nice to put up with us at all, sorry if I said anything too strong. I just can't stand to hear the U.S. knocked, I'm sure it's psychological. Janice, do you have money? Charlie, you tell her how much we owe."

Stavros repeats that masterful small gesture of palm outward, "You owe zilch. On me." There can be no argument. Standing, himself in a hurry to see the cave men (raw meat? a bone turning into a spaceship?), Rabbit experiences, among them here, in this restaurant where the Penn Park couple are paying their bill as if laying a baby to rest, keen family happiness: it prompts him to say to Janice, to cheer Nelson up further, "Remind me tomorrow to call your father about those baseball tickets."

Before Janice can intervene, Stavros says, everybody anxious now to please, "He's in the Poconos."

Janice thought when Charlie calls Harry "paleface" it's the end, from the way Harry looked over at her, his eyes a frightening icy blue, and then when Charlie let that slip about Daddy being away she knew it was; but somehow it isn't. Maybe the movie numbs them. It's so long and then that psychedelic section where he's landing on the planet before turning into a little old man in a white wig makes her head hurt, but she rides home resolved to have it out, to confess and dare him to make his move back, all he can do is run which might be a relief. She has a glass of vermouth in the kitchen to ready herself, but upstairs Nelson is shutting the door to his room and Harry is in the bathroom and when she comes out of the bathroom with the taste of toothpaste on top of the vermouth Harry is lying under the covers with just the top of his head showing. Janice gets in beside him and listens. His breathing is a sleeping tide. So she lies there awake like the moon.

In their ten though it became twenty minutes over the coffee together she had told Charlie she had thought it reckless of him to come to the restaurant when he had known she was bringing them and he said, in that way he has of going onto his dignity, his lips pushing out as if holding a lozenge and the hunch of his shoulders a bit gangsterish, that he thought that's what she wanted, that's why she told him she was going to talk them into it. At the time she thought silently, he doesn't understand women in love, just going to his restaurant, eating food that was him, had been enough an act of love for her, he didn't have to make it dangerous by showing up himself. It even coarsened it. Because once he was physically there all her caution dissolved, if instead of having coffee with her he had asked her to go to his apartment with him she would have done it and was even mentally running through the story she would have told Harry about suddenly feeling sick. But luckily he didn't ask; he finished the coffee and paid the whole bill and dropped her off under the stumpy marquee as promised. Men are strict that way, want to keep their promises to each other, women are beneath it, property. The way while making love Charlie sells her herself, murmuring about her parts, giving them the names Harry uses only in anger, she resisted at first but relaxed seeing for Charlie they were a language of love, his way of keeping himself up, selling her her own cunt. She doesn't panic as with Harry, knowing he can't hold it much longer, Charlie holds back forever, a thick sweet toy she can do anything with, her teddy bear. The fur on the back of his shoulders at first shocked her touch, something freakish, but no, that's the way many men still are. Cave men. Cave bears. Janice smiles in the dark.

In the dark of the car driving over the bridge along Weiser he asked her if Harry guessed anything. She said she thought nothing. Though something had been bugging him the last couple of days, her staying so late supposedly at the office.

"Maybe we should cool it a little."

"Oh, let him stew. His old line on me used to be I was useless, at first he was delighted I got a job. Now he thinks I neglect Nelson. I say to him, 'Give the boy a little room, he's going on thirteen and you're leaning on him worse than your own mother.' He won't even let him get a mini-bike because it's too dangerous supposedly."

Charlie said, "He sure was hostile to me."

"Not really. He's like that about Vietnam with everybody. It's what he really thinks."

"How can he think that crap? We-them, America first. It's dead."

She tried to imagine how. One of the nice things about having a lover, it makes you think about everything anew. The rest
of your life becomes a kind of movie, flat and even rather funny.
She answered at last, "Something is very real to him about it, I
don't know what it is." She went on with difficulty, for a blurring, a halting, comes over her tongue, her head, whenever she
tries to think, and one of the many beautiful things about Charlie
Stavros is he lets her tumble it out anyway. He has given her not
only her body but her voice. "Maybe he came back to me, to
Nelson and me, for the old-fashioned reasons, and wants to live
an old-fashioned life, but nobody does that anymore, and he feels
it. He put his life into rules he feels melting away now. I mean, I
know he thinks he's missing something, he's always reading the
paper and watching the news."

Charlie laughed. The blue lights of the bridge flickered on the
backs of his hands parallel on the steering wheel. "I get it. You're
his overseas commitment."

She laughed too, but it seemed a little hard of him to say, to
make a joke of the marriage that was, after all, a part of her too.
Sometimes Charlie didn't quite listen. Her father was like that: a
hurry in their blood, wind in their ears. Getting ahead, you miss
what the slow people see.

Stavros sensed the little wound and tried to heal it, patting her
thigh as they arrived at the movie house. "Space odyssey," he said.
"My idea of a space odyssey would be to get in the sack with your
ass and ball for a week." And right here, with the light beneath the
marquee slanting into the car and the agitated last late shreds of the
audience buying their tickets, he ran his paw across her breasts and
tucked his thumb into her lap. Heated and ruffled by this touch
from him, guilty and late, she rushed into the movie house – its
plum carpeting, its unnatural coldness, its display-casket of candies
– and found Nelson and Harry down front, where they had had
to sit because of her, because she had made them late so she could
eat her lover's food, the great exploding screen close above them,
their hair on fire, their ears translucent red. The backs of their
heads, innocently alike, had sprung a rush of love within her, like
coming, a push of pity that sent her scrambling across the jagged
knees of strangers to the seat her husband and son had saved.

A car moves on the curved road outside. Rugs of light are hurled across the ceiling. The refrigerator below speaks to itself, drops its own ice into its own tray. Her body feels tense as a harp, she wants to be touched. She touches herself: hardly ever did it as a girl, after marrying Harry it seemed certainly wrong, marriage should make it never necessary, just turn to the other person and he would fix it. How sad it was with Harry now, they had become locked rooms to each other, they could hear each other cry but couldn't get in, not just the baby though that was terrible, the most terrible thing ever, but even that had faded, flattened, until it seemed it hadn't been her in that room but an image of her, and she had not been alone, there had been some man in the room with her, he was with her now, not Charlie but containing Charlie, everything you do is done in front of this man and how good to have him made flesh. She imagines it in her, like something you have swallowed. Only big, big. And slow, slow as sugar melts. Except now that she'd been with him so many times she could be quick in coming, sometimes asking him just to pound away and startling herself, coming, herself her toy, how strange to have to learn to play, they used to tell her, everybody, the gym teacher, the Episcopal minister, Mother even one awful embarrassing time, not to make your body a plaything when that's just what it was, she wonders if Nelson, his bedsprings creaking, his little jigger waiting for its hair, poor child, what would he think, what must he think, such a lonely life, sitting there alone at the TV when she comes home, his mini-bike, she's lost it. Though she flutters it faster she's lost it, her heat. How silly. How silly it all is. We're born and they try to feed us and change our diapers and love us and we get breasts and menstruate and go boy-crazy and finally one or two come forward to touch us and we can't wait to get married and have some babies and then stop having them and go man-crazy this time without even knowing it until you're in too deep the flesh grows more serious as we age and then eventually that phase must be over and we ride around in cars in flowered hats for a while to Tucson or seeing the leaves turn in New Hampshire and visit our grandchildren and then get into bed like poor Mrs. Angstrom, Harry is always after her to visit her but she doesn't see why she should she never had a good word to say for her when she was healthy, groping for words while her mouth makes spittle and her eyes trying to pop from her head trying to hear herself say something malicious, and then there's the nursing home or the hospital, poor old souls like when they used to visit her father's older sister, TVs going all up and down the hall and Christmas decorations dropping needles on the linoleum, and then we die and it wouldn't have mattered if we hadn't bothered to be born at all. And all the time there are wars and riots and history happening but it's not as important as the newspapers say unless you get caught in it. Harry seems right to her about that, Vietnam or Korea or the Philippines nobody cares about them yet they must be died for, it just is that way, by boys that haven't shaved yet, the other side has boys Nelson's age. How strange it is of Charlie to care so, to be so angry, as if he's a minority, which of course he is, her father used to talk of gang fights when he was in school, us against them, Springer an English name, Daddy very proud of that, then why, she used to ask herself at school, was she so dark, olive skin, never sunburned, hair that always frizzed up and never lay flat in bangs, never knew enough until recently to let it grow long in front and pin it back, his fucking madonna Charlie calls her blasphemously though there is an ikon in his bedroom, didn't have enough body in school, but she forgives those days now, sees she was being shaped, all those years, toward Charlie. His cunt. His rich cunt, though they were never rich just respectable, Daddy gave her a little stock to put away the time Harry was acting so irresponsible, the dividend checks come in, the envelopes with windows, she doesn't like Harry to see them, they make light of his working. Janice wants to weep, thinking of how hard Harry has worked these years. His mother used to say how hard he used to work practicing basketball, dribbling, shooting; whereas she said so spitefully Nelson has no aptitude. This is silly. This thinking is getting nowhere, there is tomorrow to face, must have it out with Harry, Charlie shrugs when she asks what to do, at lunch if Daddy isn't back from the Poconos they can go over to Charlie's apartment, the light used to embarrass her but she likes it best in the day now, you can see everything, men's bottoms so innocent, even the little hole like a purse drawn tight, the hair downy and dark, all the sitting they do, the world isn't natural for them any more: this is silly. Determined to bring herself off, Janice returns her hand and opens her eyes to look at Harry sleeping, all huddled into himself, stupid of him to keep her sex locked up all these years, his fault, all his fault, it was there all along, it was his job to call it out, she does everything for Charlie because he asks her, it feels holy, she doesn't care, you have to live, they put you here you have to live, you were made for one thing, women now try to deny it burning their bras but you were made for one thing, it feels like a falling, a falling away, a deep eye opening, a coming into the deep you, Harry wouldn't know about that, he never did dare dwell on it, racing ahead, he's too fastidious, hates sex really, she was there all along, there she is, oh: not quite. She knows he knows, she opens her eyes, she sees him lying on the edge of the bed, the edge of a precipice, they are on it together, they are about to fall off, she closes her eyes, she is about to fall off: there. Oh. *Oh.* The bed complains.

Janice sinks back. They say, she read somewhere, some doctors measuring your blood pressure when you do it, things taped to your head how can anybody concentrate, it's always best when you do it to yourself. Her causing the bed to shudder has stirred Harry half-awake; he heavily rolls over and loops his arm around her waist, a pale tall man going fat. She strokes his wrist with the fingers that did it. His fault. He is a ghost, white, soft. Tried to make a box for her to put her in like they put Rebecca in when the poor little baby died. The way she held it sopping wet against her chest already dead, she could feel it, and screamed a great red scream as if to make a hole to let life back in. The movie returns upon her, the great wheel turning against the black velvet in time with the glorious symphony that did lift her for all her confusion coming into the theater. Floating now like a ballerina among the sparse planets of her life, Daddy, Harry, Nelson, Charlie, she thinks of her coming without him as a betrayal of her lover, and furtively lifts her fingertips, with their nice smell of swamp, to her lips and kisses them, thinking, *You.*

* * *

Next day, Friday, the papers and television are full of the colored riots in York, snipers wounding innocent firemen, simple men on the street, what is the world coming to? The astronauts are nearing the moon's gravitational influence. A quick thunderstorm makes up in the late afternoon over Brewer, pelts shoppers and homebound workmen into the entranceways of shops, soaks Harry's white shirt before he and his father get to huddle in the Phoenix Bar. "We missed you last night," Earl Angstrom says.

"Pop, I *told* you we couldn't make it, we took the kid out to eat and then to a movie."

"O.K., don't bite my head off. I thought you left it more up in the air than that, but never mind, don't kill a man for trying."

"I said we *might*, was all. Did she act disappointed?"

"She didn't let on. Your mother's nature isn't to let on, you know that. She knows you have your problems."

"What problems?"

"How was the movie, Harry?"

"The kid liked it, I don't know, it didn't make much sense to me, but then I felt kind of sick on something I ate. I fell dead asleep soon as we got home."

"How did Janice like it? Did she seem to have a good time?"

"Hell, I don't know. At her age, are you supposed to have a good time?"

"I hope the other day I didn't seem to be poking my nose in where it doesn't belong."

"Mom still raving about it?"

"A little bit. Now Mother, I tell her, now Mother, Harry's a big boy, Harry's a responsible citizen."

"Yeah," Rabbit admits, "maybe that's my problem," and shivers. With his shirt wet, it is cruelly cold in here. He signals for another Daiquiri. The television, sound off, is showing film clips of cops in York stalking the streets in threes and fours, then cuts to a patrol in Vietnam, boys smudged with fear and fatigue, and Harry feels badly, that he isn't there with them. Then the television moves on to the big publicity-mad Norwegian who gave up trying to cross the Atlantic in a paper boat. Even if the TV sound were turned higher what he's saying would be drowned by the noise in the bar: the excitement of the thunderstorm plus its being Friday night.

"Think you could make it over this evening?" his father asks. "It doesn't have to be for long, just fifteen minutes or so. It would mean the world to her, with Mim as good as dead, hardly ever even writing a postcard."

"I'll talk to her about it," Harry says, meaning Janice, though he thinks of Mim whoring around on the West Coast, Mim that he used to take sledding on Jackson Road, snowflakes on her hood. He pictures her at parties, waiting with a face of wax, or lying beside a swimming pool freshly oiled while under the umbrella beside her some suety gangster with a cigar in the center of his face like a secondary prick pulls it from his mouth and snarls. "But don't get her hopes up," he adds, meaning his mother. "We're sure to be over Sunday. I got to run."

The storm has passed. Sun pours through the torn sky, drying the pavement rapidly. Maplike stains: a pulped Kleenex retains an island of wet around it. Overweight bag-luggers and skinny Negro idlers emerge smiling from the shelter of a disused shoe store's entrance. The defaced BUS STOP sign, the wrappers spilled from the KEEP BREWER CLEAN can with its top like a flying saucer, the dimpled and rutted asphalt all glory, glistening, in the deluge having passed. The scattered handkerchiefs and horsetails of inky storm-cloud drift east across the ridge of Mt. Judge and the sky resumes the hazed, engendering, blank look of Pennsylvania humidity. And nervousness, that seeks to condense into anger, regathers in Rabbit.

Janice is not home when he arrives. Neither is Nelson. Coming up the walk he sees that, freshened by rain, their lawn looks greasy with crabgrass, spiky with plantain. The kid supposedly gets his dollar-fifty allowance in part for keeping it mowed but he hasn't since June. The little power mower, that had belonged to the Springers until they got one of those you ride, leans in the garage, a can of 3-in-1 beside one wheel. He oils it and sloshes in the gasoline – amber in the can, colorless in the funnel – and starts it up on the fourth pull. Its swath spits gummy hunks of wet grass, back and forth across the two square patches that form their front lawn. There is a larger lawn behind, where the clothes tree stands and where Nelson and he sometimes play catch with a softball worn down to its strings. It needs mowing too, but he wants Janice to find him out front, to give her a little guilty start to get them going.

But by the time she comes home, swinging down Vista spraying untarred grit and tucking the Falcon into the garage in that infuriating way of hers, just not quite far enough to close the door on the bumper, the blades of grass are mixing long shadows with their cut tips and Rabbit stands by their one tree, a spindly maple tethered to the earth by guy wires, his palm sore from trimming the length of the walk with the hand-clippers.

"Harry," she says, "you're outdoors! How funny of you."

And it is true, Park Villas with its vaunted quarter-acre lots and compulsory barbecue chimneys does not tempt its residents outdoors, even the children in summer: in the snug brick neighborhood of Rabbit's childhood you were always outdoors, hiding in hollowed-out bushes, scuffling in the gravel alleys, secure in the closeness of windows from at least one of which an adult was always watching. Here, there is a prairie sadness, a barren sky raked by slender aerials. A sky poisoned by radio waves. A sewer smell from underground.

"Where the hell have you been?"

"Work, obviously. Daddy always used to say never to cut grass after rain, it's all lying down."

" 'Work, obviously.' What's obvious about it?"

"Harry, you're so strange. Daddy came back from the Poconos today and made me stay after six with Mildred's mess."

"I thought he came back from the Poconos days ago. You lied. Why?"

Janice crosses the cut grass and they stand together, he and she and the tree, the spindly planted maple that cannot grow, as if bewildered by the wide raw light. The kerosene scent of someone else's Friday evening barbecue drifts to them. Their neighbors in Penn Villas are strangers, transients – accountants, salesmen, supervisors, adjusters – people whose lives to them are passing cars and the shouts of unseen children. Janice's color heightens. Her body takes on a defiant suppleness. "I forget, it was a silly lie, you were just so angry over the phone I had to say something. It seemed the easiest thing to say, that Daddy was there; you know how I am. You know how confused I get."

"How much other lying do you do to me?"

"None. That I can remember right now. Maybe little things, how much things cost, the sort of things women lie about. Women like to lie, Harry, it makes things more fun." And, flirtatious, unlike her, she flicks her tongue against her upper lip and holds it there, like the spring of a trap.

She steps toward the young tree and touches it where it is taped so the guy wires won't cut into the bark. He asks her, "Where's Nelson?"

"I arranged with Peggy for him to spend the night with Billy, since it's not a school night."

"With those dopes again. They give him ideas."

"At his age he's going to have ideas anyway."

"I half-promised Pop we'd go over tonight and visit Mom."

"I don't see why we should visit her. She's never liked me, she's done nothing but try to poison our marriage."

"Another question."

"Yes?"

"Are you fucking Stavros?"

"I thought women only *got* fucked."

Janice turns and choppily runs into the house, up the three steps, into the house with apple-green aluminum clapboards. Rabbit puts the mower back in the garage and enters by the side door into the kitchen. She is there, slamming pots around, making their dinner. He asks her, "Shall we go out to eat for a change? I know a nifty little Greek restaurant on Quince Street."

"That was just coincidence he showed up. I admit it was Charlie who recommended it, is there anything wrong with that? And you were certainly rude to him. You were incredible."

"I wasn't rude, we had a political discussion. I like Charlie. He's an O.K. guy, for a left-wing mealy-mouthed wop."

"You are really very strange lately, Harry. I think your mother's sickness is getting to you."

"In the restaurant, you seemed to know your way around the menu. Sure he doesn't take you there for lunch? Or on some of those late-work nights? You been working a lot of nights, and don't seem to get much done."

"You know nothing about what has to be done."

"I know your old man and Mildred Kroust used to do it themselves without all this overtime."

"Having the Toyota franchise is a whole new dimension.
It's endless bills of lading, import taxes, customs forms." More
fending words occur to Janice; it is like when she was little, making snow dams in the gutter. "Anyway, Charlie has lots of girls,
he can have girls any time, single girls younger than me. They all
go to bed now without even being asked, everybody's on the Pill,
they just assume it." One sentence too many.

"How do you know?"

"He tells me."

"So you *are* chummy."

"Not very. Just now and then, when he's hung or needing a
little mothering or something."

"Right – maybe he's scared of these hot young tits, maybe he
likes older women, *mamma mia* and all that. These slick Mediterranean types need a lot of mothering."

It's fascinating to her, to see him circling in; she fights the rising in her of a wifely wish to collaborate, to help him find the truth
that sits so large in her own mind she can hardly choose the words
that go around it.

"Anyway," he goes on, "those girls aren't the boss's daughter."

Yes, that is what he'd think, it was what she thought those first
times, those first pats as she was standing tangled in a net of numbers she didn't understand, those first sandwich lunches they
would arrange when Daddy was out on the lot, those first five-
o'clock whisky sours in the Atlas Bar down the street, those first
kisses in the car, always a different car, one they had borrowed
from the lot, with a smell of new car like a protective skin their
touches were burning through. That was what she thought until
he convinced her it was her, funny old clumsy her, Janice
Angstrom née Springer; it was her flesh being licked like ice
cream, her time being stolen in moments compressed as diamonds,
her nerves caught up in an exchange of pleasure that oscillated
between them in tightening swift circles until it seemed a kind of
frenzied sleep, a hypnosis so intense that later in her own bed she
could not sleep at all, as if she had napped that afternoon. His
apartment, they discovered, was only twelve minutes distant, if

you drove the back way, by the old farmers' market that was now just a set of empty tin-roofed sheds.

"What good would my being the boss's daughter do him?"

"It'd make him feel he was climbing. All these Greeks or Polacks or whatever are on the make."

"I'd never realized, Harry, how full of racial prejudice you are."

"Yes or no about you and Stavros."

"No." But lying she felt, as when a child watching the snow dams melt, that the truth must push through, it was too big, too constant: though she was terrified and would scream, it was something she must have, her confession like a baby. She felt so proud.

"You dumb bitch," he says. He hits her not in the face but on the shoulder, like a man trying to knock open a stuck door.

She hits him back, clumsily, on the side of the neck, as high as she can reach. Harry feels a flash of pleasure: sunlight in a tunnel. He hits her three, four, five times, unable to stop, boring his way to that sunlight, not as hard as he can hit, but hard enough for her to whimper; she doubles over so that his last punches are thrown hammerwise down into her neck and back, an angle he doesn't see her from that much – the chalk-white parting, the candle-white nape, the bra strap showing through the fabric of the back of the blouse. Her sobbing arises muffled and, astonished by a beauty in her abasement, by a face that shines through her reduction to this craven faceless posture, he pauses. Janice senses that he will not hit her anymore. She abandons her huddle, flops over to her side, and lets herself cry out loud – high-pitched, a startled noise pinched between sieges of windy gasping. Her face is red, wrinkled, newborn; in curiosity he drops to his knees to examine her. Her black eyes flash at this and she spits up at his face, but misjudges; the saliva falls back into her own face. For him there is only the faintest kiss of spray. Flecked with her own spit Janice cries, "I do, I *do* sleep with Charlie!"

"Ah, shit," Rabbit says softly, "of course you do," and bows his head into her chest, to protect himself from her scratching, while he half-pummels her sides, half-tries to embrace her and lift her.

"I love him. Damn you, Harry. We make love all the time."

"Good," he moans, mourning the receding of that light, that ecstasy of his hitting her, of knocking her open. Now she will become again a cripple he must take care of. "Good for you."

"It's been going on for *months*," she insists, writhing and trying to get free to spit again, furious at his response. He pins her arms, which would claw, at her sides and squeezes her hard. She stares into his face. Her face is wild, still, frozen. She is seeking what will hurt him most. "I do things for him," she says, "I never do for you."

"Sure you do," he murmurs, wanting to have a hand free to stroke her forehead, to re-enclose her. He sees the gloss of her forehead and the gloss of the kitchen linoleum. Her hair wriggles outward into the spilled wriggles of the marbled linoleum pattern, worn where she stands at the sink. A faint rotten smell here, of the sluggish sink tie-in. Janice abandons herself to crying and limp relief, and he has no trouble lifting her and carrying her in to the living-room sofa. He has zombie-strength: his shins shiver, his palm sore from the clipper handles is a stiff crescent.

She sinks lost into the sofa's breadth.

He prompts her, "He makes better love than me," to keep her confession flowing, as a physician moistens a boil.

She bites her tongue, trying to think, surveying her ruins with an eye toward salvage. Impure desires – to save her skin, to be kind, to be exact – pollute her primary fear and anger. "He's different," she says. "I'm more exciting to him than to you. I'm sure it's just mostly our not being married."

"Where do you do it?"

Worlds whirl past and cloud her eyes – car seats, rugs, tree undersides seen through windshields, the beigy-gray carpeting in the narrow space between the three green steel desks and the safe and the Toyota cutout, motel rooms with their cardboard panelling and scratchy bedspreads, his dour bachelor's apartment stuffed with heavy furniture and tinted relatives in silver frames. "Different places."

"Do you want to marry him?"

"No. *No*." Why does she say this? The possibility opens an abyss. She would not have known this. A gate she had always assumed gave onto a garden gave onto emptiness. She tries to drag

Harry down closer to her; she is lying on the sofa, one shoe off, her bruises just beginning to smart, while he kneels on the carpet, having carried her here. He remains stiff when she pulls at him, he is dead, she has killed him.

He asks, "Was I so lousy to you?"

"Oh sweetie, no. You were good to me. You came back. You work in that dirty place. I don't know what got into me, Harry, I honestly don't."

"Whatever it was," he tells her, "it must be still there." He looks like Nelson, saying this, a mulling discontented hurt look, puzzling to pry something open, to get something out. She sees she will have to make love to him. A conflicted tide moves within her – desire for this pale and hairless stranger, abhorrence of this desire, fascination with the levels of betrayal possible.

He shies, afraid of failing her; he falls back from the sofa and sits on the floor and offers to talk, to strike a balance. "Do you remember Ruth?"

"The whore you lived with when you ran away."

"She wasn't a whore exactly."

"Whatever she was, what about her?"

"A couple of years ago, I saw her again."

"Did you sleep with her?"

"Oh God no. She had become very straight. That was the thing. We met on Weiser Street, she was shopping. She had put on so much weight I didn't recognize her, I think she recognized me first, something about the way this woman looked at me; and then it hit me. Ruth. She still had this great head of hair. By then she had gone by, I followed her for a while and then she ducked into Kroll's. I gave it an even chance, I waited there at the side entrance figuring if she came out of that one I'd say hello and if she went out one of the others, O.K. I gave it five minutes. I really wasn't that interested." But in saying this, his heart beats faster, as it had beat then. "Just as I was going away she came out lugging two shopping bags and looked at me and the first thing she said was, 'Let me alone.' "

"She loved you," Janice explains.

"She did and she didn't," he says, and loses her sympathy with this complacence. "I offered to buy her a drink but all she'd let me do is walk her up toward the parking lot where the old Acme used to be. She lived out toward Galilee, she told me. Her husband was a chicken farmer and ran a string of school buses, I got the impression he was some guy older than she was, who'd had a family before. She told me they had three children, a girl and two boys. She showed me their pictures in a wallet. I asked how often she got into town and she said, 'As far as you're concerned, never.' "

"Poor Harry," Janice says. "She sounds awful."

"Well, she was, but still. She'd gotten heavy, as I said, she was sort of lost inside this other person who pretty much blended in with those other fat bag-luggers you see downtown, but at the same time, still, it was *her*."

"All right. You still love her," Janice says.

"No, I didn't, I don't. You haven't heard the worse thing she did then."

"I can't believe you never tried to get in touch with her after you came back to me. At least to see what she did about her . . . pregnancy."

"I felt I *shouldn't*." But he sees now, in his wife's dark and judging eyes, that the rules were more complicated, that there were some rules by which he should have. There were rules beneath the surface rules that also mattered. She should have explained this when she took him back.

She asks, "What was the worse thing?"

"I don't know if I should tell you."

"Tell me. Let's tell each other everything, then we'll take off all our clothes." She sounds tired. The shock of having given it all away must be sinking in. He talks to distract, as we joke with a loser at poker.

"You already said it. About the baby. I thought of that and asked her how old the girl was, her oldest child. She wouldn't tell me. I asked to see the wallet pictures again, to see if there was, you know, a resemblance. She wouldn't show them to me. She laughed at me. She was really quite nasty. She said something very strange."

"What?"

"I forget exactly. She looked me over and said I'd gotten fat.

This from *her*. Then she said, 'Run along, Rabbit. You've had your day in the cabbage patch.' Or something like that. Nobody ever calls me Rabbit, was what sort of got me. This was two years ago. I think in the fall. I haven't seen her since."

"Tell me the truth now. These ten years, haven't you had any other women?"

He runs his mind backward, encounters a few dark places, a room in a Polish-American Club where Verity was having its annual blast, a skinny flat-chested girl with a cold, she had kept her bra and sweater on; and then a weird episode at the Jersey shore, Janice and Nelson off at the amusement park, him back from the beach in his trunks, a knock at the door of the cabin, a chunky colored girl, two skinny boys escorting her, offering herself for five or seven dollars, depending what he wanted done. He had had trouble understanding her accent, had made her repeat – with downcast eyes, as the boys with her sniggered – "screwin'," "suck-off." Frightened, he had quickly shut the flimsy door on them, locked it as if they had threatened to harm him, and jerked off facing the wall; the wall smelled of damp and salt. He tells Janice, "You know, ever since that happened to Becky, I haven't been that much for sex. It comes on, wanting it, and then some-thing turns it off."

"Let me up."

Janice stands in front of the television set, the screen green ashes, a dead fire. Efficiently she undresses herself. Her dark-tipped breasts droop tubular and sway as she disengages her pantyhose. Her tan stops below her throat. Other summers they used to go to the West Brewer pool some Sundays but the kid became too big to go with his parents so none go now. They haven't gone to the Shore since the Springers discovered the Poconos. Buggy brown lakes imprisoned among dark green trees: Rabbit hates it there and never goes, never goes anywhere, takes his vacation around the house. He used to daydream about going South, Florida or Alabama, to see the cotton fields and the alligators, but that was a boy's dream and died with the baby. He once saw Texas and that has to be enough. Tongue pinched between her lips, naked Janice unbuttons his shirt, fumbling. Numbly he takes over, completes the job. The pants, the shoes last. Socks. Air knows him, air of day still lingering, summer air tingling along the skin that never knows the light. He and Janice have not made love in the light for years. She asks him in the middle of it, "Don't you love *see*ing? I used to be so embarrassed."

In twilight they eat, still naked, salami sandwiches she makes, and drink whisky. Their house stays dark, though the others around them, that mirror it, turn on their lights. These neighboring lights, and the cars that pass along Vista Crescent, throw sliding soft witnesses into their room: the open shelves lunge like parallel swords, the driftwood lamp throws a rhinoceros-shadow, the school portrait of Nelson, in its cardboard frame on the mantel, from beneath the embalming tints of its color wash, smiles. To help them see when darkness comes, Janice turns on the television set without sound, and by the bluish flicker of module models pantomiming flight, of riot troops standing before smashed supermarkets, of a rowboat landing in Florida having crossed the Atlantic, of situation comedies and western melodramas, of great gray momentary faces unstable as quicksilver, they make love again, her body a stretch of powdery sand, her mouth a loose black hole, her eyes holes with sparks in them, his own body a barren landscape lit by bombardment, silently exploding images no gentler than Janice's playful expert touches, that pass through him and do him no harm. She inverts herself and pours out upon him the months of her new knowledge; her appetite frightens him, knowing he cannot fill it, any more than Earth's appetite for death can be satisfied. Her guilt became love; her love becomes rage. The first time was too quick but the second was sweet, with work and sweat in it, and the third time strainingly sweet, a work of the spirit almost purely, and the fourth time, because there was no fourth time, sad; straddling his thighs, her cunt revealed by the flickering touch of the television to be lopsidedly agape, she bows her head, her hair tickling his belly, and drops cold tears, starpricks, upon the slack flesh that has failed her.

"Jesus," he says, "I forgot. We were supposed to go over to Mom's tonight!"

*   *   *

He dreams of driving north with Charlie Stavros, in a little scarlet Toyota. The gear shift is very thin, a mere pencil, and he is afraid of breaking it as he shifts. Also, he is wearing golf shoes, which makes operating the pedals awkward. Stavros sits in the driver's seat and, with that stolid way of muttering, his square ringed hands masterfully gesturing, discusses his problem: Lyndon Johnson has asked him to be his Vice-President. They need a Greek. He would like to accept, but doesn't want to leave Brewer. So they are negotiating to have at least the summer White House moved to Brewer. They have lots of vacant lots they could build it on, Charlie explains. Rabbit is thinking maybe this is his chance to get out of the printing plant and into a white-collar job. Services and software are where the future lies. He tells Stavros hopefully, "I can lick stamps." He shows him his tongue. They are on a superhighway heading north, into the deserted coal regions and, beyond that, the wilds of northern Pennsylvania. Yet here, in this region of woods and lakes, a strange white city materializes beside the highway; hill after hill of tall row houses white as bedsheets, crowding to the horizon, an enormous city, strange it seems to have no name. They part in a suburban region beside a drugstore and Stavros hands him a map; with difficulty Rabbit locates on it where they are. The metropolis, marked with a bull's-eye, is named, simply, The Rise.

The Rise, The Rise . . . the dream is so unpleasant he awakes, with a headache and an erection. His prick feels glassily thin and aches from all that work with Janice. The bed is empty beside him. He remembers they went to bed after two, when the television screen became a buzzing test-signal. He hears the sound of the vacuum cleaner downstairs. She is up.

He dresses in his Saturday clothes, patched chinos and apricot polo shirt, and goes downstairs. Janice is in the living room sweeping, pushing the silver tube back and forth. She glances over at him, looking old. Sex ages us. Priests are boyish, spinsters stay black-haired until after fifty. We others, the demon rots us out. She says, "There's orange juice on the table, and an egg in the pan. Let me finish this room."

From the breakfast table he surveys his house. The kitchen on one side, the living room on the other are visible. The furniture that frames his life looks Martian in the morning light: an armchair covered in synthetic fabric enlivened by a silver thread, a sofa of airfoam slabs, a low table hacked to imitate an antique cobbler's bench, a piece of driftwood that is a lamp, nothing shaped directly for its purpose, gadgets designed to repel repair, nothing straight from a human hand, furniture Rabbit has lived among but has never known, made of substances he cannot name, that has aged as in a department store window, worn out without once conforming to his body. The orange juice tastes acid; it is not even frozen orange juice but some chemical mix tinted orange.

He breaks his egg into the pan, sets the flame low, thinks guiltily of his mother. Janice turns off the vacuum, comes over, pours herself some coffee to sit opposite him with as he eats. Lack of sleep has left purple dents beneath her eyes. He asks her, "Are you going to tell him?"

"I suppose I must."

"Why? Wouldn't you like to keep him?"

"What are you saying, Harry?"

"Keep him, if he makes you happy. I don't seem to, so go ahead, until you've had your fill at least."

"Suppose I never have my fill?"

"Then I guess you should marry him."

"Charlie can never marry anybody."

"Who says?"

"He did once. I asked him why not and he wouldn't say. Maybe it has to do with his heart murmur. That was the only time we ever discussed it."

"What *do* you and he discuss? Except which way to do it next."

She might have risen to this taunt but doesn't. She is very flat, very honest and dry this morning, and this pleases him. A graver woman than he has known reveals herself. We contain chords someone else must strike. "We don't say much. We talk about funny little things, things we see from his windows, things we did as children. He loves to listen to me; when he was a boy they lived in the worst part of Brewer, a town like Mt. Judge looked marvellous to him. He calls me a rich bitch."

"The boss's daughter."

"Don't, Harry. You said that last night. You can't understand.

It would sound silly, the things we talk about. He has a gift, Charlie does, of making everything exciting – the way food tastes, the way the sky looks, the customers that come in. Once you get past that defensiveness, that tough guy act, he's quite quick and, *lov*ing, in what he sees. He felt awful last night, after you left, that he had made you say more than you meant to. He hates to argue. He loves life. He really does, Harry. He loves life."

"We all do."

"Not really. I think our generation, the way we were raised, makes it hard for us to love life. Charlie does. It's like – daylight. You want to know something?"

He agrees, "Sure," knowing it will hurt.

"Daylight love – it's the best."

"O.*K*. Relax. I said, keep the son of a bitch."

"I don't believe you."

"Only one thing. Try to keep the kid from knowing. My mother already knows, the people who visit her tell her. It's all over town. Talk about daylight."

"*Let* it be," Janice says. She rises. "Goddam your mother, Harry. The only thing she's ever done for us is try to poison our marriage. Now she's drowning in the poison of her life. She's dying and I'm glad."

"Jesus, don't say that."

"Why not? She would, if it were me. Who did she want you to marry? Tell me, who would have been wonderful enough for you? Who?"

"My sister," he suggests.

"Let me tell you something else. At first with Charlie, whenever I'd feel guilty, so I couldn't relax, I'd just think of your mother, how she's not only treated me but treated *Nel*son, her own *grand*son, and I'd say to myself, O.K., fella, sock it to me, and I'd just *come*."

"O.K., O.K. Spare me the fine print."

"I'm sick, so sick, of sparing you things. There've been a lot of days" – and this makes her too sad to confess, so that a constraint slips like a net over her face, which goes ugly under the pull – "when I was sorry you came back that time. You were a beauti-ful brainless guy and I've had to watch that guy die day by day."

"It wasn't so bad last night, was it?"

"No. It was so good I'm angry. I'm all confused."

"You've been confused from birth, kid." He adds, "Any dying I've been doing around here, you've been helping it right along." At the same time, he wants to fuck her again, to see if she can turn inside out again. For some minutes last night she turned all tongue and his mouth was glued to hers as if in an embryo the first cell division had not yet occurred.

The phone rings. Janice plucks it from its carriage on the kitchen wall and says, "Hi, Daddy. How was the Poconos? Good. I knew she would. She just needed to feel appreciated. Of course he's here. Here he is." She holds it out to Rabbit. "For you."

Old man Springer's voice is reedy, coaxing, deferential. "Harry, how's everything?"

"Not bad."

"You still game for the ball game? Janice mentioned you asked about the tickets to the Blasts today. They're in my hand, three right behind first base. The manager's been a client of mine for twenty years."

"Yeah, great. The kid spent the night at the Fosnachts, but I'll get him back. You want to meet at the stadium?"

"Let me pick you up, Harry. I'll be happy to pick you up in my car. That way we'll leave Janice yours." A note in his voice that didn't used to be there, gentle, faintly wheedling: nursing along an invalid. He knows too. The world knows. It'll be in the *Vat* next week. LINOTYPER'S WIFE LAYS LOCAL SALES REP. *Greek Takes Strong Anti-Viet Stand.*

"Tell me, Harry," Springer wheedles on, "how is your mother's health? Rebecca and I are naturally very concerned. *Very* concerned."

"My father says it's about the same. It's a slow process, you know. They have drugs now that make it even slower. I've been meaning this week to get up to Mt. Judge to see her but we haven't managed."

"When you do, Harry, give her our love. Give her our love."

Saying everything twice: he probably swung the Toyota franchise because the Japs could understand him second time around.

"O.K., sure enough. Want Janice back?"

"No, Harry, you can keep her." A joke. "I'll be by twelve-twenty, twelve-thirty."

He hangs up. Janice is gone from the kitchen. He finds her in the living room crying. He goes and kneels beside the sofa and puts his arms around her but these actions feel like stage directions followed woodenly. A button is off on her blouse and the sallow curve of breast into the bra mixes with her hot breath in his ear. She says, "You can't understand, how good he was. Not sexy or funny or anything, just *good*."

"Sure I can. I've known some good people. They make you feel good."

"They make you feel everything you do and are *is* good. He never told me how dumb I am, every hour on the hour like you do, even though he's much smarter than you could ever imagine. He would have gone to college, if he hadn't been a Greek."

"Oh. Don't they let Greeks in now? The nigger quota too big?"

"You say such sick things, Harry."

"It's because nobody tells me how good I am," he says, and stands. The back of her neck is vulnerable beneath him. One good karate chop would do it.

The driveway crackles outside; it's much too early for Springer. He goes to the window. A teal-blue Fury. The passenger door swings open and Nelson gets out. On the other side appears Peggy Gring, wearing sunglasses and a miniskirt that flashes her big thighs like a card dealer's thumbs. Unhappiness – being deserted – has made her brisk, professional. She gives Rabbit hardly a hello and her sunglasses hide the eyes that he knows from school days look northeast and northwest. The two women go into the kitchen. From the sound of Janice snuffling he guesses a confession is in progress. He goes outside to finish the yard work he began last night. All around him, in the back yards of Vista Crescent, to the horizons of Penn Villas with their barbecue chimneys and aluminum wash trees, other men are out in their yards; the sound of his mower is echoed from house to house, his motions of bending and pushing are carried outwards as if in fragments of mirror suspended from the hot blank sky. These his neighbors, they come with their furniture in vans and leave with the vans. They get together to sign futile petitions for better sewers and quicker fire protection but otherwise do not connect. Nelson comes out and asks him, "What's the matter with Mommy?"

He shuts off the mower. "What's she doing?"

"She's sitting at the table with Mrs. Fosnacht crying her eyes out."

"Still? I don't know, kid; she's upset. One thing you must learn about women, their chemistries are different from ours."

"Mommy almost never cries."

"So maybe it's good for her. Get lots of sleep last night?"

"Some. We watched an old movie about torpedo boats."

"Looking forward to the Blasts game?"

"Sure."

"But not much, huh?"

"I don't like sports as much as you do, Dad. It's all so competitive."

"That's life. Dog eat dog."

"You think? Why can't things just be nice? There's enough stuff for everybody to share."

"You think there is? Why don't you start then by sharing this lawnmowing? You push it for a while."

"You owe me my allowance." As Rabbit hands him a dollar bill and two quarters, the boy says, "I'm saving for a mini-bike."

"Good luck."

"Also, Dad –?"

"Yeah?"

"I think I should get a dollar twenty-five an hour for work. That's still under the federal minimum wage."

"See?" Rabbit tells him. "Dog eat dog."

As he washes up inside, pulling grass bits out of his cuffs and putting a Band-aid on the ball of his thumb (tender place; in high school they used to say you could tell how sexy a girl was by how fat she was here), Janice comes into the bathroom, shuts the door, and says, "I've decided to tell him. While you're at the ball game I'll tell him." Her face looks taut but pretty dried-out; patches of moisture glisten beside her nose. The tile walls amplify her sniffs. Peggy Gring's car roars outside in leaving.

"Tell who what?"

"Tell Charlie. That it's all over. That you know."

"I said, keep him. Don't do anything for today at least. Calm down. Have a drink. See a movie. See that space movie again, you slept through the best parts."

"That's cowardly. No. He and I have always been honest with each other, I must tell him the truth."

"I think you're just looking for an excuse to see him while I'm tucked away at the ball park."

"You would think that."

"Suppose he asks you to sleep with him?"

"He wouldn't."

"Suppose he does, as a graduation present?"

She stares at him boldly: dark gaze tempered in the furnace of betrayal. It comes to him: growth is betrayal. There is no other route. There is no arriving somewhere without leaving somewhere. "I would," she says.

"Where are you going to find him?"

"At the lot. He stays on until six summer Saturdays."

"What reason are you going to give him? For breaking it off."

"Why, the fact that you know."

"Suppose he asks you why you told?"

"It's obvious why I told. I told because I'm your wife."

Tears belly out between her lids and the tension of her face breaks like Nelson's when a hidden anxiety, a D or a petty theft or a headache, is confessed. Harry denies his impulse to put his arm around her; he does not want to feel wooden again. She teeters, keeping her balance while sobbing, sitting on the edge of the bathtub, while the plastic shower curtain rustles at her shoulder.

"Aren't you going to stop me?" she brings out at last.

"Stop you from what?"

"From *see*ing him!"

Given this rich present of her grief, he can afford to be cruel. Coolly he says, "No, see him if you want to. Just as long as *I* don't have to see the bastard." And, avoiding the sight of her face, he sees himself in the cabinet mirror, a big pink pale man going shapeless under the chin, his little lips screwed awry in what wants to be a smile.

The gravel in the driveway crackles again. From the bathroom window he sees the boxy dun top of Springer's spandy new Toyota wagon. To Nelson he calls, "Grandpa's here. Let's go-o." To Janice he murmurs, "Sit tight, kid. Don't commit yourself to anything." To his father-in-law, sliding in beside him, across a spaghetti of nylon safety straps, Rabbit sings, "Buy me some peanuts and crack-er-jack ..."

The stadium is on the northern side of Brewer, through a big cloverleaf, past the brick hulks of two old hosiery mills, along a three-lane highway where in these last years several roadside restaurants have begun proclaiming themselves as Pennsylvania Dutch, with giant plaster Amishmen and neon hex signs. GENUINE "*Dutch*" COOKING. *Pa. Dutch Smörgåsbord.* Trying to sell what in the old days couldn't be helped. Making a tourist attraction out of fat-fried food and a diet of dough that would give a pig pimples. They pass the country fairgrounds, where every September the same battered gyp stands return, and the farmers bring their stinking livestock, and Serafina the Egyptian Temptress will take off all her clothes for those yokels who put up a dollar extra. The first naked woman he saw was Serafina or her mother. She kept on her high heels and a black mask and bent way backwards; she spread her legs and kept a kind of token shimmy rhythm as she moved in a semi-circle so every straining head (luckily he was tall even then) could see a trace of her cleft, an exciting queasy-making wrinkle shabbily masked by a patch of hair that looked to him pasted-on. Rubbed threadbare? He didn't know. He couldn't imagine.

Springer is shaking his head over the York riots. "Sniper fire four nights in a row, Harry. What is the world coming to? We're so defenseless, is what strikes me, we're so defenseless against the violent few. All our institutions have been based on trust."

Nelson pipes up. "It's the only way they can get justice, Grandpa. Our laws defend property instead of people."

"They're defeating their own purposes, Nellie. Many a white man of good will like myself is being turned against the blacks. Slowly but surely he's being turned against them. It wasn't Vietnam beat Humphrey, it was law and order in the streets. That's the issue that the common man votes upon. Am I right or wrong, Harry? I'm such an old fogey I don't trust my own opinions any more."

One old geezer, Harry is remembering, at the side of the little stage, reached from behind and put his hand up on her pussy, shouting, "Aha!" She stopped her dance and stared out of the black mask. The tent went quiet; the geezer, surprisingly, found enough blood in himself to blush. *Aha.* That cry of triumph, as if he had snared a precious small animal, Harry never forgot. *Aha.* He slouches down and in answer to Springer says, "Things go bad. Food goes bad, people go bad, maybe a whole country goes bad. The blacks now have more than ever, but it feels like less, maybe. We were all brought up to want things and maybe the world isn't big enough for all that wanting. I don't know. I don't know anything."

Old man Springer laughs; he snorts and snarls so his little gray mouse of a mustache merges with his nostril hairs. "Did you hear about Teddy Kennedy this morning?"

"What about him? No."

"Shut your ears, Nellie. I forgot you were in the car or I wouldn't have mentioned it."

"What, Grandpa? What did he do? Did somebody shoot him?"

"Apparently, Harry" – Springer talks out of the side of his mouth, as if to shield Nelson, yet so distinctly the child can easily hear – "he dumped some girl from Pennsylvania into one of those Massachusetts rivers. Murder as plain as my face." Springer's face, from the side, is a carving of pink bone, with rosy splotches where the cheekbones put most pressure, and a bump of red on the point where the nose turns. An anxious sharp face creased all over by a salesman's constant smile. One thing at least about setting type, there's a limit on how much ass you must kiss.

"Did they get him? Is he in jail, Grandpa?"

"Ah, Nellie, they'll never put a Kennedy in jail. Palms will be greased. Evidence will be suppressed. I call it a crying shame."

Rabbit asks, "What do you mean, dumped some girl?"

"They found her in his car upside down in the water beside some bridge, I forget the name, one of those islands they have up there. It happened last night and he didn't go to the police until they were about to nab him. And they call this a democracy, Harry, is the irony of it."

"What would you call it?"

"I'd call it a police state run by the Kennedys, is what I would call it. That family has been out to buy the country since those Brahmins up in Boston snubbed old Joe. And then he put himself in league with Hitler when he was FDR's man in London. Now they've got the young widow to marry a rich Greek in case they run out of American money. Not that she's the goodie-gumdrop the papers say; those two were a match. What's your opinion, Harry? Am I talking out of line? I'm such a back number now I don't trust to hear myself talk." *Aha.*

"I'd say," Harry says, "you're right with it. You should join the kids and buy yourself a bomb to throw."

Springer looks over from driving (the yellow parabolas of a McDonald's flash by; the tinsel spinners of a Mobil station break the noon sun into trinkets) to see if he has oversold. How timid, really, people who live by people must be. Earl Angstrom was right about that at least: better make your deals with things. Springer says, hedgily smiling, showing porcelain teeth beneath the gray blur, "I'll say this for the Kennedys, however, they don't get my dander up like FDR. There was a man, Harry, so mad he died of maggots in the brain. One thing to be said for the Kennedys, they didn't try to turn the economy upside down for the benefit of the poor, they were willing to ride along with the System as it's been handed down."

Nelson says, "Billy Fosnacht says when we grow up we're going to overthrow the System."

Springer can't hear, lost in his vision of executive madness and corruption. "He tried to turn it upside down for the benefit of the black and white trash, and when that didn't work for eight years he finagled the little Japanese into attacking Pearl Harbor so he had a war to bail him out of the Depression. That's why you have these wars, believe it or not, to bail the Democrats out of their crazy economics. LBJ, now, as soon as he got his four-year guarantee, went into Vietnam where nobody wanted us, just to get the coloreds up into the economy. LBJ, he was an FDR man. Truman, the same thing in Korea. History bears me out, every time, call me an old fogey if you want to: what's your angle on it, Nelson?"

"Last night on television," the boy says, "we watched an old movie about fighting the Japs in the Pacific, this little boat sank, and the captain or whatever he was swam miles with a broken back dragging this other guy."

"That was Kennedy," Springer says. "Pure propaganda. They made that movie because Old Joe owned a lot of those studios. He sank his money into the movies when all the honest businessmen who'd put this country on the map were losing their shirts. He was in close league, the story I heard, with those Jewish Communists out there."

Rabbit tells Nelson, "That's where your Aunt Mim is now, out there with those Communists."

"She's beautiful," Nelson tells his grandfather. "Have you ever seen my Aunt Mim?"

"Not as much as I'd have liked to, Nellie. She is a striking figure, however, I know you're right there. You're right to be proud of her. Harry, your silence disturbs me. Your silence disturbs me. Maybe I'm way off base – way off. Tell me what *you* think of the state of the nation. With these riots everywhere, and this poor Polish girl, she comes from up near Williamsport, abused and drowned when the future President takes his pleasure. Pregnant, wouldn't surprise me. Nellie, you shouldn't be hearing any of this."

Harry stretches, cramped in the car, short of sleep. They are near the stadium, and a little colored boy is waving them into a lot. "I think," he says, "about America, it's still the only place."

But something has gone wrong. The ball game is boring. The spaced dance of the men in white fails to enchant, the code beneath the staccato spurts of distant motion refuses to yield its meaning. Though basketball was his sport, Rabbit remembers the grandeur of all that grass, the excited perilous feeling when a high fly was hoisted your way, the homing-in on the expanding dot, the leathery smack of the catch, the formalized nonchalance of the heads-down trot in toward the bench, the ritual flips and shrugs and the nervous courtesies of the batter's box. There was a beauty here bigger than the hurtling beauty of basketball, a beauty refined from country pastures, a game of solitariness, of waiting, waiting for the pitcher to complete his gaze toward first base and throw his lightning, a game whose very taste, of spit and dust and grass and sweat and leather and sun, was America. Sitting behind first base between his son and his father-in-law, the sun resting on his thighs, the rolled-up program in his hand, Rabbit waits for this beauty to rise to him, through the cheers and the rhythm of innings, the traditional national magic, tasting of his youth; but something is wrong. The crowd is sparse, thinning out from a cluster behind the infield to fistfuls of boys sprawling on the green seats sloped up from the outfield. Sparse, loud, hard: only the drunks, the bookies, the cripples, the senile, and the delinquents come out to the ball park on a Saturday afternoon. Their catcalls are coarse and unkind. "Ram it down his throat, Speedy!" "Kill that black bastard!" Rabbit yearns to protect the game from the crowd; the poetry of space and inaction is too fine, too slowly spun for them. And for the players themselves, they seem expert list-lessly, each intent on a private dream of making it, making it into the big leagues and the big money, the own-your-own-bowling-alley money; they seem specialists like any other, not men playing a game because all men are boys time is trying to outsmart. A gal-lant pretense has been abandoned. Only the explosions of orange felt on their uniforms, under the script *Blasts*, evoke the old world of heraldic local loyalties. Brewer versus Hazleton and who cares? Not Springer: as he watches, his lips absent-mindedly move as if sorting out old accounts. Not Nelson: the screen of reality is too big for the child, he misses television's running commentary, the audacious commercials. His politely unspoken disappointment nags at Rabbit, prevents the game from rising and filling the scared hollow Janice's confession has left in him. The eight-team leagues of his boyhood have vanished with the forty-eight-star flag. The shortstops never chew tobacco any more. The game drags on, with a tedious flurry of strategy, of pinch-hitters and intentional walks, prolonging the end. Hazleton wins, 7-3. Old man Springer sighs, getting up as if from a nap in an unnatural position. He wipes a fleck of beer from his mustache. " 'Fraid our boys didn't come through for you, Nellie," he says.

"That's O.K., Grampa. It was neat."

To Harry he says, needing to find something to sell, "That young Trexler is a comer though."

Rabbit is cross and groggy from two beers in the sun. He

doesn't invite Springer into his house, just thanks him a lot for everything. The house is silent, like outer space. On the kitchen table is a sealed envelope, addressed "Harry." The letter inside, in Janice's half-formed hand, with its unsteady slant and miserly cramping, says

> Harry dear –
>   I must go off a few days to think. Please don't try to find or follow me *please*. It is very important that we all respect each other as people and trust each other now. I was shocked by your idea that I keep a lover since I don't think this would be honest and it made me wonder if I mean anything to you at all. Tell Nelson I've gone to the Poconos with Grandmom. Don't forget to give him lunch money for the playground.
>   Love,
>   Jan

"Jan" – her name from the years she used to work at Kroll's selling salted nuts in the smock with *Jan* stitched above the pocket in script. In those days some afternoons they would go to Linda Hammacher's apartment up on Eighth Street. The horizontal rose rays as the sun set behind the great gray gas-holder. The wonder of it as she let him slip off all her clothes. Underwear more substantial then: stocking snaps to undo, the marks of elastic printed on her skin. Jan. That name suspended in her these fifteen years; the notes she left for him around the house were simply signed "J."

"Where's Mom?" Nelson asks.

"She's gone to the Poconos," Rabbit says, pulling the note back toward his chest, in case the boy tries to read it. "She's gone with Mom-mom, her legs were getting worse in this heat. I know it seems crazy, but that's how things are sometimes. You and I can eat over at Burger Bliss tonight."

The boy's face – freckled, framed by hair that covers his ears, his plump lips buttoned shut and his eyes sunk in fear of making a mistake – goes rapt, seems to listen, as when he was two and flight and death were rustling above him. Perhaps his experience then shapes what he says now. Firmly he tells his father, "She'll be back."

*   *   *

Sunday dawns muggy. The eight-o'clock news says there was scattered shooting again last night in York and the western part of the state. Edgartown police chief Dominick J. Arena is expected today formally to charge Senator Kennedy with leaving the scene of an accident. Apollo Eleven is in lunar orbit and the Eagle is being readied for its historic descent. Rabbit slept badly and turns the box off and walks around the lawn barefoot to shock the headache out of his skull. The houses of Penn Villas are still, with the odd Catholic car roaring off to mass. Nelson comes down around nine, and after making him breakfast Harry goes back to bed with a cup of coffee and the Sunday Brewer *Standard*. Snoopy on the front page of the funny papers is lying dreaming on his doghouse and soon Rabbit falls asleep. The kid looked scared. The boy's face shouts, and a soundless balloon comes out. When he awakes, the electric clock says five of eleven. The second hand sweeps around and around; a wonder the gears don't wear themselves to dust. Rabbit dresses – fresh white shirt out of respect for Sunday – and goes downstairs the second time, his feet still bare, the carpeting fuzzy to his soles, a bachelor feeling. The house feels enormous, all his. He picks up the phone book and searches out

Stavros Chas 1204EisenhwerAv

He doesn't dial, merely gazes at the name and the number as if to see his wife, smaller than a pencil dot, crawling between the letters. He dials a number he knows by heart.

His father answers. "Yes?" A wary voice, ready to hang up on a madman or a salesman.

"Pop, hi; hey, I hope you didn't wait up or anything the other night, we weren't able to make it and I couldn't even get to a phone."

A little pause, not much, just enough to let him know they were indeed disappointed. "No, we figured something came up and went to bed about the usual time. Your mother isn't one to waste herself complaining, as you know."

"Right. Well, look. About today."

His voice goes hoarse to whisper, "Harry, you must come over today. You'll break her heart if you don't."

"I will, I will, but —"

The old man has cupped his mouth against the receiver, urging hoarsely, "This may be her last, you know. Birthday."

"We're coming, Pop. I mean, some of us are. Janice has had to go off."

"Go off how?"

"It's kind of complicated, something about her mother's legs and the Poconos, she decided last night she had to, I don't know. It's nothing to worry about. Everybody's all right, she's just not here. The kid's here though." To illustrate, he calls, "Nelson!"

There is no answer.

"He must be out on his bike, Pop. He's been right around all morning. When would you like us?"

"Whenever it suits you, Harry. Late afternoon or so. Come as early as you can. We're having roast beef. Your mother wanted to bake a cake but the doctor thought it might be too much for her. I bought a nice one over at the Half-A-Loaf. Butterscotch icing, didn't that used to be your favorite?"

"It's her birthday, not mine. What should I get her for a present?"

"Just your simple presence, Harry, is all the present she desires."

"Yeah, O.K. I'll think of something. Explain to her Janice won't be coming."

"As my father, God rest, used to say, It is to be regretted, but it can't be helped."

Once Pop finds that ceremonious vein, he tends to ride it. Rabbit hangs up. The kid's bike — a rusty Schwinn, been meaning to get him a new one, both fenders rub — is not in the garage. Nor is the Falcon. Only the oil cans, the gas can, the lawnmower, the jumbled garden hose (Janice must have used it last), a lawn rake with missing teeth, and the Falcon's snow tires are there. For an hour or so Rabbit swims around the house in a daze, not knowing who to call, not having a car, not wanting to go inside with the television set. He pulls weeds in the border beds where that first excited summer of their own house Janice planted bulbs and set in plants and shrubs. Since then they have done nothing, just watched the azaleas die and accepted the daffodils and iris as they came in and let the phlox and weeds fight as these subsequent

summers wore on, nature lost in Nature. He weeds until he begins
to see himself as a weed and his hand with its ugly big moons on
the fingernails as God's hand choosing and killing, then he goes
inside the house and looks into the refrigerator and eats a carrot
raw. He looks into the phone directory and looks up Fosnacht,
there are a lot of them, and two Olivers, and it takes him a while
to figure out M is the one, M for Margaret and just the initial to
put off obscene calls, though if he were on that kick he'd soon
figure out that initials were unattached women. "Peggy, hi; this is
Harry Angstrom." He says his name with faint proud emphasis;
they were in school together, and she remembers him when he
was somebody. "I was just wondering, is Nelson over there playing with Billy? He went off on his bike a while ago and I'm wondering where to."

Peggy says, "He's not here, Harry. Sorry." Her voice is frosted
with all she knows, Janice burbling into her ear yesterday. Then
more warmly she asks, "How's everything going?" He reads the
equation, Ollie left me; Janice left you: hello.

He says hastily, "Great. Hey, if Nelson comes by tell him I
want him. We got to go to his grandmother's."

Her voice cools in saying goodbye, joins the vast glaring ice-
face of all those who know. Nelson seems the one person left
in the county who doesn't know: this makes him even more
precious. Yet, when the boy returns, red-faced and damp-haired
from hard pedalling, he tells his father, "I was at the Fosnachts."

Rabbit blinks and says, "O.K. After this, let's keep in better
touch. I'm your mother and your father for the time being." They
eat lunch, Lebanon baloney on stale rye. They walk up Emberly
to Weiser and catch a 12 bus east into Brewer. It being Sunday,
they have to wait twenty minutes under the cloudless colorless
sky. At the hospital stop a crowd of visitors gets on, having done
their duty, dazed, carrying away dead flowers and read books.
Boats, white arrowheads tipping wrinkled wakes, are buzzing in
the black river below the bridge. A colored kid leaves his foot
in the aisle when Rabbit tries to get off; he steps over it. "Big feet,"
the boy remarks to his companion.

"Fat lips," Nelson, following, says to the colored boy.

They try to find a store open. His mother was always difficult to buy presents for. Other children had given their mothers cheerful junk: dime-store jewelry, bottles of toilet water, boxes of candy, scarves. For Mom that had been too much, or not enough. Mim always gave her something she had made: a woven pot holder, a hand-illustrated calendar. Rabbit was pretty poor at making things so he gave her himself, his trophies, his headlines. Mom had seemed satisfied: lives more than things concerned her. But now what? What can a dying person desire? Grotesque prosthetic devices – arms, legs, battery-operated hearts – run through Rabbit's head as he and Nelson walk the dazzling, Sunday-stilled downtown of Brewer. Up near Ninth and Weiser they find a drugstore open. Thermos bottles, sunglasses, shaving lotion, Kodak film, plastic baby pants: nothing for his mother. He wants something big, something bright, something to get through to her. Realgirl Liquid Make-Up, Super Plenamins, Non-Smear polish remover, Nudit for the Legs. A rack of shampoo-in hair color, a different smiling cunt on every envelope: Snow Queen Blond, Danish Wheat, Killarney Russet, Parisian Spice, Spanish Black Wine. Nelson plucks him by the sleeve of his white shirt and leads to where a Sunbeam Clipmaster and a Roto-Shine Magnetic Electric Shoe Polisher nestle side by side, glossily packaged. "She doesn't wear shoes any more, just slippers," he says, "and she never cut her hair that I can remember. It used to hang down to her waist." But his attention is drawn on to a humidifier for $12.95. From the picture on the box, it looks like a fat flying saucer. No matter how immobile she gets, it would be there. Around Brewer, though, the summers are as humid as they can be anyway, but maybe in the winter, the radiators dry out the house, the wallpaper peels, the skin cracks; it might help. It would be there night and day, when he wasn't. He moves on to a Kantleek Water Bottle and a 2½ -inch reading glass and dismisses both as morbid. His insides are beginning to feel sickly. The pain of the world is a crater all these syrups and pills a thousandfold would fail to fill. He comes to the Quikease Electric Massager with Scalp Comb. It has the silhouettes of naked women on the box, gracefully touching their shoulders, Lesbians, caressing the backs of their necks, where else the box leaves to the imagination, with what looks like a hair brush on a live wire. $11.95. Bedsores. It might help. It might make her laugh, tickle, buzz: it is life. Life is a massage. And it costs a dollar less than the humidifier. Time is ticking. Nelson tugs at his sleeve and wants a maple walnut ice cream soda. While the kid is eating it, Rabbit buys a birthday card to go with the massager. It shows a rooster crowing, a crimson sun rising, and green letters shouting on the outside *It's Great to Get Up in the A.M. . . .* and on the inside . . . *to Wish You a Happy Birthday, MA!* Ma. Am. God, what a lot of ingenious crap there is in the world. He buys it anyway, because the rooster is bright orange and jubilant enough to get through to her. Her eyes aren't dim necessarily but because her tongue gropes they could be. Play it safe.

The world outside is bright and barren. The two of them, father and son, feel sharply alone, Rabbit gripping his bulky package. Where is everybody? Is there life on Earth? Three blocks down the deserted street of soft asphalt the clock that is the face of a giant flower, the center of the Sunflower Beer sign, says they are approaching four. They wait at the same corner, opposite the Phoenix Bar, where Harry's father customarily waits, and take the 16A bus to Mt. Judge. They are the only passengers; the driver tells them mysteriously, "They're about down." Up they go through the City Park, past the World War II tank and the bandshell and the tennis court, around the shoulder of the mountain. On one side of them, gas stations and a green cliff; on the other, a precipice and, distantly, a viaduct. As the kid stares out of the window, toward the next mountain over, Rabbit asks him, "Where did you go this morning? Tell me the truth."

The boy answers, finally. "Eisenhower Avenue."

"To see if Mommy's car was there?"

"I guess."

"Was it?"

"Yop."

"D'you go in?"

"Nope. Just looked up at the windows awhile."

"Did you know the number to look at?"

"One two oh four."

"You got it."

They get off at Central, beside the granite Baptist church, and walk up Jackson toward his parents' house. The streets haven't changed in his lifetime. They were built too close together for vacant lots and too solidly to tear down, of a reddish brick with purplish bruises in it, with a texture that as a child Rabbit thought of as chapped, like his lips in winter. Maples and horsechestnuts darken the stumpy front lawns, hedged by little wired barricades of barberry and box. The houses are semi-detached and heavy, their roofs are slate and their porches have brick walls and above each door of oak and bevelled glass winks a fanlight of somber churchly colors. As a child Rabbit imagined that fanlight to be a child of the windows above the Lutheran altar and therefore of God, a mauve and golden seeing sentinel posted above where he and Pop and Mom and Mim came and went a dozen times a day. Now, entering with his son, still too much a son himself to knock, he feels his parents' place as stifling. Though the clock on the living-room sideboard says only 4:20, darkness has come: dark carpets, thick drawn drapes, dead wallpaper, potted plants crowding the glass on the side that has the windows. Mom used to complain about how they had the inside half of a corner house; but when the Bolgers, their old neighbors, died, and their half went onto the market, they made no move to inquire after the price, and a young couple from Scranton bought it, the wife pregnant and barefoot and the husband something in one of the new electronics plants out along Route 422; and the Angstroms still live in the dark half. They prefer it. Sunlight fades. They sent him, Harry, out in the world to shine, but hugged their own shadows here. Their neighbor house on the other side, across two cement sidewalks with a strip of grass between them, where lived the old Methodist Mom used to fight with about who would mow the grass strip, has had a FOR SALE sign up for a year. People now want more air and land than those huddled hillside neighborhoods can give them. The house smells to Rabbit of preservative: of odors filming other odors, of layers of time, of wax and aerosol and death; of safety.

A shape, a shade, comes forward from the kitchen. He expects it to be his father, but it is his mother, shuffling, in a bathrobe, yet erect and moving. She leans forward unsmiling to accept his kiss. Her wrinkled cheek is warm; her hand steadying itself on his wrist is knobbed and cold.

"Happy birthday, Mom." He hugs the massager against his chest; it is too early to offer it. She stares at the package as if he has put a shield between them.

"I'm sixty-five," she says, groping for phrases, so that her sentences end in the middle. "When I was twenty. I told my boy friend I wanted to be shot. When I was thirty." It is not so much the strange tremulous attempt of her lips to close upon a thought as the accompanying stare, an unblinking ungathering gaze into space that lifts her eyes out of any flow and frightens Rabbit with a sense of ultimate blindness, of a blackboard from which they will all be wiped clean.

"You told Pop this?"

"Not your dad. Another. I didn't meet your dad till later. This other one, I'm glad. He's not here to see me now."

"You look pretty good to me," Rabbit tells her. "I didn't think you'd be up."

"Nelson. How do I look. To you?" Thus she acknowledges the boy. She has always been testing him, putting him on the defensive. She has never forgiven him for not being another Harry, for having so much Janice in him. *Those little Springer hands.* Now her own hands, held forgotten in front of her bathrobe belt, constantly work in a palsied waggle.

"Nice," Nelson says. He is wary. He has learned that brevity and promptness of response are his best defense.

To take attention off the kid, Rabbit asks her, "*Should* you be up?"

She laughs, an astonishing silent thing; her head tips back, her big nose glints from the facets of its tip and underside, her hand stops waggling. "I know, the way Earl talks. You'd think from the way he wants me in bed. I'm laid out already. The doctor. Wants me up. I had to bake a cake. Earl wanted. One of those tasteless paps from the Half-A-Loaf. Where's Janice?"

"Yeah, about that. She's awfully sorry, she couldn't come. She had to go off with her mother to the Poconos, it took us all by surprise."

"Things can be. Surprising."

From upstairs Earl Angstrom's thin voice calls anxiously, with a wheedler's borrowed triumph, "They're down! Eagle has landed! We're on the moon, boys and girls! Uncle Sam is on the moon!"

"That's just. The place for him," Mom says, and with a rough gesture sweeps her distorted hand back toward her ear, to smooth down a piece of hair that has wandered loose from the bun she still twists up. Funny, the hair as it grays grows more stubborn. They say even inside the grave, it grows. Open coffins of women and find the whole thing stuffed like inside of a mattress. Pubic hair too? Funny it never needs to be cut. Serafina's looked threadbare, mangy. When he touches his mother's arm to help her up the stairs to look at the moon, the flesh above her elbow is disconcerting – loose upon the bone, as on a well-cooked chicken.

The set is in Mom's bedroom at the front of the house. It has the smell their cellar used to have when they had those two cats. He tries to remember their names. Pansy. And Willy. Willy, the tom, got in so many fights his belly began to slosh and he had to be taken to the Animal Rescue. There is no picture of the moon on the tube, just crackling voices while cardboard cutouts simulate what is happening, and electronic letters spell out who in the crackle of men is speaking.

". . . literally thousands of little one and two foot craters around the area," a man is saying in the voice that used to try to sell them Shredded Ralston between episodes of Tom Mix. "We see some angular blocks out several hundred feet in front of us that are probably two feet in size and have angular edges. There is a hill in view just about on the ground track ahead of us. Difficult to estimate, but might be a half a mile or a mile."

A voice identified as Houston says, "Roger, Tranquillity. We copy. Over." The voice has that Texas authority. As if words were invented by them, they speak so lovingly. When Rabbit was stationed at Fort Larson in '53, Texas looked like the moon to him, brown land running from his knees level as a knife, purple rumpled horizon, sky bigger and barer than he could believe, first time away from his damp green Pennsylvania hills, last time too. Everybody's voice was so nice and gritty and loving, even the girls in the whorehouse. *Honeh. You didn't pay to be no two-timer.*

A voice called Columbia says, "Sounds like a lot better than it did yesterday. At that very low sun angle, it looked rough as a cob

then." As a what? The electronic letters specify: MIKE COLLINS
SPEAKING FROM COMMAND MODULE ORBITING MOON.

Tranquillity says, "It really was rough, Mike, over the targeted
landing area. It was extremely rough, cratered and large numbers
of rocks that were probably some many larger than five or ten feet
in size." Mom's room has lace curtains aged yellowish and pinned
back with tin daisies that to an infant's eyes seemed magical, rose-
and-thorns wallpaper curling loose from the wall above where the
radiator safety valve steams, a kind of plush armchair that soaks up
dust. When he was a child this chair was downstairs and he would
sock it to release torrents of swirling motes into the shaft of afternoon sun; these whirling motes seemed to him worlds, each an
earth, with him on one of them, unthinkably small, unbearably.
Some light used to get into the house in late afternoon, between
the maples. Now the same maples have thronged that light solid,
made the room cellar-dim. The bedside table supports an erect
little company of pill bottles and a Bible. The walls hold tinted
photographs of himself and Mim in high school, taken he remembers by a pushy pudgy little blue-jawed crook who called himself
a Studio and weaseled his way into the building every spring and
made them line up in the auditorium and wet-comb their hair so
their parents couldn't resist two weeks later letting them take in to
the homeroom the money for an 8 by 10 tinted print and a sheet of
wallet-sized grislies of themselves; now this crook by the somer-
sault of time has become a donor of selves otherwise forever lost:
Rabbit's skinny head pink in its translucent blond whiffle, his ears
out from his head an inch, his eyes unreally blue as marbles, even
his lower lids youthfully fleshy; and Miriam's face plump between
the shoulder-length shampoo-shining sheaves rolled under in Rita
Hayworth style, the scarlet tint of her lipstick pinned like a badge
on the starched white of her face. Both children smile out into
space, through the crook's smudged lens, from that sweat-scented
giggling gym toward their mother bedridden some day.

Columbia jokes, "When in doubt, land long."

Tranquillity says, "Well, we did."

And Houston intervenes, "Tranquillity, Houston. We have a
P twenty-two update for you if you're ready to copy. Over."

Columbia jokes again: "At your service, sir."

Houston, unamused, a city of computers working without
sleep, answers, "Right, Mike. P one one zero four thirty two
eighteen; P two one zero four thirty-seven twenty-eight and that
is four miles south. This is based on a targeted landing site. Over."

Columbia repeats the numbers.

Tranquillity says, "Our mission timer is now reading nine zero
four thirty-four forty-seven and static."

"Roger, copy. Your mission timer is now static at – say again
the time."

"Nine zero four thirty-four forty-seven."

"Roger, copy, Tranquillity. That gravity align looked good.
We see you recycling."

"Well, no. I was trying to get time sixteen sixty-five out and
somehow it proceeded on the six-twenty-two before I could do
a BRP thirty-two enter. I want to log a time here and then I'd like
to know whether you want me to proceed on torquing angles or
to go back and re-enter again before torquing. Over."

"Rog, Buzz. Stand by."

Nelson and his grandfather listen raptly to these procedures;
Mary Angstrom turns impatiently – or is it that her difficulty of
motion makes all gestures appear impatient? – and makes her
shuffling way out into the landing and down the stairs again.
Rabbit, heart trembling in its hollow, follows. She needs no help
going down the stairs. In the garishly bright kitchen she asks,
"Where did you say. Janice was?"

"In the Poconos with her mother."

"Why should I believe that?"

"Why shouldn't you?"

She stoops over, waveringly, to open the oven and look in, her
tangled wire hair making a net of light. She grunts, stands, and
states, "Janice. Stays out of my way. These days."

In his frightened, hypnotized condition, Rabbit can only, it
seems, ask questions. "Why would she do that?"

His mother stares and stares, only a movement of her tongue
between her parted lips betraying that she is trying to speak. "I
know too much," she at last brings out, "about her."

Rabbit says, "You know only what a bunch of pathetic old
gossips tell you about her. And stop bugging Pop about it, he

comes into work and bugs me." Since she does not fight back, he
is provoked to go on. "With Mim out turning ten tricks a day in
Las Vegas I'd think you'd have more to worry about than poor
Janice's private life."

"She was always," his mother brings out, "spoiled."

"Yes and Nelson too I suppose is spoiled. How would you
describe me? Just yesterday I was sitting over at the Blasts game
thinking how lousy I used to be at baseball. Let's face it. As a
human being I'm about C minus. As a husband I'm about zilch.
When Verity folds I'll fold with it and have to go on welfare. Some
life. Thanks, Mom."

"Hush," she says, expressionless, "you'll make. The cake fall,"
and like a rusty jackknife she forces herself to bend over and peer
into the gas oven.

"Sorry Mom, but Jesus I'm tired lately."

"You'll feel better when. You're my age."

The party is a success. They sit at the kitchen table with the
four places worn through the enamel in all those years. It is like it
used to be, except that Mom is in a bathrobe and Mim has become
Nelson. Pop carves the roast beef and then cuts up Mom's piece
in small bits for her; her right hand can hold a fork but cannot use
a knife. His teeth slipping down, he proposes a toast in New York
State wine to "my Mary, an angel through thick and thin"; Rabbit
wonders what the thin was. Maybe this is it. When she unwraps
her few presents, she laughs at the massager. "Is this. To keep me
hopping?" she asks, and has her husband plug it in, and rests it,
vibrating, on the top of Nelson's head. He needs this touch of
cheering up. Harry feels Janice's absence gnawing at him. When
the cake is cut the kid eats only half a piece, so Rabbit has to eat
double so not to hurt his mother's feelings. Dusk thickens: over in
West Brewer the sanitorium windows are burning orange and on
this side of the mountain the shadows sneak like burglars into the
narrow concrete space between this house and the unsold one.
Through the papered walls, from the house of the young barefoot
couple, seeps the dull bass percussion of a rock group, making the
matched tins (cookies, sugar, flour, coffee) on Mom's shelf tingle
in their emptiness. In the living room the glass face of the
mahogany sideboard shivers. Nelson's eyes begin to sink, and the

buttoned-up cupid-curves of his mouth smile in apology as he slumps forward to rest his head on the cold enamel of the table. His elders talk about old times in the neighborhood, people of the Thirties and Forties, once so alive you saw them every day and never thought to take even a photograph. The old Methodist refusing to mow his half of the grass strip. Before him the Zims with that pretty daughter the mother would shriek at every breakfast and supper. The man down the street who worked nights at the pretzel plant and who shot himself one dawn with nobody to hear it but the horses of the milk wagon. They had milk wagons then. Some streets were still soft dust. Nelson fights sleep. Rabbit asks him, "Want to head home?"

"Negative, Pop." He drowsily grins at his own wit.

Rabbit extends the joke. "The time is twenty-one hours. We better rendezvous with our spacecraft."

But the spacecraft is empty: a long empty box in the blackness of Penn Villas, slowly spinning in the void, its border beds half-weeded. The kid is frightened to go home. So is Rabbit. They sit on Mom's bed and watch television in the dark. They are told the men in the big metal spider sitting on the moon cannot sleep, so the moon-walk has been moved up several hours. Men in studios, brittle and tired from killing time, demonstrate with actual-size mockups what is supposed to happen; on some channels men in space suits are walking around, laying down tinfoil trays as if for a cookout. At last it happens. The real event. Or is it? A television camera on the leg of the module comes on: an abstraction appears on the screen. The announcer explains that the blackness in the top of the screen is the lunar night, the blackness in the lower left corner is the shadow of the spacecraft with its ladder, the whiteness is the surface of the moon. Nelson is asleep, his head on his father's thigh; funny how kids' skulls grow damp when they sleep. Like bulbs underground. Mom's legs are under the blankets; she is propped up on pillows behind him. Pop is asleep in his chair, his breathing a distant sad sea, touching shore and retreating, touching shore and retreating, an old pump that keeps going; lamplight sneaks through a crack in the windowshade and touches the top of his head, his sparse hair mussed into lank feathers. On the bright box something is happening. A snaky shape sneaks down from the upper left corner; it is a man's leg. It grows another leg, eclipses the bright patch that is the surface of the moon. A man in clumsy silhouette has interposed himself among these abstract shadows and glare. An Armstrong, but not Jack. He says something about "steps" that a crackle keeps Rabbit from understanding. Electronic letters travelling sideways spell out MAN IS ON THE MOON. The voice, crackling, tells Houston that the surface is fine and powdery, he can pick it up with his toe, it adheres to his boot like powdered charcoal, that he sinks in only a fraction of an inch, that it's easier to move around than in the simulations on Earth. From behind him, Rabbit's mother's hand with difficulty reaches out, touches the back of his skull, stays there, awkwardly tries to massage his scalp, to ease away thoughts of the trouble she knows he is in. "I don't know, Mom," he abruptly admits. "I know it's happened, but I don't feel anything yet."

II. JILL

"It's different but it's very pretty out here."
— NEIL ARMSTRONG, *July 20, 1969*

DAYS, pale slices between nights, they blend, not exactly alike, transparencies so lightly tinted that only stacked all together do they darken to a fatal shade. One Saturday in August Buchanan approaches Rabbit during the coffee break. They are part of the half-crew working the half-day; hence perhaps this intimacy. The Negro wipes from his lips the moisture of the morning whisky enjoyed outside in the sunshine of the loading platform, and asks, "How're they treatin' you, Harry?"

"They?" Harry has known the other man by sight and name for years but still is not quite easy, talking to a black; there always seems to be some joke involved, that he doesn't quite get.

"The world, man."

"Not bad."

Buchanan stands there blinking, studying, jiggling up and down on his feet engagingly. Hard to tell how old they are. He might be thirty-five, he might be sixty. On his upper lip he wears the smallest possible black mustache, smaller than a type brush. His color is ashy, without any shine to it, whereas the other shop Negro, Farnsworth, looks shoe-polished and twinkles among the printing machinery, under the steady shadowless light. "But not good, huh?"

"I'm not sleeping so good," Rabbit does confess. He has an itch, these days, to confess, to spill, he is so much alone.

"Your old lady still shackin' up across town?"

Everybody knows. Niggers, coolies, derelicts, morons. Numbers writers, bus conductors, beauty shop operators, the entire brick city of Brewer. VERITY EMPLOYEE NAMED CUCKOLD OF WEEK. *Angstrom Accepts Official Horns from Mayor.* "I'm living alone," Harry admits, adding, "with the kid."

"How about that," Buchanan says, lightly rocking. "How about that?"

Rabbit says weakly, "Until things straighten out."

"Gettin' any tail?"

Harry must look startled, for Buchanan hastens to explain, "Man has to have tail. Where's your dad these days?" The question flows from the assertion immediately, though it doesn't seem to follow.

Rabbit says, puzzled, offended, but because Buchanan is a Negro not knowing how to evade him, "He's taking two weeks off so he can drive my mother back and forth to the hospital for some tests."

"Yeass." Buchanan mulls, the two pushed-out cushions of his mouth appearing to commune with each other through a hum; then a new thought darts out through them, making his mustache jig. "Your dad is a real pal to you, that's a wonderful thing. That is a truly wonderful thing. I never had a dad like that, I knew who the man was, he was around town, but he was never my dad in the sense your dad is your dad. He was never my pal like that."

Harry hangs uncertainly, not knowing if he should commiserate or laugh. "Well," he decides to confess, "he's sort of a pal, and sort of a pain in the neck."

Buchanan likes the remark, even though he goes through peppery motions of rejecting it. "Oh, never say that now. You just be grateful you have a dad that cares. You don't know, man, how lucky you have it. Just 'cause your wife's gettin' her ass looked after elsewhere don't mean the whole world is come to some bad end. You should be havin' your tail, is all. You're a big fella."

Distaste and excitement contend in Harry; he feels tall and pale beside Buchanan, and feminine, a tingling target of fun and tenderness and avarice mixed. Talking to Negroes makes him feel itchy, up behind the eyeballs, maybe because theirs look so semi-liquid and yellow in the white and sore. Their whole beings seem lubricated in pain. "I'll manage," he says reluctantly, thinking of Peggy Fosnacht.

The end-of-break bell rings. Buchanan snaps his shoulders into a hunch and out of it as if rendering a verdict. "How about it, Harry, steppin' out with some of the boys tonight," he says. "Come on into Jimbo's Lounge around nine, ten, see what develops. Maybe nothin'. Maybe sumpthin'. You're just turnin' old, the way you're goin' now. Old and fat and finicky, and that's no way for a nice big man to go." He sees that Rabbit's instincts are to refuse; he holds up a quick palm the color of silver polish and says, "Think about it. I like you, man. If you don't show, you don't show. No sweat."

All Saturday the invitation hums in his ears. Something in what Buchanan said. He was lying down to die, had been lying down for years. His body had been telling him to. His eyes blur print in the afternoons, no urge to run walking even that stretch of tempting curved sidewalk home, has to fight sleep before supper and then can't get under at night, can't even get it up to jerk off to relax himself. Awake with the first light every morning regardless, another day scraping his eyes. Without going much of anywhere in his life he has somehow seen everything too often. Trees, weather, the molding trim drying its cracks wider around the front door, he notices every day going out, house made of green wood. No belief in an afterlife, no hope for it, too much more of the same thing, already it seems he's lived twice. When he came back to Janice that began the second time for him; poor kid is having her first time now. Bless that dope. At least she had the drive to get out. Women, fire in their crotch, won't burn out, begin by fighting off pricks, end by going wild hunting for one that still works.

Once last week he called the lot to find out if she and Stavros were reporting for work or just screwing around the clock. Mildred Kroust answered, she put him on to Janice, who whispered, "Harry, Daddy doesn't know about us, don't ever call me here, I'll call you back." And she had called him late that afternoon, at the house, Nelson in the other room watching *Gilligan's Island*, and said cool as you please, he hardly knew her voice, "Harry, I'm sorry for whatever pain this is causing you, truly sorry, but it's very important that at this point in our lives we don't let guilt feelings motivate us. I'm trying to look honestly into myself, to see who I am, and where I should be going. I want us both, Harry, to come to a decision we can live with. It's the year nineteen sixty-nine and there's no reason for two mature people to smother each other to death simply out of inertia. I'm searching for a valid identity and I suggest you do the same." After some more of this, she hung up. Her vocabulary had expanded, maybe she was watching a lot of psychiatric talk shows. The sinners shall be justified. Screw her. Dear Lord, screw her. He is thinking this on the bus.

He thinks, *Screw her*, and at home has a beer and takes a bath and puts on his good summer suit, a light gray sharkskin, and gets Nelson's pajamas out of the dryer and his toothbrush out of the bathroom. The kid and Billy have arranged for him to spend the night. Harry calls up Peggy to check it out. "Oh absolutely," she says, "I'm not going anywhere, why don't you stay and have dinner?"

"I can't I don't think."

"Why not? Something else to do?"

"Sort of." He and the kid go over around six, on an empty bus. Already at this hour Weiser has that weekend up-tempo, cars hurrying faster home to get out again, a very fat man with orange hair standing under an awning savoring a cigar as if angels will shortly descend, an expectant shimmer on the shut storefronts, girls clicking along with heads big as rose-bushes, curlers wrapped in a kerchief. Saturday night. Peggy meets him at the door with an offer of a drink. She and Billy live in an apartment in one of the new eight-story buildings in West Brewer overlooking the river, where there used to be a harness racetrack. From her living room she has a panorama of Brewer, the concrete eagle on the skyscraper Court House flaring his wings above the back of the Owl Pretzels sign. Beyond the flowerpot-red city Mt. Judge hangs smoky-green, one side gashed by a gravel pit like a roast beginning to be carved. The river coal black.

"Maybe just one. I gotta go somewhere."

"You said that. What kind of drink?" She is wearing a clingy palish-purple sort of Paisley mini that shows a lot of heavy leg. One thing Janice always had, was nifty legs. Peggy has a pasty helpless look of white meat behind the knees.

"You have Daiquiri mix?"

"I don't know, Ollie used to keep things like that, but when we moved I think it all stayed with him." She and Ollie Fosnacht had lived in an asbestos-shingled semi-detached some blocks away, not far from the county mental hospital. Ollie lives in the city now, near his music store, and she and the kid have this apartment, with Ollie in their view if they can find him. She is rummaging in a low cabinet below some empty bookcases. "I can't see any, it comes in envelopes. How about gin and something?"

"You have bitter lemon?"

More rummaging. "No, just some tonic."

"Good enough. Want me to make it?"

"If you like." She stands up, heavy-legged, lightly sweating, relieved. Knowing he was coming, Peggy had decided against sunglasses, a sign of trust to leave them off. Her walleyes are naked to him, her face has this helpless look, turned full toward him while both eyes seem fascinated by something in the corners of the ceiling. He knows only one eye is bad but he never can bring himself to figure out which. And all around her eyes this net of white wrinkles the sunglasses usually conceal.

He asks her, "What for you?"

"Oh, anything. The same thing. I drink everything."

While he is cracking an ice tray in the tiny kitchenette, the two boys have snuck out of Billy's bedroom. Rabbit wonders if they have been looking at dirty photographs. The kind of pictures kids used to have to pay an old cripple on Plum Street a dollar apiece for you can buy a whole magazine full of now for seventy-five cents, right downtown. The Supreme Court, old men letting the roof cave in. Billy is a head taller than Nelson, sunburned where Nelson takes a tan after his mother, both of them with hair down over their ears, the Fosnacht boy's blonder and curlier. "Mom, we want to go downstairs and run the mini-bike on the parking lot."

"Come back up in an hour," Peggy tells them, "I'll give you supper."

"Nelson had a peanut-butter sandwich before we left," Rabbit explains.

"Typical male cooking," Peggy says. "Where're you going this evening anyway, all dressed up in a suit?"

"Nowhere much. I told a guy I might meet him." He doesn't say it is a Negro. He should be asking her out, is his sudden frightened feeling. She is dressed to go out; but not so dolled-up it can't appear she plans to stay home tonight. He hands her her g.-and-t. The best defense is to be offensive. "You don't have any mint or limes or anything."

Her plucked eyebrows lift. "No, there are lemons in the fridge, is all. I could run down to the grocery for you." Not entirely ironical: using his complaint to weave coziness.

Rabbit laughs to retract. "Forget it, I'm just used to bars, where they have everything. At home all I ever do is drink beer."

She laughs in answer. She is tense as a schoolteacher facing her first class. To relax them both he sits down in a loose leather armchair that says *pfsshhu*. "Hey, this is nice," he announces, meaning the vista, but he spoke too early, for from this low chair the view is flung out of sight and becomes all sky: a thin bright wash, stripes like fat in bacon.

"You should hear Ollie complain about the rent." Peggy sits down not in another chair but on the flat grille where the radiator breathes beneath the window, opposite and above him, so he sees a lot of her legs — shiny skin stuffed to the point of shapelessness. Still, she is showing him what she has, right up to the triangle of underpants, which is one more benefit of being alive in 1969. Miniskirts and those magazines: well, hell, we've always known women had crotches, why not make it legal? A guy at the shop brought in a magazine that, honestly, was all cunts, in blurred bad four-color but cunts, upside down, backwards, the girls attached to them rolling their tongues in their mouths and fanning their hands on their bellies and otherwise trying to hide how silly they felt. Homely things, really, cunts. Without the Supreme Court that might never have been made clear.

"Hey, how is old Ollie?"

Peggy shrugs. "He calls. Usually to cancel his Sunday with Billy. You know he never was the family man you are."

Rabbit is surprised to be called that. He is getting too tame. He asks her, "How does he spend his time?"

"Oh," Peggy says, and awkwardly turns her body so Rabbit sees pricked out in windowlight the tonic bubbles in her drink, which is surprisingly near drunk, "he rattles around Brewer with a bunch of creeps. Musicians, mostly. They go to Philadelphia a lot, and New York. Last winter he went skiing at Aspen and told me all about it, including the girls. He came back so brown in the face, I cried for days. I could never get him outdoors, when we had the place over on Franklin Street. How do *you* spend *your* time?"

"I work. I mope around the house with the kid. We look at the boob tube and play catch in the back yard."

"Do you mope for *her*, Harry?" With a clumsy shrug of her hip the woman moves off her radiator perch, her walleyes staring to either side of him so he thinks he is her target and flinches. But she floats past him and, clattering, refills her drink. "Want another?"

"No thanks, I'm still working on this one. I gotta go in a minute."

"So soon," she croons unseen, as if remembering the beginning of a song in her tiny kitchenette. From far below their windows arises the razzing, coughing sound of the boys on the mini-bike. The noise swoops and swirls, a rude buzzard. Beyond it across the river hangs the murmur of Brewer traffic, constant like the sea; an occasional car toots, a wink of phosphorescence. From the kitch-enette, as if she had been baking the thought in the oven, Peggy calls, "She's not worth it." Then her body is at his back, her voice upon his head. "I didn't know," she says, "you loved her so much. I don't think Janice knew it either."

"Well, you get used to somebody. Anyway, it's an insult. With a wop like that. You should hear him run down the U.S. govern-ment."

"Harry, you know what I think. I'm sure you know what I think."

He doesn't. He has no idea. She seems to think he's been read-ing thoughts printed on her underpants.

"I think she's treated you horribly. The last time we had lunch together, I told her so. I said, 'Janice, your attempts to justify your-self do not impress me. You've left a man who came back to you when you needed him, and you've left your son at a point in his development when it's immensely important to have a stable home setting.' I said that right to her face."

"Actually the kid goes over to the lot pretty much and sees her there. She and Stavros take him out to eat. In a way it's like he gained an uncle."

"You're so for*giv*ing, Harry! Ollie would have *strang*led me; he's still immensely jealous. He's always asking me who my boyfriends are."

He doubts she has any, and sips his drink. Although in this county women with big bottoms usually don't go begging. Dutchmen love bulk. He says, "Well, I don't know if I did such a great job with Janice. She has to live too."

"Well Harry, if that's your reasoning, we *all* have to live." And from the way she stands there in front of him, if he sat up straight her pussy would be exactly at his nose. Hair tickles: he might sneeze. He sips the drink again, and feels the tasteless fluid expand his inner space. He might sit up at any minute, if she doesn't watch out. From the hair on her head probably a thick springy bush, though you can't always tell, some of the cunts in the magazine just had wisps at the base of their bellies, hardly an armpit's worth. Dolls. She moves away saying, "Who'll hold families together, if everybody has to live? Living is a compromise, between doing what *you* want and doing what *oth*er people want."

"What about what poor old God wants?"

The uncalled-for noun jars her from the seductive pose she has assumed, facing out the window, her backside turned to him. The dog position. Tip her over a chair and let her fuss herself with her fingers into coming while he does it from behind. Janice got so she preferred it, more animal, she wasn't distracted by the look on his face, never was one for wet kisses, when they first started going together complained she couldn't breathe, he asked her if she had adenoids. Seriously. No two alike, a billion cunts in the world, snowflakes. Touch them right they melt. What we most protect is where we want to be invaded. Peggy leaves her drink on the sill like a tall jewel and turns to him with her deformed face open. Since the word has been sprung on her, she asks, "Don't you think God is people?"

"No, I think God is everything that isn't people. I guess I think that. I don't think enough to know what I think." In irritation, he stands.

Big against the window, a hot shadow, palish-purple edges

catching the light ebbing from the red city, the dim mountain, Peggy exclaims. "Oh, you think with" – and to assist her awkward thought she draws his shape in the air with two hands, having freed them for this gesture – "your whole person."

She looks so helpless and vague there seems nothing for Harry to do but step into the outline of himself she has drawn and kiss her. Her face, eclipsed, feels large and cool. Her lips bumble on his, the spongy wax of gumdrops, yet narcotic, not quite tasteless: as a kid Rabbit loved bland candy like Dots; sitting in the movies he used to plow through three nickel boxes of them, playing with them with his tongue and teeth, playing, playing before giving himself the ecstasy of the bite. Up and down his length she bumps against him, straining against his height, touching. The strange place on her where nothing is, the strange place higher where some things are. Her haunches knot with the effort of keeping on tiptoe. She pushes, pushes: he is a cunt this one-eyed woman is coldly pushing up into. He feels her mind gutter out; she has wrapped them in a clumsy large ball of darkness.

Something scratches on the ball. A key in a lock. Then the door knocks. Harry and Peggy push apart, she tucks her hair back around her spread-legged eyes and runs heavily to the door and lets in the boys. They are red-faced and furious. "Mom, the fucking thing broke down again," Billy tells his mother. Nelson looks over at Harry. The boy is near tears. Since Janice left, he is silent and delicate: an eggshell full of tears.

"It wasn't my fault," he calls huskily, injustice a sieve in his throat. "Dad, he says it was my fault."

"You baby, I didn't say that exactly."

"You did. He did, Dad, and it wasn't."

"All I said was he spun out too fast. He always spins out too fast. He flipped on a loose stone, now the headlight is bent under and it won't start."

"If it wasn't such a cheap one it wouldn't break all the time."

"It's not a cheap one it's the best one there is almost and anyway you don't even have any –"

"I wouldn't take one if you gave it to me –"

"So who are you to talk."

"Hey, easy, easy," Harry says. "We'll get it fixed. I'll pay for it."

"Don't pay for it, Dad. It wasn't anybody's fault. It's just he's so spoiled."

"You shrimp," Billy says, and hits him, much the same way that three weeks ago Harry hit Janice, hard but seeking a spot that could take it. Harry separates them, squeezing Billy's arm so the kid clams up. This kid is going to be tough some day. Already his arm is stringy.

Peggy is just bringing it all into focus, her insides shifting back from that kiss. "Billy, these things will happen if you insist on playing so dangerously." To Harry she says, "*Damn* Ollie for getting it for him, I think he did it to spite me. He knows I hate machines."

Harry decides Billy is the one to talk to. "Hey. Billy. Shall I take Nelson back home, or do you want him to spend the night anyway?"

And both boys set up a wailing for Nelson to spend the night. "Dad you don't have to come for me or anything, I'll ride my bike home in the morning first thing, I left it here yesterday."

So Rabbit releases Billy's arm and gives Nelson a kiss somewhere around the ear and tries to find the right eye of Peggy's to look into. "Okey-doak. I'll be off."

She says, "Must you? Stay. Can't I give you supper? Another drink? It's early yet."

"This guy's waiting," Rabbit lies, and makes it around her furniture to the door.

Her body chases him. Her vague eyes shine in their tissue-paper sockets, and her lips have that loosened look kissed lips get; he resists the greedy urge to buy another box of Dots. "Harry," she begins, and seems to fall toward him, after a stumble, though they don't touch.

"Yeah?"

"I'm usually here. If – you know."

"I know. Thanks for the g.-and-t. Your view is great." He reaches then and pats, not her ass exactly, the flank at the side of it, too broad, too firm, alive enough under his palm, it turns out, to make him wonder, when her door closes, why he is going down the elevator, and out.

It is too early to meet Buchanan. He walks back through the

West Brewer side streets toward Weiser, through the dulling summer light and the sounds of distant games, of dishes rattled in kitchen sinks, of television muffled to a murmur mechanically laced with laughter and applause, of cars driven by teenagers laying rubber and shifting down. Children and old men sit on the porch steps beside the lead-colored milk-bottle boxes. Some stretches of sidewalk are brick; these neighborhoods, the oldest in West Brewer, close to the river, are cramped, gentle, barren. Between the trees there is a rigid flourishing of hydrants, meters, and signs, some of them – virtual billboards in white on green – directing motorists to superhighways whose number is blazoned on the federal shield or on the commonwealth keystone; from these obscure West Brewer byways, sidewalks and asphalt streets rumpled comfortably as old clothes, one can be arrowed toward Philadelphia, Baltimore, Washington the national capital, New York the headquarters of commerce and fashion. Or in the other direction can find Pittsburgh and Chicago. But beneath these awesome metal insignia of vastness and motion fat men in undershirts loiter, old ladies move between patches of gossip with the rural waddle of egg-gatherers, dogs sleep curled beside the cooling curb, and children with hockey sticks and tape-handled bats diffidently chip at whiffle balls and wads of leather, whittling themselves into the next generation of athletes and astronauts. Rabbit's eyes sting in the dusk, in this smoke of his essence, these harmless neighborhoods that have gone to seed. So much love, too much love, it is our madness, it is rotting us out, exploding us like dandelion polls. He stops at a corner grocery for a candy bar, an Oh Henry, then at the Burger Bliss on Weiser, dazzling in its lake of parking space, for a Lunar Special (double cheeseburger with an American flag stuck into the bun) and a vanilla milkshake, that tastes toward the bottom of chemical sludge.

The interior of Burger Bliss is so bright that his fingernails, with their big mauve moons, gleam and the coins he puts down in payment seem cartwheels of metal. Beyond the lake of light, unfriendly darkness. He ventures out past a dimmed drive-in bank and crosses the bridge. High slender arc lamps on giant flower stems send down a sublunar light by which the hurrying cars all appear purple. There are no other faces but his on the bridge.

From the middle, Brewer seems a web, to which glowing droplets adhere. Mt. Judge is one with the night. The luminous smudge of the Pinnacle Hotel hangs like a star.

Gnats bred by the water brush Rabbit's face; Janice's desertion nags him from within, a sore spot in his stomach. Ease off beer and coffee. Alone, he must take care of himself. Sleeping alone, he dreads the bed, watches the late shows, Carson, Griffin, cocky guys with nothing to sell but their brass. Making millions on sheer gall. American dream: when he first heard the phrase as a kid he pictured God lying sleeping, the quilt-colored map of the U.S. coming out of his head like a cloud. Peggy's embrace drags at his limbs. Suit feels sticky. Jimbo's Friendly Lounge is right off the Brewer end of the bridge, a half-block down from Plum. Inside it, all the people are black.

Black to him is just a political word but these people really are, their faces shine of blackness turning as he enters, a large soft white man in a sticky gray suit. Fear travels up and down his skin, but the music of the great green-and-mauve-glowing jukebox called Moonmood slides on, and the liquid of laughter and tickled muttering resumes flowing; his entrance was merely a snag. Rabbit hangs like a balloon waiting for a dart; then his elbow is jostled and Buchanan is beside him.

"Hey, man, you made it." The Negro has materialized from the smoke. His overtrimmed mustache looks wicked in here.

"You didn't think I would?"

"Doubted it," Buchanan says. "Doubted it severely."

"It was your idea."

"Right. Harry, you are right. I'm not arguing, I am rejoicing. Let's fix you up. You need a drink, right?"

"I don't know, my stomach's getting kind of sensitive."

"You need two drinks. Tell me your poison."

"Maybe a Daiquiri?"

"Never. That is a lady's drink for salad luncheons. Rufe, you old rascal."

"Yazzuh, yazzuh," comes the answer from the bar.

"Do a Stinger for the man."

"Yaz-*zuh*."

Rufe has a bald head like one of the stone hatchets in the

Brewer Museum, only better polished. He bows into the marine underglow of the bar and Buchanan leads Rabbit to a booth in the back. The place is deep and more complicated than it appears from the outside. Booths recede and lurk: darkwood cape-shapes. Along one wall, Rufe and the lowlit bar; behind and above it, not only the usual Pabst and Bud and Miller's gimcracks bobbing and shimmering, but two stuffed small deer-heads, staring with bright brown eyes that will never blink. Gazelles, could they have been gazelles? A space away, toward a wall but with enough room for a row of booths behind, a baby grand piano, painted silver with one of those spray cans, silver in circular swirls. In a room oblique-ly off the main room, a pool table: colored boys all arms and legs spidering around the idyllic green felt. The presence of any game reassures Rabbit. Where any game is being played a hedge exists against fury. "Come meet some soul," Buchanan says. Two shad-ows in the booth are a man and a woman. The man wears silver circular glasses and a little pussy of a goatee and is young. The woman is old and wrinkled and smokes a yellow cigarette that requires much sucking in and holding down and closing of the eyes and sighing. Her brown eyelids are gray, painted blue. Sweat shines below the base of her throat, on the slant bone between her breasts, as if she had breasts, which she does not, though her dress, the blood-color of a rooster's comb, is cut deep, as if she did. Before they are introduced she says "Hi" to Harry, but her eyes slit to pin him fast in the sliding of a dream.

"This man," Buchanan is announcing, "is a co-worker of mine, he works right beside his daddy at Ver-i-ty Press, an expert Lino-typist," giving syllables an odd ticking equality, a put-on or signal of some sort? "But not only that. He is an ath-e-lete of renown, a basketball player bar none, the Big O of Brewer in his day."

"Very beautiful," the other dark man says. Round specs tilt, glint. The shadow of a face they cling to feels thin in the darkness. The voice arises very definite and dry.

"Many years ago," Rabbit says, apologizing for his bulk, his bloated pallor, his dead fame. He sits down in the booth to hide.

"He has the hands," the woman states. She is in a trance. She says, "Give old Babe one of those hands, white boy." A-prickle with nervousness, wanting to sneeze on the sweetish smoke,

Rabbit lifts his right hand up from his lap and lays it on the slippery table. Innocent meat. Distorted paw. Reminds him of, on television, that show with chimpanzees synchronized with talk and music, the eerie look of having just missed the winning design.

The woman touches it. Her touch reptilian cool. Her eyes lift, brooding. Above the glistening bone her throat drips jewels, a napkin of rhinestones or maybe real diamonds; Cadillacs after all, alligator shoes, they can't put their money into real estate like whites; Springer's thrifty Toyotas not to the point. His mind is racing with his pulse. She has a silver sequin pasted beside one eye. Accent the ugly until it becomes gorgeous. Her eyelashes are great false crescents. That she has taken such care of herself leads him to suspect she will not harm him. His pulse slows. Her touch slithers nice as a snake. "Do dig that thumb," she advises the air. She caresses his thumb's curve. Its thin-skinned veined ball. Its color-less moon nail. "That thumb means sweetness and light. It is an indicator of pleasure in Sagittarius and Leo." She gives one knuckle an affectionate pinch.

The Negro not Buchanan (Buchanan has hustled to the bar to check on the Stinger) says, "Not like one of them usual little sawed-off nuggers these devils come at you with, right?"

Babe answers, not yielding her trance, "No, sir. This thumb here is extremely plausible. Under the right signs it would absolutely function. Now these knuckles here, they aren't so good, I don't get much music out of these knuckles." And she presses a chord on them, with fingers startlingly hard and certain. "But this here thumb," she goes back to caressing it, "is a real enough heartbreaker."

"All these Charlies is heartbreakers, right? Just cause they don't know how to shake their butterball asses don't mean they don't get Number One in, they gets it in real mean, right? The reason they so mean, they has so much religion, right? That big white God go tells 'em, Screw that black chick, and they really wangs away 'cause God's right there slappin' away at their butterball asses. Cracker spelled backwards is fucker, right?"

Rabbit wonders if this is how the young Negro really talks, wonders if there is a real way. He does not move, does not even bring back his hand from the woman's inspection, her touches chill as teeth. He is among panthers.

Buchanan, that old rascal, bustles back and sets before Rabbit a tall pale glass of poison and shoves in so Rabbit has to shove over opposite the other man. Buchanan's eyes check around the faces and guess it's gotten heavy. Lightly he says, "This man's wife, you know what? That woman, I never had the pleasure of meeting her, not counting those Verity picnics where Farnsworth, you all know Farnsworth now − ?"

"Like a father," the young man says, adding, "Right?"

" − gets me so bombed out of my mind on that barrel beer I can't remember anybody by face or name, where was I? Yes, that woman, she just upped and left him the other week, left him flat to go chasing around with some other gentleman, something like an I-talian, didn't you say Harry?"

"A Greek."

Babe clucks. "Honey, now what did he have you didn't? He must of had a thumb long as this badmouth's tongue." She nudges her companion, who retrieves from his lips this shared cigarette, which has grown so short it must burn, and sticks out his tongue. Its whiteness shocks Rabbit; a mouthful of luminous flesh. Though fat and pale, it does not look very long. This man, Rabbit sees, is a boy; the patch of goatee is all he can grow. Harry does not like him. He likes Babe, he thinks, even though she has dried hard, a prune on the bottom of the box. In here they are all on the bottom of the box. This drink, and his hand, are the whitest thing around. Not to think of the other's tongue. He sips. Too sweet, wicked. A thin headache promptly begins.

Buchanan is persisting, "Don't seem right to me, healthy big man living alone with nobody now to comfort him."

The goatee bobs. "Doesn't bother me in the slightest. Gives the man time to think, right? Gets the thought of cunt off his back, right? Chances are he has some hobby he can do, you know, like woodwork." He explains to Babe, "You know, like a lot of these peckerwoods have this clever thing they can do down in their basements, like stamp collecting, right? That's how they keep making it big. Cleverness, right?" He taps his skull, whose narrowness is padded by maybe an inch of tight black wool. The texture reminds Rabbit of his mother's crocheting, if she had used tiny metal thread. Her blue bent hands now helpless. Even in here, family sadness pokes at him, probing sore holes.

"I used to collect baseball cards," he tells them. He hopes to excite enough rudeness from them so he can leave. He remembers the cards' bubble–gum smell, their silken feel from the powdered sugar. He sips the Stinger.

Babe sees him make a face. "You don't have to drink that piss." She nudges her neighbor again. "Let's have one more stick."

"Woman, you must think I'm made of hay."

"I know you're plenty magical, that's one thing. Off that uptight shit, the ofay here needs a lift and I'm nowhere near spaced enough to pee-form."

"Last drag," he says, and passes her the tiny wet butt.

She crushes it into the Sunflower Beer ashtray. "This roach is hereby dead." And holds her thin hand palm up for a hit.

Buchanan is clucking. "Mother-love, go easy on yourself," he tells Babe.

The other Negro is lighting another cigarette; the paper is twisted at the end and flares, subsides. He passes it to her saying, "Waste is a sin, right?"

"Hush now. This honeyman needs to loosen up, I hate to see 'em sad, I always have, they aren't like us, they don't have the insides to accommodate it. They's like little babies that way, they passes it off to someone else." She is offering Rabbit the cigarette, moist end toward him.

He says, "No thanks, I gave up smoking ten years ago."

Buchanan chuckles, with thumb and forefinger smooths his mustache sharper.

The boy says, "They're going to live forever, right?"

Babe says, "This ain't any of that nicotine shit. This weed is kindness itself."

While Babe is coaxing him, Buchanan and the boy diagonally discuss his immortality. "My daddy used to say, Down home, you never did see a dead white man, any more'n you'd see a dead mule."

"God's on their side, right? God's white, right? He doesn't want no more Charlies up there to cut into his take, he has it just fine the way it is, him and all those black angels out in the cotton."

"Your mouth's gonta hurt you, boy. The man is the lay of the land down here."

"Whose black ass you hustling, hers or yours?"

"You just keep your smack in the heel of your shoe."

Babe is saying, "You suck it in as far as it'll go and hold it down as long as you absolutely can. It needs to mix with *you*."

Rabbit tries to comply, but coughing undoes every puff. Also he is afraid of getting "hooked," of being suddenly jabbed with a needle, of starting to hallucinate because of something dropped into his Stinger. AUTOPSY ORDERED IN FRIENDLY LOUNGE DEATH. *Coroner Notes Atypical Color of Skin.*

Watching him cough, the boy says, "He *is* beautiful. I didn't know they still came with all those corners. Right out of the crackerbox, right?"

This angers Rabbit enough to keep a drag down. It burns his throat and turns his stomach. He exhales with the relief of vomiting and waits for something to happen. Nothing. He sips the Stinger but now it tastes chemical like the bottom of that milkshake. He wonders how he can get out of here. Is Peggy's offer still open? Just to feel the muggy kiss of summer night on the Brewer streets would be welcome. Nothing feels worse than other people's good times.

Babe asks Buchanan, "What'd you have in mind, Buck?" She is working on the joint now and the smoke includes her eyes.

The fat man's shrug jiggles Rabbit's side. "No big plans," Buchanan mutters. "See what develops. Woman, way you're goin', you won't be able to tell those black keys from the white."

She plumes smoke into his face. "Who owns who?"

The boy cuts in. "Ofay doesn't dig he's a john, right?"

Buchanan, his smoothness jammed, observes, "That mouth again."

Rabbit asks loudly, "What else shall we talk about?" and twiddles his fingers at Babe for the joint. Inhaling still burns, but something is starting to mesh. He feels his height above the others as a good, a lordly, thing.

Buchanan is probing the other two. "Jill in tonight?"

Babe says, "Left her back at the place."

The boy asks, "On a nod, right?"

"You stay away, hear, she got herself clean. She's on no nod, just tired from mental confusion, from fighting her signs."

"Clean," the boy says, "what's clean? White is clean, right? Cunt is clean, right? Shit is clean, right? There's nothin' not clean the law don't go pointing its finger at it, right?"

"Wrong," Babe says. "Hate is not clean. A boy like you with hate in his heart, he needs to wash."

"Wash is what they said to Jesus, right?"

"Who's Jill?" Rabbit asks.

"Wash is what Pilate said he thought he might go do, right? Don't go saying clean to me, Babe, that's one darkie bag they had us in too long."

Buchanan is still delicately prying at Babe. "She coming in?"

The other cuts in, "She'll be in, can't keep that cunt away; put locks on the doors, she'll ooze in the letter slot."

Babe turns to him in mild surprise. "Now you loves little Jill."

"You can love what you don't like, right?"

Babe hangs her head. "That poor baby," she tells the tabletop, "just going to hurt herself and anybody standing near."

Buchanan speaks slowly, threading his way. "Just thought, man might like to meet Jill."

The boy sits up. Electricity, reflected from the bar and the streets, spins around his spectacle rims. "Gonna match 'em up," he says, "you're gonna cut yourself in on an all-honky fuck. You can out-devil these devils any day, right? You could of out-niggered Moses on the hill."

He seems to be a static the other two put up with. Buchanan is still prying at Babe across the table. "Just thought," he shrugs, "two birds with one stone."

A tear falls from her creased face to the tabletop. Her hair is done tight back like a schoolgirl's, a red ribbon in back. It must hurt, with kinky hair. "Going to take herself down all the way, it's in her signs, can't slip your signs."

"Who's that voodoo supposed to boogaboo?" the boy asks. "Whitey here got so much science he don't even need to play the numbers, right?"

Rabbit asks, "Is Jill white?"

The boy tells the two others angrily, "Cut the crooning, she'll

be here, Christ, where else would she go, right? We're the blood
to wash her sins away, right? Clean. Shit, that burns me. There's
no dirt made that cunt won't swallow. With a smile on her face,
right? Because she's *clean*." There seems to be not only a history
but a religion behind his anger. Rabbit sees this much, that the
other two are working to fix him up with this approaching cloud,
this Jill, who will be pale like the Stinger, and poisonous.

He announces, "I think I'll go soon."

Buchanan swiftly squeezes his forearm. "What you want to do
that for, Br'er Rabbit? You haven't achieved your objective,
friend."

"My only objective was to be polite." *She'll ooze in the letter slot*:
haunted by this image and the smoke inside him, he feels he can
lift up from the booth, pass across Buchanan's shoulders like a
shawl, and out the door. Nothing can hold him, not Mom, not
Janice. He could slip a posse dribbling, Tothero used to flatter him.

"You going to go off half-cocked," Buchanan warns.

"You ain't heard Babe play," the other man says.

He stops rising. "Babe plays?"

She is flustered, stares at her thin ringless hands, fiddles,
mumbles. "Let him go. Let the man run. I don't want him to hear."

The boy teases her. "Babe now, what sort of bad black act you
putting on? He wants to hear you do your thing. Your darkie
thing, right? You did the spooky card-reading bit and now you
can do the banjo bit and maybe you can do the hot momma bit
afterwards but it doesn't look like it right now, right?"

"Ease off, nigger," she says, face still bent low. "Sometime you
going to lean too hard."

Rabbit asks her shyly, "You play the piano?"

"He gives me bad vibes," Babe confesses to the two black men.
"Those knuckles of his aren't too good. Bad shadows in there."

Buchanan surprises Harry by reaching and covering her thin
bare hands with one of his broadened big pressman's hands, a ring
of milk-blue jade on one finger, battered bright copper on another.
His other arm reaches around Harry's shoulders, heavy. "Suppose
you was him," he says to Babe, "how would that make you feel?"

"Bad," she says. "As bad as I feel anyway."

"Play for me Babe," Rabbit says in the lovingness of pot, and she lifts her eyes to his and lets her lips pull back on long yellow teeth and gums the color of rhubarb stems. "Men," Babe gaily drawls. "They sure can retail the shit." She pushes herself out of the booth, hobbling in her comb-red dress, and crosses through a henscratch of applause to the piano painted as if by children in silver swirls. She signals to the bar for Rufe to turn on the blue spot and bows stiffly, once, grudging the darkness around her a smile and, after a couple of runs to burn away the fog, plays.

What does Babe play? All the good old ones. All show tunes. "Up a Lazy River," "You're the Top," "Thou Swell," "Summertime," you know. There are hundreds, thousands. Men from Indiana wrote them in Manhattan. They flow into each other without edges, flowing under black bridges of chords thumped six, seven times, as if Babe is helping the piano to remember a word it won't say. Or spanking the silence. Or saying, *Here I am, find me, find me.* Her hands, all brown bone, hang on the keyboard hushed like gloves on a table; she gazes up through blue dust to get herself into focus, she lets her hands fall into another tune: "My Funny Valentine," "Smoke Gets in Your Eyes," "I Can't Get Started," starting to hum along with herself now, lyrics born in some distant smoke, decades when Americans moved within the American dream, laughing at it, starving on it, but living it, humming it, the national anthem everywhere. Wise guys and hicks, straw boaters and bib overalls, fast bucks, broken hearts, penthouses in the sky, shacks by the railroad tracks, ups and downs, rich and poor, trolley cars, and the latest news by radio. Rabbit had come in on the end of it, as the world shrank like an apple going bad and America was no longer the wisest hick town within a boat ride of Europe and Broadway forgot the tune, but here it all still was, in the music Babe played, the little stairways she climbed and came tap-dancing down, twinkling in black, and there is no other music, not really, though Babe works in some Beatles songs, "Yesterday" and "Hey Jude," doing it rinky-tink, her own style of ice to rattle in the glass. As Babe plays she takes on swaying and leaning backwards; at her arms' ends the standards go root back into ragtime. Rabbit sees circus tents and fireworks and farmers' wagons and an empty sandy river running so slow the sole motion is catfish sleeping beneath the golden skin.

The boy leans forward and murmurs to Rabbit, "You want ass, right? You can have her. Fifty gets you her all night, all ways you can think up. She knows a lot."

Sunk in her music, Rabbit is lost. He shakes his head and says, "She's too good."

"Good, man; she got to live, right? This place don't pay her shit."

Babe has become a railroad, prune-head bobbing, napkin of jewels flashing blue, music rolling through crazy places, tunnels of dissonance and open stretches of the same tinny thin note bleeding itself into the sky, all sad power and happiness worn into holes like shoe soles. From the dark booths around voices call out in a mutter "Go Babe" and "Do it, do it." The spidery boys in the adjacent room are frozen around the green felt. Into the mike that is there no bigger than a lollipop she begins to sing, sings in a voice that is no woman's voice at all and no man's, is merely human, the words of Ecclesiastes. A time to be born, a time to die. A time to gather up stones, a time to cast stones away. Yes. The Lord's last word. There is no other word, not really. Her singing opens up, grows enormous, frightens Rabbit with its enormous black maw of truth yet makes him overjoyed that he is here; he brims with joy, to be here with these black others, he wants to shout love through the darkness of Babe's noise to the sullen brother in goatee and glasses. He brims with this itch but does not spill. For Babe stops. As if suddenly tired or insulted Babe breaks off the song and shrugs and quits.

That is how Babe plays.

She comes back to the table stooped, trembling, nervous, old.

"That was beautiful, Babe," Rabbit tells her.

"It was," says another voice. A small white girl is standing there prim, in a white dress casual and dirty as smoke.

"Hey. Jill," Buchanan says.

"Hi Buck. Skeeter, hi."

So Skeeter is his name. He scowls and looks at the cigarette of which there is not even butt enough to call a roach.

"Jilly-love," Buchanan says, standing until his thighs scrape the table edge, "allow me to introduce. Harry the Rabbit Angstrom, he works at the printing plant with me, along with his daddy."

"He has a daddy?" Jill asks, still looking at Skeeter, who will not look at her.

"Jilly, you go sit in here where I am," Buchanan says. "I'll go get a chair from Rufe."

"Down, baby," Skeeter says. "I'm splitting." No one offers to argue with him. Perhaps they are all as pleased as Rabbit to see him go.

Buchanan chuckles, he rubs his hands. His eyes keep in touch with all of them, even though Babe seems to be dozing. He says to Jill, "How about a beverage? A 7-Up? Rufe can make a lemonade even."

"Nothing," Jill says. Teaparty manner. Hands in lap. Thin arms. Freckles. Rabbit scents in her the perfume of class. She excites him.

"Maybe she'd like a real drink," he says. With a white woman here he feels more in charge. Negroes, you can't blame them, haven't had his advantages. Slave ships, cabins, sold down the river, Ku Klux Klan, James Earl Ray: Channel 44 keeps having these documentaries all about it.

"I'm under age," Jill tells him politely.

Rabbit says, "Who cares?"

She answers, "The police."

"Not up the street they wouldn't mind so much," Buchanan explains, "if the girl halfway acted the part, but down here they get a touch fussy."

"The fuzz is fussy," Babe says dreamily. "The fuzz is our fussy friends. The fuzzy motherfuckers fuss."

"Don't, Babe," Jill begs. "Don't pretend."

"You let your old black mamma have a buzz on," Babe says. "Don't I take good care of you mostly?"

"How would the police know if this kid has a drink?" Rabbit asks, willing to be indignant.

Buchanan makes his high short wheeze. "Friend Harry, they'd just have to turn their heads."

"There're cops in here?"

"Friend" — and from the way he sidles closer Harry feels he's found another father — "if it weren't for po-lice spies, poor Jimbo's wouldn't sell two beers a night. Po-lice spies are the absolute backbone of local low life. They got so many plants going, that's why they don't dare shoot in riots, for fear of killing one of their own."

"Like over in York."

Jill asks Rabbit, "Hey. You live in Brewer?" He sees that she doesn't like his being white in here, and smiles without answering. Screw you, little girl.

Buchanan answers for him. "Lady, does he live in Brewer? If he lived any more in Brewer he'd be a walking advertisement. He'd be the Owl Pretzel owl. I don't think this fella's ever gotten above Twelfth Street, have you Harry?"

"A few times. I was in Texas in the Army, actually."

"Did you get to fight?" Jill asks. Something scratchy here, but maybe like a kitten it's the way of making contact.

"I was all set to go to Korea," he says. "But they never sent me." Though at the time he was grateful, it has since eaten at him, become the shame of his life. He had never been a fighter but now there is enough death in him so that in a way he wants to kill.

"Now Skeeter," Buchanan is saying, "he's just back from Vietnam."

"That's why he so rude," Babe offers.

"I couldn't tell if he was rude or not," Rabbit confesses.

"That's nice," Buchanan says.

"He was rude," Babe says.

Jill's lemonade arrives. She is still girl enough to look happy when it is set before her: cakes at the teaparty. Her face lights up. A crescent of lime clings to the edge of the glass; she takes it off and sucks and makes a sour face. A child's plumpness has been drained from her before a woman's bones could grow and harden. She is the reddish type of fair; her hair hangs dull, without fire, almost flesh-color, or the color of the flesh of certain soft trees, yews or cedars. Harry feels protective, timidly. In her tension of small bones she reminds him of Nelson. He asks her, "What do you do, Jill?"

"Nothing much," she says. "Hang around." It had been square of him to ask, pushing. The blacks fit around her like shadows.

"Jilly's a poor soul," Babe volunteers, stirring within her buzz. "She's fallen on evil ways." And she pats Rabbit's hand as if to say, *Don't you fall upon these ways.*

"Young Jill," Buchanan clarifies, "has run away from her home up there in Connec-ticut."

Rabbit asks her, "Why would you do that?"

"Why not? Let freedom ring."

"Can I ask how old you are?"

"You can ask."

"I'm asking."

Babe hasn't let go of Rabbit's hand; with the fingernail of her index finger she is toying with the hairs on the back of his fist. It makes his teeth go cold, for her to do that. "Not so old you couldn't be her daddy," Babe says.

He is beginning to get the drift. They are presenting him with this problem. He is the consultant honky. The girl, too, unwilling as she is, is submitting to the interview. She inquires of him, only partly parrying, "How old are *you?*"

"Thirty-six."

"Divide by two."

"Eighteen, huh? How long've you been on the run? Away from your parents."

"Her daddy dead," Buchanan interposes softly.

"Long enough, thank you." Her face pales, her freckles stand out sharply: blood-dots that have dried brown. Her dry little lips tighten; her chin drifts toward him. She is pulling rank. He is Penn Villas, she is Penn Park. Rich kids make all the trouble.

"Long enough for what?"

"Long enough to do some sick things."

"Are you sick?"

"I'm cured."

Buchanan interposes, "Babe helped her out."

"Babe is a beautiful person," Jill says. "I was really a mess when Babe took me in."

"Jilly is my sweetie," Babe says, as suddenly as in playing she moves from one tune to another, "Jilly is my baby-love and I'm her mamma-love," and takes her brown hands away from Harry's to encircle the girl's waist and hug her against the rooster-comb-red of her dress; the two are women, though one is a prune and the other a milkweed. Jill pouts in pleasure. Her mouth is lovable when it moves, Rabbit thinks, the lower lip bumpy and dry as if chapped, though this is not winter but the humid height of summer.

Buchanan is further explaining. "Fact of it is, this girl hasn't got no place regular to go. Couple weeks ago, she comes in here, not knowing I suppose the place was mostly for soul, a little pretty girl like this get in with some of the brothers they would tear her apart limb by sweet limb" – he has to chuckle – "so Babe takes her right away under her wing. Only trouble with that is" – the fat man rustles closer, making the booth a squeeze – "Babe's place is none too big, and anyways . . ."

The child flares up. "Anyways I'm not welcome." Her eyes widen: Rabbit has not seen their color before, they have been shadowy, moving slowly, as if their pink lids are tender or as if, rejecting instruction and inventing her own way of moving through the world, she has lost any vivid idea of what to be look- ing for. Her eyes are green. The dry tired green, yet one of his favorite colors, of August grass.

"Jilly-love," Babe says, hugging, "you the most welcome little white baby there could be."

Buchanan is talking only to Rabbit, softer and softer. "You know, those things happen over York way, they could happen here, and how could we protect" – the smallest wave of his hand toward the girl lets the sentence gracefully hang; Harry is reminded of Stavros's gestures. Buchanan ends chuck- ling: "We be so busy keepin' holes out of our own skins. Dependin' where you get caught, being black's a bad ticket both ways!"

Jill snaps, "I'll be all right. You two stop it now. Stop trying to sell me to this creep. I don't want him. He doesn't want me. Nobody wants me. That's all right. I don't want anybody."

"Everybody wants somebody," Babe says. "I don't mind your hangin' around my place, some gentlemen mind, is all."

Rabbit says, "Buchanan minds," and this perception astonishes them; the two blacks break into first shrill, then jingling, laughter, and another Stinger appears on the table between his hands, pale as lemonade.

"Honey, it's just the visibility," Babe then adds sadly. "You make us ever so visible."

A silence grows like the silence when a group of adults is waiting for a child to be polite. Sullenly Jill asks Rabbit, "What do *you* do?"

"Set type," Rabbit tells her. "Watch TV. Babysit."

"Harry here," Buchanan explains, "had a nasty shock the other day. His wife for no good reason upped and left him."

"No reason at all?" Jill asks. Her mouth pouts forward, vexed and aggressive, yet her spark of interest dies before her breath is finished with the question.

Rabbit thinks. "I think I bored her. Also, we didn't agree politically."

"What about?"

"The Vietnam war. I'm all for it."

Jill snatches in her breath.

Babe says, "I knew those knuckles looked bad."

Buchanan offers to smooth it over. "Everybody at the plant is for it. We think, you don't hold 'em over there, you'll have those black-pajama fellas on the streets over here."

Jill says to Rabbit seriously, "You should talk to Skeeter about it. He says it was a fabulous trip. He loved it."

"I wouldn't know about that. I'm not saying it's pleasant to fight in or be caught in. I just don't like the kids making the criticisms. People say it's a mess so we should get out. If you stayed out of every mess you'd never get into anything."

"Amen," Babe says. "Life is generally shit."

Rabbit goes on, feeling himself get rabid, "I guess I don't much believe in college kids or the Viet Cong. I don't think they have any answers. I think they're minorities trying to bring down everything that halfway works. Halfway isn't all the way but it's better than no way."

Buchanan smooths on frantically. His upper lip is bubbling with sweat under his slit of a mustache. "I agree ninety-nine per cent. Enlightened self-interest is the phrase I like. The way I see, enlightened self-interest's the best deal we're likely to get down here. I don't buy pie in the sky whoever is slicing it. These young ones like Skeeter, they say All power to the people, you look around for the people, the only people around is *them*."

"Because of Toms like you," Jill says.

Buchanan blinks. His voice goes deeper, hurt. "I ain't no Tom, girl. That kind of talk doesn't help any of us. That kind of talk just shows how young you are. What I am is a man trying to get from Point A to Point B, from the cradle to the grave hurting the fewest people I can. Just like Harry here, if you'd ask him. Just like your late daddy, God rest his soul."

Babe says, hugging the stubbornly limp girl, "I just likes Jilly's spunk, she's less afraid what to do with her life than fat old smelly you, sittin' there lickin' yourself like an old cigar end." But while talking she keeps her eyes on Buchanan as if his concurrence is to be desired. Mothers and fathers, they turn up everywhere.

Buchanan explains to Jill with a nice levelness, "So that is the problem. Young Harry here lives in this fancy big house over in the fanciest part of West Brewer, all by himself, and never gets any tail."

Harry protests. "I'm not that alone. I have a kid with me."

"Man has to have tail," Buchanan is continuing.

"Play, Babe," a dark voice shouts from a dark booth. Rufe bobs his head and switches on the blue spot. Babe sighs and offers Jill what is left of Skeeter's joint. Jill shakes her head and gets out of the booth to let Babe out. Rabbit thinks the girl is leaving and discovers himself glad when she sits down again, opposite him. He sips his Stinger and she chews the ice from her lemonade while Babe plays again. This time the boys in the poolroom softly keep at their game. The clicking and the liquor and the music mix and make the space inside him very big, big enough to hold blue light and black faces and "Honeysuckle Rose" and stale smoke sweeter than alfalfa and this apparition across the way, whose wrists and forearms are as it were translucent and belonging to another order of creature; she is not yet grown. Her womanliness is attached to her, it floats from her like a little zeppelin he can almost see. And his inside space expands to include beyond Jimbo's the whole world with its arrowing wars and polychrome races, its continents shaped like ceiling stains, its strings of gravitational attraction attaching it to every star, its glory in space as of a blue marble swirled with clouds; everything is warm, wet, still coming to birth but himself and his home, which remains a strange dry place, dry and cold and emptily spinning in the void of Penn Villas like a cast-off space capsule. He doesn't want to go there but he must. He must. "I must go," he says, rising.

"Hey, hey," Buchanan protests. "The night hasn't even got itself turned around to get started yet."

"I ought to be home in case my kid can't stand the kid he's staying with. I promised I'd visit my parents tomorrow, if they didn't keep my mother in the hospital for more tests."

"Babe will be sad, you sneaking out. She took a shine to you."

"Maybe that other guy she took a shine to will be back. My guess is Babe takes a shine pretty easy."

"Don't you get nasty."

"No, I love her, Jesus. Tell her. She plays like a whiz. This has been a terrific change of pace for me." He tries to stand, but the table edge confines him to a crouch. The booth tilts and he rocks slightly, as if he is already in the slowly turning cold house he is heading toward. Jill stands up with him, obedient as a mirror.

"One of these times," Buchanan continues beneath them, "maybe you can get to know Babe better. She is one good egg."

"I don't doubt it." He tells Jill, "Sit down."

"Aren't you going to take me with you? They want you to."

"Gee. I hadn't thought to."

She sits down.

"Friend Harry, you've hurt the little girl's feelings. Nasty must be your middle name."

Jill says, "Far as creeps like this are concerned, I have no feelings. I've decided he's queer anyway."

"Could be," Buchanan says. "It would explain that wife."

"Come on, let me out of the booth. I'd *like* to take her —"

"Then help yourself, friend. On me."

Babe is playing "Time After Time." *I tell myself that I'm.*

Harry sags. The table edge is killing his thighs. "O.K., kid. Come along."

"I wouldn't dream of it."

"You'll be bored," he feels in honesty obliged to add.

"You've been had," she tells him.

"Jilly now, be gracious for the gentleman." Buchanan hastily pushes out of the booth, lest the combination tumble, and lets Harry slide out and leans against him confidentially. Geezers. His breath rises bad, from under the waxed needles. "Problem is," he explains, the last explaining he will do tonight, "it don't look that

good, her being in here, under age and all. The fuzz now, they
aren't absolutely unfriendly, but they hold us pretty tight to the
line, what with public opinion the way it is. So it's not that healthy
for anybody. She's a poor child needs a daddy, is the simple truth
of it."

Rabbit asks her, "How'd he die?"

Jill says, "Heart. Dropped dead in a New York theater lobby.
He and my mother were seeing *Hair*."

"O.K. Let's shove." To Buchanan Rabbit says, "How much
for the drinks? Wow. They're just hitting me."

"On us," is the answer, accompanied by a wave of a palm the
color of silver polish. "On the black community." He has to
wheeze and chuckle. Struggling for solemnity: "This is real big of
you, man. You're a big man."

"See you at work Monday."

"Jilly-love, you be a good girl. We'll keep in touch."

"I bet."

Disturbing, to think that Buchanan works. We all work. Day
selves and night selves. The belly hungers, the spirit hungers.
Mouths munch, cunts swallow. Monstrous. Soul. He used to try
to picture it when a child. A parasite like a tapeworm inside. A
sprig of mistletoe hung from our bones, living on air. A jellyfish
swaying between our lungs and our liver. Black men have more,
bigger. Cocks like eels. Night feeders. Their touching underbelly
smell on buses, their dread of those clean dry places where Harry
must be. He wonders if he will be sick. Poison in those Stingers,
on top of moonburgers.

Babe shifts gears, lays out six chords like six black lead slugs
slapping into the tray, and plays, "There's a Small Hotel." *With a
wishing well.*

With this Jill, then, Rabbit enters the street. On his right,
toward the mountain, Weiser stretches sallow under blue street
lights. The Pinnacle Hotel makes a tattered blur, the back of the
Sunflower Beer clock shows yellow neon petals; otherwise the
great street is dim. He can remember when Weiser with its five

movie marquees and its medley of neon outlines appeared as gaudy
as a carnival midway. People would stroll, children between them.
Now the downtown looks deserted, sucked dry by suburban
shopping centers and haunted by rapists. LOCAL HOODS ASSAULT
ELDERLY, last week's *Vat* had headlined. In the original version of
the head LOCAL had been BLACK.

They turn left, toward the Weiser Street Bridge. River
moisture cools his brow. He decides he will not be sick. Never,
even as an infant, could stand it; some guys, Ronnie Harrison for
one, liked it, throw up after a few beers or before a big game, joke
about the corn between their teeth, but Rabbit needed to keep it
down, even at the cost of a bellyache. He still carries from sitting
in Jimbo's the sense of the world being inside him; he will keep it
down. The city night air. The ginger of tar and concrete baked all
day, truck traffic lifted from it like a lid. Infrequent headlights
stroke this girl, catching her white legs and thin dress as she hangs
on the curb hesitant.

She asks, "Where's your car?"

"I don't have any."

"That's impossible."

"My wife took it when she left me."

"You didn't have two?"

"No." This is really a rich kid.

"I have a car," she says.

"Where is it?"

"I don't know."

"How can you not know?"

"I used to leave it on the street up near Babe's place off of Plum,
I didn't know it was somebody's garage entrance, and one morning they had taken it away."

"And you didn't go after it?"

"I didn't have the money for any fine. And I'm scared of the
police, they might check me out. The staties must have a bulletin
on me."

"Wouldn't the simplest thing for you be to go back to
Connecticut?"

"Oh, please," she says.

"What didn't you like about it?"

"It was all ego. Sick ego."

"Something pretty egotistical about running away, too. What'd that do to your mother?"

The girl makes no answer, but crosses the street, from Jimbo's to the beginning of the bridge. Rabbit has to follow. "What kind of car was it?"

"A white Porsche."

"Wow."

"My father gave it to me for my sixteenth birthday."

"My father-in-law runs the Toyota agency in town."

They keep arriving at this place, where a certain symmetry snips their exchanges short. Having crossed the bridge, they stand on a little pond of sidewalk squares where in this age of cars few feet tread. The bridge was poured in the Thirties – sidewalks, broad balustrades, and lamp plinths – of reddish rough concrete; above them an original light standard, iron fluted and floral toward the top, looms stately but unlit at the entrance to the bridge, illumined since recently with cold bars of violet on tall aluminum stems rooted in the center of the walkway. Her white dress is unearthly in this light. A man's name is embedded in a bronze plaque, illegible. Jill asks impatiently, "Well, how shall we do?"

He assumes she means transportation. He is too shaky still, too full of smoke and Stinger, to look beyond that. The way to the center of Brewer, where taxis prowl and doze, feels blocked. In the gloom beyond Jimbo's neon nimbus, brown shadows, local hoods, giggle in doorways, watching. Rabbit says, "Let's walk across the bridge and hope for a bus. The last one comes around eleven, maybe on Saturdays it's later. Anyway, if none comes at all, it's not too far to walk to my place. My kid does it all the time."

"I love walking," she says. She touchingly adds, "I'm strong. You mustn't baby me."

The balustrade was poured in an X-pattern echoing rail fences; these Xs click past his legs not rapidly enough. The gritty breadth he keeps touching runs tepid. Flecks as if of rock salt had been mixed into it. Not done that way anymore, not done this color, reddish, the warmth of flesh, her hair also, cut cedar color, lifting as she hurries to keep up.

"What's the rush?"

"Shhh. Dontcha hear 'em?"

Cars thrust by, rolling balls of light before them. An anvil-drop below, to the black floor of the river: white shards, boat shapes. Behind them, pattering feet, the press of pursuit. Rabbit dares stop and peek backwards. Two brown figures are chasing them. Their shadows shorten and multiply and lengthen and simplify again as they fly beneath the successive mauve angles, in and out of strips of light; one man is brandishing something white in his hand. It glitters. Harry's heart jams; he wants to make water. The West Brewer end of the bridge is forever away. LOCAL MAN STABBED DEFENDING OUT-OF-STATE GIRL. *Body Tossed From Historic Bridge.* He squeezes her arm and tries to make her run. Her skin is smooth and narrow yet tepid like the balustrade. She snaps, "Cut it out," and pulls away. He turns and finds, unexpectedly, what he had forgotten was there, courage; his body fits into the hardshell blindness of meeting a threat, rigid, only his eyes soft spots, himself a sufficient shield. *Kill.*

The Negroes halt under the near purple moon and back a step, frightened. They are young, their bodies liquid. He is bigger than they. The white flash in the hand of one is not a knife but a pocketbook of pearls. The bearer shambles forward with it. His eyewhites and the pearls look lavender in the light. "This yours, lady?"

"Oh. Yes."

"Babe sent us after."

"Oh. Thank you. Thank her."

"We scare somebody?"

"Not me. Him."

"Yeah."

"Dude scared us too."

"Sorry about that," Rabbit volunteers. "Spooky bridge."

"O.K."

"O.K." Their mauve eyeballs roll; their purple hands flip as their legs in the stitched skin of Levis seek the rhythm of leaving. They giggle together; and also at this moment two giant trailer trucks pass on the bridge, headed in opposite directions: their rectangles thunderously overlap and, having clapped the air between them, hurtle each on its way, corrosive and rumbling. The bridge trembles. The Negro boys have disappeared. Rabbit walks on with Jill.

The pot and brandy and fear in him enhance the avenue he knows too well. No bus comes. Her dress flutters in the corner of his eye as he tries, his skin stretched and his senses shuffling and circling like a cloud of gnats, to make talk. "Your home was in Connecticut."

"A place called Stonington."

"Near New York?"

"Near enough. Daddy used to go down Mondays and come back Fridays. He loved to sail. He said about Stonington it was the only town in the state that faces the open sea, everything else is on the Sound."

"And he died, you said. My mother – she has Parkinson's Disease."

"Look, do you like to talk this much? Why don't we just walk? I've never been in West Brewer before. It's nice."

"What's nice about it?"

"Everything. It doesn't have a past like the city does. So it's not so disappointed. Look at that, Burger Bliss. Isn't it beautiful, all goldy and plasticky with that purple fire inside?"

"That's where I ate tonight."

"How was the food?"

"Awful. Maybe I taste everything too much, I should start smoking again. My kid loves the place."

"How old did you say he was?"

"Twelve. Thirteen this October. He's small for his age."

"You shouldn't tell him that."

"Yeah. I try not to ride him."

"What would you ride him about?"

"Oh. He's bored by things I used to love. I don't think he's having much fun. He never goes outdoors."

"Hey. What's your name?"

"Harry."

"Hey, big Harry. Would you mind feeding me?"

"Sure, I mean No. At home? I don't know what we have in the icebox. Refrigerator."

"I mean over there, at the burger place."

"Oh, sure. Terrific. I'm sorry. I assumed you ate."

"Maybe I did, I tend to forget material details like that. But I don't think so. All I feel inside is lemonade."

She selects a Cashewburger for 85¢ and a strawberry milkshake. In the withering light she devours the burger, and he orders her another. She smiles apologetically. She has small inturned teeth, roundish and with tiny gaps between them like a printer's hairline spaces. Nice. "Usually I try to rise above eating."

"Why?"

"It's so ugly. Don't you think, it's one of the uglier things we do?"

"It has to be done."

"That's your philosophy, isn't it?" Even in this garishly lit place her face has about it something shadowy and elusive, something that's skipped a stage. Finished, she wipes her fingers one by one on a paper napkin and says decisively, "Thank you very much." He pays. She clutches the purse, but what is in it? Credit cards? Diagrams for the revolution?

He has had coffee, to keep himself awake. Be up all night fucking this poor kid. Upholding the honor of middle-aged squares. Different races. In China, they used to tell you in the Army, the women put razor blades in their cunts in case the Japanese tried rape. Rabbit's scrotum shrivels at the thought. Enjoy the walk. They march down Weiser, the store windows dark but for burglar lights, the Acme parking lot empty but for scattered neckers, the movie marquee changed from 2001 to TRUE GRIT. Short enough to get it all on. They cross the street at a blinking yellow to Emberly Avenue, which then becomes Emberly Drive, which becomes Vista Crescent. The development is dark. "Talk about spooky," she says.

"I think it's the flatness," he says. "The town I grew up in, no two houses were on the same level."

"There's such a smell of plumbing somehow."

"Actually, the plumbing is none too good."

This smoky creature at his side has halved his weight. He floats up the steps to the porchlet, knees vibrating. Her profile by his shoulder is fine and cool as the face on the old dime. The key to the door of three stepped windows nearly flies out of his hand, it feels so magical. Whatever he expects when he flicks on the inside hall light, it is not the same old furniture, the fake cobbler's bench, the sofa and the silverthread chair facing each other like two bulky drunks too tired to go upstairs. The blank TV screen in its box of metal painted with wood grain, the see-through shelves with nothing on them.

"Wow," Jill says. "This is really tacky."

Rabbit apologizes, "We never really picked out the furniture, it just kind of happened. Janice was always going to do different curtains."

Jill asks, "Was she a good wife?"

His answer is nervous; the question plants Janice back in the house, quiet in the kitchen, crouching at the head of the stairs, listening. "Not too bad. Not much on organizational ability, but until she got mixed up with this other guy at least she kept plugging away. She used to drink too much but got that under control. We had a tragedy about ten years ago that sobered her up I guess. Sobered me up too. A baby died."

"How?"

"An accident we caused."

"That's sad. Where do we sleep?"

"Why don't you take the kid's room, I guess he won't be back. The kid he's staying with, he's a real spoiled jerk, I told Nelson if it got too painful he should just come home. I probably should have been here to answer the phone. What time is it? How about a beer?"

Penniless, she is wearing a little wristwatch that must have cost two hundred at least. "Twelve-ten," she says. "Don't you want to sleep with me?"

"Huh? That's not your idea of bliss, is it? Sleeping with a creep?"

"You are a creep, but you just fed me."

"Forget it. On the white community. Ha."

"And you have this sweet funny family side. Always worrying about who needs you."

"Yeah, well it's hard to know sometimes. Probably nobody if I could face up to it. In answer to your question, sure I'd like to sleep with you, if I won't get hauled in for statutory rape."

"You're really scared of the law, aren't you?"

"I try to keep out of its way is all."

"I promise you on a Bible – do you have a Bible?"

"There used to be one somewhere, that Nelson got for going to Sunday school, when he did. We've kind of let all that go. Just promise me."

"I promise you I'm eighteen. I'm legally a woman. I am not bait for a black gang. You will not be mugged or blackmailed. You may fuck me."

"Somehow you're making me almost cry."

"You're awfully scared of me. Let's take a bath together and then see how we feel about it."

He laughs. "By then I guess I'll feel pretty gung-ho about it."

She is serious, a serious small-faced animal sniffing out her new lair. "Where's the bathroom?"

"Take off your clothes here."

The command startles her; her chin dents and her eyes go wide with fright. No reason he should be the only scared person here. Rich bitch calling his living room tacky. Standing on the rug where he and Janice last made love, Jill skins out of her clothes. She kicks off her sandals and strips her dress upward. She is wearing no bra. Her tits tug upward, drop back, give him a headless stare. She is wearing bikini underpants, black lace, in a pattern too fine to read. Not pausing a moment for him to drink her in, she pulls the elastic down with two thumbs, wriggles, and steps out. Where Janice had a springy triangle encroaching on the insides of her thighs when she didn't shave, Jill has scarcely a shadow, amber fuzz dust darkened toward the center to an upright dainty mane. The horns of her pelvis like starved cheekbones. Her belly a child's, childless. Her breasts in some lights as she turns scarcely exist. Being naked elongates her neck: a true ripeness there, in the unhurried curve from base of skull to small of back, and in the legs, which link to the hips with knots of fat and keep a plumpness all the way down. Her ankles are less slim than Janice's. But, hey, she is naked in this room, his room. This really strange creature, too trusting. She bends to pick up her clothes. She treads lightly on his carpet, as if watchful for tacks. She stands an arm's-length from him, her mouth pouting prim, a fleck of dry skin on the lower lip. "And you?"

"Upstairs." He undresses in his bedroom, where he always does; in the bathroom on the other side of the partition, water begins to cry, to sing, to splash. He looks down and has nothing of a hard-on. In the bathroom he finds her bending over to test the temperature mix at the faucet. A tuft between her buttocks. From behind she seems a boy's slim back wedged into the upside-down valentine of a woman's satin rear. He yearns to touch her, to touch the satin symmetry, and does. It stings his figertips like glass we don't expect is there. Jill doesn't deign to flinch or turn at his touch, testing the water to her satisfaction. His cock stays small but has stopped worrying.

Their bath is all too gentle, silent, liquid, and pure. They are each attentive: he soaps and rinses her breasts as if their utter cleanness challenges him to make them even cleaner; she kneels and kneads his back as if a year of working weariness were in it. She blinds him in drenched cloth; she counts the gray hairs (six) in the hair of his chest. Still even as they stand to dry each other and he looms above her like a Viking he cannot shake the contented impotence of his sensation that they are the ends of spotlight beams thrown on the clouds, that their role is to haunt this house like two bleached creatures on a television set entertaining an empty room.

She glances at his groin. "I don't turn you on exactly, do I?"

"You do, you do. Too much. It's still too strange. I don't even know your last name."

"Pendleton." She drops to her knees on the bathroom rug and takes his penis into her mouth. He backs away as if bitten.

"Wait."

Jill looks up at him crossly, looks up the slope of his slack gut, a cranky puzzled child with none of the answers in the last class of the day, her mouth slick with forbidden candy. He lifts her as he would a child, but she is longer than a child, and her armpits are scratchy and deep; he kisses her on the mouth. No gumdrops, her lips harden and she twists her thin face away, saying into his shoulder, "I don't turn anybody on, much. No tits. My mother has nifty tits, maybe that's my trouble."

"Tell me about your trouble," he says, and leads her by the hand toward the bedroom.

"Oh, Jesus, one of those. Trouble-shooters. From the look of it you're in worse shape than me, you can't even respond when somebody takes off their clothes."

"First times are hard; you need to absorb somebody a little first." He darkens the room and they lie on the bed. She offers to embrace him again, hard mouth and sharp knees anxious to have it done, but he smooths her onto her back and massages her breasts, plumping them up, circling. "These aren't your trouble," he croons. "These are lovely." Down below he feels himself easily stiffening, clotting: cream in the freezer. CLINIC FOR RUN-AWAYS OPENED. *Fathers Do Duty On Nights Off.*

Relaxing, Jill grows stringy; tendons and resentments come to the surface. "You should be fucking my mother, she really is good with men, she thinks they're the be-all and end-all. I know she was playing around, even before Daddy died."

"Is that why you ran away?"

"You wouldn't believe if I really told you."

"Tell me."

"A guy I went with tried to get me into heavy drugs."

"That's not so unbelievable."

"Yeah, but his reason was crazy. Look, you don't want to hear this crap. You're up now, why don't you just give it to me?"

"Tell me his reason."

"You see, when I'd trip, I'd see, like, you know – God. He never would. He just saw pieces of like old movies, that didn't add up."

"What kind of stuff did he give you? Pot?"

"Oh, no, listen, pot is just like having a Coke or something. Acid, when he could get it. Strange pills. He'd rob doctors' cars to get their samples and then mix them to see what happened. They have names for all these pills, purple hearts, dollies, I don't know what all. Then after he stole this syringe he'd inject stuff, he wouldn't even know what it was half the time, it was wild. I would never let him break my skin. I figured, anything went in by the mouth, I could throw it up, but anything went in my veins, I had no way to get rid of it, it could kill me. He said that was part of the kick. He was really freaked, but he had this, you know, power over me. I ran."

"Has he tried to follow you?" A freak coming up the stairs. Green teeth, poisonous needles. Rabbit's penis has wilted, listening.

"No, he's not the type. Toward the end I don't think he knew me from Adam really, all he was thinking about was his next fix. Junkies are like that. They get to be bores. You think they're talking to you or making love or whatever, and then you realize they're looking over your shoulder for the next fix. You realize you're nothing. He didn't need me to find God for him, if he met God right on the street he'd've tried to hustle Him for money enough for a couple bags."

"What did he look like?"

"Oh, about five-ten, brown hair down to his shoulders, slightly wavy when he brushed it, a neat build. Even after smack had pulled all the color from him he had a wonderful frame. His back was really marvellous, with long sloping shoulders and all these ripply little ribby bumps behind, you know, here." She touches him but is seeing the other. "He had been a runner in junior high."

"I meant God."

"Oh, God. He changed. He was different every time. But you always knew it was Him. Once I remember something like the inside of a big lily, only magnified a thousand times, a sort of glossy shining funnel that went down and down. I can't talk about it." She rolls over and kisses him on the mouth feverishly. His slowness to respond seems to excite her; she gets up in a crouch and like a raccoon drinking water kisses his chin, his chest, his navel, goes down and stays. Her mouth nibbling is so surprising he fights the urge to laugh; her fingers on the hair of his thighs tickle like the threat of ice on his skin. The hair of her head makes a tent on his belly. He pushes at her but she sticks at it: he might as well relax. The ceiling. The garage light shining upwards shows a stained patch where chimney flashing let the rain in. Must turn the garage light off. Though maybe a good burglar preventive. These junkies around steal anything. He wonders how Nelson made out. Asleep, boy sleeps on his back, mouth open, frightening; skin seems to tighten on the bone like in pictures of Buchenwald. Always tempted to wake him, prove he's O.K. Missed the eleven-o'clock news tonight. Vietnam death count, race riots probably somewhere. Funny man, Buchanan. No plan, exactly, just feeling his way, began by wanting to sell him Babe, maybe that's the way to live. Janice in bed got hot like something cooking but this kid stays cool, a prep-school kid applying what she knows. It works.

"That's nice," she says, stroking the extent of his extended cock, glistening with her spittle.

"You're nice," he tells her, "not to lose faith."

"I like it," she tells him, "making you get big and strong."

"Why bother?" he asks. "I'm a creep."

"Want to come into me?" the girl asks. But when she lies on her back and spreads her legs, her lack of self-consciousness again strikes him as sad, and puts him off, as does the way she winces when he seeks to enter; so that he grows small. Her blurred face widens its holes and says with a rising inflection, "You don't *like* me."

While he fumbles for an answer, she falls asleep. It is the answer to a question he hadn't thought to ask: was she tired? Of course, just as she was hungry. A guilty grief expands his chest muscles and presses on the backs of his eyes. He gets up, covers her with a sheet. The nights are growing cool, August covers the sun's retreat. The cold moon. Scraped wallpaper. Pumice stone under a flash bulb. Footprints stay for a billion years, not a fleck of dust blows. The kitchen linoleum is cold on his feet. He switches off the garage light and spreads peanut butter on six Saltines, making three sandwiches. Since Janice left, he and Nelson shop for what they like, keep themselves stocked in salt and starch. He eats the crackers sitting in the living room, not in the silverthread chair but the old brown mossy one, that they've had since their marriage. He chews and stares at the uninhabited aquarium of the television screen. Ought to smash it, poison, he read somewhere the reason kids today are so crazy they were brought up on television, two minutes of this, two minutes of that. Cracker crumbs adhere to the hair of his chest. Six gray. Must be more than that. What did Janice do for Stavros she didn't do for him? Only so much you can do. Three holes, two hands. Is she happy? He hopes so. Poor mutt, he somehow squelched her potential. Let things bloom. The inside of a great lily. He wonders if Jesus will be waiting for Mom, a man in a nightgown at the end of a glossy chute. He hopes so. He remembers he must work tomorrow, then remembers he mustn't, it is Sunday. Sunday, that dog of a day. Ruth used to mock him and church, in those days he could get himself up for anything. Ruth and her chicken farm, wonders if she can stand it. Hopes so. He pushes himself up from the fat chair, brushes crumbs from his chest hair. Some fall and catch further down. Wonder why it was made so curly there, springy, they could stuff mattresses with it, if people would shave, like nuns and wigs. Upstairs, the body in his bed sinks his heart like a bar of silver. He had forgotten she was on his hands. Bad knuckles. The poor kid, she stirs and tries to make love to him again, gives him a furry-mouthed French kiss and falls asleep at it again. A day's work for a day's lodging. Puritan ethic. He masturbates, picturing Peggy Fosnacht. What will Nelson think?

Jill sleeps late. At quarter of ten Rabbit is rinsing his cereal bowl and coffee cup and Nelson is at the kitchen screen door, red-faced from pumping his bicycle. "Hey, Dad!"

"Shh."

"Why?"

"Your noise hurts my head."

"Did you get drunk last night?"

"What sort of talk is that? I never get drunk."

"Mrs. Fosnacht cried after you left."

"Probably because you and Billy are such brats."

"She said you were going to meet somebody in Brewer."

She shouldn't be telling kids things like that. These divorced women, turn their sons into little husbands: cry, shit, and change Tampax right in front of them. "Some guy I work with at Verity. We listened to some colored woman play the piano and then I came home."

"We stayed up past twelve o'clock watching a wicked neat movie about guys landing somewhere in boats that open up in front, some place like Norway –"

"Normandy."

"That's right. Were you there?"

"No, I was your age when it happened."

"You could see the machine gun bullets making the water splash up all in a row, it was a blast."

"Hey, try to keep your voice down."

"Why, Dad? Is Mommy back? Is she?"

"No. Have you had any breakfast?"

"Yeah, she gave us bacon and French toast. I learned how to make it, it's easy, you just smash some eggs and take bread and fry it, I'll make you some sometime."

"Thanks. My mother used to make it."

"I hate her cooking. Everything tastes greasy. Didn't you used to hate her cooking, Dad?"

"I liked it. It was the only cooking I knew."

"Billy Fosnacht says she's dying, is she?"

"She has a disease. But it's very slow. You've seen how she is. She may get better. They have new things for it all the time."

"I hope she does die, Dad."

"No you don't. Don't say that."

"Mrs. Fosnacht tells Billy you should say everything you feel."

"I'm sure she tells him a lot of crap."

"Why do you say crap? I think she's nice, once you get used to her eyes. Don't you like her, Dad? She thinks you don't."

"Peggy's O.K. What's on your schedule? When was the last time you went to Sunday school?"

The boy circles around to place himself in his father's view. "There's a reason I rushed home. Mr. Fosnacht is going to take Billy fishing on the river in a boat some guy he knows owns and Billy asked if I could come along and I said I'd have to ask you. O.K., Dad? I had to come home anyway to get a bathing suit and clean pants, that fucking mini-bike got these all greasy."

All around him, Rabbit hears language collapsing. He says weakly, "I didn't know there was fishing in the river."

"They've cleaned it up, Ollie says. At least above Brewer. He says they stock it with trout up around Eifert's Island."

Ollie, is it? "That's hours from here. You've never fished. Remember how bored you were with the ball game we took you to."

"That was a boring game, Dad. Other people were playing it. This is something you do yourself. Huh, Dad? O.K.? I got to get my bathing suit and I said I'd be back on the bicycle by ten-thirty." The kid is at the foot of the stairs: stop him.

Rabbit calls, "What am I going to do all day, if you go off?"

"You can go visit Mom-mom. She'd rather see just you anyway." The boy takes it that he has secured permission, and pounds upstairs. His scream from the landing freezes his father's stomach. Rabbit moves to the foot of the stairs to receive Nelson in his arms. But the boy, safe on the next-to-bottom step, halts there horrified. "Dad, something moved in your bed!"

"My bed?"

"I looked in and saw it!"

Rabbit offers, "Maybe it was just the air-conditioner fan lifting the sheets."

"*Dad*." The child's pallor begins to recede as some flaw in the horror of this begins to dawn. "It had long hair, and I saw an arm. Aren't you going to call the police?"

"No, let's let the poor old police rest, it's Sunday. It's O.K., Nelson, I know who it is."

"You do?" The boy's eyes sink upon themselves defensively as his brain assembles what information he has about long-haired creatures in bed. He is trying to relate this contraption of half-facts to the figure of his father looming, a huge riddle in an undershirt, before him. Rabbit offers, "It's a girl who's run away from home and I somehow got stuck with her last night."

"Is she going to live here?"

"Not if you don't want me to," Jill's voice composedly calls from the stairs. She has come down wrapped in a sheet. Sleep has made her more substantial, her eyes are fresh wet grass now. She says to the boy, "I'm Jill. You're Nelson. Your father told me all about you."

She advances toward him in her sheet like a little Roman senator, her hair tucked under behind, her forehead shining. Nelson stands his ground. Rabbit is struck to see that they are nearly the same height. "Hi," the kid says. "He did?"

"Oh, yes," Jill goes on, showing her class, becoming no doubt her own mother, a woman pouring out polite talk in an unfamiliar home, flattering vases, curtains. "You are *very* much on his mind. You're very fortunate, to have such a loving father."

The kid looks over with parted lips. Christmas morning. He

doesn't know what it is, but he wants to like it, before it's unwrapped.

Tucking her sheet about her tighter, Jill moves them into the kitchen, towing Nelson along on the thread of her voice. "You're lucky, you're going on a boat. I love boats. Back home we had a twenty-two-foot sloop."

"What's a sloop?"

"It's a sailboat with one mast."

"Some have more?"

"Of course. Schooners and yawls. A schooner has the big mast behind, a yawl has the big one up front. We had a yawl once but it was too much work, you needed another man really."

"You used to sail?"

"All summer until October. Not only that. In the spring we all used to have to scrape it and caulk it and paint it. I liked that almost the best, we all used to work at it together, my parents and me and my brothers."

"How many brothers did you have?"

"Three. The middle one was about your age. Thirteen?"

He nods. "Almost".

"He was my favorite. Is my favorite."

A bird outside hoarsely scolds in sudden agitation. Cat? The refrigerator purrs.

Nelson abruptly volunteers, "I had a sister once but she died."

"What was her name?"

His father has to answer for him. "Rebecca."

Still Jill doesn't look toward him, but concentrates on the boy. "May I eat breakfast, Nelson?"

"Sure."

"I don't want to take the last of your favorite breakfast cereal or anything."

"You won't. I'll show you where we keep them. Don't take the Rice Krispies, they're a thousand years old and taste like floor fluff. The Raisin Bran and Alphabits are O.K., we bought them this week at the Acme."

"Who does the shopping, you or your father?"

"Oh – we share. I meet him on Pine Street after work sometimes."

"When do you see your mother?"

"A lot of times. Weekends sometimes I stay over in Charlie Stavros's apartment. He has a real gun in his bureau. It's O.K., he has a license. I can't go over there this weekend because they've gone to the Shore."

"Where's the shore?"

Delight that she is so dumb creases the corners of Nelson's mouth. "In New Jersey. Everybody calls it just the Shore. We used to go to Wildwood sometimes but Dad hated the traffic too much."

"That's one thing I miss," Jill says, "the smell of the sea. Where I grew up, the town is on a peninsula, with sea on three sides."

"Hey, shall I make you some French toast? I just learned how."

Jealousy, perhaps, makes Rabbit impatient with this scene: his son in spite of his smallness bony and dominating and alert, Jill in her sheet looking like one of those cartoon figures, Justice or Liberty or Mourning Peace. He goes outside to bring in the Sunday *Triumph*, sits reading the funnies in the sunshine on the porchlet steps until the bugs get too bad, comes back into the living room and reads at random about the Egyptians, the Phillies, the Onassises. From the kitchen comes sizzling and giggling and whispering. He is in the Garden Section (*Scorn not the modest goldenrod, dock, and tansy that grow in carefree profusion in fields and roadside throughout these August days; carefully dried and arranged, they will form attractive bouquets to brighten the winter months around the corner*) when the kid comes in with milk on his mustache and, wide-eyed, pressingly, with a new kind of energy, asks, "Hey Dad, can she come along on the boat? I've called up Billy and he says his father won't mind, only we have to hurry up. You can come too."

"Maybe *I* mind."

"*Dad*. Don't." And Harry reads his son's taut face to mean, *She can hear. She's all alone. We must be nice to her, we must be nice to the poor, the weak, the black. Love is here to stay.*

Monday, Rabbit is setting the *Vat* front page. WIDOW, SIXTY-SEVEN, RAPED AND ROBBED. *Three Black Youths Held.*

Police authorities revealed Saturday that they are
holding for questioning two black minors and Wendell
Phillips, 19, of 42B Plum Street, in connection with
the brutal assault of an unidentified sywsfyz kmlhs
the brutal assault of an unidentified elderly white
woman late Thursday night.

The conscienceless crime, the latest in a series of similar incidents in the Third
Ward, aroused residents of
the neighborhood to organize a committee of protest
which appeared before Friday's City Council session.

Nobody Safe

''Nobody's safe on the st

''Nobody's safe on the
streets any more,'' said
committee spokesman Ber-
nard Vogel to VAT report-
ers.

''Nobody's safe not even
in our own homes.''

Through the clatter Harry feels a tap on his shoulder and looks
around. Pajasek, looking worried. "Angstrom, telephone."

"Who the hell?" He feels obliged to say this, as apology for
being called at work, on Verity time.

"A woman," Pajasek says, not placated.

Who? Jill (last night her hair still damp from the boat ride tickled his belly as she managed to make him come) was in trouble.
They had kidnapped her – the police, the blacks. Or Peggy
Fosnacht was calling up to offer supper again. Or his mother had
taken a turn for the worse and with her last heartbeats had dialled
this number. He is not surprised she would want to speak to him
instead of his father, he has never doubted she loves him most. The
phone is in Pajasek's little office, three walls of frosted glass, on the
desk with the parts catalogues (these old Mergenthalers are always
breaking down) and the spindled dead copy. "Hello?"

"Hi, sweetie. Guess who."

"Janice. How was the Shore?"

"Crowded and muggy. How was it here?"

"Pretty good."

"So I hear. I hear you went out in a boat."

"Yeah, it was the kid's idea, he got me invited by Ollie. We went up the river as far as Eifert's Island. We didn't catch much, the state put some trout in but I guess the river's still too full of coal silt. My nose is so sunburned I can't touch it."

"I hear you had a lot of people in the boat."

"Nine or so. Ollie runs around with this musical crowd. We had a picnic up at the old camp meeting ground, near Stogey's Quarry, you know, where that witch lived so many years. Ollie's friends all got out guitars and played. It was nice."

"I hear *you* brought a guest too."

"Who'd you hear that from?"

"Peggy told me. Billy told her. He was all turned-on about it, he said Nelson brought a girlfriend."

"Beats a mini-bike, huh?"

"Harry, I don't find this amusing. Where did you find this girl?"

"Uh, she's a go-go dancer in here at the shop. For the lunch hour. The union demands it."

"*Where*, Harry?"

Her weary dismissive insistence pleases him. She is growing in confidence, like a child at school. He confesses, "I sort of picked her up in a bar."

"Well. That's being honest. How long is she going to stay?"

"I haven't asked. These kids don't make plans the way we used to, they aren't so scared of starving. Hey, I got to get back to the machine. Pajasek doesn't like our being called here, by the way."

"I don't intend to make a practice of it. I called you at work because I didn't want Nelson to overhear. Harry, now are you listening to me?"

"Sure, to who else?"

"I want that girl out of my home. I don't want Nelson exposed to this sort of thing."

"What sort of thing? You mean the you and Stavros sort of thing?"

"Charlie is a mature man. He has lots of nieces and nephews so he's very understanding with Nelson. This girl sounds like a little animal out of her head with dope."

"That's how Billy described her?"

"After she talked to Billy Peggy called up Ollie for a better description."

"And that was his description. Gee. They got along famously at the time. She was better-looking than those two old crows Ollie had along, I tell ya."

"Harry, you're horrible. I consider this a very negative development. I suppose I have no right to say anything about how you dispose of your sexual needs, but I will not have my son corrupted."

"He's not corrupted, she's got him to help with the dishes, that's more than we could ever do. She's like a sister to him."

"And what is she to you, Harry?" When he is slow to answer, she repeats, her voice taunting, aching, like her mother's, "Harry, what is she to you? A little wifey?"

He thinks and tells her, "Come on back to the house, I'm sure she'll go."

Now Janice thinks. Finally she states: "If I come back to the house, it'll be to take Nelson away."

"Try it," he says, and hangs up.

He sits a minute in Pajasek's chair to give the phone a chance to ring. It does. He picks it up. "Yeah?"

Janice says, near tears, "Harry, I don't like to tell you this, but if you'd been adequate I would never have left. You drove me to it. I didn't know what I was missing but now that I have it I know. I refuse to accept all the blame, I really do."

"O.K. No blame assigned. Let's keep in touch."

"I want that girl away from my son."

"They're getting along fine, relax."

"I'll sue you. I'll take you to court."

"Fine. After the stunts you've been pulling, it'll at least give the judge a laugh."

"That's my house legally. At least half of it is."

"Tell me which my half is, and I'll try to keep Jill in it."

Janice hangs up. Maybe using Jill's name had hurt. He doesn't wait for another ring this time, and leaves the cubicle of frosted glass. The trembling in his hands, which feel frightened and inflated, merges with the clatter of the machines; his body sweat is lost in the smell of oil and ink. He resettles himself at his

Mergenthaler and garbles three lines before he can put her phone call in the back of his mind. He supposes Stavros can get her legal advice. But, far from feeling Stavros as one of the enemy camp, he counts on him to keep this madwoman, his wife, under control. Through her body, they have become brothers.

Jill through the succession of nights adjusts Rabbit's body to hers. He cannot overcome his fear of using her body as a woman's – her cunt *stings*, is part of it; he never forces his way into her without remembering those razor blades – but she, beginning the damp-haired night after the boat ride, perfects ways with her fingers and mouth to bring him off. Small curdled puddles of his semen then appear on her skin, and though easily wiped away leave in his imagination a mark like an acid-burn on her shoulders, her throat, the small of her back; he has the vision of her entire slender fair flexible body being eventually covered with these invisible burns, like a napalmed child in the newspapers. And he, on his side, attempting with hands or mouth to reciprocate, is politely dissuaded, pushed away, reassured she has already come, serving him, or merely asked for the mute pressure of a thigh between hers and, after some few minutes during which he can detect no spasm of relief, thanked. The August nights are sticky and close; when they lie on their backs the ceiling of heavy air seems a foot above their faces. A car, loud on the soft tar and loose gravel, slides by. A mile away across the river a police siren bleats, a new sound, more frantic than the old rising and falling cry. Nelson turns on a light, makes water, flushes the toilet, turns out the light with a *snap* close to their ears. Had he been listening? Could he even be watching? Jill's breath saws in her throat. She is asleep.

He finds her when he comes back from work sitting and reading, sitting and sewing, sitting and playing Monopoly with Nelson. Her books are spooky: yoga, psychiatry, zen, plucked from racks at the Acme. Except to shop, she reluctantly goes outdoors, even at night. It is not so much that the police of several states are looking for her – they are looking as well for thousands like her – as that the light of common day, and the sights and streets that have been the food of Rabbit's life, seem to nauseate her. They rarely watch television, since she leaves the room when they turn the set on, though when she's in the kitchen he sometimes sneaks himself a dose of six-o'clock news. Instead, in the evenings, she and Nelson discuss God, beauty, meaning.

"Whatever men make," she says, "what they felt when they made it is there. If it was made to make money, it will smell of money. That's why these houses are so ugly, all the corners they cut to make a profit are still in them. That's why the cathedrals are so lovely; nobles and ladies in velvet and ermine dragged the stones up the ramps. Think of a painter. He stands in front of the canvas with a color on his brush. Whatever he feels when he makes the mark – if he's tired or bored or happy and proud – will be there. The same color, but we'll feel it. Like fingerprints. Like handwriting. Man is a means for turning things into spirit and turning spirit into things."

"What's the point?" Nelson asks.

"The point is ecstasy," she says. "Energy. Anything that is good is in ecstasy. The world is what God made and it doesn't stink of money, it's never tired, too much or too little, it's always exactly full. The second after an earthquake, the stones are calm. Everywhere is *play*, even in thunder or an avalanche. Out on my father's boat I used to look up at the stars and there seemed to be invisible strings between them, tuned absolutely right, playing thousands of notes I could almost hear."

"Why can't we hear them?" Nelson asks.

"Because our egos make us deaf. Our egos make us blind. Whenever we think about ourselves, it's like putting a piece of dirt in our eye."

"There's that thing in the Bible."

"That's what He meant. Without our egos the universe would be absolutely clean, all the animals and rocks and spiders and moon-rocks and stars and grains of sand absolutely doing their thing, unself-consciously. The only consciousness would be God's. Think of it, Nelson, like this: matter is the mirror of spirit. But it's three-dimensional, like an enormous room, a ballroom. And inside it are these tiny *other* mirrors tilted this way and that and throwing the light back the wrong way. Because to the big face looking in, these little mirrors are just dark spots, where He can't see Himself."

Rabbit is entranced to hear her going on like this. Her voice, laconic and dry normally, moves through her sentences as through a memorized recitation, pitched low, an underground murmur. She and Nelson are sitting on the floor with the Monopoly board between them, houses and hotels and money, the game has been going on for days. Neither gives any sign of knowing he has come into the room and is towering above them. Rabbit asks, "Why doesn't He just do away with the spots then? I take it the spots are us."

Jill looks up, her face blank as a mirror in this instant. Remembering last night, he expects her to look burned around the mouth; it had been like filling a slippery narrow-mouthed pitcher from an uncontrollable faucet. She answers, "I'm not sure He's noticed us yet. The cosmos is so large and our portion of it so small. So small and recent."

"Maybe we'll do the erasing ourselves," Rabbit offers helpfully. He wants to help, to hold his end up. Never too late for education. With Janice and old man Springer you could never have this kind of conversation.

"There is that death-wish," Jill concedes.

Nelson will talk only to her. "Do you believe in life on other planets? I don't."

"Why Nelson, how ungenerous of you! Why not?"

"I don't know, it's silly to say —"

"Say it."

"I was thinking, if there was life on other planets, they would have killed our moon men when they stepped out of the space ship. But they didn't, so there isn't."

"Don't be dumb," Rabbit says. "The moon is right down our block. We're talking about life in systems millions of light years away."

"No, I think the moon was a good test," Jill says. "If nobody bothered to defend it, it proves how little God is content with. Miles and miles of gray dust."

Nelson says, "One guy at school I know says there's people on the moon but they're smaller than atoms, so even when they grind the rocks up they won't find them. He says they have whole cities and everything. We breathe them in through our nostrils and they make us think we see flying saucers. That's what this one guy says."

"I myself," Rabbit says, still offering, drawing upon an old *Vat* feature article he set, "have some hopes for the inside of Jupiter. It's gas, you know, the surface we see. A couple of thousand miles down inside the skin there might be a mix of chemicals that could support a kind of life, something like fish."

"It's your Puritan fear of waste makes you want that," Jill tells him. "You think the other planets must be *used* for something, must be *farmed*. Why? Maybe the planets were put there just to teach men how to count up to seven."

"Why not just give us seven toes on each foot?"

"A kid at school," Nelson volunteers, "was born with an extra finger. The doctor cut it off but you can still see where it was."

"Also," Jill says, "astronomy. Without the planets the night sky would have been one rigid thing, and we would never have guessed at the third dimension."

"Pretty thoughtful of God," Rabbit says, "if we're just some specks in His mirror."

Jill waves his point away blithely. "He does everything," she says, "by the way. Not because it's what He has to do."

She can be blithe. After he told her once she ought to go outdoors more, she went out and sunbathed in just her bikini underpants, on a blanket beside the barbecue, in the view of a dozen other houses. When a neighbor called up to complain, Jill justified herself, "My tits are so small, I thought they'd think I was a boy." Then after Harry began giving her thirty dollars a week to shop with, she went and redeemed her Porsche from the police. Its garage parking fees had quadrupled the original fine. She gave her address as Vista Crescent and said she was staying the summer with her uncle. "It's a nuisance," she told Rabbit, "but Nelson ought to have a car around, at his age, it's too humiliating not to. Everybody in America has a car except you." So the Porsche came to live by their curb. Its white is dusty and the passenger-side front fender is scraped and one convertible top snap is broken. Nelson loves it so much he nearly cries, finding it there each morning. He washes it. He reads the manual and rotates the tires. That crystalline week before school begins, Jill takes him for drives out into the country, into the farmland and the mountains of Brewer County; she is teaching him how to drive.

Some days they return after Rabbit is home an hour from work. "Dad, it was a blast. We drove way up into this mountain that's a hawk refuge and Jill let me take the wheel on the twisty road coming down, all the way to the highway. Have you ever heard of shifting down?"

"I do it all the time."

"It's when you go into a lower gear instead of braking. It feels neat. Jill's Porsche has about five gears and you can really zoom around curves because the center of gravity is so low."

Rabbit asks Jill, "You sure you're handling this right? The kid might kill somebody. I don't want to be sued."

"He's very competent. And responsible. He must get that from you. I used to stay in the driver's seat and let him just steer but that's more dangerous than giving him control. The mountain was really quite deserted."

"Except for hawks, Dad. They sit on all these pine trees waiting for the guys to put out whole carcasses of cows and things. It's really grungy."

"Well," Rabbit says, "hawks got to live too."

"That's what I keep telling him," Jill says. "God is in the tiger as well as in the lamb."

"Yeah. God really likes to chew himself up."

"You know what you are?" Jill asks, her eyes the green of a meadow, her hair a finespun cedar-colored tangle dissolving into windowlight; a captured idea is fluttering in her head. "You are cynical."

"Just middle-aged. Somebody came up to me and said, 'I'm God,' I'd say, 'Show me your badge.'"

Jill dances forward, on fire with some fun and wickedness the day has left in her, and gives him a hug that dances off, a butterfly hug. "I think you're beautiful. Nelson and I both think so. We often talk about it."

"You do? That's the only thing you can think of to do, talk

about me?" He means to be funny, to keep her mood alive, but her face stops, hovers a second; and Nelson's tells him he has struck on something. What they do. In that little car. Well, they don't need much space, much contact: young bodies. The kid's faint mustache, black hairs; her cedar mane. Bodies not sodden yet like his. At that keen age the merest touch. Their brother-sister shyness, touching hands in the flicker of wet glass at the sink. If she'd offer to lay hairy old heavy him the first night, what wouldn't she do to bring the kid along; somebody has to. Why not? Chief question facing these troubled times. Why not.

Though he doesn't pursue this guilt he has startled from her, that night he does make her take him squarely, socks it into her, though she offers her mouth and her cunt is so tight it sears. She is frightened when he doesn't lose his hardness; he makes her sit up on him and pulls her satin hips down, the pelvis bones starved, and she sucks in breath sharply and out of pained astonishment pitched like delight utters, "You're wombing me!" He tries to picture it. A rosy-black floor in her somewhere, never knows where he is, in among kidneys, intestines, liver. His child bride with flesh-colored hair and cloudy innards floats upon him, stings him, sucks him up like a cloud, falls, forgives him. His love of her coats him with distaste and confusion, so that he quickly sleeps, only his first dreams jostled when she gets from bed to go wash, check on Nelson, talk to God, take a pill, whatever else she needs to do to heal the wound where his seared cock was. How sad, how strange. We make companions out of air and hurt them, so they will defy us, completing creation.

Harry's father sidles up to him at the coffee break. "How's every little thing, Harry?"

"Not bad."

"I hate like hell to nag like this, you're a grown man with your own miseries, I know that, but I'd be appreciative as hell if you'd come over some evenings and talk to your mother. She hears all sorts of malicious folderol about you and Janice now, and it would help settle her down if you could put her straight. We're no moralists, Harry, you know that; your mother and I tried to live by our own lights and to raise the two children God was good enough to give us by those same lights, but I know damn well it's a different world now, so we're no moralists, me and Mary."

"How is her health, generally?"

"Well, that's another of these problematical things, Harry. They've gone ahead and put her on this new miracle drug, they have some name for it I can never remember, L-dopa, that's right, L-dopa, it's still in the experimental stage I guess, but there's no doubt in a lot of cases it works wonders. Trouble is, also it has these side effects they don't know too much about, depression in your mother's case, some nausea and lack of appetite; and nightmares, Harry, nightmares that wake her up and she wakes me up so I can hear her heart beating, beating like a tom-tom. I never heard that before, Harry, another person's heart in the room as clear as footsteps, but that's what these L-dopa dreams do for her. But there's no doubt, her talk comes easier, and her hands don't shake that way they have so much. It's hard to know what's right, Harry. Sometimes you think, Let Nature take its course, but then you wonder, What's Nature and what isn't? Another side effect" – he draws closer, glancing around and then glancing down as his coffee slops in the paper cup and burns his fingers – "I shouldn't mention it but it tickles me, your mother says this new stuff she's taking, whatever you call it, makes her feel, how shall I say?" – he glances around again, then confides to his son – "lovey-dovey. Here she is, just turned sixty-five, lying in bed half the day, and gets these impulses so bad she says she can hardly stand it, she says she won't watch television, the commercials make it worse. She says she has to laugh at herself. Now isn't that a helluva thing? A good woman like that. I'm sorry to talk your ear off, I live alone with it too much, I suppose, what with Mim on the other side of the country. Christ knows it isn't as if you don't have your problems too."

"I don't have any problems," Rabbit tells him. "Right now I'm just holding my breath to when the kid gets back into school. His state of mind's pretty well stabilized, I'd say. One of the reasons, you know, I don't make it over to Mt. Judge as often as I should, Mom was pretty rough on Nelson when he was little and the kid is still scared of her. On the other hand I don't like to leave him alone in the house, with all these robberies and assaults all over the county, they come out into the suburbs and steal anything they can get their hands on. I was just setting an item, some woman over in Perley Township, they stole her vacuum cleaner and a hundred feet of garden hose while she was upstairs going to the bathroom."

"It's these God, damn, blacks, is what it is." Earl Angstrom lowers his voice so it turns husky, though Buchanan and Farnsworth always take their coffee break outside in the alley, with Boonie and the other drinkers. "I've always called 'em black and they call themselves blacks now and that suits me fine. They can't do a white man's job, except for a few, and take even Buck, he's never made head of makeup though he's been here the longest; so they have to rob and kill, the ones that can't be pimps and prizefighters. They can't cut the mustard and never could. This country should have taken whosever advice it was, George Washington if memory serves, one of the founding fathers, and shipped 'em all back to Africa when we had a chance. Now, Africa wouldn't take 'em. Booze and Cadillacs and white pussy, if you'll pardon my saying so, have spoiled 'em rotten. They're the garbage of the world, Harry. American Negroes are the lowest of the low. They steal and then they have the nerve to say the country owes it to 'em."

"O.K., O.K." To see his father passionate about anything disagrees with Rabbit. He shifts to the most sobering subject they have between them: "Does she mention me much? Mom."

The old man licks spittle from his lips, sighs, slumps confidingly lower, glancing down at the cooled scummed coffee in his hands. "All the time, Harry, every minute of the day. They tell her things about you and she raves against the Springers; oh, how she carries on about that family, especially the women of it. Apparently, the Mrs. is saying you've taken up with a hippie teenager, that's what drove Janice out of the house in the first place."

"No, Janice went first. I keep inviting her back."

"Well, whatever the actualities of the case are, I know you're trying to do the right thing. I'm no moralist, Harry, I know you young people nowadays have more tensions and psychological pressures than a man my age could tolerate. If I'd of had the atomic bomb and these rich-kid revolutionaries to worry about, I'd no doubt just have put a shotgun to my head and let the world roll on without me."

"I'll try to get over. I ought to talk to her," Rabbit says. He looks past his father's shoulder to where the yellow-faced wall clock jumps to within a minute of 11:10, the end of the coffee break. He knows that in all this rolling-on world his mother is the only person who *knows* him. He remembers from the night we touched the moon the nudge delivered out of her dying, but doesn't want to open himself to her until he understands what is happening inside him enough to protect it. She has something happening to her, death and L-dopa, and he has something happening to him, Jill. The girl has been living with them three weeks and is learning to keep house and to give him a wry silent look saying *I know you* when he offers to argue about Communism or kids today or any of the other sore spots where he feels rot beginning and black madness creeping in. A little wry green look that began the night he hurt her upwards and touched her womb.

His father is more with him than he suspects, for the old man draws still closer and says, "One thing it's been on my mind to say, Harry, forgive me talking out of turn, but I hope you're taking all the precautions, knock up one of these minors, the law takes a very dim view. Also, they say they're dirty as weasels and giving everybody the clap." Absurdly, as the clock ticks the last minute and the end-of-break bell rasps, the old man claps.

In his clean crisp after-work shirt he opens the front door of the apple-green house and hears guitar music from above. Guitar chords slowly plucked, and two high small voices moving through a melody. He is drawn upstairs. In Nelson's room, the two are sitting on the bed, Jill up by the pillows in a yoga position that displays the crotch of her black lace underpants. A guitar is cradled across her thighs. Rabbit has never seen the guitar before; it looks new. The pale wood shines like a woman oiled after a bath. Nelson sits beside Jill in Jockey shorts and T-shirt, craning his neck to read from the sheet of music on the bedspread by her ankles.

The boy's legs, dangling to the floor, look suddenly sinewy, long, beginning to be shaded with Janice's dark hair, and Rabbit notices that the old posters of Brooks Robinson and Orlando Cepeda and Steve McQueen on a motorcycle have been removed from the boy's walls. Paint has flaked where the Scotch tape was. They are singing, ". . . must a man wa-alk down"; the delicate thread breaks when he enters, though they must have heard his footsteps on the stairs as warning. The kid's being in his underclothes is O.K.: far from dirty as a weasel, Jill has gotten Nelson to take a shower once a day, before his father's homecoming, perhaps because her own father came home to Stonington only on Fridays and deserved a ceremony.

"Hey, Dad," Nelson says, "this is neat. We're singing harmony."

"Where did you get the guitar?"

"We hustled."

Jill nudges the boy with a bare foot, but not quick enough to halt the remark.

Rabbit asks him, "How do you hustle?"

"We stood on streetcorners in Brewer, mostly at Weiser and Seventh, but then we moved over to Cameron when a pig car slowed down to look us over. It was a gas, Dad. Jill would stop these people and tell 'em I was her brother, our mother was dying of cancer and our father had lit out, and we had a baby brother at home. Sometimes she said a baby sister. Some of the people said we should apply to welfare, but enough gave us a dollar or so so finally we had the twenty dollars Ollie promised was all he'd charge us for a forty-four dollar guitar. And he threw in the music free after Jill talked to him in the back room."

"Wasn't that nice of Ollie?"

"Harry, it really was. Don't look like that."

He says to Nelson, "I wonder what they talked about."

"Dad, there was nothing dishonest about it, these people we stopped felt better afterwards, for having got us off their conscience. Anyway, Dad, in a society where power was all to the people money wouldn't exist anyway, you'd just be given what you need."

"Well hell, that's the way your life is now."

"Yeah, but I have to beg for everything, don't I? And I never did get a mini-bike."

"Nelson, you get some clothes on and stay in your room. I want to talk to Jill a second."

"If you hurt her, I'll kill you."

"If you don't shut up, I'll make you live with Mommy and Charlie Stavros."

In their bedroom, Rabbit carefully closes the door and in a soft shaking voice tells Jill, "You're turning my kid into a beggar and a whore just like yourself," and, after waiting a second for her to enter a rebuttal, slaps her thin disdainful face with its prim lips and its green eyes drenched so dark in defiance their shade is as of tree leaves, a shuffling concealing multitude, a microscopic forest he wants to bomb. His slap feels like slapping plastic: stings his fingers, does no good. He slaps her again, gathers the dry flesh of her hair into his hand to hold her face steady, feels cold fury when she buckles and tries to slither away but, after a fist to the side of her neck, lets her drop onto the bed.

Still shielding her face, Jill hisses up at him, strangely hisses out of her little spaced inturned teeth, until her first words come. They are calm and superior. "You know why you did that, you just wanted to hurt me, that's why. You just wanted to have that kick. You don't give a shit about me and Nelson hustling. What do you care about who begs and who doesn't, who steals and who doesn't?"

A blankness in him answers when she asks; but she goes on. "What have the pig laws ever done for you except screw you into a greasy job and turn you into such a gutless creep you can't even keep your idiotic wife?"

He takes her wrist. It is fragile. Chalk. He wants to break it, to feel it snap; he wants to hold her absolutely quiet in his arms for the months while it will heal. "Listen. I earn my money one fuck-ing dollar at a time and you're living on it and if you want to go back bumming off your nigger friends, go. Get out. Leave me and my kid alone."

"You creep," she says, "you baby-killing creep."

"Put another record on," he says. "You sick bitch. You rich kids playing at life make me sick, throwing rocks at the poor dumb cops protecting your daddy's loot. You're just playing, baby. You think you're playing a great game of happy cunt but let me tell you something. My poor dumb mutt of a wife throws a better piece of ass backwards than you can manage frontwards."

"Backwards is right, she can't stand facing you."

He squeezes her chalk wrist tighter, telling her, "You have no juice, baby. You're all sucked out and you're just eighteen. You've tried everything and you're not scared of nothing and you wonder why it's all so dead. You've had it handed to you, sweet baby, that's why it's so dead. Fucking Christ you think you're going to make the world over you don't have a fucking clue what makes people run. Fear. That's what makes us poor bastards run. You don't know what fear is, do you, poor baby? That's why you're so dead." He squeezes her wrist until he can picture the linked curved bones in it bending ghostly as in an X ray; and her eyes widen a fraction, a hairspace of alarm he can see only because he is putting it there.

She tugs her wrist free and rubs it, not lowering her eyes from his. "People've run on fear long enough," Jill says. "Let's try love for a change."

"Then you better find yourself another universe. The moon is cold, baby. Cold and ugly. If you don't want it, the Commies do. They're not so fucking proud."

"What's that noise?"

It is Nelson crying, outside the door, afraid to come in. It had been the same way with him and Janice, their fights: just when they were getting something out of them, the kid would beg them to stop. Maybe he imagined that Becky had been killed in just such a quarrel, that this one would kill him. Rabbit lets him in and explains, "We were talking politics."

Nelson squeezes out in the spaces between his sobs. "Daddy, why do you disagree with everybody?"

"Because I love my country and can't stand to have it knocked."

"If you loved it you'd want it better," Jill says.

"If it was better *I'd* have to be better," he says seriously, and they all laugh, he last.

Thus, through lame laughter – she still rubs her wrists, the hand he hit her with begins to hurt – they seek to reconstitute their family. For supper Jill cooks a filet of sole, lemony, light, simmered in sunshine, skin flaky brown; Nelson gets a hamburger with wheat-germ sprinkled on it to remind him of a Nutburger. Wheatgerm, zucchini, water chestnuts, celery salt, Familia: these are some of the exotic items Jill's shopping brings into the house. Her cooking tastes to him of things he never had: candlelight, saltwater, health fads, wealth, class. Jill's family had a servant, and it takes her some nights to understand that dirtied dishes do not clear and clean themselves by magic, but have to be carried and washed. Rabbit, still, Saturday mornings, is the one to vacuum the rooms, to bundle his shirts and the sheets for the laundry, to sort out Nelson's socks and underwear for the washer in the basement. He can see, what these children cannot, dust accumulate, deterioration advance, chaos seep in, time conquer. But for her cooking he is willing to be her servant, part-time. Her cooking has renewed his taste for life. They have wine now with supper, a California white in a half-gallon jug. And always a salad: salad in Diamond County cuisine tends to be a brother of sauerkraut, fat with creamy dressing, but Jill's hands serve lettuce in an oily film invisible as health. Where Janice would for dessert offer some doughy goodie from the Half-A-Loaf, Jill concocts designs of fruit. And her coffee is black nectar compared to the watery tar Janice used to serve. Contentment makes Harry motionless; he watches the dishes be skimmed from the table, and resettles expansively in the living room. When the dishwashing machine is fed and chugging contentedly, Jill comes into the living room, sits on the tacky carpet, and plays the guitar. What does she play? "Farewell, Angelina, the sky is on fire," and a few others she can get through a stanza of. She has maybe six chords. Her fingers on the frets often tighten on strands of her hanging hair; it must hurt. Her voice is a thin instrument that quickly cracks. "All my tri-als, Lord, soon be o-over," she sings, quitting, looking up for applause.

Nelson applauds. Small hands.

"Great," Rabbit tells her and, mellow on wine, goes on, in apology for his life, "No kidding, I once took that inner light trip and all I did was bruise my surroundings. Revolution, or whatever, is just a way of saying a mess is fun. Well, it *is* fun, for a while, as long as somebody else has laid in the supplies. A mess is a luxury, is all I mean."

Jill has been strumming for him, between sentences, part helping him along, part poking fun. He turns on her. "Now you tell
us something. You tell us the story of your life."

"I've had no life," she says, and strums. "No man's daughter,
and no man's wife."

"Tell us a story," Nelson begs. From the way she laughs, showing her roundish teeth and letting her thin cheeks go dimply, they
see she will comply.

"This is the story of Jill and her lover who was *ill*," she
announces, and releases a chord. It's as if, Rabbit thinks, studying
the woman-shape of the guitar, the notes are in there already,
waiting to fly from the dovecote of that round hole. "Now Jill,"
Jill goes on, "was a comely lass, raised in the bosom of the middle
class. Her dad and mother each owned a car, and on the hood of
one was a Mercedes star. I don't know how much longer I can go
on rhyming." She strums quizzically.

"Don't try it," Rabbit advises.

"Her upbringing" – emphasis on the "ging" – "was orthodox
enough – sailing and dancing classes and *français* and all that stuff."

"Keep rhyming, Jill," Nelson begs.

"Menstruation set in at age fourteen, but even with her braces
off Jill was no queen. Her knowledge of boys was con*fined* to
boys who played tennis and whose parents with her parents
dined. Which suited her perfectly *well*, since having observed her
parents drinking and chatting and getting and spending she was in
no great hurry to become old and fat and *swell*. Ooh, that was a
stretch."

"Don't rhyme on my account," Rabbit says. "I'm getting a
beer, anybody else want one?"

Nelson calls, "I'll share yours, Dad."

"Get your own. I'll get it for you."

Jill strums to reclaim their attention. "Well, to make a boring
story short, one summer" – she searches ahead for a rhyme, then
adds, "after her daddy died."

"Uh-oh," Rabbit says, tiptoeing back with two beers.

"She met a boy who became her psycho-physical guide."

Rabbit pulls his tab and tries to hush the *pff*.

"His name was Freddy –"

He sees there is nothing to do but yank it, which he does so quickly the beer foams through the keyhole.

"And the nicest thing about him was that *she* was ready." Strum. "He had nice brown shoulders from being a lifeguard, and his bathing suit held something sometimes soft and sometimes hard. He came from far away, from romantic Rhode Island across Narragansett Bay."

"Hey," Rabbit *olés*.

"The only bad thing was, inside, the nice brown lifeguard had already died. Inside there was an old man with a dreadful need, for pot and hash and LSD and speed." Now her strumming takes a different rhythm, breaking into the middle on the offbeat.

"He was a born loser, though his race was white, and he fucked sweet virgin Jill throughout one sandy night. She fell for him" – *strum* – "and got deep into his bag of being stoned: she freaked out nearly every time the bastard telephoned. She went from popping pills to dropping acid, then" – she halts and leans forward staring at Nelson so hard the boy softly cries, "Yes?"

"He lovingly suggested shooting heroin."

Nelson looks as if he will cry: the way his eyes sink in and his chin develops another bump. He looks, Rabbit thinks, like a sulky girl. He can't see much of himself in the boy, beyond the small straight nose.

The music runs on.

"Poor Jill got scared; the other kids at school would tell her not to be a self-destructive fool. Her mother, still in mourning, was being kept bus-*ee*, by a divorced tax lawyer from nearby Wester-lee. Bad Freddy was promising her Heaven above, when all Jill wanted was his mundane love. She wanted the feel of his prick, not the prick of the needle; but Freddy would beg her, and stroke her, and sweet-talk and wheedle."

And Rabbit begins to wonder if she has done this before, that rhyme was so slick. What *has*n't this kid done before?

"She was afraid to *die*" – strum, strum, pale orange hair thrashing – "he asked her *why*. He said the world was rotten and insane; she said she had no cause to complain. He said racism was rampant, hold out your arm; she said no white man but him had ever done her any harm. He said the first shot will just be beneath the skin; she said okay, lover, put that shit right in." Strum strum *strum*. Face lifted toward them, she is a banshee, totally bled. She speaks the next line. "It was hell."

St-r-r-um. "He kept holding her head and patting her ass, and saying relax, he'd been to life-saving class. He asked her, hadn't he shown her the face of God? She said, *Yes,* thank you, but she would have been happy to settle for *less.* She saw that her lover with his tan skin and white smile was death; she feared him and loved him with every frightened breath. So what did Jill do?"

Silence hangs on the upbeat.

Nelson blurts, "What?"

Jill smiles. "She ran to the Stonington savings bank and generously with*drew*. She hopped inside her Porsche and drove *away*, and that is how come she is living with you two creeps to*day*."

Both father and son applaud. Jill drinks deep of the beer as a reward to herself. In their bedroom, she is still in the mood, artistic elation, to be rewarded. Rabbit says to her, "Great song. But you know what I didn't like about it?"

"What?"

"Nostalgia. You miss it. Getting stoned with Freddy."

"At least," she says, "I wasn't just playing, what did you call it, happy cunt?"

"Sorry I blew my stack."

"Still want me to go?"

Rabbit, having sensed this would come, hangs up his pants, his shirt, puts his underclothes in the hamper. The dress she has dropped on the floor he drapes on a hook in her half of the closet, her dirty panties he puts in the hamper. "No. Stay."

"Beg me."

He turns, a big tired man, slack-muscled, who has to rise and set type in eight hours. "I beg you to stay."

"Take back those slaps."

"How can I?"

"Kiss my feet."

He kneels to comply. Annoyed at such ready compliance, which implies pleasure, she stiffens her feet and kicks so her toenails stab his cheek, dangerously near his eyes. He pins her ankles to continue his kissing. Slightly doughy, matronly ankles. Green veins on her insteps. Nice remembered locker room taste. Vanilla going rancid.

"Your tongue between my toes," she says; her voice cracks timidly, issuing the command. When again he complies, she edges forward on the bed and spreads her legs. "Now here." She knows he enjoys this, but asks it anyway, to see what she can make of him, this alien man. His head, with its stubborn old-fashioned short haircut – the enemy's uniform, athlete and soldier; bone above the ears, dingy blond silk thinning on top – feels large as a boulder between her thighs. The excitement of singing her song, ebbing, unites with the insistent warmth of his tongue lapping. A spark kindles, a green sprig lengthens in the barren space between her legs. "A little higher," Jill says, then, her voice quite softened and crumbling, "Faster. Lovely. *Lovely*."

One day after work as he and his father are walking down Pine Street toward their before-bus drink at the Phoenix Bar, a dapper thickset man with sideburns and hornrims intercepts them. "Hey, Angstrom." Both father and son halt, blink. In the tunnel of sunshine, after their day of work, they generally feel hidden.

Harry recognizes Stavros. He is wearing a suit of little beige checks on a ground of greenish threads. He looks a touch thinner, more brittle, his composure more of an effort. Maybe he is just tense for this encounter. Harry says, "Dad, I'd like you to meet a friend of mine. Charlie Stavros, Earl Angstrom."

"Pleased to meet you, Earl."

The old man ignores the extended square hand and speaks to Harry. "Not the same that's ruined my daughter-in-law?"

Stavros tries for a quick sale. "Ruined. That's pretty strong. Humored is more how I'd put it." His try for a smile ignored, Stavros turns to Harry. "Can we talk a minute? Maybe have a drink down at the corner. Sorry to butt in like this, Mr. Angstrom."

"Harry, what is your preference? You want to be left alone with this scum or shall we brush him off?"

"Come on, Dad, what's the point?"

"You young people may have your own ways of working things out, but I'm too old to change. I'll get on the next bus. Don't let yourself be talked into anything. This son of a bitch looks slick."

"Give my love to Mom. I'll try to get over this weekend."

"If you can, you can. She keeps dreaming about you and Mim."

"Yeah, some time could you give me Mim's address?"

"She doesn't have an address, just care of some agent in Los Angeles, that's the way they do it now. You were thinking of writing her?"

"Maybe send her a postcard. See you tomorrow."

"Terrible dreams," the old man says, and slopes to the curb to wait for the 16A bus, cheated of his beer, the thin disappointed back of his neck reminding Harry of Nelson.

Inside the Phoenix it is dark and cold; Rabbit feels a sneeze gathering between his eyes. Stavros leads the way to a booth and folds his hands on the Formica tabletop. Hairy hands that have held her breasts. Harry asks, "How is she?"

"She? Oh hell, in fine form."

Rabbit wonders if this means what it seems. The tip of his tongue freezes on his palate, unable to think of a delicate way to probe. He says, "They don't have a waitress in the afternoon. I'll get a Daiquiri for myself, what for you?"

"Just soda water. Lots of ice."

"No hootch?"

"Never touch it." Stavros clears his throat, smooths back the hair above his sideburns with a flat hand that is, nevertheless, slightly trembling. He explains, "The medicos tell me it's a no-no."

Coming back with their drinks, Rabbit asks, "You sick?"

Stavros says, "Nothing new, the same old ticker. Janice must have told you, heart murmur since I was a kid."

What does this guy think, he and Janice sat around discussing him like he was their favorite child? He does remember Janice crying out he couldn't marry, expecting him, Harry, her husband, to sympathize. Oddly, he had. "She mentioned something."

"Rheumatic fever. Thank God they've got those things licked now, when I was a kid I caught every bug they made." Stavros shrugs. "They tell me I can live to be a hundred, if I take care of the physical plant. You know," he says, "these doctors. There's still a lot they don't know."

"I know. They're putting my mother through the wringer right now."

"Jesus, you ought to hear Janice go on about your mother."

"Not so· enthusiastic, huh?"

"Not so at all. She needs some gripe, though, to keep herself justified. She's all torn up about the kid."

"She left him with me and there he stays."

"In court, you know, you'd lose him."

"We'd see."

Stavros makes a small chopping motion around his glass full of soda bubbles (poor Peggy Fosnacht; Rabbit should call her) to indicate a new angle in their conversation. "Hell," he says, "I can't take him in. I don't have the room. As it is now, I have to send Janice out to the movies or over to her parents when my family visits. You know I just don't have a mother, I have a *grand*mother. She's ninety-three, speaking of living forever."

Rabbit tries to imagine Stavros's room, which Janice described as full of tinted photographs, and instead imagines Janice nude, tinted, Playmate of the month, posed on a nappy Greek sofa olive green in color, with scrolling arms, her body twisted at the hips just enough to hide her gorgeous big black bush. The crease of the centerfold cuts across her navel and one hand dangles a rose. The vision makes Rabbit for the first time hostile. He asks Stavros, "How do you see this all coming out?"

"That's what I wanted to ask *you.*"

Rabbit asks, "She going sour on you?"

"No, Jesus, *au contraire.* She's balling me ragged."

Rabbit sips, swallows that, probes for another nerve. "She miss the kid?"

"Nelson, he comes over to the lot some days and she sees him weekends anyhow, I don't know that she saw much more of him before. I don't know as how motherhood is Janice's best bag anyway. What she doesn't much care for is the idea of her baby just out of diapers shacking up with this hippie."

"She's not a hippie, especially; unless everybody that age is. And I'm the one shacking up."

"How is she at it?"

"She's balling me ragged," Rabbit tells him. He is beginning to get Stavros's measure. At first, meeting him on the street so suddenly, he felt toward him like a friend, met through Janice's body. Then first coming into the Phoenix he felt him as a sick man, a man holding himself together against odds. Now he sees him as a competitor, one of those brainy cute close-set little playmakers. O.K. So Rabbit is competing again. What he has to do is hang loose and let Stavros make the move.

Stavros hunches his square shoulders infinitesimally, has some soda, and asks, "What do you see yourself doing with this hippie?"

"She has a name. Jill."

"What's Jill's big picture, do you know?"

"No. She has a dead father and a mother she doesn't like, I guess she'll go back to Connecticut when her luck runs thin."

"Aren't you being, so to speak, her luck?"

"I'm part of her picture right now, yeah."

"And she of yours. You know, your living with this girl gives Janice an open-and-shut divorce case."

"You don't scare me, somehow."

"Do I understand that you've assured Janice that all she has to do is come back and the girl will go?"

Rabbit begins to feel it, where Stavros is pressing for the opening. The tickle above his nose is beginning up again. "No," he says, praying not to sneeze, "you don't understand that." He sneezes. Six faces at the bar look around; the little Schlitz spinner seems to hesitate. They are giving away refrigerators and ski weekends in Chile on the TV.

"You don't want Janice back now?"

"I don't know."

"You would like a divorce so you can keep living the good life? Or marry the girl, maybe, even? Jill. She'll break your balls, Sport."

"You think too fast. I'm just living day by day, trying to forget my sorrow. I've been left, don't forget. Some slick-talking kinky-haired peacenik-type Japanese-car salesman lured her away, I forget the son-of-a-bitch's name."

"That isn't exactly the way it was. She came pounding on my door."

"You let her in."

Stavros looks surprised. "What else? She had put herself out on a limb. Where could she go? My taking her in made the least trouble for everybody."

"And now it's trouble?"

Stavros fiddles his fingertips as if cards are in them; if he loses this trick, can he take the rest? "Her staying on with me gives her expectations we can't fulfill. Marriage isn't my thing, sorry. With anybody."

"Don't try to be polite. So now you've tried her in all positions and want to ship her back. Poor old Jan. So dumb."

"I don't find her dumb. I find her – unsure of herself. She wants what every normal chick wants. To be Helen of Troy. There've been hours when I gave her some of that. I can't keep giving it to her. It doesn't hold up." He becomes angry; his square brow darkens. "What do *you* want? You're sitting there twitching your whiskers, so how about it? If I kick her out, will you pick her up?"

"Kick her out and see. She can always go live with her parents."

"Her mother drives her crazy."

"That's what mothers are for." Rabbit pictures his own. His bladder gets a touch of that guilty sweetness it had when as a child he was running to school late, beside the slime-rimmed gutter water that ran down from the ice plant. He tries to explain. "Listen, Stavros. You're the one in the wrong. You're the one screwing another man's wife. If you want to pull out, pull out. Don't try to commit me to one of your fucking coalition governments."

"Back to that," Stavros says.

"Right. You intervened, not me."

"I didn't intervene, I performed a rescue."

"That's what all you hawks say." He is eager to argue about Vietnam, but Stavros keeps to the less passionate subject.

"She was desperate, fella. Christ, hadn't you taken her to bed in ten years?"

"I resent that."

"Go ahead. Resent it."

"She was no worse off than a million wives." A billion cunts, how many wives? Five hundred million? "We had relations. They didn't seem so bad to me."

"All I'm saying is, I didn't cook this up, it was delivered to me hot. I didn't have to talk her into anything, she was pushing all the way. I was the first chance she had. If I'd been a one-legged milkman, I would have done."

"You're too modest."

Stavros shakes his head. "She's some tiger."

"Stop it, you're giving me a hard-on."

Stavros studies him squarely. "You're a funny guy."

"Tell me what it is you don't like about her now."

His merely interested tone relaxes Stavros's shoulders an inch. The man measures off a little cage in front of his lapels. "It's just too – confining. It's weight I don't need. I got to keep light, on an even keel. I got to avoid stress. Between you and me, I'm not going to live forever."

"You just told me you might."

"The odds are not."

"You know, you're just like me, the way I used to be. Everybody now is like the way I used to be."

"She's had her kicks for the summer, let her come back. Tell the hippie to move on, that's what a kid like that wants to hear anyway."

Rabbit sips the dregs of his second Daiquiri. It is delicious, to let this silence lengthen, widen: he will not promise to take Janice back. The game is on ice. He says at last, because continued silence would have been unbearably rude, "Just don't know. Sorry to be so vague."

Stavros takes it up quickly. "She on anything?"

"Who?"

"This nympho of yours."

"On something?"

"You know. Pills. Acid. She can't be on horse or you wouldn't have any furniture left."

"Jill? No, she's kicked that stuff."

"Don't you believe it. They never do. These flower babies, dope is their milk."

"She's fanatic against. She's been there and back. Not that this is any of your business." Rabbit doesn't like the way the game has started to slide; there is a hole he is trying to plug and can't.

Stavros minutely shrugs. "How about Nelson? Is he acting different?"

"He's growing up." The answer sounds evasive. Stavros brushes it aside.

"Drowsy? Nervous? Taking naps at odd times? What do they do all day while you're playing hunt and peck? They must do *some*thing, fella."

"She teaches him how to be polite to scum. Fella. Let me pay for your water."

"So what have I learned?"

"I hope nothing."

But Stavros has sneaked in for that lay-up and the game is in overtime. Rabbit hurries to get home, to see Nelson and Jill, to sniff their breaths, look at their pupils, whatever. He has left his lamb with a viper. But outside the Phoenix, in the hazed sunshine held at its September tilt, traffic is snarled, and the buses are caught along with everything else. A movie is being made. Rabbit remembers it mentioned in the *Vat* (BREWER MIDDLE AMERICA? *Gotham Filmmakers Think So*) that Brewer had been chosen for a location by some new independent outfit; none of the stars' names meant anything to him, he forgot the details. Here they are. An arc of cars and trucks mounted with lights extends halfway into Weiser Street, and a crowd of locals with rolled-up shirtsleeves and bag-lugging grannies and Negro delinquents straggles into the rest of the street to get a closer look, cutting down traffic to one creeping lane. The cops that should be unsnarling the tangle are ringing the show, protecting the moviemakers. So tall, Rabbit gets a glimpse from a curb. One of the boarded-up stores near the old Baghdad that used to show M-G-M but now is given over to skin flicks (*Sepia Follies*, *Honeymoon in Swapland*) has been done up as a restaurant front; a tall salmon-faced man with taffy hair and a little bronze-haired trick emerge from this pretend-restaurant arm in arm and there is some incident involving a passerby, another painted actor who emerges from the crowd of dusty real people watching, a bumping-into, followed by laughter on the part of the first man and the woman and a slow resuming look that will probably signal when the film is all cut and projected that they are going to fuck. They do this several times. Between takes everybody waits, wisecracks, adjusts lights and wires. The girl, from Rabbit's distance, is impossibly precise: her eyes flash, her hair hurls reflections like a helmet. Even her dress scintillates. When someone, a director or electrician, stands near her, he looks dim. And it makes Rabbit feel dim, dim and guilty, to see how the spotlights carve from the sunlight a yet brighter day, a lurid pastel island of heightened reality around which the rest of us — technicians, policemen, the straggling fascinated spectators including himself — are penumbral ghosts, suppliants ignored.

Local Excavations
Unearth Antiquities

As Brewer renews itself, it discovers more about itself.

The large-scale demolition and reconstruction now taking place in the central city continues uncovering numerous artifacts of the "olden times" which yield interesting insights into our city's past.

An underground speakeasy complete with wall murals emerged to light during the creation of a parking lot at M ing the creation of a parking lot at Muriel and Greeley Streets.

Old-timers remembered the hideaway as the haunt of "Gloves" Naugel and other Prohibition figures, as also the training-ground for musicians like "Red" Wenrich of sliding trombone fame who went on to become household names on a nationwide scale.

Also old sign-boards are common. Ingeniously shaped in the forms of cows, beehives, boots, mortars, plows, they advertise "dry goods and notions," leatherwork, drugs, and medicines, produce of infinite variety. Preserved underground, most are still easily legible and date from the nineteenth century.

Amid the old fieldstone foundations,
metal tools and grindstones come to light.
Arrowheads are not uncommon.
Dr. Klaus Schoerner, vice-president of
the Brewer Historical Society, spent a

At the coffee break, Buchanan struts up to Rabbit. "How's little Jilly doing for you?"

"She's holding up."

"She worked out pretty fine for you, didn't she?"

"She's a good girl. Mixed-up like kids are these days, but we've gotten used to her. My boy and me."

Buchanan smiles, his fine little mustache spreading an em, and sways a half-step closer. "Little Jill's still keeping you company?"

Rabbit shrugs, feeling pasty and nervous. He keeps giving hostages to fortune. "She has nowhere else to go."

"Yes, man, she must be working out real fine for you." Still he doesn't walk away, going out to the platform for his whisky. He stays and, still smiling but letting a pensive considerate shadow slowly subdue his face, says, "You know, friend Harry, what with Labor Day coming on, and the kids going back to school, and all this inflation you see everywhere, things get a bit short. In the financial end."

"How many children do you have?" Rabbit asks politely. Working with him all these years, he never thought Buchanan was married.

The plump ash-gray man rocks back and forth on the balls of his feet. "Oh . . . say five, that's been counted. They look to their daddy for support, and Labor Day finds him a little embarrassed. The cards just haven't been falling for old Lester lately."

"I'm sorry," Rabbit says. "Maybe you shouldn't gamble."

"I am just tickled to death little Jilly's worked out to fit your needs," Buchanan says. "I was thinking, twenty would sure help me by Labor Day."

"Twenty dollars?"

"That is all. It is miraculous, Harry, how far I've learned to make a little stretch. Twenty little dollars from a friend to a friend would sure make my holiday go easier all around. Like I say, seeing Jill worked out so good, you must be feeling pretty good. Pretty generous. A man in love, they say, is a friend to all."

But Rabbit has already fished out his wallet and found two tens. "This is just a loan," he says, frightened, knowing he is lying, bothered by that sliding again, that sweet bladder running late to school. The doors will be shut, the principal Mr. Kleist always stands by the front doors, with their rattling chains and push bars rubbed down to the yellow of brass, to snare the tardy and clap them into his airless office, where the records are kept.

"My children bless you," Buchanan says, folding the bills away. "This will buy a world of pencils."

"Hey, whatever happened to Babe?" Rabbit asks. He finds, with his money in Buchanan's pocket, he has new ease; he has bought rights of inquiry.

Buchanan is caught off guard. "She's still around. She's still doing her thing as the young folks say."

"I wondered, you know, if you'd broken off connections."

Because he is short of money. Buchanan studies Rabbit's face, to make certain he knows what he is implying. Pimp. He sees he does, and his mustache broadens. "You want to get into that nice Babe, is that it? Tired of white meat, want a drumstick? Harry, what would your Daddy say?"

"I'm just asking how she was. I liked the way she played."

"She sure took a shine to you, I know. Come up to Jimbo's some time, we'll work something out."

"She said my knuckles were bad." The bell rasps. Rabbit tries to gauge how soon the next touch will be made, how deep this man is into him; Buchanan sees this and playfully, jubilantly slaps the palm of the hand Rabbit had extended, thinking of his knuckles. The slap tingles. Skin.

Buchanan says, "I *like* you, man," and walks away. A plum-pudding–colored roll of fat trembles at the back of his neck. Poor diet, starch. Chitlins, grits.

> fascinating hour with the VAT reporter, chatting informally concerning Brew-er's easliest days as a trading post with
>
> er's earliest days as a trading post with the Indian tribes along the Running Horse River.
>
> He showed us a pint of log huts
>
> He showed us a print of log huts

etched when the primitive settlement bore the name of Greenwich, after Greenwich, England, home of the famed observatory.

Also in Dr. Kleist's collection were many fascinating photos of Weiser Street when it held a few rude shops and inns. The most famous of these inns was the Goose and Feathers, where George Washington and his retinue tarried one night on their way west to suppress the Whisky Rebellion in 1720. suppress the Whisky Rebellion in 1799.

The first iron mine in the vicinity was the well-known Oriole Furnace, seven miles south of the city. Dr. Kleist owns a collection of original slag and spoke enthusiastically about the methods whereby these early ironmakers produced a sufficiently powerful draft in

Pajasek comes up behind him. "Angstrom. Telephone." Pajasek is a small tired bald man whose bristling eyebrows increase the look of pressure about his head, as if his forehead is being pressed over his eyes, forming long horizontal folds. "You might tell the party after this you have a home number."

"Sorry, Ed. It's probably my crazy wife."

"Could you get her to be crazy on your private time?"

Crossing from his machine to the relative quiet of the frosted-glass walls is like ascending through supportive water to the sudden vacuum of air. Instantly, he begins to struggle. "Janice, for Christ's sake, I told you not to call me here. Call me at home."

"I don't want to talk to your little answering service. Just the thought of her voice makes me go cold all over."

"Nelson usually answers the phone. She never answers it."

"I don't want to hear her, or see her, or hear about her. I can't describe to you, Harry, the disgust I feel at just the thought of that person."

"Have you been on the bottle again? You sound screwed-up."

"I am sober and sane. And satisfied, thank you. I want to know what you're doing about Nelson's back-to-school clothes. You realize he's grown three inches this summer and nothing will fit."

"Did he, that's terrific. Maybe he won't be such a shrimp after all."

"He will be as big as my father and my father is no shrimp."

"Sorry, I always thought he was."

"Do you want me to hang up right now? Is that what you want?"

"No, I just want you to call me someplace else than at work."

She hangs up. He waits in Pajasek's wooden swivel chair, looking at the calendar, which hasn't been turned yet though this is September, and the August calendar girl, who is holding two ice-cream cones so the scoops cover just where her nipples would be, one strawberry and one chocolate, *Double Dips!* being the caption, until the phone rings.

"What were we saying?" he asks.

"I must take Nelson shopping for school clothes."

"O.K., come around and pick him up any time. Set a day."

"I will not come near that house, Harry, as long as that girl is in it. I won't even go near Penn Villas. I'm sorry, it's an uncontrollable physical revulsion."

"Maybe you're pregnant, if you're so queasy. Have you and Chas been taking precautions?"

"Harry, I don't know you any more. I said to Charlie, I can't believe I lived thirteen years with that man, it's as if it never happened."

"Which reminds me, what shall we get Nelson for his birthday? He's going to be thirteen next month."

She begins to cry. "You never forgave me for that, did you? For getting pregnant."

"I did, I did. Relax. It worked out great. I'll send Nelson over to your love nest to go shopping. Name the day."

"Send him to the lot Saturday morning. I don't like him coming to the apartment, it seems too terrible when he leaves."

"Does it have to be Saturday? There was some talk of Jill driving us both down to Valley Forge; the kid and I've never seen it."

"Are you poking fun of me? Why do you think this is all so funny, Harry? This is *life*."

"I'm not, we were. Seriously."

"Well, tell her you can't. You two send Nelson over. Only send him with some money, I don't see why I should pay for his clothes."

"Buy everything at Kroll's and charge it."

"Kroll's has gone terribly downhill, you know it has. There's a nice little new shop now up near Perley, past that submarine place that used to be Chinese."

"Open another charge account. Tell him you're Springer Motors and offer a Toyota for security."

"Harry, you mustn't be so hostile. You sent me off myself. You said, that night, I'll never forget it, it was the shock of my life, 'See him if you want to, just so I don't have to see the bastard.' Those were your words."

"Hey, that reminds me, I did see him the other day."

"Who?"

"Chas. Your dark and swarthy lover."

"How?"

"He ambushed me after work. Waiting in the alley with a dagger. *Oog*, I said, you got me, you Commie rat."

"What did he want?"

"Oh, to talk about you."

"What about me? Harry, are you lying, I can't tell any more. *What* about me?"

"Whether or not you were happy."

She makes no comeback, so he goes on, "We concluded you were."

"Right," Janice says, and hangs up.

```
         the days before the Bessemer furnace.
      Old  faded  photographs  of  Weiser
   Street  show  a  prosperous-appearing
   avenue of tasteful, low brick buildings
   with  horsedrawn  trolly  tracks  promi-
   with  horse-drown  trolley  traks  prami-
   with  horsed-rawn  trolleyyyfff  etaoin
   etaoinshrdlu etaoinshrdlucmfwpvbgkqjet
```

*   *   *

He asks her, "What did you and the kid do today?"

"Oh, nothing much. Hung around the house in the morning, took a drive in the afternoon."

"Where to?"

"Up to Mt. Judge."

"The town?"

"The mountain. We had a Coke in the Pinnacle Hotel and watched a softball game in the park for a while."

"Tell me the truth. Do you have the kid smoking pot?"

"Whatever gave you that idea?"

"He's awfully fascinated with you, and I figure it's either pot or sex."

"Or the car. Or the fact that I treat him like a human being instead of a failed little athlete because he's not six feet six. Nelson is a very intelligent sensitive child who is very upset by his mother leaving."

"I know he's intelligent, thanks, I've known the kid for years."

"Harry, do you want me to leave, is that it? I will if that's what you want. I could go back to Babe except she's having a rough time."

"What kind of rough time?"

"She's been busted for possession. The pigs came into the Jimbo the other night and took about ten away, including her and Skeeter. She says they asked for a bigger payoff and the owner balked. The owner is white, by the way."

"So you're still in touch with that crowd."

"You don't want me to be?"

"Suit yourself. It's your life to fuck up."

"Somebody's been bugging you, haven't they?"

"Several people."

"Do whatever you want to with me, Harry. I can't be anything in your real life."

She is standing before him in the living room, in her cutoff jeans and peasant blouse, her hands held at her sides slightly lifted and open, like a servant waiting for a tray. Her fingers are red from washing his dishes. Moved to gallantry, he confesses, "I need your sweet mouth and your pearly ass."

"I think they're beginning to bore you."

He reads this in reverse: he bores her. Always did. He attacks: "O.K., what *about* sex, with you and the kid?"

She looks away. She has a long nose and long chin, and that dry moth mouth that he feels, seeing it in repose, when she is not watching him, as absentmindedly disdainful, as above him and wanting to flutter still higher. Summer has put only a few freckles on her, and these mostly on her forehead, which bulges gently as a milk pitcher. Her hair is twisty from being so much in those little tiny braids hippies make. "He likes me," she answers, except it is no answer.

He tells her. "We can't do that trip to Valley Forge tomorrow. Janice wants Nelson to go shopping with her for school clothes, and I should go see my mother. You can drive me if you want, or I can take the bus."

He thinks he is being obliging, but she gives him her rich-girl sneer and says, "You remind me of my mother sometimes. She thought she owned me too."

Saturday morning, she is gone. But her clothes still hang like rags in the closet. Downstairs on the kitchen table lies a note in green magic marker: *Out all day. Will drop Nelson at the lot.* ⊕ ♡ x ♃. So he takes the two bus rides all the way across Brewer. The lawns in Mt. Judge, patches of grass between cement walks, are burned; spatterings of leaves here and there in the maples are already turned gold. There is that scent in the air, of going back to school, of beginning again and reconfirming the order that exists. He wants to feel good, he always used to feel good at every turning of the year, every vacation or end of vacation, every new sheet on the calendar: but his adult life has proved to have no seasons, only changes of weather, and the older he gets, the less weather interests him.

The house next to his old house still has the FOR SALE sign up. He tries his front door but it is locked; he rings, and after a prolonged shuffle and rumble within Pop comes to the door. Rabbit asks, "What's this locked door business?"

"Sorry, Harry, there've been so many burglaries in town lately. We had no idea you were coming."

"Didn't I promise?"

"You've promised before. Not that your mother and I can blame you, we know your life is difficult these days."

"It's not so difficult. In some ways it's easier. She upstairs?"

Pop nods. "She's rarely down anymore."

"I thought this new stuff was working."

"It does in a way, but she's so depressed she lacks the will. Nine-tenths of life is will, my father used to say it, and the longer I live the more I see how right he was."

The disinfected scent of the house is still oppressive, but Harry goes up the stairs two at a time; Jill's disappearance has left him vigorous with anger. He bursts into the sickroom, saying, "Mom, tell me your dreams."

She has lost weight. The bones have shed all but the minimum connective tissue; her face is strained over the bones with an expression of far-seeing, expectant sweetness. Her voice emerges from this apparition more strongly than before, with less hesitation between words.

"I'm tormented something cruel at night, Harry. Did Earl tell you?"

"He mentioned bad dreams."

"Yes, bad, but not so bad as not being able to sleep at all. I know this room so well now, every object. At night even that innocent old bureau and that – poor shapeless armchair – they."

"They what?" He sits on the bed to take her hand, and fears the swaying under his weight will jostle and break her bones.

She says, "They want. To suffocate me."

"Those things do?"

"All things – do. They crowd in, in the queerest way, these simple homely bits of furniture I've. Lived with all my life. Dad's asleep in the next room, I can hear him snore. No cars go by. It's just me and the streetlamp. It's like being – under water. I count the seconds I have breath left for. I figure I can go forty, thirty, then it gets down to ten."

"I didn't know breathing was affected by this."

"It isn't. It's all my mind. The things I have in my mind, Hassy, it reminds me of when they clean out a drain. All that hair and sludge mixed up with a rubber comb somebody went and dropped down years ago. Sixty years ago in my case."

"You don't feel that about your life, do you? I think you did a good job."

"A good job at what? You don't even know what you're trying to do, is the humor of it."

"Have a few laughs," he offers. "Have a few babies."

She takes him up on that. "I keep dreaming about you and Mim. Always together. When you haven't been together since you got out of school."

"What do Mim and I do, in these dreams?"

"You look up at me. Sometimes you want to be fed and I can't find the food. Once I remember looking into the icebox and. A man was in it frozen. A man I never knew, just one. Of those total strangers dreams have. Or else the stove won't light. Or I can't locate where Earl put the food when he came home from shopping, I know he. Put it somewhere. Silly things. But they become so important. I wake up screaming at Earl."

"Do Mim and I say anything?"

"No, you just look up like children do. Slightly frightened but sure I'll save. The situation. This is how you look. Even when I can see you're dead."

"Dead?"

"Yes. All powdered and set out in coffins. Only still standing up, still waiting for something from me. You've died because I couldn't get the food on the table. A strange thing about these dreams, come to think of it. Though you look up at me from a child's height. You look the way you do now. Mim all full of lipstick, with one of those shiny miniskirts and boots zippered up to her knee."

"Is that how she looks now?"

"Yes, she sent us a publicity picture."

"Publicity for what?"

"Oh, you know. For herself. You know how they do things now. I didn't understand it myself. It's on the bureau."

The picture, eight by ten, very glossy, with a diagonal crease where the mailman bent it, shows Mim in a halter and bracelets and sultan pants, her head thrown back, one long bare foot – she had big feet as a child, Mom had to make the shoe salesmen go deep into the stockroom – up on a hassock. Her eyes from the way they've reshaped them do not look like Mim at all. Only something about the nose makes it Mim. The kind of lump on the end, and the nostrils: the way as a baby they would tuck in when she started to cry is the way they tuck in now when they tell her to look sexy. He feels in this picture less Mim than the men posing her. Underneath, the message pale in ballpoint pen, she had written, *Miss you all Hope to come East soon Love Mim*. A slanting cramped hand that hadn't gone past high school. Jill's message had been written in splashy upright private-school semi-printing, confident as a poster. Mim never had that.

Rabbit asks, "How old is Mim now?"

Mom says, "You don't want to hear about my dreams."

"Sure I do." He figures it: born when he was six, Mim would be thirty now: she wasn't going anywhere, not even in harem costume. What you haven't done by thirty you're not likely to do. What you have done you'll do lots more. He says to his mother: "Tell me the worst one."

"The house next door has been sold. To some people who want to put up an apartment building. The Scranton pair have gone into partnership with them and then. These two walls go up, so the house doesn't get any light at all, and I'm in a hole looking up. And dirt starts to come down on me, cola cans and cereal boxes, and then. I wake up and know I can't breathe."

He tells her, "Mt. Judge isn't zoned for high-rise."

She doesn't laugh. Her eyes are wide now, fastened on that other half of her life, the night half, the nightmare half that now is rising like water in a bad cellar and is going to engulf her, proving that it was the real half all along, that daylight was an illusion, a cheat. "No," she says, "that's not the worst. The worst is Earl and I go to the hospital for tests. All around us are tables the size of our kitchen table. Only instead of set for meals each has a kind of puddle on it, a red puddle mixed up with crumpled bedsheets so they're shaped like. Children's sandcastles. And connected with tubes to machines with like television patterns on them. And then it dawns on me these are each people. And Earl keeps saying, so proud and pleased he's brainless, 'The government is paying for it all. The government is paying for it.' And he shows me the paper you and Mim signed to make me one of – you know, *them*. Those puddles."

"That's not a dream," her son says. "That's how it is."

And she sits up straighter on the pillows, stiff, scolding. Her mouth gets that unforgiving downward sag he used to fear more than anything – more than vampires, more than polio, more than thunder or God or being late for school. "I'm ashamed of you," she says. "I never thought I'd hear a son of mine so bitter."

"It was a joke, Mom."

"Who has so much to be grateful for," she goes on implacably.

"For what? For exactly what?"

"For Janice's leaving you, for one thing. She was always. A damp washrag."

"And what about Nelson, huh? What happens to him now?" This is her falsity, that she forgets what time creates, she still sees the world with its original four corners, her and Pop and him and Mim sitting at the kitchen table. Her tyrant love would freeze the world.

Mom says, "Nelson isn't my child, you're my child."

"Well, he exists anyway, and I have to worry about him. You just can't dismiss Janice like that."

"She's dismissed you."

"Not really. She calls me up at work all the time. Stavros wants her to come back."

"Don't you let her. She'll. Smother you, Harry."

"What choices do I have?"

"Run. Leave Brewer. I never knew why you came back. There's nothing here any more. Everybody knows it. Ever since the hosiery mills went south. Be like Mim."

"I don't have what Mim has to sell. Anyway she's breaking Pop's heart, whoring around."

"He wants it that way, your father has always been looking. For excuses to put on a long face. Well, he has me now, and I'm excuse enough. Don't say no to life, Hassy. Let the dead bury the dead. Bitterness never helps. I'd rather have a postcard from you happy than. See you sitting there like a lump."

Always these impossible demands and expectations from her. These harsh dreams. "Hassy, do you ever pray?"

"Mostly on buses."

"Pray for rebirth. Pray for your own life."

His cheeks flame; he bows his head. He feels she is asking him to kill Janice, to kill Nelson. Freedom means murder. Rebirth means death. A lump, he silently resists, and she looks aside with

the corner of her mouth worse bent. She is still trying to call him
forth from her womb, can't she see he is an old man? An old lump
whose only use is to stay in place to keep the lumps leaning on
him from tumbling.

Pop comes upstairs and tunes in the Phillies game on television.
"They're a much sounder team without that Allen," he says. "He
was a bad egg, Harry, I say that without prejudice; bad eggs come
in all colors."

After a few innings, Rabbit leaves.

"Can't you stay for at least the game, Harry? I believe there's a
beer still in the refrigerator, I was going to go down to the kitchen
anyway to make Mother some tea."

"Let him go, Earl."

To protect the electrical wires, a lot of the maples along Jackson
Road have been mutilated, the center of their crowns cut out.
Rabbit hadn't noticed this before, or the new sidewalk squares
where they have taken away the little surface gutters that used to
trip you roller skating. He had been roller skating when Kenny
Leggett, an older boy from across the street, who later became a
five-minute miler, a county conference marvel, but that was later,
this day he was just a bigger boy who had hit Rabbit with an icy
snowball that winter – could have taken out an eye if it had hit
higher – this day he just tossed across Jackson Road the shout,
"Harry, did you hear on the radio? The President is dead." He said
"The President," not "Roosevelt"; there had been no other President for them. The next time this would happen, the President
would have a name: as he sat at the deafening tall machine one
Friday after lunch his father sneaked up behind him and confided,
"Harry, it just came over the radio, engraving had it on. Kennedy's
been shot. They think in the head." Both charmers dead of
violent headaches. Their smiles fade in the field of stars. We grope
on, under bullies and accountants. On the bus, Rabbit prays as his
mother told him to do: *Make the L-dopa work, give her pleasanter
dreams, keep Nelson more or less pure, don't let Stavros turn too hard on
Janice, help Jill find her way home. Keep Pop healthy. Me too. Amen.*

A man in a pink shirt drops down beside him with a stagey sigh,
after a stop on the side of the mountain, by the gas station with
the Day-Glo spinner. The man's face, turned full, clings to the side

of Rabbit's vision; after a while he defiantly returns the stare. The other man's cheeks are like his shirt pink, smooth as a boy's though his hair is gray, and his long worried eyebrows are lifted with an effort of recognition. "I *do* beg your pardon," he says, with an emphasis that curls back into his voice purringly, "but aren't you Harry –?"

"Hey, and you're Eccles. Reverend Eccles."

"Angstrom, yes? Harry Angstrom. How very wonderful. *Really.*" And Eccles takes his hand, in that plump humid grip that feels as if it will never let go. In the clergyman's eyes there is something new, a hardened yet startled something, naked like the pale base of his throat, which lacks a clerical collar. And the shirt, Rabbit sees, is a fancy shirt, with a fine white stitch-stripe and an airy semi-transparent summer weave: he remembers how the man wore not black but a subtly elegant midnight blue. Eccles still has hold of his hand. Harry pulls it free. "*Do* tell me," Eccles says, with that preening emphasis again, which Rabbit doesn't remember from ten years ago, "how things have gone for you. Are you still with –?"

"Janice."

"She didn't seem quite up to you, I can say now, frankly."

"Well, or *vice versa*. We never had another child." That had been Eccles' advice, in those first months of reconciliation, when he and Janice were starting fresh and even going to the Episcopal church together. Then Eccles had been called to a church nearer Philadelphia. They had heard a year or two later, by way of Janice's mother, that he had run into some trouble in his new parish; then nothing. And here he was again, grayer but looking no older: if anything, younger, slimmer through the middle, in self-consciously good condition, hard and tan in a way few in Brewer bother to cultivate, and with that young, startled look to his eyes. His hair is long, and curls at the back of his shirt collar. Rabbit asks him, "And what about things with *you*?" He is wondering where Eccles could have been, to board the bus at the side of the mountain. Nothing there but the gas station, a diner, a view of the viaduct, and some rich men's homes tucked up among the spruces, behind iron fences.

"*Ça va*. It goes. I've been buried; and yet I live. I've parted company with the ministry." And his jaw stays open, propped as if to emit a guffaw, though no sound comes, and those strangely purified eyes remain watchful.

"Why'd you do that?" Rabbit asks.

Eccles' chuckle, which always had something exploratory and quizzical about it, has become impudent, mocking, if not quite unafraid. "A variety of reasons. I was rather invited to, for one. I wanted to, for another."

"You no longer believe it?"

"In my fashion. I'm not sure I believed it then."

"No?" Rabbit is shocked.

"I believed," Eccles tells him, and his voice takes on an excessive modulation, a self-caressing timbre, "in certain kinds of human interrelation. I still do. If people want to call what happens in certain relationships Christ, I raise no objection. But it's not the word *I* choose to use anymore."

"How'd your father feel about this? Wasn't he a bishop?"

"My father – God rest his, et cetera – was dead when my decision was reached."

"And your wife? She was nifty, I forget her name."

"Lucy. Dear Lucy. She left me, actually. Yes, I've shed many skins." And the mouth of this pale-throated, long-haired man holds open on the possibility of a guffaw, but silently, watchfully.

"She left ya?"

"She fled my indiscretions. She remarried and lives in Wilmington. Her husband's a painfully ordinary fellow, a chemist of some sort. No indiscretions. My girls adore him. You remember my two girls."

"They were cute. Especially the older one. Since we're on the subject, Janice has left me, too."

Eccles' pale active eyebrows arch higher. "Really? Recently?"

"The day before the moon shot."

"She seemed more the left than the leaving type. Look, Harry, we should get together in a more, ah, stationary place and have a real conversation." In his leaning closer for emphasis, as the bus sways, his arm touches Rabbit's. He always had a certain surprising muscularity, but Eccles has become burlier, more himself. His fluffed-up head seems huge.

Rabbit asks him, "Uh, what do you do now?"

Again, the guffaw, the held jaw, the watchfulness. "I live in Philadelphia, basically. For a while I did youth work with the Y.M.C.A. I was a camp supervisor three summers in Vermont. Some winters, I've chosen just to read, to meditate. I think a very exciting thing is happening in Western consciousness and, laugh if you will, I'm making notes toward a book about it. What I think, in essence, is that, at long last, we're coming out of Plato's cave. How does 'Out from Plato's Cave' strike you as a title?"

"Kind of spooky, but don't mind me. What brings you back to this dirty old burg then?"

"Well, it's rather curious, Harry. You don't mind my calling you Harry? That all is beginning to seem as if it were only yesterday. What curious people we were then! The ghosts we let bedevil us! Anyway, you know the little town called Oriole, six miles south of Brewer?"

"I've been there." With his high-school basketball team, a dozen years ago. Junior year. He had one of his great nights there.

"Well, they have a summer theater, called the Oriole Players."

"Sure. We run their ads."

"That's right – you're a printer. I've heard that."

"Linotyper, actually."

"Good for you. Well, a friend of mine, he's an absurd person, *very* egotistical, but nevertheless a wonderful man, is with them as co-director, and has talked me into helping with their P.R. Public relations. It's really being a fund raiser. I was in Mt. Judge just now seeing this im*poss*ible old Mahlon Youngerman, that's Sunflower Beer of course, for a donation. He said he'd think about it. That's code for he *won't* think about it."

"It sounds a little like what you used to do."

Eccles glances at him more sharply; a defensive sleepiness masks his face. "Pearls before swine, you mean? Pushing stumbling-blocks at the Gentiles. Yes, a little, but I only do it eight hours a day. The other sixteen, I can be my own *man*."

Harry doesn't like the hungry way he says *man*, like it means too much. They are jerking and trembling down Weiser Street; Eccles looks past Harry out the window and blinks. "I *must* get off here. Could I ask you to get off with me and have me buy you a drink? There's a bar here on the corner that's not too depressing."

"No, Jesus, thanks. I got to keep riding. I got to get home. I have a kid there alone."

"Nelson."

"Right! What a memory! So thanks a lot. You look great."

"De*light*ful to see you again, Harry. Let's *do* make a more leisurely occasion sometime. Where are you living?"

"Over in Penn Villas, they put it up since you were here. Things are a little vague right now . . ."

"I understand," Eccles says, quickly, for the bus is chuffing and groaning to a stop. Yet he finds time to put his hand on Harry's shoulder, up near the neck. His voice changes quality, beseeches, becomes again a preacher's: "I think these are *mar*vellous times to be alive in, and I'd *love* to share my good news with you at your leisure."

To put distance between them, Rabbit rides the 16A six blocks further, to where it turns up Greely, and gets off there, walking back to the roasted-peanut place on Weiser to catch the bus to Penn Villas. PIG ATROCITIES STIR CAMDEN says a headline on a rack, a radical black paper out of Philly. Harry feels nervous, looking north along Weiser for a pink shirt coming after him. The place on his bare neck where Eccles touched tickles: amazing how that guy wants to cling, after all these years, with both their lives turned upside down. The bus number 12 comes and pulls him across the bridge. The day whines at the windows, a September brightness empty of a future: the lawns smitten flat, the black river listless and stinking. HOBBY HEAVEN. BUTCH CSSDY & KID. He walks down Emberly toward Vista Crescent among sprinklers twirling in unison, under television aerials raking the same four-o'clock garbage from the sky.

The dirty white Porsche is in the driveway, halfway into the garage, the way Janice used to do it, annoyingly. Jill is in the brown armchair, in her slip. From the slumped way she sits he sees she has no underpants on. She answers his questions groggily, with a lag, as if they are coming to her through a packing of dirty cotton, of fuzzy memories accumulated this day.

"Where'd you go so early this morning?"

"Out. Away from creeps like you."

"You drop the kid off?"

"Sure."

"When'd you get back?"

"Just now."

"Where'd you spend all day?"

"Maybe I went to Valley Forge anyway."

"Maybe you didn't."

"I did."

"How was it?"

"Beautiful. A gas, actually. George was a beautiful dude."

"Describe one room."

"You go in a door, and there's a four-poster bed, and a little tasselled pillow, and on it it says, 'George Washington slept here.' On the bedside tables you can still see the pills he took, to make himself sleep, when the redcoats had got him all uptight. The walls have some kind of lineny stuff on them, and all the chairs have ropes across the arms so you can't sit down on them. That's why I'm sitting on this one. Because it didn't. O.K.?"

He hesitates among the many alternatives she seems to be presenting. Laughter, anger, battle, surrender. "O.K. Sounds interesting. I'm sorry we couldn't go."

"Where did you go?"

"I went to visit my mother, after doing the housework around here."

"How is she?"

"She talks better, but seems frailer."

"I'm sorry. I'm sorry she has that disease. I guess I'll never meet your mother, will I?"

"Do you want to? You can see my father any time you want, just be in the Phoenix Bar at four-fifteen. You'd like him, he cares about politics. He thinks the System is shit, just like you do."

"And I'll never meet your wife."

"Why would you want to? What is this?"

"I don't know, I'm interested. Maybe I'm falling for you."

"Jesus, don't do that."

"You don't think much of yourself, do you?"

"Once the basketball stopped, I suppose not. My mother by the way told me I should let Janice screw herself and leave town."

"What'd you say to that?"

"I said I couldn't."

"You're a creep."

Her lack of underpants and his sense that she has already been used today, and his sense of this unique summer, this summer of the moon, slipping away forever, lead him to ask, blushing for the second time this afternoon, "You wouldn't want to make love, would you?"

"Fuck or suck?"

"Whichever. Fuck." For he has come to feel that she gives him the end of her with teeth in it as a way of keeping the other for some man not yet arrived, some man more real to her than himself.

"What about Nelson?" she asks.

"He's off with Janice, she may keep him for supper. He's no threat. But maybe you're too tired. From all that George Washington."

Jill stands and pulls her slip to her shoulder and holds it there, a crumpled bag containing her head, her young body all there below, pale as a candlestick, the breasts hardened drippings. "Fuck me," she says coolly, tossing her slip toward the kitchen, and, when under him and striving, continues, "Harry, I want you to fuck all the shit out of me, all the shit and dreariness of this shit-dreary world, hurt me, clean me out, I want you to be all of my insides, sweetheart, right up to my throat, yes, oh yes, bigger, more, shoot it all out of me, sweet oh sweet sweet creep." Her eyes dilate in surprise. Their green is just a rim, around pupils whose pure black is muddied with his shadow. "You've gotten little."

It is true: all her talk, her wild wanting it, have scared him down to nothing. She is too wet; something has enlarged her. And the waxen solidity of her young body, her buttocks spheres too perfect, feels alien to him: he grasps her across a distance clouded with Mom's dry warm bones and Janice's dark curves, Janice's ribs crescent above where the waist dipped. He senses winds playing through Jill's nerve-ends, feels her moved by something beyond him, of which he is only a shadow, a shadow of white, his chest a radiant shield crushing her. She disengages herself and kneels to tongue his belly. They play with each other in a fog. The furniture dims around them. They are on the scratchy carpet, the television screen a mother-planet above them. Her hair is in his mouth. Her ass is two humps under his eyes. She tries to come against his face but his tongue isn't that strong. She rubs her clitoris against his chin upside down until he hurts. Elsewhere she is nibbling him. He feels gutted, silly, limp. At last he asks her to drag her breasts, the tough little tips, across his genitals, that lie cradled at the join of his legs. In this way he arouses himself, and attempts to satisfy her, and does, though by the time she trembles and comes they are crying over secrets far at their backs, in opposite directions, moonchild and earthman. "I love you," he says, and the fact that he doesn't makes it true. She is sitting on him, still working like some angry mechanic who, having made a difficult fit, keeps testing it.

In the small slipping sound they make he hears their mixed liquids, imagines in the space of her belly a silver machine, spider-shaped, spun from the threads of their secretions, carefully spinning. This links them. He says, surrendering, "Oh cry. Do." He pulls her down to him, puts their cheeks together, so their tears will mix.

Jill asks him, "Why are you crying?"

"Why are you?"

"Because the world is so shitty and I'm part of it."

"Do you think there's a better one?"

"There must be."

"Well," he considers, "why the hell not?"

By the time Nelson comes home, they have both taken baths, their clothes are on, the lights are on. Rabbit is watching the six-o'clock news (the round-up tally on summer riots, the week's kill figures in Vietnam, the estimate of traffic accidents over the coming Labor Day weekend) and Jill is making lentil soup in the kitchen. Nelson spreads over the floor and furniture the unwrapped loot of his day with Janice: snappy new Jockey shorts, undershirts, stretch socks, two pairs of slacks, four sports shirts, a corduroy jacket, wide neckties, even cufflinks to go with a lavender dress shirt, not to mention new loafers and basketball sneakers.

Jill admires: "Groovy, groovier, grooviest. Nelson, I just pity those eighth-grade girls, they'll be at your mercy."

He looks at her anxiously. "You know it's square. I didn't want to, Mom made me. The stores were disgusting, all full of materialism."

"What stores did she go to?" Rabbit asked. "How the hell did she pay for all this junk?"

"She opened charge accounts everywhere, Dad. She bought herself some clothes too, a really neat thing that looks like pajamas only it's O.K. to wear to parties if you're a woman, and stuff like that. And I got a suit, kind of grayey-green with checks, really cool, that we can pick up in a week when they make the alterations. Doesn't it feel funny when they measure you?"

"Do you remember, who was the name on the accounts? Me or Springer?"

Jill for a joke has put on one of his new shirts and tied her hair in a tail behind with one of his wide new neckties. To show herself off she twirls. Nelson, entranced, can scarcely speak. At her mercy.

"The name on her driver's license, Dad. Isn't that the right one?"

"And the address here? All those bills are going to come here?"

"Whatever's on the driver's license, Dad. Don't go heavy on *me*, I told her I just wanted blue jeans. And a Che Guevara sweatshirt, only there aren't any in Brewer."

Jill laughs. "Nelson, you'll be the best-dressed radical at West Brewer Junior High. Harry, these neckties are *silk!*"

"So it's war with that bitch."

"Dad, *don't*. It wasn't my *fault*."

"I know that. Forget it. You needed the clothes, you're growing."

"And Mom really looked neat in some of the dresses."

He goes to the window, rather than continue to be heavy on the kid. He sees his own car, the faithful Falcon, slowly pull out. He sees for a second the shadow of Janice's head, the way she sits at the wheel hunched over, you'd think she'd be more relaxed with cars, having grown up with them. She had been waiting, for what? For him to come out? Or was she just looking at the house, maybe to spot Jill? Or homesick. By a tug of tension in one cheek he recognizes himself as smiling, seeing that the flag decal is still on the back window, she hasn't let Stavros scrape it off.

III. SKEETER

"We've been raped, we've been raped!"
— BACKGROUND VOICE ABOARD SOYUZ 5

ONE DAY in September Rabbit comes home from work to find another man in the house. The man is a Negro. "What the hell," Rabbit says, standing in the front hall beside the three chime tubes.

"Hell, man, it's revolution, right?" the young black says, not rising from the mossy brown armchair. His glasses flash two silver circles; his goatee is a smudge in shadow. He has let his hair grow out so much, into such a big ball, that Rabbit didn't recognize him at first.

Jill rises, quick as smoke, from the chair with the silver threads. "You remember Skeeter?"

"How could I forget him?" He goes forward a step, his hand lifted ready to be shaken, the palm tingling with fear; but since Skeeter makes no move to rise, he lets it drop back to his side, unsullied.

Skeeter studies the dropped white hand, exhaling smoke from a cigarette. It is a real cigarette, tobacco. "I like it," Skeeter says. "I like your hostility, Chuck. As we used to say in Nam, it is my meat."

"Skeeter and I were just talking," Jill says; her voice has changed, it is more afraid, more adult. "Don't I have any rights?"

Rabbit speaks to Skeeter. "I thought you were in jail or something."

"He is out on bail," Jill says, too hastily.

"Let him speak for himself."

Wearily Skeeter corrects her. "To be precise, I am way out on bail. I have jumped the blessed thing. I am, as they would say, de*sir*ed by the local swine. I have become one hot item, right?"

"It would have been two years," Jill says. "Two years for nothing, for not hurting anybody, not stealing anything, for nothing, Harry."

"Did Babe jump bail too?"

"Babe is a lady," Skeeter goes on in this tone of weary mincing precision. "She makes friends easy, right? I have no friends.
I am known far and wide for my lack of sympathetic qualities."
His voice changes, becomes falsetto, cringing. "Ah is one *baad*
niggeh." He has many voices, Rabbit remembers, and none of
them exactly his.

Rabbit tells him, "They'll catch you sooner or later. Jumping
bail makes it much worse. Maybe you would have gotten off with
a suspended sentence."

"I have one of those. Officialdom gets bored with handing
them out, right?"

"How about your being a Vietnam veteran?"

"How *about* it? I am also black and unemployed and surly,
right? I seek to undermine the state, and Ol' Massah State, he
cottons on."

Rabbit contemplates the set of shadows in the old armchair,
trying to feel his way. The chair has been with them ever since
their marriage, it comes from the Springers' attic. This nightmare
must pass. He says, "You talk a cool game, but I think you panicked, boy."

"Don't boy me."

Rabbit is startled; he had meant it neutrally, one outlaw to
another. He tries to amend: "You're just hurting yourself. Go turn
yourself in, say you never meant to jump."

Skeeter stretches luxuriously in the chair, yawns, inhales and
exhales. "It dawns upon me," he says, "that you have a white
gentleman's concept of the police and their exemplary works.
There is nothing, let me repeat no thing, that gives them more
pleasurable sensations than pulling the wings off of witless poor
black men. First the fingernails, then the wings. Truly, they are
constituted for that very sacred purpose. To keep me off your back
and under your smelly feet, right?"

"This isn't the South," Rabbit says.

"Hee-yah! Friend Chuck, have you ever considered running
for po-litical office, there can't be a county clerk left who believes
the sweet things you do. The news is, the South is everywhere.
We are fifty miles from the Mason-Dixon line where we sit, but
way up in Detroit they are shooting nigger boys like catfish in a

barrel. The news is, the cotton is in. Lynching season is on. In these Benighted States, everybody's done become a cracker." A brown hand delicately gestures from the shadows, then droops. "Forgive me, Chuck. This is just too simple for me to explain. Read the papers."

"I do. You're crazy."

Jill horns in. "The System is rotten, Harry. The laws are written to protect a tiny elite."

"Like people who own boats in Stonington," he says.

"Score one," Skeeter calls, "right?"

Jill flares. "What of it, I ran away from it, I reject it, I *shit* on it, Harry, where you're still loving it, you're eating it, you're eating my shit. My father's. Everybody's. Don't you see how you're *used?*"

"So now you want to use me. For *him*."

She freezes, white. Her lips thin to nothing. "Yes."

"You're crazy. I'd be risking jail too."

"Harry, just a few nights, until he can hustle up a stake. He has family in Memphis, he'll go there. Skeeter, right?"

"Right, sugar. Oh so right."

"It isn't just the pot bust, the pigs think he's a dealer, they say he pushes, they'll crucify him. Harry. They will."

Skeeter softly croons the start of "That Old Rugged Cross."

"Well, does he? Push."

Skeeter grins under his great ball of hair. "What can I get for you, Chuck? Goof balls, jolly beans, red devils, purple hearts. They have so much Panama Red in Philly right now they're feeding it to cows. Or want to sniff a little scag for a real rush?" From the gloom of the chair he extends his pale palms cupped as if heaped with shining poison.

So he is evil. Rabbit in his childhood used to lift, out of the same curiosity that made him put his finger into his belly-button and then sniff it, the metal waffle-patterned lid on the back yard cesspool, around the corner of the garage from the basketball hoop. Now this black man opens up under him in the same way: a pit of scummed stench impossible to see to the bottom of.

Harry turns and asks Jill, "Why are you doing this to me?"

She turns her head, gives him that long-chinned profile, a dime's worth. "I was stupid," she says, "to think you might trust me. You shouldn't have said you loved me."

Skeeter hums "True Love," the old Crosby–Grace Kelly single.

Rabbit re-asks, "Why?"

Skeeter rises from the chair. "Jesus deliver me from puking uptight honky lovers. She's doing it because I been screwing her all afternoon, right? If I go, she comes with me, hey Jill honey, right?"

She says, again thin-lipped, "Right."

Skeeter tells her, "I wouldn't take you on a bet, you poor cock-happy bitch. Skeeter splits alone." To Rabbit he says, "Toodle-oo, Chuck. Goddam green pickles, but it's been fun to watch you squirm." Standing, Skeeter seems frail, shabby in blue Levis and a colorless little Army windbreaker from which the insignia have been unstitched. His ball of hair has shrunk his face.

"Toodle-oo," Rabbit agrees, with relief in his bowels, and turns his back.

Skeeter declines to go so simply. He steps closer, he smells spicy. He says, "Throw me out. I want you to touch me."

"I don't want to."

"Do it."

"I don't want to fight you."

"I screwed your bitch."

"Her decision."

"And a lousy little cunt she was, too. Like putting your prick in a vise."

"Hear him, Jill?"

"Hey. Rabbit. That's what they used to call you, right? Your mamma's a whore, right? She goes down on old black winos behind the railroad station for fifty cents, right? If they don't have fifty cents she does it free because she likes it, right?"

Remote Mom. The quilty scent of her room, medicine, bed-warmth. Of all those years when she was well he can only remember her big bones bent above the kitchen table with its four worn places; she is not sitting down, she has already eaten, she is feeding him supper, he has come home from practice late, it is after dark, the windows are glazed from within.

"Your daddy's a queer, right? You must be too to take all this shit. Your wife couldn't stand living with a queer, it was like being balled by a mouse, right? You're a mouse down there, hey, ain't that right, gimme a feel." He reaches and Rabbit bats his hand away. Skeeter dances, delighted. "Nothin' there, right? Hey. Rabbit. Jill says you believe in God. I got news for you. Your God's a pansy. Your white God's queerer than the Queen of Spades. He sucks off the Holy Ghost and makes his son watch. Hey. Chuck. Another thing. Ain't no Jesus. He was a faggot crook, right? They bribed the Romans to get his carcass out of the tomb 'cause it smelled so bad, right?"

"All you're showing me," Rabbit says, "is how crazy you are." But a creeping sweetness, rage, is filling him solid. Sunday school images – a dead man whiter than lilies, the lavender rocks where he was betrayed by a kiss – are being revived in him.

Skeeter dances on, he is wearing big creased Army boots. He bumps Harry's shoulder, tugs the sleeve of his white shirt. "Hey. Wanna know how I know? Wanna know? Hey. I'm the real Jesus. I am *the* black Jesus, right? There is none other, no. When I fart, lightning flashes, right? Angels scoop it up in shovels of zillion-carat gold. Right? Kneel down, Chuck. Worship me. I am Jesus. Kiss my balls – they are the sun and the moon, and my pecker's a comet whose head is the white-hot heart of the glory that never does fail!" And, his head rolling like a puppet's, Skeeter unzips his fly and prepares to display this wonder.

Rabbit's time has come. He is packed so solid with anger and fear he is seeing with his pores. He wades toward the boy deliciously and feels his fists vanish, one in the region of the belly, the other below the throat. He is scared of the head, whose glasses might shatter and slash. Skeeter curls up and drops to the floor dry as a scorpion and when Rabbit pries at him he has no opening, just abrasive angles shaking like a sandpaper machine. Rabbit's hands start to hurt. He wants to pry this creature open because there is a soft spot where he can be split and killed; the curved back is too tough, though knuckles slammed at the hole of the ear do produce a garbled whimper.

Jill is screaming and with her whole weight pulling the tail of his shirt and in the ebb of his sweetness Rabbit discovers his hands and forearms somehow clawed. His enemy is cringing on the floor, the carpet that cost them eleven dollars a yard and was supposed to wear longer than the softer loop for fifteen that Janice wanted (she always said it reminded her of the stuff they use in miniature golf courses), cringing expertly, knees tucked under chin and hands over head and head tucked under the sofa as far as it will go. His Levis are rumpled up and it shocks Rabbit to see how skinny his calves and ankles are, iridescent dark spindles. Humans made of a new material. Last longer, wear more evenly. And Jill is sobbing, "Harry, no more, no more," and the door chime is saying its three syllables over and over, a scale that can't get anywhere, that can't get over the top.

The door pops open. Nelson is there, in his spiffy new school clothes, fishbone-striped sport shirt and canary-yellow slacks. Billy Fosnacht is behind him, a hairy head taller. "Hey," Skeeter says from the floor, "it's Babychuck, right?"

"Is he a burglar, Dad?"

"We could hear the furniture being smashed and everything," Billy says. "We didn't know what to do."

Nelson says, "We thought if we kept ringing the bell it would stop."

Jill tells him, "Your father lost all control of himself."

Rabbit asks, "Why should I always be the one to have control of myself?"

Getting up as if from a bin of dust, one careful limb at a time, Skeeter says, "That was to get us acquainted, Chuck. Next time I'll have a gun."

Rabbit taunts, "I thought at least I'd see some nice karate chops from basic training."

"Afraid to use 'em. Break you in two, right?"

"Daddy, who is he?"

"He's a friend of Jill's called Skeeter. He's going to stay here a couple days."

"He is?"

Jill's voice has asked.

Rabbit sifts himself for the reason. Small scraped places smart on his knuckles; overstimulation has left a residue of nausea; he notices through the haze that still softly rotates around him that the end table was upset and that the lamp whose base is driftwood lies on the carpet awry but not smashed. The patient fidelity of these things bewilders him. "Sure," he says. "Why not?"

Skeeter studies him from the sofa, where he sits bent over, nursing the punch to his stomach. "Feeling guilty, huh Chuck? A little tokenism to wash your sins away, right?"

"Skeeter, he's being generous," Jill scolds.

"Get one thing straight, Chuck. No gratitude. Anything you do, do for selfish reasons."

"Right. The kicks I get in pounding you around." But in fact he is terrified at having taken this man in. He will have to sleep with him in the house. The tint of night, Skeeter will sneak to his side with a knife shining like the moon. He will get the gun as he has promised. FUGITIVE FROM JUSTICE HOLDS FAMILY AT GUNPOINT. *Mayor Vows, No Deals*. Why has he invited this danger? To get Janice to rescue him. These thoughts flit by in a flash. Nelson has taken a step toward the black man. His eyes are sunk in their sockets with seriousness. Wait, wait. He is poison, he is murder, he is black.

"Hi," Nelson says, and holds out his hand.

Skeeter puts his skinny fingers, four gray crayons, as thick at the tips as in the middle, in the child's hand and says, "Hi there, Babychuck." He nods over Nelson's shoulder toward Billy Fosnacht. "Who's your gruesome friend?"

And everybody, everybody laughs, even Billy, even Skeeter contributes a cackle, at this unexpected illumination, that Billy *is* gruesome, with his father's skinny neck and big ears and a hint of his mother's mooncalf eyes and the livid festerings of adolescence speckling his cheeks and chin. Their laughter makes a second wave to reassure him they are not laughing at him, they are laughing in relief at the gift of truth, they are rejoicing in brotherhood, at having shared this moment, giggling and cackling; the house is an egg cracking because they are all hatching together.

But in bed, the house dark and Billy gone home, Skeeter breathing exhausted on the sofa downstairs, Rabbit repeats his question to Jill: "Why have you done this to me?"

Jill snuffles, turns over. She is so much lighter than he, she irre-
sistibly rolls down to his side. Often in the morning he wakes to
find himself nearly pushed from the bed by this inequality, her
sharp little elbows denting his flesh. "He was so pathetic," she
explains. "He talks tough but he really has nothing, he really does
want to become the black Jesus."

"Is that why you let him screw you this afternoon? Or didn't
you?"

"I didn't really."

"He lied?"

Silence. She slides an inch deeper into his side of the bed. "I
don't think it counts when you just let somebody do it to you and
don't do anything back."

"You don't."

"No, it just happens on the surface, a million miles away."

"And how about with me? Is it the same way, you don't feel
anything, it's so far away. So you're really a virgin, aren't you?"

"Shh. Whisper. No, I do feel things with you."

"What?"

She nudges closer and her arm encircles his thick waist. "I feel
you're a funny big teddy bear my Daddy has given me. He used
to bring home these extravagant Steiff toys from F.A.O. Schwarz's
in New York, giraffes six feet high that cost five hundred dollars,
you couldn't do anything with them, they'd just stand around
taking up space. Mother hated them."

"Thanks a lot." Sluggishly he rolls over to face her.

"Other times, when you're over me, I feel you're an angel.
Piercing me with a sword. I feel you're about to announce some-
thing, the end of the world, and you say nothing, just pierce me.
It's beautiful."

"Do you love me?"

"Please, Harry. Since that God thing I went through I just can't
focus that way on anybody."

"Is Skeeter out of focus for you too?"

"He's horrible. He really is. He feels all scaly, he's so bitter."

"Then why in holy hell −?"

She kisses him to stop his voice. "Shh. He'll hear." Sounds
travel freely down the stairs, through the house of thin partitions.

The rooms are quadrants of one rustling heart. "Because I must, Harry. Because whatever men ask of me, I must give, I'm not interested in holding anything for myself. It all melts together anyway, you see."

"I don't see."

"I think you do. Otherwise why did you let him stay? You had him beaten. You were killing him."

"Yeah, that was nice. I thought I was out of shape worse than I am."

"Yet now he's here." She flattens her body against his; it feels transparent. He can see through her to the blue window beyond, moonlit, giving onto the garage roof, composition shingling manufactured with a strange shadow-line, to give an illusion of thickness. She confesses, in such a whisper it may be only a thought he overhears, "He frightens me."

"Me too."

"Half of me wanted you to kick him out. More than half."

"Well," and he smiles unseen, "if he is the next Jesus, we got to keep on His good side." Her body broadens as if smiling. It has grown plain that the betrayals and excitements of the day must resolve into their making love now. He encloses her skull in his hands, caressing the spinelike ridges behind the seashell curve of her ears, palming the broad curve of the whole, this cup, sealed upon a spirit. Knowing her love is coming, he sees very clearly, as we see in the etched hour before snow. He amends, "Also, Janice has been doing some things out of the way, so I have to do things out of the way."

"To pay her back."

"To keep up with her."

The item was narrow-measure:

Sentenced for
Possession

Eight local men and one
woman were given six-month

sentences for possession of
marijuana Thursday.

The defendants appearing before Judge Milton F. Schoffer
had been apprehended in a police raid on Jimbo's Lounge,
Weiser Street, early in the
morning of August 29.

The female among them, Miss
Beatrice Greene, a well-known
local entertainer under her nom
de plume of ''Babe,'' had her
sentence suspended, with one
year's probation, as were four
of the men. Two minors were
remanded to juvenile court.

A tenth defendant, Hubert H.
Farnsworth, failed to appear in
court and forfieted bail. A war-
court and forfeited bail. A war-
ant has been issued for his arrest.

ant has been issued for his
arrest.

The proprietor of Jimbo's,
Mr. Timothy Cartney of Penn

Rabbit's ears can sense now when Pajasek is coming up behind
him with a phone call. Something weary and menacing in his step,
and then his breath has a sarcastic caress. "Angstrom, maybe we
should move your Lino into my office. Or install a phone jack out
here."

"I'll give her hell, Ed. This is the last time."

"I don't like a man's private life to interfere with his work."

"I don't either. I tell you, I'll tell her."

"Do that, Harry. Do that for good old Verity. We have a team
here, we're in a highly competitive game, let's keep up our end,
what do you say?"

Behind the frosted walls he says into the phone, "Janice, this is
the last time. I won't come to the phone after this."

"I won't be calling you after this, Harry. After this all our communications will be through lawyers."

"How come?"

"How come? How *come!*"

"How come. Come on. Just give me information. I got to get back to the machine."

"Well, for one reason how come, you've let me sit over here without ever once calling me back, and for another you've taken a darkie into the house along with that hippie, you're in*cred*ible, Harry, my mother always said it, 'He means no harm, he just has less moral sense than a skunk,' and she was right."

"He's just there a couple days, it's a funny kind of emergency."

"It must be funny. It must be hilarious. Does your mother know? So help me, I have a mind to call and tell her."

"Who told you, anyway? He never goes out of the house."

He hopes by his reasonable tone to bring hers down; she does unwind a notch. "Peggy Fosnacht. She said Billy came home absolutely bug-eyed. He said the man was on the living-room floor and the first thing he said was to insult Billy."

"It wasn't meant as an insult, it was meant to be pleasant."

"Well I wish *I* could be pleasant. I wish it very much. I've seen a lawyer and we're filing a writ for immediate custody of Nelson. The divorce will follow. As the guilty party you can't remarry for two years. Absolutely, Harry. I'm sorry. I thought we were more mature than this, I *hated* the lawyer, the whole thing is too ugly."

"Yeah, well, the law is. It serves a ruling elite. More power to the people."

"I think you've lost your mind. I honestly do."

"Hey, what did you mean, I let you sit over there? I thought that was what you wanted. Isn't Stavros still doing the sitting with you?"

"You might at least have fought a *little*," she cries, and gasps for breath between sobs. "You're so weak, you're so wishy-washy," she manages to bring out, but then it becomes pure animal sound, a kind of cooing or wheezing, as if all the air is running out of her, so he says, "We'll talk later, call me at home," and hangs up to plug the leak.

> Park, expressed shock and strong disapproval of drug use over the telephone to VAT inquiries.

> Cartney was not in the build-
> ing at the time of the arrests.
> Rumors have prevailed for
> some time concerning the sale
> of this well-known nightspot
> and gathering place to a "black
> capitalist" syndicate.

During the coffee break Buchanan comes over. Rabbit touches his wallet, wondering if the touch will go up. Escalation. Foreign aid. Welfare. He'll refuse if it does. If he asks more than twenty, let them riot in the streets. But Buchanan holds out two ten dollar bills, not the same two, but just as good. "Friend Harry," he says, "never let it be said no black man pays his debts. I'm obliged to you a thousand and one times over, them two sawbucks turned the cards right around. Would you believe two natural full houses in a row? I couldn't believe it myself, nobody could, those fools all stayed the second time like there was no tomorrow." He wads the money into Rabbit's hand, which is slow to close.

"Thanks, uh, Lester. I didn't really –"

"Expect to get it back?"

"Not so soon."

"Well, sometimes one man's in need, sometimes another man is. Spread it around, isn't that what the great ones teach us?"

"I guess they do. I haven't talked to many great ones lately."

Buchanan chuckles politely and rocks back and forth on his heels, estimating, rolling a toothpick in his lips, beneath the mustache no thicker than a toothpick. "I hear tell you're so hard up over at your place you're taking in boarders."

"Oh. That. It's just temporary, it wasn't my idea."

"I believe that."

"Uh – I'd rather it didn't get around."

"That's just what I'd rather."

Change the subject, somehow. "How's Babe now? Back in business?"

"What kind of business you think she's in?"

"You know, singing. I meant after the bust and court sentence. I just set the news item."

"I know what you meant. I know exactly. Come on down to Jimbo's, any night of the week, get better acquainted. Babe's estimation of you has shot way up, I tell you that. Not that she didn't take a shine in the first place."

"Yeah, O.K., great. Maybe I'll get down sometime. If I can get a babysitter." The idea of ever going into Jimbo's again frightens him, as does the idea of leaving Nelson, Jill, and Skeeter alone in the house. He is sinking into an underworld he used to see only from a bus. Buchanan squeezes his arm.

"We'll set something up," the Negro promises. "Oh, yeass." The hand squeezes tighter, as if pressing fingerprints through the screen of Harry's blue workshirt. "Jer-ome asked me to express an especial gratitude."

Jerome?

The yellow-faced clock ticks, the end-of-break buzzer rasps. The last to return to his machine, Farnsworth passes between the brightly lit makeup tables, a man so black he twinkles. He bobs his shaved head, wipes the whisky from his lips, and throws Harry a dazzling grin. Brothers in paternity.

He gets off the bus early, on the other side of the bridge, and walks along the river through the old brick neighborhoods burdened with great green highway signs. Peggy Fosnacht's buzzer buzzes back and when he gets off the elevator she is at the door in a shapeless blue bathrobe. "Oh, *you*," she says. "I thought it would be Billy having lost his key again."

"You alone?"

"Yes, but Harry, he'll be back from school any minute."

"I only need a minute." She leads him in, pulling her bathrobe tighter about her body. He tries to wrap his errand in a little courtesy. "How've you been?"

"I'm managing. How have you been?"

"Managing. Just."

"Would you like a drink?"

"This early in the day?"

"I'm having one."

"No, Peggy, thanks. I can only stay a minute. I got to see what's cooking back at the ranch."

"Quite a lot, I hear."

"That's what I wanted to say something about."

"Please sit down. I'm getting a crick in my neck." Peggy takes a sparkling glass of beaded fluid from the sill of the window that overlooks Brewer, a swamp of brick sunk at the foot of its mountain basking westward in the sun. She sips, and her eyes slide by on either side of his head. "You're offended by my drinking. I just got out of the bathtub. That's often how I spend my afternoons, after spending the morning with the lawyers or walking the streets looking for a job. Everybody wants younger secretaries. They must wonder why I keep my sunglasses on. I come back and take off all my clothes and get into the tub and ever so slowly put a drink inside me and watch the steam melt the ice cubes."

"It sounds nice. What I wanted to say —"

She is standing by the window with one hip pushed out; the belt of her bathrobe is loose and, though she is a shadow against the bright colorless sky, he can feel with his eyes as if with his tongue the hollow between her breasts that would still be dewy from her bath.

She prompts, "What you wanted to say —"

"Was to ask you a favor: could you kind of keep it quiet about the Negro staying with us that Billy saw? Janice called me today and I guess you've already told her, that's O.K. if you could stop it there, I don't want everybody to know. Don't tell Ollie, if you haven't already, I mean. There's a legal angle or I wouldn't bother." He lifts his hands helplessly; it wasn't worth saying, now that he's said it.

Peggy steps toward him, stabbingly, too much liquor or trying to keep the hip out seductively or just the way she sees, two of everything, and tells him, "She must be an awfully good lay, to get you to do this for her."

"The girl? No, actually, she and I aren't usually on the same wavelength."

She brushes back her hair with an approximate flicking motion that lifts the bathrobe lapel and exposes one breast; she is drunk. "Try another wavelength."

"Yeah, I'd love to, but right now, the fact is, I'm running too scared to take on anything else, and anyway Billy's about to come home."

"Sometimes he hangs around Burger Bliss for hours. Ollie thinks he's getting bad habits."

"Yeah, how *is* old Ollie? You and he getting together at all?"

She lets her hand down from her hair; the lapel covers her again. "Sometimes he comes by and fucks me, but it doesn't seem to bring us any closer."

"Probably it does, he just doesn't express it. He's too embarrassed at having hurt you."

"That's how *you* would be, but Ollie isn't like that. It would never enter his head to feel guilty. It's the artist in him, you know he really can play almost any instrument he picks up. But he's a cold little bastard."

"Yeah, I'm kind of cold too." He has stood in alarm, since she has come closer another clumsy step.

Peggy says, "Give me your hands." Her eyes fork upon him, around him. Her face unchanging, she reaches down and lifts his hands from his sides and holds them to her chest. "They're warm." He thinks, *Cold heart.* She inserts his left hand into her bathrobe and presses it around a breast. He thinks of spilling guts, of a cow's stomach tumbling out; elastically she overflows his fingers, her nipple a clot, a gumdrop stuck to his palm. Her eyes are closed – veins in her lids, crow's feet at the corners – and she is intoning, "You're not cold, you're warm, you're a warm man, Harry, a good man. You've been hurt and I want you to heal, I want to help you heal, do whatever you want with me." She is talking as if to herself, rapidly, softly, but has brought him so close he hears it all; her breath beats at the base of his throat. Her heartbeat is sticking to his palm. The skin of her brow is vexed and the piece of her body her bathrobe discloses is lumpy and strange, blind like the brow of an ox, but eased by liquor she has slid into that state where the body of the other is her own body, the body of secretive self-love that the mirror we fill and the bed we warm alone give us back; and he is enclosed in this body of love of hers and against all thought and wish he thickens all over tenderly and the one-eyed rising beneath his waist begins.

He protests "I'm not good" but is also sliding; he relaxes the hand that is holding her breast to give it air to sway in.

She insists "You're good, you're lovely" and fumbles at his fly; with the free hand he pulls aside the lapel of the bathrobe so the other breast is free and the bathrobe belt falls unknotted.

An elevator door sucks shut in the hall. Footsteps swell toward their door. They spring apart; Peggy wraps the robe around herself again. He keeps on his retinas the afterimage of a ferny triangle, broader than his palm, beneath a belly whiter than crystal, with silvery stretch-marks. The footsteps pass on by. The would-be lovers sigh with relief, but the spell has been broken. Peggy turns her back, reknots her belt. "You're keeping in touch with Janice," she says.

"Not really."

"How did you know I told her about the black?"

Funny, everybody else has no trouble saying "black." Or hating the war. Rabbit must be defective. Lobotomy. A pit opens where guilt gnaws, at the edge of his bladder. He must hurry home. "She called me to say a lawyer was starting divorce proceedings."

"Does that upset you?"

"I guess. Sort of. Sure."

"I suppose I'm dumb, I just never understood why you put up with Janice. She was never enough for you, never. I love Janice, but she is about the most childish, least sensitive woman I've ever known."

"You sound like my mother."

"Is that bad?" She whirls around; her hair floats. He has never seen Peggy so suddenly soft, so womanly frontal. Even her eyes he could take. In play, mocking the pressure of Billy impending at his back, he rubs the back of his hand across her nipples. Nibs and Dots.

"Maybe you're right. We should try out our wavelengths."

Peggy flushes, backs off, looks stony, as if an unexpected mirror has shown her herself too harshly. She pulls the blue terrycloth around her so tight her shoulders huddle. "If you want to take me out to dinner some night," she says, "I'm around," adding irritably, "but don't count your chickens."

*   *   *

Hurry, hurry. The 12 bus takes forever to come, the walk down Emberly is endless. Yet his house, third from the end of Vista Crescent, low and new and a sullen apple-green on the quarter-acre of lawn scraggly with plantain, is intact, and all around it the unpopulated stretches of similar houses hold unbroken the intensity of duplication. That the blot of black inside his house is unmirrored fools him into hoping it isn't there. But, once up the three porch steps and through the door of three stepped windows, Rabbit sees, to his right, in the living room, from behind – the sofa having been swung around – a bushy black sphere between Jill's cone of strawberry gold and Nelson's square-cut mass of Janice-dark hair. They are watching television. Skeeter seems to have reinstated the box. The announcer, ghostly pale because the adjustment is too bright and mouthing as rapidly as a vampire because there is too much news between too many commercials, enunciates, ". . . after a five-year exile spent in Communist Cuba, various African states, and Communist China, landed in Detroit today and was instantly taken into custody by waiting FBI men. Elsewhere on the racial front, the U.S. Commission on Civil Rights sharply charged that the Nixon Administration has made quote a major retreat unquote pertaining to school integration in the southern states. In Fayette Mississippi three white Klansmen were arrested for the attempted bombing of the supermarket owned by newly elected black mayor of Fayette, Charles Evers, brother of the slain civil rights leader. In New York City Episcopal spokesmen declined to defend further their controversial decision to grant two hundred thousand dollars toward black church leader James Forman's demand of five hundred million dollars in quote reparations unquote from the Christian churches in America for quote three centuries of indignity and exploitation unquote. In Hartford Connecticut and Camden New Jersey an uneasy peace prevails after last week's disturbances within the black communities of these cities. And now, an important announcement."

"Hello, hello," Rabbit says, ignored.

Nelson turns and says, "Hey Dad. Robert Williams is back in this country."

"Who the hell is Robert Williams?"

Skeeter says, "Chuck baby, he's a man going to fry your ass."

"Another black Jesus. How many of you are there?"

"By many false prophets," Skeeter tells him, "you shall know my coming, right? That's the Good Book, right?"

"It also says He's come and gone."

"Comin' again, Chuck. Gonna fry your ass. You and Nixon's, right?"

"Poor old Nixon, even his own commissions beat on him. What the hell can he do? He can't go into every ghetto and fix the plumbing himself. He can't give every copped-out junkie a million dollars and a Ph.D. Nixon, who's Nixon? He's just a typical flatfooted Chamber of Commerce type who lucked his way into the hot seat and is so dumb he thinks it's good luck. Let the poor bastard alone, he's trying to bore us to death so we won't commit suicide."

"Nixon, shit. That honky was put there by the cracker vote, right? Strom Stormtrooper is his very bag. He is Herod, man, and all us black babies better believe it."

"Black babies, black leaders, Jesus am I sick of the word black. If I said white one-eightieth as often as you say black you'd scream yourself blue. For Chrissake, forget your skin."

"I'll forget it when you forget it, right?"

"Lord I'd love to forget not only your skin but everything inside it. I thought three days ago you said you were getting out in three days."

"Dad, *don't.*" The kid's face is tense. Mom was right, too delicate, too nervous. Thinks the world is going to hurt him, so it will. The universal instinct to exterminate the weak.

Jill rises to shield the other two. Three on one: Rabbit is exhilarated. Faking and dodging, he says before she can speak, "Tell the darker of your boyfriends here I thought he promised to pull out when he got a stake. I have twenty bucks here to give him. Which reminds me of something else."

Skeeter interrupts, addressing the air. "I *love* him when he gets like this. He is the Man."

And Jill is saying her piece. "Nelson and I refuse to live with this quarrelling. Tonight after supper we want to have an organized discussion. There's a crying need for education in this household."

"Household," Rabbit says, "I'd call it a refugee camp." He persists in what he has been reminded of. "Hey, Skeeter. Do you have a last name?"

"X," Skeeter tells him. "42X."

"Sure it's not Farnsworth?"

Skeeter's body sheds its shell, hangs there outfeinted a second, before regathering hardness. "That Super Tom," he says definitively, "is not the slightest relation of mine."

"The *Vat* had your last name as Farnsworth."

"The *Vat*," Skeeter pronounces mincingly, "is a Fascist rag."

Having scored, you put your head down and run back up the floor; but with that feeling inside, of having made a mark that can't be rubbed out. "Just wondering," Rabbit smiles. He stretches out his arms as if from wall to wall. "Who wants a beer besides me?"

After supper, Nelson washes the dishes and Skeeter dries. Jill tidies up the living room for their discussion; Rabbit helps her swing the sofa back into place. On the shelves between the living room and the breakfast nook that he and Janice had kept empty Rabbit notices now a stack of tired paperbacks, their spines chafed and biased by handling. *The Selected Writings of W. E. B. Du Bois*, *The Wretched of the Earth*, *Soul on Ice*, *Life and Times of Frederick Douglass*, others, history, Marx, economics, stuff that makes Rabbit feel sick, as when he thinks about what surgeons do, or all the plumbing and gas lines there are under the street. "Skeeter's books," Jill explains. "I went into Jimbo's today for them, and his clothes. Babe had them."

"Hey Chuck," Skeeter calls from the sink, through the shelves, "know where I got those books? Over in Nam, at the Longbinh base bookstore. They love us to read, that crazy Army of yours. Teach us how to read, shoot, dig pot, sniff scag, black man's best friend, just like they say!" He snaps his towel, *pap!*

Rabbit ignores him and asks Jill, "You went in there? It's full of police, they could easy tail you."

Skeeter shouts from the kitchen, "Don't you worry Chuck,

those poor pigs've bigger niggers than me to fry. You know what happened over in York, right? Brewer's gone to make that look like the Ladies Aid ball!" *Pap!*

Nelson washing beside him asks, "Will they shoot every white person?"

"Just the big old ugly ones, mostly. You stay away from that gruesome Billy and stick next to me, Babychuck, you'll be all right."

Rabbit pulls down a book at random and reads,

> Government is for the people's progress and not for the comfort of an aristocracy. The object of industry is the welfare of the workers and not the wealth of the owners. The object of civilization is the cultural progress of the mass of workers and not merely of an intellectual elite.

It frightens him, as museums used to frighten him, when it was part of school to take trips there and to see the mummy rotting in his casket of gold, the elephant tusk filed into a hundred squinting Chinamen. Unthinkably distant lives, abysses of existence, worse than what crawls blind on ocean floors. The book is full of Skeeter's underlinings. He reads,

> Awake, awake, put on thy strength, O Zion! Reject the weakness of missionaries who teach neither love nor brotherhood, but chiefly the virtues of private profit from capital, stolen from your land and labor. Africa, awake! Put on the beautiful robes of Pan-African socialism.

Rabbit replaces the book feeling better. There are no such robes. It is all crap. "What's the discussion about?" he asks, as they settle around the cobbler's bench.

Jill says nervously, blushing, "Skeeter and Nelson and I were talking about it today after school and agreed that since there seems to be such a painful communications problem –"

"Is that what it is?" Rabbit asks. "Maybe we communicate too well."

"– a structured discussion might be helpful and educational."

"Me being the one who needs to be educated," Rabbit says.

"Not necessarily." The care with which Jill speaks makes

Rabbit feel pity; *we are too much for her*, he thinks. "You're older than we are and we respect your experience. We all agree, I think, that your problem is that you've never been given a chance to formulate your views. Because of the competitive American context, you've had to convert everything into action too rapidly. Your life has no reflective content; it's all instinct, and when your instincts let you down, you have nothing to trust. That's what makes you cynical. Cynicism, I've seen it said somewhere, is tired pragmatism. Pragmatism suited a certain moment here, the frontier moment; it did the work, very wastefully and ruthlessly, but it did it."

"On behalf of Daniel Boone," Rabbit says, "I thank you."

"It's wrong," Jill goes on gently, "when you say Americans are exploiters, to forget that the first things they exploit are themselves. You," she says, lifting her face, her eyes and freckles and nostrils a constellation, "you've never given yourself a chance to think, except on techniques, basketball and printing, that served a self-exploitative purpose. You carry an old God with you, and an angry old patriotism. And now an old wife." He takes breath to protest, but her hand begs him to let her finish. "You accept these things as sacred not out of love or faith but fear; your thought is frozen because the first moment when your instincts failed, you raced to the conclusion that everything is nothing, that zero is the real answer. That is what we Americans think, it's win or lose, all or nothing, kill or die, because we've never created the leisure in which to take thought. But now, you see, we must, because action is no longer enough, action without thought is violence. As we see in Vietnam."

He at last can speak. "There was violence in Vietnam before we ever heard of the fucking place. You can see by just the way I'm sitting here listening to this crap I'm a pacifist basically." He points at Skeeter. "*He's* the violent son of a bitch."

"But you *see*," Jill says, her voice lulling and nagging, with just a teasing ragged hem showing of the voice she uses in bed, "the reason Skeeter annoys and frightens you is you don't know a thing about his history, I don't mean his personal history so much as the history of his race, how he got to where he is. Things that threaten you like riots and welfare have jumped into the newspapers out of nowhere for you. So for tonight we thought we would just talk a little, have a kind of seminar, about Afro-American history."

"Please, Dad," Nelson says.

"Jesus. O.K. Hit me. We were beastly to the slaves so why do so few American Negroes want to give up their Cadillacs and, excuse the expression, colored televisions and go back to Africa?"

"Dad, *don't*."

Skeeter begins. "Let's forget the slavery, Chuck. It was forever ago, everybody used to do it, it was a country kind of thing, right? Though I must say, the more it began to smell like shit, the more you crackers rolled around in it, right?"

"We had more country."

"Easy, sit back. No arguments, right? You had cotton come along, right? Anybody but black folks die working those cotton swamps, right? Anyhoo, you had this war. You had these crazies up North like Garrison and Brown agitating and down South a bunch of supercrackers like Yancy and Rhett who thought they could fatten their own pie by splitting, funny thing is" – he chuckles, wheezes, Rabbit pictures him with a shaved head and sees Farnsworth – "they didn't, the Confederacy sent 'em away on a ship and elected all play-it-safes to office! Same up North with cats like Sumner. Come to the vote, people scared of the man with the idea, right? Do you know, suppose you don't, dude called Ruffin, bright as could be, invented modern agriculture or next thing to it, hated the Yankees so much he pulled the string on the first cannon at Sumter and shot himself in the head when the South lost? Wild men. Beautiful, right? So any*hoo*, Lincoln got this war, right, and fought it for a bunch of wrong reasons – what's so sacred about a *Union*, just a power trust, right? – and for another wrong reason freed the slaves, and it was done. God bless America, right? So here I begin to get mad."

"Get mad, Skeeter," Rabbit says. "Who wants a beer?"

"Me, Dad."

"Half a one."

Jill says, "I'll split it with him."

Skeeter says, "That stuff rots the soul. Mind if I burn some good Red?"

"It's not legal."

"Right. But everybody does it. All those swish cats over in Penn Park, you think they have a Martini when they come home at night? That's yesterday. They blow grass. Sincerely, it is more in than chewing gum. Over in Nam, it was the fighting boy's candy."

"O.K. Light up. I guess we've gone this far."

"There is far to go," Skeeter says, rolling his joint, from a rubber pouch he produces from within the sofa, where he sleeps, and thin yellow paper, licking it rapidly with that fat pale tongue, and twisting the ends. When he lights it, the twisted end flames. He sucks in hungrily, holds it in as if about to dive very deep, and then releases the sweet used smoke with a belch. He offers the wet end to Rabbit. "Try?"

Rabbit shakes his head, watching Nelson. The kid's eyes are bird-bright, watching Skeeter. Maybe Janice is right, he's letting the kid see too much. Still, he didn't do the leaving. And life is life, God invented it, not him. But he looks at Nelson fearful that his presence in the room will be construed as a blessing. He says to Skeeter, "Get on with your song. Lincoln won the war for the wrong reasons."

"And then he was shot, right?" Skeeter passes the joint to Jill. As she takes it her eyes ask Rabbit, *Is this what you want?* She holds it the way the experts do, not like a tobacco cigarette, something for Fred Astaire to gesture with, but reverently as food, with as many fingers as she can get around it, feeding the wet end to herself like a nipple. Her thin face goes peaceful, puts on the fat of dreams. Skeeter is saying, "So then you had these four million freed slaves without property or jobs in this economy dead on its feet thinking the halleluiah days had come. Green pastures, right? Forty acres and a mule, right? Goddam green pickles, Chuck, that was the most pathetic thing, the way those poor niggers jumped for the bait. They taught themselves to read, they broke their backs for chickenshit, they sent good men to the fuckhead Yoo Ess Senate, they set up legislatures giving Dixie the first public schools it ever had, how about that now, there's a fact for your eddi-cayshun, right? Jill honey, hand that stick back, you gonna blow yourself to the moon, that is uncut Red. And all this here while, Chuck and Babychuck, the crackers down there were frothing at the mouth and calling our black heroes baboons. Couldn't do much else as long as the Northern armies hung around, right? Baboons, monkeys, apes: these hopeful sweet blacks trying to make men of themselves, thinking they'd been called to be men at last in these the Benighted States of Amur-rika." Skeeter's face is shedding its shell of scorn and writhing as if to cry. He has taken his glasses off. He is reaching toward Jill for the marijuana cigarette, keeping his eyes on Rabbit's face. Rabbit is frozen, his mind racing. Nelson. Put him to bed. Seeing too much. His own face as he listens to Skeeter feels weak, shapeless, slipping. The beer tastes bad, of malt. Skeeter wants to cry, to yell. He is sitting on the edge of the sofa and making gestures so brittle his arms might snap off. He is crazy. "So what did the South do? They said baboon and lynched and whipped and cheated the black man of what pennies he had and thanked their white Jesus they didn't have to feed him anymore. And what did the North do? It copped out. It pulled out. It had put on all that muscle for the war and now it was wading into the biggest happiest muck of greed and graft and exploitation and pollution and slum-building and Indian-killing this poor old whore of a planet has ever been saddled with, right? Don't go sleepy on me Chuck, here comes the interesting part. The Southern assholes got together with the Northern assholes and said, Let's us do a deal. What's all this about democracy, let's have here a dollar-cracy. Why'd we ever care, free versus slave? Capital versus labor, that's where it's at, right? This poor cunt of a country's the biggest jampot's ever come along so let's eat it, friend. You screw your black labor and we'll screw our immigrant honky and Mongolian idiot labor and, *whoo-hee!* Halleluiah, right? So the Freedman's Bureau was trashed and the military governors were chased back by crackers on horses who were very big on cutting up colored girls with babies inside 'em and Tilden was cheated out of the Presidency in the one bony-fidey swindle election you can find admitted in every honky history book. Look it up, right? And that was the revolution of 1876. Far as the black man goes, that's the '76 that hurt, the one a hundred years before was just a bunch of English gents dodging taxes." Skeeter has put his glasses back on; the glass circles glitter behind a blueness of smoke. His voice has settled for irony again. "So let's all sing America the Beautiful, right? North and West, robber barons and slums. Down South, one big nigger barbecue. Hitler bless his sweet soul leastways tried to keep the ovens out of sight. Down Dixieway, every magnolia had a rope. Man, they passed laws if a nigger sneezed within three miles of a white ass his balls were chewed off by sawtoothed beagles. Some nigger didn't hop off the sidewalk and lick up the tobacco juice whenever the town trash spit, he was tucked into a chain gang and peddled to the sheriff's brother-in-law cheaper than an alligator egg. And if he dared ask for the vote the Fifteenth Amendment had flat-out given him, why, they couldn't think up ways to skin him slowly enough, they couldn't invent enough laws to express their dis-approbation, better for a poor black man to go stick his head up Great-aunt Lily's snatch than try to stick it in a polling booth. Right? Chuck, I got to hand it to you, you had it all ways. The South got slavery back at half the price, it got control of Congress back by counting the black votes that couldn't be cast, the North got the cotton money it needed for capital, and everybody got the fun of shitting on the black man and then holding their noses. You believe any of this?"

"I believe all of it," Rabbit says.

"Do you believe, do you believe I'm so mad just telling this if I had a knife right now I'd poke it down your throat and watch you gargle your life away and would love it, oh, would I love it." Skeeter is weeping. Tears and smoke mix on the skin of his face.

"O.K., O.K.," Rabbit says.

"Skeeter, don't cry," Nelson says.

"Skeeter, it was too rich, I'm going to lose it," Jill says and stands. "I'm dizzy."

But Skeeter will talk only to Harry. "What I want to say to you," he says, "what I want to make ever so clear, Chuck, is you had that chance. You could have gone some better road, right? You took that greedy turn, right? You sold us out, right? You sold yourselves out. Like Lincoln said, you paid in blood, sword for the lash and all that, and you didn't lift us up, we held out our hands, man, we were like faithful dogs waiting for that bone, but you gave us a kick, you put us down, you put us down."

"Skeeter, please don't ever give me any more of that what-ever it was, ever, ever," Jill says, drifting away.

Skeeter controls his crying, lifts his face darkened in streaks like ashes wetted down. "It wasn't just us, you sold yourselves out, right? You really had it here, you had it all, and you took that greedy mucky road, man, you made yourself the asshole of the planet. Right? To keep that capitalist thing rolling you let those asshole crackers have their way and now you's all asshole crackers, North and South however you look there's assholes, you lapped up the poison and now it shows, Chuck, you say America to you and you still get bugles and stars but say it to any black or yellow man and you get hate, right? Man the world does hate you, you're the big pig keeping it all down." He jabs blearily with his skinny finger, and hangs his head.

From upstairs, discreet as the noise a cat makes catching a bird, comes a squeezed heaving noise, Jill being sick.

Nelson asks, "Dad, shouldn't you call a doctor?"

"She'll be O.K. Go to bed. You have school tomorrow."

Skeeter looks at Rabbit; his eyeballs are fiery and rheumy. "I said it, right?"

"Trouble with your line," Rabbit tells him, "it's pure self-pity. The real question is, Where do you go from here? We all got here on a bad boat. You talk as if the whole purpose of this country since the start has been to frustrate Negroes. Hell, you're just ten per cent. The fact is most people don't give a damn *what* you do. This is the freest country around, make it if you can, if you can't, die gracefully. But Jesus, stop begging for a free ride."

"Friend, you are wrong. You are white but wrong. We fasci-nate you, white man. We are in your dreams. We are tech-nology's nightmare. We are all the good satisfied nature you put down in yourselves when you took that mucky greedy turn. We are what has been left *out* of the industrial revolution, so we are the *next* revolution, and don't you know it? You know it. Why else you so scared of me, Rabbit?"

"Because you're a spook with six loose screws. I'm going to bed."

Skeeter rolls his head loosely, touches it dubiously. In the light from the driftwood lamp his round mass of hair is seen as insubstantial, his skull narrow as the bone handle of a knife. He brushes at his forehead as if midges are there. He says, "Sweet dreams. I'm too spaced to sleep right now, I got just to sit here, nursing the miseries. Mind if I play the radio if I keep it low?"

"No."

Upstairs, Jill, a sudden warm wisp in his arms, begs with rapid breath, "Get him out of here, Harry, don't let him stay, he's no good for me, no good for any of us."

"You brought him here." He takes her talk as the exaggerating that children do, to erase their fears by spelling them out; and indeed in five minutes she is dead asleep, motionless. The electric clock burns beyond her head like a small moon's skeleton. Downstairs, a turned-down radio faintly scratches. And shortly Rabbit too is asleep. Strangely, he sleeps soundly, with Skeeter in the house.

"Harry, how about a quick one?" His father tells the bartender, as always, "Let's make it a Schlitz."

"Whisky sour," he says. Summer is over, the air-conditioning in the Phoenix has been turned off. He asks, "How's Mom doing?"

"As good as can be hoped, Harry." He nudges a conspiratorial inch closer. "That new stuff really seems to do the job, she's on her feet for hours at a time now. For my money, though, the sixty-four-thousand-dollar question is what the long-range effects will be. The doctor, he's perfectly honest about it. He says to her when we go on in to the hospital, 'How's my favorite guinea pig?' "

"What's the answer?" Rabbit abruptly asks.

His father is startled. "Her answer?"

"Anybody's."

His father now understands the question and shrugs his narrow shoulders in his faded blue shirt. "Blind faith," he suggests. In a mutter he adds, "One more bastard under the ground."

On the television above the bar men are filing past a casket, but the sound is turned off and Rabbit cannot tell if it is Everett Dirksen's lying-in-state in Washington or Ho Chi Minh's ceremonies in Hanoi. Dignitaries look alike, always dressed in mourning. His father clears his throat, breaks the silence. "Janice called your mother last night."

"Boy, I think she's cracking up, she's on the phone all the time. Stavros must be losing his muscle."

"She was very disturbed, she said you'd taken a colored man into your house."

"I didn't exactly take him, he kind of showed up. Nobody's supposed to know about it. I think he's Farnsworth's son."

"That can't be, Jerry's never married to my knowledge."

"They don't marry generally, right? They weren't allowed to as slaves."

This bit of historical information makes Earl Angstrom grimace. He takes, what for him, with his boy, is a tough line. "I must say, Harry, I'm not too happy about it either."

The funeral (the flag on the coffin has stars and stripes, so it must be Dirksen's) vanishes, and flickering in its place are shots of cannons blasting, of trucks moving through the desert, of planes soundlessly batting through the sky, of soldiers waving. He cannot tell if they are Israeli or Egyptian. He asks, "How happy is Mom about it?"

"I must say, she was very short with Janice. Suggested if she wanted to run your household she go back to it. Said she had no right to complain. I don't know what all else. I couldn't bear to listen; when women get to quarrelling, I head for the hills."

"Janice talk about lawyers?"

"Your mother didn't mention it if she did. Between you and me, Harry, she was so upset it scared me. I don't believe she slept more than two, three hours; she took twice the dose of Seconal and still it couldn't knock her out. She's worried and, pardon my crust for horning in where I have no business, Harry, so am I."

"Worried about what?"

"Worried about this new development. I'm no nigger-hater, I'm happy to work with 'em and I have for twenty years, if needs be I'll live next to 'em though the fact is they haven't cracked Mt. Judge yet, but get any closer than that, you're playing with fire, in my experience."

"What experience?"

"They'll let you down," Pop says. "They don't have any feeling of obligation. I'm not blaming a soul, but that's the fact, they'll let you down and laugh about it afterwards. They're not ethical like white men and there's no use saying they are. You asked me what experience, I don't want to go into stories, though there's plenty I could tell, just remember I was raised in the Third Ward back when it was more white than black, we mixed it up in every sense. I know the people of this county. They're good-natured people. They like to eat and drink and like to have their red-light district and their numbers, they'll elect the scum to political office time and time again; but they don't like seeing their women desecrated."

"Who's being desecrated?"

"Just that menagerie over there, the way you're keeping it, is a desecration. Have you heard from your neighbors what they think about it yet?"

"I don't even know my neighbors."

"That black boy shows his face outside, you'll get to know them; you'll get to know them as sure as I'm sitting here trying to be a friend and not a father. The day when I could whip sense into you is long by, Harry, and anyway you gave us a lot less trouble than Mim. Your mother always says you let people push you around and I always answer her, Harry knows his way around, he lands on his feet; but I'm beginning to see she may be right. Your mother may be all crippled up but she's still hard to fool, ask the man who's tried."

"When did you try?"

But this secret – had Pop played Mom false? – stays dammed behind those loose false teeth the old man's mouth keeps adjusting, pensively sucking. Instead he says, "Do us a favor, Harry, I hate like hell to beg, but do us a favor and come over tonight and talk about it. Your mother stiff-armed Janice but I know when she's been shook."

"Not tonight, I can't. Maybe in a couple of days, things'll clear up."

"Why not, Harry? We promise not to grill you or anything, Lord, I wouldn't ask for myself, it's your mother's state of mind. You know" – and he slides so close their shirt sleeves touch and

Rabbit smells the sour fog of his father's breath – "she's having the adventure now we're all going to have to have."

"Stop asking, Pop. I can't right now."

"They've gotcha in their clutches, huh?"

He stands straight, decides one whisky sour will do, and answers, "Right."

That night after supper they discuss slavery. Jill and Skeeter have done the dishes together, Rabbit has helped Nelson with his homework. The kid is into algebra this year but can't quite manage that little flip in his head whereby a polynomial cracks open into two nice equalities of x, one minus and one plus. Rabbit had been good at math, it was a game with limits, with orderly movements and a promise of completion at the end. The combination always cracked open. Nelson is tight about it, afraid to let go and swing, a smart kid but tight, afraid of maybe that thing that got his baby sister: afraid it might come back for him. They have half an hour before *Laugh-In*, which they all want to watch. Tonight Skeeter takes the big brown chair and Rabbit the one with silver threads. Jill and Nelson sit on the airfoam sofa. Skeeter has some books; they look childishly bright under his thin brown hands. School days. *Sesame Street*.

Skeeter says to Rabbit, "Chuck, I been thinking I sold out the truth last night when I said your slavery was a country thing. The fact upon reflection appears to be that your style of slavery was uniquely and e-specially bad, about the worst indeed this poor blood-soaked globe has ever seen." Skeeter's voice as he speaks exerts a steady pressure, wind rattling a dead tree. His eyes never deviate to Nelson or Jill.

Rabbit, a game student (in high school he used to get B's), asks, "What was so bad about it?"

"Let me guess what you think. You think it wasn't so bad on the plantations, right? What with banjos and all the fritters you could eat and Ol' Massah up at the big house instead of the Department of Welfare, right? Those niggers were savages anyway, their chuckleheads pure bone, and if they didn't like it, well, why didn't they just up and die in their chains like the noble old redman, right?"

"Yeah. Why didn't they?"

"I love that question. Because I have the answer. The reason is, old Tonto was so primitive farmwork made no sense to him, he was on the moon, right?, and just withered away. Now the black man, he was from West Africa, where they had agriculture. Where they had social organization. How do you think those slaves got to the coast from a thousand miles away? Black men arranged it, they wouldn't cut the white men in, they kept the pie all for themselves. Organization men, right?"

"That's interesting."

"I'm glad you said that. I am grateful for your interest."

"He meant it," Jill intercedes.

"Swallow your tongue," Skeeter says without looking toward her.

"Swallow your tongue yourself," Nelson intervenes. Rabbit would be proud of the boy, but he feels that Nelson's defense of Jill, like Skeeter's attack, are automatic: parts of a pattern the three have developed while he is away working.

"The readings," Jill prompts.

Skeeter explains. "Little Jilly and I, today, been talking, and her idea is, to make cosy nights all together more structured, right? We'd read aloud a few things, otherwise I'm apt to do all the talking, that is until you decide to dump me on the floor again."

"Let me get a beer then."

"Puts pimples on your belly, man. Let me light up some good Tijuana brass and pass it over, old athlete like you shouldn't be getting a beer gut, right?"

Rabbit neither agrees nor moves. He glances at Nelson: the kid's eyes are sunk and shiny, frightened but not to the point of panic. He is learning; he trusts them. He frowns over to stop his father looking at him. Around them the furniture – the fireplace that never holds a fire, the driftwood base like a corpse lying propped on one arm – listens. A quiet rain has begun at the windows, sealing them in. Skeeter holds his lips pinched to seal into himself the first volumes of sweet smoke, then exhales, sighing, and leans back into the chair, vanishing between the brown wings but for the glass-and-silver circles of his spectacles. He says, "He was property, right? From Virginia on, it was profit and capital absolutely. The King of England, all he cared about was tobacco cash, right? Black men just blots on the balance sheet to him. Now the King of Spain, he knew black men from way back; those Moors had run his country and some had been pretty smart. So south of the border a slave was property but he was also other things. King of Spain say, That's my subject, he has legal rights, right? Church say, That's an everlasting immortal soul there: baptize him. Teach him right from wrong. His marriage vows are sacred, right? If he rustles up the bread to buy himself free, you got to sell. This was all written in the law down there. Up here, the law said one thing: no rights. No rights. This is no man, this is one warm piece of animal meat, worth one thousand Yoo Hess Hay coldblooded clams. Can't let it marry, that might mess up selling it when the market is right. Can't let it go and testify in court, that might mess up Whitey's property rights. There was no such thing, *no* such, believe me, as the father of a slave child. That was a legal fact. Now how could the law get that way? Because they did believe a nigger was a piece of shit. And they was scared of their own shit. Man, those crackers were sick and they knew it absolutely. All those years talkin' about happy Rastus chompin' on watermelon they was scared shitless of uprisings, *up*risings, Chuck, when there hadn't been more than two or three the whole hundred years and those not amounted to a bucket of piss. They was scared rigid, right? Scared of blacks learning to read, scared of blacks learning a trade, scared of blacks on the job market, there was no place for a freedman to go, once he *was* freed, all that talk about free soil, the first thing the free-soil convention in Kansas said was we don't want no black faces here, keep 'em away from our eyeballs. The thing about these Benighted States all around is that it was never no place like other places where this happens because that happens, and some men have more luck than others so let's push a little here and give a little here; no, sir, this place was never such a place it was a *dream*, it was a state of mind from those poor fool pilgrims on, right? Some white man see a black man he don't see a man he sees a *symbol*, right? All these people around here are walking around inside their own *heads*, they don't even know if you kick somebody else it *hurts*, Jesus won't even tell 'em because the Jesus they brought over on the boats was the meanest most de-balled Jesus the good Lord ever let run around scaring people. Scared, *scared*. I'm scared of you, you scared of me, Nelson scared of us both, and poor Jilly here so scared of everything she'll run and hide herself in dope again if we don't all act like big daddies to her." He offers the smoking wet-licked reefer around. Rabbit shakes his head no.

"Skeeter," Jill says, "the selections." A prim clubwoman calling the meeting to order. "Thirteen minutes to *Laugh-In*," Nelson says. "I don't want to miss the beginning, it's neat when they introduce themselves."

"Ree-ight," Skeeter says, fumbling at his forehead, at that buzzing that seems sometimes there. "Out of this book here." The book is called *Slavery;* the letters are red, white, and blue. It seems a small carnival under Skeeter's slim hand. "Just for the fun of it, to give us something more solid than my ignorant badmouthing, right? You know, like a happening. Chuck, this gives you pretty much a pain in the ass, right?"

"No, I like it. I like learning stuff. I have an open mind."

"He turns me on, he's so true to life," Skeeter says, handing the book to Jill. "Baby, you begin. Where my finger is, just the part in little type." He announces, "These are old-time speeches, dig?"

Jill sits up straight on the sofa and reads in a voice higher than her natural voice, a nice-girl-school-schooled voice, with riding lessons in it, and airy big white-curtained rooms; territory even higher in the scale than Penn Park.

"*Think*," she reads, "*of the nation's deed, done continually and afresh. God shall hear the voice of your brother's blood, long crying from the ground; His justice asks you even now, 'America, where is thy brother?' This is the answer which America must give: 'Lo, he is there in the rice-swamps of the South, in her fields teeming with cotton and the luxuriant cane. He was weak and I seized him; naked and I bound him; ignorant, poor and savage, and I over-mastered him. I laid on his feebler shoulders my grievous yoke. I have chained him with my fetters; beat him with my whip. Other tyrants had dominion over him, but my finger was on his human flesh. I am fed with his toil; fat, voluptuous on his sweat, and tears, and blood. I stole the father, stole also the sons, and set them to toil; his wife and daughters are a pleasant spoil to me. Behold the children also of thy servant and his handmaidens — sons swarthier than their sire. Askest thou for the African? I have made him a beast. Lo, there Thou hast what is thine.'* " She hands the book back blushing. Her glance at Rabbit says, *Bear with us. Haven't I loved you?*

Skeeter is cackling. "Green pickles, that turns me on. A pleasant spoil to me, right? And did you dig that beautiful bit about the sons swarthier than their sire? Those old Yankee sticks were really bugged, one respectable fuck would have stopped the abolition movement cold. But they weren't getting it back home in the barn so they sure gave hell to those crackers getting it out in the slave shed. Dark meat is soul meat, right? That was Theodore Parker, here's another, the meanest mouth in the crowd, old William Lloyd. Nellie, you try this. Just where I've marked. Just read the words slow, don't try for any expression."

Gaudy book in hand, the boy looks toward his father for rescue. "I feel stupid."

Rabbit says, "Read, Nelson. I want to hear it."

He turns for help elsewhere. "Skeeter, you promised I wouldn't have to."

"I said we'd see how it *went*. Come on, your daddy likes it. He has an open mind."

"You're just poking fun of everybody."

"Let him off," Rabbit says. "I'm losing interest."

Jill intervenes. "Do it, Nelson, it'll be fun. We won't turn on *Laugh-In* until you do."

The boy plunges in, stumbling, frowning so hard his father wonders if he doesn't need glasses. "*No matter,*" he reads, "*though every party should be torn by dis-*, dis —"

Jill looks over his shoulder. "Dissensions."

"*— every sest —*"

"Sect."

"*— every sect dashed into fragments, the national compact dissolved —*"
Jill says, "Good!"

"Let him ride," Skeeter says, his eyes shut, nodding.

Nelson's voice gains confidence. "*— the land filled with the horrors of a civil and a servile war — still, slavery must be buried in the grave of infantry —*"

"Infamy," Jill corrects.

"– *in-fa-my, beyond the possibility of a rez, a razor* –"

"A resurrection."

"*If the State cannot survive the anti-slavery agitation, then let the State perish. If the Church must be cast down by the strugglings of Humanity, then let the Church fall, and its fragments be scattered to the four winds of heaven, never more to curse the earth. If the American Union cannot be maintained, except by immolating* – what's that?"

"Sacrificing," Jill says.

Rabbit says, "I thought it meant burn."

Nelson looks up, uncertain he should continue.

The rain continues at the windows, gently, gently nailing them in, tighter together.

Skeeter's eyes are still closed. "Finish up. Do the last sentence, Babychuck."

"*If the Republic must be blotted out from the roll of nations, by proclaiming liberty to the captives, then let the Republic sink beneath the waves of oblivion, and a shout of joy, louder than the voice of many waters, fill the universe at its extinction.* I don't understand what any of this stuff means."

Skeeter says, "It means, More Power to the People, Death to the Fascist Pigs."

Rabbit says, "To me it means, Throw the baby out with the bath." He remembers a tub of still water, a kind of dust on its dead surface. He relives the shock of reaching down through it to pull the plug. He loops back into the room where they are sitting now, within the rain.

Jill is explaining to Nelson, "He's saying what Skeeter says. If the System, even if it works for most people, has to oppress some of the people, then the whole System should be destroyed."

"Do I say that? No." Skeeter leans forward from the mossy brown wings, reaching a trembling thin hand toward the young people, all parody shaken from his voice. "That'll come anyway. That big boom. It's not the poor blacks setting the bombs, it's the offspring of the white rich. It's not injustice pounding at the door, it's impatience. Put enough rats in a 'cage the fat ones get more frantic than the skinny ones 'cause they feel more *squeezed*. No. We must look past that, past the violence, into the next stage. That it's gonna blow up we can as*sume*. That's not interesting. What comes next is what's interesting. There's got to be a great *calm*."

"And you're the black Jesus going to bring it in," Rabbit mocks. "From A.D. to A.S. After Skeeter. I should live so long. All Praise Be Skeeter's Name."

He offers to sing but Skeeter is concentrating on the other two, disciples. "People talk revolution all the time but revolution's not interesting, right? Revolution is just one crowd taking power from another and that's bullshit, that's just power, and power is just guns and gangsters, and that's boring bullshit, right? People say to me Free Huey, I say Screw Huey, he's just Agnew in blackface. World forgets gangsters like that before they're dead. No. The problem is really, when the gangsters have knocked each other off, and taken half of everybody else with them, to make use of the *space*. After the Civil War ended, there was space, only they let it fill up with that same old greedy muck, only worse, right? They turned that old dog-eat-dog thing into a divine law."

"That's what we need, Skeeter," Rabbit says. "Some new divine laws. Why doncha go up to the top of Mt. Judge and have 'em handed to you on a tablet?"

Skeeter turns that nicely carved knife-handle of a face to him slowly, says slowly, "I'm no threat to you, Chuck. You're *set*. Only thing I could do to you is kill you and that matters less than you think, right?"

Jill delicately offers to make peace. "Didn't we pick out something for Harry to read?"

"Fuck it," Skeeter says. "That won't swing now. He's giving off ugly vibes, right? He's not ready. He is immature."

Rabbit is hurt, he had only been kidding. "Come on, I'm ready, give me my thing to read."

Skeeter asks Nelson, "What say, Babychuck? Think he's ready?"

Nelson says, "You must read it right, Dad. No poking fun."

"Me? Who'd I ever poke fun of?"

"Mom. All the time you poke fun of Mom. No wonder she left you."

Skeeter gives Harry the book open to a page. "Just a little bit. Just read where I've marked."

Soft red crayon. Those Crayola boxes that used to remind him of bleachers with every head a different color. This strange return. "*I believe, my friends and fellow citizens,*" Rabbit reads solemnly, "*we are not prepared for this suffrage. But we can learn. Give a man tools and let him commence to use them, and in time he will learn a trade. So it is with voting. We may not understand it at the start, but in time we shall learn to do our duty.*"

The rain makes soft applause.

Skeeter tips his narrow head and smiles at the two children on the sofa. "Makes a pretty good nigger, don't he?"

Nelson says, "Don't, Skeeter. He didn't poke fun so you shouldn't."

"Nothing wrong with what I said, that's what the world needs, pretty good niggers, right?"

To show Nelson how tough he is, Rabbit tells Skeeter, "This is all bleeding-heart stuff. It'd be like me bellyaching that the Swedes were pushed around by the Finns in the year Zilch."

Nelson cries, "We're missing *Laugh-In!*"

They turn it on. The cold small star expands, a torrent of stripes snaps into a picture, Sammy Davis Jr. is being the little dirty old man, tapping along behind the park bench, humming that aimless sad doodling tune. He perks up, seeing there is someone sitting on the bench. It is not Ruth Buzzi but Arte Johnson, the white, the real little dirty old man. They sit side by side and stare at each other. They are like one man looking into a crazy mirror. Nelson laughs. They all laugh: Nelson, Jill, Rabbit, Skeeter. Kindly the rain fastens them in, a dressmaker patting and stitching all around the house, fitting its great wide gown.

Nights with Skeeter, they blend together. Skeeter asks him, "You want to know how a Ne-gro feels?"

"Not much."

"Dad, don't," Nelson says.

Jill, silent, abstracted, passes Rabbit the joint. He takes a tentative puff. Has hardly held a cigarette in ten years, scared to inhale. Nearly sick after the other time, in Jimbo's. You suck and hold it down. Hold it down.

"Ee-magine," Skeeter is saying, "being in a glass box, and every time you move toward something, your head gets bumped. Ee-magine being on a bus, and everybody movin' away, 'cause your whole body's covered with pustulatin' scabs, and they're scared to get the disease."

Rabbit exhales, lets it out. "That's not how it is. These black kids on buses are pushy as hell."

"You've set so much type the world is lead, right? You don't hate nobody, right?"

"Nobody." Serenely. Space is transparent.

"How you feel about those Penn Park people?"

"Which ones?"

"All those ones. All those ones live in those great big piecrust mock-Two-door houses with His and Hers Caddies parked out by the hydrangea bushes. How about all those old farts down at the Mifflin Club with all those iron gates that used to own the textile mills and now don't own anything but a heap of paper keeps 'em in cigars and girlfriends? How about those? Let 'em settle in before you answer."

Rabbit pictures Penn Park, the timbered gables, the stucco, the weedless lawns plumped up like pillows. It was on a hill. He used to imagine it on the top of a hill, a hill he could never climb, because it wasn't a real hill like Mt. Judge. And he and Mom and Pop and Mim lived near the foot of this hill, in the dark next to the Bolgers, and Pop came home from work every day too tired to play catch in the back yard, and Mom never had jewelry like other women, and they bought day-old bread because it was a penny cheaper, and Pop's teeth hurt to keep money out of the dentist's hands, and now Mom's dying was a game being played by doctors who drove Caddies and had homes in Penn Park. "I hate them," he tells Skeeter.

The black man's face lights up, shines. "Deeper."

Rabbit fears the feeling will be fragile and vanish if he looks at it but it does not; it expands, explodes. Timbered gables, driveway pebbles, golf clubs fill the sky with debris. He remembers one doctor. He met him early this summer by accident, coming up on the porch to visit Mom, the doctor hurrying out, under the fan-light that sees everything, in a swank cream raincoat though it had just started to sprinkle, that kind of dude, who produces a raincoat from nowhere when proper, all set up, life licked, tweed trousers knife-sharp over polished strapped shoes, hurrying to his next appointment, anxious to get away from this drizzling tilted street. Pop worrying his teeth like an old woman in the doorway, performing introductions, "our son Harry," pathetic pride. The doctor's irritation at being halted even a second setting a prong of distaste on his upper lip behind the clipped mustache the color of iron. His handshake also metal, arrogant, it pinches Harry's unready hand and says, *I am strong, I twist bodies to my will. I am life, I am death.* "I hate those Penn Park motherfuckers," Harry ampli-fies, performing for Skeeter, wanting to please him. "If I could push the red button to blow them all to Kingdom Come" – he pushes a button in mid-air – "I would." He pushes the button so hard he can see it there.

"Ka-boom, right?" Skeeter grins, flinging wide his sticklike arms.

"But it is," Rabbit says. "Everybody knows black pussy is beautiful. It's on posters even, now."

Skeeter asks, "How you think all this mammy shit got started? Who you think put all those hog-fat churchified old women at the age of thirty in Harlem?"

"Not me."

"It *was* you. Man, you is just who it was. From those breeding cabins on you made the black girl feel sex was shit, so she hid from it as quick as she could in the mammy bit, right?"

"Well, tell 'em it's not shit."

"They don't believe me, Chuck. They see I don't count. I have no muscle, right? I can't protect my black women, right? 'Cause you don't let me be a man."

"Go ahead. Be one."

Skeeter gets up from the armchair with the silver threads and circles the imitation cobbler's bench with a wary hunchbacked quickness and kisses Jill where she sits on the sofa. Her hands, after a startled jerk, knit together and stay in her lap. Her head does not pull back nor strain forward. Rabbit cannot see, around the eclipsing orb of Skeeter's Afro, Jill's eyes. He can see Nelson's eyes. They are warm watery holes so dark, so stricken that Rabbit would like to stick pins into them, to teach the child there is worse. Skeeter straightens from kissing, wipes the Jill-spit from his mouth. "A pleasant spoil. Chuck, how do you like it?"

"I don't mind. If she doesn't."

Jill has closed her eyes, her mouth open on a small bubble.

"She *does* mind it," Nelson protests. "Dad, don't *let* him!"

Rabbit says to Nelson, "Bedtime, isn't it?"

Physically, Skeeter fascinates Rabbit. The lustrous pallor of the tongue and palms and the soles of the feet, left out of the sun. Or a different kind of skin? White palms never tan either. The peculiar glinting luster of his skin. The something so very finely turned and finished in the face, reflecting light at a dozen polished points: in comparison white faces are blobs: putty still drying. The curious greased grace of his gestures, rapid and watchful as a lizard's motions, free of mammalian fat. Skeeter in his house feels like a finely made electric toy; Harry wants to touch him but is afraid he will get a shock.

"O.K.?"

"Not especially." Jill's voice seems to come from further away than beside him in the bed.

"Why not?"

"I'm scared."

"Of what? Of me?"

"Of you and him together."

"We're not together. We hate each other's guts."

She asks, "When are you kicking him out?"

"They'll put him in jail."

"Good."

The rain is heavy above them, beating everywhere, inserting itself in that chimney flashing that always leaked. He pictures a wide brown stain on the bedroom ceiling. He asks, "What's with you and him?"

She doesn't answer. Her lean cameo profile is lit by a flash. Seconds pass before the thunder arrives.

He asks shyly, "He getting at you?"

"Not that way anymore. He says that's not interesting. He wants me another way now."

"What way can that be?" Poor girl, crazy suspicious.

"He wants me to tell him about God. He says he's going to bring some mesc for me."

The thunder follows the next flash more closely.

"That's crazy." But exciting: maybe she can do it. Maybe he can get music out of her like Babe out of the piano.

"He is crazy," Jill says. "I'll never be hooked again."

"What can I do?" Rabbit feels paralyzed, by the rain, the thunder, by his curiosity, by his hope for a break in the combination, for catastrophe and deliverance.

The girl cries out but thunder comes just then and he has to ask her to repeat it. "All you care about is your *wife*," she shouts upward into the confusion in heaven.

Pajasek comes up behind him and mumbles about the phone. Rabbit drags himself up. Worse than a liquor hangover, must stop, every night. Must get a grip on himself. Get a grip. Get angry. "Janice, for Chrissake —"

"It isn't Janice, Harry. It's me. Peggy."

"Oh. Hi. How's tricks? How's Ollie?"

"Forget Ollie, don't ever mention his name to me. He hasn't been to see Billy in weeks or contributed *any*thing to his keep, and when he finally does show up, you know what he brings? He's a genius, you'll never guess."

"Another mini-bike."

"A puppy. He brought us a Golden Retriever puppy. Now what the hell can we do with a puppy with Billy off in school and me gone from eight to five every day?"

"You got a job. Congratulations. What do you do?"

"I type tape for Brewer Fealty over at Youngquist, they're putting all their records on computer tape and not only is the work so boring you could scream, you don't even know when you've made a mistake, it comes out just holes in this tape, all these premium numbers."

"It sounds nifty. Peggy, speaking of work, they don't appreciate my being called here."

Her voice retreats, puts on dignity. "Pardon *me*. I wanted to talk to you when Nelson wasn't around. Ollie has promised Billy to take him fishing next Sunday, not *this* Sunday, and I wondered, since it doesn't look as if you'll ever ask me, if you'd like to have dinner Saturday when you bring him over."

Her open bathrobe, that pubic patch, the silver stretchmarks, don't count your chickens. Meaning do count your chickens. "That might be great," he says.

"Might be."

"I'll have to see, I'm kind of tied up these days —"

"Hasn't that man gone yet? Kick him out, Harry. He's taking incredible advantage of you. Call the police if he won't go. Really, Harry, you're much too passive."

"Yeah. Or something." Only after shutting the office door behind him and starting to walk through the solid brightness toward his machine does he feel last night's marijuana clutch at him, drag at his knees like a tide. Never again. Let Jesus find him another way.

"Tell us about Vietnam, Skeeter." The grass is mixing with his veins and he feels very close, very close to them all: the driftwood lamp, Nelson's thatch of hair an anxious tangle, Jill's bare legs a touch unshaped at the ankles. He loves them. All. His voice moves in and out behind their eyes. Skeeter's eyes roll red toward the ceiling. Things are pouring for him through the ceiling.

"Why you want to be told?" he asks.

"Because I wasn't there."

"Think you should have been there, right?"

"Yes."

"Why would that be?"

"I don't know. Duty. Guilt."

"No sir. You want to have been there because that is where it was at, right?"

"O.K."

"It was the best place," Skeeter says, not quite as a question.

"Something like that."

Skeeter goes on, gently urging, "It was where you would have felt not so de-balled, right?"

"I don't know. If you don't want to talk about it, don't. Let's turn on television."

"*Mod Squad* will be on," Nelson says.

Skeeter explains: "If you can't fuck, dirty pictures won't do it for you, right? And then if you can, they don't do it either."

"O.K., don't tell us anything. And try to watch your language in front of Nelson."

At night when Jill turns herself to him in bed he finds the unripe hardness of her young body repels him. The smoke inside him severs his desires from his groin, he is full of flitting desires that prevent him from directly answering her woman's call, a call he helped create in her girl's body. Yet in his mind he sees her mouth defiled by Skeeter's kiss and feels her rotting with his luminous poison. Nor can he forgive her for having been rich. Yet through these nightly denials, these quiet debasements, he feels something unnatural strengthening within him that may be love. On her side she seems, more and more, to cling to him; they have come far from that night when she went down on him like a little girl bobbing for apples.

*   *   *

This fall Nelson has discovered soccer; the junior high school has a team and his small size is no handicap. Afternoons Harry comes home to find the child kicking the ball, sewn of black-and-white pentagons, again and again against the garage door, beneath the unused basketball backboard. The ball bounces by Nelson, Harry picks it up, it feels bizarrely seamed in his hands. He tries a shot at the basket. It misses clean. "The touch is gone," he says. "It's a funny feeling," he tells his son, "when you get old. The brain sends out the order and the body looks the other way."

Nelson resumes kicking the ball, vehemently, with the side of his foot, against a spot on the door already worn paintless. The boy has mastered that trick of trapping the ball to a dead stop under his knees.

"Where are the other two?"

"Inside. Acting funny."

"How funny?"

"You know. The way they act. Dopey. Skeeter's asleep on the sofa. Hey, Dad."

"What?"

Nelson kicks the ball once, twice, hard as he can, until it gets by him and he has worked up nerve to tell. "I hate the kids around here."

"What kids? I never see any. When I was a kid, we were all over the streets."

"They watch television and go to Little League and stuff."

"Why do you hate them?"

Nelson has retrieved the ball and is shuffling it from one foot to the other, his feet clever as hands. "Tommy Frankhauser said we had a nigger living with us and said his father said it was ruining the neighborhood and we'd better watch out."

"What'd you say to that?"

"I said he better watch out himself."

"Did you fight?"

"I wanted to but he's a head taller than me even though we're in the same grade and he just laughed."

"Don't worry about it, you'll shoot up. All us Angstroms are late bloomers."

"I hate them, Dad, I *hate* them!" And he heads the ball so it bounces off the shadow-line shingles of the garage roof.

"Mustn't hate anybody," Harry says, and goes in.

Jill is in the kitchen, crying over a pan of lamb chops. "The flame keeps getting too big," she says. She has the gas turned down so low the little nipples of blue are sputtering. He turns it higher and Jill screams, falls against him, presses her face into his chest, peeks up with eyes amusement has dyed deep green. "You smell of ink," she tells him. "You're all ink, so clean, just like a new newspaper. Every day, a new newspaper comes to the door."

He holds her close; her tears tingle through his shirt. "Has Skeeter been feeding you anything?"

"No, Daddy. I mean lover. We stayed in the house all day and watched the quizzes, Skeeter hates the way they always have Negro couples on now, he says it's tokenism."

He smells her breath and, as she has promised, there is nothing, no liquor, no grass, just a savor of innocence, a faint tinge of sugar, a glimpse of a porch swing and a beaded pitcher. "Tea," he says.

"What an elegant little nose," she says, of his, and pinches it. "That's right. Skeeter and I had iced tea this afternoon." She keeps caressing him, rubbing against him, making him sad. "You're elegant all over," she says. "You're an enormous snowman, twinkling all over, except you don't have a carrot for a nose, you have it here."

"Hey," he says, hopping backwards.

Jill tells him urgently, "I like you there better than Skeeter, I think being circumcised makes men ugly."

"Can you make the supper? Maybe you should go up and lie down."

"I hate you when you're so uptight," she tells him, but without hate, in a voice swinging as a child wandering home swings a basket, "can I cook the supper, I can do anything, I can fly, I can make men satisfied, I can drive a white car, I can count in French up to any number; look!" – she pulls her dress way up above her waist – "I'm a Christmas tree!"

But the supper comes to the table badly cooked. The lamb chops are rubbery and blue near the bone, the beans crunch underdone in the mouth. Skeeter pushes his plate away. "I can't eat this crud. I ain't that primitive, right?"

Nelson says, "It tastes all right, Jill."

But Jill knows, and bows her thin face. Tears fall onto her plate. Strange tears, less signs of grief than chemical condensations: tears she puts forth as a lilac puts forth buds. Skeeter keeps teasing her. "Look at me, woman. Hey you cunt, look me in the eye. What do you see?"

"I see you. All sprinkled with sugar."

"You see Him, right?"

"Wrong."

"Look over at those drapes, honey. Those ugly home-made drapes where they sort of blend into the wallpaper."

"He's not there, Skeeter."

"Look at me. *Look.*"

They all look. Since coming to live with them, Skeeter has aged; his goatee has grown bushy, his skin has taken on a captive's taut glaze. He is not wearing his glasses tonight.

"Skeeter, He's not there."

"Keep looking at me, cunt. What do you see?"

"I see – a chrysalis of mud. I see a black crab. I just thought, an angel is like an insect, they have six legs. Isn't that true? Isn't that what you want me to say?"

Skeeter tells them about Vietnam. He tilts his head back as if the ceiling is a movie screen. He wants to do it justice but is scared to let it back in. "It was where it was coming to an end," he lets out slowly. "There was no roofs to stay under, you stood out in the rain like a beast, you slept in holes in the ground with the roots poking through, and, you know, you could do it. You didn't die of it. That was interesting. It was like you learned there was life on another world. In the middle of a recon action, a little old gook in one of them hats would come out and try to sell you a chicken. There were these little girls pretty as dolls selling you smack along the road in those little cans the press photogs would throw away, right? It was very complicated, there isn't any net" – he lifts his hand – "to grab it all in."

Colored fragments pour down toward him through the hole in the ceiling. Green machines, an ugly green, eating ugly green bushes. Red mud pressed in patterns to an ooze by Amtrac treads. The emerald of rice paddies, each plant set there with its reflection in the water pure as a monogram. The color of human ears a guy from another company had drying under his belt like withered apricots, yellow. The black of the *ao dai* pajamas the delicate little whores wore, so figurine-fine he couldn't believe he could touch them though this clammy guy in a white suit kept pushing, saying, "Black GI, number one, most big pricks, Viet girls like suck." The red, not of blood, but of the Ace of Diamonds a guy in his company wore in his helmet for luck. All that luck-junk: peace-signs of melted lead, love beads, beads spelling LOVE, JESUS, MOTHER, BURY ME DEEP, Ho Chi Minh sandals cut from rubber tires for tiny feet, Tao crosses, Christian crosses, the cross-shaped bombs the Phantoms dropped on the trail up ahead, the X's your laces wore into your boots over the days, the shiny green body bags tied like long mail sacks, sun on red dust, on blue smoke, sun caught in shafts between the canopies of the jungle where dinks with Russian rifles waited quieter than orchids, it all tumbles down on him, he is overwhelmed. He knows he can never make it intelligible to these three ofays that worlds do exist beyond these paper walls.

"Just the sounds," Skeeter says. "When one of them Unfriendly mortar shells hits near your hole it is as if a wall were there that was big and solid, twenty feet thick of noise, and you is just a gushy bug. Feet up there just as soon step on you as not, it doesn't matter to them, right? It does blow your mind. And the dead, the dead are so weird, they are so – *dead*. Like a stiff chewed mouse the cat fetches up on the lawn. I mean, they are so out of it, so peaceful, there is no word for it, this same grunt last night he was telling you about his girl back in Oshkosh, making it so real you had to jack off, and the VC trip a Claymore and his legs go this way and he goes the other. It was bad. They used to say, 'A world of hurt,' and that is what it was."

Nelson asks, "What's a grunt?"

"A grunt is a leg. An eleven bush, right? He is an ordinary drafted soldier who carries a rifle and humps the boonies. The green machine is very clever. They put the draftees out in the bush to get blown and the re-ups sit back at Longbinh tellin' reporters the body count. They put old Charlie Company on some bad hills, but they didn't get me to re-up. I'd had a bushel, right?"

"I thought I was Charlie," Rabbit says.

"I thought the Viet Cong was," Nelson says.

"You are, they are, so was I, everybody is. I was Company C for Charlie, Second Battalion, 28th Infantry, First Division. We messed around all up and down the Dongnai River." Skeeter looks at the blank ceiling and thinks, I'm not doing it, I'm not doing it justice, I'm selling it short. The holy quality is hardest to get. "The thing about Charlie is," he says, "he's everywhere. In Nam, it's all Charlies, right? Every gook's a Charlie, it got so you didn't mind greasing an old lady, a little kid, they might be the ones planted punji stakes at night, they might not, it didn't matter. A lot of things didn't matter. Nam must be the only place in Uncle Sam's world where black-white doesn't matter. Truly. I had white boys die for me. The Army treats a black man truly swell, black body can stop a bullet as well as any other, they put us right up there, and don't think we're not grateful, we are indeed, we hustle to stop those bullets, we're so happy to die alongside Whitey." The white ceiling still is blank, but beginning to buzz, beginning to bend into space; he must let the spirit keep lifting him along these lines. "One boy I remember, *hate* the way you make me bring it back, I'd give one ball to forget this, hit in the dark, VC mortars had been working us over since sunset, we never should have been in that valley, lying there in the dark with his guts spilled out. I couldn't see him, hustling my ass back from the perimeter, I stepped on his insides, felt like stepping on a piece of Jell-O, worse, he screamed out and died right then, he hadn't been dead to then. Another time, four of us out on recon, bunch of their AK-47s opened up, had an entirely different sound from the M-16, more of a cracking sound, dig?, not so punky. We were pinned down. Boy with us, white boy from Tennessee, never shaved in his life and ignorant as Moses, slithered away into the bush and wiped 'em out, when we picked him up bullets had cut him in two, impossible for a man to keep firing like that. It was bad. I wouldn't have believed you could see such bad things and keep your eyeballs. These poor unfriendlies, they'd call in the napalm on 'em just up ahead, silver cans tumbling over and over, and they'd come out of the bush right at you, burning and shooting, spitting bullets and burning like a torch in some parade, come tumbling right into your hole with you, they figured the only place to get away from the napalm was inside our perimeter. You'd shoot 'em to shut off their noise. Little boys with faces like the shoeshine back at base. It got so killing didn't feel so bad, it never felt *good*, just necessary, like taking a piss. Right?"

"I don't much want to hear any more," Nelson says. "It makes me feel sick and we're missing *Samantha*."

Jill tells him, "You must let Skeeter tell it if he wants to. It's good for Skeeter to tell it."

"It happened, Nelson," Rabbit tells him. "If it didn't happen, I wouldn't want you to be bothered with it. But it happened, so we got to take it in. We all got to deal with it somehow."

"Schlitz."

"I don't know. I feel lousy. A ginger ale."

"Harry, you're not yourself. How's it going? D'ya hear anything from Janice?"

"Nothing, thank God. How's Mom?"

The old man nudges closer, as if to confide an obscenity. "Frankly, she's better than a month ago anybody would have dared to hope."

Now Skeeter does see something on the ceiling, white on white, but the whites are different and one is pouring out of a hole in the other. "Do you know," he asks, "there are two theories of how the universe was done? One says, there was a Big Bang, just like in the Bible, and we're still riding that, it all came out of nothing all at once, like the Good Book say, right? And the funny thing is, all the evidence backs it up. Now the other, which I prefer, says it only seems that way. Fact is, it says, there is a steady state, and though it is true everything is expanding outwards, it does not thin out to next to nothingness on account of the reason that through strange holes in this nothingness new somethingness comes pouring in from exactly nowhere. Now that to me has the ring of truth."

Rabbit asks, "What does that have to do with Vietnam?"

"It is the local hole. It is where the world is redoing itself. It is the tail of ourselves we are eating. It is the bottom you have to have. It is the well you look into and are frightened by your own face in the dark water down there. It is as they say Number One and Number Ten. It is the end. It is the beginning. It is beautiful, men do beautiful things in that mud. It is where God is pushing through. He's coming, Chuck, and Babychuck, and Ladychuck, let Him in. Pull down, shoot to kill. The sun is burning through. The moon is turning red. The moon is a baby's head bright red between his momma's legs."

Nelson screams and puts his hands over his ears. "I *hate* this, Skeeter. You're scaring me. I don't want God to come, I want Him to stay where He is. I want to grow up like *him*" – his father, Harry, the room's big man – "average and ordinary. I *hate* what you say about the war, it doesn't sound beautiful it sounds horrible."

Skeeter's gaze comes down off the ceiling and tries to focus on the boy. "Right," he says. "You still want to live, they still got you. You're still a slave. Let go. Let go, boy. Don't be a slave. Even *him*, you know, your Daddychuck, is learning. He's learning how to die. He's one slow learner but he takes it a day at a time, right?" He has a mad impulse. He lets it guide him. He goes and kneels before the child where he sits on the sofa beside Jill. Skeeter kneels and says, "Don't keep the Good Lord out, Nellie. One little boy like you put his finger in the dike; take it out. Let it come. Put your hand on my head and promise you won't keep the Good Lord out. Let Him come. Do that for old Skeeter, he's been hurtin' so long."

Nelson puts his hand on Skeeter's orb of hair. His eyes widen, at how far his hand sinks down. He says, "I don't want to hurt you, Skeeter. I don't want anybody to hurt anybody."

"Bless you, boy." Skeeter in his darkness feels blessing flow down through the hand tingling in his hair like sun burning through a cloud. Mustn't mock this child. Softly, stealthily, parting vines of craziness, his heart approaches certainty.

Rabbit's voice explodes. "Shit. It's just a dirty little war that has to be fought. You can't make something religious out of it just because you happened to be there."

Skeeter stands and tries to comprehend this man. "Trouble with you," he sees, "you still cluttered up with common sense. Common sense is bullshit, man. It gets you through the days all right, but it leaves you alone at *night*. I keeps you from *knowing*. You just don't *know*, Chuck. You don't even know that now is all the time there is. What happens to you, is all that happens, right? You are *it*, right? You. Are. It. I've come down" – he points to the ceiling, his finger a brown crayon – "to tell you that, since along these two thousand years somewhere you've done gone and forgotten again, right?"

Rabbit says, "Talk sense. Is our being in Vietnam wrong?"

"Wrong? Man, how can it be wrong when that's the way it is? These poor Benighted States just being themselves, right? Can't stop bein' yourself, somebody has to do it for you, right? Nobody that big around. Uncle Sam wakes up one morning, looks down at his belly, sees he's some cockroach, what can he do? Just keep bein' his cockroach self, is all. Till he gets stepped on. No such shoe right now, right? Just keep doing his cockroach thing. I'm not one of these white lib-er-als like that cracker Fulldull or that Charlie McCarthy a while back gave all the college queers a hard-on, think Vietnam some sort of mistake, we can fix it up once we get the cave men out of office, it is *no* mistake, right, any President comes along falls in love with it, it is lib-er-al-ism's very wang and ding-dong pussy. Those crackers been lickin' their mother's ass so long they forgotten what she looks like frontwards. What is lib-er-alism? Bringin' joy to the world, right? Puttin' enough sugar on dog-eat-dog so it tastes good all over, right? Well now what could be nicer than Vietnam? We is keepin' that coast open. Man, what is we all about if it ain't keepin' things open? How can money and jizz make their way if we don't keep a few cunts like that open? Nam is an act of love, right? Compared to Nam, beatin' Japan was flat-out ugly. We was ugly fuckers then and now we is truly a civilized spot." The ceiling agitates; he feels the gift of tongues descend to him. "We is *the* spot. Few old fools like the late Ho may not know it, we is what the world is begging *for*. Big beat, smack, black cock, big-assed cars and billboards, we is into *it*. Jesus come down, He come down here. These other countries, just bullshit places, right? We got the *ape* shit, right? Bring down Kingdom Come, we'll swamp the world in red-hot real American blue-green ape shit, right?"

"Right," Rabbit says.

Encouraged, Skeeter sees the truth: "Nam," he says, "Nam the spot where our heavenly essence is pustulatin'. Man don't like Vietnam, he don't like America."

"Right," Rabbit says. "*Right.*"

The two others, pale freckled faces framed in too much hair, are frightened by this agreement. Jill begs, "Stop. Everything hurts." Skeeter understands. Her skin is peeled, the poor girl is wide open to the stars. This afternoon he got her to drop some mescaline. If she'll eat mesc, she'll snort smack. If she'll snort, she'll shoot. He has her.

Nelson begs, "Let's watch television."

Rabbit asks Skeeter, "How'd you get through your year over there without being hurt?"

These white faces. These holes punched in the perfection of his anger. God is pouring through the white holes of their faces; he cannot stanch the gushing. It gets to his eyes. They had been wicked, when he was a child, to teach him God was a white man. "I *was* hurt," Skeeter says.

BEATITUDES OF SKEETER

(written down in Jill's confident, rounded, private-school hand, in green felt pen, playfully one night, on a sheet of Nelson's notebook filler)

> Power is bullshit.
> Love is bullshit.
> Common sense is bullshit.
> Confusion is God's very face.
> Nothing is interesting save eternal sameness.
> There is no salvation, 'cepting through Me.

Also from the same night, some drawings by her, in crayons Nelson found for her; her style was cute, linear, arrested where some sophomore art class had left it, yet the resemblances were clear. Skeeter of course was the spade. Nelson, his dark bangs and side-sheaves exaggerated, the club, on a stem of a neck. Herself, her pale hair crayoned in the same pink as her sharp-chinned face, the heart. And Rabbit, therefore, the diamond. In the center of the diamond, a tiny pink nose. Sleepy small blue eyes with worried eyebrows. An almost invisible mouth, lifted as if to nibble. Around it all, green scribbles she had to identify with an affectionate pointing arrow and a balloon: "in the rough."

One of these afternoons, when Nelson is home from soccer practice and Harry is home from work, they all cram into Jill's Porsche and drive out into the county. Rabbit has to have the front seat; Nelson and Skeeter squeeze into the half-seats behind. Skeeter scuttles blinking from the doorway to the curb and inside the car says, "Man, been so long since I been out in the air, it hurts my lungs." Jill drives urgently, rapidly, with the arrogance of the young; Rabbit keeps slapping his foot on the floor, where there is no brake. Jill's cool profile smiles. Her little foot in a ballet slipper feeds gas halfway through curves, pumps up speed enough just to pinch them past a huge truck – a raging, belching house on wheels – before another hurtling the other way scissors them into oblivion, on a straight stretch between valleys of red earth and pale corn stubble. The country is beautiful. Fall has lifted that heavy Pennsylvania green, the sky is cleared of the suspended summer milk, the hills edge into shades of amber and flaming orange that in another month will become the locust-husk tint that crackles underfoot in hunting season. A brushfire haze floats in the valleys like fog on a river's skin. Jill stops the car beside a whitewashed fence and an apple tree. They get out into a cloud of the scent of fallen apples, overripe. At their feet apples rot in the long dank grass that banks a trickling ditch, the grass still powerfully green; beyond the fence a meadow has been scraped brown by grazing, but for clumps where burdock fed by cow dung grows high as a man. Nelson picks up an apple and bites on the side away from wormholes. Skeeter protests, "Child, don't put your mouth on that garbage!" Had he never seen a fruit eaten in nature before?

Jill lifts her dress and jumps the ditch to touch one of the rough warm whitewashed slats of the fence and to look between them into the distance, where in the dark shelter of trees a sandstone farmhouse glistens like a sugar cube soaked in tea and the wide gaunt wheel of an old farm wagon, spokes stilled forever, waits beside a rusty upright that must be a pump. She remembers rusty cleats that waited for the prow line of visiting boats on docks in Rhode Island and along the Sound, the whole rusty neglected salt-bleached barnacled look of things built where the sea laps, summer sun on gull-gray wood, docks, sheds, metal creaking with the motion of the water, very distant from this inland overripeness. She says, "Let's go."

And they cram back into the little car, and again there are the trucks, and the gas stations, and the "Dutch" restaurants with neon hex signs, and the wind and the speed of the car drowning out all smells and sounds and thoughts of a possible other world. The open sandstone country south of Brewer, the Amish farms printed on the trimmed fields like magazine covers, becomes the ugly hills and darker valleys north of the city, where the primitive iron industry had its day and where the people built with brick – tall narrow-faced homes with gables and dormers like a buzzard's shoulders, perched on domed lawns behind spiked retaining walls. The soft flowerpot-red of Brewer hardens up here, ten miles to the north, to a red dark like oxblood. Though it is not yet the coal regions, the trees feel darkened by coal dust. Rabbit begins to remember accounts, a series run in the *Vat*, of strange murders, axings and scaldings and stranglings committed in these pinched valleys with their narrow main streets of oxblood churches and banks and Oddfellows' halls, streets that end with, as with a wrung neck, a sharp turn over abandoned railroad tracks into a sunless gorge where a stream the color of tarnished silver is now and then crossed by a damp covered bridge that rattles as it swallows you.

Rabbit and Nelson, Skeeter and Jill, crushed together in the little car, laugh a lot during this drive, laugh at nothing, at the silly expression on the face of a bib-overalled hick as they barrel past, at pigs dignified in their pens, at the names on mailboxes (Hinnershitz, Focht, Schtupnagel), at tractor-riding men so fat nothing less wide than a tractor seat would hold them. They even laugh when the little car, though the gas gauge stands at ½, jerks, struggles, slows, stops as if braked. Jill has time only to bring it to the side of the road, out of traffic. Rabbit gets out to look at the engine; it's in the back, under a tidy slotted hood, a tight machine whose works are not open and tall and transparent as with a Linotype, but are tangled and greasy and closed. The starter churns but the engine will not turn over. The chain of explosions that works by faith is jammed. He leaves the hood up to signal an emergency. Skeeter, crouching down in the back, calls, "Chuck, know what you're doin' with that hood, you're callin' down the fucking fuzz!"

Rabbit tells him, "You better get out of the back. We get hit from behind, you've had it. You too Nelson. Out."

It is the most dangerous type of highway, three-lane. The commuter traffic out from Brewer shudders past in an avalanche of dust and noise and carbon monoxide. No Good Samaritans stop. The Porsche has stalled atop an embankment seeded with that feathery finespun ground-cover the state uses to hold steep soil: crown vetch. Below, swifts are skimming a shorn cornfield. Rabbit and Nelson lean against the fenders and watch the sun, an hour above the horizon, fill the field with stubble-shadows, ridges subtle as those of corduroy. Jill wanders off and gathers a baby bouquet of the tiny daisylike asters that bloom in the fall, on stems so thin they form a cirrus hovering an inch or two above the earth. Jill offers the bouquet to Skeeter, to lure him out. He reaches to bat the flowers from her hand; they scatter and fall in the grit of the roadside. His voice comes muffled from within the Porsche. "You honky cunt, this all a way to turn me in, nothing wrong with this fucking car, right?"

"It won't go," she says; one aster rests on the toe of one ballet slipper. Her face has shed expression.

Skeeter's voice whines and snarls in its metal shell. "Knew I should never come out of that house. Jill honey, I know why. Can't stay off the stuff, right? No will at all, right? Easier than having any will, hand old Skeeter over to the law, hey, right?"

Rabbit asks her, "What's he saying?"

"He's saying he's scared."

Skeeter is shouting, "Get them dumb honkies out of the way, I'm making a run for it. How far down on the other side of that fence?"

Rabbit says, "Smart move, you'll really stick out up here in the boondocks. Talk about a nigger in the woodpile."

"Don't you nigger me, you honky prick. Tell you one thing, you turn me in I'll get you all greased if I have to send to Philly to do it. It's not just me, we're everywhere, hear? Now you fuckers get this car to *go*, hear me? Get it to *go*."

Skeeter issues all this while crouched down between the leather backs of the bucket seats and the rear window. His panic is disgusting and may be contagious. Rabbit lusts to pull him out of his shell into the sunshine, but is afraid to reach in; he might get stung. He slams the Porsche door shut on the churning rasping voice, and at the rear of the car slams down the hood. "You two stay here. Calm him down, keep him in the car. I'll walk to a gas station, there must be one up the road."

He runs for a while, Skeeter's venomous fright making his own bladder burn. After all these nights together betrayal is the Negro's first thought. Maybe natural, three hundred years of it. Rabbit is running, running to keep that black body pinned back there, so it won't panic and flee. Like running late to school. Skeeter has become a duty. Late, late. Then an antique red flying-horse sign suspended above sunset-dyed fields. It is an old-fashioned garage: an unfathomable work space black with oil, the walls precious with wrenches, fan belts, peen hammers, parts. An old Coke machine, the kind that dispenses bottles, purrs beside the hydraulic lift. The mechanic, a weedy young man with a farmer's drawl and black palms, drives him in a jolting tow truck back up the highway. The side window is broken; air whistles there, hungrily gushes.

"Seized up," is the mechanic's verdict. He asks Jill, "When'd you last put oil in it?"

"Oil? Don't they do it when they put the gas in?"

"Not unless you ask."

"You dumb mutt," Rabbit says to Jill.

Her mouth goes prim and defiant. "Skeeter's been driving the car too."

Skeeter, while the mechanic was poking around in the engine and pumping the gas pedal, uncurled from behind the seats and straightened in the air, his glasses orange discs in the last of the sun. Rabbit asks him, "How far've you been taking this crate?"

"Oh," the black man says, fastidious in earshot of the mechanic, "here and there. Never recklessly. I wasn't aware," he minces on, "the automobile was your property."

"It's just," he says lamely, "the waste. The carelessness."

Jill asks the mechanic, "Can you fix it in an hour? My little brother here has homework to do."

The mechanic speaks only to Rabbit. "The enchine's destroyed. The pistons have fused to the cylinders. The nearest place to fix a car like this is probably Pottstown."

"Can we leave it with you until we arrange to have somebody come for it?"

"I'll have to charge a dollar a day for the parking."

"Sure. Swell."

"And that'll be twenty for the towing."

He pays. The mechanic tows the Porsche back to the garage. They ride with him, Jill and Harry in the cab ("Careful now," the mechanic says as Jill slides over, "I don't want to get grease on that nice white dress"), Skeeter and Nelson in the little car, dragged backwards at a slant. At the garage, the mechanic phones for a cab to take them into West Brewer. Skeeter disappears behind a smudged door and flushes the toilet repeatedly. Nelson settles to watching the mechanic unhitch the car and listens to him talk about "enchines." Jill and Harry walk outside. Crickets are shrilling in the dark cornfields. A quarter-moon, with one sick eye, scuds above the flying horse sign. The garage's outer lights are switched off. He notices something white on her slipper. The little flower that fell has stuck there. He stoops and hands it to her. She kisses it to thank him, then, silently lays it to rest in a trash barrel full of oil-wiped paper towels and punctured cans. "Don't get your dress greasy." Car tires crackle; an ancient fifties Buick, with those tailfins patterned on B-19s, pulls into their orbit. The taxi driver is fat and chews gum. On the way back to Brewer, his head bulks as a pyramid against the oncoming headlights, motionless but for the rhythm of chewing. Skeeter sits beside him. "Beautiful day," Rabbit calls forward to him.

Jill giggles. Nelson is asleep on her lap. She toys with his hair, winding it around her silent fingers.

"Fair for this time of the year," is the slow answer.

"Beautiful country up here. We hardly ever get north of the city. We were driving around sightseeing."

"Not too many sights to see."

"The engine seized right up on us, I guess the car's a real mess."

"I guess."

"My daughter here forgot to put any oil in it, that's the way young people are these days, ruin one car and on to the next. Material things don't mean a thing to 'em."

"To some, I guess."

Skeeter says sideways to him, "Yo' sho' meets a lot ob nice folks hevin' en acci-dent lahk dis, a lot ob naas folks way up no'th heah."

"Yes, well," the driver says, and that is all he says until he says to Rabbit, having stopped on Vista Crescent, "Eighteen."

"Dollars? For ten miles?"

"Twelve. And I got to go back twelve now."

Rabbit goes to the driver's side to pay, while the others run into the house. The man leans out and asks, "Know what you're doing?"

"Not exactly."

"They'll knife you in the back every time."

"Who?"

The driver leans closer; by street-lamplight Rabbit sees a wide sad face, sallow, a whale's lipless mouth clamped in a melancholy set, a horseshoe-shaped scar on the meat of his nose. His answer is distinct: "Jigaboos."

Embarrassed for him, Rabbit turns away and sees – Nelson is right – a crowd of children. They are standing across the Crescent, some with bicycles, watching this odd car unload. This crowd phenomenon on the bleak terrain of Penn Villas alarms him: as if growths were to fester on the surface of the moon.

   The incident emboldens Skeeter. His skin has dared the sun again. Rabbit comes home from work to find him and Nelson shooting baskets in the driveway. Nelson bounces the ball to his father and Rabbit's one-handed set from twenty feet out swishes. Pretty. "Hey," Skeeter crows, so all the homes in Penn Villas can hear, "where'd you get that funky old style of shooting a basket-ball? You were tryin' to be comical, right?"
   "Went in," Nelson tells him loyally.
   "Shit, boy, a one-armed dwarf could have blocked it. T'get that shot off you need a screen two men thick, right? You gotta jump and shoot, jump and *shoot.*" He demonstrates; his shot misses but looks right: the ball held high, a back-leaning ascent into the air, a soft release that would arch over any defender. Rabbit tries it, but finds his body heavy, the effort of lifting jarring. The ball flies badly. Says Skeeter, "You got a white man's lead gut, but I adore those hands." They scrimmage one on one; Skeeter is quick and slick, slithering by for the layup on the give-and-go to Nelson again and again. Rabbit cannot stop him, his breath begins to ache in his chest, but there are moments when the ball and his muscles and the air overhead and the bodies competing with his all feel taut and unified and defiant of gravity. Then the October chill bites into his sweat and he goes into the house. Jill has been sleeping upstairs. She sleeps more and more lately, a dazed evad-ing sleep that he finds insulting. When she comes downstairs, in that boring white dress, brushing back sticky hair from her cheeks, he asks roughly, "Dja do anything about the car?"
   "Sweet, what would I do?"
   "You could call your mother."
   "I can't. She and Stepdaddy would make a thing. They'd come for me."
   "Maybe that's a good idea."
   "Stepdaddy's a creep." She moves past him, not focusing, into the kitchen. She looks into the refrigerator. "You didn't shop."

"That's your job."

"Without a car?"

"Christ, you can walk up to the Acme in five minutes."

"People would see Skeeter."

"They see him anyway. He's outside horsing around with Nelson. And evidently you've been letting him drive all around Pennsylvania." His anger recharges itself: *lead gut.* "Goddammit, how can you just run an expensive car like that into the ground and just let it *sit?* There's people in the world could live for ten years on what that car cost."

"Don't, Harry. I'm weak."

"O.K. I'm sorry." He tugs her into his arms. She rocks sadly against him, rubbing her nose on his shirt. But her body when dazed has an absence, an unconnectedness, that feels disagreeable against his skin. He itches to sneeze.

Jill is murmuring, "I think you miss your wife."

"That bitch. Never."

"She's like anybody else, caught in this society. She wants to be alive while she is alive."

"Don't you?"

"Sometimes. But I know it's not enough. It's how they get you. Let me go now. You don't like holding me, I can feel it. I just remembered, some frozen chicken livers behind the ice cream. But they take forever to thaw."

Six-o'clock news. The pale face caught behind the screen, unaware that his head, by some imperfection in reception at 26 Vista Crescent, is flattened, and his chin rubbery and long, sternly says, "Chicago. Two thousand five hundred Illinois National Guardsmen remained on active duty today in the wake of a day of riots staged by members of the extremist faction of the Students for a Democratic Society. Windows were smashed, cars overturned, policemen assaulted by the young militants whose slogan is" – sad, stern pause; the bleached face lifts toward the camera, the chin stretches, the head flattens like an anvil – "Bring the War Home." Film cuts of white-helmeted policemen flailing at nests of arms and legs, of long-haired girls being dragged, of sudden bearded faces shaking fists that want to rocket out through the television screen; then back to clips of policemen swinging clubs, which seems balletlike and soothing to Rabbit. Skeeter, too, likes it. "Right on!" he cries. "Hit that honky snob again!" In the commercial break he turns and explains to Nelson, "It's beautiful, right?"

Nelson asks, "Why? Aren't they protesting the war?"

"Sure as a hen has balls they are. What those crackers protesting is they gotta wait twenty years to get their daddy's share of the pie. They want it *now*."

"What would they do with it?"

"Do, boy? They'd *eat* it, that's what they'd do."

The commercial — an enlarged view of a young woman's mouth — is over. "Meanwhile, within the courtroom, the trial of the Chicago Eight continued on its turbulent course. Presiding Judge Julius J. Hoffman, no relation to Defendant Abbie Hoffman, several times rebuked Defendant Bobby Seale, whose outbursts contained such epithets as" — again, the upward look, the flattened head, the disappointed emphasis — "pig, fascist, and racist." A courtroom sketch of Seale is flashed.

Nelson asks, "Skeeter, do you like *him?*"

"I do not much cotton," Skeeter says, "to establishment niggers."

Rabbit has to laugh. "That's ridiculous. He's as full of hate as you are."

Skeeter switches off the set. His tone is a preacher's, ladylike. "I am by no means full of hate. I am full of love, which is a dynamic force. Hate is a paralyzing force. Hate freezes. Love strikes and liberates. Right? Jesus liberated the money-changers from the temple. The new Jesus will liberate the new money-changers. The old Jesus brought a sword, right? The new Jesus will also bring a sword. He will be a living flame of love. Chaos is God's body. Order is the Devil's chains. As to Robert Seale, any black man who has John Kennel Badbreath and Leonard Birdbrain giving him fund-raising cocktail parties is one house nigger in my book. He has gotten into the power bag, he has gotten into the publicity bag, he has debased the coinage of his soul and is thereupon as they say irrelevant. We black men came here without names, we are the future's organic seeds, seeds have no names, right?"

"Right," Rabbit says, a habit he has acquired.

Jill's chicken livers have burned edges and icy centers.

Eleven-o'clock news. A gauzy-bearded boy, his face pressed so hard against the camera the focus cannot be maintained, screams, "Off the pigs! All power to the people!"

An unseen interviewer mellifluously asks him, "How would you describe the goals of your organization?"

"Destruction of existing repressive structures. Social control of the means of production."

"Could you tell our viewing audience what you mean by 'means of production'?"

The camera is being jostled; the living room, darkened otherwise, flickers. "Factories. Wall Street. Technology. All that. A tiny clique of capitalists is forcing pollution down our throats, and the SST and the genocide in Vietnam and in the ghettos. All that."

"I see. Your aim, then, by smashing windows, is to curb a runaway technology and create the basis for a new humanism."

The boy looks off-screen blearily, as the camera struggles to refocus him. "You being funny? You'll be the first up against the wall, you —" And the blip showed that the interview had been taped.

Rabbit says, "Tell me about technology."

"Technology," Skeeter explains with exquisite patience, the tip of his joint glowing red as he drags, "is horseshit. Take that down, Jilly."

But Jill is asleep on the sofa. Her thighs glow, her dress having ridden up to a sad shadowy triangular peep of underpants.

Skeeter goes on, "We are all at work at the mighty labor of forgetting everything we know. We are sewing the apple back on the tree. Now the Romans had technology, right? And the barbarians saved them from it. The barbarians were their saviors. Since we cannot induce the Eskimos to invade us, we have raised a generation of barbarians ourselves, pardon me, *you* have raised them,

Whitey has raised them, the white American middle-class and its imitators the world over have found within themselves the divine strength to generate millions of subhuman idiots that in less benighted ages only the inbred aristocracies could produce. Who were those idiot kings?"

"Huh?" says Rabbit.

"Merovingians, right? Slipped my mind. They were dragged about in ox carts gibbering and we are now blessed with motorized gibberers. It is truly written, we shall blow our minds, and dedicate the rest to Chairman Mao. Right?"

Rabbit argues, "That's not quite fair. These kids have some good points. The war aside, what about pollution?"

"I am getting weary," Skeeter says, "of talking with white folk. You are defending your own. These rabid children, as surely as Agnew Dei, desire to preserve the status quo against the divine plan and the divine wrath. They are Antichrist. They perceive God's face in Vietnam and spit upon it. False prophets: by their proliferation you know the time is nigh. Public shamelessness, ingenious armor, idiocy revered, all laws mocked but the laws of bribery and protection: we are Rome. And I am the Christ of the new Dark Age. Or if not me, then someone exactly like me, whom later ages will suppose to have been me. Do you believe?"

"I believe." Rabbit drags on his own joint, and feels his world expand to admit new truths as a woman spreads her legs, as a flower unfolds, as the stars flee one another. "I do believe."

Skeeter likes Rabbit to read to him from the *Life and Times of Frederick Douglass*. "You're just gorgeous, right? You're gone to be our big nigger tonight. As a white man, Chuck, you don't amount to much, but niggerwise you groove." He has marked sections in the book with paper clips and a crayon.

Rabbit reads, "*The reader will have noticed that among the names of slaves that of Esther is mentioned. This was the name of a young woman who possessed that which was ever a curse to the slave girl – namely, personal beauty. She was tall, light-colored, well formed, and made a fine* appearance. *Esther was courted by 'Ned Roberts,' the son of a favorite slave of Colonel Lloyd, and who was as fine-looking a young man as Esther was a woman. Some slaveholders would have been glad to have promoted the marriage of two such persons, but for some reason Captain Anthony disapproved of their courtship. He strictly ordered her to quit the society of young Roberts, telling her that he would punish her severely if he ever found her again in his company. But it was impossible to keep this couple apart. Meet they would and meet they did.* Then we skip." The red crayon mark resumes at the bottom of the page; Rabbit hears drama entering his voice, early morning mists, a child's fear. "*It was early in the morning, when all was still, and before any of the family in the house or kitchen had risen. I was, in fact, awakened by the heart-rendering shrieks and piteous cries of poor Esther. My sleeping-place was on the dirt floor of a little rough closet which opened into the kitchen –*"

Skeeter interrupts, "You can smell that closet, right? Dirt, right, and old potatoes, and little bits of grass turning yellow before they can grow an inch, right? Smell that, he *slept* in there."

"Hush," Jill says.

"*– and through the cracks in its unplaned boards I could distinctly see and hear what was going on, without being seen. Esther's wrists were firmly tied, and the twisted rope was fastened to a strong iron staple in a heavy wooden beam above, near the fireplace. Here she stood on a bench, her arms tightly drawn above her head. Her back and shoulders were perfectly bare. Behind her stood old master, cowhide in hand, pursuing his barbarous work with all manner of harsh, coarse, and tantalizing epithets. He was cruelly deliberate, and protracted the torture as one who was delighted with the agony of his victim. Again and again he drew the hateful scourge through his hand, adjusting it with a view of dealing the most pain-giving blow his strength and skill could inflict. Poor Esther had never before been severely whipped. Her shoulders were plump and tender. Each blow, vigorously laid on, brought screams from her as well as blood. 'Have mercy! Oh, mercy!' she cried. 'I won't do so no more.' But her piercing cries seemed only to increase his fury.*" The red mark stops but Rabbit sweeps on to the end of the chapter. "*The whole scene, with all its attendant circumstances, was revolting and shocking to the last degree, and when the motives for the brutal castigation are known, language has no power to convey a just sense of its dreadful criminality. After laying on I dare not say how many stripes, old master untied his suffering victim. When let down*

she could scarcely stand. From my heart I pitied her, and child as I was,
and new to such scenes, the shock was tremendous. I was terrified, hushed,
stunned, and bewildered. The scene here described was often repeated, for
Edward and Esther continued to meet, notwithstanding all efforts to pre-
vent their meeting."

Skeeter turns to Jill and slaps her sharply, as a child would, on
the chest. "Don't hush me, you cunt."

"I wanted to hear the passage."

"How'd it turn you on, cunt?"

"I liked the way Harry read it. With feeling."

"Fuck your white feelings."

"Hey, easy," Rabbit says, helplessly, seeing that violence is due.

Skeeter is wild. Keeping his one hand on her shoulder as a brace,
with the other he reaches to her throat and rips the neck of
her white dress forward. The cloth is tough; Jill's head snaps far
forward before the rip is heard. She recoils back into the sofa,
her eyes expressionless; her little tough-tipped tits bounce in
the torn V.

Rabbit's instinct is not to rescue her but to shield Nelson. He
drops the book on the cobbler's bench and puts his body between
the boy and the sofa. "Go upstairs."

Nelson, stunned, bewildered, has risen to his feet; he moans,
"He'll *kill* her, Dad." His cheeks are flushed, his eyes are sunk.

"No he won't. He's just high. She's all right."

"Oh shit, shit," the child repeats in desperation; his face caves
into crying.

"Hey there Babychuck," Skeeter calls. "You want to whip me,
right?" Skeeter hops up, does a brittle bewitched dance, strips off
his shirt so violently one cuff button flies off and strikes the lampshade. His skinny chest, naked, is stunning in its articulation: every
muscle sharp in its attachment to the bone. Rabbit has never seen
such a chest except on a crucifix. "What's next?" Skeeter shouts.
"Wanna whup my bum, right? Here it is!" His hands have undone
his fly button and are on his belt, but Nelson has fled the room.
His sobbing comes downstairs, diminishing.

"O.K., that's enough," Rabbit says.

"Read a little bitty bit more," Skeeter begs.

"You get carried away."

"That damn child of yours, thinks he owns this cunt."

"Stop calling her a cunt."

"Man, wasn't this Jesus gave her one." Skeeter cackles.

"You're horrible," Jill tells him, drawing the torn cloth together.

He flips one piece aside. "Moo."

"Harry, help me."

"Read the book, Chuck, I'll be good. Read me the next paper clip."

Above them, Nelson's footsteps cross the floor. If he reads, the boy will be safe. "*Alas*, that the one?"

"That'll do. Little Jilly, you love me, right?"

"*Alas, this immense wealth, this gilded splendor, this profusion of luxury, this exemption from toil, this life of ease, this sea of plenty, were not the pearly gates they seemed –*"

"You're my pearly gate, girl."

"*The poor slave, on his hard pine plank, scantily covered with his thin blanket, slept more soundly than the feverish voluptuary who reclined upon his downy pillow. Food to the indolent is poison, not sustenance. Lurking beneath the rich and tempting viands were invisible spirits of evil, which filled the self-deluded gormandizer with aches and pains, passions uncontrollable, fierce tempers, dyspepsia, rheumatism, lumbago, and gout, and of these the Lloyds had a full share.*"

Beyond the edge of the page Skeeter and Jill are wrestling; in gray flashes her underpants, her breasts are exposed. Another flash, Rabbit sees, is her smile. Her small spaced teeth bare in silent laughter; she is liking it, this attack. Seeing him spying, Jill starts, struggles angrily out from under, hugs the rags of her dress around her, and runs from the room. Her footsteps flicker up the stairs. Skeeter blinks at her flight; he resettles the great pillow of his head with a sigh. "Beautiful," is the sigh. "One more, Chuck. Read me the one where he fights back." His carved chest melts into the beige sofa; its airfoam is covered in a plaid of green and tan and red that have rubbed and faded toward a single shade.

"You know, I gotta get up and go to work tomorrow."

"You worried about your little dolly? Don't you worry about that. The thing about a cunt, man, it's just like a Kleenex, you use it and throw it away." Hearing silence, he says, "I'm just kidding, right? To get your goat, O.K.? Come on, let's put it back together, the next paper clip. Trouble with you, man, you're all the time married. Woman don't like a man who's nothin' but married, they want some soul that keeps 'em guessing, right? Woman stops guessing, she's dead."

Rabbit sits on the silverthread chair to read. "*Whence came the daring spirit necessary to grapple with a man who, eight-and-forty hours before, could, with the slightest word, have made me tremble like a leaf in a storm, I do not know; at any rate, I was resolved to fight, and what was better still, I actually was hard at it. The fighting madness had come upon me, and I found my strong fingers firmly attached to the throat of the tyrant, as heedless of consequences, at the moment, as if we stood equals before the law. The very color of the man was forgotten. I felt supple as a cat, and was ready for him at every turn. Every blow of his was parried, though I dealt no blows in return. I was strictly on the defensive, preventing him from injuring me, rather than trying to injure him. I flung him on the ground several times when he meant to have hurled me there. I held him so firmly by the throat that his blood followed my nails. He held me, and I held him.*"

"Oh I love it, it grabs me, it kills me," Skeeter says, and he gets up on one elbow so his body confronts the other man's. "Do me one more. Just one more bit."

"I gotta get upstairs."

"Skip a couple pages, go to the place I marked with double lines."

"Why doncha read it to yourself?"

"It's not the same, right? Doin' it to yourself. Every school kid knows that, it's not the same. Come on, Chuck. I been pretty good, right? I ain't caused no trouble, I been a faithful Tom, give the Tom a bone, read it like I say. I'm gonna take off all my clothes, I want to hear it with my pores. Sing it, man. Do it. Begin up a little, where it goes *A man without force.*" He prompts again, "*A man without force,*" and is fussing with his belt buckle.

"*A man without force,*" Rabbit intently reads, "*is without the essential dignity of humanity. Human nature is so constituted, that it cannot honor a helpless man, though it can pity him, and even this it cannot do long if signs of power do not arise.*"

"Yes," Skeeter says, and the blur of him is scuffling and

slithering, and a patch of white flashes from the sofa, above the white of the printed page.

"*He can only understand,*" Rabbit reads, finding the words huge, each one a black barrel his voice echoes in, "*the effect of this combat on my spirit, who has himself incurred something, or hazarded something, in repelling the unjust and cruel aggressions of a tyrant. Covey was a tyrant and a cowardly one withal. After resisting him, I felt as I had never felt before.*"

"Yes," Skeeter's voice calls from the abyss of the unseen beyond the rectangular island of the page.

"*It was a resurrection from the dark and pestiferous tomb of slavery, to the heaven of comparative freedom. I was no longer a servile coward, trembling under the frown of a brother worm of the dust, but my long-cowed spirit was roused to an attitude of independence. I had reached a point at which I was* not afraid to die." Emphasis.

"Oh yes. Yes."

"*This spirit made me a freeman in* fact, *though I still remained a slave in* form. *When a slave cannot be flogged, he is more than half free.*"

"A-men."

"*He has a domain as broad as his own manly heart to defend, and he is really 'a power on earth.'* "

"Say it. Say it."

"*From this time until my escape from slavery, I was never fairly whipped. Several attempts were made, but they were always unsuccessful. Bruised I did get, but the instance I have described was the end of the brutification to which slavery had subjected me.*"

"Oh, you do make one lovely nigger," Skeeter sings.

Lifting his eyes from the page, Rabbit sees there is no longer a patch of white on the sofa, it is solidly dark, only moving in a whispering rhythm that wants to suck him forward. His eyes do not dare follow down to the hand the live line of reflected light lying the length of Skeeter's rhythmic arm. Long as an eel, feeding. Rabbit stands and strides from the room, dropping the book as if hot, though the burning eyes of the stippled Negro on the cover are quick to follow him across the hard carpet, up the varnished stairs, into the white realm where an overhead frosted fixture burns on the landing. His heart is hammering hard.

*   *   *

Light from the driftwood lamp downstairs floods the little maple from underneath, its leaves red like your fingers on a flashlight face. Its turning head half-fills their bedroom window. In bed Jill turns to him pale and chill as ice. "Hold me," she says. "Hold me, hold me, hold me," so often it frightens him. Women are crazy, they contain this ancient craziness, he is holding wind in his arms. He feels she wants to be fucked, any way, without pleasure, but to pin her down. He would like to do this for her but he cannot pierce the fright, the disgust between them. She is a mermaid gesturing beneath the skin of the water. He is floating rigid to keep himself from sinking in terror. The book he has read aloud torments him with a vision of bottomless squalor, of dead generations, of buried tortures and lost reasons. Rising, working, there is no reason any more, no reason for anything, no reason why not, nothing to breathe but a sour gas bottled in empty churches, nothing to rise by; he lives in a tight well whose dank sides squeeze and paralyze him, no, it is Jill tight against him, trying to get warm, though the night is hot. He asks her, "Can you sleep?"

"No. Everything is crashing."

"Let's try. It's late. Shall I get another blanket?"

"Don't leave me for even a second. I'll fall through."

"I'll turn my back, then you can hug me."

Downstairs, Skeeter flicks the light off. Outside, the little maple vanishes like a blown-out flame. Within himself, Rabbit completes his motion into darkness, into the rhythmic brown of the sofa. Then terror returns and squeezes him shut like an eyelid.

Her voice sounds tired and wary, answering. "Brewer Fealty, Mrs. Fosnacht. May I help you?"

"Peggy? Hi, it's Harry Angstrom."

"So it is." A new sarcastic note. "I *don't* believe it!" Overexpressive. Too many men.

"Hey, remember you said about Nelson and Billy going fishing this Sunday and inviting me for Saturday dinner?"

"Yes, Harry, I do remember."

"Is it too late? For me to accept?"

"Not at all. What's brought this about?"

"Nothing special. Just thought it might be nice."

"It will be nice. I'll see you Saturday."

"Tomorrow," he clarifies. He would have talked on, it was his lunch hour, but she cuts the conversation short. Press of work. Don't count your chickens.

After work as he walks home from the bus stop on Weiser, two men accost him, at the corner where Emberly Avenue becomes a Drive, beside a red-white-and-blue mailbox. "Mr. Angstrom?"

"Sure."

"Might we talk to you a minute? We're two of your neighbors." The man speaking is between forty and fifty, plump, in a gray suit that has stretched to fit him, with those narrow lapels of five years ago. His face is soft but pained. A hard little hook nose at odds with the puffy patches below his eyes. His chin is two damp knobs set side by side, between them a dimple where the whiskers hide from the razor. He has that yellow Brewer tint and an agile sly white-collar air. An accountant, a schoolteacher. "My name is Mahlon Showalter. I live on the other side of Vista Crescent, the house, you probably noticed, with the new addition in back we added on last summer."

"Oh, yeah." He recalls distant hammering but had not noticed; he really only looks at Penn Villas enough to see that it isn't Mt. Judge: that is, it is nowhere.

"I'm in computers, the hardware end," Showalter says. "Here's my card." As Rabbit glances at the company name on it Showalter says, "We're going to revolutionize business in this town, file that name in your memory. This here is Eddie Brumbach, he lives around the further crescent, Marigold, up from you."

Eddie presents no card. He is black-haired, shorter and younger than Harry. He stands the way guys in the Army used to, all buttoned in, shoulders tucked back, an itch for a fight between their shoulder blades. Only in part because of his brush cut, his head looks flattened on top, like the heads on Rabbit's television set. When he shakes hands, it reminds him of somebody else. Who? One side of Brumbach's face has had a piece of jawbone removed, leaving a dent and an L-shaped red scar. Gray eyes like dulled tool tips. He says with ominous simplicity, "Yessir."

Showalter says, "Eddie works in the assembly shop over at Fessler Steel."

"You guys must have quit work early today," Rabbit says.

Eddie tells him, "I'm on night shift this month."

Showalter has a way of bending, as if dance music is playing far away and he wants to cut in between Rabbit and Eddie. He is saying, "We made a decision to talk to you, we appreciate your patience. This is my car here, would you like to sit in it? It's not too comfortable, standing out like this."

The car is a Toyota; it reminds Harry of his father-in-law and gets a whole set of uneasy feelings sliding. "I'd just as soon stand," he says, "if it won't take long," and leans on the mailbox to make himself less tall above these men.

"It won't take long," Eddie Brumbach promises, hitching his shoulders and coming a crisp step closer.

Showalter dips his shoulder again as if to intervene, looks sadder around the eyes, wipes his soft mouth: "Well no, it needn't. We don't mean to be unfriendly, we just have a few questions."

"Friendly questions," Rabbit clarifies, anxious to help this man, whose careful slow voice is pure Brewer; who seems, like the city, bland and broad and kind, and for the time being depressed.

"Now some of us," Showalter goes on, "were discussing, you know, the neighborhood. Some of the kids have been telling us stories, you know, about what they see in your windows."

"They've been looking in my windows?" The mailbox blue is hot; he stops leaning and stands. Though it is October the sidewalk has a flinty glare and a translucent irritability rests upon the pastel asphalt rooftops, the spindly young trees, the low houses like puzzles assembled of wood and cement and brick and fake-fieldstone siding. He is trying to look through these houses to his own, to protect it.

Brumbach bristles, thrusts himself into Rabbit's attention. "They haven't had to look in any windows, they've had what's going on pushed under their noses. And it don't smell good."

Showalter intervenes, his voice wheedling like a woman's, buttering over. "No now, that's putting it too strong. But it's true, I guess, there hasn't been any particular secret. They've been coming and going in that little Porsche right along, and I notice now he plays basketball with the boy right out front."

"He?"

"The black fella you have living with you," Showalter says, smiling as if the snag in their conversation has been discovered, and all will be clear sailing now.

"And the white girl," Brumbach adds. "My younger boy came home the other day and said he saw them screwing right on the downstairs rug."

"Well," Rabbit says, stalling. He feels absurdly taller than these men, he feels he might float away while trying to make out the details of what the boy had seen, a little framed rectangle hung in his head like a picture too high on the wall. "That's the kind of thing you see, when you look in other people's windows."

Brumbach steps neatly in front of Showalter, and Rabbit remembers who his handshake had been reminiscent of: the doctor giving Mom the new pills. *I twist bodies to my will. I am life, I am death.* "Listen, brother. We're trying to raise children in this neighborhood."

"Me too."

"And that's something else. What kind of pervert are you bringing up there? I feel sorry for the boy, it's the fact, I do. But what about the rest of us, who are trying to do the best we can? This is a decent white neighborhood," he says, hitting "decent" weakly but gathering strength for, "that's why we live here instead of across the river over in Brewer where they're letting 'em run wild."

"Letting who run wild?"

"You know fucking well who, read the papers, these old ladies can't even go outdoors in broad daylight with a pocketbook."

Showalter, supple, worried, sidles around and intrudes himself. "White neighborhood isn't exactly the point, we'd welcome a self-respecting black family, I went to school with blacks and I'd work right beside one any day of the week, in fact my company has a recruitment program, the trouble is, their own leaders tell them not to bother, tell them it's a sellout, to learn how to make an honest living." This speech has slid further than he had intended; he hauls it back. "If he acts like a man I'll treat him like a man, am I way out of line on that, Eddie?"

Brumbach puffs up so his shirt pocket tightens on his cigarette pack; his forearms bend at his sides as if under the pull of their veins. "I fought beside the colored in Vietnam," he says. "No problems."

"Hey that's funny you're a Viet veteran too, this guy we're kind of talking about –"

"No problems," Brumbach goes on, "because we all knew the rules."

Showalter's hands glide, flutter, touch his narrow lapels in a double downward caress. "It's the girl and the black together," he says quickly, to touch it and get away.

Brumbach says, "Christ those boogs love white ass. You should have seen what went on around the bases."

Rabbit offers, "That was yellow ass, wasn't it? Gook ass?"

Showalter tugs at his arm and takes him aside, some steps from the mailbox. Harry wonders if anybody ever mails a letter in it, he passes it every day and it seems mysterious as a fire hydrant, waiting for its moment that may never come. He never hears it clang. In Mt. Judge people were always mailing Valentines. Brumbach at his little distance stared into space, at TV-aerial level, knowing he's being discussed. Showalter says, "Don't keep riding him."

Rabbit calls over to Brumbach, "I'm not riding you, am I?"

Showalter tugs harder, so Harry has to bend his ear to the man's little beak and soft unhappy mouth. "He's not that stable. He feels very threatened. It wasn't my idea to get after you, I said to him, The man has his rights of privacy."

Rabbit tries to play the game, whispers. "How many more in the neighborhood feel like him?"

"More than you'd think. I was surprised myself. These are reasonable good people, but they have blind spots. I believe if they didn't have children, if this wasn't a children's neighborhood, it'd be more live and let live."

But Rabbit worries they are being rude to Brumbach. He calls over, "Hey, Eddie. I tell you what."

Brumbach is not pleased to be called in; he had wanted Showalter to settle. Rabbit sees the structure: one man is the negotiator, the other is the muscle. Brumbach barks, "What?"

"I'll keep my kid from looking in your windows, and you keep yours from looking in mine."

"We had a name over there for guys like you. Wiseass. Sometimes just by mistake they got fragged."

"I'll tell you what else," Rabbit says. "As a bonus, I'll try to remember to draw the curtains."

"You better do fucking more than pull the fucking curtains," Brumbach tells him, "you better fucking barricade the place."

Out of nowhere a mail truck, red, white, and blue, with a canted windshield like a display case, squeaks to a stop at the curb; hurriedly, not looking at any of them, a small man in gray unlocks the mailbox front and scoops a torrent, hundreds it seems, of letters into a gray sack, locks it shut, and drives away.

Rabbit goes close to Brumbach. "Tell me what you want. You want me to move out of the neighborhood."

"Just move the black out."

"It's him and the girl together you don't like; suppose he stays and the girl goes?"

"The black goes."

"He goes when he stops being my guest. Have a nice supper."

"You've been warned."

Rabbit asks Showalter, "You hear that threat?"

Showalter smiles, he wipes his brow, he is less depressed. He has done what he could. "I told you," he says, "not to ride him. We came to you in all politeness. I want to repeat, it's the circumstances of what's going on, not the color of anybody's skin. There's a house vacant abutting me and I told the realtor, I said as plain as I say to you, 'Any colored family, with a husband in the house, can get up the equity to buy it at the going market price, let them have it by all means. By all means.' "

"It's nice to meet a liberal," Rabbit says, and shakes his hand.

"My wife keeps telling me I'm a conservative."

And, because he likes him, because he likes anybody who fought in Vietnam where he himself should have been fighting, had he not been too old, too old and fat and cowardly, he offers to shake Brumbach's hand too.

The cocky little man keeps his arms stiff at his sides. Instead he turns his head, so the ruined jaw shows. The scar is not just a red L, Rabbit sees it is an ampersand, complicated by faint lines where skin was sewn and overlapped to repair a hole that would always be, that would always repel eyes. Rabbit makes himself look at it. Brumbach's voice is less explosive, almost regretful, sad in its steadiness. "I earned this face," he says. "I got it over there so I could have a decent life here. I'm not asking for sympathy, a lot of my buddies made out worse. I'm just letting you know, after what I seen and done, no wiseass is crowding me in my own neighborhood."

Inside the house, it is too quiet. The television isn't going. Nelson is doing homework at the kitchen table. No, he is reading one of Skeeter's books. He has not gotten very far. Rabbit asks, "Where are they?"

"Sleeping. Upstairs."

"Together?"

"I think Jill's on your bed, Skeeter's in mine. He says the sofa stinks. He was awake when I got back from school."

"How did he seem?"

Though the question touches a new vein, Nelson answers promptly. For all the shadows between them, they have lately grown toward each other, father and son. "Jumpy," he answers, into the book. "Said he was getting bad vibes lately and hadn't slept at all last night. I think he had taken some pills or something. He didn't seem to see me, looking over my head, kind of, and kept calling me Chuck instead of Babychuck."

"And how's Jill?"

"Dead asleep. I looked in and said her name and she didn't move. Dad —"

"Spit it out."

"He *gives* her things." The thought is too deep in him to get out easily; his eyes sink in after it, and his father feels him digging, shy, afraid, lacking the right words, not wanting to offend his father.

Harry prompts, "Things."

The boy rushes into it. "She never laughs any more, or takes any interest in anything, just sits around and sleeps. Have you looked at her skin, Dad? She's gotten so pale."

"She's naturally fair."

"Yeah, I know, but it's more than that, she looks *sick*. She doesn't eat hardly anything and throws up sometimes anyway. Dad, don't let him keep doing it to her, whatever it is. Stop him."

"How can I?"

"You can kick him out."

"Jill's said she'll go with him."

"She won't. She hates him too."

"Don't you like Skeeter?"

"Not really. I know I should. I know you do."

"I do?" Surprised, he promises Nelson, "I'll talk to him. But you know, people aren't property, I can't control what they want to do together. We can't live Jill's life for her."

"We *could*, if you wanted to. If you cared at all." This is as close as Nelson has come to defiance; Rabbit's instinct is to be gentle with this sprouting, to ignore it.

He points out simply, "She's too old to adopt. And you're too young to marry."

The child frowns down into the book, silent.

"Now tell me something."

"O.K." Nelson's face tenses, prepared to close; he expects to be asked about Jill and sex and himself. Rabbit is glad to disappoint him, to give him a little space here.

"Two men stopped me on the way home and said kids had been looking in our windows. Have you heard anything about this?"

"Sure."

"Sure what?"

"Sure they do."

"Who?"

"All of them. Frankhauser, and that slob Jimmy Brumbach, Evelyn Morris and those friends of hers from Penn Park, Mark Showalter and I guess his sister Marilyn though she's awful little –"

"When the hell do they do this?"

"Different times. When they come home from school and I'm at soccer practice, before you get home, they hang around. I guess sometimes they come back after dark."

"They see anything?"

"I guess sometimes."

"They talk to you about it? Do they tease you?"

"I guess. Sometimes."

"You poor kid. What do you tell 'em?"

"I tell 'em to fuck off."

"Hey. Watch your language."

"That's what I tell 'em. You asked."

"And do you have to fight?"

"Not much. Just sometimes when they call me something."

"What?"

"Something. Never mind, Dad."

"Tell me what they call you."

"Nigger Nellie."

"Huh. Nice kids."

"They're just kids, Dad. They don't mean anything. Jill says ignore them, they're ignorant."

"And do they kid you about Jill?"

The boy turns his face away altogether. His hair covers his neck, yet even from the back he would not be mistaken for a girl: the angles in the shoulders, the lack of brushing in the hair. The choked voice is manly: "I don't want to talk about it anymore; Dad."

"O.K. Thanks. Hey. I'm sorry. I'm sorry you have to live in the mess we all make."

The choked voice exclaims, "Gee I wish Mom would come back! I know it can't happen, but I wish it." Nelson thumps the back of the kitchen chair and then rests his forehead where his fist struck; Rabbit ruffles his hair, helplessly, on his way past, to the refrigerator to get a beer.

* * *

The nights close in earlier now. After the six-o'clock news there is darkness. Rabbit says to Skeeter, "I met another veteran from Vietnam today."

"Shit, the world's filling up with Nam veterans so fast there won't be nobody else soon, right? Never forget, got into a lighthouse up near Tuy Hoa, white walls all over, everybody been there one time or another and done their drawings. Well, what blew my mind, absolutely, was somebody, Charlie or the unfriendlies, Arvin never been near this place till we handed it to 'em, somebody on that other side had done a whole wall's worth of Uncle Ho himself, Uncle Ho being buggered, Uncle Ho shitting skulls, Uncle Ho doing this and that, it was downright disrespectful, right? And I says to myself, those poor dinks being screwed the same as us, we is all in the grip of crazy old men thinkin' they can still make history happen. History isn't going to happen any more, Chuck."

"What is going to happen?" Nelson asks.

"A bad mess," Skeeter answers, "then, most probably, Me."

Nelson's eyes seek his father's, as they do now when Skeeter's craziness shows. "Dad, shouldn't we wake up Jill?"

Harry is into his second beer and his first joint; his stockinged feet are up on the cobbler's bench. "Why? Let her sleep. Don't be so uptight."

"No suh," Skeeter says, "the boy has a good plan there, where is that fucking little Jill? I do feel horny."

Nelson asks, "What's horny?"

"Horny is what I feel," Skeeter answers. "Babychuck, go drag down that no-good cunt. Tell her the menfolk needs their vittles."

"Dad —"

"Come on, Nellie, quit nagging. Do what he asks. Don't you have any homework? Do it upstairs, this is a grown-up evening."

When Nelson is gone, Rabbit can breathe. "Skeeter, one thing I don't understand, how do you feel about the Cong? I mean are they right, or wrong, or what?"

"Man by man, or should I say gook by gook, they are very beautiful, truly. So brave they must be tripping, and a lot of them no older than little Nellie, right? As a bunch, I never could dig what they was all about, except that we was white or black as the case may be, and they was yellow, and had got there first, right? Otherwise I can't say they made a great deal of sense, since the people they most liked to castrate and string up and bury in ditches alive and make that kind of scene with was yellow like them, right? So I would consider them one more facet of the confusion of false prophecy by which you may recognize My coming in this the full-ness of time. However. However, I confess that politics being part of this boring power thing do not much turn me on. Things human turn me on, right? You too, right, Chuck? Here she is."

Jill has drifted in. Her skin looks tight on her face.

Rabbit asks her, "Hungry? Make yourself a peanut-butter sandwich. That's what we had to do."

"I'm not hungry."

Trying to be Skeeter, Rabbit goads her. "Christ, you should be. You're skinny as a stick. What the hell kind of piece of ass are you, there's nothing there anymore? Why you think we keep you here?"

She ignores him and speaks to Skeeter. "I'm in need," she tells him.

"Shee-yut, girl, we're all in need, right? The whole world's in need, isn't that what we done agreed on, Chuck? The whole benighted world is in need of Me. And Me, I'm in need of some-thing else. Bring your cunt over here, white girl."

Now she does look toward Rabbit. He cannot help her. She has always been out of his class. She sits down on the sofa beside Skeeter and asks him gently, "What? If I do it, will you do it?"

"Might. Tell you what, Jill honey. Let's do it for the man."

"What man?"

"*The* man. That man. Victor Charlie over there. He wants it. What you think he's keepin' us here for? To *breed*, that's what for. Hey. Friend Harry?"

"I'm listening."

"You like being a nigger, don't ya?"

"I do."

"You want to be a good nigger, right?"

"Right." The sad rustling on the ceiling, of Nelson in his room, feels far distant. Don't come down. Stay up there. The smoke mixes with his veins and his lungs are a branching tree.

"O.K.," Skeeter says. "Now here's how. You is a big black man sittin' right there. You is chained to that chair. And I, I is white as snow. Be-hold." And Skeeter, with that electric scuttling suddenness, stands, and pulls off his shirt. In the room's deep dusk his upper half disappears. Then he scrabbles at himself at belt-level and his lower half disappears. Only his glasses remain, silver circles. His voice, disembodied, is the darkness. Slowly his head, a round cloud, tells against the blue light from the streetlamp at the end of the Crescent. "And this little girl here," he calls, "is black as coal. An ebony virgin torn from the valley of the river Niger, right? Stand up, honey, show us your teeth. Turn clean around." The black shadows of his hands glide into the white blur Jill is, and guide it upward, as a potter guides a lump of clay upward on the humming wheel, into a vase. She keeps rising, smoke from the vase. Her dress is being lifted over her head. "Turn around, honey, show us your rump." A soft slap gilds the darkness, the whiteness revolves. Rabbit's eyes, enlarged, can sift out shades of light and dark, can begin to model the bodies six feet from him, across the cobbler's bench. He can see the dark crack between Jill's buttocks, the faint dent her hip muscle makes, the shadowy mane between her starved hipbones. Her belly looks long. Where her breasts should be, black spiders are fighting: he sorts these out as Skeeter's hands. Skeeter is whispering to Jill, murmuring, while his hands flutter like bats against the moon. He hears her say, in a voice sifted through her hair, a sentence with the word "satisfy" in it.

Skeeter cackles: forked lightning. "Now," he sings, and his voice has become golden hoops spinning forward, an auctioneer who is a juggler, "we will have a demon-stray-shun of o-bee-deeyance, from this little coal-black lady, who has been broken in by expert traders working out of Nashville, Tennessee, and who is guaranteed by them ab-so-lutily to give no trouble in the kitchen, hallway, stable *or* bedroom!" Another soft slap, and the white clay dwindles; Jill is kneeling, while Skeeter still stands. A most delicate slipping silvery sound touches up the silence now;

but Rabbit cannot precisely see. He needs to see. The drift-wood lamp is behind him. Not turning his head, he gropes and switches it on.

Nice.

What he sees reminds him, in the first flash, of the printing process, an inked plate contiguous at some few points to white paper. As his eyes adjust, he sees Skeeter is not black, he is a gentle brown. These are smooth-skinned children being gently punished, one being made to stand and the other to kneel. Skeeter crouches and reaches down a long hand, fingernails like baby rose petals, to shield Jill's profile from the glare. Her eyelids remain closed, her mouth remains open, her breasts cast no shadow they are so shallow, she is feminine most in the swell of her backside spread on her propping heels and in the white lily of a hand float-ing beside his balls as if to receive from the air a baton. An inch or two of Skeeter's long cock is un-enclosed by her face, a purplish inch bleached to lilac, below his metallic pubic explosion, the shape and texture of his goatee. Keeping his protective crouch, Skeeter turns his face sheepishly toward the light; his eyeglasses glare opaquely and his upper lip lifts in imitation of pain. "Hey man, what's with that? Cut that light."

"You're beautiful," Rabbit says.

"O.K., strip and get into it, she's full of holes, right?"

"I'm scared to," Rabbit confesses: it is true, they seem not only beautiful but in the same vision an interlocked machine that might pull him apart.

Though the slap of light left her numb, this confession pierces Jill's trance; she turns her head, Skeeter's penis falling free, a bright string of moisture breaking. She looks at Harry, past him; as he reaches to switch off the light mercifully, she screams. In the cor-ner of his vision, he saw it too: a face. At the window. Eyes like two cigarette burns. The lamp is out, the face is vanished. The window is a faintly blue rectangle in a black room. Rabbit runs to the front door and opens it. The night air bites. October. The lawn looks artificial, lifeless, dry, no-color: a snapshot of grass. Vista Crescent stretches empty but for parked cars. The maple is too slender to hide anyone. A child might have made it across the front of the house along the flowerbeds and be now in the garage.

The garage door is up. And, if the child is Nelson, a door from the garage leads into the kitchen. Rabbit decides not to look, not to give chase; he feels that there is no space for him to step into, that the vista before him is a flat, stiff, cold photograph. The only thing that moves is the vapor of his breathing. He closes the door. He hears nothing move in the kitchen. He tells the living room, "Nobody."

"Bad," Skeeter says. His prick has quite relaxed, a whip between his legs as he squats. Jill is weeping on the floor; face down, she has curled her naked body into a knot. Her bottom forms the top half of a valentine heart, only white; her flesh-colored hair fans spilled over the sullen green carpet. Rabbit and Skeeter together squat to pick her up. She fights it, she makes herself roll over limply; her hair streams across her face, clouds her mouth, adheres like cobwebs to her chin and throat. A string as of milkweed spittle is on her chin; Rabbit wipes her chin and mouth with his handkerchief and, for weeks afterward, when all is lost, will take out this handkerchief and bury his nose in it, in its scarcely detectable smell of distant ocean.

Jill's lips are moving. She is saying, "You promised. You promised." She is talking to Skeeter. Though Rabbit bends his big face over hers, she has eyes only for the narrow black face beside him. There is no green in her eyes, the black pupils have eclipsed the irises. "It's such dumb hell," she says, with a little whimper, as if to mock her own complaint, a Connecticut housewife who knows she exaggerates. "Oh Christ," she adds in an older voice and shuts her eyes. Rabbit touches her; she is sweating. At his touch, she starts to shiver. He wants to blanket her, to blanket her with his body if there is nothing else, but she will talk only to Skeeter. Rabbit is not there for her, he only thinks he is here.

Skeeter asks down into her, "Who's your Lord Jesus, Jill honey?"

"You are."

"I am, right?"

"Right."

"You love me more'n you love yourself?"

"Much more."

"What do you see when you look at me, Jill honey?"

"I don't know."

"You see a giant lily, right?"

"Right. You promised."

"Love my cock?"

"Yes."

"Love my jism, sweet Jill? Love it in your veins?"

"Yes. Please. Shoot me. You promised."

"I your Savior, right? Right?"

"You promised. You must. Skeeter."

"O.K. Tell me I'm your Savior."

"You are. Hurry. You did promise."

"O.K." Skeeter explains hurriedly. "I'll fix her up. You go upstairs, Chuck. I don't want you to see this."

"I want to see it."

"Not this. It's bad, man. Bad, bad, bad. It's shit. Stay clean, you in deep enough trouble on account of me without being party to this, right? Split. I'm begging, man."

Rabbit understands. They are in country. They have taken a hostage. Everywhere out there, there are unfriendlies. He checks the front door, staying down below the three windows echoing the three chime-tones. He sneaks into the kitchen. Nobody is there. He slips the bolt across, in the door that opens from the garage. Sidling to make his shadow narrow, he climbs upstairs. At Nelson's door he listens for the sound of unconscious breathing. He hears the boy's breath rasp, touching bottom. In his own bed-room, the streetlamp prints negative spatters of the maple leaves on his wallpaper. He gets into bed in his underwear, in case he must rise and run; as a child, in summer, he would have to sleep in his underwear when the wash hadn't dried on the line. Rabbit listens to the noises downstairs – clicking, clucking kitchen noises, of a pan being put on the stove, of a bit of glass clinking, of footsteps across the linoleum, the sounds that have always made him sleepy, of Mom up, of the world being tended to. His thoughts begin to dissolve, though his heart keeps pounding, waves breaking on Jill's white valentine, stamped on his retinas like the sun. Offset versus letterpress, offset never has the bite of the other, looks greasy, the wave of the future. She slips into bed beside him; her valentine nestles cool against his belly and silken limp cock. He has been asleep. He asks her, "Is it late?"

Jill speaks very slowly. "Pretty late."

"How do you feel?"

"Better. For now."

"We got to get you to a doctor."

"It won't help."

He has a better idea, so obvious he cannot imagine why he has never thought of it before. "We got to get you back to your father."

"You forget. He's dead."

"Your mother, then."

"The car's dead."

"We'll get it out of hock."

"It's too late," Jill tells him. "It's too late for you to try to love me."

He wants to answer, but there is a puzzling heavy truth in this that carries him under, his hand caressing the inward dip of her waist, a warm bird dipping toward its nest.

Sunshine, the old clown. So many maple leaves have fallen that morning light slants in baldly. A headache grazes his skull, his dream (Pajasek and he were in a canoe, paddling upstream, through a dark green country; their destination felt to be a distant mountain striped and folded like a tablecloth. "When can I have my silver bullet?" Rabbit asked him. "You promised." "Fool," Pajasek told him. "Stupid." "You know so much more," Rabbit answered, nonsensically, and his heart opened in a flood of light) merges with the night before, both unreal. Jill sleeps dewily beside him; at the base of her throat, along her hairline, sweat has collected and glistens. Delicately, not to disturb her, he takes her wrist and turns it so he can see the inside of her freckled arm. They might be bee-stings. There are not too many. He can talk to

Janice. Then he remembers that Janice is not here, and that only Nelson is their child. He eases from the bed, amused to discover himself in underwear, like those times when Mom had left his pajamas on the line to dry.

After breakfast, while Jill and Skeeter sleep, he and Nelson rake and mow the lawn, putting it to bed for the winter. He hopes this will be the last mowing, though in fact the grass, parched in high spots, is vigorously green where a depression holds moisture, and along a line from the kitchen to the street – perhaps the sewer connection is broken and seeping, that is why the earth of Penn Villas has a sweetish stink. And the leaves – he calls to Nelson, who has to shut off the razzing mower to listen, "How the hell does such a skinny little tree produce so many leaves?"

"They aren't all *its* leaves. They blow in from the other trees."

And he looks, and sees that his neighbors have trees, saplings like his, but some already as tall as the housetops. Someday Nelson may come back to this, his childhood neighborhood, and find it strangely dark, buried in shade, the lawns opulent, the homes venerable. Rabbit hears children calling in other yards, and sees across several fences and driveways kids having a Saturday scrimmage, one voice piping, "I'm free, I'm free," and the ball obediently floating. This isn't a bad neighborhood, he thinks, this could be a nice place if you gave it a chance. And around the other houses men with rakes and mowers mirror him. He asks Nelson, before the boy restarts the mower, "Aren't you going to visit your mother today?"

"Tomorrow. Today she and Charlie were driving up to the Poconos, to look at the foliage. They went with some brother of Charlie's and his wife."

"Boy, she's moving right in." A real Springer. He smiles to himself, perversely proud. The legal stationery must be on the way. And then he can join that army of the unattached, of Brewer geezers. Human garbage, Pop used to say. He better enjoy Vista Crescent while he has it. He resumes raking, and listens for the mower's razzing to resume. Instead, there is the lurch and rattle of the starter, repeated, and Nelson's voice calling, "Hey Dad. I think it's out of gas."

A Saturday, then, of small sunlit tasks, acts of caretaking and commerce. He and Nelson stroll with the empty five-gallon can up to Weiser Street and get it filled at the Getty station. Returning, they meet Jill and Skeeter emerging from the house, dressed to kill. Skeeter wears stovepipe pants, alligator shoes, a maroon turtleneck and a peach-colored cardigan. He looks like the newest thing in golf pros. Jill has on her mended white dress and a brown sweater of Harry's; she suggests a cheerleader, off to the noon pep rally before the football game. Her face, though thin, and the skin of it thin and brittle like isinglass, has a pink flush; she seems excited, affectionate. "There's some salami and lettuce in the fridge for you and Nelson to make lunch with if you want. Skeeter and I are going into Brewer to see what we can do about this wretched car. And we thought we might drop in on Babe. We'll be back late this after. Maybe you should visit your mother this afternoon, I feel guilty you never do."

"O.K., I might. You O.K.?" To Skeeter: "You have bus fare?"

In his clothes Skeeter puts on a dandy's accent; he thrusts out his goatee and says between scarcely parted teeth, "Jilly is loaded. And if we run short, your name is good credit, right?" Rabbit tries to recall the naked man of last night, the dangling penis, the jutting heels, the squat as by a jungle fire, and cannot; it was another terrain.

Serious, a daylight man, he scolds: "You better get back before Nelson and I go out around six. I don't want to leave the house empty." He drops his voice so Nelson won't hear. "After last night, I'm kind of spooked."

"What happened last night?" Skeeter asks. "Nothin' spooky that I can remember, we'se all jest folks, livin' out life in these Benighted States." He has put on all his armor, nothing will get to him.

Rabbit tests it: "You're a *baad* nigger."

Skeeter smiles in the sunshine with angelic rows of teeth; his spectacles toss halos higher than the TV aerials. "Now you're singing my song," he says.

Rabbit asks Jill, "You O.K. with this crazyman?"

She says lightly, "He's my sugar daddy," and puts her arm through his, and linked like that they recede down Vista Crescent, and vanish in the shuffle of picture windows.

Rabbit and Nelson finish the lawn. They eat, and toss a football around for a while, and then the boy asks if he can go off and
join the scrimmage whose shouts they can hear, he knows some
of the kids, the same kids who look into windows but that's O.K.,
Dad; and really it does feel as though all can be forgiven, all will
sink into Saturday's America like rain into earth, like days into
time. Rabbit goes into the house and watches the first game of the
World Series, Baltimore outclassing the Mets, for a while, and
switches to Penn State outclassing West Virginia at football, and,
unable to sit still any longer with the bubble of premonition
swelling inside him, goes to the phone and calls his home. "Hi
Pop, hey. I thought of coming over this after but the kid is outside playing a game and we have to go over to Fosnachts tonight
anyhow, so can she wait until tomorrow? Mom. Also I ought to
get hot on changing the screens around to storm windows, it felt
chilly last night."

"She can wait, Harry. Your mother does a lot of waiting these
days."

"Yeah, well." He means it's not his fault, he didn't invent old
age. "When is Mim coming in?"

"Any day now, we don't know the exact day. She'll just arrive,
is how she left it. Her old room is ready."

"How's Mom sleeping lately? She still having dreams?"

"Strange you should ask, Harry. I always said, you and your
mother are almost psychic. Her dreams are getting worse. She
dreamed last night we buried her alive. You and me and Mim
together. She said only Nelson tried to stop it."

"Gee, maybe she's warming up to Nelson at last."

"And Janice called us this morning."

"What about? I'd hate to have Stavros's phone bill."

"Difficult to say, what about. She had nothing concrete that
we could fathom, she just seems to want to keep in touch. I think
she's having terrible second thoughts, Harry. She says she's
exceedingly worried about you."

"I bet."

"Your mother and I spent a lot of time discussing her call;
you know our Mary, she's never one to admit when she's disturbed —"

"Pop, there's somebody at the door. Tell Mom I'll be over tomorrow, absolutely."

There had been nobody at the door. He had suddenly been unable to keep talking to his father, every word of the old man's dragging with reproach. But having lied frightens him now; "nobody" has become an evil presence at the door. Moving through the rooms stealthily, he searches the house for the kit Skeeter must use to fix Jill with. He can picture it from having watched television: the syringe and tourniquet and the long spoon to melt the powder in. The sofa cushions divulge a dollar in change, a bent paperback of *Soul on Ice*, a pearl from an earring or pocketbook. Jill's bureau drawers upstairs conceal nothing under the underwear but a box of Tampax, a packet of hairpins, a half-full card of Enovid pills, a shy little tube of ointment for acne. The last place he thinks to look is the downstairs closet, fitted into an ill-designed corner beside the useless fireplace, along the wall of stained pine where the seascape hangs that Janice bought at Kroll's complete with frame, one piece in fact with its frame, a single shaped sheet of plastic, Rabbit remembers from hanging it on the nail. In this closet, beneath the polyethylene bags holding their winter clothes, including the mink stole old man Springer gave Janice on her twenty-first birthday, there is a squat black suitcase, smelling new, with a combination lock. Packed so Skeeter could grab it and run from the house in thirty seconds. Rabbit fiddles with the lock, trying combinations at random, trusting to God to make a very minor miracle, then, this failing, going at it by system, beginning 111, 112, 113, 114, and then 211, 212, 213, but never hits it, and the practical infinity of numbers opens under him dizzyingly. Some dust in the closet starts him sneezing. He goes outdoors with the Windex bottle for the storm windows.

This work soothes him. You slide up the aluminum screen, putting the summer behind you, and squirt the inside window with the blue spray, give it those big square swipes to spread it thin, and apply the tighter rubbing to remove the film and with it the dirt; it squeaks, like birdsong. Then slide the winter window down from the slot where it has been waiting since April and repeat the process; and go inside and repeat the process, twice: so that at last four flawless transparencies permit outdoors to come indoors, other houses to enter yours.

Toward five o'clock Skeeter and Jill return, by taxi. They are jubilant; through Babe they found a man willing to give them six hundred dollars for the Porsche. He drove them up-county, he examined the car, and Jill signed the registration over to him.

"What color was he?" Rabbit asks.

"He was green," Skeeter says, showing him ten-dollar bills fanned in his hand.

Rabbit asks Jill, "Why'd you split it with *him?*"

Skeeter says, "I dig hostility. You want your cut, right?" His lips push, his glasses glint.

Jill laughs it off. "Skeeter's my partner in crime," she says.

"You want my advice, what you should do with that money?" Rabbit says. "You should get a train ticket back to Stonington."

"The trains don't run any more. Anyway, I thought I'd buy some new dresses. Aren't you tired of this ratty old white one? I had to pin it up in the front and wear this sweater over it."

"It suits you," he says.

She takes up the challenge in his tone. "Something bugging you?"

"Just your sloppiness. You're throwing your fucking life away."

"Would you like me to leave? I could now."

His arms go numb as if injected: his hands feel heavy, his palms tingly and swollen. Her nibbling mouth, her apple hardness, the sea-fan of her cedar-colored hair on their pillows in the morning light, her white valentine of packed satin. "No," he begs, "don't go yet."

"Why not?"

"You're under my skin." The phrase feels unnatural on his lips, puffs them like a dry wind in passing; it must have been spoken for Skeeter, for Skeeter cackles appreciatively.

"Chuck, you're learning to be a loser. I love it. The Lord loves it. Losers gonna grab the earth, right?"

Nelson returns from the football game with a bruised upper lip, his smile lopsided and happy. "They give you a hard time?" Rabbit asks.

"No, it was fun. Skeeter, you ought to play next Saturday, they asked who you were and I said you used to be a quarterback for Brewer High."

"Quarterback, shit, I was *full* back, I was so small they couldn't find me."

"I don't mind being small, it makes you quicker."

"O.K.," his father says, "see how quick you can take a bath. And for once in your life brush your hair."

Festively Jill and Skeeter see them off to the Fosnachts. Jill straightens Rabbit's tie, Skeeter dusts his shoulders like a Pullman porter. "Just think, honey," Skeeter says to Jill, "our little boy's all growed up, his first date."

"It's just dinner," Rabbit protests. "I'll be back for the eleven-o'clock news."

"That big honky with the sideways eyes, she may have something planned for dessert."

"You stay as late as you want," Jill tells him. "We'll leave the porch light on and won't wait up."

"What're *you* two going to do tonight?"

"Jes' read and knit and sit cozy by the fire," Skeeter tells him.

"Her number's in the book if you need to get ahold of me. Under just M."

"We won't disturb you," Jill tells him.

Nelson unexpectedly says, "Skeeter, lock the doors and don't go outside unless you have to."

The Negro pats the boy's brushed hair. "Wouldn't dream of it, chile. Ol' tarbaby, he just stay right here in his briar patch."

Nelson says suddenly, panicking, "Dad, we shouldn't go."

"Don't be dumb." They go. Orange sunlight stripes with long shadows the spaces of flat lawn between the low houses. As Vista Crescent curves, the sun moves behind them and Rabbit is struck, seeing their elongated shadows side by side, by how much like himself Nelson walks: the same loose lope below, the same faintly tense stillness of the head and shoulders above. In shadow the boy, like himself, is as tall as the giant at the top of the beanstalk, treading the sidewalk on telescoping legs. Rabbit turns to speak. Beside him, the boy's overlong dark hair bounces as he strides to keep up, lugging his pajamas and toothbrush and change of underwear and sweater in a paper grocery bag for tomorrow's boat ride, an early birthday party. Rabbit finds there is nothing to say, just mute love spinning down, love for this extension of himself downward into time when he will be in the grave, love cool as the flame of sunlight burning level among the stick-thin maples and fallen leaves, themselves flames curling.

And from Peggy's windows Brewer glows and dwindles like ashes in a gigantic hearth. The river shines blue long after the shores turn black. There is a puppy in the apartment now, a fuzzy big-pawed Golden that tugs at Rabbit's hand with a slippery nipping mouth; its fur, touched, is as surprising in its softness as ferns. Peggy has remembered he likes Daiquiris; this time she has mix and the electric blender rattles with ice before she brings him his drink, half froth. She has aged a month: a pound or two around her waist, two or three more gray hairs showing at her parting. She has gathered her hair back in a twist, rather than letting it straggle around her face as if she were still in high school. Her face looks pushed-forward, scrubbed, glossy. She tells him wearily, "Ollie and I may be getting back together."

She is wearing a blue dress, secretarial, that suits her more than that paisley that kept riding up her pasty thighs. "That's good, isn't it?"

"It's good for Billy." The boys, once Nelson arrived, went down the elevator again, to try to repair the mini-bike in the basement. "In fact, that's mostly the reason; Ollie is worried about Billy. With me working and not home until dark, he hangs around with that bad crowd up toward the bridge. You know, it's not like when we were young, the temptations they're exposed to. It's not just cigarettes and a little feeling up. At thirteen now, they're ready to go."

Harry brushes froth from his lips and wishes she would come away from the window so he could see all of the sky. "I guess they figure they might be dead at eighteen."

"Janice says you like the war."

"I don't like it; I defend it. I wasn't thinking of that, they have a lot of ways to die now we didn't have. Anyway, it's nice about you and Ollie, if it works out. A little sad, too."

"Why sad?"

"Sad for me. I mean, I guess I blew my chance, to —"

"To what?"

"To cash you in."

Bad phrase, too harsh, though it had been an apology. He has lived with Skeeter too long. But her blankness, the blankness of her silhouette as Peggy stands in her habitual pose against the windows, suggested it. A blank check. A woman is blank until you fuck her. Everything is blank until you fuck it. Us and Vietnam, fucking and being fucked, blood is wisdom. Must be some better way but it's not in nature. His silence is leaden with regret. She remains blank some seconds, says nothing. Then she moves into the space around him, turns on lamps, lifts a pillow into place, plumps it, stoops and straightens, turns, takes light upon her sides, is rounded into shape. A lumpy big woman but not a fat one, clumsy but not gross, sad with evening, with Ollie or not Ollie, with having a lengthening past and less and less future. Three classes behind his, Peggy Gring had gone to high school with Rabbit and had seen him when he was good, had sat in those hot bleachers screaming, when he was a hero, naked and swift and lean. She has seen him come to nothing. She plumps down in the chair beside his and says, "I've been cashed in a lot lately."

"You mean with Ollie?"

"Others. Guys I meet at work. Ollie minds. That may be why he wants back in."

"If Ollie minds, you must be telling him. So you must want him back in too."

She looks into the bottom of her glass; there is nothing there but ice. "And how about you and Janice?"

"Janice who? Let me get you another drink."

"Wow. You've become a gentleman."

"Slightly."

As he puts her gin-and-tonic into her hand, he says, "Tell me about those other guys."

"They're O.K. I'm not that proud of them. They're human. I'm human."

"You do it but don't fall in love?"

"Apparently. Is that terrible?"

"No," he says. "I think it's nice."

"You think a lot of things are nice lately."

"Yeah. I'm not so uptight. Sistah Peggeh, I'se seen de light."

The boys come back upstairs. They complain the new head-light they bought doesn't fit. Peggy feeds them, a casserole of chicken legs and breasts, poor dismembered creatures simmering. Rabbit wonders how many animals have died to keep his life going, how many more will die. A barnyard full, a farmful of thumping hearts, seeing eyes, racing legs, all stuffed squawking into him as into a black sack. No avoiding it: life does want death. To be alive is to kill. Dinner inside them, they stuff themselves on television: Jackie Gleason, *My Three Sons*, *Hogan's Heroes*, *Petticoat Junction*, *Mannix*. An orgy. Nelson is asleep on the floor, radio-active light beating on his closed lids and open mouth. Rabbit carries him into Billy's room, while Peggy tucks her own son in. "Mom, I'm not sleepy." "It's past bedtime." "It's Saturday night." "You have a big day tomorrow." "When is *he* going home?" He must think Harry has no ears. "When he wants to." "What are you going to do?" "Nothing that's any of your business." "*Mom*." "Shall I listen to your prayers?" "When he's not listening." " Then you say them to yourself tonight."

Harry and Peggy return to the living room and watch the week's news roundup. The weekend commentator is fairer-haired and less severe in expression than the weekday one. He says there has been some good news this week. American deaths in Vietnam were reported the lowest in three years, and one twenty-four-hour period saw no American battle deaths at all. The Soviet Union made headlines this week, agreeing with the U.S. to ban atomic weapons from the world's ocean floors, agreeing with Red China to hold talks concerning their sometimes bloody border disputes, and launching Soyuz 6, a linked three-stage space spectacular bringing closer the day of permanent space stations. In Washington, Hubert Humphrey endorsed Richard Nixon's handling of the Vietnam war and Lieutenant General Lewis B. Hershey, crusty and controversial head for twenty-eight years of this nation's selective service system, was relieved of his post and promoted to four-star general. In Chicago, riots outside the courtroom and riotous behavior within continued to charac-terize the trial of the so-called Chicago Eight. In Belfast,

Protestants and British troops clashed. In Prague, Czechoslovakia's revisionist government, in one of its sternest moves, banned citizens from foreign travel. And preparations were under way: for tomorrow's Columbus Day parades, despite threatened protests from Scandinavian groups maintaining that Leif Ericson and not Columbus was the discoverer of America, and for Wednesday's Moratorium Day, a nationwide outpouring of peaceful protest. "Crap," says Rabbit. Sports. Weather. Peggy rises awkwardly from her chair to turn it off. Rabbit rises, also stiff. "Great supper," he tells her. "I guess I'll get back to the ranch."

The television off, they stand rimmed by borrowed light: the bathroom door down the hall left ajar for the boys, the apartment-house corridor a bright slit beneath the door leading out, the phosphorescence of Brewer through the windows. Peggy's body, transected and rimmed by those remote fires, does not quite fit together; her arm jerks up from darkness and brushes indifferently at her hair and seems to miss. She shrugs, or shudders, and shadows slip from her. "Wouldn't you like," she asks, in a voice not quite hers, originating in the dim charged space between them, and lighter, breathier, "to cash me in?"

Yes, it turns out, yes he would, and they bump, and fumble, and unzip, and she is gumdrops everywhere, yet stately as a statue, planetary in her breadth, a contour map of some snowy land where he has never been; not since Ruth has he had a woman this big. Naked, she makes him naked, even kneeling to unlace his shoes, and then kneeling to him in the pose of Jill to Skeeter, so he has glided across a gulf, and stands where last night he stared. He gently unlinks her, lowers her to the floor, and tastes a salty swamp between her legs. Her thighs part easily, she grows wet readily, she is sadly unclumsy at this, she has indeed been to bed with many men. In the knowing way she handles his prick he feels their presences, feels himself competing, is put off, goes soft. She leaves off and comes up and presses the gumdrop of her tongue between his lips. Puddled on the floor, they keep knocking skulls and ankle bones on the furniture legs. The puppy, hearing their commotion, thinks they want to play and thrusts his cold nose and scrabbling paws among their sensitive flesh; his fern-furry busy bustlingness tickles and hurts. This third animal among them re-excites Rabbit; observing this, Peggy leads him down her hall, the dark crease between her buttocks snapping tick-tock with her walk. Holding her rumpled dress in front of her like a pad, she pauses at the boys' door, listens, and nods. Her hair has gone loose. The puppy for a while whimpers at their door and claws the floor as if to dig there; then he is eclipsed by the inflammation of their senses and falls silent beneath the thunder of their blood. Harry is afraid with this unknown woman, of timing her wrong, but she tells him, "One sec." Him inside her, she does something imperceptible, relaxing and tensing the muscles of her vagina, and announces breathily "Now." She comes one beat ahead of him, a cool solid thump of a come that lets him hit home without fear of hurting her: a fuck innocent of madness. Then slides in that embarrassment of afterwards – of returning discriminations, of the other re-emerging from the muddle, of sorting out what was hers and what was yours. He hides his face in the hot cave at the side of her neck. "Thank you."

"Thank you yourself," Peggy Fosnacht says, and, what he doesn't especially like, grabs his bottom to give her one more deep thrust before he softens. Both Jill and Janice too ladylike for that. Still, he is at home.

Until she says, "Would you mind rolling off? You're squeezing the breath out of me."

"Am I so heavy?"

"After a while."

"Actually, I better go."

"Why? It's only midnight."

"I'm worried about what they're doing back at the house."

"Nelson's here. The others, what do you care?"

"I don't know. I care."

"Well they don't care about you and you're in bed with someone who does."

He accuses her: "You're taking Ollie back."

"Have any better ideas? He's the father of my child."

"Well that's not my fault."

"No, nothing's your fault," and she tumbles around him, and they make solid sadly skillful love again, and they talk and he dozes a little, and the phone rings. It shrills right beside his ear.

A woman's arm, plump and elastic and warm, reaches across his face to pluck it silent. Peggy Gring's. She listens, and hands it to him with an expression he cannot read. There is a clock beside the telephone; its luminous hands say one-twenty. "Hey. Chuck? Better get your ass over here. It's bad. Bad."

"Skeeter?" His throat hurts, just speaking. Fucking Peggy has left him dry.

The voice at the other end hangs up.

Rabbit kicks out of the bedcovers and hunts in the dark for his clothes. He remembers. The living room. The boys' door opens as he runs down the hall naked. Nelson's astonished face takes in his father's nakedness. He asks, "Was it Mom?"

"Mom?"

"On the phone."

"Skeeter. Something's gone wrong at the house."

"Should I come?"

They are in the living room, Rabbit stooping to gather his clothes scattered over the floor, hopping to get into his underpants, his suit pants. The puppy, awake again, dances and nips at him.

"Better stay."

"What can it be, Dad?"

"No idea. Maybe the cops. Maybe Jill getting sicker."

"Why didn't he talk longer?"

"His voice sounded funny, I'm not sure it was our phone."

"I'm coming with you."

"I told you to stay here."

"I *must*, Dad."

Rabbit looks at him and agrees, "O.K. I guess you must."

Peggy in blue bathrobe is in the hall; more lights are on. Billy is up. His pajamas are stained yellow at the fly, he is pimply and tall. Peggy says, "Shall I get dressed?"

"No. You're great the way you are." Rabbit is having trouble with his tie: his shirt collar has a button in the back that has to be undone to get the tie under. He puts on his coat and stuffs the tie into his pocket. His skin is tingling with the start of sweat and his penis murmuringly aches. He has forgotten to do the laces of his shoes and as he kneels to do them his stomach jams into his throat.

"How will you get there?" Peggy asks.

"Run," Rabbit answers.

"Don't be funny, it's a mile and a half. I'll get dressed and drive you."

She must be told she is not his wife. "I don't want you to come. Whatever it is, I don't want you and Billy to get involved."

"Mo-*om*," Billy protests from the doorway. But he is still in stained pajamas whereas Nelson is dressed, but for bare feet. His sneakers are in his hand.

Peggy yields. "I'll get you my car keys. It's the blue Fury, the fourth slot in the line against the wall. Nelson knows. No, Billy. You and I will stay here." Her voice is factual, secretarial.

Rabbit takes the keys, which come into his hand as cold as if they have been in the refrigerator. "Thanks a lot. Or have I said that before? Sorry about this. Great dinner, Peggy."

"Glad you liked it."

"We'll let you know what's what. It's probably nothing, the son of a bitch is probably just stoned out of his mind."

Nelson has put his socks and sneakers on. "Let's *go*, Dad. Thank you very much, Mrs. Fosnacht."

"You're both very welcome."

"Thank Mr. Fosnacht in case I can't go on the boat tomorrow."

Billy is still trying. "Mo-*om*, let me."

"No."

"Mom, you're a bitch."

Peggy slaps her son: pink leaps up on his cheek in stripes like fingers, and the child's face hardens beyond further controlling. "Mom, you're a whore. That's what the bridge kids say. You'll lay anybody."

Rabbit says, "You two take it easy," and turns; they flee, father and son, down the hall, down the steel stairwell, not waiting for an elevator, to a basement of parked cars, a polychrome lake caught in a low illumined grotto. Rabbit blinks to realize that even while he and Peggy were heating their little mutual darkness a cold fluorescent world surrounded them in hallways and down stairwells and amid unsleeping pillars upholding their vast building. The universe is unsleeping, neither ants nor stars sleep, to die will be to be forever wide awake. Nelson finds the blue car for him. Its

dashlights glow green at ignition. Almost silently the engine comes
to life, backs them out, sneaks them along past the stained grotto
walls. In a corner by the brickwork of a stairwell the all-chrome
mini-bike waits to be repaired. An asphalt exitway becomes a
parking lot, becomes a street lined with narrow houses and great
green signs bearing numbers, keystones, shields, the names of unat-
tainable cities. They come onto Weiser; the traffic is thin, sinister.
The stoplights no longer regulate but merely wink. Burger Bliss is
closed, though its purple oven glows within, plus a sallow residue
of ceiling tubes to discourage thieves and vandals. A police car nips
by, bleating. The Acme lot at this hour has no horizon. Are
the few cars still parked on it abandoned? Or lovers? Or ghosts
in a world so thick with cars their shadows like leaves settle
everywhere? A whirling light, insulting in its brilliance, materializes in Rabbit's rear-view mirror and as it swells acquires the
overpowering grief of a siren. The red bulk of a fire engine plunges
by, sucking the Fury toward the center of the street, where the
trolley-track bed used to be. Nelson cries, "Dad!"
    "Dad what?"
    "Nothing, I thought you lost control."
    "Never. Not your Dad."
    The movie marquee, unlit and stubby, is announcing, BACK BY
REQST – 2001. All these stores along Weiser have burglar lights on
and a few, a new defense, wear window grilles.
    "Dad, there's a glow in the sky."
    "Where?"
    "Off to the right."
    He says, "That can't be us. Penn Villas is more ahead."
    But Emberly Avenue turns right more acutely than he had ever
noticed, and the curving streets of Penn Villas do deliver them
toward a dome of rose-colored air. People, black shapes, race on
silent footsteps, and cars have run to a stop diagonally against the
curbs. Down where Emberly meets Vista Crescent, a policeman
stands, rhythmically popping into brightness as the twirling fire-
engine lights pass over him. Harry parks where he can drive no
further and runs down Vista, after Nelson. Fire hoses lie across the
asphalt, some deflated like long canvas trouser legs and some fat as
cobras, jetting hissingly from their joints. The gutter gnashes with

swirling black water and matted leaves; around the sewer drain, a whirlpool widens out from the clogged center. Two houses from their house, they encounter an odor akin to leaf-smoke but more acrid and bitter, holding paint and tar and chemicals; one house away, the density of people stops them. Nelson sinks into the crowd and vanishes. Rabbit shoulders after him, apologizing, "Excuse me, this is my house, pardon me, my house." He says this but does not yet believe it. His house is masked from him by heads, by searchlights and upward waterfalls, by rainbows and shouts, by something magisterial and singular about the event that makes it as hard to see as the sun. People, neighbors, part to let him through. He sees. The garage is gone; the charred studs still stand, but the roof has collapsed and the shingles smolder with spurts of blue-green flame amid the drenched wreckage on the cement floor. The handle of the power mower pokes up intact. The rooms nearest the garage, the kitchen and the bedroom above it, the bedroom that had been his and Janice's and then his and Jill's, flame against the torrents of water. Flame sinks back, then bursts out again, through roof or window, in tongues. The apple-green aluminum clapboards do not themselves burn; rather, they seem to shield the fire from the water. Abrupt gaps in the shifting weave of struggling elements let shreds show through of the upstairs wallpaper, of the kitchen shelves; then these gaps shut at a breath of wind. He scans the upstairs window for Jill's face, but glimpses only the stained ceiling. The roof above, half the roof, is a field of smoke, smoke bubbling up and coming off the shadow-line shingles in serried billows that look combed. Smoke pours out of Nelson's windows, but that half of the house is not yet aflame, and may be saved. Indeed, the house burns spitefully, spitting, stinkingly: the ersatz and synthetic materials grudge combustion its triumph. Once in boyhood Rabbit saw a barn burn in the valley east of Mt. Judge; it was a torch, an explosion of hay outstarring the sky with embers. Here there is no such display.

There is space around him. The spectators, the neighbors, in honor of his role, have backed off. Months ago Rabbit had seen that bright island of moviemakers and now he is at the center of this bright island and still feels peripheral, removed, nostalgic, numb. He scans the firelit faces and does not see Showalter or Brumbach. He sees no one he knows.

The crowd stirs, *ooh*. He expects to see Jill at the window, ready to leap, her white dress translucent around her body. But the windows let only smoke escape, and the drama is on the ground. A policeman is struggling with a slight lithe figure; Harry thinks eagerly, *Skeeter*, but the struggle pivots, and it is Nelson's white face. A fireman helps pin the boy's arms. They bring him away from the house, to his father. Seeing his father, Nelson clamps shut his eyes and draws his lips back in a snarl and struggles so hard to be free that the two men holding his arms seem to be wildly operating pump handles. "She's *in* there, Dad!"

The policeman, breathing hard, explains, "Boy tried to get into the house. Says there's a girl in there."

"I don't know, she must have gotten out. We just got here."

Nelson's eyes are frantic; he screeches everything. "Did Skeeter *say* she was with *him?*"

"No." Harry can hardly get the words out. "He just said things were bad."

In listening, the fireman and policeman loosen their grip, and Nelson breaks away to run for the front door again. Heat must meet him, for he falters at the porchlet steps, and he is seized again, by men whose slickers make them seem beetles. This time, brought back, Nelson screams up at Harry's face: "You fucking asshole, you've let her die. I'll kill you. I'll kill *you*." And, though it is his son, Harry crouches and gets his hands up ready to fight.

But the boy cannot burst the grip of the men; he tells them in a voice less shrill, arguing for his release, "I know she's in there. Let me go, please. Please let me go. Just let me get her out, I know I can. I *know* I can. She'd be upstairs asleep. She'd be easy to lift. Dad, I'm sorry. I'm sorry I swore at you. I didn't mean it. Tell them to let me. Tell them about Jill. Tell them to get her out."

Rabbit asks the firemen, "Wouldn't she have come to the window?"

The fireman, an old rodent of a man, with tufty eyebrows and long yellow teeth, ruminates as he talks. "Girl asleep in there, smoke might get to her before she properly woke up. People don't realize what a deadly poison smoke is. That's what does you in, the smoke not the fire." He asks Nelson, "O.K. to let go, sonny? Act your age now, we'll send men up the ladder."

One beetle-backed fireman chops at the front door. The glass from the three panes shatters and tinkles on the flagstones. Another fireman emerges from the other side of the roof and with his ax picks a hole above the upstairs hall, about where Nelson's door would be. Something invisible sends him staggering back. A violet flame shoots up. A cannonade of water chases him back over the roof ridge.

"They're not doing it right, Dad," Nelson moans. "They're not getting her. I know where she is and they're not *get*ting her, Dad!" And the boy's voice dies in a shuddering wail. When Rabbit reaches toward him he pulls away and hides his face. The back of his head feels soft beneath the hair: an overripe fruit.

Rabbit reassures him, "Skeeter would've gotten her out."

"He *would*n't of, Dad! He wouldn't *care*. All he cared about was *himself*. And all you cared about was *him*. Nobody cared about *Jill*." He writhes in his father's fumbling grasp.

A policeman is beside them. "You Angstrom?" He is one of the new style of cops, collegiate-looking: pointed nose, smooth chin, sideburns cut to a depth Rabbit still thinks of as antisocial.

"Yes."

The cop takes out a notebook. "How many persons were in residence here?"

"Four. Me and the kid —"

"Name?"

"Nelson."

"Any middle initial?"

"F for Frederick." The policeman writes slowly and speaks so softly he is hard to hear against the background of crowd murmur and fire crackle and water being hurled. Harry has to ask, "What?"

The cop repeats, "Name of mother?"

"Janice. She's not living here. She lives over in Brewer."

"Address?"

Harry remembers Stavros's address, but gives instead, "Care of Frederick Springer, 89 Joseph Street, Mt. Judge."

"And who is the girl the boy mentioned?"

"Jill Pendleton, of Stonington, Connecticut. Don't know the street address."

"Age?"

"Eighteen or nineteen."

"Family relationship?"

"None."

It takes the cop a very long time to write this one word. Something is happening to a corner of the roof; the crowd noise is rising, and a ladder is being lowered through an intersection of searchlights.

Rabbit prompts: "The fourth person was a Negro we called Skeeter. *S-k*-double-*e-t-e-r*."

"Black male?"

"Yes."

"Last name?"

"I don't know. Could be Farnsworth."

"Spell please."

Rabbit spells it and offers to explain. "He was just here temporarily."

The cop glances up at the burning ranch house and then over at the owner. "What were you doing here, running a commune?"

"No, Jesus; listen. I'm not for any of that. I voted for Hubert Humphrey."

The cop studies the house. "Any chance this black is in there now?"

"Don't think so. He was the one that called me, it sounded as if from a phone booth."

"Did he say he'd set the fire?"

"No, he didn't even say there was a fire, he just said things were bad. He said the word 'bad' twice."

"Things were bad," the cop writes, and closes his notepad. "We'll want some further interrogation later." Reflected firelight gleams peach-color off of the badge in his cap. The corner of the house above the bedroom is collapsing; the television aerial, that they twice adjusted and extended to cut down ghosts from their neighbors' sets, tilts in the leap of flame and slowly swings downward like a skeletal tree, still clinging by some wires or brackets to its roots. Water vaults into what had been the bedroom. A lavish cumulus of yellow smoke pours out, golden-gray, rich as icing squeezed from the sugary hands of a pastry cook.

The cop casually allows, "Anybody in there was cooked a half-hour ago."

Two steps away, Nelson is bent over to let vomit spill from his mouth. Rabbit steps to him and the boy allows himself to be touched. He holds him by the shoulders; it feels like trying to hold out of water a heaving fish that wants to go back under, that needs to dive back under or die. His father brings back his hair from his cheeks so it will not be soiled by vomit; with his fist he makes a feminine knot of hair at the back of the boy's hot soft skull. "Nellie, I'm sure she got out. She's far away. She's safe and far away."

The boy shakes his head *No* and retches again; Harry holds him for minutes, one hand clutching his hair, the other around his chest. He is holding him up from sinking into the earth. If Harry were to let go, he would sink too. He feels precariously heavier on his bones; the earth pulls like Jupiter. Policemen, spectators, watch him struggle with Nelson but do not intervene. Finally a cop, not the interrogating one, does approach and in a calm Dutch voice asks, "Shall we have a car take the boy somewhere? Does he have grandparents in the county?"

"Four of them," Rabbit says. "Maybe he should go to his mother."

"*No!*" Nelson says, and breaks loose to face them. "You're not getting me to go until we know where Jill is." His face shines with tears but is sane: he waits out the next hour standing by his father's side.

The flames are slowly smothered, the living-room side of the house is saved. The interior of the kitchen side seems a garden where different tints of smoke sprout; formica, vinyl, nylon, linoleum each burn differently, yield their curdling compounds back to earth and air. Firemen wet down the wreckage and search behind the gutted walls. Now the upstairs windows stare with searchlights, now the lower. A skull full of fireflies. Yet still the crowd waits, held by a pack sense of smell; death is in heat. Intermittently there have been staticky calls over the police radios and one of them has fetched an ambulance; it arrives with a tentative sigh of its siren. Scarlet lights do an offbeat dance on its roof. A strange container, a green rubber bag or sheet, is taken into the house, and brought back by three grim men in slickers. The ambulance receives the shapeless package, is shut with that punky sound only the most expensive automobile doors make, and – again, the tentative sigh of a siren just touched – pulls away. The crowd thins after it. The night overflows with the noise of car motors igniting and revving up.

Nelson says, "Dad."

"Yeah."

"That was her, wasn't it?"

"I don't know. Maybe."

"It was *some*body."

"I guess."

Nelson rubs his eyes; the gesture leaves swipes of ash, Indian markings. The child seems harshly ancient.

"I need to go to bed," he says.

"Want to go back to the Fosnachts?"

"No." As if in apology he explains, "I hate Billy." Further qualifying, he adds, "Unless you do." Unless you want to go back and fuck Mrs. Fosnacht again.

Rabbit asks him, "Want to see your mother?"

"I can't, Dad. She's in the Poconos."

"She should be back by now."

"I don't want to see her now. Take me to Jackson Road."

There is in Rabbit an engine murmuring *Undo, undo,* which wants to take them back to this afternoon, beginning with the moment they left the house, and not do what they did, not leave, and have it all unhappen, and Jill and Skeeter still there, in the house still there. Beneath the noise of this engine the inner admission that it did happen is muffled; he sees Nelson through a gauze of shock and dares ask, "Blame me, huh?"

"Sort of."

"You don't think it was just bad luck?" And though the boy hardly bothers to shrug Harry understands his answer: luck and God are both up there and he has not been raised to believe in anything higher than his father's head. Blame stops for him in the human world, it has nowhere else to go.

The firemen of one truck are coiling their hoses. A policeman, the one who asked after Nelson, comes over. "Angstrom? The chief wants to talk to you where the boy can't hear."

"Dad, ask him if that was Jill."

The cop is tired, stolid, plump, the same physical type as – what was his name? – Showalter. Kindly patient Brewerites. He lets out the information, "It was a cadaver."

"Black or white?" Rabbit asks.

"No telling."

Nelson asks, "Male or female?"

"Female, sonny."

Nelson begins to cry again, to gag as if food is caught in his throat, and Rabbit asks the policeman if his offer is still good, if a cruiser might take the boy to his grandparents' house in Mt. Judge. The boy is led away. He does not resist; Rabbit thought he might, might insist on staying with his father to the end. But the boy, his hair hanging limp and his tears flowing unchecked, seems relieved to be at last in the arms of order, of laws and limits. He doesn't even wave from the window of the silver-blue West Brewer cruiser as it U-turns in Vista Crescent and heads away from the tangle of hoses and puddles and red reflections. The air tastes sulphuric. Rabbit notices that the little maple was scorched on the side toward the house; its twigs smolder like cigarettes.

As the firemen wind up their apparatus, he and the police chief sit in the front of an unmarked car. Harry's knees are crowded by the radio apparatus on the passenger's side. The chief is a short man but doesn't look so short sitting down, with his barrel chest crossed by a black strap and his white hair crew-cut close to his scalp and his nose which was once broken sideways and has accumulated broken veins in the years since. He says, "We have a death now. That makes it a horse of another color."

"Any theories how the fire started?"

"I'll ask the questions. But yes. It was set. In the garage. I notice a power mower in there. Can of gas to go with it?"

"Yeah. We filled the can just this afternoon."

"Tell me where you were this evening."

He tells him. The chief talks on his car radio to the West Brewer headquarters. In less than five minutes they call back. But in the total, unapologetic silence the chief keeps during these minutes, a great lump grows in Rabbit, love of the law. The radio sizzles its words like bacon frying: "Mrs. Fosnacht confirms suspect's story. Also a minor boy in dwelling as additional witness."

"Check," the chief says, and clicks off.

"Why would I burn my own house down?" Rabbit asks.

"Most common arsonist is owner," the chief says. He studies Rabbit thoughtfully; his eyes are almost round, as if somebody took a stitch at the corner of each lid. "Maybe the girl was pregnant by you."

"She was on the Pill."

"Tell me about her."

He tries, though it is hard to make it seem as natural as it felt. Why did he permit Skeeter to move in on him? Well, the question was more, Why not? He tries, "Well, when my wife walked out on me, I kind of lost my bearings. It didn't seem to matter, and anyway he would have taken Jill with him, if I'd kicked him out. I got so I didn't mind him."

"Did he terrorize you?"

He tries to make these answers right. Out of respect for the law. "No. He educated us." Harry begins to get mad. "Some law I don't know about against having people live with you?"

"Law against harboring," the chief tells him, neglecting to write on his pad. "Brewer police report a Hubert Johnson out on default on a possession charge."

Rabbit's silence is not what he wants. He makes it clearer what he wants. "You in ignorance over the existence of this indictment and defiance of court?" He makes it even clearer. "Shall I accept your silence as a profession of ignorance?"

"Yes." It is the only opening. "Yes, I knew nothing about Skeeter, not even his last name."

"His present whereabouts, any ideas?"

"No idea. His call came through from it sounded like a phone booth but I couldn't swear to it."

The cop puts his broad hand over the notebook as if across the listening mouth of a telephone receiver. "Off the record. We've been watching this place. He was a little fish, a punk. We hoped he would lead us to something bigger."

"What bigger? Dope?"

"Civil disturbance. The blacks in Brewer are in touch with Philly, Camden, Newark. We know they have guns. We don't want another York here, now do we?" Again, Rabbit's silence is not what he wants. He repeats, "Now do we?"

"No, of course not. I was just thinking. He talked as if he was beyond revolution; he was kind of religious-crazy, not gun-crazy."

"Any idea why he set this fire?"

"I don't think he did. It isn't his style."

The pencil is back on the notebook. "Never mind about style," the chief says. "I want facts."

"I don't have any more facts than I've told you. Some people in the neighborhood were upset because Skeeter was living with us, two men stopped me on the street yesterday and complained about it, I can give you their names if you want."

The pencil hovers. "They complained. Any specific threats of arson?"

&. Wiseasses get fragged. *You better fucking barricade the whole place.* "Nothing that specific."

The chief makes a notation, it looks like *n.c.*, and turns the notebook page. "The black have sexual relations with the girl?"

"Look, I was off working all day. I'd come back and we'd cook supper and help the kid with his homework and sit around and talk. It was like having two more kids in the house, I don't know what they did every minute. Are you going to arrest me, or what?"

A fatherly type himself, the chief takes a smiling long time answering. Rabbit sees that his nose wasn't broken by accident, somewhere in the alleys of time he had asked for it. His snow-soft hair is cut evenly as a powderpuff, with a pink dent above the ears where the police cap bites. His smile broadens enough to crease his cheek. "Strictly speaking," he says, "this isn't my beat. I'm acting on behalf of my esteemed colleague the sheriff of Furnace Township, who rolled over and went back to sleep. Offhand I'd say we're doing a good enough business in the jails without putting solid citizens like you in there. We'll have some more questions later." He flips the notebook shut and flips the radio on to put out a call, "All cars, Brewer police copy, be on the lookout, Negro, male, height approx five-six, weight approx one-twenty-five, medium dark-skinned, hair Afro, name Skeeter, that is Sally, Katherine, double Easter –" He does not turn his head when Rabbit opens the car door and walks away.

So again in his life the net of law has slipped from him. He knows he is criminal, yet is never caught. Sickness sinks through his body like soot. The firemen wet down the smoking wreckage, the clot of equipment along Vista Crescent breaks up and flows away. The house is left encircled in its disgrace with yellow flashers on trestles warning people off. Rabbit walks around the lawn, so lately a full stage, sodden and pitted by footprints, and surveys the damage.

The burning was worse on the back side: the fixtures of the bedroom bathroom dangle in space from stems of contorted pipe. The wall that took the bed headboard is gone. Patches of night-blue sky show through the roof. He looks in the downstairs windows and sees, by flashing yellow light, as into a hellish fun house, the sofa and the two chairs, salted with fallen plaster, facing each other across the cobbler's bench. The driftwood lamp is still upright. On the shelves giving into the breakfast nook, Skeeter's books squat, soaked and matted. Where the kitchen was, Harry can see out through the garage to an N of charred 2 by 4s. The sky wants to brighten. Birds – birds in Penn Villas, where? there are no trees old enough to hold them – flicker into song. It is cold now, colder than in the heart of the night, when the fire was alive. The sky pales in the east, toward Brewer. Mt. Judge develops an outline in the emulsion of pre-dawn gray. A cloud of birds migrating crosses the suburb southward. The soot is settling on Harry's bones. His eyelids feel like husks. In his weariness he hallucinates; as in the seconds before we sleep, similes seem living organisms. The freshening sky above Mt. Judge is Becky, the child that died, and the sullen sky to the west, the color of a storm sky but flawed by stars, is Nelson, the child that lives. And he, he is the man in the middle.

He walks up to his battered front door, brushes away the glass shards, and sits down on the flagstone porchlet. It is warm, like a hearth. Though none of his neighbors came forward to speak to him, to sparkle on the bright screen of his disaster, the neighborhood presents itself to his gaze unapologetically, naked in the gathering light, the pastel roof shingles moist in patches echoing the pattern of rafters, the back-yard bathing pools and swing sets whitened by dew along with the grass. A half-moon rests cockeyed in the blanched sky like a toy forgotten on a floor. An old man in a noisy green raincoat, a geezer left behind as a watchman, walks over and speaks to him. "This your home, huh?"

"This is it."

"Got some other place to go?"

"I suppose."

"Body a loved one?"

"Not exactly."

"That's good news. Cheer up, young fella. Insurance'll cover most of it."

"Do I have insurance?"

"Had a mortgage?"

Rabbit nods, remembering the little slippery bankbook, imagining it burned.

"Then you had insurance. Damn the banks all you will, they look after their own, you'll never catch them damn Jews short."

This man's presence begins to seem strange. It has been months since anything seemed as strange as this man's presence. Rabbit asks him, "How long you staying here?"

"I'm on duty till eight."

"Why?"

"Fire procedure. Prevent looting." The two of them look wonderingly at the dormant houses and cold lawns of Penn Villas. As they look, a distant alarm rings and an upstairs light comes on, sallow, dutiful. Still, looting these days is everywhere. The geezer asks him, "Anything precious in there, you might want to take along?" Rabbit doesn't move. "You better go get some sleep, young fella."

"What about you?" Rabbit asks.

"Fella my age doesn't need much. Sleep long enough soon enough. Anyway, I like the peacefulness of these hours, have ever since a boy. Always up, my dad, he was a great boozer and a late sleeper, used to wallop the bejesus out of me if I made a stir mornings. Got in the habit of sneaking out to the birds. Anyway, double-hour credit, time outdoors on this shift. Don't always put it in, go over a certain amount, won't get any social security. Kill you with kindness, that's the new technique."

Rabbit stands up, aching; pain moves upward from his shins through his groin and belly to his chest and out. A demon leaving. Smoke, mist rise. He turns to his front door; swollen by water, axed, it resists being opened. The old man tells him, "It's my responsibility to keep any and all persons out of this structure. Any damage you do yourself, you're the party responsible."

"You just told me to take out anything precious."

"You're responsible, that's all I'm saying. I'm turning my back. Fall through the floor, electrocute yourself, don't call for help. Far as I'm concerned, you're not there. See no evil is the way I do it."

"That's the way I do it too." Under pressure the door pops open. Splintered glass on the other side scrapes white arcs into the hall floor finish. Rabbit begins to cry from smoke and the smell. The house is warm, and talks to itself; a swarm of small rustles and snaps arises from the section on his left; settling noises drip from the charred joists and bubble up from the drenched dark rubble where the floor had been. The bed's metal frame has fallen into the kitchen. On his right, the living room is murky but undamaged. The silver threads of the Lustrex chair gleam through an acid mist of fumes; the television set's green blank waits to be turned on. He thinks of taking it, it is the one resaleable item here, but no, it is too heavy to lug, he might drop himself through the floor, and there are millions like it. Janice once said we should drop television sets into the jungle instead of bombs, it would do as much good. He thought at the time the idea was too clever for her; even then Stavros was speaking through her.

She always loved that dumb bench. He remembers her kneeling beside it early in their marriage, rubbing it with linseed oil, short keen strokes, a few inches at a time, it made him feel horny watching. He takes the bench under his arm and, discovering it to be so light, pulls the driftwood lamp loose from its socket and takes that too. The rest the looters and insurance adjusters can have. You never get the smell of smoke out. Like the smell of failure in a life. He remembers the storm windows, Windexing their four sides, and it seems a fable that his life was ever centered on such details. His house slips from him. He is free. Orange light in long stripes, from sun on the side of him opposite from the side the sun was on when he and Nelson walked here a long night ago, stretches between the low strange houses as he walks down Vista Crescent with the table and the lamp tugging under his arms. Peggy's Fury is the only car still parked along the curb: a teal-blue tailfinned boat the ebb has stranded. He opens the door, pushes the seat forward to put the bench in the back, and finds someone there. A Negro. Asleep. "What the hell," Rabbit says.

Skeeter awakes blind and gropes for his glasses on the rubber floor. "Chuck baby," he says, looking up with twin circles of glass. His Afro is flattened on one side. Bad fruit. "All by yourself, right?"

"Yeah." The little car holds a concentration of that smell which in the mornings would spice the living room, give it animal substance, sleep's sweetness made strong.

"How long's it been light?"

"Just started. It's around six. How long've you been here?"

"Since I saw you and Babychuck pull in. I called you from a booth up on Weiser and then watched to see if you'd go by. The car wasn't you but the head was, right, so I snuck along through the back yards and got in after you parked. The old briar patch theory, right? Shit if I didn't fall asleep. Hey get in man, you're lettin' in the air."

Rabbit gets in and sits in the driver's seat, listening without turning his head, trying to talk without moving his mouth. Penn Villas is coming to life; a car just passed. "You ought to know," he says, "they're looking for you. They think you set it."

"Count on the fuzz to fuck up. Why would I go burn my own pad?"

"To destroy evidence. Maybe Jill — what do you call it? — O.D.'d."

"Not on the scag she was getting from me, that stuff was so cut sugar water has more flash. Look, Chuck, that up at your house was honky action. Will you believe the truth, or shall I save my breath for the pigpen?"

"Let's hear it."

Skeeter's voice, unattached to his face, is deeper than Harry remembers, with a hypnotic rasping lilt that reminds him of childhood radio. "Jill sacked out early and I made do with the sofa, right? Since getting back on the stuff she wasn't putting out any of her own, and anyway I was pretty spaced and beat, we went twice around the county unloading that bullshit car. Right? So I wake up. There was this rattling around. I placed it coming from the kitchen, right? I was thinkin' it was Jill coming to bug me to shoot her up again, instead there was this *whoosh* and soft *woomp*, reminded me of an APM hitting in the bush up the road, only it wasn't up any road, I say to myself *The war is come home*. Next thing there's this slam of a door, garage door from the rumble of it, and I flip to the window and see these two honky cats makin' tail across the lawn, across the street, into between those houses there, and disappear, right? They had no car I could see. Next thing, I smell smoke."

"How do you know these were white men?"

"Shit, you know how honkies run, like with sticks up their ass, right?"

"Could you identify them if you saw them again?"

"I ain't identifying Moses around here. My skin is fried in this county, right?"

"Yeah," Rabbit says. "Something else you should know. Jill is dead."

The silence from the back seat is not long. "Poor bitch, doubt if she knows the difference."

"Why didn't you get her out?"

"Hell, man, there was *heat*, right? I thought lynching time had come, I didn't know there wasn't twelve hundred crackers out there, I was in no shape to take care of some whitey woman, let Whitey take care of his own."

"But nobody stopped you."

"Basic training, right? I eluded as they say my pursuers."

"They didn't want to hurt you. It was me, they were trying to tell *me* something. People around here don't lynch, don't be crazy."

"Crazy, you've been watching the wrong TV channel. How about those cats in Detroit?"

"How about those dead cops in California? How about all this Off the Pigs crap you brothers have been pushing? I should take you in. The Brewer cops would love to see you, they love to re-educate crazy coons."

Two more cars swish by; from the height of a milk truck the driver looks down curiously. "Let's drive," Skeeter says.

"What's in it for me?"

"Nothing much, right?"

The car starts at a touch. The motor is more silent than their tires swishing in the puddles along Vista Crescent, past the apple-green ruin and the man in the green raincoat dozing on the doorstep. Rabbit heads out the curved streets to where they end, to where they become truck tracks between muddy house foundations. He finds a lost country lane. Tall rows of poplars, a neglected potholed surface. Skeeter sits up. Rabbit waits for the touch of metal on the back of his neck. A gun, a knife, a needle: they always have something. Poison darts. But there is nothing, nothing but the fluctuating warmth of Skeeter's breathing on the back of his neck. "How could you let her die?" he asks.

"Man, you want to talk guilt, we got to go back hundreds of years."

"I wasn't there then. But you were there last night."

"I was severely disadvantaged."

Harry's head is light with lack of sleep; he knows he shouldn't be making decisions. "Tell you what. I'll drive you ten miles south and you take it from there."

"That's cutting it fine, man, but let's say sold. One embarrassment remains. We brothers call it bread."

"You just got six hundred for selling her car."

"My wallet back next to that sofa, every mothering thing, right?"

"How about that black suitcase in the closet?"

"Say. You been snooping, or what?"

"I have maybe thirty dollars," Rabbit says. "You can have that. I'll keep this ride from the cops but then that's quits. Like you said, you've had it in this county."

"I shall return," Skeeter promises, "only in glory."

"When you do, leave me out of it."

Miles pass. A hill, a cluster of sandstone houses, a cement factory, a billboard pointing to a natural cave, another with a huge cutout of a bearded Amishman. Skeeter in yet another of his voices, the one that sounds most like a white man and therefore in Rabbit's ears most human, asks, "How'd Babychuck take it, Jill's being wasted?"

"About like you'd expect."

"Broken up, right?"

"Broken up."

"Tell him, there's a ton of cunt in the world."

"I'll let him figure that out himself."

They come to a corner where two narrow roads meet in sunlight. On the far side of a tan cut cornfield a whitewashed stone house sends up smoke. A wooden arrow at the intersection says Galilee 2. Otherwise it could be nowhere. A jet trail smears in the sky. Pennsylvania spreads south silently, through green and brown. A dry stone conduit underlies the road here; a roadside marker is a metal keystone rusted blank. Rabbit empties his wallet into Skeeter's pink palm and chokes off the impulse to apologize for its not being more. He wonders now what would be proper. A Judas kiss? They have scarcely touched since the night they wrestled and Harry won. He holds out his hand to shake farewell. Skeeter studies it as if like Babe he will tell a fortune, takes it into both his slick narrow hands, tips it so the meaty pink creases are skyward, contemplates, and solemnly spits into the center. His saliva being as warm as skin, Harry at first only knows it has happened by seeing: moisture full of bubbles like tiny suns. He chooses to take the gesture as a blessing, and wipes his palm dry on his pants. Skeeter tells him, "Never did figure your angle."

"Probably wasn't one," is the answer.

"Just waiting for the word, right?" Skeeter cackles. When he laughs there is that complexity about his upper lip white men don't have, a welt in the center, a genial seam reminding Rabbit of the stitch of flesh that holds the head of your cock to the shaft. As Harry backs Peggy's Fury around in the strait intersection, the young black waits by a bank of brown weed stalks. In the rear-view mirror, Skeeter looks oddly right, blends right in, even with the glasses and goatee, hanging empty-handed between fields of stubble where crows settle and shift, gleaning.

COL. EDWIN E. ALDRIN, JR.: *Now you're clear. Over toward me. Straight down, to your left a little bit. Plenty of room. You're lined up nicely. Toward me a little bit. Down. O.K. Now you're clear. You're catching the first hinge. The what hinge? All right, move. Roll to the left. O.K., now you're clear. You're lined up on the platform. Put your left foot to the right a little bit. O.K., that's good. More left. Good.*

NEIL ARMSTRONG: *O.K., Houston, I'm on the porch.*

IV. MIM

RABBIT is at his machine. His fingers feather, the matrices rattle on high, the molten lead comfortably steams at his side.

ARSON SUSPECTED IN PENN VILLAS BLAZE

Out-of-Stater Perishes

West Brewer police are still collecting testimony from neighbors in connection with the mysterious fire that destroyed the handsome Penn Villas residence of Mr. and Mrs. Harold Angstrom.

A guest in the home, Mill Jiss

A guest in the home, Miss Jill Pendleton, 18, of Stonington, Connecticut, perished of smoke inhalation and burns. Rescue attempts by valiant firemen were to no avail.

Miss Pendleton was pronounced dead on arrival at the Sister of Mercy Homeopathic Sisters of Mercy Homeopathic Hospital in Brewer.

A man reported seen in the vicinity of the dwelling, Hubert Johnson last of Plum Street, is being sought for questioning. Mr. Johnson is also known as "Skeeter" and sometimes gives his last name as Farnsworth.

Furnace Township fire chief Raymond "Buddy" Fessler told VAT reporters, "The fire was set I'm pretty sure, but we have no evidence of a Molotov cocktail or anything of that nature. This was not a bombing in the ordinary sense."

**Neighbors are baffled by the
event, reporting nothing unusual
about the home but the skulking
presence of a black man thought**

Pajasek taps him on the shoulder.

"If that's my wife," Rabbit says. "Tell her to bug off. Tell her I'm dead."

"It's nobody on the phone, Harry. I need to have a word with you privately. If I may."

That "if I may" is what puts the chill into Harry's heart. Pajasek is imitating somebody higher up. He shuts his frosted-glass door on the clatter and with a soft thump sits at his desk; he slowly spreads his fingers on the mass of ink-smirched papers there. "More bad news, Harry," he says. "Can you take it?"

"Try me."

"I hate like Jesus to put this into you right on top of your misfortune with your home, but there's no use stalling. Nothing stands still. They've decided up top to make Verity an offset plant. We'll keep an old flatbed for the job work, but the *Vat* said either go offset or have them print in Philly. It's been in the cards for years. This way, we'll be geared up to take other periodicals, there's some new sheets starting up in Brewer, a lot of it filth in my book but people buy it and the law allows it, so there you are." From the way he sighs, he thinks he's made his point. His forehead, seen from above, is global; the worried furrows retreat to the horizon of the skull, where the brass-pale hair begins, wisps brushed straight back.

Rabbit tries to help him. "So no Linotypers, huh?"

Pajasek looks up startled; his eyebrows arch and drop and there is a moment of spherical smoothness, with a long clean highlight from the fluorescent tubes overhead. "I thought I made that point. That's part of the technical picture, that's where the economy comes. Offset, you operate all from film, bypass hot metal entirely. Go to a cathode ray tube, Christ, it delivers two thousand lines a minute, that's the whole *Vat* in seven minutes. We can keep a few men on, retrain them to the computer tape, we've worked the deal out with the union, but this is a sacrifice, Harry, from the management point of view. I'm afraid you're far down the list. Nothing to do with your personal life, understand me – strictly seniority. Your Dad's secure, and Buchanan, Christ, let him go we'd have every do-good outfit in the city on our necks, it's not the way *I'd* do things. If they'd come to me I would have told them, that man is half-soused from eleven o'clock on every morning, they're all like that, I'd just as soon have a moron with mittens on as long he was white —"

"O.K.," Rabbit says. "When do I knock off?"

"Harry, this hurts me like hell. You learned the skill and now the bottom's dropping out. Maybe one of the Brewer dailies can take you on, maybe something in Philly or up in Allentown, though what with papers dropping out or doubling up all over the state there's something of a glut in the trade right now."

"I'll survive. What did Kurt Schrack do?"

"Who he?"

"You know. The *Schockelschtuhl* guy."

"Christ, him. That was back in B.C. As I remember he bought a farm north of here and raises chickens. If he's not dead by now."

"Right. Die I guess would be the convenient thing. From the management point of view."

"Don't talk like that, Harry, it hurts me too much. Give me credit for some feelings. You're a young buck, for Chrissake, you got the best years still ahead of you. You want some fatherly advice? Get the hell out of the county. Leave the mess behind you. Forget that slob you married, no offense."

"No offense. About Janice, you can't blame her, I wasn't that great myself. But I can't go anywhere, I got this kid."

"Kid, schmid. You can't live your life that way. You got to reason outwards from Number One. To you, you're Number One, not the kid."

"That's not how it feels, exactly," Rabbit begins, then sees from the sudden gleaming globe of Pajasek's head bent to study the smirched slips on his desk that the man doesn't really want to talk, he wants Harry to go. So Rabbit asks, "So when do I go?"

Pajasek says, "You'll get two months' pay plus the benefits you've accumulated, but the new press is coming in this weekend, faster than we thought. Everything moves faster nowadays."

"Except me," Rabbit says, and goes. His father, in the bright

racket of the shop, swivels away from his machine and gives him
the thumbs down sign questioningly. Rabbit nods, thumbs down.
As they walk down Pine Street together after work, feeling
ghostly in the raw outdoor air after their day's immersion in fluor-
escence, Pop says, "I've seen the handwriting on the wall all along,
whole new philosophy operating at the top now at Verity, one of
the partner's sons came back from business school somewhere full
of beans and crap. I said to Pajasek, 'Why keep me on, I have less
than a year before retirement?' and he says, 'That's the reason.' I
said to him, 'Why not let me go and give my place to Harry?' and
he says, 'Same reason.' He's running scared himself, of course. The
whole economy's scared. Nixon's getting himself set to be the new
Hoover, these moratorium doves'll be begging for LBJ to come
back before Tricky Dick's got done giving their bank accounts a
squeeze!"

Pop talks more than ever now, as if to keep Harry's mind
cluttered; he clings to him like sanity. It has been a dreadful three
days. All Sunday, on no sleep, he drove back and forth in Peggy's
borrowed Fury through Brewer between Mt. Judge and Penn
Villas, through the municipal headache of the Columbus Day
parade. The monochrome idyll of early morning, Skeeter dwindling to a brown dot in brown fields, became a four-color nightmare of martial music, throbbing exhaustion, bare-thighed girls
twirling bolts of lightning, iridescent drummers pounding a tattoo
on the taut hollow of Harry's stomach, cars stalled in the side-
streets, Knights of Columbus floats, marching veterans, American
flags. Between entanglements with this monster celebration, he
scavenged in warm ashes and trucked useless stained and soaked
furniture, including a charred guitar, to the garage at the back of
the Jackson Road place. He found no wallet near the sofa, and no
black bag in the closet. Jill's bureau had been along the wall of
which only charred 2 by 4s remained, yet he prodded the ashes for
a scrap of the six hundred dollars. Back on Jackson Road, insurance investigators were waiting for him, and the sheriff of
Furnace Township, a little apple-cheeked old man, in suspenders
and a soft felt hat, who was mostly interested in establishing that
his failure to be present at the fire could in no way be held against
him. He was quite deaf, and every time someone in the room

spoke he would twirl around and alertly croak, "Let's put *that* on the record too! I want everything out in the open, everything on the record!"

Worst of all, Harry had to talk to Jill's mother on the telephone. The police had broken the news to her and her tone fluctuated between a polite curiosity about how Jill came to be living in this house and a grieved outrage seeking its ceiling, a bird cramped in a cage of partial comprehension.

"She was staying with me, yes, since before Labor Day," Rabbit told her, over the downstairs phone, in the dark living room, smelling of furniture polish and Mom's medicine. "Before that she had been bumming around in Brewer with a crowd of Negroes who hung out at a restaurant they've closed down since. I thought she'd be better off with me than with them."

"But the police said there *was* a Negro."

"Yeah. He was a friend of hers. He kind of came and went." Each time he was made to tell this story, he reduced the part Skeeter played, beginning with having to lie about driving him south that morning, until the young black man has become in his backwards vision little more substantial than a shadow behind a chair. "The cops say he might have set the fire but I'm sure he didn't."

"How are you sure?"

"I just am. Look, Mrs. —"

"Aldridge." And this, of all things, her second husband's name, set her to crying.

He fought through her sobbing. "Look, it's hard to talk now, I'm dead beat, my kid's in the next room, if we could talk face to face, I could maybe explain —"

The outrage tested a wing. "*Explain!* Can you explain her back to life?"

"No, I guess not."

The politeness returned. "My husband and I are flying to Philadelphia tomorrow morning and renting a car. Perhaps we should meet."

"Yeah. I'd have to take off from work, except for the lunch hour."

"We'll meet at the West Brewer police station," the distant

voice said with surprising firmness, a sudden pinch of authority. "At noon."

Rabbit had never been there before. The West Brewer Borough Hall was a brick building with white trim, set diagonally on a plot of grass and flower beds adjacent to the tall madhouse, itself really an addition to the original madhouse, a granite mansion built a century ago by one of Brewer's iron barons. All this land had belonged to that estate. Behind the borough hall stretched a long cement-block shed with a corrugated roof; some doors were open and Rabbit saw trucks, a steamroller, the spidery black machine that tars roads, the giant arm that lifts a man in a basket to trim branches away from electric wires. These appliances of a town's housekeeping seemed to him part of a lost world of blameless activity; he would never be allowed to crawl back into that world. Inside the town hall, there were wickets where people could pay their utilities bills, paneled doors labelled in flaking gold Burgess and Assessor and Clerk. Gold arrows pointed downstairs to the Police Department. Rabbit saw too late that he could have entered this half-basement from the side, saving himself the curious gaze of ten town employees. The cop behind the green-topped counter looked familiar, but it took a minute for the sideburns to register. The collegiate type. Harry was led down a hall past mysterious rooms; one brimmed with radio equipment, another with filing cabinets, a third gave on a cement stairway leading still further down. The dungeon. Jail. Rabbit wanted to run down into this hole and hide but was led into a fourth room, with a dead green table and metal folding chairs. The broken-nosed chief was in here and a woman who, though hollow with exhaustion and slow-spoken with pills, was Connecticut. She had more edge, more salt to her manner, than Pennsylvania women. Her hair was not so much gray as grayed; her suit was black. Jill's pensive thin face must have come from her father, for her mother had quite another kind, a roundish eager face with pushy lips that when she was happy must be greedy. Rabbit flicked away the impression of a peppy little dog: wideset brown eyes, a touch of jowl, a collar of pearls at her throat. *Nifty tits*, Jill had said, but her mother's cupped and braced bosom struck Rabbit in this moment of sexless and sorrowing encounter as a militant prow, part of a uniform's padding. He regretted that he had not enough praised Jill here, her boyish chest with its shallow faint shadows, where she had felt to herself shy and meager and yet had been soft enough in his mouth and hands, quite soft enough, and abundant, as grace is abundant, that we do not measure, but take as a presence, that abounds. In his mist, he heard the chief grunt introductions: Mr. and Mrs. Aldridge. Rabbit remembered in Jill's song the tax lawyer from Westerly, but the man remained blank for him; he had eyes only for the woman, for this wrong-way reincarnation of Jill. She had Jill's composure, less fragilely; even her despairing way of standing with her hands heavy at her sides, at a loss, was Jill's. Rabbit wondered, Has she come from identifying the remains? What was left but blackened bones? Teeth. A bracelet. A flesh-colored swatch of hair. "Hey," he said to her, "I'm sick about this."

"Yes-s." Her bright eyes passed over his head. "Over the phone, I was so stupid, you mentioned explaining."

Had he? What had he wanted to explain? That it was not his fault. Yet Nelson thought it was. For taking her in? But she was unsheltered. For fucking her? But it is all life, sex, fire, breathing, all combination with oxygen, we shimmer at all moments on the verge of conflagration, as the madhouse windows tell us. Rabbit tried to remember. "You had asked about Skeeter, why I was sure he hadn't set the fire."

"Yes. Why were you?"

"He loved her. We all did."

"You all used her?"

"In ways."

"In your case" – strange precision, clubwoman keeping a meeting within channels, the vowels roughened by cigarettes and whisky, weathered in the daily sunslant of cocktails – "as a concubine?"

He guessed at what the word meant. "I never forced it," he said. "I had a house and food. She had herself. We gave what we had."

"You are a beast." Each word was too distinct; the sentence had been lying in her mind and had warped and did not quite fit.

"O.K., sure," he conceded, refusing to let her fly, to let that caged outrage escape her face and scream. Stepdaddy behind her coughed and shifted weight, preparing to be embarrassed. Harry's guts felt suspended and transparent, as before a game. He was matched against this glossy woman in a way he was never matched with Jill. Jill had been too old for him, too wise, having been born so much later. This little pug, her money and rasping clubwoman voice aside, was his generation, he could understand what she wanted. She wanted to stay out of harm's way. She wanted to have some fun and not be blamed. At the end she wanted not to have any apologizing to do to any heavenly committee. Right now she wanted to tame the ravenous miracle of her daughter's being cast out and destroyed. Mrs. Aldridge touched her cheeks in a young gesture, then let her hands hang heavy beside her hips.

"I'm sorry," she said. "There are always . . . circumstances. I wanted to ask, were there any . . . effects."

"Effects?" He was back with blackened bones, patterns of teeth, melted bracelets. He thought of the bracelets girls in high school used to wear, chains with name-tags, Dorene, Margaret, Mary Ann.

"Her brothers asked me . . . some memento . . ."

Brothers? She had said. Three. One Nelson's age.

Mrs. Aldridge stepped forward, bewildered, hoping to be helpful. "There was a car."

"They sold the car," Rabbit said, too loudly. "She ran it without oil and the engine seized up and she sold it for junk."

His loudness alarmed her. He was still indignant, about the waste of that car. She took a step backward, protesting, "She loved the car."

She didn't love the car, she didn't love anything we would have loved, he wanted to tell Mrs. Aldridge, but maybe she knew more than he, she was there when Jill first saw the car, new and white, her father's gift. Rabbit at last found in his mind an "effect." "One thing I did find," he told Mrs. Aldridge, "her guitar. It's pretty well burned, but —"

"Her guitar," the woman repeated, and perhaps having forgotten that her daughter played brought her eyes down, made her round face red and brought the man over to comfort her, a man blank like men in advertisements, his coat impeccable and in the breast pocket a three-folded maroon handkerchief. "I have *noth*-ing," she wailed, "she didn't even leave me a *note* when she *left*."

And her voice had shed its sexy roughness, become high and helpless; it was Jill again, begging, *Hold me, help me, I'm all shit inside, everything is crashing in.*

Harry turned from the sight. The chief, leading him out the side door, said, "Rich bitch, if she'd given the girl half a reason to stay home she'd be alive today. I see things like this every week. All our bad checks are being cashed. Keep your nose clean, Angstrom, and take care of your own." A coach's paternal punch on the arm, and Harry was sent back into the world.

"Pop, how about a quick one?"

"Not today, Harry, not today. We have a surprise for you at home. Mim's coming."

"You sure?" The vigil for Mim is months old; she keeps sending postcards, always with a picture of a new hotel on them.

"Yep. She called your mother this morning from New York City, I talked to your mother this noon. I should have told you but you've had so much on your mind I thought, Might as well save it. Things come in bunches, that's the mysterious truth. We get numb and the Lord lets us have it, that's how His mercy works. You lose your wife, you lose your house, you lose your job. Mim comes in the same day your mother couldn't sleep a wink for nightmares, I bet she's been downstairs all day trying to tidy up if it kills her, you wonder what's next." But he has just said it: Mom's death is next. The number 16A bus joggles, sways, smells of exhaust. The Mt. Judge way, there are fewer Negroes than toward West Brewer. Rabbit sits on the aisle; Pop, by the window, suddenly hawks and spits. The spittle runs in a weak blur down the dirty glass. "Goddammit, but that burns me," he explains, and Rabbit sees they have passed a church, the big gray Presbyterian at Weiser and Park: on its steps cluster some women in overcoats, two young men with backwards collars, nuns and schoolchildren carrying signs and unlit candles protesting the war. This is Moratorium Day. "I don't have much use for Tricky Dick and never have," Pop is explaining, "but the poor devil, he's trying to do the decent thing over there, get us out so the roof doesn't fall in until after we leave, and these queer preachers so shortsighted they can't see across the pulpit go organizing these parades that all they do is convince the little yellow Reds over there they're winning. If I were Nixon I'd tax the bejesus out of the churches, it'd take some of the burden off the little man. Old Cushing up there in Boston must be worth a hundred million just by his lonesome."

"Pop, all they're saying is they want the killing to stop."

"They've got you too, have they? Killing's not the worst thing around. Rather shake the hand of a killer than a traitor."

So much passion, where he now feels none, amuses Harry, makes him feel protected, at home. It has been his salvation, to be home again. The same musty teddy-bear smells from the carpet, the same embrace of hot air when you open the cellar door, the same narrow stairs heading up off the living room with the same loose baluster that lost its dowel and has to be renailed again and again, drying out in the ebb of time; the same white-topped kitchen table with the four sets of worn spots where they used to eat. An appetite for boyish foods has returned: for banana slices on cereal, for sugar doughnuts though they come in boxes with cellophane windows now instead of in waxpaper bags, for raw carrots and cocoa, at night. He sleeps late, so he has to be wakened for work; in Penn Villas, in the house where Janice never finished making curtains, he would be the one the sun would usually rouse first. Here in Mt. Judge familiar gloom encloses him. The distortions in Mom's face and speech, which used to distress him during his visits, quickly assimilate to the abiding reality of her presence, which has endured all these years he has been absent and which remains the same half of the sky, sealing him in – like the cellar bulkhead out back, of two heavy halves. As a child he used to crouch on the cement steps beneath them and listen to the rain. The patter above seemed to be pitting his consciousness lovingly and mixing its sound with the brusque scrape and stride of Mom working in the kitchen. She still, for spells, can work in the kitchen. Harry's being home, she claims, is worth a hundred doses of L–dopa.

The one disturbing element, new and defiant of assimilation, is Nelson. Sullen, grieving, strangely large and loutish sprawled on the caneback davenport, his face glazed by some television of remembrance: none of them quite know what to do about him.

He is not Harry, he is sadder than Harry ever was, yet he demands
the privileges and indulgence of Harry's place. In the worn shadows of the poorly lit half-house on Jackson Road, the Angstroms
keep being startled by Nelson's ungrateful presence, keep losing
him. "Where's Nellie?" "Where did the kid get to?" "Is the child
upstairs or down?" are questions the other three often put to one
another. Nelson stays in his temporary room – Mim's old room –
for hours of listening to rock-pop-folk turned down to a murmur.
He skips meals without explaining or apologizing, and is making
a scrapbook of news items the Brewer papers have carried about
their fire. Rabbit discovered this scrapbook yesterday, snooping in
the boy's room. Around the clippings the boy had drawn with
various colors of ballpoint flowers, peace signs, Tao crosses, musical notes, psychedelic rainbows, those open-ended swirling
doodles associated with insanity before they became commercial.
Also there are two Polaroid snaps of the ruin; Billy took them
Monday with a new camera his father had given him. The photos, brownish and curling, show a half-burned house, the burned
half dark like a shadow but active in shape, eating the unburned
half, the garage studs bent like matchsticks in an ashtray. Looking
at the photographs, Rabbit smells ash. The smell is real and not
remembered. In Nelson's closet he finds the source, a charred guitar. So that is why it wasn't in the garage when he looked for it, to
give to Jill's mother. She is back in Connecticut now, let the poor
kid keep it. His father can't reach him, and lives with him in his
parents' house as an estranged, because too much older, brother.

He and his father see, walking up Jackson Road, a strange car
parked in front of number 303, a white Toronado with orange-
on-blue New York plates. His father's lope accelerates; "There's
Mim!" he calls, and it is. She is upstairs and comes to the head of
the stairs as they enter beneath the fanlight of stained glass; she
descends and stands with them in the murky little foyer. It is Mim.
It isn't. It has been years since Rabbit has seen her. "Hi," Mim says,
and kisses her father dryly, on the cheek. They were never, even
when the children were little, much of a family for kissing. She

would kiss her brother the same way, dismissingly, but he holds her, wanting to feel the hundreds of men who have held her before, this his sister whose diapers he changed, who used to hold his thumb when they'd go for Sunday walks along the quarry, who once burst out *oh I love you* sledding with him, the runners whistling on the dark packed slick, the street waxy with snow still falling. Puzzled by his embrace, Mim kisses him again, another peck on the same cheek, and then firmly shrugs his arms away. A competence in that. She feels lean, not an ounce extra but all woman; swimming must do it, in hotel pools, late hours carve the fat away and swimming smooths what's left. She appears to wear no makeup, no lipstick, except for her eyes, which are inhuman, Egyptian, drenched in peacock purple and blue, not merely outlined but re-created, and weighted with lashes he expects to stick fast when she blinks. These marvellously masked eyes force upon her pale mouth all expressiveness; each fractional smile, sardonic crimping, attentive pout, and abrupt broad laugh follows its predecessor so swiftly Harry imagines a coded tape is being fed into her head and producing, rapid as electronic images, this alphabet of expressions. She used to have buck teeth but that has been fixed. Her nose, her one flaw, that kept her off the screen, that perhaps kept her from fame, is still long, with a faceted lump of cartilage at the end, exactly like Mom's nose, but now that Mim is thirty and never going to be a screen beauty seems less a flaw, indeed saves her face from looking like others and gives it, between the peacock eyes and the actressy-fussy mouth, a lenient homeliness. And this, Rabbit guesses, would extend her appeal for men, though now she would get barroom criers, with broken careers and marriages, rather than hard-hearted comers who need an icy showpiece on their arm. In the style of the Sixties her clothes are clownish: bell-bottom slacks striped horizontally as if patched from three kinds of gingham; a pinstripe blouse, mannish but for the puff sleeves; shoes that in color and shape remind him of Donald Duck's bill; and hoop earrings three inches across. Even in high school Mim had liked big earrings; they made her look like a gypsy or Arab then, now, with the tan, Italian. Or Miami Jewish. Her hair is expensively tousled honey-white, which doesn't offend him; not since junior high has she worn it the color it was, the mild brown she once called, while he leaned in her doorway watching her study herself in the mirror, "Protestant rat."

Pop busies his hands, touching her, hanging up his coat, steering her into the dismal living room. "When did you get here? Straight from the West Coast? You fly straight to Idlewild, they do it non-stop now, don't they?"

"Pop, they don't call it Idlewild any more. I flew in a couple days ago, I had some stuff in New York to do before I drove down. Jersey was breathtaking, once you got past the oil tanks. Everything still so green."

"Where'd you get the car, Mim? Rent it from Hertz?" The old man's washed-out eyes sparkle at her daring, at her way with the world.

Mim sighs. "A guy lent it to me." She sits in the caneback rocker and puts her feet up on the very hassock that Rabbit as a child had once dreamed about: he dreamed it was full of dollar bills to solve all their problems. The dream had been so vivid he had tested it; the stitched scar of his incision still shows. The stuffing had been disagreeable fiber deader than straw.

Mim lights a cigarette. She holds it in the exact center of her mouth, exhales twin plumes around it, frowns at the snuffed match.

Pop is enchanted by the routine, struck dumb. Rabbit asks her, "How does Mom seem to you?"

"Good. For someone who's dying."

"She make sense to you?"

"A lot of it. The guy who doesn't make much sense to me is you. She told me what you've been doing. Lately."

"Harry's had a hell of a time lately," Pop chimes in, nodding as if to mesh himself with this spinning wheel, his dazzling daughter. "Today in at Verity, get this, they gave him his notice. They kept me on and canned a man in his prime. I saw the handwriting on the wall but I didn't want it to be me who'd tell him, it was their meatloaf, let them deliver it, bastards, a man gives them his life and gets a boot in the fanny for his pains."

Mim closes her eyes and lets a look of weary age wash over her and says, "Pop, it's fantastic to see you. But don't you want to go up and look in on Mom for a minute? She may need to be led to the pot, I asked her but with me she could be shy still."

Pop rises quickly, obliging; yet then he stands in a tentative crouch, offering to say away her brusqueness. "You two have a language all your own. Mary and I, we used to marvel, I used to say to her, There couldn't ever have been a brother and a sister closer than Harry and Miriam. These other parents used to tell us, you know, about kids fighting, we didn't know what they were talking about, we'd never had an example. I swear to God above we never heard a loud word between the two of you. A lot of boys, all of six when Mim arrived, might have expressed resentment, you know, settled in with things pretty much his own way up to then: not Harry. Right from the start, right from that first summer, we could trust you alone with him, alone in the house, Mary and I off to a movie, about the only way to forget your troubles in those days, go off to a motion picture." He blinks, gropes among these threads for the one to pull it all tight. "I swear to God, we've been lucky," he says, then weakens it by adding, "when you look at some of the things that can happen to people," and goes up; his tears spark as he faces the bulb burning at the head of the stairs, before cautiously returning his eyes to the treads.

Did they ever have a language of their own? Rabbit can't remember it, he just remembers them being here together, in this house season after season, for grade after grade of school, setting off down Jackson Road in the aura of one holiday after another, Hallowe'en, Thanksgiving, Christmas, Valentine's Day, Easter, in the odors and feel of one sports season succeeding another, football, basketball, track; and then him being out and Mim shrunk to a word in his mother's letters; and then him coming back from the Army and finding her grown up, standing in front of the mirror, ready for boys, maybe having had a few, tinting her hair and wearing hoop earrings; and then Janice took him off; and then both of them were off and the house empty of young life; and now both of them are here again. The smoke from her cigarette seems what the room needs, has needed a long time, to chase these old furniture and sickness smells away. He is sitting on the piano stool; he perches forward and reaches toward her. "Gimme a weed."

"I thought you stopped."

"Years ago. I don't inhale. Unless it's grass."

"Grass yet. You've been living it up." She fishes in her purse, a big bright patchy bag that matches her slacks, and tosses him a cigarette. It is menthol, with a complicated filter tip. Death is easily fooled. If the churches don't work, a filter will do.

He says, "I don't know what I've been doing."

"I would say so. Mom talked to me for an hour. The way she is now, that's a lot of talking."

"What d'ya think of Mom now? Now that you have all this perspective."

"She was a great woman. With nowhere to put it."

"Well, is where you put it any better?"

"It involves less make-believe."

"I don't know, you look pretty fantastic to me."

"Thanks."

"What'd she say? Mom."

"Nothing you don't know, except Janice calls her a lot."

"I knew that. She's called a couple times since Sunday, I can't stand it to talk to her."

"Why not?"

"She's too wild. She doesn't make any sense. She says she's getting a divorce but never starts it, she says she'll sue me for burning her house and I tell her I only burned my half. Then she says she'll come get Nelson but never comes, I wish the hell she would."

"What does it mean to you, her being wild like this?"

"I think she's losing her buttons. Probably drinking like a fish."

Mim turns her profile to blunt the cigarette in the saucer serving as an ashtray. "It means she wants back in." Mim knows things, Rabbit realizes proudly. Wherever you go in some directions, Mim has been there. The direction where she hasn't been is the one that has Nelson in it, and the nice hot slap of the slug being made beside your left hand. But these are old directions, people aren't going that way any more. Mim repeats, "She wants you back."

"People keep telling me that," Rabbit says, "but I don't see much evidence. She can find me if she wants to."

Mim crosses her pants legs, aligns the stripes, and lights another cigarette. "She's trapped. Her love for this guy is the biggest thing she has, it's the first step out she's taken since she drowned that baby. Let's face it, Harry. You kids back here in the sticks still believe in ghosts. Before you screw you got to square it with old Jack Frost, or whatever you call him. To square skipping out with herself she has to make it a big deal. So. Remember as kids those candy jars down at Spottsie's you reached inside of to grab the candy and then you couldn't get your fist out? If Janice lets go to pull her hand out she'll have no candy. She wants it out, but she wants the candy too; no, that's not exactly it, she wants the *idea* of what she's made out of the candy in her own mind. So. Somebody has to break the jar for her."

"I don't want her back still in love with this greaseball."

"That's how you have to take her."

"The son of a bitch, he even has the nerve, sitting there in these snappy suits, he must make three times what I do just cheating people, he has the fucking nerve to be a dove. One night we all sat in this restaurant with him and me arguing across the table about Vietnam and them playing touch-ass side by side. You'd like him, actually, he's your type. A gangster."

Patiently Mim is sizing him up: one more potential customer at the bar. "Since when," she asks, "did you become such a war lover? As I remember you, you were damn glad to wriggle out of that Korean thing."

"It's not all war I love," he protests, "it's *this* war. Because nobody else does. Nobody else understands it."

"Explain it to me, Harry."

"It's a, it's a kind of head fake. To keep the other guy off balance. The world the way it is, you got to do something like that once in a while, to keep your options, to keep a little space around you." He is using his arms to show her his crucial concept of space. "Otherwise, he gets so he can read your every move and you're dead."

Mim asks, "You're sure there is this other guy?"

"Sure I'm sure." The other guy is the doctor who shakes your hand so hard it hurts. *I know best.* Madness begins in that pinch.

"You don't think there might just be a lot of little guys trying to get a little more space than the system they're under lets them have?"

"Sure there are these little guys, billions of 'em" – billions, millions, too much of everything – "but then also there's this big guy trying to put them all into a big black bag. He's crazy, so so must we be. A little."

She nods like a type of doctor herself. "That fits," she says. "Be crazy to keep free. The life you been leading lately sounds crazy enough to last you a while."

"What did I do wrong? I was a fucking Good Samaritan. I took in these orphans. Black, white, I said Hop aboard. Irregardless of color or creed, Hop aboard. Free eats. I was the fucking Statue of Liberty."

"And it got you a burned-down house."

"O.K. That's other people. That's their problem, not mine. I did what felt right." He wants to tell her everything, he wants his tongue to keep pace with this love he feels for this his sister; he wants to like her, though he feels a forbidding denseness in her, of too many conclusions reached when he wasn't there. He tells her, "I learned some things."

"Anything worth knowing?"

"I learned I'd rather fuck than be blown."

Mim removes a crumb, as of tobacco but the cigarette is filtered, from her lower lip. "Sounds healthy," she says. "Rather unAmerican, though."

"And we used to read books. Aloud to each other."

"Books about what?"

"I don't know. Slaves. History, sort of."

Mim in her stripey clown costume laughs. "You went back to school," she says. "That's sweet." She used to get better marks than he did, even after she began with boys: A's and B's against his B's and C's. Mom at the time told him girls had to be smarter, just to pull even. Mim asks, "So what'd you learn from these books?"

"I learned" – he gazes at a corner of a room, wanting to get this right: he sees a cobweb above the sideboard, gesturing in some ceiling wind he cannot feel – "this country isn't perfect." Even as he says this he realizes he doesn't believe it, any more than he believes at heart that he will die. He is tired of explaining himself. "Speaking of sweet," he says, "how is *your* life?"

"*Ça va.* That's French for, It goes. *Va bene.*"

"Somebody keeping you, or is it a new one every night?"

She looks at him and considers. A glitter of reflexive anger snipes at her mask of eye makeup. Then she exhales and relaxes, seeming to conclude, Well he's my brother. "Neither. I'm a career girl, Harry. I perform a service. I can't describe it to you, the way it is out there. They're not bad people. They have rules. They're not very interesting rules, nothing like Stick your hand in the fire and make it up to Heaven. They're more like, Ride the exercise bicycle the morning after. The men believe in flat stomach muscles and sweating things out. They don't want to carry too much fluid. You could say they're puritans. Gangsters are puritans. They're narrow and hard because off the straight path you don't live. Another rule they have is, Pay for what you get because anything free has a rattlesnake under it. They're survival rules, rules for living in the desert. That's what it is, a desert. Look out for it, Harry. It's coming East."

"It's here. You ought to see the middle of Brewer; it's all parking lots."

"But the things that grow here you can eat, and the sun is still some kind of friend. Out there, we hate it. We live underground. All the hotels are underground with a couple of the windows painted blue. We like it best at night, about three in the morning, when the big money comes to the crap table. Beautiful faces, Harry. Hard and blank as chips. Thousands flow back and forth without any expression. You know what I'm struck by back here, looking at the faces? How soft they are. God they're soft. *You* look so soft to me, Harry. You're soft still standing and Pop's soft curling under. If we don't get Janice propped back under you you're going to curl under too. Come to think of it, Janice is not soft. She's hard as a nut. That's what I never liked about her. I bet I'd like her now. I should go see her."

"Sure. Do. You can swap stories. Maybe you could get her a job on the West Coast. She's pretty old but does great things with her tongue."

"That's quite a hang-up you have there."

"I just said, nobody's perfect. How about you? You have some specialty, or just take what comes?"

She sits up. "She really hurt you, didn't she?" And eases back. She stares at Harry interested. Perhaps she didn't expect in him such reserves of resentful energy. The living room is dark though the noises that reach them from outside say that children are still playing in the sun. "You're all soft," she says, lulling, "like slugs under fallen leaves. Out there, Harry, there are no leaves. People grow these tan shells. I have one, look." She pulls up her pinstripe blouse and her belly is brown. He tries to picture the rest and wonders if her pussy is tinted honey-blonde to match the hair on her head. "You never see them out in the sun but they're all tan, with flat stomach muscles. Their one flaw is, they're still soft inside. They're like those chocolates we used to hate, those chocolate creams, remember how we'd pick through the Christmas box they'd give us at the movie theater, taking out only the square ones and the caramels in cellophane? The other ones we hated, those dark brown round ones on the outside, all ooky inside. But that's how people are. It embarrasses everybody but they need to be milked. Men need to be drained. Like boils. Women too for that matter. You asked me my specialty and that's it, I milk people. I let them spill their insides on me. It can be dirty work but usually it's clean. I went out there wanting to be an actress and that's in a way what I got, only I take on the audience one at a time. In some ways it's more of a challenge. So. Tell me some more about your life."

"Well I was nursemaid to this machine but now they've retired the machine. I was nursemaid to Janice but she upped and left."

"We'll get her back."

"Don't bother. Then I was nursemaid to Nelson and he hates me because I let Jill die."

"She let herself die. Speaking of that, that's what I do like about these kids: they're trying to kill it. Even if they kill themselves in the process."

"Kill what?"

"The softness. Sex, love; me, mine. They're doing it in. I have no playmates under thirty, believe it. They're burning it out with dope. They're going to make themselves hard clean through. Like, oh, cockroaches. That's the way to live in the desert. Be a cock-roach. It's too late for you, and a little late for me, but once these kids get it together, there'll be no killing them. They'll live on poison."

Mim stands; he follows. For all that she was a tall girl and is enlarged by womanhood and makeup, her forehead comes to his chin. He kisses her forehead. She tilts her face up, slime-blue eyelids shut, to be kissed again. Pop's loose mouth under Mom's chiselled nose. He tells her, "You're a cheerful broad," and pecks her dry cheek. Perfumed stationery. A smile in her cheek pushes his lips. She is himself, with the combination jiggled.

She gives him a sideways hug, patting the fat around his waist. "I swing," Mim confesses. "I'm no showboat like Rabbit Angstrom, but in my quiet way I swing." She tightens the hug, and linked like that they walk to the foot of the stairs, to go up and console their parents.

Next day, Thursday, when Pop and Harry come home, Mim has Mom and Nelson downstairs at the kitchen table, having tea and laughing. "Dad," Nelson says, the first time since Sunday morning he has spoken to his father without first being spoken to, "did you know Aunt Mim worked at Disneyland once? Do Abraham Lincoln for him, please do it again."

Mim stands. Today she wears a knit dress, short and gray; in black tights her legs show skinny and a little knock-kneed, the same legs she had as a kid. She wobbles forward as to a lectern, removes an imaginary piece of paper from a phantom breast pocket, and holds it wavering a little below where her eyes would focus if they could see. Her voice as if on rustling tape within her throat emerges: "Fow-er scow-er and seven yaars ago –"

Nelson is falling off the chair laughing; yet his careful eyes for a split second check his father's face, to see how he takes it. Rabbit laughs, and Pop emits an appreciative snarl, and even Mom: the bewildered foolish glaze on her features becomes intentionally foolish, amused. Her laughter reminds Rabbit of the laughter of a child who laughs not with the joke but to join the laughter of others, to catch up and be human among others. To keep the laughter swelling Mim sets out two more cups and saucers in the jerky trance of a lifesize Disney doll, swaying, nodding, setting one cup not in its saucer but on the top of Nelson's head, even to keep the gag rolling pouring some hot water not in the teacup but onto the table; the water runs, steaming, against Mom's elbow. "Stop, you'll scald her!" Rabbit says, and seizes Mim, and is shocked by the tone of her flesh, which for the skit has become plastic, not hers, flesh that would stay in any position you twisted it to. Frightened, he gives her a little shake, and she becomes human, his efficient sister, wiping up, swishing her lean tail from table to stove, taking care of them all.

Pop asks, "What kind of work did Disney have you do, Mim?"

"I wore a little Colonial get-up and led people through a rep-lica of Mt. Vernon." She curtseys and with both hands in artificial unison points to the old gas stove, with its crusty range and the crazed mica window in the oven door. "The Fa-ther of our Coun-try," she explains in a sweet, clarion, idiot voice, "was himself nev-er a fa-ther."

"Mim, you ever get to meet Disney personally?" Pop asks.

Mim continues her act. "His con-nu-bi-al bed, which we see before us, measures five feet four and three-quarter inches from rail to rail, and from head-board to foot-board is two inch-es under sev-en feet, a gi-ant's bed for those days, when most gentle-men were no bigger than warming pans. Here" – she plucks a plastic fly swatter off the fly-specked wall – "you see a warm-ing pan."

"If you ask me," Pop says to himself, having not been answered, "it was Disney more than FDR kept the country from going under to the Commies in the Depression."

"The ti-ny holes," Mim is explaining, holding up the fly-swatter, "are de-signed to let the heat e-scape, so the fa-ther of our coun-try will not suf-fer a chill when he climbs into bed with his be-lov-ed Mar-tha. Here" – Mim gestures with two hands at the Verity Press giveaway calendar on the wall, turned to October, a grinning jack-o-lantern – "is Mar-tha."

Nelson is still laughing, but it is time to let go, and Mim does. She pecks her father on the forehead and asks him, "How's the Prince of Pica today? Remember that, Daddy? When I thought pica was the place where they had the leaning tower."

"North of Brewer somewhere," Nelson tells her, "I forget the exact place, there's some joint that calls itself the Leaning Tower of Pizza." The boy waits to see if this is funny, and though the grown-ups around the table laugh obligingly, he decides that it wasn't, and shuts his mouth. His eyes go wary again. "Can I be excused?"

Rabbit asks sharply, "Where're you going?"

"My room."

"That's Mim's room. When're you going to let her have it?"

"Any time."

"Whyncha go outdoors? Kick the soccer ball around, do something positive, for Chrissake. Get the self-pity out of your system."

"Let. Him alone," Mom brings out.

Mim intercedes. "Nelson, when will you show me your famous mini-bike?"

"It's not much good, it keeps breaking down." He studies her, his possible playmate. "You can't ride it in clothes like that."

"Out West," she says, "everybody rides motorcycles in trendy knits."

"Did you ever ride a motorcycle?"

"All the time, Nelson. I used to be den mother for a pack of Hell's Angels. We'll ride over and look at your bike after supper."

"It's not the kid's bike, it's somebody else's," Rabbit tells her.

"It'll be dark after supper," Nelson tells Mim.

"I love the dark," she says. Reassured, he clumps upstairs, ignoring his father. Rabbit is jealous. Mim has learned, these years out of school, what he has not: how to manage people.

Shakily, Mom lifts her teacup, sips, sets it down. A perilous brave performance. She is proud of something; he can tell by the way she sits, upright, her neck cords stretched. Her hair has been brushed tight about her head. Tight and almost glossy. "Mim," she says, "went calling today."

Rabbit asks, "On who?"

Mim answers. "On Janice. At Springer Motors."

"Well." Rabbit pushes back from the table, his chair legs scraping. "What did the little mutt have to say for herself?"

"Nothing. She wasn't there."

"Where was she?"

"He said seeing a lawyer."

"Old man Springer said that?" Fear slides into his stomach, nibbling. The law. The long white envelope. Yet he likes the idea of Mim going over there and standing in one of her costumes in front of the Toyota cutout, a gaudy knife into the heart of the Springer empire. Mim, their secret weapon.

"No," she tells him, "not old man Springer. Stavros."

"You saw Charlie there? Huh. How does he look? Beat?"

"He took me out to lunch."

"Where?"

"I don't know, some Greek place in the black district."

Rabbit has to laugh. People dead and dying all around him, he has to let it out. "Wait'll he tells her that."

Mim says, "I doubt he will."

Pop is slow to follow. "Who're we talking about, Mim? That slick talker turned Janice's head?"

Mom's face gropes; her eyes stretch as if she is strangling while her mouth struggles to frame a droll thought. In suspense they all fall silent. "Her lover," she pronounces. A sick feeling stabs Rabbit.

Pop says, "Well I've kept my trap shut throughout this mess, don't think Harry there wasn't a temptation to meddle but I kept my peace, but a lover in my book is somebody who loves somebody through thick and thin and from all I hear this smooth operator is just after the ass. The ass and the Springer name. Pardon the expression."

"I think," Mom says, faltering though her face still shines. "It's nice. To know Janice has."

"An ass," Mim finally completes for her. And it seems to Rabbit wicked that these two, Pop and Mim, are corrupting Mom on the edge of the grave. Coldly he asks Mim, "What'd you and Chas talk about?"

"Oh," Mim says, "things." She shrugs her knitted hip off the kitchen table, where she has been perched as on a bar stool. "Did you know, he has a rheumatic heart? He could kick off at any minute."

"Fat chance," Rabbit says.

"That type of operator," Pop says, snarling his teeth back into place, "lives to be a hundred, while they bury all the decent natural Americans. Don't ask me why it works that way, the Lord must have His reasons."

Mim says, "I thought he was sweet. And quite intelligent. And *much* nicer about you all than you are about him. He was very thoughtful about Janice, he's probably the first person in thirty years to give her some serious attention as a *person*. He sees a lot in her."

"Must use a microscope," Rabbit says.

"And *you*," Mim says, turning, "he thinks you're about the biggest spook he's ever met. He can't understand why if you want Janice back you don't come and get her back."

Rabbit shrugs. "Too proud or lazy. I don't believe in force. I don't like contact sports."

"I did tell him, what a gentle brother you were."

"Never hurt a fly if he could help it, used to worry me," Pop says. "As if we'd had a girl and didn't know it. Isn't that the truth, Mother?"

Mom gets out, "Never. All boy."

"In that case, Charlie says," Mim goes on.

Rabbit interrupts: " 'Charlie' yet."

" 'In that case,' he said, 'why is he for the war?' "

"Fuck," Rabbit says. He is more tired and impatient than he knew. "Anybody with any sense at all is for the damn war. They want to fight, we *got* to fight. What's the alternative? What?"

Mim tries to ride down her brother's rising anger. "His theory is," she says, "you like any disaster that might spring you free. You liked it when Janice left, you liked it when your house burned down."

"And I'll like it even more," Rabbit says, "when you stop seeing this greasy creep."

Mim gives him the stare that has put a thousand men in their place. "Like you said. He's my type."

"A gangster, right. No wonder you're out there screwing yourself into the morgue. You know where party chicks like you wind up? In coroners' reports, when you take too many sleeping pills when the phone stops ringing, when the gangsters find playmates in not such baggy condition. You're in big trouble, Sis, and the

Stavroses of the world are going to be no help. They've put you where you are."

"*Maa*-om," Mim cries, out of old instinct appealing to the frail cripple nodding at the kitchen table. "Tell Harry to lay *off*." And Rabbit remembers, it's a myth they never fought; they often did.

When Pop and Harry return from work the next day, Harry's last day on the job, the Toronado with New York plates is not in front of the house. Mim comes in an hour later, after Rabbit has put the supper chops in the oven; when he asks her where she's been, she drops her big stripey bag on the old davenport and answers, "Oh, around. Revisiting the scenes of my childhood. The downtown is really sad now, isn't it? All black-topped parking lots and Afro-topped blacks. And linoleum stores. I did one nice thing, though. I stopped at that store on lower Weiser with the lefty newspapers for sale and bought a pound of peanuts. Believe it or not Brewer is the only place left you can get good peanuts in the shell. Still warm." She tosses him the bag, a wild pass; he grabs it left-handed and as they talk in the living room he cracks peanuts. He uses a flowerpot for the shells.

"So," he says. "You see Stavros again?"

"You told me not to."

"Big deal, what I tell you. How was he? Still clutching his heart?"

"He's touching. Just the way he carries himself."

"Boo hoo. You analyze me some more?"

"No, we were selfish, we talked about ourselves. He saw right through me. We were halfway into the first drink and he looks me up and down through those tinted glasses and says, 'You work the field don't you?' Gimme a peanut."

He tosses a fistful overhanded; they pelt her on the chest. She is wearing a twitchy little dress that buttons down the front and whose pattern imitates lizardskin. When she puts her feet up on the hassock he sees clear to the crotch of her pantyhose. She acts lazy and soft; her eyes have relented, though the makeup shines as if freshly applied. "That's all you did?" he asks. "Eat lunch."

"Th-that's all, f-f-folks."

"What're you tryin' to prove? I thought you came East to help Mom."

"To help her help *you*. How can I help *her*, I'm no doctor."

"Well, I really appreciate your help, fucking my wife's boy-friend like this."

Mim laughs at the ceiling, showing Harry the horseshoe curve of her jaw's underside, the shining white jugular bulge. As if cut by a knife the laugh ends. She studies her brother gravely, impu-dently. "If you had a choice, who would you rather went to bed with him, her or me?"

"Her. Janice, I can always have too, I mean it's possible; but you, never."

"I know," Mim gaily agrees. "Of all the men in the world, you're the only one off bounds. You and Pop."

"And how does that make me seem?"

She focuses hard on him, to get the one-word answer. "Ridi-culous."

"That's what I thought. Hey, Jesus. Did you really give Stavros a bang today? Or're you just getting my goat? Where would you go? Wouldn't Janice miss him at the office?"

"Oh – he could say he was out on a sale or something," Mim offers, bored now. "Or he could tell her to mind her own busi-ness. That's what European men do." She stands, touches all the buttons in the front of her lizardskin dress to make sure they're done. "Let's go visit Mom." Mim adds, "Don't fret. Years ago, I made it a rule never to be with a guy more than three times. Unless there was some percentage in getting involved."

That night Mim gets them all dressed and out to dinner, at the Dutch smörgåsbord diner north toward the ball park. Though Mom's head waggles and she has some trouble cutting the crust of her apple pie, she manages pretty well and looks happy: how come he and Pop never thought of getting her out of the house? He resents his own stupidity, and tells Mim in the hall, as they go in to their beds – she is back in her old room, Nelson sleeps with him now – "You're just little Miss Fix-It, aren't you?"

"Yes," she snaps, "and you're just big Mister Muddle." She begins undoing her buttons in front of him, and closes her door only after he has turned away.

Saturday morning she takes Nelson in her Toronado over to the Fosnachts; Janice has arranged with Mom that she and Peggy will do something all day with the boys. Though it takes twenty minutes to drive from Mt. Judge to West Brewer, Mim is gone all morning and comes back to the house after two. Rabbit asks her, "How was it?"

"What?"

"No, seriously. Is he that great in the sack, or just about average in your experience? My theory for a while was there must be something wrong with him, otherwise why would he latch on to Janice when he can have all these new birds coming up?"

"Maybe Janice has wonderful qualities."

"Let's talk about him. Relative to your experience." He imagines that all men have been welded into one for her, faces and voices and chests and hands welded into one murmuring pink wall, as once for him the audience at those old basketball games became a single screaming witness that was the world. "To your wide experience," he qualifies.

"Why don't you tend your own garden instead of hopping around nibbling at other people's?" Mim asks. When she turns in that clown outfit, her lower half becomes a gate of horizontal denim stripes.

"I have no garden," he says.

"Because you didn't tend it at all. Everybody else has a life they try to fence in with some rules. You just do what you feel like and then when it blows up or runs down you sit there and pout."

"Christ," he says, "I went to work day after day for ten years."

Mim tosses this off. "You felt like it. It was the easiest thing to do."

"You know, you're beginning to remind me of Janice."

She turns again; the gate opens. "Charlie told me Janice is fantastic. A real wild woman."

Sunday Mim stays home all day. They go for a drive in Pop's old Chevy, out to the quarry, where they used to walk. The fields that used to be dusted white with daisies and then yellow with goldenrod are housing tracts now; of the quarry only the great gray hole in the ground remains. The Oz-like tower of sheds and chutes where the cement was processed is gone, and the mouth of the cave where children used to hide and frighten themselves is sealed shut with bulldozed dirt and rusted sheets of corrugated iron. "Just as well," Mom pronounces. "Awful things. Used to happen there. Men and boys." They eat at the aluminum diner out on Warren Street, with a view of the viaduct, and this meal out is less successful than the last. Mom refuses to eat. "No appetite," she says, yet Rabbit and Mim think it is because the booths are close and the place is bright and she doesn't want people to see her fumble. They go to a movie. The movie page of the *Vat* advertises: *I Am Curious Yellow*, *Midnight Cowboy*, a double bill of *Depraved* and *The Circus* (Girls Never Played Games Like This Before!), a Swedish X-film titled *Yes*, and *Funny Girl*. *Funny Girl* sounds like more of the same but it has Barbra Streisand; there will be music. They make it late to the 6:30 show. Mom falls asleep and Pop gets up and walks around in the back of the theater and talks to the usher in a penetrating whine until one of the scattered audience calls out "*Shh*." On the way out, the lights on, a trio of hoods give Mim such an eye Rabbit gives them back the finger. Blinking in the street, Mom says, "That was nice. But really Fanny. Was very ugly. But stylish. And a gangster. She always knew Nick Arnstein was a gangster. Everybody. Knew it."

"Good for her," Mim says.

"It isn't the gangsters who are doing the country in," Pop says. "If you ask me it's the industrialists. The monster fortunes. The Mellons and the du Ponts, those are the cookies we should put in jail."

Rabbit says, "Don't get radical, Pop."

"I'm no radical," the old man assures him, "you got to be rich to be radical."

Monday, a cloudy day, is Harry's first day out of work. He is awake at seven but Pop goes off to work alone. Nelson goes with him; he still goes to school in West Brewer and switches buses on Weiser. Mim leaves the house around eleven, she doesn't say where to. Rabbit scans the want ads in the Brewer *Standard*. Accountant. Administrative Trainee. Apprentice Spray Painter.

Auto Mechanic. Bartender. The world is full of jobs, even with Nixon's Depression. He skips down through Insurance Agents and Programmers to a column of Salesmen and then turns to the funnies. Goddam *Apartment 3-G*: he feels he's been living with those girls for years now, when is he going to see them with their clothes off? The artist keeps teasing him with bare shoulders in bathrooms, naked legs in the foreground with the crotch coming just at the panel edge, glimpses of bra straps being undone. He calculates: after two months' pay from Verity he has thirty-seven weeks of welfare and then he can live on Pop's retirement. It is like dying now: they don't let you fall though, they keep you up forever with transfusions, otherwise you'll be an embarrassment to them. He skims the divorce actions and doesn't see himself and goes upstairs to Mom.

She is sitting up in the bed, her hands quiet on the quilted coverlet, an inheritance from her own mother. The television is also quiet. Mom stares out of the window at the maples. They have dropped leaves enough so the light in here seems harsh. The sad smell is more distinct: fleshly staleness mingled with the pepper-mint of medicine. To spare her the walk down the hall they have put a commode over by the radiator. To add a little bounce to her life, he sits down heavily on the bed. Her eyes with their film of clouding pallor widen; her mouth works but produces only saliva. "What's up?" Harry loudly asks. "How's it going?"

"Bad dreams," she brings out. "L-dopa does things. To the system."

"So does Parkinson's Disease." This wins no response. He tries, "What do you hear from Julia Arndt? And what's-er-name, Mamie Kellog? Don't they still come visiting?"

"I've outlasted. Their interest."

"Don't you miss their gossip?"

"I think. It scared them when. It all came true."

He tries, "Tell me one of your dreams."

"I was picking scabs. All over my body. I got one off and under-neath. There were bugs, the same. As when you turn over a rock."

"Wow. Enough to make you stay awake. How do you like Mim's being here?"

"I do."

"Still full of sauce, isn't she?"

"She tries to be. Cheerful."

"Hard as nails, I'd say."

"Inch by inch," Mom says.

"Huh?"

"That was on one. Of the children's programs. Earl leaves the set on and makes me watch. Inch by inch."

"Yeah, go on."

"Life is a cinch. Yard by yard. Life is hard."

He laughs appreciatively, making the bed bounce more. "Where do you think I went wrong?"

"Who says. You did?"

"Mom. No house, no wife, no job. My kid hates me. My sister says I'm ridiculous."

"You're. Growing up."

"Mim says I've never learned any rules."

"You haven't had to."

"Huh. Any decent kind of world, you wouldn't need all these rules."

She has no ready answer for this. He looks out of her windows. There was a time – the year after leaving, even five years after – when this homely street, with its old-fashioned high crown, its sidewalk blocks tugged up and down by maple roots, its retaining walls of sandstone and railings of painted iron and two-family brickfront houses whose siding imitates gray rocks, excited Rabbit with the magic of his own existence. These mundane surfaces had given witness to his life; this cup had held his blood; here the universe had centered, each downtwirling maple seed of more account than galaxies. No more. Jackson Road seems an ordinary street anywhere. Millions of such American streets hold millions of lives, and let them sift through, and neither notice nor mourn, and fall into decay, and do not even mourn their own passing but instead grimace at the wrecking ball with the same gaunt façades that have outweathered all their winters. However steadily Mom communes with these maples – the branches' misty snake-shapes as inflexibly fixed in these two windows as the leading of stained glass – they will not hold back her fate by the space of a breath; nor, if they are cut down tomorrow to widen Jackson Road at last,

will her staring, that planted them within herself, halt their vanishing. And the wash of new light will extinguish even her memory of them. Time is our element, not a mistaken invader. How
stupid, it has taken him thirty-six years to begin to believe that.
Rabbit turns his eyes from the windows and says, to say something,
"Having Mim home sure makes Pop happy"; but in his silence
Mom, head rolling on the pillow, her nostrils blood-red in contrast with the linen, has fallen asleep.

He goes downstairs and makes himself a peanut-butter sandwich. He pours himself a glass of milk. He feels the whole house
as balanced so that his footsteps might shake Mom and tumble her
into the pit. He goes into the cellar and finds his old basketball and,
more of a miracle still, a pump with the air needle still screwed into
the nozzle. In their frailty things keep faith. The backboard is still
on the garage but years have rusted the hoop and loosened the
bolts, so the first hard shots tilt the rim sideways. Nevertheless he
keeps horsing around and his touch begins to come back. Up and
soft, up and soft. Imagine it just dropping over the front of the rim,
forget it's a circle. The day is very gray so the light is nicely even.
He imagines he's on television; funny, watching the pros on the
box how you can tell, from just some tone of their bodies as they
go up, if the shot will go in. Mim comes out of the house, down
the back steps, down the cement walk, to him. She is wearing a
plain black suit, with wide boxy lapels, and a black skirt just to the
knee. An outfit a Greek would like. Classic widow. He asks her,
"That new?"

"I got it at Kroll's. They're outlandishly behind the coasts, but
their staid things are half as expensive."

"You see friend Chas?"

Mim puts down her purse and removes her white gloves and
signals for the ball. He used to spot her ten points at Twenty-one
when he was in high school. As a girl she had speed and a knock-
kneed moxie at athletics, and might have done more with it if he
hadn't harvested all the glory already. "Friend Janice too," she says,
and shoots. It misses but not by much.

He bounces it back. "More arch," he tells her. "Where'd you
see Jan?"

"She followed us to the restaurant."

"You fight?"

"Not really. We all had Martinis and *retsina* and got pretty well smashed. She can be quite funny about herself now, which is a new thing." Her grease-laden eyes squint at the basket. "She says she wants to rent an apartment away from Charlie so she can have Nelson." This shot, the ball hits the crotch and every loose bolt shudders looser.

"I'll fight her all the way on that."

"Don't get uptight. It won't come to that."

"Oh it won't. Aren't you a fucking little know-it-all?"

"I try. One more shot." Her breasts jog her black lapels as she shoves the dirty ball into the air. A soft drizzle has started. The ball swishes the net, if the net had been there.

"How could you give Stavros his bang if Janice was there?"

"We sent her back to her father."

He had meant the question to be rude, not for it to be answered. "Poor Janice," he says. "How does she like being out-tarted?"

"I said, don't get uptight. I'm flying back tomorrow. Charlie knows it and so does she."

"Mim. You can't, so soon. What about them?" He gestures at the house. From the back, it has a tenement tallness, a rickety hangdog wood-and-tar-shingle backside mismatched to its solid street face. "You'll break their hearts."

"They know. My life isn't here, it's there."

"You have nothing there but a bunch of horny hoods and a good chance of getting V.D."

"Oh, we're clean. Didn't I tell you? We're all obsessed with cleanliness."

"Yeah. Mim. Tell me something else. Don't you ever get tired of fucking? I mean" – to show the question is sincere, not rude – "I'd think you would."

She understands and is sisterly honest. "Actually, no. I don't. As a girl I would have thought you would but now being a woman I see you really don't. It's what we do. It's what people do. It's a connection. Of course, there are times, but even then, there's something nice. People want to be nice, haven't you noticed? They don't like being shits, that much; but you have to find some way out of it for them. You have to help them."

Her eyes in their lassos of paint seem, outdoors, younger than they have a right to be. "Well, good," he says weakly; he wants to take her hand, to be helped. As her brother, once, he had been afraid she would fall in the quarry if he let go and he had let go and she had fallen and now says it's all right, all things must fall. She laughs and goes on, "Of course I was never squeamish like you. Remember how you hated food that was mixed up, when the pea-juice touched the meat or something? And that time I told you all food had to be mushed like vomit before you could swallow it, you hardly ate for a week."

"I don't remember that. Stavros is really great, huh?"

Mim picks up her white gloves from the grass. "He's nice." She slaps her palm with the gloves, studying her brother. "Also," she says.

"What?" He braces for the worst, the hit that will leave nothing there.

"I bought Nelson a mini-bike. Nobody in this Godforsaken household seems to remember it, but tomorrow is his birthday. He's going to be thirteen, for Cry-eye. *A teenager.*"

"You can't do that, Mim. He'll kill himself. It's not legal on the streets here."

"I'm having it delivered over to the Fosnachts' building. They can share it on the parking lot, but it'll be Nelson's. The poor kid deserves *some*thing for what you put him through."

"You're a super aunt."

"And you're so dumb you don't even know it's raining." In the darkening drizzle she sprints, still knock-kneed and speedy, up the walk through their narrow backyard, up the stairs of their spindly back porch. Harry hugs the ball and follows.

In his parents' house Rabbit not only reverts to peanut-butter sandwiches and cocoa and lazing in bed when the sounds of Pop and Nelson leaving have died; he finds himself faithfully mas-turbating. The room itself demands it: a small long room he used to imagine as a railway car being dragged through the night. Its sin-gle window gives on the sunless passageway between the houses. As a boy in this room he could look across the space of six feet at the drawn shade of the room that used to be little Carolyn Zim's. The Zims were night owls. Some nights, though he was three grades ahead of her, Carolyn would go to bed later than he, and he would strain to see in the chinks of light around her shade the glimmer of her undressing. And by pressing his face to the chill glass by his pillow he could look at a difficult diagonal into Mr. and Mrs. Zim's room and one night glimpsed a pink commotion that may have been intercourse. But nearly every morning the Zims could be heard at breakfast fighting and Mom used to wonder how long they would stay together. People that way plainly wouldn't be having intercourse. In those days this room was full of athletes, mostly baseball players, their pictures came on school tablet covers, Musial and DiMag and Luke Appling and Rudy York. And for a while there had been a stamp collection, weird to remember, the big blue album with padded covers and the waxpaper mounts and the waxpaper envelopes stuffed with a tumble of Montenegro and Sierra Leone cancelleds. He imagined then that he would travel to every country in the world and send Mom a postcard from every one, with these stamps. He was in love with the idea of travelling, with running, with geography, with Parcheesi and Safari and all board games where you roll the dice and move; the sense of a railroad car was so vivid he could almost see his sallow overhead light, tulip-shaped, tremble and sway with the motion. Yet travelling became an offense in the game he got good at.

The tablet covers were pulled from the wall while he was in the Army. The spots their tacks left were painted over. The tulip of frosted glass was replaced by a fluorescent circle that buzzes and flickers. Mom converted his room to her junk room: an old push-treadle Singer, a stack of *Reader's Digest*s and *Family Circle*s, a bridge lamp whose socket hangs broken like a chicken's head by one last tendon, depressing pictures of English woods and Italian palaces where he has never been, the folding cot from Sears on which Nelson slept in his father's room while Mim was here. When Mim left Tuesday, the kid, dazed by his good fortune in owning a mini-bike over in West Brewer, moved back into her room, abandoning Rabbit to memories and fantasies. He always has to imagine somebody, masturbating. As he gets older real people aren't exciting enough. He tried imagining Peggy Fosnacht, because she had been recent, and good, all gumdrops; but remembering her reminds him that he has done nothing for her, has not called her since the fire, has no desire to, left her blue Fury in the basement and had Nelson give her the key, scared to see her, blames her, she seduced him, the low blue flame that made her want to be fucked spread and became the fire. From any thought of the fire his mind darts back singed. Nor can he recall Janice; but for the bird-like dip of her waist under his hand in bed she is all confused mocking darkness where he dare not insert himself. He takes to conjuring up a hefty coarse Negress, fat but not sloppy fat, muscular and masculine, with a trace of a mustache and a chipped front tooth. Usually she is astraddle him like a smiling Buddha, slowly rolling her ass on his thighs, sometimes coming forward so her big cocoa-colored breasts swing into his face like boxing gloves with sensitive tips. He and this massive whore have just shared a joke, in his fantasy; she is laughing and good humor is rippling through his chest; and the room they are in is no ordinary room but a kind of high attic, perhaps a barn, with distant round windows admitting dusty light and rafters from which ropes hang, almost a gallows. Though she is usually above him, and he sometimes begins on his back, imagining his fingers are her lips, for the climax he always rolls over and gives it to the bed in the missionary position. He has never been able to shoot off lying on his back; it feels too explosive, too throbbing, too blasphemous upwards. God is on that side of him, spreading His feathered wings as above a crib. Better turn and pour it into Hell. You nice big purple-lipped black cunt. Gold tooth.

When this good-humored goddess of a Negress refuses, through repeated conjuration, to appear vividly enough, he tries imagining Babe. Mim, during her brief stay, told him offhand, at the end of his story, that what he should have done was sleep with Babe; it had been all set up, and it was what his subconscious wanted. But Babe in his mind has stick fingers cold as ivory, and there is no finding a soft hole in her, she is all shell. And the puckers on her face have been baked there by a wisdom that withers him. He has better luck making a movie that he is not in, imagining two other people, Stavros and Mim. How did they do it? He sees her white Toronado barrelling up the steepness of Eisenhower Avenue, stopping at 1204. The two of them get out, the white doors slam punkily, they go in, go up, Mim first. She would not even turn for a preliminary kiss; she would undress swiftly. She would stand in noon windowlight lithe and casual, her legs touching at the knees, her breasts with their sunken nipples and bumpy aureoles (he has seen her breasts, spying) still girlish and undeveloped, having never nursed a child. Stavros would be slower in undressing, stolid, nursing his heart, folding his pants to keep the crease for when he returns to the lot. His back would be hairy: dark whirlpools on his shoulder blades. His cock would be thick and ropily veined, ponderous but irresistible in rising under Mim's deft teasing; he hears their wisecracking voices die; he imagines afternoon clouds dimming the sepia faces of the ancestral Greeks on the lace-covered tables; he sees the man's clotted cock with the column of muscle on its underside swallowed by Mim's rat-furred vagina (no, she is not honey-blonde here), sees her greedy ringless fingers press his balls deeper up, up into her ravenous stretched cunt; and himself comes. As a boy, Rabbit had felt it as a space-flight, a squeezed and weightless toppling over onto his head but now it is a mundane release as of anger, a series of muffled shouts into the safe bedsheet, rocks thrown at a boarded window. In the stillness that follows he hears a tingling, a submerged musical vibration slowly identifiable as the stereo set of the barefoot couple next door, in the other half of the house.

One night while he is letting his purged body drift in listening Jill comes and bends over and caresses him. He turns his head to kiss her thigh and she is gone. But she has wakened him; it was her presence, and through this rip in her death a thousand details are loosed; tendrils of hair, twists of expression, her frail voice quavering into pitch as she strummed. The minor details of her person that slightly repelled him, the hairlines between her teeth, her doughy legs, the apple smoothness of her valentine bottom, the something prim and above-it-all about her flaky-dry mouth, the unwashed white dress she kept wearing, now return and become the body of his memory. Times return when she merged on the bed with moonlight, her young body just beginning to learn to feel, her nerve endings still curled in like fernheads in the spring, green, a hardness that repelled him but was not her fault, the gift

of herself was too new to give. Pensive moments of her face return
to hurt him. A daughterly attentiveness he had bid her hide. Why?
He had retreated into protest and did not wish her to call him out.
He was not ready, he had been affronted. Let black Jesus have her;
he had been converted to a hardness of heart, a billion cunts and
only one him. He tries to picture, what had been so nice, Jill and
Skeeter as he actually saw them once in hard lamplight, but in fantasy now Rabbit rises from the chair to join them, to be a father
and lover to them, and they fly apart like ink and paper whirling
to touch for an instant on the presses. JILL COMES AGAIN. *Angstrom
Senses Presence.* She breathes upon him again as he lies in his boyhood bed and this time he does not make the mistake of turning
his face, he very carefully brings his hand up from his side to touch
the ends of her hair where it must hang. Waking to find his hand
in empty mid-air he cries; grief rises in him out of a parched stomach, a sore throat, singed eyes; remembering her daughterly blind
grass-green looking to him for more than shelter he blinds himself,
leaves stains on the linen that need not be wiped, they will be invisible in the morning. Yet she had been here, her very breath and
presence. He must tell Nelson in the morning. On this dreamlike
resolve he relaxes, lets his room, with hallucinatory shuddering, be
coupled to an engine and tugged westward toward the desert,
where Mim is now.

"That bitch," Janice said. "How many times did you screw
her?"

"Three times," Charlie said. "That ended it. It's one of her
rules."

This ghost of conversation haunts Janice this night she cannot
sleep. Harry's witch of a sister has gone back to whoring but her
influence is left behind in Charlie like a touch of disease. They had
it so perfect. Lord they had never told her, not her mother or father
or the nurses at school, only the movies had tried to tell her but
they couldn't show it, at least not until recently, how perfect it
could be. Sometimes she comes just thinking about him and then
other times they last forever together, it is beautiful how slow he

can be, murmuring all the time to her, selling her herself. They call it a piece of ass and she never understood why until Charlie, it wasn't on her front so much where she used to get mad at Harry because he couldn't make their bones touch or give her the friction she needed long enough so then he ended blaming her for not being with him, it was deeper inside, where the babies happened, where everything happens, she remembers how, was it with Nelson or poor little Becky, they said push and it was embarrassing like forcing it when you haven't been regular, but then the pain made her so panicky she didn't care what came out, and what came out was a little baby, all red-faced and cross as if it had been interrupted doing something else in there inside her. Stuff up your ass, she had hated to hear people say it, what men did to each other in jail or in the Army where the only women are yellow women screaming by the roadside with babies in their arms and squatting to go to the bathroom anywhere, disgusting, but with Charlie it is a piece of ass she is giving him, he is remaking her from the bottom up, the whole base of her feels made new, it's the foundation of life. Yet afterwards, when she tries to say this, how he remakes her, he gives that lovable shrug and pretends it was something anybody could do, a trick like that little trick he does with matches to amuse his nephews, making them always pick the last one up, instead of the sad truth which is that nobody else in the whole wide (Harry was always worrying about how wide the world was, caring about things like how far stars are and the moon shot and the way the Communists wanted to put everybody in a big black bag so he couldn't breathe) world but Charlie could do that for her, she was made for him from the beginning of time without exaggeration. When she tries to describe this to him, how unique they are and sacred, he measures a space of silence with his wonderful hands, just the way his thumbs are put together takes the breath out of her, and slips the question like a cloak from his shoulders.

She asked, "How could you do that to me?"

He shrugged. "I didn't do it to you. I did it to her. I screwed her."

"Why? Why?"

"Why not? Relax. It wasn't that great. She was cute as hell at lunch, but as soon as we got into bed her thermostat switched off. Like handling white rubber."

"Oh, Charlie. Talk to me, Charlie. Tell me why."

"Don't lean on me, tiger."

She had made him make love to her. She had done everything for him. She had worshipped him, she had wanted to cry out her sorrow that there wasn't more she could do, that bodies were so limited. Though she had extracted her lover's semen from him, she failed to extract testimony that his sense of their love was as absolute as her own. Terribly – complainingly, preeningly – she had said, "You know I've given up the world for you."

He had sighed, "You can get it back."

"I've destroyed my husband. He's in all the newspapers."

"He can take it. He's a showboat."

"I've dishonored my parents."

He had turned his back. With Harry it had been usually she who turned her back. Charlie is hard to snuggle against, too broad; it is like clinging to a rock slippery with hair. He had, for him, apologized: "Tiger, I'm bushed. I've felt rotten all day."

"Rotten how?"

"Deep down rotten. Shaky rotten."

And feeling him slip away from her into sleep had so enraged her she had hurled herself naked from bed, shrieked at him the words he had taught her in love, knocked a dead great-aunt from a bureau top, announced that any decent man would at least have *offered* to marry her now knowing she would never accept, did things to the peace of the apartment that now reverberate in her insomnia, so the darkness shudders between pulses of the headlights that tirelessly pass below on Eisenhower Avenue. The view from the back of Charlie's apartment is an unexpected one, of a bend in the Running Horse River like a cut in fabric, of the elephant-colored gas tanks in the boggy land beside the dump, and, around a church with twin blue domes she never knew was there, a little cemetery with iron crosses instead of stones. The traffic out front never ceases. Janice has lived near Brewer all her life but never in it before, and thought all places went to sleep at ten, and was surprised how this city always rumbles with traffic, like her heart which even through dreams keeps pouring out its love.

She awakes. The curtains at the window are silver. The moon is a cold stone above Mt. Judge. The bed is not her bed, then she remembers it has been her bed since, when? July it was. For some reason she sleeps with Charlie on her left; Harry was always on her right. The luminous hands of the electric clock by Charlie's bedside put the time at after two. Charlie is lying face up in the moonlight. She touches his cheek and it is cold. She puts her ear to his mouth and hears no breathing. He is dead. She decides this must be a dream.

Then his eyelids flutter as if at her touch. His eyeballs in the faint cold light seem unseeing, without pupils. Moonlight glints in a dab of water at the far corner of the far eye. He groans, and Janice realizes this is what has waked her. A noise not freely given but torn from some heavy mechanism of restraint deep in his chest. Seeing that she is up on an elbow watching, he says, "Hi, tiger. Jesus it hurts."

"What hurts, love? Where?" Her breath rushes from her throat so fast it burns. All the space in the room, from the corners in, seems a crystal a wrong move from her will shatter.

"Here." He seems to mean to show her but cannot move his arms. Then his whole body moves, arching upward as if twitched by something invisible outside of him. She glances around the room for the unspeaking presence tormenting them, and sees again the lace curtains stamped, interwoven medallions, on the blue of the streetlamp, and against the reflecting blue of the bureau mirroring the square blank silhouettes of framed aunts, uncles, nephews. The groan comes again, and the painful upward arching: a fish hooked deep, in the heart.

"Charlie. Is there any pill?"

He makes words through his teeth. "Little white. Top shelf. Bathroom cabinet."

The crowded room pitches and surges with her panic. The floor tilts beneath her bare feet; the nightie she put on after her disgraceful scene taps her burning skin scoldingly. The bathroom door sticks. One side of the frame strikes her shoulder, hard. She cannot find the light cord, her hand flailing in the darkness; then she strikes it and it leaps from her touch and while she waits for it to swing back down out of the blackness Charlie groans again, the

worst yet, the tightest-sounding. The cord finds her fingers and
she pulls; the light pounces on her eyes, she feels them shrink so
rapidly it hurts yet she doesn't take the time to blink, staring for
the little white pills. She confronts in the cabinet a sick man's
wealth. All the pills are white. No, one is aspirin; another is yellow and transparent, those capsules that hold a hundred little
bombs to go off against hayfever. Here: this one must be it; though
the little jar is unlabelled the plastic squeeze lid looks important.
There is tiny red lettering on each pill but she can't take the time
to read it, her hands shake too much, they must be right; she tilts
the little jar into her palm and five hurry out, no, six, and she wonders how she can be wasting time counting and tries to slide some
back into the tiny round glass mouth but her whole body is beating so hard her joints have locked to hold her together. She looks
for a glass and sees none and takes the square top of the Water Pik
and very stupidly lets the faucet water run to get cold, wetting her
palm in turning it off, so the pills there blur and soften and stain
the creased skin they are cupped in. She has to hold everything,
pills and slopping Water Pik lid, in one hand to free the other to
close the bathroom door to keep the light caged away from
Charlie. He lifts his large head a painful inch from the pillow and
studies the pills melting in her hand and gets out, "Not those. *Little
white.*" He grimaces as if to laugh. His head sinks back. His throat
muscles go rigid. The noise he makes now is up an octave, a woman's noise. Janice sees she does not have time to go back and search
again, he is being tuned too high. She sees that they are beyond
chemicals; they are pure spirits, she must make a miracle. Her body
feels leaden on her bones, she remembers Harry telling her she has
the touch of death. But a pressure from behind like a cuff on the
back of her head pitches her forward with a keening cry pitched
like his own and she presses herself down upon his body that has
been so often pressed upon hers; he has become a great hole nothing less large than she wild with love can fill. She wills her heart to
pass through the walls of bone and give its rhythm to his. He grits
his teeth "Christ" and strains upward against her as if coming and
she presses down with great calm, her body a sufficiency, its
warmth and wetness and pulse as powerful as it must be to stanch
this wound that is an entire man, his length and breadth loved, his

level voice loved and his clever square hands loved and his whirlpools of hair loved and his buffed fingernails loved and the dark gooseflesh bag of his manhood loved and the frailty held within him like a threat and lock against her loved. She is a gateway of love gushing from higher ground; she feels herself dissolving piece by piece like a little mud dam in a sluice. She feels his heart kick like pinned prey and keeps it pinned. Though he has become a devil, widening now into a hole wider than a quarry and then gathering into a pain-squeezed upward thrust as cold as an icicle she does not relent; she widens herself to hold his edges in, she softens herself to absorb the spike of his pain. She will not let him leave her. There is a third person in the room, this person has known her all her life and looked down upon her until now; through this other pair of eyes she sees she is weeping, hears herself praying, *Go, Go*, to the devil thrashing inside this her man. "Go!" she utters aloud.

Charlie's body changes tone. He is dead. No, at his mouth she eavesdrops on the whistle of his breathing. Sudden sweat soaks his brow, his shoulders, his chest, her breasts, her cheek where it was pressed against his cheek. His legs relax. He grunts, "O.K." She dares slide from him, tucking the covers, which she had torn down to bare his chest, back up to his chin.

"Shall I get the real pills now?"

"In a minute. Yes. Nitroglycerin. What you brought me was Coricidin. Cold pills."

She sees that his grimace had meant to be laughter, for he does smile now. Harry is right. She is stupid.

To ease the hurt look from her face Stavros tells her, "Rotten feeling. Pressure worse than a fist. You can't breathe, move anything makes it worse, you feel your own heart. Like some animal skipping inside you. Crazy."

"I was scared to leave you."

"You did great. You brought me back."

She knows this is true. The mark upon her as a giver of death has been erased. As in fucking, she has been rendered transparent, then filled solid with peace. As if after fucking, she takes playful inventory of his body, feels the live sweat on his broad skin, traces a finger down the line of his nose.

He repeats, "Crazy," and sits up in bed, cooling himself, gasping safe on the shore. She snuggles at his side and lets her tears out like a child. Absently, still moving his arms gingerly, he fumbles with the ends of her hair as it twitches on his shoulder.

She asks, "Was it me? My throwing that awful fit about Harry's sister? I could have killed you."

"Never." Then he admits, "I need to keep things orderly or they get to me."

"My being here is disorderly," she says.

"Never mind, tiger," he says, not quite denying, and tugs her hair so her head jerks.

Janice gets up and fetches the right pills. They had been there all along, on the top shelf; she had looked on the middle shelf. He takes one and shows her how he puts it under his tongue to dissolve. As it dissolves he makes that mouth she loves, lips pushed forward as if concealing a lozenge. When she turns off the light and gets into bed beside him, he rolls on his side to give her a kiss. She does not respond, she is too full of peace. Soon the soft rhythm of his unconscious breathing rises from his side of the bed. On her side, she cannot sleep. Awake in every nerve she untangles her life. The traffic ebbs down below. She and Charlie float motionless above Brewer; he sleeps on the wind, his heart hollow. Next time she might not be able to keep him up. Miracles are granted but we must not lean on them. This love that has blown through her has been a miracle, the one thing worthy of it remaining is to leave. Spirits are insatiable but bodies get enough. She has had enough, he has had enough; more might be too much. She might begin to kill. He calls her tiger. Toward six the air brightens. She sees his square broad forehead, the wiry hair in its tidy waves, the nose so shapely a kind of feminine vanity seems to be bespoken, the mouth even in sleep slightly pouting, a snail-shine of saliva released from one corner. Angel, buzzard, floating, Janice sees that in the vast volume of her love she has renounced the one possible imperfection, its object. Her own love engulfs her; she sinks down through its purity swiftly fallen, all feathers.

* * *

Mom has the phone by her bed; downstairs Rabbit hears it ring, then hears it stop, but some time passes before she makes him understand it is for him. She cannot raise her voice above a kind of whimper now, but she has a cane, an intimidating knobby briar Pop brought home one day from the Brewer Salvation Army store. She taps on the floor with it until attention comes up the stairs. She is quite funny with it, waving it around, thumping. "All my life," she says. "What I wanted. A cane."

He hears the phone ring twice and then only slowly the tapping of the cane sinks in; he is vacuuming the living-room rug, trying to get some of the fustiness up. In Mom's room, the smell is more powerful, the perverse vitality of rot. He has read somewhere that what we smell are just tiny fragments of the thing itself tickling a plate in our nose, a subtler smoke. Everything has its cloud, a flower's bigger than a rock's, a dying person's bigger than ours. Mom says, "For you." The pillows she is propped on have slipped so she sits at a slant. He straightens her and, since the word "Janice" begins with a sound difficult for her throat muscles to form, she is slow to make him understand who it is.

He freezes, reaching for the phone. "I don't want to talk to her."

"Why. Not."

"O.K., O.K." It is confusing, having to talk here, Janice's voice filling his ear while Mom and her rumpled bed fill his vision. Her blue-knuckled hands clasp and unclasp; her eyes, open too wide, rest on him in a helpless stare, the blue irises ringed with a thin white circle like a sucked Life Saver. "Now what?" he says to Janice.

"You could at least not be rude right away," she says.

"O.K., I'll be rude later. Let me guess. You're calling to tell me you've finally gotten around to getting a lawyer."

Janice laughs. It's been long since he heard it, a shy noise that tries to catch itself halfway out, like a snagged yo-yo. "No," she says, "I haven't gotten around to that yet. Is that what you're waiting for?" She is harder to bully now.

"I don't know what I'm waiting for."

"Is your mother there? Or are you downstairs?"

"Yes. Up."

"You sound that way. Harry – Harry, are you there?"

"Sure. Where else?"

"Would you like to meet me anyplace?" She hurries on, to make it business. "The insurance men keep calling me at work, they say you haven't filled out any of the forms. They say we ought to be making some decisions. I mean about the house. Daddy already is trying to sell it for us."

"Typical."

"And then there's Nelson."

"You don't have room for him. You and your greaseball."

His mother looks away, shocked; studies her hands, and by an effort of will stops their idle waggling. Janice has taken a quick high breath. He cannot bump her off the line today. "Harry, that's another thing. I've moved out. It's all decided, everything's fine. I mean, that way. With Charlie and me. I'm calling from Joseph Street, I've spent the last two nights here. Harry?"

"I'm listening. I'm right here. Whatcha think – I'm going to run away?"

"You have before. I was talking to Peggy yesterday on the phone, she and Ollie are back together, and *he* had heard you had gone off to some other state, a newspaper in Baltimore had given you a job."

"Fat chance."

"And Peggy said she hadn't heard from you at all. I think she's hurt."

"Why should she be hurt?"

"She told me why."

"Yeah. She would. Hey. This is a lot of fun chatting, but did you have anything definite you want to say? You want Nelson to come live with the Springers, is that it? I suppose he might as well, he's –" He is going to confess that the boy is unhappy, but his mother is listening and it would hurt her feelings. Considering her condition, she has really put herself out for Nelson this time.

Janice asks, "Would you like to see me? I mean, would it make you too mad, looking at me?"

And he laughs; his own laugh is unfamiliar in his ears. "It might," he says, meaning it might not.

"Oh, let's," she says. "You want to come here? Or shall I come

606 RABBIT ANGSTROM

there?" She understands his silence, and confirms, "We need a third place. Maybe this is stupid, but what about the Penn Villas house? We can't go in, but we need to look at it and decide what to do; I mean somebody's offering to buy it, the bank talked to Daddy the other day."

"O.K. I got to make Mom lunch now. How about two?"

"And I want to give you something," Janice is going on, while Mom is signalling her need to be helped to the commode; her blue hand tightens white around the gnarled handle of the cane.

"Don't let her wriggle," is her advice, when he hangs up, "her way. Around you." Sitting on the edge of the bed, Mom thumps the floor with her cane for emphasis, drawing an arc with the tip as illustration.

After putting the lunch dishes in the drainer Harry prepares for a journey. For clothes, he decides on the suntans he is wearing and has worn for two weeks straight, and a fresh white shirt as in his working days, and an old jacket he found in a chest in the attic: his high school athletic jacket. It carries MJ in pistachio green on an ivory shield on the back, and green sleeves emerge from V-striped shoulders. The front zips. Zipped, it binds across his chest and belly, but he begins that way, walking down Jackson Road under the chill maples; when the 12 bus lets him out at Emberly, the warmer air of this lower land lets him unzip, and he walks jauntily flapping along the curving street where the little ranch houses have pumpkins on their porchlets and Indian corn on their doors.

His own house sticks out from way down Vista Crescent: black coal in a row of candies. His station wagon is parked there. The American flag decal is still on the back window. It looks aggressive, fading.

Janice gets out of the driver's seat and stands beside the car looking lumpy and stubborn in a camel-colored loden coat he remembers from winters past. He had forgotten how short she is, how the dark hair has thinned back from the tight forehead, with that oily shine that puts little bumps along the hairline. She has abandoned the madonna hairdo, wears her hair parted way over on one side, unflatteringly. But her mouth seems less tight; her lips have lost the crimp in the corners and seem much readier to laugh, with less to lose, than before. His instinct, crazy, is to reach out and

pet her – do something, like tickle behind her ear, that you would
do to a dog; but they do nothing. They do not kiss. They do not
shake hands. "Where'd you resurrect that corny old jacket? I'd forgotten what awful school colors we had. Ick. Like one of those
fake ice creams."

"I found it in an old trunk in my parents' attic. They've kept
all that stuff. It still fits."

"Fits who?"

"A lot of my clothes got burned up." This note of apology
because he sees she is right, it was an ice-cream world he made his
mark in. Yet she too is wearing something too young for her, with
a hairdo reverting to adolescence, parted way over like those South
American flames of the Forties. Chachacha.

She digs into a side pocket of the loden coat awkwardly. "I said
I had a present for you. Here." What she hands him twinkles and
dangles. The car keys.

"Don't you need it?"

"Not really. I can drive one of Daddy's. I don't know why I
ever thought I did need it, I guess at first I thought we might escape
to somewhere. California. Canada. I don't know. We never even
considered it."

He asks, "You're gonna stay at your parents'?"

Janice looks up past the jacket to him, seeking his face. "I can't
stand it, really. Mother nags so. You can see she's been primed
not to say anything to me, but it keeps coming out, she keeps
using the phrase 'public opinion.' As if she's a Gallup poll. And
Daddy. For the first time, he seems pathetic to me. Somebody is
opening a Datsun agency in one of the shopping centers and
he feels really personally threatened. I thought," Janice says, her
dark eyes resting on his face lightly, ready to fly if what she
sees there displeases her, "I might get an apartment somewhere.
Maybe in Peggy's building. So Nelson could walk to school in
West Brewer again. I'd have Nelson, of course." Her eyes dart
away.

Rabbit says, "So the car is sort of a swap."

"More of a peace offering."

He makes the peace sign, then transfers it to his head, as
horns. She is too dumb to get it. He tells her, "The kid is pretty

miserable, maybe you ought to take him. Assuming you're through with Whatsisname."

"We're through."

"Why?"

Her tongue flicks between her lips, a mannerism that once struck him as falsely sensual but seems inoffensive now, like licking a pencil. "Oh," Janice says. "We'd done all we could together. He was beginning to get jittery. Your sweet sister didn't help, either."

"Yeah. I guess we did a number on him." The "we" – him, her, Mim, Mom; ties of blood, of time and guilt, family ties. He does not ask her for more description. He has never understood exactly about women, why they have to menstruate for instance, or why they feel hot some times and not others, and how close the tip of your prick comes to their womb or whether the womb is a hollow place without a baby in it or what, and instinct disposes him to consign Stavros to that same large area of feminine mystery. He doesn't want to bring back any lovelight into her eyes, that are nice and quick and hard on him, the prey.

Perhaps she had prepared to tell him more, how great her love was and how pure it will remain, for she frowns as if checked by his silence. She says, "You must help me with Nelson. All he'll talk to me about is this terrible mini-bike your sister bought him."

He gestures at the burned green shell. "My clothes weren't the only thing went up in that."

"The girl. Were she and Nelson close?"

"She was sort of a sister. He keeps losing sisters."

"Poor baby boy."

Janice turns and they look together at where they lived. Some agency, the bank or the police or the insurance company, has put up a loose fence of posts and wire around it, but children have freely approached, picking the insides clean, smashing the windows, storm windows and all, in the half that still stands. Some person has taken the trouble to bring a spray can of yellow paint and has hugely written NIGGER on the side. Also the word KILL. The two words don't go together, so it is hard to tell which side the spray can had been on. Maybe there had been two spray cans. Demanding equal time. On the broad stretch of aluminum clapboards below the windows, where in spring daffodils come up and in summer phlox goes wild, yellow letters spell in half-script, *Pig Power = Clean Power*. Also there is a peace sign and a swastika, apparently from the same can. And other people, borrowing charred sticks from the rubble, have come along and tried to edit and add to these slogans and symbols, making Pig into Black and Clean into Cong. It all adds up no better than the cluster of commercials TV stations squeeze into the chinks between programs. A clown with a red spray can has scrawled between two windows TRICK OR TREAT.

Janice asks, "Where was she sleeping?"

"Upstairs. Where we did."

"Did you love her?" For this her eyes leave his face and contemplate the trampled lawn. He remembers that this camel coat has a detachable hood for winter, that snaps on.

He confesses to her, "Not like I should have. She was sort of out of my class." Saying this makes him feel guilty, he imagines how hurt Jill would be hearing it, so to right himself he accuses Janice: "If you'd stayed in there, she'd still be alive somewhere."

Her eyes lift quickly. "No you don't. Don't try to pin *that* rap on me, Harry Angstrom. Whatever happened in there was your trip." Her trip drowns babies; his burns girls. They were made for each other. She offers to bring the truth into neutral. "Peggy says the Negro was doping her, that's what Billy says Nelson told him."

"She wanted it, he said. The Negro."

"Strange he got away."

"Underground Railroad."

"Did you help him? Did you see him after the fire?"

"Slightly. Who says I did?"

"Nelson."

"How did he know?"

"He guessed."

"I drove him south into the county and let him off in a cornfield."

"I hope he's not ever going to come back. I'd call the police, I mean, I would if –" Janice lets the thought die, premature.

Rabbit feels heightened and frozen by this giant need for tact;

he and she seem to be slowly revolving, afraid of jarring one another
away. "He promised he won't." Only in glory.

Relieved, Janice gestures toward the half-burned house. "It's
worth a lot of money," she says. "The insurance company wants
to settle for eleven thousand. Some man talked to Daddy and
offered nineteen-five as is. I guess the lot is worth eight or nine by
itself, this is becoming such a fashionable area."

"I thought Brewer was dying."

"Only in the middle."

"I tell you what. Let's sell the bastard."

"Let's."

They shake hands. He twirls the car keys in front of her face.
"Lemme drive you back to your parents'."

"Do we have to go there?"

"You could come to my place and visit Mom. She'd love to
see you. She can hardly talk now."

"Let's save that," Janice says. "Couldn't we just drive around?"

"Drive around? I'm not sure I still know how to drive."

"Peggy says you drove her Chrysler."

"Gee. A person doesn't have many secrets in this county."

As they drive east on Weiser toward the city, she asks, "Can
your mother manage the afternoon alone?"

"Sure. She's managed a lot of them."

"I'm beginning to like your mother, she's quite nice to me,
over the phone, when I can understand what she's saying."

"She's mellowing. Dying I guess does that to you." They cross
the bridge and drive up Weiser in the heart of Brewer, past the
Wallpaper Boutique, the roasted peanut newsstand, the expanded
funeral home, the great stores with the façades where the pale
shadow of the neon sign for the last owner underlies the hopeful
bright sign the new owners have put up, the new trash disposal
cans with tops like flying saucers, the blank marquees of the deserted movie palaces. They pass Pine Street and the Phoenix Bar. He
announces, "I ought to be out scouting printshops for a job, maybe
move to another city. Baltimore might be a good idea."

Janice says, "You look better since you stopped work. Your
color is better. Wouldn't you be happier in an outdoor job?"

"They don't pay. Only morons work outdoors anymore."

"I would keep working at Daddy's. I think I should."

"What does that have to do with me? You're going to get an apartment, remember?"

She doesn't answer again. Weiser is climbing too close to the mountain, to Mt. Judge and their old homes. He turns left on Summer Street. Brick three-stories with fanlights; optometrists' and chiropractors' signs. A limestone church with a round window. He announces, "We could buy a farm."

She makes the connection. "Because Ruth did."

"That's right, I'd forgotten," he lies, "this was her street." Once he ran along this street toward the end and never got there. He ran out of steam after a few blocks and turned around. "Remember Reverend Eccles?" he asks Janice. "I saw him this summer. The Sixties did a number on him, too."

Janice says, "And speaking of Ruth, how did you enjoy Peggy?"

"Yeah, how about that? She's gotten to be quite a girl about town."

"But you didn't go back."

"Couldn't stomach it, frankly. It wasn't her, she was great. But all this fucking, everybody fucking, I don't know, it just makes me too sad. It's what makes everything so hard to run."

"You don't think it's what *makes* things run? Human things."

"There must be something else."

She doesn't answer.

"No? Nothing else?"

Instead of answering, she says, "Ollie is back with her now, but she doesn't seem especially happy."

It is easy in a car; the STOP signs and corner groceries flicker by, brick and sandstone merge into a running screen. At the end of Summer Street he thinks there will be a brook, and then a dirt road and open pastures; but instead the city street broadens into a highway lined with hamburger diners, and drive-in sub shops, and a miniature golf course with big plaster dinosaurs, and food-stamp stores and motels and gas stations that are changing their names, Humble to Getty, Atlantic to Arco. He has been here before.

Janice says, "Want to stop?"

"I ate lunch. Didn't you?"

"Stop at a motel," she says.

"You and me?"

"You don't have to *do* anything, it's just we're wasting gas this way."

"Cheaper to waste gas than pay a motel, for Chrissake. Anyway don't they like you to have luggage?"

"They don't care. Anyway I think I did put a suitcase in the back, just in case."

He turns and looks and there it is, the tatty old brown one still with the hotel label on from the time they went to the Shore, *Wildwood Cabins*. The same suitcase she must have packed to run to Stavros with. "Say," he says. "You're full of sexy tricks now, aren't you?"

"Forget it, Harry. Take me home. I'd forgotten about you."

"These guys who run motels, don't they think it's fishy if you check in before suppertime? What time is it, two-thirty."

"Fishy? What's fishy, Harry? God, you're a prude. Everybody knows people screw. It's how we all got here. When're you going to grow up, even a little bit?"

"Still, to march right in with the sun pounding down –"

"Tell him I'm your wife. Tell him we're exhausted. It's the truth, actually. I didn't sleep two hours last night."

"Wouldn't you rather go to my parents' place? Nelson'll be home in an hour."

"Exactly. Who matters more to you, me or Nelson?"

"Nelson."

"Nelson or your mother?"

"My mother."

"You are a sick man."

"There's a place. Like it?"

Safe Haven Motel the sign says, with slats strung below it claiming

QUEEN SIZE BEDS
ALL COLOR TVS
SHOWER & BATH
TELEPHONES
"MAGIC FINGERS"

A neon VACANCY sign buzzes dull red. The office is a little brick tollbooth; there is a drained swimming pool with a green tarpaulin over it. At the long brick façade bleakly broken by doorways several cars already park; they seem to be feeding, metal cattle at a trough. Janice says, "It looks crummy."

"That's what I like about it," Rabbit says. "They might take us."

But as he says this, they have driven past. Janice asks, "Seriously, haven't you ever done this before?"

He tells her, "I guess I've led a kind of sheltered life."

"Well, it's by now," she says, of the motel.

"I could turn around."

"Then it'd be on the wrong side of the highway."

"Scared?"

"Of what?"

"Me." Racily Rabbit swings into a Garden Supplies parking lot, spewing gravel, brakes just enough to avoid a collision with oncoming traffic, crosses the doubled line, and heads back the way they came. Janice says, "If you want to kill yourself, go ahead, but don't kill me; I'm just getting to like being alive."

"It's too late," he tells her. "You'll be a grandmother in a couple more years."

"Not with you at the wheel."

But they cross the double line again and pull in safely. The VACANCY sign still buzzes. Ignition off. Lever at P. The sun shimmers on the halted asphalt. "You can't just *sit* here," Janice hisses. He gets out of the car. Air. Globes of ether, pure nervousness, slide down his legs. There is a man in the little tollbooth, along with a candy bar machine and a rack of black-tagged keys. He has wet-combed silver hair, a string tie with a horseshoe clasp, and a cold. Placing the registration card in front of Harry, he pats his chafed nostrils with a blue bandana. "Name and address and license plate number," he says. He speaks with a Western twang.

"My wife and I are really bushed," Rabbit volunteers. His ears are burning; the blush spreads downward, his undershirt feels damp, his heart jars his hand as it tries to write, *Mr. and Mrs. Harold Angstrom.* Address? Of course, he must lie. He writes unsteadily, *26 Vista Crescent, Penn Villas, Pa.* Junk mail and bills are being forwarded to him from that address. Wonderful service, the postal. Put yourself in one of those boxes, sorted from sack to sack, finally there you go, *plop*, through the right slot out of millions. A miracle that it works. Young punk revolutionaries, let them try to get the mail through, through rain and sleet and dark of night. The man with the string tie patiently leans on his Formica desk while Rabbit's thoughts race and his hand jerks. "License plate number, that's the one that counts," he peaceably drawls. "Show me a suitcase or pay in advance."

"No kidding, she is my wife."

"Must be on honeymoon straight from haah school."

"Oh, this." Rabbit looks down at his peppermint-and-cream Mt. Judge athletic jacket, and fights the creeping return of his blush. "I haven't worn this for I don't know how many years."

"Looks to almost fit," the man says, tapping the blank space for the plate number. "Ah'm in no hurry if you're not," he says.

Harry goes to the show window of the little house and studies the license plate and signals for Janice to show the suitcase. He lifts an imaginary suitcase up and down by the handle and she doesn't understand. Janice sits in their Falcon, mottled and dimmed by window reflections. He pantomimes unpacking; he draws a rectangle in the air; he exclaims, "God, she's dumb!" and she belatedly understands, reaching back and lifting the bag into view through the layers of glass between them. The man nods; Harry writes his plate number (U20–692) on the card and is given a numbered key (17). "Toward the back," the man says, "more quaat away from the road."

"I don't care if it's quiet, we're just going to sleep," Rabbit says; key in hand, he bursts into friendliness. "Where're you from, Texas? I was stationed there with the Army once, Fort Larson, near Lubbock."

The man inserts the card into a rack, looking through the lower half of his bifocals, and clucks his tongue. "You ever get up around Santa Fe?"

"Nope. Never. Sorry I didn't."

"That's my idea of a *goood* place," the man tells him.

"I'd like to go someday. I really would. Probably never will, though."

"Don't say that, young buck like you, and your cute little lady."

"I'm not so young."

"You're yungg," the man absentmindedly insists, and this is so nice of him, this and handing over the key, people are so nice generally, that Janice asks Harry as he gets back into the car what he's grinning about. "And what took so long?"

"We were talking about Santa Fe. He advised us to go."

The door numbered 17 gives on a room surprisingly long, narrow but long. The carpet is purple, and bits of backlit cardboard here and there undercut the sense of substance, as in a movie lobby. A fantasy world. The bathroom is at the far end, the walls are of cement-block painted rose, imitation oils of the ocean are trying to adorn them, two queen-sized beds look across the narrow room at a television set. Rabbit takes off his shoes and turns on the set and gets on one bed. A band of light appears, expands, jogs itself out of diagonal twitching stripes into *The Dating Game*. A colored girl from Philly is trying to decide which of three men to take her out on a date; one man is black, another is white, the third is yellow. The color is such that the Chinese man is orange and the colored girl looks bluish. The reception has a ghost so that when she laughs there are many, many teeth. Janice turns it off. Like him she is in stocking feet. They are burglars. He protests, "Hey. That was interesting. She couldn't see them behind that screen so she'd have to tell from their voices what color they were. If she cared."

"You *have* your date," Janice tells him.

"We ought to get a color television, the pro football is a lot better."

"Who's this we?"

"Oh – me and Pop and Nelson and Mom. And Mim."

"Why don't you move over on that bed?"

"You *have* your bed. Over there."

She stands there, firm-footed on the wall-to-wall carpet without stockings, nice-ankled. Her dull wool skirt is just short enough to show her knees. They have boxy edges. Nice. She asks, "What is this, a put-down?"

"Who am I to put you down? The swingingest broad on Eisenhower Avenue."

"I'm not so sure I like you anymore."

"I didn't know I had that much to lose."

"Come on. Shove over."

She throws the old camel loden coat over the plastic chair beneath the motel regulations and the fire inspector's certificate. Being puzzled darkens her eyes on him. She pulls off her sweater and as she bends to undo her skirt the bones of her shoulders ripple in long quick glints like a stack of coins being spilled. She hesitates in her slip. "Are you going to get under the covers?"

"We could," Rabbit says, yet his body is as when a fever leaves and the nerves sink down like veins of water into sand. He cannot begin to execute the energetic transitions contemplated: taking off his clothes, walking that long way to the bathroom. He should probably wash in case she wants to go down on him. Then suppose he comes too soon and they are back where they've always been. Much safer to lie here enjoying the sight of her in her slip; he had been lucky to choose a little woman, they keep their shape better than big ones. She looked older than twenty at twenty but doesn't look that much older now, at least angry as she is, black alive in her eyes. "You can get in but don't expect anything, I'm still pretty screwed up." Lately he has lost the ability to masturbate; nothing brings him up, not even the image of a Negress with nipples like dowel-ends and a Hallowe'en pumpkin instead of a head.

"I'll say," Janice says. "Don't expect anything from me either. I just don't want to have to shout between the beds."

With heroic effort Rabbit pushes himself up and walks the length of the rug to the bathroom. Returning naked, he holds his clothes in front of him and ducks into the bed as if into a burrow, being chased. He feels particles of some sort bombarding him. Janice feels skinny, strange, snaky-cool, the way she shivers tight against him immediately; the shock on his skin makes him want to sneeze. She apologizes: "They don't heat these places very well."

"Be November pretty soon."

"Isn't there a thermostat?"

"Yeah. I see it. Way over in the corner. You can go turn it up if you want."

"Thanks. The man should do that."

Neither moves. Harry says, "Hey. Does this remind you of Linda Hammacher's bed?" She was the girl who when they were all working at Kroll's had an apartment in Brewer she let Harry and Janice use.

"Not much. That had a view."

They try to talk, but out of sleepiness and strangeness it only comes in spurts. "So," Janice says after a silence wherein nothing happens. "Who do you think you are?"

"Nobody," he answers. He snuggles down as if to kiss her breasts but doesn't; their presence near his lips drugs him. All sorts of winged presences exert themselves in the air above their covers.

Silence resumes and stretches, a ballerina in the red beneath his eyelids. He abruptly asserts, "The kid really hates me now."

Janice says, "No he doesn't." She contradicts herself promptly, by adding, "He'll get over it." Feminine logic: smother and out-last what won't be wished away. Maybe the only way. He touches her low and there is moss, it doesn't excite him, but it is re-assuring, to have that patch there, something to hide in.

Her body irritably shifts; him not kissing her breasts or any-thing, she puts the cold soles of her feet on the tops of his. He sneezes. The bed heaves. She laughs. To rebuke her, he asks inno-cently, "You always came with Stavros?"

"Not always."

"You miss him now?"

"No."

"Why not?"

"You're here."

"But don't I seem sad, sort of?"

"You're making me pay, a little. That's all right."

He protests, "I'm a mess," meaning he is sincere: which per-haps is not a meaningful adjustment over what she had said. He feels they are still adjusting in space, slowly twirling in some gor-geous ink that filters through his lids as red. In a space of silence, he can't gauge how much, he feels them drift along sideways deeper into being married, so much that he abruptly volunteers, "We must have Peggy and Ollie over sometime."

"Like hell," she says, jarring him, but softly, an unexpected joggle in space. "You stay away from her now, you had your crack at it."

After a while he asks her – she knows everything, he realizes – "Do you think Vietnam will ever be over?"

"Charlie thought it would, just as soon as the big industrial interests saw that it was unprofitable."

"God, these foreigners are dumb," Rabbit murmurs.

"Meaning Charlie?"

"All of you." He feels, gropingly, he should elaborate. "Skeeter thought it was the doorway into utter confusion. There would be this terrible period, of utter confusion, and then there would be a wonderful stretch of perfect calm, with him ruling, or somebody exactly like him."

"Did you believe it?"

"I would have liked to, but I'm too rational. Confusion is just a local view of things working out in general. That make sense?"

"I'm not sure," Janice says.

"You think Mom ever had any lovers?"

"Ask her."

"I don't dare."

After another while, Janice announces, "If you're not going to make love, I might as well turn my back and get some sleep. I was up almost all night worrying about this – reunion."

"How do you think it's going?"

"Fair."

The slither of sheets as she rotates her body is a silver music, sheets of pale noise extending outward unresisted by space. There was a grip he used to have on her, his right hand cupping her skull through her hair and his left hand on her breasts gathering them together, so the nipples were an inch apart. The grip is still there. Her ass and legs float away. He asks her, "How do we get out of here?"

"We put on our clothes and walk out the door. But let's have a nap first. You're talking nonsense already."

"It'll be so embarrassing. The guy at the desk'll think we've been up to no good."

"He doesn't care."

"He does, he *does* care. We could stay all night to make him feel better, but nobody else knows where we are. They'll worry."

"Stop it, Harry. We'll go in an hour. Just shut up."

"I feel so guilty."

"About what?"

"About everything."

"Relax. Not everything is your fault."

"I can't accept that."

He lets her breasts go, lets them float away, radiant debris. The space they are in, the motel room long and secret as a burrow, becomes all interior space. He slides down an inch on the cool sheet and fits his microcosmic self limp into the curved crevice between the polleny offered nestling orbs of her ass; he would stiffen but his hand having let her breasts go comes upon the familiar dip of her waist, ribs to hip bone, where no bones are, soft as flight, fat's inward curve, slack, his babies from her belly. He finds this inward curve and slips along it, sleeps. He. She. Sleeps. O.K.?

RABBIT IS RICH

"At night he lights up a good cigar, and climbs into the little old 'bus, and maybe cusses the carburetor, and shoots out home. He mows the lawn, or sneaks in some practice putting, and then he's ready for dinner."
— George Babbitt, of the Ideal Citizen

The difficulty to think at the end of day,
When the shapeless shadow covers the sun
And nothing is left except light on your fur ...
—Wallace Stevens, "A Rabbit as King of the Ghosts"

I

RUNNING out of gas, Rabbit Angstrom thinks as he stands behind
the summer-dusty windows of the Springer Motors display room
watching the traffic go by on Route 111, traffic somehow thin and
scared compared to what it used to be. The fucking world is running out of gas. But they won't catch him, not yet, because there
isn't a piece of junk on the road gets better mileage than his
Toyotas, with lower service costs. Read *Consumer Reports*, April
issue. That's all he has to tell the people when they come in. And
come in they do, the people out there are getting frantic, they
know the great American ride is ending. Gas lines at ninety-nine
point nine cents a gallon and ninety per cent of the stations to be
closed for the weekend. The governor of the Commonwealth of
Pennsylvania calling for five-dollar minimum sales to stop the panicky topping-up. And truckers who can't get diesel shooting at
their own trucks, there was an incident right in Diamond County,
along the Pottsville Pike. People are going wild, their dollars are
going rotten, they shell out like there's no tomorrow. He tells
them, when they buy a Toyota, they're turning their dollars into
yen. And they believe him. A hundred twelve units new and used
moved in the first five months of 1979, with eight Corollas, five
Coronas including a Luxury Edition Wagon, and that Celica that
Charlie said looked like a Pimpmobile unloaded in these first three
weeks of June already, at an average gross mark-up of eight hundred dollars per sale. Rabbit is rich.

He owns Springer Motors, one of the two Toyota agencies in
the Brewer area. Or rather he co-owns a half-interest with his wife
Janice, her mother Bessie sitting on the other half inherited when
old man Springer died five years back. But Rabbit feels as though
he owns it all, showing up at the showroom day after day, riding
herd on the paperwork and the payroll, swinging in his clean suit
in and out of Service and Parts where the men work filmed with

oil and look up white-eyed from the bulb-lit engines as in a kind
of underworld while he makes contact with the public, the community, the star and spearpoint of all these two dozen employees
and hundred thousand square feet of working space, which seem
a wide shadow behind him as he stands there up front. The wall
of imitation boards, really sheets of random-grooved Masonite,
around the door into his office is hung with framed old clippings
and team portraits, including two all-county tens, from his days as
a basketball hero twenty years ago – no, more than twenty-five
years now. Even under glass, the clippings keep yellowing, something in the chemistry of the paper apart from the air, something
like the deepening taint of sin people used to try to scare you with.
ANGSTROM HITS FOR 42. *"Rabbit" Leads Mt. Judge Into Semi-Finals.*
Resurrected from the attic where his dead parents had long kept
them, in scrapbooks whose mucilage had dried so they came loose
like snakeskins, these clippings thus displayed were Fred Springer's
idea, along with that phrase about an agency's reputation being the
shadow of the man up front. Knowing he was dying long before
he did, Fred was getting Harry ready to be the man up front. When
you think of the dead, you got to be grateful.

Ten years ago when Rabbit got laid off as a Linotyper and reconciled with Janice, her father took him on as salesman and when
the time was ripe five years later had the kindness to die. Who
would have thought such a little tense busy bird of a man could
get it up for a massive coronary? Hypertense: his diastolic had been
up around one-twenty for years. Loved salt. Loved to talk
Republican, too, and when Nixon left him nothing to say he had
kind of burst. Actually, he had lasted a year into Ford, but the skin
of his face was getting tighter and the red spots where the cheek
and jaw bones pressed from underneath redder. When Harry
looked down at him rouged in the coffin he saw it had been coming, dead Fred hadn't much changed. From the way Janice and her
mother carried on you would have thought a mixture of Prince
Valiant and Moses had bit the dust. Maybe having already buried
both his own parents made Harry hard. He looked down, noticed
that Fred's hair had been parted wrong, and felt nothing. The great
thing about the dead, they make space.

While old man Springer was still prancing around, life at the lot was hard. He kept long hours, held the showroom open on winter nights when there wasn't a snowplow moving along Route 111, was always grinding away in that little high-pitched grinder of a voice about performance guidelines and washout profits and customer servicing and whether or not a mechanic had left a thumbprint on some heap's steering wheel or a cigarette butt in the ashtray. When he was around the lot it was like they were all trying to fill some big skin that Springer spent all his time and energy imagining, the ideal Springer Motors. When he died that skin became Harry's own, to stand around in loosely. Now that he is king of the lot he likes it here, the acre of asphalt, the new-car smell present even in the pamphlets and pep talks Toyota mails from California, the shampooed carpet wall to wall, the yellowing basketball feats up on the walls along with the plaques saying Kiwanis and Rotary and C of C and the trophies on a high shelf won by the Little League teams the company sponsors, the ample square peace of this masculine place spiced by the girls in billing and reception that come and go under old Mildred Kroust, and the little cards printed with HAROLD C. ANGSTROM on them and CHIEF SALES REPRESENTATIVE. The man up front. A center of sorts, where he had been a forward. There is an airiness to it for Harry, standing there in his own skin, casting a shadow. The cars sell themselves, is his philosophy. The Toyota commercials on television are out there all the time, preying on people's minds. He likes being part of all that; he likes the nod he gets from the community, that had overlooked him like dirt ever since high school. The other men in Rotary and Chamber turn out to be the guys he played ball with back then, or their ugly younger brothers. He likes having money to float in, a big bland good guy is how he sees himself, six three and around two fifteen by now, with a forty-two waist the suit salesman at Kroll's tried to tell him until he sucked his gut in and the man's thumb grudgingly inched the tape tighter. He avoids mirrors, when he used to love them. The face far in his past, crewcut and thin-jawed with sleepy predatory teen-age eyes in the glossy team portraits, exists in his present face like the chrome bones of a grille within the full front view of a car and its fenders. His nose is still small and straight, his eyes maybe less sleepy. An ample blown-dry-looking businessman's haircut masks his eartips and fills in where his temples are receding. He didn't much like the counterculture with all its drugs and draft-dodging but he does like being allowed within limits to let your hair grow longer than those old Marine cuts and to have it naturally fluff out. In the shaving mirror a chaos of wattles and slack cords blooms beneath his chin in a way that doesn't bear study. Still, life is sweet. That's what old people used to say and when he was young he wondered how they could mean it.

Last night it hailed in Brewer and its suburbs. Stones the size of marbles leaped up from the slant little front yards and drummed on the tin signs supporting flickering neon downtown; then came a downpour whose puddles reflected a dawn gray as stone. But the day has turned breezy and golden and the patched and white-striped asphalt of the lot is dry, late in the afternoon of this longest Saturday in June and the first of calendar summer. Usually on a Saturday Route 111 is buzzing with shoppers pillaging the malls hacked from the former fields of corn, rye, tomatoes, cabbages, and strawberries. Across the highway, the four concrete lanes and the median divider of aluminum battered by many forgotten accidents, stands a low building faced in dark clinker brick that in the years since Harry watched its shell being slapped together of plywood has been a succession of unsuccessful restaurants and now serves as the Chuck Wagon, specializing in barbecued take-outs. The Chuck Wagon too seems quiet today. Beyond its lot littered with flattened take-out cartons a lone tree, a dusty maple, drinks from a stream that has become a mere ditch. Beneath its branches a picnic table rots unused, too close to the overflowing dumpster the restaurant keeps by its kitchen door. The ditch marks the bound of a piece of farmland sold off but still awaiting its development. This shapely old maple from its distance seems always to be making to Harry an appeal he must ignore.

He turns from the dusty window and says to Charlie Stavros, "They're running scared out there."

Charlie looks up from the desk where he is doing paperwork, the bill of sale and NV-1 on a '74 Barracuda 8 they finally moved for twenty-eight hundred yesterday. Nobody wants these old guzzlers, though you got to take them on trade-in. Charlie handles the used cars. Though he has been with Springer Motors twice as long as Harry, his desk is in a corner of the showroom, out in the open, and the title on his card is SENIOR SALES REPRESENTATIVE. Yet he bears no grudge. He sets down his pen even with the edge of his papers and in response to his boss asks, "Did you see in the paper the other day where some station owner and his wife somewhere in the middle of the state were pumping gas for a line and one of the cars slips its clutch and crushes the wife against the car next in line, broke her hip I think I read, and while the husband was holding her and begging for help the people in the cars instead of giving him any help took over the pumps and gave themselves free gas?"

"Yeah," Harry says, "I guess I heard that on the radio, though it's hard to believe. Also about some guy in Pittsburgh who takes a couple of two-by-fours with him and drives his back wheels up on them so as to get a few more cents' worth of gas in his tank. That's fanatical."

Charlie emits a sardonic, single-syllabled laugh, and explains, "The little man is acting like the oil companies now. I'll get mine, and screw you."

"I don't blame the oil companies," Harry says tranquilly. "It's too big for them too. Mother Earth is drying up, is all."

"Shit, champ, you never blame anybody," Stavros tells the taller man. "Skylab could fall on your head right now and you'd go down saying the government had done its best."

Harry tries to picture this happening and agrees, "Maybe so. They're strapped these days like everybody else. About all the feds can do these days is meet their own payroll."

"That they're guaranteed to do, the greedy bastards. Listen, Harry. You know damn well Carter and the oil companies have rigged this whole mess. What does Big Oil want? Bigger profits. What does Carter want? Less oil imports, less depreciation of the dollar. He's too chicken to ration, so he's hoping higher prices will do it for him. We'll have dollar-fifty no-lead before the year is out."

"And people'll pay it," Harry says, serene in his middle years. The two men fall silent, as if arrived at a truce, while the scared traffic kicks up dust along the business strip of Route 111 and the unbought Toyotas in the showroom exude new-car smell. Ten

years ago Stavros had an affair with Harry's wife Janice. Harry
thinks of Charlie's prick inside Janice and his feeling is hostile and
cozy in almost equal proportions, coziness getting the edge. At the
time he took his son-in-law on, old man Springer asked him if he
could stomach working with him, Charlie. Rabbit didn't see why
not. Sensing he was being asked to bargain, he said he'd work with
him, not under him. *No question of that, you'd be under me only, as
long as I'm among the living*, Springer had promised: *you two'll work
side by side.* Side by side then they had waited for customers in all
weathers and bemoaned their boss's finickiness and considered
monthly which of the used cars on inventory would never move
and should be wholesaled to cut carrying costs. Side by side they
had suffered with Springer Motors as the Datsun franchise came
into the Brewer area, and then those years when everyone was
buying VWs and Volvos, and now the Hondas and Le Car presenting themselves as the newest thing in cute economy. In these
nine years Harry added thirty pounds to his frame while Charlie
went from being a chunky Greek who when he put on his shades
and a checked suit looked like an enforcer for the local numbers
racket to a shrivelled little tipster-type. Stavros had always had a
tricky ticker, from rheumatic fever when he was a boy. Janice had
been moved by this, this weakness hidden within him, his squarish chest. Now like a flaw ramifying to the surface of a crystal his
infirmity has given him that dehydrated prissy look of a reformed
rummy, of a body preserved day to day by taking thought. His eyebrows that used to go straight across like an iron bar have dwindled
in to be two dark clumps, disconnected, almost like the charcoal
dabs clowns wear. His sideburns have gone white so the top of his
tightly wavy hair looks dyed in a broad stripe. Each morning at
work Charlie changes his lavender-tinted black hornrims for ones
with amber lenses the instant he's indoors, and walks through the
day's business like a grizzled old delicate ram who doesn't want to
slip on a crag and fall. *Side by side, I promise you.* When old man
Springer promised that, when he turned his full earnestness on
anything, the pink patches in his face glowed red and his lips tightened back from his teeth so you thought all the more of his skull.
Dirty yellow teeth loaded with gum-line fillings, and his sand-
colored mustache never looked quite even, or quite clean.

The dead, Jesus. They were multiplying, and they look up begging you to join them, promising it is all right, it is very soft down here. Pop, Mom, old man Springer, Jill, the baby called Becky for her little time, Tothero. Even John Wayne, the other day. The obituary page every day shows another stalk of a harvest endlessly rich, the faces of old teachers, customers, local celebrities like himself flashing for a moment and then going down. For the first time since childhood Rabbit is happy, simply, to be alive. He tells Charlie, "I figure the oil's going to run out about the same time I do, the year two thousand. Seems funny to say it, but I'm glad I lived when I did. These kids coming up, they'll be living on table scraps. We had the meal."

"You've been sold a bill of goods," Charlie tells him. "You and a lot of others. Big Oil has enough reserves located right now to last five hundred years, but they want to ooze it out. In the Delaware Bay right now I heard there's seventeen supertankers, seventeen, at anchor waiting for the prices to go up enough for them to come into the South Philly refineries and unload. Meanwhile you get murdered in gas lines."

"Stop driving. Run," Rabbit tells him. "I've begun this jogging thing and it feels great. I want to lose thirty pounds." Actually his resolve to run before breakfast every day, in the dew of the dawn, lasted less than a week. Now he contents himself with trotting around the block after supper sometimes to get away from his wife and her mother while they crab at each other.

He has touched a sore point. Charlie confides as if to the NV-1 form, "Doctor tells me if I try any exercise he washes his hands."

Rabbit is abashed, slightly. "Really? That's not what that Doctor Whatsisname used to say. White. Paul Dudley White."

"He died. Exercise freaks are dropping down dead in the parks like flies. It doesn't get into the papers because the fitness industry has become big bucks. Remember all those little health-food stores hippies used to run? You know who runs 'em now? General Mills."

Harry doesn't always know how seriously to take Charlie. He does know, in relation to his old rival, that he is hearty and huge, indisputably preferred by God in this chance matter of animal health. If Janice had run off with Charlie like she wanted to she'd be nothing but a nursemaid now. As is, she plays tennis three, four times a week and has never looked sharper. Harry keeps wanting to downplay himself around Charlie, protecting the more fragile man from the weight of his own good fortune. He keeps silent, while Charlie's mind works its way back from the shame and shadow of his doctor washing his hands, back into memory's reserves of energy. "Gasoline," he suddenly says, giving it that Greek cackle, almost a wheeze. "Didn't we used to burn it up? I had an Imperial once with twin carburetors and when you took off the filter and looked down through the butterfly valve when the thing was idling it looked like a toilet being flushed."

Harry laughs, wanting to ride along. "Cruising," he says, "after high school got out, there was nothing to do but cruise. Back and forth along Central, back and forth. Those old V-8s, what do you think they got to the gallon? Ten, twelve miles? Nobody ever thought to keep track."

"My uncles still won't drive a little car. Say they don't want to get crumpled if they meet a truck."

"Remember Chicken? Funny more kids weren't killed than were."

"Cadillacs. If one of his brothers got a Buick with fins, my father had to have a Cadillac with bigger fins. You couldn't count the taillights, it looked like a carton of red eggs."

"There was one guy at Mt. Judge High, Don Eberhardt, 'd get out on the running board of his Dad's Dodge when it was going down the hill behind the box factory and steer from out there. All the way down the hill."

"First car I bought for myself, it was a '48 Studebaker, with that nose that looked like an airplane. Had about sixty-five thousand miles on it, it was the summer of '53. The dig-out on that baby! After a stoplight you could feel the front wheels start to lift, just like an airplane."

"Here's a story. One time when we were pretty newly married I got sore at Janice for something, just being herself probably, and drove to West Virginia and back in one night. Crazy. You couldn't do that now without going to the savings bank first."

"Yeah," Charlie says slowly, saddened. Rabbit hadn't wanted to sadden him. He could never figure out, exactly, how much the man had loved Janice. "She described that. You did a lot of roaming around then."

"A little. I brought the car back though. When she left me, she took the car and kept it. As you remember."

"Do I?"

He has never married, and that says something flattering, to Janice and therefore to Harry, the way it's worked out. A man fucks your wife, it puts a new value on her, within limits. Harry wants to restore the conversation to the cheerful plane of dwindling energy. He tells Stavros, "Saw a kind of funny joke in the paper the other day. It said, You can't beat Christopher Columbus for mileage. Look how far he got on three galleons." He pronounces the crucial word carefully, in three syllables; but Charlie doesn't act as if he gets it, only smiles a one-sided twitch of a smile that could be in response to pain.

"The oil companies made us do it," Charlie says. "They said, Go ahead, burn it up like madmen, all these highways, the shopping malls, everything. People won't believe it in a hundred years, the sloppy way we lived."

"It's like wood," Harry says, groping back through history, which is a tinted fog to him, marked off in centuries like a football field, with a few dates – 1066, 1776 – pinpointed and a few faces – George Washington, Hitler – hanging along the sidelines, not cheering. "Or coal. As a kid I can remember the anthracite rattling down the old coal chute, with these red dots they used to put on it. I couldn't imagine how they did it, I thought it was something that happened in the ground. Little elves with red brushes. Now there isn't any anthracite. That stuff they strip-mine now just crumbles in your hand." It gives him pleasure, makes Rabbit feel rich, to contemplate the world's wasting, to know that the earth is mortal too.

"Well," Charlie sighs. "At least it's going to keep those chinks from ever having an industrial revolution."

That seems to wrap it up, though Harry feels they have let something momentous, something alive under the heading of energy, escape. But a lot of topics, he has noticed lately, in private conversation and even on television where they're paid to talk it up, run dry, exhaust themselves, as if everything's been said in this hemisphere. In his inner life too Rabbit dodges among more blanks than there used to be, patches of burnt-out gray cells where there used to be lust and keen dreaming and wide-eyed dread; he falls asleep, for instance, at the drop of a hat. He never used to understand the phrase. But then he never used to wear a hat and now, at the first breath of cold weather, he does. His roof wearing thin, starlight showing through.

You Asked For It, We Got It, the big paper banner on the showroom window cries, in tune with the current Toyota television campaign. The sign cuts a slice from the afternoon sun and gives the showroom a muted aquarium air, or that of a wide sunken ship wherein the two Coronas and the acid-green Corolla SR-5 liftback wait to be bought and hoisted into the air on the other side of the glass and set down safe on the surface of the lot and Route 111 and the world of asphalt beyond.

A car swings in from this world: a fat tired '71 or '2 Country Squire wagon soft on its shocks, with one dented fender hammered out semi-smooth but the ruddy rustproofing underpaint left to do for a finish. A young couple steps out, the girl milky-pale and bare-legged and blinking in the sunshine but the boy roughened and reddened by the sun, his jeans dirt-stiffened by actual work done in the red mud of the county. A kind of crate of rough green boards has been built into the Squire's chrome roof rack and from where Rabbit is standing, a soft wedge shot away, he can see how the upholstery and inner padding have been mangled by the station wagon's use as a farm truck. "Hicks," Charlie says from his desk. The pair comes in shyly, like elongated animals, sniffing the air-conditioned air.

Feeling protective, God knows why, Charlie's snipe ringing in his ears, Harry walks toward them, glancing at the girl's hand to see if she wears a wedding ring. She does not, but such things mean less than they used to. Kids shack up. Her age he puts at nineteen or twenty, the boy a bit older – the age of his own son. "Can I help you folks?"

The boy brushes back his hair, showing a low white forehead. His broad baked face gives him a look of smiling even when he isn't. "We chust came in for some information." His accent bespeaks the south of the county, less aggressively Dutch than the north, where the brick churches get spiky and the houses and barns are built of limestone instead of sandstone. Harry figures them for leaving some farm to come into the city, with no more need to haul fenceposts and hay bales and pumpkins and whatever else this poor heap was made to haul. Shack up, get city jobs, and spin around in a little Corolla. We got it. But the boy could be just scouting out prices for his father, and the girlfriend be riding along, or not even be a girlfriend, but a sister, or a hitchhiker. A little touch of the hooker about her looks. The way her soft body wants to spill from these small clothes, the faded denim shorts and purple Paisley halter. The shining faintly freckled flesh of her shoulders and top arms and the busy wanton abundance of her browny-red many-colored hair, carelessly bundled. A buried bell rings. She has blue eyes in deep sockets and the silence of a girl from the country used to letting men talk while she holds a sweet-and-sour secret in her mouth, sucking it. An incongruous disco touch in her shoes, with their high cork heels and ankle straps. Pink toes, painted nails. This girl will not stick with this boy. Rabbit wants this to be so; he imagines he feels an unwitting swimming of her spirit upward toward his, while her manner is all stillness. He feels she wants to hide from him, but is too big and white, too suddenly womanly, too nearly naked. Her shoes accent the length of her legs; she is taller than average, and not quite fat, though tending toward chunky, especially around the chest. Her upper lip closes over the lower with a puffy bruised look. She is bruisable, he wants to protect her; he relieves her of the pressure of his gaze, too long by a second, and turns to the boy.

"This is a Corolla," Harry says, slapping orange tin. "The two-door model begins at thirty-nine hundred and will give you highway mileage up to forty a gallon and twenty to twenty-five city driving. I know some other makes advertise more but believe me you can't get a better buy in America today than this jalopy right here. Read *Consumer Reports*, April issue. Much better than average on maintenance and repairs through the first four years. Who in this day and age keeps a car much longer than four years? In four years we may all be pushing bicycles the way things are going. This particular car has four-speed synchromesh transmission, fully transistorized ignition system, power-assisted front disc brakes, vinyl reclining bucket seats, a locking gas cap. That last feature's getting to be pretty important. Have you noticed lately how all the auto-supply stores are selling out of their siphons? You can't buy a siphon in Brewer today for love nor money, guess why. My mother-in-law's old Chrysler over in Mt. Judge was drained dry the other day in front of the hairdresser's, she hardly ever takes the buggy out except to go to church. People are getting rough. Did you notice in the paper this morning where Carter is taking gas from the farmers and going to give it to the truckers? Shows the power of a gun, doesn't it?"

"I didn't see the paper," the boy says.

He is standing there so stolidly Harry has to move around him with a quick shuffle-step, dodging a cardboard cutout of a happy customer with her dog and packages, to slap acid-green. "Now if you want to replace your big old wagon, that's some antique, with another wagon that gives you almost just as much space for half the running expense, this SR-5 has some beautiful features – a *five*-speed transmission with an overdrive that really saves fuel on a long trip, and a fold-down split rear seat that enables you to carry one passenger back there and still have the long space on the other side for golf clubs or fenceposts or whatever. I don't know why Detroit never thought it, that split seat. Here we're supposed to be Automobile Heaven and the foreigners come up with all the ideas. If you ask me Detroit's let us all down, two hundred million of us. I'd much rather handle native American cars but between the three of us they're junk. They're cardboard. They're pretend."

"Now what are those over there?" the boy asks.

"That's the Corona, if you want to move toward the top of the line. Bigger engine – twenty-two hundred ccs. Instead of sixteen. More of a European look. I drive one and love it. I get about thirty miles to the gallon on the highway, eighteen or so in Brewer. Depends on how you drive, of course. How heavy a foot you have. Those testers for *Consumer Reports*, they must really give it the gun, their mileage figures are the one place they seem off to me. This liftback here is priced at sixty-eight five, but remember you're buying yen for dollars, and when trade-in time comes you get your yen back."

The girl smiles at "yen." The boy, gaining confidence, says,

"And this one here now." The young farmer has touched the Celica's suave black hood. Harry is running out of enthusiasm. Interested in that, the kid wasn't very interested in buying.

"You've just put your hand on one super machine," Harry tells him. "The Celica GT Sport Coupe, a car that'll ride with a Porsche or an MG any day. Steel-belted radials, quartz crystal clock, AM/FM stereo – all standard. *Standard*. You can imagine what the extras are. This one has power steering and a sun roof. Frankly, it's pricey, pretty near five figures, but like I say, it's an investment. That's how people buy cars now, more and more. That old Kleenex mentality of trade it in every two years is gone with the wind. Buy a good solid car now, you'll have something for a long while, while the dollars if you keep 'em will go straight to Hell. Buy good goods, that's my advice to any young man starting up right now."

He must be getting too impassioned, for the boy says, "We're chust looking around, more or less."

"I understand that," Rabbit says quickly, pivoting to face the silent girl. "You're under absolutely no pressure from me. Picking a car is like picking a mate – you want to take your time." The girl blushes and looks away. Generous paternal talkativeness keeps bubbling up in Harry. "It's still a free country, the Commies haven't gotten any further than Cambodia. No way I can make you folks buy until you're good and ready. It's all the same to me, this product sells itself. Actually you're lucky there's such a selection on the floor, a shipment came in two weeks ago and we won't have another until August. Japan can't make enough of these cars to keep the world happy. Toyota is number-one import all over the globe." He can't take his eyes off this girl. Those chunky eye-sockets reminding him of somebody. The milky flecked shoulders, the dent of flesh where the halter strap digs. Squeeze her and you'd leave thumbprints, she's that fresh from the oven. "Tell me," he says, "which size're you thinking of? You planning to cart a family around, or just yourselves?"

The girl's blush deepens. Don't marry this chump, Harry thinks. His brats will drag you down. The boy says, "We don't need another wagon. My dad has a Chevy pick-up, and he let me take the Squire over when I got out of high school."

"A great junk car," Rabbit concedes. "You can hurt it but you can't kill it. Even in '71 they were putting more metal in than they do now. Detroit is giving up the ghost." He feels he is floating – on their youth, on his money, on the brightness of this June afternoon and its promise that tomorrow, a Sunday, will be fair for his golf game. "But for people planning to tie the knot and get serious you need something more than a nostalgia item, you need something more like this." He slaps orange tin again and reads irritation in the cool pallor of the girl's eyes as they lift to his. Forgive me, baby, you get so fucking bored standing around in here, when the time comes you tend to run off at the mouth.

Stavros, forgotten, calls from his desk, across the showroom space awash in sun shafts slowly approaching the horizontal, "Maybe they'd like to take a spin." He wants peace and quiet for his paperwork.

"Want to test drive?" Harry asks the couple.

"It's pretty late," the boy points out.

"It'll take a minute. You only pass this way once. Live it up. I'll get some keys and a plate. Charlie, are the keys to the blue Corolla outside hanging on the pegboard or in your desk?"

"I'll get 'em," Charlie grunts. He pushes up from his desk and, still bent, goes into the corridor behind the waist-high partition of frosted glass – a tacky improvement ordered by Fred Springer toward the end of his life. Behind it, three hollow flush doors in a wall of fake-walnut pressboard open into the offices of Mildred Kroust and the billing girl, whoever she is that month, with the office of the Chief Sales Representative between them. The doors are usually ajar and the girl and Mildred keep crossing back and forth to consult. Harry prefers to stand out here on the floor. In the old days there were just three steel desks and a strip of carpet; the one closed door marked the company toilet with its dispenser of powdered soap you turned upside down to get any out of. Reception now is off in another separate cubicle, adjoining the waiting room where few customers ever wait. The keys Charlie needs hang, among many others, some no longer unlocking anything in this world, on a pegboard darkened by the touch of greasy fingertips beside the door on the way to Parts: Parts, that tunnel of loaded steel shelves whose sliding window overlooks the clangorous cavern of Service. No reason for Charlie to go except he knows where things are and you don't want to leave customers alone for a moment and feeling foolish, they're apt to sneak away. More timid than deer, customers. With nothing to say between them, the boy, the girl, and Harry can hear the faint strained wheeze of Charlie's breathing as he comes back with the demonstrator Corolla keys and the dealer's plate on its rusty spring clip. "Want me to take these youngsters out?" he asks.

"No, you sit and rest," Harry tells him, adding, "You might start locking up in back." Their sign claims they are open Saturdays to six but on this ominous June day of gas drought quarter of should be close enough. "Back in a minute."

The boy asks the girl, "Want to come or stay here?"

"Oh, *come*," she says, impatience lighting up her mild face as she turns and names him. "Jamie, Mother expects me *back*."

Harry reassures her, "It'll just take a minute." Mother. He wishes he could ask her to describe Mother.

Out on the lot, bright wind is bringing summer in. The spots of grass around the asphalt sport buttery dabs of dandelion. He clips the plate to the back of the Corolla and hands the boy the keys. He holds the seat on the passenger side forward so the girl can get into the rear; as she does so the denim of her shorts permits a peek of cheek of ass. Rabbit squeezes into the death seat and explains to Jamie the trinkets of the dashboard, including the space where a tape deck could go. They are, all three passengers, on the tall side, and the small car feels stuffed. Yet with imported spunk the Toyota tugs them into rapid motion and finds its place in the passing lane of Route 111. Like riding on the back of a big bumblebee; you feel on top of the buzzing engine. "Peppy," Jamie acknowledges.

"And smooth, considering," Harry adds, trying not to brake on the bare floor. To the girl he calls backwards, "You O.K.? Shall I slide my seat forward to give more room?" The way the shorts are so short now you wonder if the crotches don't hurt. The stitching, pinching up.

"No I'm all right, I'll sit sideways."

He wants to turn and look at her but at his age turning his head is not so easy and indeed some days he wakes with pains all through the neck and shoulders from no more cause than his dead weight on the bed all night. He tells Jamie, "This is the sixteen hundred cc., they make a twelve hundred base model but we don't like to handle it, I'd hate to have it on my conscience that somebody was killed because he didn't have enough pick-up to get around a truck or something on these American roads. Also we believe in carrying a pretty full complement of options; without 'em you'll find yourself short-changed on the trade-in when the time comes." He manages to work his body around to look at the girl. "These Japanese for all their good qualities have pretty short legs," he tells her. The way she has to sit, her ass is nearly on the floor and her knees are up in the air, these young luminous knees inches from his face.

Unself-consciously she is pulling a few long hairs away from her mouth where they have blown and gazing through the side window at this commercial stretch of greater Brewer. Fast-food huts in eye-catching shapes and retail outlets of everything from bridal outfits to plaster birdbaths have widened the aspect of this, the old Weisertown Pike, with their parking lots, leaving the odd surviving house and its stump of a front lawn sticking out painfully. Competitors – Pike Porsche and Renault, Diefendorfer Volkswagen, Old Red Barn Mazda and BMW, Diamond County Automotive Imports – flicker their FUEL ECONOMY banners while the gasoline stations intermixed with their beckoning have shrouded pumps and tow trucks parked across the lanes where automobiles once glided in, were filled, and glided on. An effect of hostile barricade, late in the day. Where did the shrouds come from? Some of them quite smartly tailored, in squared-off crimson canvas. A new industry, gas pump shrouds. Among vacant lakes of asphalt a few small stands offer strawberries and early peas. A tall sign gestures to a cement-block building well off the road; Rabbit can remember when this was a giant Mister Peanut pointing toward a low shop where salted nuts were arrayed in glass cases, Brazil nuts and hazelnuts and whole cashews and for a lesser price broken ones, Diamond County a great area for nuts but not that great, the shop failed. Its shell was broken and doubled in size and made into a nightclub and the sign repainted, keeping the top hat but Mister Peanut becoming a human reveller in white tie and trails. Now after many mutilations this sign has been turned into an ill-fitted female figure, a black silhouette with no bumps indicating clothing, her head thrown back and the large letters D I S C O falling in bubbles as if plucked one by one from her cut throat. Beyond such advertisements the worn green hills hold a haze of vapor and pale fields bake as their rows of corn thicken. The inside of the Corolla is warming with a mingled human smell. Harry thinks of the girl's long thigh as she stretched her way into the back seat and imagines he smells vanilla. Cunt would be a good flavor of ice cream, Sealtest ought to work on it.

The silence from the young people troubles him. He prods it. He says, "Some storm last night. I heard on the radio this morning the underpass at Eisenhower and Seventh was flooded for over an hour."

Then he says, "You know it seems gruesome to me, all these gas stations closed up like somebody has died."

Then he says, "Did you see in the paper where the Hershey company has had to lay off nine hundred people because of the truckers' strike? Next thing we'll be in lines for Hershey bars."

The boy is intently passing a Freihofer's Bakery truck and Harry responds for him: "The downtown stores are all pulling out. Nothing left in the middle of the city now but the banks and the post office. They put that crazy stand of trees in to make a mall but it won't do any good, the people are still scared to go downtown."

The boy is staying in the fast lane, and in third gear, either for the pep or because he's forgotten there is a fourth. Harry asks him, "Getting the feel of it, Jamie? If you want to turn around, there's an intersection coming up."

The girl understands. "Jamie, we better turn around. The man wants to get home for supper."

As Jamie slows to ease right at the intersection, a Pacer — silliest car on the road, looks like a glass bathtub upside-down — swings left without looking. The driver is a fat spic in a Hawaiian shirt. The boy slaps the steering wheel in vain search for the horn. Toyota indeed has put the horn in a funny place, on two little arcs a thumb's reach inside the steering-wheel rim; Harry reaches over quick and toots for him. The Pacer swerves back into its lane, with a dark look back above the Hawaiian shirt. Harry directs, "Jamie, I want you to take a left at the next light and go across the

highway and take the next left you can and that'll bring us back."
To the girl he explains, "Prettier this way." He thinks aloud,
"What can I tell you about the car I haven't? It has a lot of locks.
Those Japanese, they live on top of each other and are crazy about
locks. Don't kid yourselves, we're coming to it, I won't be here to
see it, but you will. When I was a kid nobody ever thought to lock
their house and now everybody does, except my crazy wife. If she
locked the door she'd lose the key. One of the reasons I'd like to
go to Japan – Toyota asks some of their dealers but you got to have
a bigger gross than I do – is to see how you lock up a paper house.
At any rate. You can't get the key out of the ignition without
releasing this catch down here. The trunk in back releases from this
lever. The locking gas cap you already know about. Did either of
you hear about the woman somewhere around Ardmore this week
who cut into a gas line and the guy behind her got so mad he
sneaked his own locking gas cap onto her tank so when she got to
the pump the attendant couldn't remove it? They had to tow her
away. Serve the bitch right, if you ask me."

They have taken their two lefts and are winding along a road
where fields come to the edge so you can see the clumps of red
earth still shiny from where the plow turned them, and where what
businesses there are – LAWNMOWERS SHARPENED, PA. DUTCH
QUILTS – seem to stem from an earlier decade than those along
Route 111, which runs parallel. On the banks of the road, between
mailboxes some of which are painted with a heart or hex design,
crown vetch is in violet flower. At a crest the elephant-colored gas
tanks of Brewer lift into view, and the brick-red rows as they climb
Mt. Judge and smudge its side. Rabbit dares ask the girl, "You
from around here?"

"More toward Galilee. My mother has a farm."

And is your mother's name Ruth? Harry wants to ask, but doesn't,
lest he frighten her, and destroy for himself the vibration of excitement, of possibility untested. He tries to steal another peek at her,
to see if her white skin is a mirror, and if the innocent blue in her
eyes is his own, but his bulk restrains him, and the tightness of the
car. He asks the boy, "You follow the Phillies, Jamie? How about
that seven-zip loss last night? You don't see Bowa commit an error
that often."

"Is Bowa the one with the big salary?"

Harry will feel better when he gets the Toyota out of this moron's hands. Every turn, he can feel the tires pull and the sudden secret widen within him, circle upon circle, it's like seed: seed that goes into the ground invisible and if it takes hold cannot be stopped, it fulfills the shape it was programmed for, its destiny, sure as our death, and shapely. "I think you mean Rose," he answers. "He's not been that much help, either. They're not going anywhere this year, Pittsburgh's the team. Pirates or Steelers, they always win. Take this left, at the yellow blinker. That'll take you right across One Eleven and then you swing into the lot from the back. What's your verdict?"

From the side the boy has an Oriental look – a big stretch of skin between his red ear and red nose, puffy eyes whose glitter gives away nothing. People who gouge a living out of the dirt are just naturally mean, Harry has always thought. Jamie says, "Like I said we were looking around. This car seems pretty small but maybe that's chust what you're used to."

"Want to give the Corona a whirl? That interior feels like a palace after you've been in one of these, you wouldn't think it would, it's only about two centimeters wider and five longer." He marvels at himself, how centimeters trip off his tongue. Another five years with these cars and he'll be talking Japanese. "But you better get used," he tells Jamie, "to a little scaling down. The big old boats have had it. People trade 'em in and we can't give 'em away. Wholesale half of 'em, and the wholesalers turn 'em into windowboxes. The five hundred trade-in I'd allow you on yours is just a courtesy, believe me. We like to help young people out. I think it's a helluva world we're coming to, where a young couple like yourselves can't afford to buy a car or own a home. If you can't get your foot on even the bottom rung of a society geared like this, people are going to lose faith in the system. The Sixties were a lark in the park compared to what we're going to see if things don't straighten out."

Loose stones in the back section of the lot crackle. They pull into the space the Corolla came from and the boy can't find the button to release the key until Harry shows him again. The girl leans forward, anxious to escape, and her breath stirs the colorless hairs on Harry's wrist. His shirt is stuck to his shoulder blades, he discovers standing to his height in the air. All three of them straighten slowly. The sun is still bright but horsetails high in the sky cast doubt upon the weather for tomorrow's golf game after all. "Good driving," he says to Jamie, having given up on any sale. "Come back in for a minute and I'll give you some literature." Inside the showroom the sun strikes the paper banner and makes the letters ᴛI ᴛoꓛ ꟼW show through. Stavros is nowhere to be seen. Harry hands the boy his Cʜɪᴇꜰ card and asks him to sign the customer register.

"Like I said —" the boy begins.

Harry has lost patience with this escapade. "It doesn't commit you to a blessed thing," he says. "Toyota'll send you a Christmas card is all it means. I'll do it for you. First name James —?"

"Nunemacher," the boy says warily, and spells it. "R. D. number two, Galilee."

Harry's handwriting has deteriorated over the years, gained a twitch at the end of his long arm, which yet is not long enough for him to see clearly what he writes. He owns reading glasses but it is his vanity never to wear them in public. "Done," he says, and all too casually turns to the girl. "O.K. young lady, how about you? Same name?"

"No way," she says, and giggles. "You don't want me."

A boldness sparks in the cool flat eyes. In that way of women she has gone all circles, silly, elusive. When her gaze levels there is something sexy in the fit of her lower lids, and the shadow of insufficient sleep below them. Her nose is slightly snub. "Jamie's our neighbor, I just came along for the ride. I was going to look for a sundress at Kroll's if there was time."

Something buried far back glints toward the light. Today's slant of sun has reached the shelf where the trophies Springer Motors sponsors wait to be awarded; oval embossments on their weightless white-metal surfaces shine. Keep your name, you little cunt, it's still a free country. But he has given her his. She has taken his card from Jamie's broad red hand and her eyes, childishly alight, slip from its lettering to his face to the section of far wall where his old headlines hang yellowing, toasted brown by time. She asks him, "Were you ever a famous basketball player?"

The question is not so easy to answer, it was so long ago. He tells her, "In the dark ages. Why do you ask, you've heard the name?"

"Oh no," this visitant from lost time gaily lies. "You just have that look."

When they have gone, the Country Squire swaying off on its soupy shocks, Harry uses the toilet down past Mildred Kroust's door along the corridor half of frosted glass and meets Charlie coming back from locking up. Still, there is pilferage, mysterious discrepancies eating into the percentages. Money is like water in a leaky bucket: no sooner there, it begins to drip. "Whajja think of the girl?" Harry asks the other man, back in the showroom.

"With these eyes, I don't see the girls anymore. If I saw 'em, with my condition I couldn't do anything about it. She looked big and dumb. A lot of leg."

"Not so dumb as that hick she was with," Harry says. "God when you see what some girls are getting into it makes you want to cry."

Stavros's dark dabs of eyebrows lift. "Yeah? Some could say it was the other way around." He sits down to business at his desk. "Manny get to talk to you about that Torino you took on trade?"

Manny is head of Service, a short stooping man with black pores on his nose, as if with that nose he burrows through each day's dirty work. Of course he resents Harry, who thanks to his marriage to Springer's daughter skates around in the sun of the showroom and accepts clunky Torinos on trade-in. "He told me the front end's out of alignment."

"Now he thinks in good conscience it should have a valve job. He also thinks the owner turned back the odometer."

"What could I do, the guy had the book right in his hand, I couldn't give him less than book value. If I don't give 'em book value Diefendorfer or Pike Porsche sure as hell will."

"You should have let Manny check it out, he could have told at a glance it had been in a collision. And if he spotted the odometer monkey business put the jerk on the defensive."

"Can't he weight the front wheels enough to hide the shimmy?"

Stavros squares his hands patiently on the olive-green top of his desk. "It's a question of good will. The customer you unload that Torino on will never be back, I promise you."

"Then what's your advice?"

Charlie says, "Discount it over to Ford in Pottsville. You had a cushion of nine hundred on that sale and can afford to give away two rather than get Manny's back up. He has to mark up his parts to protect his own department and when they're Ford parts you're carrying a mark-up already. Pottsville'll put a coat of wax on it and make some kid happy for the summer."

"Sounds good." Rabbit wants to be outdoors, moving through the evening air, dreaming of his daughter. "If I had my way," he tells Charlie, "we'd wholesale the American makes out of here as fast as they come in. Nobody wants 'em except the blacks and the spics, and even they got to wake up some day."

Charlie doesn't agree. "You can still do well in used, if you pick your spots. Fred used to say every car has a buyer somewhere, but you shouldn't allow more on any trade-in than you'd pay cash for that car. It *is* cash, you know. Numbers are cash, even if you don't handle any lettuce." He tips back his chair, letting his palms screech with friction on the desktop. "When I first went to work for Fred Springer in '63 we sold nothing but second-hand American models, you never saw a foreign car this far in from the coast. The cars would come in off the street and we'd paint 'em and give 'em a tune-up and no manufacturer told us what price to attach, we'd put the price on the windshield in shaving cream and wipe it off and try another if it didn't move inside a week. No import duty, no currency devaluation; it was good clean dog eat dog."

Reminiscence. Sad to see it rotting Charlie's brain. Harry waits respectfully for the mood to subside, then asks as if out of the blue, "Charlie, if I had a daughter, what d'you think she'd look like?"

"Ugly," Stavros says. "She'd look like Bugs Bunny."

"It'd be fun to have a daughter, wouldn't it?"

"Doubt it." Charlie lifts his palms so the legs of his chair slap to the floor. "What d'you hear from Nelson?"

Harry turns vehement. "Nothing much, thank God," he says.

"The kid never writes. Last we heard he was spending the summer out in Colorado with this girl he's picked up." Nelson attends college at Kent State, in Ohio, off and on, and has a year's worth of credits still to go before he graduates, though the boy was twenty-two last October.

"What kind of girl?"

"Lordy knows, I can't keep track. Each one is weirder than the last. One had been a teen-age alcoholic. Another told fortunes from playing cards. I think that same one was a vegetarian, but it may have been somebody else. I think he picks 'em to frustrate me."

"Don't give up on the kid. He's all you've got."

"Jesus, what a thought."

"You just go ahead. I want to finish up here. I'll lock up."

"O.K., I'll go see what Janice has burned for supper. Want to come take pot luck? She'd be tickled to see you."

"Thanks, but *Manna mou* expects me." His mother, getting decrepit herself, lives with Charlie now, in his place on Eisenhower Avenue, and this is another bond between them, since Harry lives with his mother-in-law.

"O.K. Take care, Charlie. See you in Monday's wash."

"Take care, champ."

The day is still golden outside, old gold now in Harry's lengthening life. He has seen summer come and go until its fading is one in his heart with its coming, though he cannot yet name the weeds that flower each in its turn through the season, or the insects that also in ordained sequence appear, eat, and perish. He knows that in June school ends and the playgrounds open, and the grass needs cutting again and again if one is a man, and if one is a child games can be played outdoors while the supper dishes tinkle in the mellow parental kitchens, and the moon is discovered looking over your shoulder out of a sky still blue, and a silver blob of milkweed spittle has appeared mysteriously on your knee. Good luck. Car sales peak in June: for a three-hundred-car-a-year dealer like Harry this means upwards of twenty-five units, with twenty-one accounted for already and six selling days to go. Average eight hundred gross profit times twenty-five equals twenty grand minus the twenty-five per cent they estimate for salesmen's compensation

both salary and incentives leaves fifteen grand minus between eight
and ten for other salaries those cute little cunts come and go in
billing one called Cissy a Polack a few years ago they got as far as
rubbing fannies easing by in that corridor and the rent that Springer
Motors pays itself old man Springer didn't believe in owning anything the banks could own but even he had to pay off the mortgage eventually boy the rates now must kill anybody starting up
and the financing double-digit interest Brewer Trust been doing
it for years and against the twelve per cent you got to figure the
two or three per cent that comes back as loss reserves nobody likes
to call it kick-back and the IRS calls it taxable earnings and the
upkeep the electricity that Sun 2001 Diagnostic Computer Manny
wants would use a lot of juice and the power tools they can't even
turn a nut on a wheel anymore it has to be pneumatic *rrrrrt* and
the heat thank God a few months' reprieve from that the fucking
Arabs are killing us and the men won't wear sweaters under the
coveralls the young mechanics are the worst they say they lose feeling in their fingertips and health insurance there's another killer up
and up the hospitals keeping people alive that are really dead like
some game they're playing at Medicaid's expense and the advertising he often wonders how much good it does a rule of thumb
he read somewhere is one and a half per cent of gross sales but if
you look at the Auto Sales page of the Sunday paper you never saw
such a jumble just the quiet listing of the prices and the shadow of
the dealer like old man Springer said the man he gets known to be
at Rotary and in the downtown restaurants and the country club
really he should be allowed to take all that off as business expenses the four seventy-five a week he pays himself doesn't take
into account the suits to make himself presentable he has to buy
three or four a year and not at Kroll's anymore he doesn't like that
salesman who measured his fat waist Webb Murkett knows of a
little shop on Pine Street that's as good as hand tailoring and then
the property taxes and the kids keep throwing stones or shooting
BBs at the glass signs outside we ought to go back to wood grouted wood but national Toyota has its specifications, where was he,
let's say nine total monthly expenses variable and invariable that
leaves four net profit and deduct another thousand from that for
inflation and pilferage and the unpredictable that's always there

you still have three, fifteen hundred for Ma Springer and fifteen hundred for Janice and him plus the two thousand salary when his poor dead dad used to go off to the print shop at quarter after seven every morning for forty dollars a week and that wasn't considered bad money then. Harry wonders what his father would think if he could only see him now, rich.

His 1978 Luxury Edition liftback five-door Corona is parked in its space. Called Red Metallic, it is a color more toward brown, like tired tomato soup. If the Japanese have a weakness it is their color sense: their Copper Metallic to Harry's eyes is a creosote brown, the Mint Green Metallic something like what he imagines cyanide to be, and what they called Beige a plain lemon yellow. In the war there used to be all these cartoons showing the Japanese wearing thick glasses and he wonders if it can be true, they don't see too well, all their colors falling in between the stripes of the rainbow. Still, his Corona is a snug machine. Solid big-car feel, padded tilt steering wheel, lumbar support lever for adjustable driver comfort, factory-installed AM/FM/MPX four-speaker radio. The radio is what he enjoys, gliding through Brewer with the windows up and locked and the power-boosted ventilation flowing through and the four corners of the car dinging out disco music as from the four corners of the mind's ballroom. Peppy and gentle, the music reminds Rabbit of the music played on radios when he was in high school, "How High the Moon" with the clarinet breaking away, the licorice stick they used to call it, "Puttin' on the Ritz": city music, not like that country music of the Sixties that tried to take us back and make us better than we are. Black girls with tinny chiming voices chant nonsense words above a throbbing electrified beat and he likes that, the thought of those black girls out of Detroit probably, their boyfriends goofing off on the assembly line, in shimmery tinsel dresses throbbing one color after another as the disco lights spin. He and Janice ought to visit at least the place down Route 111 D I S C O he noticed today for the hundredth time, never dared go in. In his mind he tries to put Janice and the colored girls and the spinning lights all together and they fly apart. He thinks of Skeeter. Ten years ago this small black man came and lived with him and Nelson for a crazy destructive time. Now Skeeter is dead, he learned just this April. Someone anonymous sent him, in a long stamped envelope such as anybody can buy at the post office, addressed in neat block ballpoint printing such as an accountant or a schoolteacher might use, a clipping in the familiar type of the Brewer *Vat*, where Harry had been a Linotyper until Linotyping became obsolete:

FORMER RESIDENT
SLAIN IN PHILLY

Hubert Johnson, formerly of Brewer, died of gunshot wounds in General Municipal Hospital, Philadelphia, after an alleged shoot-out with police officers.

Johnson was purported to have fired the first shots without provocation upon officers investigating reported violations of sanitation and housing laws in a religious commune supposedly headed by Johnson, whose Messiah Now Freedom Family included a number of black families and young persons.

Numerous complaints had been occasioned among neighbors by their late singing and abrasive behavior. The Messiah Now Freedom Family was located on Columbia Avenue.

Johnson Wanted

Johnson, last of Plum Street, city, was remembered locally as ''Skeeter'' and also went under the name of Farnsworth. He was wanted here under several complaints, local officials confirmed.

Philadelphia police lieutenant Roman Surpitski informed reporters that he and his men had no choice but to return fire upon Johnson. Fortunately, no officers and no other ''commune'' members suffered wounds in the exchange.

The office of outgoing Mayor Frank Rizzo declined to comment upon the incident. ''We don't come up against as many of these crazies as we used to,'' Lieutenant Surpitski volunteered.

The clipping had been accompanied by no note. Yet the sender must have known him, known something of his past, and be watching him, as the dead supposedly do. Creepy. Skeeter dead, a certain light was withdrawn from the world, a daring, a promise that all would be overturned. Skeeter had foretold this, his death young. Harry last had seen him heading across a field of corn stubble, among crows gleaning. But that had been so long ago the paper in his hand this last April felt little different from any other news item or from those sports clippings hanging framed in his showroom, about himself. Your selves die too. That part of him subject to Skeeter's spell had shrivelled and been overlaid. In his life he had known up close no other black people and in truth had been beyond all fear and discomfort flattered by the attentions of this hostile stranger descended like an angel; Harry felt he was seen by this furious man anew, as with X-rays. Yet he was surely a madman and his demands inordinate and endless and with him dead Rabbit feels safer.

As he sits snug in his sealed and well-assembled car the venerable city of Brewer unrolls like a silent sideways movie past his closed windows. He follows 111 along the river to West Brewer, where once he lived with Skeeter, and then cuts over the Weiser Street Bridge renamed after some dead mayor whose name nobody ever uses and then, to avoid the pedestrian mall with fountains and birch trees the city planners put in the broadest two blocks of Weiser to renew the downtown supposedly (the joke was, they planted twice as many trees as they needed, figuring half would die, but in fact almost all of them thrived, so they have a kind of forest in the center of town, where a number of muggings have taken place and the winos and junkies sleep it off), Harry cuts left on Third Street and through some semi-residential blocks of mostly ophthalmologists' offices to the diagonal main drag called Eisenhower, through the sector of old factories and railroad yards. Railroads and coal made Brewer. Everywhere in this city, once the fifth largest in Pennsylvania but now slipped to seventh, structures speak of expended energy. Great shapely stacks that have not issued smoke for half a century. Scrolling cast-iron light stanchions not lit since World War II. The lower blocks of Weiser given over to the sale of the cut-rate and the X-rated and the only new emporium a big windowless enlargement in white brick of Schoenbaum Funeral Directors. The old textile plants given over to discount clothing outlets teeming with a gimcrack cheer of banners FACTORY FAIR and slogans *Where the Dollar Is Still a Dollar.* These acres of dead railroad track and car shops and stockpiled wheels and empty boxcars stick in the heart of the city like a great rusting dagger. All this had been cast up in the last century by what now seem giants, in an explosion of iron and brick still preserved intact in this city where the sole new buildings are funeral parlors and government offices, Unemployment and Join the Army.

Beyond the car yards and the underpass at Seventh that had been flooded last night, Eisenhower Avenue climbs steeply through tight-built neighborhoods of row houses built solid by German workingmen's savings and loans associations, only the fanlights of stained glass immune to the later layers of aluminum awning and Permastone siding, the Polacks and Italians being squeezed out by the blacks and Hispanics that in Harry's youth were held to the low blocks down by the river. Dark youths thinking in languages of their own stare from the triangular stone porches of the old corner grocery stores.

The vanished white giants as they filled Brewer into its grid named these higher streets that Eisenhower crosses for fruits and the seasons of the year: Winter, Spring, Summer, but no Fall Street. For three months twenty years ago Rabbit lived on Summer with a woman, Ruth Leonard. There he fathered the girl he saw today, if that was his daughter. There is no getting away; our sins, our seed, coil back. The disco music shifts to the Bee Gees, white men who have done this wonderful thing of making themselves sound like black women. "Stayin' Alive" comes on with all that amplified throbbleo and a strange nasal whining underneath: the John Travolta theme song. Rabbit still thinks of him as one of the Sweathogs from Mr. Kotter's class but for a while back there last summer the U.S.A. was one hundred per cent his, every twat under fifteen wanting to be humped by a former Sweathog in the back seat of a car parked in Brooklyn. He thinks of his own daughter getting into the back seat of the Corolla, bare leg up to her ass. He wonders if her pubic hair is ginger in color like her mother's was. That curve where a tender entire woman seems an inch away around a kind of corner, where no ugly penis hangs like sausage on the rack, blue-veined. Her eyes his blue: wonderful to think that he has been turned into cunt, a secret message carried by genes all that way through all these comings and goings all these years, the bloody tunnel of growing and living, of staying alive. He better stop thinking about it, it fills him too full of pointless excitement. Some music does that.

Some car with double headlights, a yellow LeMans with that big vertical bar in the middle of the grille, is riding his tail so close he eases over behind a parked car and lets the bastard by: a young blonde with a tipped-up tiny profile is driving. How often that seems to be the case these days, some pushy road-hog you hate turns out to be a little girl at the wheel, who must be somebody's daughter and from the lackadaisical glassy look on her face has no idea of being rude, just wants to get there. When Rabbit first began to drive the road was full of old fogeys going too slow and now it seems nothing but kids in a hell of a hurry, pushing. Let 'em by, is his motto. Maybe they'll kill themselves on a telephone pole in the next mile. He hopes so.

His route takes him up into the area of the stately Brewer High School, called the Castle, built in 1933, the year of his birth is how he remembers. They wouldn't build it now, no faith in education, indeed they say with zero growth rate approaching there aren't enough students to fill the schools now, they are closing a lot of the elementary schools down. Up this high the city builders had run out of seasons and went to tree names. Locust Boulevard east of the Castle is lined with houses with lawns all around, though the strips between are narrow and dark and rhododendrons die for lack of sun. The better-off live up here, the bone surgeons and legal eagles and middle management of the plants that never had the wit to go south or have come in since. When Locust begins to curve through the municipal park its name changes to Cityview Drive, though with all the trees that have grown up in time there isn't much view left; Brewer can be seen all spread out really only from the Pinnacle Hotel, now a site of vandalism and terror where once there had been dancing and necking. Something about spics they don't like to see white kids making out, they surround the car and smash the windshield with rocks and slit the clothes off the girl while roughing up the boy. What a world to grow up in, especially for a girl. He and Ruth walked up to the Pinnacle once or twice. The railroad tie steps probably rotted now. She took off her shoes because the high heels dug into the gravel between the railroad ties, he remembers her city-pale feet lifting ahead of him under his eyes, naked just for him it seemed. People satisfied with less then. In the park a World War II tank, made into a monument, points its guns at tennis courts where the nets, even the ones made of playground fencing, keep getting ripped away. The strength these kids use, just to destroy. Was he that way at that age? You want to make a mark. The world seems indestructible and won't let you out. Let 'em by.

There is a stoplight and, turning left, Harry passes between houses gabled and turreted the way they did early in the century when men wore straw hats and made ice cream by hand and rode bicycles, and then there is a shopping center, where a four-theater movie complex advertises on its sign high up where vandals can't reach it to steal letters ALIEN MOONRAKER MAIN EVENT ESCAPE FROM ALCATRAZ. None of them does he want to see though he likes the way Streisand's hair frizzes up and that Jewish nose, not just the nose, there is Jewishness in the thrust of her voice that thrills him, must have to do with being the chosen people, they do seem more at home here on Earth, the few he knows, more full of bounce. Funny about Streisand, if she isn't matched up with an Egyptian like Sharif it's with a super Waspy-looking type like Ryan O'Neal; same thing with Woody Allen, nothing Jewish about Diane Keaton, though her hair does frizz come to think of it.

The music stops, the news comes on. A young female voice reads it, with a twang like she knows she's wasting our time. Fuel, truckers. Three-Mile Island investigations continue. Date for Skylab fall has been revised. Somoza in trouble too. Stay of execution of convicted Florida killer denied. Former leader of Great Britain's Liberal Party acquitted of charges of conspiring to murder his former homosexual lover. This annoys Rabbit, but his indignation at this pompous pansy's getting off scot-free dissolves in his curiosity about the next criminal case on the news, this of a Baltimore physician who was charged with murdering a Canada goose with a golf club. The defendant claims, the disinterested female voice twangs on, that he had accidentally struck the goose with a golf ball and then had dispatched the wounded creature with a club to end its misery. The voice concludes, "A mercy killing, or murder most foul?" He laughs aloud, in the car, alone. He'll have to try to remember that, to tell the gang at the club tomorrow. Tomorrow will be a sunny day, the woman reassures him, giving the weather. "And now, the Number One Hit coast to coast, 'Hot Stuff,' by the Queen of Disco, Donna Summer!"

> *Sittin' here eatin' my heart out waitin'*
> *Waitin' for some lover to call. . . .*

Rabbit likes the chorus where the girls in the background chime in, you can picture them standing around some steamy city corner chewing gum and who knows what else:

> *Hot stuff*
> *I need hot stuff*
> *I want some hot stuff*
> *I need hot stuuuuuff!*

Still he liked Donna Summer best in the days when she was doing those records of a woman breathing and panting and sighing like she was coming. Maybe it wasn't her, just some other slim black chick. But he thinks it was her.

The road takes on a number, 422, and curves around the shoulders of Mt. Judge, with a steep drop on the right side and a view of the viaduct that once brought water to the city from the north of the county across the black breadth of the Running Horse River. Two gas stations mark the beginning of the borough of Mt. Judge; instead of keeping on 422 toward Philadelphia Harry steers his Corona off the highway onto Central by the granite Baptist church and then obliquely up Jackson Street and after three blocks right onto Joseph. If he stays on Jackson two more blocks he will pass his old house, one number in from the corner of Maple, but since Pop passed on, after holding on without Mom for a couple of years, doing all the yardwork and vacuuming and meals by himself until his emphysema just got too bad and you'd find him sitting in a chair all curled over like a hand sheltering a guttering candle-flame from the wind, Rabbit rarely drives by: the people he and Mim had sold it to had painted the wood trim an awful grape color and hung an ultraviolet plant light in the big front window. Like these young couples in Brewer who think anything goes on a row house, however cute, and they're doing the world a favor by taking it on. Harry hadn't liked the guy's accent, hair-cut, or leisure suit; he had liked the price he had paid, though: fifty-eight thousand for a place that had cost Mom and Pop forty-two hundred in 1935. It made a nice bundle even with Mim taking her half with her back out to Nevada and the real-estate agents' and lawyers' fees, they just step in everywhere where money's chang-ing hands. He had begged Janice at the time to use the twenty grand to buy a new house, just for them, maybe over in Penn Park in West Brewer, five minutes from the lot. But no, Janice didn't think they should desert Mother: the Springers had taken them in when they had no house, their own house had burned, and their marriage had hit rock bottom and what with Harry being promised to head up new car sales at about the time Pop died and Nelson having had so many shocks already in his life and so many bad aftereffects still smoldering at that end of Brewer, the inquest for Jill and a police investigation and her parents thinking of suing all the way from Connecticut and the insurance company taking forever to come through with the claim because there were suspi-cious circumstances and poor Peggy Fosnacht having to swear Harry had been with her and so couldn't have set it himself, what with all this it seemed better to lie low, to hide behind the Springer name in the big stucco house, and the weeks had become months and the months years without the young Angstroms going into another place of their own, and then with Fred dying so sud-denly and Nelson going off to college there seemed more room and less reason than ever to move. The house, 89 Joseph, always reminds Harry under its spreading trees with its thready lawn all around of the witch's house made out of candy, penuche for the walls and licorice Necco wafers for the thick slate roof. Though the place looks big outside the downstairs is crammed with furni-ture come down through Ma Springer's people the Koerners and the shades are always half drawn; except for the screened-in back porch and the little upstairs room that had been Janice's when she was a girl and then Nelson's for those five years before he went away to Kent, there isn't a corner of the Springer house where Harry feels able to breathe absolutely his own air.

He circles around into the alley of bluestone grit and puts the Corona into the garage beside the '74 navy-blue Chrysler Newport that Fred got the old lady for her birthday the year before he died and that she drives around town with both hands tight on the wheel, with the look on her face as if a bomb might go off under the hood. Janice always keeps her Mustang convertible parked out front by the curb, where the maple drippings can ruin the top faster. When the weather gets warm she leaves the top down for nights at a time so the seats are always sticky. Rabbit swings down the overhead garage door and carries up the cement walk through the back yard like twin car headlights into a tunnel his strange consciousness of having not one child now but two.

Janice greets him in the kitchen. Something's up. She is wearing a crisp frock with pepperminty stripes but her hair is still scraggly and damp from an afternoon of swimming at the club pool. Nearly every day she has a tennis date with some of her girlfriends at the club they belong to, the Flying Eagle Tee and Racquet, a newish organization laid out on the lower slopes of Mt. Judge's woodsy brother mountain with the Indian name, Mt. Pemaquid, and then kills the rest of the afternoon lying at poolside gossiping or playing cards and getting slowly spaced on Spritzers or vodka-and-tonics. Harry likes having a wife who can be at the club so much. Janice is thickening through the middle at the age of forty-three but her legs are still hard and neat. And brown. She was always dark-complected and with July not even here she has the tan of a savage, legs and arms almost black like some little Polynesian in an old Jon Hall movie. Her lower lip bears a trace of zinc oxide, which is sexy, even though he never loved that stubborn slotlike set her mouth gets. Her still-wet hair pulled back reveals a high forehead somewhat mottled, like brown paper where water has been dropped and dried. He can tell by the kind of heat she is giving off that she and her mother have been fighting. "What's up now?" he asks.

"It's been wild," Janice says. "She's in her room and says we should eat without her."

"Yeah well, she'll be down. But what's to eat? I don't see anything cooking." The digital clock built into the stove says 6:32.

"Harry. Honest to God I was going to shop as soon as I came back and changed out of tennis things but then this postcard was here and Mother and I have been at it ever since. Anyway it's summer, you don't want to eat too much. Doris Kaufmann, I'd give anything to have her serve, she says she never has more than a glass of iced tea for lunch, even in the middle of winter. I thought maybe soup and those cold cuts I bought that you and Mother refuse to touch, they have to be eaten sometime. And the lettuce is coming on in the garden now so fast we must start having salads before it gets all leggy." She had planted a little vegetable garden in the part of the back yard where Nelson's swing set used to be, getting a man from down the block to turn the earth with his Rototiller, the earth miraculously soft and pungent beneath the crust of winter and Janice out there enthusiastic with her string and rake in the gauzy shadows of the budding trees; but now that summer is here and the leafed-out trees keep the garden in the shade and the games at the club have begun she has let the plot go to weeds.

Still, he cannot dislike this brown-eyed woman who has been his indifferent wife for twenty-three years this past March. He is rich because of her inheritance and this mutual knowledge rests adhesively between them like a form of sex, comfortable and sly. "Salad and baloney, my favorite meal," he says, resigned. "Lemme have a drink first. Some window-shoppers came in to the lot today just as I was leaving. Tell me what postcard."

As he stands by the refrigerator making a gin-and-bitter-lemon, knowing these sugary mixers add to the calories in the alcohol and help to keep him overweight but figuring that this Saturday evening meal in its skimpiness will compensate and maybe he'll jog a little afterwards, Janice goes in through the dark dining room into the musty front parlor where the shades are drawn and Ma Springer's sulking spirit reigns, and brings back a postcard. It shows a white slope of snow under a stark blue wedge of sky; two small dark hunched figures are tracing linked S's on the slanted snow, skiing. GREETINGS FROM COLORADO red cartoon letters say across the sky that looks like blue paint. On the opposite side a familiar scrawled hand, scrunched as if something in the boy had been squeezed too tight while his handwriting was coming to birth, spells out:

> Hi Mom & Dad & Grandmom:
>   These mts. make Mt. Judge
> look sick! No snow tho,
> just plenty of grass (joke).
> Been learning to hang glide.
> Job didn't work out, guy was
> a bum. Penna. beckons.
> OK if I bring Melanie
> home too? She could get
> job and be no troble. Love,
>   Nelson

"Melanie?" Harry asks.

"That's what Mother and I have been fighting about. She doesn't want the girl staying here."

"Is this the same girl he went out there with two weeks ago?"

"I was wondering," Janice says. "She had a name more like Sue or Jo or something."

"Where would she sleep?"

"Well, either in that front sewing room or Nelson's room."

"*With* the kid?"

"Well really, Harry, I wouldn't be utterly surprised. He *is* twenty-two. When have you gotten so Puritanical?"

"I'm not being Puritanical, just practical. It's one thing to have these kids go off into the blue and go hang gliding or whatever else and another to have them bring all their dope and little tootsies back to the nest. This house is awkward upstairs, you know that. There's too much hall space and you can't sneeze or fart or fuck without everybody else hearing; it's been bliss, frankly, with just us and Ma. Remember the kid's radio all through high school to two in the morning, how he'd fall asleep to it? That bed of his is a little single, what are we supposed to do, buy him and Melody a double bed?"

"Melanie. I don't know, she can sleep on the floor. They all have sleeping bags. You can try putting her in the sewing room but I know she won't stay there. We wouldn't have." Her blurred dark eyes gaze beyond him into time. "We spent all our energy sneaking down hallways and squirming around in the back seats of cars and I thought we could spare our children that."

"We have a child, not children," he says coldly, as the gin expands his inner space. They had children once, but their infant daughter Becky died. It was his wife's fault. The entire squeezed and cut-down shape of his life is her fault; at every turn she has been a wall to his freedom. "Listen," he says to her, "I've been trying to get out of this fucking depressing house for years and I don't want this shiftless arrogant goof-off we've raised coming back and pinning me in. These kids seem to think the world exists to serve them but I'm sick of just standing around waiting to be of service."

Janice stands up to him scarcely flinching, armored in her country-club tan. "He is our son, Harry, and we're not going to turn away a guest of his because she is female in sex. If it was a boyfriend of Nelson's you wouldn't be at all this excited, it's the fact that it's a *girl*friend of Nelson's that's upsetting you, a girlfriend of *Nelson*'s. If it was a girlfriend of *yours*, the upstairs wouldn't be too crowded for you to fart in. This is my son and I want him here if he wants to be here."

"I don't have any girlfriends," he protests. It sounds pitiful. Is Janice saying he should have? Women, once sex gets out in the open, they become monsters. You're a creep if you fuck them and a creep if you don't. Harry strides into the dining room, making the glass panes of the antique breakfront shudder, and calls up the dark stained stairs that are opposite the breakfront, "Hey Bessie, come on down! I'm on your side!"

There is a silence as from God above and then the creak of a bed being relieved of a weight, and reluctant footsteps slither across the ceiling toward the head of the stairs. Mrs. Springer on her painful dropsical legs comes down talking: "This house is legally mine and that girl is not spending one night under a roof Janice's father slaved all his days to keep over our heads."

The breakfront quivers again; Janice has come into the dining room. She says in a voice tightened to match her mother's,

"Mother, you wouldn't be keeping this enormous roof over your head if it weren't for Harry and me sharing the upkeep. It's a great sacrifice on Harry's part, a man of his income not having a house he can call his own, and you have no right to forbid Nelson to come home when he wants to, *no* right, Mother."

The plump old lady groans her way down to the landing three steps shy of the dining-room floor and hesitates there saying, in a voice tears have stained, "Nellie I'm happy to see whenever he deems fit, I love that boy with all my soul even though he hasn't turned out the way his grandfather and I had hoped."

Janice says, angrier in proportion as the old lady makes herself look pathetic, "You're always bringing Daddy in when he can't speak for himself but as long as he was alive he was *very* hospitable and tolerant of Nelson and his friends. I remember that cookout Nelson had in the back yard for his high-school graduation when Daddy had had his first stroke already, I went upstairs to see if it was getting too rowdy for him and he said with his wry little smile" – tears now stain her own voice too – " 'The sound of young voices does my old heart good.' "

That slippery-quick salesman's smile of his, Rabbit can see it still. Like a switchblade without the click.

"A cookout in the back yard is one thing," Mrs. Springer says, thumping herself in her dirty aqua sneakers down the last three steps of the stairs and looking her daughter level in the eye. "A slut in the boy's bed is another."

Harry thinks this is pretty jazzy for an old lady and laughs aloud. Janice and her mother are both short women; like two doll's heads mounted on the same set of levers they turn identically chocolate-eyed, slot-mouthed faces to glare at his laugh. "We don't know the girl is a slut," Harry apologizes. "All we know is her name is Melanie instead of Sue."

"You said you were on my side," Mrs. Springer says.

"I am, Ma, I am. I don't see why the kid has to come storming home; we gave him enough money to get him started out there, I'd like to see him get some kind of grip on the world. He's not going to get it hanging around here all summer."

"Oh, money," Janice says. "That's all you ever think about. And what have *you* ever done except hang around here? Your father got you one job and my father got you another, I don't call that any great adventure."

"That's not all I think about," he begins lamely, of money, before his mother-in-law interrupts.

"Harry doesn't want a home of his own," Ma Springer tells her daughter. When she gets excited and fearful of not making herself understood her face puffs up and goes mottled. "He has such disagreeable associations from the last time you two went out on your own."

Janice is firm, younger, in control. "Mother, you know nothing about it. You know nothing about life period. You sit in this house and watch idiotic game shows and talk on the phone to what friends you have that are still alive and then sit in judgment on Harry and me. You know *nothing* of life now. You have no *idea*."

"As if playing games at a country club with the nickel rich and coming home tiddled every night is enough to make you wise," the old lady comes back, holding on with one hand to the knob of the newel post as if to ease the pain in her ankles. "You come home," she goes on, "too silly to make your husband a decent supper and then want to bring this tramp into a house where I do all the housekeeping, even if I can scarcely stand to stand. I'm the one that would be here with them, you'd be off in that convertible. What will the neighbors make of it? What about the people in the church?"

"I don't care even if they care, which I dare say they won't," Janice says. "And to bring the church into it is ridiculous. The last minister at St. John's ran off with Mrs. Eckenroth and this one now is so gay I wouldn't let my boy go to his Sunday school, if I had a boy that age."

"Nellie didn't go that much anyway," Harry recalls. "He said it gave him headaches." He wants to lower the heat between the two women before it boils over into grief. He sees he must break this up, get a house of his own, before he runs out of gas. Stone outside, exposed beams inside, and a sunken living room: that is his dream.

"Melanie," his mother-in-law is saying, "what kind of name is that? It sounds colored."

"Oh Mother, don't drag out all your prejudices. You sit and

giggle at the Jeffersons as if you're one of them and Harry and Charlie unload all their old gas-hogs on the blacks and if we take their money we can take what else they have to offer too."

Can Melanie actually be black? Harry is asking himself, thrilled. Little cocoa babies. Skeeter would be so pleased.

"Anyway," Janice is going on, looking frazzled suddenly, "nobody's said the girl is black, all we know is she hang glides."

"Or is that the other one?" Harry asks.

"If she comes, I go," Bessie Springer says. "Grace Stuhl has all those empty rooms now that Ralph's passed on and she's more than once said we should team up."

"Mother, I find that humiliating, that you've been begging Grace Stuhl to take you in."

"I haven't been begging, the thought just naturally occurred to the both of us. I'd expect to be bought out here, though, and the values in the neighborhood have been going way up since they banned the through truck traffic."

"Mother. Harry *hates* this house."

He says, still hoping to calm these waters, "I don't hate it, exactly; I just think the space upstairs —"

"Harry," Janice says. "Why don't you go out and pick some lettuce from the garden like we said? Then we'll eat."

Gladly. He is glad to escape the house, the pinch of the women, their heat. Crazy the way they flog at each other with these ghosts of men, Daddy dead, Nelson gone, and even Harry himself a kind of ghost in the way they talk of him as if he wasn't standing right there. Day after day, mother and daughter sharing that same house, it's not natural. Like water blood must run or grow a scum. Old lady Springer always plump with that sausage look to her wrists and ankles but now her face puffy as well like those movie stars whose cheeks they stuff cotton up into to show them getting older. Her face not just plumper but wider as if a screw turning inside is spreading the sides of her skull apart, her eyes getting smaller, Janice heading the same way though she tries to keep trim, there's no stopping heredity. Rabbit notices now his own father talking in his own brain sometimes when he gets tired.

Bitter lemon fading in his mouth, an aluminum colander pleasantly light in his hand, he goes down the brick back steps into grateful space. He feels the neighborhood filter through to him and the voices in his brain grow still. Dark green around him is damp with coming evening, though this long day's lingering brightness surprises his eye above the shadowy masses of the trees. Rooftops and dormers notch the blue as it begins to blush brown; here also electric wires and television aerials mar with their scratches the soft beyond, a few swallows dipping as they do at day's end in the middle range of air above the merged back yards, where little more than a wire fence or a line of hollyhocks marks the divisions of property. When he listens he can hear the sounds of cooking clatter or late play, alive in this common realm with a dog's bark, a bird's *weep weep*, the rhythmic far tapping of a hammer. A crew of butch women has moved in a few houses down and they're always out in steel-toed boots and overalls with ladders and hammers fixing things, they can do it all, from rain gutters to cellar doors: terrific. He sometimes waves to them when he jogs by in twilight but they don't have much to say to him, a creature of another species.

Rabbit swings open the imperfect little gate he constructed two springs ago and enters the fenced rectangle of silent vegetable presences. The lettuce flourishes between a row of bean plants whose leaves are badly bug-eaten and whose stems collapse at a touch and a row of feathery carrot tops all but lost in an invasion of plantain and chickweed and purselane and a pulpy weed with white-and-yellow flowers that grows inches every night. It is easy to pull, its roots let go docilely, but there are so many he wearies within minutes of pulling and shaking the moist earth free from the roots and laying bundles of the weed along the chicken-wire fence as mulch and as barrier to the invading grasses. Grass that won't grow in the lawn where you plant it comes in here wild to multiply. Seed, so disgustingly much of it, Nature such a cruel smotherer. He thinks again of the dead he has known, the growingly many, and of the live child, if not his then some other father's, who visited him today with her long white legs propped up on cork heels, and of the other child, undoubtedly his, the genes show even in that quick scared way he looks at you, who has threatened to return. Rabbit pinches off the bigger lettuce leaves (but not the ones at the base so big as to be tough and bitter) and looks into his heart for welcome, welcoming love for his son. He finds instead a rumple of apprehensiveness in form and texture like a towel tumbled too soon from the dryer. He finds a hundred memories, some vivid as photographs and meaningless, snapped by the mind for reasons of its own, and others mere facts, things he knows are true but has no snapshot for. Our lives fade behind us before we die. He changed the boy's diapers in the sad apartment high on Wilbur Street, he lived with him for some wild months in an apple-green ranch house called 26 Vista Crescent in Penn Villas, and here at 89 Joseph he watched him become a high-school student with a wispy mustache that showed when he stood in the light, and a headband like an Indian's instead of getting a haircut, and a fortune in rock records kept in the sunny room whose drawn shades are above Harry's head now. He and Nelson have been through enough years together to turn a cedar post to rot and yet his son is less real to Harry than these crinkled leaves of lettuce he touches and plucks. Sad. Who says? The calm eyes of the girl who showed up at the lot today haunt the growing shadows, a mystery arrived at this time of his own numb life, death taking his measure with the invisible tapping of that neighborhood hammer: each day he is a little less afraid to die. He spots a Japanese beetle on a bean plant leaf and with a snap of his fingernail – big fingernails, with conspicuous cuticle moons – snaps the iridescent creature off. Die.

Back in the house, Janice exclaims, "You've picked enough for six of us!"

"Where'd Ma go?"

"She's in the front hall, on the telephone to Grace Stuhl. Really, she's impossible. I really think senility is setting in. Harry, what shall we *do*?"

"Ride with the punches?"

"Oh, great."

"Well honey it *is* her house, not ours and Nelson's."

"Oh, drop dead. You're no help." An illumination rises sluggishly within her sable, gin-blurred eyes. "You don't want to be any help," she announces. "You just like to see us fight."

* * *

The evening passes in a stale crackle of television and suppressed resentment. *Waitin' for some lover to call.* . . . Ma Springer, having condescended to share with them at the kitchen table some lumpy mushroom soup Janice has warmed and the cold cuts slightly sweaty from waiting too long in the refrigerator and all that salad he picked, stalks upstairs to her own room and shuts the door with a firmness that must carry out into the neighborhood as far as the butch women's house. A few cars, looking for hot stuff, prowl by on Joseph Street, with that wet-tire sound that makes Harry and Janice feel alone as on an island. For supper they opened a half-gallon of Gallo Chablis and Janice keeps drifting into the kitchen to top herself up, so that by ten o'clock she is lurching in that way he hates. He doesn't blame people for many sins but he does hate uncoördination, the root of all evil as he feels it, for without coördination there can be no order, no connecting. In this state she bumps against doorframes coming through and sets her glass on the sofa arm so a big translucent lip of contents slops up and over into the fuzzy gray fabric. Together they sit through *Battlestar Galactica* and enough of *The Love Boat* to know it's not one of the good cruises. When she gets up to fill her glass yet again he switches to the Phillies game. The Phillies are being held to one hit by the Expos, he can't believe it, all that power. On the news, there is rioting in Levittown over gasoline, people are throwing beer bottles full of gasoline; they explode, it looks like old films of Vietnam or Budapest but it is Levittown right down the road, north of Philadelphia. A striking trucker is shown holding up a sign saying To Hell With Shell. And Three-Mile Island leaking radioactive neutrons just down the road in the other direction. The weather for tomorrow looks good, as a massive high continues to dominate from the Rocky Mountain region eastward all the way to Maine. Time for bed.

Harry knows in his bones, it has been borne in on him over the years, that on the nights of the days when Janice has fought with her mother and drunk too much she will want to make love. The first decade of their marriage, it was hard to get her to put out, there were a lot of things she wouldn't do and didn't even know were done and these seemed to be the things most on Rabbit's mind, but then with the affair with Charlie Stavros opening her up

at about the time of the moon shot, and the style of the times proclaiming no holds barred, and for that matter death eating enough
into her body for her to realize it wasn't such a precious vessel and
there wasn't any superman to keep saving it for, Harry has no complaints. Indeed what complaints there might be in this line would
come from her about him. Somewhere early in the Carter administration his interest, that had been pretty faithful, began to wobble and by now there is a real crisis of confidence. He blames it on
money, on having enough at last, which has made him satisfied all
over; also the money itself, relaxed in the bank, gets smaller in real
value all the time, and this is on his mind, what to do about it,
along with everything else: the Phils, and the dead, and golf. He
has taken the game up with a passion since they joined the Flying
Eagle, without getting much better at it, or at least without giving
himself any happier impression of an absolute purity and power
hidden within the coiling of his muscles than some lucky shots in
those first casual games he played once did. It is like life itself in
that its performance cannot be forced and its underlying principle
shies from being permanently named. *Arms like ropes*, he tells himself sometimes, with considerable success, and then, when that
goes bad, *Shift the weight*. Or, *Don't chicken-wing it*, or, *Keep the angle*,
meaning the angle between club and arms when wrists are cocked.
Sometimes he thinks it's all in the hands, and then in the shoulders, and even in the knees. When it's in the knees he can't control it. Basketball was somehow more instinctive. If you thought
about merely walking down the street the way you think about
golf you'd wind up falling off the curb. Yet a good straight drive
or a soft chip stiff to the pin gives him the bliss that used to come
thinking of some woman, imagining if only you and she were
alone on a warm island.

Naked, Janice bumps against the doorframe from their bathroom back into their bedroom. Naked, she lurches onto the bed
where he is trying to read the July issue of *Consumer Reports* and thrusts
her tongue into his mouth. He tastes Gallo, baloney, and toothpaste while his mind is still trying to sort out the virtues and
failings of the great range of can openers put to the test over five
close pages of print. The Sunbeam units were most successful at
opening rectangular and dented cans and yet pierced coffee cans

with such force that grains of coffee spewed out onto the counter. Elsewhere, slivers of metal were dangerously produced, magnets gripped so strongly that the contents of the cans tended to spatter, blades failed to reach deep lips, and one small plastic insert so quickly wore away that the model (Ekco C865K) was judged Not Acceptable. Amid these fine discriminations Janice's tongue like an eyeless eager eel intrudes and angers him. Ever since in her late thirties she had her tubes burned to avoid any more bad side effects from the Pill, a demon of loss (never any more children never ever) has given her sexuality a false animation, a thrust somehow awry. Her eyes as her face backs off from the kiss he has resisted, squirming, have in them no essential recognition of him, only a glaze of liquor and blank unfriendly wanting. By the light by which he had been trying to read he sees the hateful aged flesh at the base of her throat, reddish and tense as if healed from a burn. He wouldn't see it so clearly if he didn't have his reading glasses on. "Jesus," he says, "at least let's wait till I turn out the light."

"I like it on." Her insistence is slurred. "I like to see all the gray hair on your chest."

This interests him. "Is there much?" He tries to see, past his chin. "It's not gray, it's just blond, isn't it?"

Janice pulls the bedsheet down to his waist and crouches to examine him hair by hair. Her breasts hang down so her nipples, bumply in texture like hamburger, sway an inch above his belly. "You do here, and here." She pulls each gray hair.

"Ouch. Damn you, Janice. *Stop*." He pushes his stomach up so her nipples vanish and her breasts are squashed against her own frail ribs. Gripping the hair of her head in one fist in his rage at being invaded, the other hand still holding the magazine in which he was trying to read about magnets gripping, he arches his spine so she is thrown from his body to her side of the bed. In her boozy haze mistaking this for love play, Janice tugs the sheet down still lower on him and takes his prick in a fumbling, twittering grip. Her touch is cold from having just washed her hands in the bathroom. The next page of *Consumer Reports* is printed on blue and asks, *Summer cooling, 1979: air-conditioner or fan?* He tries to skim the list of advantages and disadvantages peculiar to each (*Bulky and heavy to install* as opposed to *Light and portable*, *Expensive to run* as against

Inexpensive to run, the fan seems to be scoring all the points) but can't quite disassociate himself from the commotion below his waist, where Janice's anxious fingers seem to be asking the same question over and over, without getting the answer they want. Furious, he throws the magazine against the wall behind which Ma Springer sleeps. More carefully, he removes his reading glasses and puts them in his bedside table drawer and switches off the bedside lamp.

His wife's importunate flesh must then compete with the sudden call to sleep that darkness brings. It has been a long day. He was awake at six-thirty and got up at seven. His eyelids have grown too thin to tolerate the early light. Even now near midnight he feels tomorrow's early dawn rotating toward him. He recalls again the blue-eyed apparition who seemed to be his and Ruth's genes mixed; he is reminded then from so long ago of that Ruth whom he fucked upwards the first time, saying "Hey" in his surprise at her beauty, her body one long underbelly erect in light from the streetlamp outside on Summer Street, his prick erect in her ripe, ripe loveliness above him, *Hey*, it seems a melancholy falling that an act so glorious has been dwindled to this blurred burrowing of two old bodies, one drowsy and one drunk. Janice's rummaging at his prick has become hostile now as it fails to rise; her attention burns upon it like solar rays focused by a magnifying glass upon a scrap of silk, kids used to kill ants that way. Harry watched but never participated. We are cruel enough without meaning to be. He resents that in her eagerness for some dilution of her sense of being forsaken, having quarrelled with her mother, and perhaps also afraid of their son's return, Janice gives him no space of secrecy in which blood can gather as it did behind his fly in ninth-grade algebra sitting beside Lotty Bingaman who in raising her hand to show she had the answers showed him wisps of armpit hair and pressed the thin cotton of her blouse tighter against the elastic trusswork of her bra, so its salmon color strained through. Then the fear was the bell would ring and he would have to stand with this hard-on.

He resolves to suck Janice's tits, to give himself a chance to pull himself together, this is embarrassing. A pause at the top, you need a pause at the top to generate momentum. His spit glimmers within her dark shape above him; the headboard of their bed is placed between two windows shaded from the light of sun and moon alike by a great copper beech whose leaves yet allow a little streetlight through.

"That feels nice." He wishes she wouldn't say this. Nice isn't enough. Without some shadow of assault or outrage it becomes another task, another duty. To think, all along, that Lotty was sitting there itching to be fucked. It wasn't just him. She was holding a dirty yearning between her legs just like the lavatory walls said, those drawings and words put there by the same kids who magnified the ants to death, that little sticky pop they died with, you could hear it, did girls too make a little sticky noise when they opened up? The thought of her *knowing* when she raised her hand that her blouse was tugged into wrinkles all pointing to the tip of her tit and that an edge of bra peeped out through the cotton armhole with those little curly virgin hairs and that he was watching for it all to happen does make blood gather. In the fumbly worried dark, with Ma Springer sleeping off her sulk a thickness of plaster away, Harry as if casually presents his stiffened prick to Janice's hand. *Hot stuuuuff.*

But wanderings within her own brain have blunted her ardor and her touch conveys this, it is too heavy, so in a desperate mood of self-rescue he hisses "Suck" in her ear, "Suck." Which she does, turning her back, her head heavy on his belly. Diagonal on the bed he stretches one arm as if preparing to fly and caresses her ass, these lower globes of hers less spherical than once they were, and the fur between more findable by his fingers. She learned to blow when she went away with Stavros but doesn't really get her head into it, nibbles more, the top inch or two. To keep himself excited he tries to remember Ruth, that exalted "Hey" and the way she swallowed it once, but the effort brings back with such details the guilt of their months together and, betrayal betrayed, his desertion and the final sour sorrow of it all.

Janice lets him slide from her mouth and asks, "What are you thinking about?"

"Work," he lies. "Charlie worries me. He's taking such good care of himself you hate to ask him to do anything. I seem to handle most of the customers now."

"Well why not? You give yourself twice the salary he gets and he's been there forever."

"Yeah, but I married the boss's daughter. He could have, but didn't."

"Marriage wasn't our thing," Janice says.

"What was?"

"Never mind."

Absentmindedly he strokes her long hair, soft from all that swimming, as it flows on his abdomen. "Pair of kids came into the lot late today," he begins to tell her, then thinks better of it. Now that her sexual push is past, his prick has hardened, the competing muscles of anxiety having at last relaxed. But she, she is relaxed all over, asleep with his prick in her face. "Want me inside?" he asks softly, getting no answer. He moves her off his chest and works her inert body around so they lie side by side and he can fuck her from behind. She wakes enough to cry "Oh" when he penetrates. Slickly admitted, he pumps slowly, pulling the sheet up over them both. Not hot enough yet for the fan versus air-conditioner decision, both are tucked around the attic somewhere, back under the dusty eaves, strain your back lifting it out, he has never liked the chill of air-conditioning even when it was only to be had at the movies and thought to be a great treat drawing you in right off the hot sidewalk, the word COOL in blue-green with icicles on the marquee, always seemed to him healthier to live in the air God gave however lousy and let your body adjust, Nature can adjust to anything. Still, some of these nights, sticky, and the cars passing below with that wet-tire sound, the kids with their windows open or tops down and radios blaring just at the moment of dropping off to sleep, your skin prickling wherever it touched cloth and a single mosquito alive in the room. His prick is stiff as stone inside a sleeping woman. He strokes her ass, the crease where it nestles against his belly, must start jogging again, the crease between its halves and that place within the crease, opposite of a nipple, dawned on him gradually over these years that she had no objection to being touched there, seemed to like it when she was under him his hand beneath her bottom. He touches himself too now and then to test if he is holding hard; he is, thick as a tree where it comes up out of the grass, the ridges of the roots, her twin dark moons swallowing and letting go, a little sticky sound. The long slack oily curve of her side, ribs to hip bone, floats under his fingertips idle as a gull's glide. Love has lulled her, liquor has carried her off. Bless that dope. "Jan?" he whispers. "You awake?" He is not displeased to be thus stranded, another consciousness in bed is a responsibility, a snag in the flow of his thoughts. Further on in that issue an article *How to shop for a car loan* he ought to look at for professional reasons though it's not the sort of thing that interests him, he can't get it out of his head how they noticed those coffee grounds that jump out of the can when punctured. Janice snores: a single rasp of breath taken underwater, at some deep level where her nose becomes a harp. Big as the night her ass unconscious wraps him all around in this room where dabs of streetlight sifted by the beech shuffle on the ceiling. He decides to fuck her, the stiffness in his cock is killing him. His hard-on was her idea anyway. The Japanese beetle he flicked away comes into his mind as a model of delicacy. Hold tight, dream girl. He sets three fingers on her flank, the pinky lifted as in a counting game. He is stealthy so as not to wake her but single in his purpose, quick, and pure. The climax freezes his scalp and stops his heart, all stealthy; he hasn't come with such a thump in months. So who says he's running out of gas?

"I hit the ball O.K.," Rabbit says next afternoon, "but damned if I could score." He is sitting in green bathing trunks at a white outdoor table at the Flying Eagle Tee and Racquet Club with the partners of his round and their wives and, in the case of Buddy Inglefinger, girlfriend. Buddy had once had a wife too but she left him for a telephone lineman down near West Chester. You could see how that might happen because Buddy's girlfriends are sure a sorry lot.

"When did you *ever* score?" Ronnie Harrison asks him so loudly heads in the swimming pool turn around. Rabbit has known Ronnie for thirty years and never liked him, one of those locker-room show-offs always soaping himself for everybody to see and giving the JVs redbellies and out on the basketball court barging around all sweat and elbows trying to make up in muscle what he lacked in style. Yet when Harry and Janice joined Flying Eagle there old Ronnie was, with a respectable job at Schuylkill Mutual and this nice proper wife who taught third grade for years and must be great in bed, because that's all Ronnie ever used to talk about, he was like frantic on the subject, in the locker room. His kinky brass-colored hair, that began to thin right after high school, is pretty thoroughly worn through on top now, and the years and respectability have drained some pink out of him; the skin from his temples to the corners of his eyes is papery and bluish, and Rabbit doesn't remember that his eyelashes were white. He likes playing golf with Ronnie because he loves beating him, which isn't too hard: he has one of those herky-jerky punch swings short stocky guys gravitate toward and when he gets excited he tends to roundhouse a big banana right into the woods.

"I heard Harry was a big scorer," Ronnie's wife Thelma says softly. She has a narrow forgettable face and still wears that quaint old-fashioned kind of one-piece bathing suit with a little pleated skirt. Often she has a towel across her shoulders or around her ankles as if to protect her skin from the sun; except for her sun-burnt nose she is the same sallow color all over. Her wavy mousy hair is going gray strand by strand. Rabbit can never look at her without wondering what she must do to keep Harrison happy. He senses intelligence in her but intelligence in women has never much interested him.

"I set the B-league county scoring record in 1951," he says, to defend himself, and to defend himself further adds, "Big deal."

"It's been broken long since," Ronnie feels he has to explain. "By blacks."

"Every record has," Webb Murkett interposes, being tactful. "I don't know, it seems like the miles these kids run now have shrunk. In swimming they can't keep the record books up to date." Webb is the oldest man of their regular foursome, fifty and then some – a lean thoughtful gentleman in roofing and siding contracting and supply with a calming gravel voice, his long face broken into longitudinal strips by creases and his hazel eyes almost lost under an amber tangle of eyebrows. He is the steadiest golfer, too. The one unsteady thing about him, he is on his third wife;

this is Cindy, a plump brown-backed honey still smelling of high
school, though they have two little ones, a boy and a girl, ages five
and three. Her hair is cut short and lies wet in one direction, as if
surfacing from a dive, and when she smiles her teeth look unnaturally even and white in her tan face, with pink spots of peeling
on the roundest part of her cheeks; she has an exciting sexually
neutral look, though her boobs slosh and shiver in the triangular
little hammocks of her bra. The suit is one of those minimal black
ones with only a string or two between the nape of her neck and
where her ass begins to divide, a cleft more or less visible depending on the sag of her black diaper. Harry admires Webb. Webb
always swings within himself, and gets good roll.

"Better nutrition, don't you think that's it?" Buddy Inglefinger's girl pipes up, in a little-girl reedy voice that doesn't go with
her pushed-in face. She is some kind of physical therapist, though
her own shape isn't too great. The girls Buddy brings around are a
good lesson to Harry in the limits of being single – hard little secretaries and restaurant hostesses, witchy-looking former flower
children with grizzled ponytails and flat chests full of Navajo jewelry, overweight assistant heads of personnel in one of those grim
new windowless office buildings a block back from Weiser where
they spend all day putting computer print-outs in the wastebasket.
Women pickled in limbo, their legs chalky and their faces slightly
twisted, as if they had been knocked into their thirties by a sideways
blow. They remind Harry somehow of pirates, jaunty and maimed,
though without the eye patches. What the hell was this one's name?
She had been introduced around not a half hour ago, but when
everybody was still drunk on golf.

Buddy brought her, so he can't let her two cents hang up there
while the silence gets painful. He fills in, "My guess is it's mostly
in the training. Coaches at even the secondary level have all these
techniques that in the old days only the outstanding athlete would
discover, you know, pragmatically. Nowadays the outstanding
isn't that outstanding, there's a dozen right behind him. Or her."
He glances at each of the women in a kind of dutiful tag. Feminism
won't catch him off guard, he's traded jabs in too many singles
bars. "And in countries like East Germany or China they're
pumping these athletes full of steroids, like beef cattle, they're

hardly human." Buddy wears steel-rimmed glasses of a style that only lathe operators used to employ, to keep shavings out of their eyes. Buddy does something with electronics and has a mind like that, too precise. He goes on, to bring it home, "Even golf. Palmer and now Nicklaus have been trampled out of sight by these kids nobody has heard of, the colleges down south clone 'em, you can't keep their names straight from one tournament to the next."

Harry always tries to take an overview. "The records fall because they're there," he says. "Aaron shouldn't have been playing, they kept him in there just so he could break Ruth's record. I can remember when a five-minute mile in high school was a miracle. Now girls are doing it."

"It is amazing," Buddy's girl puts in, this being her conversation, "what the human body can do. Any one of us women here could go out now and pick up a car by the front bumper, if we were motivated. If say there was a child of ours under the tires. You read about incidents like that all the time, and at the hospital where I trained the doctors could lay the statistics of it right out on paper. We don't use half the muscle-power we have."

Webb Murkett kids, "Hear that, Cin? Gas stations all closed down, you can carry the Audi home. Seriously, though. I've always marvelled at these men who know a dozen languages. If the brain is a computer think of all the gray cells this entails. There seems to be lots more room in there, though."

His young wife silently lifts her hands to twist some water from her hair, that is almost too short to grab. This action gently lifts her tits in their sopping black small slings and reveals the shape of each erect nipple. A white towel is laid across her lap as if to relieve Harry from having to think about her crotch. What turns him off about Buddy's girl, he realizes, is not only does she have pimples on her chin and forehead but on her thighs, high on the inside, like something venereal. Georgene? Geraldine? She is going on in that reedy too-eager voice, "Or the way these yogas can lift themselves off the ground or go back in time for thousands of years. Edgar Cayce has example after example. It's nothing supernatural, I can't believe in God, there's too much suffering, they're just using human powers we all have and never develop. You should all read the Tibetan Book of the Dead."

"Really?" Thelma Harrison says dryly. "Who's the author?"

Now silence does invade their group. A greenish reflective wobble from the pool washes ghostly and uneasy across their faces and a child gasping as he swims can be heard. Then Webb kindly says, "Closer to home now, we've had a spooky experience lately. I bought one of these Polaroid SX-70 Land Cameras as kind of a novelty, to give the kids a charge, and all of us can't stop being fascinated, it is super*na*tural, to watch that image develop right under your eyes."

"The kind," Cindy says, "that spits it out at you like this." She makes a cross-eyed face and thrusts out her tongue with a *thrupp*-ing noise. All the men laugh, and laugh.

"*Consumer Reports* had something on it," Harry says.

"It's magical," Cindy tells them. "Webb gets really turned on." When she grins her teeth look stubby, the healthy gums come so babyishly low.

"Why is my glass empty?" Janice asks.

"Losers buy," Harry virtually shouts. Such loudness years ago would have been special to male groups but now both sexes have watched enough beer commercials on television to know that this is how to act, jolly and loud, on weekends, in the bar, beside the barbecue grill, on beaches and sundecks and mountainsides. "Winners bought the first round," he calls needlessly, as if among strangers or men without memories, while several arms flail for the waitress.

Harry's team lost the Nassau, but he feels it was his partner's fault. Buddy is such a flub artist, even when he hits two good shots he skulls the chip and takes three putts to get down. Whereas Harry as he has said hit the ball well, if not always straight: arms like ropes, start down slow, and *look at the ball* until it seems to swell. He ended with a birdie, on the long par-five that winds in around the brook with its watercress and sandy orange bottom almost to the clubhouse lawn; and that triumph – the wooden gobbling sound the cup makes when a long putt falls! – eclipses many double bogeys and suffuses with a limpid certainty of his own omnipotence and immortality the sight of the scintillating chlorinated water, the sunstruck faces and torsos of his companions, and the undulant shadow-pitted flank of Mt. Pemaquid where its forest begins above the shaven bright stripes of the fairways. He feels brother to this mountain in the day's declining sunlight. Mt. Pemaquid has only been recently tamed; for the two centuries while Mt. Judge presided above the metropolitan burgeoning of Brewer, the mountain nearby yet remained if not quite a wilderness a strange and forbidding place, where resort hotels failed and burned down and only hikers and lovers and escaping criminals ventured. The developers of the Flying Eagle (its name plucked from a bird, probably a sparrow hawk, the first surveyor spotted and took as an omen) bought three hundred acres of the lower slopes cheap; as the bulldozers ground the second-growth ash, poplar, hickory, and dogwood into muddy troughs that would become fairways and terraced tennis courts, people said the club would fail, the county already had the Brewer Country Club south of the city for the doctors and the Jews and ten miles north the Tulpehocken Club behind its fieldstone walls and tall wrought-iron fencing for the old mill-owning families and their lawyers and for the peasantry several nine-hole public courses tucked around in the farmland. But there was a class of the young middle-aged that had arisen in the retail businesses and service industries and software end of the new technology and that did not expect liveried barmen and secluded cardrooms, that did not mind the pre-fab clubhouse and sweep-it-yourself tennis courts of the Flying Eagle; to them the polyester wall-to-wall carpeting of the locker rooms seemed a luxury, and a Coke machine in a cement corridor a friendly sight. They were happy to play winter rules all summer long on the immature, patchy fairways and to pay for all their privileges the five hundred, now risen to six-fifty, in annual dues, plus a small fortune in chits. Fred Springer for years had angled for admission to the Brewer C.C. – the Tulpehocken was as out of reach as the College of Cardinals, he knew that – and had failed; now his daughter Janice wears whites and signs chits just like the heiresses of Sunflower Beer and Frankhauser Steel. Just like a du Pont. At the Flying Eagle Harry feels exercised, cleansed, cherished; the biggest man at the table, he lifts his hand and a girl in the restaurant uniform of solid green blouse and checked skirt of white and green comes and takes his order for more drinks on this Sunday of widespread gas dearth. She doesn't ask his name; the people here know it. Her own name is stitched *Sandra* on her blouse pocket; she has milky skin like his daughter but is shorter, and the weary woman she will be is already moving into her face.

"Do you believe in astrology?" Buddy's girl abruptly asks Cindy Murkett. Maybe she's a Lesbian, is why Harry can't remember her name. It was a name soft around the edges, not Gertrude.

"I don't know," Cindy says, the widened eyes of her surprise showing very white in her mask of tan. "I look at the horoscope in the papers sometimes. Some of the things they say ring so true, but isn't there a trick to that?"

"It's no trick, it's ancient science. It's the most ancient science there is."

This assault on Cindy's repose agitates Harry so he turns to Webb and asks if he watched the Phillies game last night.

"The Phillies are dead," Ronnie Harrison butts in.

Buddy comes up with the statistic that they've lost twenty-three of their last thirty-four games.

"I was brought up a Catholic," Cindy is saying to Buddy's girl in a voice so lowered Harry has to strain to hear. "And the priests said such things are the work of the Devil." She fingers as she confides this the small crucifix she wears about her throat on a chain so fine it has left no trace in her tan.

"Bowa's being out has hurt them quite a lot," Webb says judiciously, and pokes another cigarette into his creased face, lifting his rubbery upper lip automatically like a camel. He shot an 84 this afternoon, with a number of three-putt greens.

Janice is asking Thelma where she bought that lovely bathing suit. She must be drunk. "You can't find that kind at all in Kroll's anymore," Rabbit hears her say. Janice is wearing an old sort of Op-pattern blue two-piece, with a white cardigan bought to go with her tennis whites hung capelike over her shoulders. She holds a cigarette in her hand and Webb Murkett leans over to light it with his turquoise propane lighter. She's not so bad, Harry thinks, remembering how he fucked her in her sleep. Or was it, for she seemed to moan and stop snoring afterwards. Compared to Thelma's passive sallow body Janice's figure has energy, edge, the bones of the knees pressing their shape against the skin as she leans forward to accept his light. She does this with a certain accustomed grace. Webb respects her, as Fred Springer's daughter.

Harry wonders where his own daughter is this afternoon, out in the country. Doing some supper chore, having come back from feeding chickens or whatever. Sundays in the sticks aren't so different, animals don't know about holidays. Would she have gone to church this morning? Ruth had no use for that. He can't picture Ruth in the country at all. For him, she was city, those solid red brick rows of Brewer that take what comes. The drinks come. Grateful cries, like on the beer commercials, and Cindy Murkett decides to earn hers by going for another swim. When she stands, the backs of her thighs are printed in squares and her skimpy black bathing suit bottom, still soaked, clings in two thin arcs well below two dimples symmetrically set in her fat like little whirlpools; the sight dizzies Harry. Didn't he used to take Ruth to the public pool in West Brewer? Memorial Day. There was the smell of grass pressed under your damp towel spread out in the shade of the trees away from the tile pool. Now you sit in chairs of enamelled wire that unless you have a cushion print a waffle pattern on the backs of your thighs. The mountain is drawing closer. Sun reddening beyond the city dusts with gold the tips of trees high like a mane on the crest of Pemaquid and deepens the pockets of dark between each tree in the undulating forest that covers like deep-piled carpet the acreage between crest and course. Along the far eleventh fairway men are still picking their way, insect-sized. As his eyes are given to these distances Cindy flat-dives and a few drops of the splash prick Harry's naked chest, that feels broad as the basking mountain. He frames in his mind the words, *I heard a funny story on the radio yesterday driving home.* . . .

". . . if I had your nice legs," Ronnie's plain wife is concluding to Janice.

"Oh but you still have a waist. Creeping middle-itis, that's what I've got. Harry says I'm shaped like a pickle." Giggle. First she giggles, then she begins to lurch.

"He looks asleep."

He opens his eyes and announces to the air, "I heard a funny story on the radio yesterday driving home."

"Fire Ozark," Ronnie is insisting loudly. "He's lost their respect, he's demoralizing. Until they can Ozark and trade Rose away, the Phillies are D, E, A, D, dead."

"I'm listening," Buddy's awful girlfriend tells Harry, so he has to go on.

"Oh just some doctor down in Baltimore, the radio announcer said he was hauled into court for killing a goose on the course with a golf club."

"Course on the golf with a goose club," Janice giggles. Some day what would give him great pleasure would be to take a large round rock and crush her skull in with it.

"Where'd you hear this, Harry?" Webb Murkett asks him, coming in late but politely tilting his long head, one eye shut against the smoke of his cigarette.

"On the radio yesterday, driving home," Harry answers, sorry he has begun.

"Speaking of yesterday," Buddy has to interrupt, "I saw a gas line five blocks long. That Sunoco at the corner of Ash and Fourth, it went down Fourth to Buttonwood, Buttonwood to Fifth, Fifth back to Ash, and then a new line beginning the other side of Ash. They had guys directing and everything. I couldn't believe it, and cars were still getting into it. Five fucking blocks long."

"Big heating-oil dealer who's one of our clients," Ronnie says, "says they have plenty of crude, it's just they've decided to put the squeeze on gasoline and make more heating oil out of it. The crude. In their books winter's already here. I asked the guy what was going to happen to the average motorist and he looked at me funny and said, 'He can go screw himself instead of driving every weekend to the Jersey Shore.'"

"Ronnie, Harry's trying to tell a story," Thelma says.

"It hardly seems worth it," he says, enjoying now the prolonged focus on him, the comedy of delay. Sunshine on the mountain. The second gin is percolating through his system and elevating his spirits. He loves this crowd, his crowd, and the crowds at the other tables too, that are free to send delegates over and mingle with theirs, everybody knowing everybody else, and the kids in the pool, that somebody would save even if that caramel-colored lifeguard-girl popping bubble gum weren't on duty, and loves the fact that this is all on credit, the club not taking its bite until the tenth of every month.

Now they coax him. "Come on, Harry, don't be a prick," Buddy's girl says. She's using his name now, he has to find hers. Gretchen. Ginger. Maybe those aren't actually pimples on her thighs, just a rash from chocolate or poison oak. She looks allergic, that pushed-in face, like she'd have trouble breathing. Defects come in clumps.

"So this doctor," he concedes, "is hauled into court for killing a goose on the course with a golf club."

"What club?" Ronnie asks.

"I knew you'd ask that," Harry says. "If not you, some other jerk."

"I'd think a sand wedge," Buddy says, "right at the throat. It'd clip the head right off."

"Too short in the handle, you couldn't get close enough," Ronnie argues. He squints as if to judge a distance. "I'd say a five or even an easy four would be the right stick. Hey Harry, how about that five-iron I put within a gimme on the fifteenth from way out on the other side of the sand trap? In deep rough yet."

"You nudged it," Harry says.

"Heh?"

"I saw you nudge the ball up to give yourself a lie."

"Let's get this straight. You're saying I cheated."

"Something like that."

"Let's hear the story, Harry," Webb Murkett says, lighting another cigarette to dramatize his patience.

Ginger was in the ballpark. Thelma Harrison is staring at him with her big brown sunglasses and that is distracting too. "So the doctor's defense evidently was that he had hit the goose with a golf ball and injured it badly enough he had to put it out of its misery. Then this announcer said, it seemed cute at the time, she was a female announcer –"

"Wait a minute sweetie, I don't understand," Janice says. "You mean he threw a golf ball at this goose?"

"Oh my God," Rabbit says, "am I ever sorry I got started on this. Let's go home."

"No *tell* me," Janice says, looking panicked.

"He didn't *throw* the ball, the goose was on the fairway probably by some pond and the guy's drive or whatever it was —"

"Could have been his second shot and he shanked it," Buddy offers.

His nameless girlfriend looks around and in that fake little-girl voice asks, "Are geese allowed on golf courses? I mean, that may be stupid, Buddy's the first golfer I've gone out with —"

"You call *that* a golfer?" Ronnie interrupts.

Buddy tells them, "I've read somewhere about a course in Alaska where these caribou wander. Maybe it's Sweden."

"I've heard of moose on courses in Maine," Webb Murkett says. Lowering sun flames in his twisted eyebrows. He seems sad. Maybe he's feeling the liquor too, for he rambles on, "Wonder why you never hear of a Swedish golfer. You hear of Bjorn Borg, and this skier Stenmark."

Rabbit decides to ride it through. "So the announcer says, 'A mercy killing, or murder most foul?'"

"Ouch," someone says.

Ronnie is pretending to ruminate, "Maybe you'd be better off with a four-wood, and play the goose off your left foot."

"Nobody heard the punch line," Harry protests.

"I heard it," Thelma Harrison says.

"We all heard it," Buddy says. "It's just very distressing to me," he goes on, and looks very severe in his steel-rimmed glasses, so the women at first take him seriously, "that nobody here, I mean *no*body, has shown any sympathy for the goose."

"Somebody sympathized enough to bring the man to court," Webb Murkett points out.

"I discover myself," Buddy complains sternly, "in the midst of a crowd of people who while pretending to be liberal and tolerant are really anti-goose."

"Who, me?" Ronnie says, making his voice high as if goosed. Rabbit hates this kind of humor, but the others seem to enjoy it, including the women.

Cindy has returned glistening from her swim. Standing there with her bathing suit slightly awry, she tugs it straight and blushes in the face of their laughter. "Are you talking about me?" The little cross glints beneath the hollow of her throat. Her feet look pale on the poolside flagstones. Funny, how pale the tops of feet stay.

Webb gives his wife's wide hips a sideways hug. "No, honey. Harry was telling us a shaggy goose story."

"Tell me, Harry."

"Not now. Nobody liked it. Webb will tell you."

Sandra in her green and white uniform comes up to them. "Mrs. Angstrom."

The words shock Harry, as if his mother has been resurrected.

"Yes," Janice answers matter-of-factly.

"Your mother is on the phone."

"Oh Lordie, what now?" Janice stands, lurches slightly, composes herself. She takes her beach towel from the back of her chair and wraps it around her hips rather than walk in merely a bathing suit past dozens of people into the clubhouse. "What do you think it is?" she asks Harry.

He shrugs. "Maybe she wants to know what kind of baloney we're having tonight."

A dig in that, delivered openly. The awful girlfriend titters. Harry is ashamed of himself, thinking in contrast of Webb's sideways hug of Cindy's hips. This kind of crowd will do a marriage in if you let it. He doesn't want to get sloppy.

In defiance Janice asks, "Honey, could you order me another vod-and-ton while I'm gone?"

"No." He softens this to, "I'll think about it," but the chill has been put on the party.

The Murketts consult and conclude it may be time to go, they have a thirteen-year-old babysitter, a neighbor's child. The same sunlight that ignited Webb's eyebrows lights the halo of fine hairs standing up from the goosebumps on Cindy's thighs. Not bothering with any towel around her, she saunters to the ladies' locker room to change, her pale feet leaving wet prints on the gray flagstones. Wait, wait, the Sunday, the weekend cannot be by, a golden sip remains in the glass. On the transparent tabletop among the wire chairs drinks have left a ghostly clockwork of rings refracted into visibility by the declining light. What can Janice's mother want? She has called out to them from a darker older world he remembers but wants to stay buried, a world of constant clothing and airless front parlors, of coal bins and narrow houses with spite-fully drawn shades, where the farmer's drudgery and the mill-worker's ruled land and city. Here, clean children shivering with their sudden emergence into the thinner element are handed towels by their mothers. Cindy's towel hangs on her empty chair. To be Cindy's towel and to be sat upon by her: the thought dries Rabbit's mouth. To stick your tongue in just as far as it would go while her pussy tickles your nose. No acne in that crotch. Heaven. He looks up and sees the shaggy mountain shouldering into the sun still, though the chairs are making long shadows, lozenge checker-boards. Buddy Inglefinger is saying to Webb Murkett in a low voice whose vehemence is not ironical, "Ask yourself sometime who benefits from inflation. The people in debt benefit, society's losers. The government benefits because it collects more in taxes without raising the rates. Who doesn't benefit? The man with money in his pocket, the man who's paid his bills. That's why" – Buddy's voice drops to a conspiratorial hiss – "that man is vanishing like the red Indian. Why should I work," he asks Webb, "when the money is taken right out of my pocket for the benefit of those who don't?"

Harry is thinking his way along the mountain ridge, where clouds are lifting like a form of steam. As if in driven motion Mt. Pemaquid cleaves the summer sky and sun, though poolside is in shadow now. Thelma is saying cheerfully to the girlfriend, "Astrology, palm-reading, psychiatry – I'm for all of it. Anything that helps get you through." Harry is thinking of his own parents. They should have belonged to a club. Living embattled, Mom feuding with the neighbors, Pop and his union hating the men who owned the printing plant where he worked his life away, both of them scorning the few kin that tried to keep in touch, the four of them, Pop and Mom and Hassy and Mim, against the world and a certain guilt attaching to any reaching up and outside for a friend. *Don't trust anybody: Andy Mellon doesn't, and I don't.* Dear Pop. He never got out from under. Rabbit basks above that old remembered world, rich, at rest.

Buddy's voice nags on, aggrieved. "Money that goes out of one pocket goes into somebody else's, it doesn't just evaporate. The big boys are getting rich out of this."

A chair scrapes and Rabbit feels Webb stand. His voice comes from a height, gravelly, humorously placating. "Become a big boy yourself I guess is the only answer."

"Oh sure," Buddy says, knowing he is being put off.

A tiny speck, a bird, the fabled eagle it might be, no, from the motionlessness of its wings a buzzard, is flirting in flight with the ragged golden-green edge of the mountain, now above it like a speck on a Kodak slide, now below it out of sight, while a blue-bellied cloud unscrolls, endlessly, powerfully. Another chair is scraped on the flagstones. His name, "Harry," is sharply called, in Janice's voice.

He lowers his gaze at last out of glory and as his eyes adjust his forehead momentarily hurts, a small arterial pain; perhaps with such a negligible unexplained ache do men begin their deaths, some slow as being tumbled by a cat and some fast as being struck by a hawk. Cancer, coronary. "What did Bessie want?"

Janice's tone is breathless, faintly stricken. "She says Nelson's come. With this girl."

"Melanie," Harry says, pleased to have remembered. And his remembering brings along with it Buddy's girlfriend's name. Joanne. "It was nice to have met you, Joanne," he says in parting, shaking her hand. Making a good impression. Casting his shadow.

As Harry drives them home in Janice's Mustang convertible with the top down, air pours over them and lends an illusion of urgent and dangerous speed. Their words are snatched from their mouths. "What the fuck are we going to do with the kid?" he asks her.

"How do you mean?" With her dark hair being blown back, Janice looks like a different person. Eyes asquint against the rush of wind and her upper lip lifted, a hand held near her ear to keep her rippling silk head scarf from flying away. Liz Taylor in *A Place in the Sun*. Even the little crow's-feet at the corner of her eye look glamorous. She is wearing her tennis dress and the white cashmere cardigan.

"I mean is he going to get a job or what?"

"Well Harry. He's still in college."

"He doesn't act like it." He feels he has to shout. "I wasn't so fucking fortunate as to get to college and the guys that did didn't goof off in Colorado hang gliding and God knows what until their father's money ran out."

"You don't know what they did. Anyway times are different. Now you be nice to Nelson. After the things you put him through —"

"Not just me."

"— after what he went through you should be grateful he *wants* to come home. Ever."

"I don't know."

"You don't know *what?*"

"This doesn't feel good to me. I've been too happy lately."

"Don't be irrational," Janice says.

She is not, this implies. But one of their bonds has always been that her confusion keeps pace with his. As the wind pours past he feels a scared swift love for something that has no name. Her? His life? The world? Coming from the Mt. Pemaquid direction, you see the hillside borough of Mt. Judge from a spread-out angle altogether different from what you see coming home from the Brewer direction: the old box factory a long lean-windowed slab down low by the dried-up falls, sent underground to make electricity, and the new supertall Exxon and Mobil signs on their tapered aluminum poles along Route 422 as eerie as antennae arrived out of space. The town's stacked windows burn orange in the sun that streams level up the valley, and from this angle great prominence gathers to the sandstone spire of the Lutheran church where Rabbit went to Sunday school under crusty old Fritz Kruppenbach, who pounded in the lesson that life has no terrors for those with faith but for those without faith there can be no salvation and no peace. *No* peace. A sign says THICKLY SETTLED. As the Mustang slows, Harry is moved to confess to Janice, "I started to tell you last night, this young couple came into the lot yesterday and the girl reminded me of Ruth. She would be about the right age too. Slimmer, and not much like her in her way of talking, but there was, I don't know, something."

"Your imagination is what it was. Did you get the girl's name?"

"I asked, but she wouldn't give it. She was cute about it, too. Kind of flirty, without anything you could put your finger on."

"And you think that girl was your daughter."

From her tone he knows he shouldn't have confessed. "I didn't say that exactly."

"Then what did you say? You're telling me you're still thinking of this bag you fucked twenty years ago and now you and she have a darling little *baby*." He glances over and Janice no longer suggests Elizabeth Taylor, her lips all hard and crinkled as if baked in her fury. Ida Lupino. Where did they go, all the great Hollywood bitches? In town for years there had been just a Stop sign at the corner where Jackson slants down into Central but the other year after the burgess's own son smashed up a car running the sign the borough put in a light, that is mostly on blink, yellow this way and red the other. He touches the brake and takes the left turn. Janice leans with the turn to keep her mouth close to his ear. "You are crazy," she shouts. "You *always* want what you don't have instead of what you *do*. Getting all cute and smiley in the face thinking about this *girl* that doesn't exist while your *real* son, that you had with your *wife*, is waiting at home right now and you saying you wished he'd stay in Colorado."

"I do wish that," Harry says – anything to change the subject even slightly. "You're wrong about my wanting what I don't have. I pretty much like what I have. The trouble with that is, then you get afraid somebody will take it from you."

"Well it's not going to be Nelson, he wants nothing from you except a little love and he doesn't get that. I don't know *why* you're such an unnatural father."

So they can finish their argument before they reach Ma Springer's he has slowed their speed up Jackson, under the shady interlock of maples and horsechestnuts, that makes the hour feel later than it is. "The kid has it in for me," he says mildly, to see what this will bring on.

It re-excites her. "You keep saying that but it's not *true*. He *loves* you. Or did." Where the sky shows through the mingled tree tops there is still a difference of light, a flickering that beats upon their faces and hands mothlike. In a sullen semi-mollified tone she says, "One thing definite, I don't want to hear any more about your darling illegitimate daughter. It's a disgusting idea."

"I know. I don't know why I mentioned it." He had mistaken the two of them for one and entrusted to her this ghost of his alone. A mistake married people make.

"Dis*gus*ting!" Janice cries.

"I'll never mention it again," he promises.

They ease into Joseph, at the corner where the fire hydrant still wears, faded, the red-white-and-blue clown outfit that school-children three Junes ago painted on for the Bicentennial. Polite in his freshened dislike of her, he asks, "Shall I put the car in the garage?"

"Leave it out front, Nelson may want it."

As they walk up the front steps his feet feel heavy, as if the world has taken on new gravity. He and the kid years ago went through something for which Rabbit has forgiven himself but which he knows the kid never has. A girl called Jill died when Harry's house burned down, a girl Nelson had come to love like a sister. At least like a sister. But the years have piled on, the surviving have patched things up, and so many more have joined the dead, undone by diseases for which only God is to blame, that it no longer seems so bad, it seems more as if Jill just moved to another town, where the population is growing. Jill would be twenty-eight now. Nelson is twenty-two. Think of all the blame God has to shoulder.

Ma's front door sticks and yields with a shove. The living room is dark and duffel bags have been added to its clutter of padded furniture. A shabby plaid suitcase, not Nelson's, sits on the stair landing. The voices come from the sunporch. These voices lessen Harry's gravity, seem to refute the world's rumors of universal death. He moves toward the voices, through the dining room and then the kitchen, into the porch area conscious of himself as slightly too drunk to be cautious enough, overweight and soft and a broad target.

Copper-beech leaves crowd at the porch screen. Faces and bodies rise from the aluminum and nylon furniture like the cloud of an explosion with the sound turned down on TV. More and more in middle age the world comes upon him like images on a set with one thing wrong with it, like those images the mind entertains before we go to sleep, that make sense until we look at them closely, which wakes us up with a shock. It is the girl who has risen most promptly, a curly-headed rather sturdy girl with shining brown eyes halfway out of her head and a ruby-red dimpling smile lifted from a turn-of-the-century valentine. She has on jeans that have been through everything and a Hindu sort of embroidered shirt that has lost some sequins. Her handshake surprises him by being damp, nervous.

Nelson slouches to his feet. His usual troubled expression wears a mountaineer's tan, and he seems thinner, broader in the shoulders. Less of a puppy, more of a mean dog. At some point in Colorado or at Kent he has had his hair, which in high school used to fall to his shoulders, cut short, to give a punk look. "Dad, this is my friend Melanie. My father. And my mother. Mom, this is Melanie."

"Pleased to meet you both," the girl says, keeping the merry red smile as if even these plain words are prelude to a joke, to a little circus act. That is what she reminds Harry of, those somehow unreal but visibly brave women who hang by their teeth in circuses, or ride one-footed the velvet rope up to fly through the spangled air, though she is dressed in that raggy look girls hide in now. A strange wall or glare has instantly fallen between himself and this girl, a disinterest that he takes to be a gesture toward his son.

Nelson and Janice are embracing. *Those little Springer hands*, Harry remembers his mother saying, as he sees them press into the back of Janice's tennis dress. Tricky little paws, something about the curve of the stubby curved fingers that hints of sneaky strength. No visible moons to the fingernails and the ends look nibbled. A habit of sullen grievance and blank stubbornness has descended to Nelson from Janice. The poor in spirit.

Yet when Janice steps aside to greet Melanie, and father and son are face to face, and Nelson says, "Hey, Dad," and like his father Harry wonders whether to shake hands or hug or touch in any way, love floods clumsily the hesitant space.

"You look fit," Harry says.

"I feel beat."

"How'd you get here so soon?"

"Hitched, except for a stretch after Kansas City where we took a bus as far as Indianapolis." Places where Rabbit has never been, restless though his blood is. The boy tells him, "The night before last we spent in some field in western Ohio, I don't know, after Toledo. It was weird. We'd gotten stoned with the guy who picked us up in this van all painted with designs, and when he dumped us off Melanie and I were really disoriented, we had to keep talking to each other so we wouldn't panic. The ground was colder than you'd think, too. We woke up frozen but at least the trees had stopped looking like octopuses."

"Nelson," Janice cries, "something dreadful could have happened to you! To the two of you."

"Who cares?" the boy asks. To his grandmother, Bessie sitting in her private cloud in the darkest corner of the porch, he says, "You wouldn't care, would you Mom-mom, if I dropped out of the picture?"

"Indeed I would," is her stout response. "You were the apple of your granddad's eye."

Melanie reassures Janice, "People are basically very nice." Her voice is strange, gurgling as if she has just recovered from a fit of laughter, with a suspended singing undertone. Her mind seems focused on some faraway cause for joy. "You only meet the difficult ones now and then, and they're usually all right as long as you don't show fear."

"What does your mother think of your hitchhiking?" Janice asks her.

"She hates it," Melanie says, and laughs outright, her curls shaking. "But she lives in California." She turns serious, her eyes shining on Janice steadily as lamps. "Really though, it's ecologically sound, it saves all that gas. More people should do it, but everybody's afraid."

A gorgeous frog, is what she looks like to Harry, though her body from what you can tell in those flopsy-mopsy clothes is human enough, and even exemplary. He tells Nelson, "If you'd budgeted your allowance better you'd've been able to take the bus all the way."

"Buses are boring, Dad, and full of creeps. You don't *learn* anything on a bus."

"It's true," Melanie chimes in. "I've heard terrible stories from
girlfriends of mine, that happened to them on buses. The drivers
can't do anything, they just drive, and if you look at all, you know,
what they think of as hippie, they egg the guys on it seems."

"The world is no longer a safe place," Ma Springer announces
from her dark corner.

Harry decides to act the father. "I'm glad you made it," he tells
Nelson. "I'm proud of you, getting around the way you do. If
I'd seen a little more of the United States when I was your age, I'd
be a better citizen now. The only free ride I ever got was when
Uncle sent me to Texas. Lubbock, Texas. They'd let us out," he
tells Melanie, "Saturday nights, in the middle of a tremendous cow
pasture. Fort Larson, it was called." He is overacting, talking too
much.

"Dad," Nelson says impatiently, "the country's the same now
wherever you go. The same supermarkets, the same plastic shit for
sale. There's nothing to see."

"Colorado was a disappointment to Nelson," Melanie tells
them, with her merry undertone.

"I liked the state, I just didn't care for the skunks who live in
it." That aggrieved stunted look on his face. Harry knows he will
never find out what happened in Colorado, to drive the kid back
to him. Like those stories kids bring back from school where it was
never them who started the fight.

"Have these children had any supper?" Janice asks, working up
her mother act. You get out of practice quickly.

Ma Springer with unexpected complacence announces, "Melanie made the most delicious salad out of what she could find in
the refrigerator and outside."

"I love your garden," Melanie tells Harry. "The little gate.
Things grow so beautifully around here." He can't get over the
way she warbles everything, all the while staring at his face as if
fearful he will miss some point.

"Yeah," he says. "It's depressing, in a way. Was there any
baloney left?"

Nelson says, "Melanie's veggy, Dad."

"Veggy?"

"Vegetarian," the boy explains in his put-on whine.

"Oh. Well, no law against that."

The boy yawns. "Maybe we should hit the hay. Melanie and I got about an hour's sleep last night."

Janice and Harry go tense, and eye Melanie and Ma Springer. Janice says, "I better make up Nellie's bed."

"I've already done it," her mother tells her. "And the bed in the old sewing room too. I've had a lot of time by myself today, it seems you two are at the club more and more."

"How was church?" Harry asks her.

Ma Springer says unwillingly, "It was not very inspiring. For the collection music they had brought out from St. Mary's in Brewer one of those men who can sing in a high voice like a woman."

Melanie smiles. "A countertenor. My brother was once a countertenor."

"Then what happened?" Harry asks, yawning himself. He suggests, "His voice changed."

Her eyes are solemn. "Oh no. He took up polo playing."

"He sounds like a real sport."

"He's really my half-brother. My father was married before."

Nelson tells Harry, "Mom-mom and I ate what was left of the baloney, Dad. We ain't no veggies."

Harry asks Janice, "What's there left for me? Night after night, I starve around here."

Janice waves away his complaint with a queenly gesture she wouldn't have possessed ten years ago. "I don't know, I was thinking we'd get a bite at the club, then Mother called."

"I'm not sleepy," Melanie tells Nelson.

"Maybe she ought to see a little of the area," Harry offers. "And you could pick up a pizza while you're out."

"In the West," Nelson says, "they hardly have pizzas, everything is this awful Mexican crap, tacos and chili. Yuk."

"I'll phone up Giordano's, remember where that is? A block beyond the courthouse, on Seventh?"

"Dad, I've lived my whole life in this lousy county."

"You and me both. How does everybody feel about pepperoni? Let's get a couple, I bet Melanie's still hungry. One pepperoni and one combination."

"Jesus, Dad. We keep telling you, Melanie's a vegetarian."

"Oops. I'll order one plain. You don't have any bad feelings about cheese, do you Melanie? Or mushrooms. How about with mushrooms?"

"I'm full," the girl beams, her voice slowed it seems by its very burden of delight. "But I'd love to go with Nelson for the ride, I really like this area. It's so lush, and the houses are all kept so neat."

Janice takes this opening, touching the girl's arm, another gesture she might not have dared in the past. "Have you seen the upstairs?" she asks. "What we normally use for a guest room is across the hall from Mother's room, you'd share a bathroom with her."

"Oh, I didn't expect a room at all. I had thought just a sleeping bag on the sofa. Wasn't there a nice big sofa in the room where we first came in?"

Harry assures her, "You don't want to sleep on that sofa, it's so full of dust you'll sneeze to death. The room upstairs is nice, honest; if you don't mind sharing with a dressmaker's dummy."

"Oh no," the girl responds. "I really just want a tiny corner where I won't be in the way, I want to go out and get a job as a waitress."

The old lady fidgets, moving her coffee cup from her lap to the folding tray table beside her chair. "I made all my dresses for years but once I had to go to the bifocals I couldn't even sew Fred's buttons on," she says.

"By that time you were rich anyway," Harry tells her, jocular in his relief at the bed business seeming to work out so smoothly. Old lady Springer, when you cross her there's no end to it, she never forgets. Harry was a little hard on Janice early in the marriage and you can still see resentment in the set of Bessie's mouth. He dodges out of the sunporch to the phone in the kitchen. While Giordano's is ringing, Nelson comes up behind him and rummages in his pockets. "Hey," Harry says, "what're ya robbing me for?"

"Car keys. Mom says take the car out front."

Harry braces the receiver between his shoulder and ear and fishes the keys from his left pocket and, handing them over, for the first time looks Nelson squarely in the face. He sees nothing of himself there except the small straight nose and a cowlick in one eyebrow that sends a little fan of hairs the wrong way and seems to express a doubt. Amazing, genes. So precise in all that coiled coding they can pick up a tiny cowlick like that. That girl had had Ruth's tilt, exactly: a little forward push of the upper lip and thighs, soft-tough, comforting.

"Thanks, Pops."

"Don't dawdle. Nothing worse than cold pizza."

"What was that?" a tough voice at the other end of the line asks, having at last picked up the phone.

"Nothing, sorry," Harry says, and orders three pizzas – one pepperoni, one combination, and one plain in case Melanie changes her mind. He gives Nelson a ten-dollar bill. "We ought to talk sometime, Nellie, when you get some rest." The remark goes with the money, somehow. Nelson makes no answer, taking the bill.

When the young people are gone, Harry returns to the sun-porch and says to the women, "Now that wasn't so bad, was it? She seemed happy to sleep in the sewing room."

"Seems isn't being," Ma Springer darkly says.

"Hey that's right," Harry says. "Whaddid you think of her any-way? The girlfriend."

"Does she feel like a girlfriend to you?" Janice asks him. She has at last sat down, and has a small glass in her hand. The liquid in the glass he can't identify by its color, a sickly but intense red like old-fashioned cream soda or the fluid in thermometers.

"Whaddeya mean? They spent last night in a field together. God knows how they shacked up in Colorado. Maybe in a cave."

"I'm not sure that follows anymore. They try to be friends in a way we couldn't when we were young. Boys and girls."

"Nelson does not look contented," Ma Springer announces heavily.

"When did he ever?" Harry asks.

"As a little boy he seemed very hopeful," his grandmother says.

"Bessie, what's your analysis of what brought him back here?"

The old lady sighs. "Some disappointment. Some thing that got too big for him. I'll tell you this though. If that girl doesn't behave herself under our roof, I'm moving out. I talked to Grace Stuhl about it after church and she's more than willing, poor soul, to have me move in. She thinks it might prolong her life."

"Mother," Janice asks, "aren't you missing *All in the Family?*"

"It was to be a show I've seen before, the one where this old girlfriend of Archie's comes back to ask for money. Now that it's summer it's all reruns. I did hope to look at *The Jeffersons* though, at nine-thirty, before this hour on Moses, if I can stay awake. Maybe I'll go upstairs to rest my legs. When I was making up Nellie's little bed, a corner hit a vein and it won't stop throbbing." She stands, wincing.

"Mother," Janice says impatiently, "I would have made up those beds if you'd just waited. Let me go up with you and look at the guest room."

Harry follows them out of the sunporch (it's getting too tragic in there, the copper beech black as ink, captive moths beating their wings to a frazzle on the screens) and into the dining room. He likes the upward glimpse of Janice's legs in the tennis dress as she goes upstairs to help her mother make things fit and proper. Ought to try fucking her some night when they're both awake. He could go upstairs and give her a hand now but he is attracted instead to the exotic white face of the woman on the cover of the July *Consumer Reports*, that he brought downstairs this morning to read in the pleasant hour between when Ma went off to church and he and Janice went off to the club. The magazine still rests on the arm of the Barcalounger, that used to be old man Springer's evening throne. You couldn't dislodge him, and when he went off to the bathroom or into the kitchen for his Diet Pepsi the chair stayed empty. Harry settles into it. The girl on the cover is wearing a white bowler hat on her white-painted face above the lapels of a fully white tuxedo; she is made up in red, white, and blue like a clown and in her uplifted hand has a dab of gooey white face cleaner. Jism, models are prostitutes, the girls in blue movies rub their faces in jism. *Broadway tests face cleansers* it says beneath her, for face cleansers are one of the commodities this month's issue is testing, along with cottage cheese (how unclean is it?

it is rather unclean), air-conditioners, compact stereos, and can openers (why do people make rectangular cans anyway?). He turns to finish with the air-conditioners and reads that if you live in a high-humidity area (and he supposes he does, at least compared to Arizona) almost all models tend to drip, some enough *to make them doubtful choices for installation over a patio or walkway.* It would be nice to have a patio, along with a sunken living room like Webb Murkett does. Webb and that cute little cunt Cindy, always looking hosed down. Still, Rabbit is content. This is what he likes, domestic peace. Women circling with dutiful footsteps above him and the summer night like a lake lapping at the windows. He has time to read about compact stereos and even try the piece on car loans before Nelson and Melanie come back out of this night with three stained boxes of pizza. Quickly Harry snatches off his reading glasses, for he feels strangely naked in them.

The boy's face has brightened and might even be called cheerful. "Boy," he tells his father, "Mom's Mustang really can dig when you ask it to. Some jungle bunny in about a '69 Caddy kept racing his motor and I left him standing. Then he tailgated me all the way to the Running Horse Bridge. It was scary."

"You came around that way? Jesus, no wonder it took so long."

"Nelson was showing me the city," Melanie explains, with her musical smile, that leaves the trace of a hum in the air as she moves with the flat cardboard boxes toward the kitchen. Already she has that nice upright walk of a waitress.

He calls after her, "It's a city that's seen better days."

"I think it's beauti-ful," her answer floats back. "The people paint their houses in these different colors, like something you'd see in the Mediterranean."

"The spics do that," Harry says. "The spics and the wops."

"Dad, you're really prejudiced. You should travel more."

"Naa, it's all in fun. I love everybody, especially with my car windows locked." He adds, "Toyota was going to pay for me and your mother to go to Atlanta, but then some agency toward Harrisburg beat our sales total and they got the trip instead. It was a regional thing. It bothered me because

I've always been curious about the South: love hot weather."

"Don't be so chintzy, Dad. Go for your vacation and pay your
way."

"Vacations, we're pretty well stuck with that camp up in the
Poconos." Old man Springer's pride and joy.

"I took this course in sociology at Kent. The reason you're so
tight with your money, you got the habit of poverty when you
were a child, in the Depression. You were traumatized."

"We weren't that bad off. Pop got decent money, printers
were never laid off like some of the professions. Anyway who says
I'm tight with my money?"

"You owe Melanie three dollars already. I had to borrow from
her."

"You mean those three pizzas cost thirteen dollars?"

"We got a couple of sixpacks to go with them."

"You and Melanie can pay for your own beer. We never drink
it around here. Too fattening."

"Where's Mom?"

"Upstairs. And another thing. Don't leave your mother's car
out front with the top down. Even if it doesn't rain, the maples
drop something sticky on the seats."

"I thought we might go out again."

"You're kidding. I thought you said you got only an hour's
sleep last night."

"Dad, lay off the crap. I'm going on twenty-three."

"Twenty-three, and no sense. Give me the keys. I'll put the
Mustang out back in the garage."

"*Mo-om*," the boy shouts upwards. "Dad won't let me drive
your car!"

Janice is coming down. She has put on her peppermint dress
and looks tired. Harry tells her, "All I asked was for him to put it
in the garage. The maple sap gets the seats sticky. He says he wants
to go out again. Christ, it's nearly ten o'clock."

"The maples are through dripping for the year," Janice says. To
Nelson she merely says, "If you don't want to go out again maybe
you should put the top up. We had a terrible thunderstorm two
nights ago. It hailed, even."

"Why do you think," Rabbit asks her, "your top is all black and spotty? The sap or whatever it is drips down on the canvas and can't be cleaned off."

"Harry, it's not your car," Janice tells him.

"Piz–za," Melanie calls from the kitchen, her tone bright and pearly. "*Mangiamo, prego!*"

"Dad's really into cars, isn't he?" Nelson asks his mother. "Like they're magical, now that he sells them."

Harry asks her, "How about Ma? She want to eat again?"

"Mother says she feels sick."

"Oh great. One of her spells."

"Today was an exciting day for her."

"Today was an exciting day for me too. I was told I'm a tight-wad and think cars are magical." This is no way to be, spiteful. "Also, Nelson, I birdied the eighteenth, you know that long dog-leg? A drive that just cleared the creek and kept bending right, and then I hit an easy five-iron and then wedged it up to about twelve feet and sank the damn putt! Still have your clubs? We ought to play." He puts a paternal hand on the boy's back.

"I sold them to a guy at Kent." Nelson takes an extra-fast step, to get out from under his father's touch. "I think it's the stupidest game ever invented."

"You must tell us about hang gliding," his mother says.

"It's neat. It's very quiet. You're in the wind and don't feel a thing. Some of the people get stoned beforehand but then there's the danger you'll think you can really fly."

Melanie has sweetly set out plates and transferred the pizzas from their boxes to cookie sheets. Janice asks, "Melanie, do you hang glide?"

"Oh no," says the girl. "I'd be terrified." Her giggling does not somehow interrupt her lustrous, caramel–colored stare. "Pru used to do it with Nelson. I never would."

"Who's Pru?" Harry asks.

"You don't know her," Nelson tells him.

"I know I don't. I know I don't know her. If I knew her I wouldn't have to ask."

"I think we're all cross and irritable," Janice says, lifting a piece of pepperoni loose and laying it on a plate.

Nelson assumes that plate is for him. "Tell Dad to quit leaning on me," he complains, settling to the table as if he has tumbled from a motorcycle and is sore all over.

In bed, Harry asks Janice, "What's eating the kid, do you think?"

"I don't know."

"Something is."

"Yes."

As they think this over they can hear Ma Springer's television going, chewing away at Moses from the Biblical sound of the voices, shouting, rumbling, with crescendos of music between. The old lady falls asleep with it on and sometimes it crackles all night, if Janice doesn't tiptoe in and turn it off. Melanie had gone to bed in her room with the dressmaker's dummy. Nelson came upstairs to watch *The Jeffersons* with his grandmother and by the time his parents came upstairs had gone to bed in his old room, without saying goodnight. Sore all over. Rabbit wonders if the young couple from the country will come into the lot tomorrow. The girl's pale round face and the television screen floating unwatched in Ma Springer's room become confused in his mind as the exalted music soars. Janice is asking, "How do you like the girl?"

"Melanie baby. Spooky. Are they all that way, of that genera-tion, like a rock just fell on their heads and it was the nicest exper-ience in the world?"

"I think she's trying to ingratiate herself. It must be a difficult thing, to go into a boyfriend's home and make a place for your-self. I wouldn't have lasted ten minutes with your mother."

Little she knows, the poison Mom talked about her. "Mom was like me," Harry says. "She didn't like being crowded." New people at either end of the house and old man Springer's ghost sit-ting downstairs on his Barcalounger. "They don't act very lovey," he says. "Or is that how people are now? Hands off."

"I think they don't want to shock us. They know they must get around Mother."

"Join the crowd."

Janice ponders this. The bed creaks and heavy footsteps slither on the other side of the wall, and the excited cries of the television set are silenced with a click. Burt Lancaster just getting warmed up. Those teeth: can they be his own? All the stars have them crowned. Even Harry, he used to have a lot of trouble with his molars and now they're snug, safe and painless, in little jackets of gold alloy costing four hundred fifty each.

"She's still up," Janice says. "She won't sleep. She's stewing." In the positive way she pronounces her *s*'s she sounds more and more like her mother. We carry our heredity concealed for a while and then it pushes through. Out of those narrow DNA coils.

In a stir of wind as before a sudden rain the shadows of the copper-beech leaves surge and fling their ragged interstices of streetlight back and forth across the surfaces where the ceiling meets the far wall. Three cars pass, one after the other, and Harry's sense of the active world outside sliding by as he lies here safe wells up within him to merge with the bed's nebulous ease. He is in his bed, his molars are in their crowns. "She's a pretty good old sport," he says. "She rolls with the punches."

"She's waiting and watching," Janice says in an ominous voice that shows she is more awake than he. She asks, "When do I get my turn?"

"Turn?" The bed is gently turning, Stavros is waiting for him by the great display window that brims with dusty morning light. *You asked for it.*

"You came last night, from the state I was in this morning. Me and the sheet."

The wind stirs again. Damn. The convertible is still out there with the top down. "Honey, it's been a long day." Running out of gas. "Sorry."

"You're forgiven," Janice says. "Just." She has to add, "I might think I don't turn you on much anymore."

"No, actually, over at the club today I was thinking how much sassier you look than most of those broads, old Thelma in her little skirt and the awful girlfriend of Buddy's."

"And Cindy?"

"Not my type. Too pudgy."

"Liar."

You got it. He is dead tired yet something holds him from the black surface of sleep, and in that half-state just before or after he sinks he imagines he hears lighter, younger footsteps slither outside in the hall, going somewhere in a hurry.

Melanie is as good as her word, she gets a job waitressing at a new restaurant downtown right on Weiser Street, an old restaurant with a new name, The Crêpe House. Before that it was the Café Barcelona, painted tiles and paella, iron grillwork and gazpacho; Harry ate lunch there once in a while but in the evening it had attracted the wrong element, hippies and Hispanic families from the south side instead of the white-collar types from West Brewer and the heights along Locust Boulevard, that you need to make a restaurant go in this city. Brewer never has been much for Latin touches, not since Carmen Miranda and all those Walt Disney Saludos Amigos movies. Rabbit remembers there used to be a Club Castanet over on Warren Avenue but the only thing Spanish had been the name and the frills on the waitresses' uniforms, which had been orange. Before the Crêpe House had been the Barcelona it had been for many years Johnny Frye's Chophouse, good solid food day and night for the big old-fashioned German eaters, who have eaten themselves pretty well into the grave by now, taking with them tons of pork chops and sauerkraut and a river of Sunflower Beer. Under its newest name, Johnny Frye's is a success; the lean new race of downtown office workers comes out of the banks and the federal offices and the deserted department stores and makes its way at noon through the woods the city planners have inflicted on Weiser Square and sits at the little tile tables left over from the Café Barcelona and dabbles at glorified pancakes wrapped around minced whatever. Even driving through after a movie at one of the malls you can see them in there by candlelight, two by two, bending toward each other over the crêpes earnest as hell, on the make, the guys in leisure suits with flared open collars and the girls in slinky dresses that cling to their bodies as if by static electricity, and a dozen more just like them

standing in the foyer waiting to be seated. It has to do with diet,
Harry figures – people now want to feel they're eating less, and a
crêpe sounds like hardly a snack whereas if they called it a pancake
they would have scared everybody away but kids and two-ton
Katrinkas. Harry marvels that this new tribe of customers exists,
on the make, and with money. The world keeps ending but new
people too dumb to know it keep showing up as if the fun's just
started. The Crêpe House is such a hit they've bought the decrepit
brick building next door and expanded into the storerooms, leaving the old cigar store, that still has a little gas pilot to light up by
by the cash register, intact and doing business. To staff their new
space the Crêpe House needed more waitresses. Melanie works
some days the lunch shift from ten to six and other days she goes
from five to near one in the morning. One day Harry took Charlie
over to lunch for him to see this new woman in the Angstrom life,
but it didn't work out very well: having Nelson's father show up
as a customer with a strange man put roses of embarrassment in
Melanie's cheeks as she served them in the midst of the lunchtime
mob.

"Not a bad looker," Charlie said on that awkward occasion,
gazing after the young woman as she flounced away. The Crêpe
House dresses its waitresses in a kind of purple colonial mini, with
a big bow in back that switches as they walk.

"You can see that?" Harry said. "I can't. It bothers me, actually.
That I'm not turned on. The kid's been living with us two weeks
now and I should be climbing the walls."

"A little old for wall-climbing, aren't you, chief? Anyway there
are some women that don't do it for some men. That's why they
turn out so many models."

"As you say she has all the equipment. Big knockers, if you look."

"I looked."

"The funny thing is, she doesn't seem to turn Nelson on either,
that I can see. They're buddies all right; when she's home they
spend hours in his room together playing his old records and talking about God knows what, sometimes they come out of there it
looks like he's been crying, but as far as Jan and I can tell she sleeps
in the front room, where we put her as a sop to old lady Springer
that first night, never thinking it would stick. Actually Bessie's

kind of taken with her by now, she helps with the housework more than Janice does for one thing; so at this point wherever Melanie sleeps I think she'd look the other way."

"They've *got* to be fucking," Stavros insisted, setting his hands on the table in that defining, faintly menacing way he has: palms facing, thumbs up.

"You'd think so," Rabbit agreed. "But these kids now are spooky. These letters in long white envelopes keep arriving from Colorado and they spend a lot of time answering. The postmark's Colorado but the return address printed on is some dean's office at Kent. Maybe he's flunked out."

Charlie scarcely listened. "Maybe I should give her a buzz, if Nelson's not ringing her bell."

"Come on, Charlie. I didn't say he's not, I just don't get that vibe around the house. I don't think they do it in the back of the Mustang, the seats are vinyl and these kids today are too spoiled." He sipped his Margarita and wiped the salt from his lips. The bartender here was left over from the Barcelona days, they must have a cellarful of tequila. "To tell you the truth I can't imagine Nelson screwing anybody, he's such a sourpussed little punk."

"Got his grandfather's frame. Fred was sexy, don't kid yourself. Couldn't keep his hands off the clerical help, that's why so many of them left. Where'd you say she's from?"

"California. Her father sounds like a bum, he lives in Oregon after being a lawyer. Her parents split a time ago."

"So she's a long way from home. Probably needs a friend, along more mature lines."

"Well I'm right there across the hall from her."

"You're family, champ. That doesn't count. Also you don't appreciate this chick and no doubt she twigs to that. Women do."

"Charlie, you're old enough to be her father."

"Aah. These Mediterranean types, they like to see a little gray hair on the chest. The old *mastoras*."

"What about your lousy ticker?"

Charlie smiled and put his spoon into the cold spinach soup that Melanie had brought. "Good a way to go as any."

"Charlie, you're crazy," Rabbit said admiringly, admiring yet once again in their long relationship what he fancies as the other man's superior grip upon the basic elements of life, elements that Harry can never settle in his mind.

"Being crazy's what keeps us alive," Charlie said, and sipped, closing his eyes behind his tinted glasses to taste the soup better. "Too much nutmeg. Maybe Janice'd like to have me over, it's been a while. So I can feel things out."

"Listen, I can't have you over so you can seduce my son's girl-friend."

"You said she wasn't a girlfriend."

"I said they didn't act like it, but then what do I know?"

"You have a pretty good nose. I trust you, champ." He changed the subject slightly. "How come Nelson keeps showing up at the lot?"

"I don't know, with Melanie off at work he doesn't have much to do, hanging around the house with Bessie, going over to the club with Janice swimming till his eyes get pink from the chlorine. He shopped around town a little for a job but no luck. I don't think he tried too hard."

"Maybe we could fit him in at the lot."

"I don't want that. Things are cozy enough around here for him already."

"He going back to college?"

"I don't know. I'm scared to ask."

Stavros put down his soup spoon carefully. "Scared to ask," he repeated. "And you're paying the bills. If my father had ever said to anybody he was scared of anything to do with me, I think the roof would have come off the house."

"Maybe scared isn't the word."

"Scared is the word you used." He looked up squinting in what seemed to be pain through his thick glasses to perceive Melanie more clearly as, in a flurry of purple colonial flounces, she set before Harry a *Crêpe con Zucchini* and before Charlie a *Crêpe aux Champignons et Oignons*. The scent of their vegetable steam remained like a cloud of perfume she had released from the frills of her costume before flying away. "Nice," Charlie said, not of the food. "Very nice." Rabbit still couldn't see it. He thought of her body without the frills and got nothing in the way of feeling except a certain fear, as if seeing a weapon unsheathed, or gazing upon an inflexible machine with which his soft body should not become involved.

But he feels obliged one night to say to Janice, "We haven't had Charlie over for a while."

She looks at him curiously. "You want to? Don't you see enough of him at the lot?"

"Yeah but you don't see him there."

"Charlie and I had our time, of seeing each other."

"Look, the guy lives with his mother who's getting to be more and more of a drag, he's never married, he's always talking about his nieces and nephews but I don't think they give him shit actually –"

"All right, you don't have to sell it. I *like* seeing Charlie. I must say I think it's creepy that you encourage it."

"Why shouldn't I? Because of that old business? I don't hold a grudge. It made you a better person."

"Thanks," Janice says dryly. Guiltily he tries to count up how many nights since he's given her an orgasm. These July nights, you get thirsty for one more beer as the Phillies struggle and then in bed feel a terrific weariness, a bliss of inactivity that leads you to understand how men can die willingly, gladly, into an eternal release from the hell of having to perform. When Janice hasn't been fucked for a while, her gestures speed up, and the thought of Charlie's coming intensifies this agitation. "What night?" she asks.

"Whenever. What's Melanie's schedule this week?"

"What does that have to do with it?"

"He might as well meet her properly. I took him over to the crêpe place for lunch and though she tried to be pleasant she was rushed and it didn't really work out."

"What would 'work out' mean, if it did?"

"Don't give me a hard time, it's too fucking humid. I've been thinking of asking Ma to go halves with us on a new air-conditioner, I read where a make called Friedrich is best. I mean 'work out' just as ordinary human interchange. He kept asking me embarrassing questions about Nelson."

"Like what? What's so embarrassing about Nelson?"

"Like whether or not he was going to go back to college and why he kept showing up at the lot."

"Why shouldn't he show up at the lot? It was his grandfather's. And Nelson's always loved cars."

"Loves to bounce 'em around, at least. The Mustang has a whole new set of rattles, have you noticed?"

"I hadn't noticed," Janice says primly, pouring herself more Campari. In an attempt to cut down her alcohol intake, to slow down creeping middle-itis, she has appointed Campari-and-soda her summer drink; but keeps forgetting to put in the soda. She adds, "He's used to those flat Ohio roads."

Out at Kent Nelson had bought some graduating senior's old Thunderbird and then when he decided to go to Colorado sold it for half what he paid. Remembering this adds to Rabbit's suffocating sensation of being put upon. He tells her, "They have the fifty-five-mile-an-hour speed limit out there too. The poor country is trying to save gas before the Arabs turn our dollars into zinc pennies and that baby boy of yours does fifty-five in second gear."

Janice knows he is trying to get her goat now, and turns her back with that electric swiftness, as of speeded-up film, and heads toward the dining-room phone. "I'll ask him for next week," she says. "If that'll make you less bitchy."

Charlie always brings flowers, in a stapled green cone of paper, that he hands to Ma Springer. After all those years of kissing Springer's ass he knows his way around the widow. Bessie takes them without much of a smile; her maiden name was Koerner and she never wholly approved of Fred's taking on a Greek, and then her foreboding came true when Charlie had an affair with Janice with such disastrous consequences, around the time of the moon landing. Well, nobody is going to the moon much these days.

The flowers, unwrapped, are roses the color of a palomino horse. Janice puts them in a vase, cooing. She has dolled up in a perky daisy-patterned sundress for the occasion, that shows off her brown shoulders, and wears her long hair up in the heat, to remind them all of her slender neck and to display the gold necklace of tiny overlapping fish scales that Harry gave her for their twentieth wedding anniversary three years ago. Paid nine hundred dollars for it then, and it must be worth fifteen hundred now, gold going crazy the way it is. She leans forward to give Charlie a kiss, on the mouth and not the cheek, thus effortlessly reminding those who watch of how these two bodies have travelled within one another. "Charlie, you look too thin," Janice says. "Don't you know how to feed yourself?"

"I pack it in, Jan, but it doesn't stick to the ribs anymore. You look terrific, on the other hand."

"Melanie's got us all on a health kick. Isn't that right, Mother? Wheat germ and alfalfa sprouts and I don't know what all. Yogurt."

"I feel better, honest to God," Bessie pronounces. "I don't know though if it's the diet or just having a little more life around the house."

Charlie's square fingertips are still resting on Janice's brown arm. Rabbit sees the phenomenon as he would something else in nature – a Japanese beetle on a leaf, or two limbs of a tree rubbing together in the wind. Then he remembers, descending into the molecules, what love feels like: huge, skin on skin, planets impinging.

"We all eat too much sugar and sodium," Melanie says, in that happy uplifted voice of hers, that seems unconnected to what is below, like a blessing no one has asked for. Charlie's hand has snapped away from Janice's skin; he is all warrior attention; his profile in the gloom of this front room through which all visitors to this household must pass shines, low-browed and jut-jawed, the muscles around the hollow of his jaw pulsing. He looks younger than at the lot, maybe because the light is poorer.

"Melanie," Harry says, "you remember Charlie from lunch the other day, doncha?"

"Of course. He had the mushrooms and capers."

"Onions," Charlie says, his hand still poised to take hers.

"Charlie's my right-hand man over there, or I'm his is I guess how he'd put it. He's been moving cars for Springer Motors since –" He can't think of a joke.

"Since they were called horseless buggies," Charlie says, and takes her hand in his. Watching, Harry marvels at her young hand's narrowness. We broaden all over. Old ladies' feet: they look like little veiny loaves of bread, rising. Away from her spacey stare Melanie is knit as tight together as a new sock. Charlie is moving in on her. "How are you, Melanie? How're you liking these parts?"

"They're nice," she smiles. "Quaint, almost."

"Harry tells me you're a West Coast baby."

Her eyes lift, so the whites beneath the irises show, as she looks toward her distant origins. "Oh yes. I was born in Marin County. My mother lives now in a place called Carmel. That's to the south."

"I've heard of it," Charlie says. "You've got some rock stars there."

"Not really, I don't think. . . . Joan Baez, but she's more what you'd call traditional. We live in what used to be our summer place."

"How'd that happen?"

Startled, she tells him. "My father used to work in San Francisco as a corporation lawyer. Then he and my mother broke up and we had to sell the house on Pacific Avenue. Now he's in Oregon learning to be a forester."

"That's a sad story, you could say," Harry says.

"Daddy doesn't think so," Melanie tells him. "He's living with a lovely girl who's part Yakima Indian."

"Back to Nature," Charlie says.

"It's the only way to go," Rabbit says. "Have some soybeans." This is a joke, for he is passing them Planter's dry-roasted cashews in a breakfast bowl, nuts that he bought on impulse at the grocery next to the state liquor store fifteen minutes ago, running out in the rattling Mustang to stoke up for tonight's company. He had been almost scared off by the price on the jar, $2.89, up 30¢ from the last time he'd noticed, and reached for the dry-roasted peanuts instead. Even these, though, were over a dollar, $1.09, peanuts that you used to buy a big sack of unshelled for a quarter when he was a boy, so he thought, What the hell's the point of being rich, and took the cashews after all.

He is offended when Charlie glances down and holds up a fastidious palm, not taking any. "No salt," Harry urges. "Loaded with protein."

"Never touch junk," Charlie says. "Doc says it's a no-no."

"Junk!" he begins to argue.

But Charlie is keeping the pressure on Melanie. "Every winter, I head down to Florida for a month. Sarasota, on the Gulf side."

"What's that got to do with California?" Janice asks, cutting in.

"Same type of Paradise," Charlie says, turning a shoulder so as to keep speaking directly to Melanie. "It's my meat. Sand in your shoes, that's the feeling, wearing the same ragged cut-offs day after day. This is over on the Gulf side. I hate the Miami side. The only way you'd get me over on the Miami side would be inside an alligator. They have 'em, too: come up out of these canals right onto your lawn and eat your pet dog. It happens a lot."

"I've never been to Florida," Melanie says, looking a little glazed, even for her.

"You should give it a try," Charlie says. "It's where the real people are."

"You mean we're *not* real people?" Rabbit asks, egging him on, helping Janice out. This must hurt her. He takes a cashew between his molars and delicately cracks it, prolonging the bliss. That first fracture, in there with tongue and spit and teeth. He loves nuts. Clean eating, not like meat. In the Garden of Eden they ate nuts and fruit. Dry-roasted, the cashew burns a little. He prefers them salted, soaked in sodium, but got this kind in deference to Melanie; he's being brainwashed about chemicals. Still, some chemical must have entered into this dry-roasting too, there's nothing you can eat won't hurt you down here on earth. Janice must just hate this.

"It's not just all old people either," Charlie is telling Melanie. "You see plenty of young people down there too, just living in their skins. Gorgeous."

"Janice," Mrs. Springer says, pronouncing it *Chaniss*. "We should go on the porch and you should offer people drinks." To Charlie she says, "Melanie made a lovely fruit punch."

"How much gin can it absorb?" Charlie asks.

Harry loves this guy, even if he is putting the make on Melanie in front of Janice. On the porch, when they've settled on the aluminum furniture with their drinks and Janice is in the kitchen stirring at the dinner, he asks him, to show him off, "How'd you like Carter's energy speech?"

Charlie cocks his head toward the rosy-cheeked girl and says, "I thought it was pathetic. The man was right. I'm suffering from a crisis in confidence. In him."

Nobody laughs, except Harry. Charlie passes the ball. "What did you think of it, Mrs. Springer?"

The old lady, called onto the stage, smooths the cloth of her lap and looks down as if for crumbs. "He seems a well-intentioned Christian man, though Fred always used to say the Democrats were just a tool for the unions. Still and all. Some businessman in there might have a better idea what to do with the inflation."

"He *is* a businessman, Bessie," Harry says. "He grows peanuts. His warehouse down there grosses more than we do."

"I thought it was sad," Melanie unexpectedly says, leaning forward so her loose gypsyish blouse reveals cleavage, a tube of air between her braless breasts, "the way he said people for the first time think things are going to get worse instead of better."

"Sad if you're a chick like you," Charlie says. "For old crocks like us, things are going to get worse in any case."

"You believe that?" Harry asks, genuinely surprised. He sees his life as just beginning, on clear ground at last, now that he has a margin of resources, and the stifled terror that always made him restless has dulled down. He wants less. Freedom, that he always thought was outward motion, turns out to be this inner dwindling.

"I believe it, sure," Charlie says, "but what does this nice girl here believe? That the show's over? How *can* she?"

"I believe," Melanie begins. "Oh, I don't know – Bessie, help me."

Harry didn't know she calls the old lady by her first name. Took him years of living with her to work up to feeling easy about that, and it wasn't really until after one day he had accidentally walked in on her in her bathroom, Janice hogging theirs.

"Say what's on your mind," the old woman advises the younger. "Everybody else is."

The luminous orbs of Melanie's eyes scout their faces in a sweep that ends in an upward roll such as you see in images of saints. "I believe the things we're running out of we can learn to do without. I don't need electric carving knives and all that. I'm more upset about the snail darters and the whales than about iron ore and oil." She lingers on this last word, giving it two syllables, and stares at Harry. As if he's especially into oil. He decides what he resents about her is she seems always to be trying to hypnotize him. "I mean," she goes on, "as long as there are growing things, there's still a world with endless possibilities."

The hum beneath her words hangs in the darkening space of the porch. Alien. Moonraker.

"One big weed patch," Harry says. "Where the hell is Nelson, anyway?" He is irked, he figures, because this girl is out of this world and that makes his world feel small. He feels sexier even toward fat old Bessie. At least her voice has a lot of the county, a lot of his life, in it. That time he blundered into the bathroom he didn't see much; she shouted, sitting on the toilet with her skirt around her knees, and he heard her shout and hardly saw a thing, just a patch of flank as white as a butcher's marble counter.

Bessie answers him dolefully, "I believe he went out for a reason. Janice would know."

Janice comes to the doorway of the porch, looking snappy in her daisies and an orange apron. "He went off around six with Billy Fosnacht. They should have been back by now."

"Which car'd they take?"

"They had to take the Corona. You were at the liquor store with the Mustang."

"Oh great. What's Billy Fosnacht doing around anyway? Why isn't he in the volunteer army?" He feels like making a show, for Charlie and Melanie, of authority.

There is authority, too, in the way Janice is holding a wooden stirring spoon. She says, to the company in general, "They say he's doing very well. He's in his first year of dental school up somewhere in New England. He wants to be a, what do they call it –?"

"Ophthalmologist," Rabbit says.

"Endodontist."

"My God," is all Harry can say. Ten years ago, the night his house had burned, Billy had called his mother a bitch. He had seen Billy often since, all the years Nelson was at Mt. Judge High, but

had never forgotten that, how Peggy had then slapped him, this
little boy just thirteen years old, the marks of her fingers leaping
up pink on the child's delicate cheek. Then he had called her a
whore, Harry's jism warm inside her. Later that night Nelson had
vowed to kill his father. *You fucking asshole, you've let her die. I'll kill
you. I'll kill you.* Harry had put up his hands to fight. The misery
of life. It has carried him away from the faces on the porch. In the
silence he hears from afar a neighbor woman's hammer knocking.
"How are Ollie and Peggy?" he asks, his voice rough even after
clearing it. Billy's parents have dropped from his sight, as the
Toyota business lifted him higher in the social scale.

"About the same," Janice says. "Ollie's still at the music store.
They say Peggy's gotten into causes." She turns back to her stirring.

Charlie tells Melanie, "You should book yourself on a flight to
Florida when you get fed up around here."

"What's with you and Florida?" Harry asks him loudly. "She
says she comes from California and you keep pushing Florida at
her. There's no connection."

Charlie pulls at his spiked pink punch and looks like a pathetic old guy, the skin pegged ever tighter to the planes of his skull.
"We can make a connection."

Melanie calls toward the kitchen, "Janice, can I be of any
help?"

"No dear, thanks; it's all but done. Is everybody starving? Does
anybody else want their drink freshened?"

"Why not?" Harry asks, feeling reckless. This bunch isn't going
to be fun, he'll have to make his fun inside. "How about you,
Charlie?"

"Forget it, champ. One's my limit. The doctors tell me even
that should be a no-no, in my condition." Of Melanie he asks,
"How's your Kool-Aid holding up?"

"Don't call it Kool-Aid, that's rude," Harry says, pretending
to joust. "I admire anybody of this generation who isn't polluting
their system with pills and booze. Ever since Nelson got back, the
sixpacks come and go in the fridge like, like coal down a chute."
He feels he has said this before, recently.

"I'll get you some more," Melanie sings, and takes Charlie's glass, and Harry's too. She has no name for him, he notices. Nelson's father. Over the hill. Out of this world.

"Make mine weak," he tells her. "A g-and-t."

Ma Springer has been sitting there with thoughts of her own. She says to Stavros, "Nelson has been asking me all these questions about how the lot works, how much sales help there is, and how the salesmen are paid, and so on."

Charlie shifts his weight in his chair. "This gas crunch's got to affect car sales. People won't buy cows they can't feed. Even if so far Toyota's come along smelling pretty good."

Harry intervenes. "Bessie, there's no way we can make room for Nelson on sales without hurting Jake and Rudy. They're married men trying to feed babies on their commissions. If you want I could talk to Manny and see if he can use another kid on clean-up –"

"He doesn't want to work on clean-up," Janice calls sharply from the kitchen.

Ma Springer confirms, "Yes, he told me he'd like to see what he could do with sales, you know he always admired Fred so, idolized him you might say –"

"Oh come *on*," Harry says. "He never gave a damn about either of his grandfathers once he hit about tenth grade. Once he got onto girls and rock he thought everybody over twenty was a sap. All he wanted was to get the hell out of Brewer, and I said, O.K., here's the ticket, go to it. So what's he pussy-footing around whispering to his mother and grandmother now for?"

Melanie brings in the two men's drinks. Waitressly erect, she holds a triangulated paper napkin around the dewy base of each. Rabbit sips his and finds it strong when he asked for it weak. A love message, of sorts?

Ma Springer puts one hand on each of her thighs and points her elbows out, elbows all in folds like little pug dog faces. "Now Harry –"

"I know what you're going to say. You own half the company. Good for you, Bessie, I'm glad. If it'd been me instead of Fred I'd've left it all to you." He quickly turns to Melanie and says, "What they really should do with this gas crisis is bring back the trolley cars. You're too young to remember. They ran on tracks but the power came from electric wires overhead. Very clean. They went everywhere when I was a kid."

"Oh, I know. They still have them in San Francisco."

"Harry, what I wanted to say —"

"But you're *not* running it," he continues to his mother-in-law, "and never have, and as long as I am, Nelson, if he wants a start there, can hose down cars for Manny. I don't want him in the sales room. He has none of the right attitudes. He can't even straighten up and smile."

"I thought those were cable cars," Charlie says to Melanie.

"Oh they just have those on a few hills. Everybody keeps saying how dangerous they are, the cables snap. But the tourists expect them."

"Harry. Dinner," Janice says. She is stern. "We won't wait for Nelson any more, it's after eight."

"Sorry if I sound hard," he says to the group as they rise to go eat. "But look, even now, the kid's too rude to come home in time for dinner."

"Your own son," Janice says.

"Melanie, what do you think? What's his plan? Isn't he heading back to finish college?"

Her smile remains fixed but seems flaky, painted-on. "Nelson may feel," she says carefully, "that he's spent enough time at college."

"But where's his degree?" He hears his own voice in his head as shrill, sounding trapped. "Where's his degree?" Harry repeats, hearing no answer.

Janice has lit candles on the dining table, though the July day is still so light they look wan. She had wanted this to be nice for Charlie. Dear old Jan. As Harry walks to the table behind her he rests his eyes on what he rarely sees, the pale bared nape of her neck. In the shuffle as they take places he brushes Melanie's arm, bare also, and darts a look down the ripe slopes loosely concealed by the gypsy blouse. Firm. He mutters to her, "Sorry, didn't mean to put you on the spot just now. I just can't figure out what Nelson's game is."

"Oh you didn't," she answers crooningly. Ringlets fall and tremble; her cheeks flame within. As Ma Springer plods to her place at the head of the table, the girl peeks up at Harry with a glint he reads as sly and adds, "I think one factor, you know, is Nelson's becoming more security-minded."

He can't quite follow. Sounds like the kid is going to enter the Secret Service.

Chairs scrape. They wait while a dim tribal memory of grace flits overhead. Then Janice dips her spoon into her soup, tomato, the color of Harry's Corona. Where is it? Out in the night, with the kid at the wheel making every joint rattle. They rarely sit in this room – even with the five of them now they eat around the kitchen table – and Harry is newly aware of, propped on the sideboard where the family silver is stored, tinted photos of Janice as a high-school senior with her hair brushed and rolled under in a page-boy to her shoulders, of Nelson as an infant propped with his favorite teddy bear (that had one eye) on a stagy sunbathed window seat of this very house, and then Nelson as himself a high-school senior, his hair almost as long as Janice's, but less brushed, looking greasy, and his grin for the cameraman lopsided, half-defiant. In a gold frame broader than his daughter and grandson got, Fred Springer, misty-eyed and wrinkle-free courtesy of the portrait studio's darkroom magic, stares in studied three-quarters profile at whatever it is the dead see.

Charlie asks the table, "Did you see where Nixon gave a big party at San Clemente in honor of the moon-landing anniversary? They should keep that guy around forever, as an example of what sheer gall can do."

"He did some good things," Ma Springer says, in that voice of hers that shows hurt, tight and dried-out, somehow. Harry is sensitive to it after all these years.

He tries to help her, to apologize if he had been rough with her over who ran the company. "He opened up China," he says.

"And what a can of worms that's turned out to be," Stavros says. "At least all those years they were hating our guts they didn't cost us a nickel. This party of his wasn't cheap either. Everybody was there – Red Skelton, Buzz Aldrin."

"You know I think it broke Fred's heart," Ma Springer pronounces. "Watergate. He followed it right to the end, when he could hardly lift his head from the pillows, and he used to say to me, 'Bessie, there's never been a President who hasn't done worse. They just have it in for him because he isn't a glamour boy. If that had been Roosevelt or one of the Kennedys,' he'd say, 'you would never have heard "boo" about Watergate.' He believed it, too."

Harry glances at the gold-framed photograph and imagines it nodded. "I believe it," he says. "Old man Springer never steered me wrong." Bessie glances at him to see if this is sarcasm. He keeps his face motionless as a photograph.

"Speaking of Kennedys," Charlie puts in – he really is talking too much, on that one Kool-Aid – "the papers are sure giving Chappaquiddick another go-around. You wonder, how much more can they say about a guy on his way to neck who drives off a bridge instead?"

Bessie may have had a touch of sherry, too, for she is working herself up to tears. "Fred," she says, "would never settle on its being that simple. 'Look at the result,' he said to me more than once. 'Look at the result, and work backwards from that.'" Her berry-dark eyes challenge them to do so, mysteriously. "What was the result?" This seems to be in her own voice. "The result was, a poor girl from up in the coal regions was killed."

"Oh Mother," Janice says. "Daddy just had it in for Democrats. I loved him dearly, but he was absolutely hipped on that."

Charlie says, "I don't know, Jan. The worst things I ever heard your father say about Roosevelt was that he tricked us into war and died with his mistress, and it turns out both are true." He looks in the candlelight after saying this like a cardsharp who has snapped down an ace. "And what they tell us now about how Jack Kennedy carried on in the White House with racketeers' molls and girls right off the street Fred Springer in his wildest dreams would never have come up with." Another ace. He looks, Harry thinks, like old man Springer in a way: that hollow-templed, well-combed look. Even the little dabs of eyebrows sticking out like toy artillery.

Harry says, "I never understood what was so bad about Chappaquiddick. He *tried* to get her out." Water, flames, the tongues of God: a man is helpless.

"What was bad about it," Bessie says, "was he put her in."

"What do you think about all this, Melanie?" Harry asks, playing cozy to get Charlie's goat. "Which party do you back?"

"Oh the parties," she exclaims in a trance. "I think they're both evil." *Ev-il*: a word in the air. "But on Chappaquiddick a friend of mine spends every summer on the island and she says she wonders why more people don't drive off that bridge, there are no guard rails or anything. This is lovely soup," she adds to Janice.

"That spinach soup the other day was terrific," Charlie tells Melanie. "Maybe a little heavy on the nutmeg."

Janice has been smoking a cigarette and listening for a car door to slam. "Harry, could you help me clear? You might want to carve in the kitchen."

The kitchen is suffused with the strong, repugnant smell of roasting lamb. Harry doesn't like to be reminded that these are living things, with eyes and hearts, that we eat; he likes salted nuts, hamburger, Chinese food, mince pie. "You know I can't carve lamb," he says. "Nobody can. You're just having it because you think it's what Greeks eat, showing off for your old lover boy."

She hands him the carving set with the bumpy bone handles. "You've done it a hundred times. Just cut parallel slices perpendicular to the bone."

"Sounds easy. You do it if it's so fucking easy." He is thinking, stabbing someone is probably harder than the movies make it look, cutting underdone meat there's plenty of resistance, rubbery and tough. He'd rather hit her on the head with a rock, if it came to that, or that green glass egg Ma has as a knickknack in the living room.

"Listen," Janice hisses. A car door has slammed on the street. Footsteps pound on a porch, their porch, and the reluctant front door pops open with a bang. A chorus of voices around the table greet Nelson. But he keeps coming, searching for his parents, and finds them in the kitchen. "Nelson," Janice says. "We were getting worried."

The boy is panting, not with exertion but the shallow-lunged panting of fear. He looks small but muscular in his grape-colored tie-dyed T-shirt: a burglar dressed to shinny in a window. But caught, here, in the bright kitchen light. He avoids looking Harry in the eye. "Dad. There's been a bit of a mishap."

"The car. I knew it."

"Yeah. The Toyota got a scrape."

"My Corona. Whaddeya mean, a scrape?"

"Nobody was hurt, don't get carried away."

"Any other car involved?"

"No, so don't worry, nobody's going to *sue*." The assurance is contemptuous.

"Don't get smart with *me*."

"O.K., O.K., Jesus."

"You drove it home?"

The boy nods.

Harry hands the knife back to Janice and leaves the kitchen to address the candlelit group left at the table – Ma at the head, Melanie bright-eyed next to her, Charlie on Melanie's other side, his square cufflink reflecting a bit of flame. "Everybody keep calm. Just a mishap, Nelson says. Charlie, you want to come carve some lamb for me? I got to look at this."

He wants to put his hands on the boy, whether to give him a push or comfort he doesn't know; the actual touch might demonstrate which, but Nelson stays just ahead of his father's fingertips, dodging into the summer night. The streetlights have come on, and the Corona's tomato color looks evil by the poisonous sodium glow – a hollow shade of black, its metallic lustre leeched away. Nelson in his haste has parked it illegally, the driver's side along the curb. Harry says, "This side looks fine."

"It's the *other* side, Dad." Nelson explains: "See Billy and I were coming back from Allenville where his girlfriend lives by this windy back road and because I knew I was getting late for supper I may have been going a little fast, I don't know, you can't go too fast on those back roads anyway, they wind too much. And this woodchuck or whatever it was comes out in front of me and in trying to avoid it I get off the road a little and the back end slides into this telephone pole. It happened so fast, I couldn't believe it."

Rabbit has moved to the other side and by lurid light views the damage. The scrape had begun in the middle of the rear door and deepened over the little gas-cap door; by the time the pole reached the tail signal and the small rectangular sidelight, it had no trouble ripping them right out, the translucent plastic torn and shed like

Christmas wrapping, and inches of pretty color-coded wiring exposed. The urethane bumper, so black and mat and trim, that gave Harry a small sensuous sensation whenever he touched the car home against the concrete parking-space divider at the place on the lot stencilled ANGSTROM, was pulled out from the frame. The dent even carried up into the liftback door, which would never seat exactly right again.

Nelson is chattering, "Billy knows this kid who works in a body shop over near the bridge to West Brewer and he says you should get some real expensive rip-off place to do the estimate and then when you get the check from the insurance company give it to him and he can do it for less. That way there'll be a profit everybody can split."

"A profit," Harry repeats numbly.

Nails or rivets in the pole have left parallel longitudinal gashes the length of the impact depression. The chrome-and-rubber stripping has been wrenched loose at an angle, and behind the wheel socket on this side – hooded with a slightly protruding flare like an eyebrow, one of the many snug Japanese details he has cherished – a segment of side strip has vanished entirely, leaving a chorus of tiny holes. Even the many-ribbed hubcap is dented and besmirched. He feels his own side has taken a wound. He feels he is witnessing in evil light a crime in which he has collaborated.

"Oh come *on*, Dad," Nelson is saying. "Don't make such a big deal of it. It'll cost the insurance company, not you, to get it fixed, and anyway you can get a new one for almost nothing, don't they give you a terrific discount?"

"Terrific," Rabbit says. "You just went out and smashed it up. My Corona."

"I didn't *mean* to, it was an *ac*cident, shit. What do you want me to do, piss blood? Get down on my knees and cry?"

"Don't bother."

"Dad, it's just a *thing*; you're looking like you lost your best friend."

A breeze, too high to touch them, ruffles the treetops and makes the streetlight shudder on the deformed metal. Harry sighs. "Well. How'd the woodchuck do?"

II

ONCE that first weekend of riots and rumors is over, the summer isn't so bad; the gas lines never get so long again. Stavros says the oil companies have the price hike they wanted for now, and the government has told them to cool it or face an excess profits tax. Melanie says the world will turn to the bicycle, as Red China has already done; she has bought herself a twelve-speed Fuji with her waitress's wages, and on fair days pedals around the mountain and down, her chestnut curls flying, through Cityview Park into Brewer. Toward the end of July comes a week of record heat; the papers are full of thermal statistics and fuzzy photographs of the time at the turn of the century when the trolley tracks warped in Weiser Square, it was so hot. Such heat presses out from within, against our clothes; we want to break out, to find another self beside the sea or in the mountains. Not until August will Harry and Janice go to the Poconos, where the Springers have a cottage they rent to other people for July. All over Brewer, air-conditioners drip onto patios and into alleyways.

On an afternoon of such hot weather, with his Corona still having bodywork done, Harry borrows a Caprice trade-in from the lot and drives southwest toward Galilee. On curving roads he passes houses of sandstone, fields of corn, a cement factory, a bill-board pointing to a natural cave (didn't natural caves go out of style a while ago?), and another billboard with a great cutout of a bearded Amishman advertising "Authentic Dutch Smörgåsbord." Galilee is what they call a string town, a hilly row of houses with a feed store at one end and a tractor agency at the other. In the middle stands an old wooden inn with a deep porch all along the second story and a renovated restaurant on the first with a window full of credit card stickers to catch the busloads of tourists that come up from Baltimore, blacks most of them, God knows what they hope to see out here in the sticks. A knot of young locals is hanging around in front of the Rexall's, you never used to see that in farm country, they'd be too busy with the chores. There is an old stone trough, a black-lacquered row of hitching posts, a glossy new bank, a traffic island with a monument Harry cannot make out the meaning of, and a small brick post office with its bright silver letters GALILEE up a side street that in a block dead-ends at the edge of a field. The woman in the post office tells Harry where the Nunemacher farm is, along R. D. 2. By the landmarks she gives him – a vegetable stand, a pond rimmed with willows, a double silo close to the road – he feels his way through the tummocks and swales of red earth crowded with shimmering green growth, merciless vegetation that allows not even the crusty eroded road embankments to rest barren but makes them bear tufts and mats of vetch and honeysuckle vines and fills the stagnant hot air with the haze of exhaled vapor. The Caprice windows are wide open and the Brewer disco station fades and returns in twists of static as the land and electrical wires obtrude. NUNEMACHER is a faded name on a battered tin mailbox. The house and barn are well back from the road, down a long dirt lane, brown stones buried in pink dust.

Rabbit's heart rises in his chest. He cruises the road, surveying the neighboring mailboxes; but Ruth gave him, when he once met her by accident in downtown Brewer a dozen years ago, no clue to her new name, and the girl a month ago refused to write hers in his showroom ledger. All he has to go by, other than Nunemacher's being his daughter's neighbor, if she is his daughter, is Ruth's mentioning that her husband besides being a farmer ran a fleet of school buses. He was older than she and should be dead now, Harry figures. The school buses would be gone. The mailboxes along this length of road say BLANKENBILLER, MUTH, and BYER. It is not easy to match the names with the places, as glimpsed in their hollows, amid their trees, at the end of their lanes of grass and dirt. He feels conspicuous, gliding along in a magenta Caprice, though no other soul emerges from the wide landscape to observe him. The thick-walled houses hold their inhabitants in, this hazy mid-afternoon too hot for work. Harry drives down a lane at random and stops and backs around in the beaten, rutted space between the buildings while some pigs he passed in their pen set up a commotion of snorting and a fat woman in an apron comes out of a door of the house. She is shorter than Ruth and younger than Ruth would be now, with black hair pulled tight beneath a Mennonite cap. He waves and keeps going. This was the Blankenbillers, he sees by the mailbox as he pulls onto the road again.

The other two places are nearer the road and he thinks he might get closer on foot. He parks on a widened stretch of shoulder, packed earth scored by the herringbone of tractor tire treads. When he gets out of the car, the powerful sweetish stench of the Blankenbillers' pigsty greets him from a distance, and what had seemed to be silence settles into his ear as a steady dry hum of insects, an undercoat to the landscape. The flowering weeds of mid-summer, daisies and Queen Anne's lace and chicory, thrive at the side of the road and tap his pants legs as he hops up onto the bank. In his beige summerweight salesman's suit he prowls behind a hedgerow of sumac and black gum and wild cherry overgrown with poison ivy, shining leaves of it big as valentines and its vines having climbed to the tips of strangled trees. The roughly shaped sandstones of a tumbled old wall lie within this hedgerow, hardly one upon another. At a gap where wheeled vehicles have been driven through he stands surveying the cluster of buildings below him – barn and house, asbestos-sided chicken house and slat-sided corn crib, both disused, and a newish building of cement-block with a roof of corrugated overlapped Fiberglas. Some kind of garage, it looks like. On the house roof has been mounted a copper lightning rod oxidized green and an H-shaped television aerial, very tall to catch the signals out here. Harry means only to survey, to relate this layout to the Nunemacher spread across the next shaggy rise, but a soft clinking arising from somewhere amid the buildings, and the ripples a little runnel makes pouring itself into a small pond perhaps once for ducks, and an innocent clutter of old tractor seats and axles and a rusted iron trough in a neglected patch between the woodpile and the mowed yard lure him downward like a species of music while he churns in his head the story he will tell if approached and challenged. This soft dishevelled farm feels like a woman's farm, in need of help. An unreasonable expectancy brings his heart up to the pitch of the surrounding insect-hum.

Then he sees it, behind the barn, where the woods are encroaching upon what had once been a cleared space, sumac and cedar in the lead: the tilted yellow shell of a school bus. Its wheels and windows are gone and the snub hood of its cab has been torn away to reveal a hollow space where an engine was cannibalized; but like a sunken galleon it testifies to an empire, a fleet of buses whose proprietor has died, his widow left with an illegitimate daughter to raise. The land under Rabbit seems to move, with the addition of yet another citizen to the subterrain of the dead.

Harry stands in what once had been an orchard, where even now lopsided apple and pear trees send up sprays of new shoots from their gutted trunks. Though the sun burns, wetness at the root of the orchard grass has soaked his suede shoes. If he ventures a few steps farther he will be in the open and liable to be spotted from the house windows. There are voices within the house he can hear now, though they have the dim steady rumble that belongs to voices on radio or television. A few steps farther, he could distinguish these voices. A few steps farther still, he will be on the lawn, beside a plaster birdbath balanced off-center on a pillar of blue-tinted fluting, and then he will be committed to stride up bravely, put his foot on the low cement porch, and knock. The front door, set deep in its socket of stone, needs its green paint refreshed. From the tattered composition shingles of its roof to the dreary roller shades that hang in its windows the house exhales the tired breath of poverty.

What would he say to Ruth if she answered his knock?

Hi. You may not remember me . . .

Jesus. I wish I didn't.

No, wait. Don't close it. Maybe I can help you.

How the hell would you ever help me? Get out. Honest to God, Rabbit, just looking at you makes me sick.

I have money now.

I don't want it. I don't want anything that stinks of you. When I did need you, you ran.

O.K., O.K. But let's look at the present situation. There's this girl of ours —

Girl, she's a woman. Isn't she lovely? I'm so proud.

Me too. We should have had lots. Great genes.

Don't be so fucking cute. I've been here for twenty years, where have you been?

It's true, he could have tried to look her up, he even knew she lived around Galilee. But he hadn't. He hadn't wanted to face her, the complicated and accusing reality of her. He wanted to hold her in his mind as just fucked and satisfied, lifting white and naked above him on an elbow. Before he drifted off to sleep she got him a drink of water. He does not know if he loved her or not, but with her he had known love, had experienced that cloudy inflation of self which makes us infants again and tips each moment with a plain excited purpose, as these wands of grass about his knees are tipped with packets of their own fine seeds.

A door down below slams, not on the sides of the house he can see. A voice sounds the high note we use in speaking to pets. Rabbit retreats behind an apple sapling too small to hide him. In his avidity to see, to draw closer to that mysterious branch of his past that has flourished without him, and where lost energy and lost meaning still flow, he has betrayed his big body, made it a target. He crowds so close to the little tree that his lips touch the bark of its crotch, bark smooth as glass save where darker ridges of roughness at intervals ring its gray. The miracle of it: how things grow, always remembering to be themselves. His lips have flinched back from the unintended kiss. Living microscopic red things – mites, aphids, he can see them – will get inside him and multiply.

"Hey!" a voice calls. A woman's voice, young on the air, frightened and light. Could Ruth's voice be so young after so many years?

Rather than face who it is, he runs. Up through the heavy orchard grass, dodging among the old fruit trees, breaking through as if a sure lay-up waits on the other side of the ragged hedgerow, onto the red tractor path and back to the Caprice, checking to see if he tore his suit as he trots along, feeling his age. He is panting; the back of his hand is scratched, by raspberries or wild rose. His heart is pounding so wildly he cannot fit the ignition key into the lock. When it does click in, the motor grinds for a few revolutions before catching, overheated from waiting in the sun. The female voice calling "Hey" so lightly hangs in his inner ear as the motor settles to its purr and he listens for pursuing shouts and even the sound of a rifle. These farmers all have guns and think nothing of using them, the years he worked as a typesetter for the *Vat* hardly a week went by without some rural murder all mixed in with sex and booze and incest.

But the haze of the country around Galilee hangs silent above the sound of his engine. He wonders if his figure had been distinct enough to be recognized, by Ruth who hadn't seen him since he'd put on all this weight or by the daughter who has seen him once, a month ago. They report this to the police and use his name it'll get back to Janice and she'll raise hell to hear he's been snooping after this girl. Won't wash so good at Rotary either. Back. He must get back. Afraid of getting lost the other way, he dares back around and head back the way he came, past the mailboxes. He decides the mailbox that goes with the farm he spied on down in its little tousled valley with the duck pond is the blue one saying BYER. Fresh sky blue, painted this summer, with a decal flower, the sort of decoration a young woman might apply.

Byer. Ruth Byer. His daughter's first name Jamie Nunemacher never pronounced, that Rabbit can recall.

He asks Nelson one night, "Where's Melanie? I thought she was working days this week."

"She is. She's gone out with somebody."

"Really? You mean on a date?"

The Phillies have been rained out tonight and while Janice and her mother are upstairs watching a *Waltons* rerun he and the kid find themselves in the living room, Harry leafing through the August *Consumer Reports* that has just come (*"Are hair dyes safe?"* *"Road tests: 6 pickup trucks"* *"An alternative to the $2000 funeral"*) while the boy is looking into a copy of a book he has stolen from Fred Springer's old office at the lot, which has become Harry's. He doesn't look up. "You could call it a date. She just said she was going out."

"But *with* somebody."

"Sure."

"That's O.K. with you? Her going out with somebody?"

"Sure. Dad, I'm trying to read."

The same rain that has postponed the Phils against the Pirates at Three Rivers Stadium has swept east across the Commonwealth and beats on the windows here at 89 Joseph Street, into the low-spreading branches of the copper beech that is the pride of the grounds, and at times thunderously upon the roof and spouting of the front porch roof. "Lemme see the book," Harry begs, and from within the Barcalounger holds out a long arm. Nelson irritably tosses over the volume, a squat green handbook on automobile dealership written by some crony of old man Springer's who had an agency in Paoli. Harry has looked into it once or twice: mostly hot air, hotshot stuff geared to the greater volume you can expect in the Philly area. "This tells you," he tells Nelson, "more than you need to know."

"I'm trying to understand," Nelson says, "about the financing."

"It's very simple. The bank owns the new cars, the dealer owns the used cars. The bank pays Mid-Atlantic Toyota when the car leaves Maryland; also there's something called holdback that the manufacturer keeps in case the dealer defaults on parts purchases, but that he rebates annually, and that to be frank about it has the effect of reducing the dealer's apparent profit in case he gets one of these wiseass customers who takes a great interest in the numbers and figures he can jew you down. Toyota insists we sell everything at their list so there's not much room for finagling, and that saves you a lot of headaches in my opinion. If they don't like the price they can come back a month later and find it three hundred bucks higher, the way the yen is going. Another wrinkle about financing, though, is when the customer takes out his loan where we send him – Brewer Trust generally, and though this magazine right here had an article just last month about how you ought to shop around for loans instead of going where the agency recommends it's a hell of a hassle actually to buck the system, just to save maybe a half of a per cent – the bank keeps back a percentage for our account, supposedly to cover the losses of selling repossessed vehicles, but in fact it amounts to a kickback. Follow me? Why do you care?"

"Just interested."

"You should have been interested when your granddad Springer was around to be talked to. He ate this crap up. By the time he had sold a car to a customer the poor bozo thought he was robbing old Fred blind when the fact is the deal had angles to it like a spider web. When he wanted Toyota to give him the franchise, he claimed sixty thousand feet of extra service space that was just a patch of weeds, and then got a contractor who owed him a favor to throw down a slab and put up an uninsulated shell. That shop is still impossible to heat in the winter, you should hear Manny bitch."

Nelson asks, "Did they used to ever chop the clock?"

"Where'd you learn that phrase?"

"From the book."

"Well. . . ." This isn't so bad, Harry thinks, talking to the kid sensibly while the rain drums down. He doesn't know why it makes him nervous to see the kid read. Like he's plotting something. They say you should encourage it, reading, but they never say why. "You know chopping the clock is a felony. But maybe in the old days sometimes a mechanic, up in the dashboard anyway, kind of had his screwdriver slip on the odometer. People who buy a used car know it's a gamble anyway. A car might go twenty thousand miles without trouble or pop a cylinder tomorrow. Who's to say? I've seen some amazing wear on cars that were running like new. Those VW bugs, you couldn't kill 'em. The body so rotten with rust the driver can see the road under his feet but the engine still ticking away." He tosses the chunky green book back. Nelson fumbles the catch. Harry asks him, "How do you feel, about your girlfriend's going out with somebody else?"

"I've told you before, Dad, she's not my girlfriend, she's my friend. Can't you have a friend of the opposite sex?"

"You can try it. How come she settled on moving back here with you then?"

Nelson's patience is being tried but Harry figures he might as well keep pushing, he's not learning anything playing the silent game. Nelson says, "She needed to blow the scene in Colorado and I was coming east and told her my grandmother's house had a lot of empty rooms. She's not been any trouble, has she?"

"No, she's charmed old Bessie right out of her sneakers. What was the matter with the scene in Colorado, that she needed to blow it?"

"Oh, you know. The wrong guy was putting a move on her, and she wanted to get her head together."

The rain restates its theme, hard, against the thin windows. Rabbit has always loved that feeling, of being inside when it rains. Shingles in the attic, pieces of glass no thicker than cardboard keeping him dry. Things that touch and yet not.

Delicately Harry asks, "You *know* the guy she's out with?"

"Yes, Dad, and so do you."

"Billy Fosnacht?"

"Guess again. Think older. Think Greek."

"Oh my God. You're kidding. That old crock?"

Nelson watches him with an alertness, a stillness of malice. He is not laughing, though the opportunity has been given. He explains, "He called up the Crêpe House and asked her, and she thought Why not? It gets pretty boring around here, you have to admit. Just for a meal. She didn't promise to go to bed with him. The trouble with your generation, Dad, you can only think along certain lines."

"Charlie Stavros," Harry says, trying to get a handle on it. The kid seems in a pretty open mood. Rabbit dares go on, "You remember he saw your mother for a while."

"I remember. But everybody else around here seems to have forgotten. You all seem so cozy now."

"Times change. You don't think we should be? Cozy."

Nelson sneers, sinking lower into the depths of the old sofa. "I don't give that much of a damn. It's not my life."

"It was," Harry says. "You were right there. I felt sorry for you, Nelson, but I couldn't think what else to do. That poor girl Jill —"

"Dad —"

"Skeeter's dead, you know. Killed in a Philadelphia shootout. Somebody sent me a clipping."

"Mom wrote me that. I'm not surprised. He was crazy."

"Yeah, and then not. You know he said he'd be dead in ten years. He really did have a certain —"

"Dad. Let's cool this conversation."

"O.K. Suits me. Sure."

Rain. So sweet, so solid. In the garden the smallest scabs of earth, beneath the lettuce and lopsided bean leaves perforated by Japanese beetles, are darkening, soaking, the leaves above them glistening, dripping, in the widespread vegetable sharing of this secret of the rain. Rabbit returns his eyes to his magazine from studying Nelson's stubborn clouded face. The best type of four-slice toaster, he reads, is the one that has separate controls for each pair of toast slots. Stavros and Melanie, can you believe? Charlie had kept saying he had liked her style.

As if in apology for having cut his father off when the rain was making him reminiscent, Nelson breaks the silence. "What's Charlie's title over there, anyway?"

"Senior Sales Rep. He's in charge of the used cars and I take care of the new. That's more or less. In practice, we overlap. Along with Jake and Rudy, of course." He wants to keep reminding the kid of Jake and Rudy. No rich men's sons, they give a good day's work for their dollar.

"Are you satisfied with the job Charlie does for you?"

"Absolutely. He knows the ropes better than I do. He knows half the county."

"Yeah, but his health. How much energy you think he has?"

The question has a certain collegiate tilt to it. He hasn't asked Nelson enough about college, maybe that's the way through to him. All these women around, it's too easy for Nelson to hide. "Energy? He has to watch himself and take it easy, but he gets the job done. People don't *like* to be hustled these days, there was too much of that, the way the car business used to be. I think a salesman who's a little – what's the word? – laid back, people trust more. I don't mind Charlie's style." He wonders if Melanie does. Where are they, in some restaurant? He pictures her face, bright-eyed almost like a thyroid bulge and her cheeks that look always rouged, rosy with exertion even before she bought the Fuji, her young face dense and smooth as she smiles and keeps smiling opposite old Charlie's classic con-man's profile, as he puts his move on her. And then later that business down below, his thick cock that blue-brown of Mediterranean types and, he wonders if her hair there is as curly as the hair on her head, in and out, he can't believe it will happen, while the rest of them sit here listening to the rain.

Nelson is saying, "I was wondering if something couldn't be done with convertibles." A heavy shamed diffidence thickens his words so they seem to drop one by one from his face, downturned where he sits in the tired gray sofa with his muskrat cut.

"Convertibles? How?"

"You know, Dad, don't make me say it. Buy 'em and sell 'em. Detroit doesn't make 'em anymore, so the old ones are more and more valuable. You could get more than you paid for Mom's Mustang."

"If you don't wreck it first."

This reminder has the effect Rabbit wants. "Shit," the boy exclaims, defenseless, darting looks at every corner of the ceiling looking for the escape hatch, "I didn't wreck your damn precious Corona, I just gave it a little dent."

"It's still in the shop. Some dent."

"I didn't do it on purpose, Christ, Dad, you act like it was some divine chariot or something. You've gotten so uptight in your old age."

"Have I?" He asks sincerely, thinking this might be information.

"Yes. All you think about is money and *things*."

"That's not good, is it?"

"No."

"You're right. Let's forget about the car. Tell me about college."

"It's yukky," is the prompt response. "It's Dullsville. People think because of that shooting ten years ago it's some great radical place but the fact is most of the kids are Ohio locals whose idea of a terrific time is drinking beer till they throw up and having shaving cream fights in the dorms. Most of 'em are going to go into their father's business anyway, they don't care."

Harry ignores this, asking, "You ever have reason to go over to the big Firestone plant? I keep reading in the paper where they kept making those steel-belted radial five hundreds even after they kept blowing up on everybody."

"Typical," the boy tells him. "All the products you buy are like that. All the American products."

"We used to be the best," Harry says, staring into the distance as if toward a land where he and Nelson can perfectly agree.

"So I'm told." The boy looks downward into his book.

"Nelson, about work. I told your mother we'd make a summer job for you over there on wash-up and maintenance. You'd learn a lot, just watching Manny and the boys."

"Dad, I'm too old for wash-up. And maybe I need more than a summer job."

"Are you trying to tell me you'd drop out of college with one lousy year to go?"

His voice has grown loud and the boy looks alarmed. He stares at his father open-mouthed, the dark ajar spot making with his two eyesockets three holes, in a hollow face. The rain drums on the porch roof spout. Janice and her mother come down from *The Waltons* weeping. Janice wipes at her eyes with her fingers and laughs. "It's so stupid, to get carried away. It was in *People* how all the actors couldn't stand each other, that's what broke up the show."

"Well, they have lots of reruns," Ma Springer says, dropping onto the gray sofa beside Nelson, as if this little trip downstairs has been all her legs can bear. "I'd seen that one before, but still they get to you."

Harry announces, "The kid here says he may not go back to Kent."

Janice had been about to walk into the kitchen for a touch of Campari but freezes, standing. She is wearing just her short see-through nightie over underpants in the heat. "You knew that, Harry," she says.

Red bikini underpants, he notices, that show through as dusty pink. At the height of the heat wave last week she got her hair cut in Brewer by a man Doris Kaufmann goes to. He exposed the back of her neck and gave her bangs; Harry isn't used to them yet, it's as if a strange woman was slouching around here nearly naked. He almost shouts, "The hell I did. After all the money we've put into his education?"

"Well," Janice says, swinging so her body taps the nightie from within, "maybe he's got what he can out of it."

"I don't get all this. There's something fishy going on. The kid comes home with no explanation and his girlfriend goes out with Charlie Stavros while he sits here hinting to me I should can Charlie so I can hire him instead."

"Well," Ma Springer pronounces peacefully, "Nelson's of an age. Fred made space for you, Harry, and I know if he was here he'd make space for Nelson."

In on the dining-room sideboard, dead Fred Springer listens to the rain, misty-eyed.

"Not at the top he wouldn't," Harry says. "Not to somebody who quits college a few lousy credits short of graduating."

"Well Harry," Ma Springer says, as calm and mellow as if the TV show had been a pipe of pot, "some would have said you weren't so promising when Fred took you on. More than one person advised him against it."

Out in the country, under the ground, old Farmer Byer mourns his fleet of school buses, rotting in the rain.

"I was a forty-year-old man who'd lost his job through no fault of his own. I sat and did Linotype as long as there was Linotype."

"You worked at your father's trade," Janice tells him, "and that's what Nelson's asking to do."

"Sure, *sure*," Harry shouts, "when he gets out of college if that's what he wants. Though frankly I'd hoped he'd want more. But what is the *rush*? What'd he come home for anyway? If I'd ever been so lucky at his age to get to a state like Colorado I'd sure as hell have stayed at least the summer."

Sexier than she can know, Janice drags on a cigarette. "Why don't you want your own son home?"

"He's too *big* to be home! What's he running from?" From the look on their faces he may have hit on something, he doesn't know what. He's not sure he wants to know what. In the silence that answers him he listens again to the downpour, an incessant presence at the edge of their lamplight domain, gentle, insistent, unstoppable, a million small missiles striking home and running in rivulets from the face of things. Skeeter, Jill, and the Kent State Four are out there somewhere, bone dry.

"Forget it," Nelson says, standing up. "I don't want any job with this creep."

"What's he so hostile for?" Harry beseeches the women. "All

I've said was I don't see why we should fire Charlie so the kid can peddle convertibles. In time, sure. In 1980, even. Take over, young America. Eat me up. But one thing at a time, Jesus. There's tons of time."

"Is there?" Janice asks strangely. She does know something. Cunts always know something.

He turns to her directly. "You. I'd think *you'd* be loyal to Charlie at least."

"More than to my own son?"

"I'll tell you this. I'll tell you all this. If Charlie goes, I go." He struggles to stand, but the Barcalounger has a sticky grip.

"Hip, hip hooray," Nelson says, yanking his denim jacket from the clothes tree inside the front door and shrugging it on. He looks humpbacked and mean, a rat going out to be drowned.

"Now he's going out to wreck the Mustang." Harry struggles to his feet and stands, taller than them all.

Ma Springer slaps her knees with open palms. "Well this discussion has ruined my mood. I'm going to heat up water for a cup of tea, the damp has put the devil in my joints."

Janice says, "Harry, say goodnight to Nelson nicely."

He protests, "He hasn't said goodnight nicely to me. I was down here trying to talk nicely to him about college and it was like pulling teeth. What's everything such a secret for? I don't even know what he's majoring in now. First it was pre-med but the chemistry was too hard, then it was anthropology but there was too much to memorize, last I heard he'd switched to social science but it was too much bullshit."

"I'm majoring in geography," Nelson admits, nervous by the door, tense to scuttle.

"Geography! That's something they teach in the third grade! I never heard of a grownup studying geography."

"Apparently it's a great specialty out there," Janice says.

"Whadde they do all day, color maps?"

"Mom, I got to split. Where's your car keys?"

"Look in my raincoat pocket."

Harry can't stop getting after him. "Now remember the roads around here are slippery when wet," he says. "If you get lost just call up your geography professor."

"Charlie's taking Melanie out really bugs you, doesn't it?" Nelson says to him.

"Not at all. What bugs me is why it doesn't bug you."

"I'm queer," Nelson tells him.

"Janice, what have I done to this kid to deserve this?"

She sighs. "Oh, I expect you know."

He is sick of these allusions to his tainted past. "I took care of him, didn't I? While you were off screwing around who was it put his breakfast cereal on the table and got him off to school?"

"My daddy did," Nelson says in a bitter mincing voice.

Janice intervenes. "Nellie, why don't you go now if you're going to go? Did you find the keys?"

The child dangles them.

"You're committing automotive suicide," Rabbit tells her. "This kid is a car killer."

"It was just a fucking *dent*," Nelson cries to the ceiling, "and he's going to make me suffer and *suf*fer." The door slams, having admitted a sharp gust of the aroma of the rain.

"Now who else would like some tea?" Ma Springer calls from the kitchen. They go in to her. Moving from the stuffy over-furnished living room to the kitchen with its clean enamelled surfaces provides a brighter perspective on the world. "Harry, you shouldn't be so hard on the boy," his mother-in-law advises. "He has a lot on his mind."

"Like what?" he asks sharply.

"Oh," Ma says, still mellow, setting out plates of comfort, Walton-style, "the things young people do."

Janice has on underpants beneath her nightie but no bra and in the bright light her nipples show inside the cloth with their own pink color, darker, more toward wine. She is saying, "It's a hard age. They seem to have so many choices and yet they don't. They've been taught by television all their lives to want this and that and yet when they get to be twenty they find money isn't so easy to come by after all. They don't have the opportunities even we had."

This doesn't sound like her. "Who have *you* been talking to?" Harry asks scornfully.

Janice is harder to put down than formerly; she tidies her bangs with a fiddling raking motion of her fingers and answers, "Some

of the girls at the club, their children have come home too and
don't know what to do with themselves. It even has a name now,
the back-to-the-nest something."

"Syndrome," he says; he is being brought round. He and Pop
and Mom sometimes after Mim had been put to bed would settle
like this around the kitchen table, with cereal or cocoa if not tea.
He feels safe enough to sound plaintive. "If he'd just *ask* for help,"
he says, "I'd try to give it. But he doesn't ask. He wants to take
without asking."

"And isn't that just human nature," Ma Springer says, in a
spruced-up voice. The tea tastes to her satisfaction and she adds as
if to conclude, "There's a lot of sweetness in Nelson, I think he's
just a little overwhelmed for now."

"Who isn't?" Harry asks.

In bed, perhaps it's the rain that sexes him up, he insists they
make love, though at first Janice is reluctant. "I would have taken
a bath," she says, but she smells great, deep jungle smell, of precious rotting mulch going down and down beneath the ferns.
When he won't stop, crazy to lose his face in this essence, the cool
stern fury of it takes hold of her and combatively she comes,
thrusting her hips up to grind her clitoris against his face and then
letting him finish inside her beneath him. Lying spent and adrift
he listens again to the rain's sound, which now and then quickens
to a metallic rhythm on the window glass, quicker than the throbbing in the iron gutter, where ropes of water twist.

"I like having Nelson in the house," Harry says to his wife. "It's
great to have an enemy. Sharpens your senses."

Murmurously beyond their windows, yet so close they might
be in the cloud of it, the beech accepts, leaf upon leaf, shelves and
stairs of continuous dripping, the rain.

"Nelson's not your enemy. He's your boy and needs you more
now than ever though he can't say it."

Rain, the last proof left to him that God exists. "I feel," he says,
"there's something I don't know."

Janice admits, "There is."

"What is it?" Receiving no answer, he asks then, "How do you
know it?"

"Mother and Melanie talk."

"How bad is it? Drugs?"

"Oh Harry no." She has to hug him, his ignorance must make him seem so vulnerable. "Nothing like that. Nelson's like you are, underneath. He likes to keep himself pure."

"Then what the fuck's up? Why can't I be told?"

She hugs him again, and lightly laughs. "Because you're not a Springer."

Long after she has fallen into the steady soft rasping of sleep he lies awake listening to the rain, not willing to let it go, this sound of life. You don't have to be a Springer to have secrets. Blue eyes so pale in the light coming into the back seat of that Corolla. Janice's taste is still on his lips and he thinks maybe it wouldn't be such a good idea for Sealtest. Twice as he lies awake a car stops outside and the front door opens: the first time from the quietness of the motor and the lightness of the steps on the porch boards, Stavros dropping off Melanie; the next time, not many minutes later, the motor brutally raced before cut-off and the footsteps loud and defiant, must be Nelson, having had more beers than was good for him. From the acoustical quality surrounding the sounds of this second car Rabbit gathers that the rain is letting up. He listens for the young footsteps to come upstairs but one set seems to trap the other in the kitchen, Melanie having a snack. The thing about vegetarians, they seem always hungry. You eat and eat and it's never the right food. Who told him that, once? Tothero, he seemed so old there at the end but how much older than Harry is now was he? Nelson and Melanie stay in the kitchen talking until the eavesdropper wearies and surrenders. In his dream, Harry is screaming at the boy over the telephone at the lot, but though his mouth is open so wide he can see all his own teeth spread open like in those dental charts they marked your cavities on that looked like a scream, no sound comes out; his jaws and eyes feel frozen open and when he awakes it seems it has been the morning sun, pouring in hungrily after the rain, that he has been aping.

The display windows at Springer Motors have been recently washed and Harry stands staring through them with not a fleck of dust to show him he is not standing outdoors, in an air-conditioned outdoors, the world left rinsed and puddled by last night's rain, with yet a touch of weariness in the green of the tree across Route 111 behind the Chuck Wagon, a dead or yellow leaf here and there, at the tips of the crowded branches that are dying. The traffic this weekday flourishes. Carter keeps talking about a windfall tax on the oil companies' enormous profits but that won't happen, Harry feels. Carter is smart as a whip and prays a great deal but his gift seems to be the old Eisenhower one of keeping much from happening, just a little daily seepage.

Charlie is with a young black couple wrapping up the sale of a trade-in, unloading a '73 Buick eight-cylinder two-tone for three K on good folks too far behind in the rat race to know times have changed, we're running out of gas, the smart money is into foreign imports with sewing-machine motors. They even got dressed up for the occasion, the wife wears a lavender suit with the skirt old-fashionedly short, her calves hard and high up on her skinny bow legs. They really aren't shaped like we are; Skeeter used to say they were the latest design. Her ass is high and hard along the same lines as her calves as she revolves gleefully around the garish old Buick, in the drench of sunshine, on the asphalt still wet and gleaming. A pretty sight, out of the past. Still it does not dispel the sour unease in Harry's stomach after his short night's sleep. Charlie says something that doubles them both up laughing and then they drive the clunker off. Charlie comes back to his desk in a corner of the cool showroom and Harry approaches him there.

"How'd you dig Melanie last night?" He tries to keep the smirk out of his voice.

"Nice girl." Charlie keeps his pencil moving. "Very straight."

Harry's voice rises indignantly. "What's straight about her? She's kooky as a bluebird, for all I can see."

"Not so, champ. Very level head. She's one of those women you worry about, that they see it all so clearly they'll never let themselves go."

"You're telling me she didn't let herself go with you."

"I didn't expect her to. At my age – who needs it?"

"You're younger than I am."

"Not at heart. You're still learning."

It is as when he was a boy in grade school, and there seemed to be a secret everywhere, flickering up and down the aisles, bouncing around like the playground ball at recess, and he could not get his hands on it, the girls were keeping it from him, they were too quick. "She mention Nelson?"

"A fair amount."

"Whatcha think is going on between them?"

"I think they're just buddies."

"You don't think anymore they got to be fucking?"

Charlie gives up, slapping his desk and pushing back from his paperwork. "Hell, I don't know how these kids have it organized. In our day if you weren't fucking you'd move on. With them it may be different. They don't want to be killers like we were. If they *are* fucking, from the way she talks about him it has about the charge of cuddling a teddy bear before you go to sleep."

"She sees him that way, huh? Childish."

"Vulnerable is the way she'd put it."

Harry offers, "There's some piece missing here. Janice was dropping hints last night."

Stavros delicately shrugs. "Maybe it's back in Colorado. The piece."

"Did she say anything specific?"

Stavros ponders before answering, pushing up his amber glasses with a forefinger and then resting that finger on the bridge of his nose. "No."

Harry tries outright grievance. "I can't figure out what the kid *wants*."

"He wants to get started at the real world. I think he wants in around here."

"I *know* he wants in, and I don't *want* him in. He makes me uncomfortable. With that sorehead look of his he couldn't sell —"

"Coke in the Sahara," Charlie finishes for him. "Be that as it may, he's Fred Springer's grandson. He's *engonaki*."

"Yeah, both Janice and Bessie are pushing, you saw that the other night. They're driving me wild. We have a nice symmetrical arrangement here, and how many cars'd we move in July?"

Stavros checks a sheet of paper under his elbow. "Twenty-nine, would you believe. Thirteen used, sixteen new. Including three of those Celica GTs for ten grand each. I didn't think it would go, not against all the little sports coming out of Detroit at half the price. Those Nips, they know their market research."

"So to hell with Nelson. There's only one month left in the summer anyway. Why screw Jake and Rudy out of sales commission just to accommodate a kid too spoiled to take a job in the shop? He wouldn't even have had to dirty his hands, we could have put him in Parts."

Stavros says, "You could put him on straight salary here on the floor. I'd take him under my wing."

Charlie doesn't seem to realize he is the one to get pushed out. You try to defend somebody and he undermines you while you're doing it. But Charlie sees the problem after all; he expresses it: "Look. You're the son-in-law, you can't be touched. But me, the old lady is my connection here, and it's sentimental at that, she likes me because I remind her of Fred, of the old days. Sentiment doesn't beat out blood. I'm in no position to hang tough. If you can't beat 'em, join 'em. Furthermore I think I can talk to the kid, do something for him. Don't worry, he'll never stick in this business, he's too twitchy. He's too much like his old man."

"I see no resemblance," Harry says, though pleased.

"You wouldn't. I don't know, it seems to be hard these days, being a father. When I was a kid it seemed simple. Tell the kid what to do and if he doesn't do it sock him one. Here's my thought. When you and Jan and the old lady are taking your weeks in the Poconos, has Nelson been planning to come along?"

"They've asked him, but he didn't seem too enthusiastic. As a kid he was always lonely up there. Jesus, it'd be hell, in that little space. Even around the house every time you come into a room it seems he's sitting there with a beer."

"Right. Well how about buying him a suit and tie and letting him come in here? Give him the minimum wage, no commission and no draw. He wouldn't be getting on your nerves, or you on his."

"How could I be getting on his nerves? He walks all over me. He takes the car all the time and tries to make me feel guilty besides."

Charlie doesn't dignify this with an answer; he knows too much of the story.

Harry admits, "Well, it's an idea. Then he'd be going back to college?"

Charlie shrugs. "Let's hope. Maybe you can make that part of the bargain."

Looking down upon the top of Charlie's fragile wavy-haired skull, Rabbit cannot avoid awareness of his own belly, an extensive, suit-straining slope; he has become a person and a half, where the same years have pared Charlie's shape, once stocky, bit by bit. He asks him, "You really want to do this for Nelson?"

"I like the kid. To me, he's just another basket case. At his age now they're all basket cases."

A couple has parked out in the glare and is heading for the showroom doors, a well-dressed Penn Park sort of pair that will probably collect the literature and sneak off to buy a Mercedes, as an investment. "Well, it's your funeral," Harry tells Charlie. Actually it might be nice all around. Melanie wouldn't be left alone in that big house all by herself. And it occurs to him that this all may be Melanie's idea, and Charlie's way of keeping his move on her alive.

In bed Melanie asks Nelson, "What are you learning?"

"Oh, stuff." They have decided upon her bed in the front room for these weeks when the old people are in the Poconos. Melanie in the month and more of her tenancy here has gradually moved the headless dress dummy to a corner and hidden some of the Springers' other ugly possessions – slid some rolled-up hall carpeting beneath the bed, tucked a trunkful of old curtains and a broken foot-pedalled Singer into the back of the closet, already crammed with outgrown and outmoded clothes in polyethylene cleaner bags. She has Scotch-taped a few Peter Max posters to the walls and made the room her own. They have used Nelson's room up to now, but his childhood bed is single and in truth he feels inhibited there. They had not intended to sleep together at all in this house but out of their long and necessary conversations it had been inevitable they sink into it. Melanie's breasts are indeed, as Charlie had noticed at a glance, large; their laden warm sway sometimes sickens Nelson, reminding him of a more shallow-breasted other, whom he has abandoned. He elaborates: "Lots of things. There's all these pressures that don't show, like between the agency and the manufacturer. You got to buy sets of their special tools, for thousands of dollars, and they keep loading their base models with what used to be extras, where the dealer used to make a lot of his profit. Charlie told me a radio used to cost the dealer about thirty-five dollars and he'd add about one-eighty on to the sales price. See then by the manufacturer getting greedy and taking these options away from the dealer the dealers have to think up more gimmicks. Like undercoating. And rustproofing. There's even a treatment they'll give the vinyl upholstery to keep it from wearing supposedly. All that stuff. It's all cutthroat but kind of jolly at the same time, all these little pep talks people keep giving each other. My grandfather used to have a performance board but Dad's let it drop. You can tell Charlie thinks Dad's really lazy and sloppy the way he runs things."

She pushes herself more upright in the bed, her breasts sluggish and luminous in the half-light the maples filter from the sodium lamps on Joseph Street. There is that something heavy and maternal and mystical in her he cannot escape. "Charlie's asked me out on another date," she says.

"Go," Nelson advises, enjoying the altered feeling of the bed, Melanie's lifting her torso above him deepening the rumpled trough in which he lies. When he was a little child and Mom and Dad were living in that apartment high on Wilbur Street and they would come visit here he would be put to bed in this very room, his grandmother's hair all black then but the patterns of light carved on the ceiling by the window mullions just the same as they are now. Mom-mom would sing him songs, he remembers, but he can't remember what they were. In Pennsylvania Dutch, some of them. *Reide, reide, Geile.* . . .

Melanie pulls a hairpin from the back of her head and fishes with it in the ashtray for a dead roach that may have a hit or two left in it. She holds it to her red lips and lights it; the paper flares. When she lifted her arm to pull the hairpin, the hair in her armpit, unshaved, has flared in Nelson's field of vision. Despite himself, to no purpose, his prick with little knocks of blood begins to harden down in the trough of childish warmth. "I don't know," Melanie says. "I think with them away, he's psyched to score."

"How do you feel about that?"

"Not so great."

"He's a pretty nice guy," Nelson says, snuggling deeper beside her abstracted body, enjoying the furtive growth of his erection. "Even if he did screw Mom."

"Suppose it kills him, how would I feel then? I mean, one of the reasons for my coming with you was to clean my head of all this father-figure shit."

"You came along because Pru told you to." Saying the other's name is delicious, a cool stab in the warmth. "So I wouldn't get away."

"Well, yeah, but I wouldn't have if I hadn't had reasons of my own. I'm glad I came. I like it here. It's like America used to be. All these brick houses built so solid, one against the other."

"I hate it. Everything's so humid and stuffy and, so *closed*."

"You really feel that Nelson?" He likes it when she kind of purrs his name. "I thought you acted frightened, in Colorado. There was too much space. Or maybe it was the situation."

Nelson loses Colorado in awareness of his erection, like a piece of round-ended ridged ivory down there, and of the womanly thick cords in her throat swelling as she sucks one last hit from the tiny butt held tight against her painted lips. Melanie always wears makeup, lipstick and touches of red to her cheeks to make her complexion less olive, where Pru never wore any, her lips pale as her brow, and everything about her face precise and dry as a photograph. Pru: the thought of her is a gnawing in his stomach, like somebody rolling a marble around over grits of sand. He says, "Maybe what I mind about around here is Dad." At the thought of Dad the abrasion intensifies. "I can't stand him, the way he sits there in the living room hogging the Barcalounger. He" – he can hardly find words, the discomfort is so great – "just sits there in the middle of the whole fucking world, taking and taking. He doesn't know anything the way Charlie does. What did he ever do, to build up the lot? My granddad was grubbing his way up while my father wasn't doing anything but being a lousy husband to my mother. That's all he's done to deserve all this money: be too lazy and shiftless to leave my mother like he wanted to. I think he's queer. You should have seen him with this black guy I told you about."

"You loved your granddad, didn't you Nelson?" When she's high on pot her voice gets husky and kind of trancy, like one of these oracles sitting over her tripod they talked about in anthro at Kent. Kent: more sand rubbing in his stomach.

"He liked *me*," Nelson insists, writhing a little and noticing with his hand that his erection has slightly wilted, possessing no longer the purity of ivory but the compromised texture of flesh and blood. "He wasn't always criticizing me because I wasn't some great shakes athlete and ten feet tall."

"I've never heard your father criticize you," she says, "except when you cracked up his car."

"Goddam it I *did*n't crack it up, I just dented the bastard and he's going through this whole big deal, weeks in the body shop while I'm supposed to feel guilty or inept or something. And there *was* an animal in the road, some little thing I don't know what it was, a woodchuck, I would have seen the stripes if it had been a skunk, I don't know why they don't make these dumb animals with longer legs, it *waddled*. Right into the headlights. I wish I'd killed it. I wish I'd smashed up all Dad's cars, the whole fucking inventory."

"This is really crazy talk Nelson," Melanie says from within her amiable trance. "You need your father. We all need fathers. At least yours is where you can find him. He's not a bad man."

"He *is* bad, really bad. He doesn't know what's up, and he doesn't *care*, and he thinks he's so great. That's what gets me, his *hap*piness. He is so fucking *hap*py." Nelson almost sobs. "You think of all the misery he's caused. My little sister dead because of him and then this Jill he let die."

Melanie knows these stories. She says in a patient singsong, "You mustn't forget the circumstances. Your father's not God." Her hand follows down inside the bedsheet where his has been exploring. She smiles. Her teeth are perfect. She's had orthodontia, and poor Pru never did, her people were too poor, so she hates to smile, though the irregularity isn't really that noticeable, just a dog tooth slightly overlapping on one side. "You're feeling frustrated right now," Melanie tells him, "because of your situation. But your situation is not your father's fault."

"It *is*," Nelson insists. "Everything's his fault, it's his fault I'm so fucked up, and he en*joys* it, the way he looks at me sometimes, you can tell he's really eating it up, that I'm fucked up. And then the way Mom waits on him, like he's actually *done* something for her, instead of the other way around."

"Come on Nelson, let it go," Melanie croons. "Forget everything for now. I'll help you." She flips down the sheet and turns her back. "Here's my ass. I love being fucked from behind when I have a buzz on. It's like I'm occupying two planes of being."

Melanie hardly ever tries to come when they make love, takes it for granted she is serving the baby male and not herself. With Pru, though, the woman was always trying, breathing "Wait" in his ear and squirming around with her pelvis for the right contact, and even when he couldn't wait and failed, this was somehow more flattering. Remembering Pru this way he feels the nibble of guilt in the depths of his stomach take a sharper bite, like the moment in *Jaws* when the girl gets pulled under.

Water. Rabbit distrusts the element though the little brown hourglass-shaped lake that laps the gritty beach in front of the Springers' old cottage in the Poconos seems friendly and tame, and he swims in it every day, taking a dip before breakfast, before Janice is awake, and while Ma Springer in her quilty bathrobe fusses at the old oil stove to make the morning coffee. On weekdays when there aren't so many people around he walks down across the coarse imported sand wrapped in a beach towel and, after a glance right and left at the cottages that flank theirs back in the pines, slips into the lake naked. What luxury! A chill silver embrace down and through his groin. Gnats circling near the surface shatter and reassemble as he splashes through them, cleaving the plane of liquid stillness, sending ripples right and left toward muddy rooty banks city blocks away. A film of mist sits visible on the skin of the lake if the hour is early enough. He was never an early-to-rise freak but sees the point of it now, you get *into* the day at the start, before it gets rolling, and roll with it. The film of mist tastes of evening chill, of unpolluted freshness in a world waking with him. As a kid Rabbit never went to summer camps, maybe Nelson is right they were too poor, it never occurred to them. The hot cracked sidewalks and dusty playground of Mt. Judge were summer enough, and the few trips to the Jersey Shore his parents organized stick up in his remembrance as almost torture, the hours on poky roads in the old Model A and then the mud-brown Chevy, his sister and mother adding to the heat the vapors of female exasperation, Pop dogged at the wheel, the back of his neck sweaty and scrawny and freckled while the flat little towns of New Jersey threw back at Harry distorted echoes of his own town, his own life, for which he was homesick after an hour. Town after town numbingly demonstrated to him that his life was a paltry thing, roughly duplicated by the millions in settings where houses and porches and trees mocking those in Mt. Judge fed the illusions of other little boys that their souls were central and important and invisibly cherished. He would look at the little girls on the sidewalks they drove alongside wondering which of them he would marry, for his idea of destiny was to move away and marry a girl from another town. The traffic as they neared the Shore became thicker, savage, metropolitan. Cars, he has always found cars, their glitter, their exhalations, cruel. Then at last arriving in a burst of indignities – the parking lot full, the bathhouse attendant rude – they would enter upon a few stilted hours on the alien beach whose dry sand burned the feet and scratched in the crotch and whose wet ribs where the sea had receded had a deadly bottomless smell, a smell of vast death. Every found shell had this frightening faint stink. His parents in bathing suits alarmed him. His mother didn't look obscenely fat like some of the other mothers but bony and long and hard, and as she stood to call him or little Mim back from the suspect crowds of strangers or the dangerous rumor of undertow her arms seemed to be flapping like featherless wings. Not Rabbit then, he would be called as "Hassy! Hassy!" And his father's skin where the workclothes always covered it seemed so tenderly white. He loved his father for having

such whiteness upon him, secretly, a kind of treasure; in the bath-
house he and Pop changed together rapidly, not looking at one
another, and at the end of the day changed again. The ride back
to Diamond County was always long enough for the sunburn to
start hurting. He and Mim would start slapping each other just to
hear the other yell and to relieve the boredom of this wasted day
that could have been spent among the fertile intrigues and perfected connections of the Mt. Judge playground.

In his memory of these outings they always seem to be climbing toward the ocean as toward a huge blue mountain. Sometimes
at night before falling to sleep he hears his mother say with a hiss,
"Hassy." He sees now that he is rich that these were the outings
of the poor, ending in sunburn and stomach upset. Pop liked crab-
cakes and baked oysters but could never eat them without throwing up. When the Model A was tucked into the garage and little
Mim tucked into bed Harry could hear his father vomiting in a far
corner of the yard. He never complained about vomiting or about
work, they were just things you had to do, one more regularly
than the other.

So as a stranger to summer places Rabbit had come to this
cottage Fred Springer had bought rather late in his life, after the
Toyota franchise had made him more than a used-car dealer, after
his one child was married and grown. Harry and Janice used to
come for just visits of a week. The space was too small, the tensions would begin to rub through, with Nelson bored and bug-
eaten after the first day or so. You can only go visit Bushkill Falls
so often, climbing up and down those steps admiring the ferns.

When old man Springer died Harry became the man of the
place and at last understood that Nature isn't just something that
pushes up through the sidewalk cracks and keeps the farmers
trapped in the sticks but is an elixir, a luxury that can be bought
and fenced off and kept pure for the more fortunate, in an impure
age. Not that this five-room, dark-shingled cottage, which Ma
Springer rents for all but these three weeks of August, taking the
Labor Day gravy and renting into hunting season if she can, was
in any league with the gabled estates and lodges and resort hotels
that are all around them tumbling down or being broken up by
developers; but it has two acres of woods behind it and a dock and

rowboat of its own, and holds out to Harry the possibility that life can be lived selectively, as one chooses from a menu, or picks a polished fruit from a bowl. Here in the Poconos food, exercise, and sleep, no longer squeezed into the margins of the day, swell to a sumptuous importance. The smell of fresh coffee drifting to greet him as he walks still wet back from his swim; the kiss of morning fog through a rusted window screen; the sight of Janice with bare brown feet wearing the same tennis shorts and kid's black T-shirt day after day; the blue jay switching stances on the porch rail; the smooth rose-veined rock holding shut the upstairs door that has lost its latch; the very texture of root-riddled mud and reeds where the fresh cedar dock pilings have been driven: he feels love for each phenomenon and not for the first time in his life seeks to bring himself into harmony with the intertwining simplicities that uphold him, that were woven into him at birth. There must be a good way to live.

He eases off on the gin and snacks. He swims and listens to Ma Springer reminisce over the morning coffee and goes down into the village with Janice each day to shop. At night they play three-handed pinochle by the harsh light of bridge lamps, the light feeling harsh because when he had first come to this place they lit kerosene lamps, with fragile interior cones of glowing ash, and went to bed soon after dark, the crickets throbbing. He does not like to fish, nor does he much like playing tennis with Janice against one of the other couples that have access to the lake community's shared court, an old rectangle of clay in the pines, the edges coated with brown needles and the chicken-wire fencing drooping like wet wash. Janice plays every day at the Flying Eagle, and beside her efficient grace he feels cumbersome and out of it. The ball hops at him with a speed his racket cannot match. Her black T-shirt has on it in faded 3-D script the word *Phillies*; it is a shirt he bought Nelson on one of their excursions to Veterans Stadium, and the boy left it behind when he went away to Kent, and Janice in her middle-aged friskiness found it and made it hers. Typical of the way things have gone, that the kid's growing up should seem a threat and a tragedy to him and to her an excuse to steal a T-shirt. Not that it would fit Nelson anymore. It fits her fine; he feels her beside him in the corner of his eye nimbler and

freer than he in her swarthy thick-middled old girl's shape with
her short hair and bouncing bangs. The ball arcs back steadily from
her racket while he hits it too hard or else, trying to "stroke" it
like she tells him, pops it weakly into the net. "Harry, don't try to
steer it," she says. "Keep your knees bent. Point your hip toward
the net." She has had a lot of lessons. The decade past has taught
her more than it has taught him.

What has he done, he wonders as he waits to receive the serve,
with this life of his more than half over? He was a good boy to his
mother and then a good boy to the crowds at the basketball games,
a good boy to Tothero his old coach, who saw in Rabbit something special. And Ruth saw in him something special too, though
she saw it winking out. For a while Harry had kicked against
death, then he gave in and went to work. Now the dead are so
many he feels for the living around him the camaraderie of survivors. He loves these people with him, penned in among the lines
of the tennis court. Ed and Loretta: he's an electrical contractor
from Easton specializing in computer installations. Harry loves the
treetops above their heads, and the August blue above these. What
does he know? He never reads a book, just the newspaper to have
something to say to people, and then mostly human interest
stories, like where the Shah is heading next and how sick he really
is, and that Baltimore doctor. He loves Nature, though he can
name almost nothing in it. Are these pines, or spruces, or firs? He
loves money, though he doesn't understand how it flows to him,
or how it leaks away. He loves men, uncomplaining with their pot
bellies and cross-hatched red necks, embarrassed for what to talk
about when the game is over, whatever the game is. What a
threadbare thing we make of life! Yet what a marvellous thing the
mind is, they can't make a machine like it, though some of these
computers Ed was telling about fill rooms; and the body can do a
thousand things there isn't a factory in the world can duplicate the
motion. He used to love screwing, though more and more he's
willing just to think about it and let the younger people mess with
it, meeting in their bars and cars, amazing how many of them there
are now, just walking down the street or getting into a movie line
he often seems to be the oldest guy in sight. At night when he's
with Janice, she needing a touch of cock to lead her into sleep, he

tries to picture what will turn him on, and he's running out of pictures; the last that works is of a woman on all fours being fucked
by one man while she blows another. And it's not clear in the picture if Harry is doing the fucking or is the man being blown, he
is looking at all three from the outside, as if up on a screen at one
of these movie theaters on upper Weiser with titles like *Harem
Girls* and *All the Way*, and the woman's sensations seem nearer to
him than the man's, the prick in your mouth like a small wet zucchini, plus the other elsewhere, in and out, in and out, a kind of
penance at your root. Sometimes he prays a few words at night
but a stony truce seems to prevail between himself and God.

    He begins to run. In the woods, along the old logging roads
and bridle trails, he ponderously speeds in tennis shoes first, orange
with clay dust, and then in gold-and-blue Nikes bought at a sporting goods shop in Stroudsburg especially for this, running shoes
with tipped-up soles at toe and heel, soles whose resilient circlets
like flattened cleats lift him powerfully as, growing lighter and
quicker and quieter, he runs. At first he feels his weight like some
murderous burden swaddled about his heart and lungs and his
thigh muscles ache in the morning so that he staggers in leaving
the bed and laughs aloud in surprise. But as over the days, running
after supper in the cool of the early evening while all the light has
not ebbed from the woods, he accustoms his body to this new
demand, his legs tighten, his weight seems less, his chest holds
more air, the twigs fly past his ears as if winged on their own, and
he extends the distance he jogs, eventually managing the mile and
a half to the waist of the hourglass, where the gates of an old estate
bar the way. Carbon Castle the locals call the estate, built by a coal
baron from Scranton and now little utilized by his scattered and
dwindled descendants, the swimming pool drained, the tennis
courts overgrown, energy gone. The glass eyes of the stuffed deer
heads in the hunting lodge stare through cobwebs; the great main
house with its precipitous slate roofs and diamond-paned windows
is boarded up, though ten years ago one of the grandsons tried
to make of it a commune, the villagers say. The young people
vandalized the place, the story runs, and sold off everything they
could move, including the two bronze brontosaurs that guarded
the main entrance, emblems of the Coal Age. The heavy iron gates

to Carbon Castle are double-chained and padlocked; Rabbit touches the forbidding metal, takes a breath for a still second while the world feels still to be rushing on, pouring through the tremble of his legs, then turns and jogs back, casting his mind wide, so as to become unconscious of his heaving body. There is along the way an open space, once a meadow, now spiked with cedars and tassle-headed weeds, where swallows dip and careen, snapping up insects revived in the evening damp. Like these swallows Rabbit, the blue and gold of his new shoes flickering, skims, above the earth, above the dead. The dead stare upwards. Mom and Pop are lying together again as for so many years on that sway-backed bed they'd bought second-hand during the Depression and never got around to replacing though it squeaked like a tricycle left out in the rain and was so short Pop's feet stuck out of the covers. Papery-white feet that got mottled and marbled with veins finally: if he'd ever have exercised he might have lived longer. Tothero down there is all eyes, eyes big as saucers staring out of his lopsided head while his swollen tongue hunts for a word. Fred Springer, who put Harry where he is, eggs him on, hunched over and grimacing like a man with a poker hand so good it hurts. Skeeter, who that newspaper clipping claimed had fired upon the Philly cops first even though there were twenty of them in the yard and hallways and only some pregnant mothers and children on the commune premises, Skeeter black as the earth turns his face away. The meadow ends and Harry enters a tunnel, getting dark now, the needles a carpet, he makes no sound, Indians moved without sound through trees without end where a single twig snapping meant death, his legs in his fatigue cannot be exactly controlled but flail against the cushioned path like arms of a loose machine whose gears and joints have been bevelled by wear. Becky, a mere seed laid to rest, and Jill, a pale seedling held from the sun, hang in the earth, he imagines, like stars, and beyond them there are myriads, whole races like the Cambodians, that have drifted into death. He is treading on them all, they are resilient, they are cheering him on, his lungs are burning, his heart hurts, he is a membrane removed from the hosts below, their filaments caress his ankles, he loves the earth, he will never make their mistake and die.

The last hundred feet, up their path to the tilting front porch,

Rabbit sprints. He opens the front screen door and feels the punky floorboards bounce under him. The milk-glass shades of the old kerosene lamps, increasingly valuable as antiques, tremble, like the panes in the breakfront back on Joseph street. Janice emerges barefoot from the kitchen and says, "Harry, you're all red in the face."

"I'm. All. Right."

"Sit down. For heaven's sakes. What are you training for?"

"The big bout," he pants. "It feels great. To press against. Your own limitations."

"You're pressing too hard if you ask me. Mother and I thought you got lost. We want to play pinochle."

"I got to take. A shower. The trouble with running is. You get all sweaty."

"I still don't know what you're trying to prove." With that Phillies shirt on she looks like Nelson, before he needed to shave.

"It's now or never," he tells her, the blood of fantasy rushing through his brain. "There's people out to get me. I can lie down now. Or fight."

"*Who's* out to get you?"

"You should know. You hatched him."

The hot water here runs off a little electric unit and is scalding for a few minutes and then cools with lightning speed. Harry thinks, A good way to kill somebody would be to turn off the cold water while they're in the shower. He dances out before the hot expires totally, admires the wet prints of his big feet on the bare pine floors of this attic-shaped upstairs, and thinks of his daughter, her feet in those cork-soled platforms. With her leggy pallor and calm round face she glows like a ghost but unlike the dead shares the skin of this planet with him, breathes air, immerses herself in water, moves from element to element, and grows. He goes into the bedroom he and Janice have here and dresses himself in Jockey shorts, an alligator shirt, and soft Levis all washed and tumble-dried at the laundromat behind the little Acme in the village. Each crisp item seems another tile of his well-being he is fitting into place. As he sits on the bed to put on fresh socks a red ray of late sun slices through a gap in the pines and falls knifelike across his toes, the orangish corns and the little hairs between the joints and the nails translucent like the thin sheets in furnace peepholes. There are feet that have done worse than his, on a lot of women's in summer sandals you notice how the little toes have been bent under by years of pointy high-heeled shoes, and the big toes pushed over so the joint sticks out like a broken bone; thank God since he is a man that has never had to happen to him. Nor to Cindy Murkett either, come to think of it: toes side by side like candies in a box. Suck. That lucky stiff Webb. Still. It's good to be alive. Harry goes downstairs and adds the fourth element to his happiness; he lights a fire. Ma Springer, riding shrewdly with the times, has bought a new wood stove. Its bright black flue pipe fits snugly into the smudged old fireplace of ugly fieldstones. Old man Springer had installed baseboard electric heat when the cottage was connected for electricity, but his widow begrudges the expense of turning it on, even though by August the nights bring in a chill from the lake. The stove comes from Taiwan and is clean as a skillet, installed just this summer. Harry lays some rough sticks found around the cottage on top of a crumpled Sports page from the Philadelphia *Bulletin* and watches them catch, watches the words EAGLES READY ignite and blacken, the letters turning white on the crinkling ash; then he adds some crescent-shaped scraps of planed fruitwood a local furniture-maker sells by the bushel outside his factory. This fire greets the dark as Janice and her mother, the dishes done, come in and get out the pinochle deck.

As she deals, Ma Springer says, the words parcelled out in rhythm with the cards, "Janice and I were saying, really we don't think it's so wise, for you to be running like this, at your age."

"My age is the age to do it. Now's the time to start taking care of myself, I've had a free ride up to now."

"Mother says you should have your heart checked first," Janice says. She has put on a sweater and jeans but her feet are still bare. He glances at them under the card table. Pretty straight, the toes are. Not too much damage, considering. Bony and brown and boyish. He likes it, that up here in the Poconos she looks so often like a boy. His playmate. As when a child he would stay over at a playmate's house.

"Your father, you know," Ma Springer is telling him, "was taken off by his heart."

"He'd been suffering for years," Harry says, "with a lot of things. He was seventy. He was ready to go."

"You may not think so when your time comes."

"I've been thinking about all the dead people I know lately," Harry says, looking at his cards. Ace, ten, king, and jack of spades, but no queen. No pinochle either therefore. No runs. No four of anything. A raft of low clubs. "I pass."

"Pass," Janice says.

"I'll take it at twenty-one," Ma Springer sighs, and lays down a run in diamonds, and the nine, and a queen of spades to go with the jack.

"Wow," Harry tells her. "What power."

"Which dead, Harry?" Janice asks.

She is afraid he means Becky. But he really rarely thinks of their dead infant, and then pleasantly, as of a brief winter day's sun on last night's snowfall, though her name was June. "Oh, Pop and Mom mostly. Wondering if they're watching. You do so much to get your parents' attention for so much of your life, it seems weird to be going on without them. I mean, who cares now?"

"A lot of people care," Janice says, clumsily earnest.

"You don't know what it feels like," he tells her. "You still have your mother."

"For just a little while yet," Bessie says, playing an ace of clubs. Gathering in the trick with a deft rounding motion of her hand, she pronounces, "Your father now was a good worker, who never gave himself airs, but your mother I must confess I never could abide. A sharp tongue, in a plain body."

"Mother. Harry loved his mother."

Bessie snaps down the ace of hearts. "Well that's right and proper I guess, at least they say it is, for a boy to like his mother. But I used to feel sorry for him when she was alive. She drove him to have an uncommon high opinion of himself and yet could give him nothing to grab a hold of, the way Fred and I could you."

She talks of Harry as if he too is dead. "I'm still here, you know," he says, flipping on the lowest heart he has.

Bessie's mouth pinches in and her face slightly bloats as her black eyes stare down at her cards. "I know you're still here, I'm not saying anything I won't say to your face. Your mother was an unfortunate woman who caused a lot of devilment. You and Janice when you were starting out would never have had such a time of it if it hadn't been for Mary Angstrom, and that goes for ten years ago too. She thought too much of herself for what she was." Ma has that fanatic tight look about the cheeks women get when they hate one another. Mom didn't think that much of Bessie Springer either — *little upstart married to that crook, a woman without enough brains to grease a saucepan living in that big house over on Joseph Street looking down her nose. The Koerners were dirt farmers and not even the good dirt, they farmed the hills.*

"Mother, Harry's mother was bedridden all through that time the house burned down. She was dying."

"Not so dying she didn't stir up a lot of mischief before she went. If she'd have let you two work out your relations with these others there would never have been a separation and all the grief. She was envious of the Koerners and had been since Day One. I knew her when she was Mary Renninger two classes ahead of me in the old Thad Stevens School before they built the new high school where the Morris farm used to be, and she thought too much of herself then. The Renningers weren't country people, you see, they came right out of Brewer and had that slum mentality, that cockiness. Too tall for her sex and too big for her britches. Your sister, Harry, got all her looks from your father's side. Your father's father they say was one of those very fair Swedes, a plasterer." With a thump of her thumb she lays down the ace of diamonds.

"You can't lead trump until after the third trick," Harry reminds her.

"Oh, foolish." She takes the ace back and stares at her cards through the unbecoming though fashionable eyeglasses she bought recently — heavy blue shell frames hinged low to S-shaped temples and with a kind of continuous false eyebrow of silvery inlay. They aren't even comfortable, she has to keep touching the bridge to push them up on her little round nose.

Her agony is so great pondering the cards, Harry reminds her, "You only need one point to make your bid. You've already made it."

"Yes, well . . . make all you can while you can, Fred used

to say." She fans her cards a little wider. "Ah. I thought I had another one of those." She lays down a second ace of clubs.

But Janice trumps it. She pulls in the trick and says, "Sorry, Mother. I only had a singleton of clubs, how could you know?"

"I had a feeling as soon as I put down that ace. I had a premonition."

Harry laughs; you have to love the old lady. Cabined with these two women, he has grown soft and confiding, as when he was a little boy and asked Mom where ladies went wee-wee. "I used to sometimes wonder," he confides to Bessie, "if Mom had ever, you know, been false to Pop."

"I wouldn't have put it past her," she says, grim-lipped as Janice leads out her own aces. Her eyes flash at Harry. "See, if you'd have let me play that diamond she wouldn't have gotten in."

"Ma," he says, "you can't take every trick, don't be so greedy. I know Mom must have been sexy, because look at Mim."

"What do you hear from your sister?" Ma asks to be polite, staring down at her cards again. The shadows thrown by her ornate spectacle frames score her cheeks and make her look old, dragged down, where there is no anger to swell the folds of her face.

"Mim's fine. She's running this beauty parlor in Las Vegas. She's getting rich."

"I never believed half of what people said about her," Ma utters absently.

Now Janice has run through her aces and plays a king of spades to the ace she figures Harry must have. Since she joined up with that bridge-and-tennis bunch of witches over at the Flying Eagle, Janice isn't as dumb at cards as she used to be. Harry plays the expected ace and, momentarily in command, asks Ma Springer, "How much of my mother do you see in Nelson?"

"Not a scrap," she says with satisfaction, whackingly trumping his ten of spades. "Not a whit."

"What can I do for the kid?" he asks aloud. It is as if another has spoken, through him. Fog blowing through a window screen.

"Be patient," Ma answers, triumphantly beginning to run out the trumps.

"Be loving," Janice adds.

"Thank God he's going back to college next month."

Their silence fills the cottage like cool lake air. Crickets.

He accuses, "You both know stuff I don't."

They do not deny it.

He gropes. "What do you both think of Melanie, really? I think she depresses the kid."

"I dare say the rest are mine," Ma Springer announces, laying down a raft of little diamonds.

"Harry," Janice tells him. "Melanie's not the problem."

"If you ask me," Ma Springer says, so firmly they both know she wants the subject changed, "Melanie is making herself altogether too much at home."

On television Charlie's Angels are chasing the heroin smugglers in a great array of expensive automobiles that slide and screech, that plunge through fruit carts and large panes of glass and finally collide one with another, and then another, tucking into opposing fenders and grilles in a great slow-motion climax of bent metal and arrested motion and final justice. The Angel who has replaced Farrah Fawcett-Majors gets out of her crumpled Malibu and tosses her hair: this becomes a freeze-frame. Nelson laughs in empathetic triumph over all those totalled Hollywood cars. Then the more urgent tempo and subtly louder volume of the commercial floods the room; a fresh palette of reflected light paints the faces, chubby and clownish side by side, of Melanie and Nelson as they sit on the old sofa of gray nappy stuff cut into a pattern and gaze at the television set where they have placed it in the rearranged living room, where the Barcalounger used to be. Beer bottles glint on the floor beneath their propped-up feet; hanging drifts of sweetish smoke flicker in polychrome as if the ghosts of Charlie's Angels are rising to the ceiling. "Great smash-up," Nelson pronounces, with difficulty rising and fumbling the television off.

"I thought it was stupid," Melanie says in her voice of muffled singing.

"Oh shit, you think everything is stupid except what's his name, Kerchief."

"G. I. Gurdjieff." She has a prim mode of withdrawal, into mental regions where she knows he cannot reach. At Kent it became clear there were realms real for others not real to him – not just languages he didn't know, or theorems he couldn't grasp, but drifting areas of unprofitable knowledge where nevertheless profits of a sort were being made. Melanie was mystical, she ate no meat and felt no fear, the tangled weedy gods of Asia spelled a harmony to her. She lacked that fury against limits that had been part of Nelson since he had known he would never be taller than five nine though his father was six three, or perhaps before that since he had found himself helpless to keep his father and mother together and to save Jill from the ruin she wanted, or perhaps before that since he had watched grownups in dark suits and dresses assembling around a small white coffin, with silvery handles and something sparkly in the paint, that they told him held what had been his baby sister, born and then allowed to die without anybody asking *him*; nobody ever asked him, the grownup world was like that, it just ground on, and Melanie was part of that world, smugly smiling out at him from within that bubble where the mystery resided that amounted to power. It would be nice, as long as he was standing, to take up one of the beer bottles and smash it down into the curly hair of Melanie's skull and then to take the broken half still in his hand and rotate it into the smiling plumpnesses of her face, the great brown eyes and cherry lips, the mocking implacable Buddha calm. "I don't care what the fuck his dumb name is, it's all bullshit," he tells her instead.

"You should read him," she says. "He's wonderful."

"Yeah, what does he say?"

Melanie thinks, unsmiling. "It's not easy to sum up. He says there's a Fourth Way. Besides the way of the yogi, the monk, and the fakir."

"Oh, great."

"And if you go this way you'll be what he calls awake."

"Instead of asleep?"

"He was very interested in somehow grasping the world as it is. He believed we all have plural identities."

"I want to go out," he tells her.

"Nelson, it's ten o'clock at night."

"I promised I might meet Billy Fosnacht and some of the guys down at the Laid-Back." The Laid-Back is a new bar in Brewer, at the corner of Weiser and Pine, catering to the young. It used to be called the Phoenix. He accuses her, "You go out all the time with Stavros leaving me here with nothing to do."

"You could read Gurdjieff," she says, and giggles. "Anyway I haven't gone out with Charlie more than four or five times."

"Yeah, you work all the other nights."

"It isn't as if we ever *do* anything, Nelson. The last time we sat and watched television with his mother. You ought to see her. She looks younger than he does. All black hair." She touches her own dark, vital, springy hair. "She was wonderful."

Nelson is putting on his denim jacket, bought at a shop in Boulder specializing in the worn-out clothes of ranch hands and sheep herders. It had cost twice what a new one would have cost. "I'm working on a deal with Billy. One of the other guys is going to be there. I gotta go."

"Can I come along?"

"You're working tomorrow, aren't you?"

"You know I don't care about sleep. Sleep is giving in to the body."

"I won't be late. Read one of your books." He imitates her giggle.

Melanie asks him, "When have you last written to Pru? You haven't answered any of her recent letters."

His rage returns; his tight jacket and the very wallpaper of this room seem to be squeezing him smaller and smaller. "How can I, she writes twice every fucking day, it's worse than a newspaper. Christ, she tells me her temperature, what she's eaten, when she's taken a crap practically —"

The letters are typewritten, on stolen Kent stationery, page after page, flawlessly.

"She thinks you're interested," Melanie says in reproach. "She's lonely and apprehensive."

Nelson gets louder. "*She's* apprehensive! What does she have to be apprehensive about? Here I am, good as gold, with you such a goddam watchdog I can't even go into town for a beer."

"Go."

He is stabbed by guilt. "Honest, I did promise Billy; he's going to bring this kid whose sister owns a '76 TR convertible with only fifty-five thousand miles on it."

"Just go," Melanie says quietly. "I'll write to Pru and explain how you're too busy."

"Too busy, too busy. Who the hell am I doing all this for except for fucking silly-ass Pru?"

"I don't know, Nelson. I honestly don't know what you're doing or who you're doing it for. I do know that I found a job, according to our plan, whereas you did nothing except finally bully your poor father into making up a job for you."

"My *poor* father! *Poor* father! Listen who do you think put him where he is? Who do you think owns the company, my mother and grandmother own it, my father is just their front man and doing a damn lousy job of it too. Now that Charlie's run out of moxie there's nobody over there with any drive or creativity at all. Rudy and Jake are stooges. My father's running that outfit into the ground; it's sad."

"You can say all that, Nelson, and that Charlie's run out of moxie which I think I'm in a better position than you to know, but you haven't shown me much capacity for responsibility."

He hears, though frustrated and guilty to the point of tears, a deliberate escalation in her "capacity for responsibility" in answer to his mention of "creativity." Against the Melanies of the world he will always come in tongue-tied. "Bullshit" is all he can say.

"You have a lot of *feel*ings, Nelson," she tells him. "But feelings aren't actions." She stares at him as if to hypnotize him, batting her eyes once.

"Oh Christ. I'm doing exactly what you and Pru wanted me to do."

"You see, that's how your mind works, putting everything off on others. We didn't *want* you to *do* anything specific, we just wanted you to cope like an adult. You couldn't seem to do it out there so you came back here to put yourself in phase with reality. I don't see that you've done it." When she bats her eyelids like that, her head becomes a doll's, all hollow inside. Fun to smash. "Charlie says," Melanie says, "you're overanxious as a salesman; when the people come in, they're scared away."

"They're scared away by the lousy tinny Japanese cars that cost a fortune because of the shit-eating yen. I wouldn't buy one, I don't see why anybody else should buy one. It's Detroit. Detroit has let everybody down, millions of people depending for jobs on Detroit's coming up with some decent car design and the assholes won't do it."

"Don't swear so much, Nelson. It doesn't impress me." As she gazes steadily up at him her eyeballs show plenty of white; he pictures the also plentiful white orbs of her breasts and he doesn't want this quarrel to progress so far she won't comfort him in bed. She hasn't ever sucked him off but he bets she does it for Charlie, that's the only way these old guys can get it up. Smiling that hollow-headed Buddha smile, Melanie says, "You go off and play with the other little boys, I'll stay here and write Pru and won't tell her you said her ass is silly. But I'm getting very tired, Nelson, of covering for you."

"Well who asked you to? You're getting something out of it too." In Colorado she had been sleeping with a married man who was also the partner of the crumb Nelson was supposed to spend the summer working for, putting up condominiums in ski country. The man's wife was beginning to make loud noises though she had been around herself and the other guy Melanie was seeing had visions of himself as a cocaine supplier to the beautiful people at Aspen and yet lacked the cool and the contacts, and seemed headed for jail or an early grave depending on which foot he tripped over first. Roger the guy's name was and Nelson had liked him, the way he sidled along like a lanky yellow hound who knows he's going to be kicked. It had been Roger who had gotten them into hang gliding, Melanie too prudent but Pru surprisingly willing to try, joking about how this would be one way to solve all their problems. Her face so slender in the great white crash helmet they rented you at the Highlands base, up on the Golden Horn, in the second before the launch into astonishing, utterly quiet space she would give him that same wry sharp estimating look sideways he had seen the first time she had decided to sleep with him, in her little studio apartment in that factorylike high-rise over in Stow, her picture window above a parking lot. He had met Melanie first, in a course they both took called the

Geography of Religions: Shintō, shamanism, the Jains, all sorts of antique superstitions thriving, according to the maps, in overlapping patches, like splotches of disease, and in some cases even spreading, the world was in such a desperate state. Pru was not a student but a typist for the Registrar's office over in Rockwell Hall; Melanie had gotten to know her during a campaign by the Students' League for a Democratic Kent to create discontent among the university employees, especially the secretaries. Most of such friendships withered when the next cause came along but Pru had stuck. She wanted something. Nelson had been drawn to her grudging crooked smile, as if she too had trouble spinning herself out for display, not like these glib kids who had gone from watching TV straight to the classroom with never a piece of the world's real weather to halt their tongues. And also her typist's hard long hands, like the hands of his grandmother Angstrom. She had taken her portable Remington west with her in hopes of finding some free-lance work out of Denver, so she typed her letters telling him when she went to sleep and when she woke up and when she felt like vomiting, whereas he has to respond in his handwriting that he hates, it is such a childish-looking scrawl. The fluent perfection of her torrent of letters overwhelms him, he couldn't have known she would be the source of such a stream. Girls write easier than boys somehow: he remembers the notes in green ink Jill used to leave around the house in Penn Villas. And he remembers, suddenly, more of the words of the song Mom-mom used to sing: "*Reide, reide, Geile / Alle Schtunn en Meili / Geht's iwwer der Schtumbe / Fallt's Bubbli nunner!*" with the last word, where Baby falls down, *nunner*, not sung but spoken, in a voice so solemn he always laughed.

"What am I getting out of it, Nelson?" Melanie asks with that maddening insistent singingness.

"Kicks," he tells her. "Safe kicks, too, the kind you like. Controlling me, more or less. Charming the old folks."

Her voice relaxes and she sounds sad. "I think that's wearing thin. Maybe I've talked too much to your grandmother."

"Could be." As he stands there he feels some advantage return to him. This is his house, his town, his inheritance. Melanie is an outsider here.

"Well, I *liked* her," she says, strangely using the past tense. "I'm always drawn to older people."

"She makes more sense at least than Mom and Dad."

"What do you want me to tell Pru if I write?"

"I don't *know*." His shoulders shiver in his jacket as if the taut little coat is an electric contact; he feels his face cloud, even his breath grow hot. Those white envelopes, the white of the crash helmet she put on, the white of her belly. Space would open up immensely under you after you launched but was not menacing somehow, the harness holding you tight and the trees falling away smaller along the grassy ski trails and tilted meadows below and the great nylon wing responsive to every tug on the control bar. "Tell her to hold on."

Melanie says, "She's *been* holding on, Nelson, she can't keep holding on forever. I mean, it *shows*. And I can't stay on here much longer either. I have to visit my mother before I go back to Kent."

Everything seems to complicate, physically, in front of his mouth, so he is conscious of the effort of breathing. "And *I* gotta get to the Laid-Back before everybody leaves."

"Oh, go. Just go. But tomorrow I want you to help me start tidying up. They'll be back Sunday and you haven't once weeded the garden or mowed the lawn."

Driving Ma Springer's cushy old Newport up Jackson to where Joseph Street intersects, the first thing Harry sees is his tomato-red Corona parked in front, looking spandy-new and just washed besides. They had got it fixed at last. It was cute of the kid to have had it washed. Loving, even. A surge of remorse for all the ill will he has been bearing Nelson gives a quickening countercurrent to the happiness he feels at being back in Mt. Judge, on a sparkling Sunday noon late in August with the dry-grass smell of football in the air and the maples thinking of turning gold. The front lawn, even that awkward little section up by the azalea bushes and the strip between the sidewalk and the curb where roots are coming to the surface and hand-clippers have to be used, has been mowed. Harry knows how those hand-clippers begin to chafe in the palm.

When the boy comes out on the porch and down to the street to help with the bags, Harry shakes Nelson's hand. He thinks of kissing him but the start of a frown scares him off; his impulse to be extra friendly flounders and drowns amidst the clutter of greetings. Janice embraces Nelson and, more lightly, Melanie. Ma Springer, overheated from the car ride, allows herself to be kissed on the cheek by both young people. Both are dressed up, Melanie in a peach-colored linen suit Harry didn't know she owned and Nelson in a gray sharkskin he knows the boy didn't have before. A new suit to be a salesman in. The effect is touchingly trimmer; in the tilt of the child's combed head his father is startled to see a touch of the dead Fred Springer, con artist.

Melanie looks taller than he remembers: high heels. In her pleased croon of a voice she explains, "We went to church," turning toward Ma Springer. "You had said over the phone you might try to make the service and we thought we'd surprise you in case you did."

"Melanie, I couldn't get them up in time," Bessie says. "They were just a pair of lovebirds up there."

"The mountain air, nothing personal," Rabbit says, handing Nelson a duffel bag full of dirty sheets. "It was supposed to be a vacation and I wasn't going to get up at dawn the last day we were there just so Ma could come make cow eyes at that fag."

"He didn't seem that faggy, Dad. That's just how ministers talk."

"To me he seemed pretty radical," Melanie says. "He went on about how the rich have to go through a camel's eye." To Harry she says, "You look *thin*ner."

"He's been running, like an idiot," Janice says.

"Also not having to eat lunch at a restaurant every day," he says. "They give you too much. It's a racket."

"Mother, be careful of the curb," Janice says sharply. "Do you want an arm?"

"I've been managing this curb for thirty years, you don't need to tell me it's here."

"Nelson, help Mother up the steps," Janice nevertheless says.

"The Corona looks great," Harry tells the boy. "Better than new." He suspects, though, that that annoying bias in the steering will still be there.

"I really got on 'em about it, Dad. Manny kept giving it bottom priority because it was yours and you weren't here. I told him
by the time you *were* here I wanted that car *done*, period."

"Take care of the paying customers first," Harry says, vaguely
obliged to defend his service chief.

"Manny's a jerk," the boy calls over his shoulder as he steers
his grandmother and the duffel bag through the front door, under
the stained-glass fanlight that holds among leaded foliate shapes the
number 89.

Toting suitcases, Harry follows them in. This house had faded
in his mind. "Oh boy," he breathes. "Like an old shoe."

Ma is dutifully admiring the neatness, the flowers from the border beds arranged in vases on the sideboard and dining-room table,
the vacuumed rugs and the laundered antimacassars on the nappy
gray sofa and matching easy chair. She touches the tufted chenille.
"These pieces haven't looked so good since Fred fought with the
cleaning woman, old Elsie Lord, and we had to let her go."

Melanie explains, "If you use a damp brush, with just a dab of
rug cleaner –"

"Melanie, you know how to do a job," Harry says. "The only
trouble with you, you should have been a man." This comes out
rougher than he had intended, but a sudden small vexation had
thrown him off balance when he stepped into the house. His
house, yet not his. These stairs, those knickknacks. He lives here
like a boarder, a rummy old boarder in his undershirt, too fuddled
to move. Even Ruth has her space. He wonders how his round-
faced girl is doing, out in that overgrown terrain, in her sandstone
house with its scabby green door.

Ma Springer is sniffing the air. "Something smells sweet," she
says. "It must be the rug cleaner you used."

Nelson is at Harry's elbow, closer than he usually gets. "Dad,
speaking of jobs, I have something I want to show you."

"Don't show me anything till I get these bags upstairs. It's
amazing how much crap you need just to walk around in sneakers in the Poconos."

Janice bangs the kitchen door, coming in from the outside.
"Harry, you should see the garden, it's all beautifully weeded! The
lettuce comes up to my knees, the kohlrabi has gotten *enor*mous!"

Harry says to the young people, "You should have eaten some, the kohlrabi gets pulpy if you let it grow too big."

"It *never* has any taste, Dad," Nelson says.

"Yeah. I guess nobody much likes it except me." He likes to nibble, is one reason he's fat. While growing up he had many sensitive cavities and now that he has his molars crowned eating has become perhaps too much of a pleasure. No more twinges, just everlasting gold.

"Kohlrabi," Melanie is saying dreamily, "I wondered what it was, Nelson kept telling me turnips. Kohlrabi is rich in vitamin C."

"How're the crêpes cooking these days?" Harry asks her, trying to make up for having told the girl she should have been a man. He may have hit on something, though; in her a man's normal bossiness has had to turn too sweet.

"Fine. I've given them my notice and the other waitresses are going to give me a party."

Nelson says, "She's turned into a real party girl, Dad. I hardly ever saw her when we were here together. Your pal Charlie Stavros keeps taking her out, he's even coming for her this afternoon."

You poor little shnook, Rabbit thinks. Why is the kid standing so close? He can hear the boy's worried breath.

"He's taking me to Valley Forge," Melanie explains, bright-eyed, those bright eyes concealing what mischief, Rabbit may never know now. The girl is pulling out. "I'm about to leave Pennsylvania and I really haven't seen any of the sights, so Charlie's being nice enough to take me to some of the places. Last weekend we went into Amish country and saw all the buggies."

"Depressing damn things, aren't they?" Harry says, going on, "Those Amish are mean bastards – mean to their kids, to their animals, to each other."

"Dad –"

"If you're going as far as Valley Forge you might as well go look at the Liberty Bell, see if it still has a crack in it."

"We weren't sure it was open Sundays."

"Philly in August is a sight to see anyhow. One big swamp of miserable humanity. They cut your throat for a laugh down there."

"Melanie, I'm so sorry to hear you're leaving," Janice intervenes smoothly. It sometimes startles Harry, how smooth Janice can be in her middle age. Looking back, he and Jan were pretty rough customers – kids with a grudge, and not much style. No style, in fact. A little dough does wonders.

"Yeah," the guest of their summer says, "I should visit my family. My mother and sisters, I mean, in Carmel. I don't know if I'll go up to see my father or not, he's gotten so *strange*. And then back to college. It's been wonderful staying here, you were all so kind. I mean, considering that you didn't even *know* me."

"No problem," Harry says, wondering about her sisters, if they all have such eyes and ruby lips. "You did it yourself; you paid your way." Lame, lame. Never could talk to her.

"I know Mother will really miss your company," Janice says, and calls over, "Isn't that right, Mother?"

But Ma Springer is examining the china in her breakfront, to see if anything has been stolen, and doesn't seem to hear.

Harry asks Nelson abruptly, "So what did you want to show me in such a hurry?"

"It's over at the lot," the boy says. "I thought we could drive over when you came back."

"Can't I even have lunch first? I hardly had any breakfast, with all this talk of making church. Just a couple of Pecan Sandies that the ants hadn't gotten to." His stomach hurts to think of it.

"I don't think there is that much for lunch," Janice says.

Melanie offers, "There's some wheat germ and yogurt in the fridge, and some Chinese vegetables in the freezer."

"I have no appetite," Ma Springer announces. "And I want to try my own bed. Without exaggerating I don't believe I had more than three hours' sleep in a row all that time up there. I kept hearing the raccoons."

"She's just sore about missing church," Rabbit tells the others. He feels trapped by all this fuss of return. There is a tension here that wasn't here before. You never return to the same place. Think of the dead coming back on Resurrection Day. He goes out through the kitchen into his garden and eats a kohlrabi raw, tearing off the leaves with his hands and stripping the skin from the bland crisp bulb with his front teeth. The butch women up the street are still hammering away – what can they be building? How did that poem used to go? *Build thee more stately something O my soul.* Lotty Bingaman would have known, waving her hand in the air. The air feels nice. A flatter noon than earlier, the summer settling to its dust. The trees have dulled down from the liquid green of June and the undertone of insect hum has deepened to a constant dry rasp, if you listen. The lettuce is tall and seedy, the beans are by, a carrot he pulls up is stubby as a fat man's prick, all its push gone upwards into greens. Back in the kitchen Janice has found some salami not too dried-out to eat and has made sand-wiches for him and Nelson. This excursion to the lot seems bound to happen, when Harry had hoped to get over to the club this after-noon and see if the gang has missed him. He can see them gathered by the shuddering bright pool of chlorinated aqua, laughing, Buddy and his dog of the month, the Harrisons, foxy old Webb and his little Cindy. Little Cindy Blackbottom Babytoes. Real sunlight people, not these shadows in the corners of Ma's glum house. Charlie honks out front but doesn't come in. Embarrassed, and he should be, the babysnatcher. Harry looks at Janice to see how she takes it when the front door slams. Not a flicker. Women are tough. He asks her, "So what're *you* going to do this afternoon?"

"I was going to tidy up the house, but Melanie seems to have done it all. Maybe I'll go over to the club and see if I can get into a game. At least I could swim." She swam at Hourglass Lake, and in truth does look more supple through the middle, longer from hips to breasts. Not a bad little bride, he sometimes thinks, sur-prised by their connivance in this murky world of old blood and dark strangers.

"How'd you like that, about Charlie and Melanie?" he asks.

She shrugs, imitating Charlie. "I like it fine, why not? More power to him. You only live once. They say."

"Whyn't you go over and Nellie and I'll come join you after I look at this thing of his, whatever it is?"

Nelson comes into the kitchen, mouth ajar, eyes suspicious.

Janice says, "Or I could come with you and Nelson to the lot and then we all three could go to the club together and save gas by using only the one car."

"Mom, it's *business*," Nelson protests, and from the way his face clouds both parents see that they had better let him have his way. His gray suit makes him seem extra vulnerable, in the way of children placed in unaccustomed clothes for ceremonies they don't understand.

So Nelson and Harry, behind the wheel of his Corona for the first time in a month, drive through the Sunday traffic the route they both know better than the lines in their palms, down Joseph to Jackson to Central and around the side of the mountain. Harry says, "Car feels a little different, doesn't it?" This is a bad start; he tries to patch it with, "Guess a car never feels the same after it's been banged up."

Nelson bridles. "It was just a dent, it didn't have anything to do with the front end, that's where you'd feel the difference if there was any."

Harry holds his breath and then concedes, "Probably imagining it."

They pass the view of the viaduct and then the shopping center where the four-theater complex advertises AGATHA MANHATTAN MEATBALLS AMITYVILLE HORROR. Nelson asks, "Did you read the book, Dad?"

"What book?"

"*Amityville Horror.* The kids at Kent were all passing it around."

Kids at Kent. Lucky stiffs. What he could have done with an education. Been a college coach somewhere. "It's about a haunted house, isn't it?"

"Dad, it's about Satanism. The idea is some previous occupant of the house had conjured up the Devil and then he wouldn't go away. Just an ordinary-looking house on Long Island."

"You believe this stuff?"

"Well – there's evidence that's pretty hard to get around."

Rabbit grunts. Spineless generation, no grit, nothing solid to tell a fact from a spook with. Satanism, pot, drugs, vegetarianism. Pathetic. Everything handed to them on a platter, think life's one big TV, full of ghosts.

Nelson reads his thoughts and accuses: "Well *you* believe all that stuff they say in church and that's really sick. You should have seen it, they were giving out communion today and it was incredible, all these people sort of patting their mouths and looking serious when they come back from the altar rail. It was like something out of anthropology."

"At least," Harry says, "it makes people like your grandmother feel better. Who does this Amityville horror make feel better?"

"It's not sup*posed* to, it's just something that *hap*pened. The people in the house didn't want it to happen either, it just *did*." From the pitch of his voice the kid is feeling more in a corner than Rabbit had intended. He doesn't want to think about the invisible anyway; every time in his life he's made a move toward it somebody has gotten killed.

In silence father and son wind along Cityview Drive, with its glimpses through trees grown too tall of the flowerpot-colored city that German workers built on a grid laid out by an English surveyor and where now the Polacks and spics and blacks sit crammed in listening to each other's television sets jabber through the walls, and each other's babies cry, and each other's Saturday nights turn ugly. Tricky to drive now, all these bicycles and mopeds and worst of all the roller skaters in jogging shorts with earphones on their heads, looking like boxers, all doped up, roller-skating as though they owned the street. The Corona coasts along Locust, where the doctors and lawyers hole up in their long brick single-family dwellings, set back and shady, with retaining walls and plantings of juniper fighting the slope of the ground, and passes on the right Brewer High, that he thought of as a kid as a castle, the multiple gyms and rows of lockers you wouldn't believe, receding to infinity it seemed, the few times he went there, the times the Mt. Judge varsity played the Brewer JV squad, more or less for laughs (theirs). He thinks of telling Nelson about this, but knows the kid hates to have him reminisce about his sporting days. Brewer kids, Rabbit remembers in silence, were mean, with something dirty-looking about their mouths, as if they'd all just sucked raspberry popsicles. The girls fucked and some of the really vicious types smoked things called reefers in those days. Now even Presidents' kids, that Ford son and who knows about Chip, fuck and smoke reefers. Progress. In a way, he sees now, he grew up in a safe pocket of the world, like Melanie said, like one of those places you see in a stream where the twigs float backward and accumulate along the mud.

As they swing down into the steep part of Eisenhower, Nelson breaks the silence and asks, "Didn't you used to live up on one of these cross streets?"

"Yeah. Summer. For a couple of months, ages ago. Your mother and I were having some problems. What makes you ask?"

"I just remembered. Like when you feel you've been someplace before, only it must have been in a dream. When I'd miss you real bad Mom used to put me in the car and we'd drive over here and look at some house hoping you'd come out. It was in a row that all looked alike to me."

"And did I? Come out."

"Not that I can ever remember. But I don't remember much about it, just being there in the car, and Mom having brought some cookies along to keep me entertained, and her starting to cry."

"Jesus, I'm sorry. I never knew about this before, that she drove you over."

"Maybe it just happened once. But it feels like more than once. I remember her being so big."

Eisenhower flattens out and they pass without comment number 1204, where Janice years later had fled to Charlie Stavros, and where Nelson used to come on his bicycle and look up at the window. The kid had been desperate for a mini-bike at the time, and Mim had finally gotten him one, but he hadn't used it much, a sadness had attached to it, it was a piece of junk somewhere now. Funny about feelings, they seem to come and go in a flash yet outlast metal.

Down over the abandoned car yards they go, through the factory outlet district, and left on Third, then right on lower Weiser, past white windowless Schoenbaum Funeral Directors, and then over the bridge. The traffic is mostly composed of old ladies poking back from their restaurant lunch they owed themselves after church and of carloads of kids already beered-up heading for the ballgame in the stadium north of Brewer where the Blasts play. Left on Route 111. D I S C O. Fuel Economy. They have forgotten to turn on the radio, so distracting has the tension between them been. Harry clears his throat and says, "So Melanie's getting set to go back to college. You must be too."

Silence. The subject of college is hot, too hot to touch. He should have been asking the kid what he's been learning at the lot. SPRINGER MOTORS. They pull in. Three weeks since Harry's seen it, and as with the house there's been a pollution. That Caprice he sometimes drove when the Corona was out of action isn't there, must have been sold. Six new Corollas are lined up next to the highway in their sweet and sour colors. Harry can never quite get over how small their wheels look, almost like tricycle wheels compared to the American cars he grew up with. Still, they're the guts of the line: buy cheap, most people are still poor, face it. You don't get something for nothing but hope springs eternal. Like a little sea of melting candy his cars bake in the sun. Since it's Sunday Harry parks right next to the hedge that struggles up front around the entrance and that collects at its roots all the stray wrappers and napkins that blow across 111 from the Chuck Wagon. The display windows need washing again. A paper banner bearing the slogan of the new TV campaign, OH WHAT A FEELING, fills the top half of the lefthand pane. The showroom has two new Celicas, one black with a yellow side stripe and one blue with a white one. Under the OH WHAT A FEELING poster, featuring some laughing cunt in a bathing suit splashing around in some turquoise pool with an Alp or Rocky in the background, lurks something different, a little low roachlike car that is no Toyota. Harry has no key; Nelson lets them in the double glass door with his. The strange car is a TR-6 convertible, polished up for sale but unmistakably worn, the windshield dull with the multiplied scratches of great mileage, the fender showing that slight ripple where metal has been bruised and healed. "What the hell is this?" Harry asks, lifted to a great height by the comparative lowness of this intruding automobile.

"Dad, that's my idea we talked about, to sell convertibles. Honest, hardly anybody makes 'em anymore, even Jaguar has quit, they're bound to go up and up. We're asking fifty-five hundred and already a couple of guys have almost bought it."

"Why'd the owner get rid of it if it was worth so much? What'd you give him on the trade?"

"Well, it wasn't a trade-in exactly —"

"What was it, exactly?"

"We bought it —"

"You *bought* it!"

"A friend of Billy Fosnacht's has this sister who's marrying some guy who's moving to Alaska. It's in great shape, Manny went all over it."

"Manny and Charlie let you go ahead with this?"

"Why wouldn't they? Charlie's been telling me how he and old man Springer used to do all these crazy things, they'd give away stuffed animals and crates of oranges and have these auctions with girls in evening gowns where the highest bid got the car even if it was only five dollars — guys from car rodeos used to come —"

"That was the good old days. These are the bad new days. People come in here looking for Toyotas, they don't want some fucking British sports car —"

"But they will, once we have the name."

"We *have* a name. Springer Motors, Toyota and used. That's what we're known for and that's what people come in here for." He hears his voice straining, feels that good excited roll of anger building in him, like in a basketball game when you're down ten points and less than five minutes left on the clock and you've just taken one too many elbows in the ribs, and all the muscles go loose suddenly and something begins lifting you and you know nothing is impossible, with faith. He tries to hold himself back, this is a fragile kid and his son. Still, this has been his lot. "I don't remember discussing any convertibles with you."

"One night, Dad, we were sitting in the living room just the two of us, only you got sore about the Corona and changed the subject."

"And Charlie really gave you the green light?"

"Sure; he kind of shrugged. With you gone he had the new cars to manage, and this whole shipment came in early —"

"Yeah. I saw. That close to the road they'll pick up all the dust."

"— and anyway Charlie's not my boss. We're equals. I told him Mom-mom had thought it was a good idea."

"Oh. You talked to Ma Springer about this?"

"Well not exactly at the time, she was off with you and Mom, but I know she wants me to plug into the lot, so it'll be three generations and all that stuff."

Harry nods. Bessie will back the kid, they're both black-eyed Springers. "O.K., I guess no harm done. How much you pay for this crate?"

"He wanted forty-nine hundred but I jewed him down to forty-two."

"Jesus. That's way over book. Did you look at the book? Do you know what the book is?"

"Dad of course I know what the fucking book is, the point is convertibles don't go by the book, they're like antiques, there's only so many and there won't be any more. They're what they call collectibles."

"You paid forty-two for a '76 TR that cost six new. How many miles on it?"

"A girl drove it, they don't drive a car hard."

"Depends on the girl. Some of these tootsies I see on the road are really pushing. How many miles did you say?"

"Well, it's kind of hard to say; this guy who went to Alaska was trying to fix something under the dashboard and I guess he didn't know which —"

"Oh boy. O.K., let's see if we can unload it for wholesale and chalk it up to experience. I'll call Hornberger in town tomorrow, he still handles TR and MG, maybe he'll take it off our hands as a favor."

Harry realizes why Nelson's short haircut troubles him: it reminds him of how the boy looked back in grade school, before all that late Sixties business soured everything. He didn't know how short he was going to be then, and wanted to become a baseball pitcher like Jim Bunning, and wore a cap all summer that pressed his hair in even tighter to his skull, that bony freckled unsmiling face. Now his necktie and suit seem like that baseball cap to be the costume of doomed hopes. Nelson's eyes brighten as if at the approach of tears. "Take if off our hands for cost? Dad, I *know* we can sell it, and clear a thousand. And there's two more."

"Two more TRs?"

"Two more convertibles, out back." By now the kid is scared, white in the face so his eyelids and eartips look pink. Rabbit is scared too, he doesn't want any more of this, but things are rolling, the kid has to show him, and he has to react. They walk back along the corridor past the parts department, Nelson leading the way and picking a set of car keys off the pegboard fastened next to the metal doorframe, and then they let themselves into the great hollow space of the garage, so silent on Sunday, a bare-girdered ballroom with its good warm stink of grease and acetylene. Nelson switches off the burglar alarm and pushes against the crash bar of the back door. Air again. Brewer far across the river, the tip of the tall courthouse with its eagle in concrete relief peeking above the forest of weeds, thistle and poke, at the lot's unvisited edge. This back area is bigger than it should be and always makes Rabbit think somehow of Paraguay. Making a little island of their own on the asphalt, two extinct American convertibles sit: a '72 Mercury Cougar, its top a tattered cream and its body that intense pale scum-color they called Nile Green, and a '74 Olds Delta 88 Royale, in color the purply-red women wore as nail polish in the days of spy movies. They were gallant old boats, Harry has to admit to himself, all that stretched tin and aerodynamical razzmatazz, headed down Main Street straight for a harvest moon with the old accelerator floored. He says, "These are here on spec, or what? I mean, you haven't paid for them yet." He senses that even this is the wrong thing to say.

"They're bought, Dad. They're ours."

"They're mine?"

"They're not yours, they're the *com*pany's."

"How the hell'd you work it?"

"What do you mean, how the hell? I just asked Mildred Kroust to write the checks and Charlie told her it was O.K."

"Charlie said it was O.K.?"

"He thought we'd all *agreed*. Dad, cut it out. It's not such a big deal. That's the idea here, isn't it – buy cars and sell 'em at a profit?"

"Not those crazy cars. How much were they?"

"I bet we make six, seven hundred on the Merc and more on the Olds. Dad, you're too uptight. It's only money. Was I supposed to have any responsibility while you were away, or not?"

"How much?"

"I forget exactly. The Cougar was about two thousand and the Royale, some dealer toward Pottsville that Billy knows had it but

I thought we should be able to offer, you know, a selection, it came to I think around two-five."

"Two thousand five hundred dollars."

Just repeating the numbers slowly makes him feel good, in a bad kind of way. Any debt he ever owed Nelson is being paid back now. He goes at it again. "Two thousand five hundred good American —"

The child almost screams. "We'll get it back, I promise! It's like antiques, it's like gold! You can't lose, Dad."

Harry can't stop adding. "Forty-two hundred for the little chop-clock TR, four thousand five hundred —"

The boy is begging. "Leave me alone, I'll do it myself. I've already put an ad in the paper, they'll be gone in two weeks. I promise."

"You promise. You'll be back in college in two weeks."

"Dad. I won't."

"You won't?"

"I want to quit Kent and stay here and work." This little face all frightened and fierce, so pale his freckles seem to be coming forward and floating on the surface, like flecks in a mirror.

"Jesus, that is all I need," Harry sighs.

Nelson looks at him shocked. He holds up the car keys. His eyes blur, his lower lip is unsteady. "I was going to let you drive the Royale for fun."

Harry says, "Fun. You know how much gas these old hot rods burn? You think people today with gas a dollar a gallon are going to want these eight-cylinder inefficient guzzlers just to feel the wind in their hair? Kid, you're living in a dream world."

"They don't *care*, Dad. People don't *care* that much about money anymore, it's all shit anyway. Money is shit."

"Maybe to you but not to me I'll tell you that now. Let's keep calm. Think of the parts. These things sure as hell need some work, the years they've been around. You know what six-, seven-year-old parts cost these days, when you can get 'em at all? This isn't some fancy place dealing in antiques, we sell Toyotas. To*yo*tas."

The child shrinks beneath his thunder. "Dad, I won't buy any more, I promise, until these sell. These'll sell, I promise."

"You'll promise me nothing. You'll promise me to keep your nose out of my car business and get your ass back to Ohio. I hate to be the one telling you this, Nelson, but you're a disaster. You've gotta get yourself straightened out and it isn't going to happen here."

He hates what he's saying to the kid, though it's what he feels. He hates it so much he turns his back and tries to get back into the door they came out of but it has locked behind them, as it's supposed to do. He's locked out of his own garage and Nelson has the keys. Rabbit rattles the knob and thumps the metal door with the heel of his hand and even as in a blind scrimmage knees it; the pain balloons and coats the world in red so that though he hears a car motor start up not far away he doesn't connect it to himself until a squeak of rubber and a roar of speed slam metal into metal. That black gnashing cuts through the red. Rabbit turns around and sees Nelson backing off for a second go. Small parts are still settling, tinkling in the sunshine. He thinks the boy might now aim to crush him against the door where he is paralyzed but that is not the case. The Royale rams again into the side of the Mercury, which lifts up on two wheels. The pale green fender collapses enough to explode the headlight; the lens rim flies free.

Seeing the collision coming, Harry expected it to happen in slow motion, like on television, but instead it happened comically fast, like two dogs tangling and then thinking better of it. The Royale's motor dies. Through the windshield's granular fracture Nelson's face looks distorted, twisted by tears, twisted small. Rabbit feels a wooden sort of choked hilarity rising within him as he contemplates the damage. Pieces of glass finer than pebbles, bright grit, on the asphalt. Shadows on the broad skins of metal where shadows were not designed to be. The boy's short haircut looking like a round brush as he bends his face to the wheel sobbing. The whisper of Sunday traffic continuing from the other side of the building. These strange awkward blobs of joy bobbing in Harry's chest. Oh what a feeling.

*   *   *

Within a week, at the club, it has become a story he tells on himself. "Five thousand bucks' worth of metal, *crunch*. I had this terrible impulse to laugh, but the kid was in there crying, they were *his* cars after all, the way he saw it. The only thing I could think of to do was go stand by the Olds with my arms out like *this*." He spreads his arms wide, under the benign curve of the mountain. "If the kid'd come out swinging my gut would've been wide open. But sure enough he stumbles out all blubbery and I take him into my arms." He demonstrates the folding, consoling motion. "I haven't felt so close to Nelson since he was about two. What makes me really feel rotten, he was right. His ad for the convertibles ran that same Sunday and we must have had twenty calls. The TR was gone by Wednesday, for fifty-five Cs. People aren't counting their pennies anymore, they're throwin' 'em out the window."

"Like the Arabs," Webb Murkett says.

"Jesus, those Arabs," Buddy Inglefinger says. "Wouldn't it be bliss just to nuke 'em all?"

"Did you see what gold did last week?" Webb smiles. "That's the Arabs dumping their dollars in Europe. They smell a rat."

Buddy asks, "D'you see in today's paper where some investigation out of Washington showed that absolutely the government rigged the whole gas shortage last June?"

"We knew it at the time, didn't we?" Webb asks back, the red hairs that arc out of his eyebrows glinting.

Today is the Sunday before Labor Day, the day of the members-only fourball. Their foursome has a late starting time and they are having a drink by the pool waiting, with their wives. With some of their wives: Buddy Inglefinger has no wife, just that same dumb pimply Joanne he's been dragging around all summer, and Janice this morning said she'd go with her mother to church and show up at the club around drink time, for the after-the-fourball banquet. This is strange. Janice loves the Flying Eagle even more than he does. But ever since Melanie left the house this last Wednesday something is cooking. Charlie has taken two weeks off now that Harry is back from the Poconos, and with Nelson being persona non grata around the lot the Chief Sales Representative has his hands full. There is always a little uptick at the end of summer, what with the fall models being advertised and raised prices already in the wind and the standing inventory beginning to look like a bargain, what with inflation worse and worse. There always comes in September a parched brightness to the air that hits Rabbit two ways, smelling of apples and blackboard dust and marking the return to school and work in earnest, but then again reminding him he's suffered another promotion, taken another step up the stairs that has darkness at the head.

Cindy Murkett hoists herself out of the pool. Dry sun catches in every drop beaded on her brown shoulders, so tan the skin bears a flicker of iridescence. Her boyishly cut hair is plastered in a fringe of accidental feathers halfway down the back of her skull. Standing on the flagstones, she tilts her head to twist water from this hair. Hair high inside her thigh merges with the black triangle of her string bikini. Walking over to their group, Cindy leaves plump wet footprints, heel and sole pad and tiny round toes. Little circular darkdab sucky toes.

"You think gold is still a good thing to buy?" Harry asks Webb, but the man has turned his narrow creased face to gaze up at his young wife. The fat eaves of her body drip onto his lap, the checks of his golf pants, darkening their lime green by drops. From the length of those eyebrow hairs of Webb's that curve out it's a wonder some don't stab him in the eye. He hugs her hips sideways; the Murketts look framed as for an ad against the green sweep of Mt. Pemaquid. Behind them a diver knifes supply into the chlorine. Harry's eyes sting.

Thelma Harrison has been listening to his story, its sad undertone. "Nelson must have been desolated by what he'd done," she says.

He likes the word "desolated," so old-fashioned, coming from this mousy sallow woman who somehow keeps the lid on that jerk Harrison. "Not so's you'd notice," he says. "We had that moment right after it happened, but he's been mean as hell to everybody since, especially since I made the mistake of telling him his ad had produced some results. He wants to keep coming to the lot but I told him to stay the hell away. You know what he did borders on crazy."

Thelma offers, "Maybe there's more on his mind than he can

tell you." The sun must be right behind his head from the way she shields her eyes to look up at him, even though she has on her sunglasses, big rounded brown ones that darken at the top like windshields. They hide the top half of her face so her lips seem to move with a strange precise independence; though thin, they have a dozen little curves that might fit sweetly around Harrison's thick prick, if you try to think what her hold on him might be, though this is hard to imagine. She's such a schoolteacher with her little pleated skirt and studied way of holding herself and pronouncing words. For all of her lotions her nose is pink and the pinkness spreads into the area below her eyes, that her sunglasses all but hide.

In his floating wifeless state beside the pool, near the bottom of his g-and-t with its wilted sprig of mint, waiting for his fourball to start, he finds Thelma's solemn staring mottled look a bit befuddling. "Yeah," he says, eyes on the sprig. "Janice keeps suggesting that. But she won't tell me what it might be."

"Maybe she can't," Thelma says, pressing her legs together tighter and tugging the skirt of her bathing suit down over an inch of thigh. She has these little purple veins women her age get but Harry can't see why she'd be self-conscious with an old pot-bellied pal like him.

He tells her, "He doesn't seem to want to go back to college so maybe he's flunked out and never told us. But wouldn't we have gotten a letter from the dean or something? These letters from Colorado, boy, we see plenty of them."

"You know Harry," Thelma tells him, "a lot of fathers Ronnie and I know complain how the boys don't *want* to come into the family business. They have these businesses and no one to carry them on. It's a tragedy. You should be glad Nelson does care about cars."

"All he cares about is smashing 'em up," Harry says. "It's his revenge." He lowers his voice to confide, "I think one of the troubles between me and the kid is every time I had a little, you know, slip-up, he was there to see it. That's one of the reasons I don't like to have him around. The little twerp knows it, too."

Ronnie Harrison, trying to put some kind of a move on poor old Joanne, looks up and shouts across to his wife, "What's the old hotshot trying to sell ya, hon? Don't let him do a number on ya."

Thelma ignores her husband with a dim smile and tells Harry matter-of-factly, "I think that's more in you than in Nelson. I'm wondering, could he be having girl trouble? Nelson."

Harry is wondering if another g-and-t might erase a little headache that's beginning. Drinking in the middle of the day always does that to him. "Well I can't see how. These kids, they just drift in and out of each other's beds like a bunch of gerbils. This girl he brought with him, Melanie, they didn't seem to have any contact really, in fact were getting pretty short with each other toward the end. She took some kind of a crazy shine to Charlie Stavros, of all people."

"Why 'of all people'?" Her smile is less dim, its thin curves declare that she knows Charlie had been Janice's lover, in the time before this club existed.

"Well he's old enough to be her father for one thing and he has one foot in the grave for another. He had rheumatic fever as a kid and it left him with a bum ticker. You ought to see him toddle around the lot now, it's pathetic."

"Having an ailment doesn't mean you want to give up living," she says. "You know I have what they call lupus; that's why I try to protect myself against the sun and can't get nice and tan like Cindy."

"Oh. Really?" Why is she telling him this?

Thelma from a wryness in her smile sees that she's presumed. "Some men with heart murmurs live forever," she says. "And now the girl and Charlie are out of the county together."

This is a new thought also. "Yeah, but in totally different directions. Charlie goes to Florida and Melanie's visiting her family on the West Coast." But he remembers Charlie talking up Florida to her at the dinner table and he finds the possibility that they are together depressing. You can't trust anybody not to fuck. He turns his head to let the sun strike the skin of his face; his eyes close, the lids glowing red. He should be practicing chipping for the fourball instead of lying here drowning in these voices. He heard on the radio driving over that a hurricane is approaching Florida.

Ronnie Harrison's voice, close at hand, shouts, "What's that hon, you say I'm going to live forever? You bet your sweet bippy I am!"

Rabbit opens his eyes and sees that Ronnie has changed the position of his chair to make room for Cindy Murkett, who is at home enough now among them all not to fuss covering her lap with the towel the way she did earlier in the summer; she just sits there on the wire grid of her poolside chair naked but for a few black strings and the little triangles they hold in place, letting her boobs wobble the way they will as she pushes back the wet hair from her ears and temples, not once but several times, self-conscious at that. In her happiness with Webb she is letting her weight slip up, there is almost too much baby fat; when she stands, Harry knows, the pattern of the chair bottom will be printed in the backs of her thighs like a waffle iron releasing two warm slabs of dark dough. Still, that wobble: to lick and suck and let them fall first one and then the other into your eyesockets. He closes his eyes. Ronnie Harrison is trying to entrance Joanne and Cindy simultaneously with a story that involves a lot of deep-pitched growling as the hero-self talks back to the villain-other. What a conceited shit.

Webb Murkett leans forward to tell Harry, "In answer to your question, yes, I think gold is an excellent buy. It's up over sixty per cent in less than a year and I see no reason for it not to appreciate at the same rate as long as the world energy situation holds. The dollar is bound to keep leaking, Harry, until they figure out how to get gasoline cheap out of grain alcohol, which'll put us back in the driver's seat. Grain we've got."

From the other side of the group, Buddy Inglefinger calls over, "Nuke 'em, I say; let's take their oil from the Arabs the same way we took it from the Eskimos." Joanne gives this an obligatory giggle, Ronnie's story having been overridden for a minute. Buddy sees Harry as his straight man and calls, "Hey Harry, did you see in *Time* where people stuck with their big old American cars are giving 'em to charity and taking a deduction or leaving 'em on the street to be stolen so they can collect the insurance? It said some dealer somewhere is giving you a free Chevette if you buy a Cadillac Eldorado."

"We don't get *Time*," Harry tells him coolly. Looked at a certain way, the world is full of twerps. Oh but to close your eyes and just flicker out with your tongue for Cindy's nipples as she swung them back and forth, back and forth, teasing.

Joanne tries to join in: "Meanwhile the President is floating down the Mississippi."

"What else can the poor schmuck do?" Harry asks her, himself feeling floating and lazy and depressed.

"Hey Rabbit," Harrison calls, "whaddidya think when he was attacked by that killer rabbit?"

This gets enough of a laugh so they stop teasing him. Thelma speaks softly at his side. "Children are hard. Ron and I have been lucky with Alex, once we gave him an old television set he could take apart he's known what he's wanted to do, electronics. But now our other boy Georgie sounds a lot like your Nelson, though he's a few years younger. He thinks what his father does is gruesome, betting against people that they're going to die, and Ron can't make him understand how life insurance is really such a small part of the whole business."

"They're disillusioned," Webb Murkett asserts in that wise voice of tumbling gravel. "They've seen the world go crazy since they were age two, from JFK's assassination right through Vietnam to the oil mess now. And here the other day for no good reason they blow up this old gent Mountbatten."

"Huh," Rabbit grunts, doubting. According to Skeeter the world was never a pleasant place.

Thelma intervenes, saying, "Harry was saying about how Nelson wants to come into the car business with him, and his negative feelings about it."

"Be the very worst thing you could do for him," Webb says. "I've had five kids, not counting the two tykes Cindy has given me, bless her for it, and when any of them mentioned the roofing business to me I'd say, 'Go get a job with another roofer, you'll never learn a thing staying with me.' I couldn't give 'em an order, and if I did they wouldn't obey it anyway. When those kids turned twenty-one, boy or girl, I told each one of them, 'It's been nice knowing you, but you're on your own now.' And not one has ever sent me a letter asking for money, or advice, or anything. I get a Christmas card at Christmastime if I'm lucky. One once said to me, Marty the oldest, he said, 'Dad, thanks for being such a bastard. It's made me fit for life.'"

Harry contemplates his empty glass. "Webb, whaddeya think? Should I have another drink or not? It's fourball, you can carry the team."

"Don't do it, Harry, we need you. You're the long knocker. Stay sober."

He obeys, but can't shake his depression, thinking of Nelson. Thanks for being such a bastard. He misses Janice. With her around, his paternity is diluted, something the two of them did together, conniving, half by accident, and can laugh together about. When he contemplates it by himself, bringing a person into the world seems as terrible as pushing somebody into a furnace. By the time they finally get out onto the golf course, green seems a shade of black. Every blade of grass at his feet is an individual life that will die, that has flourished to no purpose. The fairway springy beneath his feet blankets the dead, is the roof of a kingdom where his mother stands at a cloudy sink, her hands red and wearing sleeves of soap bubbles when she lifts them out to give him some sort of warning. Between her thumb and knobby forefinger, the hands not yet badly warped by Parkinson's, a bubble pops. Mountbatten. And this same week their old mailman has died, Mr. Abendroth, a cheerful overweight man with his white hair cut in a whiffle, dead of a thrombosis at sixty-two. Ma Springer had heard about it from the neighbors, he'd been bringing the neighborhood their bills and magazines ever since Harry and Janice had moved in; it had been Mr. Abendroth who had delivered last April that anonymous envelope containing the news that Skeeter was dead. As he held that clipping that day the letters of type like these blades of grass drew Harry's eyes down, down into a blackness between them, as the ribs of a grate reveal the unseen black river rushing in the sewer. The earth is hollow, the dead roam through caverns beneath its thin green skin. A cloud covers the sun, giving the grass a silver sheen. Harry takes out a seven-iron and stands above his ball. Hit *down*. One of the weaknesses of Harry's game is he cannot make himself take a divot, he tries with misapplied tenderness to skim it off the turf, and hits it thin. This time he hits the ball fat, into a sand bunker this side of the tenth green. Must have rocked forward onto his toes, another fault. His practice swing is always smooth and long but when the pressure is on anxiety and hurry enter in. "You dummy," Ronnie Harrison shouts over at him. "What'd you do that for?"

"To annoy you, you creep," Rabbit tells him. In a fourball one of the foursome must do well on every hole or the aggregate suffers. Harry here had the longest drive. Now look at him. He wriggles his feet to root himself in the sand, keeping his weight back on his heels, and makes himself swing through with the wedge, pick it up and swing it *through*, blind faith, usually he picks it clean in his timidity and flies it over the green but in this instance with his fury at Ronnie and his glum indifference it all works out: the ball floats up on its cushioning spray of sand, bites, and crawls so close to the pin the three others of his foursome cackle and cheer. He sinks the putt to save his par. Still, the game seems long today, maybe it's the gin at noon or the end-of-summer doldrums, but he can't stop seeing the fairways as chutes to nowhere or feeling he should be somewhere else, that something has happened, *is* happening, that he's late, that an appointment has been made for him that he's forgotten. He wonders if Skeeter had this feeling in the pit of his stomach that moment when he decided to pull his gun out and get blasted, if he had that feeling when he woke on the morning of that day. Tired flowers, goldenrod and wild carrot, hang in the rough. The millions of grass blades shine, ready to die. This is what it all comes to, a piece of paper that itself turns yellow, a news item you cut out and mail to another with no note. File to forget. History carves these caverns with a steady drip-drip. Dead Skeeter roams below, cackling. Time seeps up through the blades of grass like a colorless poison. He is tired, Harry, of summer, of golf, of the sun. When he was younger and just taking up the game twenty years ago and even when he took it up again eight years or so ago there were shots that seemed a miracle, straight as an edge of glass and longer than any power purely his could have produced, and it was for the sake of collaboration with this power that he kept playing, but as he improved and his handicap dwindled from sky's-the-limit to a sane sixteen, these super shots became rarer, even the best of his drives had a little tail or were struck with a little scuff, and a shade off line one way or another, and the whole thing became more like work, pleasant work but work, a matter of approximations in the realm of the imperfect, with nothing breaking through but normal healthy happiness. In pursuit of such happiness Harry feels guilty, out on the course as the shadows lengthen, in the company of these three men, who away from their women loom as as boring as they must appear to God.

Janice is not waiting for him in the lounge or beside the pool when at last around 5:45 they come in from playing the par-5 eighteenth. Instead one of the girls in their green and white uniforms comes over and tells him that his wife wants him to call home. He doesn't recognize this girl, she isn't Sandra, but she knows his name. Everybody knows Harry at the Flying Eagle. He goes into the lounge, his hand lifted in continuous salute to the members there, and puts the same dime he's been using as a ball marker on the greens into the pay phone and dials. Janice answers after a single ring.

"Hey come on over," he begs. "We miss you. I played pretty good, the second nine, once I worked a g-and-t out of my system. With our handicap strokes Webb figures our best ball to be a sixty-one, which ought to be good for an alligator shirt at least. You should have seen my sand shot on the third."

"I'd like to come over," Janice says, her voice sounding so careful and far away the idea crosses his mind she's being held for ransom and so must be careful what she says, "but I can't. There's somebody here."

"Who?"

"Somebody you haven't met yet."

"Important?"

She laughs. "I believe so."

"Why are you being so fucking mysterious?"

"Harry, just come."

"But there's going to be the banquet, and the prizes. I can't desert my foursome."

"If you won any prize Webb can give it to you later. I can't keep talking forever."

"This better be good," he warns her, hanging up. What can it be? Another accident for Nelson, the police have come for him. The kid has a criminal slouch. Harry goes back to the pool and tells the others, "Crazy Janice says I have to come home but she won't say why."

The women's faces show concern but the men are on their second round of drinks now and feeling no pain. "Hey Harry," Buddy Inglefinger shouts. "Before you go, here's one you might not have heard up in the Poconos. Why did the Russian ballet dancer defect to the U.S.A.?"

"I don't know, why?"

"Because Communism wasn't Goodunov."

The obliging laughter of the three women, as they all gaze upward in the reddening slant sun toward Harry's face, is like some fruit, three different ripenesses on the same branch, still hanging there when he turns his back. Cindy has put on over her bare shoulders a peach-colored silken shirt and in the V of its throat her little gold cross twinkles; he hadn't noticed it when she was nearly naked. He changes out of his golf shoes in the locker room and instead of showering just takes the hanger holding the sports coat and slacks he was going to put on for the banquet out to the parking lot on his arm. The Corona still doesn't feel right. He hears on the radio the Phillies have eked out a victory in Atlanta, 2–1. The gang never mentions the Phillies anymore, they're in fifth place, out of it. Get out of it in this society and you're as good as dead, an embarrassment. Not Goodunov. Keep Our City Clean. The radio announcer is not that wiseass woman but a young man with a voice like bubbles of fat in water, every syllable. Hurricane David has already left six hundred dead in the Caribbean region, he says, and, finally, life may exist, some scientists are coming to believe, on Titan, Saturn's largest moon. Harry passes the old box factory and enjoys yet once again the long view of the town of Mt. Judge you get coming in the Route 422 way. The row houses ascending the slope of the mountain like stairs, their windows golden with setting sun like holes in a Hallowe'en pumpkin. Suppose he had been born on Titan instead, how different would he feel down deep? He thinks of those cindery lunar surfaces, the chunky men in their white suits hopping, the footprints they left in the dust there forever. He remembers how when they'd come visiting the Springers or after the fire the first years they lived here he and Nelson used to watch *Lost in Space* together on the gray sofa, how they'd squirm and groan when Doctor Smith did some dumb imperilling egotistical thing, and only that manly-voiced robot and the little boy Will with enough sense to pull the thing off, the spaceship fighting free of man-eating plants or whatever the week's villains were. He wonders now if Nelson saw himself as Will, saving the grownups from themselves, and he wonders where the boy actor is now, what he is, Rabbit hopes not a junkie the way so many of these child stars seem to end up. That was good solid space they were lost in, not this soupy psychedelic space they have on TV now, all tricks with music and lights, tricks he associates with the movie *2001*, an unpleasant association since that was the time Janice ran off with Charlie and all hell broke loose on the home front. The problem is, even if there is a Heaven how can there be one we can stand forever? On Earth, when you look up from being bored, things have changed, you're that much closer to the grave, and that's exciting. Imagine climbing up and up into that great tree of night sky. Dizzying. Terrible. Rabbit didn't even like to get too high into these little Norway maples around town, though with the other kids as witnesses he pushed himself up, gripping tighter and tighter as the branches got smaller. From a certain angle the most terrifying thing in the world is your own life, the fact that it's yours and nobody else's. A loop is rising in his chest as in a rope when you keep twisting. Whatever can have happened bad enough to make Janice miss the fourball banquet?

He accelerates along Jackson as the streetlights come on, earlier each day now. Janice's Mustang is out along the curb with the top down, she must have gone somewhere after church, she wouldn't take Bessie to church with the top down. Inside the front door, a wealth of duffel bags and suitcases has been deposited in the living room as by a small army. In the kitchen there is laughter and light. The party comes to meet him halfway, in the shadowy no-man's land between the staircase and the breakfront. Ma Springer and Janice are overtopped by a new female, taller, with a smoothly parted head of hair from which the kitchen light

RABBIT ANGSTROM

strikes an arc of carrot color, where Melanie's hair would have caught in its curls a straggly halo. He had grown used to Melanie. It is Nelson who speaks. "Dad, this here is Pru," the "this here" a little scared joke.

"Nelson's fiancée," Janice amplifies in a voice tense but plump, firmly making the best of it.

"Is that a fact?" Harry hears himself ask. The young woman saunters forward, a slender slouching shape, and he takes the bony hand she extends. In the lingering daylight that the dining-room windows admit she stands plain, a young redhead past girlhood, with arms too long and hips too wide for the boniness of her face, an awkward beauty, her body helplessly not only hers but somehow theirs, overcommitted, with a look about her of wry, slightly twisted resignation, of having been battered by life young as she is, but the battering having not yet reached her eyes, which are clear green, though guarded. As she entrusts her hand to his her smile is a fraction slow, as if inside she must make certain there is something to smile at, but then comes forth eagerly enough, with a crimp in one corner. She wears a baggy brown sweater and the new looser style of jeans, bleach spattered across the thighs. Her hair, swept back behind her ears to form a single fanning sheaf down her back, looks ironed, it is so straight, and dyed, it is so vivid a pallid red.

"I wouldn't say fiancée exactly," Pru says, directly to Harry. "There's no ring, look." She holds up a naked trembling hand.

Harry in his need to get a fix on this new creature glances from Nelson right through Janice, whom he can grill later in bed, to Ma Springer. Her mouth is clamped shut; if you tapped her she'd ring like a gong, rigid in her purple church dress. Nelson's mouth is ajar. He is a sick man fascinated by the ministration of doctors around him, his illness at last confessed and laid open to cure. In Pru's presence he looks years younger than when Melanie was about, a nervous toughness melted all away. It occurs to Harry that this girl is older than the boy, and another, deeper, instinctive revelation pounds in upon him even as he hears himself saying, as humorous paternal host, "Well in any case it's nice to meet you, Pru. Any friend of Nelson's, we put up with around here." This maybe falls flat, so he adds, "I bet you're the girl's been sending all those letters."

Her eyes glance down, the demure plane of her cheek reddened as if he's slapped her. "Too many I suppose," she says.

"No bother to me," he assures her, "I'm not the mailman. He recently upped and died, by the way. Not your fault, though."

She lifts her eyes, a flourishing green.

Pru is pregnant. One of the few advantages of not having been born yesterday is that a man acquires, like a notion of tomorrow's weather from the taste of the evening air, some sense of the opposite sex's physiology, its climate. She has less waist than a woman so young should, and that uncanny green clarity of her eyes and a soft slowed something in her motions as she turns away from Harry's joke to take a cue from Nelson bespeak a burden beyond disturbing, a swell beneath the waves. In her third or fourth month, Rabbit guesses. And with this guess a backwards roll of light illumines the months past. And the walls of this house, papered with patterns sunk into them like stains, change meaning, containing this seed between them. The fuzzy gray sofa and the chair that matches and the Barcalounger and the TV set (an Admiral) and Ma Springer's pompous lamps of painted porcelain and tarnished brass and the old framed watercolors sunk to the tint of dust from never being looked at, the table runners Ma once crocheted and her collection of brittle bright knickknacks stored on treble corner shelves nicked and sanded to suggest antique wood but stemming from an era of basement carpentry in Fred Springer's long married life: all these souvenirs of the dead bristle with new point, with fresh mission, if as Harry imagines this intruder's secret is a child to come.

He feels swollen. His guess has been like a fist into him. As was not the case with Melanie he feels kinship with this girl, is touched by her, turned on: *he* wants to be giving her this baby.

In bed he asks Janice, "How long have you known?"

"Oh," she says, "about a month. Melanie let some of the cat out of the bag and then I confronted Nelson with it. He was relieved to talk, he cried even. He just didn't want *you* to know."

"Why not?" He is hurt. He is the boy's father.

Janice hesitates. "I don't know, I guess he was afraid you'd be mad. Or laugh at him."

"Why would I laugh at him? The same thing happened to me."

"He doesn't know that, Harry."

"How could he not? His birthday keeps coming around seven months after our anniversary."

"Well, yes." In her impatience she sounds much like her mother, setting the heel of her voice into each word. The bed creaks as she flounces in emphasis. "Children don't *want* to know these things, and by the time they're old enough to care it's all so long ago."

"When did he knock the girl up, does he remember that much?"

"Weren't you funny, guessing so quickly she was in a family way? We weren't going to tell you for a while."

"Thanks. It was the first thing that hit me. That baggy sweater. That, and that she's taller than Nelson."

"Harry, she isn't. He's an inch taller, he's told me himself, it's just that his posture is so poor."

"And how much older is she? You can see she's older."

"Well, a year or less. She was a secretary in the Registrar's office –"

"Yeah and why wasn't he fucking another student? What does he have to get mixed up in the secretarial pool for?"

"Harry, you should talk to *them* if you want to know every in and out of it all. You know though how he used to say how phony these college girls were, he never felt comfortable in that atmosphere. He's from business people on my side and working people on yours and there hasn't been much college in his background."

"Or in his future from the way it looks."

"It's not such a bad thing the girl can do a job. You heard her say at supper she'd like him to go back to Kent and finish, and she could take in typing in their apartment."

"Yeah and I heard the little snot say he wanted no part of it."

"You won't get him to go back by shouting at him."

"I didn't shout."

"You got a look on your face."

"Well, Jesus. Because the kid gets a girl pregnant he thinks he's entitled to run Springer Motors."

"Harry, he doesn't want to run it, he just wants a place in it."

"You can't give him a place without taking a place from some-body else."

"Mother and I think he should have a place," Janice says, so definitely it seems her mother has spoken, out of the dark air of this bedroom where the old lady's presence was always felt as a rumble of television or a series of snores coming through the wall.

He reverts to his question, "When did he get her pregnant?"

"Oh, when these things happen, in the spring. She missed her first period in May, but they waited till they got to Colorado to do the urine test. It was positive and Pru told him she wasn't going to get an abortion, she didn't believe in them and too many of her friends had had their insides messed up."

"In this day and age, she said all that."

"Also I believe there's Catholicism in her background, on her mother's side."

"Still, she looks like she has some common sense."

"Maybe it was common sense talking. If she goes ahead and has the baby then Nelson has to do something."

"Poor little devil. How come she got pregnant in the first place? Don't they all have the Pill, and loops, and God knows what else now? I was reading in *Consumer Reports* about these tempo-rary polyurethane tube ties."

"Some of these new things are getting a bad name in the papers. They give you cancer."

"Not at her age they wouldn't. So then she sat out there in the Rocky Mountains hatching this thing while Melanie kept him on a short leash around here."

Janice is growing sleepy, whereas Harry fears he will be awake forever, with this big redhead out of the blue across the hall. Ma Springer had made it clear she expected Pru to sleep in Melanie's old room and had stomped upstairs to watch *The Jeffersons*. The old crow had just sat there pretty silent all evening, looking like a boiler with too much pressure inside. She plays her cards tight. Harry nudges Janice's sleepy soft side to get her talking again.

She says, "Melanie said Nelson became very hard to manage, once the test came back positive – running around with a bad crowd out there, making Pru take up hang gliding. Then when he saw she wouldn't change her mind all he wanted to do was run back here. They couldn't talk him out of it, he went and quit this good job he had with a man building condominiums. Melanie I guess had some reasons of her own to get away so she invited herself along. Nelson didn't want her to but I guess the alternative was Pru letting her parents and us know what the situation was and instead of that he begged for time, trying to get some kind of nest ready for her here and maybe still hoping it would all go away, I don't know."

"Poor little Nelson," Harry says. Sorrow for the child bleeds upward to the ceiling with its blotches of streetlight shuffling through the beech. "This has been Hell for him."

"Well Melanie's theory was not Hell enough; she didn't like the way he kept going out with Billy Fosnacht and his crowd instead of facing us with the facts and telling us why he really wanted to go to work at the lot."

Harry sighs. "So when's the wedding?"

"As soon as it can be arranged. I mean, it's her fifth month. Even you spotted it."

Even you, he resents this, but doesn't want to tell Janice of the instinctive bond he has with this girl. Pru is like his mother, awkward and bony, with big hands, but less plain.

"One of the reasons I took Mother to church this morning was so we could have a word with Reverend Campbell."

"That fag? Lordy-O."

"Harry you know nothing about him. He's been uncommonly sweet to Mother and he's really done a lot for the parish."

"The little boys' choir especially, I bet."

"You are so un-open. Mother with all her limitations is more open than you." She turns her face away and says into her pillow, "Harry, I'm very tired. All this upsets me too. Was there anything else you wanted to ask?"

He asks, "Does he love the girl, do you think?"

"You've seen her. She's striking."

"I can see that, but can Nelson? You know they say history repeats but it never does, exactly. When we got married everybody was doing it but now when these kids hang back and just live together it must be a bigger deal. I mean, marriage must be more frightening."

Janice turns her head back again and offers, "I think it's good, that she's a little older."

"Why?"

"Well, Nelson needs steadying."

"A girl who gets herself knocked up and then pulls this right-to-life act isn't my idea of steady. What kind of parents does she come from anyway?"

"They're just average people in Ohio. I think the father works as a steamfitter."

"A-*ha*," he says. "Blue collar. She's not marrying Nelson, she's marrying Springer Motors."

"Just like you did," Janice says.

He should resent this but he likes it, her new sense of herself as a prize. He lays his hand in that soft place where her waist dips. "Listen," he says, "when I married you you were selling salted nuts at Kroll's and my parents thought your dad was a shifty character who was going to wind up in jail."

But he didn't, he wound up in Heaven. Fred Springer made that long climb into the tree of the stars. Lost in space. Now Janice is following, his touch tipping her into sleep just as he feels below his waist a pulsing that might signal a successful erection. Nothing like the thought of fucking money. He doesn't fuck her enough, his poor dumb moneybags. She has fallen asleep naked. When they were newly married and for years thereafter she wore cotton nighties that made her look like that old-fashioned Time to Retire ad, but sometime in the Seventies she began to come to bed in just her skin, her little still-tidy snake-smooth body brown wherever the tennis dress didn't cover, with a fainter brown belly where that Op-pattern two-piece bathing suit exposed her middle. How quickly Cindy's footprints dried on the flagstones behind her today! The strange thing is he can never exactly picture fucking her, it is like looking into the sun. He turns on his back, frustrated yet relieved to be alone in the quiet night where his mind can revolve all that is new. In middle age you are carrying the world in a sense and yet it seems out of control more than ever, the self that you had as a boy all scattered and distributed like those pieces of bread in the miracle. He had been struck in Kruppenbach's Sunday School by the verse that tells of the

clean-up, twelve baskets full of the fragments. Keep Your City
Clean. He listens for the sound of footsteps slithering out of
Melanie's – no, Pru's – room, she'd come a long way today and
had met a lot of new faces, what a hard thing for her this evening
must have been. While Ma and Janice had scraped together supper, another miracle of sorts, the girl had sat there in the bamboo
basket chair brought in from the porch and they all eased around
her like cars easing past an accident on the highway. Harry could
hardly take his eyes from this grown woman sitting there so
demure and alien and perceptibly misshapen. She breathed that air
he'd forgotten, of high-school loveliness, come uninvited to
bloom in the shadow of railroad overpasses, alongside telephone
poles, within earshot of highways with battered aluminum center
strips, out of mothers gone to lard and fathers ground down by
gray days of work and more work, in an America littered with bot-
tlecaps and pull-tabs and pieces of broken muffler. Rabbit remembered such beauty, seeing it caught here in Pru, in her long downy
arms and skinny bangled wrists and the shining casual fall of her
hair, caught as a stick snags the flow of a stream with a dimpled
swirl. Janice sighs in her sleep. A car swishes by, the radio trailing
disco through the open window. Labor Day Eve, the end of
something. He feels the house swell beneath him, invading presences crowding the downstairs, the dead awakened. Skeeter, Pop,
Mom, Mr. Abendroth. The photograph of Fred Springer fading
on the sideboard fills with the flush of hectic color Fred carried on
his cheeks and where the bridge of his nose pressed. Harry buries
his mind in the girls of Mt. Judge High as they were in the Forties,
the fuzzy sweaters and dimestore pearls, the white blouses that let
the beige shadow of the bra show through, the skirts, always skirts,
long as gowns when the New Look was new, swinging in the
locker-lined halls, and then out along the pipe rail that guarded
the long cement wells that let light into the basement windows
of the shop and home ec. and music rooms, the long skirts in
rows, the saddle shoes and short white socks in rows, the girls
exhaling winter breath like cigarette smoke, their pea jackets,
nobody wore parkas then, the dark lipstick of those girls, looking
all like Rita Hayworth in the old yearbooks. The teasing of their
skirts, open above their socks, come find me if you can, the wild

fact of pubic hair, the thighs timidly parted in the narrow space of cars, the damp strip of underpants, Mary Ann his first girl, her underpants down around her saddle shoes like an animal trap, the motor running to keep the heater on in Pop's new blue Plymouth, that they let him borrow one night a week in spite of all Mim's complaining and sarcasm. Mim a flat-chested brat until about seventeen when she began to have her own secrets. Between Mary Ann's legs a locker-room humidity and flesh smell turned delicate, entrusted to him. Married another while he was in the Army. Invited another into that secret space of hers, he couldn't believe it. Lost days, buried at the back of his brain, deep inside, gray cells of which millions die every day he has read somewhere, taking his life with them into blackout, his only life, trillions of electric bits they say, makes even the biggest computer look sick: having found and entered again that space he notices his prick has stayed hard and grown harder, the process there all along, little sacs of blood waiting for the right deep part of the brain to come alive again. Left-handedly, on his back so as not to disturb Janice, he masturbates, remembering Ruth. Her room on Summer. The first night, him having run, all that sad craziness with dead Tothero, then the privacy of this room. This island, their four walls, her room. Her fat white body out of her clothes and her poking fun of his Jockey underpants. Her arms seemed thin, thin, pulling him down and rising above him, one long underbelly erect in light.

Hey.

Hey.

You're pretty.

Come on. Work.

He shoves up and comes, the ceiling close above him, his body feeling curved as if tied to a globe that is growing, growing as his seed bucks up against the sheet. More intense than pumping down into darkness. Weird behavior for an old guy. He stealthily slides from the bed and gropes after a handkerchief in a drawer, not wanting the scrape to wake Janice or Ma Springer or this Pru, cunts all around him. Back in bed, having done his best, though it's always queer where the wet is, maybe it doesn't come out when you feel it does, he composes himself for sleep by thinking of his daughter, her pale round face floating in what appeared to be a milky serene disposition. A voice hisses, *Hassy.*

The Reverend Archie Campbell comes visiting a few nights later, by appointment. He is short and slight, but his voice compensates by being deep and mellow; he enunciates with such casual smiling sonorousness that his sentences seem to keep travelling around a corner after they are pronounced. His head is too big for his body. His lashes are long and conspicuous and he sometimes shuts his eyes as if to display the tremor in his closed lids. He wears his backwards collar with a flimsy black buttonless shirt and a seersucker coat. When he smiles, thick lips like Carter's reveal small even teeth, like seeds in a row, stained by nicotine.

Ma Springer offers him a cup of coffee but he says, "Dear me, no thank you, Bessie. This is my third call this evening and any more caffeine intake will positively give me the shakes." The sentence travels around a corner and disappears up Joseph Street.

Harry says to him, "A real drink then, Reverend. Scotch? A g-and-t? It's still summer officially."

Campbell glances around for their reaction – Nelson and Pru side by side on the gray sofa, Janice perched on a straight chair brought in from the dining room, Ma Springer uneasy on her legs, her offer of coffee spurned. "Well as a matter of fact yes," the minister drawls. "A touch of the sauce might be sheer bliss. Harry, do you have vodka, perchance?"

Janice intervenes, "Way in the back of the corner cupboard, Harry, the bottle with the silver label."

He nods. "Anybody else?" He looks at Pru especially, since in these few days of living with them she's shown herself to be no stranger to the sauce. She likes liqueurs; she and Nelson the other day brought back from a shopping expedition along with the beer sixpacks Kahlúa, Cointreau, and Amaretto di Saronno, chunky little bottles, there must have been between twenty and thirty dollars invested in that stuff. Also they have found in the corner cupboard some crème de menthe left over from a dinner party Harry and Janice gave for the Murketts and Harrisons last February and a little bright green gleam of it appears by Pru's elbow at surprising times, even in the morning, as she and Ma watch *Edge of Night*. Nelson says he wouldn't turn down a beer. Ma Springer says she's going to have coffee anyway, she even has decaffeinated if the rector would prefer. But Archie sticks to his guns, with a perky little bow of thanks to her and a wink all around. The guy is something of a card, Rabbit can see that. Probably the best way to play it, at this late date A.D. They had figured him for the gray easy chair that matches the sofa, but he foxes them by pulling out the lopsided old Syrian hassock from behind the combination lamp and table, where Ma keeps some of her knickknacks, and squatting down. Thus situated, the minister grins up at them all and, nimble as a monkey, fishes a pipe from his front coat pocket and stuffs its bowl with a brown forefinger.

Janice gets up and goes with Harry into the kitchen while he makes the drinks. "That's some little pastor you've got there," he tells her softly.

"Don't be snide."

"What's snide about that?"

"Everything." She pours herself some Campari in an orange-juice glass and without comment fills with crème de menthe one of the set of eight little cylindrical liqueur glasses that came as a set with a decanter she had bought at Kroll's years ago, about the same time they joined the Flying Eagle. They hardly ever have used them. When Harry returns to the living room with Campbell's vodka-and-tonic and Nelson's beer and his own g-and-t Janice follows him in and sets this cylinder of gaudy green on the end table next to Pru's elbow. Pru gives no sign of noticing.

Reverend Campbell has persuaded Ma Springer to take the Barcalounger, where Harry had anticipated sitting, and to raise up its padded extension for her legs. "I must say," she says, "that does wonders for the pressure in my ankles."

Thus laid back the old lady looks vulnerable, and absurdly reduced in importance within the family circle. Janice, seeing her mother stretched out helpless, volunteers, "Mother, I'll fetch you your coffee."

"And that plate of chocolate-chip cookies I set out. Though I don't suppose anybody with liquor wants cookies too."

"I do, Mom-mom," Nelson says. He wears a different expression since Pru arrived – the surly clotted look has relaxed into an expectant emptiness, a wide-eyed docility that Harry finds just as irritating.

Since the minister declined to take the gray easy chair, Harry must. As he sinks into it his legs stretch out, and Campbell without rising jumps the hassock and himself together a few feet to one side, like a bullfrog hopping, pad and all, to avoid being touched by Harry's big suede shoes. Grinning at his own agility, the little man resonantly announces, "Well now. I understand somebody here wants to get married."

"Not me, I'm married already," Rabbit says quickly, as a joke of his own. He has the funny fear that Campbell, one of whose little hands (they look grubby, like his teeth) rests on the edge of the hassock inches from the tips of Harry's shoes, will suddenly reach down and undo the laces. He moves his feet over, some more inches away.

Pru had smiled sadly at his joke, gazing down, her green-filled glass as yet untouched. Seated beside her, Nelson stares forward, solemnly unaware of the dabs of beer on his upper lip. A baby eating: Rabbit remembers how Nelson used to batter with the spoon, held left-handed in his fist though they tried to get him to take it in his right, on the tray of the high chair in the old apartment on Wilbur Street, high above the town. He was never one of the messier babies, though – always wanting to be good. Harry wants to cry, gazing at the innocently ignored mustache of foam on the kid's face. They're selling him down the river. Pru touches her glass furtively, without giving it a glance.

Ma Springer's voice sounds weary, rising from the Barca-lounger. "Yes they'd like to have it be in the church, but it won't be one of your dressy weddings. Just family. And as soon as convenient, even next week we were thinking." Her feet in their dirty aqua sneakers, with rounded toes and scuffed rims of white rubber, look childish and small off the floor, up on the padded extension.

Janice's voice sounds hard, cutting in. "Mother there's no need for such a rush. Pru's parents will need time to make arrangements to come from Ohio."

Her mother says, with a flip of her tired hand toward Pru, "She says her folks may not be bothering to come."

The girl blushes, and tightens her touch on the glass, as if to pick it up when attention has moved past her. "We're not as close as this family is," she says. She lifts her eyes, with their translucent green, to the face of the minister, to explain, "I'm one of seven. Four of my sisters are married already, and two of those marriages are on the rocks. My father's sour about it."

Ma Springer explains, "She was raised Catholic."

The minister smiles broadly. "Prudence seems such a Protestant name."

The blush, as if quickened by a fitful wind, deepens again. "I was baptized Teresa. My friends in high school used to think I was prudish, that's where Pru came from."

Campbell giggles. "*Really!* That's *fas*cinating!" The hair on the top of his head, Rabbit sees, is getting thin, young as he is. Thank God that's one aspect of aging Harry doesn't have to worry about: good lasting heads of hair on both sides of his family, though Pop's toward the end had gone through gray to yellow, finer than cornsilk, and too dry to comb. They say the mother's genes determine. One of the things he never liked about Janice was her high forehead, like she might start to go bald. Nelson's too young to tell yet. Old man Springer used to slick his hair back so he always looked like a guy in a shirt collar ad, even on Saturday mornings, and in the coffin they got the parting all wrong; the newspaper obituary had reversed the photo in doing the halftone and the mortician had worked from that. With Mim, one of the first signs of her rebellion as he remembers was she bleached stripes into her hair, "Protestant rat" she used to call the natural color, in tenth grade, and Mom would get after her saying, "Better that than look like a skunk." It was true, with those blonde pieces Mim did look tough, suddenly – besmirched. That's life, besmirching yourself. The young clergyman's voice is sliding from syllable to syllable smoothly, his surprising high giggle resettled in the back of his throat. "Bessie, before we firm up particulars like the date and the guest list, I think we should investigate some basics. Nelson and Teresa: do you love one another, and are you both prepared to make the eternal commitment that the church understands to exist at the heart of Christian marriage?"

The question is a stunner. Pru says "Yes" in a whisper and takes the first sip from her glass of crème de menthe.

Nelson looks so glazed his mother prompts, "Nelson."

He wipes his mouth and whines, "I *said* I'd do it, didn't I? I've been here all summer trying to work things out. I'm not going back to school, I'll never graduate now, because of this. What more do you people want?"

All flinch into silence but Harry, who says, "I thought you didn't like Kent."

"I didn't, much. But I'd put in my time and would just as soon have gotten the degree, for what it's worth, which isn't much. All summer, Dad, you kept bugging me about college and I wanted to say, O.K., O.K., you're right, but you didn't know the story, you didn't know about *Pru*."

"Don't marry me then," Pru says quickly, quietly.

The boy looks sideways at her on the sofa and sinks lower into the cushions. "I'd just as soon," he says. "It's time I got serious."

"We can get married and still go back for a year and have you finish." Pru has transferred her hands to her lap and with them the little glass of green; she gazes down into it and speaks steadily, as if she is drawing up out of its tiny well words often rehearsed, her responses to Nelson's complaints.

"Naa," Nelson says, shamed. "That seems silly. If I'm gonna be married, let's really do it, with a job and clunky old station wagon and a crummy ranch house and all that drill. There's nothing I can get at Kent'll make me better at pushing Dad's little Japanese kiddy cars off on people. If Mom and Mom-mom can twist his arm so he'll take me in."

"Jesus, how you distort!" Harry cries. "We'll all take you in, how can we help but? But you'd be worth a helluva lot more to the company and what's more to your*self* if you'd finish up at college. Because I keep saying this I'm treated around here like a monster." He turns to Archie Campbell, forgetting how low the man is sitting and saying over his head, "Sorry about all this chitchat, it's hardly up your alley."

"No," the young man mellifluously disagrees, "it's part of the picture." Of Pru he asks, "What would be *your* preference, of where to live for the coming year? The first year of married life, all the little books say, sets the tone for all the rest."

With one hand Pru brushes back her long hair from her shoulders as if angry. "I don't have such happy associations with Kent," she allows. "I'd be happy to begin in a fresh place."

Campbell's pipe is filling the room with a sweetish tweedy perfume. Probably less than thirty and there's nothing they can throw at him that he hasn't fielded before. A pro: Rabbit can respect that. But how did he let himself get queer?

Ma Springer says in a spiteful voice, "You may wonder now why they don't wait that year."

The small man's big head turns and he beams. "No, I hadn't wondered at that."

"She's got herself in a family way," the old lady declares, needlessly.

"With Nelson's help, of course," the minister smiles.

Janice tries to intervene: "Mother, these things happen."

Ma snaps back, "Don't tell me. I haven't forgotten it happened to you."

"*Mother.*"

"This is horrible," Nelson announces from the sofa. "What'd we drag this poor guy in here for anyway? Pru and I didn't ask to be married in a church, I don't believe any of that stuff anyway."

"You don't?" Harry is shocked, hurt.

"No, Dad. When you're dead, you're dead."

"You are?"

"Come off it, you know you are, everybody knows it down deep."

"Nobody knows for sure," Pru points out in a quiet voice.

Nelson asks her furiously, "How many dead people have you seen?"

Even as a child, Harry remembers, Nelson's face would get white around the gills when he was angry. He would get nervous stomach aches, and clutch at the edge of the banister on his way upstairs to get his books. They would send him off to school anyway. Harry still had his job at Verity and Janice was working part-time at the lot and they had no babysitter. School was the babysitter.

Reverend Campbell, puffing unruffled on his aromatic pipe, asks Pru another question. "How do your parents feel about your being married outside of the Roman faith?"

That tender blush returns, deepening the green of her eyes. "Only my mother was a Catholic actually, and I think by the time I came along she had pretty much given up. I was baptized but never confirmed, though there was this confirmation dress my sisters had worn. Daddy had beaten it out of her I guess you could say. He didn't like having all the children to feed."

"What was his denomination?"

"He was a nothing."

Harry remembers out loud, "Nelson's grandfather came from a Catholic background. *His* mother was Irish. My dad's side, I'm talking about. Hell, what I think about religion is —"

All eyes are upon him.

"— is without a little of it, you'll sink."

Saying this, he gazes toward Nelson, mostly because the child's vivid pale-gilled face falls at the center of his field of vision. That muskrat haircut: it suggests to Harry a convict's shaved head that has grown out. The boy sneers. "Well don't sink, Dad, whatever you do."

Janice leans forward to speak to Pru in that mannerly mature woman's bosomy voice she can produce now. "I *wish* you could persuade your parents to come to the wedding."

Ma Springer says, trying a more placating tone, since she has got the minister here and the conference is not delivering for her, "Around here the Episcopalians are thought the next thing to the Catholics anyway."

Pru shakes her head, her red hair flicking, a creature at bay. She says, "My parents and I don't talk much. They didn't approve of something I did before I met Nelson, and they wouldn't approve of this, the way I am now."

"What did you do?" Harry asks.

She doesn't seem to have heard, saying as if to herself, "I've learned to take care of myself without them."

"I'll say this," Campbell says pleasantly, his pipe having gone dead and its relighting having occupied his attention for the last minute. "I'm experiencing some difficulty wrapping my mind around" – the phrase brings out his mischievous grin, stretched like that guy's on *Mad* – "performing a church ceremony for two persons one of whom belongs to the Church of Rome and the other, he has just told us, is an atheist." He gives a nod to Nelson. "Now the bishop gives us more latitude in these matters than we used to have. The other day I married a divorced Japanese man, but with an Episcopal background, to a young woman who originally wanted the words 'Universal Mother' substituted for 'God' in the service. We talked her out of that. But in this case, good people, I really don't see much indication that Nelson and his *very* charming fiancée are at all prepared for, or desirous of, what you might call our brand of magic." He releases a great cloud of smoke and closes his lips in that prissy satisfied way of pipe-smokers, waiting to be contradicted.

Ma Springer is struggling as if to rise from the Barcalounger. "Well no grandson of Fred Springer is going to get married in a Roman Catholic church!" Her head falls back on the padded headrest. Her gills look purple.

"Oh," Archie Campbell says cheerfully. "I don't think my dear friend Father McGahern could handle them either. The young lady was never even confirmed. You know," he adds, knitting his hands at one knee and gazing into space, "a lot of wonderful, dynamic marriages have been made in City Hall. Or a Unitarian-Universalist service. My friend Jim Hancock of the fellowship in Maiden Springs has more than once taken some of our problem betrothals."

Rabbit jumps up. Something awful is being done here, he doesn't know exactly what, or to whom. "Anybody besides me for another drink?"

Without looking at Harry, Campbell holds out a glass which has become empty, as has Pru's little glass of crème de menthe. The green of it has all gone into her eyes. The minister is telling her, and Nelson, "Truly, under some circumstances, even for the most devout it can be the appropriate recourse. At a later date, the wedding can be consecrated in a church; we see a number now of these reaffirmations of wedding vows."

"Why don't they just keep living in sin right here?" Harry asks. "We don't mind."

"We do indeed," Ma says, sounding smothered.

"Hey Dad," Nelson calls, "could you bring me another beer?"

"Get it yourself. My hands are full." Yet he stops in front of Pru and takes up the little liqueur glass. "Sure it's good for the baby?"

She looks up with an unexpected coldness. He was feeling so fatherly and fond and from her eyes he is a dumb traffic cop. "Oh yes," she tells him. "It's the beer and wine that are bad; they bloat you."

By the time Rabbit returns from the kitchen, Campbell is allowing himself to be brought around. He has what they want: a church wedding, a service acceptable in the eyes of the Grace Stuhls of this world. Knowing this, he is in no hurry. Beneath the girlish lashes his eyes are as dark as Janice's and Ma's, the Koerner eyes. Ma Springer is holding forth, the little rounded toes of her aqua sneakers bouncing. "You must take what the boy says with a grain of salt. At his age I didn't know what I believed myself, I thought the government was foolish and the gangsters had the right idea. This was back in Prohibition days."

Nelson looks at her with his own dark eyes, sullen. "Mom-mom, if it matters so much to you, I don't care that much, one way or another."

"What does Pru think?" Harry asks, giving her her poison. He wonders if the girl's frozen stiffness of manner, and those little waits while her smile gets unstuck, aren't simply fear: it is she who is growing another life within her body, and nobody else.

"I think," she responds slowly, so quietly the room goes motionless to hear, "it would be nicer in a church."

Nelson says, "I know I sure don't want to go down to that awful new concrete City Hall they've built behind where the Bijou used to be, some guy I know was telling me the contractor raked off a million and there's cracks in the cement already."

Janice in her relief says, "Harry, I could use some more Campari."

Campbell lifts his replenished glass from his low place on the hassock. "Cheers, good people." He states his terms: "The customary procedure consists of at least three sessions of counseling and Christian instruction after the initial interview. This I suppose we can consider the interview." As he addresses Nelson particularly, Harry hears a seductive note enrich the great mellow voice. "Nelson, the church does not expect that every couple it marries be a pair of Christian saints. It does ask that the participants have some understanding of what they are undertaking. *I* don't take the vows; you and Teresa do. Marriage is not merely a rite; it is a sacrament, an invitation from God to participate in the divine. And the invitation is not for one moment only. Every day you share is meant to be sacramental. Can you feel a meaning in that? There were wonderful words in the old prayer book; they said that marriage was not 'to be entered into unadvisedly or lightly; but reverently, discreetly, advisedly, soberly, and in the fear of God.' " He grins, having intoned this, and adds, "The new prayer book omits the fear of God."

Nelson whines, "I *said*, I'd go along."

Janice asks, a little prim, "How long would these sessions of instructions take?" It is like she is sitting, in that straight-backed dining-room chair, on an egg that might hatch too soon.

"Oh," Campbell says, rolling his eyes toward the ceiling, "I should think, considering the various factors, we could get three of them in in two weeks. I just happen, the officious clergyman said, to have my appointment book here." Before reaching into the breast pocket of the seersucker coat, Campbell taps out the bowl of his pipe with a finicky calm that conveys to Harry the advantages of being queer: the world is just a gag to this guy. He walks on water; the mud of women and making babies never dirties his shoes. You got to take off your hat: nothing touches him. That's real religion.

Some rebellious wish to give him a poke, to protest the smooth bargain that has been struck, prompts Harry to say, "Yeah, we want to get 'em in before the baby comes. He'll be here by Christmas."

"God willing," Campbell smiles, adding, "He or she."

"January," Pru says in a whisper, after putting down her glass. Harry can't tell if she is pleased or displeased by the gallant way he keeps mentioning the baby that everybody else wants to ignore. While the appointments are being set up she and Nelson sit on that sofa like a pair of big limp Muppets, with invisible arms coming up through the cushions into their torsos and heads.

"Fred had his birthday in January," Ma Springer announces, grunting as she tries to get out of the Barcalounger, to see the minister off.

"Oh Mother," Janice says. "One twelfth of the world has January birthdays."

"*I* was born in January," Archie Campbell says, rising. He grins to show his seedy teeth. "In my case, after much prayerful effort. My parents were *an*cient. It's a wonder I'm here at all."

The next day a warm rain is beginning to batter the yellowing leaves down from the trees in the park along Cityview Drive as Harry and Nelson drive through Brewer to the lot. The kid is still persona non grata but he's asked to check on the two convertibles he crunched, one of which, the Royale, Manny is repairing. The '72 Mercury, hit twice from the side, was more severely damaged, and parts are harder to get. Rabbit's idea had been when the kid went off to school to sell it for junk and write off the loss. But he didn't have the heart not to let the boy look at the wrecks at least. Then Nelson is going to borrow the Corona and visit Billy Fosnacht before he goes back to Boston to become an endodontist. Harry had a root canal job once; it felt like they were tickling the underside of his eyeball. What a hellish way to make a living. Maybe there's no entirely good way. The Toyota's windshield wipers keep up a steady rubbery singsong as the Brewer traffic slows, brake lights burning red all along Locust Boulevard. The Castle has started up again and yellow school buses loom ahead in the jam. Harry switches the wipers from Fast to Intermittent and wishes he still smoked cigarettes. He wants to talk to the kid.

"Nelson."

"Unhh?"

"How do you feel?"

"O.K. I woke up with a soreness in my throat but I took two of those five-hundred-milligram vitamin Cs Melanie talked Bessie into getting."

"She was really a health nut, wasn't she? Melanie. We still have all that Granola in the kitchen."

"Yeah, well. It was part of her act. You know, mystical gypsy. She was always reading this guru, I forget his name. It sounded like a sneeze."

"You miss her?"

"Melanie? No, why would I?"

"Weren't you kind of close?"

Nelson avoids the implied question. "She was getting pretty grouchy toward the end."

"You think she and Charlie went off together?"

"Beats me," the boy says.

The wipers, now on Intermittent, startle Rabbit each time they switch across, as if someone other than he is making decisions in this car. A ghost. Like in that movie about Encounters of the Third Kind the way the truck with Richard Dreyfuss in it begins to shake all over and the headlights behind rise up in the air instead of pulling off to one side. He readjusts the knob from Intermittent to Slow. "I didn't mean your physical health, exactly. I meant more your state of mind. After last night."

"You mean about that sappy minister? I don't mind going over to listen to his garbage a couple times if it'll satisfy the Springer honor or whatever."

"I guess I mean more about the marriage in general. Nellie, I don't want to see you railroaded into anything."

The boy sits up a little in the side of Harry's vision; the yellow buses ahead pull into the Brewer High driveway and the line of cars begins to move again, slowly, beside a line of parked cars whose rooftops are spattered with leaves the rain has brought down. "Who says I'm being railroaded?"

"Nobody says it. Pru seems a fine girl, if you're ready for marriage."

"You don't think I'm ready. You don't think I'm ready for anything."

He lets the hostility pass, trying to talk meditatively, like Webb Murkett. "You know, Nelson, I'm not sure any man is ever a hundred per cent ready for marriage. I sure as hell know I wasn't, from the way I acted toward your mother."

"Yeah, well," the boy says, in a voice a little crumbled, from his father's not taking the bait. "She got her own back."

"I never could hold that against her. Or Charlie either. You ought to understand. After we got back together that time, we've both been pretty straight. We've even had a fair amount of fun together, in our dotage. I'm just sorry we had so much working out to do, with you still on the scene."

"Yeah, well." Nelson's voice sounds breathy and tight, and he keeps looking at his knees, even when Harry hangs that tricky left turn onto Eisenhower Avenue. The boy clears his throat and volunteers, "It's the times, I guess. A lot of the kids I got to know at Kent, they had horror stories worse than any of mine."

"Except that thing with Jill. They couldn't top that, I bet." He doesn't quite chuckle. Jill is a sacred name to the boy; he will never talk about it. Harry goes on clumsily, as the car gains momentum downhill and the spic and black kids strolling uphill to school insolently flirt with danger, daring him to hit them, his fenders brushing their bodies, "There's something that doesn't feel right to me in this new development. The girl gets knocked up, O.K., it takes two to tango, you have some responsibility there, nobody can deny it. But then as I understand it she flat out refuses to get the abortion, when one of the good things that's come along in twenty years along with a lot that's not so good is you can go have an abortion now right out in the open, in a hospital, safe and clean as having your appendix out."

"So?"

"So why didn't she?"

The boy makes a gesture that Rabbit fears might be an attempt to grab the wheel; his grip tightens. But Nelson is merely waving to indicate a breadth of possibilities. "She had a lot of reasons. I forget what all they were."

"I'd like to hear them."

"Well for one thing she said she knew of women who had their insides all screwed up by abortions, so they could *never* have a baby. You say it's easy as an appendix but you've never had it done. She didn't *believe* in it."

"I thought she wasn't that much of a Catholic."

"She wasn't, she isn't, but still. She said it wasn't natural."

"What's natural? In this day and age with all these contraceptives getting knocked up like that isn't natural."

"Well she's *shy*, Dad. They don't call her Pru for nothing. Going to a doctor like that, and having him scrape you out, she just didn't want to do it."

"You bet she didn't. Shy. She wanted to have a baby, and she wasn't too shy to manage that. How much younger're you than she?"

"A year. A little more. What does it matter? It wasn't just a baby she wanted to have, it was *my* baby. Or so she said."

"That's sweet. I guess. What did you think about it?"

"I thought it was O.K., probably. It was her body. That's what they all tell you now, it's their body. I didn't see much I could do about it."

"Then it's sort of her funeral, isn't it?"

"How do you mean?"

"I mean," Harry says, in his indignation honking at some kids at the intersection of Plum Street who saunter right out toward him, this early in the school year the crossing guards aren't organized yet, "so she decides to keep pregnant till there's no correcting it while this other girl babysits for you, and your mother and grandmother and now this nance of a minister all decide when and how you're going to marry the poor broad. I mean, where do you come in? Nelson Angstrom. I mean, what do *you* want? Do you know?" In his frustration he hits the rim of the steering wheel with the heel of his hand, as the avenue dips down beneath the blackened nineteenth-century stones of the underpass at Eisenhower and Seventh, that in a bad rainstorm is flooded but not today. The arch of this underpass, built without a keystone, by masons all long dead, is famous, and from his earliest childhood has reminded Rabbit of a crypt, of death. They emerge among the drooping wet pennants of low-cost factory outlets.

"Well, I want —"

Fearing the kid is going to say he wants a job at Springer Motors, Harry interrupts: "You look scared, is all I see. Scared to say No to any of these women. I've never been that great at saying No either, but just because it runs in the family doesn't mean you have to get stuck. You don't necessarily have to lead my life, I guess is what I want to say."

"Your life seems pretty comfy to me, frankly." They turn

down Weiser, the forest of the inner-city mall a fogged green smear in the rearview mirror.

"Yeah, well," Harry says, "it's taken me a fair amount of time to get there. And by the time you get there you're pooped. The world," he tells his son, "is full of people who never knew what hit 'em, their lives are over before they wake up."

"Dad, you keep talking about yourself but I don't see what it has to do with *me*. What *can* I do with Pru except marry her? She's not so bad, I mean I've known enough girls to know they all have their limits. But she's a person, she's a friend. It's as if you want to deny her to me, as if you're jealous or something. The way you keep mentioning her baby."

This kid should have been spanked at some point. "I'm not jealous, Nelson. Just the opposite. I feel sorry for you."

"Don't feel sorry for me. Don't waste your feelings on me."

They pass Schoenbaum Funeral Directors. Nobody out front in this rain. Harry swallows and asks, "Don't you want out, if we could rig it somehow?"

"How could we rig it? She's in her fifth month."

"She could go ahead have the baby without you marrying her. These adoption agencies are crying for white babies, you'd be doing somebody else a favor."

"Pru would never consent."

"Don't be too sure. We could ease the pain. She's one of seven, she knows the value of a dollar."

"Dad, this is crazy talk. You're forgetting this baby is a person. An Angstrom!"

"Jesus, how could I forget that?"

The light at the foot of Weiser, before the bridge, is red. Harry looks over at his son and gets an impression of something freshly hatched, wet and not quite unfolded. The light turns green. A bronze plaque on a pillar of pebbled concrete names the mayor for whom the bridge was named but it is raining too hard to read it.

He starts up again, "Or you could just, I don't know, not make any decision, just disappear for a while. I'd give you the money for that."

"Money, you're always offering me money to stay away."

"Maybe because when I was your age I wanted to get away and I couldn't. I didn't have the money. I didn't have the sense. We tried to send you away to get some sense and you've thumbed your nose at it."

"I haven't thumbed my nose, it's just that there's not that much out there. It isn't what you think, Dad. College is a rip-off, the professors are teaching you stuff because they're getting paid to do it, not because it does you any good. They don't give a fuck about geography or whatever any more than you do. It's all phony, they're there because parents don't want their kids around the house past a certain age and sending them to college makes them look good. 'My little Johnny's at Haavahd.' 'My little Nellie's at Kent.' "

"Really, that's how you see it? In my day kids *wanted* to get out in the world. We were scared but not so scared we kept running back to Mama. And Grandmama. What're you going to do when you run out of women to tell you what to do?"

"Same thing you'll do. Drop dead."

D I S C O. Datsun. Fuel Economy. Route 111 has a certain beauty in the rain, the colors and the banners and the bluish asphalt of the parking lots all run together through the swish of traffic, the beat of wipers. Rubbery hands flailing, *Help, help.* Rabbit has always liked rain, it puts a roof on the world. "I just don't like seeing you *caught*," he blurts out to Nelson. "You're too much *me*."

Nelson gets loud. "I'm not you! I'm not caught!"

"Nellie, you're caught. They've got you and you didn't even squeak. I hate to see it, is all. All I'm trying to say is, as far as I'm concerned you don't have to go through with it. If you want to get out of it, I'll help you."

"I don't want to be helped that way! I *like* Pru. I like the way she looks. She's great in bed. She needs me, she thinks I'm neat. She doesn't think I'm a baby. You say I'm caught but I don't feel caught, I feel like I'm becoming a man!"

Help, help.

"Good," Harry says then. "Good luck."

"Where I want your help, Dad, you won't give it."

"Where's that?"

"Here. Stop making it so hard for me to fit in at the lot."

They turn into the lot. The tires of the Corona splash in the gutter water rushing toward its grate along the highway curb. Stonily Rabbit says nothing.'

III

A NEW SHOP has opened on Weiser Street in one of those scruffy blocks between the bridge and the mall, opposite the enduring old variety store that sells out-of-town newspapers, warm unshelled peanuts, and dirty magazines for queers as well as straights. From the look of it the new store too might be peddling smut, for its showcase front window is thoroughly masked by long thin blond Venetian blinds, and the lettering on its windows is strikingly discreet. Gold letters rimmed in black and very small simply say FISCAL ALTERNATIVES and below that, smaller yet, *Old Coins, Silver and Gold Bought and Sold*. Harry passes the place by car every day, and one day, there being two empty metered spaces he can slide into without holding up traffic, he parks and goes in. The next day, after some business at his bank, the Brewer Trust two blocks away, he comes out of Fiscal Alternatives with thirty Krugerrands purchased for $377.14 each, including commission and sales tax, coming to $11,314.20. These figures had been run off inside by a girl with platinum hair; her long scarlet fingernails didn't seem to hamper her touch on the hand computer. She was the only person visible, at her long glass-topped desk, with beige sides and swivel chair to match. But there were voices and monitoring presences in other rooms, back rooms into which she vanished and from which she emerged with his gold. The coins came in cunning plastic cylinders of fifteen each, with round blue-tinted lids that suggested dollhouse toilet seats; indeed, bits of what seemed toilet paper were stuffed into the hole of this lid to make the fit tight and to conceal even a glimmer of the sacred metal. So heavy, the cylinders threaten to tear the pockets off his coat as Harry hops up Ma Springer's front steps to face his family. Inside the front door, Pru sits knitting on the gray sofa and Ma Springer has taken over the Barcalounger to keep her legs up while some quick-lipped high yellow from Philly is giving her the six-o'clock news. Mayor Frank Rizzo has once again denied charges of police brutality, he says, in a rapid dry voice that pulls the rug out from every word. Used to be Philadelphia was a distant place where no one dared visit, but television has pulled it closer, put its muggy murders and politics right next door. "Where's Janice?" Harry asks.

Ma Springer says, "Shh."

Pru says, "Janice took Nelson over to the club, to fill in with some ladies' doubles, and then I think they were going to go shopping for a suit."

"I thought he bought a new suit this summer."

"That was a business suit. They think he needs a three-piece suit for the wedding."

"Jesus, the wedding. How're you liking your sessions with what's–his–name?"

"I don't mind them. Nelson hates them."

"He says that just to get his grandmother going," Ma Springer calls, twisting to push her voice around the headrest. "I think they're really doing him good." Neither woman notices the hang of his coat, though it feels like a bull's balls tugging at his pockets. It's Janice he wants. He goes upstairs and snuggles the two dense, immaculate cylinders into the back of his bedside table, in the drawer where he keeps a spare pair of reading glasses and the rubber tip on a plastic handle he is supposed to massage his gums with to keep out of the hands of the periodontist and the pink wax earplugs he stuffs in sometimes when he has the jitters and can't tune out the house noise. In this same drawer he used to keep condoms, in that interval between when Janice decided the Pill was bad for her and when she went and had her tubes burned, but that was a long while ago and he threw them all away, the whole tidy tin box of them, after an indication, the lid not quite closed, perhaps he imagined it, that Nelson or somebody had been into the box and filched a couple. From about that time on he began to feel crowded, living with the kid. As long as Nelson was socked into baseball statistics or that guitar or even the rock records that threaded their sound through all the fibers of the house, his occupation of the room down the hall was no more uncomfortable than the persistence of Rabbit's own childhood in an annex of his

brain; but when the stuff with hormones and girls and cars and
beers began, Harry wanted out of fatherhood. Two glimpses mark
the limits of his comfort in this matter of men descending from
men. When he was about twelve or thirteen he walked into his
parents' bedroom in the half-house on Jackson Road not expecting his father to be there, and the old man was standing in front
of his bureau in just socks and an undershirt, innocently fishing in
a drawer for his undershorts, that boxer style that always looked
sad and dreary to Harry anyway, and here was his father's bare
behind, such white buttocks, limp and hairless, mute and helpless
flesh that squeezed out shit once a day and otherwise hung there
in the world like linen that hadn't been ironed; and then when
Nelson was about the same age, a year older he must have been
for they were living in this house already and they moved when
the kid was thirteen, Harry had wandered into the bathroom not
realizing Nelson would be stepping out of the shower and had
seen the child frontally: he had pubic hair and, though his body
was still slim and pint-sized, a man-sized prick, heavy and oval,
unlike Rabbit's circumcised and perhaps because of this looking
brutal, and big. Big. This was years before the condoms were
stolen. The drawer rattles, stuck, and Harry tries to ease it in, hearing that Janice and Nelson have come into the house, making the
downstairs resound with news of tennis and clothing stores and of
the outer world. Harry wants to save his news for Janice. To
knock her out with it. The drawer suddenly eases shut and he
smiles, anticipating her astonished reception of his precious, lustrous, lead-heavy secret.

As with many anticipated joys it does not come exactly as envisioned. By the time they climb the stairs together it is later than
it should be, and they feel unsettled and high. Dinner had to be
early because Nelson and Pru were going over to Soupy, as they
both call Campbell, for their third session of counseling. They
returned around nine-thirty with Nelson in such a rage they had
to break out the dinner wine again while with a beer can in hand
he did an imitation of the young minister urging the church's way
into the intimate space between these two. "He keeps talking
about the church being the be-riide of Ke-riist. I kept wanting to
ask him, Whose little bride are you?"

"Nelson," Janice said, glancing toward the kitchen, where her mother was making herself Ovaltine.

"I mean, it's ob*scene*," Nelson insisted. "What does He do, fuck the church up the ass?"

Pru laughed, Harry noticed. Did Nelson do that to her? It was about the last thing left a little out of the ordinary for these kids, blowing all over the magazines these days, giving head they call it, there was that movie *Shampoo* where Julie Christie who you associate with costume dramas all decked out in bonnets announced right on the screen she wanted to blow Warren Beatty, actually said it, and it wasn't even an X, it was a simple R, with all these teen-age dating couples sitting there holding hands as sweetly as if it was a return of *Showboat* with Kathryn Grayson and Howard Keel, the girls laughing along with the boys. Pru's long-boned mute body does not declare what it does, nor her pale lips, that in repose have a dry, pursed look, an expression maybe you learn in secretarial school. *Great in bed*, Nelson had said.

"I'm sorry, Mom, but he really pisses me off. He gets me to say these things I don't believe and then he grins and acts jolly like it's all some kind of crappy joke. Mom-mom, how can you and those other old ladies stand him?"

Bessie had come in from the kitchen, her mug of Ovaltine steaming as she stared it steady and her hair pinned tight up against her skull with a net over it all, for bed. "Oh," she said, "he's higher than some, and lower than others. At least he doesn't choke us on all the incense like the one that became a Greek Orthodox priest finally. And he did a good job of getting the diehards to accept the new form. My tongue still sticks at some of the responses."

Pru offered, "Soupy seemed quite proud that the new service doesn't have 'obey.'"

"People never did obey, I guess they might as well leave it out," Ma said.

Janice seemed determined to have a go at Nelson herself. "Really you shouldn't put up such resistance, Nelson. The man is leaning over backwards to give us a church service, and I think from the way he acts he sincerely likes you. He really does have a feel for young people."

"Does he ever," Nelson said, soft enough for Ma Springer not to hear, then mimicking loudly, "Dear Mater and Pater were *ain*-cient. It's such a *whun*der I got here at all. In case you *whun*der why I have this *toad*stool look."

"You shouldn't mind people's physical appearance," Janice said.

"Oh but Mater, one simply *does*." For some while they went on in this way, it was as good as television, Nelson imitating Soupy's mellow voice, Janice pleading for reason and charity, Ma Springer drifting in some world of her own where the Episcopal Church has presided since Creation; but Harry felt above them all, a golden man waiting to take his wife upstairs and show her their treasure. When the joking died, and a rerun of *M*A*S*H* came on that Nelson wanted to see, the young couple looked tired and harried suddenly, sitting there on the sofa, being beaten into one. Already each took an accustomed place, Pru over on the end with the little cherry side table for her crème de menthe and her knit-ting, and Nelson on the middle cushion with his feet in their button-soled Adidas up on the reproduction cobbler's bench. Now that he didn't go to the lot he didn't bother to shave every day, and the whiskers came in as reddish bristle on his chin and upper lip but his cheeks were still downy. To hell with this scruffy kid. Rabbit has decided to live for himself, selfishly at last.

When Janice comes back from the bathroom naked and damp inside her terrycloth robe, he has locked their bedroom door and arranged himself in his underpants on the bed. He calls in a husky and insinuating voice, "Hey. Janice. Look. I bought us something today."

Her dark eyes are glazed from all that drinking and parenting downstairs; she took the shower to help clear her head. Slowly her eyes focus on his face, which must show an intensity of pleasure that puzzles her.

He tugs open the sticky drawer and is himself startled to see the two tinted cylinders sliding toward him, still upright, still there. He would have thought something so dense with preciousness would broadcast signals bringing burglars like dogs to a bitch in heat. He lifts one roll out and places it in Janice's hand; her arm dips with the unexpected weight, and her robe, untied, falls open.

Her thin brown used body is more alluring in this lapsed sheath of rough bright cloth than a girl's; he wants to reach in, to where the shadows keep the damp fresh.

"What is it, Harry?" she asks, her eyes widening.

"Open it," he tells her, and when she fumbles too long at the transparent tape holding on the toilet-seat-shaped little lid he pries it off for her with his big fingernails. He removes the wad of tissue paper and spills out upon the quilted bedspread the fifteen Krugerrands. Their color is redder than gold in his mind had been. "Gold," he whispers, holding up close to her face, paired in his palm, two coins, showing the two sides, the profile of some old Boer on one and a kind of antelope on the other. "Each of these is worth about three hundred sixty dollars," he tells her. "Don't tell your mother or Nelson or anybody."

She does seem bewitched, taking one into her fingers. Her nails scratch his palm as she lifts the coin off. Her brown eyes pick up flecks of yellow. "Is it all right?" Janice asks. "Where on earth did you get them?"

"A new place on Weiser across from the peanut store that sells precious metals, buys and sells. It was simple. All you got to do is produce a certified check within twenty-four hours after they quote you a price. They guarantee to buy them back at the going rate any time, so all you lose is their six per cent commission and the sales tax, which at the rate gold is going up I'll have made back by next week. Here. I bought two stacks. Look." He takes the other thrillingly hefty cylinder from the drawer and undoes the lid and spills those fifteen antelopes slippingly upon the bedspread, thus doubling the riches displayed. The spread is a lightweight Pennsylvania Dutch quilt, small rectangular patches sewed together by patient biddies, graded from pale to dark to form a kind of dimensional effect, of four large boxes having a lighter and darker side. He lies down upon its illusion and places a Krugerrand each in the sockets of his eyes. Through the chill red pressure of the gold he hears Janice say, "My God. I thought only the government could have gold. Don't you need a license or anything?"

"Just the bucks. Just the fucking bucks, Wonder Woman." Blind, he feels amid the pure strangeness of the gold his prick firming up and stretching the fabric of his Jockey shorts.

"Harry. How much did you spend?"

He wills her to lift down the elastic of his underpants and suck, suck until she gags. When she fails to read his mind and do this, he removes the coins and gazes up at her, a dead man reborn and staring. No coffin dark greets his open eyes, just his wife's out-of-focus face, framed in dark hair damp and stringy from the shower and fringy across the forehead so that Mamie Eisenhower comes to mind. "Eleven thousand five hundred more or less," he answers. "Honey, it was just sitting in the savings account drawing a lousy six per cent. At only six per cent these days you're losing money, inflation's running about twelve. The beauty of gold is, it loves bad news. As the dollar sinks, gold goes up. All the Arabs are turning their dollars into gold. Webb Murkett told me all about it, the day you wouldn't come to the club."

She is still examining the coin, stroking its subtle relief, when he wants her attention to turn to him. He hasn't had a hard-on just blossom in his pants since he can't remember when. Lotty Bingaman days. "It's pretty," Janice admits. "Should you be supporting the South Africans though?"

"Why not, they're making jobs for the blacks, mining the stuff. The advantage of the Krugerrand, the girl at this fiscal alternatives place explained, is it weighs one troy ounce exactly and is easier to deal with. You can buy Mexican pesos if you want, or there's a little Canadian maple leaf, though there she said it's so fine the gold dust comes off on your hands. Also I liked the look of that deer on the back. Don't you?"

"I do. It's exciting," Janice confesses, at last looking at him, where he lies tumescent amid scattered gold. "Where are you going to keep them?" she asks. Her tongue sneaks forward in thought, and rests on her lower lip. He loves her when she tries to think.

"In your great big cunt," he says, and pulls her down by the lapels of her rough robe. Out of deference to those around them in the house – Ma Springer just a wall's thickness away, her television a dim rumble, the Korean War turned into a joke – Janice tries to suppress her cries as he strips the terrycloth from her willing body and the coins on the bedspread come in contact with her skin. The cords of her throat tighten; her face darkens as she strains

in the grip of indignation and glee. His underwear off, the overhead light still on, his prick up like a jutting piece of pink wreckage, he calms her into lying motionless and places a Krugerrand
on each nipple, one on her navel, and a number on her pussy,
enough to mask the hair with a triangle of unsteady coins overlapping like snake scales. If she laughs and her belly moves the
whole construction will collapse. Kneeling at her hips, Harry holds
a Krugerrand by the edge as if to insert it in a slot. "*No!*" Janice
protests, loud enough to twitch Ma Springer awake through the
wall, loud enough to jar loose the coins so some do spill between
her legs. He hushes her mouth with his and then moves his mouth
south, across the desert, oasis to oasis, until he comes to the ferny
jungle, which his wife lays open to him with a humoring toss of
her thighs. A kind of interest compounds as, seeing red, spilled
gold pressing on his forehead, he hunts with his tongue for her clitoris. He finds what he thinks is the right rhythm but doesn't feel
it take; he thinks the bright overhead light might be distracting her
and risks losing his hard-on in hopping from the bed to switch it
off over by the door. Turning then in the half-dark he sees she has
turned also, gotten up onto her knees and elbows, a four-legged
moonchild of his, her soft cleft ass held high to him in the gloom
as her face peeks around one shoulder. He fucks her in this position gently, groaning in the effort of keeping his jism in, letting
his thoughts fly far. The pennant race, the recent hike in the factory base price of Corollas. He fondles her underside's defenseless
slack flesh, his own belly massive and bearing down. Her back
looks so breakable and brave and narrow – the long dent of its
spine, the cross-bar of pallor left by her bathing-suit bra. Behind
him his bare feet release a faraway sad odor. Coins jingle, slithering in toward their knees, into the depressions their interlocked
weights make in the mattress. He taps her ass and asks, "Want to
turn over?"

"Uh-huh." As an afterthought: "Want me to sit on you first?"

"Uh-huh." As an afterthought: "Don't make me come."

Harry's skin is bitten as by ice when he lies on his back. The
coins: worse than toast crumbs. So wet he feels almost nothing,
Janice straddles him, vast and globular in the patchy light that
filters from the streetlight through the big copper beech. She picks

up a stray coin and places it glinting in her eye, as a monocle. Lording it over him, holding him captive, she grinds her wet halves around him; self to self, bivalve and tuber, this is what it comes to. "Don't come," she says, alarmed enough so that her mock-monocle drops to his tense abdomen with a thud. "Better get underneath," he grunts. Her body then seems thin and black, silhouetted by the scattered circles, reflecting according to their tilt. Gods bedded among stars, he gasps in her ear, then she in his.

After this payoff, regaining their breaths, they can count in the semi-dark only twenty-nine Krugerrands on the rumpled bedspread, its landscape of ridged green patches. He turns on the overhead light. It hurts their eyes. By its harshness their naked skins seem also rumpled. Panic encrusts Harry's drained body; he does not rest until, naked on his knees on the rug, a late strand of spunk looping from his reddened glans, he finds, caught in the crack between the mattress and the bed side-rail, the precious thirtieth.

He stands with Charlie gazing out at the bleak September light. The tree over beyond the Chuck Wagon parking lot has gone thin and yellow at its top; above its stripped twigs the sky holds some diagonal cirrus, bands of fat in bacon, promising rain tomorrow. "Poor old Carter," Harry says. "D'ya see where he nearly killed himself running up some mountain in Maryland?"

"He's pushing," Charlie says. "Kennedy's on his tail." Charlie has returned from his two weeks' vacation with a kiss of Florida tan undermined by a weak heart and the days intervening. He did not come from Florida directly. Simultaneously with his return Monday a card sent from Ohio arrived at Springer Motors, saying in his sharply slanted book-keeper's hand,

> Hi Gang –
>   Detoured on way
> back from Fla. thru Gt.
> Smokies. Southern belles,
> mile after mile. Now near
> Akron, exploded radial

> capital of the world. Fuel
> economy a no-no out here,
> big fins & V–8s still reign.
> Miss you all lots.   Chas.

The joke especially for Harry was on the other side: a picture of a big flat-roofed building like a quarter of a pie, identified as KENT STATE STUDENT COMPLEX, *embracing the largest open-stack library in northeastern Ohio.*

"Sort of pushing yourself these days, aren't you?" Harry asks him. "How was Melanie all that while?"

"Who says I was with Melanie?"

"You did. With that card. Jesus, Charlie, a young kid like that grinding your balls could kill you."

"What a way to go, huh champ? You know as well as I do it's not the chicks that grind your balls, it's these middle-aged broads time is running out on."

Rabbit remembers his bout with Janice amid their gold, yet still remains jealous. "Whajja do in Florida with her?"

"We moved around. Sarasota, Venice, St. Pete's. I couldn't talk her out of the Atlantic side so we drove over from Naples on 75, old Alligator Alley, and did the shmeer – Coral Gables, Ocean Boulevard, up to Boca and West Palm. We were going to take in Cape Canaveral but ran out of time. The bimbo didn't even bring a bathing suit, the one we bought her was one of these new ones with the sides wide open. Great figure. Don't know why you didn't appreciate her."

"I *could*n't appreciate her, it was Nelson brought her into the house. It'd be like screwing your own daughter."

Charlie has a toothpick left over from lunch downtown, a persimmon-colored one, and he dents his lower lip with it as he gazes out the tired window. "There's worse things," he offers bleakly. "How's Nelson and the bride-to-be?"

"Pru." Harry sees that Charlie is set to guard the details of his trip, to make him pull them out one by one. Miles of Southern belles. Fuck this guy. Rabbit has secrets too. But, thinking this, he can picture only a farm, its buildings set down low in a hollow.

"Melanie had a lot to say about Pru."

"Like what?"

"Like she thinks she's weird. Her impression is that shy as she seems she's a tough kid up from a really rocky upbringing and isn't too steady on her feet, emotionally speaking."

"Yeah well, some might say a girl who gets her kicks screwing an old crow like you is pretty weird herself."

Charlie looks away from the window straight up into his eyes, his own eyes behind their tinted spectacles looking watery. "You shouldn't say things like that to me, Harry. Both of us getting on, two guys just hanging in there ought to be nice to each other."

Harry wonders from this if Charlie knows how threatened his position is, Nelson on his tail.

Charlie continues, "Ask me whatever you want about Melanie. Like I said, she's a good kid. Solid, emotionally. The trouble with you, champ, is you have screwing on the brain. My biggest kick was showing this young woman something of the world she hadn't seen before. She ate it up – the cypresses, that tower with the chimes. She said she'd still take California though. Florida's too flat. She said if this Christmas I could get my ass out to Carmel she'd be happy to show me around. Meet her mother and whoever else is around. Nothing heavy."

"How much – how much future you think you two have?"

"Harry, I don't have much future with anybody." His voice is whispery, barely audible. Harry would like to take it and wire-brush it clean.

"You never know," he reassures the smaller man.

"You *know*," Stavros insists. "You know when your time is running out. If life offers you something, take it."

"O.K., O.K. I will. I do. What'd your poor old *Manna mou* do, while you were bombing around with Bimbo in the Everglades?"

"Well," he says, "funny thing there. A female cousin of mine, five or so years younger, I guess has been running around pretty bad, and her husband kicked her out this summer, and kept the kids. They lived in Norristown. So Gloria's been living in an apartment by herself out on Youngquist a couple blocks away and was happy to babysit for the old lady while I was off and says she'll do it again any time. So I have some freedom now I didn't used to have." Everywhere, it seems to Harry, families are breaking up and different pieces coming together like survivors in one great big lifeboat, while he and Janice keep sitting over there in Ma Springer's shadow, behind the times.

"Nothing like freedom," he tells his friend. "Don't abuse it now. You asked about Nelson. The wedding's this Saturday. Immediate family only. Sorry."

"Wow. Poor little Nellie. Signed, sealed, and delivered."

Harry hurries by this. "From what Janice and Bessie let drop the mother will probably show up. The father's too sore."

"You should see Akron," Charlie tells him. "I'd be sore too if I had to live there."

"Isn't there a golf course out there where Nicklaus holds a tournament every year?"

"What I saw wasn't any golf course."

Charlie has come back from his experiences tenderized, nostalgic it seems for his life even as he lives it. So aged and philosophical he seems, Harry dares ask him, "What'd Melanie think of me, did she say?"

A very fat couple are prowling the lot, looking at the little cars, testing by their bodies, sitting down on air beside the driver's doors, which models might be big enough for them. Charlie watches this couple move among the glittering roofs and hoods a minute before answering. "She thought you were neat, except the women pushed you around. She thought about you and her balling but got the impression you and Janice were very solid."

"You disillusion her?"

"Couldn't. The kid was right."

"Yeah how about ten years ago?"

"That was just cement."

Harry loves the way he ticks this off, Janice's seducer; he loves this savvy Greek, dainty of heart beneath his coat of summer checks. The couple have wearied of trying on cars for size and get into their old car, a '77 Pontiac Grand Prix with cream hardtop, and drive away. Harry asks suddenly, "How do you feel about it? Think we can live with Nelson over here?"

Charlie shrugs, a minimal brittle motion. "Can he live with me? He wants to be a cut above Jake and Rudy, and there aren't that many cuts in an outfit like this."

"I've told them, Charlie, if you go I go."

"You can't go, Chief. You're family. Me, I'm old times. I can go."

"You know this business cold, that's what counts with me."

"Ah, this isn't selling. It's like supermarkets now: it's shelf-stacking, and ringing it out at the register. When it was all used, we used to try to fit a car to every customer. Now it's take it or leave it. With this seller's market there's no room to improvise. Your boy had the right idea: go with convertibles, antiques, something with a little amusement value. I can't take these Jap bugs seriously. This new thing called the Tercel we're supposed to start pushing next month, have you seen the stats? One point five liter engine, twenty-inch tires. It's like those little cars they used to have on merry-go-rounds for the kids who were too scared to ride the horses."

"Forty-three m.p.g. on the highway, that's the stat people care about, the way the world's winding."

Charlie says, "You don't see too many bugs down in Florida. The old folks are still driving the big old hogs, the Continentals, the Toronados, they paint 'em white and float around. Of course the roads, there isn't a hill in the state and never any frost. I've been thinking about the Sun Belt. Go down there and thumb my nose at the heating-oil bills. Then they get you on the air-conditioning. You can't escape."

Harry says, "Sodium wafers, that's the answer. Electricity straight from sunlight. It's about five years off, that's what *Consumer Reports* was saying. Then we can tell those Arabs to take their fucking oil and grease their camels with it."

Charlie says, "Traffic fatalities are up. You want to know why they're up? Two reasons. One, the kids are pretty much off drugs now and back into alcohol. Two, everybody's gone to compacts and they crumple like paper bags."

He chuckles and twirls the flavored toothpick against his lower lip as the two men gaze out the window at the river of dirty tin. An old low-slung station wagon pulls into the lot but it has no wooden rack on top; though Harry's heart skips, it is not his daughter. The station wagon noses around and heads out into 111 again, just casing. Burglaries are up. Harry asks Charlie, "Melanie really thought about" — he balks at "balling," it is not his generation's word — "going to bed with me?"

"That's what the lady said. But you know these kids, they come right out with everything we used to keep to ourselves. Doesn't mean there's more of it. Probably less as a matter of fact. By the time they're twenty-five they're burnt out."

"I was never attracted to her, to tell you the truth. Now this new girl of Nelson's —"

"I don't want to hear about it," Charlie says, pivoting to go back to his desk. "They're about to get married, for Chrissake."

Running. Harry has continued the running he began up in the Poconos, as a way of getting his body back from those sodden years when he never thought about it, just ate and did what he wanted, restaurant lunches downtown in Brewer plus the Rotary every Thursday, it begins to pack on. The town he runs through is dark, full of slanty alleys and sidewalks cracked and tipped from underneath, whole cement slabs lifted up by roots like crypt lids in a horror movie, the dead reach up, they catch at his heels. He keeps moving, pacing himself, overriding the protest of his lungs and fashioning of his stiff muscles and tired blood a kind of machine that goes where the brain directs, uphill past the wide-eaved almost Chinese-looking house where the butch women hammer, their front windows never lit, must watch a lot of television or else snuggle into whatever it is they do early or else saving electricity, women won't get paid the same as men until ERA passes, at least having a nest of them moving into the neighborhood not like blacks or Puerto Ricans, they don't breed.

Norway maples shade these streets. Not much taller than when he was a boy. Grab a low branch and hoist yourself up into a hornets' nest. Split the seeds and stick them to your nose to make yourself a rhinoceros. Panting, he cuts through their shadow. A slim pain cuts through his high left side. Hold on, heart. Old Fred Springer popped off in a blaze of red, anyway Rabbit has always imagined the last thing you'd see in a heart attack would be a bright flash of red. Amazing, how dark these American houses are, at nine o'clock at night. A kind of ghost town, nobody else on the sidewalk, all the chickens in their coop, only a brownish bit of glow showing through a window crack here and there, night light in a child's room. His mind strides on into a bottomless sorrow, thinking of children. Little Nellie in his room newly moved into Vista Crescent, his teddies stacked in a row beside him, his eyes like theirs unable to close, scared of dying while asleep, thinking of baby Becky who did fall through, who did die. A volume of water still stood in the tub many hours later, dust on the unstirring gray surface, just a little rubber stopper to lift and God in all His strength did nothing. Dry leaves scrape and break underfoot, the sound of fall, excitement in the air. The Pope is coming, and the wedding is Saturday. Janice asks him why is his heart so hard toward Nelson. Because Nelson has swallowed up the boy that was and substituted one more pushy man in the world, hairy wrists, big prick. Not enough room in the world. People came north from the sun belt in Egypt and lived in heated houses and now the heat is being used up, just the oil for the showroom and offices and garage has doubled since '74 when he first saw the Springer Motors books and will double in the next year or two again and when you try to cut it down to where the President says, the men in the garage complain, they have to work with their bare hands, working on a concrete slab they can wear thick socks and heavy soles, he thought at one point he should get them all that kind of golf glove that leaves the fingertips bare but it would have been hard to find ones for the right hand, guys under thirty now just will not work without comfort and all the perks, a whole new ethic, soft, socialism, heat tends to rise in a big space like that and hang up there amid the crossbraces, if they built it now they'd put in twenty inches of insulation. If the Pope is so crazy about babies why doesn't *he* try to keep them warm?

He is running along Potter Avenue now, still uphill, saving the downhill for the homeward leg, along the gutter where the water from the ice plant used to run, an edge of green slime, life tries to get a grip anywhere, on earth that is, not on the moon, that's another thing he doesn't like about the thought of climbing through the stars. Once clowning on the way to school along the gutter that now is dry he slipped on the slime and fell in, got his knickers soaked, those corduroy knickers they used to make you wear, *swish swish*, and the long socks, incredible how far back he goes now, he can remember girls in first grade still wearing high-button shoes: Margaret Schoelkopf, she was so full of life her nose would start to bleed for no reason. When he fell in the gutter of ice-plant water his knickers were so wet he had to run home crying and change, he hated being late for school. Or for anywhere, it was something Mom drummed into him, she didn't so much care where he went but he had to be home on time, and for most of his life this sensation would overtake him, anywhere, in the locker room, on a 16A bus, in the middle of a fuck, that he was late for somewhere and he was in terrible dark trouble, a kind of tunnel would open in his mind with Mom at the end of it with a switch. *Do you want a switching Hassy?* she would ask him as if asking if he wanted dessert, the switches came off the base of the little pear tree in the narrow back yard on Jackson Road; angry yellowjackets would hover over the fallen rotting fruit. Lately he no longer ever feels he is late for somewhere, a strange sort of peace at his time of life: a thrown ball at the top of its arc is for a second still. His gold is rising in value, ten dollars an ounce or so in the papers every day, ten times thirty is three hundred smackers without his lifting a finger, you think how Pop slaved. Janice putting that monocle on was a surprise, the only trouble with her in bed is she still doesn't like to blow, something mean about her mouth and always was, Melanie had those funny saucy stubborn cherry lips, a wonder Charlie didn't pop his aorta in some motel down there in the sands, how lovely it is when a woman forgets herself and opens her mouth to laugh or exclaim so wide you see the whole round cavern the ribbed pink roof and the tongue like a rug in a hall and the butterfly-shaped blackness in the back that goes down into the throat, Pru did that the other day in the kitchen at something Ma Springer said, her smile usually wider on one side than the other and a bit cautious like she might get burned, but all the girls coming up now blew, it was part of the culture, taken for granted, fuck-and-suck movies they call them, right out in the open, you take your date, ADULT FILMS NEW EACH FRIDAY in the old Baghdad on upper Weiser where in Rabbit's day they used to go see Ronald Reagan being co-pilot against the Japs. Lucky Nelson, in a way. Still he can't envy him. A worn-out world to find his way in. Funny about mouths, they must do so much, and don't tell what went into them, even a minute later. One thing he does hate is seeing bits of food, rice or cereal or whatever, hanging in the little hairs of a face during a meal. Poor Mom in those last years.

His knees are jarring. His big gut jounces. Each night he tries to extend his run among the silent dark houses, through the cones of the streetlights, under the ice-cold lopsided moon, that the other night driving home in the Corona he happened to see through the tinted upper part of the windshield and for a second thought, My God, it *is* green. Tonight he pushes himself as far as Kegerise Street, a kind of alley that turns downhill again, past black-sided small factories bearing mysterious new names like Lynnex and Data Development and an old stone farmhouse that all the years he was growing up had boarded windows and a yard full of tumbledown weeds milkweed and thistle and a fence of broken slats but now was all fixed up with a little neat sign outside saying *Albrecht Stamm Homestead* and inside all sorts of authentic hand-made furniture and quaint kitchen equipment to show what a farmhouse was like around 1825 and in cases in the hall photographs of the early buildings of Mt. Judge before the turn of the century but not anything of the fields when the area of the town was in large part Stamm's farm, they didn't have cameras that far back or if they did didn't point them at empty fields. Old man Springer had been on the board of the Mt. Judge Historical Society and helped raise the funds for the restoration, after he died Janice and Bessie thought Harry might be elected to take his place on the board but it didn't happen, his checkered past haunting him. Even though a young hippie couple lives upstairs and leads the visitors through, to Harry the old Stamm place is full of ghosts, those old farmers lived weird lives, locking their crazy sisters in the attic and strangling the pregnant hired girl in a fit of demon rum and hiding the body in the potato bin so that fifty years later the skeleton comes to light. Next door the Sunshine Athletic Association used to be, that Harry as a boy had thought was full of athletes, so he hoped he could some day belong, but when twenty years ago he did get inside it smelled of cigar butts and beer gone flat in the bottom of the glass. Then through the Sixties it fell into dilapidation and disrepute, the guys who drank and played cards in there getting older and fewer and more morose. So when the building came up for sale the Historical Society bought it and tore it down and made where it was into a parking lot for the visitors who came by to the Stamm Homestead on their way to Lancaster to look at the Amish or on their way to Philadelphia to look at the Liberty Bell. You wouldn't think people could find it tucked away on what used to be Kegerise Alley but an amazing number do, white-haired most of them. History. The more of it you have the more you have to live it. After a little while there gets to be too much of it to memorize and maybe that's when empires start to decline.

Now he is really rolling, the alley slants down past the body shop and a chicken house turned into a little leather-working plant, these ex-hippies are everywhere, trying to hang on, they missed the boat but had their fun, he has pushed through the first wave of fatigue, when you think you can't drag your body another stride, your thighs pure pain. Then second wind comes and you break free into a state where your body does it by itself, a machine being ridden, your brain like the astronaut in the tip of the rocket, your thoughts just flying. If only Nelson would get married and go away and come back rich twenty years from now. Why can't these kids get out on their own instead of crawling back? Too crowded out there. The Pope, Jesus, you have to hope he isn't shot, just like America to have some nut take a shot to get his name in the papers, that Squeaky Fromme who used to lay the old cowboys for the Manson ranch, all the ass that Manson had you'd think it would have made him nicer since it's being sexually frustrated that causes war, he read somewhere. He knows how the Pope feels about contraception though, he could never stand rubbers, even when they gave them to you free in the Army, this month's *Consumer Reports* has an article on them, page after page, all this testing, some people apparently prefer bright-colored ones with ribs and little nubbins to give the woman an added tickle inside, did the staffers on the magazine all ask the secretaries to screw or what, some people even liked ones made out of sheep intestine, the very thought of it makes him crawl down there, with

names like Horizon Nuda and Klingtie Naturalamb, Harry could-
n't read to the end of the article, he was so turned off. He wonders about his daughter, what she uses, country methods they used
to kid about in school, squat on a cornstalk, she looked pretty virginal in that one glimpse of her and who wouldn't be, surrounded by rubes? Ruth would set her straight, what pigs men are. And
that barking dog would be a discouragement too.

    There is a longer way home, down Jackson to Joseph and over,
but tonight he takes the shortcut, diagonally across the lawn of the
big stone Baptist church, he likes the turf under his feet for a
minute, the church façade so dark, to the concrete steps that take
you down onto Myrtle, and on past the red, white, and blue post
office trucks parked in a row at the back platform, the American
flag hanging limp and bright over the fake gable out front, used to
be you shouldn't fly the flag at night but now all the towns do it
with a spotlight, waste of electricity, soaking up the last dribble of
energy flying the flag. Myrtle leads into Joseph from the other end.
They will be sitting around waiting for him, watching the boob
tube or going on about the wedding, getting silly about it now
that it's so close and Soupy has declared all systems go, they've
invited Charlie Stavros after all and Grace Stuhl and a batch of
other biddies and a few friends from the Flying Eagle and it turns
out Pru or Teresa as they call her in the announcement they want
to send out has an aunt and uncle in Binghamton, New York,
who will come down even if the father is some sorehead who
wants to strangle his daughter and put her in the potato bin. In he
will come and Janice will make her usual crack about him killing
himself with a heart attack, it's true he does get very red in his
white face, he can see in the mirror in the foyer, with his blue eyes,
Santa Claus without the whiskers, and has to bend over the back
of a chair gasping for a while to get his breath, but that's part of
the fun, giving her a scare, poor mutt what would she do without
him, have to give up the Flying Eagle and everything, go back to
selling nuts in Kroll's. In he will come and there Pru will be
sitting on the sofa right next to Nelson like the police officer who
takes the criminal from one jail to another on the train without
letting the handcuffs show, the one thing Harry is fearful of now
that Pru is in the family is stinking up the room with his sweat.

Tothero had it that time in the Sunshine, an old man's sour sad body smell, and getting out of bed in the morning sometimes Harry surprises it on himself, this faraway odor like a corpse just beginning to sweeten. Middle age is a wonderful country, all the things you thought would never happen are happening. When he was fifteen, forty-six would have seemed the end of the rainbow, he'd never get there, if a meaning of life was to show up you'd think it would have by now.

Yet at moments it seems it has, there are just no words for it, it is not something you dig for but sits on the top of the table like an unopened dewy beer can. Not only is the Pope coming but the Dalai Lama they bounced out of Tibet twenty years ago is going around the U.S.A. talking to divinity schools and appearing on TV talk shows, Harry has always been curious about what it would feel like to *be* the Dalai Lama. A ball at the top of its arc, a leaf on the skin of a pond. A water strider in a way is what the mind is like, those dimples at the end of their legs where they don't break the skin of the water quite. When Harry was little God used to spread in the dark above his bed like that and then when the bed became strange and the girl in the next aisle grew armpit hair He entered into the blood and muscle and nerve as an odd command and now He had withdrawn, giving Harry the respect due from one well-off gentleman to another, but for a calling card left in the pit of the stomach, a bit of lead true as a plumb bob pulling Harry down toward all those leaden dead in the hollow earth below.

The front lights of Ma Springer's big shadowy stucco house blaze, they are all excited by the wedding, Pru now has a constant blush and Janice hasn't played tennis for days and Bessie evidently gets up in the middle of the night and goes downstairs to watch on the bigger TV the old Hollywood comedies, men in big-brimmed hats and little mustaches, women with shoulders broader than their hips swapping wisecracks in newspaper offices and deluxe hotel suites, Ma must have seen these movies first when she had all black hair and the Brewer downtown was a great white way. Harry jogs in place to let a car pass, one of those crazy Mazdas with the Wankel engine like a squirrel wheel, Manny says they'll never get the seal tight enough, crosses from curb to curb under the streetlight, notices Janice's Mustang isn't parked out front, sprints down the brick walk and up the porch steps, and at last on the porch, under the number 89, stops running. His momentum is such that the world for a second or two streams on, seeming to fling all its trees and housetops outward against star-spangled space.

In bed Janice says, "Harry."

"What?" After you run your muscles have a whole new pulled, sheathed feel and sleep comes easy.

"I have a little confession to make."

"You're screwing Stavros again."

"Don't be so rude. No, did you notice the Mustang wasn't left out front as usual?"

"I did. I thought, 'How nice.'"

"It was Nelson who put it out back, in the alley. We really ought to clean out that space in the garage some day, all these old bicycles nobody uses. Melanie's Fuji is still in there."

"O.K., good. Good for Nelson. Hey, are you going to talk all night, or what? I'm beat."

"He put it there because he didn't want you to see the front fender."

"Oh no. That son of a bitch. That little son of a bitch."

"It wasn't his fault exactly, this other man just kept coming, though I guess the Stop sign was on Nelson's street."

"Oh Christ."

"Luckily both hit their brakes, so it really was just the smallest possible bump."

"The other guy hurt?"

"Well, he said something about whiplash, but then that's what people are trained to say now, until they can talk to their lawyer."

"And the fender is mashed?"

"Well, it's tipped in. The headlight doesn't focus the same place the other does. But it's fine in the daytime. It's really hardly more than a scratch."

"Five hundred bucks' worth. At least. The masked fender-bender strikes again."

"He really was terrified to tell you. He made me promise I wouldn't, so you can't say anything to him."

"I can't? Then why are you telling me? How can I go to sleep now? My head's pounding. It's like he has it in a vise."

"Because I didn't want you noticing by yourself and making a scene. Please, Harry. Just until after the wedding. He's really very embarrassed about it."

"The fuck he is, he loves it. He has my head in a vise and he just keeps turning the screw. That he'd do it to *your* car, after you've been knocking yourself out for him, that's really gratitude."

"Harry, he's about to get married, he's in a state."

"Well, shit, now I'm in a state. Where're some clothes? I got to go outside and see the damage. That flashlight in the kitchen, did it ever get new batteries?"

"I'm sorry I told you. Nelson was right. He said you wouldn't be able to handle it."

"Oh did he say that? Our own Mr. Cool."

"So just settle down. I'll take care of the insurance forms and everything."

"And who do you think pays for the increase in our insurance rates?"

"We do," she says. "The two of us."

St. John's Episcopal Church in Mt. Judge is a small church that never had to enlarge, built in 1912 in the traditional low-sided steep-roofed style, of a dark gray stone hauled from the north of the county, whereas the Lutheran church was built of local red sandstone, and the Reformed, next to the fire station, of brick. Ivy has been encouraged to grow around St. John's pointed windows. Inside, it is dark, with knobby walnut pews and dados and, on the walls between stained-glass windows of Jesus in violet robes making various gestures, marble plaques in memory of the dead gentry who contributed heavily here, in the days when

Mt. Judge was a fashionable suburb. WHITELAW. STOVER. LEG-
GETT. English names in a German county, gone to give tone to
the realms of the departed after thirty years as wardens and vestrymen. Old man Springer had done his bit but the spaces between
the windows were used up by then.

Though the wedding is small and the bride an Ohio working-
man's daughter, yet in the eyes of passersby the gathering would
make a bright brave flurry before the church's rust-red doors, on
the verge of four o'clock this September the twenty-second.
A person or persons driving past this Saturday afternoon on the
way to the MinitMart or the hardware store would have a pang of
wanting to be among the guests. The organist with his red robe
over his arm is ducking into the side door. He has a goatee. A
little grubby guy in green coveralls like a troll is waiting for Harry
to show up so he can get paid for the flowers, Ma said it was only
decent to decorate the altar at least, Fred would have died to see
Nellie married in St. John's with a bare altar. Two bouquets of
white mums and baby's breath come to $38.50, Rabbit pays him
with two twenties, it was a bad sign when the banks started paying out in twenties instead of tens, and yet the two-dollar bill still
isn't catching on. People are superstitious. This wasn't supposed
to be a big wedding but in fact it's costing plenty. They've had to
take three rooms over at the Four Seasons Motel on Route 422:
one for the mother of the bride, Mrs. Lubell, a small scared soul
who looks like she thinks they'll all stick forks into her if she drops
her little smile for a second; and another for Melanie, who came
across the Commonwealth with Mrs. Lubell from Akron in a bus,
and for Pru, who has been displaced from her room – Melanie's
old room and before that the sewing dummy's – by the arrival
from Nevada of Mim, whom Bessie and Janice didn't want in the
house at all but Harry insisted, she's his only sister and the only
aunt Nelson has got; and the third room for this couple from
Binghamton, Pru's aunt and uncle, who were driving down today
but hadn't checked in by three-thirty, when the shuttle service
Harry has been running in the Corona picked up the two girls and
the mother to bring them to the church. His head is pounding.
This mother bothers him, her smile has been on her face so long
it's as dry as a pressed flower, she doesn't seem to belong to his

generation at all, she's like an old newspaper somebody has used as a drawer liner and then in cleaning house you lift out and try to read; Pru's looks must have all come from the father's side. At the motel the woman kept worrying that the messages they were leaving at the front desk for her tardy brother and sister-in-law weren't clear enough, and began to cry, so her smile got damp and ruined. A case of Mumm's second-best champagne waits back in the Joseph Street kitchen for the little get-together afterwards that nobody would call a reception; Janice and her mother decided they should have the sandwiches catered by a grandson of Grace Stuhl's who would bring along this girlfriend in a serving uniform. And then they ordered a cake from some wop over on Eleventh Street who was charging one hundred and eighty-five American dollars for a cake, a *cake* – Harry couldn't believe it. Every time Nelson turns around, it costs his father a bundle.

Harry stands for a minute in the tall ribbed space of the empty church, reading the plaques, hearing Soupy's giggle greet the three dolled-up women off in a side room, one of those out-of-sight chambers churches have where the choir puts itself into robes and the deacons count the collection plates and the communion wine is stored where the acolytes won't drink it and the whole strange show is made ready. Billy Fosnacht was supposed to be best man but he's up at Tufts so a friend of theirs from the Laid-Back called Slim is standing around with a carnation in his lapel waiting to usher. Uncomfortable from the way this young man's slanted eyes brush across him, Rabbit goes outside to stand by the church doors, whose rust-red paint in the September sun gives back heat so as to remind him of standing in his fresh tan uniform on a winter day in Texas at the side of the barracks away from the wind, that incessant wind that used to pour from that great thin sky across the treeless land like the whine of homesickness through this soldier who had never before been away from Pennsylvania.

Standing there thus for a breath of air, in this pocket of peace, he is trapped in the position of a greeter, as the guests suddenly begin to arrive. Ma Springer's stately dark-blue Chrysler pulls up, grinding its tires on the curb, and the three old ladies within claw at the door handles for release. Grace Stuhl has a translucent wart off-center on her chin but she hasn't forgotten how to dimple. "I bet but for Bessie I'm the only one here went to your wedding too," she tells Harry on the church porch.

"Not sure I was there myself," he says. "How did I act?"

"Very dignified. Such a tall husband for Janice, we all said."

"And he's kept his looks," adds Amy Gehringer, the squattest of these three biddies. Her face is enlivened with rouge and a flaking substance the color of Russian salad dressing. She pokes him in the stomach, hard. "Even added to them some," the old lady wisecracks.

"I'm trying to take it off," he says, as if he owes her something. "I go jogging most every night. Don't I, Bessie?"

"Oh it frightens me," Bessie says. "After what happened to Fred. And you know there wasn't an ounce extra on him."

"Take it easy, Harry," Webb Murkett says, coming up behind with Cindy. "They say you can injure the walls of your intestines, jogging. The blood all rushes to the lungs."

"Hey Webb," Harry says, flustered. "You know my mother-in-law."

"My pleasure," he says, introducing himself and Cindy all around. She is wearing a black silk dress that makes her look like a young widow. Would that she were, Jesus. Her hair has been fluffed up by a blow-dryer so it doesn't have that little-headed wet-otter look that he loves. The top of her dress is held together with a pin shaped like a bumblebee at the lowest point of a plunging V-shaped scoop.

And Bessie's friends are staring at gallant Webb with such enchantment Harry reminds them, "Go right in, there's a guy there leading people to their seats."

"I want to go right up front," Amy Gehringer says, "so I can get a good look at this young minister Bessie raves so about."

"'Fraid this screwed up golf for today," Harry apologizes to Webb.

"Oh," Cindy says, "Webb got his eighteen in already, he was over there by eight-thirty."

"Who'd you get to take my place?" Harry asks, jealous and unable to trust his eyes not to rest on Cindy's tan décolletage. The tops of tits are almost the best part, nipples can be repulsive. Just above the bumblebee a white spot that even her bikini bra hides from the sun shows. The little cross is up higher, just under the sexy hollow between her collarbones. What a package.

"The young assistant pro went around with us," Webb confides. "A seventy-three, Harry. A seventy-*three*, with a ball into the pond on the fifteenth, he hits it so far."

Harry is hurt but he has to greet the Fosnachts, who are pushing behind. Janice didn't want to invite them, especially after they decided not to invite the Harrisons, to keep it all small. But since Nelson wanted Billy as best man Harry thought they had no choice, and also even though Peggy has let herself slide there is that aura about a woman who's once upon a time taken off all her clothes for you however poorly it turned out. What the hell, it's a wedding, so he bends down and kisses Peggy to one side of the big wet hungry mouth he remembers. She is startled, her face broader than he remembers. Her eyes swim up at him in the wake of the kiss, but since one of them is a walleye he never knows which to search for expression.

Ollie's handshake is limp, sinewy, and mean: a mean-spirited little loser, with ears that stick out and hair like dirty straw. Harry crunches his knuckles together a little, squeezing. "How's the music racket, Ollie? Still tootling?" Ollie is one of these reedy types, common around Brewer, who can pick out a tune on anything but never manage to make it pay. He works in a music store, Chords 'n' Records, renamed Fidelity Audio, on Weiser Street near the old Baghdad, where the adult movies show now.

Peggy, her voice defensive from the kiss, says, "He sits in on synthesizer sometimes with a group of Billy's friends."

"Keep at it, Ollie, you'll be the Elton John of the Eighties. Seriously, how've you both been? Jan and I keep saying, we got to have you two over." Over Janice's dead body. Funny, just that one innocent forlorn screw, and Janice holds a grudge, where he's forgiving as hell of Charlie, just about his best friend in the world in fact.

And here is Charlie. "Welcome to the merger," Harry kids.

Charlie chuckles, his shrug small and brief. He knows the tide is running against him, with this marriage. Still, he has some reserve within him, some squared-off piece of philosophy that keeps him from panicking.

"You seen the bridesmaid?" Harry asks him. Melanie.

"Not yet."

"The three of 'em went over into Brewer last night and got drunk as skunks, to judge from Nelson. How's that for a way to act on the night before your wedding?"

Charlie's head ticks slowly sideways in obliging disbelief. This elderly gesture is jarred, however, when Mim, dressed in some crinkly pants outfit in chartreuse, with ruffles, grabs him from behind around the chest and won't let go. Charlie's face tenses in fright, and to keep him from guessing who it is Mim presses her face against his back so that Harry fears all her makeup will rub off on Charlie's checks. Mim comes on now any hour of the day or night made up like a showgirl, every tint and curl exactly the way she wants it; but really all the creams and paints in a world of jars won't counterfeit a flexible skin, and rimming your eyes in charcoal may be O.K. for these apple-green babies that go to the disco but at forty it makes a woman look merely haunted, staring, the eyes lassoed. Her teeth are bared as she hangs on, wrestling Charlie from behind like an eleven-year-old with Band-Aids on her knees. "Jesus," Charlie grunts, seeing the hands at his chest with their purple nails long as grasshoppers, but slow to think back through all the women he has known who this might be.

Embarrassed for her, worried for him, Harry begs, "C'mon, Mim."

She won't let go, her long-nosed tarted-up face mussed and distorted as she maintains the pressure of her grip. "Gotcha," she says. "The Greek heartbreaker. Wanted for transporting a minor across state lines and for misrepresenting used cars. Put the handcuffs on him, Harry."

Instead Harry puts his hands on her wrists, encountering bracelets he doesn't want to bend, thousands of dollars' worth of gold on her bones, and pulls them apart, having set his own body into the jostle for leverage, while Charlie, looking grimmer every second, holds himself upright, cupping his fragile heart within. Mim is wiry, always was. Pried loose at last, she touches herself rapidly here and there, putting each hair and ruffle back into place.

"Thought the boogyboo had gotten you, didn't you Charlie?" she jeers.

"Pre-owned," Charlie tells her, pulling his coat sleeves taut to restore his dignity. "Nobody calls them used cars anymore."

"Out west we call them shitboxes."

"Shh," Harry urges. "They can hear you inside. They're about to get started." Still exhilarated by her tussle with Charlie, and amused by the disapproving conscientious man her brother has become, Mim wraps her arms around Harry's neck and hugs him hard. The frills and pleats of her fancy outfit crackle, crushing against his chest. "Once a bratty little sister," she says in his ear, "always a bratty little sister."

Charlie has slipped into the church. Mim's eyelids, shut, shine in the sunlight like smears left by some collision of greased vehicles – often on the highways Harry notices the dark swerves of rubber, the gouges of crippled metal left to mark where something unthinkable had suddenly happened to someone. Though it happened the day's traffic continues. *Hold me, Harry*, she used to cry out, little Mim in her hood between his knees as their sled hit the cinders spread at the bottom of Jackson Road, and orange sparks flew. Years before, a child had died under a milk truck sledding here and all the children were aware of this: that child's blank face leaned toward them out of each snowstorm. Now Harry sees a glisten in Mim's eyelids as in the backs of the Japanese beetles that used to cluster on the large dull leaves of the Bolgers' grape arbor out back. Also he sees how her earlobes have been elongated under the pull of jewelry and how her ruffles shudder as she pants, out of breath after her foolery. She is sinking through all her sins and late nights toward being a pathetic hag, he sees, one of those women you didn't believe could ever have been loved, with only Mom's strong bones in her face to save her. He hesitates, before going in. The town falls away from this church like a wide flight of stairs shuffled together of roofs and walls, a kind of wreck wherein many Americans have died.

He hears the side door where the organist hurried in open, and peeks around the corner, thinking it might be Janice needing him. But it is Nelson who steps out, Nelson in his cream-colored three-piece marrying suit with pinched waist and wide lapels, that looks too big for him, perhaps because the flared pants almost cover the heels of his shoes. Three hundred dollars, and when will he ever wear it again?

As always when he sees his son unexpectedly Harry feels shame. His upper lip lifts to call out in recognition, but the boy doesn't look his way, just appears to sniff the air, looking around at the grass and down toward the houses of Mt. Judge and then up the other way at the sky at the edge of the mountain. *Run*, Harry wants to call out, but nothing comes, just a stronger scent of Mim's perfume at the intake of breath. Softly the child closes the door again behind him, ignorant that he has been seen.

Behind the ajar rust-red portal the church is gathering in silence toward its eternal deed. The world then will be cloven between those few gathered in a Sunday atmosphere and all the sprawling fortunate Saturday remainder, the weekday world going on about its play. From childhood on Rabbit has resented ceremonies. He touches Mim on the arm to take her in, and over the spun glass of her hairdo sees a low-slung dirty old Ford station wagon with the chrome roof rack heightened by rough green boards crawl by on the street. He isn't quick enough to see the passengers, only gets a glimpse of a fat angry face staring from a back window. A fat mannish face yet a woman's.

"What's the matter?" Mim asks.

"I don't know. Nothing."

"You look like you've seen a ghost."

"I'm worrying about the kid. How do *you* feel about all this?"

"Me. Aunt Mim? It seems all right. The chick will take charge."

"That's good?"

"For a while. You must let go, Harry. The boy's life is his, you live your own."

"That's what I've been telling myself. But it feels like a copout."

They go in. A pathetic little collection of heads juts up far down front. This mysterious slant-eyed Slim, smoothly as if he were a professional usher, escorts Mim down the aisle to the second pew and indicates with a graceful sly gesture where Harry should settle in the first, next to Janice. The space has been waiting. On Janice's other side sits the other mother. Mrs. Lubell's profile is pale; like her daughter she is a redhead but her hair has been rinsed to colorless little curls, and she never could have had Pru's height and nice rangy bearing. She looks, Harry can't help thinking it, like a cleaning lady. She gives over to him her desiccated but oddly perfect smile, a smile such as flickered from the old black-and-white movie screens, coy and certain, a smile like a thread of pure melody, that when she was young must have seemed likely to lift her life far above where it eventually settled. Janice has pulled back her head to whisper with her mother in the booth behind. Mim has wound up in the same pew as Ma Springer and her biddies. Stavros sits with the Murketts in the third pew, he has Cindy's neckline to look down when he gets bored, let him see what country-club tits look like after all those stuffed grape leaves. In willful awkwardness the Fosnachts were seated or seated themselves across the aisle, on what would have been the bride's side if there had been enough to make a side, and are quarrelling in whispers between themselves: much hissed emphasis from Peggy and stoic forward-gazing mutter from Ollie. The organist is doodling through the ups and downs of some fugue to give everybody a chance to cough and recross their legs. The tip of his little ruddy goatee dips about an inch above the keyboard during the quiet parts. The way he slaps and tugs at the stops reminds Harry of the old Linotype he used to operate, the space adjuster and how the lead jumped out hot, all done with computer tapes now. To the left of the altar one of the big wall panels with rounded tops opens, it is a secret door like in a horror movie, and out of it steps Archie Campbell in a black cassock and white surplice and stole. He flashes his *What? Me worry?* grin, those sudden seedy teeth.

Nelson follows him out, head down, looking at nobody.

Slim slides up the aisle, light as a cat, to stand beside him. He must be a burglar in his spare time. He stands a good five inches taller than Nelson. Both have these short punk haircuts. Nelson's hair makes a whorl in back that Harry knows so well his throat goes dry, something caught in it.

Peggy Fosnacht's last angry whisper dies. The organ has been silent this while. With both plump hands lifted, Soupy bids them all stand. To the music of their rustle Melanie leads in Pru, from another side room, along the altar rail. The secret knowledge shared by all that she is pregnant enriches her beauty. She wears an ankle-length crêpey dress that Ma Springer calls oatmeal in color and Janice and Melanie call champagne, with a brown sash they decided to leave off her waist lest they have to tie it too high. It must have been Melanie who wove the little wreath of field flowers, already touched by wilt, that the bride wears as a crown. There is no train or veil save an invisible aura of victory. Pru's face, downcast and purse-lipped, is flushed, her carroty hair brushed slick down her back and tucked behind her ears to reveal their crimped soft shell shapes hung with tiny hoops of gold. Harry could halt her with his arm as she paces by but she does not look at him. Melanie gives all the old folks a merry eye; Pru's long red-knuckled fingers communicate a tremble to her little bouquet of baby's breath. Now her bearing as she faces the minister is grave with that gorgeous slowed composure of women carrying more than themselves.

Soupy calls them Dearly Beloved. The voice welling up out of this little man is terrific, Harry had noticed it at the house, but here, in the nearly empty church, echoing off the walnut knobs and memorial plaques and high arched rafters, beneath the tall central window of Jesus taking off into the sky with a pack of pastel apostles for a launching pad, the timbre is doubled, enriched by a rounded sorrowful something Rabbit hadn't noticed hitherto, gathering and pressing the straggle of guests into a congregation, subduing any fear that this ceremony might be a farce. Laugh at ministers all you want, they have the words we need to hear, the ones the dead have spoken. *The union of husband and wife*, he announces in his great considerate organ tones, *is intended by God for their mutual joy*, and like layers of a wide concealing dust the syllables descend, *prosperity, adversity, procreation, nurture*. Soupy bats his eyelids between phrases, is his only flaw. Harry hears a faint groan behind him: Ma Springer standing on her legs too long. Mrs. Lubell over past Janice has removed a grubby-looking handkerchief from her purse and dabs at her face with it. Janice is smiling. There is a dark dent at the corner of her lips. With a little white hat on her head like a flower she looks Polynesian.

Ringingly Soupy addresses the rafters: "If any of you can show just cause why they may not lawfully be married, speak now; or else for ever hold your peace."

Peace. A pew creaks. The couple from Binghamton. Dead Fred Springer. Ruth. Rabbit fights down a crazy impulse to shout out. His throat feels raw.

The minister now speaks to the couple direct. Nelson, from hanging lamely over on the side, his eyes murky in their sockets and the carnation crooked in his lapel, moves closer to the center, toward Pru. He is her height. The back of his neck looks so thin and bare above his collar. That whorl.

Pru has been asked a question. In an exceedingly small voice she says she will.

Now Nelson is being questioned and his father's itch to shout out, to play the disruptive clown, has become something else, a prickling at the bridge of his nose, a pressure in the two small ducts there.

Woman, wife, covenant, love her, comfort her, honor and keep her, sickness, health, forsaking all others as long as you both shall live?

Nelson in a voice midway in size between Soupy's and Pru's says he will.

And the burning in his tear ducts and the rawness scraping at the back of his throat have become irresistible, all the forsaken poor ailing paltry witnesses to this marriage at Harry's back roll forward in hoops of terrible knowing, an impalpable suddenly sensed mass of human sadness concentrated burningly upon the nape of Nelson's neck as he and the girl stand there mute while the rest of them grope and fumble in their thick red new prayer books after the name and number of a psalm announced; Soupy booms angelically above their scattered responses, *wife, a fruitful vine*, to which Rabbit cannot contribute, *the man who fears the Lord*, because he is weeping, weeping, washing out the words, the page, which has become as white and blank as the nape of Nelson's poor mute frail neck. Janice looks up at him in jaunty surprise under her white hat and Mrs. Lubell with that wistful cleaning-lady smile passes over her grubby handkerchief. He shakes his head No, he is too big, he will overwhelm the cloth with his effluvia; then takes it anyway, and tries to blot this disruptive tide. There is this place the tears have unlocked that is endlessly rich, a spring.

"May you live to see your children's children," Soupy intones in his huge mellow encompassing fairy's voice. "May peace be upon Israel," he adds.

And outside, when it is done, the ring given, the vows taken in the shaky young voices under the towering Easter-colored window of Christ's space shot and the Lord's Prayer mumbled through and the pale couple turned from the requisite kiss (poor Nellie, couldn't he be just another inch taller?) to face as now legally and mystically one the little throng of their blood, their tribe, outside in the sickly afternoon, clouds having come with the breeze that flows toward evening, the ridiculous tears dried in long stains on Harry's face, then Mim comes into his arms again, a sisterly embrace, all sorts of family grief since the days he held her little hand implied, the future has come upon them darkly, his sole seed married, marriage that daily doom which she may never know; lean and crinkly in his arms she is getting to be a spinster, even a hooker can be a spinster, think of all she's had to swallow all these years, his baby sister, crying in imitation of his own tears, out here where the air quickly dries them, and the after-church smiles of the others flicker about them like butterflies born to live a day.

Oh this day, this holiday they have made just for themselves from a mundane Saturday, this last day of summer. What a great waste of gas it seems as they drive in procession to Ma Springer's house through the slanted streets of the town. Harry and Janice in the Corona follow Bessie's blue Chrysler in case the old dame plows into something, with Mim bringing Mrs. Lubell in Janice's Mustang, its headlight still twisted, behind. "What made you cry so much?" Janice asks him. She has taken off her hat and fiddled her bangs even in the rearview mirror.

"I don't know. Everything. The way Nellie looked from the back. The way the backs of kids' heads *trust* you. I mean they really *liked* that, this little dumb crowd of us gathered to watch."

He looks sideways at her silence. The tip of her little tongue rests on her lower lip, not wanting to say the wrong thing. She says, "If you're so full of tears you might try being less mean about him and the lot."

"I'm not mean about him and the lot. He doesn't give a fuck about the lot, he just wants to hang around having you and your

mother support him and the easiest way to put a face on that is
to go through some sort of motions over at the lot. You know
how much that caper of his with the convertibles cost the firm?
Guess."

"He says you got him so frustrated he went crazy. He says you
knew you were doing it, too."

"Forty-five hundred bucks, that was what those shitboxes cost.
Plus now all the parts Manny's had to order and the garage time
to fix 'em, you can add another grand."

"Nelson said the TR sold right off."

"That was a fluke. They don't make TRs anymore."

"He says Toyotas have had their run at the market, Datsun and
Honda are outselling them all over the East."

"See, that's why Charlie and me don't want the kid over at the
lot. He's full of negative thinking."

"Has Charlie said he doesn't want Nelson over at the lot?"

"Not in so many words. He's too much of a nice guy."

"I never noticed he was such a nice guy. Nice in that way. I'll
ask him over at the house."

"Now don't go lighting into poor Charlie, just because he's
moved on to Melanie. I don't know what he's ever said about
Nelson."

"Moved *on*! Harry, it's been ten years. You *must* stop living in
the past. If Charlie wants to make a fool of himself chasing after some
twenty-year-old it couldn't matter to me less. Once you've achieved
closure with somebody, all you have is good feelings for them."

"What's this achieving closure? You've been looking at too
many talk shows."

"It's a phrase people use."

"Those hussies you hang out with over at the club. Doris
Kaufmann. Fuck her." It stung him, that she thinks he lives in the
past. Why should he be the one to cry at the wedding? Mr. Nice
Guy. Mr. Tame Guy. To Hell with them. "Well at least Charlie's
avoiding marriage so that makes him less of a fool than Nelson,"
he says, and switches on the radio to shut off their conversation.
The four-thirty news: earthquake in Hawaii, kidnapping of two
American businessmen in El Salvador, Soviet tanks patrolling the
streets of Kabul in the wake of last Sunday's mysterious change of

leadership in Afghanistan. In Mexico, a natural-gas pact with the United States signals possible long-term relief for the energy crisis. In California, ten days of brush fire have destroyed more acres than any such fire since 1970. In Philadelphia, publishing magnate Walter Annenberg has donated fifty thousand dollars to the Catholic Archdiocese to help defray costs of the controversial platform from which Pope John Paul the Second is scheduled to celebrate Mass on October the third. Annenberg, the announcer gravely concludes, is a Jew.

"Why did they tell us that?" Janice asks.

God, she is dumb still. The realization comforts him. He tells her, "To make us alleged Christians feel lousy we've all been such cheapskates about the Pope's platform."

"I must say," Janice says, "it does seem extravagant, to build such a thing you're only going to use once."

"That's life," Harry says, pulling up to the curb along Joseph Street. There are so many cars in front of number 89 he has to park halfway up the block, in front of the house where the butch ladies live. One of them, a hefty youngish woman wearing an Army surplus fatigue jacket, is lugging a big pink roll of foil-backed insulation up onto the front porch.

"My son got married today," Harry calls out to her, on impulse.

His butch neighbor blinks and then calls back, "Good luck to her."

"Him."

"I meant the bride."

"O.K., I'll tell her."

The expression on the woman's face, slit-eyed like a cigar-store Indian, softens a little; she sees Janice getting out of the car on the other side, and calls to her, in a shouting mood now, "Jan, how do *you* feel about it?"

Janice is so slow to answer Harry answers for her, "She feels great. Why wouldn't she?" What he can't figure out about these butch ladies is not why they don't like him but why he wants them to, why just the distant sound of their hammering has the power to hurt him, to make him feel excluded.

Somehow, this Slim person, driving a canary-yellow Le Car with its name printed a foot high on the side, has made it from the church

with bride, groom, and Melanie ahead of Harry and Janice; and Ollie
and Peggy too, in their cinnamon-brown '73 Dodge Dart with a
Fiberglas-patched fender; and even Soupy has beat their time,
because his snappy little black Opel Manta with vanity plate
STJOHN is also parked by the curb this side of the maple that Ma
Springer has been seeing from her front bedroom for over thirty
years. These guests already crowd the living room, while this flustered little fat girl in a stab at a waitress uniform tries to carry around
those hors d'oeuvres that are costing a fortune, muddled things that
look like cheese melted on Taco Chips with a sprig of parsley added;
Harry dodges through, elbows lifted out of old basketball habit in
case somebody tries to put a move on him, to get the champagne in
the kitchen. Bottles of Mumm's at twelve dollars apiece even at case
price fill the whole second shelf of the fridge, stacked 69-style, foil
heads by heavy hollow butts, beautiful. CHAMPAGNE PROVIDED AT
SHOTGUN WEDDING, he thinks. *Angstrom Foots Bill.* Grace Stuhl's
grandson turns out to be a big beefy kid, can't weigh less than two
hundred fifty, with a bushy pirate's beard, and he has teeny weenies
frying in a pan on the stove and something wrapped in bacon in the
oven. Also a beer he took from the fridge open on the counter. The
noise in the living room keeps growing, and the front door keeps
opening, Stavros and the Murketts following Mim and Ma's brood
in, and all the fools come gabbling when the first cork pops. Boy,
it's like coming, it can't stop, the plastic hollow-stemmed champagne glasses Janice found at the Acme are on the round Chinese
tray on the counter behind Grace Stuhl's grandson's beer, too far
away for Harry to reach without some of the tawny foam spilling
onto the linoleum. The glasses as he fills them remind him of the
gold coins, precious down through the ages, and a latch inside him
lifts to let his sorrow out. What the hell, we're all going down the
chute together. Back in the living room, in front of the breakfront,
Ma Springer proposes a nervous little toast she's worked up, ending with the Pennsylvania Dutch, "*Dir seid nur eins: halt es selle weg.*"

"What does that mean, Mom-mom?" Nelson asks, afraid
something's being put over on him, such a child beside the blushing full-grown woman he's crazily gone and married.

"I was going to say," Bessie says irritably. "You are now one:
keep it that way."

Everybody cheers, and drinks, if they haven't already.

Grace Stuhl glides a step forward, into the circle of space cleared by the breakfront, maybe she was a great dancer fifty years ago, a certain type of old lady keeps her ankles and her feet small, and she is one. "Or as they always used to say," she proposes, "*Bussie waiirt ows, kocha dut net*. Kissing wears out, cooking don't."

The cheers are louder. Harry pops another bottle and settles on getting drunk. Those melted Taco Chips aren't so bad, if you can get them to your mouth before they break in your fingers, and the little fat girlfriend has an amazing bosom. All this ass, at least there's no shortage of that, it just keeps arriving. It seems an age since he lay awake disturbed by the entrance into this house of Pru Lubell, now Teresa Angstrom. Harry finds himself standing next to her mother. He asks her, "Have you ever been to this part of the world before?"

"Just passing through from time to time," she says, in a wisp of a voice he has to bend over to hear, as at a deathbed. How softly Pru had spoken her vows at the ceremony! "My people are from Chicago, originally."

"Well, your daughter does you proud," he tells her. "We love her already." He sounds to himself, saying this, like an impersonator; life, just as we first thought, is playing grownup.

"Teresa tries to do the right thing," her mother says. "But it's never been easy for her."

"It hasn't?"

"She takes after her father's people. You know, always going to extremes."

"Really?"

"Oh yes. Stubborn. You daren't go against them."

Her eyes widen. He feels with this woman as if he and she have been set to making a paper chain together, with inadequate glue, and the links keep coming unstuck. It is not easy to hear in this room. Soupy and that Slim are giggling now together.

"I'm sorry your husband can't be here," Harry says.

"You wouldn't be if you knew him," Mrs. Lubell replies serenely, and waggles her plastic glass as if to indicate how empty it is.

"Lemme get you some more." Rabbit realizes with a shock that she is his proper date: old as she seems this woman is about his age and instead of naked in dreamland with stacked chicks like Cindy Murkett and Grace Stuhl's grandson's girlfriend he should be in mental bed with the likes of Mrs. Lubell. He retreats into the kitchen to look after the champagne supply and finds Nelson and Melanie busy at the bottles. The countertop is strewn with those little wire cages each cork comes trapped in.

"Dad, there may not be *enough*," Nelson whines.

These two. "Why don't you kids switch to milk?" he suggests, taking a bottle from the boy. Heavy and green and cold, like money. The label engraved. His own poor dead dad never drank such bubbly in his life. Seventy years of beer and rusty water. To Melanie he says, "That expensive bike of yours is still in the garage."

"Oh I know," she says, innocently staring. "If I took it back to Kent someone would steal it." Her bulging brown eyes show no awareness that he has been curt, feeling betrayed by her.

He tells her, "You ought to go out and say hello to Charlie."

"Oh, we've *said* hello." Did she leave the motel room he was paying for to go shack up with Charlie? Harry can't follow it all. As if to make things right Melanie says, "I'll tell Pru she can use the bike if she wants. It's wonderful exercise for those muscles."

What muscles? Back in the living room, nobody has been kind enough to take his place beside the mother of the bride. As he refills her readily proffered glass he says to her, "Thanks for the handkerchief. Back in the church."

"It must be hard," she says, looking up at him more cozily now, "when there's only one."

There's not only one, he wants to tell her, drunker than he intended. There's a dead little sister lying buried in the hill above us, and a long-legged girl roaming the farmland south of Galilee. Who does she remind him of, Mrs. Lubell, when she flirts her head like that, looking up? Thelma Harrison, beside the pool. The Harrisons maybe should have been invited, but then you get into things like Buddy Inglefinger's feelings being hurt. And Ronnie would have been gross. The organist with the goatee (who invited *him*?) has joined Soupy and Slim now and something in the gaiety there leads the minister to remember his duty to others. He comes and joins Harry and the mother, a Christian act.

"Well," Harry blurts to him. "What's done is done, huh?"

Becky a skeleton by now, strange to think. The nightie they buried her in turned to cobwebs. Her little toenails and fingernails bits of confetti scattered on the satin.

Reverend Campbell's many small tobacco-darkened teeth display themselves in a complacent smile. "The bride looked lovely," he tells Mrs. Lubell.

"She gets her height from her father's people," she says. "And her straight hair. Mine just curls naturally, where Frank's sticks up all over his head, he can never get it to lay down. Teresa's isn't quite that stubborn, since she's a girl."

"Just lovely," Soupy says, his smile getting a glaze.

Harry asks the man, "How does that Opel of yours do for mileage?"

He takes out his pipe to address the question. "Up and down on these hills isn't exactly optimum, is it? I'd say twenty-five, twenty-six at best. I do a lot of stopping and starting and with nothing but short trips the carbon builds up."

Harry tells him, "You know the Japanese make these cars even though Buick sells 'em. I heard they may not be importing any after the 1980 model. That's going to put a squeeze on parts."

Soupy is amused, his twinkling eyes tell Mrs. Lubell. Toward Harry he slides these eyes with mock severity and asks, "Are you trying to sell me a Toyota?"

Mom getting to be a skeleton too, come to think of it. Those big bones in the earth like dinosaur bones.

"Well," Harry says, "we have a new little front-wheel drive called the Tercel, don't know where they get these names from but never mind, it gets over forty m.p.g. on the highway and is plenty of car for a single man."

Waiting for the Resurrection. Suppose it never comes?

"But suppose I get *mar*ried," the small man protests, "and have an *enor*mous brood!"

"And indeed you should," Mrs. Lubell unexpectedly pipes up. "The priests are leaving the church in droves because they've got the itch. All this sex, in the movies, books, everywhere, even on the television if you stay up late enough, no wonder they can't resist. Be grateful you don't have that conflict."

"I have often thought," Soupy tells her in a muted return of his great marrying voice, "I might have made an excellent priest. I *adore* structure."

Rabbit says, "Just now in the car we heard that Annenberg down in Philadelphia gave the Catholics fifty thousand so they could put up this platform for the Pope without all this squawking from the civil liberties people."

Soupy sniffs. "Do you know how much publicity that fifty thousand is going to get him? It's a bargain."

Slim and the organist seem to be discussing clothes, fingering each other's shirts. If he has to talk to the organist Harry can ask why he didn't play "Here Comes the Bride."

Mrs. Lubell says, "They wanted the Pope to come to Cleveland but I guess he had to draw the line somewhere."

"I hear he's going to some farm way out in nowhere," Harry says.

Soupy touches the mother of the bride on the wrist and tips his head so as to show to Harry the beginnings of his bald spot. "Mr. Annenberg is our former ambassador to the Court of St. James in England. The story goes that when presenting his credentials to the Queen she held out her hand to be kissed and he shook it instead and said, 'How're ya doin', Queen?'"

His growl is good. Mrs. Lubell laughs outright, a titter jumps from her to her shame, for she quickly covers her mouth with her knuckles. Soupy loves it, giving her back a deep laugh as from a barrel-chested old fart. If that's the way they're going to carry on Rabbit figures he can leave them to it, and using Soupy as a pick makes his move away. He scouts over the gathered heads looking for an opening. It's always slightly dark in the living room, no matter how many lights are on or what the time of day; the trees and the porch cut down the sun. He'd like a house some day with lots of light, splashing in across smart square surfaces. Why bury yourself alive?

Ma Springer has Charlie locked in a one-on-one over by the breakfront, her face puffy and purplish like a grape with the force of the unheard words she is urging into his ear; he politely bows his tidy head, once broad like a ram's but now whittled to an old goat's, nodding almost greedily, like a chicken pecking up grains of corn. Up front, silhouetted against the picture window, the Murketts are holding forth with the Fosnachts, old Ollie no doubt letting these new folks know what a clever musical fellow he is and Peggy gushing, backing him up, holding within herself the knowledge of what a shiftless rat he amounts to domestically. The Murketts belong to the new circle in Harry's life and the Fosnachts to the old and he hates to see them overlap; even if Peggy was a pretty good lay that time he doesn't want those dismal old high-school tagalongs creeping into his country-club set, yet he can see flattery is doing it, flattery and champagne, Ollie ogling Cindy (don't you wish) and Peggy making cow-eyed moos all over Murkett, she'll flop for anybody, Ollie must be very unsatisfying, one of those very thin reedy pricks probably. Harry wonders if he'd better not go over there and break it up, but foresees a wall of razzing he feels too delicate to push through, after all those tears in church, and remembering Becky and Pop and Mom and even old Fred who aren't here. Mim is on the sofa with Grace Stuhl and that other old biddy Amy, and Christ if they aren't having a quiet little ball, the two of them recalling Mim as a child to herself, the Diamond County accent and manner of expressing things making her laugh every minute, and she reminding them, all painted and done up in flowerpot foil, of the floozies they sit and watch all day and night on television, the old souls don't even know they are floozies, these celebrity women playing *Beat the Clock* or *Hollywood Squares* or giving Merv or Mike or Phil the wink sitting in those talk show soft chairs with their knees sticking up naked, they all got there on their backs, nobody cares anymore, the times have caught up with Mim and put her on the gray sofa with the church folk. Nelson and Melanie and Grace Stuhl's lout of a grandson are still in the kitchen and the girlfriend, after going around with the teeny weenies under her tits in a tricky little warmer with a ketchup dip, seems to have given up and joined them; they have in there the little portable Sony Janice sometimes watches the Carol Burnett reruns on as she makes supper, and from the sound of it – cheers, band music – these useless drunken kids have turned on the Penn State–Nebraska game. Meanwhile there's Pru in her champagne-colored wedding dress, the little wreath off her head now, standing alone over by the three-way lamp examining that heavy green glass bauble of Ma Springer's, with the teardrop of air sealed inside, turning it over and over under the wan light with her long pink hands, where a wedding ring now gleams. Laughter explodes from the Fosnacht-Murkett group, which Janice has joined. Webb pushes past Harry toward the kitchen, his fingers full of plastic glasses. "How about that crazy Rose?" he says, going by, to say something.

Pete Rose has been hitting over .600 lately and only needs four more hits to be the first player ever to get two hundred hits in ten major league seasons. But it doesn't mean that much, the Phillies are twelve and a half games out. "What a showboat," Rabbit says, what they used to say about him, nearly thirty years ago.

Perhaps in her conspicuous pregnancy Pru is shy of pushing through the crowd to join the others of her generation in the kitchen. Harry goes to her side and stoops down to kiss her demure warm cheek before she is aware; champagne makes it easy. "Aren't you supposed to kiss the bride?" he asks her.

She turns her head and gives him that smile that hesitates and then suddenly spreads, one corner tucked awry. Her eyes have taken green from contemplating the glass, that strange glossy egg Harry has more than once thought would be good to pound into Janice's skull. "Of course," she says. Held against her belly the bauble throws from its central teardrop a pale blade of light. He senses that she had been aware of his approaching in the side of her vision but had held still like a deer in danger. Among these strange people, her fate sealed by a ceremony, of course she is afraid. Rabbit tries to comfort his daughter-in-law: "I bet you're beat. Don't you get sleepy as hell? As I remember it Janice did."

"You feel clumsy," Pru allows, and with both hands replaces the green glass orb on the round table that is like a wooden leaf all around the stem of the standing lamp. Abruptly she asks, "Do you think I'll make Nelson happy?"

"Oh sure. The kid and I had a good long talk about it once. He thinks the world of you."

"He doesn't feel trapped?"

"Well, frankly, that's what I was curious about, 'cause in his position I might. But honest to God, Teresa, it doesn't seem to bother him. From little on up he's always had this sense of fairness and in this case he seems to feel fair is fair. Listen. Don't you worry yourself. The only thing bothering Nelson these days is his old man."

"He thinks the world of you," she says, her voice very small, in case this echo is too impudent.

Harry snorts; he loves it when women sass him, and any sign of life from this one is gratefully received. "It'll all work out," he promises, though Teresa's aura of fright remains intense and threatens to spread to him. When the girl dares a full smile you see her teeth needed braces and didn't get them. The taste of champagne keeps reminding him of poor Pop. Beer and rusty water and canned mushroom soup.

"Try to have some fun," he tells Pru, and cuts across the jammed room, around the boisterous Murkett-Fosnacht-Janice crowd, to the sofa where Mim sits between the two old ladies. "Are you being a bad influence on my little sister?" he asks Amy Gehringer.

While Grace Stuhl laughs at this Amy struggles to get to her feet. "Don't get up on my account," Rabbit tells her. "I just came over to see if I could get any of you anything."

"What I need," Amy grunts, still floundering, so he pulls her up, "I must get for myself."

"What's that?" he asks.

She looks at him a little glassily, like Melanie when he told her to drink milk. "A call of nature," Amy answers, "you could say."

Grace Stuhl holds up a hand that when he takes it, to pull her up, feels like a set of worn stones in a sack of the finest driest paper, strangely warm. "I better say goodbye to Becky," she says.

"She's over there talking the ear off Charlie Stavros," Harry tells her.

"Yes, and probably saying too much by now." She seems to know the subject; or does he imagine that? He drops down onto the sofa beside Mim wearily.

"So," she says.

"Next I gotta marry you off," he says.

"I've been asked, actually, now and then."

"And whajja say?"

"At my age it seemed like too much trouble."

"Your health good?"

"I make it good. No more smoking, notice?"

"How about those crazy hours you keep, staying up to watch Ol' Blue Eyes? I knew he was called Ol' Blue Eyes, by the way. I just didn't know *which* Ol' Blue Eyes, I thought a new one might have come along." When he had called her long-distance to invite her to the wedding she said she had a date with a very dear friend to see Ol' Blue Eyes and he had asked, *Who's Ol' Blue Eyes?* She said *Sinatra, ya dummy, where've you been all your life?* and he answered, *You know where I've been, right here* and she said, *Yeah, it shows.* God, he loves Mim; in the end there's nothing to understand you like your own blood.

Mim says, "You sleep it off during the day. Anyway I'm out of the fast lane now, I'm a businesswoman." She gestures toward the other side of the room. "What's Bessie trying to do, keep me from talking to Charlie? She's been at him an hour."

"I don't know what's going on."

"You never did. We all love you for it."

"Drop dead. Hey how do you like the new Janice?"

"What's new about her?"

"Don't you see it? More confident. More of a woman, somehow."

"Hard as a nut, Harry, and always will be. You were always feeling sorry for her. It was a wasted effort."

"I miss Pop," he suddenly says.

"You're getting more and more like him. Especially from the side."

"He never got a gut like mine."

"He didn't have the teeth for all those munchies you like."

"You notice how this Pru looks like him a little? And Mom's big red hands. I mean, she seems more of an Angstrom than Nelson."

"You guys like tough ladies. She's pulled off a trick I didn't think could be pulled off anymore."

He nods, imagining through her eyes his father's toothless profile closing in upon his own. "She's running scared."

"And how about you?" Mim asks. "What're *you* doing these days, to feed the inner man?"

"I play golf."

"And still fuck Janice?"

"Sometimes."

"You two. Mother and I didn't give it six months, the way she trapped you."

"Maybe I trapped myself. And what's up with you? How does money work, out in Vegas? You really own a beauty parlor, or you just a front for the big guys?"

"I own thirty-five per cent. That's what I got for being a front for the big guys."

He nods again. "Sounds familiar."

"You fucking anybody else? You can tell me, I'll be on that plane tomorrow. How about the broad bottom over there with the Chinesey eyes?"

He shakes his head. "Nope. Not since Jill. That shook me up."

"O.K., but ten years, that's not normal, Harry. You're letting them turn you into a patsy."

"Remember," he asks, "how we used to go sledding on Jackson Road? I often think about it."

"That happened maybe once or twice, it never *snows* around here, for Cry-eye. Come out to Lake Tahoe; now there's *snow*. We'll go over to Alta or Taos; you should see me ski. Come on out by yourself, we'll fix you up with somebody really nice. Blonde, brunette, redhead, you name it. Good clean small-town girl too; nothing crude."

"Mim," he says, blushing, "you're the limit," and thinks of telling her how much he loves her, but there is a commotion at the front door.

Slim and the organist are leaving together and they encounter there a dowdy couple who have been ringing the disconnected doorbell for some time. From the look of them they are selling encyclopaedias, except that people don't do that in pairs, or going door-to-door for the Jehovah's Witnesses, except that instead of *The Watchtower* they are holding on to a big silver-wrapped wedding present. This is the couple from Binghamton. They took the wrong turn off the Northeast Extension and found themselves lost in West Philadelphia. The woman sheds tears of relief and exhaustion once inside the foyer. "Blocks and blocks of

blacks," the man says, telling their story, still staggered by the wonder of it.

"*Oh*," Pru cries from across the room, "Uncle Rob!" and
throws herself into his arms, home at last.

Ma Springer has made the Poconos place available to the young
couple for a honeymoon in these golden last weeks of warm
weather – the birches beginning to turn, the floats and canoes
pulled in from the lake. All of it wasted on the kid, they'll be lucky
if he doesn't burn the cottage down frying his brain and his genes
with pot. But it's not Harry's funeral. Now that Nelson is married
it's like a door has been shut in his mind, a debt has been finally
paid, and his thoughts are turning again to that farm south of here
where another child of his may be walking, walking and waiting
for her life to begin.

One evening when nothing she likes is on television Ma calls a
little conference in the living room, easing her legs wrapped around
with flesh-colored bandages (a new thing her doctor has prescribed;
when Harry tries to visualize an entire creature made out of the flesh
the bandage manufacturers are matching, it would make the Hulk
look healthy) up on the hassock and letting the man of the house
have the Barcalounger. Janice sits on the sofa with a post-dinner nip
of some white creamy poison fermented from coconut milk the
kids have brought into the house, looking girlish beside her mother, with her legs tucked up under her. Nice taut legs. She's kept
those and he has to take his hat off to her, tiddly half the time or
not. What more can you ask of a wife in a way than that she stick
around and see with you what happens next?

Ma Springer announces, "We must settle now what to do with
Nelson."

"Send him back to college," Harry says. "She had an apartment
out there, they can both move into one."

"He doesn't want to go," Janice tells them, not for the first
time.

"And why the hell not?" Harry asks, the question still exciting
to him, though he knows he's beaten.

"Oh Harry," Janice says wearily, "nobody knows. You didn't go to college, why should he?"

"That's the reason. Look at me. I don't want him to live my life. I'm living it and that's enough."

"Darling, I said that from his point of view, not to argue with you. Of course Mother and I would have preferred he had graduated from Kent and not got so involved with this secretary. But that's not the way it is."

"He can't go back to college with a wife as if nothing happened," Bessie states. "They knew her out there as one of the employees and I think he'd be embarrassed. He needs a job."

"Great," Harry says, enjoying being perverse, letting the women do the constructive thinking. "Maybe his father-in-law can get him a job out in Akron."

"You saw the mother," Ma Springer says. "There's no help there."

"Uncle Rob was a real swinger, though. What does he do up in the shoe factory? Punch the holes for the laces?"

Janice imitates her mother's flat, decided rhythm. "Harry. Nelson must come to work at the lot."

"Oh Christ. Why? *Why?* This is a huge country. It has old factories, new factories, farms, stores, why can't the lazy brat get a job at one of *them*? All those summers he was back from Kent he never got a job. He hasn't had a job since that paper route when he was fourteen and needed to buy Beatles records."

Janice says, "Going up to the Poconos a month every summer meant he couldn't get anything too serious, he used to complain about it. Besides, he did do some things. He babysat for a time there, and he helped that high-school teacher who was building his own home, with the solar panels and the cellar full of rocks that stored heat."

"Why doesn't he go into something like that? That's where the future is, not selling cars. Cars have had it. The party's over. It's going to be all public transportation twenty years from now. Ten years from now, even. Why doesn't he take a night course and learn how to program a computer? If you look at the want ads, that's all there is, computer programmers and electronic engineers. Remember when Nelson rigged up all those hi-fi components and even had speakers hooked up on the sunporch? He could do all that, what happened?"

"What happened is, he grew up," Janice says, finishing off the coconut liqueur, tilting her head back so far her throat shows the pale rings that when her head is held normally are wrinkles. Her tongue probes the bottom of the glass. With Nelson and Pru part of the household, Janice drinks more freely; they sit around getting silly and waiting up for Johnny Carson or *Saturday Night Live*, her smoking has gotten back up to over a pack a day in spite of Harry's nagging to get her to quit. Now in this discussion she's acting as if he is some natural disturbance they must let boringly run its course.

He is getting madder. "I *offered* to take him on in Service, there's the department they can always use an extra man, Manny'd have him trained as a full-fledged mechanic in no time. You know what mechanics pull down an hour now? Seven bucks, and it costs me over eight to pay 'em that what with all this fringe stuff. And once they can work faster than the flat rate they get bonuses. Our top men take home over fifteen thousand a year and a couple of them aren't much older than Nelson."

"Nelson doesn't want," Janice says, "to be a grease monkey any more than you do."

"Happiest days of my life," he lies, "were spent working with my hands."

"It isn't easy," Ma Springer decides to tell them, "being old, and a widow. In everything I do, after I pray about it, I try to ask myself, 'Now what would Fred want?' And I know with absolute certainty in this instance he would want little Nellie to come work on the lot if that's what the boy desired. A lot of these young men now wouldn't want such a job, they don't have the thick skins a salesman has to have, and it's not so glamorous, unless you began by following the hind end of a horse around all day the way the people of my generation did."

Rabbit bristles, impatient. "Bessie, every generation has its problems, we all start behind the eight ball. Face the facts. How much you gonna pay Nelson? How much salary, how much commission? You know what a dealer's profit margin is. Three per cent, three lousy little per cent, and that's being cut down to nothing by a lot of new overhead you can't pass on the customer with these fixed prices Toyota has. Oil going up takes everything up with it; in the five years I've been in charge heating costs have doubled, electricity is way up, delivery costs are up, plus all these social security hikes and unemployment to pay so the bums in this country won't have to give up their yacht or whatever, half the young people in the country go to work just enough to collect unemployment, and now the interest on the inventory is going out of sight. It's just like the Weimar thing, people's savings are being washed right down the tube, everybody agrees there's a recession coming to curl your hair. The economy is *shot*, Ma, we can't hack it, we don't have the discipline the Japs and Germans do, and on top of this you want me to hire a piece of dead weight who happens to be my son."

"In answer to your question," Ma says, grunting a little as she shifts the sorer leg on the hassock, "the minimum wage is going to be three-ten an hour so if he works forty hours a week you'll have to give him a hundred twenty-five a week, and then the bonuses you'd have to figure on the usual formula, isn't it now something like twenty per cent of the gross profit on the sale, and then going to twenty-five over a certain minimum? I know it used to be a flat five per cent of the net amount of the sale, but Fred said you couldn't do that with foreign cars for some reason."

"Bessie, with all respect, and I love you, but you are crazy. You pay Nelson five hundred a month to start with and set commissions on top of that he's going to be taking home a thousand a month for bringing in the company only twenty-five hundred. To pay Nelson that amount it should mean he sells, depending on the proportion of new to used, between seven to ten cars a month for an agency that doesn't move twenty-five a month overall!"

"Well, maybe with Nelson there you'll move more," Ma says.

"*Dreamer*," Harry says to her. "Detroit's getting tooled up finally to turn out subcompacts a dime a dozen, and there's going to be stiffer import taxes any day now. Twenty-five a month is optimum, honest to God."

"The people that remember Fred will like to see Nelson there," she insists.

Janice says, "Nelson says the mark-up on the new Toyotas is at least a thousand dollars."

"That's a loaded model, with all the extras. The people who buy Toyotas aren't into extras. Basic Corollas are what we sell mostly, four to one. And even on the bigger models the carrying costs amount to a couple hundred per unit with money going to Hell the way it is."

She is obstinate and dumb. "A thousand a car," she says, "means he has to sell only five a month, the way you figure it."

"What about Jake and Rudy!" he cries. "How could the kid sell even five without cutting into Jake and Rudy? Listen, if you two want to know who your loyal employees are, it's Jake and Rudy. They work all the shit hours you ask 'em to, on the floor nights and weekends, they moonlight to make up for all the low hours you tell 'em to stay away, Rudy runs a little bike repair shop out of his garage, in this day and age, everybody else begging for handouts, they're still taking a seventy-five base and a one-fifty draw. You can't turn guys like that out in the cold."

"I wasn't thinking so much of Jake and Rudy," Ma Springer says, with a frown resting one ankle on top of the other. "How much now does Charlie make?"

"Oh no you don't. We've been through this. Charlie goes, I go."

"Just for my information."

"Well, Charlie pulls down around three-fifty a week – rounds out to over twenty thousand a year with the bonuses."

"Well, then," Ma Springer pronounces, easing the ankle back to where it was, "you'd actually save money, taking Nelson on instead. He has this interest in the used cars, and that's Charlie's department, hasn't it been?"

"Bessie, I can't believe this. Janice, talk to her about Charlie."

"We've talked, Harry. You're making too much of it. Mother has talked to me and I thought it might do Charlie good to make a change. She also talked to Charlie and he agreed."

Harry is disbelieving. "*When* did you talk to Charlie?"

"At the reception," Ma Springer admits. "I saw you looking over at us."

"Well my God, whajja say?"

This is some old lady, Rabbit thinks, sneakers, Ace bandages, cotton dress up over her knees, puffy throat, funny silver-browed eyeglasses, and all. Once in a while, in the winters since old Fred cashed in, she has visited the lot wearing the mink coat he gave her for their twenty-fifth wedding anniversary, and there was a glitter on that fur like needles of steel, like a signal crackling out of mission control. She says, "I asked him how his health was."

"The way we worry about Charlie's health you'd think he was in a wheelchair."

"Janice has told me, even ten years ago he was taking nitro-glycerine. For a man only in his thirties then, that's not good."

"Well what did *he* say, how his health was?"

"Fair," Ma Springer answers, giving it the local two syllables, *Fai-ir*. "Janice herself claims you complain he doesn't do his share anymore, just sits huddled at the desk playing with paperwork he should leave for Mildred to do."

"Did I say all that?" He looks at Janice, his betrayer. He has always thought of her darkness as a Springer trait but of course old man Springer was fair, thin-skinned pink; it is her mother's blood, the Koerners', that has determined her coloring.

She flicks her cigarette at the ashtray impatiently. "More than once," she says.

"Well I didn't mean your mother should go fire the guy."

"Fire was never used as a word," Ma Springer says. "Fred would never have fired Charlie, unless his personal life got all out of hand."

"You got to go pretty far to get out of hand these days," Harry says, resenting that this is the case. He had tried to have fun too early.

Ma Springer rolls her weight uncomfortably on the sofa. "Well I must say, this chasing that girl out to Ohio —"

"He took her to Florida, too," Harry says, so quickly both women stare at him with their button-black eyes. It's true, it galls him more than it should, since he could never warm to Melanie himself and had nowhere to take her anyhow.

"We talked about Florida," Ma Springer says. "I asked him if now that winter's coming he mightn't be better off down there. Amy Gehringer's son-in-law, that used to work in an asbestos plant in New Jersey until they got that big scare, has retired down there on the compensation, and he's under fifty. She says he tells her there are a lot of young people coming down there now, to get away from the oil crisis, it's not just the old people like in all the jokes, and of course there are jobs to be had there too. Charlie's clever. Fred recognized that from the start."

"He has this mother, Ma. An old Greek lady who can't speak English and who's never been out of Brewer hardly."

"Well maybe it's time she was. You know people think we old people are such sticks in the mud but Grace Stuhl's sister, older than she is, mind you, and buried two husbands right in the county, went out to visit her son in Phoenix and loved it so she's bought her own little condominium and even, Grace was telling me, her burial plot, that's how much she pulled up her roots."

"Charlie's not like you, Harry," Janice explains. "He's not scared of change."

He could take that green glass egg and in one stride be at the sofa and pound it down into her dense skull. Instead he ignores her, saying to Ma, "I still haven't heard exactly what you said to Charlie, and he said to you."

"Oh, we reminisced. We talked about the old days with Fred and we agreed that Fred would want Nellie to have a place at the lot. He was always one for family, Fred, even when family let him down."

That must mean him, Rabbit thinks. Letting that shifty little wheeler-dealer down is about the last thing on his conscience.

"Charlie understands family," Janice interposes, in that smooth matronly voice she can do now, imitating her mother. "All the time I was, you know, seeing him, he was absolutely ready to stand aside and have me go back."

Bragging about her affair to her own mother. The world is falling apart fast.

"And so," Ma Springer sighs – she is wearying of this, her legs hurt and aren't improving, old people need their privacy – "we tried to come to an understanding of what Fred would want and came up with this idea of a leave for Charlie, for six months with half pay, and then at the end we'd see how Nellie was working out. In the meantime if the offer of another job comes Charlie's way he's to be free to take it, and then we'll settle at that point with two months' pay as a bonus, plus whatever his Christmas bonus would be for all of 1979. This wasn't just worked out at the party, I was over there today while you were playing golf."

He had been carrying an 83 into the last hole and then hooked into the creek and took an 8. It seems he'll never break 90 there, unless he does it in his sleep. Webb Murkett's relaxed swing is getting on his nerves. "Sneaky," he says. "I thought you didn't trust yourself to drive the Chrysler in Brewer traffic anymore."

"Janice drove me over."

"Aha." He asks his wife, "How did Charlie like seeing you there on this mission of mercy?"

"He was sweet. This has all been between him and Mother. But he knows Nelson is our son. Which is more than you seem to."

"No, no, I know he is, that's the trouble," Harry tells her. To old lady Springer he says, "So you're paying Charlie thousands to hand Nelson a job he probably can't do. Where's the savings for the firm in that? And you're going to lose sales without Charlie, I don't have half the contacts around town he does. Not just Greeks, either. Being single he's been in a lot of bars, that's where you win people's trust around here."

"Well, it may be." Ma Springer gets herself to her feet and stamps each one softly on the carpet, testing if either is asleep. "It may all be a mistake, but in this life you can't always be afraid of mistakes. I never liked that about Charlie, that he was unwilling to get married. It bothered Fred too, I know. Now I must get myself upstairs and see my Angels. Though it's not been the same since Farrah left."

"Don't I get a vote?" Harry asks, almost yelling, strapped as he feels into the Barcalounger. "I vote against it. I don't *want* to be bothered with Nelson over there."

"Well," Ma says, and in her long pause he has time to appreciate how big she is, how broad from certain angles, like a tree trunk seen suddenly in terms of all the toothpicks it would make, all those meals and days gone into this bulk, the stiff heavy seesaw of her hips, the speckled suet of her arms, "as I understand Fred's will, he left the lot to me and Janice, and I think we're of a mind."

"Two against three, Harry, in any case," Janice says, with a winning smile.

"Oh screw you," he says. "Screw Springer Motors. I suppose if I don't play dead doggie you two'll vote to can me too."

They don't deny it. While Ma's steps labor up the staircase, Janice, beginning to wear that smudged look she gets when the day's intake catches up with her, gets to her feet and tells him confidentially, "Mother thought you'd take it worse than you did. Want anything from the kitchen? This CocoRibe is really addictive."

October first falls on a Monday. Autumn is starting to show its underside: out of low clouds like a row of torn mattresses a gray rain is knocking the leaves one by one off the trees. That lonely old maple behind the Chuck Wagon across Route 111 is bare now down to its lower branches, which hang on like a monk's fringe. Not a day for customers: Harry and Charlie gaze together through the plate-glass windows where the posters now say COMING, ALL NEW COROLLAS • *New 1.8-liter engine* • *New aerodynamic styling* • *Aluminum wheels on SR5 models* • *Removable sunroof/moonroof* • *Best selling car in the world!* Another paper banner proclaims THE COROLLA TERCEL • *First Front-Wheel Drive Toyota* • *Toyota's Lowest Price & Highest Mileage* • *33 Est. MPG* • *43 EPA Estimated Highway MPG.* "Well," Harry says, after clearing his throat, "the Phillies went out with a bang." By shutting out the Montreal Expos on the last day of the season, 2–0, they enabled Pittsburgh to win the championship of the National League East.

"I was rooting for the Expos," Charlie says.

"Yeah, you hate to see Pittsburgh win again. They're so fucking jivey. All that Family crap."

Stavros shrugs. "Well, a team of blacks like that, you need a slogan. They all grew up on television commercials, the box was the only mother they had. That's the tragedy of blacks these days."

It relieves Harry, to hear Charlie talk. He came in half expecting to find him crushed. "At least the Eagles screwed the Steelers," he says. "That felt good."

"They were lucky. That fumble going into the end zone. Bradshaw you can expect to throw some interceptions, but you don't expect Franco Harris to fumble going into the end zone."

Harry laughs aloud, in remembered delight. "How about that barefoot rookie kicker the Eagles got? Wasn't that beautiful?"

Charlie says, "Kicking isn't football."

"A forty-eight-yard field goal barefoot! That guy must have a big toe like a rock."

"For my money they can ship all these old soccer players back to Argentina. The contact in the line, that's football. The Pit. That's where the Steelers will get you in the end. I'm not worried about the Steelers."

Harry sniffs anger here and changes the subject, looking out at the weather. Drops on the glass enlarge and then abruptly dart down, dodgingly, leaving trails. The way he wept. Ever since earliest childhood, his consciousness dawning by the radiators in the old half-house on Jackson Road, it has been exciting for Harry to stand near a window during a rain, his face inches from the glass and dry, where a few inches away everything is wet. "Wonder if it's going to rain on the Pope." The Pope is flying into Boston that afternoon.

"Never. He'll just wave his arms and the sky'll be full of blue-birds. Bluebirds and horseshit."

Though no Catholic, Harry feels this is a bit rude; no doubt about it, Charlie is prickly this morning. "Ja see those crowds on television? The Irish went wild. One crowd was over a million, they said."

"Micks are dumb," Charlie says, and starts to turn away. "I gotta get hot on some NV-1s."

Harry can't let him go. He says, "And they gave the old Canal back last night."

"Yeah. I get sick of the news. This country is sad, everybody can push us around."

"You were the guy wanted to get out of Vietnam."

"That was sad too."

"Hey."

"Yeah?"

"I hear you had a talk with Ma Springer."

"The last of a long series. She's not so sad. She's tough."

"Any thoughts about where you're going to be going?" Nelson and Pru are due back from the Poconos Friday.

"Nowhere, for a while. See a few movies. Hit a few bars."

"How about Florida, you're always talking about Florida."

"Come on. I can't ask the old lady to move down there. What would she do, play shuffleboard?"

"I thought you said you had a cousin taking care of her now."

"Gloria. I don't know, something's cooking there. She and her husband may be getting back together. He doesn't like scrambling his own eggs in the morning."

"Oh. Sorry." Harry pauses. "Sorry about everything."

Charlie shrugs. "What can *you* do?"

This is what he wants to hear; relief bathes him like a kind of light. When you feel better, you see better; he sees all the papers, wrappers and take-out cup lids that have blown across the highway from the Chuck Wagon, lying in the bushes just outside the window, getting soaked. He says, "I could quit myself."

"That's crazy, champ. What would you do? Me, I can sell anywhere, that's no worry. Already I've had some feelers. News travels fast in this business. It's a hustling business."

"I told her, 'Ma, Charlie's the heart of Springer Motors. Half the clients come in because of him. More than half.'"

"I appreciate your putting in a word. But you know, there comes a time."

"I guess." But not for Harry Angstrom. Never, never.

"How about Jan? What'd *she* have to say about giving me the gate?"

A tough question. "Not much, that I heard. You know she can't stand up to the old lady; never could."

"If you want to know what I think cooked my goose, it was that trip with Melanie. That cooled it with both the Springer girls."

"You think Janice still cares that much?"

"You don't stop caring, champ. You still care about that little girl whose underpants you saw in kindergarten. Once you care, you always care. That's how stupid we are."

A rock in space, is the image these words bring to Rabbit's mind. He is interested in space, and scans the paper every day for more word on these titanic quasars on the edge of everything, and in the Sunday section studies the new up-close photos of Jupiter, expecting to spot a clue that all those scientists have missed; God might have a few words to say yet. In the vacuum of the heart love falls forever. Janice jealous of Charlie, we get these ideas and can't let go, it's been twenty years since he slept with Ruth but whenever in some store downtown or along Weiser he sees from behind a woman with gingery hair bundled up carelessly with a few loops flying loose, his heart bumps up. And Nelson, he was young at the time but you're never too young to fall, he loved Jill and come to think of it Pru has some of the hippie style, long hair flat down the back and that numb look daring you to hurt her, though Jill of course was of a better class, she was no Akron steamfitter's daughter. Harry says to Charlie, "Well at least now you can run out to Ohio from time to time."

Charlie says, "There's nothing out there for me. Melanie's more like a daughter. She's smart, you know. You ought to hear her go on about transcendental meditation and this crazy Russian philosopher. She wants to go on and get a Ph.D. if she can worm the money out of her father. He's out there on the West Coast fucking Indian maidens."

Coast to coast, Rabbit thinks, we're one big funhouse. It's done with mirrors. "Still," he tells Charlie, "I wish I had some of your freedom."

"You got freedom you don't even use. How come you and Jan keep living in that shabby old barn with her mother? It's not doing Jan any good, it's keeping her childish."

Shabby? Harry had never thought of the Springer place as shabby: old-fashioned maybe but with big rooms full of the latest and best goods, just the way he saw it the first time, when he began to take Janice out, the summer they were both working at Kroll's. Everything looked new and smelled so clean, and in the side room off the living room a long wrought-iron table held a host of tropical plants, a jungle of their own that seemed the height of luxury. Now the table stands there hollow and you can see where it's stained the hardwood floor with rusty drippings. And he thinks of the gray sofa and the wallpaper and watercolors that haven't changed since the days he used to pick Jan up for a night of heavy petting in the back of the old Nash he bought in the Army and maybe it is shabby. Ma doesn't have the energy she did and what she does with all her money nobody knows. Not buy new furniture. And now that it's fall the copper beech outside their bedroom window is dropping its nuts, the little triangular seedpods explode and with all the rustling and crackling it's not so easy to sleep. That room has never been ideal. "Childish, huh?"

"Speaking of which," Charlie says, "remember those two kids who came in at the beginning of the summer, the girl that turned you on? The boy came back Saturday, while you were out on the golf course, I can't think of his name."

"Nunemacher."

"Right. He bought that orange Corolla liftback with standard transmission out on the lot. No trade-in, and these new models coming in, I quoted him two hundred off the list. I thought you'd want me to be nice to him."

"Right. Was the girl with him?"

"Not that I could see."

"And he didn't trade in that Country Squire?"

"You know these farmers, they like to keep junk in their yards. Probably hitch it up to a band saw."

"My God," Harry says. "Jamie bought the orange Corolla."

"Well come on, it's not that much of a miracle. I asked him why he waited so long and he said he thought if he waited to fall the '79s would be down in price a little. And the dollar would be worth less. The yen too as it turns out."

"When's he taking delivery?"

"He said around noon tomorrow. That's one of the NV-1s I gotta do."

"Shit. That's when I have Rotary."

"The girl wasn't with him, what do you care? You talk about me; she was younger than Melanie. That girl might have been as young as sixteen, seventeen."

"Nineteen is what she'd be," Rabbit says. "But you're right. I don't care." Rain all around them leads his heart upward by threads; he as well as Charlie has his options.

* * *

Tuesday after Rotary with the drinks still working in him Harry goes back to the lot and sees the orange Corolla gone and can hardly focus with happiness, God has kissed him out of space. Around four-thirty, with Rudy on the floor and Charlie over in Allenville trying to wrap up a used-car package with a dealer there to clear the books a little before Nelson takes over, he eases out of his office and down the corridor and out through the shop where Manny's men are still whacking metal but their voices getting louder as the bliss of quitting time approaches and out the back door, taking care not to dirty his shirt cuffs on the crash bar, and out into air. Paraguay. On this nether portion of the asphalt the Mercury with its mashed-in left side and fender and grille still waits upon a decision. It turns out Charlie was able to unload the repaired Royale for thirty-six hundred to a young doctor from Royersford, he wasn't even a regular doctor but one of these homeopathic or holistic doctors as they call it now who looks at your measles and tells you to eat carrots or just hum at a certain pitch for three hours a day, he must be doing all right because he snapped up that old Olds, said a guy he admired at college had driven one like it and he'd always wanted one just that color, evidently – that purply-red nail-polish color. Harry squeezes himself into his Corona the color of tired tomato soup and slides out of the lot softly and heads down 111 the way away from Brewer, toward Galilee. Springer Motors well behind him, he turns on the radio and that heavy electrified disco beat threatens to pop the stereo speakers. Tinny sounds, wiffling sounds, sounds like a kazoo being played over the telephone come at him from the four corners of the vinyl-upholstered interior, setting that hopeful center inside his ribs to jingling. He thinks back to the Rotary luncheon and Eddie Pastorelli of Pastorelli Realty with his barrel chest and stiff little bow legs now, that used to do the 440 in less than fifty seconds, giving them a slide show on the proposed planned development of the upper blocks of Weiser, which were mostly parking lots and bars these days, and little businesses like vacuum-cleaner repair and pet supplies that hadn't had the capital to move out to the malls, Eddie trying to tell them that some big glass boxes and a corkscrew-ramped concrete parking garage are going to bring the shoppers back in spite of all the spic kids roaming around with transistors glued to their ears and knives up their wrists. Harry has to laugh, he remembers Eddie when he was a second-string guard for Hemmigtown High, a meaner greaseball never stayed out of reform school. Donna Summer comes on singing, *Dim all the lights sweet darling* . . . When you see pictures of her she's much less black than you imagine, a thin-cheeked yellow staring out at you like what are you going to do about it. The thing about those Rotarians, if you knew them as kids you can't stop seeing the kid in them, dressed up in fat and baldness and money like a cardboard tuxedo in a play for high-school assembly. How can you respect the world when you see it's being run by a bunch of kids turned old? That's the joke Rabbit always enjoys at Rotary. With a few martinis inside him Eddie can be funny as hell, when he told that joke about the five men in the airplane the tip of his nose bent down like it was on a little string and his laugh came out as an old woman's wheeze. *Knapsack! hee hee hee.* Rabbit must try to remember and try it out on the gang at the Flying Eagle. Five men: a hippie, a priest, a policeman, and Henry Kissinger, the smartest man in the world. But who was the fifth? Donna Summer says to turn her brown body white, at least that's what he thinks she's said, you can't be sure with all this disco *wowowow*, some doped-up sound engineer wiggling the knobs to give that sound, the words don't matter, it's that beat pushed between your ribs like a knife, making the soul jingle.

Houses of sandstone. A billboard pointing to a natural cave. He wonders who goes there anymore, natural caves a thing of the past, like waterfalls. Men in straw hats. Women with not even their ankles showing. Natural wonders. That smartass young female announcer – he hasn't heard her for a while, he thought maybe the station had fired her, too sassy or got pregnant – comes on and says that the Pope has addressed the UN and is stopping in Harlem on his way to Yankee Stadium. Harry saw the cocky little guy on television last night, getting soaked in Boston in his white robes, you had to admire his English, about his seventh language, and who was the deadpan guy standing there holding the umbrella over him? Some Vatican bigwig, but Pru didn't seem to know any more than he did, what's the good of being raised a Catholic? In Europe, gold rose today to a new high of four hundred forty-four dollars an ounce while the dollar slipped to new lows. The station fades and returns as the road twists among the hilly fields. Harry calculates, up eighty dollars in less than three weeks, thirty times eighty is two thousand four hundred, when you're rich you get richer, just like Pop used to say. In some of the fields the corn stands tall, others are stubble. He glides through the ugly string town of Galilee, on the lookout for the orange Corolla. No need to ask at the post office this time. The vegetable stand is closed for the season. The pond has some geese on it, he doesn't remember those, migrating already, the green little turds they leave all over the fairways, maybe that was the reason that doctor . . . He turns off the radio. BLANKENBILLER. MUTH. BYER. He parks on the same widened spot of red dirt road shoulder. His heart is pounding, his hands feel swollen and numb, resting on the steering wheel. He turns off the ignition, digging himself in deeper. It's not as if he's doing anything illegal. When he gets out of the car, the pigsty whiff isn't in the air, the wind is from the other direction, and there is no insect hum. They have died, millions. Across the silence cuts the far-off whine and snarl of a chain saw. The new national anthem. *Oho say can you saw* . . . The woods are a half-mile off and can't be part of the Byer farm. He begins to trespass. The hedgerow that has swallowed the stone wall is less leafy, he is less hidden. A cool small wind slips through the tangled black gum and wild cherry and licks his hands. Poison ivy leaves have turned, a Mercurochrome red, some of them half-dyed as if dipped. As he ventures down through the old orchard, a step at a time, he treads on fallen apples lying thick in the grass grown to hay. Mustn't turn an ankle, lie up here and rot as well. Poor trees, putting out all this wormy fruit for nothing. Perhaps not nothing from their point of view, when men didn't exist they were doing the same. Strange thought. Harry looks down upon the farmhouse now, the green door, the birdbath on its pale blue pillar. Smoke is rising from the chimney; the nostalgic smell of burning wood comes to him. So close, he gets behind a dying apple tree with a convenient fork at the height of his head. Ants are active in the velvety light brown rot inside the trunk, touching noses, telling the news, hurrying on. The tree trunk is split open like an unbuttoned overcoat but still carries life up through its rough skin to the small round leaves that tremble where the twigs are young and smooth. Space feels to drop away not only in front of him but on all sides, even through the solid earth, and he wonders what he is doing here in his good beige suit, his backside exposed to any farmer with a shotgun who might be walking along in the field behind him and his face posed in this fork like a tin can up for target practice were anybody to look up from the buildings below, he who has an office with his name on the door and CHIEF SALES REPRESENTATIVE on his business cards and who a few hours back was entertaining other men in suits with the expense and complications of his son's wedding, the organist going off with this Slim and the couple turning up so late he thought they were Jehovah's Witnesses; and for some seconds of panic cannot answer himself why, except that out here, in the air, nameless, he feels purely alive. Then he remembers: he hopes to glimpse his daughter. And what if he were to gather all his nerve and go down and knock at the green door in its deep socket of wall and she were to answer? She would be in jeans this time of year, and a sweatshirt or sweater. Her hair would be less loose and damp than in its summer do, maybe pulled back and held by a rubber band. Her eyes, widely spaced, would be pale blue little mirrors.

Hi. You don't remember me –

Sure I do. You're the car dealer.

I'm more than that, I think.

Like what?

Is your mother's name by any chance Ruth Byer?

Well . . . yes.

And has she ever talked to you about your father?

My father's dead. He used to run the school buses for the township.

That wasn't your father. I'm your father.

And that broad pale face in which he saw his own would stare at him furious, disbelieving, fearful. And if he did at last make her believe, she would be angry at him for taking from her the life she had lived and substituting for it one she could never live now. He sees that these fields where his seed may have taken hold hold nothing of harvest for him but, if he seizes it, the space at his back to escape in. Yet he stands, in his tired summer suit – time to have it cleaned and stored in the big plastic clothes bag until next April – transfixed by the motionlessness of the scene below, but for the rising smoke. His heart races in steady alarm at his having strayed so far off track. You have a life and there are these volumes on either side that go unvisited; some day soon as the world winds he will lie beneath what he now stands on, dead as those insects whose sound he no longer hears, and the grass will go on growing, wild and blind.

His idling heart jumps at a rustle close behind him in the orchard. He has lifted his arms and framed the first words of his self-explanation before he sees that the other presence is not a person but a dog, an old-looking collie with one red eye and its coat loaded with burrs. Rabbit is uncomfortable with dogs anyway and knows collies to be especially nervous and prone to attack, Lassie to the contrary. This dog is blacker than Lassie. It stands the length of a long putt away, head cocked, the hair behind its ears electric, set to bark.

"Hi," Harry says, his voice a hoarse shade above a whisper, lest it carry down to the house.

The collie cocks its narrow head at a sharper tilt, as if to favor the sore eye, and the long white hair around its throat like a bib riffles where the breeze flattens it.

"You a good doggie?" Harry asks. He envisions the distance to the car, sees himself running, the dog at his legs in two seconds, the tearing of cloth, the pointed yellowish canines, the way dogs lift that black split upper lip to bare the little front teeth in hate; he feels his ankle pinned as if between two grinding cogwheels, his fall, his arms up in a futile attempt to save his face.

But the dog makes a decision in its narrow skull. Its dropped tail cautiously wags, and it lopes forward with that horrible silent lightness of four-footed animals through the orchard grass. It sniffs at Harry's knees and then leans against his legs, allowing its neck to be scratched as Harry keeps up a whispered patter. "Nice boy, good girl, where'd you get all these burrs, *baaad* burrs." Don't let them smell your terror. You sure know you're out in the country when you meet dogs running around without collars just like bears.

Distantly, a car door slams. The sound echoes off the barn wall so that at first he looks in the wrong spot. Then he sees through the fork of the apple tree, about a six-iron away allowing for the slope, the orange Corolla in the big bare spot between the house and the garage, which has the yellow shell of the school bus behind it.

So a wild hope is confirmed, but most of his mind stays with the opaque bundle of muscle and teeth at his knees, how to keep it from barking, how to keep it from biting. Tiny brains, change in a second, a collie belonging to old Mrs. Zug down Jackson Road lived in a barrel, snapped one time when nobody expected it, Harry still has the faint white scar on two middle fingers, pulling them loose felt like skinning a carrot, he can still feel it.

The dog too hears the car door slam and, flattening its ears, rockets down through the orchard. Around the Corolla it sets up a barking that is frantic but remote, delayed by echo and space. Harry seizes the moment to scurry back to a tree farther away. From there he sees the car's driver step out, lanky Jamie, no longer wearing dirty dungarees but pinkish bell-bottoms and a red turtle-neck shirt. The collie jumps up and down, greeting, apologizing for barking at the unfamiliar car. The boy's drawl drifts up through the orchard, doing singsong dog talk, the words indistinct. Rabbit drops his eyes a moment to the earth, where two yellowjackets are burrowing into a rotten apple. When he looks again, a girl, his girl, her round white face unmistakable, her hair shorter than in June, steps out of the Corolla's passenger side and hunkers down to the dog, mingling herself with its flurry. She turns her face away from a thrust of the dog's muzzle and stares upwards at the exact spot from which Harry, frozen, watches. He sees when she stands that she is dressed trimly, in dark brown skirt and russet sweater, a lit-tle plaid jacket squaring up her shoulders so she looks sharp, col-legiate, a city girl. Still there is that certain languor of her legs as she takes a stride or two toward the house. Her voice lifts in call-ing. Both their young faces have turned to the house, so Rabbit takes the opportunity to retreat to yet a farther tree, slimmer than the one previous. But he is close to the tangled hedgerow now and perhaps against this invisible in his light brown suit, camou-flaged among pieces of sky.

Down below, echoing off the stucco and cinder-block walls, the cries of greeting and pleasure have a melancholy, drifting sound. From out of the house, following a thin slam of its door, a fat elderly woman has emerged, moving under the burden of her own weight so cautiously that the collie, herding, nudges her forward, encircling her legs. This might be the woman he glimpsed in the old station wagon when it went by the church on the day of the wedding, but it cannot be Ruth, for her hair, that had been a kind of soft and various wiry fire, is an iron cap of gray fitted to her head, and her body is enormous, so big her clothes from this distance seem wide as a sail. In pants and shirt this person advances plodding to admire the new car. There is no exchange of kisses, but from the way they all rotate and slide one past another these three are well acquainted. Their voices drift to Harry unintelligibly.

The boy demonstrates the liftback. The girl taps the old woman, as if to say, *Go on*; she is being teased. Then they fish from the car's interior two tall brown paper bags, groceries, and the collie dog, bored with these proceedings, lifts its head and points its nose in the direction where Harry, his heart thunderous, is holding as still as the man concealed in the tangled lines of those puzzle drawings that used to be in Sunday papers.

The dog begins to bark and races up into the orchard toward him; Harry has no choice but to turn and run. Perhaps he makes it through the hedgerow before the people look up and see him. They call out for the dog – "Fritzie! Fritzie!" – in two female voices. Twigs scratch his hands; the loose stones of the old wall nearly trip him, and scuff one shoe. Now he flies. The red earth marred by tractor treads skims underfoot. Yet the dog, he sees glancing behind, will overtake him before he can reach the car; already the creature, its hair and ears swept flat by its speed, has broken through the hedgerow and is streaming along beside the corn stubble. Oh Christ. Rabbit stops, wraps his arms around his face, and waits. The house is out of sight below the rise of land; he is all alone with this. He hears the dog's claws rattle past him in momentum and a bark dies to a growl in its throat. He feels his legs being nosed through his trousers, then leaned on. The dog doesn't want to bring him down but to gather him in, to herd him also.

"Nice Fritzie," Harry says. "Good Fritzie. Let's go to my car. Let's trot along." Foot by careful foot he consumes the little distance to the shoulder of the road, the dog bumping and sniffing him all the way. The cries from the house, invisible, persist raggedly; the collie's tail, uncertainly wagging, pats Harry's calves while the long skull inquires upward with its sick red eye. Harry pulls his hands up to the level of his lapels. Dirty yellow drooly teeth would skin his fingers like a carrot grater. He tells Fritzie, "You're a beautiful girl, a wonderful girl," and eases around the back of the Corona. The chain saw is still zipping along. He opens the driver's door and slides in. Slams it. The collie stands on the overgrown banking of red earth looking puzzled, her shepherding come to an end. Harry finds the car key in his pocket, the engine starts. His heart is still pounding. He leans over toward the passenger's window and scrabbles his fingers on the glass. "Hey Fritzie!" he shouts and keeps up the scrabbling until the dog starts to bark again. *Bark. Bark bark bark.* Laughing, Rabbit pops the clutch and digs out, the thing inside his chest feeling fragile and iridescent like a big soap bubble. Let it pop. He hasn't felt so close to breaking out of his rut since Nelson smashed those convertibles.

Webb Murkett is handy about the house; he has a cellar full of expensive power tools and subscribes to magazines with titles like *Fine Woodworking* and *Homecraft*. In every corner of the garrison colonial he and Cindy have shared for the seven years of their marriage there are hand-made refinements of rounded, stained, and varnished wood – shelves, cabinets, built-in lazy susans with as many compartments as a seashell – expressing the patience and homelovingness of the house's master. There is a way of working with rotten wood, and making it as solid as marble, and like marble swirled and many-shaded; this art is on display in the base of several lamps and in a small bowl holding an untouched spiral of cigarettes on the butler's-tray table, which Webb has also fashioned, down to its gleaming copper hinges shaped like butterflies. Some of these objects must have come from the homes of Webb's previous marriages, and Harry wonders what these phantom women have kept, that so much remains. Webb's previous marriages are represented in his great long sunken living room only by color photographs, in ensemble frames of unusual proportion that Webb himself has cut and grooved and cemented together of Lucite, of children too old to be his and Cindy's, caught in a moment of sunshine on the flagstone stoop of another suburban house, or in a sailboat against the blue of a lake that the Kodak chemicals are permitting to fade to yellow, or at a moment of marriage or graduation – for some of these children were now adult, older than Nelson, and infants of a third generation stare out unsmiling, propped on a pillow or held in firm young arms, from among the many smiles of these family groups. Harry has several times in Webb's house slyly searched these photos for the sight of a former wife; but though there are women beheaded or sliced to a splinter by the edge of a frame or another picture, and here and there an unidentifiable mature hand and forearm intrudes behind a set of children's heads, no face seems preserved of the vanished mistresses of all this fleeting family happiness.

When Webb and Cindy entertain, built-in speakers bathe the downstairs rooms in a continuous sweetness of string music and spineless arrangements, of old show tunes or mollified rock classics, voiceless and seamless and with nagging dental associations for Harry. Behind a mahogany bar that Webb salvaged from the tavern of a farmer's hotel being demolished in Brewer and then transported with its brass rail to a corner of his living room, he has constructed a kind of altar to booze, two high doors with rounded tops that meet in a point and shelves that come forward on a lazy-tongs principle with not only the basic whisky, gin, and vodka but exotic drinks like rum and tequila and sake and all the extras you could want from bitters to powdered Old-fashioned mix in little envelopes. And the bar has its own small refrigerator, built in. Much as he admires Webb, Harry thinks when he gets his own dream house he will do without the piped music and such elaborate housing for the liquor.

The bathroom, though, enchants him, with its little enamelled dishes of rosebud-shaped soap, its furry blue toilet seat cover, and its dazzling mirror rimmed with naked light bulbs like actors have in their dressing rooms. Everything in here that doesn't shine is tinted and scented. The toilet paper, very dulcet, is printed with old comic strips, each piece a panel. Poor Popeye, eating shit instead of spinach. And the towels have W and M and L for Lucinda intertwined in such a crusty big monogram he hates to think what it would do to Cindy's sweet underparts if she forgot and rubbed herself hard. But Harry wonders if this downstairs bathroom is ever used by the Murketts and their rather pasty-looking little kids or is set up primarily for guests. Certain mysterious artifacts in it – a big sort of sugar bowl, white, with a knobbed lid painted with two women dressed in filmy gowns sitting on clouds or a sofa that fades into nothing, and their feet in pink ballerina shoes and their ankles crossed and the toes of one woman touching the other's and one bare arm of each interwined above the knob, yet when the lid is lifted utterly empty, so empty you feel nothing has ever been put inside; and a pink plastic hand on a stick, meant maybe for a comic backscratcher; and an egg-shaped jar a third full of lavender crystalline salts; and a kind of tiny milkman's carrier of what he takes to be bath oils; and a flexible plastic cylinder holding a pastel rainbow of powder puffs like a stack of pancakes – all seem put there, on the set of open shelves hung on two black dowels between the bathtub and the toilet, for exhibit more than use. To think of little Cindy though, pouring that oil into her bath and then just soaking there, playing with herself with the backscratcher, her nipples poking through the blanket of soapsuds. Harry feels sexy. In the mirror that makes things too vivid his eyes stare with a pallor almost white, like the little frost-flowers that appear on the skin of a car in the morning, and his lips look bluish. He is drunk. He has had two tequila fizzes before dinner, as much Gallo Chablis as he could grab during the meal, and a brandy and a half afterwards. In the middle of the second brandy the need to urinate came upon him like yet another pressure of happiness, added to his health and prosperity and the privilege of being there sitting across a coffee table from Cindy watching her body rotate within the strange coarse cloth of the exotic Arab-looking thing she is wearing, her wrists and her feet, bare but for sandals, as exciting in this outfit as the insides of her thighs in a bikini. Besides himself and Janice the Murketts have invited the Harrisons and for a new thrill the moronic Fosnachts, whom they just met at Nelson's wedding two weeks ago. Harry doesn't suppose the Murketts know he and Peggy had a fling years back when Ollie had done one of his copouts, but maybe they do, people know more than you ever think they do, and it turns out it doesn't much matter. Look at what you read every week in *People* magazine, and you still keep watching television, the actors all dope addicts and adulterers. He has an urge to peek into the medicine cabinet framed by the rim of showbiz bulbs and waits until a gale of laughter from the drunken bunch in the living room arises to drown out any possible *click* of him opening the mirror-door. *Click.* The cabinet has more in it than he would have supposed: thick milk-glass jars of skin cream and flesh-tint squeeze bottles of lotion and brown tubes of suntan lotion, Parepectolin for diarrhea, Debrox for ear wax control, menthol Chloraseptic, that mouthwash called Cēpacol, several kinds of aspirin, both Bayer and Anacin, and Tylenol that doesn't make your stomach burn, and a large chalky bottle of liquid Maalox. He wonders which of the Murketts needs Maalox, they both always look so relaxed and at peace. The pink poison ivy goo would be downstairs handy for the kids, and the Band-Aids, but how about the little flat yellow box of Preparation H for hemorrhoids? Carter of course has hemorrhoids, that grim over-motivated type who wants to do everything on schedule ready or not, pushing, pushing, but old Webb Murkett with that gravelly voice and easy swing, like the swing you see crooners use at celebrity tournaments, unwrapping one of those little wax bullets and poking it up his own asshole? You have to go into a squat and the place is not easy to find, Rabbit remembers from his own experience, years ago, when he was sitting all day at the Linotype on that hard steel bench, under tension, the matrices rattling down in response to the touch of his fingertips, every slip a ruined slug, everybody around him unhappy, the kid still small, his own life closed in to a size his soul had not yet shrunk to fit. And what of these amber pill bottles with *Lucinda R. Murkett* typed in pale blue script face on the prescription labels? White pills, lethally small. He should have brought his reading glasses. Harry is tempted to lift one of these containers off its shelf in hopes of deciphering what illness might have ever found its way into that plump and supple and delectable body, but a superstitious fear of fingerprints restrains him. Medicine cabinets are tragic, he sees by this hard light, and closes the door so gently no one will hear the click. He returns to the living room.

They are discussing the Pope's visit, loudly. "Did you *see*," Peggy Fosnacht is shouting, "what he said in Chicago yesterday about *sex*!" The years since Harry knew her have freed her to stop wearing dark glasses to hide her walleye and to be sloppy in her person and opinions both; she's become the kind of woman who looks permanently out of press, as a protest of sorts. "He said everything outside marriage was *wrong*. Not just if you're married, but *before* you're married too. What does that man *know*? He doesn't know anything about *life*, life as she is lived."

Webb Murkett offers in a soft voice, trying to calm his guest down, "I liked what Earl Butz said some years ago. 'He no play-a the game, he no make-a the rules.' " Webb is wearing a maroon turtleneck under a coarse yarny gray sweater that has something to do, Rabbit thinks, with Scandinavian fishermen. The way the neck is cut. Harry and Ronnie came in suits; Ollie was with-it enough to know you don't wear suits out even on a Saturday night anymore. He came in tight faded jeans and an embroidered shirt that made him look like a cowboy too runty to be on the range.

"No play-a the game!" Peggy Fosnacht yells. "See if you're a pregnant slum mother and can't get an abortion legally if you think it's such a game."

Rabbit says to her, "Webb's agreeing with you," but she doesn't hear him, babbling on headlong, face flushed by wine and the exciting class of company, her hairdo coming uncurled like taffy softening in the sun.

"Did any of you watch except me – I can't stop watching, I get so furious – the performance he put on in Philly where he said absolutely No to women priests? And he kept smiling, what really got my goat, he kept smiling while spouting all this sexist crap about only men in the priesthood and how it was the conviction of the church and God's decision and all that, so solly. He's so *smooth* about it, I think is what gets to me, at least somebody like Nixon or Hitler had the decency to be frantic."

"He is one smooth old Polack," Ollie says, uneasy at this outburst by his wife. He is into cool, you can see. Music, dope. Just on the fringes, but enough to give you the pitch.

"He sure can kiss those nigger babies," Ronnie Harrison comes in with, maybe trying to help. It's fascinating to Rabbit how long those strands of hair are Ronnie is combing over his bald spot these days, if you pulled one the other way it would go below his ear. In this day and age why fight it? There's a bald look, go for it. Blank and pink and curved, like an ass. Everybody loves an ass. Those wax bullets in the yellow box – could they have been for Cindy? Sore there from, but would Webb? Harry has read somewhere that male homosexuals have a lot of trouble with hemorrhoids. Amazing the things they try to put up – fists, light bulbs. He squirms on his cushion.

"I think he's very sexy," Thelma Harrison states. Everything she says sounds like a schoolteacher, enunciated. He looks at her through the enhancing lens of liquor: thin lips and that unhealthy yellowy color. Harry can hardly ever look at her without seeing Ronnie's prick, flat like a board on the upper side it's so thick. "He is a beautiful man," Thelma insists. Her eyes are half-shut. She's had a glass or two too many herself. Her throat rises absolutely straight, like a person trying not to hiccup. He has to look down the front of her dress, velvet that mousy blue of old movie seats, the way she's holding herself. Nothing much there. That little stocky guy in white with all those gold buttons and different funny hats, to see him as sexy you'd have to be a nun. Ronnie is stocky like that, actually. She likes thick men. He looks down the front of her dress again. Maybe more there than you'd think.

Janice is saying, she has known Peggy for ages and is trying to save her from herself, "What I liked today, I don't know if you were watching, Peggy, was when he came out on the balcony of that cathedral in Washington, before he went to the White House, to this crowd that was shouting, 'We want the Pope, we want the Pope,' and he came out on the balcony waving and shouted, 'John Paul Two, he wants you!' Actually."

"Actually" because the men had laughed, it was news to them. Three of them had been out on the Flying Eagle course today, summer had made one last loop back to Diamond County, bringing out fat buds on the magnolias by the sixth tee. Their fourth had been the young assistant pro, the same kid who had shot a 73 the day Nelson got married. He hits a long ball, Webb was right, but Harry doesn't like his swing: too wristy. Give him a few years around his waist he'll be hooking everything. Buddy Inglefinger had been dropped, lately; his golf was a drag and the wives didn't like his tarty girlfriends. But Ollie Fosnacht is no substitute. The only thing he plays is the synthesizer, and his sloppy wife won't stop blabbering.

"I'd *like* to find it amusing," Peggy says, hoisting her voice above the laughter, "but to me the issues he's trampling on are too damn serious."

Cindy Murkett unexpectedly speaks. "He's been a priest in a Communist country; he's used to taking a stand. What is it that offends you, Peggy, if you're not a Catholic and don't have to listen?"

A hush has surrounded her words because they all except the Fosnachts know that she was Catholic until she married Webb. Peggy senses this now but like a white sad heifer having charged in one direction cannot turn herself around. "You're Catholic?" she bluntly asks.

Cindy tips her chin up, not used to this kind of spotlight, the baby of their group. "I was raised as one," she says.

"So was my daughter-in-law, it turns out," Harry volunteers. He is amused by the idea of his having a daughter-in-law at all, a new branch of his wealth. And he hopes to be distracting. He hates to see women fight, he'd be happy to get these two off the spot. Cindy comes up from that swimming pool like a wet dream, and Peggy was kind enough to lay him when he was down.

But no one is distracted. "When I married a divorced man," Cindy explains levelly to the other woman, "I couldn't take communion anymore. But I still go to Mass sometimes. I still believe." Her voice softens saying this, for she is the hostess, younger though she is.

"And do you use birth control?" Peggy asks.

Back to nowhere, Fosnachts. Harry is just as pleased; he liked his little crowd the way it was.

Cindy hesitates. She can go all girlish and slide and giggle away from the question, or she can sit still and get dignified. With just the smallest of dignified smiles she says, "I'm not sure that's any of your business."

"Nor the Pope's either, that's my point!" Peggy sounds triumphant, but even she must be feeling the battle slipping away. She will not be invited here again.

Webb, always the gentleman, perches on the arm of the easy chair in which cumbersome Peggy has set herself up as anti-Pope and leans down a deft inch to say to his guest alone, "I think Cindy's point, as I understand it, is that John Paul is addressing the doctrinal issues for his fellow Catholics while bringing good will to every American."

"He can keep his good will along with the doctrine as far as I'm concerned," Peggy says, trying to shut up but unable. Rabbit remembers how her nipples had felt like gumdrops and how sad her having gotten good at screwing since Ollie left her had seemed to him at the time, ten years ago.

Cindy attacks a little now, "But he sees the trouble the church has got into since Vatican Two. The priests —"

"The church is in trouble because it's a monument to a lie, run by a bunch of antiquated chauvinists who don't know *any*thing. I'm sorry," Peggy says, "I'm talking too much."

"Well, this is America," Harry says, coming to her rescue, somewhat, "Let's all sock it to each other. Today I said goodbye to the only friend I've ever had, Charlie Stavros."

Janice says, "Oh, Harry," but nobody else takes him up on it. The men were supposed to say *they* were his friends.

Webb Murkett tilts his head, his eyebrows working toward Ronnie and Ollie. "Did either of you see in the paper today where Nixon finally bought a house in Manhattan? Right next to David Rockefeller. I'm no great admirer of tricky Dick's, but I must say the way he's been excluded from apartment houses in a great city is a disgrace to the Constitution."

"If he'd been a spade," Ronnie begins, "every civil rights —"

"Well how would *you* like," Peggy Fosnacht has to say, "a lot of secret service men checking your handbag every time you came back from the store?"

The chair Peggy sits in is squared-off ponderous modern with a pale fabric thick as plywood; it matches another chair and a long sofa set around that kind of table with no overhang to the top they call a Parsons table, which is put together in alternating blocks of light and dark wood with a curly knotty grain such as they make golf club heads of. The entire deep space of the room, which Webb added on when he and Cindy acquired this house in the pace-setting development of Brewer Heights, gently brims with appointments chosen all to harmonize. Its tawny wallpaper has vertical threads of texture in it like the vertical folds of the slightly darker pull drapes, and reproductions of Wyeth watercolors lit by spots on track lighting overhead echo with scratchy strokes the same tints, and the same lighting reveals little sparkles, like mica on a beach, in the overlapping arcs of the rough-plastered ceiling. When Harry moves his head these sparkles in the ceiling change location, wave upon wave of hidden silver. He announces, "I heard a kind of funny story at Rotary the other day involving Kissinger. Webb, I don't think you were there. There were these five guys in an airplane that was about to crash – a priest, a hippie, a policeman, somebody else, and Henry Kissinger. And only four parachutes."

Ronnie says, "And at the end the hippie turns to the priest and says, 'Don't worry, Father. The Smartest Man in the World just jumped out with my knapsack.' We've all heard it. Speaking of which, Thel and I were wondering if you'd seen this." He hands him a newspaper clipping, from an Ann Landers column printed in the Brewer *Standard*, the respectable paper, not the *Vat*. The second paragraph is marked in tidy ballpoint. "Read it aloud," Ronnie demands.

He doesn't like being given orders by sweaty skinheads like Harrison when he's come out for a pleasant low-key time with the Murketts, but all eyes are on him and at least it gets them off the Pope. He explains, more to the Fosnachts than the others, since the Murketts seem to be in on the joke already, "It's a letter to Ann Landers from somebody. The first paragraph tells about a news story about some guy whose pet python bit him in the stomach and wouldn't let go, and when the paramedics came he yelled at them to get out of his apartment if they're going to hurt his snake." There is a little laughter at that and the Fosnachts, puzzled, try to join in. The next paragraph goes:

> The other news story was about a Washington,
> D.C., physician who beat a Canadian goose to death

with his putter on the 16th green of a country club.
(The goose honked just as he was about to sink
one.) The reason for printing those letters was to
demonstrate that truth is stranger than fiction.

Having read this aloud, he explains to the Fosnachts, "The reason they're razzing me with this is last summer I heard about the
same incident on the radio and when I tried to tell them about it
at the club they wouldn't listen, nobody believed me. Now here's
proof it happened."

"You chump, *that's* not the point," Ronnie Harrison says.

"The point is, Harry," Thelma says, "it's so *different*. You said
he was from Baltimore and this says he was from Washington.
You said the ball hit the goose accidentally and the doctor put him
out of his misery."

Webb says, "Remember − 'A mercy killing, or murder most
foul?' That really broke me up."

"You didn't show it at the time," Harry says, pleased however.

"According to Ann Landers, then, it *was* murder most foul,"
Thelma says.

"Who cares?" Ronnie says, getting ugly. This clipping was
clearly her idea. Her touch on the ballpoint too.

Janice has been listening with that glazed dark look she gets
when deep enough into the booze. She and Webb have been trying some new imported Irish liqueur called Greensleeves. "Well
not if the goose honked," she says.

Ollie Fosnacht says, "I can't believe a goose honking would
make that much difference on a putt."

All the golfers there assure him it would.

"Shit," he says, "in music, you do your best work at two in the
morning, stoned half out of your mind and a lot of drunks acting
up besides."

His mention of music reminds them all that in the background
Webb's hidden speakers are incessantly performing; a Hawaiian
melody at the moment, with Vibra-Harp.

"Maybe it wasn't a goose," Harry says. "Maybe it was a very
little caddy with feathers."

"That's music," Ronnie sneers, of Ollie's observation. "Hey
Webb, how come there isn't any beer in this place?"

"There's beer, there's beer. Miller Lite and Heineken's. What can I get everybody?"

Webb acts a little jumpy, and Rabbit worries that the party is in danger of flattening out. He misses, whom he never thought he would, Buddy Inglefinger, and tries to say the kind of thing Buddy would if he were here. "Speaking of dead geese," he says, "I noticed in the paper the other day where some anthropologist or something says about a fourth of the animal species on earth right now will be extinct by the year 2000."

"Oh *don't,*" Peggy Fosnacht protests loudly, shaking herself ostentatiously, so the fat on her upper arms jiggles. She is wearing a short-sleeved dress, out of season. "Don't mention the year 2000, just the thought of it gives me the *creeps.*"

Nobody asks her why.

Rabbit at last says, "Why? You'll still be alive."

"No I won't," she says flatly, wanting to make an argument even of that.

The heated flush the papal argument roused in Cindy still warms her throat and upper chest, that with its tiny gold cross sits half-exposed by the unbuttoned two top buttons or string-latches of the Arab-style robe, her tapering forearms looking child-ishly fragile within its wide sleeves, her feet bare but for the thinnest golden sandals below the embroidered hem. In the com-motion as Webb takes drink orders and Janice wobbles up to go to the john, Harry goes over and sits on a straight chair beside their young hostess. "Hey," he says, "I think the Pope's pretty great. He really knows how to use TV."

Cindy says, with a sharp quick shake of her face as if stung, "I don't like a lot of what he says either, but he's got to draw the line somewhere. That's his job."

"He's running scared," Rabbit offers. "Like everybody else."

She looks at him, her eyes a bit Chinesey like Mim said, the fatty pouches of her lower lids giving her a kind of squint, as if she's been beaten or is suffering from ragweed, so she twinkles even as she's being serious, her pupils large in this shadowy center of the room away from the track lighting. "Oh, I can't think of him that way, though you're probably right. I've still too much parochial school in me." The ring of brown around her pupils is smooth chocolate, without flecks or fire. "Webb's so gentle, he never pushes me. After Betsey was born, and we agreed he's been father enough, Webb, I couldn't make myself use a diaphragm, it seemed so evil, and he didn't want me on the Pill, what he'd read about it, so he offered to get himself fixed, you know, like the men are paid to do in India, what do they call it, a vasectomy. Rather than have him do that and do God knows what to his psyche, I went impulsively one day and got myself fitted for the diaphragm, I still don't know if I'm putting it in right when I do it, but poor Webb. You know he had five other children by his other wives, and they're both after his money *con*stantly. Neither has married though they're living with men, that's what I would call immoral, to keep bleeding him that way."

This is more than Harry had bargained for. He tries to confess back at her. "Janice had her tubes cauterized the other year, and I must say, it's great not to have to worry about it, whenever you want it, night or day, no creams or crap or anything. Still, sometimes she starts crying, for no reason. At being sterile at forty-three."

"Well of course, Harry. I would too." Cindy's lips are long and in their lipstick lie together with a wised-up closeness of fit, a downward tug at the end of sentences, he has never noticed before tonight.

"But you're a baby," he tells her.

Cindy gives him a wise slanting look and almost toughly says, "I'm getting there, Harry. I'll be thirty this April."

Twenty-nine, she must have been twenty-two when Webb started fucking her, what a sly goat, he pictures her body all brown with its little silken slopes and rolls of slight excess inside the rough loose garment, shadowy spaces you could put your hand in, for the body to breathe in that desert heat, it goes with the gold threads on her feet and the bangles around her wrists, still small and round as a child's, veinless. The vehemence of his lust dries his mouth. He stands to go after his brandy but loses his balance so his knee knocks against Peggy Fosnacht's ponderous square chair. She is not in it, she is standing at the top of the two steps that lead upward out of the living room, with the out-of-date dull plaid coat she came in draped around her shoulders. She looks down at them like one placed above and beyond, driven away.

Ollie, though, is seated around the Parsons table waiting for Webb to bring the beer and oblivious of his wife's withdrawal. Ronnie Harrison, so drunk his lips are wet and the long hair he brushes across his bald spot stands up in a loop, asks Ollie, "How goes the music racket these days? I hear the guitar craze is over now there's no more revolution."

"They're into flutes now, it's weird. Not just the girls, but guys too, who want to play jazz. A lot of spades. A spade came in the other day wanted to buy a platinum flute for his daughter's eighteenth birthday, he said he read about some Frenchman who had one. I said, 'Man, you're crazy. I can't begin to guess what a flute like that would cost.' He said, 'I don't give a flying fuck, man,' and showed me this roll of bills, there must have been an inch of hundred-dollar bills in it. At least those on top were hundreds."

Any more feeling-out with Cindy would be too much for now; Harry sits down heavily on the sofa and joins the male conversation. "Like those gold-headed putters a few years ago. Boy I bet *they've* gone up in value."

Like Peggy, he is ignored. Harrison is boring in. These insurance salesmen: they have that way of putting down their heads and just boring in until it's either scream or say, sure, you'll take out another fifty thousand of renewable life.

Ronnie says to Ollie, "How about electric stuff? You see this guy on television even has an electric violin. That stuff must cost."

"An arm and a leg," Ollie says, looking up gratefully as Webb sets a Heineken's on a light square of the table in front of him. "Just the amplifiers take you into the thousands," he says, pleased to be talking, pleased to sound rich. Poor sap, when most of his business is selling thirteen-year-old dumplings records to make them wet their pants. What did Nelson used to call it? Lollipop music. Nelson used to be serious about the guitar, that one he saved from the fire and then the one they got him with a big pearl plate on the face, but the chords stopped coming from his room after school when he got his driver's license.

Ronnie has tilted his head to bore in at a different angle. "You know I'm in client service at Schuylkill Mutual and my boss told me the other day, 'Ron, you cost this company eight thousand seven hundred last year.' That's not salary, that's benefits. Retirement, health insurance, participation options. How do you handle that in your operation? If you don't have employer-financed insurance and retirement in this day and age, you're in the soup. People expect it and without it they won't perform."

Ollie says, "Well, I'm my own employer in a way. Me and my partners —"

"How about Keogh? You gotta have Keogh."

"We try to keep it simple. When we started out —"

"You gotta be kidding, Ollie. You're just robbing yourself. Schuylkill Mutual offers a terrific deal on Keogh, and we could plug you in, in fact we advise plugging you in, on the corporate end so not a nickel comes out of your personal pocket, it comes out of the corporate pocket and there's that much less for Uncle to tax. These poor saps carrying their own premiums with no company input are living in the dark ages. There's nothing shady about rigging it this way, we're just using the laws the government has put there. They *want* people to take advantage, it all works to up the gross national product. You know what I mean by Keogh, don't you? You're looking kind of blank."

"It's something like social security."

"A thousand times better. Social security's just a rip-off to benefit the freeloaders now; you'll never see a penny of what you put in. In the Keogh plan, up to seventy-five hundred goes untaxed, every year; you just set it aside, with our help. Our usual suggestion is, depending on circumstances — how many dependents you got? —"

"Two, if you count the wife. My son Billy's out of college and up in Massachusetts studying specialized dentistry."

Ronnie whistles. "Boy, you were smart. Limiting yourself to one offspring. I saddled myself with three and only these last few years am I feeling out of the woods. The older boy, Alex, has taken to electronics but the middle boy, Georgie, needed special schools from the start. Dyslexia. I'd never heard of it, but I'll tell you I've heard of it now. Couldn't make any goddam sense at all out of anything written, and you'd never know it from his conversation.

He could outtalk me at this job, that's for certain, but he can't see it. He wants to be an artist, Jesus. There's no money there, Ollie, you know that better than I do. But even with just the one kid, you don't want him to starve if you were suddenly out of the picture, or the good woman either. Any man in this day and age carrying less than a hundred, a hundred fifty thousand dollars straight life just isn't being realistic. A decent funeral alone costs four, five grand."

"Yeah, well —"

"Lemme get back to the Keogh a minute. We generally recommend a forty-sixty split, take the forty per cent of seventy-five hundred in straight life premiums, which generally comes to close to the hundred thou, assuming you pass the exam that is. You smoke?"

"Off and on."

"Uh-oh. Well, lemme give you the name of a doctor who gives an exam everybody can live with."

Ollie says, "I think my wife wants to go."

"You're kidding, Foster."

"Fosnacht."

"You're kidding. This is Saturday night, man. You got a gig or something?"

"No, my wife — she needs to go to some anti-nuclear meeting tomorrow morning at some Universalist church."

"No wonder she's down on the Pope then. I hear the Vatican and Three-Mile Island are hand-in-glove, just ask friend Harry here. Ollie, here's my card. Could I have one of yours please?"

"Uh —"

"That's O.K. I know where you are. Up there next to the fuck movies. I'll come by. No bullshit, you really owe it to yourself to listen to some of these opportunities. People keep saying the economy is shot but it isn't shot at all from where I sit, it's booming. People are begging for shelters."

Harry says, "Come on, Ron. Ollie wants to go."

"Well, I don't exactly but Peggy —"

"Go. Go in peace, man." Ronnie stands and makes a ham-handed blessing gesture. "Gott pless Ameri-ca," he pronounces in a thick slow foreign accent, loud, so that Peggy, who has been conferring with the Murketts, patching things up, turns her back. She too went to high school with Ronnie and knows him for the obnoxious jerk he is.

"Jesus, Ronnie," Rabbit says to him when the Fosnachts have gone. "What a snow job."

"Ahh," Ronnie says. "I wanted to see how much garbage he could eat."

"I've never been that crazy about him either," Harry confesses. "He treats old Peggy like dirt."

Janice, who has been consulting with Thelma Harrison about something, God knows what, their lousy children, overhears this and turns and tells Ronnie, "Harry screwed her years ago, that's why he minds Ollie." Nothing like a little booze to freshen up old sore points.

Ronnie laughs to attract attention and slaps Harry's knee. "You screwed that big pig, funny eyes and all?"

Rabbit pictures that heavy glass egg with the interior teardrop of air back in Ma Springer's living room, its smooth heft in his hand, and imagines himself making the pivot from pounding it into Janice's stubborn dumb face to finishing up with a one-handed stuff straight down into Harrison's pink brainpan. "It seemed a good idea at the time," he has to admit, uncrossing his legs and stretching them in preparation for an extended night. The Fosnachts' leaving is felt as a relief throughout the room. Cindy is tittering to Webb, clings briefly to his coarse gray sweater in her rough loose Arab thing, like a loving pair advertising vacations abroad. "Janice had run off at the time with this disgusting Greek smoothie Charlie Stavros," Harry explains to anybody who will listen.

"O.K. O.K.," Ronnie says, "you don't need to tell us. We've all heard the story, it's ancient history."

"What isn't so ancient, you twerpy skinhead, is I had to kiss Charlie goodbye today because Janice and her mother got him canned from Springer Motors."

"Harry likes to say that," Janice said, "but it was as much Charlie's idea as anybody's."

Ronnie is not so potted he misses the point. He tips his head and looks at Janice with a gaze that from Harry's angle is mostly furry white eyelashes. "You got your old boyfriend fired?" he asks her.

Harry amplifies, "All so my shiftless son who won't even finish college with only one year to go can take over this job he's no more qualified for than, than –"

"Than Harry was," Janice finishes for him – in the old days she would never have been quick with sass like that – and giggles. Harry has to laugh too, even before Ronnie does. His cock isn't the only thick thing about Harrison.

"This is what I like," Webb Murkett says in his gravelly voice above them. "Old friends." He and Cindy side by side stand presiding above their circle as the hour settles toward midnight. "What can I get anybody? More beer? How about a light highball? Scotch? Irish? A CC and seven?" Cindy's tits jut out in that caftan or burnoose or whatever like the angle of a tent. Desert silence. Crescent moon. Put the camel to bed. "We-ell," Webb exhales with such pleasure he must be feeling that Greensleeves, "and what did we think of the Fosnachts?"

"They won't do," Thelma says. Harry is startled to hear her speak, she has been so silent. If you close your eyes and pretend you're blind, Thelma has the nicest voice. He feels melancholy and mellow, now that the invasion from the pathetic world beyond the Flying Eagle has been repelled.

"Ollie's been a sap from Day One," he says, "but she didn't used to be such a blabbermouth. Did she, Janice?"

Janice is cautious, defending her old friend. "She always had a tendency," she says. "Peggy never thought of herself as attractive, and that was a problem."

"You did, huh?" Harry accuses.

She stares at him, having not followed, her face moistened as by a fine spray.

"Of *course* she did," Webb gallantly intervenes, "Jan is mighty attractive, at least to this old party," and goes around behind her chair and puts his hands on her shoulders, close to her neck so that her shoulders hunch.

Cindy says, "She was a lot pleasanter just chatting with me and Webb at the door. She said she sometimes just gets carried away."

Ronnie says, "Harry and Janice I guess see a lot of 'em. I'll have a brew as long as you're up, Webb."

"We don't at all. Nelson's best friend is their obnoxious son Billy, is how they got to the wedding. Webb, could you make that two?"

Thelma asks Harry, her voice softly pitched for him alone, "How *is* Nelson? Have you heard from him in his married state?"

"A postcard. Janice has talked to them on the phone a couple times. She thinks they're bored."

Janice interrupts, "I don't think, Harry. He *told* me they're bored."

Ronnie offers, "If you've done all your fucking before marriage, I guess a honeymoon can be a drag. Thanks, Webb."

Janice says, "He said it's been chilly in the cabin."

"Too lazy no doubt to carry the wood in from the stack outside," Harry says. "Yeah, thanks." The *pffft* of opening a can isn't near as satisfying since they put that safety tab on to keep idiots from choking themselves.

"Harry, he told us they've been having a fire in the wood stove all day long."

"Burning it all up so somebody else can chop. He's his mamma's boy."

Thelma, tired perhaps of the tone the Angstroms keep setting, lifts her voice and bends her face far back, exposing a startling length of sallow throat. "Speaking of the cold, Webb. Are you and Cindy going away at all this winter?" They usually go to an island in the Caribbean. The Harrisons once went with them, years ago. Harry and Janice have never been.

Webb has been circling behind Thelma getting a highball for someone. "We've talked about it," he tells Thelma. Through the haze of beer laid over brandy there seems an enchanting conspiracy between her bent-back throat and Webb's arched and lowered voice. Old friends, Harry thinks. Fit like pieces of a puzzle. Webb bends down and reaches over her shoulder to put a tall weak Scotch-and-soda on a dark square in front of her. "I'd like to go," he is going on, "where they have a golf course. You can get a pretty fair deal, if you shop around for a package."

"Let's all go," Harry announces. "The kid's taking over the lot Monday, let's get the hell out of here."

"Harry," Janice says, "he's not taking over the lot, you're being irrational about this. Webb and Ronnie are shocked, to hear you talk about your son this way."

"They're not shocked. *Their* kids are eating 'em alive too. I want to go to the Caribbean and play golf this winter. Let's bust out. Let's ask Buddy Inglefinger to be the fourth. I hate the winter around here – there's no snow, you can't ice-skate, it's just boring and raw, month after month. When I was a kid, there was snow all the time, what ever happened to it?"

"We had a ton of snow in '78," Webb observes.

"Harry, maybe it's time to go home," Janice tells him. Her mouth has turned to a slot, her forehead under her bangs is shiny.

"I don't want to go home. I want to go to the Caribbean. But first I want to go to the bathroom. Bathroom, home, Caribbean, in that order." He wonders if a wife like that ever dies of natural causes. Never, those dark wiry types, look at her mother, still running the show. Buried poor old Fred and never looked back.

Cindy says, "Harry, the downstairs john is plugged, Webb just noticed. Somebody must have used too much toilet paper."

"Peggy Gring, that's who," Harry says, standing and wondering why the wall-to-wall carpeting has a curve to it, like the deck of a ship falling away on all sides. "First she attacks the Pope, then she abuses the plumbing."

"Use the one in our bedroom," Webb says to him. "At the head of the stairs, turn left, past the two closet doors with the slats."

". . . wiping away her tears . . . ," Rabbit hears Thelma Harrison saying dryly as he leaves. Up the two carpeted steps, his head floating far above his feet. Then down a hall and up stairs in different-colored carpeting, a dirty lime, more wear, older part of the house. Someone else's upstairs always has that hush. Tired nights, a couple talking softly to themselves. The voices below him fade. Turn left, Webb had said. Slatted doors. He stops and peeks in. Female clothes, strips of many colors, fragrant of Cindy. Get her down there in that sand, who can say, talking to him about her diaphragm already. He finds the bathroom. Every light in it is lit. What a waste of energy. Going down with all her lights blazing, the great ship America. This bathroom is smaller than the one downstairs, and of a deeper tint, wall tiles and wallpaper and shag carpeting and towels and tinted porcelain all brown, with touches of tangerine. He undoes his fly and in a stream of blissful relief fills one of this room's bright bowls with gold. His bubbles multiply like coins. He and Janice took their Krugerrands from the bedside table drawer and together went downtown and into the Brewer Trust with them and nestled them in their little cylinders like blue-tinted dollhouse toilets into their stout long safe-deposit box and in celebration had drinks with their lunch at the Crêpe House before he went back to the lot. Because he was never circumcised he tends to retain a drop or two, and pats his tip with a piece of lemon-yellow toilet paper, plain, the comic strips were to amuse guests. Who was Thelma saying would wipe away her tears? The shocking flash of long white throat, muscular, the swallowing muscles developed, she must have something, to hold Harrison. Maybe she meant Peggy using toilet paper to wipe away her tears had clogged the toilet. Cindy's eyes had had a glisten, too shy to like arguing like that with poor Peggy, telling him instead about her diaphragm, Jesus, inviting him to think about it, her sweet red dark deep, could she mean it? *Getting there, Harry:* her voice more wised-up and throaty than he ever noticed before, her eyes pouchy, sexy when women's lower lids are like that, up a little like eggcups, his daughter's lids he noticed that day did that. All around in here are surfaces that have seen Cindy stark naked. Harry looks at his face in this less dazzling mirror, fluorescent tubes on either side, and his lips look less blue, he is sobering up for the drive home. Oh but blue still the spaces in his eyes, encircling the little black dot through which the world flows, a blue with white and gray mixed in from the frost of his ancestors, those beefy blonds in horned helmets pounding to a pulp with clubs the hairy mammoth and the slant-eyed Finns amid snows so pure and widespread their whiteness would have made eyes less pale hurt. Eyes and hair and skin, the dead live in us though their brains are dust and their eyesockets of bone empty. His pupils enlarge as he leans closer to the mirror, making a shadow, seeking to see if there truly is a soul. That's what he used to think ophthalmologists were looking at when they pressed that little hot periscope of a flashlight tight against your eye. What they saw, they never told him. He sees nothing but black, out of focus, because his eyes are aging.

He washes his hands. The faucet is one of those single-handed Lavomaster mixers with a knob on the end of the handle like a clown's nose or big pimple, he can never remember which way is hot and which cold, what was wrong with the old two faucets that said H and C? The basin, though, is good, with a wide lip of several ledges to hold soap without its riding off, these little ridges most basins have now don't hold anything, dinky cheap pseudo-marble, he supposes if you're in the roofing industry you know plumbing suppliers who can still provide the good stuff, even though there's not much market for it. The curved lavender bar he has right in his hands must have lost its lettering making lather for Cindy's suntanned skin, suds in her crotch, her hair must be jet black there, her eyebrows are: you should look at a woman's eyebrows not the hair on her head for the color of her pussy. This bathroom has not been so cleaned up for guests as the downstairs one, *Popular Mechanics* on the straw hamper next to the toilet, the towels slung crooked on the plastic towel holders and a touch of damp to them, the Murketts showering just a few hours ago for this party. Harry considers opening this bathroom cabinet as he did the other one but thinking of fingerprints notices the chrome rim and refrains. Nor does he dry his hands, for fear of touching the towel Webb used. He has seen that long yellow body in the Flying Eagle locker room. The man has moles all across his back and shoulders that probably aren't contagious but still.

He can't return downstairs with wet hands. That shit Harrison would make some crack. *Ya still got scum on your hands, ya jerkoff.* Rabbit stands a moment in the hall, listening to the noise of the party rise, a wordless clatter of voices happy without him, the women's the most distinct, a kind of throbbing in it like the melody you sometimes hear in a ragged engine idling, a song so distinct you expect to hear words. The hall is carpeted here not in lime but in a hushed plum, and he moves to follow its color to the threshold of the Murketts' bedroom. Here it happens. It hollows out Harry's stomach, makes him faintly sick, to think what a lucky stiff Webb is. The bed is low in modern style, a kind of tray with sides of reddish wood, and the covers had been pulled up hastily rather than made. Had it just happened? Just before the showers before the party that left the towels in the bathroom damp? In

mid-air above the low bed he imagines in afterimage her damp
and perfect toes, those sucky little dabtoes whose print he has often
spied on the Flying Eagle flagstones, here lifted high to lay her cunt
open, their baby dots mingling with the moles on Webb's back.
It hurts, it isn't *fair* for Webb to be so lucky, not only to have a
young wife but no old lady Springer on the other side of the walls.
Where do the Murketts put their kids? Harry twists his head to see
a closed white door at the far other end of the plum carpet. There.
Asleep. He is safe. The carpet absorbs his footsteps as, silent as a
ghost, he follows its color into the bedroom. A cavernous space,
forbidden. Another shadowy presence jars his heart: a man in blue
suit trousers and rumpled white shirt with cuffs folded back and a
loosened necktie, looking overweight and dangerous, is watching
him. Jesus. It is himself, his own full-length reflection in a large
mirror placed between two matching bureaus of wood bleached
so that the grain shows through as through powder. The mirror
faces the foot of the bed. Hey. These two. It hasn't been just his
imagination. They fuck in front of a mirror. Harry rarely sees himself head to toe except when he's buying a suit at Kroll's or that
little tailor on Pine Street. Even there you stand close in to the
three-way mirrors and there's not this weird surround of space, so
he's meeting himself halfway across the room. He looks mussed
and criminal, a burglar too overweight for this line of work.

Doubled in the mirror, the calm room holds few traces of the
Murketts' living warmth. No little lacy bits of underwear lying
around smelling of Cindy-cunt. The curtains are a thick red striped
material like a giant clown's pants ballooning, and they have window shades of that room-darkening kind that he keeps asking
Janice to get; now that the leaves are letting go the light barrels
through the copper beech right into his face at seven in the morning, he's making nearly fifty thousand a year and this is how he has
to live, he and Janice will never get themselves organized. The far
window here with its shade drawn for a nap must overlook the
pool and the stand of woods everybody has up here in this development between the houses, but Harry doesn't want to get himself that deep into the room, already he's betraying hospitality. His
hands have dried, he should go down. He is standing near a corner of the bed, its mute plane lower than his knees, the satiny

peach bedspread tugged smooth in haste, and he impulsively, remembering the condoms he used to keep in a parallel place, steps to the curly maple bedside table and ever so stealthily pulls out the small drawer. It was open an inch anyway. No diaphragm, that would be in the bathroom. A ballpoint pen, an unlabelled box of pills, some match folders, a few receipts tossed in, a little yellow memo pad with the roofing company logo on it and a diagonally scrawled phone number, a nail clippers, some paper clips and golf tees, and – his thumping heart drowns out the mumble of the party beneath his feet. At the back of the drawer are tucked some black-backed Polaroid instant photos. That SX-70 Webb was bragging about. Harry lifts the little stack out delicately, turns it over, and studies the photos one by one. Shit. He should have brought his reading glasses, they're downstairs in his coat pocket, he must get over pretending he doesn't need them.

The top photo, flashlit in this same room, on this same satiny bedspread, shows Cindy naked, lying legs spread. Her pubic hair is even darker than he imagined, the shape of it from this angle a kind of T, the upright of the T infolded upon a redness as if sore, the underside of her untanned ass making a pale blob on either side. At arm's length he holds the glazed picture closer to the bed-side light; his eyes water with the effort to see everything, every crease, every hair. Cindy's face, out of focus beyond her breasts, which droop more to either side than Harry would have hoped, smiles with nervous indulgence at the camera. Her chin is doubled, looking so sharply down. Her feet look enormous. In the next shot, she has turned over, showing a relaxed pair of buttocks, fish-white with an eyelike widening staring from the crack. For the next couple of photos the camera has switched hands, and old Webb, stringy and sheepish, stands as Harry has often seen him after a shower, except without the hard-on, which he is helping with his hand. Not a great hard-on, pointing to ten o'clock, not even ten but more like a little after nine, but then you can't expect a guy over fifty to go for high noon, leave that to the pimply teen-agers: when Rabbit was fourteen in soc sci class, a spot of sun, the shadow of Lotty Bingaman's armpit as she raised her hand with a pencil in it, that sweet strain of cloth and zipper against thick blood. Webb has length but not much bulk at the base; still, there

he is, game and even with the pot belly and gnarled skinny legs
and shit-eating expression somehow debonair, not a hair on his
wavy head out of place. The next shots were in the nature of
experiments, by natural light, the shades must have all been up,
bold to the day: slabby shapes and shelves of flesh interlocked and
tipped toward violet by the spectrum of underexposure. Harry
deciphers one bulge as Cindy's cheek, and then the puzzle fits, she
is blowing him, that purply stalk is his prick rooted in her stretched
lips and the fuzzy foreground is Webb's chest hair as he takes the
picture. In the next one he has improved the angle and light
and the focus is perfect on the row of one eye's black lashes.
Beyond the shiny tan tip of her nose, her fingers, boneless and
blue-knuckled, with stubby nails, hold the veined thing in its
place, her little finger lifted as on a flute. What was Ollie saying
about flutes? For the next shot Webb had the idea of using the
mirror; he is standing sideways with the camera squarely where his
face ought to be and Cindy's own dear face impaled, as she kneels
naked, on this ten-o'clock hook of his. Her profile is snub-nosed
and her nipples jut out stiff. The old bastard's tricks have turned
the little bitch on. But her head seems so small and round and
brave, stuck on his prick like a candy apple. Harry wants in the
next picture to see come like toothpaste all over her face like in
the fuck movies, but Webb has turned her around and is fucking
her from behind, his prick vanished in the fish-white curve of her
ass and his free hand steadying her with his thumb sunk where her
asshole would be; her tits hang down pear-shaped in their weight
and her legs next to Webb's appear stocky. She's getting there. She
will get fatter. She will turn ugly. She is looking into the mirror
and laughing. Perhaps in the difficulty of keeping her balance
while Webb's one hand operates the camera, Cindy laughed at
that moment a big red laugh like a girl on a poster, with this yellow prick in her from behind. The light in the room must have
been dying that day for the flesh of both the Murketts appears
golden and the furniture reflected in the mirror is dim in blue
shadow as if underwater. This is the last picture; there were eight
and a camera like this takes ten. *Consumer Reports* had a lot to say
a while ago about the SX-70 Land Camera but never did explain
what the SX stood for. Now Harry knows. His eyes burn.

The party noise below is lessening, perhaps they are listening for a sound from upstairs, wondering what has happened to him. He slips the Polaroids back into the drawer, face down, black backs up, and tries to slide shut the drawer to the exact inch it was open by. The room otherwise is untouched; the mirror will erase his image instantly. The only clue remaining, he has given himself an aching great erection. He can't go downstairs like this: he tries to tear his mind loose from that image of her open mouth laughing at the sight of herself being fucked, who would have thought sweet Cindy could be so dirty? It takes some doing to realize that other boys are like you are, that dirty, and then to realize that girls can go right along with it takes more than one lifetime to assimilate. Rabbit tries to fling away that laugh, out of his mind, but it has no more carry to it than a handkerchief. He tries to displace what he has just seen with his other secrets. His daughter. His gold. His son coming down from the Poconos tomorrow to claim his place at the lot. That does it, the thing is wilting. Holding gloomy Nelson firmly in his mind, Harry goes into the bathroom and turns on the faucet as if washing his hands in case somebody down below is listening while he undoes his belt and tucks himself properly into his underpants. What is killing, he has seen her laugh that same laugh at poolside, at something he or Buddy Inglefinger or even some joker from outside their group altogether has just said. She'd go down on anybody.

As he descends the stairs his head still feels to be floating on a six-foot string attached to his big shoes. The gang in the long living room has realigned itself in a tighter circle about the Parsons table. There seems to be no place for him. Ronnie Harrison looks up. "My God, whatcha been doin', jacking off?"

"I'm not feeling so great," Rabbit says, with dignity.

"Your eyes look red," Janice says. "Have you been crying again?"

They are too excited by the topic among themselves to tease him long. Cindy doesn't even turn around. The nape of her neck is thick and brown, soft and impervious. Treading to them on spongy steps across the endless pale carpeting, he pauses by the fireplace mantel to notice what he had failed to notice before, two Polaroid snaps propped up, one each of the Murketts' little

children, the five-year-old boy with an outsize fielder's mitt standing sadly on the bricks of their patio, and the three-year-old girl on
this same hazily bright summer afternoon, before the parents took
a nap, squinting with an obedient and foolish half-smile up toward
some light-source that dazzles her. Betsey is wearing both pieces
of a play-muddied little bikini and Webb's shadow, arms lifted to
his head as if to scare her with horns, fills one corner of the exposed
square of film. These are the missing two shots from that pack
of ten.

"Hey, Harry, how about the second week of January?" Ronnie hoots at him.

They have all been discussing a shared trip to the Caribbean,
and the women are as excited about it as the men.

It is after one when he and Janice drive home. Brewer Heights
is a development of two-acre lots off the highway to Maiden
Springs, a good twenty minutes from Mt. Judge. The road sweeps
down in stylish curves; the developer left trees, and six hours
ago when they drove up this road each house was lit in its bower
of unbulldozed woods like displays in the façade of a long gray
department store. Now the houses, all but the Murketts', are dark.
Dead leaves swirl in the headlights, pour from the trees in the fall
wind as if from bushel baskets. The seasons catch up to you. The
sky gets streaky, the trees begin to be bare. Harry can think of
little to say, intent upon steering on these winding streets called
drives and boulevards. The stars flickering through the naked
swaying treetops of Brewer Heights yield to the lamp-lit straight-
away of the Maiden Springs Pike. Janice drags on a cigarette; the
glow expands in the side of his vision, and falls away. She clears
her throat and says, "I suppose I should have stuck up more for
Peggy, she being an old friend and all. But she did talk out of turn,
I thought."

"Too much women's lib."

"Too much Ollie maybe. I know she keeps thinking of leaving him."

"Aren't you glad we have all that behind us?"

He says it mischievously, to hear her grapple with whether they did or didn't, but she answers simply, "Yes."

He says nothing. His tongue feels trapped. Even now, Webb is undressing Cindy. Or she him. And kneeling. Harry's tongue seems stuck to the floor of his mouth like those poor kids every winter who insist on touching their tongues to iron railings.

Janice tells him, "Your idea of taking this trip in a bunch sure took hold."

"It'll be fun."

"For you men playing golf. What'll *we* do all day?"

"Lie in the sun. There'll be things. They'll have tennis courts." This trip is precious to him, he speaks of it gingerly.

Janice drags again. "They keep saying now how sunbathing leads to cancer."

"No faster than smoking."

"Thelma has this condition where she shouldn't be in the sun at all, it could kill her she's told me. I'm surprised she's so keen on going."

"Maybe she won't be in the morning on second thought. I don't see how Harrison can afford it, with that kid of theirs in defective school."

"Can we I wonder? Afford it. On top of the gold."

"Honey, of course. The gold's already gone up more than the trip will cost. We're so pokey, we should have taken up travelling years ago."

"You never wanted to go anywhere, with just me."

"Of course I did. We were running scared. We had the Poconos to go to."

"I was wondering, it might mean leaving Nelson and Pru just at the time."

"Forget it. The way she hung on to Nelson, she'll hang on to this baby till the end of January. Till Valentine's Day."

"It seems mean," she says. "And then leaving Nelson at the lot alone with too much responsibility."

"It's what he wanted, now he's got it. What can happen? Jake and Rudy'll be around. Manny'll run his end."

Her cigarette glows once more, and then with that clumsy scrabbling motion that always annoys him she stubs it out. He hates having the Corona ashtray dirty, it smells for days even after you've emptied it. She sighs. "I wish in a way it was just us going, if we must go."

"We don't know the ropes. Webb does. He's been there before, I think he's been going since long before Cindy, with his other wives."

"You can't mind Webb," she admits. "He's nice. But to tell the truth I could do without the Harrisons."

"I thought you had a soft spot for Ronnie."

"That's you."

"I hate him," Rabbit says.

"You like him, all that vulgarity. He reminds you of basketball days. Anyway it's not just him. Thelma worries me."

"How can she? She's a mouse."

"I think she's very fond of you."

"I never noticed. How can she be?" Stay off Cindy, he'll let it all out. He tries to see those photographs again, hair by hair in his mind's eye, and already they are fading. The way their bodies looked golden at the end, like gods.

Janice says with a sudden surprising stiffness, "Well, I don't know what you think's going to happen down there but we're not going to have any funny stuff. We're too *old*, Harry."

A pick-up truck with its high beams glaring tailgates him blindingly and then roars around him, kids' voices jeering.

"The drunks are out," he says, to change the subject.

"What were you *doing* up there in the bathroom so long anyway?" she asks.

He answers primly, "Waiting for something to happen that didn't."

"Oh. Were you sick?"

"Heading toward it, I thought. That brandy. That's why I switched to beer."

Cindy is so much on his mind he cannot understand why Janice fails to mention her, it must be deliberate. All that blowing, Lord. There's birth control. White gobs of it pumping in, being swallowed; those little round teeth and the healthy low baby gums that show when she laughs. Webb on front and him from behind, or the other way around, Harry doesn't care. Ronnie operating the camera. His prick has reawaked, high noon once more in his life, and the steering wheel as they turn into Central Street caresses its swollen tip through the cloth. Janice should appreciate this: if he can get it up to their room intact.

But her mind has wandered far from sex, for as they head down through the cones of limb-raddled light along Wilbur she says aloud, "Poor Nelson. He seemed so young, didn't he, going off with his bride?"

This town they know so well, every curb, every hydrant, where every mailbox is. It gives way before them like a veil, its houses dark, their headlights low. "Yeah," he agrees. "You sometimes wonder," he hears himself go on, "how badly you yourself fucked up a kid like that."

"We did what we could," Janice says, firm again, sounding like her mother. "We're not God."

"Nobody is," Rabbit says, scaring himself.

IV

THE HOSTAGES have been taken. Nelson has been working at Springer Motors for five weeks. Teresa is seven months pregnant and big as a house, a house within a house as she slops around Mom-mom's in those maternity slacks with Spandex in front and some old shirts of Dad's he let her have. When she walks down the upstairs hall from the bathroom she blocks out all the light, and when she tries to help in the kitchen she drops a dish. Because there are five of them now they have had to dip into the good china Mom-mom keeps in the breakfront and the dish Pru dropped was a good one. Though Mom-mom doesn't say much you can see by the way her throat gets mottled it's a deal for her, the kind of thing that is a big deal for old ladies, going on about those dishes that she and Fred bought fifty years ago together at Kroll's when the trolley cars ran all up and down Weiser every seven minutes and Brewer was a hot shit kind of place.

What Nelson can't stand about Pru, she farts. And lying on her back in bed because she can't sleep on her stomach, she snores. A light but raspy little rhythmic noise he can't ignore, lying there in the front room with the streetlights eating away at the window-shades and the cars roaring by on the street below. He misses his quiet old room at the back of the house. He wonders if Pru has what they call a deviated septum. Until he married her, he didn't notice that her nostrils aren't exactly the same size: one is more narrow than the other, as if her thin pointy hooked nose with its freckles had been given a sideways tweak when it was still soft back there in Akron. And then she keeps wanting to go to bed early at just the hour after dinner when the traffic outside picks up and he is dying to go out, over to the Laid-Back for a brew or two or even just down to the Superette on Route 422 to check out some new faces after the claustrophobia of hanging around the lot all day trying to deal around Dad and then coming home and having to deal around him some more, his big head grazing the ceiling and his silly lazy voice laying down the law on everything, if you listen, putting Nelson down, looking at him so nervously, with that sad-eyed little laugh, *Did I say that?*, when he thinks he's said something funny. The trouble with Dad is he's lived in a harem too long, Mom and Mom-mom doing everything for him. Any other man around except Charlie who was dying in front of your eyes and those goons he plays golf with, he gets nasty. Nobody except Nelson in the world seems to realize how nasty Harry C. Angstrom is and the pressure of it sometimes makes Nelson want to scream, his father comes into the room all big and fuzzy and sly when he's a killer, a body-count of two to his credit and his own son next if he can figure out how to do it without looking bad. Dad doesn't like to look bad anymore, that was one thing about him in the old days you could admire, that he didn't care that much how he looked from the outside, what the neighbors thought when he took Skeeter in for instance, he had this crazy dim faith in himself left over from basketball or growing up as everybody's pet or whatever so he could say Fuck You to people now and then. That spark is gone, leaving a big dead man on Nelson's chest. He tries to explain it to Pru and she listens but she doesn't understand.

At Kent she was slender and erect and quick in her way of walking, her terrific long carrotty hair up in a sleek twist when it wasn't let flat down her back looking ironed. Going to meet her up at the new part of Rockwell around five, a student out of water, he would feel enlarged to be taking this working woman a year older than he away from the typewriters and files and cool bright light; the administration offices seemed a piece of the sky of the world's real business that hung above the tunnels of the classes he wormed through every day. Pru had none of that false savvy, she knew none of the names to drop, the fancy dead, and could talk only about what was alive now, movies and records and what was on TV and the scandals day to day at work, who burst into tears and who had been propositioned by one of the deans. One of the other secretaries at work was fucking the man she worked for without much liking him but out of a kind of flip indifference to her own life and body and it thrilled Nelson to think how that could be Pru just as well, there was a tightness to lives in Pennsylvania that loosened out here and let people drift where they would. It thrilled him how casually tough she was, with that who-cares? way of walking beside him, smelling of perfume, and a softer scent attached to her clothes, beneath all those trees they kept bragging about at Kent, that and all those gyms in the Student Center Complex and having the biggest campus bus system in the world, all that bullshit heaped on to try to make people forget the only claim to fame Kent State would ever have, which was May 4, 1970, when the Guardsmen fired from Blanket Hill. As far as Nelson was concerned they could have shot all those jerks. When in '77 there was all that fuss about Tent City Nelson stayed in his dorm. He didn't know Pru then. At one of the bars along Water Street she would get into the third White Russian and tell him horror stories of her own growing up, beatings and rages and unexplained long absences on her father's part and then the tangled doings of her sisters as they matured sexually and began to kick the house down. His tales seemed pale in comparison. Pru made him feel better about being himself. With so many of the students he knew, including Melanie, he felt mocked, outsmarted by them at some game he didn't want to play, but with Pru Lubell, this secretary, he did not feel mocked. They agreed about things, basic things. They knew that at bottom the world was brutal, no father protected you, you were left alone in a way not appreciated by these kids horsing around on jock teams or playing at being radicals or doing the rah-rah thing or their own thing or whatever. That Nelson saw it was all bullshit gave him for Pru a certain seriousness. Across the plywood booth tables of the working-man's-type bar in north Akron they used to go to in her car – she had a car of her own, a salt-rotted old Plymouth Valiant, its front fender flapping like a flag, and this was another thing he liked about her, her being willing to drive such an ugly old clunker, and having worked for the money to pay for it – Nelson could tell he looked pretty good. In terms of the society she knew he was a step up. And so was she, in terms of this environment, the local geography. Not only a car but an apartment, small but all her own, with a stove she cooked her own dinners on, and liquor she would pour for him after putting on a record. From their very first date, not counting the times they were messing around with Melanie and her freaky SLDK friends, Pru had taken him back to her apartment house in this town called Stow, assuming without making any big deal of it that fucking was what they were both after. She came with firm quick thrusts that clipped him tight and secure into his own coming. He had fucked other girls before but hadn't been sure if they had come. With Pru he was sure. She would cry out and even flip a little, like a fish that flashes to the surface of a gloomy lake. And afterwards cooking him up something to eat she would walk around naked, her hair hanging down her back to about the sixth bump on her spine, even though there were a lot of windows across the apartment courtyard she could be seen from. Who cares? She liked being looked at, actually, in the dancing spots they went to some nights, and in private let him look at her from every angle, her big smooth body like that of a doll whose arms and legs and head stayed where you set them. His intense gratitude for all this, where another might have casually accepted, added to his value in her eyes until he was locked in, too precious to let go of, ever.

Now she sits all day watching the afternoon soaps with Mommom and sometimes Mom, *Search for Tomorrow* on Channel 10 and then *Days of Our Lives* on 3 and back to 10 for *As the World Turns* and over to 6 for *One Life to Live* and then 10 again for *The Guiding Light*, Nelson knows the routine from all those days before they let him work at the lot. Now Pru farts because of some way the baby is displacing her insides and drops things and says she thinks his father is perfectly nice.

He has told her about Becky. He told her about Jill. Pru's response is, "But that was long ago."

"Not to me. It is to him. He's forgotten, the silly shit, just to look at him you can see he's forgotten. He's forgotten everything he ever did to us. The stuff he did to Mom, incredible, and I don't know the half of it probably. He's so smug and *sat*isfied, is what gets me. If I could *just once* make him see himself for the shit he is, I maybe could let it go."

"What good would it do, Nelson? I mean, your father's not perfect, but who is? At least he stays home nights, which is more than mine ever did."

"He's gutless, that's why he stays home. Don't you think he wouldn't like to be out chasing pussy every night? Just the way he used to look at Melanie. It isn't any great love of Mom that holds him back, I tell you that. It's the lot. Mom has the whip hand now, no thanks to herself."

"Why, honey. I think from what I've seen your parents are quite fond of each other. Couples that have stayed together that long, they must have something."

To dip his mind into this possibility disgusts Nelson. The wall-paper, its tangled pattern of things moving in and out of things, looks evil. As a child he was afraid of this front room where now they sleep, across the hall from the mumble of Mom–mom's tele-vision. Cars passing on Joseph Street, underneath the bare maple limbs, wheel sharp-edged panels around the walls, bright shapes rapidly altering like in those computer games that are everywhere now. When a car brakes at the corner, a patch of red shudders across the wallpaper and a pale framed print of a goateed farmer with a wooden bucket at some stone well: this fading print has always hung here. The farmer too had seemed evil to the child's eyes, a leering devil. Now Nelson can see the figure as merely foolish, sentimental. Still, the taint of malevolence remains, caught somewhere in the transparency of the glass. The red shudders, and winks away; a motor guns, and tires dig out. Go: the fury of this unseen car, escaping, becoming a mere buzz in the distance, grati-fies Nelson vicariously.

He and Pru are lying in the old swaybacked bed he used to share with Melanie. He thinks of Melanie, unpregnant, free, having a ball at Kent, riding the campus buses, taking courses in Oriental religion. Pru is dead sleepy, lying there in an old shirt of Dad's buttoned at the breasts and unbuttoned over her belly. He had offered her some shirts of his, now that he has this job he has had to buy shirts, and she said they were too small and pinched. The room is hot. The furnace is directly under it and heat rises, there's nothing they can do about it, here it is the middle of November and they still sleep under a sheet. He is wide awake and will be for hours, agitated by his day. Those friends of Billy's are after him to buy some more convertibles and though the Olds Delta 88 Royale did sell for $3600 to that doctor Dad says and says

Manny backs him up on this that by the time you figure in the deductible on the insurance and the carrying costs there really wasn't any profit.

And now the Mercury is in the shop though the insurance man wanted to declare it totalled, he said that would be simplest with a virtual antique like this, parts at a premium and the front end screwed up like somebody had done it deliberately; Manny estimates that the repair costs are going to come in four to five hundred above the settlement check, they can't give you more than car book value, and when he asked Manny if some of the mechanics couldn't do it in their spare time he said, looking so solemn, his brow all furrowed and the black pores in his nose jumping out at you, *Kid, there is no spare time, these men come in here for their bread and butter*, implying he didn't, a rich man's son. Not that Dad backs him up in any of this, he takes the attitude the kid's being taught a lesson, and enjoys it. The only lesson Nelson's being taught is that everybody is out for their own little pile of dollars and nobody can look up to have any vision. He'll show them when he sells that Mercury for forty-five hundred or so, he knows a lot of guys at the Laid-Back money like that is nothing to. This Iranian thing is going to scare gas prices even higher but it'll blow over, they won't dare keep them long, the hostages. Dad keeps telling him how it costs three to five dollars a day every day to carry a car in inventory but he can't see why, if it's just sitting there on a lot you already own, the company even pays rent to itself, he's discovered, to gyp the government.

Pru beside him starts to snore, her head propped up on two pillows, her belly shiny like one of those puffballs you find in the woods attached to a rotten stump. Downstairs Mom and Dad are laughing about something, they've been high as kites lately, worse than kids, going out a lot more with that crummy crowd of theirs, at least kids have the excuse there isn't much else to do. He thinks of those hostages in Tehran and it's like a pill caught in his throat, one of those big dry vitamins Melanie was always pushing on him, when it won't go down or come up. Take a single big black helicopter in there on a moonless night, commandos with blackened faces, a little piano wire around the throats of those freaky radical Arabs, *uuglh, arg*, you'd have to whisper, women and children first, and lift them all away. Drop a little tactical A-bomb on a minaret as a calling card. Or else a tunnel or some sort of boring machine like James Bond would have. That fantastic scene in *Moonraker* when he's dumped from the plane without a parachute and free-falls into one of the bad guys and steals his, can't be much worse than hang gliding. By the moonlight Pru's belly-button is casting a tiny shadow, it's been popped like inside out, he never knew a pregnant woman naked before, he had no idea it was that bad. Like a cannonball, that hit from behind and stuck.

Once in a while they get out. They have friends. Billy Fosnacht has gone back to Tufts but the crowd at the Laid-Back still gathers, guys and these scumbags from around Brewer still hanging around, with jobs in the new electronics plants or some govern-ment boondoggle or what's left of the downtown stores; you go into Kroll's these days, where Mom met Dad in prehistoric days, you go in through that forest where Weiser Square used to be and it's like the deserted deck of a battleship just after the Japs bombed Pearl Harbor, a few scared salesladies standing around cut off at the waist by the On Sale tables. Mom used to work at the salted nut and candy section but they don't have one anymore, probably figured out after thirty years and six people died of worms it wasn't sanitary. But if there hadn't been a nut counter Nelson wouldn't exist, or would exist as somebody else, which doesn't make sense. He and Pru don't know all their friends' first names, they have first names like Cayce and Pam and Jason and Scott and Dody and Lyle and Derek and Slim, and if you show up at the Laid-Back enough you get asked along to some of their parties. They live in places like those new condos with stained rough-planking walls and steep-pitched roofs like a row of ski lodges thrown up on the side of Mt. Pemaquid out near the Flying Eagle, or like those city mansions of brick and slate with lots of ironwork and chimneys that the old mill money built along the north end of Youngquist or out beyond the car yards and now are broken up into apartments, where they haven't been made into nursing homes or office buildings for cutesy outfits like handcrafted-leather shops and do-it-yourself framers and young architects spe-cializing in solar panels and energy saving and young lawyers with fluffy hair and bandit mustaches along with their business suits, that charge their young clients a flat fee of three hundred dollars whether it's for a divorce or beating a possession rap. In these neighborhoods health-food stores have sprung up, and little long restaurants in half-basements serving vegetarian or macrobiotic or Israeli cuisine, and bookstores with names like Karma Paperbacks, and little shops heavy on macramé and batik and Mexican wedding shirts and Indian silk and those drifter hats that make everybody look like the part of his head with the brain in it has been cut off. Old machine shops with cinder-block sides now sell pieces of unpainted furniture you put together yourselves, for these apartments where everybody shares.

The apartment Slim shares with Jason and Pam is on the third floor of a tall old house on the high side of Locust, blocks beyond the high school, in the direction of Maiden Springs. A big bay of three four-paned windows overlooks the deadened heart of the city: where once the neon outlines of a boot, a peanut, a top hat, and a great sunflower formed a garland of advertisement above Weiser Square now only the Brewer Trust's beacons trained on its own granite façade mark the center of the downtown: four great pillars like four white fingers stuck in a rich black pie, the dark patch made by the planted trees of the so-called shopping mall. From this downtown the standard sodium-yellow lamps of the city streets spread outward, a rectilinear web receding down toward the curving river and on into suburbs whose glow flattens to a horizon swallowed by hills that merge with the clouds of night. Slim's front bay windows have in their upper panes the stained-glass transom lights, those simplified flowers of pieces of purple and amber and milky green, that are along with pretzels Brewer's pride. But the old floors of parqueted oak have been covered wall-to-wall with cheap shag carpeting speckled like pimento, and hasty plasterboard partitions have divided up the generous original rooms. The high ceilings have been lowered, to save heat, and reconstituted in soft white panels of something like pegboard. Nelson sits on the floor, his head tipped back, a can of beer cold between his ankles; he has shared two joints with Pru and the little holes in the ceiling are trying to tell him something, an area of them seems sharp and vivid and aggressive, like the blackheads on Manny's nose the other day, and then this look fades and another area takes it up, as if a jellyfish of intensity is moving transparently across the ceiling. Behind him on the wall is a large grimacing poster of Ilie Nastase. Slim belongs to a tennis club out next to the Hemmigtown Mall and loves Ilie Nastase. Nastase is beaded with sweat, his legs thick as posts. Hairy, knotty posts. The stereo is playing Donna Summer, something about a telephone, very loud. Out in the center of the room between Nelson and some potted ferns and broad-leaved plants like Mommom used to have in that side room off the living room (he remembers sitting with his father looking at them some day when an awful thing had happened, a thing enormous and hollow under them while the leaves of the plants drank the sunlight as these bigger plants too must do when the sun comes slanting in the tall bay windows) there is a space and in this space Slim is dancing like a snake on a string with another skinny boy with a short haircut called Lyle. Lyle has a narrow skull with hollows at the back and wears tight jeans and some long-sleeved shirt like a soccer shirt with a broad green stripe down the middle. Slim is queer and though Nelson isn't supposed to mind that he does. He also minds that there are a couple of slick blacks making it at the party and that one little white girl with that grayish kind of sharp-chinned Polack face from the south side of Brewer took off her shirt while dancing even though she has no tits to speak of and now sits in the kitchen with still bare tits getting herself sick on Southern Comfort and Pepsi. At these parties someone is always in the bathroom being sick or giving themselves a hit or a snort and Nelson minds this too. He doesn't mind any of it very much, he's just tired of being young. There's so much wasted energy to it. He sees on the ceiling that the jellyfish intensity flitting across the holes is energy such as flows through the binary bits of computers but he can't take it any further than that. At Kent he was curious about computer science but in just the introductory course Math 10061 in Merrill Hall the math got to be too much for him, all those Jewish kids and Koreans with faces flat as platters just breezing along like it was plain as day, what a function was, it didn't seem to be anything you could actually point to, just the general idea somehow of the equation, another jellyfish, but how to extract it out? It beat him. So he figured he might as well come home and share the wealth. His father was holding him on his lap that day, the sensation of a big warm sad-smelling body all around and under his has stayed with him along with a memory of a beam of sunlight eating into the crescent edge of a furry leaf in that iron table of green plants, it must have been around when Becky died. Mom-mom can't last forever and when she kicks the bucket that leaves him and Mom in charge of the lot, with Dad up front like one of those life-size cardboard cutouts you used to see in car showrooms before cardboard became too expensive. Those blacks mooching around so superior, that decided cool way they have of saying hello, daring you to outstare them, not taking responsibility for anything though, makes him itch with anger, though the joints should be working him around toward mellow by now. Maybe another beer. Then he remembers the beer between his knees, it's cold and heavy because it's full and fresh from Slim's fridge, and takes a sip. Nelson studies his hand carefully because it feels holding the can as though he has a mitten on.

Why doesn't Dad just die? People that age get diseases. Then he and Mom. He knows he can manage Mom.

He's not that young, he's turned twenty-three, and what makes him feel foolish among these people, he's married. Nobody else here looks married. There is sure nobody else pregnant, that it shows. It makes him feel put on display, as a guy who didn't know better. To be fair to her Pru didn't want to come out, she was willing to sit over there like one of these green plants basking in the light of the television set, watching *The Love Boat* and then *Fantasy Island* with poor old Mom-mom, she's been fading lately, Dad and Mom used to sit home with her but now like tonight they're out somewhere with that Flying Eagle crowd, incredible how irresponsible grownups so-called get when they think they're ahead of the game, Mom has told him all about their crazy gold, maybe he should have offered to stay home, him and Pru with Mom-mom, she's the one with all the cards after all, but by that time Pru had gotten herself dolled up thinking she owed Nelson a little social life because he was working so hard and always housebound with her – families, doing everything for each other out of imagined obligation and always getting in each other's way, what a tangle. Then once Pru got here and got a buzz on, the madwoman of

Akron took over, she decided to play to the hilt the token pregnant woman, throwing her weight around, dancing in shoes she
really shouldn't even be walking in, thick-soled wedgy platforms
held on by thin green plastic strapping like that gimp the playground supervisors at the Mt. Judge Rec Field used to have you
braid lanyards for a whistle out of, there was even he remembers
a way of weaving called butterflies, you could make a keyholder
this way as if kids ever had keys to hold. Maybe she's doing it out
of spite. But he has undergone an abandonment of his own and
enjoys watching her from a distance of his own, through the
smoke. She has flash, Pru, flash and glitter in this electric-green
beltless dress she bought herself at a new shop over on Locust
where the old retired people are being forced out by gentrifica-
tion, the middle class returning to the cities. Sleeves wide as wings
lift when she whirls and that cannonball of a stomach sticks out
tugging up her dress in front to show more of the orange elastic
stockings the doctor told her to wear to save her young veins. Her
shiny platforms can barely shuffle on the shag carpeting but she
leaves them on, showing she can do it, more spite at him; her body
as if skewered through a spot between her shoulder blades writhes
to the music while her arms lift shimmery green and her fantastic
long hair snaps in a circle, again and again.

Nelson cannot dance, which is to say he will not, for all dancing is now is standing in place and letting the devil of the music
enter you, which takes more faith than he's got. He doesn't want
to appear a fool. Now Dad, Dad would do it if he were here, just
like when Jill was there he gave himself to Skeeter and never looked
back even when all the worst had happened, such a fool he really
believes there is a God he is the apple of the eye of. The dots on
the ceiling don't let Nelson take this glimpse higher than this and
he returns his eyes to Pru, painfully bright in the dazzle dress, its
flow like a jewel turned liquid, her face asleep in the music above
her belly, which is solid and not hers alone but also his, so he is
dancing too. He hates for a second that in himself which cannot do
it, just as he could not join in the flickering mind play of computer science and college generally and could not be the floating
easy athlete his father had been. The dark second passes, dissolved
by the certainty that some day he will have his revenge on them all.

Pru's partner for some of the dancing has been one of the sassy
Brewer blacks, the bigger one, in bib overalls and cowboy boots,
and then Slim comes out of a twirl over by the potted plants with
Lyle and swings into orbit with Pru, who keeps at it whether or
not anybody is there, up and down, little flips of her hands, and a
head toss. Her face does look asleep. That hooked nose of hers
sharp in profile. People keep touching her belly, as if for luck: in
spinning and snapping their fingers their loose fingers trail across
the sacred bulge where something that belongs to him too is
lodged. But how to fend off their touches, how to protect her and
keep her clean? She is too big, he would look like a fool, she likes
the dirt, she came out of it. Once she drove him past her old home
in Akron, she never took him in, what a sad row, houses with
wooden porches with old refrigerators on them. Melanie would
have been better, her brother played polo. At least Pru should take
off her shoes. He sees himself rising up to tell her but in truth feels
too stoned to move, obliged to sit here and mellow between the
fluffy worms of the carpet and the worm holes of the ceiling. The
music has gas bubbles in it, popping in the speakers, and Donna
Summer's zombie voice slides in and out of itself, doubling, taking all parts. *Stuck on you, stuck like glue.* The fairy that Slim stopped
dancing with offers Pru a toke and she sucks the wet tip of the
joint and holds it down deep without losing a beat of the music,
belly and feet keeping that twitch. Nelson sees that to an Akron
slum kid like this Brewer is a city of hicks and she's showing them
all something.

A girl he noticed before, she came here with some big red-
faced clod who actually wore a coat and tie to this brawl, comes
and sits on the floor beside Nelson under Ilie Nastase and takes the
beer from between his ankles to sip from it. Her smiling pale
round face looks a little lost here but willing to please. "Where do
you live?" she asks, as if picking up with him a conversation begun
with someone else.

"In Mt. Judge?" He thinks that's the answer.

"In an apartment?"

"With my parents and my grandmother."

"Why is that?" Her face shines amiably with sweat. She has
been drinking too. But there is a calm about her he is grateful for.

Her legs stretch out beside his in white pants that look radiant where that jellyfish of strangeness moves across them.

"It's cheaper." He softens this. "We thought no point in look-ing for a place until the baby comes."

"You have a wife?"

"There she is." He gestures toward Pru.

The girl drinks her in. "She's terrific."

"You could say that."

"What does *that* tone of voice mean?"

"It means she's bugging the shit out of me."

"Should she be bouncing like that? I mean, the baby."

"Well, they say exercise. Where do *you* live?"

"Not far. On Youngquist. Our apartment isn't near as grand as this, we're on the first floor back, overlooking a little yard where all the cats come. They say our building might be going condo."

"That good or bad?"

"Good if you have the money, bad if you don't I guess. We just started working in town and my – my man wants to go to col-lege when we get our stake."

"Tell him, Forget it. I've been to college and it's absolute horse poop." She has a pleasant puffy look to her upper lip and he's sorry to see, from the way she holds her mouth, that he's left her no-thing to say. "What do you work at?" he asks her.

"I'm a nurses' aide in an old people's home. I doubt if you know it, Sunnyside out toward the old fairgrounds."

"Isn't it depressing?"

"People say that but I don't mind it. They talk to me, that's mostly what people want, company."

"You and this man aren't married?"

"Not yet. He wants to get further along in life. I think it's good. We might want to change our minds."

"Smart. That chick in green out there got herself knocked up and I had no choice." Not much answer to this either. Yet the girl doesn't show boredom, like so many people do with him. At the lot he watches Jake and Rudy prattle away and he envies how they do it without feeling idiotic. This strange face hangs opposite his calmly, mildly attentive, the eyes a blue paler than you almost ever see and her skin milky and her nose slightly tipped up and her gingery hair loosely bundled to the back. Her ears are exposed and pierced but unadorned. In his stoned condition the squarish white folds of these ears seem very vivid. "You say you just moved to town," Nelson says. "Where'd you move from?"

"Near Galilee. Know where that is?"

"More or less. When I was a kid we went down there to the drag race strip a couple times."

"You can hear the engines from our place, on a quiet night. My room is on the side and I used to always hear them."

"Where we live there's always traffic going by. My room used to be out in back but now it's up front." Dear little ears, small like his, though nothing else about her is small, especially. Her thighs really fill those bright white pants. "What does your father do, he a farmer?"

"My father's dead."

"Oh. Sorry."

"No, it was hard, but he was getting along. He was a farmer, you're right, and he had the school bus contract for the township."

"Still, that's too bad."

"I have a wonderful mother though."

"What's wonderful about her?"

In his stupidity he keeps sounding combative. But she doesn't seem to mind. "Oh. She's just very understanding. And can be very funny. I have these two brothers –"

"You do?"

"Yes, and she's never tried to make me feel I should back down or anything because I'm a girl."

"Well why would she?" He feels jealous.

"Some mothers would. They think girls should be quiet and smart. Mine says women get more out of life. With men, it's if you don't win every time, you're nothing."

"Some momma. She has it all figured."

"And she's fatter than I am and I love her for that."

You're not fat, you're just nice, he wants to tell her. Instead he says, "Finish up the beer. I'll get us another."

"No thanks – what's your name?"

"Nelson." He should ask her hers but the words stick.

"Nelson. No thanks, I just wanted a sip. I should go see what Jamie's doing. He's in the kitchen with some girl –"

"Who's showing her tits."

"That's right."

"My theory on that is, those that got real tits to show don't." He glances down. The vertical ribs of her russet knit sweater are pushed slightly apart as they pass over the soft ample shelf there. Below that the white cloth of her slacks, taut in wrinkles where belly meets thighs in a triangle, has a radiance that manifests the diagonal run of the threads, the way the cloth was woven and cut. Below that her feet are bare, with a pinkness along the outer edge of each big toe fresh from the pressure of her discarded shoes.

The girl has been made to blush by this survey of her body. "What do you do since college, Nelson?"

"I just veg out. No, actually, I sell cars. Not your ordinary tacky cars but special old convertibles, that nobody makes anymore. Their value is going to go up and up, it *has* to."

"Sounds exciting."

"It is. Jesus, the other day in the middle of town I saw this white Thunderbird parked, with red leather seats, the guy still had the top down though it's getting pretty cold, and I nearly flipped. It looked like a yacht. When they turned out those things there wasn't all this penny-pinching."

"Jamie and I just bought a Corolla. It's in his name but I'm the one that uses it, there isn't any bus that goes out to the fairgrounds anymore and Jamie has a job he can walk to, in this place that makes bug-killers, you know, those electric grids with a purple light that people put outdoors by their pools or barbecues."

"Sounds groovy. Must be a slack season for him though."

"You'd think so but it's not, they're busy making them for next year, and they ship all over the South."

"Huh." Maybe they've had enough of this conversation. He doesn't want to hear any more about Jamie's bug-killers.

But the girl keeps going, she's relaxed with him now, and so young everything is new to her. Nelson guesses she's three or four years younger than he is. Pru is over a year older, and that irritates him right now, along with her defiant dancing and her pregnancy and all these blacks and queers she's not afraid of. "So I really should put in my half," she is explaining, "even though he makes twice what I do. His parents and my mother loaned us the down payment equally though I know she couldn't afford it. Next year if I can get a part-time job somewhere I want to begin nurse's training. Those RNs make a fortune doing just what I'm doing now, except they're allowed to give injections."

"Jesus, you want to spend your whole life around sick people?"

"I like taking care of things. On the farm until my father died there were always chickens and animals. I used to shear my own sheep even."

"Huh." Nelson has always been allergic to animals.

"Do you dance, Nelson?" she asks him.

"No. I sit and drink beer and feel sorry for myself." Pru is bouncing around now with a Puerto Rican or something. Manny has a couple of them working for him in the shop now. He doesn't know what disease they get as kids, but their cheeks have worse than pocks – like little hollow cuts all over.

"Jamie won't dance either."

"Ask one of the fairies. Or just go do it by yourself, somebody'll pick you up."

"I love to dance. Why do you feel sorry for yourself?"

"Oh . . . my father's a prick." He doesn't know why this popped out of his mouth. Something about the goody-goody way in which the girl speaks of her own parents. But in thinking of his father, what strikes Nelson about the large bland face that appears to his inner eye is a mournful helplessness. His father's face bloats like an out-of-focus close-up in some war movie in the scramble of battle before floating away. Big and white and vague as on that day when he held him on his lap, when the world was too much for the two of them.

"You shouldn't say that," the girl says, and stands. Luminous long legs. Her thighs make a kind of lap even when she stands. Her pink-rimmed bare feet sunk in the shag rug so close nearly kill him, they are so sexy. What did she say that for? Making him feel guilty and scolded. Her own father is dead. She makes him feel he's killed his. She can go fuck. She goes and dances, standing shy along the wall for a minute and then moving in, loosening. He doesn't want to watch and get envious; he heaves himself up, to get another beer and steal another look at the girl in the kitchen. Sad, tits by themselves, on a woman sitting up. Little half-filled purses. This Jamie's face and hands are broad and scraped-looking and he has loosened his tie to let his bull neck breathe. Another girl is reading his palm; they are all sitting around a little porcelain kitchen table, with spots worn black where place settings were, which reminds Nelson of something. What? A poster in here is of Marlon Brando in the black-leather get-up of *The Wild One*. Another shows Alice Cooper with his green eyelids and long fingernails. The refrigerator with its cool shelves of yogurt in paper cups and beer in sharply lettered sixpacks seems an island of decent order amid all this. Nelson is reminded of the lot, its rows of new Toyotas, and his stomach sinks. Sometimes at the lot, standing in the showroom with no customers in sight, he feels return to him from childhood that old fear of being in the wrong place, of life being run by rules nobody would share with him. He returns to the big front room with its fake ceiling and thinks that Pru looks ridiculously older than the other dancers: a little frizzy-haired girl called Dody Weinstein interning in teen fashions at Kroll's and Slim and this Lyle in the soccer shirt back together again and Pam their hostess in a big floppy muu-muu her body is having fits within, while the wan lights of Brewer fall away beyond the bay window, and the girl without a name waits in her white pants to be picked up while she stands to one side shivering from side to side in time to the music. *One night in a lifetime, one life in a night.* She looks a little self-conscious but happy to be here, out of the sticks. The black bubbles in the speakers pop faster and faster, and his wife with her cannonball gut is about to fall flat on her face. He goes to Pru and pulls her by her wrist away. Her spic thug of a partner dead-pan writhes to the girl in white pants and picks her up. *Babe it's gotta be tonight, babe it's gotta be tonight.* Nelson is squeezing Pru's wrist to hurt. She is unsteady, pulled out of the music, and this further angers him, his wife getting tipsy. Defective equipment breaking down on purpose just to show him up. Her brittle imbalance makes him want to smash her completely.

"You're *hurt*ing me," she says. Her voice arrives, tiny and dry, from a little box suspended in air behind his ear. As she tries to pull her wrist away her bangles pinch his fingers, and this is infuriating.

He wants to get her somewhere out of this. He pulls her across a hallway looking for a wall to prop her up against. He finds one, in a small side room; the light-switch plate beside her shoulder has been painted like an open-mouthed face with an off-on tongue. He puts his own face up against Pru's and hisses, "Listen. You shape up for Chrissake. You're going to hurt yourself if you don't shape up. And the baby. What're you tryin' to do, shake him loose? Now you calm down."

"I am calm. You're the one that's not calm, Nelson." Their eyes are so close her eyes threaten to swallow his with their blurred green. "And who says it's going to be a him?" Pru gives him her lopsided smirk. Her lips are painted vampire red in the new style and it's not becoming, it emphasizes her hatchet face, her dead calm bloodless look. That blank defiance of the poor: you can't scare them enough.

He pleads, "You shouldn't be drinking and smoking pot at all, you'll cause genetic damage. You know that."

She forms her words in response slowly. "Nelson. You don't give a shit about genetic damage."

"You silly bitch. I do. Of course I do. It's my kid. Or is it? You Akron kids'll fuck anybody."

They are in a strange room. Flamingos surround them. Whoever lives in this side room with its view of the brick wall across two narrow sideyards has collected flamingos as a kind of joke. A glossy pink stuffed satin one drapes its ridiculous long black legs over the back of the sofabed, and hollow plastic ones with stick legs are propped along the walls on shelves. There are flamingos worked into ashtrays and coffee mugs and there are little 3-D tableaux of the painted pink birds with lakes and palms and sunsets, souvenirs of Florida. For one souvenir a trio of them were gathered in knickers and Scots caps on a felt putting green. Some of the bigger ones wear on their hollow drooping beaks those limp candylike sunglasses you can get in five and dimes. There are hundreds, other gays must give them to him, it has to be Slim who lives in here, that sofabed wouldn't be enough for Jason and Pam.

"It is," Pru promises. "You know it is."

"I don't know. You're acting awfully whorey tonight."

"I didn't want to come, remember? You're the one always wants to go out."

He begins to cry: something about Pru's face, that toughness out of Akron closed against him, her belly bumping his, that big doll-like body he used to love so much, that she might just as easily have entrusted to another, its clefts, its tufts, and might just as easily take from him now, he is nothing to her. All their tender times, picking her up on the hill and walking under the trees, and the bars along Water Street, and his going ahead and letting her out there in Colorado make such a sucker of him while he stewed in Diamond County, nothing. He is nothing to her like he was nothing to Jill, a brat, a bug to be humored, and look what happened. Love feels riddled through all his body like rot, down clear to his knees spongy as punk. "You'll do damage to yourself," he sobs; tears add their glitter to the green of her dress at the shoulder, yet his own crumpled face hangs as clear in the back of his brain as a face on a TV screen.

"You're strange," Pru tells him, her voice breathier now, a whispery rag stuffed in his ear.

"Let's get out of this creepy place."

"That girl you were talking to, what did she say?"

"Nothing. Her boyfriend makes bug-killers."

"You talked together a long time."

"She wanted to dance."

"I could see you pointing and looking at me. You're ashamed of my being pregnant."

"I'm not. I'm proud."

"The fuck you are, Nelson. You're embarrassed."

"Don't be so hard. Come on, let's split."

"See, you are embarrassed. That's all this baby is to you, an embarrassment."

"Please come. What're you trying to do, make me get down on my knees?"

"Listen, Nelson. I was having a perfectly good time dancing and you come out and pull this big macho act. My wrist still hurts. Maybe you broke it."

He tries to lift her wrist to kiss it but she stiffly resists: at times she seems to him, body and soul, a board, flat, with that same

abrasive grain. And then the fear comes upon him that this flatness
is her, that she is not withholding depths within but there are
no depths, this is what there is. She gets on a track sometimes and
it seems she can't stop. His pulling at her wrist again, only to kiss
it but she doesn't want to see that, has made her altogether mad,
her face all pink and pointy and rigid. "You know what you
are?" She tells him, "You're a little Napoleon. You're a *twerp*,
Nelson."

"Hey don't."

The space around her vampire lips is tight and her voice is a
dead level engine that won't stop. "I didn't really know you. I've
been watching how you act with your family and you're very
spoiled. You're spoiled and you're a bully, Nelson."

"Shut up." He mustn't cry again. "I was never spoiled, just the
opposite. You don't know what my family did to me."

"I've heard about it a thousand times and to me it never
sounded like any big deal. You expect your mother and poor old
grandmother to take care of you no matter what you do. You're
horrid about your father when all he wants is to love you, to have
a halfway normal son."

"He didn't want me to work at the lot."

"He didn't think you were ready and you weren't. You aren't.
You aren't ready to be a father either but that's my mistake."

"Oh, even you make mistakes." The green she is wearing is
a hateful color, shimmery electric arsenic like a big fat black
hooker would wear to get attention on the street. He turns his eyes
away and sees over on a bureau top some bendable toy flamingos
have been arranged in a copulating position, one on top of the
other's back, and another pair in what he supposes is a blow job,
but the droopy beaks spoil the effect.

"I make plenty," Pru is going on, "why wouldn't I, nobody
has ever taught me anything. But I'll tell you one thing Nelson
Angstrom I'm going to have this baby no matter what you do.
You can go to Hell."

"I can, huh?"

"Yes." She has to weaken it. Her very belly seems to soften
against his, nestling. "I don't want you to but you can. I can't stop
you and you can't stop me, we're two people even if we did get

married. You never wanted to marry me and I shouldn't have let you, it turns out."

"I did though, I did," he says, fearful that confessing this will make his face crumple again.

"Then stop being a bully. You bullied me to come here and now you're bullying me to go. I like these people. They have better senses of humor than the people in Ohio."

"Let's stay then." There are things other than flamingos in the room – hideous things, he sees. A plaster cast of Elvis Presley with votive candles in red cups at its base. An aquarium without fish in it but full of Barbie dolls and polyplike plastic things he thinks are called French ticklers. Tacked-up postcards of women in tinsel triangles somersaulting, mooning, holding giant breasts in their silver-gloved hands, postcards from Germany printed on those tiny ridges that hold two views, one coy and one obscene, depending on how you move your head. The room all over has the distinctness and variousness of vomit that still holds whole green peas and orange carrot dice from the dinner of an hour ago. He can't stop looking.

As he moves from one horror to the next Pru slips away, giving his hand a squeeze that may be apologetic for all they've said. What have they said? In the kitchen the girl with bare tits has put on a T-shirt saying ERA, Jamie has taken off his coat and his necktie. Nelson feels very tall, so tall he can't hear what he himself is saying, but it doesn't matter, and they all laugh. In a dark bedroom off the kitchen someone is watching the eleven-thirty special report from Iran, time slips by in that rapid spasmodic skid of party time. When Pru returns to him asking to go she is dead pale, a ghost with the lipstick on her face like movie blood and worn in the center where her lips meet. Things are being dyed blue by something in his head and her teeth look crooked as she tells him almost inaudibly that she has taken off her shoes like he wanted her to and now she can't find them. She plops down on a kitchen chair and stretches her orange legs out so her belly thrusts up like a prick and laughs with all those around her. What pigs. Nelson in searching for her shoes finds instead in the side room of horrible tinsel and flamingos the girl in white pants asleep on the sofabed. With her face slack she looks even younger than before. Her hand curls beside her snub nose pale palm up. The calm and mildly freckled bulge of her forehead sleeps without a crease. Only her hair holds that deep force of a woman, unbundled from its pins and many-colored in the caves and ridges of its tangle. He wants to cover her up but sees no blanket, just the French ticklers and Barbie dolls brilliant in their aquarium. A sliver of milky bare skin peeps where her russet knit sweater has ridden up from the waist of her slacks. Nelson looks down and wonders, Why can't a woman just be your friend, even with the sex? Why do you have to keep dealing with all this ego, giving back hurt just to defend yourself? Gazing down at that milky bit of skin, he forgets what he came in here to find. He needs to urinate, he realizes.

And in the bathroom after his bladder has emptied in those unsteady dribbles that mean it's been allowed to get too full he becomes fascinated by a big slick book sitting on the hamper, belonging to Slim most likely, an album printed of photographs and posters from the Nazi days in Germany, beautiful blond boys in rows singing and a handsome fat man in a white uniform loaded with medals and Hitler looking young and lean and gallant, gazing toward some Alps. Having this here is some kind of swish thing like those tinselled cards showing women as so ugly and there seems no protection against all the ugliness that is in the world, no protection for that girl asleep or for him. Pru has found her horrible green platform shoes and in the kitchen is sitting in a straight chair while that Puerto Rican she picked up with like little knife cuts all over his face kneels at her feet doing up the little buckles on the straps like gimp. When she stands she acts rocky, what have they been giving her? She lets herself be slipped into that velvet jacket she used to wear in fall and spring at Kent, red so with the bright green dress she looks like Christmas six weeks early, all wrapped up. Jason is dancing in that front room where now Jamie and the girl with ERA across her pathetic tits are trying it out too, so they say their goodbyes to Pam and Slim, Pam giving Pru a kiss on the cheek woman to woman as if whispering the code word in her ear and Slim putting his hands together in front of his chest and bowing Buddha-style. That slanty look to his eyes, Nelson wonders if it's natural or comes with doing perverted things. The jellyfish of intensity crawls across Slim's lips. Last little waves and smiles and the door closes on the party noise.

The door to the apartment is an old-fashioned heavy one of yellow oak. He and Pru on this third-floor landing are sealed into something like silence. Rain is tapping on the black skylight of chicken-wire glass above their heads.

"Still think I'm a twerp?" he asks.

"Nelson, why don't you grow up?"

The solid wooden banister on the right does a dizzying double loop down the two flights to the first floor. Looking down, Nelson can see the tops of two plastic garbage cans set in the basement far below. Impatiently Pru passes him on the left, fed up with him and anxious to be out in the air, and afterwards he remembers her broad hip bumping into his and his anger at what seemed her willful clumsiness, but not if he gives her a bit of hip back, a little vengeful shove. On the left of the stairwell there is no banister, and the plaster wall here is marred by ragged nail holes where the renovators stripped away what must have been panelling. So when Pru in those wedgy platforms turns her ankle, there is nothing for her to hold on to; she gives a little grunt but her pale face is impassive as in the old days of hang gliding, at the moment of launch. Nelson grabs for her velvet jacket but she is flying beyond his reach, her legs no longer under her; he sees her face skid past these nail holes as she twists toward the wall, clawing for support there, where there is none. She topples then twisting sideways, headfirst, the metal-edged treads ripping at her belly. It is all so fast yet his brain has time to process a number of sensations — the touch of her velvet humming in his fingertips, the scolding bump her hip gave him, his indignation at her clunky shoes and the people who stripped the staircase of its banister, all precisely layered in his mind. Distinctly he sees the patch of darker orange reinforcing at the crotch of her tights like the center of a flagrant green flower as her dress is flung wide with her legs by first impact. Her arms keep trying to brace her slithering body and one arm ends at an angle when she stops, about halfway down the steep flight, a shoe torn loose on a string of gimp, her head hidden beneath the splayed mass of her beautiful hair and all her long form still.

Fallt's Bubbli nunner!

In soft sweeps the rain patters on the skylight. Music leaks through the walls from the party. The noise of her fall must have been huge, for the yellow oak door pops open at once and people thunder all around, but the only sound Nelson heard was a squeak Pru gave when she first hit like one of those plastic floating bath toys suddenly accidentally stepped on.

Soupy is in fine form at the hospital, kidding the nurses and staff and moving through this white world in his black clothes like a happy germ, an exception to all the rules. He comes forward as if to embrace Ma Springer but at the last second holds back and gives her instead a somewhat jaunty swat on the shoulder. To Janice and Harry he gives his mischievous small-toothed grin; to Nelson he turns a graver, but still bright-eyed, face. "She looks just dandy, except for the cast on her arm. Even there she was fortunate. It's the left arm."

"She's left-handed," Nelson tells him. The boy is grouchy and stoops with lack of sleep. He was with her at the hospital from one to three and now at nine-thirty is back again. He called the house around one-fifteen and nobody answered and that has been added to his twenty years of grievances. Mom-mom had been in the house but had been too old and dopey to hear the phone through her dreams and his parents had been out with the Murketts and Harrisons at the new strip joint along Route 422 beyond the Four Seasons toward Pottstown and then had gone back to the Murketts' for a nightcap. So the family didn't hear the news until Nelson, who had crawled into his empty bed at three-thirty, awoke at nine. On the ride over to the hospital in his mother's Mustang he claimed he hadn't fallen asleep until the birds began to chirp.

"What birds?" Harry said. "They've all gone south."

"Dad, don't bug me, there are these black sort of birds right outside the window."

"Starlings," Janice offered, peacemaking.

"They don't chirp, they scrawk," Harry insisted. "*Scrawk, scrawk.*"

"Doesn't it stay dark late now?" Ma Springer interposed. It's aging her, this constant tension between her son-in-law and her grandson.

Nelson sitting there all red-eyed and snuffly and stinking of last night's vapors did annoy Harry, short of sleep and hungover himself. He fought down the impulse to say *Scrawk* again. At the hospital, he asks Soupy, "How'd you get here so soon?" genuinely admiring. Snicker all you want, the guy *is* magical somehow.

"The lady herself," the clergyman gaily announces, doing a little side-step that knocks a magazine to the floor from a low table where too many are stacked. *Woman's Day. Field and Stream.* A hospital of course wouldn't get *Consumer Reports*. A killing article in there a while ago about medical costs and the fantastic mark-up on things like aspirin and cold pills. Soupy stoops to retrieve the magazine and comes up slightly breathless. He tells them, "Evidently, after they calmed the dear girl down and set her arm and reassured her that the fetus appeared unaffected she still felt such concern that she woke up at seven a.m. and knew Nelson would be asleep and didn't know who to call. So she thought of *me*." Soupy beams. "I of course was still wrapped in the arms of Morpheus but got my act together and told her I'd rush over between Holy Communion and the ten o'clock service and, behold, here I am. *Ecce homo.* She wanted to pray with me to keep the baby, she'd been praying *con*stantly, and at least to this point in time as they used to say it seems to have *worked*!" His black eyes click from one to another face, up and down and across. "The doctor who received her went off duty at eight but the nurse in attendance *sol*emnly swore to me that for all of the mother's bruises that little heartbeat in there is just as strong as ever, and *no* signs of vaginal bleeding or anything nasty like that. That Mother Nature, she is one tough old turkey." He has chosen Ma Springer to tell this to. "Now I *must* run, or the hungry sheep will look up and be not fed. Visiting hours here don't really begin until one p.m., but I'm *sure* the authorities wouldn't object if you took a quick peek. Tell them I gave you my blessing." And his hand reflexively lifts, as if to give them a blessing. But instead he lays the hand on the sleeve of Ma Springer's glistening fur coat. "If you *can't* make the service," he entreats, "*do* come for the meeting afterwards. It's the meeting to advise the vestry on the new tracker organ, and a lot of pennypinchers are coming out of the woods. They put a dollar a week into the plate all year, and their vote is as good as mine or thine." He flies away, scattering the V-for-peace sign down the hall.

Boy, these boys do love misery, Harry thinks. Well, it's a turf nobody else wants. St. Joseph's Hospital is in the tatty north-central part of Brewer where the old Y.M.C.A. was before they tore it down for yet another drive-in bank and where the old wooden railroad bridge has been rebuilt in concrete that started to crack immediately. They used to talk about burying the tracks along through here in a tunnel but then the trains pretty much stopped running and that solved that. Janice had had Rebecca June here when the nurses were all nuns, they may still be nuns but now there's no way of telling. The receptionist for this floor wears a salmon-colored pants suit. Her swollen bottom and slumping shoulders lead the way. Half-open doors reveal people lying ema-ciated under white sheets staring at the white ceiling, ghosts already. Pru is in a four-bed room and two women in gauzy hospital johnnies scatter back into their beds, ambushed by early visitors. In the fourth bed an ancient black woman sleeps. Pru her-self is all but asleep. She still wears flecks of last night's mascara but the rest of her looks virginal, especially the fresh white cast from elbow to wrist. Nelson kisses her lightly on the lips and then, sit-ting in the one bedside chair while his elders stand, sockets his face in the space on the bed edge next to the curve of Pru's hip. What a baby, Harry thinks.

"Nelson was wonderful," Pru is telling them. "So caring." Her voice is more musical and throaty than Harry has ever heard it. He wonders if just lying down does that to a woman: changes the angle of her voice box.

"Yeah, he felt sick about it," Harry says. "We didn't hear the story till this morning."

Nelson lifts his head. "They were at a *strip* joint, can you imag-ine?"

"Jesus," Harry says to Janice. "Who's in charge here? What does he want us to do, sit around the house all the time aging gracefully?"

Ma Springer says, "Now we can only stay a minute, I want to get to church. It wouldn't look right I think just to go to the meet-ing like Reverend Campbell said."

"Go to that meeting, Ma," Harry points out, "they'll hit you up for a fortune. Tracker organs don't grow on trees."

Janice says to Pru, "You poor sweetie. How bad is the arm?"

"Oh, I wasn't paying that much attention to what the doctor said." Her voice floats, she must be full of tranquilizers. "There's a bone on the outside, with a funny name —"

"Femur," Harry suggests. Something about all this has jazzed him up, made him feel nerved-up and defiant. Those strippers last night, some of them young enough to be his daughter. The Gold Cherry, the place was called.

Nelson lifts his head again from burrowing in Pru's side. "That's in the *thigh*, Dad. She means the humerus."

"Ha ha," Harry says.

Pru seems to moan. "Ulna," she supplies. "He said it was just a simple fracture."

"How long's it gonna be on?" Harry asks.

"He said six weeks if I do what he says."

"Off by Christmas," Harry says. Christmas is a big thing in his mind this year, for beyond it, and the mop-up of New Year's, they're going to take their trip, they have the hotel, the plane reservations, they were discussing it all last night again, after the excitement of the strippers.

"You poor sweetie," Janice repeats.

Pru begins to sing, without music. But the words come out as if sung. "Oh my God, I don't mind, I'm glad for it, I deserve to be punished somehow. I honestly believe" — she keeps looking straight at Janice, with an authority they haven't seen from her before — "it's God telling me this is the price He asks for my not losing the baby. I'm glad to pay it, I'd be glad if every bone in my body was broken, I really wouldn't care. Oh my God, when I felt my feet weren't under me and I knew there wasn't anything for me to do but fall down those horrible stairs, the thoughts that ran through my head! You must know."

Meaning Janice must know what it's like to lose a baby. Janice kind of yelps and falls on the bedridden girl so hard Harry winces, and plucks at her back to pull her off. Feeling the rock of plaster against her breasts, Janice arches her spine under his hands; through the cloth her skin feels taut as a drum, and hot. But Pru shows no pain, smiling her crooked careful smile and keeping her eyelids with their traces of last night's blue closed serenely, accepting the older woman's weight upon her. The hand not captured in a cast Pru sneaks around to pat Janice's back; her fingers come close to Harry's own. Pat, they go, pat pat. He thinks of Cindy Murkett's round fingers and marvels how much more childish and grublike they look than these, bony though young and reddened at the knuckles: his mother's hands had that tough scrubbed look. Janice can't stop sobbing, Pru can't stop patting, the two other women patients awake in the room can't stop glancing over. Moments this complicated rub Harry the wrong way. He feels rebuked, since the official family version is that the baby's dying at Janice's hands was all his fault. Yet now the truth seems declared that he was just a bystander. Nelson, pushed to one side by his mother's assault of grief, sits up and stares, poor frazzled kid. These damn women so intent on communing should leave us out of it entirely. At last Janice rights herself, having snuffled so hard her upper lip is wet with snot.

Harry hands her his handkerchief.

"I'm so happy," she says with a big runny sniff, "for Pru."

"Come on, shape up," he mutters, taking back the handkerchief.

Ma Springer soothes the waters with, "It does seem a miracle, all the way down those stairs and nothing worse. Up that high in those old Brewer houses the stairs were just for the servants."

"I didn't go all the way down," Pru says. "That's how I broke my arm, stopping myself. I don't remember any pain."

"Yeah," Harry offers. "Nelson said you were feeling no pain."

"Oh no, no." Her hair spread out across the pillow by Janice's embrace makes her look like she is falling through white space, singing. "I'd hardly had anything, the doctors all say you shouldn't, it was those terrible tall platforms they're making us all wear. Isn't that the dumbest style? I'm going to burn them up, absolutely, as soon as I get back."

"When will that be now?" Ma asks, shifting her black purse to the other hand. She has been dressed for church since before Nelson woke up and the fuss began. She's a slave to that church, God knows what she gets out of it.

"Up to a week, he said," Pru says. "To keep me quiet and, you know, to make sure. The baby. I woke up this morning with what I thought were contractions and they scared me so I called Soupy. He was wonderful."

"Yes, well," Ma says.

Harry hates the way they all keep calling it the baby. More like a piglet or a wobbly big frog at this stage, as he pictures it. What if she had lost it, wouldn't it have lived? They keep five-month preemies alive now and pretty soon you'll have life in a test tube start to finish. "We gotta get Ma to church," he announces. "Nelson, you want to wake up and come or stay here and sleep?" The boy's head had gone back down onto the hospital mattress again. He used to fall asleep at the kitchen table that way.

"Harry," Janice says. "Don't be so rough on everybody."

"He thinks we're all silly about the baby," Pru says dreamily, dimly teasing.

"No, hey: I think it's great about the baby." He bends over to kiss her goodbye for now and wants to whisper in her ear about all the babies he has had, dead and alive, visible and invisible. Instead he tells her, straightening, "Keep cool. We'll be back after this when we can stay longer."

"Don't not play golf," she says.

"Golf's shot. They don't like you to walk on the greens after a certain point."

Nelson is asking her, "What do you want me to do, go or stay?"

"Go, Nelson, for heaven's sake. Let me get some sleep."

"You know, I'm sorry last night if I said anything. I was skunked. When they told me last night they didn't think you'd lose the baby I was so relieved I cried. Honest." He would cry again but his face clouds with embarrassed awareness that the others have listened. That's why we love disaster, Harry sees, it puts us back in touch with guilt and sends us crawling back to God. Without a sense of being in the wrong we're no better than animals. Suppose the baby had aborted at the very moment he was watching that olive chick with the rolling tongue tug down her tinsel underpants to her knees and peek at the audience from behind her shoulder while tickling her asshole with that ostrich feather: he'd feel terrible.

Pru waves her husband's quavery words and all their worried faces away. "I'm *fine*. I love all of you so much." Her hair streams outward as she waits to sink into sleep, into more wild prayer, into the dreaming fluids of her own bruised belly. Her stumpy wing of snow-white plaster lifts a few inches from her chest in farewell. They leave her to the company of ex-nuns and shuffle back through the hospital corridors, their footsteps clamorous amid their silent determination to save their quarrels for the car.

"A week!" Harry says, as soon as they're rolling in the Mustang. "Does anybody have any idea how much a week in a hospital costs these days?"

"Dad, how can you keep thinking about money all the time?"

"Somebody has to. A week is a thousand dollars minimum. *Mini*mum."

"You *have* Blue Cross."

"Not for daughter-in-laws I don't. Not for you either, once you're over nineteen."

"Well I don't know," Nelson says, "but I don't like her being in a ward with all those other women barfing and moaning all night. One of 'em was even black, did you notice?"

"How did you get so prejudiced? Not from me. Anyway that's not a ward, that's what you call a semi-private," Harry says.

"I want my wife to have a private room," Nelson says.

"Is that a fact? You want, you want. And who's going to foot the bill, big shot? Not you."

Ma Springer says, "I know when I had my diverticulitis, Fred wouldn't hear of anything but a private room for me. And it was a corner room at that. A wonderful view of the arboretum, the magnolias just in bloom."

Janice asks, "How about at the lot, isn't he under the group insurance there?"

Harry tells her, "Maternity benefits don't start till you've worked for Springer Motors nine months."

"A broken arm isn't what I'd call maternity," Nelson says.

"Yeah but if it weren't for her maternity she'd be out walking around with it."

"Maybe Mildred could look into it," Janice suggests.

"O.K.," he concedes, with ill grace. "I don't know what our exact policy is."

Nelson should let it go at that. Instead he says, leaning forward from the back seat so his voice presses on Harry's ear, "Without Mildred and Charlie there isn't much you do know exactly. I mean —"

"I know what you mean and I know a lot more about the car business than you ever will at the rate you're going, if you don't stop futzing around with these old Detroit hotrods that lose us a bundle and start focusing on the line we carry."

"I wouldn't mind if they were Datsuns or Hondas, but frankly Dad, Toyotas —"

"The Toyota franchise is what old Fred Springer landed and Toyotas are what we sell. Bessie, why doncha slap the kid around a little? I can't reach him."

His mother-in-law's voice comes from the back seat after a pause. "I was wondering if I should go to church after all. I know his heart's set on a big drive for the organ and there aren't too many that enthusiastic. If I show up I might get made a committee head and I'm too old for that."

"Didn't Teresa seem sweet?" Janice asks aloud. "It seemed like she'd grown up overnight."

"Yeah," Harry says, "and if she'd fallen down all two flights she'd be older than we are."

"Jesus, Dad," Nelson says. "Who *do* you like?"

"I like everybody," Harry says. "I just don't like getting boxed in."

The way from St. Joseph's to Mt. Judge is to keep going straight over the railroad tracks and then continue right on Locust past Brewer High and on through Cityview Park and then left past the shopping mall as usual. On a Sunday morning the people out in cars are mostly the older American type, the women with hair tinted blue or pink like the feathers of those Easter chicks before they outlawed it and the men gripping the steering wheel with two hands like the thing might start to buck and bray: with no-lead up to a dollar thirteen at some city stations thanks to the old Ayatollah they have to try to squeeze value out of every drop. Actually, people's philosophy seems to be they'll burn it while it's here and when it's fourth down and twenty-seven Carter can punt. The four features at the mall cinema are BREAKING AWAY STARTING OVER RUNNING and "10." He'd like to see "10," he knows from the ads this Swedish-looking girl has her hair in corn rows like a black chick out of Zaire. One world: everybody fucks everybody. When he thinks of all the fucking there's been in the world and all the fucking there's going to be, and none of it for him, here he sits in this stuffy car dying, his heart just sinks. He'll never fuck anybody again in his lifetime except poor Janice Springer, he sees this possibility ahead of him straight and grim as the known road. His stomach, sour from last night's fun, binds as it used to when he was running to school late. He says suddenly to Nelson, "How the hell could you let her fall, why didn't you keep ahold of her? What were you *doing* out so late anyway? When your mother was pregnant with you we never went *any*where."

"Together at least," the boy says. "You went a lot of places by yourself the way I heard it."

"Not when she was pregnant with *you*, we sat there night after night with the boob tube, *I Love Lucy* and all that family comedy, didn't we Bessie? And we weren't snorting any dope, either."

"You don't snort dope, you smoke it. Coke is what you snort."

Ma Springer responds slowly to his question. "Oh I don't know how you and Janice managed exactly," she says wearily, in a voice that is looking out the window. "The young people are different now."

"I'll say they are. You fire somebody to give 'em a job and they knock the product."

"It's an O.K. product if all you want is to get from here to there," Nelson begins.

Harry interrupts furiously, thinking of poor Pru lying there with a snivelling baby burying his head in her side instead of a husband, of Melanie slaving away at the Crêpe House for all those creeps from the banks that lunch downtown, of his own sweet hopeful daughter stuck with that big red-faced Jamie, of poor little Cindy having to put on a grin at being fucked from behind so old Webb can have his kicks with his SX-70, of Mim going down on all those wop thugs out there all those years, of Mom plunging her old arms in gray suds and crying the kitchen blues until Parkinson's at last took mercy and got her upstairs for a rest, of all the women put upon and wasted in the world as far as he can see so little punks like this can come along. "Let me tell you something about Toyotas," he calls back at Nelson. "They're put together by little yellow guys in white smocks that work in one plant cradle to grave and go crazy if there's a fleck of dust in the fuel injector system and those jalopies Detroit puts out are slapped together by jigaboos wearing headphones pumping music into their ears and so zonked on drugs they don't know a slothead screw from a lug nut and furthermore are taught by the NAACP to hate the company. Half the cars come through the Ford assembly line are deliberately sabotaged, I forget where I read all this, it wasn't *Consumer Reports*."

"Dad, you're so prejudiced. What would Skeeter say?"

Skeeter. In quite another voice Harry says, "Skeeter was killed in Philly last April, did I tell ya?"

"You *keep* telling me."

"I'm not blaming the blacks on the assembly line, I'm just saying it sure makes for lousy cars."

Nelson is on the attack, frazzled and feeling rotten, poor kid. "And who are you to criticize me and Pru for going out to see some friends when you were off with yours seeing those ridiculous exotic dancers? How could you stand it, Mom?"

Janice says, "It wasn't as bad as I'd thought. They keep it within bounds. It really wasn't any worse than it used to be at the old fairgrounds."

"Don't answer him," Harry tells her. "Who's he to criticize?"

"The funny thing," Janice goes on, "is how Cindy and Thelma and I could agree which girl was the best and the men had picked some girl entirely different. We all liked this tall Oriental who was very graceful and artistic and *they* liked, Mother, the men liked some little chinless blonde who couldn't even dance."

"She had that look about her," Harry explains. "I mean, she meant it."

"And then that tubby dark one that turned you on. With the feather."

"Olive-complected. She was nice too. The feather I could have done without."

"Mom-mom doesn't want to hear all this disgusting stuff," Nelson says from the back seat.

"Mom-mom doesn't mind," Harry tells him. "Nothing fazes Bessie Springer. Mom-mom loves life."

"Oh I don't know," the old lady says with a sigh. "We didn't have such things when we might have been up to it. Fred I remember used to bring home the *Playboy* sometimes, but to me it seemed more pathetic than not, these eighteen-year-old girls that are really just children except for their bodies."

"Well who isn't?" Harry asks.

"Speak for yourself, Dad," Nelson says.

"No now, I meant," Ma insists, "you wonder what their parents raised them for, seeing them all naked just the way they were born. And what the parents must think." She sighs. "It's a different world."

Janice says, "I guess at this same place Monday nights they have ladies' night with male strippers. And they say really the young men become frightened, Doris Kaufmann was telling me, the women grab for them and try to get up on the stage after them. The women over forty they say are the worst."

"That's so sick," Nelson says.

"Watch your mouth," Harry tells him. "Your mother's over forty."

"*Dad.*"

"Well I wouldn't behave like that," she says, "but I can see how some might. I suppose a lot of it depends on how satisfying the husband you have is."

"*Mo-om,*" the boy protests.

They have swung around the mountain and turned up Central and by the electric clock in the dry cleaner's window it is three of ten. Harry calls back, "Looks like we'll make it, Bessie!"

The town hall has its flag at half-mast because of the hostages. At the church the people in holiday clothes are still filing in, beneath the canopy of bells calling with their iron tongues, beneath the wind-torn gray clouds of this November sky with its scattered silver. Letting Ma out of the Mustang, Harry says, "Now don't pledge the lot away, just for Soupy's organ."

Nelson asks, "How will you get home, Mom-mom?"

"Oh, I guess I can get a ride with Grace Stuhl's grandson, he generally comes for her. Otherwise it won't kill me to walk."

"Oh Mother," Janice says. "You could never walk it. Call us at the house when the meeting's over if you haven't a ride. We'll be home." The club is down to minimal staff now; they serve only packaged sandwiches and half the tennis court nets are down and already they have relocated the pins to temporary greens. A sadness in all this plucks at Rabbit. Driving home with just Janice and Nelson he remembers the way they used to be, just the three of them, living together, younger. The kid and Janice still have it between them. He's lost it. He says aloud, "So you don't like Toyotas."

"It's not a question of like, Dad, there isn't that much about 'em to like or dislike. I was talking to some girl at the party last night who'd just bought a Corolla, and all we could talk about was the old American cars, how great they were. It's like Volvos, they don't have it anymore either, it's not something anybody can control. It's like, you know, time of life."

The boy is trying to be conversational and patch things up; Harry keeps quiet, thinking, Time of life, the crazy way you're going, zigzagging around and all those drugs, you'll be lucky to get to my time of life.

"Mazdas," Nelson says. "That's what I'd want to have an agency in. That rotary engine is *so* much more efficient than the four-cycle piston, you could run this country on half the gas, once they get the seal perfected."

"Go over and ask Abe Chafetz for a job then. I heard he was going broke, the Mazdas have so many bugs. Manny says they'll never get the seal right."

Janice says, placating, "I think the Toyota ads on television are very clever and glamorous."

"Oh the *ads* have charisma," Nelson says. "The ads are terrific. It's the cars I'm talking about."

"Don't you love," Harry asks, "that new one with Scrooge, the way he cackles and goes off into the distance?" He cackles, and Janice and Nelson laugh, and for the last block home, down Joseph Street beneath the bare maples, their three heads entertain common happy memories, of Toyota commercials, of men and women leaping, average men and women, their clothes lifted in cascading slow-motion folds like angels' robes, like some intimate violence of chemical mating or hummingbird wing magnified and laid bare in its process, leaping and falling, grinning and then in freeze-frame hanging there, defying gravity.

"We got to get out of here," Harry says hoarsely to Janice in their bedroom some days later, on the eve of Pru's return from her week of grace in the hospital. It is night; the copper beech, stripped of its leaves and clamorous pods, admits more streetlight into their room than in summer. One or two of the panes in the window on the side nearer the street, the side where Rabbit sleeps, hold imperfections, patches of waviness or elongated bubbles, scarcely visible to the eye of day but which at night hurl onto the far wall, with its mothlike shadows of medallion pattern, dramatic amplifications, the tint of each pane also heightened in the enlargement, so that an effect of stained glass haunts the area above Janice's jumbled mahogany dresser descended from the Koerners, beside the four-panelled door that locks out the world. Ten years of habitancy, in the minutes or hours between when the bedside lamps are extinguished and sleep is achieved, have borne these luminous rectangles into Harry's brain as precious entities, diffuse jewels pressed from the air, presences whose company he will miss if he leaves this room. He must leave it. Intermixed with the abstract patterns the imperfect panes project are the unquiet shadows of the beech branches as they shudder and sway in the cold outside.

"Where would we go?" Janice asks.

"We'd buy a house like everybody else," he says, speaking in a low hoarse voice as if Ma Springer might overhear this breath of treachery through the wall and the mumble and soft roar of her television set as a crisis in her program is reached, then a commercial bursts forth, and another crisis begins to build. "On the other side of Brewer, closer to the lot. That drive through the middle of town every day is driving me crazy. Wastes gas, too."

"Not Penn Villas," she says. "You'll never get me back into Penn Villas."

"Me neither. What about Penn Park though? With all those nice divorce lawyers and dermatologists? I've always kind of dreamed, ever since we used to play them in basketball, of living over there somewhere. Some house with at least stone facing on the front, and maybe a sunken living room, so we can entertain the Murketts in decent style. It's awkward having anybody back here, Ma goes upstairs after dinner but the place is so damn gloomy, and now we're going to be stuck with Nelson and his crew."

"He was saying, they plan to get an apartment when things work out."

"Things aren't going to work out, with his attitude. You know that. The ride is free here and with him around we wouldn't feel so rotten leaving your mother. This is our chance." His hand has crept well up into her nightie; in his wish to have his vision shared he grips her breasts, familiar handfuls, a bit limp like balloons deflating with her age; but still thanks to all that tennis and swimming and old Fred Springer's stingy lean genes her body is holding up better than most. Her nipples stiffen, and his prick with no great attention paid to it is hardening on the sly. "Or maybe," he pursues, his voice still hoarse, "one of those mock-Tudor jobbies that look like piecrust and have those steep pitched roofs like witches' houses. Jesus, wouldn't Pop be proud, seeing me in one of those?"

"Could we afford it," Janice asks, "with the mortgage rates up around thirteen per cent now?"

He shifts his hand down the silvery slick undulations of her belly to the patch of her hair, that seems to bristle at his touch. He ought to eat her sometime. Bed her down on her back with her legs hanging over the side and just kneel and chew her cunt until she came. He used to when they were courting in that apartment of the other girl's with its view of the old gray gas tanks by the river, kneel and just graze in her ferny meadow for hours, nose, eyelids rubbing up against the wonder of it. Any woman, they deserve to be eaten once in a while, they don't come so your mouth is full like with an oyster, how do whores stand it, cock after cock, cuts down on VD, but having to swallow, must amount to pints in the course of a week. Ruth hated it that time, but some cunts now if you read the sex tapes in *Oui* lap it up, one said it tasted to her like champagne. Maybe it wouldn't be the living room that would be sunken, it could be the den, just somewhere where there's a carpeted step down or two, so you know you're in a modern home. "That's the beauty of inflation," he says seductively to Janice. "The more you owe, the better you do. Ask Webb. You pay off in shrunken dollars, and the interest Uncle Sam picks up as an income tax deduction. Even after buying the Krugerrands and paying the September taxes we have too much money in the bank, money in the bank is for dummies now. Sock it into the down payment for a house, we'd be letting the bank worry about the dollar going down and have the house appreciating ten, twenty per cent a year at the same time." Her cunt is moistening, its lips growing loose.

"It seems hard on Mother," Janice says in that weak voice she gets, lovemaking. "She'll be leaving us this place some day and I know she expects we'd stay in it with her till then."

"She'll live for another twenty years," Harry says, sinking his middle finger in. "In twenty years you'll be well over sixty."

"And wouldn't it seem strange to Nelson?"

"Why? It's what he wants, me out of the way. I depress the kid."

"Harry, I'm not so sure it's you that's doing it. I think he's just scared."

"What's he got to be scared of?"

"The same thing you were scared of at his age. Life."

Life. Too much of it, and not enough. The fear that it will end some day, and the fear that tomorrow will be the same as yesterday. "Well he shouldn't have come home if that's the way he was going to feel," Harry says. He's losing his erection.

"He didn't know," Janice says. He can feel, his finger still in her, that her mind too is drifting away from their flesh, into sad realms of family. "He didn't know you'd be so hard on him. Why are you?"

Fucking kid not thirteen years old and tried to take Jill from him, back in Penn Villas after Janice had gone. "He's hard on me," Harry says. He has ceased to whisper. Ma Springer's television set, when he listens, is still on – a rumbling, woofing, surging noise less like human voices than a noise Nature would make in the trees or along the ocean shore. She has become a fan of the ABC eleven-thirty special report on the hostages and every morning tells them the latest version of nothing happening. Khomeini and Carter both trapped by a pack of kids who need a shave and don't know shit, they talk about old men sending young men off to war, if you could get the idiotic kids out of the world it might settle down to being a sensible place. "He gets a disgruntled look on his face every time I open my mouth to talk. Everything I try to tell him at the lot he goes and does the opposite. Some guy comes in to buy this Mercury that was the other one of the convertibles the kid wrecked that time and offers a snowmobile on the trade-in. I thought it was a joke until the other day I go in and the Mercury's gone and this little yellow Kawasaki snowmobile is sitting up in the front row with the new Tercels. I hit the roof and Nelson tells me to stop being so uptight, he allowed the guy four hundred on it and it'll give us more publicity than twice that in ads, the crazy lot that took a snowmobile on trade-in."

Janice makes a soft noise that were she less tired would be laughter. "That's the kind of thing Daddy used to do."

"And then behind my back he's taken on about ten grand's worth of old convertibles that get about ten miles to the gallon nobody'll want and this caper with Pru is running up a fucking fortune. There's no *bene*fits covering her."

"Shh. Mother can hear."

"I *want* her to hear, she's the one giving the kid all his high and mighty ideas. Last night, you hear them cooking up how he's going to have his own car for him and Pru, when that old Newport of hers just sits in the garage six days out of seven?" A muffled sound of chanting comes through the papered wall, Iranians outside the Embassy demonstrating for the benefit of the TV cameras. Rabbit's throat constricts with frustration. "I got to get out, honey."

"Tell me about the house," Janice says, taking his hand in hers and returning it to her pussy. "How many rooms would it have?"

He begins to massage, dragging his fingers along the crease on one side, then the other, of the triangle, and then bisecting with a thoughtful stroke, looking for the fulcrum, the nub, of it. Cindy's

hair had looked darker than Janice's, less curly, alive maybe
with needles of light like the fur of Ma Springer's old coat. "We
wouldn't need a lot of bedrooms," he tells Janice, "just a big one
for us, with a big mirror you can see from the bed —"

"A mirror! Where'd you get the idea of a mirror?"

"Everybody has mirrors now. You watch yourself making love
in them."

"Oh, Harry. I couldn't."

"I think you could. And then at least another bedroom, in case
your mother has to come live with us, or we have guests, but not
next to ours, with at least a bathroom between so we don't hear
her television, and downstairs a kitchen with all new equipment
including a Cuisinart —"

"I'm scared of them. Doris Kaufmann says for the first three
weeks she had hers everything came out mush. One night it was
pink mush and the next night green mush was the only difference."

"You'll learn," he croons, drawing circles on her front, circles
that widen to graze her breasts and beaver and then diminish to
feather into her navel like the asshole of that olive bitch along 422,
"there are instruction books, and a refrigerator with an automatic
ice-maker, and one of those wall ovens that's at the height of your
face so you don't have to bend over, and I don't know about all
this microwave, I was reading somewhere how they fry your
brains even if you're in the next room . . ." Moist, she is so moist
her cunt startles him, touching it, like a slug underneath a leaf in
the garden. His prick undergoes such a bulbous throb it hurts.
". . . and this big sunken living room with lights along the side
where we can give parties."

"Who would we give these parties for?" Her voice is sinking
into the pillow like the dust of a mummy's face, so weak.

"Oh . . ." His hand continues to glide, around and around,
carrying the touch of wetness up to her nipples and adorning
first one then the other with it like tinsel on the tips of a Christmas
tree. ". . . everybody. Doris Kaufmann and all those other tennis
Lesbians at the Flying Eagle, Cindy Murkett and her trusty sidekick
Buddy Inglefinger, all the nice girls who work their pretty asses off
for a better America down at the Gold Cherry, all the great macho
guys in the service and parts department of Springer Motors —"

Janice giggles, and simultaneously the front door downstairs slams. After visiting Pru, Nelson has been going to that bar that used to be the Phoenix and bumming around with that creepy crowd that kills time there. It oppresses Harry, this freedom: if the kid has been excused from evening floor duty to visit Pru for the week then he has no business going out getting stewed on the time. If the kid was so shook up when she took her tumble he ought to be doing something better than this out of gratitude or penance or whatever. His footsteps below sound drunken, one plunked down on top of the other, bump, bump, across the living room between the sofa and the Barcalounger and past the foot of the stairs, making the china in the sideboard tingle, on into the kitchen for one more beer. Harry's breath comes quick and short, thinking of that surly puzzled face sucking the foam out of one more can: drinking and eating up the world, and out of sheer spite at that. He feels the boy's mother at his side listening to the footsteps and puts her hand on his prick; in expert reflex her fingers pump the loose skin of the sides. Simultaneous with Nelson's footsteps below as he treads back into the living room toward the Barcalounger, Harry thrusts as hard as if into the olive chick's ass into the socket Janice's wifely hand makes and speeds up his hypnotic tracing of rapid smooth circles upon the concave expectancy of her belly, assuring her hoarsely, of the house he wants, "You'll love it. You'll love it."

Nelson says to Pru, as they drive together into Brewer in Ma Springer's stately old navy-blue Chrysler, "Now guess what. He's talked Mom into them getting a house. They've looked at about six so far, she told me. They all seem too big to her but Dad says she should learn to think big. I think he's flipping out."

Pru says, quietly, "I wonder how much it has to do with us moving in." She had wanted them to find an apartment of their own, in the same general neighborhood as Slim and Jason and Pam, and couldn't understand Nelson's need to live with his grandmother.

A defensive fury begins to warm him. "I don't see why, any decent father would be glad to have us around. There's plenty of room, Mom-mom shouldn't live by herself."

"I think maybe it's natural," his wife offers, "in a couple that age, to want your own space."

"What's natural, to leave old ladies to die all alone?"

"Well, we're in the house now."

"Just temporarily."

"That's what I thought at first, Nelson, but now I don't believe you want us to have a place of our own. I'd be too much for you, just the two of us, you and me."

"I hate ticky-tacky apartments and condos."

"It's all right, I'm not complaining. I'm at home there now. I like your grandmother."

"I hate crummy old inner-city blocks getting all revitalized with swish little stores catering to queers and stoned interracial couples. It all reminds me of Kent. I came back here to get away from all that phony stuff. Somebody like Slim acts so counter-culture sniffing coke and taking mesc and all that, you know what he does for a living? He's a biller for Diamond County Light and Power, he stuffs envelopes and is going to be Head Stuffer if he keeps at it for ten more years, how's that for Establishment?"

"He doesn't pretend to be a revolutionary, he just likes nice clothes and other boys."

"People ought to be con*sis*tent," Nelson says, "it isn't *fair* to milk the society and then sneer at it at the same time. One of the reasons I liked you better than Melanie was she was so sold on all this radical stuff and I didn't think you were."

"I didn't know," Pru says, even more quietly, "that Melanie and I were competing for you. How much sexual *was* there between you two this summer?"

Nelson stares ahead, sorry his confiding has led to this. The Christmas lights are up in Brewer already, red and green and shivering tinsel looking dry and wilted above the snowless streets, the display a shadow of the seasonal glory he remembers as a boy, when there was abundant energy and little vandalism. Then each lamppost wore a giant wreath of authentic evergreen cut in the local hills and a lifelike laughing Santa in a white-and-silver sleigh

and a line of eight glassy-eyed reindeer coated in what seemed real
fur were suspended along cables stretched from the second story
of Kroll's to the roof of the cigar-store building that used to be
opposite. The downtown windows from below Fourth up to
Seventh were immense with painted wooden soldiers and camels
and Magi and golden organ pipes intertwined with clouds of spun
glass and at night the sidewalks were drenched with shoppers and
carols overflowing from the heated stores into air that prickled like
a Christmas tree and it was impossible not to believe that somewhere, in the dark beyond the city, baby Jesus was being born.
Now, it was pathetic. City budget had been cut way back and half
the downtown stores were shells.

Pru insists, "Tell me. I know there was some."

"How do you know?"

"I know."

He decides to attack: let these young wives get the upper hand
now they'll absolutely take over. "You don't know anything," he
tells her, "the only thing you know is how to hang on to that damn
thing inside you, *that* you're really good at. Boy."

Now she stares ahead, the sling on her arm a white blur in the
corner of his vision. His eyes are stung by perforations of festive
light in the December darkness. Let her play the martyr all she
wants. You try to speak the truth and all you get is grief.

Mom-mom's old car feels silky but sluggish under him: all that
metal they used to put in, even the glove compartment is lined
with metal. When Pru goes silent like this, a kind of taste builds
up in his throat, the taste of injustice. He didn't ask her to con-
ceive this baby, nobody did, and now that he's married her she has
the nerve to complain he isn't getting her an apartment of her
own, give them one thing they instantly want the next. Women.
They are holes, you put one thing in after another and it's never
enough, you stuff your entire life in there and they smile that
crooked little sad smile and are sorry you couldn't have done better, when all is said and done. He's gotten in plenty deep already
and she's not getting him in any deeper. Sometimes when he looks
at her from behind he can't believe how big she has grown, hips
wide as a barn getting set to hatch not some little pink being but
a horny-hided white rhinoceros no more in scale with Nelson

than the mottled man in the moon, that's what cunts do to you when Nature takes over: go out of control.

The build-up of the taste in his throat is too great; he has to speak. "Speaking of fucking," he says, "what about *us?*"

"I don't think we're supposed to this late. Anyway I feel so ugly."

"Ugly or not, you're mine. You're my old lady."

"I get so sleepy, you can't imagine. But you're right. Let's do something tonight. Let's go home early. If somebody asks us back from the Laid-Back to their place let's not go."

"See if we had an apartment like you're so crazy for *we'd* have to ask people back. At least at Mom-mom's you're safe from that."

"I do feel safe there," she says, sighing. Meaning what? Meaning he shouldn't be bringing her out at night: he's married now, he works, he's not supposed to have any fun. Nelson dreads work, he wakes every workday morning with a gnawing in his stomach like he's the one with something inside him, that white rhinoceros. Those convertibles staring at him unbought every day and the way Jake and Rudy can't get over his taking that little Kawasaki, as if it's some great joke he's deliberately played on Dad, when he hadn't meant it that way at all, the guy had been so plead-ing and Nelson was anxious to get the Mercury off the lot, it reminded him every time he saw it of that time Dad had been so scoffing, wouldn't even listen, it wasn't *fair*, he had had to ram the two cars together to wipe that you've-got-to-be-kidding smirk off his face.

On that showroom floor it's like a stage where he hasn't quite learned the lines yet. Maybe it's the stuff he's been taking, too much coke burns the septum out and now they say pot really does rot your brain cells, the THC gets tucked in the fatty tissue and makes you stupid for months, all these teen-age boys coming through with breasts now because something was suppressed when they were turning on at age thirteen, Nelson has these visions lately though he's standing upright with his eyes open, people with holes where their noses should be because of too much coke, or Pru lying there in the hospital with this pink-eyed baby rhinoceros, maybe it has to do with that cast on her arm, dirty and crumbling at the edges now, the gauze underneath the plaster fraying through. And Dad. He's getting bigger and bigger, never jogs anymore, his skin glows like his pores are absorbing food out of the air.

One of the books Nelson had as a child, with those stiff shiny cartoon covers and a black spine like electrical tape, had a picture in it of a giant, his face all bumpy and green with hairs coming out of it here and there, and smiling – that made it worse, that the giant was grinning, looking in, with those blubbery lips and separated teeth giants have, looking into some cave where two children, a boy and a girl, brother and sister probably, who were the heroes of the story are crouching, silhouettes in shadow, you see only the backs of their heads, they are *you*, looking out, hunted, too scared to move a muscle or breathe a breath as the great bumpy gleeful face fills the sunny mouth of the cave. That's how he sees Dad these days: he Nelson is in a tunnel and his father's face fills the far end where he might get out into the sun. The old man doesn't even know he's doing it, it comes on with that little nibbly sorry smile, a flick of dismissal as he pivots away, disappointed, that's it, he's disappointed his father, he should be something other than he is, and now at the lot all the men, not just Jake and Rudy but Manny and his mechanics all grimy with grease, only the skin around their eyes white, staring, see that too: he is not his father, lacks that height, that tossing off that Harry Angstrom can do. And no witness but Nelson stands in the universe to proclaim that his father is guilty, a cheat and coward and murderer, and when he tries to proclaim it nothing comes out, the world laughs as he stands there with open mouth silent. The giant looks in and smiles and Nelson sinks back deeper into the tunnel. He likes that about the Laid-Back, the tunnel snugness of it, and the smoke and the booze and the joints passed from hand to hand under the tables, and the acceptance, the being all in the smoky tunnel together, rats, losers, who cares, you didn't have to listen to what anybody said because nobody was going to buy a Toyota or insurance policy or anything anyway. Why don't they make a society where people are given what they need and do what they want to do? Dad would say that's fantastic but it's how animals live all the time.

"I still think you fucked Melanie," Pru says, in her dried-up slum cat's flat voice. One track and that's it.

Without braking Nelson swings the big Chrysler around the corner where that shaggy park blocks the way down Weiser Street. Pine Street has been made one way and he has to approach it from around the block so Pru doesn't have too far to walk. "Oh, what if I did?" he says. "You and I weren't married, what does it matter now?"

"It doesn't matter because of *you*, we all know you'll grab anything you can get you're so greedy, it matters because she was my *friend*. I trusted her. I trusted you both."

"For Chrissake, don't snivel."

"I'm not snivelling." But he foresees how she will sit there beside him in the booth sulking and not saying anything, not listening to anything but that kicking in her belly, her broken arm making her look even more ridiculous, belly and sling and all, and picturing it that way makes him feel a little sorry for her, until he tells himself it's his way of taking care of her, bringing her along when a lot of guys wouldn't.

"Hey," he says gruffly. "Love you."

"Love you, Nelson," she responds, lifting the hand not in a sling from her lap as he lifts one of his from the wheel to give hers a squeeze. Funny, the fatter the middle of her is getting the thinner and drier her hands and face seem.

"We'll leave after two beers," he promises. Maybe the girl in white pants will be there. She sometimes comes in with that big dumb Jamie and Nelson can tell it is she who gets them here; she digs the scene and he doesn't.

The Laid-Back under this new name is such a success that parking along Pine is hard to find; he wants to spare Pru at least a long walk in the cold, though the doctor says exercise is good. He hates the cold. When he was little he had loved December because it had Christmas in it toward the end and he was so excited by all the things there were to get in the world that he never noticed how the dark and cold closed in, tighter and tighter. And now Dad is taking Mom off for this fancy holiday on some island with these putrid other couples, to lie there and bask while Nelson freezes and holds the fort at the lot; it's not fair. The girl doesn't always wear white slacks, the last time he saw her she had on one of that new style of skirt with the big slit down the side. There is a space in front of the long low brick building that used to be the Verity Press, between an old two-tone Fairlane and a bronze Honda station wagon, that looks big enough, just. The trick of tight parking is to swing your back bumper square into the other guy's headlights and don't leave yourself too far out from the curb or you'll be forever jockeying in. And don't be afraid to cut it tight on the left, you always have more room than you think. He pulls so close to the Fairlane Pru speaks up sharply, "Nelson."

He says, "I see him, I *see* him, shut up and let me concentrate." He intends, with that heavy Chrysler's veloured steering wheel – a ratio on the power steering you could turn a cruise ship with – to snap the car into its slot slick as a skater stopping on ice. God, figure skaters' costumes are sexy, the way their little skirts flip up when they skate ass-backwards, and he remembers, straining to see the Honda's rather low little headlights, how that girl's slit skirt fell away to show a whole long load of shining thigh before she arranged herself on the barstool, having given Nelson a brief shy smile of recognition. Mom-mom's ponderous Chrysler slips into reverse and his anticipation of ideal liquid motion is so strong he does not hear the subtle grinding of metal on metal until it has proceeded half the car's length and Pru is yelping, Jesus, like she's having the baby now.

Webb Murkett says gold has gone about as far as it can go for now: the little man in America has caught the fever and when the little man climbs on the bandwagon the smart money gets off. Silver, now that's another story: the Hunt brothers down in Texas are buying up silver futures at the rate of millions a day, and big boys like that must know something. Harry decides to change his gold into silver.

Janice was going to come downtown anyway to do some Christmas shopping, so he meets her at the Crêpe House (which she still calls Johnny Frye's) for lunch, and then they can go to the Brewer Trust with the safe-deposit key and take out the thirty Krugerrands Harry bought for $11,314.20 three months before. In the cubicle the bank lets you commune with your safe-deposit box in, he fishes out from behind the insurance policies and U.S. Savings Bonds the two blue-tinted cylinders like dollhouse toilets, and passes them into Janice's hands, one into each, and smiles when her face acknowledges with renewed surprise the heft, the weight of the gold. Solid citizens by this extra degree, then, the two of them walk out between the great granite pillars of the Brewer Trust into the frail December sunlight and cross through the forest, where the fountains are dry and the concrete park benches are spray-painted full of young people's names, and on down the east side of Weiser past two blocks of stores doing scattered Christmas business. Underfed little Puerto Rican women are the only ones scuttling in and out of the cut-rate entranceways, and kids who ought to be in school, and bleary retirees in dirty padded parkas and hunter's hats, with whiskery loose jaws; the mills have used these old guys up and spit them out.

The tinsel of the wreaths hung on the aluminum lampposts tingles, audibly shivering, as Harry passes each post. Gold, gold, his heart sings, feeling the weight balanced in the two deep pockets of his overcoat and swinging in time with his strides. Janice hurries beside him with shorter steps, a tidy dense woman warm in a sheepskin coat that comes down to her boots, clutching several packages whose paper rattles in this same wind that stirs the tinsel. He sees them together in the flecked scarred mirror next to a shoestore entrance: him tall and unbowed and white of face, her short and dark and trotting beside him in boots of oxblood leather zippered tight to her ankles, with high heels, so they thrust from her swinging coat with a smartness of silhouette advertising as clear as his nappy black overcoat and Irish bog hat that he is all set, that they are all set, that their smiles as they walk along can afford to discard the bitter blank glances that flicker toward them on the street, then fall away.

Fiscal Alternatives with its long thin Venetian blinds is in the next block, a block that once had the name of disreputable but with the general sinking of the downtown is now no worse than the next. Inside, the girl with platinum hair and long fingernails smiles in recognition of him, and pulls a plastic chair over from the waiting area for Janice. After a telephone call to some far-off trading floor, she runs some figures through her little computer and tells them, as they sit bulky in their coats at the corner of her desk, that the price of gold per ounce had nearly touched five hundred earlier this morning but now she can offer them no more than $488.75 per coin, which will come to – her fingers dance unhampered by her nails; the gray display slot of the computer staggers forth with its bland magnetic answer – $14,662.50. Harry calculates inwardly that he has made a thousand a month on his gold and asks her how much silver he can buy for that now. The young woman slides out from under her eyelashes a glance as if she is a manicurist deciding whether or not to admit that she does, in the back room, also give massages. At his side Janice has lit a cigarette, and her smoke pours across the desk and pollutes the relationship this metallic temptress and Harry have established.

The girl explains, "We don't deal in silver bullion. We only handle silver in the form of pre-'65 silver dollars, which we sell under melt value."

"Melt value?" Harry asks. He had pictured a tidy ingot that would slip into the safe-deposit box snug as a gun into a holster.

The salesgirl is patient, with something sultry about her dispassion. Some of the silky weightiness of precious metals has rubbed off onto her. "You know, the old-fashioned cartwheel" – she makes an illustrative circle with daggerlike forefinger and thumb – "the U.S. Mint put out until fifteen years ago. Each one contains point seventy-five troy ounces of silver. Silver this noon was going for" – she consults a slip on her desk, next to the vanilla push-dial telephone – "$23.55 a troy ounce, which would make each coin, irrespective of collector value, worth" – the calculator again – "$17.66. But there's some wear on some of the coins, so were you and your wife to decide to buy now I could give you a quote under that."

"These are old coins?" Janice asks, that Ma Springer edge in her voice.

"Some are, some aren't," the girl answers coolly. "We buy them by weight from collectors who have sifted through them for collector value."

This isn't what Harry had pictured, but Webb had sworn that silver was where the smart money was. He asks, "How many could we buy with the gold money?"

A flurry of computation follows; $14,662.50 would convert to the magical number of 888. Eight hundred eighty-eight silver dollars priced at $16.50 each, including commission and Pennsylvania sales tax. To Rabbit eight hundred eighty-eight seems like a lot of anything, even matchsticks. He looks at Janice. "Sweetie. Whaddeya think?"

"Harry, I don't know what to think. It's your investment."

"But it's our money."

"You don't want to just keep the gold."

"Webb says silver could double, if they don't return the hostages."

Janice turns to the girl. "I was just wondering, if we found a house we wanted to put a down payment on, how liquid is this silver?"

The blonde speaks to Janice with new respect, at a softer pitch, woman to woman. "It's very liquid. Much more so than collectibles or land. Fiscal Alternatives guarantees to buy back whatever it sells. These coins today, if you brought them in, we'd pay" – she consults the papers on her desk again – "thirteen fifty each."

"So we'd be out three dollars times eight hundred eighty-eight," Harry says. His palms have started to sweat, maybe it's the overcoat. Make a little profit in this world and right away the world starts scheming to take it from you. He wishes he had the gold back. It was so pretty, that little delicate deer on the reverse side.

"Oh, but the way silver's been going," the girl says, pausing to scratch at some fleck of imperfection adjacent to the corner of her lips, "you could make that up in a week. I think you're doing the smart thing."

"Yeah, but as you say, suppose the Iran thing gets settled," Harry worries. "Won't the whole bubble burst?"

"Precious metals aren't a bubble. Precious metals are the ultimate security. I myself think what's brought the Arab money into gold was not so much Iran as the occupation of the Great Mosque. When the Saudis are in trouble, then it's *really* a new ballgame."

A new ballgame, hey. "O.K.," he says, "let's do it. We'll buy the silver."

Platinum-hair seems a bit surprised, for all of her smooth sales talk, and there is a long hassle over the phone locating so many coins. At last some boy she calls Lyle brings in a gray cloth sack like you would carry some leftover mail in; he is swaying with the effort and grunts right out, lifting the sack up onto her desk, but then he has a slender build, with something faggy about him, maybe his short haircut. Funny how that's swung completely around: the squares let their hair grow now and the fags and punks are the ones with butches. Harry wonders what they're doing in the Marines, probably down to their shoulders. This Lyle goes off, after giving Harry a suspicious squint like he's bought not only the massage but the black-leather-and-whip trick too.

At first Harry and Janice think that only the girl with the platinum hair and all but perfect skin may touch the coins. She pushes her papers to one side of her desk and struggles to lift a corner of the bag. Dollars spill out. "Damn." She sucks at a fingernail. "You can help count if you would." They take off their coats and dig in, counting into stacks of ten. Silver is all over the desk, hundreds of Miss Libertys, some thinned by wear, some as chunky as if virgin from the mint. Handling such a palpable luxury of profiles and slogans and eagles makes Janice titter, and Harry knows what she means: playing in the mud. The muchness. The stacks proliferate and are arranged in ranks of ten times ten. The bag at last yields its final coin, with a smidgeon of lint the girl flicks away. Unsmiling, she waves her red-tipped hand across her stacks. "I have three hundred and ninety."

Harry taps his stacks and reports, "Two forty."

Janice says of hers, "Two hundred fifty-eight." She beat him. He is proud of her. She can become a teller if he suddenly dies.

The calculator is consulted: 888. "Exactly right," the girl says, as surprised as they. She performs the paperwork, and gives Harry back two quarters and a ten-dollar bill in change. He wonders if he should hand it back to her, as a tip. The coins fit into three cardboard boxes the size of fat bricks. Harry puts them one on top of another, and when he tries to lift all three Janice and the girl both laugh aloud at the expression on his face.

"My God," he says. "What do they weigh?"

The platinum-headed girl fiddles at her computer. "If you take each one to be a troy ounce at least, it comes to seventy-four pounds. There are only twelve ounces troy measure in a pound."

He turns to Janice. "You carry one."

She lifts one and it's his turn to laugh, at the look on her face, her eyelids stretched wide. "I can't," she says.

"You must," he says. "It's only up to the bank. Come on, I gotta get back to the lot. Whajja play all that tennis for if you don't have any muscles?"

He is proud of that tennis; he is performing for the blonde girl now, acting the role of eccentric Penn Park nob. She suggests, "Maybe Lyle could walk up with you."

Rabbit doesn't want to be seen on the street with that fag. "We can manage." To Janice he says, "Just imagine you're pregnant. Come on. Let's go." To the girl he says, "She'll be back for her packages." He picks up two of the boxes and pushes the door open with his shoulder, forcing Janice to follow. Out in the cold sunlight and shimmering wind of Weiser Street he tries not to grimace, or to return the stares of those who glance wonderingly at the two small boxes clutched so fiercely in his two hands at the level of his fly.

A black man in a blue watch cap, with bloodshot eyes like marbles dropped in orange juice, halts on the pavement and stumbles a step toward Harry. "Hey buddy you wanna hep out a fren' – " Something about these blacks they really zero in on Rabbit. He pivots to shield the silver with his body, and its swung weight tips him so he has to take a step. In moving off, he doesn't dare look behind him to see if Janice is following. But standing on the curb next to a bent parking meter he hears her breathing and feels her struggle to his side.

"This coat is so heavy too," she pants.

"Let's cross," he says.

"In the middle of the block?"

"Don't argue," he mutters, feeling the puzzled black man at his back. He pushes off the curb, causing a bus halfway down the block to hiss with its brakes. In the middle of the street, where the double white line has wobbled in summer's soft tar, he waits for Janice to catch up. The girl has given her the mail sack to carry the third box of silver in, but rather than sling it over her shoulder Janice carries it cradled in her left arm like a baby. "How're you doing?" he asks her.

"I'll manage. Keep moving, Harry."

They reach the far curb. The peanut store now not only has porno magazines inside but has put an array of them on a rack outside. Young muscular oiled boys pose singly or in pairs under titles such as DRUMMER and SKIN. A Japanese in a three-piece pinstripe suit and gray bowler hat steps smartly out of the door, folding a *New York Times* and a *Wall Street Journal* together under his arm. How did the Japanese ever get to Brewer? As the door eases shut, the old circus smell of warm roasted peanuts drifts out to the cold sidewalk. Harry says to Janice. "We could put all three boxes in the bag and I could lug it over my shoulder. You know, like Santa Claus. Ho ho."

A small crowd of pocked dark street kids mixed with shaggy rummies in their winter layered look threatens to collect around them as they confer. Harry tightens his grip on his two boxes. Janice hugs her third and says, "Let's push on this way. The bank's only a block more." Her face is flushed and bitten by the cold, her eyes squinting and watering and her mouth a determined slot.

"A good block and a half," he corrects.

Past then the Brewer Wallpaper Company with its display rolls stiffening in the dusty windows like shrouds, past Blimline's Sandwiches and Manderbach Wholesale Office Supplies and a narrow place jammed with flat boxes called Hobby Heaven, past the cigar store with its giant rusting Y-B sign and the ornately iron-barred windows of the old Conrad Weiser Oyster House that now promises *Live Entertainment* in desperate red letters on its dark doors, across Fourth Street when the light at last turns green, past the long glass-block-inlaid façade of the Acme they say is going out of business at the end of the year, past Hollywood Beauty Supplies and Imperial Floor Coverings and Zenith Auto Parts and Accessories with its sweetish baked smell of fresh tires and window of chrome tailpipes they go, man and wife, as the wind intensifies and the sparkling sidewalk squares grow in size.

The squared-off weight in Harry's hands has become a hostile thing, burning his palms, knocking against his crotch. Now when he would almost welcome being robbed he feels that the others on this west side of the street are shying from them, as somehow menacing, distorted into struggling shapes by the force-fields of their dense boxes. He keeps having to wait for Janice to catch up, while his own burden, double hers, pulls at his arms. The tinsel wound around the aluminum lampposts vibrates furiously. He is sweating across his back beneath his expensive overcoat and his shirt collar keeps drying to a clammy cold edge. During these waits he stares up Weiser toward the mauve and brown bulk of Mt. Judge; in his eyes as a child God had reposed on the slopes of that mountain, and now he can imagine how through God's eyes from that vantage he and Janice might look below: two ants trying to make it up the sides of a bathroom basin.

They pass a camera store advertising Agfa film, the Hexerei Boutique with its mannequins flaunting their nippleless boobs through transparent blouses and vests of gold mail, a Rexall's with pastel vibrators among the suggested Christmas gifts in the windows festooned with cotton and angel hair, the Crêpe House with its lunching couples, the locally famous cigar store saved as an act of historical preservation, and a new store called PedalEase specializing in male and female footwear for jogging and tennis and even racquetball and squash, that young couples or pairs of young singles do together these days, to judge from the big cardboard blow-ups in the window. The Dacron-clad girl's honey-colored hair lifts like air made liquid as she laughingly strokes a ball on easy feet. Next, at last, the first of the four great granite columns of the Brewer Trust looms. Harry leans his aching back against its Roman breadth while waiting for Janice to catch up. If she's robbed in this gap between them it will cost them a third of $14,652 or nearly $5000 but at this point the risk doesn't seem so real. Some distance away he sees spray-painted on the back of one of the concrete benches in the mall of trees a slogan SKEETER LIVES. If he could go closer he could be sure that's what it says. But he cannot move. Janice arrives beside his shoulder. Red-faced, she looks like her mother. "Let's not stand here," she pants. Even the circumference of the pillar seems a lengthy distance as she leads him around it and pushes ahead of him through the revolving doors.

Christmas carols are pealing within the great vaulted interior. The high groined ceiling is painted blue here in every season, with evenly spaced stars of gold. When Harry sets his two boxes down on one of the shelves where you write checks, his relieved body seems to rise toward this false sky. The teller, a lady in an orchid pants suit, smiles to be readmitting them to their safe-deposit box so soon. Their box is a four by four – narrower, they discover, than the boxes of silver dollars three rows abreast. Hearts still laboring, their hands still hurting, Harry and Janice are slow to grasp the disparity, once the frosted glass door has sealed them into the cubicle. Harry several times measures the width of one paper lid against the breadth of tin before concluding, "We need a bigger box." Janice is delegated to go back out into the bank and request one. Her father had been a good friend of the manager. When she returns, it is with the news that there has been a run lately on safe-deposit boxes, that the best the bank could do was put the Angstroms on a list. The manager that Daddy knew has retired. The present one seemed to Janice very young, though he wasn't exactly rude.

Harry laughs. "Well we can't sell 'em back to Blondie down there, it'd cost us a fortune. Could we dump everything back in the bag and stuff it in?"

Crowded together in the cubicle, he and Janice keep bumping into each other, and he scents rising from her for the first time a doubt that he has led them well in this new inflated world; or perhaps the doubt he scents arises from him. But there can be no turning back. They transfer silver dollars from the boxes to the bag. When the silver clinks loudly, Janice winces and says, "*Shh.*"

"Why? Who'll hear?"

"The people out there. The tellers."

"What do they care?"

"I care," Janice says. "It's stifling in here." She takes off her sheepskin coat and in the absence of a hook to hang it on drops it folded to the floor. He takes off his black overcoat and drops it on top. Sweat of exertion has made her hair springier; her bangs have curled back to reveal that high glossy forehead that is so much her, now and twenty years ago, that he kisses it, tasting salt. He wonders if people have ever screwed in these cubicles and imagines that a vault would be a nice place, one of those primped-up young tellers and a lecherous old mortgage officer, put the time-lock on to dawn and ball away. Janice feeds stacks of coins into the coarse

gray pouch furtively, suppressing the clink. "This is so embarrassing," she says, "suppose one of those ladies comes in," as if the
silver is naked flesh; and not for the first time in twenty-three years
he feels a furtive rush of loving her, caught with him as she is in
the tight places life affords. He takes one of the silver dollars and
slips it down the neck of her linen blouse into her bra. As he fore-
saw, she squeals at the chill and tries to suppress the squeal. He
loves her more, seeing her unbutton her blouse a button and
frowningly dig into her bra for the coin; old as he is it still excites
him to watch women fiddle with their underwear. Make our own
coat hook in here.

After a while she announces, "It simply will *not* go in." Stuff
and adjust as they will, hardly half of the bagged coins can be made
to fit. Their insurance policies and Savings Bonds, Nelson's birth
certificate and the never-discarded mortgage papers for the house
in Penn Villas that burned down – all the scraps of paper preserved
as evidence of their passage through an economy and a certain
legal time – are lifted out and reshuffled to no avail. The thick
cloth of the bag, the tendency of loose coins to bunch in a clump,
the long slender shape of the gray tin box frustrate them as side by
side they tug and push, surgeons at a hopeless case. The eight hundred eighty-eight coins keep escaping the mouth of the sack and
falling onto the floor and rolling into corners. When they have
pressed the absolute maximum into the box, so its tin sides bulge,
they are still left with three hundred silver dollars, which Harry
distributes among the pockets of his overcoat.

When they emerge from the cubicle, the friendly teller in her
orchid outfit offers to take the loaded box off his hands. "Pretty
heavy," he warns her. "Better let me do it." Her eyebrows arch;
she backs off and leads him into the vault. They go through a great
door, its terraced edges gleaming, into a space walled with small
burnished rectangles and floored in waxy white. Not a good place
to fuck, he was wrong about that. She lets him slide his long box
into the empty rectangle. R.I.P. Harry is in a sweat, bent over
with effort. He straightens up and apologizes, "Sorry we loaded it
up with so much crap."

"Oh no," the orchid lady says. "A lot of people nowadays . . .
all this burglary."

"What happens if the burglars get in here?" he jokes.

This is not funny. "Oh . . . they *can't*."

Outside the bank, the afternoon has progressed, and shadows from the buildings darken the glitter of tinsel. Janice taps one of his pockets playfully, to hear him jingle. "What are you going to do with all these?"

"Give 'em away to the poor. That bitch down the street, that's the last time I buy anything from her." Cold cakes his face as his sweat dries. Several guys he knows from Rotary come out of the Crêpe House looking punchy on lunch and he gives them the high sign, while striding on. God knows what's happening over on the lot without him, the kid may be accepting roller skates for trade-in.

"You could use the safe at the lot," Janice suggests. "They could go into one of these." She hands him one of the empty cardboard boxes.

"Nelson will steal 'em," he says. "He knows the combination now too."

"Harry. What a thing to say."

"You know how much that scrape he gave your mother's Chrysler is going to cost? Eight hundred fucking bucks minimum. He must have been out of his head. You could see poor Pru was humiliated, I wonder how long she'll let things cook before she gets smart and asks for a divorce. That'll cost us, too." His overcoat, so weighted, drags his shoulders down. He feels, as if the sidewalk now is a downslanted plane, the whole year dropping away under him, loss after loss. His silver is scattered, tinsel. His box will break, the janitor will sweep up the coins. It's all dirt anyway. The great sad lie told to children that is Christmas stains Weiser end to end, and through the murk he glimpses the truth that to be rich is to be robbed, to be rich is to be poor.

Janice recalls him to reality, saying, "Harry, please. Stop looking so tragic. Pru loves Nelson, and he loves her. They won't get a divorce."

"I wasn't thinking about that. I was thinking about how silver's going to go down."

"Oh, what do we care if it does? Everything's just a gamble anyway."

Bless that dope, still trying. The daughter of old Fred Springer, local high roller. Rolled himself into a satin-lined coffin. In the old days they used to bury the silver and put the corpses in slots in the wall.

"I'll walk down to the car with you," Janice says, worried-wifely. "I have to get my packages back from that bitch as you call her. How much did you want to go to bed with her by the way?" Trying to find a topic he'll enjoy.

"Hardly at all," he confesses. "It's terrifying in fact, how little. Did you get a look at her fingernails? Sccr-*ratch*."

The week between the holidays is a low one for car sales: people feel strapped after Christmas, and with winter coming, ice and salt on the road and fenderbenders likely, they are inclined to stick with the heap they have. Ride it out to spring is the motto. At least the snowmobile's been moved around to the back where nobody can see it, instead of its sitting there like some kind of cousin of those new little front-wheel-drive Tercels. Where do they get their names? Sounds like an Edsel. Even Toyota, it has too many *o*'s, makes people think of "toy." Datsun and Honda, you don't know where they're coming from. Datsun could be German from the sound of it, data, rat-tat-tat, rising sun. The Chuck Wagon across Route 111 isn't doing much of a business either, now that it's too cold to eat outdoors or in the car, unless you leave the motor running, people die doing that every winter, trying to screw. The build-up is terrific though of hoagie wrappers and milkshake cartons blowing around in the lot, with the dust. Different kind of dust in December, grayer and grittier than summer dust, maybe the colder air, less lift in it, like cold air holds less water, that's why the insides of the storm windows now when you wake up in the morning have all that dew. Think of all the problems. Rust. Dry rot. Engines that don't start in the morning unless you take off the distributor cap and wipe the wires. Without condensation the world might last forever. On the moon, for example, there's no problem. Or on Mars either it turns out. New Year's, Buddy Inglefinger is throwing the blast this year, guess he was afraid of dropping out of sight with the old gang, getting the wind up about the trip to the islands they're taking without inviting him. Wonder who his hostess is going to be, that flat-chested sourpuss with straight black hair running some kind of crazy shop in Brewer or that girl before her, with the rash on the inside of her thighs and even between her breasts you could see in a bathing suit, what *was* her name? Ginger. Georgene. He and Janice just want to make an appearance to be polite, you get to a certain age you know nothing much is going to happen at parties, and leave right after midnight. Then six more days and, *powie*, the islands. Just the six of them. Little Cindy down there in all that sand. He needs a rest, things are getting him down. Sell less than a car a day in this business not counting Sundays and you're in trouble. All this tin getting dusty and rusty, the chrome developing pimples. Metal corrodes. Silver dropped two dollars an ounce the minute he bought it from that bitch.

Nelson, who has been in the shop with Manny fussing over the repairs to the Chrysler, the kid wanting a break on the full $18.50 customer rate and Manny explaining over and over like to a moron how if you shave the rate for agency employees it shows up in the books and affects everybody's end-of-the-month incentive bonus, comes over and stands by his father at the window.

Harry can't get used to the kid in a suit, it makes him seem even shorter somehow, like one of those midget emcees in a tuxedo, and with his hair shaped longer now and fluffed up by Pru's blow-drier after every shower Nellie seems a little mean-eyed dude Harry never knew. Janice used to say when the boy was little how he had Harry's ears with that crimp in the fold at the tip like one of the old-fashioned train conductors had taken his punch, but the tips of Nelson's are neatly covered by soft shingles of hair and Harry hasn't bothered to study his own since at about the age of forty he came out of that adolescent who-am-I vanity trip. He just shaves as quick as he can now and gets away from the mirror. Ruth had sweetly small tightly folded ears, he remembers. Janice's get so tan on top an arch of tiny dark spots comes out. Her father's lobes got long as a Chinaman's before he died. Nelson has a hot-looking pimple almost due to pop in the crease above his nostril,

Harry notices in the light flooding through the showroom window. The slant of sun makes all the dust on the plate glass look thick as gold leaf this time of year, the arc of each day is so low. The kid is trying to be friendly. Come on. Unbend.

Harry asks him, "You stay up to watch the 76ers finish?"

"Naa."

"That Gervin for San Antonio was something, wasn't he? I heard on the radio this morning he finished with forty-six points."

"Basketball is all goons, if you ask me."

"It's changed a lot since my day," Rabbit admits. "The refs used to call travelling once in a while at least; now, Christ, they eat up half the floor going in for a lay-up."

"I like hockey," Nelson says.

"I know you do. When you have the damn Flyers on there's nowhere in the house you can go to get away from the yelling. All those apes in the crowd go for is to see a fight break out and someone's teeth get knocked out. Blood on the ice, that's the drawing card." This isn't going right; he tries another topic. "What do you think about those Russkis in Afghanistan? They sure gave themselves a Christmas present."

"It's stupid," Nelson says. "I mean, Carter's getting all upset. It's no worse than what we did in Vietnam, it's not even as bad because at least it's right next door and they've had a puppet government there for years."

"Puppet governments are O.K., huh?"

"Well *ev*erybody has 'em. All of South America is our puppet governments."

"I bet that'd be news to the spics."

"At least the Russians, Dad, *do* it when they're going to do it. We *try* to do it and then everything gets all bogged down in politics. We can't do *any*thing anymore."

"Well not with young people talking like you we can't," Harry says to his son. "How would you feel about going over and fighting in Afghanistan?"

The boy chuckles. "Dad, I'm a married man. And way past draft age besides."

Can this be? Harry doesn't feel too old to fight, and he's going to be forty-seven in February. He's always been sort of sorry they didn't send him to Korea when they had him in the Army, though at the time he was happy enough to hunker down in Texas. They had a funny straight-on way of looking at the world out there: money, booze, and broads, and that was it. Down to the bones. What is it Mim likes to say? God didn't go west, He died on the trail. To Nelson he says, "You mean you got married to stay out of the next war?"

"There won't be any next war, Carter will make a lot of noise but wind up letting them have it, just like he's letting Iran have the hostages. Actually, Billy Fosnacht was saying the only way we'll get the hostages back is if Russia invades Iran. Then they'd give us the hostages and sell us the oil because they need our wheat."

"Billy Fosnacht – that jerk around again?"

"Just for vacation."

"No offense, Nelson, but how can you stand that pill?"

"He's my friend. But I know why you can't stand him."

"Why can't I?" Harry asks, his heart rising to what has become a confrontation.

Turning full toward his father beside the gold-dusted pane, the boy's face seems to shrink with hate, hate and fear of being hit for what he is saying. "Because Billy was there the night you were screwing his mother while Skeeter was burning up Jill in the house we should have been in, protecting her."

That night. Ten years ago, and still cooking in the kid's head, alive like a maggot affecting his growth. "That still bugs you, doesn't it?" Rabbit says mildly.

The boy doesn't hear, his eyes lost in those sockets sunk as if thumbs had gripped too deep in clay, trying to pick up a lump. "You let Jill die."

"I didn't, and Skeeter didn't. We don't know who burnt the house down but it wasn't us. It was the neighbors, their idea of a Welcome Wagon. You got to let it go, kid. Your mother and me have let it go."

"I know you have." The sound of Mildred Kroust's electric typewriter rattles muffled in the distance, a couple in maroon parkas is stalking around in the lot checking the price stickers taped inside the windows, the boy stares as if stunned by the sound of his father's voice trying to reach him.

"The past is the past," Harry goes on, "you got to live in the present. Jill was headed that way no matter what the rest of us did. The first time I saw her, she had the kiss of death on her face."

"I know that's what you want to think."

"It's the only way to think. When you're my age you'll see it. At my age if you carried all the misery you've seen on your back you'd never get up in the morning." A flicker of something, a split second when he feels the boy actually listening, encourages Harry to urge his voice deeper, more warmly. "Once that baby of yours shows up," he tells the boy, "you'll have your hands full. You'll have a better perspective."

"You want to know something?" Nelson asks in a rapid dead voice, looking through him with lifted eyes the slant light has stolen color from.

"What?" Rabbit's heart skips.

"When Pru fell down those stairs. I'm not sure if I gave her a push or not. I can't remember."

Harry laughs, scared. "Of course you didn't push her. Why would you push her?"

"Because I'm as crazy as you."

"We're not crazy, either of us. Just frustrated, sometimes."

"Really?" This seems information the kid is grateful for.

"Sure. Anyway, everybody survived. When is he due? He or she." Fear rolls off this kid so thick Harry doesn't want to keep talking to him. The way his eyes looked transparent that instant, all the brown lifted out.

Nelson lowers his eyes, surly again. "They think about three more weeks."

"That's great. We'll be back in plenty of time. Look, Nelson. Maybe I haven't done everything right in my life. I know I haven't. But I haven't committed the greatest sin. I haven't laid down and died."

"Who says that's the greatest sin?"

"Everybody says it. The church, the government. It's against Nature, to give up, you've got to keep moving. That's the thing about you. You're not moving. You don't want to be here, selling old man Springer's jalopies. You want to be out *there*, learning something." He gestures toward the west, beyond West Brewer. "How to hang glide, or run a computer, or whatever."

He has talked too much and closed up the space that opened in Nelson's resistance for a second. Nelson accuses: "You don't want me here."

"I want you where you're happy and that's not here. Now I didn't want to say anything but I've been going over the figures with Mildred and they're not that hot. Since you came here and Charlie left, gross sales are down about eleven per cent over last year, this same period, November–December."

The boy's eyes water. "I *try*, Dad. I try to be friendly and semi-aggressive and all that when the people come in."

"I know you do, Nelson. I know you do."

"I can't go out and *drag* 'em in out of the cold."

"You're right. Forget what I said. The thing about Charlie was, he had connections. I've lived in this county all my life except those two years in the Army and I don't have that kind of connections."

"I know a *lot* of people my age," Nelson protests.

"Yeah," Harry says, "you know the kind of people who sell you their used-up convertibles for a fancy price. But Charlie knows the kind of people who actually come in and buy a car. He expects 'em to; he's not surprised, they're not surprised. Maybe it's being Greek, I don't know. No matter what they say about you and me, kid, we're not Greek."

This joking doesn't help; the boy has been wounded, deeper than Harry wanted. "I don't think it's me," Nelson says. "It's the economy."

The traffic on Route 111 is picking up; people are heading home in the gloom. Harry too can go; Nelson is on the floor till eight. Climb into the Corona and turn on the four-speaker radio and hear how silver is doing. Hi ho, Silver. Harry says, in a voice that sounds sage in his own ears, almost like Webb Murkett's, "Yeah, well, that has its wrinkles. This oil thing is hurting the Japanese worse than it is us, and what hurts them should be doing us good. The yen is down, these cars cost less in real dollars than they did last year, and it ought to be reflected in our sales." That look on Cindy's face in the photograph, Harry can't get it out of his mind: an anxious startled kind of joy, as if she was floating away in a balloon and had just felt the earth lurch free. "Numbers," he tells Nelson in stern conclusion. "Numbers don't lie, and they don't forgive."

New Year's Day was when Harry and Janice had decided to go to Ma Springer with their news, which they had been keeping to themselves for nearly a week. Dread of how the old lady might react had prompted the postponement, plus a groping after ceremony, a wish to show respect for the sacred bonds of family by announcing the break on a significant day, the first of a new decade. Yet now that the day is here, they feel hungover and depleted from having stayed at Buddy Inglefinger's until three in the morning. Their tardy departure had been further prolonged by an uproarious commotion over cars in the driveway – a car that wouldn't start, belonging to Thelma Harrison's Maryland cousin, who was visiting. There was a lot of boozy shouting and falling-down helpfulness in the headlights as jump cables were found and Ronnie's Volvo was jockeyed nose to nose with the cousin's Nova, everybody poking their flashlight in to make sure Ronnie was connecting positive to positive and not going to blow out the batteries. Harry has seen jump cables actually melt in circumstances like this. Some woman he hardly knew had a mouth big enough to put the head of a flashlight in it, so her cheeks glowed like a lampshade. Buddy and his new girl, a frantic skinny six-footer with frizzed-out hair and three children from a broken marriage, had made some kind of punch of pineapple juice and rum and brandy, and the taste of pineapple still at noon keeps returning. On top of Harry's headache Nelson and Pru, who stayed home with Mom-mom last night watching on television straight from Times Square Guy Lombardo's brother now that Guy Lombardo is dead, are hogging the living room watching the Cotton Bowl Festival Parade from Texas, so he and Janice have to take Ma Springer into the kitchen to get some privacy. A deadly staleness flavors the new decade. As they sit down at the kitchen table for their interview, it seems to him that they have already done this, and are sitting down to a rerun.

Janice, her eyes ringed by weariness, turns to him in his daze and says, "Harry, you begin."

"Me?"

"My goodness, what can this be?" Ma asks, pretending to be cross but pleased by the formality, the two of them touching her elbows and steering her in here. "You're acting like Janice is pregnant but I know she had her tubes tied."

"Cauterized," Janice says softly, pained.

Harry begins. "Bessie, you know we've been looking at houses."

Playfulness snaps out of the old lady's face as if pulled by a rubber band. The skin at the corners of her set lips is crossed and recrossed, Harry suddenly sees, by fine dry wrinkles. In his mind his mother-in-law has stayed as when he first met her, packed into her skin; but unnoticed by him Bessie's hide has loosened and cracked like putty in a cellar window, has developed the complexity of paper crumpled and then smoothed again. He tastes pineapple. A small black spot of nausea appears and grows as if rapidly approaching down the great parched space of her severe, expectant silence.

"Now," he must go on, swallowing, "we think we've found one we like. A little stone two-story over in Penn Park. The realtor thinks it might have been a gardener's cottage that somebody sold off when the estates were broken up and then was enlarged to fit a better kitchen in. It's on a little turnaround off Franklin Drive behind the bigger houses; the privacy is great."

"It's only twenty minutes away, Mother."

Harry can't stop studying, in the cold kitchen light, the old woman's skin. The dark life of veins underneath that gave her her flushed swarthy look that Janice inherited has been overlaid with a kind of dust of fine gray threads, wrinkles etched on the lightstruck flat of the cheek nearest him like rows and rows of indecipherable writing scratched on a far clay cliff. He feels himself towering, giddy, and all of his poor ashamed words strike across a great distance, a terrible widening as Ma listens motionless to her doom. "Virtually next door," he says to her, "and with three bedrooms upstairs, I mean there's a little room that the kids who lived there had used as a kind of clubhouse, two bedrooms though absolutely, and we'd be happy to put you up any time if it came to that, for as long as needs be." He feels he is blundering: already he has the old lady living with them again, her TV set muttering on the other side of the wall.

Janice breaks in: "Really, Mother, it makes much more sense for Harry and me at this point of our lives."

"But I had to talk her into it, Ma; it was my idea. When you and Fred very kindly took us in after we got back together I never thought of it as for forever. I thought of it as more of a stop-gap thing, until we got our feet back under us."

What he had liked about it, he sees now, was that it would have made it easy for him to leave Janice: just walk out under the streetlights and leave her with her parents. But he hadn't left her, and now cannot. She is his fortune.

She is trying to soften her mother's silence. "Also as an investment, Mother. Every couple we know owns their own house, even this bachelor we were with last night, and a lot of the men earn less than Harry. Property's the only place to put money if you have any, what with inflation and all."

Ma Springer at last does speak, in a voice that keeps rising in spite of herself. "You'll have this place when I'm gone, if you could just wait. Why can't you wait a little yet?"

"Mother, that's ghoulish when you talk like that. We don't want to wait for *your* house; Harry and I want our house *now*." Janice lights a cigarette, and has to press her elbow onto the table-top to hold the match steady.

Harry assures the old lady, "Bessie, you're going to live forever." But having seen what's happening to her skin he knows this isn't true.

Wide-eyed suddenly, she asks, "What's going to happen to this house then?"

Rabbit nearly laughs, the old lady's expression is so childlike, taken with the pitch of her voice. "It'll be fine," he tells her. "When they built places like this they built 'em to last. Not like the shacks they slap up now."

"Fred always wanted Janice to have this house," Ma Springer states, staring with eyes narrowed again at a place just between Harry's and Janice's heads. "For her security."

Janice laughs now. "Mother, I have plenty of security. We told you about the gold and silver."

"Playing with money like that is a good way to lose it," Ma says. "I don't want to leave this house to be auctioned off to some Brewer Jew. They're heading out this way, you know, now that the blacks and Puerto Ricans are trickling into the north side of town."

"Come on, Bessie," Harry says, "what do you care? Like I said, you got a lot of life ahead of you, but when you're gone, you're gone. Let go, you got to let some things go for other people to worry about. The Bible tells you that, it says it on every page. Let go; the Lord knows best."

Janice from her twitchy manner thinks he is saying too much. "Mother, we might come back to the house –"

"When the old crow is dead. Why didn't you and Harry tell me my presence was such a burden? I tried to stay in my room as much as I could. I went into the kitchen only when it looked like nobody else was going to make the meal –"

"Mother, stop it. You've been lovely. We both love you."

"Grace Stuhl would have taken me in, many's the times she offered. Though her house isn't half the size of this and has all those front steps." She sniffs, so loudly it seems a cry for help.

Nelson shouts in from the living room, "Mom-mom, when's lunch?"

Janice says urgently, "See, Mother. You're forgetting Nelson. He'll be here, with his *family*."

The old lady sniffs again, less tragically, and replies with pinched lips and a level red-rimmed gaze, "He may be or he may not be. The young can't be depended on."

Harry tells her, "You're right about that all right. They won't fight and they won't learn, just sit on their asses and get stoned."

Nelson comes into the kitchen holding a newspaper, today's Brewer *Standard*. He looks cheerful for once, on his good night's sleep. He has folded the paper to a quiz on Seventies trivia and asks them all, "How many of these people can you identify? Renée Richards, Stephen Weed, Megan Marshack, Marjoe Gortner, Greta Rideout, Spider Sabich, D. B. Cooper. I got six out of seven, Pru got only four."

"Renée Richards was Patty Hearst's boyfriend," Rabbit begins.

Nelson sees the state his grandmother's face is in and asks, "What's happening here?"

Janice says, "We'll explain later, sweetie."

Harry tells him, "Your mother and I have found a house we're going to move to."

Nelson stares from one to the other of his parents and it seems he might scream, the way he goes white around the gills. But instead he pronounces quietly, "What a copout. What a fucking pair of copout artists. Well screw you both. Mom, Dad. Screw you."

And he returns to the living room where the rumble of drums and trombones merges with the mumble of unheard words as he and Pru confer within the tunnel of their young marriage. The kid had felt frightened. He felt left. Things are getting too big for him. Rabbit knows the feeling. For all that is wrong between them there are moments when his heart and Nelson's might be opposite ends of a single short steel bar, he knows so exactly what the kid is feeling. Still, just because people are frightened of being alone doesn't mean he has to sit still and be everybody's big fat patsy like Mim said.

Janice and her mother are holding hands, tears blurring both faces. When Janice cries, her face loses shape, dissolves to the ugly child she was. Her mother is saying, moaning as if to herself, "Oh I knew you were looking but I guess I didn't believe you'd actually go ahead and buy one when you have this free. Isn't there any adjustment we could make here so you could change your minds or at least let me get adjusted first? I'm too old, is the thing, too old to take on responsibility. The boy means well in his way but he's all *ferhuddled* for now, and the girl, I don't know. She wants to do it all but I'm not sure she can. To be honest, I've been dreading the baby, I've been trying to remember how it was with you and Nelson, and for the life of me I can't. I remember the milk didn't come the way they thought it should, and the doctor was so rude to you about it Fred had to step in and have a word."

Janice is nodding, nodding, tears making the side of her nose shine, the cords on her throat jumping out with every sob. "Maybe we could wait, though we said we'd pass papers, if you feel that way at least wait until the baby comes."

There is a rhythm the two of them are rocking to, hands clasped on the table, heads touching. "Do what you must, for your own happiness," Ma Springer is saying, "the ones left behind will manage. It can't do worse than kill me, and that might be a blessing."

She is turning Janice into a mess: face blubbery and melting, the pockets beneath her eyes liverish with guilt, Janice is leaning hard into her mother, giving in on the house, begging for forgiveness, "Mother we thought, Harry was certain, you'd feel less alone, with –"

"With a worry like Nelson in the house?"

Tough old turkey. Harry better step in before Janice gives it all away. His throat hardens. "Listen, Bessie. You asked for him, you got him."

Free! Macadam falls away beneath the wheels, a tawny old fort can be glimpsed as they lift off the runway beneath the rounded riveted edge of one great wing, the gas tanks of South Philadelphia are reduced to a set of white checkers. The wheels thump, retracted, and cruel photons glitter on the aluminum motionless beside the window. The swift ascent of the plane makes their blood weighty; Janice's hand sweats in his. She had wanted him to have the window seat, so she wouldn't have to look. There is marsh below, withered tan and blue with saltwater. Harry marvels at the industrial buildings beyond the Delaware: flat gravel roofs vast as parking lots and parking lots all inlaid with glittering automobile roofs like bathroom floors tiled with jewels. And in junkyards of cars the effect is almost as brilliant. The NO SMOKING sign goes off. Behind the Angstroms the voices of the Murketts and the Harrisons begin to chatter. They all had a drink at an airport bar, though the hour was eleven in the morning. Harry has flown before, but to Texas with the Army and dealers' conferences in Cleveland and Albany: never aloft on vacation like this, due east into the sun.

How quickly, how silently, the 747 eats up the toy miles below! Sun glare travels with the plane across lakes and rivers in a second's glinting. The winter has been eerily mild thus far, to spite the Ayatollah; on golf courses the greens show as living discs and ovals amid the white beans of the traps and on the fairways he can spot moving specks, men playing. Composition tennis courts are dominoes from this height, drive-in movies have the shape of a fan, baseball diamonds seem a species of tattered money. Cars move very slowly and with an odd perfection, as if the roads hold tracks. The houses of the Camden area scatter, relenting to disclose a plowed field or an estate with its prickly mansion and its eye of a swimming pool tucked into mist-colored woods; and then within another minute, still climbing, Harry is above the dark carpet of the Jersey Pines, scored with yellow roads and patches of scraping but much of it still unmarred, veins of paler unleafed trees following the slope of land and flow of water among the darker evergreens, the tints of competition on earth made clear to the eye so hugely lifted. Janice lets go of his hand and gives signs of having swallowed her terror.

"What do you see?" she asks.

"The Shore."

It is true, in another silent stride the engines had inched them to the edge of the ocean of trees and placed underneath them a sandy strip, separated from the mainland by a band of flashing water and filled to a precarious fullness with linear summer cities, etched there by builders who could not see, as Harry can, how easily the great shining shoulder of the ocean could shrug and immerse and erase all traces of men. Where the sea impinges on the white sand a frill of surf slowly waves, a lacy snake pinned in place. Then this flight heads over the Atlantic at an altitude from which no whitecaps can be detected in the bluish hemisphere below, and immensity becomes nothingness. The plane, its earnest droning without and its party mutter and tinkle within, becomes all of the world there is.

An enamelled stewardess brings them lunch, sealed on a tray of blond plastic. Though her makeup is thickly applied Harry thinks he detects beneath it, as she bends close with a smile to ask what beverage he would prefer, shadowy traces of a hectic night. They fuck on every layover, he has read in *Club* or *Oui*, a separate boyfriend in every city, twenty or thirty men, these women the

fabulous horny sailors of our time. Ever since the airport he has
been amazed by other people: the carpeted corridors seemed
thronged with freaks, people in crazy sizes and clothes, girls with
dead-white complexions and giant eyeglasses and hair frizzed
out to fill a bushel basket, black men swaggering along in long fur
coats and hip-hugging velvet suits, a tall pale boy in a turban and
a down vest, a dwarf in a plaid tam-o'-shanter, a woman so obese
she couldn't sit in the molded plastic chairs of the waiting areas
and had to stand propping herself on a three-legged aluminum
cane. Life outside Brewer was gaudy, wild. Everyone was a clown
in costume. Rabbit and his five companions were in costume too,
flimsy summer clothes under winter overcoats. Cindy Murkett is
wearing high-heeled slides on naked ankles; Thelma Harrison
pads along in woolly socks and tennis sneakers. They all keep
laughing among themselves, in that betraying Diamond County
way. Harry doesn't mind getting a little high, but he doesn't want
to sacrifice awareness of the colors around him, of the revelation
that outside Brewer there is a planet without ruts worn into it. In
such moments of adventure he is impatient with his body, that its
five windows aren't enough, he can't get the world all in. Joy
makes his heart pound. God, having shrunk in Harry's middle
years to the size of a raisin lost under the car seat, is suddenly great
again, everywhere like a radiant wind. Free: the dead and the living alike have been left five miles below in the haze that has
annulled the earth like breath on a mirror.

Harry turns from the little double-paned airplane window of
some tinted soft substance that has been scratched again and again
horizontally as by a hail of meteorites. Janice is leafing through the
airline magazine. He asks her, "How do you think they'll do?"

"Who?"

"Your mother and Nelson and Pru, who else?"

She flips a glossy page. Her mother is in that set of the lips, as
if they have just pronounced a mournful truth and will not take it
back. "I expect better than when we're there."

"They say anything to you about the house?"

Harry and Janice passed papers two days ago, a Tuesday. The
day before, Monday the seventh, they had sold their silver back
to Fiscal Alternatives. The metal, its value driven up by panic

buying in the wake of Afghanistan by heavy holders of petrodollars, stood at $36.70 that day, making each of the silver dollars, bought for $16.50 including sales tax, worth $23.37, according to the calculations of the platinum-haired young woman. Janice, who had not worked all these years off and on at her father's lot for nothing, slid the hand computer toward herself and after some punching politely pointed out that if silver stood at $36.70 a troy ounce, then seventy-five per cent of that would give a melt value of $27.52. Well, the young woman pointed out, you couldn't expect Fiscal Alternatives to sell at less than melt value and not buy back for less too. She was less soignée than formerly; the tiny imperfection at one corner of her lips had bloomed into something that needed to be covered with a little circular Band-Aid. But after a phone call to some office deeper than hers, hidden by more than a sheet of thin Venetian blinds, she conceded that they could go to $24 even. Times 888 came to $21,312, or a profit in less than a month of $6,660. Harry wanted to keep eight of the handsome old cartwheels as souvenirs and this reduced the check to $21,120, a more magical number anyway. From the Brewer Trust safe-deposit box and the safe at Springer Motors they retrieved their cumbersome riches, taking care this time to minimize portage by double-parking the Corona on Weiser Street. The next day, while silver was dropping to $31.75 an ounce, they signed, at this same Brewer Trust, a twenty-year mortgage for $62,400 at 13½ per cent, 1½ per cent below the current prime rate, with a one-point fee of $624 and a three-year renegotiation proviso. The little stone house, once a gardener's cottage, in Penn Park cost $78,000. Janice wanted to put down $25,000, but Harry pointed out to her that in inflationary times debt is a good thing to have, that mortgage interest is tax-deductible, and that six-month $10,000-minimum money market certificates are paying close to 12 per cent these days. So they opted for the 20 per cent minimum of equity, or $15,600, which the bank, considering the excellent credit standing in the community of Mr. Angstrom and his family, was pleased to allow. Stepping out between the monumental pillars into the winter daylight blinking, Janice and Harry owned a house, and the day after tomorrow would fly into summer. For years nothing happens;

then everything happens. Water boils, the cactus blooms, cancer declares itself.

Janice replies, "Mother seems resigned. She told me a long story about how her parents, who were better regarded, you know, in the county than the Springers, offered to have her and Daddy come stay with them while he was still studying accountancy and he said, No, if he couldn't put a roof over a wife he shouldn't have taken a wife."

"She should tell that story to Nelson."

"I wouldn't push at Nelson too hard these days. Something's working at him from inside."

"I don't push at him, he's pushing me. He's pushed me right out of the house."

"It may be our going off has frightened him. Made it more real, that he has these responsibilities."

"About time the kid woke up. What do you think poor Pru makes of all this?"

Janice sighs, a sound lost in the giant whispering that upholds them. Little dull nozzles above their heads hiss oxygen. Harry wants to hear that Pru hates Nelson, that she is sorry she has married him, that the father has made the son look sick. "Oh, I don't think she knows what to make," Janice says. "We have these talks sometimes and she knows Nelson is unhappy but still has this faith in him. The fact of it is Teresa was so anxious to get away from her own people in Ohio she can't afford to be too picky about the people she's gotten in with."

"She still keeps putting away that crème de menthe."

"She's a little heedless but that's how you are at that age. You think whatever happens, you can manage; the Devil won't touch you."

He nudges her elbow with his comfortingly, to show he remembers. The Devil touched her twenty years ago. The guilt they share rests in their laps like these safety belts, holding them fast, chafing only when they try to move.

"Hey you two lovebirds." Ronnie Harrison's loud shallow voice breaks upon them from above; he is looking down with his boozy breath from the backs of their seats. "Deal us in, you can neck at home." For the rest of the flight's three droning hours they party with the other four, swapping seats, standing in the aisle, moving around in the 747's wide body as if it were Webb Murkett's long living room. They stoke themselves with drinks and reminisce about times they have already shared as if, were silence and forgetfulness once to enter, the bubble of this venture together would pop and all six would go tumbling into the void that surrounds and upholds the shuddering skin of the plane. Cindy seems, in this confusion, amiable but remote, a younger sister, or another passenger swept up into their holiday mood. She perches forward on the edge of her reclined window seat to catch each gust of jocularity; it is hard to believe that her outer form, clothed in a prim black suit with a floppy white cravat that reminds Harry of George Washington, has secret places, of folds and fur and moist membranes, where a diaphragm can go, and that entry into these places is the purpose of his trip and his certain destination.

The plane drops; his stomach clenches; the pilot's omnipotent Texas voice comes on and tells them to return to their seats and prepare for arrival. Harry asks Janice now that she's loose on booze if she wouldn't like the window seat but she says No, she doesn't dare to look until they land. Through his patch of scratched Plexiglas he sees a milky turquoise sea mottled with purple-green shadows cast from underneath, islands beneath the surface. A single sailboat. Then a ragged arm of rocky land in a sleeve of white beach. Small houses with red corrugated roofs rise toward him. The wheels of the plane groan and unwind down and lock in place. They are skimming a swamp. He thinks to pray but his thoughts scatter; Janice is grinding the bones of his fingers together. A house with a wind sock, an unmanned bulldozer, branchless trees that are palms flash by; there is a thud, a small swerve, a loud hiss, and a roar straining backwards, a screaming straining. It stops, they slow, they are on the ground, and a low pink air terminal is wheeled into view as the 747 taxis close. The passengers move, suddenly sweating, clutching their winter coats and groping for sunglasses, toward the exits. At the head of the silver stairs down to the macadam, the tropical air, so warm, moist, and forgiving, composed all of tiny little circles, strikes Rabbit's face as if gusted from an atomizer; but Ronnie Harrison ruins the moment by exclaiming distinctly, behind his ear, "Oh boy. That's better than a blow job." And, worse even than Ronnie's smearing his voice across so precious a moment of first encounter with a new world, the women laugh, having been meant to overhear. Janice laughs, the dumb mutt. And the stewardess, her enamel gone dewy in the warmth by the door where she poses saying goodbye, goodbye, promiscuously smiles.

Cindy's laugh skips girlishly above the others and is quickly followed by her drawled word, "Ronnie." Rabbit is excited amid his disgust, remembering those Polaroids tucked in a drawer.

As the days of the vacation pass, Cindy turns the same mahogany brown she wears in the summer, by the pool at the Flying Eagle, and comes up dripping from the beryl Caribbean in the same bikini of black strings, only with salt-glisten on her skin. Thelma Harrison burns badly the first day, and has some pain connected with that quiet ailment of hers. She spends the whole second day in their bungalow, while Ronnie bounces in and out of the water and supervises the fetching of drinks from the bar built on the sand entirely of straw. Old black ladies move up and down the beach offering beads and shells and sunclothes for sale, and on the morning of the third day Thelma buys from one of them a wide-brimmed straw hat and a pink ankle-length wrapper with long sleeves, and thus entirely covered, with sun block on her face and a towel across the tops of her feet, she sits reading in the shade of the sea-grape trees. Her face in the shade of her hat seems sallow and thin and mischievous, when she glances toward Harry as he lies in the sun. Next to her, he tans least easily, but he is determined to keep up with the crowd. The ache of a sunburn reminds him nostalgically of the muscle aches after athletic exertion. In the sea, he doggy-paddles, secretly afraid of sharks.

The men spend each morning on the golf course that adjoins the resort, riding in canopied carts down sere fairways laid out between brambly jungles from which there is no recovery; indeed, in looking for lost balls there is a danger of stepping into a deep hole. The substance of the island is coral, pitted with caves. At night, there is entertainment, set in a rigid weekly cycle. They arrived on a Thursday, the evening of the crab races, and on the next night witnessed a limbo dance, and on the next, a Saturday, themselves danced to a steel band. Every night there is music to dance to, beside the Olympic-length pool under stars that seem closer down here, and that hang in the sky with a certain menace, fragments of a frozen explosion. Some of the constellations are strange; Webb Murkett, who knows stars from his years in the Navy – he enlisted in '45, when he was eighteen, and crossed the Pacific on an aircraft carrier as the war was ending – points out the Southern Cross, and a ghostly blur in the sky he says is another galaxy altogether; and they can all see that the Big Dipper stands on its handle here in a way never seen in southeastern Pennsylvania.

Oh, that little Cindy, browner at every dinnertime, just begging for love. You can see it in her teeth, they are getting so white, and the way she picks an oleander blossom from the bush outside their bungalow every night to wear in her hair all fluffy from swimming so much, and the swarthiness of her toes that makes the nails look pale as petals also. She wears on her dark skin white dresses that shine from far across the swimming pool – lit from underneath at night as if it has swallowed the moon – when she is coming back from the ladies' room beyond the bamboo bar. She claims she is getting fatter, too: those piña coladas and banana Daiquiris and rum punches, all those calories, shameless. Yet she never turns a drink down, none of them do; from the Bloody Marys that fortify the golfers for their morning on the course to the last round of Stingers after midnight, they keep a gentle collective buzz on. Janice wonders, "Harry, what's the final tab going to look like? You keep signing for everybody."

He tells her, "Relax. Might as well spend it as have it eaten up by inflation. Did you hear Webb saying that the dollar now is worth exactly half what it was ten years ago in 1970? So these are fifty-cent dollars; relax." The expense in his mind is part of a worthy campaign, to sleep with Cindy before their seven days are over. He feels it coming, coming upon all of them, the walls between them are wearing thin, he knows exactly when Webb will clear his throat or how he will light his cigarette, eye-glance and easy silence are hour by hour eroding constraint, under sun and under stars they stretch out their six bodies on the folding chaises, with vinyl strapping, that are everywhere. Their hands touch passing drinks and matches and suntan lotion, they barge in and out of one another's bungalows; indeed Rabbit has seen Thelma Harrison bare-assed by accident returning their Solarcaine one afternoon. She had been lying on the bed letting her burned skin breathe and hustled into the bathroom at the sound of his voice at the door, but not quick enough. He saw the crease between her cheeks, the whole lean sallow length of her fleeing, and handed the Solarcaine to Ronnie, himself naked, without comment or apology, they were half-naked with each other all the day long, but for Thelma huddled under the sea-grape: Janice rubbing Coppertone into the criss-crossing creases of Webb's red neck, Ronnie's heavy cock bulging the front of his obscene little European-style trunks, sweet Cindy untying a black string to give her back an even tan and showing the full nippled silhouette of one boob when she reached up for her Planter's Punch from the tray of them the boy had brought. These blacks down here are silkier than American blacks, blacker, their bodies moving to a gentler beat. Toward four o'clock, the shadows of the sea-grape coming forward like knobby fingers onto the sand, the men's faces baked red despite the canopies on the golf carts, they move their act from the beach (the rustling of palm trees gets on Harry's nerves; at night he keeps thinking it's raining, and it never is) to the shaded area beside the Olympic pool, where young island men in white steward's jackets circle among them taking drink orders and the hard white pellet of the sun slowly lowers toward the horizon of the sea, which it meets promptly at six, in a perfunctory splash of purples and pinks. Stupefied, aching with pleasure, Harry stares at the way, when Cindy rolls her body into a new position on the chaise, the straps have bitten laterally into her delicious fat, like tire treads in mud. Thelma sits among them swaddled and watchful, Webb drones on, Ronnie is making some new friends at the bamboo bar. It's the salesman in him, he has to keep trying his pitch. His voice balloons above the rippling as a single fair child, waterlogged and bored, dives and paddles away the time to dinner. Janice, much as he loves her now and then, down here is a piece of static, getting between Harry and what signals Cindy may be sending; luckily Webb keeps her entertained, talking to her as one member of the lesser Brewer gentry to another, about

that tireless subject of money. "You think fourteen per cent is catastrophic, in Israel they live with a hundred eleven per cent, a
color television set costs eighteen hundred dollars. In Argentina
it's a hundred fifty per cent per year, believe me I kid you not. In
Tokyo a pound of steak costs twenty dollars and in Saudi Arabia
a pack of cigarettes goes for a fin. Five dollars a pack. You may
think we're hurting but the U.S. consumer still gets the best deal
to be had in any industrialized nation." Janice hangs on his words
and bums his cigarettes. Her hair since summer has grown long
enough to pull back in a little stubby ponytail; she sits by his feet,
dabbling her legs in the pool. The hair on Webb's long skinny legs
spirals around like the stripes on a barber pole, and his face with
its wise creases has tanned the color of lightly varnished pine. It
occurs to Harry that she used to listen to her father bullshit this
way, and likes it.

By Sunday night they are bored with the routine around the
resort and hire a taxi to take them across the island to the casino.
In the dark they pass through villages where black children are
invisible until their eye-whites gleam beside the road. A herd of
goats trotting with dragging rope halters materializes in the headlights of the taxi. Shuttered cabins up on cinder blocks reveal by
an open door that they are taverns, with bottle-crammed shelves
and a sheaf of standing customers. An old stone church flings
candlelight from its pointed windows, which have no glass, and
the moan of one phrase of a hymn, that is swiftly left behind. The
taxi, a '69 Pontiac with a lot of voodoo dolls on the dashboard,
drives ruthlessly, on the wrong side of the road, for this was an
English colony. The truncated cone-shapes of abandoned sugar
mills against the sky full of stars remember the past, all those dead
slaves, while Janice and Thelma and Cindy chatter in the surging
dark about people left behind in Brewer, about Buddy
Inglefinger's newest awful girlfriend with all that height and all
those children, Buddy's such a victim-type, and about impossible
Peggy Fosnacht, whom rumor has reported to be very hurt that
she and Ollie weren't asked along on this trip to the Caribbean,
even though everybody knows they could never afford it.

The casino is attached to another beach resort, grander than
theirs. Boardwalks extend out over the illuminated coral shelf.

There are worlds within worlds, Harry thinks. Creatures like broken bags of noodles wave upward from within the golden-green slipslop. He has come out here to clear his head. He got hooked on blackjack and in an attempt to recoup his losses by doubling and redoubling his bets cashed three hundred in Traveller's Checks and, while his friends marvelled, lost it all. Well, that's less than half the profit on the sale of one Tercel, less than three per cent of what Nelson's pranks have cost. Still, Harry's head throbs and he feels shaky and humiliated. The black dealer didn't even glance up when, cleaned out, he pushed away from the garish felt of the table. He walks along the boards toward the black horizon, as the tropical air soothes his hot face with microscopic circular kisses. He imagines he could walk to South America, that has Paraguay in it; he thinks fondly of that area of tall weeds behind the asphalt of the lot, and of that farm he has always approached as a spy, through the hedgerow that grew up over the tumbled sandstone wall. The grass in the orchard will be flattened and bleached by winter now, smoke rising from the lonely house below. Another world.

Cindy is beside him suddenly, breathing in rhythm with the slipslop of the sea. He fears their moment has come, when he is far from ready; but she says in a dry commiserating voice, "Webb says you should always set a limit for yourself before you sit down, so you won't get carried away."

"I wasn't carried away," Harry tells her. "I had a theory." Perhaps she figures that his losses have earned a compensation and she is it. Her brown arms are set off by a crocheted white shawl; with the flower behind her ear she looks flirty. What would it be like, to press his own high heavy face down into those apple-hard roundnesses of hers, cheeks and brow and nose-tip, and her alert little life-giving slits, long-lipped mouth and dark eyes glimmering with mischief like a child's? Slipslop. Will their faces fit? Her eyes glance upward toward his and he gazes away, at the tropical moon lying on its side at an angle you never see in Pennsylvania. As if accidentally, while gazing out to sea, he brushes his fingertips against her arm. An electric warmth seems to linger from her Sunday in the sun. Kelp slaps the pilings of the catwalk, a wave collapses its way along the beach, his moment to pounce is here.

Something too firm in the protuberances of her face holds him off, though she is lightly smiling, and tips her face up, as if to make it easier for him to slip his mouth beneath her nose.

But footsteps rumble toward them and Webb and Janice, almost running, their hands in the confused mingled lights of moon and subaqueous spots and blazing casino beyond seeming linked, then released, come up to this angle of the boardwalk and announce excitedly that Ronnie Harrison is burning up the crap table inside. "Come and see, Harry," Janice says. "He's at least eight hundred ahead."

"That Ronnie," Cindy says, in a tone of girlish dry reproach, and the casino lights glow through her long skirt as she hurries toward these lights, her legs silhouetted beneath her dark wide ass.

They get back to their own resort after two. Ronnie stayed too long at the crap table and wound up only a few bucks better than even. He and Janice fall asleep on the long ride back, while Thelma sits tensely in Rabbit's lap and Webb and Cindy sit up front with the driver, Webb asking questions about the island that the man answers in a reluctant, bubbling language that is barely English. At the gate to their resort a uniformed guard lets them in. Everything down here is guarded, theft is rampant, thieves and even murderers pour outward from the island's dark heart to feed on its rim of rich visitors. Guest bungalows are approached along paths of green-painted concrete laid down on the sand, under muttering palm trees, between bushes of papery flowers that attract hummingbirds in the morning. While the men confer as to what hour tomorrow's golf should be postponed to, the three women whisper at a little distance, at the point in the concrete walk where the paths to their separate bungalows diverge. Janice, Cindy, and Thelma are tittering and sending glances this way, glances flickering birdlike in the moon-glazed warm night. Cindy's shawl glimmers like a splotch of foam on surging water. But in the end, making the hushed grove of palms ring with cries of "'Night. 'Night," each wife walks to her own bungalow with her husband. Rabbit fucks Janice out of general irritation and falls asleep hoping that morning will be indefinitely postponed.

But it comes on schedule, in the form of bars of sunlight the window louvers cast on to the floor of hexagonal tiles, while the little yellow birds they have that song about down here follow the passage of clinking breakfast trays along the concrete paths. It is not so bad, once he stands up. The body was evolved for adversity. As has become his custom he takes a short, cautious swim off the deserted beach, where last night's plastic glasses are still propped in the sand. It is the one moment of the day or night when Harry is by himself, not counting the old couples, with the wives needing an arm to make their way down across the sand, who also like an early swim. The sea between soft breakers seems the color of a honeydew melon, that pale a green. Floating on his back he can see, on the roads along the scraggly steep hills that flank the bay, those to whom this island is no vacation, blacks in scraps of bright cloth, strolling to work, some of the women toting bundles and even buckets on their heads. They really do that. Their voices carry on fresh morning air, along with the slap and swoosh and fizz of warm saltwater sliding and receding at his feet. The white sand is spongy, and full of holes where crabs breathe. He has never seen sand this white, minced coral fine as sugar. The early sun sits lightly on his sensitive shoulders. This is it, health. Then the girl with the breakfast tray comes to their door – their bungalow number is 9 – and Janice in her terrycloth bathrobe opens the louvered door and calls "*Har*ry" out across the beach where an old black rummy in khaki pants is already sweeping up seaweed and plastic glasses, and the party, the hunt, is on again.

He plays golf badly today; when he is tired he tends to overswing, and to flip his hands instead of letting the arms ride through. Keep the wrist-cock, don't waste it up at the top. Don't sway onto your toes, imagine your nose pressed against a pane of glass. Think railroad tracks. Follow through. These tips are small help today; it seems a long morning's slog between hungry wings of coral jungle, up to greens as bumpy as quilts, though he supposes it's a miracle of sorts to have greens at all under this sun. He hates Webb Murkett, who is sinking everything inside of twenty feet today. Why should this stringy old bullshitter hog that fantastic little cunt and take the Nassau besides? Harry misses Buddy Inglefinger, to feel superior to. Ronnie's sparse scalp and naked high forehead look like a peeling pink egg when he stoops to his shot. Swings like an ape, all the hair off his head gone into his arms, how can

Thelma stand him? Women, they'll put up with anything for the sake of a big prick evidently. Harry can't stop thinking of that three hundred dollars he blew last night, that his father would have slaved six weeks for. Poor Pop, he didn't live to see money get unreal.

But things look up in the afternoon, after a couple of piña coladas and a crabmeat-salad sandwich. They all decide to rent three Sunfishes, and they pair up so that he and Cindy go out together. He has never sailed, so she stands up to her tits in the water fussing with the rudder while he sits high and dry holding the ropes that pull this striped three-cornered sail, that doesn't look to him firmly attached enough, flapping this way and that while one aluminum pipe rubs against another. The whole thing feels shaky. They have you wear a kind of black rubber pad around your middle and in hers Cindy looks pretty cute with that short otter haircut, butch, like one of those female cops on TV or a frogwoman. He has never before noticed how dark and thick her eyebrows are; they knit toward each other and almost touch until the rudder catch clicks in finally. Then she gives a grunt and up she jumps, flat on her front so her tits squeeze out sideways, the untanned parts of them white as Maalox, her legs kicking in the water to bring her ass all black and shiny aboard, she is too much woman for this little boat, it is tilting like crazy. He pulls her by the arm and the aluminum pole at the bottom of the sail swings and hits him on the back of the head. Hard. He is stunned. She has grabbed the rope from him while still holding on to the rudder handle and keeps shouting, "The centerboard, the centerboard," until he figures out what she means. This splintery long wood fin under his leg should go in that slot. He gets it out from under him and shoves it in. Instead of congratulating him, Cindy says, "Shit." The little Fiberglas shell is parallel to the beach, where an arc of bathers has gathered to watch, and each wave is slopping them closer in. Then the wind catches the sail and flattens it taut, so the aluminum mast creaks, and they slowly bob out over the breaking waves toward the point of land on the right where the bay ends.

Once you get going you don't feel how fast you're moving, the water having no landmarks. Harry is toward the front, crouching way over in case the boom swings at his head again. Sitting yoga-style in her stout rubber gasket, the center strip of her bikini barely covering her opened-up crotch, Cindy tends the tiller and for the first time smiles. "Harry, you don't have to keep holding on to the top of the centerboard, it doesn't have to be pulled until we hit the beach." The beach, the palms, the bungalows have been reduced to the size of a postcard.

"Should we be this far out?"

She smiles again. "We're not far out." The sailing gear tugs at her hands, the boat tips. The water out here is no longer the pale green of a honeydew melon but a green like bile, black in the troughs.

"We're not," he repeats.

"Look over there." A sail scarcely bigger than the flash of a wave. "That's Webb and Thelma. They're much further out than we are."

"Are you sure that's them?"

Cindy takes pity. "We'll come about when we're closer to those rocks. You know what come about means, Harry?"

"Not exactly."

"We'll change direction. The boom will swing, so watch your head."

"Do you think there are any sharks?" Still, he tells himself, there is an intimacy to it, just the two of them, the same spray hitting his skin and hers, the wind and water sounds that drown out all others, the curve of her shoulder shining like metal in the light of that hard white sun that makes the sun he grew up under seem orange and bloated in memory.

"Did you see *Jaws II*?" she asks back.

"D'you ever get the feeling everything these days is sequels?" he asks in turn. "Like people are running out of ideas." He feels so full of fatigue and long-held lust as to be careless of his life, amid this tugging violence of elements. Even the sun-sparkle on the water feels cruel, a malevolence straight from Heaven, like those photons beating on the wings of the airplane flying down.

"Coming about," Cindy says. "Hard alee."

He crouches, and the boom misses. He sees another sail out here with them, Ronnie and Janice, headed for the horizon. She seems to be at the back, steering. When did she learn? Some

summer camp. You have to be rich from the start to get the full
benefits. Cindy says, "Now Harry, you take over. It's simple. That
little strip of cloth at the top of the mast is called a telltale. It tells
what direction the wind is coming from. Also, look at the waves.
You want to keep the sail at an angle to the wind. What you don't
want is to see the front edge of the sail flapping. That's called
luffing. It means you're headed directly into the wind, and then
you must head off. You push the tiller away from you, away from
the sail. You'll feel it, I promise. The tension between the tiller
and the line – it's like a scissors, sort of. It's fun. Come on, Harry,
nothing can happen. Change places with me." They manage the
maneuver, while the boat swings like a hammock beneath their
bulks. A little cloud covers the sun, dyeing the water dark, then
releasing it back into sunshine with a pang. Harry takes hold of the
tiller and gropes until the wind takes hold with him. Then, as she
says, it's fun: the sail and tiller tugging, the invisible sea breeze
pushing, the distances not nearly so great and hopeless once you
have control. "You're doing fine," Cindy tells him, and from the
way she sits with legs crossed facing ahead he can see the underside of all five toes of one bare foot, the thin blue skin here wrinkled, the littlest dear toe bent into the toe next to it as if trying to
hide. She trusts him. She loves him. Now that he has the hang of
it he dares to heel, pulling the mainsheet tighter and tighter, so the
waves spank and his palm burns. The land is leaping closer, they
are almost safe when, in adjusting his aim toward the spot on the
beach where Janice and Ronnie have already dragged their
Sunfish up, he lets out the sail a touch and the wind catches it full
from behind; the prow goes under abruptly in a furious surging
film; heavily the whole shell slews around and tips; he and Cindy
have no choice but to slide off together, entangled with line. A
veined translucence closes over his head. *Air* he thinks wildly and
comes up in sudden shade, the boat looming on edge above them.
Cindy is beside him in the water. Gasping, wanting to apologize,
he clings briefly to her. She feels like a shark, slimy and abrasive.
Their two foam-rubber belts bump underwater. Each hair in her
eyebrows gleams in the strange light here, amid shadowed waves
and the silence of stilled wind, only a gentle slipslap against the
hollow hull. With a grimace she pushes him off, takes a deep

breath, and disappears beneath the boat. He tries to follow but his belt roughly buoys him back. He hears her grunting and splashing on the other side of the upright keel, first pulling at, then standing on the centerboard until the Sunfish comes upright, great pearls of water exploding from it as the striped sail sweeps past the sun. Harry heaves himself on and deftly she takes the boat in to shore.

The episode is inglorious, but they all laugh about it on the beach, and in his self-forgiving mind their underwater embrace has rapidly dried to something tender and promising. The slither of two skins, her legs fluttering between his. The few black hairs where her eyebrows almost meet. The hairs of her crotch she boldly displayed sitting yoga-style. It all adds up.

Lunch at the resort is served by the pool or brought by tray to the beach, but dinner is a formal affair within a vast pavilion whose rafters drip feathery fronds yards long and at whose rear, beside the doors leading into the kitchen, a great open barbecue pit sends flames roaring high, so that shadows twitch against the background design of thatch and carved masks, and highlights spark in the sweating black faces of the assistant chefs. The head chef is a scrawny Belgian always seen sitting at the bar between meals, looking sick, or else conferring in accents of grievance with one of the prim educated native women who run the front desk. Monday night is the barbecue buffet, with a calypso singer during the meal and dancing to electrified marimbas afterward; but all six of the holidayers from Diamond County agree they are exhausted from the night at the casino and will go to bed early. Harry after nearly drowning in Cindy's arms fell asleep on the beach and then went inside for a nap. While he was sleeping, a sudden sharp tropical rainstorm drummed for ten minutes on his tin roof. When he awoke, the rain had passed, and the sun was setting in a band of orange at the mouth of the bay, and his pals had been yukking it up in the bar ever since the shower an hour ago. Something is cooking. They seem, the three women, very soft-faced by the light of the candle set on the table in a little red netted hurricane lamp, amid papery flowers that will be wilted before the meal is over. They keep touching one another, their sisterhood strengthened and excited down here. Cindy is wearing a yellow hibiscus in her hair tonight, and that Arab thing, unbuttoned halfway

down. She more than once reaches past Webb's drink and stringy
brown hands as they pose on the tablecloth to touch Janice on a
wrist, remembering "that fresh colored boy behind the bar today,
I told him I was down here with my husband and he shrugged like
it made no difference whatsoever!" Webb looks sage, letting the
currents pass around him, and Ronnie sleepy and puffy but still
full of beans, in that grim play-maker way of his. Harry and Ronnie
were on the Mt. Judge basketball varsity together and more than
once Rabbit had to suppress a sensation that though he was the
star the coach, Marty Tothero, liked Ronnie better, because he
never quit trying and was more "physical" around the backboards.
The world runs on push. Rabbit's feeling about things has been
that if it doesn't happen by itself it's not worth making happen.
Still, that Cindy. A man could kill for a piece of that. Pump it in,
and die like a male spider. The calypso singer comes to their table
and sings a long dirty song about the Big Bamboo. Harry doesn't
understand all the allusions but the wives titter after every verse.
The singer smiles and the song smiles but his bloody eyes glitter
like those of a lizard frozen on the wall and his skull when bent
over the guitar shows gray wool. An old act. A dying art. Harry
doesn't know if they are supposed to tip him or just applaud. They
applaud and quick as a lizard's tongue his hand flickers out to take
the bill that Webb, leaning back, has offered. The old singer
moves on to the next table and begins that one about Back to back,
and Belly to belly. Cindy giggles, touches Janice on the forearm,
and says, "I bet all the people back in Brewer will think we've
swapped down here."

"Maybe we should then," Ronnie says, unable to suppress a
belch of fatigue.

Janice, in that throaty mature woman's voice cigarettes and age
have given her but that Harry is always surprised to hear she has,
asks Webb, who sits beside her, gently, "How do you feel about
that sort of thing, Webb?"

The old fox knows he has the treasure to barter and takes his
time, pulling himself up in his chair to release an edge of coat he's
sitting on, a kind of dark blue captain's jacket with spoked brass buttons, and takes his pack of Marlboro Lights from his side pocket.
Rabbit's heart races so hard he stares down at the table, where the

bloody bones, ribs and vertebrae, of their barbecue wait to be cleared away. Webb drawls, "Well, after two marriages that I'd guess you'd have to say were not fully successful, and some of the things I've seen and done before, after, and between, I must admit a little sharing among friends doesn't seem to me so bad, if it's done with affection and respect. Respect is the key term here. Every party involved, and I mean every party, has to be willing, and it should be clearly understood that whatever happens will go no further than that particular occasion. Secret affairs, that's what does a marriage in. When people get romantic."

Nothing romantic about him, the king of the Polaroid pricks. Harry's face feels hot. Maybe it's the spices in the barbecue settling, or the length of Webb's sermon, or a blush of gratitude to the Murketts, for arranging all this. He imagines his face between Cindy's thighs, tries to picture that black pussy like a curved snug mass of eyebrow hairs, flattened and warmed to fragrance from being in underpants and framed by the white margins the bikini bottom had to cover to be decent. He will follow her slit down with his tongue, her legs parting with that same weightless slither he felt under water today, down and in, and around the corner next to his nose will be that whole great sweet ass he has a thousand times watched jiggle as she dried herself from swimming in the pool at the Flying Eagle, under the nappy green shadow of Mt. Pemaquid. And her tits, the fall of them forward when she obediently bends over. Something is happening in his pants, like the stamen of one of these floppy flowers on the tablecloth jerking with shadow as the candle-flame flickers.

"Down the way," the singer sings at yet another table, "where the nights are gay, and the sun shines daily on the moun-tain-top." Black hands come and smoothly clear away the dark bones and distribute dessert menus. There is a walnut cake they offer here that Harry especially likes, though there's nothing especially Caribbean about it, it's probably flown in from Fort Lauderdale.

Thelma, who is wearing a sort of filmy top you can see her cocoa-colored bra through, is gazing into middle distance like a schoolteacher talking above the heads of her class and saying, " . . . simple female curiosity. It's something you hardly ever see discussed in all these articles on female sexuality, but I think it's what's

behind these male strippers rather than any real desire on the part
of the women to go to bed with the boys. They're just curious
about the penises, what they look like. They *do* look a lot different from each other, I guess."

"That how you feel?" Harry asks Janice. "Curious?"

She lowers her eyes to the guttering hurricane lamp. She murmurs, "Of course."

"Oh I'm not," Cindy says, "not the shape. I don't think I am.
I really am not."

"You're very young," Thelma says.

"I'm thirty," she protests. "Isn't that supposed to be my sexual
prime?"

As if rejoining her in the water, Harry tries to take her side.
"They're ugly as hell. Most of the pricks I've seen are."

"You don't see them erect," Thelma lightly points out.

"Thank God for that," he says, appalled, as he sometimes is, by
this coarse crowd he's in – by human coarseness in general.

"And yet he loves his own," Janice says, keeping that light and
cool and as it were scientific tone that has descended upon them,
in the hushed dining pavilion. The singer has ceased. People at
other tables are leaving, moving to the smaller tables at the edge
of the dance floor by the pool.

"I don't love it," he protests in a whisper. "I'm stuck with it."

"It's you," Cindy quietly tells him.

"Not just the pricks," Thelma clarifies, "it has to be the whole
man who turns you on. The way he carries himself. His voice, the
way he laughs. But it all refers to that, I guess."

Pricks. Can it be? They let the delicate subject rest, as dessert
and coffee come. Revitalized by food and their talk, they decide
after all to sit with Stingers and watch the dancing a while, under
the stars that on this night seem to Harry jewels of a clock that
moves with maddening slowness, measuring out the minutes until
he sinks himself in Cindy as if a star were to fall and sizzle into this
Olympic-sized pool. Once, on some far lost summer field of
childhood, someone, his mother it must have been though he cannot hear her voice, told him that if you stare up at the night sky
while you count to one hundred you are bound to see a shooting
star, they are in fact so common. But though he now leans back

from the Stinger and the glass table and the consolatory, conspiratory murmur of his friends until his neck begins to ache, all the stars above him hang unbudging in their sockets. Webb Murkett's gravelly voice growls, "Well, kiddies. As the oldest person here, I claim the privilege of announcing that I'm tired and want to go to bed." And as Harry turns his face from the heavens there it is, in a corner of his vision, vivid and brief as a scratched match, a falling star, doused in the ocean of ink. The women rise and gather their skirts about them; the marimbas, after a consultation of fluttering, fading notes, break into "Send in the Clowns." This plaintive pealing is lost behind them as they move along the pool, and past the front desk where the haggard, alcoholic resort manager is trying to get through long-distance to New York, and across the hotel's traffic circle with its curbs of whitewashed coral, down into the shadowy realm of concrete paths between bushes of sleeping flowers. The palms above them grow noisy as the music fades. The *shoosh* of surf draws nearer. At the moonlit point where the paths diverge into three, goodnights are nervously exchanged but no one moves; then a woman's hand reaches out softly and takes the wrist of a man not her husband. The others follow suit, with no person looking at another, a downcast and wordless tugging serving to separate the partners out and to draw them down the respective paths to each woman's bungalow. Harry hears Cindy giggle, at a distance, for it is not her hand with such gentle determination pulling him along, but Thelma's.

She has felt him pull back, and tightens her grip, silently. On the beach, he sees, a group has brought down a hurricane lamp, with their drinks; the lamp and their cigarettes glow red in the shadows, while the sea beyond stretches pale as milk beyond the black silhouette of a big sailboat anchored in the bay, under the half-moon tilted onto its back. Thelma lets go of his arm to fish in her sequinned purse for the bungalow key. "You can have Cindy tomorrow night," she whispers. "We discussed it."

"O.K., great," he says lamely, he hopes not insultingly. He is figuring, this means that Cindy wanted that pig Harrison, and

Janice got Webb. He had been figuring Janice would have to take Ronnie, and felt sorry for her, except from the look of him he'd fall asleep soon, and Webb and Thelma would go together, both of them yellowy stringy types. Thelma closes the bungalow door behind them and switches on a straw globe light above the bed. He asks her, "Well, are tonight's men the first choice for you ladies or're you just getting the second choice out of the way?"

"Don't be so competitive, Harry. This is meant to be a loving sharing sort of thing, you heard Webb. One thing we absolutely agreed on, we're not going to carry any of it back to Brewer. This is all the monkey business there's going to be, even if it kills us." She stands there in the center of her straw rug rather defiantly, a thin-faced sallow woman he scarcely knows. Not only her nose is pink in the wake of her sunburn but patches below her eyes as well: a kind of butterfly is on her face. Harry supposes he should kiss her, but his forward step is balked by her continuing firmly, "I'll tell you one thing though, Harry Angstrom. You're *my* first choice."

"I am?"

"Of course. I adore you. *Adore* you."

"Me?"

"Haven't you ever sensed it?"

Rather than admit he hasn't, he hangs there foolishly.

"Shit," Thelma says. "Janice did. Why else do you think we weren't invited to Nelson's wedding?" She turns her back, and starts undoing her earring before the mirror, that just like the one in his and Janice's bungalow is framed in woven strips of bamboo. The batik hanging in here is of a tropical sunset with a palm in the foreground instead of the black-mammy fruit-seller he and Janice have, but the batik manufacturer is the same. The suitcases are the Harrisons', and the clothes hanging on the painted pipe that does for a closet. Thelma asks, "You mind using Ronnie's toothbrush? I'll be a while in there, you better take the bathroom first."

In the bathroom Harry sees that Ronnie uses shaving cream, Gillette Foamy, out of a pressure can, the kind that's eating up the ozone so our children will fry. And that new kind of razor with the narrow single-edge blade that snaps in and out with a click on the television commercials. Harry can't see the point, it's just more waste, he still uses a rusty old two-edge safety razor he bought for $1.99 about seven years ago, and lathers himself with an old imitation badger-bristle on whatever bar of soap is handy. He shaved before dinner after his nap so no need now. Also the Harrisons use chlorophyll Crest in one of those giant tubes that always buckles and springs a leak when he and Janice try to save a couple pennies and buy one. He wonders whatever happened to Ipana and what was it *Consumer Reports* had to say about toothpastes a few issues back, probably came out in favor of baking soda, that's what he and Mim used to have to use, some theory Mom had about the artificial flavoring in toothpaste contributing to tartar. The trouble with consumerism is, the guy next door always seems to be doing better at it than you are. Just the Harrisons' bathroom supplies make him envious. Plain as she is, Thelma carries a hefty medicine kit, and beauty aids, plus a sun block called Eclipse, and Solarcaine. Vaseline, too, for some reason. Tampax, in a bigger box than Janice ever buys. And a lot of painkiller, aspirin in several shapes and Darvon and more pills in little prescription bottles than he would have expected. People are always a little sicker than you know. Harry debates whether he should take his leak sitting down to spare Thelma the sound of its gross splashing and rejects the idea, since she's the one wants to fuck him. It streams noisily into the bowl it seems forever, embarrassingly, all those drinks at dinner. Then he sits down on the seat anyway, to let out a little air. Too much shellfish. He imagines he can smell yesterday's crabmeat and when he stands he tests with a finger down there to see if he stinks. He decides he does. Better use a washcloth. He debates which washcloth is Ronnie's, the blue or the brown. He settles on the brown and scrubs all his undercarriage, everything that counts. Getting ready for the ball. He erases his scent by giving the cloth a good rinsing no matter whose it is.

When he steps back into the room Thelma is down to her underwear, cocoa bra and black panties. He didn't expect this, nor to be so stirred by it. Breasts are strange: some look bigger in clothes than they are and some look smaller. Thelma's are the second kind; her bra is smartly filled. Her whole body, into her forties, has kept that trim neutral serviceability nurses and grade-school teachers surprise you with, beneath their straight faces. She laughs, and holds out her arms like a fan dancer. "Here I am. You look shocked. You're such a sweet prude, Harry — that's one of the things I adore. I'll be out in five minutes. Try not to fall asleep."

Clever of her. What with the sleep debt they're all running down here and the constant booze and the trauma in the water today — his head went under and a bottomless bile-green volume sucked at his legs — he was weary. He begins to undress and doesn't know where to stop. There are a lot of details a husband and wife work out over the years that with a strange woman pop up all over again. Would Thelma like to find him naked in the bed? Or on it? For him to be less naked than she when she comes out of the bathroom would be rude. At the same time, with this straw-shaded light swaying above the bed on so bright, he doesn't want her to think seeing him lying there on display that he thinks he's a *Playgirl* centerfold. He knows he could lose thirty pounds and still have a gut. In his underpants he crosses to the bamboo-trimmed bureau in the room and switches on the lamp there whose cheap wooden base is encrusted with baby seashells glued on. He takes off his underpants. The elastic waistband has lost its snap, the only brand of this type to buy is Jockey, but those cut-rate stores in Brewer don't like to carry it, quality is being driven out everywhere. He switches off the light over the bed and in shadow stretches himself out, all of him, on top of the bedspread, as he is, as he was, as he will be before the undertakers dress him for the last time, not even a wedding ring to relieve his nakedness; when he and Janice got married men weren't expected to wear wedding rings. He closes his eyes to rest them for a second in the red blankness there, beneath his lids. He has to get through this, maybe all she wants to do is talk, and then somehow be really rested for tomorrow night. Getting there . . . . That slither under-water . . . .

Thelma with what breaks upon him like the clatter of an earth-quake has come out of the bathroom. She is holding her under-clothes in front of her, and with her back to him she sorts the underpants into the dirty pile the Harrisons keep beside the bureau, behind the straw wastebasket, and the bra, clean enough, back into the drawer, folded. This is the second time in this trip, he thinks drowsily, that he has seen her ass. Her body as she turns eclipses the bureau lamp and the front of her gathers shadow to itself; she advances timidly, as if wading into water. Her breasts sway forward as she bends to turn the light he switched off back on. She sits down on the edge of the bed.

His prick is still sleepy. She takes it into her hand. "You're not circumcised."

"No, they somehow weren't doing it at the hospital that day. Or maybe my mother had a theory, I don't know. I never asked. Sorry."

"It's lovely. Like a little bonnet." Sitting on the edge of the bed, more supple naked than he remembers her seeming with clothes on, Thelma bends and takes his prick in her mouth. Her body in the lamplight is a pale patchwork of faint tan and peeling pink and the natural yellowy tint of her skin. Her belly puckers into flat folds like stacked newspapers and the back of her hand as it holds the base of his prick with two fingers shows a dim lightning of blue veins. But her breath is warm and wet and the way that in lamp-light individual white hairs snake as if singed through the mass of dull brown makes him want to reach out and stroke her head, or touch the rhythmic hollow in her jaw. He fears, though, inter-rupting the sensations she is giving him. She lifts a hand quickly to tuck back a piece of her hair, as if to let him better see.

He murmurs, "Beautiful." He is growing thick and long but still she forces her lips each time down to her fingers as they en-circle him at his base. To give herself ease she spreads her legs; between her legs, one of them lying aslant across the bed edge, he sees emerging from a pubic bush more delicate and reddish than he would have dreamed a short white string. Unlike Janice's or Cindy's as he imagined it, Thelma's pussy is not opaque; it is a fuzz transparent upon the bruise-colored labia that with their tongue of white string look so lacking and defenseless Harry could cry. She too is near tears, perhaps from the effort of not gagging. She backs off and stares at the staring eye of his glans, swollen free of his foreskin. She pulls up the bonnet again and says crooningly, teasingly, "Such a serious little face." She kisses it lightly, once, twice, flicking her tongue, then bobs again, until it seems she must come up for air. "God," she sighs. "I've wanted to do that for so

long. Come. Come, Harry. Come in my mouth. Come in my
mouth and all over my face." Her voice sounds husky and mad
saying this and all through her words Thelma does not stop gazing at the little slit of his where a single cloudy tear has now
appeared. She licks it off.

"Have you really," he asks timidly, "liked me for a while?"

"Years," she says. "Years. And you never noticed. You shit.
Always under Janice's thumb and mooning after silly Cindy. Well
you know where Cindy is now. She's being screwed by my husband. He didn't want to, he said he'd rather go to bed with me."
She snorts, in some grief of self-disgust, and plunges her mouth
down again, and in the pinchy rush of sensation as he feels forced
against the opening of her throat he wonders if he should accept
her invitation.

"Wait," Harry says. "Shouldn't I do something for you first? If
I come, it's all over."

"If you come, then you come again."

"Not at my age. I don't think."

"Your age. Always talking about your age." Thelma rests her
face on his belly and gazes up at him, for the first time playful, her
eyes at right angles to his disconcertingly. He has never noticed
their color before: that indeterminate color called hazel but in the
strong light overhead, and brightened by all her deep-throating,
given a tawny pallor, an unthinking animal translucence. "I'm too
excited to come," she tells him. "Anyway, Harry, I'm having my
period and they're really bloody, every other month. I'm scared
to find out why. In the months in between, these terrible cramps
and hardly any show."

"See a doctor," he suggests.

"I see doctors all the time, they're useless. I'm dying, you know
that, don't you?"

"Dying?"

"Well, maybe that's too dramatic a way of putting it. Nobody
knows how long it'll take, and a lot of it depends upon me. The
one thing I'm absolutely supposed not to do is go out in the sun.
I was crazy to come down here, Ronnie tried to talk me out
of it."

"Why did you?"

"Guess. I tell you, I'm crazy, Harry. I got to get you out of my system." And it seems she might make that sob of disgusted grief again, but she has reared up her head to look at his prick. All this talk of death has put it half to sleep again.

"This is this lupus?" he asks.

"Mmm," Thelma says. "Look. See the rash?" She pulls back her hair on both sides. "Isn't it pretty? That's from being so stupid in the sun Friday. I just wanted so badly to be like the rest of you, not to be an invalid. It was terrible Saturday. Your joints ache, your insides don't work. Ronnie offered to take me home for a shot of cortisone."

"He's very nice to you."

"He loves me."

His prick has stiffened again and she bends to it. "Thelma." He has not used her name before, this night. "Let me do something to you. I mean, equal rights and all that."

"You're not going down into all that blood."

"Let me suck these sweet things then." Her nipples are not bumply like Janice's but perfect as a baby's thumb-tips. Since it is his treat now he feels free to reach up and switch off the light over the bed. In the dark her rashes disappear and he can see her smile as she arranges herself to be served. She sits cross-legged, like Cindy did on the boat, women the flexible sex, and puts a pillow in her lap for his head. She puts a finger in his mouth and plays with her nipple and his tongue together. There is a tremble running through her like a radio not quite turned off. His hand finds her ass, its warm dents; there is a kind of glassy texture to Thelma's skin where Janice's has a touch of fine, fine sandpaper. His prick, lightly teased by her fingernails, has come back nicely. "Harry." Her voice presses into his ear. "I want to do something for you so you won't forget me, something you've never had with anybody else. I suppose other women have sucked you off?"

He shakes his head yes, which tugs the flesh of her breast.

"How many have you fucked up the ass?"

He lets her nipple slip from his mouth. "None. Never."

"You and Janice?"

"Oh God no. It never occurred to us."

"Harry. You're not fooling me?"

How dear that was, her old-fashioned "fooling." From talking to all those third-graders. "No, honestly. I thought only queers ... Do you and Ronnie?"

"All the time. Well, a lot of the time. He loves it."

"And you?"

"It has its charms."

"Doesn't it hurt? I mean, he's big."

"At first. You use Vaseline. I'll get ours."

"Thelma, wait. Am I up to this?"

She laughs a syllable. "You're up." She slides away into the bathroom and while she is gone he stays enormous. She returns and anoints him thoroughly, with an icy expert touch. Harry shudders. Thelma lies down beside him with her back turned, curls forward as if to be shot from a cannon, and reaches behind to guide him. "Gently."

It seems it won't go, but suddenly it does. The medicinal odor of displaced Vaseline reaches his nostrils. The grip is tight at the base but beyond, where a cunt is all velvety suction and caress, there is no sensation: a void, a pure black box, a casket of perfect nothingness. He is in that void, past her tight ring of muscle. He asks, "May I come?"

"Please do." Her voice sounds faint and broken. Her spine and shoulder blades are taut.

It takes only a few thrusts, while he rubs her scalp with one hand and clamps her hip steady with the other. Where will his come go? Nowhere but mix with her shit. With sweet Thelma's sweet shit. They lie wordless and still together until his prick's slow shrivelling withdraws it. "O.K.," he says. "Thank you. That I won't forget."

"Promise?"

"I feel embarrassed. What does it do for you?"

"Makes me feel full of you. Makes me feel fucked up the ass. By lovely Harry Angstrom."

"Thelma," he admits, "I can't believe you're so fond of me. What have I done to deserve it?"

"Just existed. Just shed your light. Haven't you ever noticed, at parties or at the club, how I'm always at your side?"

"Well, not really. There aren't that many sides. I mean, we see you and Ronnie —"

"Janice and Cindy noticed. They knew you were who I'd want."

"Uh – not to, you know, milk this, but what is it about me that turns you on?"

"Oh darling. Everything. Your height and the way you move, as if you're still a skinny twenty-five. The way you never sit down anywhere without making sure there's a way out. Your little provisional smile, like a little boy at some party where the bullies might get him the next minute. Your good humor. You *believe* in people so – Webb, you hang on his words where nobody else pays any attention, and Janice, you're so proud of her it's pathetic. It's not as if she can *do* anything. Even her tennis, Doris Kaufmann was telling us, really –"

"Well it's nice to see her have fun at something, she's had a kind of dreary life."

"See? You're just terribly generous. You're so grateful to be anywhere, you think that tacky club and that hideous house of Cindy's are heaven. It's wonderful. You're so glad to be alive."

"Well, I mean, considering the alternative –"

"It kills me. I love you *so much* for it. And your hands. I've always loved your hands." Having sat up on the edge of the bed, she takes his left hand, lying idle, and kisses the big white moons of each fingernail. "And now your prick, with its little bonnet. Oh Harry I don't care if this kills me, coming down here, tonight is worth it."

That void, inside her. He can't take his mind from what he's discovered, that nothingness seen by his single eye. In the shadows, while humid blue moonlight and the rustle of palms seep through the louvers by the bed, he trusts himself to her as if speaking in prayer, talks to her about himself as he has talked to none other: about Nelson and the grudge he bears the kid and the grudge the boy bears him, and about his daughter, the daughter he thinks he has, grown and ignorant of him. He dares confide to Thelma, because she has let him fuck her up the ass in proof of love, his sense of miracle at being himself, himself instead of somebody else, and his old inkling, now fading in the energy crunch, that there was something that wanted him to find it, that he was here on earth on a kind of assignment.

"How lovely to think that," Thelma says. "It makes you" – the word is hard for her to find – "radiant. And sad." She gives him advice on some points. She thinks he should seek out Ruth and ask her point-blank if that is his daughter, and if so is there anything he can do to help? On the subject of Nelson, she thinks the child's problem may be an extension of Harry's; if he himself did not feel guilty about Jill's death and before that Rebecca's, he would feel less threatened by Nelson and more comfortable and kindly with him. "Remember," she says, "he's just a young man like you once were, looking for his path."

"But he's not like me!" Harry protests, having come at last into a presence where the full horror of this truth, the great falling-off, will be understood. "He's a goddam little Springer, through and through."

Thelma thinks he's more like Harry than he knows. Wanting to learn to hang glide – didn't he recognize himself in that? And the thing with two girls at once. Wasn't he, possibly, a bit jealous of Nelson?

"But I never had the impulse to screw Melanie," he confesses. "Or Pru either, much. They're both out of this world, somehow."

Of course, Thelma says. "You shouldn't want to fuck them. They're your daughters. Or Cindy either. You should want to fuck *me*. I'm your generation, Harry. I can *see* you. To those girls you're just an empty heap of years and money."

And, as they drift in talk away from the constellations of his life, she describes her marriage with Ronnie, his insecurities and worries beneath that braggart manner that she knows annoys Harry. "He was never a star like you, he never had that for a moment." She met him fairly well along in her twenties, when she was wondering if she'd die a spinster schoolteacher. Being old as she was, with some experience of men, and with a certain gift for letting go, she was amused by the things he thought of. For their honeymoon breakfast he jerked off into the scrambled eggs and they ate his fried jism with the rest. If you go along with everything on that side of Ronnie, he's wonderfully loyal, and docile, you could say. He has no interest in other women, she knows this for a fact, a curious fact even, given the nature of men. He's been a perfect father. When he was lower down on the totem pole at Schuylkill

Mutual, he lost twenty pounds, staying awake nights worrying. Only in these last few years has the weight come back. When the first diagnosis of her lupus came through, he took it worse than she did, in a way. "For a woman past forty, Harry, when you've had children. . . . If some Nazi or somebody came to me and they'd take either me or little Georgie, say – he's the one that's needed most help, so he comes to mind – it wouldn't be a hard choice. For Ronnie I think it might be. To lose me. He thinks what I do for him not every woman would. I suspect he's wrong but there it is." And she admits she likes his cock. But what Harry might not appreciate, being a man, is that a big one like Ronnie's doesn't change size that much when it's hard, just the angle changes. It doesn't go from being a little bonneted sleeping baby to a tall fierce soldier like this. She has worked him up again, idly toying as she talks, while the night outside their louvered window has grown utterly still, the last drunken shout and snatch of music long died, nothing astir but the incessant sighing of the sea and the piping of some high-pitched cricket they have down here. Courteously he offers to fuck her through her blood, and she refuses with an almost virginal fright, so that he wonders if on the excuse of her flow she is not holding this part of herself back from him, aloof from her love and shamelessness, pure for her marriage. She has explained, "When I realized I was falling in love with you, I was so *mad* at myself, I mean it couldn't contribute to *any*thing. But then I came to see that something must be missing between me and Ronnie, or maybe in any life, so I tried to accept it, and even quietly enjoy it, just watching you. My little hairshirt." He has not kissed her yet on the mouth, but now having guessed at her guilty withholding of herself from being simply fucked he does. Guilt he can relate to. Her lips feel cool and dry, considering. Since she will not admit him to her cunt, as compromise he masturbates her while sitting on her face, glad he thought of washing where he did. Her tongue probes there and her fingers, as cool on top of his as if still filmed with Vaseline, guide his own as they find and then lose and find again the hooded little center that is *her*. She comes with a smothered cry and arches her back so this darkness at the center of her pale and smooth and unfamiliar form rises hungrily under his eyes, a cloud with a mouth, a fish lunging upwards out of water. Getting her breath, she returns the kindness and with him watches the white liquid lift and collapse in glutinous strings across her hand. She rubs his jism on her face, where it shines like sun lotion. The stillness outside is beginning to brighten, each leaf sharp in the soft air. Drunk on fatigue and self-exposure, he begs her to tell him something that he can do to her that Ronnie has never done. She gets into the bathtub and has him urinate on her. "It's hot!" she exclaims, her sallow skin drummed upon in designs such as men and boys drill in the snow. They reverse the experience, Thelma awkwardly straddling, and having to laugh at her own impotence, looking for the right release in the maze of her womanly insides. Above him as he waits her bush has a masculine jut, but when her stream comes, it dribbles sideways; women cannot *aim*, he sees. And her claim of heat seems to him exaggerated; it is more like coffee or tea one lets cool too long at the edge of the desk and then must drink in a few gulps, this side of tepid. Having tried together to shower the ammoniac scent of urine off their skins, Thelma and Harry fall asleep among the stripes of dawn now welling through the louvers, they sleep as if not a few more stolen hours but an entire married life of sanctioned intimacy stretches unto death before them.

A savage rattling at the door. "Thelma. Harry. It's *us*." Thelma puts on a robe to answer the knocking while Rabbit hides beneath the sheet and peeks. Webb and Ronnie stand there in the incandescence of another day. Webb is resplendent in grape-colored alligator shirt and powder-blue plaid golf pants. Ronnie wears last night's dinner clothes and needs to get inside. Thelma shuts the door and hides in the bathroom while Harry dresses in last night's rumpled suit, not bothering to knot the necktie. He still smells of urine, he thinks. He runs to his own bungalow to change into a golf outfit. Black girls, humming, pursued by yellow birds, are carrying tinkling breakfast trays along the cement paths. Janice is in the bathroom, running a tub.

He shouts out, "You O.K.?"

She shouts back, "As O.K. as you are," and doesn't emerge.

On the way out, Harry stuffs an unbuttered croissant and some scalding sips of coffee into his mouth. The papery orange and magenta flowers beside the door hurt his head. Webb and Ronnie are waiting for him where the green cement paths meet. Among the three men, as they push through their golf, there is much banter and good humor, but little eye-contact. When they return from the course around one o'clock, Janice is sitting by the Olympic pool in the same off-white linen suit she wore down in the airplane. Linen wrinkles terribly. "Harry, Mother phoned. We have to go back."

"You're kidding. Why?" He is groggy, and had pictured a long afternoon nap, to be in shape for tonight. Also his foreskin was tender after last night's workout and slightly chafed every time he swung, thinking of Cindy, hoping her vagina would be non-frictional. His golf, threaded through vivid after-images of Thelma's underside and a ticklish awareness of his two businesslike partners as silently freighted with mental pictures of their own, was mysteriously good, his swing as it were emptied of impurities, until fatigue caught him on the fifteenth hole with three balls sliced along the identical skyey groove into the lost-ball terrain of cactus and coral and scrub growth. "What's happened? The baby?"

"No," Janice says, and by the easy way she cries he knows she's been crying off and on all morning, here in the sun. "It's *Nel*son. He's run off."

"He has? I better sit down." To the black waiter who comes to their glass table under its fringed umbrella he says, "Piña colada, Jeff. Better make that two. Janice?" She blearily nods, though there is an empty glass already before her. Harry looks around at the faces of their friends. "Jeff, maybe you should make that six." He has come to know the ropes in this place. The other people sitting around the pool look pale, newly pulled from the airplane.

Cindy has just come out of the pool, her shoulders blue-black, the diaper-shape of her bikini bottom wetly adhering. She tugs the cloth to cover the pale margin of skin above, below. She is getting fatter, day by day. Better hurry, he tells himself. But it is too late. Her face when she turns, towelling her back with a contortion that nearly pops one tit out of its triangular sling, is solemn. She and Thelma have heard Janice's story already. Thelma is sitting at the table in that ankle-length wrapper, the same dusty-pink as her nose, that she bought down here along with the wide straw hat. The big brown sunglasses she brought from home, tinted darker at the top, render her expressionless. Harry takes the chair at the table next to her. His knee accidentally touches one of hers; she pulls it away at once.

Janice is telling him, through tears, "He and Pru had a fight Saturday night, he wanted to go into Brewer for a party with that Slim person and Pru said she was too pregnant and couldn't face those stairs again, and he went by himself." She swallows. "And he didn't come back." Her voice is all roughened from swallowing the saltwater of the tears. With scrapings that hurt Harry's head Webb and Ronnie pull chairs to their table in its tight circle of shade. When Jeff brings their round of drinks Janice halts her terrible tale and Ronnie negotiates for lunch menus. He, like his wife, wears sunglasses. Webb wears none, trusting to his bushy brows and the crinkles of his flinty eyes, which gaze at Janice like those of some encouraging old fart of a father.

Her cheeks are drenched with the slime of distress and Harry has to love her for her ugliness. "I told you the kid was a rat," he tells her. He feels vindicated. And relieved, actually.

"He didn't come back," Janice all but cries, looking only at him, not at Webb, with that smeared lost balked expression he remembers so well from their earliest days, before she got cocky. "But Mother didn't want to b-bother us on our vacation and P-Pru thought he just needed to blow off steam and pretended not to be worried. But Sunday after going to church with Mother she called this Slim and Nelson had never showed up!"

"Did he have a car?" Harry asks.

"Your Corona."

"Oh boy."

"I think just scrambled eggs for me," Ronnie tells the waitress who has come. "Loose. You understand? Not too well done."

This time Rabbit deliberately seeks to touch Thelma's knee with his under the table but her knee is not there for him. Like Janice down here she has become a piece of static. The waitress is at his shoulder and he is wondering if he might dare another crab-meat-salad sandwich or should play it safe with a BLT. Janice's face, which the movement of the sun overhead is hoisting out of shadow, goes wide in eyes and mouth as she might shriek. "Harry you *can't* have lunch, you *must* get dressed and out of here! I packed for you, everything but the gray suit. The woman at the front desk was on the phone for me nearly an hour, trying to get us back to Philadelphia but it's impossible this time of year. There's not even anything to New York. She got us two seats on a little plane to San Juan and a room at the hotel airport so we can get a flight to the mainland first thing in the morning. Atlanta and then Philadelphia."

"Why not just use our regular reservations Thursday? What good's an extra day going to do?"

"I cancelled them. Harry, you didn't talk to Mother. She's wild, I've never heard her like this, you know how she always makes sense. I called back to tell her the plane on Wednesday and she didn't think she could drive the Philadelphia traffic to meet us, she burst into tears and said she was too old."

"Cancelled." It is sinking in. "You mean we can't stay here tonight because of something Nelson has done?"

"Finish your story, Jan," Webb urges. Jan, is it now? Harry suddenly hates people who seem to *know*; they would keep us blind to the fact that there is nothing to know. We are each of us filled with a perfect blackness.

Janice gulps again, and snuffles, calmed by Webb's voice. "There's nothing to finish. He didn't come back Sunday or Monday and none of these friends they have in Brewer had seen him and Mother finally couldn't stand it anymore and called this morning, even though Pru kept telling her not to bother us, it was her husband and she took the responsibility."

"Poor kid. Like you said, she thought she could work miracles." He tells her, "I don't *want* to leave before tonight."

"Stay here then," Janice says. "I'm going."

Harry looks over at Webb for some kind of help, and gets instead a sage and useless not-my-funeral grimace. He looks at Cindy but she is gazing down into her piña colada, her eyelashes in sharp focus. "I still don't understand the rush," he says. "Nobody's died."

"Not yet," Janice says. "Is that what you need?"

A rope inside his chest twists to make a kink. "Son of a fuck-ing bitch," he says, and stands, bumping his head on the fringed edge of the umbrella. "When'd you say this plane to San Juan is?"

Janice snuffles, guilty now. "Not until three."

"O.K." He sighs. In a way this is a relief. "I'll go change and bring the suitcases. Could one of you guys at least order me a hamburger? Cindy. Thel. See you around." The two ladies let themselves be kissed, Thelma primly on the lips, Cindy on her apple-firm cheek, toasty from the sun.

Throughout their twenty-four-hour trip home Janice keeps crying. The taxi ride past the old sugar mills, through the goat herds and the straggling black towns and the air that seems to be blowing them kisses; the forty-minute hop in a swaying two-engine prop plane to Puerto Rico, over mild green water beneath whose sparkling film lurk buried reefs and schools of sharks; the stopover in San Juan where everybody is a real spic; the long stunned night of porous sleep in a hotel very like that motel on Route 422 where Mrs. Lubell stayed so long ago; and in the morning two seats on a jet to Atlanta and then Philly: through all this Janice is beside him with her cheeks glazed, eyes staring ahead, her eyelashes tipped with tiny balls of dew. It is as if all the grief that swept through him at Nelson's wedding now at last has reached Janice's zone, and he is calm and emptied and as cold as the void suspended beneath the airplane's shuddering flight. He asks her, "Is it just Nelson?"

She shakes her head so violently the fringe of bangs bobs. "*Ev*erything," she blurts, so loud he fears the heads just glimpsable in the seats ahead might turn around.

"The swapping?" he pursues softly.

She nods, not so violently, pinching her lower lip in a kind of turtle mouth her mother sometimes makes.

"How *was* Webb?"

"Nice. He's always been nice to me. He respected Daddy." This sets the tears to flowing again. She takes a deep breath to steady herself. "I felt so sorry for you, having Thelma when you wanted Cindy so much." With that there is no stopping her crying.

He pats her hands, which are loosely fisted together in her lap around a damp Kleenex. "Listen, I'm sure Nelson's all right, wherever he is."

"He" – she seems to be choking, a stewardess glances down as she strides by, this is embarrassing – "*hates* himself, Harry."

He tries to ponder if this is true. He snickers. "Well he sure screwed me. Last night was my dream date."

Janice sniffs and rubs each nostril with the Kleenex. "Webb says she's not as wonderful as she looks. He talked a lot about his first two wives."

Beneath them, through the scratched oval of Plexiglas, there is the South, irregular fields and dry brown woods, more woods than he would have expected. Once he had dreamed of going south, of resting his harried heart amid all that cotton, and now there it is under him, like the patchwork slope of one big hill they are slowly climbing, fields and woods and cities at the bends and mouths of rivers, streets eating into green, America disgraced and barren, mourning her hostages. They are flying too high for him to spot golf courses. They play all winter down here, swinging easy. The giant motors he is riding whine. He falls asleep. The last thing he sees is Janice staring ahead, wide awake, the bulge of tears compounding the bulge of her cornea. He dreams of Pru, who bursts while he is trying to manipulate her limbs, so there is too much water, he begins to panic. He is changing weight and this wakes him up. They are descending. He thinks back to his night with Thelma, and it seems in texture no different from the dream. Only Janice is real, the somehow catastrophic creases in her linen sleeve and the muddy line of her jaw, her head slumped as from a broken neck. She fell asleep, the same magazine open in her lap that she read on the way down. They are descending over Maryland and Delaware, where horses run and the du Ponts are king. Rich women with little birdy breasts and wearing tall black boots in from the hunt. Walking past the butler into long halls past marble tables they flick with their whips. Women he will never fuck. He has risen as high as he can, the possibility of such women is falling from him, falling with so many other possibilities as he descends. No snow dusts the dry earth below, rooftops and fields and roads where cars are nosing along like windup toys in invisible grooves. Yet from within those cars they are speeding, and feel free. The river flashes its sheet of steel, the plane tilts alarmingly, the air nozzles hissing above him may be the last thing he hears,

Janice is awake and bolt upright. *Forgive me*. Fort Mifflin hulks just under their wheels, their speed is titanic. *Please, God*. Janice is saying something into his ear but the thump of the wheels drowns it out. They are down, and taxiing. He gives a squeeze to Janice's damp hand, that he didn't realize he was holding. "What did you say?" he asks her.

"That I love you."

"Oh, really? Well, same here. That trip was fun. I feel satisfied."

In the long slow trundle to their gate, she asks him shyly, "Was Thelma better than me?"

He is too grateful to be down to lie. "In ways. How about Webb?"

She nods and nods, as if to spill the last tears from her eyes.

He answers for her, "The bastard was great."

She leans her head against his shoulder. "Why do you think I've been crying?"

Shocked, he admits, "I thought about Nelson."

Janice sniffs once more, so loudly that one man already on his feet, arranging a Russian-style fur cap upon his sunburned bald head, briefly stares. She concedes, "It was, mostly," and she and Harry clasp hands once more, conspirators.

At the end of miles of airport corridor Ma Springer is standing apart from the cluster of other greeters. In the futuristic perspectives of this terminal she looks shrunken and bent, wearing her second-best coat, not the mink but a black cloth trimmed with silver fox, and a little cherry-red brimless hat with folded-back net that might get by in Brewer but appears quaint here, among the cowboys and the slim kids of indeterminate sex with their cropped hair dyed punk-style in pastel feathers and the black chicks whose hair is frizzed up in structures like three-dimensional Mickey Mouse ears. Hugging her, Rabbit feels how small the old lady, once the terror of his young manhood, has become. Her former look of having been stuffed tight with Koerner pride and potential indignation has fled, leaving her skin collapsed in random folds and bloodless. Deep liverish gouges underscore her eyes, and her wattled throat seems an atrocious wreck of flesh.

She can hardly wait to speak, backing a step away to give her voice room to make its impact. "The baby came last night. A girl, seven pounds and some. I couldn't sleep a wink, after getting her to the hospital and then waiting for the doctor to call." Her voice is shaky with blame. The airport Muzak, a tune being plucked on the strings of many coördinated violins, accompanies her announcement in such triumphant rhythm that Harry and Janice have to suppress smiles, not even daring to step closer in the jostle and shuffle, the old lady is so childishly, precariously intent on the message she means to deliver. "And then all the way down on the Turnpike, trucks kept tooting their horns at me, tooting these big foghorns they have. As if there were someplace else I could go; I couldn't drive the Chrysler off the *road*," Bessie says. "And after Conshohocken, on the Expressway, it's really a wonder I wasn't killed. I never saw so much traffic, though I thought at noon it would be letting up, and you know the signs, they aren't at all clear even if you have good eyes. All the way along the river I kept praying to Fred and I honestly believe it was him that got me here, I couldn't have done it alone."

And, her manner plainly implies, she will never attempt anything like it again; Janice and Harry find her at the terminus of the last great effort of her life. Henceforth, she is in their hands.

V

YET MA SPRINGER wasn't so totally thrown by events that she didn't have the wit to call up Charlie Stavros and have him come back to the lot. His own mother took a turn for the worse in December – her whole left side feels numb, so even with a cane it frightens her to walk – and as Charlie predicted his cousin Gloria went back to Norristown and her husband, though Charlie wouldn't give it a year; so he has been pretty well tied down. This time it's Harry who's come back with a tan. He gives Charlie a two-handed handclasp, he's so happy to see him at Springer Motors again. The Greek sales rep doesn't look that hot, how-ever: those trips to Florida were like a paint job. He looks pale. He looks as if you pricked his skin he'd bleed gray. He stands hunched over protecting his chest like he'd smoked three packs a day all his life, though Charlie like most Mediterranean types has never really had the self-destructive habits you see in northern Europeans and Negroes. Harry wouldn't have given him such an all-out handshake this way a week ago, but since fucking Thelma up the ass he's felt freer, more in love with the world again.

"The old *mastoras*. You look great," he exuberantly lies to Charlie.

"I've felt better," Charlie tells him. "Thank God it hasn't been any kind of a winter so far." Harry can see, through the plate-glass window, a snowless, leafless landscape, the dust of all seasons swirling and drifting, intermixed with the paper refuse from the Chuck Wagon that has blown across Route 111. A new banner is up: THE ERA OF COROLLA. *Toyota = Total Economy*. Charlie vol-unteers, "It's pretty damn depressing, watching *Manna mou* head straight downhill. She gets out of bed just to go to the bathroom and keeps telling me I ought to get married."

"Good advice, maybe."

"Well, I made a little move on Gloria in that direction, and it may be what scared her back to her husband. That guy, what a shit. She'll be back."

"Wasn't she a cousin?"

"All the better. Peppy type. About four eleven, little heavy in the rumble seat, not quite classy enough for you, champ. But cute. You should see her dance. I hadn't been to those Hellenic Society Saturday nights for years, she talked me into it. I loved to watch her sweat."

"You say she'll be back."

"Yeah but not for me. I've missed that boat." He adds, "I've missed a lot of boats."

"Who hasn't?"

Charlie rolls a toothpick in the center of his lower lip. Harry doesn't like to look at him closely; he's become one of those old Brewer geezers who go into cigar stores to put ten dollars on the numbers and hang around the magazine racks waiting for a conversation. "You've caught a few," he ventures to tell Harry.

"No, listen. Charlie. I'm in rotten shape. A kid who's disappeared and a new house with no furniture in it." Yet these facts, species of emptiness and new possibility, excite and please him more than not.

"The kid'll turn up," Charlie says. "He's just letting off steam."

"That's what Pru says. You never saw anybody so calm, considering. We went up to the hospital last night after getting in from the islands and, Jesus, is she happy about that baby. You'd think she was the first woman in the history of the world to pull this off. I guess she was worried about the kid being normal, after that fall she took a while ago."

"Worried about herself, more likely. Girl like that who's been knocked around a lot by life, having a baby's the one way they can prove to themselves they're human. What're they thinking of calling it?"

"She doesn't want to call it after her mother, she wants to name it after Ma. Rebecca. But she wants to wait to hear from Nelson, because, you know, that was his sister's name. The infant that, you know, didn't make it."

"Yeah." Charlie understands. Inviting bad luck. The sound of Mildred Kroust's typewriter bridges their silence. In the shop one of Manny's men is pounding an uncoöperative piece of metal. Charlie asks, "What're you going to do about the house?"

"Move in, Janice says. She surprised me, the way she talked to her mother. Right in the car driving home. She told her she was welcome to move in with us but she didn't see why she couldn't have a house of her own like other women her age and since Pru and the baby were obviously going to have to stay she doesn't want her to feel crowded in her own home. Bessie, that is."

"Huh. About time Jan stood on her own two feet. Wonder who she's been talking to?"

Webb Murkett, it occurs to Harry, through a tropical night of love; but things always work best between him and Charlie when they don't go too deep into Janice. He says, "The trouble with having the house is we have no furniture of our own. And everything costs a fucking fortune. A simple mattress and box spring and steel frame to set it on for six hundred dollars; if you add a headboard that's another six hundred. Carpets! Three, four thousand for a little Oriental, and they all come out of Iran and Afghanistan. The salesman was telling me they're a better investment than gold."

"Gold's doing pretty well," Charlie says.

"Better than we are, huh? Have you had a chance to look at the books?"

"They've looked better," Charlie admits. "But nothing a little more inflation won't cure. Young couple came in here Tuesday, the first day I got the call from Bessie, and bought a Corvette convertible Nelson had laid in. Said they wanted a convertible and thought the dead of winter would be a good time to buy one. No trade-in, weren't interested in financing, paid for it with a check, a regular checking account. Where do they get the money? Neither one of 'em could have been more than twenty-five. Next day, yesterday, kid came in here in a GMC pick-up and said he'd heard we had a snowmobile for sale. It took us a while to find it out back but when we did he got that light in his eyes so I began by asking twelve hundred and we settled at nine seventy-five. I said to him, There isn't any snow, and he said, That's all right, he was moving up to Vermont, to wait out the nuclear holocaust. Said Three-Mile Island really blew his mind. D'y'ever notice how Carter can't say 'nuclear'? He says 'nookier.' "

"You really got rid of that snowmobile? I can't believe it."

"People don't care about economizing anymore. Big Oil has sold capitalism down the river. What the czar did for the Russians, Big Oil is doing for us."

Harry can't take the time to talk economics today. He apologizes, "Charlie, I'm still on vacation in theory, to the end of the week, and Janice is meeting me downtown, we got a thousand things to do in connection with this damn house of hers."

Charlie nods. "Amscray. I got some sorting out to do myself. One thing nobody could accuse Nelson of is being a neatness freak." He shouts after Harry as he goes into the corridor for his hat and coat, "Say hello to Grandma for me!"

Meaning Janice, Harry slowly realizes.

He ducks into his office, where the new 1980 company calendar with its photo of Fujiyama hangs on the wall. He makes a mental note to himself, not for the first time, to do something about those old clippings that hang outside on the pressed-board partition, they're getting too yellow, there's a process he's heard about where they photograph old halftones so they look white as new, and can be blown up to any size. Might as well blow them up big, it's a business expense. He takes from old man Springer's heavy oak coat-rack with its four little bow legs the sheepskin overcoat Janice got him for Christmas and the little narrow-brim suede hat that goes with it. At his age you wear a hat. He went all through last winter without a cold, because he had taken to wearing a hat. And vitamin C helps. Next it'll be Geritol. He hopes he didn't cut Charlie short but he found talking to him today a little depressing, the guy is at a dead end and turning cranky. Big Oil doesn't know any more what's up than Little Oil. But then from Harry's altitude at this moment anyone might look small and cranky. He has taken off; he is flying high, on his way to an island in his life. He takes a tube of Life Savers (Butter Rum) from his top lefthand desk drawer, to sweeten his breath in case he's kissed, and lets himself out through the back of the shop. He is careful with the crash bar: a touch of grease on this sheepskin and there's no getting it off.

* * *

Nelson having stolen his Corona, Harry has allocated to himself a grape-blue Celica Supra, the "ultimate Toyota," with padded dash, electric tachometer, state-of-the-art four-speaker solid-state AM/FM/MPX stereo, quartz-accurate digital clock, automatic overdrive transmission, cruise control, computer-tuned suspension, ten-inch disc brakes on all four wheels, and quartz halogen hi-beam headlights. He loves this smooth machine. The Corona for all its dependable qualities was a stodgy little bug, whereas this blue buzzard has charisma. The blacks along lower Weiser really stared yesterday afternoon when he drove it home. After Janice and he had brought Ma back to 89 Joseph in the Chrysler (which in fact even Harry found not so easy to steer, after a week of being driven in taxis on the wrong side of the road), they put her to bed and came into town in the Mustang, Janice all hyper after her standing up for herself about the house, to Schaechner Furniture, where they looked at beds and ugly easy chairs and Parsons tables like the Murketts had, only not so nice as theirs, the wood grain not checkerboarded. They couldn't make any decisions; when the store was about to close she drove him over to the lot so he could have a car too. He picked this model priced in five digits. Blacks stared out from under the neon signs, JIMBO's *Friendly* LOUNGE and LIVE ENTERTAINMENT and ADULT ADULT ADULT, as he slid by in virgin blue grapeskin; he was afraid some of them lounging in the cold might come running out at a stoplight and scratch his hood with a screwdriver or smash his windshield with a hammer, taking vengeance for their lives. On a number of walls now in this part of town you can see spray-painted SKEETER LIVES, but they don't say where.

He has lied to Charlie. He doesn't have to meet Janice until one-thirty and it is now only 11:17 by the Supra's quartz clock. He is driving to Galilee. He turns on the radio and its sound is even punkier, richer, more many-leaved and many-layered, than that of the radio in the old Corona. Though he moves the dial from left to right and back again he can't find Donna Summer, she went out with the Seventies. Instead there is a guy singing hymns, squeezing the word "Jesus" until it drips. And that kind of mellow mixed-voice backup he remembers from the records when

he was in high school: the jukeboxes where you could see the
record fall and that waxy rustling cloth, organdy or whatever, the
girls went to dances in, wearing the corsage you gave them. The
corsage would get crushed as the dancing got closer and the girls'
perfumes would be released from between their powdery breasts
as their bodies were warmed and pressed by partner after partner,
in the violet light of the darkened gym, crêpe-paper streamers
drooping overhead and the basketball hoops wreathed with paper
flowers, all those warm bodies softly bumping in anticipation of
the cold air stored in cars outside, the little glowing dashboard
lights, the body heat misting the inside of the windshield, the
organdy tugged and mussed, chilly fingers fumbling through coats
and pants and underpants, clothes become a series of tunnels, Mary
Ann's body nestling toward his hands, the space between her legs
so different and mild and fragrant and safe, a world apart. And
now, the news, on the half hour. That wise-voiced young woman
is long gone from this local station, Harry wonders where she is
by now, doing go-go or assistant vice-president at Sunflower
Beer. The new announcer sounds like Billy Fosnacht, fat-lipped.
President Carter has revealed that he personally favors a boycott
of the 1980 Moscow Olympics. Reaction from athletes is mixed.
Indian Prime Minister Indira Gandhi has backed off from yesterday's apparently pro-Soviet stance on Afghanistan. On the
crowded campaign trail, U.S. Representative Philip Crane of
Illinois has labelled as "foolish" Massachusetts Senator Edward
Kennedy's proposal that the Seabrook, New Hampshire, proposed nuclear plant be converted to coal. In Japan, former Beatle
Paul McCartney was jailed on charges of possessing eight ounces
of marijuana. In Switzerland, scientists have succeeded in pro-
gramming bacteria to manufacture the scarce human protein
interferon, an anti-viral agent whose artificial production may
usher in an era as beneficial to mankind as the discovery of peni-
cillin. Meanwhile, if the fillings in your teeth cost more, it's
because the price of gold hit eight hundred dollars an ounce in
New York City today. Fuck. He sold too soon. Eight hundred
times thirty equals twenty-four thousand, that's up nearly ten
grand from fourteen six, if he'd just held on, damn that Webb
Murkett and his silver. And the 76ers continue their winning

ways, 121 to 110 over the Portland Trail Blazers at the Spectrum last night. Poor old Eagles out of their misery, Jaworski went down flinging. And now, to continue our program of Nice Music for Nice Folks, the traditional melody "Savior, Keep a Watch Over Me." Harry turns it off, driving to the purr of the Supra.

He knows the way now. Past the giant Amishman pointing to the natural cave, through the narrow town with its Purina feed-store sign and old inn and new bank and hitching posts and trac-tor agency. The corn stubble of the fields sticks up pale, all the gold bleached from it. The duck pond has frozen edges but a wide center of black water, so mild has the winter been. He slows past the Blankenbiller and Muth mailboxes, and turns down the driveway where the box says BYER. His nerves are stretched so nothing escapes his vision, the jutting stones of the two beaten reddish tracks that make the old road, the fringe of dried weeds each still bearing the form its green life assumed in the vanished summer, the peeling pumpkin-colored school bus husk, a rusting harrow, a small springhouse whitewashed years ago, and then the shabby farm buildings, corn crib and barn and stone house, approached from a new angle, for the first time from the front. He drives the Celica into the space of packed dirt where he once saw the Corolla pull in; in turning off the engine and stepping from the car he sees the ridge from which he spied, a far scratchy line of black cherry and gum trees scarcely visible through the apple trees of the orchard, farther away than it had felt, the odds were no one had ever seen him. This is crazy. Run.

But, as with dying, there is a moment that must be pushed through, a slice of time more transparent than plate glass; it is in front of him and he takes the step, drawing heart from that loving void Thelma had confided to him. In his sheepskin coat and silly small elf hat and three-piece suit of pinstriped wool bought just this November at that tailor of Webb's on Pine Street, he walks across the earth where silted-over flat sandstones once formed a walk. It is cold, a day that might bring snow, a day that feels hollow. Though it is near noon no sun shows through, not even a silver patch betrays its place in the sky, one long ribbed under-belly of low gray clouds. A drab tall thatch of winter woods rears up on his right. In the other direction, beyond the horizon, a chain saw sounds stuck. Even before, removing one glove, he raps with a bare hand on the door, where paint a poisonous green is coming loose in long curving flakes, the dog inside the house hears his footsteps scrape stone and sets up a commotion of barking.

Harry hopes the dog is alone, its owner out. There is no car or pick-up truck in the open, but one might be parked in the barn or the newish garage of cement blocks with a roof of corrugated overlapped Fiberglas. Inside the house no light burns that he can see, but then it is near noon, though the day is dull and growing darker. He peers in the door and sees himself reflected with his pale hat in another door, much like this one, with two tall panes of glass, the thickness of a stone wall away. Beyond the old panes a hallway with a tattered striped runner recedes into unlit depths. As his eyes strain to see deeper his nose and ungloved hand sting with the cold. He is about to turn away and return to the warm car when a shape materializes within the house and rushes, puffed up with rage, toward him. The black-haired collie leaps and leaps again against the inner door, frantic, trying to bite the glass, those ugly little front teeth a dog has, inhuman, and the split black lip and lavender gums, unclean. Harry is paralyzed with fascination; he does not see the great shape materialize behind Fritzie until a hand clatters on the inner door latch.

The fat woman's other hand holds the dog by the collar; Harry helps by opening the green outer door himself. Fritzie recognizes his scent and stops barking. And Rabbit recognizes, buried under the wrinkles and fat but with those known eyes blazing out alive, Ruth. So amid a tumult of wagging and the whimpers of that desperate doggy need to reclaim a friend, the two old lovers confront one another. Twenty years ago he had lived with this woman, March to June. He saw her for a minute in Kroll's eight years later, and she had spared him a few bitter words, and now a dozen years have poured across them both, doing their damage. Her hair that used to be a kind of dirty fiery gingery color is flattened now to an iron gray and pulled back in a bun like the Mennonites wear. She wears wide denim dungarees and a man's red lumberjack shirt beneath a black sweater with unravelled elbows and dog hairs and wood chips caught in the greasy weave. Yet this is Ruth. Her upper lip still pushes out a little, as if with an incipient blister, and

her flat blue eyes in their square sockets still gaze at him with a
hostility that tickles him. "What do you want?" she asks. Her
voice sounds thickened, as by a cold.

"I'm Harry Angstrom."

"I can see that. What do you want here?"

"I was wondering, could we talk a little? There's something
I need to ask you."

"No, we can't talk a little. Go away."

But she has released the dog's collar, and Fritzie sniffs at his
ankles and his crotch and writhes in her urge to jump up, to impart
the scarcely bearable joy locked in her narrow skull, behind her
bulging eyes. Her bad eye still looks sore. "Good Fritzie," Harry
says. "Down. Down."

Ruth has to laugh, that quick ringing laugh of hers, like change
tossed onto a counter. "Rabbit, you're cute. Where'd you learn
her name?"

"I heard you all calling her once. A couple times I've been here,
up behind those trees, but I couldn't get up my nerve to come any
closer. Stupid, huh?"

She laughs again, a touch less ringingly, as if she is truly amused.
Though her voice has roughened and her bulk has doubled and
there is a down including a few dark hairs along her cheeks and
above the corners of her mouth, this is really Ruth, a cloud his life
had passed through, solid again. She is still tall, compared to Janice,
compared to any of the women of his life but Mim and his mother.
She always had a weight about her; she joked the first night when
he lifted her that this would put him out of action, a weight that
pushed him off, along with something that held him fast, an air of
being willing to play, in the little space they had, and though the
time they had was short. "So you were scared of us," she says. She
bends slightly, to address the dog. "Fritzie, shall we let him in for
a minute?" The dog's liking him, a dim spark of dog memory
setting her tail wagging, has tipped the balance.

The hall inside smells decidedly of the past, the way these old
farm houses do. Apples in the cellar, cinnamon in the cooking, a
melding of the old plaster and wallpaper paste, he doesn't know.
Muddy boots stand in a corner of the hall, on newspapers spread
there, and he notices that Ruth is in stocking feet — thick gray

men's work socks, but sexy nonetheless, the silence of her steps, though she is huge. She leads him to the right, into a small front parlor with an oval rug of braided rags on the floor and a folding wooden lawn chair mixed in with the other furniture. The only modern piece is the television set, its overbearing rectangular eye dead for the moment. A small wood fire smolders in a sandstone fireplace. Harry checks his shoes before stepping onto the rag rug, to make sure he is not tracking in dirt. He removes his fancy little sheepskin hat.

As if regretting this already, Ruth sits on the very edge of her chair, a cane-bottomed rocker, tipping it forward so her knees nearly touch the floor and her arm can reach down easily to scratch Fritzie's neck and keep her calm. Harry guesses he is supposed to sit opposite, on a cracked black leather settee beneath two depressing sepia studio portraits, a century old at least they must be, in matching carved frames, of a bearded type and his buttoned-up wife, both long turned to dust in their coffins. But before sitting down he sees across the room, by the light of a window whose deep sill teems with potted African violets and those broad-leafed plants people give for Mother's Days, a more contemporary set of photographs, color snapshots that line one shelf of a bookcase holding rows of the paperback mysteries and romances Ruth used to read and apparently still does. That used to hurt him about her in those months, how she would withdraw into one of those trashy thrillers set in England or Los Angeles though he was right there, in the flesh, a living lover. He crosses to the bookcase and sees her, younger but already stout, standing before a corner of this house within the arm of a man older, taller, and stouter than she: this must have been Byer. A big sheepish farmer in awkward Sunday clothes, squinting against the sunlight with an expression like that of the large old portraits, his mouth wistful in its attempt to satisfy the camera. Ruth looks amused, her hair up in a bouffant do and still gingery, amused that for this sheltering man she is a prize. Rabbit feels, for an instant as short and bright as the click of a shutter, jealous of these lives that others led: this stout plain country couple posing by a chipped corner of brown stucco, on earth that from the greening state of the grass suggests March or April. Nature's old tricks. There are other photographs, color prints of combed and smiling adolescents, in those cardboard frames high-school pictures come in. Before he can examine them, Ruth says sharply, "Who said you could look at those? Stop it."

"It's your family."

"You bet it is. Mine and not yours."

But he cannot tear himself away from the images in flashlit color of these children. They gaze not at him but past his right ear, each posed identically by the photographer as he worked his school circuit May after May. A boy and the girl at about the same age – the senior photo – and then in smaller format a younger boy with darker hair, cut longer and parted on the other side of his head from his brother. All have blue eyes. "Two boys and a girl," Harry says. "Who's the oldest?"

"What the hell do you care? God, I'd forgotten what a pushy obnoxious bastard you are. Stuck on yourself from cradle to grave."

"My guess is, the girl is the oldest. When did you have her, and when did you marry this old guy? How can you stand it, by the way, out here in the boondocks?"

"I stand it fine. It's more than anybody else ever offered me."

"I didn't have much to offer anybody in those days."

"But you've done fine since. You're dressed up like a pansy."

"And you're dressed up like a ditchdigger."

"I've been cutting wood."

"You operate one of those chain saws? Jesus, aren't you afraid you'll cut off a finger?"

"No, I'm not. The car you sold Jamie works fine, if that's what you came to ask."

"How long have you known I've been at Springer Motors?"

"Oh, always. And then it was in the papers when Springer died."

"Was that you drove past in the old station wagon the day Nelson got married?"

"It might have been," Ruth says, sitting back in her rocking chair, so it tips the other way. Fritzie has stretched out to sleep. The wood fire spits. "We pass through Mt. Judge from time to time. It's a free country still, isn't it?"

"Why would you do a crazy thing like that?" She loves him.

"I'm not saying I did anything. How would I know Nelson was getting married at that moment?"

"You saw it in the papers." He sees she means to torment him. "Ruth, the girl. She's mine. She's the baby you said you couldn't stand to have the abortion for. So you had it and then found this old chump of a farmer who was glad to get a piece of young ass and had these other two kids by him before he kicked the bucket."

"Don't talk so rude. You're not proving anything to me except what a sad case I must have been ever to take you in. You are Mr. Bad News, honest to God. You're nothing but me, me and gimme, gimme. When I *had* something to give you I gave it even though I knew I'd never get anything back. Now thank God I have nothing to give." She limply gestures to indicate the raggedly furnished little room. Her voice in these years has gained that country slowness, that stubborn calm with which the country withholds what the city wants.

"Tell me the truth," he begs.

"I just did."

"About the girl."

"She's younger than the older boy. Scott, Annabelle, and then Morris in '66. He was the afterthought. June 6, 1966. Four sixes."

"Don't stall, Ruth, I got to get back to Brewer. And don't lie. Your eyes get all watery when you lie."

"My eyes are watery because they can't stand looking at you. A regular Brewer sharpie. A dealer. The kind of person you used to hate, remember? And fat. At least when I knew you you had a body."

He laughs, enjoying the push of this; his night with Thelma has made his body harder to insult. "*You*," he says, "are calling *me* fat?"

"I am. And how did you get so red in the face?"

"That's my tan. We just got back from the islands."

"Oh Christ, the islands. I thought you were about to have a stroke."

"When did your old guy pack it in? Whajja do, screw him to death?"

She stares at him a time. "You better go."

"Soon," he promises.

"Frank passed away in August of '76, of cancer. Of the colon. He hadn't even reached retirement age. When I met him he was younger than we are now."

"O.K., sorry. Listen, stop making me be such a prick. Tell me about our girl."

"She's *not* our girl, Harry. I *did* have the abortion. My parents arranged it with a doctor in Pottsville. He did it right in his office and about a year later a girl died afterwards of complications and they put him in jail. Now the girls just walk into the hospital."

"And expect the taxpayer to pay," Harry says.

"Then I got a job as the day cook in a restaurant over toward Stogey's Quarry to the east of here and Frank's cousin was the hostess for that time and one thing led to another pretty fast. We had Scott in late 1960, he just turned nineteen last month, one of these Christmas babies that always get cheated on presents."

"Then the girl when? Annabelle."

"The next year. He was in a hurry for a family. His mother had never let him marry while she was alive, or anyway he blamed her."

"You're lying. I've seen the girl; she's older than you say."

"She's eighteen. Do you want to see birth certificates?"

This must be a bluff. But he says, "No."

Her voice softens. "Why're you so hepped on the girl anyway? Why don't you pretend the boy's yours?"

"I have one boy. He's enough" – the phrase just comes – "bad news." He asks, brusquely, "And where *are* they? Your boys."

"What's it to you?"

"Nothing much. I was just wondering how come they're not around, helping you with this place."

"Morris is at school, he gets home on the bus after three. Scott has a job in Maryland, working in a plant nursery. I told both him and Annie, Get out. This was a good place for me to come to and hide, but there's nothing here for young people. When she and Jamie Nunemacher got this scheme of going and living together in Brewer, I couldn't say No, though his people were dead set against it. We had a big conference, I told them that's how young people do now, they live together, and aren't they smart? They know I'm an old whore anyway, I don't give a fuck what they think. The neighbors always let us alone and we let them alone. Frank and old Blankenbiller hadn't talked for fifteen years, since he began to take me out." She sees she has wandered, and says, "Annabelle won't be with the boy forever. He's nice enough, but . . ."

"I agree," Rabbit says, as if consulted. Ruth is lonely, he sees, and willing to talk, and this makes him uneasy. He shifts his weight on the old black sofa. Its springs creak. A shift in the air outside has created a downdraft that sends smoke from the damp fire curling into the room.

She glances to the dead couple in their frames like carved coffins above his head and confides, "Even when Frank was healthy, he had to have the buses to make ends meet. Now I rent the big fields and just try to keep the bushes down. The bushes and the oil bills." And it is true, this room is so cold he has not thought of taking his heavy coat off.

"Yes well," he sighs. "It's hard." Fritzie, wakened by some turn in the dream that had been twitching the ends of her paws, stands and skulks over to him as if to bark, and instead drops down to the rug again, coiling herself trustfully at his feet. With his long arm Harry reaches to the bookcase and lifts out the photograph of the daughter. Ruth does not protest. He studies the pale illumined face in its frame of maroon cardboard: backed by a strange background of streaked blue like an imitation sky, the girl gazes beyond him. Round and polished like a fruit by the slick silk finish of the print, the head, instead of revealing its secret, becomes more enigmatic, a shape as strange as those forms of sea life spotlit beneath the casino boardwalk. The mouth is Ruth's, that upper lip he noticed at the lot. And around the eyes, that squared-off look, though her brow is rounder than Ruth's and her hair, brushed to a photogenic gloss, less stubborn. He looks at the ear, for a nick in the edge like Nelson has; her hair would have to be lifted. Her nose is so delicate and small, the nostrils displayed by a slight upturn of the tip, that the lower half of her face seems heavy, still babyish. There is a candor to her skin and a frosty light to the eyes that could go back to those Swedes in their world of snow; he glimpsed it in the Murketts' bathroom mirror. His blood. Harry finds himself reliving with Annabelle that moment when her turn came in the unruly school line to enter the curtained corner of the gym and, suddenly blinded, to pose for posterity, for the yearbook, for boyfriend and mother, for time itself as it wheels on unheeding by: the opportunity come to press your face up against blankness and, by thinking right thoughts, to become a star. "She looks like me."

Ruth laughs now. "You're seeing things."

"No kidding. When she came to the lot that first time, something hit me – her legs, maybe, I don't know. Those aren't your legs." Which had been thick, twisting like white flame as she moved naked about their room.

"Well, Frank had legs too. Until he let himself get out of shape, he was on the lanky side. Over six foot, when he straightened up, I'm a sucker for the big ones I guess. Then neither of the boys inherited his height."

"Yeah, Nelson didn't get mine, either. A shrimp just like his mother."

"You're still with Janice. You used to call her a mutt," Ruth reminds him. She has settled into this situation comfortably now, leaning back in the rocker and rocking, her stocking feet going up on tiptoe, then down on the heels, then back on tiptoe. "Why am I telling you all about my life when you don't say a thing about yours?"

"It's pretty standard," he says. "Don't be sore at me because I stayed with Janice."

"Oh Christ no. I just feel sorry for her."

"A sister," he says, smiling. Women are all sisters, they tell us now.

Fat has been added to Ruth's face not in smooth scoops but in lumps, so when she lifts her head her eye sockets seem built of bony welts. A certain forgiving mischief has lifted her armored glance. "Annie was fascinated by you," she volunteers. "She several times asked me if I'd ever heard of you, this basketball hero. I said we went to different high schools. She was disappointed when you weren't there when she and Jamie went back to pick up the car finally. Jamie had been leaning to a Fiesta."

"So you don't think Jamie is the answer for her?"

"For now. But you've seen him. He's common."

"I hope she doesn't –"

"Go my way? No, it'll be all right. There aren't whores any-more, just healthy young women. I've raised her very innocent. I always felt *I* was very innocent, actually."

"We all are, Ruth."

She likes his saying her name, he should be careful about say-ing it. He puts the photograph back and studies it in place, Annabelle between her brothers. "How about money?" he asks, trying to keep it light. "Would some help her? I could give it to you so it, you know, wouldn't come out of the blue or anything. If she wants an education, for instance." He is blushing, and Ruth's silence doesn't help. The rocker has stopped rocking.

At last she says, "I guess this is what they call deferred payments."

"It's not for you, it would be for her. I can't give a lot. I mean, I'm not that rich. But if a couple thousand would make a differ-ence —"

He lets the sentence hang, expecting to be interrupted. He can't look at her, that strange expanded face. Her voice when it comes has the contemptuous confident huskiness he heard from her ages ago, in bed. "Relax. You don't have to worry, I'm not going to take you up on it. If I ever get really hard up here I can sell off a piece of road frontage, five thousand an acre is what they've been getting locally. Anyway, Rabbit. Believe me. She's not yours."

"O.K., Ruth. If you say so." In his surge of relief he stands.

She stands too, and having risen together their ghosts feel their inflated flesh fall away; the young man and woman who lived illi-citly together one flight up on Summer Street, across from a big limestone church, stand close again, sequestered from the world, and as before the room is hers. "Listen," she hisses up at him, rad-iantly is his impression, her distorted face gleaming. "I wouldn't give you the satisfaction of that girl being yours if there was a mil-lion dollars at stake. I raised her. She and I put in a lot of time together here and where the fuck were you? You saw me in Kroll's that time and there was no follow-up, I've known where you were all these years and you didn't give a simple shit what had happened to me, or my kid, or *any*thing."

"You were married," he says mildly. *My kid*: something odd here.

"You bet I was," she rushes on. "To a better man than you'll ever be, sneer all you want. The kids have had a wonderful father and they know it. When he died we just carried on as if he was still around, he was that strong. Now I don't know what the hell is going on with you in your little life up there in Mt. Judge —"

"We're moving," he tells her. "To Penn Park."

"Swell. That's just where you belong, with those phonies. You should have left that mutt of yours twenty years ago for her good as well as your own, but you didn't and now you can stew in it; stew in it but *leave my Annie alone*. It's *creepy*, Harry. When I think of you thinking she's your daughter it's like rubbing her all over with shit."

He sighs through his nose. "You still have a sweet tongue," he says.

She is embarrassed; her iron hair has gone straggly and she presses it flat with the heels of her hands as if trying to crush something inside her skull. "I shouldn't say something like that but it's *fright*ening, having you show up in your fancy clothes wanting to claim my daughter. You make me think, if I hadn't had the abortion, if I hadn't let my parents have their way, it might have all worked out differently, and we could *have* a daughter now. But you —"

"I know. You did the right thing." He feels her fighting the impulse to touch him, to cling to him, to let herself be crushed into his clumsy arms as once. He looks for a last topic. Awkwardly he asks, "What're you going to do, when Morris grows up and leaves home?" He remembers his hat and picks it up, pinching the soft new crown in three fingers.

"I don't know. Hang on a little more. Whatever happens, land won't go down. Every year I last it out here is money in the bank."

He sighs through his nose again. "O.K., if that's how it is. I'll run then. Really no soap on the girl?"

"Of course not. Think it through. Suppose she *was* yours. At this stage it'd just confuse her."

He blinks. Is this an admission? He says, "I never was too good at thinking things through."

Ruth smiles at the floor. The squarish dent above her cheekbone, seen this way from above, was one of the first things he noticed about her. Chunky and tough but kindly, somehow. Another human heart, telling him he was a big bunny, out by the parking meters in the neon light, the first time they met. Trains still ran through the center of Brewer then. "Men don't have to be," she says. "They don't get pregnant."

The dog became agitated when they both stood and Ruth's voice became louder and angry, and now Fritzie leads them from the room and waits, tail inquisitively wagging, with her nose at the crack of the door leading outside. Ruth opens it and the storm door wide enough for the dog to pass through but not Harry. "Want a cup of coffee?" she asks.

He told Janice one o'clock at Schaechner's. "Oh Jesus, thanks, but I ought to get back to work."

"You came here just about Annabelle? You don't want to hear about me?"

"I *have* heard about you, haven't I?"

"Whether I have a boyfriend or not, whether I ever thought about you?"

"Yeah, well, I'm sure that'd be interesting. From the sound of it you've done terrifically. Frank and Morris and, who's the other one?"

"Scott."

"Right. And you have all this land. Sorry, you know, to have left you in such a mess way back then."

"Well," Ruth says, with a considering slowness in which he imagines he can hear her late husband speaking. "I guess we make our own messes."

She seems now not merely fat and gray but baffled: straw on her sweater, hair on her cheeks. A shaggy monster, lonely. He longs to be out that double door into the winter air, where nothing is growing. Once he escaped by telling her, *I'll be right back*, but now there is not even that to say. Both know, what people should never know, that they will not meet again. He notices on the hand of hers that grips the doorknob a thin gold ring all but lost in the flesh of one finger. His heart races, trapped.

She has mercy on him. "Take care, Rabbit," she says. "I was just kidding about the outfit, you look good." Harry ducks his head as if to kiss her cheek but she says, "No." By the time he has taken a step off the concrete porch, her shadow has vanished from the double door's black glass. The gray of the day has intensified, releasing a few dry flakes of snow that will not amount to anything, that float sideways like flecks of ash. Fritzie trots beside him to the glossy grape-blue Celica, and has to be discouraged from jumping into the back seat.

Once on his way, out the driveway and past the mailboxes that say BLANKENBILLER and MUTH, Harry pops a Life Saver into his mouth and wonders if he should have called her bluff on the birth certificates. Or suppose Frank had had another wife, and Scott was his child by that marriage? If the girl was as young as Ruth said, wouldn't she still be in high school? But no. Let go. Let it go. God doesn't want him to have a daughter.

Waiting in the overheated front room of Schaechner's surrounded by plush new furniture, Janice looks petite and prosperous and, with her Caribbean tan, younger than forty-three. When he kisses her, on the lips, she says, "Mmm. Butter Rum. What are you hiding?"

"Onions for lunch."

She dips her nose close to his lapel. "You smell of smoke."

"Uh, Manny gave me a cigar."

She hardly listens to his lies, she is breathy and electric with news of her own. "Harry, Melanie called Mother from Ohio. Nelson is with her. Everything's all right."

As Janice continues, he can see her mouth move, her bangs tremble, her eyes widen and narrow, and her fingers tug in excitement at the pearl strand the lapels of her coat disclose, but Rabbit is distracted from the exact sense of what she is saying by remembering, when he bent his face close to old Ruth's in the light of the door, a glitter there, on the tired skin beneath her eyes, and by the idiotic thought, which it seems he should bottle and sell, that our tears are always young, the saltwater stays the same from cradle, as she said, to grave.

The little stone house that Harry and Janice bought for $78,000, with $15,600 down, sits on a quarter-acre of bushy land

tucked in off a macadamized dead end behind two larger examples
of what is locally known as Penn Park Pretentious: a tall mock-
Tudor with gables like spires and red-tiled roofs and clinker bricks
sticking out at crazy melted angles, and a sort of neo-plantation
manse of serene thin bricks the pale yellow of lemonade, with a
glassed-in sunporch and on the other side a row of Palladian windows, where Harry guesses the dining room is. He has been out
surveying his property, looking for a sunny patch where a garden
might be dug in this spring. The spot behind Ma Springer's house
on Joseph Street had been too shady. He finds a corner that might
do, with some cutting back of oak limbs that belong to his neighbor. The earth generally in this overgrown, mature suburb is well-
shaded; his lawn is half moss, which this mild winter has dried but
left exposed and resilient still. He also finds a little cement fish pond
with a blue-painted bottom, dry and drifted with pine needles.
Someone had once sunk seashells in the wet cement of the slanting rim. The things you buy when you buy a house. Doorknobs,
windowsills, radiators. All his. If he were a fish he could swim in
this pond, come spring. He tries to picture that moment when
whoever it was, man, woman, or child or all three, had set these
shells here, in the summer shade of trees a little less tall than these
above him now. The weak winter light falls everywhere in his yard,
webbed by the shadows from leafless twigs. He senses standing here
a silt of caring that has fallen from purchaser to purchaser. The
house was built in that depressed but scrupulous decade when
Harry was born. Suave gray limestone had been hauled from the
quarries in the far north of Diamond County and dressed and fitted
by men who took the time to do it right. At a later date, after the
war, some owner broke through the wall facing away from the curb
and built an addition of clapboards and white-blotched brick. Paint
is peeling from the clapboards beneath the Andersen windows of
what is now Janice's kitchen. Harry makes a mental note to trim
back the branches that brush against the house, to cut down the
dampness. Indeed there are several trees here that might be turned
altogether into firewood, but until they leaf out in the spring he
can't be sure which should go. The house has two fireplaces, one
in the big long living room and the other, off the same flue, in the
little room behind, that Harry thinks of as a den. His den.

He and Janice moved in yesterday, a Saturday. Pru was coming home from the hospital with the baby and if they were not there she could take their Joseph Street bedroom, with its own bathroom, away from the street. Also they thought the confusion might mask for Janice's mother the pain of their escape. Webb Murkett and the others got back from the Caribbean Thursday night as planned, and Saturday morning Webb brought one of his roofer's trucks with extension ladders roped to both sides and helped them move. Ronnie Harrison, that fink, said he had to go into the office to tackle the backlog of paperwork that had built up during his vacation; he had worked Friday night to midnight. But Buddy Inglefinger came over with Webb, and it didn't take the three men more than two hours to move the Angstroms. There wasn't much furniture they could call their own, mostly clothes, and Janice's mahogany bureau, and some cardboard boxes of kitchen equipment that had been salvaged when the previous house they could call their own had burned down in 1969. All of Nelson's stuff, they left. One of the butch women came out onto her porch and waved goodbye; so news travels in a neighborhood, even when the people aren't friendly. Harry had always meant to ask them what it was like, and why. He can see not liking men, he doesn't like them much himself, but why would you like women any better, if you were one? Especially women who hammer all the time, just like men.

From Schaechner's on Thursday afternoon he and Janice had bought, and got them to deliver on Friday, a new color Sony TV (Rabbit hates to put any more money into Japanese pockets but he knows from *Consumer Reports* that in this particular line they can't be touched for quality) and a pair of big padded silvery-pink wing chairs (he has always wanted a wing chair, he hates drafts on his neck, people have died from drafts on their necks) and a Queen-size mattress and box springs on a metal frame, without headboard. This bed he and Webb and Buddy carry upstairs to the room at the back, with a partially slanted ceiling but space for a mirror if they want it on the blank wall next to the closet door, and the chairs and TV go not into the living room, which is too big to think about furnishing at first, but into the much cozier room just off it, the den. Always he has wanted a den, a room where people would have trouble getting at him. What he especially loves about this little room, besides the fireplace and the built-in shelves where you could keep either books or Ma's knickknacks and china when she dies, with liquor in the cabinets below, and even room for a little refrigerator when they get around to it, are the wall-to-wall carpeting of a kind of green-and-orange mix that reminds him of cheerleaders' tassels and the little high windows whose sashes crank open and shut and are composed of leaded lozenge-panes such as you see in books of fairy tales. He thinks in this room he might begin to read books, instead of just magazines and newspapers, and begin to learn about history, say. You have to step down into the den, one step down from the hardwood floor of the living room, and this small difference in plane hints to him of many reforms and consolidations now possible in his life, like new shoots on a tree cropped back.

Franklin Drive is the elegant street their dead-end spur cuts off of; 14½ Franklin Drive is their postal address, and the spur itself has no street name, they should call it Angstrom Way. Webb suggested Angstrom Alley, but Harry has had enough of alleys in his Mt. Judge years, and resents Webb's saying this. First he tells you to sell gold too soon, then he fucks your wife, and now he puts your house down. Harry has never lived at so low a number as 14½ before. But the mailman in his little red, white, and blue jeep knows where they are. Already they've received mail here: flyers to RESIDENT collected while they were in the Caribbean, and Saturday around one-thirty, after Webb and Buddy were gone, while Janice and Harry in the kitchen were arranging spoons and pans they'd forgotten they owned, the letter slot clacked and a postcard and a white envelope lay on the front hall's bare floor. The envelope, one of the long plain stamped ones you buy at the post office, had no return address and was postmarked Brewer. It was addressed to just MR. HARRY ANGSTROM in the same slanting block printing that had sent him last April the clipping about Skeeter. Inside this new envelope the clipping was very small, and the same precise hand that had addressed it had schoolteacherishly inscribed in ballpoint along the top edge, *From "Golf Magazine"* *Annual "Roundup."* The item read:

A COSTLY BIRDIE
Dr. Sherman Thomas cooked his
own goose when he killed one of
the Canadian variety at Congres-
sional CC. The court levied a
$500 fine for the act.

Janice forced a laugh, reading at his side, there in the echoing
bare hallway, that led through a white arch into the long living
room.

He looked over at her guiltily and agreed with her unspoken
thought. "Thelma."

Her color had risen. A minute before, they had been in sentimental raptures over an old Mixmaster that, plugged in again after
ten years in Ma Springer's attic, had whirred. Now she blurted,
"She'll never let us alone. Never."

"Thelma? Of course she will, that was the deal. She was very
definite about it. Weren't you, with Webb?"

"Oh of course, but words don't mean anything to a woman in
love."

"Who? You with Webb?"

"No, you goon. Thelma. With you."

"She told me, she loves Ronnie. Though I don't see how she
can."

"He's her bread and butter. You're her dream man. You really
turn her on."

"You sound amazed," he said accusingly.

"Oh, you don't *not* turn me on, I can see what she sees, it's
just . . ." She turned away to hide her tears. Everywhere he
looked, women were crying. ". . . . the in*tru*sion. To know that
that was her that sent that other thing way back then, to think of
her watching us all the time, waiting to pounce . . . They're evil
people, Harry. I don't want to see any of them anymore."

"Oh come on." He had to hug her, there in the hollow hall.
He likes it now when she gets all flustered and frowny, her breath
hot and somehow narrow with grief; she seems most his then,
the keystone of his wealth. Once when she got like this, her fear
contaminated him and he ran; but in these middle years it is so
clear to him that he will never run that he can laugh at her, his

stubborn prize. "They're just like us. That was a holiday. In real life they're very square."

Janice was vehement. "I'm *furious* with her, doing such a flirtatious thing, so soon after. They'll never let us alone, never, now that we have a house. As long as we were at Mother's we were protected."

And it was true, the Harrisons and the Murketts and Buddy Inglefinger and the tall new girlfriend with her frizzy hair now up in corn rows and juju beads like the woman in *"10"* did come over last night, the Angstroms' first night in their new house, bearing bottles of champagne and brandy, and stayed until two, so Sunday feels sour and guilty. Harry has no habits yet in this house; without habits and Ma Springer's old furniture to cushion him, his life stretches emptily on all sides, and it seems that moving in any direction he's bound to take a fall.

The other piece of mail that came Saturday, the postcard, was from Nelson.

> Hi Mom & Dad –
>   Spring Semester begins the
> 28th so am in good shape. Need
> certified check for $1087 (397
> instrucional fee, 90 general fee,
> 600 surcharge for non Ohio
> students) plus living expenses.
> $2000–2500 shd. be enuff.
> Will call when you have phone.
> Melanie says Hi. Love, Nelson

On the other side of the card was a modern brick building topped by big slatted things like hot air vents, identified as *Business Administration Building, Kent State University*. Harry asked, "What about Pru? The kid's a father and doesn't seem to know it."

"He knows it. He just can't do everything at once. He's told Pru over the phone he'll drive back as soon as he's registered and look at the baby and leave us the car he took. Though maybe, Harry, we could just let him use it for now."

"That's *my* Corona!"

"He's doing what you wanted him to do, go back to college. Pru understands."

"She understands she's linked up with a hopeless loser," Harry said, but his heart wasn't in it. The kid was no threat to him for now. Harry was king of the castle.

And today is Super Sunday. Janice tries to get him up for church, she is driving Mother, but he is far too hungover and wants to return to the warm pocket of a dream he had been having, a dream involving a girl, a young woman, he has never met before, with darkish hair, they have met somehow at a party and are in a little bathroom together, not speaking but with a rapport, as if just having had sex or about to have sex, between them, sex very certain and casual between them but not exactly happening, the floor of many small square tiles at an angle beneath them, the small space of the bathroom cupped around them like the little chrome bowl around the flame of the perpetual cigar lighter at the old tobacco store downtown, the bliss of a new relationship, he wants it to go on and on but is awake and can't get back. This bedroom, its bright slanted ceiling, is strange. They must get curtains soon. Is Janice up to this? Poor mutt, she's never had to do much. He makes what breakfast he can of a single orange in the nearly empty refrigerator, plus some salted nuts left over from the party last night, plus a cup of instant coffee dissolved with hot water straight from the tap. This house too, like Webb's, has those single-lever faucets shaped like a slender prick stung on the tip by a bee. The refrigerator went with the place and, one of the things that sold him, has an automatic ice-maker that turns out crescent-shaped cubes by the bushel. Even though the old Mixmaster works he hasn't forgotten his promise to Janice to buy her a Cuisinart. Maybe the trouble she has getting meals on the table related to its being Ma Springer's old-fashioned kitchen. He roams through his house warily exulting in the cast-iron radiators, the brass window catches, the classy little octagonal bathroom tiles, and the doors with key-lock knobs; these details of what he has bought shine out in the absence of furniture and will soon sink from view as the days here clutter them over. Now they are naked and pristine.

Upstairs, in a slanting closet off of what once must have been a boys' bedroom – its walls pricked with dozens of thumbtack holes and marred with ends of Scotch tape used to hold posters –

he finds stacks of *Playboys* and *Penthouses* from the early Seventies.
He fetches from out beside the kitchen steps, under the slowly
revolving electric meter, one of the big green plastic trash barrels
he and Janice bought yesterday at Shur Valu; but before disposing
of each magazine Rabbit leafs through it, searching out the center spreads month after month, year after year, as the airbrushing
recedes and the pubic hair first peeks and then froths boldly forth
and these young women perfect as automobile bodies let their
negligees fall open frontally and revolve upon their couches of
leopard skin so subscribers' eyes at last can feast upon their full
shame and treasure. An invisible force month after month through
each year's seasons forces gently wider open their flawless thighs
until somewhere around the bicentennial issues the Constitutional
triumph of open beaver is attained, and the buxom boldly gazing
girls from Texas and Hawaii and South Dakota yield up to the
lights and lens a vertical rosy aperture that seems to stare back, out
of a blood-flushed nether world, scarcely pretty, an ultimate of
disclosure which yet acts as a barrier to some secret beyond,
within, still undisclosed as the winter light diminishes at the silent
window. Outside, a squirrel is watching, its gray back arched, its
black eye alert. Nature, Harry sees, is everywhere. This tree that
comes so close to the house he thinks is a cherry, its bark in rings.
The squirrel, itself spied, scurries on. The full load of magazines
makes the trash barrel almost too heavy to lift. A ton of cunt. He
lugs it downstairs. Janice comes back after two, having had lunch
with her mother and Pru and the baby.

"Everybody seemed cheerful," she reports, "including Baby."

"Baby have a name yet?"

"Pru asked Nelson about Rebecca and he said absolutely not.
Now she's thinking of Judith. That's her mother's name. I told
them to forget Janice, I never much liked it for myself."

"I thought she hated her mother."

"She doesn't hate her, she doesn't much respect her. It's her
father she hates. But he's been on the phone to her a couple of
times and been very, what's the word, conciliatory."

"Oh great. Maybe he can come and help run the lot. He can
do our steam fitting. How does Pru feel about Nelson's running
off, just on the eve?"

Janice takes off her hat, a fuzzy violet loose-knit beret she wears in winter and that makes her look with the sheepskin coat like some brown-faced boy of a little soldier off to the wars. Her hair stands up with static electricity. In the empty living room she has nowhere to drop her hat, and throws it onto a white windowsill. "Well," she says, "she's interesting about it. For just now she says she's just as glad he isn't around, it would be one more thing to cope with. In general she feels it's something he had to do, to get his shit together – that's her expression. I think she knows she pushed him. Once he gets his degree, she thinks, he'll be much more comfortable with himself. She doesn't seem at all worried about losing him for good or anything."

"Huh. Whaddeya have to do to get blamed for something these days?"

"They're very tolerant of each other," Janice says, "and I think that's nice." She heads upstairs, and Harry follows her up, closely, afraid of losing her in the vast newness of their house.

He asks, "She gonna go out there and live with him in an apartment or what?"

"She thinks her going out there with the baby would panic him right now. And of course for Mother it'd be much nicer if she stayed."

"Isn't Pru at all miffed about Melanie?"

"No, she says Melanie will watch after him for her. They don't have this jealousy thing the way we do, if you can believe them."

"If."

"Speaking of which." Janice drops her coat on the bed and bends over, ass high, to unzip her boots. "Thelma had left a message with Mother about whether or not you and I wanted to come over to their house for a light supper and watch the Super Bowl. I guess the Murketts will be there."

"And you said?"

"I said No. Don't worry, I was quite sweet. I said we were having Mother and Pru over here to watch the game on our brand-new Sony. It's true. I invited them." In stocking feet she stands and puts her hands on the hips of her black church suit as if daring him to admit he would rather go out and be with that racy crowd than stay home with his family.

"Fine," he says. "I haven't really seen –"

"Oh, and quite a sad thing. Mother got it from Grace Stuhl, who's good friends apparently with Peggy Fosnacht's aunt. While we were down there Peggy went into her doctor's for a check-up and by nighttime he had her in the hospital and a breast taken off."

"My God." Breast he had sucked. Poor old Peggy. Flicked away by God's fingernail. Life is too big for us, in the end.

"They of course said they got it all but then they always say that."

"She seemed lately headed for something unfortunate."

"She's been grotesque. I should call her, but not today."

Janice is changing into dungarees to do housecleaning. She says the people have left the place filthy but he can't see it, except for the *Playboy*s. She has never been much of a neatness freak wherever they have lived before. Uncurtained winter light bouncing off the bare floors and blank walls turns her underwear to silver and gives her shoulders and arms a quick life as of darting fish before they disappear into an old shirt of his and a moth-eaten sweater. Behind her their new bed, unmade, hasn't been fucked on yet, they were too drunk and exhausted last night. In fact they haven't since that night on the island. He asks her irritably what about *his* lunch.

Janice asks, "Oh, didn't you find something in the fridge?"

"There was one orange. I ate it for breakfast."

"I know I bought eggs and sliced ham but I guess Buddy and what's-her-name – "

"Valerie."

"Wasn't her hair wild? do you think she takes drugs? – ate it all up in that omelette they made after midnight. Isn't that a sign of drugs, an abnormal appetite for food? I know there's some cheese left, Harry. Couldn't you make do with cheese and crackers until I go out and buy something for Mother later? I don't know what's open Sundays around here, I can't keep running back to the Mt. Judge Superette and using up gas."

"No," he agrees, and makes do with cheese and crackers and a Schlitz that is left over from the three sixpacks Ronnie and Thelma brought over. Webb and Cindy brought the brandy and champagne. All afternoon he helps Janice clean, Windexing windows and wiping woodwork while she mops floors and even scours the kitchen and bathroom sinks. They have a downstairs bathroom here but he doesn't know where to buy toilet paper printed with comic strips. Janice has brought her mother's waxing machine in the Mustang along with some Butcher's paste and he wipes the wax on the long blond living-room floor, each whorl of wood grain and slightly popped-up nail and old scuff of a rubber heel his, his house. As he lays the wax on with circular swipes Rabbit keeps chasing the same few thoughts in his brain, stupid as brains are when you do physical work. Last night he kept wondering if the other two couples had gone ahead and swapped, Ronnie and Cindy doing it the second time, after he and Janice had left and they *did* act cozy, as if the four of them made the innermost circle of the party and the Angstroms and poor Buddy and that hungry Valerie were second echelon or third worlders somehow. Thelma got pretty drunk for her, her sallow skin gleaming to remind him of Vaseline, though when he thanked her for sending the clipping about the goose she stared at him and then sideways at Ronnie and then back at him as if he had rocks in his head. He guesses it'll all come out, what happened down there afterwards, people can't keep a good secret, but it pains him to think that Thelma would let Webb do to her everything the two of them did or that Cindy really wanted to go with Ronnie again and would lift up her heavy breast with a motherly hand so that loud-mouthed jerk could suck and tell about it, with his scalp bare like that he's such a baby, Harrison. No point in keeping secrets, we'll all be dead soon enough, already we're survivors, the kids are everywhere, making the music, giving the news. Ever since that encounter with Ruth he's felt amputated, a whole world half-seen in the corner of his eye snuffed out. Janice and the waxing machine are whining and knocking behind him and the way his brain is going on reminds him of some article he read last year in the paper or *Time* about some professor at Princeton's theory that in ancient times the gods spoke to people directly through the left or was it the right half of their brains, they were like robots with radios in their heads telling them everything to do, and then some-how around the time of the ancient Greeks or Assyrians the sys-tem broke up, the batteries too weak to hear the orders, though there are glimmers still and that is why we go to church, and what with all these jigaboos and fags roller-skating around with transistorized earmuffs on their heads we're getting back to it. How at night just before drifting off he hears Mom's voice clear as a whisper from the corner of the room saying *Hassy*, a name as dead as the boy that was called that is dead. Maybe the dead are gods, there's certainly something kind about them, the way they give you room. What you lose as you age is witnesses, the ones that watched from early on and cared, like your own little grandstand. Mom, Pop, old man Springer, baby Becky, good old Jill (maybe that dream had to do with the time he took her in so suddenly, except her hair wasn't dark, it was so intense, the dream, there's nothing like a new relationship), Skeeter, Mr. Abendroth, Frank Byer, Mamie Eisenhower just recently, John Wayne, LBJ, JFK, Skylab, the goose. With Charlie's mother and Peggy Fosnacht cooking. And his daughter Annabelle Byer snuffed out with that whole world he was watching in the corner of his eye like those entire planets obliterated in *Star Wars*. The more dead you know it seems the more living there are you don't know. Ruth's tears, when he was leaving: maybe God is in the universe the way salt is in the ocean, giving it a taste. He could never understand why people can't drink saltwater, it can't be any worse than mixing Coke and potato chips.

Behind him he hears Janice knocking her waxer clumsily against the baseboards at every sweep and it comes to him why they're being so busy, they're trying not to panic here in this house, where they shouldn't be at all, so far from Joseph Street. Lost in space. Like what souls must feel when they awaken in a baby's body so far from Heaven: not only scared so they cry but guilty, guilty. A huge hole to fill up. The money it'll take to fill these rooms with furniture when they had it all free before: he's ruined himself. And the mortgage payments: $62,400 at 13½ per cent comes to nearly $8500 interest alone, $700 a month over twenty years nibbling away at the principal until he's sixty-six. What did Ruth say about her youngest, 6/6/66? Funny about numbers, they don't lie but do play tricks. Three score and ten, all the things he'll never get to do now: to have Cindy arrange herself in the pose of one of those *Penthouse* sluts on a leopard skin and get down in front of her on all fours and just eat and eat and eat.

Last night Buddy turned to him so drunk his silver-rimmed eyeglasses were steamed and said he knew it was crazy, he knew what people would say about her being too tall and having three children and all, but Valerie really did it for him. She is the one, Harry. With tears in his eyes he said that. The big news from over at the Flying Eagle was Doris Kaufmann's planning to get married again. To a guy Rabbit used to know slightly, Don Eberhardt, who had gotten rich buying up inner-city real estate when nobody wanted it, before the gas crunch. Life is sweet, that's what they say.

Light still lingers in the windows, along the white window-sills, at five when they finish, the days this time of year lengthening against the grain. The planets keep their courses no matter what we do. In the freshly waxed hall by the foot of the stairs he touches Janice underneath her chin where the flesh is soft but not really repulsive and suggests a little nap upstairs, but she gives him a kiss warm and competent, the competence cancelling out the warmth, and tells him, "Oh Harry, that's a sweet idea but I have no idea when they might be coming, it's all mixed up with a lie-down Mother was going to have, she really does seem frailer, and the baby's feeding time, and I haven't even shopped yet. Isn't the Super Bowl on?"

"Not till six, it's on the West Coast. There's a pre-game thing on at four-thirty but it's all hoopla, you can only take so much. I wanted to watch the Phoenix Open at two-thirty, but you were so damn frantic to clean up just because your mother's coming over."

"You should have said something. I could have done it myself."

While she goes off in the Mustang he goes upstairs, because there isn't any place downstairs to lie down. He hopes to see the squirrel again, but the animal is gone. He thought squirrels hibernated, but maybe this winter is too mild. He holds his hands over a radiator, his, and with pride and satisfaction feels it breathing heat. He lies down on their new bed with the Amish quilt they brought from Mt. Judge and almost without transition falls asleep.

In his dream he and Charlie are in trouble at the agency, some crucial papers with numbers on them are lost, and where the new cars should be in the showroom there are just ragged craters, carefully painted with stripes and stars, in the concrete floor. He awakes realizing he is running scared. There has been another explosion, muffled: Janice closing the door downstairs. It is after six. "I had to drive out almost to the ballpark before I found this MinitMart that was open. They didn't have fresh anything of course, but I got four frozen Chinese dinners that the pictures of on the box looked good."

"Isn't crap like that loaded with chemicals? You don't want to poison Pru's milk."

"And I bought you lots of baloney and eggs and cheese and crackers so stop your complaining."

The nap, that at first waking had felt as if somebody had slugged him in the face with a ball of wet clothes, begins to sink into his bones and cheer him up. Darkness has erased the staring depth of day; the windows might be black photographic plates in their frames. Thelma and Nelson are out there circling, waiting to move in. Janice bought thirty dollars' worth at the MinitMart and as she fills the bright refrigerator he sees in a corner there are two more beers that escaped the vultures last night. She even brought him a jar of salted peanuts for all of $1.29 to watch the game with. The first half sways back and forth. He is rooting for the Steelers to lose, he hates what they did to the Eagles and in any case doesn't like overdogs; he pulls for the Rams the way he does for the Afghan rebels against the Soviet military machine.

At half-time a lot of girls in colored dresses and guys that look like fags in striped jerseys dance while about a thousand pieces of California brass imitate the old Big Bands with an off-key blare; these kids try to jitterbug but they don't have the swing, that one-beat wait back on your heels and then the twirl. They do a lot of disco wiggling instead. Then some little piece of sunshine with an Andrews-sisters pageboy sings "Sentimental Journey" but it doesn't have that Doris Day wartime Forties soul, how could it? No war. These kids were all born, can you believe it, around 1960 at the earliest and, worse yet, are sexually mature. On the "a-all aboard" they snake together in what is supposed to be the Chattanooga

Choo-choo and then produce, out there in cloudless California, flashing sheets like tinfoil that are supposed to be solar panels. "Energy is people," they sing. "People are en-er-gy!" Who needs Khomeini and his oil? Who needs Afghanistan? Fuck the Russkis. Fuck the Japs, for that matter. We'll go it alone, from sea to shining sea.

Tired of sitting in his den alone with a hundred million other boobs watching, Harry goes into the kitchen for that second beer, Janice sits at a card table her mother parted with as a loan grudgingly, even though she never plays cards except in the Poconos. "Where are our guests?" he asks.

Janice is sitting there helping the Chinese dinners warm up in the oven and reading a copy of *House Beautiful* she must have bought at the MinitMart. "They must have fallen asleep. They're up a good deal of the night, in a way it's a mercy, Harry, we're not there anymore."

He trims his lips in upon a bitter taste in the beer. Grain gone bad. Men love their poison. "Well I guess living in this house with just you is the way for me to lose weight. I never get fed."

"You'll get fed," she says, turning a slick page.

Jealous of the magazine, of the love for this house he feels growing in her, he complains, "It's like waiting for a shoe to drop."

She darts a dark, not quite hostile look up at him. "I'd think you've had enough shoes drop lately to last ten years."

From her tone he supposes she means something about Thelma but that had been far from his mind, for now.

Their guests don't arrive until early in the fourth quarter, just after Bradshaw, getting desperate, has thrown a bomb to Stallworth; receiver and defender go up together and the lucky stiff makes a circus catch. Rabbit still feels the Rams are going to win it. Janice calls that Ma and Pru are here. Ma Springer is all chattery in the front hall, taking off her mink, about the drive through Brewer, where hardly any cars were moving because she supposes of the game. She is teaching Pru to drive the Chrysler and Pru did very well once they figured out how to move the seat back: she hadn't realized what long legs Pru has. Pru, pressing a pink-wrapped bundle tight to her chest out of the cold, looks worn and thin in the face but more aligned, like a bed tugged smooth. "We would have been here earlier but I was typing a letter to Nelson and wanted to finish," she apologizes.

"It worries me," Ma is going on, "they used to say it brought bad luck to take a baby out visiting before it was baptized."

"Oh Mother," Janice says; she is eager to show her mother the cleaned-up house and leads her upstairs, even though the only lights are some 40-watt neo-colonial wall sconces in which the previous owners had let many of the bulbs die.

As Harry resettles himself in one of his silvery-pink wing chairs in front of the game, he can hear the old lady clumping on her painful legs directly above his head, inspecting, searching out the room where she might some day have to come and stay. He assumes Pru is with them, but the footsteps mingling on the ceiling are not that many, and Teresa comes softly down the one step into his den and deposits into his lap what he has been waiting for. Oblong cocooned little visitor, the baby shows her profile blindly in the shuddering flashes of color jerking from the Sony, the tiny stitchless seam of the closed eyelid aslant, lips bubbled forward beneath the whorled nose as if in delicate disdain, she knows she's good. You can feel in the curve of the cranium she's feminine, that shows from the first day. Through all this she has pushed to be here, in his lap, his hands, a real presence hardly weighing anything but alive. Fortune's hostage, heart's desire, a granddaughter. His. Another nail in his coffin. His.

RABBIT AT REST

CHAPTERS

Rabbit basks above that old remembered world, rich, at rest.
                                        −Rabbit Is Rich

Food to the indolent is poison, not sustenance.
                    −Life and Times of Frederick Douglass

I. FL

STANDING amid the tan, excited post-Christmas crowd at the Southwest Florida Regional Airport, Rabbit Angstrom has a funny sudden feeling that what he has come to meet, what's floating in unseen about to land, is not his son Nelson and daughter-in-law Pru and their two children but something more ominous and intimately his: his own death, shaped vaguely like an airplane. The sensation chills him, above and beyond the terminal air-conditioning. But, then, facing Nelson has made him feel uneasy for thirty years.

The airport is relatively new. You drive to it off Exit 21 of Interstate 75 down three miles of divided highway that for all the skinny palms in rows and groomed too-green flat-bladed grass at its sides seems to lead nowhere. There are no billboards or self-advertising roadside enterprises or those low houses with cooling white-tile roofs that are built by the acre down here. You think you've made a mistake. An anxious red Camaro convertible is pushing in the rearview mirror.

"Harry, there's no need to speed. We're early if anything."

Janice, Rabbit's wife, said this to him on the way in. What rankled was the tolerant, careful tone she has lately adopted, as if he's prematurely senile. He looked over and watched her tuck back a stubborn fluttering wisp of half-gray hair from her sun-toughened little brown nut of a face. "Honey, I'm being tail-gated," he explained, and eased back into the right lane and let the speedometer needle quiver back below sixty-five. The Camaro convertible passed in a rush, a cocoa-brown black chick in a gray felt stewardess's cap at the wheel, her chin and lips pushing forward, not giving him so much as a sideways glance. This rankled, too. From the back, the way they've designed the trunk and bumper, a Camaro seems to have a mouth, two fat metal lips parted as if to hiss. So maybe Harry's being spooked began then.

The terminal when it shows up at last is a long low white building like a bigger version of the sunstruck clinics – dental, chiropractic, arthritic, cardiac, legal, legal-medical – that line the boulevards of this state dedicated to the old. You park at a lot only a few steps away from the door of sliding brown glass: the whole state babies you. Inside, upstairs, where the planes are met, the spaces are long and low and lined in tasteful felt gray like that cocky stewardess's cap and filled with the kind of music you become aware of only when the elevator stops or when the dentist stops drilling. Plucked strings, no vocals, music that's used to being ignored, a kind of carpet in the air, to cover up a silence that might remind you of death. These long low tasteful spaces, as little cluttered by advertisements as the highway, remind Rabbit of something. Air-conditioning ducts, he thinks at first, and then crypts. These are futuristic spaces like those square tunnels in movies that a trick of the camera accelerates into spacewarp to show we're going from one star to the next. *2001*, will he be alive? He touches Janice at his side, the sweated white cotton of her tennis dress at the waist, to relieve his sudden sense of doom. Her waist is thicker, has less of a dip, as she grows into that barrel body of women in late middle age, their legs getting skinny, their arms getting loose like cooked chicken coming off the bone. She wears over the sweaty tennis dress an open-weave yellow cardigan hung unbuttoned over her shoulders against the chill of airport air-conditioning. He is innocently proud that she looks, in her dress and tan, even to the rings of pallor that sunglasses have left around her eyes, like these other American grandmothers who can afford to be here in this land of constant sunshine and eternal youth.

"Gate A5," Janice says, as if his touch had been a technical question. "From Cleveland by way of Newark," she says, with that businesswoman efficiency she has taken on in middle age, especially since her mother died seven years ago, leaving her the lot, Springer Motors and its assets, one of only two Toyota agencies in the Brewer, Pennsylvania, area: the family all still speak of it as "the lot," since it began as a used-car lot owned and run by Fred Springer, dead Fred Springer, who is reincarnated, his widow Bessie and daughter Janice have the fantasy, in Nelson, both being wiry shrimps with something shifty about them. Which is why Harry and Janice spend half the year in Florida – so Nelson can have free run of the lot. Harry, Chief Sales Representative for over ten years, with him and Charlie Stavros managing it all between them, wasn't even mentioned in Ma Springer's will, for all the years he lived with her in her gloomy big house on Joseph Street and listened to her guff about what a saint Fred was and her complaining about her swollen ankles. Everything went to Janice, as if he was an unmentionable incident in the Springer dynasty. The house on Joseph Street, that Nelson and his family get to live in just for covering the upkeep and taxes, must be worth three hundred thousand now that the yuppies are moving across the mountain from northeast Brewer into the town of Mt. Judge, not to mention the cottage in the Poconos where even the shacks in the woods have skyrocketed, and the lot land alone, four acres along Route 111 west of the river, might bring close to a million from one of the hi-tech companies that have come into the Brewer area this last decade, to take advantage of the empty factories, the skilled but depressed laboring force, and the old-fashionedly cheap living. Janice is rich. Rabbit would like to share with her the sudden chill he had felt, the shadow of some celestial airplane, but a shell she has grown repels him. The dress at her waist when he touched it felt thick and unresponsive, a damp hide. He is alone with his premonition.

A crowd of welcomers has collected this Tuesday after Christmas in this last year of Ronald Reagan's reign. A little man with that hunched back and awkward swiftness Jews often seem to have dodges around them and shouts behind him to his wife, as if the Angstroms weren't there, "Come *on*, Grace!"

Grace, Harry thinks. A strange name for a Jewish woman. Or maybe not. Biblical names, Rachel, Esther, but not always: Barbra, Bette. He is still getting used to the Jews down here, learning from them, trying to assimilate the philosophy that gives them such a grip on the world. That humpbacked old guy in his pink checked shirt and lipstick-red slacks racing as if the plane coming in was the last train out of Warsaw. When Harry and Janice were planning the move down here their advisers on Florida, mostly Charlie Stavros and Webb Murkett, told them the Gulf side was the Christian coast as opposed to the Jewish Atlantic side but Harry hasn't noticed that really; as far as his acquaintanceship goes all Florida is as Jewish as New York and Hollywood and Tel Aviv. In their condo building in fact he and Janice are pets of a sort, being gentiles: they're considered cute. Watching that little guy, seventy if he's a day, breaking into a run, hopping zigzag through the padded pedestal chairs so he won't be beaten out at the arrival gate, Harry remorsefully feels the bulk, two hundred thirty pounds the kindest scales say, that has enwrapped him at the age of fifty-five like a set of blankets the decades have brought one by one. His doctor down here keeps telling him to cut out the beer and munchies and each night after brushing his teeth he vows to but in the sunshine of the next day he's hungry again, for anything salty and easy to chew. What did his old basketball coach, Marty Tothero, tell him toward the end of his life, about how when you get old you eat and eat and it's never the right food? Sometimes Rabbit's spirit feels as if it might faint from lugging all this body around. Little squeezy pains tease his ribs, reaching into his upper left arm. He has spells of feeling short of breath and mysteriously full in the chest, full of some pressing essence. When he was a kid and had growing pains he would be worried and the grownups around him laughed them off on his behalf; now he is unmistakably a grownup and must do his own laughing off.

A colorful octagonal nook of a shop selling newspapers and magazines and candy and coral souvenirs and ridiculous pastel T-shirts saying what bliss southwestern Florida is interrupts the severe gray spaces of the airport. Janice halts and says, "Could you wait here a sec till I see if they have the new *Elle*? And maybe I should go back and use the Ladies while I have the chance, the traffic going home might be terrible what with the weather continuing so beachy."

"*Now* you think of it," he says. "Well, *do* it if you're going to do it." The little Mamie Eisenhower bangs she still wears have grown skimpy with the years and curly with the humidity and saltwater and make her look childish and stubborn and cute, actually, along with the sun wrinkles.

"We still have ten minutes at least, I don't know what that jerk was in such a hurry about."

"He was just in love with life," Harry tells her, and obediently waits. While she's in the Ladies he cannot resist going into the shop and buying something to nibble, a Planter's peanut-brittle bar for forty-five cents. Planter's Original Peanut Bar, the wrapper says. It was broken in two somewhere in transit and he thinks of saving one half to offer his two grandchildren when they're all together in the car heading home. It would make a small hit. But the first half is so good he eats the second and even dumps the sweet crumbs out of the wrapper into his palm and with his tongue licks them all up like an anteater. Then he thinks of going back and buying another for his grandchildren and him to share in the car – "Look what Grandpa has!" as they turn onto Interstate 75 – but doesn't trust himself not to eat it all and makes himself stand and look out the window instead. This airport has been designed with big windows viewing the runways, so if there's a crash everybody can feast upon it with their own eyes. The fireball, the fuselage doing a slow skidding twirl, shedding its wings. As he tries with his tongue to clean the sticky brittle stuff, the caramelized sugar and corn syrup, from between his teeth – all his still, thank God, and the front ones not even crowned – Rabbit stares out through the glass at the wide blank afternoon. The runway tapering to a triangle, the Florida flatness turning brown as thatch beyond the green reach of a watering system. Winter, the shadow of it that falls down here, hasn't hit yet. Every day the temperature has been in the eighties. After four winters in Florida he knows how the wind off the Gulf can cut into you on the first tee if you have an early starting time and the sweaters can be shed only as the sun climbs toward noon, but this December except for that one cold snap in the middle of the month has been like early September in Pennsylvania – hot, and only the horse chestnuts turning and only a certain weary dryness in the air and the buzz of cicadas to suggest that summer is over.

As the candy settles in his stomach a sense of doom regrows its claws around his heart: little prongs like those that hold fast a diamond solitaire. There has been a lot of death in the newspapers lately. Max Robinson the nation's first and only black national anchorman and Roy Orbison who always wore black and black sunglasses and sang "Pretty Woman" in that voice that could go high as a woman's and then before Christmas that Pan Am Flight 103 ripping open like a rotten melon five miles above Scotland and dropping all these bodies and flaming wreckage all over the golf course and the streets of this little town like Glockamorra, what was its real name, Lockerbie. Imagine sitting there in your seat being lulled by the hum of the big Rolls-Royce engines and the stewardesses bringing the clinking drinks caddy and the feeling of having caught the plane and nothing to do now but relax and then with a roar and giant ripping noise and scattered screams this whole cozy world dropping away and nothing under you but black space and your chest squeezed by the terrible unbreathable cold, that cold you can scarcely believe is there but that you sometimes actually feel still packed into the suitcases, stored in the unpressurized hold, when you unpack your clothes, the dirty underwear and beach towels with the merciless chill of death from outer space still in them. Just yesterday some jet flying from Rochester to Atlanta tore open at thirty-one thousand feet, a fourteen-inch hole the newspaper said, and was lucky to land in West Virginia. Everything falling apart, airplanes, bridges, eight years under Reagan of nobody minding the store, making money out of nothing, running up debt, trusting in God.

Harry has flown in his life to dealers' conferences here and there and that great time nine years ago with two other couples to the Caribbean, but to Florida he and Janice always drive, so they have the car there. Nelson will probably bitch because there's only one, though it's a Camry station wagon that takes six comfortably; Nelson likes to do his own thing, going off on mysterious errands that take hours. Nelson. A real sore spot. Harry's tongue begins to sting, so he stops working at a jagged bit of corn-syrup sweetness stuck behind an eye tooth.

And also in the Fort Myers *News-Press* this morning an item about a pregnant woman over in Fort Lauderdale shot in an attempted robbery yesterday. Must have been black but the paper didn't say so, they don't now. She died but they saved the baby by Caesarean section. And then there was also on the front page this interview with a guy convicted of picking up a twelve-year-old girl and getting her to smoke dope and raping her and then burning her alive somehow and now complaining about the cockroaches and rats in the cell on death row and telling the reporter, "I've always tried to do the best I can, but I'm no angel. And I'm no killer either." His saying this made Harry laugh, it rang a kind of bell with him. No angel yet no killer either. Not like this guy

Bundy who murdered dozens of women in dozens of states and has been stalling his execution for ten years in Tallahassee down here. And Hirohito too is taking his time. Harry can remember when Hirohito was right up there with Hitler and Mussolini in the war propaganda.

And he has never forgot how, thirty years ago it will be this June, his baby daughter Rebecca June drowned and when he went back to the apartment alone there was still this tubful of tepid gray water that had killed her. God hadn't pulled the plug. It would have been so easy for Him, Who set the stars in place. To have it unhappen. Or to delete from the universe whatever it was that exploded that Pan Am 747 over Scotland. Those bodies with hearts pumping tumbling down in the dark. How much did they know as they fell, through air dense like tepid water, tepid gray like this terminal where people blow through like dust in an air duct, to the airline we're all just numbers on the computer, one more or less, who cares? A blip on the screen, then no blip on the screen. Those bodies tumbling down like wet melon seeds.

A star has appeared in the daytime sky, in the blue beneath the streaks of stratocirrus, an airplane glinting, lowering, heading straight toward them. This glint, he thinks, holds his near and dear: Nelson his son, his left-handed daughter-in-law called Pru though she was christened Teresa, Judy his eight-year-old granddaughter, and Roy his four-year-old grandson, born the same fall Harry and Janice began to spend half the year in Florida. The baby actually was named after both fathers, Harold Roy, but everybody calls him Roy, something Harry could resent since Roy Lubell is a sorehead laid-off Akron steamfitter who didn't even come to the wedding and never did shit for his seven hungry kids. Pru still seems hungry and in that she reminds Harry of himself. The star grows, has become a saucer shape glinting in a number of points, a winged aluminum machine aglide and enlarging above the sulky flat scrubland and horizon thready with palms. He imagines the plane exploding as it touches down, ignited by one of its glints, in a ball of red flame shadowed in black like you see on TV all the time, and he is shocked to find within himself, imagining this, not much emotion, just a cold thrill at being a witness, a kind of bleak wonder at the fury of chemicals, and relief that he hadn't been on the plane himself but was instead safe on this side of the glass, with his faint pronged sense of doom.

Janice is at his side again. She is breathless, excited. "Harry, *hurry*," she says. "They're *here*, ten minutes early, there must have been a tail wind from Newark. I came out of the Ladies and went down to the gate and couldn't find you, you weren't *there*. Where *were* you?"

"Nowhere. Just standing here by the window." That plane he had mentally exploded hadn't been their plane at all.

Heart thumping, his breath annoyingly short, he strides after his little wife down the wide gray carpeting. Her pleated tennis skirt flicks at the brown backs of her thighs and her multilayered white Nikes look absurdly big at the end of her skinny legs, like Minnie Mouse in her roomy shoes, but Janice's getup is no more absurd than many in this crowd of greeters: men with bankers' trim white haircuts and bankers' long grave withholding faces wearing Day-Glo yellow-green tank tops stencilled CORAL POINT or CAPTIVA ISLAND and tomato-red bicycle shorts and Bermudas patterned with like fried eggs and their permed and thick-middled women in these ridiculous one-piece exercise outfits like long flannel underwear in pink or blue, baby colors on Kewpie-doll shapes, their costumes advertising the eternal youth they have found like those skiers and tennis players and golfers now who appear on television laden with logos like walking billboards. The hunchbacked little Jewish guy in such a hurry has already met his loved one, a tall grinning woman, a Rachel or Esther with frizzed-out hair and a big pale profile, carrying over one arm her parka from Newark, her plump dumpy mother on the other side of her, Grace was her name, while the old man with angry choppy gestures is giving the women the latest version of his spiel, they listening with half an ear each to this newest little thing he feels very strongly about. Rabbit is curious to see that this grown daughter, a head taller than her parents, appears to have no mate. A tall black man, slick-looking in a three-piece gray suit, but nothing of a dude, carrying himself with a businesslike Waspy indifference to his appearance and lugging one of those floppy big bags that smart travellers use and that hog all the overhead rack space, is trailing unnaturally close behind. But he can't be a relation, he must be just trying to pass, like that black chick in the red Camaro coming in off 75. Everybody tailgating, that's the way we move along now.

Harry and Janice reach Gate A5. People get off of airplanes in clots, one self-important fusspot with three bags or some doddery old dame with a cane bunching those behind them. You wonder if we haven't gone overboard in catering to cripples. "There they are," Janice pronounces at last, adding under her breath to Harry quickly, "Nelson looks exhausted."

Not so much exhausted, Rabbit thinks, as shifty. His son is carrying his own son on his left arm, and Nelson's right eye squints, the lid seeming to quiver, as if a blow might come from that unprotected side. Roy must have fallen asleep on the flight, for his head leans against his father's neck seeking a pillow there, his eyes open with that liquid childish darkness but his plump mouth mute, gleaming with saliva, in shock. Harry goes forward as soon as the ropes allow to lift the burden from his son, but Nelson seems reluctant to let go, as if the child's own grandfather is a kidnapper; Roy, too, clings. With a shrug of exasperation Harry gives up and leans in close and kisses Roy's velvety cheek, finer than velvet, still feverish with sleep, and shakes his own son's small and clammy hand. In recent years Nelson has grown a mustache, a tufty brown smudge not much wider than his nose. His delicate lips underneath it never seem to smile. Harry looks in vain into this fearful brown-eyed face for a trace of his blue-eyed own. Nelson has inherited Janice's tense neatness of feature, with her blur of evasion or confusion in the eyes; the puzzled look sits better on a woman than a man. Worse, Janice's high forehead and skimpy fine hair have become in Nelson a distinctly growing baldness. His receding temples have between them a transparent triangle of remaining hair soon to become an island, a patch, and at the back of his head, when he turns to kiss his mother, a swath of skin is expanding. He has chosen to wear a worn blue denim jacket down on the plane, over a crisp dressy shirt, though, pink stripes with white collar and cuffs, so he seems half cocked, like a married rock star or a weekend gangster. One earlobe bears a tiny gold earring.

"Mmmm-*wah!*" Janice says to cap her hello kiss; she has learned to make such noises down here, among the overexpressive Jewish women.

Harry carefully greets Judith and Pru. Going to be nine in less than a month, the skinny girl is a sketch of a woman, less than life-size and not filled in. A redhead like her mother. Lovely complexion, cheeks rosy under the freckles, and the details of her face — lashes, eyebrows, ears, nostril-wings, lips quick to lift up on her teeth — frighteningly perfect, as if too easy to smash. When he bends to kiss her he sees in front of her ear the sheen of childhood's invisible down. She has Pru's clear green eyes and carrot-colored hair but nothing as yet in her frail straight frame and longish calm face of the twist that life at some point gave Pru, making her beauty even when she was twenty-four slightly awkward, limping as it were, a look that has become more wry and cumbersome with the nine years of marriage to Nelson. She likes Harry and he likes her though they have never found a way around all these others to express it. "What a pair of beauties," he says now, of the mother and daughter.

Little Judy wrinkles her nose and says, "Grandpa's been eating candy again, for shame on him. I could smell it, something with peanuts in it, I can tell. He even has some little pieces stuck between his teeth. For shame."

He had to laugh at this attack, at the accuracy of it, and the Pennsylvania-Dutch way the little girl said, "for shame." Local accents are dying out, but slowly, children so precisely imitate their elders. Judy must have overheard in her house Nelson and Pru and maybe Janice talking about his weight problem and rotten diet. If they were talking, his health problems might be worse than he knows. He must look bad.

"Shit," he says, in some embarrassment. "I can't get away with anything any more. Pru, how's the world treating you?"

His daughter-in-law surprises him by, as he bends dutifully forward to kiss her cheek, kissing him flush on the mouth. Her lips have a wry regretful shy downward twist but are warm, warm and soft and big as cushions in the kiss's aftermath within him. Since he first met her in the shadows of Ma Springer's house that long-ago summer — a slender slouching shape thrust into the midst of their lives, Nelson's pregnant Roman Catholic girlfriend from Ohio, a Kent State University secretary named Teresa Lubell, suddenly become the carrier of Harry's genes into eternity — Pru has broadened without growing heavy in that suety Pennsylvania way. As if invisible pry bars have slightly spread her bones and new calcium been wedged in and the flesh gently stretched to fit, she now presents more front. Her face, once narrow like Judy's, at moments looks like a flattened mask. Always tall, she has in the years of becoming a hardened wife and matron allowed her long straight hair to be cut and teased out into bushy wings a little like the hairdo of the Sphinx. Her hips and shoulders too have widened, beneath the busy pattern − brown and white and black squares and diamond-shapes arranged to look three-dimensional − of the checked suit she put on for the airplane, a lightweight suit wrinkled by the three hours of sitting and babysitting. A stuffed blue shoulder bag is slung across one shoulder and her arms and hands clutch a gray wool topcoat, two children's jackets, several slippery children's books based on morning television shows, a Cabbage Patch doll with its bunchy beige face, and an inflated plastic dinosaur. She has big hands, with pink, cracked knuckles. Harry's mother had hands like that, from washing clothes and dishes. How did Pru get them, in this age of appliances? He stands gazing at her in a half-second's post-kiss daze. Having a wife and children soon palled for him, but he never fails to be excited by having, in the flesh, a daughter-in-law.

She says, slangily, to mask the initial awkwardness when they meet, "You're lookin' good, Harry. The sunny South agrees with you."

What did that frontal kiss mean? Its slight urgency. Some sad message there. She and Nelson never did quite fit.

"Nobody else thinks so," he says, and grabs at her shoulder bag. "Lemme help you carry some of this stuff, I'll take the bag." He begins to pull it off.

Pru shifts the coat and toys to extend her arm to let him take it but at the same time asks him, "Should you?"

Harry asks, "Why does everybody treat me like some God-damn kind of invalid?" but he is asking the air; Pru and Janice are hugging with brisk false enthusiasm and Nelson is plodding ahead down the long gray corridor with Roy back to sleep on his shoulder. Harry is irritated to see that though Nelson has a careful hair-cut that looks only a few days old the barber left one of those tails, like a rat's tail, uncut and hanging down over the boy's collar, under the spreading bald spot. How old does he think he is, seventeen? Little Judy trails her father but Nelson is not waiting or looking back. The girl is just old enough to sense that in her nice proper airplane outfit she should not sacrifice all dignity and run to catch up. She wears a navy-blue winter coat over a pink summer dress; its pink hem shows below the coat, and then her bare legs, which look long, longer than when he saw her last in early November. But it is the back of her head that kills him, her shiny carrot-colored hair braided into a pigtail caught into a showy stiff white ribbon. Something of her mother's Catholic upbringing in that ribbon, decking out the Virgin or the baby Jesus or Whoever to go on parade, to go on a ride in the sky. The sleek back of Judy's head, the pigtail bouncing as she tries not to run, so docilely, so unthinkingly wears the showy ribbon her mother put there that Harry smiles. Hurrying his stride, he catches up and reaches down and says, "Hey there, good-lookin'," and takes the hand she with a child's reflex lifts to be taken. Her hand is as surprisingly moist as her mother's lips were warm. Her head with its bone-white parting is higher than his waist. She complains to her mother, Harry has heard from Janice, about being the tallest girl in her section of the third grade. The mean boys tease her.

"How's school going?" he asks.

"I hate it," Judy tells him. "There are all these kids think they're big shots. The girls are the absolute worst."

"Do you ever think *you're* a big shot?"

She ponders this. "Some boys are always getting after me but I tell them to fuck off."

He clucks his tongue. "That's pretty rough language for the third grade."

"Not really," she says. "Even the teacher says 'damn' sometimes when we get her going."

"How do you get her going?"

Judy smiles upward, her mother's quick wide-mouthed smile without the crimp. "Sometimes we all hum so she can't see our mouths move. A couple weeks ago when she tried to make us all sing Christmas carols one of these big-shot boys I told you about

said it was against his parents' religion and his father was a lawyer
and would sue everybody."

"He sounds like a pain in the ass," Rabbit says.

"Grandpa. Don't talk dirty."

"That's not dirty, that's just saying where it hurts. If you say
somebody's a pain in the bottom it sounds dirtier. Hey. Here's the
place I bought that peanut candy you smelled. Want some?"

"You better ask Mom first."

Harry turns and lets the two mothers, walking hip to hip and
heads bowed in consultation, catch up. "Pru," he says, "will it rot
any teeth if I buy Judy a candy bar?"

She looks up, distracted, but remembers to smile at him. "I
guess it won't kill her this once, though Nelson and I try to discourage junk in their diet."

"Whatever you get her, Harry," Janice adds, "you ought to get
Roy."

"But Roy's asleep and half her size."

"He'll know, though," Pru says, "if you play favorites. He's just
now coming out from under her shadow."

Little Judy, casting a shadow? Did he cast a shadow over Mim?
Mim certainly got far enough away from Diamond County, if that
was a statement. Got into the fast lane in Las Vegas and stayed.

"Don't be forever," Janice tells Harry. "Or else give me the
keys so we can get into the car. They have two more bags they
made them check in Newark. Nelson's probably down there
already."

"Yeah, what's his idea, rushing on ahead like that? Who's he
sore at?"

"Probably me," Pru says. "I've given up trying to figure out
why."

Harry digs into one pocket of his plaid golf slacks, comes up
with only a few tees and a plastic ball marker with two blue Vs
on it, for Valhalla Village, and then into the other to find the
knobbly notched bunch of keys on the ring. Saying "Heads up,"
he tosses them toward Janice. Her hands jump together in a
womanly panic and the keys sail past them and hit her in the
stomach. Just this little effort, the search and the toss, leaves him
weary, as if the arm he lifted was soggy wash. The spontaneity and

fun have been taken out of buying his granddaughter a treat. She chooses not a Planter's Peanut Bar as he had envisioned but a Sky Bar, which he thinks might be truly bad for her teeth, those five different gooey fillings in the five humped segments of pure chocolate. He digs into the hip pocket of his pants, so old their plaid is sun-faded and the hem of each pocket is darkened by the sweat off his hands over the years, and pulls out his wallet and hangs for a while over the candy rack, uncertain whether or not to get himself another sugary rectangle of stuck-together nuts, wondering if this time he would be lucky enough to get one not broken in the wrapper, deciding against it because he eats too much, too much junk as Pru said, Pru and his doctor down here, old Dr. Morris, and then at the last possible split-second, with the black woman at the counter within the octagonal shop already counting out his change from a dollar for the Sky Bar, deciding to buy the peanut brittle after all. It is not so much the swallowing and ingesting he loves as the gritty-edgy feeling of the first corner in his mouth, the first right-angled fragment, slowly dissolving. To his surprise and indignation not only does he now receive no change from the dollar but owes the black woman – a severe matte undiluted color you rarely see in the U.S., dull as slate, must be a Haitian or Dominican, Florida is full of these boat people – a nickel more, for the state tax. Airport prices, they nail you where there's no competition. Without competition, you get socialism and everybody free-loading and economies like they have in Cuba and Haiti. He pauses to glance at the magazines on the rack. The top row holds the skin mags, sealed in plastic, pieces of printed paper hiding details of the open-mouthed girls, open-mouthed as if perpetually astonished by their own tangible assets, *Hustler*, *Gallery*, *Club*, *Penthouse*, *Oui*, *Live*, *Fox*. He imagines himself buying one, braving the Haitian woman's disapproval – all these Caribbean types are evangelical fundamentalists, tin-roofed churches where they shout for the world to end now – and sneaking the magazine home and while Janice is asleep or cooking or out with one of her groups studying to satiety the spread shots and pink labia and boosted tits and buttocks tipped up from behind so the shaved cunt shows, with its sad little anatomy like some oyster, and sadly foreseeing that he will not be enough aroused, boredom will become his main feeling, and embarrassment at the expenditure. Four dollars twenty-five they are asking these days, promising *Sexy Sirens in the Sauna* and *Cara Lott Gets Hot* and *Oral Sex: A Gourmet's Guide*. How disgusting we are, when you think about it – disposable meat, but hell-bent on gratification.

"Come *on*, Grandpa – what's taking so long?"

They hurry after the others, who have vanished. Judy's shiny beribboned head makes him nervous, popping up first on one side of him and then the other, like the car keys he was a little slow to find, Janice calls him doddery when she can't even catch, the clumsy mutt. If their granddaughter gets kidnapped from his side she'll really call him doddery. "Easy does it," he tells Judy at the top of the escalator, "pick a step and stay on it. Don't get on a crack," and at the bottom, "O.K., step off, but not too soon, don't panic, it'll happen, O.K., good."

"I go on escalators all the time at the malls," she tells him, making up at him a little pinched rebuking mouth with beads of melted chocolate at the corners.

"Where the hell is everybody?" he asks her, for amid all the tan loud presences that throng the lower, higher-ceilinged floor of the Southwest Florida Regional Airport, less ductlike and cryptlike but still echoing with a muffled steely doom that worries at his stomach, there is nobody he knows, strangers as total as if he has descended into Hell.

"Are we lost, Grandpa?"

"We can't be," he tells her.

In their sudden small plight he is newly aware of her preciousness, the jewel-cut of her eyes and eyelashes, the downy glaze in front of her ears and the gleam of each filament of her luxuriant hair, pulled taut into a thick pigtail adorned with an unreal stiff white ribbon. For the first time he sees she is also wearing symmetrical white barrettes, shaped like butterflies. Judy looks up toward his face and fights crying at the vagueness she sees there. "This coat is too hot," she complains.

"I'll carry it," he says. He folds its cloth weight over his arm and she is like a butterfly herself now, in her pink dress. Her green eyes have gone wide in this gray airport's bustling limbo, under reddish-brown eyebrows one of which near the flat bulge of her little freckled nose has a little cowlick fanning the hairs the wrong way; Nelson has that cowlick, and inherited it from Harry, who used to lick his middle finger and try to slick it down in the high-school boys' lavatory mirror. Amazing, that a thing so tiny could pass on. Maybe the only immortality we get, a little genetic quirk going on and on like a computerized number in your monthly bank statement. Ghostly empty shapes, people he doesn't know, push and stream past the two of them. They are an island surrounded by jokes and noisy news and embraces; people tanned that deep set-tled mahogany that comes only from months and months of Florida embrace newcomers the color of wallpaper paste. Harry says, so Judy will hear her grandfather say something and not just stand there numbly, "They must be over at the baggage."

He looks up and sees above their heads the sign saying BAG-GAGE and takes her moist little hand and tugs her toward the crowd around the baggage belt, which is already moving. But neither Pru nor Janice nor Nelson nor Roy is there, as far as they can see. Face after face refuses to cohere into a known face. His eyes, always good, trouble him now in artificially lit places. The blue shoulder bag Pru let him carry for her is heavier than he would have thought; she must have packed bricks. His shoulder and eyes burn.

"I guess," he ventures, though it seems unlikely, "they're already at the car." He taps his pocket for the lump of keys, doesn't feel it, begins to panic, then remembers how he tossed them to Janice. Of course. Confidently now he approaches the brown glass exit doors, but the wrong one pops its seal and slides open when his body trips the electric eye. The wrong one as far as he is con-cerned; Judy was pulling him in the right direction, where a slice of hot outdoor air swiftly widens. Sun has broken through the milky stratocirrus. It bounces off the waxy leaves of the nameless tropical plants flourishing near his knees. It winks blindingly from a mass of moving cars, a brutal river of them rushing along the access strip just beyond the curb. He holds Judy's hand tighter, in case she decides to jump off the curb, we're all full of crazy imp-ulses. They cross to a lake of shimmering cars, the lot where he parked. Where, exactly? He finds he's forgotten. He is utterly empty of the car's location.

A Camry Deluxe wagon, pearl-gray metallic, with the more potent 24-valve 2.5-liter V-6 engine. He was still so sore at being tailgated by that red Camaro and at Janice criticizing his driving that he wasn't paying any attention to where they parked. He remembers the zebra crosswalk, and the little landscaped mound of center strip where some sun-starved college kid had propped his knapsack and pillowed his head on it to soak up a few rays, and the fussy old guy who thought he was in charge gesturing at you which way the exit and the booth where you pay was, putting too much into it like that husband at the airport gabbing at his wife, Grace, as if she had no sense, meeting that frizzy-haired long-toothed smiling Jewish princess taller than either of them, but he doesn't remember which of these rows he parked the car in. He parked it in the patch of dead blank brain cells like all of our brains will be when we're dead unless the universe has cooked up some truly elaborate surprise. *The National Enquirer* which Janice sometimes brings home from the Winn Dixie keeps reporting people's near-death experiences, but for Harry they're too close to the little green men in the UFOs. Even if they're true it's not much comfort. Judy's hand has slipped out of his as he stands puzzling on the strip of grass on the edge of the parking lot, that broad-bladed grass that grows everywhere down here, watered by sprinklers, they call it St. Augustine. It doesn't feel like real grass to him, too matted and broad, kind of crunchy underfoot. His chest begins to hurt. A sly broad pain, a kind of band under the skin, tightly sewn there.

Judy's voice floats up to him like a thin lifeline. "What color is the car, Grandpa?"

"Oh, you know," he says, keeping his sentences short, so as not to stir up his pain. "Pale gray. Metallic finish. The same color as about half the cars in the world. Don't you panic. It'll come to me where I left it."

The poor kid is losing it, in her fight not to cry. "Daddy'll drive off!" she blurts out.

"Leaving you and me? Why would he do that? He won't do that, Judy."

"He gets real mad sometimes, for no real reason."

"He probably has some reason he doesn't tell you. How about you? You ever get mad?"

"Not like Daddy. Mom says he should see a doctor."

"I guess we all should, now and then." Rabbit's sense of doom is trickling like cold water through his stomach. Doctors. His own doctor is bringing his son into the practice, so if he drops dead the kid will take right over, won't miss a Medicare form. You fill a slot for a time and then move out; that's the decent thing to do: make room. He scans the ranks of glinting metal in their slots for a strip of gray that will ring a bell, and wonders if he is misremembering the color – he has owned so many cars in his life, and sold so many more. He announces, "I think I left it over on the left. In about the third row. What happened, Judy, was there was this old guy kind of directing things, waving which way everybody should go, and the bastard distracted me. Don't you hate bossy people like that, who know everything better than you do?"

The little girl's glossy red head mutely nods at his side, too worried for words.

Rabbit rattles on, to chase their clouds away, "Whenever somebody tells me to do something my instinct's always to do the opposite. It's got me into a lot of trouble, but I've had a lot of fun. This bossy old guy was pointing one direction so I went the other and found a space." And for a second, in a kind of window between two tightenings of the band across his chest, he *sees* the space: next to a cream-colored van, a Ford Bivouac with those watery-blue Minnesota plates, parked sloppily over the white line, another cause for irritation. He had to ease in carefully so as to leave Janice room enough to open her door on the right and not rub fenders with the maroon Galaxy on the left. And now he sees from far off in the shimmering Florida heat a strip of cream risen above the other metallic rooftops. Third row, about a wedge shot in. He says in triumph, "Judy, I *see* it. Let's *go*," and takes her hand again, lest her small perfection be crushed by one of the automobiles cruising the rows looking for a spot. In some of these big white Caddys and Oldses the tiny old driver can hardly see over the hood out the windshield, just clinging to the wheel, body all shrunk and bent by osteoporosis; it hasn't got him yet, he's still six feet three as far as he knows, at least his pants don't drag on the floor, but he hears Janice talk about it, it's been on TV a fair amount, that commercial with the two women on the train, it

affects women more than men, their smaller bones, she takes calcium pills along with all the other vitamin pills next to her orange
juice at breakfast. God, is she healthy. She'll live forever just to
spite him.

He and little Judith arrive across the hazardous hot asphalt at
the pearl-gray Camry, which is his, he knows, from Janice's tennis racket and cover on the back seat, flung in there separately –
the dumb mutt, what's the use of a cover if you don't put the
racket in it? But nobody is here and the car is locked and Harry
threw away the keys. The little girl begins to cry. Luckily he has
a handkerchief in the hip pocket of his faded plaid golf pants. He
lowers Pru's blue bag with its load of bricks to the asphalt and puts
the little winter coat he has been carrying on top of the car roof,
as if to stake a claim, and kneels down and wipes the bits of melted Sky Bar from Judy's lips and then the tears from her cheeks. He
too wouldn't mind having a cry, squatting here next to the car's
sunstruck metallic flank, his knees complaining on top of everything else, and the small girl's hot panicked breath adding to the
heat. In her distress her freckled nose has begun to run and her
mouth taken on a hardness, a stiffness in the upper lip he associates with Nelson when the boy is frightened or angry.

"We can either stay here and let the others find us," Harry
explains to his granddaughter, "or we can go back and look for
them. Maybe we're too tired and hot to do anything but stay here.
We could play a game seeing how many different states' license
plates we can find."

This breaks her sniffling into a wet little laugh. "Then we'd get
lost again." Her eyelids are reddened by the friction of tears and
tiny flakes of light shine in her green irises like the microscopic
facets that give metallic paint its tinselly quality.

"Look," he tells her. "Here's Minnesota, with its little clump
of pine trees. Ten Thousand Lakes, it says. Score one for
Grandpa."

Judy merely smiles this time, not granting him a laugh, she
knows he's trying to get her to forgive his mistake in losing the
others.

"It's not us who are lost, we know where we are," he says. "It's
them." He stops crouching beside her, the hoity-toity little snip,

and stands up, to uncreak his knees, and also to ease the crowded feeling in his chest.

He sees them. Just this side of the zebra crossing, coming this way, struggling with suitcases. He first sees Nelson, carrying Roy on his shoulders like a two-headed monster, and then Pru's head of red hair puffed out like the Sphinx, and Janice's white tennis dress. Harry, up to his chest in car roofs, waves his arm back and forth like a man on a desert island. Janice waves back, a quick toss of her hand as if he's far from what they're talking about.

But when they're all reunited Nelson is furious. His face is pale and his upper lip stiff and bristling. "Jesus Christ, Dad, where did you disappear to? We went all the way back upstairs to that stupid candy store when you didn't show up in the baggage area."

"We were there, weren't we, Judy?" Harry says, marvelling at his son's growing baldness, exposed mercilessly by the Florida sunlight beating down through the thinned strands, and at his mustache, a mouse-colored stray blur like those fuzzballs that collect under furniture. He has noticed these developments before in recent years but they still have the power to astonish him, along with the crow's feet and bitter cheek lines time has etched in his child's face, sharp in the sunlight. "We didn't take more than a minute in the candy store and came right down the escalator to the baggage place," Rabbit says, pleased to be remembering so exactly, exactly visualizing the two candy bars, the extra nickel he had to fish up for the black counter woman's upturned silver-polish-colored palm, the skin magazines with the girls' open mouths, the interleaved teeth of the escalator steps he was afraid Judy might catch her foot on. "We must have slipped by each other in the crowd," he adds, trying to be helpful and innocuous. His son frightens him.

Janice unlocks the Camry. The baking heat of its interior, released like a ghost, brushes past their faces. They put the suitcases in the way-back. Pru lifts the groggy boy off Nelson's shoulders and arranges him in the shadows of the back seat; Roy's thumb is stuck in his mouth and his dark eyes open for an unseeing second. Nelson, his hands at last freed, slaps the top of the Camry and cries in his agony of irritation, "God *damn* it, Dad, we've been *fran*tic, because of you! We thought you might have

lost her!" There is a look Nelson gets when he's angry or frightened that Harry has always thought of as "white around the gills"
– a tension draining color from the child's face and pulling his eyes
back into his head. He gets the look from his mother, and Janice
got it from hers, dark plump old Bessie, who was a hot-tempered
Koerner, she liked to tell them.

"We stuck right together," Rabbit says calmly. "And don't
dent my fucking car. You've damaged enough cars in your life."

"Yeah, and you've damaged enough lives in yours. Now
you're kidnapping my goddamn daughter!"

"I can't believe this," Harry begins. A cold arrow of pain suddenly heads down his left arm, through the armpit. He blinks.
"My own granddaughter" is all he can organize himself to say.

Janice, looking at his face, asks, "What's the matter, Harry?"

"Nothing," he tells her sharply. "Just this crazy kid.
Something's bugging him and I can't believe it's me." A curious
gaseous weight, enveloping his head and chest, has descended in
the wake of the sudden arrow. He slumps down behind the wheel,
feeling faintly disoriented but determined to drive. When you're
retired, you get into your routines and other people, even so-
called loved ones, become a strain. This entire other family loads
itself into place behind him. Pru swings her nice wide ass in her
three-dimensional checked suit into the back seat next to sleeping
Roy, and Nelson climbs in on the other side, right behind Harry,
so he can feel the kid's breath on the back of his neck. He turns
his head as far as he can and says to Nelson, in the corner of his
eye, "I resent the word 'kidnap.'"

"Resent it, then. That's what it felt like. Suddenly we looked
around and you weren't there."

Like Pan Am 103 on the radar screen. "We knew where we
were, didn't we, Judy?" Harry calls backward. The girl has slithered over her parents and brother into the way-back with the luggage. Harry can see the silhouette of her head with its pigtail and
angular ribbon in the rearview mirror.

"I didn't know where I was but I knew you did," she answers
loyally, casting forward the thin thread of her voice.

Nelson tries to apologize. "I didn't mean to get so pissed," he
says, "but if you knew what a hassle it is to have *two* children, the

hassle of travelling all day, and then to have your own father steal
one of them —"

"I didn't *steal* her, for Chrissake," Harry says. "I bought her a
Sky Bar." He can feel his heart racing, a kind of gallop with an
extra kick in one of the legs. He starts up the Camry and puts it
in drive and then brakes when the car jerks forward and puts it
into reverse, trying not to make contact, as he eases out, with the
side of the Minnesota Bivouac, its protruding side mirror and its
racing stripe in three tones of brown.

"Harry, would you like me to drive?" Janice asks.

"No," he says. "Why would I?"

She hesitates; without looking, he can see, in the hesitation, her
little pointed tongue poke out of her mouth and touch her upper
lip in that way she has when she tries to think, he knows her so
well. He knows her so well that making conversation with her is
like having a struggle with himself. "You just had a look on your
face a minute ago," she says. "You looked —"

"White around the gills," he supplies.

"Something like that."

The old guy who thinks he's directing the show directs them
down the arrows painted on the asphalt toward the tollbooth. The
car ahead of theirs in line, a tan Honda Accord with New Jersey
plates, GARDEN STATE, has backs of the head in it that look familiar: it's that jumpy little guy who hopped through the chairs back
in the waiting room, good old Grace up beside him, and in the
back seat the frizzy-headed daughter and another passenger, a head
even taller and the frizz even tighter — the black guy in the Waspy
business suit Harry had assumed had nothing to do with them.
The old guy is gabbing and gesturing and the black guy is nodding
just like Harry used to do with Fred Springer. It's bad enough
even when your father-in-law is the same color. Harry is so interested he nearly coasts into the back of the Honda. "Honey,
brake," Janice says, and out of the blur of her white tennis dress
in the corner of his eye she holds out to him fifty cents for the
parking-lot charge. An Oriental kid stone-deaf inside his
Walkman earmuffs takes the two quarters with a hand jumping
along with some beat only he can hear, and the striped bar goes
up, and they are free, free to go home.

"Well," Harry says, back on the weird brief highway, "it's a helluva thing, to have your own son accuse you of *kid*napping. And as to the big deal of having two children, it can't be that much worse than having one. Either way, your freedom's gone."

Actually Nelson has, unwittingly or not, touched a sore point, for Harry and Janice did have two children. Their dead child lives on with them as a silent glue of guilt and shame, an inexpungeable sourness at the bottom of things. And Rabbit suspects himself of having an illegitimate daughter, three years younger than Nelson, by a woman called Ruth, who wouldn't admit it the last time Harry saw her.

Nelson goes on, helpless in the grip of his hardened resentments, "You go run off with Judy all palsy-walsy and haven't said boo to little Roy."

"Say boo? – I'd wake him up, saying boo, he's been asleep all the time, it's like he's drugged. And how much longer you gonna let him suck his thumb? Shouldn't he be outgrowing it by now?"

"What does it matter to you if he sucks his thumb? How is it hurting you?"

"He'll get buck teeth."

"Dad, that's an old wives' tale. Pru asked our pediatrician and he said you don't suck your thumb with your teeth."

Pru says quietly, "He did say he should outgrow it soon."

"What makes you so *down* on everything, Dad?" Nelson whines, unable it seems to find another pitch. The kid is itching and his voice can't stop scratching. "You used to be a pretty laid-back hombre; now everything you say is kind of negative."

Rabbit wants to lead the boy on, to see how bad he can make him look in front of the women. "Rigid," he smilingly agrees. "The older you get, the more you get set in your ways. Nobody at Valhalla Village sucks their thumb. There may even be a rule against it, like swimming in the pool without a bathing cap. Like swimming with an earring on. Tell me something. What's the significance of an earring when you're married with two children?"

Nelson ignores the question in dignified silence, making his father look bad.

They are breezing along, between shoulders of unreal grass, the palms clicking by like telephone poles. Pru says from the back seat, to change the subject, "I can never get over how flat Florida is."

"It gets a little rolling," Harry tells her, "away from the coasts. Ranch and orange-grove country. Rednecks and a lot of Mexicans. We could all go for a drive inland some day. See the real Florida."

"Judy and Roy are dying to see Disney World," Nelson says, trying to become reasonable.

"Too far," his father swiftly tells him. "It'd be like driving to Pittsburgh from Brewer. This is a big state. You need reservations to stay overnight and this time of year there aren't any. Absolutely impossible."

This flat statement renders them all wordless. Through the rushing noise of the air-conditioning fan and the humming of the tires Harry hears from the way-back that for a second time in this first half-hour he has made his granddaughter cry. Pru turns and murmurs to her. Harry shouts back, "There's lots else to do. We can go to that circus museum in Sarasota again."

"I *hate* the circus museum," he hears Judy's small voice say.

"We've never been to the Edison house in Fort Myers," he announces, speaking now as patriarch, to the entire carful. "The people at the condo say it's fascinating, he even invented television it turns out."

"And the beach, baby," Pru softly adds. "You know how you love the beach at the Shore." In a less maternal voice she tells Janice and Harry, "She's a lovely swimmer now."

"Driving to the Jersey Shore used to be absolutely the most boring thing we did," Nelson tells his parents, trying to get down out of his dark cloud into a family mode, willing now in recollection to be a child again.

"Driving is boring," Rabbit pontificates, "but it's what we do. Most of American life is driving somewhere and then driving back wondering why the hell you went."

"Harry," Janice says. "You're going too fast again. Do you want to take 75, or push on to Route 41?"

* * *

Of all the roads Harry has seen in his life, Route 41, the old Tamiami Trail, is the most steadily depressing. It is wider than commercial-use, unlimited-access highways tend to be up north, and somehow the competitive roadside enterprise looks worse in constant sunlight, as if like plastic garbage bags it will never rot away. WINN DIXIE. PUBLIX. Eckerd Drugs. K Mart. Wal-Mart. TACO BELL. ARK PLAZA. Joy Food Store. Starvin' Marvin Discount Food Wine and Beer. Among the repeating franchises selling gasoline and groceries and liquor and drugs all mixed together in that peculiar lawless way they have down here, low pale buildings cater especially to illness and age. Arthritic Rehabilitation Center. Nursefinder, Inc. Cardiac Rehabilitation Center. Chiropractix. Legal Offices – Medicare and Malpractice Cases a Speciality. Hearing Aids and Contact Lenses. West Coast Knee Center. Universal Prosthetics. National Cremation Society. On the telephone wires, instead of the sparrows and starlings you see in Pennsylvania, lone hawks and buzzards sit. Banks, stylish big structures in smoked glass, rise higher than the wires with their glossy self-advertisements. First Federal. Southeast. Barnett Bank with its Superteller. C & S proclaiming All Services, servicing the millions and billions in money people bring down here along with their decrepit bodies, the loot of all those lifetimes flooding the sandy low land, floating these big smoked-glass superliners.

Alongside 41, between the banks and stores and pet suppliers and sprinkler installers, miles of low homes are roofed with fat white cooling tile. A block or two back from the highway in the carbon-monoxide haze tall pink condos like Spanish castles or Chinese pagodas spread sideways like banyan trees. Banyan trees fascinate Harry down here, the way they spread by dropping down vines that take root; they look to him like enormous chewing gum on your shoe. Easy Drugs. NU-VIEW. Ameri-Life and Health. Starlite Motel. JESUS CHRIST IS LORD. His carful of family grows silent and dazed as he drives the miles, stopping now and then at the overhead lights that signal an intersecting road, a secondary road heading west to beaches and what mangrove swamps survive and east to the scruffy prairie being skinned in great square tracts for yet more development. Development! We're being developed to death. Each turning off of Route 41 takes some people home, to their little niche in the maze, their own parking spot and hard-bought place in the sun. The sun is low enough over the Gulf now to tinge everything pink, the red of the stoplights almost invisible. At the Angstroms' own turnoff, two more miles of streets unfold, some straight and some curving, through blocks of single-family houses with half-dead little front yards ornamented by plumes of pampas grass and flowering bushes on vacation from flowering in this dry butt-end of the year. Janice and Harry at first thought they might purchase one of these pale one-story houses lurking behind their tropical bushes and orange trees, caves of coolness and dark, with their secret pools out back behind the garages with their automatic doors, but such houses reminded them unhappily of the house they had in Penn Villas that saw so much marital misery and strangeness before it burned down, half of it, so they settled for a two-bedroom condominium up high in the air, on the fourth floor, overlooking a golf course from a narrow balcony screened by the top branches of Norfolk pines. Of all the addresses where Harry has lived in his life – 303 Jackson Road; Btry A, 66th FA Bn, Fort Larson, Texas; 447 Wilbur Street, Apt. #5; whatever the number on Summer Street was where he parked himself with Ruth Leonard that spring long ago; 26 Vista Crescent; 89 Joseph Street for ten years, courtesy of Ma Springer; 14½ Franklin Drive – this is the highest number by far: 59600 Pindo Palm Boulevard, Building B, #413. He hadn't been crazy about the thirteen, in fact he thought builders didn't put that number in things, but maybe people are less superstitious than they used to be. When he was a kid there was all sorts of worry, not altogether playful, about black cats and spilled salt and opening umbrellas in the house and kicking buckets and walking under ladders. The air was thought then to have eyes and ears and to need placating.

VALHALLA VILLAGE: a big grouted sign, the two words curved around a gold ring of actual brass, inlaid and epoxied-over to discourage vandalous thieves. You turn in at the security booth, get recognized by the guard there, park in one of two spaces with your condo number stencilled right on the asphalt, use your key on the outer door of Building B, punch out the code number to open the inner door, take the elevator, and walk to your left. The corridor is floored in peach-colored carpet and smells of air freshener, to mask the mildew that creeps into every closed space in Florida. A crew comes through three times a week vacuuming and the rug gets lathered and the walls worked once a month, and there are plastic bouquets in little things like basketball hoops next to every numbered door and a mirror across from the elevator plus a big runny-colored green and golden vase on a table shaped like a marble half-moon, but it is still not a space in which you want to linger.

With their suitcases bumping the walls of silver and peach and Janice and Pru still gamely gabbing and little Roy being made to walk on his own two feet now that he's awake for once and crying about it at every step, Harry feels they are disturbing a mortuary calm, though in fact most everybody behind these doors has contrived something to do in the afternoon, golf or tennis or a beauty-parlor appointment or a bus trip to the Everglades. You live life here as if your condo is just home base, a sort of air-conditioned anteroom to the sunny mansion of all outdoors. Stay inside, you might start to mildew. Around five-thirty, an eerie silence of many simultaneous naps descends, but at four o'clock it's too early for that.

The door to 413 has a double lock operated with two keys, one of which also opens the outer door downstairs. With the impatient mass of his entire family and its baggage pressing behind him, Harry fumbles a bit, his hand jumping the way it does when he's feeling crowded in the chest, his notched key scratching at the wiggly small slot, but then it fits and turns and clicks and the door swings open and he is home. This place could belong to one of millions of part-time Floridians but in fact is his, his and Janice's. You enter in a kind of foyer, a closet door to the left and on the right see-through shelves of stained wood Janice has loaded with birds and flowers she made out of shells in a class she took that first year down here, when she was still enthusiastic about shells. Enthusiasm about shells doesn't last, nor does taking Spanish lessons so you can talk to the help. It's a phase the greenhorns, the fresh snowbirds, must go through. Baby scallops make feathers and petals, augurs do as bird beaks, slipper shells are like little boats.

The shelves, which also hold a few of Ma Springer's knickknacks, including a big green glass egg with a bubble inside it, separate the foyer from the kitchen, with the dining room beyond it; straight ahead lies the living-room area, where they have the TV and the comfortable wicker chairs and a low round glass table they often eat dinner from, if a show they care about is on. To the left, a square-armed blond sofa can be folded out for a bed and a hollow door leads to the master bedroom, which has a bathroom and a storage area where Janice keeps an ironing board she never uses and an exercise bicycle she rides when she thinks she's getting overweight, to Nelson's old tapes of the Bee Gees that he outgrew long ago. The guest bedroom is entered off the living room, to the right, and has its own bathroom that backs up to the kitchen plumbing. The arrangement other years has been that Nelson and Pru take this room with a cot for the baby and Judith sleeps on the foldout sofa, but Harry is not sure this arrangement is still proper. The little ones have grown: Roy perhaps is too big and observant to share a bedroom with his parents and the girl is getting to be enough of a lady to deserve a little privacy.

He explains his plan: "This year I thought we might put the cot in the storage room for Judy, she can use our bathroom and then shut the door, and give Roy the living-room sofa."

The small boy gazes upward at his grandfather while his thumb sneaks toward his mouth. He has a flubby sort of mouth that Rabbit associates with the Lubells; neither the Angstroms nor the Springers have bunched-up fat lips like that, like a row of plump berries run together, but Teresa's father, in the one time Harry met him, visiting Akron because he went to Cleveland for a dealer conference anyway, did, if you could see around the two days' beard and the cigarette always in the guy's fat mouth. It's as if Pru's worthless creep of a father has been disguised as a child and sent to spy on them all. The kid takes in everything and says nothing. Harry speaks down to him roughly: "Yeah, what's the matter with that?"

The thumb roots in deeper and the child's eyes, darker even than Nelson's and Janice's, shine with distrust. Judy offers to explain: "He's scared to be alone in this room all by himself, the baby."

Pru tries to help. "Sweetie, Mommy and Daddy would be right in that other room, where you used to sleep before you became so grown up."

Nelson says, "You might have discussed it first with us, Dad, before you switched everything around."

"Discuss it, when is there a chance to discuss anything with you? Every time I call the lot you're not there, or the line is busy. I used to get Jake or Rudy at least, now all I get is some fruity-voiced pal of yours you've hired."

"Yeah, Lyle tells me how you grill him about everything."

"I don't grill him, I'm just trying to act interested. I still have an interest up there, even if you do think you're running it half the year."

"*Half* the year! *All* the year, from what Mom says."

Janice intervenes: "What Mom says is her legs hurt after all that sitting in the car and she's thinking of moving the cocktail hour ahead if this is how we're all going to talk for five days. Nelson, your father was trying to be considerate about the sleeping arrangements. He and I discussed it. Judy, which would you rather, the sofa or the ironing room?"

"I didn't mind the old way," she says.

Little Roy is trying to follow the drift of this discussion and removes his thumb enough for his flubby lips to mouth something Rabbit does not understand. Whatever he's saying, it makes Roy's eyes water to think of it. "Eee*eee*" is all Harry hears, at the end of the sentence.

Pru translates: "He says she gets to watch TV."

"What a disgusting baby tattletale," says Judy, and quick as a dragonfly darting over water she skims across the carpet and with an open hand whacks her little brother on the side of his spherical head. Pru cuts his hair in a kind of inverted bowl-shape. As when a faucet gasps emptily for a second after being turned on, his outrage silences him a moment, though his mouth is open. His yell when it comes arrives at full volume; against its sonic background Judy explains to them all, with a certain condescending air, "Just Johnny Carson sometimes when everybody else was asleep, and *Saturday Night Live* once that I can remember."

Harry asks her, "So you'd rather stay in here with the lousy TV than have a little cozy room of your own?"

"It doesn't have any windows," she points out shyly, not wanting to hurt his feelings.

"Fine, *fine*," Harry says. "I don't give a fuck where anybody sleeps," and in demonstration of his indifference strides into his own bedroom, past the king-size bed they bought down here, with its padded headboard covered in quilted satin and a matching jade-green coverlet that is as hard to fold up as the ones in hotels, into the little windowless room and picks up the folding cot, with its sheets and baby-blue Orlon blanket on it, and lugs it through the doorways, banging the frames and one of the wicker armchairs in the living room, into the guest bedroom. He is embarrassed: he overestimated how fast Judy was growing, he had wanted to embower her as his princess, he doesn't know little girls, his one daughter died and his other is not his.

Janice says, "Harry, you mustn't overexert yourself, the doctor said."

"The doctor said," he mocks. "All he ever sees is people over seventy-five and he says to me just what he says to them."

But he is breathing hard, and Pru hastens after him to spare him the effort of straightening the folding leg, a U-shape of metal tubing, that has come unclicked and folded underneath, and pulls taut the sheets and blanket. Back in the living room, Harry says to Nelson, who is holding little Roy in his arms again, "*Now* are you and the brat happy?"

For answer Nelson turns to Janice and says, "Jesus, Mom, I don't know as I can stand five days of this."

But then when they all get settled – the suitcases unpacked into bureaus, Judy and Roy fed milk and cookies and changed into bathing suits and taken to the heated Valhalla Village pool by their mother and Janice, who has to sign them in – Harry and Nelson sit each with a beer at the round glass table and try to be friends. "So," Harry says, "how's the car business?"

"You know as well as I do," Nelson says. "You see the stat sheets every month." He has developed a nervous irritable habit of grimacing and hunching his shoulders, as though somebody behind him might be about to knock him on the head. He smokes a cigarette as if he's feeding himself something through a tube, constantly fiddling with the shape of the ash on the edge of a white clamshell he has borrowed from Janice's collection.

"How do you like the '89s?" Harry asks, determined not to put it off, now that he and the boy are alone. "I haven't seen the actual cars yet, just the brochures. Beautiful brochures. How many millions you think those ad agencies get for making up those brochures? I was looking at the Corolla one trying to figure out if they really *had* driven that sedan and that wagon up into the mountains or were just faking it, and I had to laugh. The cars were posed on snow but there were no tracks showing how they got there! Look at it sometime."

Nelson is not much amused. He shapes his ash into a perfect cone and then suddenly stabs it out, twisting the butt vehemently. His hands shake more than a young man's should. He sips his beer, leaving shreds of foam on his tufty mustache, and, looking level at his father, says, "You asked me what I thought of the '89s. The same thing I thought about the '88s. Dull, Dad. Boxy. They're still giving us cars that look like gas-misers when there's been a gas glut for ten years. Americans want to go back to fins and convertibles and the limo look and these Japs are still trying to sell these tidy little boxes. And not cheap, either. That's what hurts. The lousy dollar against the yen. Why should people pay seventeen grand for a GTS when in the same range you can get a Mustang or Beretta GT or Mazda MX-6?"

"A Celica doesn't cost seventeen grand," Harry says. "Mine back home listed at less than fifteen."

"Get a few options and it does."

"Don't push the options at people – you get a name in the county for loading. People come in determined to have a stripped model, you should sell 'em one without making 'em feel they're being cheapskates."

"Tell it to California," Nelson says. "Practically all they want to part with are loaded models. The automatic notchbacks, the All-Trac Turbos. You want a basic ST or GT, it takes months for the order to come through. Luxury is where the bigger profit is, all the way up the line back to Tokyo. You have to try to sell what they send us – the one machine they make that's really moving, the Camry, you can't wheedle enough out of the bastards. They treat us like dirt, Dad. They see us as soft. Soft lazy Americans, over the hill. Ten more years, they'll have bought the whole country. Some television show I was watching, they already own all of Hawaii and half of L.A. and Nevada. They're buying up thousands of acres of desert in Nevada! What're they going to do with it? Set off Japanese atom bombs?"

"Don't get down on the Japanese like that, Nelson. We've done fine riding along with the Japanese."

"Riding along, you said it. Like riding along in the back seat of a Tercel. You always talk of them with such awe, like they're super-men. They're not. Some of their design, you get away from the little safe dependable cheapie family car, is a disaster. The Land Cruiser is a dog, it doesn't begin to compete with the Cherokee, and neither does the 4-Runner, it was so underpowered they had to come with a V-6 engine that turns out to be a guzzler – fourteen miles to the gallon, I was reading in *Consumer Reports*. And that van! It's ridiculous. Where the engine is, up between the front seats, the only way to get to the front from the back is get all the way out and climb back in. In the winter in Pennsylvania, people don't like to do that. So many customers have been complaining, I drove one myself the other day just to see, and even though I'm no giant, boy, did I feel squeezed in – no foot room to speak of, and no place to put your elbow. And zilch acceleration: pull into a fast-moving highway you'll get rear-ended. The wind pushed me all over 422, the damn thing is so tall – I could hardly step up into it."

That's right, Harry is thinking, *you're no giant*. Nelson seems to him strangely precise and indignant and agitated, like a nicely made watch with one tooth off a cogwheel or a gummy spot in the lubrication. The kid keeps sniffing, and lights another ciga-rette, after not enjoying the one he just snuffed out. He keeps touching his nose, as if his mustache hurts. "Well," Harry says, taking a relaxed tone to try to relax his son, "vans were never the bread and butter, and Toyota knows they have a lemon. They're getting a total revamp out by '91. How do you like the new Cressida?"

"It stinks, in my humble. There's nothing new about it. Oh, it's bigger, a bit, and the engine is up from two point eight to three point oh, and twenty-four valves instead of twelve, so you get more oomph, but for a basic twenty-one K you *expect* a little oomph — my *God*. The dashboard is a disaster. The climate-control panel slides out like a drawer and won't budge unless the ignition's on, which is ridiculous, number one, and two, they kept from last year's model their crazy idea of two sets of audio controls so you have all these extra buttons when already there's enough for an airplane cockpit. It costs luxury, Dad, and it drives luxury you could say, but it looks cheap inside and pseudo-Audi outside. Toyota, let's face it, has about the styling imagination of a gerbil. Their cars don't *express* anything. Good cars, classic cars — the Thirties Packards, the little Jags with the long hood and spoked wheels, the Fifties finned jobbies, even the VW bug — ex*pressed* something, made a statement. Toyotas don't express anything but playing it safe and stealing other people's ideas. Look at their pickup. The pickup used to be hot, but now they've let Ford and GM right back into the market. Look at the MR-2. It doesn't sell for shit now."

Harry argues, "High insurance is hurting everybody's two-seaters. Toyota puts out a good solid machine. They handle well and they last, and people know that and respect it."

Nelson cuts him short. "And they're so damn dictatorial — they tell you exactly what to charge, what to put in the windows, what your salespeople should wear, how many square feet of this and that you have to have to be good enough to lick their bazoo. When I took over I was surprised at all the crap you and Charlie had been swallowing all those years. They expect you to be their *robot*."

Now Rabbit is fully offended. "Welcome to the real world, kid. You're going to be part of some organization or other in this life. Toyota's been good to us and good to your grandfather and don't you forget it. I can remember Fred Springer when he first got the Toyota franchise saying he felt like a kid at Christmas all year round." The women in the family are always saying Nelson is a throwback to his grandfather and Harry hopes by mentioning dead Fred to bring the boy back into line. All this blaspheming Toyota makes Harry uneasy.

But Nelson goes on, "Grandpa was a *dealer*, Dad. He loved to make deals. He used to tell about it: you came up short on some and made out like a bandit on others and it was *fun*. There was some *play* in the situation, some space for creativity. Unloading the trade-ins is about the only spontaneous creative thing left in the business now, and Toyota tells you they don't want a bunch of ugly American junk up front on the lot, you almost have to sell the used cars on the sly. At least you can cut an extra grand or so if you get a dummy; selling new is just running the cash register. I don't call that selling, just standing at the checkout counter."

"Not bad for forty-five thou plus benefits." What Nelson makes a year now. Harry and Janice quarrel about it; he says it's too much, she says he has a family to support. "When I was your age," he tells the boy, perhaps not for the first time, "I was pulling down thirteen five a year as a Linotyper and came home dirty every night. The job gave me headaches and ruined my eyes. I used to have perfect eyes."

"That was *then*, Dad, this is *now*. You were still in the industrial era. You were a blue-collar slave. People don't make money an hour at a time any more; you just get yourself in the right position and it *comes*. I know guys, lawyers, guys in real estate, no older than me and not as smart who pull in two, three hundred K on a single transaction. You must know a lot of retired money down here. It's *easy* to be rich, that's what this country is all about."

"These must be the guys doing all that selling-off of Nevada to the Japanese you're so upset about. What're you so hungry for money for anyway? You live mortgage-free in that house your mother gives you, you must be saving a bundle. Speaking of used cars – "

"Dad, I hate to break the news to you, but forty thousand just isn't a fuck of a lot if you want to live with any style."

"Jesus, how much style do you and Pru need? Your house is free, all you do is cover heat and taxes – "

"The taxes on that barn have crept up to over four grand. Mt. Judge real estate is *way* up since the new baby boom, even a semi-detached over toward that slummy end of Jackson Road where you used to live goes for six figures. Also the federal tax reform didn't do a thing for my bracket, you got to be rich to get the benefits. Lyle was showing me on a spread sheet – "

"That's something else I wanted to ask you about. Whose idea was it to replace Mildred Kroust with this guy?"

"Dad, she'd been with Springer Motors forever – "

"I know, that was the point. She could do it all in her sleep."

"She couldn't, actually, though she *was* asleep a lot of the time. She never could handle computers, for one thing. Oh sure, she tried, but one little scramble or error message'd show up on the screen she'd blame the machine and call up the company to send a repairman over at a hundred twenty an hour when all that was wrong was she couldn't read the manual and had hit the wrong key. She was *ancient*. You should have let her go when she reached retirement age."

The apartment door furtively clicks open. "Just me," Janice's voice calls. "Pru and the babies wanted to stay at the pool a little longer and I thought I'd come back and start dinner. I thought we'd just have odds and ends tonight; I'll see if there's any soup to warm up. Keep talking, boys." She doesn't intrude upon them; her footsteps head into the kitchen. She must imagine they are having a healing talk, father to son. In fact Harry is looking at Nelson as if the boy is a computer. There is a glitch, a secret. He talks too much, too rapidly. Nellie used to be taciturn and sullen and now he keeps spilling out words, giving more answer than there was question. Something is revving him up, something is wrong. Harry says, of Mildred Kroust, "She wasn't that old, actually, was she? Sixty-eight? Sixty-nine?"

"Dad, she was in her seventies and counting. Lyle does all she ever used to do and comes in only two or three days a week."

"He's doing it all different, I can see on the stat sheets. That was the thing I wanted to ask you about, the figures on the used in the November set."

For some reason, the kid has gone white around the gills again. He pokes his cigarette through the hole at the beer pull-tab and then crushes the can in one hand, no big trick now that they're made of paper-thin aluminum. He rises from his chair and seems to be heading toward his mother, who has been knocking things around in the kitchen.

"*Janice!*" Harry shouts, turning his head with difficulty, his neck stiff with fat.

She stands in the kitchen entryway in a wet black bathing suit and a purple wraparound skirt, to make herself decent for the elevator. She looks a touch foozled: she cracked open the Campari bottle before leading the others down to the pool and must have hurried back to give herself another slug. Her skimpy hair is wet and stringy. "What?" she says, responding guiltily to the urgent sound of Harry's voice.

"Where did that latest batch of sheets from the lot go? Weren't they sitting over on the desk?"

This desk is one they bought cheap down here, in a hurry to furnish their place, in the same style as the end tables flanking the blond fold-out sofa and their bedroom bureaus – white-painted wood with the legs slashed at intervals with gold paint to imitate bamboo joints. It has only three shallow drawers that stick in the humidity and some cubby holes up top where bills and invitations get lost. The desktop, of some glazed marmoreal stuff like petrified honey-vanilla ice cream, is generally covered by a drift of unanswered letters and bank statements and statements from their stockbrokers and money management fund and golf scorecards and Xeroxed announcements from the Village Activities Committee, called VAC since life down here is supposedly a perpetual vacation. Also Janice has a way of tearing out clippings from health magazines and *The National Enquirer* and the Fort Myers *News-Press* and then forgetting who she meant to send them to. She looks frightened.

"Were they?" she asks. "Maybe I threw them out. Your idea, Harry, is just pile everything on it and it'll still be there next year when you want it."

"These just came in last week. They were November's financial summaries."

Her mouth pinches in and her face seems to click shut on a decision she will stick to blindly no matter what happens, the way women will. "I don't know where they went to. What I especially hate are your old golf cards drifting around. Why do you keep them?"

"I write tips to myself on them, what I learned on that round. Don't change the subject, Janice. I want those Goddamn stat sheets."

Nelson stands beside his mother at the mouth of the kitchen, the crushed can in his hand. Without the denim jacket his shirt looks even more sissified, with its delicate pink stripes and white French cuffs and round-pointed white collar. The boy and Janice are near the same height, with tense small cloudy faces. Both look furtive. "No big deal, Dad," Nelson says in a dry-mouthed voice. "You'll be getting the December summaries in a couple of weeks." When he turns toward the refrigerator, to get himself another beer, he gives Rabbit a heartbreaking view of the back of his head – the careful rat's tail, the curved sliver of earring, the growing bald spot.

And when Pru comes back from the pool with the children, all of them in rubber flipflops and hugging towels around their shoulders and their hair pasted flat against their skulls, the two small children shivering gleefully, their lips bluish, their miniature fingers white and wrinkled from the water, Harry sees Pru in a new way, as the weakest link in a conspiracy against him. That cushiony frontal kiss she gave him at the airport. The pelvis that in her high-cut but otherwise demure white bathing suit looks so gently pried wider by the passing years.

Their fifth winter down here, this is, and Harry still wakes amazed to find himself actually in Florida, beside the Gulf of Mexico. If not exactly beside it, within sight of it, at least he was until that new row of six-story condos with ornamental turrets and Spanish-tile roofs shut out the last distant wink of watery horizon. When he and Janice bought the place in 1984 you could still see from their balcony snatches of the Gulf, a dead-level edge to the world over the rooftops and broken between the raw new towers like the dots and dashes of Morse code, and in their excitement they bought a telescope and tripod at a nautical shop at the mall a mile down Pindo Palm Boulevard. In its trembling little circle of vision, that first winter, they would catch a sailboat with its striped spinnaker bellying out or a luxury yacht with tall white sides peeling back the waves silently or a fishing charter with its winglike gaffing platforms or, farthest out, a world unto itself, a rusty gray oil freighter headed motionlessly toward Mobile or New Orleans or back toward Panama or Venezuela. In the years since, their view of the water has been built shut, skyscraper hotels arising along the shore, constructions the color of oatmeal or raspberry whip or else sheer glass like vertical distillations, cold and pure, of the Gulf's blue-green.

Where these towers arise had once been nothing but sand and mangrove swamp and snaky tidal inlets slipping among the nets of roots and dimpling where an alligator or a water moccasin glided; and then a scattering of white-painted houses and unpainted shacks in feeble imitation of the South to the north, scratching out some cotton and grazing some cattle on the sandy soil, sending north shuffling herds of beef on the hoof to the starving rebel troops in the Civil War; and then houses closer together, some of brick and wrought iron and of limestone and granite barged in from Alabama quarries. Then, in the era after Reconstruction, to this appendage of the South came the railroads and the rich and the sick and the hopeful misfits, this being frontier in an unexpected direction. Busts followed booms; optimism kept washing in. Now, with the jets and Social Security and the national sun-worship, they can't build onto it fast enough, this city called Deleon, named after some Spanish explorer killed for all his shining black breastplate by the poisoned arrow of a Seminole in 1521 near here or a place like it, and pronounced *Deel*yun by the locals, as if they are offering to deal you in. The past glimmers like a dream at the back of Harry's mind as he awakes; in his semi-retirement he has taken to reading history. It has always vaguely interested him, that sinister mulch of facts our little lives grow out of before joining the mulch themselves, the fragile brown rotting layers of previous deaths, layers that if deep enough and squeezed hard enough make coal as in Pennsylvania. On quiet evenings, while Janice sits on the sofa sipping herself into stupidity with some lamebrain TV show, he lies on the bed leaning back against its padded satiny headboard with a book, staring dizzily down into the past as if high in a jade-green treehouse.

The sound that breaks into his dreams and dispels them is the rasp of golf greens being mowed, and then the scarcely less mechanical weeping noise of the seagulls gathering on the freshly watered fairways, where the earthworms are surfacing to drink. The head of their bed is by the big glass sliding doors, left open a crack to take in the winter-morning cool, in these few months when the air-conditioner is non-essential; so the cool salt air, sweetened with the scent of fresh fairways, reminds his face of where he is, this mass-produced paradise where Janice's money has taken him. She is not in the bed, though her warmth still greets his knee as he spreadeagles into her space. In deference to his height of six three, they have at last bought a king-size bed, so for the first time in his life his feet do not hang over the bottom and force him to sleep on his belly like a dead man floating. It took him a long time to get used to it, his feet not hooking onto the mattress this way but instead being forced to bend at the ankle or else point sideways. He gets foot cramps. He tries to sleep on his side, slightly curled up; it gives his mouth space to breathe and his belly room to slop into, and it frightens his frail heart less than hanging face down over the thickness of the mattress. But his arms don't know where to go. A hand crooked under his head loses cir- culation at the wrist and its numbness awakes him, tingling as if with an electric shock. If he lies on his back, Janice says, he snores. She snores herself now, now that they are approaching elderly, but he tries not to blame her for it: poor mutt, she can't help what she does when asleep, snoring and sometimes farting so bad he has to bury his nose in the pillow and remind himself she's only human. Poor women: they have a lot of leaks down there, their bodies are too complicated. He hears her now in the kitchen, talking in an unreal high needling sort of voice, the way we talk to children.

Rabbit listens for the lower younger voice of the children's mother to chime in but instead hears, close to his head, a bird cheeping in the Norfolk pine whose branches can be touched from their balcony. He still can't get over Norfolk pines, the way they look like the plastic trees you buy for Christmas, the branches spaced like slats and each one of them a plume perfect as a bird's feather and the whole tree absolutely conical in shape. The bird's cheeping sounds like a piece of moist wood being rhythmically made to squeak against another. Most nature in Florida has a man- ufactured quality. Wall-to-wall carpet, green outdoor carpeting on the cement walks, crunchy St. Augustine grass in the space between the walks, all of it imposed on top of the sand, the dirty-gray sand that sprays over your shoes when you take a divot down here.

Today is Wednesday, he has a golf date, his usual foursome, tee-off time at nine-forty: the thought gives him a reason to get out of bed and not just lie there forever, trying to remember his dream. In his dream he had been reaching out toward something his sleeping eyes didn't let him see through his lids, something round and shadowy and sad, big-bellied with the vague doom he tries to suppress during the daytime.

Up, Rabbit examines the phony-looking branches of the Norfolk pine to see if he can see the noisy bird. He expects from the self-importance of the sound a cockatoo or toucan at least, a squawky tropical something with foot-long tailfeathers hanging down, but all he sees is a small brown bird such as flicker all around in Pennsylvania. Maybe it *is* a Pennsylvania bird, a migrant down here just like him. A snowbird.

He goes into the bathroom and brushes his teeth and urinates. Funny, it used to make a throaty splash in the toilet bowl, now a kind of grudging uncertain stream comes out, he has to rise once and sometimes even twice in the night, sitting on the toilet like a woman; what with the foreskin folded over sleepily he can never be sure which direction it will come out in, bad as a woman, they can't aim either. He shaves and weighs himself. He's gained a pound. Those Planter's Peanut Bars. He moves to leave the bedroom and realizes he can't. In Florida he sleeps in his underwear; pajamas get twisted around him and around two in the morning feel so hot they wake him up, along with the pressure in his bladder. With Pru and the kids here he can't just wander into the kitchen in his underwear. He hears them out there, bumping into things. He either should put on his golf pants and a polo shirt or find his bathrobe. He decides on the bathrobe, a burgundy red with gray lapels, as being more – what's that word that keeps coming up in medieval history? – seigneurial. Hostly. Grandpaternal. It makes a statement, as Nelson would say.

By the time Rabbit opens the door, the first fight of the day has begun in the kitchen. Precious little Judy is unhappy; salt tears redden the rims of her lids though she is trying, shaky-voiced, not to cry. "But half the kids in my school have been. Some of them have even been twice, and they don't even have grandparents living in Florida!" She can't reach Disney World.

Janice is explaining, "It's really a whole separate trip, sweetheart. You should fly to Orlando if you want to go. To go from here – "

"'d be like driving to Pittsburgh," Harry finishes for her.

"Daddy promised!" the child protests, with such passion that her four-year-old brother, holding a spoon suspended in his fist above a bowl of Total he is mushing without eating, sobs in sympathy. Two drops of milk fall from his slack lower lip.

"Dull driving, too," Harry continues. "Stoplights all down Route 27. We come that way sometimes, driving down."

Pru says, "Daddy didn't mean this time, he meant some other time when we have more days."

"He said *this* time," the child insists. "He's always breaking promises."

"Daddy's very busy earning money so you can have all the things you want," Pru tells her, taking the prim tone of one woman losing patience with another. She too is wearing a bathrobe, a little quilted shorty patterned with violet morning glories and their vines. Her freckled thighs have that broad bland smoothness of car fenders. Her feet are long and bony, pink in their toe-joints and papery-white on top, in cork-soled lipstick-red clogs. Her toenail polish is chipped, and Rabbit finds that pretty sexy too.

"Oh, *yeahhh*," the child replies, with a furious sarcastic emphasis Harry doesn't understand. Family life, life with children, is something out of his past, that he has not been sorry to leave behind; it was for him like a bush in some neglected corner of the back yard that gets overgrown, a lilac bush or privet some bindweed has invaded from underneath with leaves so similar and tendrils so tightly entwining it gives the gardener a headache in the sun to try to separate bad growth from good. Anyway he basically had but the one child, Nelson, one lousy child, though he was reading somewhere the other day that a human male produces enough sperm to populate not just the planet Earth but Mars and Venus as well, if they could support life. It's a depressing thought, too planetary, like that unreachable round object in his dream, that the whole point of his earthly existence has been to produce little Nellie Angstrom, so he in turn could produce Judy and Roy, and so on until the sun burns out.

Now Nelson is stirred up and sucked into the kitchen by the fuss. He must have heard himself being talked about, and comes in from the guest bedroom, barechested and unshaven in rumpled smoky-blue pajama bottoms that look expensive. Unease infiltrates Harry's abdomen with this observation of Nelson's expensive tastes, something he is trying to remember about numbers, something he can't reach. Janice said the boy looked exhausted and he does look thin, with faint shadows flickering between his ribs. There is a touch of aggression about the bare chest, something territorial, taken with Pru's shorty robe. The pajama game. Doris Day and, who was it, John Raitt? Despite the quality of his pajamas, Nelson looks haggard and scruffy and mean, with the unshaven whiskers and that tufty little mustache like what dead Fred Springer used to wear and his thinning hair standing up in damp spikes. Rabbit remembers how deeply Nelson used to sleep as a child, how hot and moist his skull on the pillow would feel. "What's this about promises?" the boy asks angrily, staring at a space between Judy and Pru. "I never promised to go up to Orlando this trip."

"Daddy, there's nothing to *do* in this dumb part of Florida. I *hat*ed that circus museum last year, and then on the way back the traffic was so miserable Roy threw up in the Kentucky Fried Chicken parking lot!"

"Route 41 does a job on you," Harry admits.

"There's *tons* to do," Nelson says. "Go swim in the pool. Go play shuffleboard." He runs dry almost immediately and looks in panic at his mother.

Janice says to Judy, "The Village has tennis courts where you and I can go and hit balls."

"*Roy*'ll have to come and he always *spoils* it," the little girl complains, the vision of it freshening her tears again.

" – and there's the beach – " Janice goes on.

Judy replies, just making objections now, "Our teacher says the sun gives you skin damage and the earlier you get it the more cancer you'll get later on."

"Don't be such a fucking smart-ass," Nelson says to her. "Your grandmother's trying to be nice."

His remark makes the child's tears spill, out through the curved lashes onto her cheeks like the silvery jerking tracks rain makes on windowpanes. "I *was*n't being –" she tries to get out.

At her age, this girl should be happier than she is, Harry thinks. "Sure you were," he tells her. "And why not? It's *boring*, going somewhere with family, away from your friends. We all remember what it's like, we used to drag your daddy to the Jersey Shore, and then make him go up to the Poconos and have hay-fever up in those Godawful dark pines. Torture! The things we do to each other in the name of fun! O.K. Here's my plan. Anybody want to hear my plan?"

The little girl nods. The others, even Roy who's been carefully shaping his Total mush into a kind of pyramid with the back of his spoon, watch him as if he is a conjurer. It's not so hard, to get back into the swing of family life. You just have to come out of yourself a little. It's like basketball was, those first two or three minutes, when amid the jamming and yelling and body heat and crowd noise you realized that you were going to have to *do it yourself*, nobody was going to do it for you. "Today I got to play golf," he begins.

"Great," Nelson says. "That's a big help. You're not going to make Judy caddy, if that's your plan. You'll bend her spine out of shape."

"Nellie, you're getting paranoid," Harry tells him. The boy's been trying ever since that business with Jill twenty years ago to protect women against his father. His son is the only person in the world who sees him as dangerous. Harry feels the day's first twinge in the chest, a little playful burning like a child flirting with a lit match. "That wasn't my plan, no, but why not sometime? She could carry my lightweight bag, I'd take out two of the woods and one of the wedges and she and I could walk a couple holes some late afternoon when the tee times are over. I could show her the swing. But in the foursome, actually, we ride carts. I'd rather we walked, for the exercise, but the other bozos insist. Actually, they're great guys, they all have grandchildren, they'd love Judy. She could ride in my place." He can picture it, her sitting there like a slim little princess, Bernie Drechsel with his cigar in his mouth at the wheel of the electric cart.

He is losing his conjurer's audience, thinking out loud this way. Roy drops his spoon and Pru squats down to pick it up, her shorty robe flaring out over one thigh. A lacy peep of jet-black bikini underpants. A slightly shiny vaccination oval high up. Nelson groans. "Out with it, Dad. I got to go to the *bath*room." He blows his nose on a paper towel. Why is his nose always running? Harry has read somewhere, maybe *People* on the death of Rock Hudson, that that's one of the first signs of AIDS.

Harry says, "No more circus museum. Actually, they've closed it. For renovations." He had noticed a story about it in the Sarasota paper a week or so ago, headlined *Circus Redux*. He hates that word, you see it everywhere, and he doesn't know how to pronounce it. Like arbitrageur and perestroika. "My plan was this. Today, I got to play golf but tonight there's Bingo in the dining hall and I thought the kids or at least Judy would enjoy that, and we could all use a real meal for a change. Tomorrow, we could either go to this Lionel Train and Seashell Museum that Joe Gold says is just terrific, or in the other direction, south, there's the Edison house. I've always been kind of curious about it but it may be a little advanced for the kids, I don't know. Maybe the invention of the telephone and the phonograph doesn't seem too exciting to kids raised on all this computerized crap they have now."

"Dad," Nelson says in his pained voice, sniffing, "it's not even that exciting to *me*. Isn't there someplace out on Route 41 where they could go play video games? Or miniature golf. Or the beach and swimming pool, Jesus. I thought we came down here to re*lax*, and you're making some kind of educational ordeal of it. Come *on*. Lay *off*."

Rabbit is hurt. "Lay off, I was just trying to create a little structure," he says.

Pru intervenes in his defense. "Nelson, the children can't spend all day in the pool, they'll get too much ultraviolet."

Janice says, "This hot weather is bound to turn cool this time of year. It's flukey."

"It's the greenhouse effect," Nelson says, turning to go to the bathroom, showing that disgusting rat's tail at the back of his head, the glint of earring. How queer *is* the kid? "The greedy consumer society has wrecked the ozone and we'll all be fried by the year 2000," Nelson says. "Look!" He points to the Fort Myers *News-Press* someone has laid on the kitchen table. The main headline is *1988: the dry look*, and a cartoon shows a crazed-looking yellow sun wringing out some clouds for a single drop of water. Janice must have brought the paper in from the corridor, though all she cares about is the *Lifestyles* section. Who's fucking who, who's divorcing who. Normally she stays in bed and lets her husband be the one to bring the paper in from the corridor. *Lifestyles* keeps.

Pru hands back Roy's spoon to him and takes away his dreadful little bowl of Total mush, congealed like dogfood left out overnight. "Want a 'nana?" she asks in a cooing coaxing sexy voice. "A nice 'nana if Mommy peeled and sliced it?"

Janice confesses, "Teresa, I'm not sure we have any bananas. In fact I know we don't. Harry hates fruit though he should eat it and I meant to do a big shopping yesterday for you and Nelson but the tennis game I was in went to the third set and then it was time to go to the airport." She brightens; her voice goes up in volume; she tries to become another conjurer. "That's what we can do this morning while Grandpa plays his golf! We can all go to Winn Dixie and do an *enor*mous shopping!"

"Count me out," Nelson yells from the bathroom. "I'd like to borrow the car sometime, though."

What does he want a car for, the little big shot?

Judy's tears have dried and she has snuck into the living room, where the *Today* show is doing its last recap of the news and weather. Willard Scott, beamed in from Nome, Alaska, has Jane and Bryant in stitches.

Pru is looking into the cupboards and begging Roy, "How about some Sugar Pops, honey? Grandpa and Grandma have lots of Sugar Pops. And jars of dry-roasted peanuts and cashews. Harry, do you know that nuts are loaded with cholesterol?"

"Yeah, people keep telling me that. But then I read some article said the body needs cholesterol and the whole scare's been engineered by the chicken lobby." Janice, in a pink alligator shirt and a pair of magenta slacks like the women wear down here to go shopping in, has wedged herself in at the kitchen table with the

News-Press and a sliced–open bagel and plastic container of cream cheese. In her Florida phase she has taken to bagels. Lox, too. She has pulled out the *Lifestyles* section of the newspaper and Harry, still able to read type in any direction from his days as a Linotyper, sees sideways the headline (they use a "down" style and lots of *USA Today*-style color graphics)

Manwatchers
name the men
with the most

and in caps at the top HUGE LOSS and 'WORKING' ON ANOTHER WEDDING. He cranks his head to look at the page the right way and sees that they mean *Working Girl* star Melanie Griffith and the survivors of the Armenian tragedy and their "unique type of grief." Funny how your wife reading the newspaper makes every item in it look fascinating, and then when you look yourself it all turns dull. The Braun Aromaster percolator, with a little sludgy coffee lukewarm in its glass half, sits at the end of the counter, past where Pru is still standing trying to find something Roy might eat. To let Harry ease his belly by, she goes up on her toes and with a little soft grunt under her breath presses her thighs tight against the counter edge. All this family closeness is almost like an African hut where everybody sleeps and screws in full view of everybody else. But, then, Harry asks himself, what has Western man done with all his precious privacy anyway? To judge from the history books, nothing much except invent the gun and psychoanalysis.

Down here it's necessary to keep bread and cookies in a drawer holding a big tin box to keep out ants, even up on the fourth floor. It's awkward to pull the drawer out and then lift the lid but he does, finding a couple of empty cookie bags, one for Double-Stuf Oreos and one for Fruit Newtons, which his grandchildren left with nothing but crumbs inside, and one and a half stale sugar doughnuts that even they disdained to consume. Rabbit takes them and his mug full of sludgy coffee and squeezes back past Pru, concentrating on the sensation in his groin as her shorty robe grazes it, and with a wicked impulse gives the kitchen table a nudge with the back of his thighs to get Janice's full cup of coffee rocking so it will slosh and spill. "*Harry*," she says, quickly lifting the newspaper. "Shit."

The sound of the shower running leaks into the kitchen. "Why the hell's Nelson so jittery?" he asks the women aloud.

Pru, who must know the answer, doesn't give it, and Janice says, mopping with a Scott Towel Pru hands her, "He's under *stress*. It's a much more competitive car world than it was ten years ago and Nelson's doing it all himself, he doesn't have Charlie to hide behind like you did."

"He could have kept Charlie on but he didn't want to, Charlie was willing to stay part-time," he says, but nobody answers him except Roy, who looks at him and says, "Grampa looks ridiculous."

"Quite a vocabulary," Harry compliments Pru.

"He doesn't know what he's saying, he hears these expressions on television," she says, brushing back hair from her forehead with a touching two-handed gesture she has developed to go with the hairdo.

The theme of the kitchen decor is aqua, a creamy frigid color that looked a little subtler in the paint chart Janice and he consulted four years ago, when they had the place repainted. He wondered at the time how it would wear but Janice thought it would be lighthearted and slightly daring, like their buying a condominium at all. Even the refrigerator and the Formica countertops are aqua, and looking at it all, with the creatures and flowers of seashells Janice has loaded the open shelves toward the foyer with, makes him feel panicky, shortens his breath. Being underwater is one of his nightmares. A simple off-white like the Golds next door have would have been less oppressive. He takes his mug and the doughnut-and-a-half and the rest of the *News-Press* into the living room and settles on the sofa side of the round glass table, since Judy occupies the wicker armchair that faces the television set. The pictures on the front page are of Donald Trump (*Male call: the year's hottest*), the grimacing sun wringing the clouds (*Rainfall 33% off average; year is driest since 1927*), and Fort Myers' mayor Wilbur Smith, looking like a long-haired kid younger even than Nelson, quoted saying that football star Deion Sanders' recent arrest for assault and battery on a police officer could be partially blamed upon the unruly crowd that had gathered to watch the incident. There is a story about an annual government book-length report on automobiles and consumer complaints: in a gray box highlighting *The best by the book,* under all four categories, subcompacts, compacts, intermediate, and minivans, there isn't a Toyota listed. He feels a small pained slipping in his stomach.

"Harry, you *must* eat a solid breakfast," Janice calls, "if you're going to play golf right through lunch. Dr. Morris told you coffee on an empty stomach is about the worst thing you can do for hypertension."

"If there's anything makes me hypertense," he calls back, "it's women telling me all the time what to eat." As he bites into the stale doughnut the sugar patters down on the paper and dusts the crimson lapels of his seigneurial bathrobe.

Janice continues to Pru, "Have you been giving any thought to Nelson's diet? He doesn't look like he's eating anything."

"He never did eat much," Pru says. "He must be where Roy gets his pickiness from."

Judy has found among all the channels of network and cable an old Lassie movie; Harry moves to the end of the sofa to get an angle on it. The collie nudges awake the lost boy asleep in the haystack and leads him home, down a dirt road toward a purple Scottish sunset. The music swells like an ache in the throat; Harry smiles sheepishly at Judy through his tears. Her eyes, that did their crying earlier, are dry. Lassie is not part of her childhood past, lost forever.

He tells her when the frog leaves his throat, "I got to go play golf, Judy. Think you can manage here today with these rude folks?"

She studies him seriously, not quite sure of the joke. "I guess so."

"They're good people," he says, not sure this is true. "How would you like to go Sunfishing some time?"

"What's Sunfishing?"

"It's sailing in a little boat. We'd go off one of the hotel beaches in Deleon. They're supposed to be just for the guests but I know the guy who runs the concession. I play golf with his father."

Her eyes don't leave his face. "Have you ever done it, Grandpa? Sunfishing."

"Sure. A coupla times." Once, actually; but it was a vivid lesson. With Cindy Murkett in her black bikini that showed the hairs in her crotch. Her breasts slipsloppy in their little black sling. The wind tugging, the water slapping, the sun wielding its silent white hammer on their skins, the two of them alone and nearly naked.

"Sounds neat," Judy ventures, adding, "I got a prize in my camp swimming class for staying underwater the longest." She returns her gaze to the television, rapidly flicking through the channels with the hand control – channel-surfing, kids call it.

Harry tries to imagine the world seen through her clear green eyes, every little thing vivid and sharp and new, packed full of itself like a satin valentine. His own vision feels fogged no matter which glasses he puts on, for reading or far vision. He wears the latter only for movies and night driving, and refuses to get bifocals; glasses worn for more than an hour at a time hurt his ears. And the lenses are always dusty and the things he looks at all seem tired; he's seen them too many times before. A kind of drought has settled over the world, a bleaching such as overtakes old color prints, even the ones kept in a drawer.

Except, strangely, the first fairway of a golf course before his first swing. This vista is ever fresh. There, on the tee's earth platform, standing in his large white spiked Footjoys and blue sweat socks, drawing the long tapered steel wand of his Lynx Predator driver from the bag, he feels tall again, tall the way he used to on a hardwood basketball floor when after those first minutes his growing momentum and lengthening bounds and leaps reduced the court to childlike dimensions, to the size of a tennis court and then a Ping-Pong table, his legs unthinkingly eating the distances up, back and forth, and the hoop with its dainty skirtlike net dipping down to be there on the layups. So, in golf, the distances, the hundreds of yards, dissolve to a few effortless swings if you find the inner magic, the key. Always, golf for him holds out the hope of perfection, of a perfect weightlessness and consummate ease, for now and again it does happen, happens in three dimensions, shot after shot. But then he gets human and tries to force it, to make it happen, to get ten extra yards, to steer it, and it goes away, grace you could call it, the feeling of collaboration, of being bigger than he really is. When you stand up on the first tee it is there, it comes back from wherever it lives during the rest of your life, endless possibility, the possibility of a flawless round, a round without a speck of bad in it, without a missed two-footer or a flying right elbow, without a pushed wood or pulled iron; the first fairway is in front of you, palm trees on the left and water on the right, flat as a picture. All you have to do is take a simple pure swing and puncture the picture in the middle with a ball that shrinks in a second to the size of a needle-prick, a tiny tunnel into the absolute. That would be *it*.

But on his practice swing his chest gives a twang of pain and this makes him think for some reason of Nelson. The kid jangles in his mind. As he stands up to the ball he feels crowded but is impatient and hits it outside in, trying too hard with his right hand. The ball starts out promisingly but leaks more and more to the right and disappears too close to the edge of the long scummy pond of water.

" 'Fraid that's alligator territory," Bernie says sadly. Bernie is his partner for the round.

"Mulligan?" Harry asks.

There is a pause. Ed Silberstein asks Joe Gold, "What do you think?"

Joe tells Harry, "I didn't notice that *we* took any mulligans."

Harry says, "You cripples don't hit it far enough to get into trouble. We always give mulligans on the first drive. That's been our tradition."

Ed says, "Angstrom, how're you ever going to live up to your potential if we keep babying you with mulligans?"

Joe says, "How much potential you think a guy with a gut like that still has? I think his potential has all gone to his colon."

While they are thus ribbing him Rabbit takes another ball from his pocket and tees it up and, with a stiff half-swing, sends it safely but ingloriously down the left side of the fairway. Perhaps not quite safely: it seems to hit a hard spot and keeps bouncing toward a palm tree. "Sorry, Bernie," he says. "I'll loosen up."

"Am I worried?" Bernie asks, putting his foot to the electric-cart pedal a split-second before Harry has settled into the seat beside him. "With your brawn and my brains, we'll cream these oafs."

Bernie Drechsel, Ed Silberstein, and Joe Gold are all older than Harry, and shorter, and usually make him feel good about himself. With them, he is a big Swede, they call him Angstrom, a comical pet gentile, a big pale uncircumcised hunk of American white bread. He in turn treasures their perspective; it seems more manly than his, sadder and wiser and less shaky. Their long history has put all that suffering in its pocket and strides on. Harry asks Bernie, as the cart rolls over the tamped and glistening grass toward their balls, "Whaddeya think about all this fuss about this Deion Sanders? In the paper this morning he even has the mayor of Fort Myers making excuses for him."

Bernie shifts the cigar in his mouth an inch and says, "It's cruel, you know, to take these black kids out of nowhere and give 'em all this publicity and turn them into millionaires. No wonder they go crazy."

"The paper says the crowd kept the cops from giving him room. He had flipped out at some salesclerk who said he had stolen a pair of earrings. He even took a pop at her."

"I don't know about Sanders," Bernie says, "but a lot of it's drugs. Cocaine. The stuff is everywhere."

"You wonder what people see in it," Rabbit says.

"What they see in it," Bernie says, stopping the cart and resting his cigar on the edge of the plastic ledge for holding drinks or beer cans, "is instant happiness." He squares up to his second shot with that awful stance of his, his feet too close together, his bald head dipping down in a reverse weight-shift, and punches the ball with a four-iron: all arms and wrists. It stays straight, though, and winds up within an easy chip in front of the elevated green. "There are two routes to happiness," he continues, back at the wheel of the cart. "Work for it, day after day, like you and I did, or take a chemical shortcut. With the world the way it is, these kids take the shortcut. The long way looks too long."

"Yeah, well, it *is* long. And then when you've gone the distance, where's the happiness?"

"Behind you," the other man admits.

"What interests me about Sanders and kids like that," Rabbit says, as Bernie speeds along down the sun-baked fairway, dodging fallen brown fronds and coconuts, "is I had a little taste of it once. Athletics. Everybody cheering, loving you. Wanting a piece."

"Sure you did. It sticks out all over. Just the way you waggle the club. 'Fraid you made the palm tree, though. You're stymied, my friend." Bernie stops the cart, a little close to the ball for Harry's comfort.

"I think I can hook it around."

"Don't try it. Chip it out. You know what Tommy Armour says: take your stroke in a situation like this, and go for the green on the next one. Don't attempt a miracle."

"Well, you're already up there for a sure bogey. Let me try to bend it on." The palm tree is one of those whose trunk looks like a giant braid. It breathes on him, with its faint rustle, its dim smell like that of a friendly attic full of dried-out old school papers and love letters. There's a lot of death in Florida, if you look. The palms grow by the lower branches dying and dropping off. The hot sun hurries the life cycles along. Harry takes his stance with his hip almost touching the jagged rough trunk, hoods the five-iron, and imagines the curving arc of the miracle shot and Bernie's glad cry of congratulation.

But in fact the closeness of the tree and maybe of Bernie in the cart inhibits his swing and he pulls the ball with the hooded club, so it hits the top of the next palm along the fairway and drops straight down into the short rough. The rough, though, in Florida isn't like the rough up north; it's just spongy pale grass a half-inch longer than fairway. They tailor these courses for the elderly and lame. They baby you down here.

Bernie sighs. "Stubborn," he says as Harry gets back in. "You guys think the world will melt if you whistle." Harry knows that "guys" is polite for "goys." The thought that he might be wrong, that obstacles won't melt if he whistles, renews that dull internal ache of doom he felt in the airport. As he stands up to his third shot with an eight-iron, Bernie's disapproval weighs on his arms and causes him to hit a bit fat, enough to take the click out of the ball and leave it ten yards short.

"Sorry, Bernie. Chip up close and get your par." But Bernie fluffs the chip – all wrists again, and too quick – and they both get sixes, losing the hole to Ed Silberstein's routine bogey. Ed is a wiry retired accountant from Toledo, with dark upright hair and a slender thrusting jaw that makes him look as if he's about to smile all the time; he never seems to get the ball more than ten feet off the ground, but he keeps it moving toward the hole.

"You guys looked like Dukakis on that one," he crows. "Blowing it."

"Don't knock the Duke," Joe says. "He gave us honest government for a change. The Boston pols can't forgive him for it." Joe Gold owns a couple of liquor stores in some city in Massachusetts called Framingham. He is stocky and sandy and wears glasses so thick they make his eyes look like they're trying to escape from two little fishbowls, jumping from side to side. He and his wife, Beu, Beu for Beulah, are very quiet condo neighbors next door; you wonder what they do all the time in there, that never makes any noise.

Ed says, "He wimped out when it counted. He should have stood up and said, 'Sure, I'm a liberal, and damn proud of it.'"

"Yeah, how would that have played in the South and the Midwest?" Joe asks. "In California and Florida for that matter with all these old farts who all they want to hear is 'No more taxes'?"

"Lousy," Ed admits. "But he wasn't going to get their votes anyway. His only hope was to get the poor excited. Knock away that three-footer, Angstrom. I've already written down your six."

"I need the practice," Harry says, and strokes it, and watches it rim out on the left edge. Not his day. Will he ever have a day again? Fifty-five and fading. His own son can't stand to be in the same room with him. Ruth once called him Mr. Death.

"He was going for those Reagan Democrats," Joe continues explaining. "Except there aren't any Reagan Democrats, there're just cut-and-dried rednecks. Now that I'm down south here, I understand better what it's all about. It's all about blacks. One hundred thirty years after Abe Lincoln, the Republicans have got the anti-black vote and it's bigger than any Democratic Presidential candidate can cope with, barring a massive depression or a boo-boo the size of Watergate. Ollie North doesn't do it. Reagan being an airhead didn't do it. Face it: the bulk of this country is scared to death of the blacks. That's the one gut issue we've got."

After that episode with Skeeter twenty years ago Rabbit has had mixed feelings about blacks and whenever the subject comes up he tends to hold his tongue lest he betray himself one way or another. "Bernie, what do you think?" Harry asks while they're watching the two others hit from the second tee, a 136-yard par-three over that same scummy pond. He finds Bernie the wisest of the three, the most phlegmatic and slowest to speak. He never came back totally from some open-heart surgery he had a few years ago. He moves cumbersomely, has emphysema and a bit of a humpback and the slack look of a plump man who lost weight because his doctor told him to. His color isn't good, his lower lip in profile looks loose.

"I think," he says, "Dukakis tried to talk intelligently to the American people and we aren't ready for it. Bush talked to us like we were a bunch of morons and we ate it up. Can you imagine, the Pledge of Allegiance, read my lips – can you imagine such crap in this day and age? Ailes and those others, they made him into a beer commercial – head for the mountains." Bernie sang this last phrase, his voice quavery but touchingly true. Rabbit is impressed by this ability Jews seem to have, to sing and to dance, to give themselves to the moment. They sing at seder, he knows, because Bernie and Fern had them to a seder one April just before heading north. Passover. The angel of death passed over. Harry had never understood the word before. Let this cup pass from me. Bernie concludes, "To my mind there are two possibilities about Bush – he believed what he was saying, or he didn't. I don't know which is more terrifying. He's what we call a *pisher*."

"Dukakis always looked like he was sore about something," Rabbit offers. This is as close as he can bring himself to admit that, alone in this foursome, he voted for Bush.

Bernie maybe guesses it. He says, "After eight years of Reagan I would have thought more people would have been sore than were. If you could ever get the poor to vote in this country, you'd have socialism. But people want to think rich. That's the genius of the capitalist system: either you're rich, or you want to be, or you think you ought to be."

Rabbit liked Reagan. He liked the foggy voice, the smile, the big shoulders, the way his head kept wagging during the long pauses, the way he floated above the facts, knowing there was more to government than facts, and the way he could change direction while saying he was going straight ahead, pulling out of Beirut, getting cozy with Gorby, running up the national debt.

The strange thing was, except for the hopeless down-and-outers, the world became a better place under him. The Communists fell apart, except for in Nicaragua, and even there he put them on the defensive. The guy had a magic touch. He was a dream man. Harry dares say, "Under Reagan, you know, it was like anesthesia."

"Ever had an operation? A real operation."

"Not really. Tonsils when I was a kid. Appendix when I was in the Army. They took it out in case I was sent to Korea. Then I was never sent."

"I had a quadruple bypass three years ago."

"I know, Bern. I remember your telling me. But you look great now."

"When you come out of anesthesia, it hurts like hell. You can't believe you can live with such pain. To get at your heart, they split your whole rib cage open. They crack you open like a coconut. And they pull the best veins they can find out of your upper leg. So when you come out of it your groin's killing you as well as your chest."

"Wow." Harry inappropriately laughs, since while Bernie was talking to him on the cart Ed, with that pompous fussy setup he has, laying his hands on the club finger by finger like he's doing flower arrangement, and then peeking toward the hole five or six times before swinging, as if he's trying to shake loose cobwebs or a tick in his collar, looked up during the swing so the topped ball scuttered into the water, skipping three times before sinking, leaving three expanding, interlocking sets of rings on the water. Alligator food.

"Six hours I was on the table," Bernie is urging into his ear. "I woke up and I couldn't move. I couldn't even open my eyelids. They *freeze* you, so your blood flow is down to almost nothing. I was like locked into a black coffin. No. It's like I *was* the coffin. And then out of this blackness I hear this weird voice, with a thick Indian accent, the Pakistani anesthetist."

Joe Gold, with his partner's ball in the water, tries to hit it too quick, to get a ball in play, jerking the club back in two stages like he does and then roundhousing with that flat swing stocky guys tend to have. He pushes the shot off so he catches the pot bunker on the right.

Bernie is doing a high, spacy, Pakistani voice. " 'Ber-nie, Ber-nie,' this voice says, so honest to God I think maybe it's the voice of God, 'oper-ation a suc-cess!' "

Harry has heard the story before but laughs anyway. It's a good, scary story about the edge of death.

" 'Ber-nie, Ber-nie,' " Bernie repeats, "like it came out of the clouds to Abraham, to go cut Isaac's throat."

Harry asks, "Shall we keep the same order?" He feels he disgraced himself on the previous hole.

"You go first, Angstrom. I think it shakes you up too much to hit last. Go for it. Show these nudniks how it's done."

This is what Rabbit hoped to hear. He takes a seven-iron and tries to think of five things: keeping his head down, keeping his backswing from being too long, moving his hip while the club is still at the top, keeping his downswing smooth, and keeping the clubface square on the ball, at that point on the sphere where a clockface says 3:15. From the whistly magic way the ball vanishes from the center of his held-down vision he knows the hit is sweet; they all together watch the dark dot rise, hover that little ghostly extra bit that gives the distance, and then drop straight down on the green, a hair to the left but what looks pin high, the ball bouncing right with the slant of the bowl-shaped green.

"Beauty," Ed has to admit.

"How about a mulligan?" Joe asks. "We'll give you one this time."

Bernie asks, pushing himself out of the cart, "What iron was that?"

"Seven."

"Gonna hit 'em like that, my friend, you should use an eight."

"Think I'm past the hole?"

"Way past. You're on the back edge."

Some partner. There's no satisfying him. Like Marty Tothero nearly forty years ago. Get twenty-five points a game, Marty wanted thirty-five and would talk about a missed layup. The soldier in Harry, the masochistic Christian, respects men like this. It's total uncritical love, such as women provide, that makes you soft and does you in.

"For me, I think a choked-up six," Bernie says.

But in trying to take something off the shot he takes off too much and leaves it short, over the water but on the bank where it's hard to manage a stance. "Tough chip from there," Harry says, unable to resist a gentle needle. He still blames Bernie for parking the cart so close on that attempted deliberate hook.

Bernie accepts the needle. "Especially after that last shitty chip of mine, huh?" he says, pushing his cut-up, deflated, hump-backed old body into the cart, Harry having slid over into the driver's seat. The guy who's on the green has earned the right to drive. Harry feels momentum building, they're going to cream these oafs. He glides over the water on an arched wooden bridge with red rubber treads laid over the planks. "From where you are," Bernie tells him as they get out, "the green slopes down. Hit your putt too hard, you'll slide miles beyond."

Ed with a ball in the water is out of it. Bernie's stance on the steep bank is so awkward he whiffs the ball once, shanks it sideways on his next swing, and picks up. But sandy Joe Gold, in his element, waggles his feet to plant himself and manages a good blast shot out of the pot bunker. With Bernie's advice preying on his mind, inter-fering with his own instincts, Harry strokes his long approach putt tentatively and leaves it four feet short. He marks it with a Valhalla Village marker while Joe two-putts for his bogey. Joe takes his time and gives Harry too long to study his four-footer. He sees a break, then doesn't see it. In trying to avoid lipping out on the left like he did on the last hole, he loses his par putt, very makable, an inch to the right. "Son of a son of a *bitch*," he says, frustration pressing from behind his eyes so hard he thinks he might burst into tears. "On in one, and a fucking three-putt."

"It happens," Ed says, writing down the 4 with his trained accountant's primness. "Tie hole."

"Sorry, Bern," Harry says, climbing back into the cart, on the passenger side.

"I screwed you up," his partner says. "Should have kept my yap shut about the green being downhill." He unwraps another cigar and, pushing the pedal, leans back into a long day.

Not Harry's day. The Florida sun seems not so much a single ball overhead but a set of klieg lights that pursue you everywhere with an even white illumination. Even directly under palm trees and right up against the twelve-foot pine fences that separate the Village from the rest of the world, the sun finds you, reddening the tip of Rabbit's nose and baking his forearms and the back of his non-gloved hand, which is already dotted with little white bumps of keratosis. He carries a tube of number-15 sunscreen in his golf bag and is always dabbing it on but the ultraviolet gets through anyway, cooking his squamous cells into skin cancer. The three men he plays with never use anything and just get a comfortable tan, even the bald top of Bernie's head, as smooth as an ostrich egg with only a few small specks on it as he bends over his shots with that awful reverse-shift, squeezed-feet stance of his. Harry feels Bernie's steady, mechanically repeating ineptitude – short shots, chunked chips – a burden today, since he can't quite carry him, and wonders why somebody who exudes suffering wisdom the way Bernie does never learns a thing about golf or even seems to try. To him, Harry supposes, it's just a game, a way of killing time in the sun at this stage of his life. Bernie was a boy once and then a man making money and children (a carpet business in Queens; two daughters who married nice solid guys and a son who went to Princeton and the Wharton School in Philadelphia and became a hostile-takeover specialist on Wall Street) and now he's at the other end of life's rainbow, and this is what you do: Bernie endures retirement fun in Florida the way he's endured his entire life, sucking that same acrid wet-cigar taste out of it. He doesn't see what Harry sees in the game – infinity, an opportunity for infinite improvement. Rabbit doesn't see it himself today. Around the eleventh hole – a dogleg par-five that he butchers, slicing his second shot, a four-wood, so wildly it winds up in a condo's side yard, between some plastic trash cans and a concrete slab with some rusting steel clothes-line poles sunk in it (a German shepherd chained to the clothesline barks at him, lunging toward him so the taut wire sings, and Gold and Silberstein loafing in their cart cackle, and Bernie chomps deeper and looks morose), taking the out-of-bounds drop for a four while the dog keeps barking and barking, trying to hit a three-iron so hard he digs six inches behind and sprays sand all over his shoes and into the tops of his socks, pulling the next

iron to the left into a bed of parched and shedding azaleas beside
the twelfth tee, taking a drop for another stroke, skulling the chip
clear across over the green (all three playing partners keeping a
ghastly silence now, shocked, mourning for him, or is it holding
in their glee?), plunking the next sand shot against the trap lip so
it dribbles back, and picking up in disgust, and even hitting himself on the knee when after raking he flips the sand rake to one
side – after this hole, the game and day begin to eat him into a state
of depression. The grass looks greasy and unreal, every other palm
tree is dying from the drought and dropping stiff brown fronds,
the condos line every fairway like tall stucco outhouses, and even
the sky, where your eyes can usually find relief, is dirtied by jet
trails that spread and wander until they are indistinguishable from
God's pure clouds.

The hours pile on, noon comes and goes, the klieg lights begin
to dim but the heat is turned up higher. They finish at quarter to
three, Harry and Bernie twenty dollars down – both sides of a five-
dollar nassau plus the eighteen and a press on the second nine that
they lost. "We'll get 'em next time," Harry promises his partner,
not really believing it.

"You weren't quite yourself today, my friend," Bernie admits.
"You got girlfriend trouble or something?"

Horny, Jews are: he once read a history of Hollywood about
their womanizing. Harry Cohn, Groucho Marx, the Warner
Brothers, they went crazy out there with the sunshine and swimming pools and all the Midwestern shiksas who'd do anything to
be movie stars – participate in orgies, blow a mogul while he was
talking on the telephone – yet his golf partners are all married to
the same women, forty, fifty years, women with big dyed hair and
thick bangles and fat brown upper arms who can't stop talking
when you see them all dolled up at dinner, Bernie and Ed and Joe
sitting smilingly silent beside them as if all this talking their women
do is sex, which it must be – pep, life. How do they do it? Wear
life like a ready-made suit that fits exactly. "I guess I told you,"
Harry tells Bernie, "my son and his family are visiting."

"There's your problem, Angstrom: you felt guilty horsing
around with us. You should have been entertaining your loved
ones."

"Yeah, entertain 'em. They just got here yesterday and are acting bored already. They want us to live next door to Disney World."

"Take 'em to Jungle Gardens. Up in Sarasota, down 41 from the Ringling Museum. Fern and I go there two, three times a winter and never get bored. I could watch those flamingos sleep for hours – how do they do it? Balanced on one leg two feet long and thinner than my finger." He holds up a finger and it seems thick. "Thinner than that," he swears.

"I don't know, Bernie. When I'm around, my kid acts like he doesn't want my own grandchildren to have anything much to do with me. The little boy, he's four, is pretty much a stranger, but the girl and I could get along. She's almost nine. I was even thinking I should bring her out in a cart sometime and let her try to hit the ball. Or maybe rent a Sunfish, Ed, if your son over at the Bayview could write me up as a guest."

The foursome is having beers and free munchies in Club Nineteen, next to the pro shop, on the bottom floor of Building A of Valhalla Village. The darkness inside – the dark panels and beams in the style of an English pub – is intensified by the subtropical brightness outside, at the round white tables under umbrellas saying *Coors*. You can hear the splashing from the pool, between Buildings A and B, and the throbbing of a generator housed on the other side of the wall, beyond the rest rooms and dart boards and video games. At night sometimes Harry imagines he can hear the generator throbbing through all the intervening apartments, carpets, air-conditioners, conversations, mattresses, and peach-colored hall wallpaper. Somehow the noise curves around and clings to the walls and comes in his big sliding window, the crack that's left open to the Gulf air.

"No problem," Ed says, as he totals their scores. "Just show up at the front desk and ask for Gregg Silvers. That's what he calls himself, don't ask me why. They'll let you walk through the lobby and downstairs to the changing rooms. I don't advise wearing bathing suits into the lobby; they try to discourage that. Do you have a day I can tell him to expect you?"

Harry gets the impression this may be a realer favor than he thought, a bigger deal than it's worth. "Friday, if ever," he says.

"Does Gregg have to know for sure? Tomorrow I thought we'd head up Sarasota way."

"Jungle Gardens," Bernie insists.

"Lionel Train Museum," Joe Gold contributes. "And right across from the Ringling Museum there's Bellm's Cars and Music of Yesterday, is I think what they call it. Over a thousand music machines, can you imagine? Antique cars from 1897, I never knew there were cars then. You're in the car business, aren't you, Angstrom? You and your boy. You'll both go ape in there."

"I don't know," Harry begins, groping to express the curious cloud that Nelson carries with him, that dampens any outing.

"Harry, this is interesting," Ed says. "Giving you a seven, two over par for handicap purposes, on the eleventh where you picked up, and a courtesy six on the sixteenth where you put two balls in the water, you scored an even ninety even so. You weren't playing as bad as it looked. Waste a few less drives and long irons, and you'll be in the eighties every time."

"I couldn't get my ass into it, I couldn't re*lease*," Harry says. "I couldn't let go." He has an unaskable question for these three wise Jewish men: how about death? He asks them, "Hey, how about that Pan Am jet?"

There is a pause. "It has to be a bomb," Ed says. "When you've got splinters of steel driven right through leather luggage and wreckage strewn across fifty miles of Scotland, it has to be a bomb."

Bernie sighs, "It's them again. The Shiiteheads."

"Arabs," Joe Gold says. A patriotic glee lights his wobbling eyes. "Once we got proof, the F-111s'll be flying into Libya again. What we ought to do is keep going right into Eye-ran and stick it to the old Ayatollah."

But their tongues are less quick than usual; Harry has made them uneasy, with what he hadn't meant to be so much a political question. With Jews, everything in the papers comes back to Israel.

"I mean," he says, "how the hell do you think it feels? Sitting there and having the plane explode?"

"Well, I bet it wakes you up," Ed says.

"They didn't feel a thing," Bernie says, considerately, sensing Harry's personal worry. "Zero. It was over that quick."

Joe says to Harry, "You know what the Israelis say, don't you, Angstrom? 'If we got to have enemies, thank God they're Arabs.' "

Harry has heard this before but tries to laugh. Bernie says, "I think Angstrom could use a new partner. I depress him."

"It wasn't you, Bernie. I came depressed."

Club Nineteen puts out a wonderful array of nibbles, in little china bowls monogrammed with Valhalla Village's logo, two sea-blue intertwined V's. Not just dry-roasted peanuts and almonds and hazelnuts but tiny pretzel sticks and salted pumpkin seeds and tight curls resembling Corn Chips, only finer and sharper in the mouth in that blissful instant while the tongue works one around to be crunched between the molars. The other men take only a pinch of this starchy salty salad now and then but soon the bowl is empty, Rabbit doing eighty per cent of the eating.

"That crap's loaded with sodium," Bernie warns him.

"Yeah, but it's good for the soul," Harry says, about as religious a remark as he dares put forth. "Who else is ready for another beer?" he asks. "Losers buy this round."

He is beginning to feel expansive: his dark mood is thinning like a squirt of ink in alcohol's gentle solvent. He waves for the waiter and asks him to bring along with four more beers another bowl of munchies. The waiter, a faunlike young Hispanic with an earring bigger than Nelson's and gold chains on both wrists, nods in a timid way; Harry must seem enormous to him, menacingly white and pink and sodden with sodium-retained water. The whole quartet must seem loud and potentially unruly: ugly old gringos. Another squirt of ink. Harry feels heavy again. Good times in Florida are never as good as those boozy late afternoons at his old club back in Diamond County, the Flying Eagle, before Buddy Inglefinger married that lanky crazy hippie Valerie and moved to Royersford and Thelma Harrison got too sick with lupus ever to show up and they dropped their membership and Cindy Murkett got fat and Webb divorced her so you never saw anybody any more. In Florida the people are so cautious, as if on two beers they might fall down and break a hip. The whole state is brittle.

"Your boy play golf?" Joe is asking him.

"Not really. He's never had the temperament. Or the time, he says." And, Rabbit might have added, he never really invited him.

"What does he do, for fun?" Ed asks. These men, it dawns on Harry, are being polite. By ordering another round of beers he has stretched the nineteenth-hole camaraderie beyond where it's effortless. These guys' sexy elderly wives are waiting. Gossip to catch up on. Letters from dutiful, prospering children to read. Interest to add up. Torah to study.

"Beats me," Harry says. "Hangs around with a bunch of Brewer creeps, swinging singles sort of. I never see him having much fun. He never went in for sports."

"The way you talk about him," Bernie said, "he could be the father and you the son."

Rabbit agrees enthusiastically; with a boost from the second beer he almost has a vision. "Yeah, and a delinquent son at that. That's how he sees me, an old juvenile delinquent. His wife looks miserable." Where did that come from? Was it true? *Help me, guys. Tell me how you've got on top of sex and death so they don't bother you.* He goes on, "The whole family, the two kids too, seem on edge. I don't know what's up."

"Your wife, does she know what's up?"

That mutt. Harry ignores the question. "Just last night I tried to talk to the kid in a friendly fashion and all he did was bitch about Toyotas. The company that feeds us, that saved him and his old man and his shady little crook of a grandfather from being bums, and all he does is complain about how Toyotas aren't Lamborghinis! Jesus, that beer went down fast. It felt like the Gobi Desert out there."

"Harry, you don't want another beer."

"You want to get home and tell your family about Bellm's. B, E, L, L, M, apostrophe, S. I know it sounds like I can't spell. Every old car you could imagine. From before steering wheels. Before gears, even."

"To be honest, guys, I've never been that much into cars. I drive 'em, I sell 'em, but I've never really understood the damn things. To me they're all alike. Great if they go, lousy if they don't." The other men are standing up.

"I want to see you out here tomorrow afternoon with your little granddaughter. Teach her the basics. Head down, slow take-away."

That was Bernie talking; Ed Silberstein tells him:

"Work on shortening that backswing, Harry. You don't need all that above the shoulders. The hit is right in here, right by your pecker. Best advice I ever had from a golf pro was, Imagine you're hitting it with your pecker."

They have sensed his silent cry for help, for consolation, and are becoming more Jewish on Harry's behalf, it seems to him as he sits there.

Bernie has pushed up from the table and towers over Harry with his gray skin, his loose dewlaps full of shadows. "We have an expression," he says downward. "*Tsuris*. Sounds to me, my friend, like you got some *tsuris*. Not full-grown yet, not *gehoketh tsuris*, but *tsuris*."

Pleasantly dazed with alcohol, his chest distantly stinging, the tip of his nose beginning to feel sunburn, Harry has no inclination to move, though the world around him is in motion. Two young college-kid hotshots who were pressing them from behind all afternoon have finished and are making the video games over by the rest rooms warble, zing, whistle, and bleat. Animated automatons in many colors appear and disappear on the screen. He sees his white fingers, with the big moons on their fingernails, absent-mindedly dabble at the bottom of the bowl of munchies, as if he is trying to pick up the intertwined V's. The junk food has been consumed. He cannot be absolutely sure, in memory, if the waiter ever brought a new bowl.

Joe Gold, his hair a sandy mane, his magnified eyes surging back and forth within his squarish spectacles, bends down a bit, as if rooting his feet again in a trap, and says, "Here's a Jewish joke for you. Abe meets Izzy after a long time no see. He asks, 'How many children do you have?' Izzy says, 'None.' Abe says, 'None! So what do you do for aggravation?'"

Their laughter seems speeded-up, like the action in a beer commercial; their mockery in its unnatural unison holds a pre-monition for Harry, that he has wasted the day, that now he must hurry, hurry to catch up, like when he used to run late to school

with a watery flutter in his stomach. The three other men, returning to their solid domestic arrangements, in farewell cuff at him,
even pinch the nape of his neck, as if to rouse him from a spiritual torpor. In Florida, he thinks, even friendship has a thin, provisional quality, since people might at any minute buy another
condominium and move to it, or else up and die.

You leave the clubs with the pro shop, and the shoes. Rabbit
walks in his moccasins, worn so loose his feet move in them without seeming to rub leather, across the parking lot and a striped
piece of driveway and one of the complex's little traffic islands
covered in green outdoor carpeting to the entryway of Building
B. He uses his key and punches in the code on the panel in the
narrow space where two closed-circuit television cameras are
watching him, pulls the door – it doesn't buzz, it goes *ding ding
ding* like a fire truck backing up – and takes the elevator to the
fourth floor. In 413, his home away from home, Janice and Pru
and the kids are playing Hearts, that is three of them are and Roy
is holding a fistful of cards while his mother tells him what to do
and which to discard. His face has a puffy look as though it's been
an afternoon of frustrations and disappointments. They all greet
Harry as if he's going to rescue them from death by boredom, but
he feels so beat all he wants to do is lie down and let his body soak
in nothingness. He asks, "Where's Nelson?"

It's not the right question, at least in front of the kids. Janice
and Pru glance toward one another and then Pru volunteers,
"He's out doing a few errands in the car." Down here they only
have one car, the Camry, leaving Harry's Celica back in Penn
Park. It works out, since most everything they need – drugs, magazines, haircuts, bathing suits, tennis balls – they can find within
the Valhalla complex. The little food commissary in Building C
charges airport prices, so Janice usually does a big shopping once
a week at the Winn Dixie a half-mile down Pindo Palm Boulevard. About once a week also they visit their bank in downtown
Deleon, on a plaza two blocks back from the beachfront where
elevator music is always playing, both inside the bank and outside;

they must have speakers hidden in the trees. Maybe twice a month they go to a movie at a cineplex in a giant mall over on Palmetto Palm Boulevard two miles away. But days at a stretch go by when the car just sits there in its parking slot, attracting rust and white splotches of birdshit.

"What kind of errands does he have to do?"

"Oh Harry," Janice says. "People need things. He doesn't like the kind of beer you buy. He likes a special kind of dental floss, tape instead of thread. And he likes to drive around; he gets claustrophobic."

"We all get claustrophobic," he tells her. "Most of us don't go stealing cars about it."

"You look exhausted. Did you lose?"

"How'd you guess?"

"You always lose. He plays with these three Jewish men," she explains to her daughter-in-law, "and they always take twenty dollars off of him."

"Don't be so prejudiced, you sound like your mother. And for your information I win as often as not."

"I never hear about it when you do. They keep telling you how good you are, and then take your money."

"You dope, one of them lost twenty dollars *with* me, he was my partner!"

Serenely she says, just like her mother, addressing nobody in particular, "They probably give it back to him; they're all in cahoots."

It occurs to him that she is saying these disagreeable and absurd things as a distraction from Nelson's rude and mysterious absence.

Judy says, "Grandpa, come take Roy's hand and play. He doesn't know how to even hold the cards and he's being fussy."

Roy obligingly proves her point by throwing the cards down on the round glass table, much as this morning he threw the spoon. "I hate games," he says, with a curious precision, like one of those old-fashioned dolls that would say a little speech when you pulled a string that came out of their backs.

Judy swiftly whomps him, with the hand not holding her cards. She chops with her fist at his shoulders and neck, and when he squalls in self-defense explains to him, "You messed up the trick

so now nobody can play. And I was going to shoot the moon!"
Pru neatly fans her hand face down on the table and with the other
arm, a downy arm of long loving bones, pulls the wailing little boy
against her chest; seeing this, Judy flares into jealousy, goes pink-
eyed the way women do before they decide to cry, and races off
toward Harry and Janice's bedroom.

Pru smiles wanly, looking exhausted herself. "Everybody's
tired and cranky," she sort of sings, over the top of Roy's head so
Judy can hear it too.

Janice stands, a bit wobbly for a second. She knocks the glass
table with her shin, and next to her abandoned hand of Hearts an
orange-juice glass half full of Campari shivers, the scarlet circlet of
it, making him think of the pond when Ed's ball skipped in. She
is back into her tennis dress. Dried sweat-stains on its side and
beneath the arms are outlined like continents on a very faint map.
"Maybe we made them do too much," she explains to Harry.
"We did this enormous shopping, went to lunch at Burger King,
came back here, Pru took them for swimming and shuffleboard
for two hours, and then Judy and I went over to the tennis courts
and knocked the ball around."

"How'd she do?" he asks.

Janice laughs as if surprised. "Terrific, actually. She's going to
be a jock, just like you."

Rabbit goes into his bedroom. If nobody but Janice were here,
he would lie on this bed, push his eyes through a few pages of the
history book she gave him for Christmas, close his eyes on the
sound of the bird dryly chirping in the Norfolk pine, and succumb
to the great heaviness of being. But Judy has beat him to his own
king-size bed with its jade-green fitted coverlet. She is curled
up and hiding her face. He lies down close to the edge and lets
her press her knees against his presence. He admires her hair,
the amazing protein perfection of it, the long pale strands that in
sun deepen to a shiny orange. "Better rest up for Bingo tonight,"
he says.

"If Roy goes I'm not going," she says.

"Don't be down on Roy," he tells her. "He's a good scout."

"He's *not*. I was going to shoot the moon. I'd already took the
Queen of Spades, and I had the Ace of Hearts and the Jack and

some others and then he ruins it all and Mommy thinks that's so cute. He gets all the attention and everything ever since he was born, just because he's a boy!"

He admits, "It's tough. I was in your shoes, except it was reversed. I had a sister instead of a brother."

"Didn't you hate her?" She removes her face from her folded arms and stares up at him with rubbed-looking green eyes.

He answers, "No. I guess, to be honest, I loved her. I loved Mim." The truth of this shocks him: he realizes how few others in his life he has loved so bluntly, without something of scorn, as his little wiry Mim. Her face seemed a narrower, harder version of his, with the same short upper lip, only a brunette, and a girl. Himself transposed into quite another key, and yet the melody recognizable. He remembers the sticky grip of her fingers in his when Mom and Pop would lead them on their Sunday walk, up the mountain to the Pinnacle Hotel and then back along the edge of the quarry; Mim hung on and roused protectiveness in him and perhaps used it up for everybody else, for every other female. Mim as his own blood sister had a certain unforced claim over him no woman since has been able to establish.

"Was she younger than you or older?"

"Younger. Younger even than me than Roy is than you. But she was a girl and girls are less ornery than boys. Though I guess Mim was ornery in her way. Once she got to be sixteen, she put my parents through hell."

"Grandpa, what's 'ornery'?"

"Oh, you know. Mean. Contrary. Rebellious."

"Like Daddy?"

"I don't think of your daddy as ornery, just, what's the word? – uptight. People get to him more than they do to most people. He's sensitive." Formulating even this much thickens his tongue and blurs his mind. "Judy, let's have a contest. You lie over there and I'll lie here and we'll see who can fall asleep soonest."

"Who'll be the judge?"

"Your mother," he says, letting his moccasins fall from his feet onto the floor over the edge of the bed. He closes his eyes on the posterlike Florida sunshine and in the intimate red of his brain envisions swooping on a bicycle down Jackson Road and then Potter Avenue with Mim on the handlebars of his rattly old blue Elgin, she maybe six and he twelve, if they hit a rock or pothole she'll go flying with him and the bike on top of her grinding her into the asphalt and ruining her pretty face forever, a woman's face is her fortune, but in her faith in him she sings, he can't remember the song, just the sensation of snatches of words flicked back into his ears as her long black hair whips against his eyes and mouth, making the bicycle ride more dangerous still. He led Mim into danger but always led her out. Shoo-fly pie. That was one of the songs she used to sing around the house, day after day until it drove them all crazy. *Shoo-fly pie and apple pan dowdy, makes your eyes light up, your tummy say "howdy!"* And then she would do a thing with her eyes that would make the whole rest of the family laugh.

He feels Judy ease her weight from his side and with that exaggerated, creaking stealth of small children move around the foot of the bed and out of the room. The door clicks, female voices whisper. Their whispers merge with a dream, involving an enormous scoop-shaped space, an amphitheater, an audience somehow for whom he is performing, though there is no other person in the dream, just this sense of presence, of echoing august dreadfully serious presence. He wakes frightened, with dribble down from one corner of his mouth. He feels like a drum that has just been struck. The space he was dreaming of he now recognizes as his rib cage, as if he has become his own heart, a huffing puffing pumping man at mid-court, waiting for the whistle and the high-reaching jump-off. At some point in his sleep his chest began to ache, a stale sorrowful ache he associates with the pathetically bad way he played golf this afternoon, unable to concentrate, unable to loosen up. He wonders how long he has slept. The poster of sunshine and palm tops and distant pink red-roofed buildings pasted on the outer skin of the sliding windows has dulled in tint, gone shadowy, and the sounds of golf, its purposeful concussions alternating with intent silence and involuntary cries of triumph or disappointment, have subsided. And in the air outside, like the fluttering tinsel above a used-car lot, birds of many makes are calling to each other to wrap up the day. This hour or two before supper, when play – the last round of Horse at the basket out by the garage in the alley – used to be most intense, has become nap time as he slowly sinks toward earth with his wasting muscles and accumulating fat. He must lose some weight.

Only Judy is in the living room. She is flicking silently back and forth between channels. Faces, black in *The Jeffersons*, white in *Family Ties*, imploringly pop into visibility and then vanish amid shots of beer cans plunged into slow-motion waterfalls, George Bush lugging a gun through Texas underbrush, a Florida farmer gesturing toward his burnt fields, a Scotland Yard detective doing a little lecture with a diagram of an airplane's hold. "What's he saying?" Harry asks, but even as he asks, the image is gone, replaced by another, of a manatee being implanted with an electronic tracking device by a male pony-tailed manatee-conservation freak. An impatient rage within the child, a gluttony for images, brushes the manatee away. "Two channels back," Harry begs. "About the Pan Am plane."

"It was a bomb, silly," Judy says. "It had to be."

Children, they believe that headlines always happen to other people. "For Chrissake, cool it with the channel-changer. Lemme get a beer and I'll show you a neat card game. Where is everybody?"

"Grandma went to her women's group, Mom put Roy down for his nap."

"Your daddy –?" He thinks midway he shouldn't bring it up, but the words are out.

Judy shrugs and finishes the sentence. "Hasn't checked in yet."

It turns out she already knows how to play Rummy. In fact, she catches him with his hand full of three-of-a-kinds he was waiting to lay down when he had gin. Caught. Their laughter brings Pru out of her bedroom, in little white shorts her widened hips have stretched into horizontal wrinkles. Her face has taken wrinkles from the pillow, and seems a bit blurred and bloated by sleep, or a spell of crying. How suggestible female flesh is. Her feet are long and bare, with that chipped toenail polish. He asks his daughter-in-law, "What's up?"

She too shrugs. "I guess we'll go to dinner when Janice comes back. I'll feed Roy some applesauce to hold him."

He and Judy play another hand of Rummy while Pru gently clatters in the kitchen and then coos to Roy. Evening down here comes without much ceremony; suddenly the air beyond the balcony is gray as if with fine fog, and sea-scent drifts in through the sliding doors, and the sounds of birds and golf have gone away. This is peace. He resents it when Janice comes back, with that aggressive glow her women's group gives her. "Oh Harry, you men have been so awful! Not only were we considered chattel, but all those patriarchal religions tried to make us feel guilty about menstruating. They said we were un*clean*."

"Sorry," he says. "That was a crummy thing to do."

"That was Eve's basic sin, the lady professor told us," Janice goes on, half to Pru. "Something about apples being the color of blood, I couldn't quite follow it."

Harry interrupts, "By any chance are either of you two Eves like me, sort of starving?"

"We bought you lots of healthy snacks," Pru says. "Apricots dried without sulphur, unsalted banana chips."

"Is that what that stuff was in little plastic bags? I thought it might be for Chinese food and I shouldn't touch it."

"Yes," Janice decides, "let's just go to dinner. We'll leave a note for Nelson. Pru, any old dress. Evenings, they won't seat shorts and men without jackets."

The Mead Hall, on the floor of Building B above Club Nineteen, is a combination restaurant and function room. On the one hand, there are menus with choices and prices, and waitresses in brief gold outfits echoing Valhalla's ring-gold theme, that figures here and there in the decor when the interior decorator remembered it, and there is even a wine steward in a summer tux and a kind of bicycle lock around his neck; on the other hand, as you go in a bulletin board is loaded with announcements and leaflets and tinted sheets about this or that set of lessons or lecture or concert or square dance or travelogue you could attend in the area, and all the time you're eating, on Wednesday and Saturday nights, Bingo goes on on the other side of the room, run from a stage and microphone somewhat out of sight behind an enormous flanged pillar that holds up the room's starry curved ceiling. The ceiling is a skylight for part of its breadth. That strange, scooping, personified space in his dream: could it have been simply this hall, conjured up because his stomach wanted food? Rabbit feels like Marty

Tothero, looking at the menu, faced for the thousandth time with the same old choices among steak and veal, pork and ham, shrimps and scallops, swordfish Cajun style and fillets of sole stuffed with mussels, mushrooms, and artichoke hearts.

The pillar on two of its broad sides bears giant muddy ceramic murals about the Vikings: broadswords and horned helmets and dragon-headed ships protrude from the enamelled mass in its numerous blotchy colors, but the men wielding and wearing and sailing these protrusions are swallowed up in a crazy weave of arms and legs and lightning bolts, a kind of bloody basketwork in honor of history. "Seventy-one," the lugubrious male voice hidden behind the pillar intones. It repeats, "Seven one."

It is hard to carry on a conversation with the numbers blaring from the loudspeakers. Pru mothers Roy and coaxes a little baked potato and a single stir-fried shrimp into him. Janice talks Judy into ordering a lobster and then has to show her how to crack it, how to push out the big curved piece of white meat with a finger up through the poor boiled creature's ass, how to suck the little tail segments, the same way you suck artichoke leaves. Rabbit, who has ordered eye-of-round steak, can hardly bear to watch; to him, eating lobster – its many little feathery legs, its eyes on stalks, its antennae roasted red like the rest – is nightmarish, a descent back into the squirmy scrabbly origins of life. Crabs, too, and oysters and clams: all around him in Florida he sees old people stuffing their faces with this filthy gluey unspeakable stuff, and telling you furthermore it's good for you, better than steak and hamburger, which is what he usually orders, though he doesn't mind a breaded pork chop or piece of veal, or a slice of ham with a pineapple ring or some moon-shaped snitzes of baked apple and on the side some greasy Dutch fries like a slipping stack of poker chips. That's how ham comes in Pennsylvania. You can't get sausage down here, at least not the spicy pork sausage he was raised on, or scrapple drenched in maple syrup, or apple pie with enough cinnamon in it, or shoo-fly pie at all. Janice went to a nutrition group a few winters ago and came back telling him how he was clogging his arteries with all this fat and dough. So for a while there was a rash of salads and low-cal pasta and fish and fowl back in the condominium; but whenever he gets into the Mead Hall he can order what he wants. With steak, you have to specify well-done or it comes rubbery and blue-rare. Disgusting. All the things that satisfy your appetite and seem so beautiful are disgusting when you don't have the appetite. Disposable meat.

Judy's perfect little hands are shiny with lobster. She asks her mother something and he can see Pru's mouth move in response but the Godlike voice blocks their words right out with its solemn "Twenty-seven. Two seven."

"What're you saying, sweetie?" he asks, embarrassed. Is his hearing going, or do people talk a little differently, more rapidly and softly, than they used to? On these TV shows that have British actors, there are stretches, especially when they put on the lower-class accents, where he can't understand a fucking word. And movies, especially in the love scenes, when the stars are establishing their coolness with the teen-age audience, just tossing the phrases away.

Pru explains, "She's worried about Daddy not getting anything to eat," and makes her wry one-sided mouth. Is this grimace a communication to him, a little lament, inviting him to conspire with her against Nelson?

Judy's shiny green eyes turn up toward her grandfather, as if she expects him to make an unsympathetic response. Instead he tells her, "Don't you worry, Judy. People can get served here until nine, and then at Club Nineteen downstairs they have sandwiches until midnight. And you saw Route 41: there's tons of eating places in Florida for your poor hungry daddy."

The girl's lower lip trembles and she gets out, "He might not have any money."

"Why wouldn't he have any money?"

The girl explains, "A lot of times he doesn't have any money. Bills come and even men come to the house and Mommy can't pay them." Her eyes shift over to her mother's face as she realizes she has said too much.

Pru looks away, wiping a crumb of potato from the corner of Roy's lips. "Things have been a bit tight," she admits almost inaudibly.

Harry wants to pursue it. "Really? That can't be. He's making fifty grand a year, with the benefits and bonuses. My father used to support us all on less than two thousand."

"Harry," Janice breaks in, in a voice that sounds like her moth-er's, toward the end, when the old widow got into the habit of laying down the law, "people now need more things than your father did. That was a simpler world. I remember it, I was there too. What did we use to do for fun, when we went out for a date? Go to the movies for seventy-five cents apiece or maybe the miniature-golf course out on 422 for even less. And then a soda at the Pensupreme, and that was considered a very adequate good time."

More than adequate, he remembers, if in the car after all that kissing and bare tit it took to warm her up Janice let him into her-self, her inside warm and wet and softly grainy like a silk slipper. If she was having her period or feeling virtuous, she might hold him in her hand while he supplied the motion and the come, white as lobster meat. A shocking white, really, and tough to mop up. What he loved best in the car with Janice was when she'd sit on him, her ass in his hands and her tits in his face. And tidily take his come away with her. Like mailing a letter.

Her mind on a track far distant from his, she is going on, "Nelson has to have good suits to make a good presentation of himself at the lot, and children now aren't just content with blocks and a ball, they have to have these video games –"

"Jesus – fifty thousand buys a lot of video games, he'll have enough to open an arcade soon if that's what he's spending it all on."

"Well, you joke, but that big barn of Mother's, it's no end of expense, isn't that the case, Pru?"

Hauled back from a politely smiling daze, Pru grins and admits, "It eats up the dollars."

They are hiding something from him, Harry sees. The unseen man portentously intones, "Fifty-six. Five six," and a quavery old voice, so frantic it nearly chokes itself, croaks, "Bingo!" *Eff one eleven*, Joe Gold had said. Fly 'em into Libya.

Harry says, "Well I don't know what the hell's going on."

No one contradicts him.

Roy is falling asleep with a sliver of shrimp shell on his slack lower lip. Harry has a sudden hankering for pecan pie. He tries to tease Judy into having dessert to keep him company. "Key-lime pie," he croons to her. "You can only get it in Florida. The chance of a lifetime."

"What makes it so special?"

He isn't quite sure. He lies. "Tiny delicate limes that only grow on the Florida Keys. Anywhere else is too coarse for them, too cold and mean."

She consents but then only picks nibbles off the crust at the back, so he, having sold it to her, has to eat it for her, on top of his pecan pie topped by a big oozing dip of butter-pecan ice cream. Nelson's absence grows bigger as their meal wears on. Janice and Pru have decaf coffee and, preoccupied, dying to talk to each other, watch Harry finish Judy's dessert. In a way, gluttony is an athletic feat, a stretching exercise. *Makes your tummy say "howdy!"* The waitress in her pleats of gold finally comes with the check and as he signs it with their condo number he feels like a god casually dispatching thunderbolts; the sum will appear on his monthly statement, next year, when the world has moved greatly on. How full he feels, stepping into the night air! A majestic float of a man, in a parade of dependents. Harry carries Roy, who fell asleep during dessert. Janice and Pru hold Judy one by each hand and, because she has been good during the boring long meal, allow her to swing herself between them, giggling as they grunt with the strain.

Between Buildings A and B, several of the overhead sodium lights on their tall burnished wands of aluminum have been mysteriously smashed: they're out there, the criminals, watching and waiting for the security guards to nod, so the fortress of sleeping retirees can be stormed. In this gap of unillumination, the stars leap down at them out of the black warm sky. At night Florida recovers something of its old subtropical self, before men tamed its teeming flatness. Being here is exciting, like being on the deck of a ship; the air tastes of salt, of rotting palm thatch, of swamp. The stars are moister here, more plummy. The St. Augustine grass has its strange spongy matted texture and each blade seems darkly metallic; the lawn snugly conceals round sprinkler heads. The skin that men have imposed on nature is so thin it develops holes, which armadillos wriggle through, the pathetic intricate things appearing in the middle of Pindo Palm Boulevard at dawn and being squashed flat by the first rush of morning traffic, they don't even have the sense to curl up into balls but jump straight into the air. Harry, Roy's breath moist on his neck and the child's head heavy as a stone on his shoulder, looks up at the teeming sky and thinks, *There is no mercy.* The stark plummy stars press down and the depth of the galactic void for an instant makes him feel suspended upside down. The entrance to Building B looms alluringly with its cab-ined yellow glow. The five Angstroms each cope in their way with the sore place inside them, Nelson's gnawing absence. They fumble through the protected entrances, the elevator, the peach-and-silver hallway, avoiding each other's eyes in embarrassment.

As her mother tucks her brother in, Judy settles before the tele-vision and flicks from *The Wonder Years* to *Night Court* to a French movie, starring that lunky Depardieu who is in all of them, this time about a man who comes to a village and usurps another man's identity, including his wife. In a moment's decision the young widow, besmirched and lonely, accepts him as her husband, and this thrills Harry; there ought to be a law that we change ident-ities and families every ten years or so. But Judy keeps flicking away from the story and Pru finally yells at the kid and tells her to get ready for bed on the sofa, they'll all clear out of the living room for her sake, though why she didn't accept Grandma and Grandpa's nice offer of a little room of her own is beyond her, Pru's, understanding. The girl breaks into tears and this is a relief for all of them, giving vent to their common unspoken sense of abandonment.

Janice tells Harry, "You go to bed, hon. You look beat. I'm too jazzed up by the coffee to sleep, Pru and I will sit in the kitchen."

"I thought the coffee was decaf." He had looked forward to having her, her little firm brown body, in bed beside him; with these other people here they don't have a second to themselves. His memories had stirred him. Fifty-two years old and she still has a solid ass. Not like Thelma, who's been losing it lately.

"That's what I ordered," Janice says, "but I never trust them really. I think a lot of the time now they just tell you it's decaf to shut you up."

"Don't sit up too late." On an impulse he adds to reassure her, "The kid's all right, he's just having some kind of a toot."

Pru glances at him in surprise, as if he's said more than he knows.

He feels goaded to elaborate: "Both me and Toyota give him a royal pain in the ass for some reason."

Again, he is not contradicted.

Fantasies about America produced two strongly contradictory conclusions that in the end came to the same point of injecting some caution into the golden dreams, he reads in bed. It's a history book Janice gave him for Christmas, by a woman historian yet, about the Dutch role in the American Revolution, which he hadn't thought up to now had been much. *According to one school, America was too big, too divided, ever to become a single country, its communications too distended for the country ever to be united.* Just that sentence makes him feel enormous, slack, distended. The beautiful thing about history is it puts you right to sleep. He looks back up the page for something amusing he remembered reading last night. *Climate in the New World, according to a best-selling French treatise translated into Dutch in 1775, made men listless and indolent; they might become happy but never stalwart. America, affirmed this scholar, "was formed for happiness, but not for empire."* Another European scholar reported that *the native Indians "have small organs of generation" and "little sexual capacity."*

Maybe if Nelson had been bigger he'd be happier. But being big doesn't automatically make you happy. Harry was big enough, and look at him. At times the size of his reflection in a clothing-store mirror or plate-glass window startles him. Appalls him, really: taking up all that space in the world. He pushes on for a few more pages: *Expectation of lucrative commerce . . . Combat at sea . . . tangled issue . . . increased tension . . . neutral bottoms . . . French vigorously . . . Debate in the provincial states . . . Unlimited convoy would become another test of ego as a* casus belli. He rereads this last sentence twice before realizing he has no idea what it means, his brain is making those short-circuit connections as in dreams. He turns out the light. This conjures up a thin crack of light under the door like a phosphorescent transmitter, emitting sounds. He hears Janice and Pru murmuring, a clink of glass, a footstep, and then a buzzer rasping, and hasty footsteps, a woman's voice in the nervous pitch you use for talking over a loudspeaker, not trusting it, and then in a later fold of his restless, distended consciousness the door opening, Nelson's voice, deep among the women's, and most dreamlike of all, laughter, all of them laughing.

A gnashing sound, the greens being mowed by kids on those big ugly reel mowers. Excited seagulls weeping. The Norfolk pine, its branches as regularly spaced as the thin metal balusters of his balcony rail. Amazing. He is still in Florida, still alive. Morning-chilly salt air wafts from the Gulf through the two-inch crack that the sliding door was left open. Janice is asleep in bed beside him. The warmth of her body is faintly rank; night sweat has pasted dark wiggly hairs to the nape of her neck. Her hair is least gray at the nape, a secret nest of her old dark silky self. She sleeps on her stomach turned away from him, and if the night is cool pulls the covers off him onto herself, and if hot dumps them on top of him, all this supposedly in her sleep. Rabbit eases from the king-size bed, goes into their bathroom with its rose-colored one-piece Fiberglas tub and shower stall, and urinates into the toilet of a matching rose porcelain. He sits down, as it is quieter, splashing against the front of the bowl. He brushes his teeth but is too curious to shave; if he takes the time to shave Janice might get away from him and hide among the others as she has been doing. He slides back into bed, stealthily but hoping that the unavoidable rustling of sheets and the soft heaving of the mattress might wake her. When it doesn't, he nudges her shoulder. "Janice?" he whispers. "Dreamboat?"

Her voice comes muffled. "What? Leave me alone."

"What time 'dyou come to bed?"

"I didn't dare look. One."

"Where had Nelson been? What was his explanation?"

She says nothing. She wants him to think she has fallen back to sleep. He waits. Lovingly, he caresses her shoulder. His glimpse of that French movie last night had stirred him with the idea of a wife as a total stranger, of moving right in, next to her little warm brown body. A wife can be as strange as a whore, that's the beauty of male-female relations. She says, still without turning her head, "Harry, touch me once more and I'll kill you."

He thinks this over and decides upon counteraggression. "Where the hell had he been?" he asks.

She rolls over, giving up. Her breath has stale tobacco in it. She has given up smoking supposedly but whenever she's around Nelson with his Camels and Pru with her Pall Malls she takes it up again. "He didn't know exactly. Just driving around. He said he needed to get out, Florida is so claustrophobic."

The kid is right: life down here is confined to the narrow paths you make. To Winn Dixie, to the Loew's cineplex and the shops in the Palmetto Palm Mall, to the doctor's, to the pro shop and back. Between these paths there's somehow nothing, a lot of identical palm trees and cactus and thirsty lawn and empty sunshine, hotels you're not staying at and beaches you're not admitted to and inland areas where there's never any reason to go. In Pennsylvania, at least in Diamond County, everything has been paved solid by memory and in any direction you go you've already been there.

Licking her lips and making a face as if her throat aches, Janice goes on, "He drove on 41 as far as what sounds like Naples and stopped at a restaurant when he got hungry and called us but the phone didn't answer, I wondered at the time if we shouldn't have waited to go over but you said you were starving –"

"That's right. Blame me."

"I wasn't, honey. It wasn't just you. The children were antsy and worried and I thought, Life must go on, dinner will distract us; but then he says he did call just about when we were heading out the door and where he was one beer led to another and on the way back he got a little lost, you know yourself how if you miss the Pindo Palm turnoff everything looks identical, for miles."

"I can't believe it," Harry says. He feels rage coming to boil in his chest and sits up in bed to relieve the pressure. "Without so much as a fucking word to anybody he disappears for, what, eight hours? He is really becoming crazy. He's always been moody but this is crazy behavior. The kid needs help."

Janice says, "He was perfectly sober when he came back and brought a bunch of those little tiny stuffed alligators they make for souvenirs; Pru and I had to laugh. One for each of the children and even one for you, where they've made it stand and put a golf club in its little feet." She flicks the blanket back from his lap and touches his drowsy penis in his open pajama fly. "How're we doing down there? We never make love any more."

But now he is out of the mood. He slaps her hand primly and tugs up the blanket and says, "We just *did* make love. Before Christmas."

"*Way* before Christmas," Janice says, not moving her head, and for a second he has the mad hope she will turn the blanket down again and simply, quickly, take his prick in her mouth, like Thelma used to do almost first thing when they would secretly meet in this last decade; but blowing has never been Janice's style. She has to be very drunk, and he never did like her drunk, a kind of chaos wells up within her that threatens him, that threatens to swamp the whole world. She says, "O.K. for you, buster," to register with him that she's been rejected, in case he wants her later, and pushes out of her side of the bed. Her damp nightie is stuck up above her waist and before she tugs it down he admires the taut pale buttocks above the tan backs of her thighs. Guiltily he hears her flush the toilet in the bathroom and with an angry rattle and rush of water start to run the shower. He pictures exactly how she looks stepping out of the shower, with her hair in a transparent shower cap and her bottom rosy and her pussy all whitened with dew, and regrets that they must live, he and his little dark woman, his stubborn shy mutt of a Springer, in a world of mostly missed signals. Down here they have been thrown together more than at any time of their lives and they have coped by turning their backs and growing thicker skins. He plays golf three or four times a week and she has her tennis and her groups and her errands. When she comes back from the bathroom, in a terrycloth robe, he is still in the bed, reading in his book about British interference with Dutch merchant ships and France needing to build up her decayed fleet with Baltic timber delivered by Dutch vessels, in case Janice wants to try at sex again, but now from the other end of the condo the sounds of children can be heard, and of Pru hushing them in her burdened maternal voice.

Harry says to Janice, "Let's try to concentrate on Judy and Roy today. They seem sort of woebegone, don't they?"

She doesn't answer, guardedly. She takes his remark as a slam at Nelson's parenting. Maybe it is. Nelson's the one who needs parenting; he always did and never got enough. When you don't get enough of something at the right biological moment, Rabbit has read somewhere, you keep after it until you die. He asks, "What do you and Pru talk about all the time?"

She answers, thin-lipped, "Oh, women things. You'd find them boring." Janice always gets a funny intense frowny look on her face when she's dressing herself. Even if it's just slacks and a blouse to go to Winn Dixie in, she pinches off an accusatory stare into the mirror, to face down the worst.

"Maybe so," he agrees, ending the conversation, and knowing this will make Janice want to continue it.

Sure enough, she volunteers, "She's worried about Nelson," and falters for the next words, the tip of her tongue sneaking out and pressing on her upper lip in the effort of thought.

But Rabbit says curtly, "Who wouldn't be?" He turns his back to put on his underpants. He still wears Jockey shorts. Ruth was amused by them that night ages ago, and he always thinks of it. Today he wants to be a grandfather and tries to dress for the role. Long eggshell-colored linen pants with cuffs, instead of his dirty old plaid bell-bottom golf slacks, and instead of a polo knit a real shirt, 100-per-cent cotton, with blue pinstripes and short sleeves. He looks at himself in the mirror that Janice's image has vacated and is stunned, deep inside, by the bulk of what he sees – face swollen to a kind of moon, with his little sunburned nose and icy eyes and nibbly small mouth bunched in the center, above the jowls, boneless jowls that come up and put a pad of fat even in front of his ears, where Judy has a silky shine. Talk about Nelson – Harry's own hair, its blondness dirtied and dulled by gray, is thinning back from his temples. Tall as he is, there is no carrying the slope under his shirt as anything other than a loose gut, a paunch that in itself must weigh as much as a starving Ethiopian child. He must start to cut down. He can feel, every motion he makes, his weight tugging at his heart – that singeing sensation he gets as if a child inside him is playing with lighted matches.

On the breakfast table, today's *News-Press* has the color photograph of a tiny sickly one-year-old girl who died last night for lack of a liver transplant. Her name was Amber. Also a headline saying that according to Scotland Yard Pan Am Flight 103 was definitely bombed, just like Ed Silberstein and Judy say. Fragments of metal. Luggage compartment. Plastic explosive, can be molded into any form, probably a high-performance Czech type called Semtex: Harry can hardly bear to read about it, the thought of all those conscious bodies suddenly with nothing all around them, freezing, *Ber-nie, Ber-nie,* and Lockerbie a faint spatter of stars below, everything in one split second upside-down and void of mercy. Also the mayor of Fort Myers now thinks his police acted properly in the arrest of Deion Sanders. Also *Deadly pollution infects Lake Okeechobee.* Also *Partly cloudy, Highs in low to mid-80s.* "Today's the day," he announces, "Grandpa's going to take you to amazing places!"

Judy and Roy look doubtful but not entirely.

Janice says, "Harry, have another of these cherry Danishes before they go stale. We bought them thinking mostly of the children but they both say they hate red runny things."

"Why do you want to kill me with carbos?" he asks, but eats the Danish anyway, and cleans up the sweet sugary crumbs with his fingertips.

Pru, tall from Harry's seated angle, her hips level with his eyes, hesitantly asks, "Would you two possibly enjoy having the grandchildren to yourselves for this expedition? Nelson couldn't get to sleep last night and kept me pretty much up too. I just can't face a day in the car." She does look pale and drawn, the kid keeping her up all night with his whining and whatever else. Even her freckles look pale, and her lips, that felt so soft and warm at the airport, are resigned and tight and wryly pulled down on one side.

Janice says, "Of course, dear. You get some sleep and then maybe you and Nellie could do something healthy and fun. If you use the Valhalla pool remind him he's supposed to shower before *and* after and not to do any diving."

Judy laughs and interrupts: "Daddy does belly flops."

Roy says, "Daddy does *not* flop. You flop."

"Hey Jesus," Harry tells them, "don't start fighting yet. We aren't even in the car."

In the car by nine-thirty, provisioned with a triple-barrelled package of Double Stuf Oreos and a sixpack of Classic Coke, they begin the long day that for years to come will be known in fond family legend as The Day Grandpa Ate the Parrot Food, though it wasn't exactly for parrots, and he didn't eat much of it. They start by driving down Route 41 (PATIOLAND, Kissin' Kuzzins, Easy Drugs, LAND OF SLEEP) to Fort Myers and visiting the Thomas Alva Edison Winter Home, which nearly does them in. They park the Camry and pass underneath a giant banyan tree, a tree (a helpful sign tells them) given to Edison when it was a twig by some financial giant of the time, Harvey Firestone or Henry Ford, and that has since become the biggest banyan tree outside of India, where a single such gigantic tree may shelter an entire bazaar. Banyans spread by dangling down roots and making new trunks that become like crutches as the limbs spread out and out – these creepy trees will go for miles if nobody stops them. Harry wonders, *How do they die?*

It turns out you can't just walk around the house and grounds, you have to join a tour, for five bucks a pop. Judy and Roy both freak out when that's explained to them. They see themselves surrounded by busloads of old retired people wearing baseball caps and flip-up sunglasses and carrying those little sticks that open out into a kind of saddle to be one-legged chairs. Several wrecks in wheelchairs join their accumulating tour group as it waits to begin. Judy, looking prematurely long-legged in short pink shorts, with funny red shadows of blusher on her cheekbones, says, "I don't *care* about any dumb grounds, I want to see the machine that makes lightning," and Roy, his loose little mouth dyed by Oreo chocolate, stares with his glazed brown eyes as if he's going to melt in the heat.

Harry tells Judy, "I don't think there's any machine that makes lightning, just the very first light bulb ever invented." He tells Roy, "I'll carry you if you get too tired."

At some signal he misses, so they get caught in the back, everybody including the wheelchairs pushes out of the shed into a space of dusty gray earth and outdoor jungle stuffiness and knifelike leaf shadows. Their guide is a prissy old blue-haired girl in a billed cap reciting what she's memorized. First she points out to them *Kigelia pinnata*, the sausage tree of Africa. "The fruit resembles a sausage and that is why the name. It is not edible, but is used as a medicine by the natives of Africa and because of their superstitious nature they worship the tree for its healing power. Just across

Memory Garden is the fried-egg tree. The flower looks very much like an egg, sunny side up. It was planted there just in case you like eggs with your sausage."

The group politely laughs. Some of the old folks indeed laugh more than politely, as if this is the funniest thing they've ever in their long lives heard. When do the gray cells start winking out in significant numbers? When will it start happening to him, Harry wonders. Or has it already? You don't know what you don't know. A void inside, a void outside. Their guide, heartened by the good audience response, points out more funny trees – the dynamite tree, *Hura crepitans*, whose fruit explodes when it is ripe, and the very rare *Cecropia* of South America, the sloth tree, indeed the *only* mature *Cecropia palmata* in the United States, whose leaves have the texture of chamois skin and *never* disintegrate. Harry wonders, Why did God bother to do all these tricks, off by Himself in the Amazon jungle? "They are chocolate brown on one side and white on the other and because of their unusual shapes and lasting qualities are in great demand for dried floral arrangements. You can purchase these leaves in our gift shop." So He did it so people would have something to buy in gift shops.

Next we come to *Enterolobium cyclocarpum*, known as the ear tree. "The seed pods," the guide recites, "resemble the human ear." The crowd, warmed up now to laugh at almost any ridiculous thing God does, titters, and the guide allows herself a self-congratulatory smile; she knows these trees, these words, and these docile senile tourists backwards and forwards.

A little human hand tugs Harry's with a chamoislike softness of its own. He bends down to little Judy's exquisite, tarted-up, green-eyed face. He sees that Pru allowed her to put on a little lipstick, too. To sweeten this outing for her, to make it seem an occasion. Going sightseeing with Grandpa and Grandma. You'll always remember this. When they're gone to their reward. "Roy wants to know," Judy says as softly as she can, but anxiety driving her voice up, "how soon it's over."

"It's just begun," Harry says.

Janice begins to whisper with them. Her attention span is as poor as theirs. "Could we make a break for it before they make us cross the street?"

"It's a one-way tour," Harry says. "Come on, everybody. Let's stick with it."

He picks up little Roy, whose body weight has been doubled by boredom, and carries him, and they all cross the street, a street that in the very old days was a cow trail and that "Mr. Edison," as the woman keeps calling him, simpering like he's some big-dicked boyfriend of hers, took it into his head to line with royal palms. "These royal palms grow wild sixty miles of us on the fringe of the Everglades; however, it was much easier, in 1900, to bring them in from Cuba by great sailboats than to drag them by ox teams through our virtually impenetrable Florida swamplands."

On winding paths they drag themselves, dodging wheelchairs, trying not to step on the little beds of cactus and flowers that line the paths, trying to hear their guide as her voice fades in and out of its scratchy groove, trying to take an interest in the embowering green enigmas that Edison brought from afar in his heavily financed search for a substitute rubber. Here are the kapok tree and the Java plum, the cannonball tree from Trinidad and the mango from India, the lipstick tree and the birdseye bush, the sweetheart orchid, which is *not* as many people think a parasite, and the lychee nut, whose fruit is much sought after by the Chinese. Harry's legs ache, and the small of his back, and that suspect area behind his left ribs, which gives him a twinge, but he cannot put Roy down because the kid is asleep: he must be one of the sleepingest four-year-olds in the world. Janice and Judy have conspiratorially separated from the group and wandered ahead to the Edison house, a house brought in four sailing schooners from Maine in 1886, the first prefabricated house in the world you could say, a house without a kitchen because Edison didn't like the smell of cooking food, a house with a wide veranda on all four sides and with the first modern pool in Florida, of blue cement reinforced not with steel but with bamboo and not a crack or leak in it to this day. Marvels! So much endeavor, ingenuity, oddity, and bravery has been compressed into history: Harry can hardly stand under the weight of it all, bending his bones, melting his mind, pressing like a turnscrew on the segments of his skull, giving him a fantastic itch under his shoulder blades, where his 100-per-cent cotton blue-pinstriped shirt has moistened and then dried. He catches up to Janice, his heart twanging, and softly begs her, "Scratch." Softly so as not to wake the child.

"Where?" She shifts her cigarette, a Pall Mall she must have borrowed from Pru, to the other hand and rakes at his back, up, down, to the right and left as he directs, until the demon feels exorcised. This jungly garden of old Edison's is a devilish place. His breathing is bothered; he makes a determined effort not to hyperventilate. The commotion wakes Roy and he drowsily announces, "I got to go pee."

"I bet you do," Harry says, and tells him, "You can't go behind any of these bushes, they're all too rare."

"The *scarlet dombeya wallichi* is known as the pink ball tree of India," the guide is telling her less unruly students with a lilt. "It has a very heavy fragrance. Mrs. Edison loved birds and always kept canaries, parakeets, and parrots. These birds live out of doors the year around and love it here."

"How does she know they love it here?" Judy asks her grandparents, a bit noisily, so that several venerable heads turn. "She's not a parrot."

"Who says she's not?" Harry whispers.

"I got to go pee," Roy repeats.

"Yeah well, your need to pee isn't the exact fucking center of the universe," Harry tells him. He is badly out of practice in this fathering business, and never was that great at it.

Janice offers, "I'll take him back along the path, there were bathrooms in the building we came in at."

Judy is alarmed to see these two escaping. "I want to come with!" she cries, so loudly the tour guide stops her recital for a moment. "Maybe I got to go pee too!"

Harry grabs her hand and holds it tight and even gives it a sadistic squeeze. "And maybe you don't," he says. "Come on, stick it out. Go with the flow, for Chrissake. You'll miss the world's oldest Goddamn light bulb."

A woman in a wheelchair, not so crippled her hair isn't dyed orange and permed into more curlicues than a monkey's ass, looks over and gives them a glare. *Knowing when to quit,* Harry thinks. *Nobody knows when to quit.* Their guide has lifted her voice up a notch and is saying, "Here is the sapodilla of the American tropics. From the sap of this tree comes chicle, used in making chewing gum."

"Hear that?" Harry asks Judy, out of breath with the social tension of this endless tour and sorry about the hurtful squeeze. "The tree Chiclets come from."

"What are Chiclets?" Judy asks, looking up at him with a little new nick of a squint taken in those clear green eyes. She is sore, slightly, and wary of him now. He has nicked her innocence. Can it be she's never heard of Chiclets? Have they really gone the way of penny candy, of sugar-soaked Fosnacht doughnuts, of those little red ration tokens you had to use during the war? All as real as yesterday to Harry. Realer.

"Mr. Edison planted this chewing-gum tree for children," the guide is going on. "He loved his children and his grandchildren very much and spent long hours with them, though because of his deafness he had to do most of the talking." There is a murmur of laughter, and she preens, stretching her neck and pursing her lips, as if she hadn't expected this, though she must have, she has done this spiel so often she must have their reactions taped down to every stray chuckle. Now she leads her herd of oldsters, shuffling and bobbing solemnly in their splashy playclothes, toward a link fence and a new phase of their five-dollar pilgrimage. They are about to cross the road lined with the unnaturally straight and concrete-colored palm trunks that Edison, the amazing great American, floated in from Cuba when the century was an infant. But she can't let them cross without socking them with one more cute plant. "The shrub with the long red tassels is the chenille plant from the Bismarck Islands. The chenille is French and means caterpillar. You can readily see the meaning for the name of the plant."

"Yukko, *cat*erpillars," little Judy pipes up to Harry, and he recognizes this as a female attempt to rebridge the space between them, and he feels worse than ever about that hurtful squeeze. He wonders why he did it, why he tends to do mean things like that, to women mostly, as if blaming them for the world as it is, full of chenille plants and without mercy. He feels fragile, on the edge of lousy. That bad child inside his chest keeps playing with matches.

The guide announces, "We are now going across the street to the laboratory where Mr. Edison did his last experimental work."

They do at last cross over and, in Edison's breezy old laboratories, among dusty beakers and siphons and alembics and big belted black machinery, are reunited with Janice and Roy. The tour guide points out the cot where Edison used to take the ten-minute catnaps that enabled him to sit and dream in his big deaf head for hours on end, and the piece of goldenrod rubber on his desk, made from goldenrod grown right here in Fort Myers and still flexible after all these years. Finally, the guide frees them to roam, marvel, and escape. Driving north, Harry asks the three others, "So, what did you like best?"

"Going pee," Roy says.

"You're dumb," Judy tells him and, to show that she's not, answers, "I liked best the phonograph where to hear because he was deaf he rested his teeth on this wooden frame and you can see the marks his teeth made. That was interesting."

"*I* was interested," Harry says, "in all those failures he had in developing the storage battery. You wouldn't think it would be so tough. How many – nine *thou*sand experiments?"

Route 41 drones past the windows. Banks. Food and gas. Arthritis clinics. Janice seems preoccupied. "Oh," she says, trying to join in, "I guess the old movie machines. And the toaster and waffle iron. I hadn't realized he had invented those, you don't think of them as needing to be invented. You wonder how different the world would be if he hadn't lived. That one man."

Harry says, authoritatively, he and Janice in the front seat like puppet grandparents, just the heads showing, playing for their little audience of two in the back seat, "Hardly at all. It was all there in the technology, waiting to be picked up. If we hadn't done it the Swiss or somebody would have. The only modern invention that wasn't inevitable, I once read somewhere, was the zipper."

"The zipper!" Judy shrieks, as if she has decided, since this day with her grandparents looks as though it will never end, to be amused.

"Yeah, it's really very intricate," Harry tells her, "all those little slopes and curves, the way they fit. It's on the principle of a wedge, an inclined plane, the same way the Pyramids were built." Feeling he may have wandered rather far, venturing into the terrible empty space where the Pyramids were built, he announces,

"Also, Edison had backing. Look at who his friends were down there. Ford. Firestone. The giant fat cats. He got his ideas to sell them to them. All this talk about his love for mankind, I had to laugh."

"Oh yes," Janice says, "I liked the old car with daffodil-rubber tires."

"Goldenrod," Harry corrects. "Not daffodil."

"I meant goldenrod."

"I like daffodil better," Judy says from the back seat. "Grandpa, how did you like our tour lady, the awful way she talked, making that mouth like she had a sourball in it?"

"I thought she was very kind of sexy," Harry says.

"Sexy!" little Judy shrieks.

"I'm hungry," Roy says.

"Me too, Roy," says Janice. "Thank you for saying that."

They eat at a McDonald's where, for some legal reason – fear of lawsuits, the unapologetic cashier thinks when they ask her about it – the door is locked out to the playground, with its spiral slide and its enticing plastic man with a head, even bigger than Edison's, shaped like a hamburger. Roy throws a fit at the locked door and all through lunch has these big liquid googies of grief to snuffle back up into his nose. He likes to pour salt out of the shaker until he has a heap and then rub the French fries in it, one by one. The French fries and about a pound of salt are all the kid eats; Harry finishes his Big Mac for him, even though he doesn't much care for all the Technicolor glop McDonald's puts on everything – pure chemicals. Whatever happened to the old-fashioned plain hamburger? Gone wherever the Chiclet went. A little Bingo game is proceeding in a corner; you have to walk right through it on your way to the bathrooms, these old people in booths bent over their cards while a young black girl in a McDonald's brown uniform gravely reads off the numbers with a twang. "Twainty-sevvn . . . Fohty-wuhunn . . ."

Back in the hot car, Harry sneaks a look at his watch. Just noon. He can't believe it, it feels like four in the afternoon. His bones ache, deep inside his flesh. "Well now," he announces, "we have some choices." He unfolds a map he carries in the glove compartment. *Figure out where you're going before you go there*: he was told that a long time ago. "Up toward Sarasota there's the Ringling Museum but it's closed, something called Bellm's Cars of Yesterday but maybe we did enough old cars back at Edison's, and this Jungle Gardens which a guy I play golf with really swears by."

Judy groans and little Roy, taking his cue from her, begins his trembly-lower-lip routine. "Please, Grandpa," she says, sounding almost maternal, "not caterpillar trees again!"

"It's not just plants, the plants are the *least* of it, they have leopards and these crazy birds. Real leopards, Roy, that'd claw your eyes out if you let 'em, and flamingos that fall asleep standing on one leg – Bernie, this friend of mine, can't get over it, the way they can sleep standing on this one skinny leg!" He holds up a single finger to convey the wonder of it. How ugly and strange a single finger is – its knuckle-wrinkles, its whorly print, its pretty useless nail. Both the children in the back seat look flushed, the way Nelson used to when he'd be coming down with a cold – a smothery frantic look in the eyes. "Or," Rabbit says, consulting the map, "here's something called Braden Castle Ruins. How do you two sports like ruins?" He knows the answer, and cinches his point with, "Or we could all go back to the condo and take a nap." He learned this much selling cars: offer the customer something he doesn't want, to make what he half-wants look better. He peeks over at Janice, a bit miffed by her air of detachment. Why is she making this all his show? She's a grandparent too.

She rouses and says, "We can't go back so soon – they may be still resting."

"Or whatever," he says. Brawling. Fucking. There is something hot and disastrous about Nelson and Pru that scares the rest of them. Young couples give off this heat; they're still at the heart of the world's business, making babies. Old couples like him and Janice give off the musty smell of dead flower stalks, rotting in the vase.

Judy suggests, "Let's go to a *movie*."

"Yeah. Movie," Roy says, for these two words doing quite a good accidental imitation of a grown-up voice, as if they've taken on a hitchhiker in the back seat.

"Let's make a deal," Harry proposes. "We'll drive up and nip into Jungle Gardens, and if there's a guided tour or you think it'll depress you we'll nip right out again, the hell with 'em. Otherwise we'll go through and see the flamingos and then buy a Sarasota paper and see what's at the movies. Roy, you big enough to sit through a whole movie?" He starts the engine and gets into gear.

Judy says, "He cried so hard during *Dumbo* Mommy had to take him out."

"Dumbo's mommy . . ." Roy begins to explain, then starts to cry.

"Yeah," Harry says, turning onto 41 again, casting back his voice, rolling along. "That's a tough one, out there in that little prison car. The business with their trunks, remember? But it all works out. Roy, you should have stayed to the end. If you don't stay to the end the sadness sticks with you."

"He becomes a *star*," Judy tells her brother spitefully. "He shoots peanuts at all the bad clowns. You missed all that."

"That Disney," Harry says, half to Janice, half for their little audience. "He packed a punch. You had to have been raised in the Depression to take it. Even Nelson, your daddy, couldn't stand *Snow White* when it came around in rerun."

"Daddy doesn't like anything," Judy confides. "Just his dumb friends."

"What friends?" Rabbit asks her.

"Oh, I don't know their names. Slim and like that. Mommy hates them and won't go out any more."

"She won't, huh?"

"She says she's scared."

"Scared! Scared of what?"

"Harry," Janice mutters beside him. "Don't pump the children."

"Scared of Slim," Roy says, trying it out for sound.

Judy thumps him. "No, Daddy is not scared of Slim, you dumbo, he's scared of those other men."

"What other men?" Harry asks.

"*Harry*," Janice says.

"Forget I asked," he calls back, his words lost in the squall as Roy grabs Judy's hair and won't let go. In reaching back to pull them apart Janice rips a seam of her blouse; he can hear the threads break even though at that moment he is being passed by an

eighteen-wheeler whose shuddering white sides say MAYFLOWER
MEANS MOVING and create an aerodynamic condition that sucks
him sideways so he has to fight the Camry's wheel. The Japanese
don't build for the full range of American conditions. Like Nelson
said about the van, the wind pushing him all over 422. Still, you
got to sell something in life. You can't just sit there and crab. We
can't all sell Lamborghinis.

Jungle Gardens works out better than anyone dared hope. A big
shop full of shells and corny artifacts like that stuff of Janice's back
on the condo shelves opens into a miniature outdoors. You can go
one way to the Reptile Show and the Gardens of Christ and the
other to the Bird Show. They all turn toward the Bird Show, and
watch tattered, disgruntled-looking parrots ride bicycles and see-
saws and hop through hoops. Then a curving cement path, Jungle
Trail, leads them along: you shuffle obediently past mossy roots and
trickling rocks and at each turn confront some fresh mild wonder
– a trio of spider monkeys with long hairy arms and little worried
faces, then a cageful of finches whirring up and down, roost to
roost, like the tireless works of a complicated clock, then a bo-tree
such as Buddha was illuminated under. Rabbit wonders how the
Dalai Lama is doing, after all that exile. Do you still believe in God,
if people keep telling you you *are* God?

The four Angstroms come to Mirror Lake, where mute swans
float, and Flamingo Lagoon, where, as Bernie Drechsel promised,
flocks of flamingos, colored that unreal orange-pink color, sleep
while standing up, like big feathery lollypops, each body a ball, the
idle leg and the neck and head somehow knitted in, balanced on
one pencil-thin leg and wide weird leathern foot. Others, almost as
marvellous, are awake and stirring, tenderly treading. "Look how
they drink," Harry tells his grandchildren, lowering his voice as if
in the presence of something sacred. "Upside down. Their bills are
scoops that work upside down." And they stand marvelling, the
four human beings, as if the space between farflung planets has been
abolished, so different do these living things loom from themselves. The Earth is many planets, that intersect only at moments.
Even among themselves, slices of difference interpose, speaking
the same language though they do, and lacking feathers, and all
drinking right side up.

After the flamingos, the path takes them to a snack bar in a pavilion, and a shell-and-butterfly exhibit, and a goldfish pond, and a cage of black leopards just as Harry had promised Roy. The black-eyed child stares at the animals' noiseless pacing as if into the heart of a whirlpool that might suck him down. A small machine such as those that in Harry's youth supplied a handful of peanuts or pistachio nuts in almost every gas station and grocery store is fixed to a pavilion post near an area where peacocks restlessly drag their extravagant feathers across the dust. Here he makes his historic blunder. As his three kin move ahead he fishes in his pocket for a dime, inserts it, receives a handful of brown dry objects, and begins to eat them. They are not exactly peanuts, but perhaps some Florida delicacy, and taste so dry and stale as to be bitter; but who knows how long these machines wait for customers? When he offers some to Judy, though, she looks at them, smells them, and stares up into his face with pure wonderment. "Grandpa!" she cries. "That's to feed the birds! Grandma! He's been eating birdfood! Little brown things like rabbit turds!"

Janice and Roy gather around to see, and Harry holds open his hand to display the shaming evidence. "I didn't know," he weakly says. "There's no sign or anything." He is suffused with a curious sensation; he feels faintly numb and sick but beyond that, beyond the warm volume enclosed by his skin, the air is swept by a universal devaluation; for one flash he sees his life as a silly thing it will be a relief to discard.

Only Judy actually laughs, a laughter that turns forced, out of her fine-featured little face with its perfect teeth; Janice and Roy just look sad, and a bit puzzled.

Judy says, "Grandpa, that's the *dumb*est thing I ever saw anybody do!"

He smiles and nods at his inflated height above her; he feels short of breath and tight bands of pain pulse across his chest. In his mouth an acid taste intensifies. He turns his hand, his puffy keratotic hand, long-fingered enough to hold a basketball from above, and scatters the pellets where the peacocks can eat them. A dirty white one dragging its filmy tail through the dust eyes the turd-like food but doesn't peck. Maybe it was human food after all. Still, his day has taken a blow, and as they move along the path only

Judy is gleeful; her prattle eclipses a sudden anguished crying, the noise peacocks make, behind them.

Wearying of Jungle Gardens, they move along a path that pas-ses yet another piece of this same all-purpose lake, and a cage where a lonely ocelot dozes, and cactus gardens, and a black pool advertising a water monitor but where they see nothing, perhaps because they don't know what a water monitor is, and cages of parrots and macaws whose brilliant plumage and ornate bills seem to weigh them down. It's hell, to be a creature. You are trapped in yourself, the genetic instructions, more strictly than in a cage. At the last cage a scraggly tall emu and a rhea are snapping at the wires of the fencing with a doleful soft leathery clack of their bills. Their long-lashed great eyes stare through the diagonal wire squares. *Clip. Tap. Clip*, say their sad persistent bills, to no avail. Are they catching insects human beings cannot see? Are they delirious, like old rummies?

Harry retastes the acid pellets and the yellow-and-red glop McDonald's puts on hamburgers, with the little limp green pickle, and wishes to God he could stop eating. Janice comes to his side and touches the back of his hanging hand with the back of hers. "It was a natural mistake," she says.

"That's the kind I make," he says. "Natural ones."

"Harry, don't be so down."

"Am I?"

"You keep thinking about Nelson," she tells him. So that's what has been preoccupying her. Her, not him.

"I was thinking about emus," he confesses.

Janice says, "Let's go see if the kids want anything in the sou-venir shop and then go buy a paper. I'm dying to be somewhere air-conditioned." In the souvenir shop they buy Judy a lovely glossy top shell and Roy a strikingly black-and-white murex, with rough prongs that he instantly begins to scrape along smooth sur-faces – the painted rail leading back to the parking lot, and the Camry itself if Harry hadn't reached down and grabbed the little slob by his boneless little arm. Harry hates shells. Whenever he sees them he can't help thinking of the blobby hungry sluggy creatures who inhabit them, with hearts and mouths and anuses and feelers and feeble eyes, underneath the sea, a murky cold world halfway to death. He really can't stand the thought of underwater, the things haunting it, eating each other, drilling through shells, sucking each other's stringy guts out.

The interior of the car has grown broiling hot in their absence. The Florida sun has burned away those thin clouds like aging jet trails and left only a waste of pure blue above the palms and the Spanish tiles. The heat and the pressure of family life have stupefied the kids; they hardly beg for a treat when he stops at a Joy Food and Gas and buys a Sarasota *Sentinel*. The movie they all decide upon is *Working Girl* at two-forty-five at some "park" that turns out to be miles away, shimmering flat Florida miles full of big white soupy power-steered American cars being driven by old people so shrunken they can hardly see over the hood. Any time you get somewhere down here without a head-on collision is a tribute to the geriatric medicine in this part of the world, the pep pills and vitamin injections and blood thinners.

Though Judy swears Roy has been to the movies before, he doesn't seem to understand you can't just talk up as in your own living room. He keeps asking why, with a plaintive inflection: "*Why* she take off her clothes?" "*Why* she so mad at that man?" Harry likes it, in the movie, when you see that Melanie Griffith in her whorehouse underwear has a bit of honest fat to her, not like most of these Hollywood anorectics, and when she bursts in upon her boyfriend with the totally naked girl, like herself supposed to be Italian but not like her aspiring to be a Wall Street wheeler-dealer, riding the guy in the astride position, her long bare side sleek as the skin of a top shell and her dark-nippled boobs right on screen for a good five seconds. But the plot, and the farce of the hero and heroine worming their way into the upper-crust wedding, he feels he saw some forty years ago with Cary Grant or Gary Cooper and Irene Dunne or Jean Arthur. When Roy loudly asks, "*Why* don't we go now?" he is willing to go out into the lobby with him, so Janice and Judy can see the picture to the end in peace.

He and Roy split a box of popcorn and try a video game called Annihilation. Though he always thought of himself as pretty good on eye-hand coördination, Harry can't hit a single space monster as it twitches and wiggles past in computer graphics. Roy, so small he has to be held up to the control panel until his twitching, wiggling weight gives Harry a pain across his shoulders, isn't any better. "Well, Roy," he sums up, when he gets his breath back, "if it was all up to us, the world would be taken over by space monsters." The boy, more accustomed to his grandfather now, stands close, and his breath smells buttery from the popcorn, making Harry slightly queasy: this thin unconscious stream of childish breath reminds him of the overhead vent in an airplane.

When the crowd comes out of Cinema 3, Janice announces, "I think I need a job. Wouldn't you like me better, Harry, if I was a working girl?"

"Which state would you work in?"

"Pennsylvania, obviously. Florida is for vacations."

He doesn't like the idea. It has something fishy and uncomfortable about it, like that batch of November stats from Springer Motors. "What work would you do?"

"I don't know. Not work at the lot, Nelson hates us to get in his way. Sell something, maybe. My father was one and my son is one so why shouldn't I be one? A salesperson."

Rabbit doesn't know what to answer. After all these years of his grudgingly sticking with her, he can't imagine him begging her to stick with him, though this is his impulse. He changes conversational partners. "Judy. How did the movie come out?"

"Good. The man from the wedding believed her story and she got an office of her own with a window and her nasty boss broke her leg and lost the man they both liked."

"Poor Sigourney," Harry says. "She should have stuck with the gorillas." He stands way above his own little herd in the theater lobby, where the ushers move back and forth with green garbage bags and red velvet ropes, getting ready for the five-o'clock shows. "So, guys. What shall we do next? How about miniature golf? How about driving up to St. Petersburg, over this fantastic long bridge they have?"

Roy's lower lip starts to tremble, and he has such trouble getting his words out that Judy translates for him. "He says he wants to go home."

"Who doesn't?" Janice concurs. "Grandpa was just teasing. Haven't you learned that about your grandfather yet, Roy? He's a terrible tease."

Is he? Harry has never thought of himself that way. He sometimes says a thing to try it out, like a head fake, to open up a little
space.

Judy smiles knowingly. "He pretends to be mean," she says.

"Grrr," Grandpa says.

Forty minutes of southwestern Florida rush-hour traffic bring
them to the Deleon exit and Pindo Palm Boulevard and the nicely
guarded entrance of Valhalla Village. Up in 413, Pru and Nelson
look bathed and refreshed and act as if nothing has ever happened.
They listen to the travellers' tales, foremost the incredible story of
how Grandpa ate the grungy birdfood, and Pru sets about making
dinner, telling Janice to take the weight off her legs, and Nelson
settles on the sofa with a child on each knee in front of the local
evening news, giving Harry a pang of jealousy and a sensation of
injustice. The surly kid spends the whole day balling this big redhead and then is treated like a hero by these two brats Harry went
and knocked himself out for.

Rabbit sits in the chair across the glass table from the sofa and delicately needles his son. "Ja catch up finally on your sleep?" he asks.

Nelson gets the dig and looks over at him with his dark swarmy
eyes a little flat across the top, like a cross cat's. "I went into a place
to get a bite to eat last night and stayed at the bar too long," he
tells his father.

"Ya do that often?"

With a roll of his eyeballs Nelson indicates the children's heads
right under his face, watching television but perhaps also listening.
Little pitchers. "Naa," he allows. "Just when I'm tense it helps to
take off once in a while. Pru understands. Nothing happens."

Rabbit holds up a generous hand. "None of my business, right?
You're twenty-one plus. It's just you could have called. I mean, a
considerate person would have called. None of us could enjoy
dinner, not knowing what had happened to you. We could
hardly eat."

"I *tried* to call, Dad, but I don't have your number down here
memorized and the place I was in some sleazeball had stolen the
phone book."

"That's your story this evening? This morning your mother
told me you did call here but we were down to dinner."

"That, too. I tried once from a phone along the highway and then in this place there was no phone book."

"Where was the place? Think I'd know it?"

"No idea where," Nelson says, and smiles into the television flicker. "I get lost down here, it's like one big business strip. One nice thing about Florida, it makes Pennsylvania look unspoiled."

The local news commentator is giving the manatee update. "Manatee herds continue to populate both warm-weather feeding areas and traditional winter refuges as fair weather and eighty-degree temperatures continue. A general waterways alert is out: boaters, cut your throttle to half-speed. Throughout the weekend, encounters with manatees remain likely in widely varied habitats around Southwest Florida."

"They say that," Rabbit says, "but I never encounter one."

"That's because you're never on the water," Nelson says. "It's stupid, to be down here like you are and not own a boat."

"What do I want a boat for? I hate the water."

"You'd get to love it. You could fish all over the Gulf. You don't have enough to do, Dad."

"Who wants to fish, if you're halfway civilized? Dangling some dead meat in front of some poor brainless thing and then pulling him up by a hook in the roof of his mouth? Cruellest thing people do is fish."

The blond newscaster, with his hair moussed down so it's stiff as a wig, tells them, "An adult manatee with calf was reported at midday on Wednesday heading inland along Cape Coral's Bimini Canal about one-half mile from the Bimini Basin. Sightings like this indicate that while a large number of the Caloosahatchee herd have moved back out into the open waters of the river and back bays, some animals may still be encountered in and near sheltered waterways. To report dead or injured manatees, call 1-800-342-1821." The number rolls across some footage of a manatee family sluggishly rolling around in the water. "And," he concludes in that sonorous way television announcers have when they see the commercial break coming, "to report a manatee sighting, call the Manatee Hotline at 332-3092."

To refresh his rapport with Judy, Rabbit calls over, "How'd you like to have a single big tooth like that mamma manatee?"

But the girl doesn't seem to hear, her fair little face radiantly riveted on one of those ads with California raisins singing and dancing like black men. In a row like the old Mouseketeers. Where are
they now? Middle-aged parents themselves. Jimmie died years
ago, he remembers reading. Died young. It happens. Roy is sucking his thumb and nodding off against Nelson's chest. Nelson is
still wearing the white-collared, pink-striped shirt he wore down
in the plane, as if he doesn't own anything as foolish as a short-
sleeved shirt.

"Tomorrow," Rabbit loudly promises he doesn't know who,
"I'll get out on the water. Judy and I will rent a Sunfish. I have it
all set up with Ed Silberstein's son over at the Bayview Hotel."

"I don't know," Nelson says. "How safe *are* those things?"

Rabbit is insulted. "They're like toys, for Chrissake. If they tip
over, you just stand on the centerboard and up they come. Kids
ten, eleven years old race them over in the Bay all the time."

"Yeah, but Judy's not even nine yet, not for a couple weeks.
And no offense, Dad, you're way into double digits. And no sailor,
from what you just said."

"O.K., *you* do something with your kids tomorrow. *You* entertain 'em. I spent over eight hours at it today and dropped around
eighty bucks."

Nelson tells him, "You're supposed to *want* to do things like
that. You're their dear old *grand*father, remember?" He softens,
slightly. "Sunfishing's a nice idea. Just make sure she wears a life
jacket."

"Why don't you all come along? You, Pru, Sleeping Beauty
here. It's a helluva beach. They keep it clean."

"Maybe we will, if I can. I'm expecting a call or two."

"From the lot? Can't they even manage for half a week?"

Nelson is drifting away, hiding behind the distraction of television. One of the new Toyota ads is playing, with the black-
woman car salesman. At the end, she and the customer jump into
the air and are frozen there. "No," Nelson is saying, so softly
Rabbit can hardly hear. "It's a contact I made down here."

"A contact? What about?"

Nelson puts his finger to his lip, to signal they should not wake
Roy.

Rabbit gets out his needle again. "Speaking of digits, I keep trying to remember what seemed off about that November statement. Maybe the number of used seemed down for this time of year. Usually it's up, along with the new models."

"Money's scared, with Reagan going out," Nelson answers, ever so softly. "Also, Lyle's put in a new accounting system, maybe they were deferred into the next month and will show up in the December stats. Don't worry about it, Dad. You and Mom just enjoy Florida. You've worked hard all your life. You've earned a rest."

And the boy, as if to seal in the possibility of irony, kisses little Judy on the top of her shiny-sleek, carrot-colored head. The blue light from the set penetrates the triangular patch of thinning hair between Nelson's deepening temples. A hostage he's given to fortune. Your children's losing battle with time seems even sadder than your own.

"Dinner, guys and gals," Pru calls from Janice's aqua kitchen.

Her meal is a more thought-out affair than Janice's ever are, with a spicy clear sort of minestrone soup to begin, and a salad on a separate plate, and a fresh white fish, broiled on the stove grill attachment that Janice never takes the trouble to use. Janice has become a great warmer-up of leftovers in the microwave, and a great buyer over at Winn Dixie of frozen meatloaves and stuffed peppers and seafood casseroles in their little aluminum pans that can be tossed into the trashmasher dirty. She was always a minimal housewife and now the technology has caught up with her. The vegetables Pru serves, wild rice and little tender peas and baby onions, have a delicate pointed taste that Harry feels is aimed at him, a personal message the others consume without knowing. "Delicious," he tells Pru.

Janice explains to Harry, "Pru went into this little narrow fish store behind Eckerd's where I never thought to go. Our generation," she explains to Pru, "didn't have that much to do with fish. Except I remember Daddy used to bring home a quart of shucked Chesapeake oysters as a treat for himself sometimes."

Pru tells Harry in her personally aimed, slightly scratchy Ohio voice, "Oily deepwater fish, bluefish especially, have lots of EPA in their oil, that's a kind of acid that actually thins your blood and lowers the triglyceride level."

She would take care of me, Harry thinks. Pleasurably he complains, "What's everybody always worried about my cholesterol level for? I must look awful."

"You're a big guy," Pru says, and the assessment pierces him like a love dart, "and as we all age the proportion of fat in our bodies goes up, and the amount of LDL, that's low-density lipoprotein, the bad kind of fat, goes up and that of the high-density, good kind stays the same, so the ratio goes up, and the danger of Apo B attaching to your arteries goes up with it. And we don't exercise the way people used to, when everybody had farms, so the fats don't get burned up."

"Teresa, you know so *much*," Janice says, not quite liking being upstaged and using Pru's baptismal name as a tiny check, to keep her in place.

The other woman lowers her eyes and drops her voice. "You remember, I took that course at the Brewer Penn State extension. I was thinking, when Roy gets into school full-time, I should have something to do, and thought maybe nutrition, or dietetics . . ."

"*I* want to get a job, too," Janice says, annoying Harry with her intrusion into Pru's demure lecture about his very own, he felt, fatty insides. "The movie we saw this afternoon, all these women working in New York skyscrapers, made me so *jea*lous." Janice didn't use to dramatize herself. Ever since her mother died and they bought this condo, she has been building up an irritating confidence, an assumption that the world is her stage and her performance is going pretty well. Around Valhalla Village, she is one of the younger women and on several committees. Just not being senile is considered great down here. When they went to the Drechsels' seder, she turned out to be the youngest and had to ask the four questions.

Harry jealously asks Pru, "Does Nelson get the benefit of all this nutrition?"

Pru says, "He doesn't need it, really – he hardly ever eats, and he has all this nervous energy. He could *use* more lipids. But the children – they say now that after two in most American children the cholesterol level is too high. When they did autopsies on young men killed in the Korean War, three-quarters of them had too much fat in their coronary arteries."

Harry's chest is beginning to bind, to ache. His insides are like the sea to him, dark and wet and full of things he doesn't want to think about.

Nelson has done nothing to contribute to this conversation but sniff occasionally. The kid's nose seems to run all the time, and the line of bare skin above his mouse-colored mustache looks chafed. Now he pushes back from his half-eaten fish and announces complacently, "The way I figure, if one thing doesn't kill you, another will." Though he rests his palms on the edge of the table, his hands are trembling, the nerves snapping.

"It's not *what* we worry about, it's *when*," his father tells him.

Janice looks alarmed, her eyes shuttling from one to the other. "Let's all be cheerful," she says.

For dessert, Pru serves them frozen yogurt – much better for you than ice cream, with no cholesterol at all. When the meal is done, Harry hangs around the kitchen counter long enough to dig into the cookie drawer and stuff himself with three quick vanilla Cameos and a broken pretzel. Down here they don't have the variety of pretzels you get in Brewer but Sunshine sells a box of thick ones that are not too tasteless. He has an impulse to help Janice with the dishes and suppresses it; it's just throwing plates into the dishwasher and what else did she contribute to the meal? His feet hurt from all that walking they did today; he has a couple of toes that over the years have twisted enough in his shoes to dig their nails into each other if he doesn't keep them cut close. Pru and Roy and Nelson retreat into their room and he sits a while and watches while Judy, the remote control in hand, bounces back and forth between *The Cosby Show*, some ice capades, and a scare documentary about foreigners buying up American businesses, and then between *Cheers* and a drama about saving a fourteen-year-old girl from becoming a prostitute like her mother. So many emergencies, Harry thinks, so much canned laughter, so many actors' tears, all this effort to be happy, to be brave, to be loved, all this wasted effort. Television's tireless energy gnaws at him. He sighs and laboriously rises. His body sags around his heart like a tent around a pole. He tells Judy, "Better pack it in, sweetie. Another big day tomorrow: we're going to go to the beach and sailing." But his voice comes out listless, and perhaps that is the saddest loss time brings, the lessening of excitement about any-thing. These four guests are a strain; he looks forward to their departure Saturday, the last day of 1988.

Judy continues to stare at the screen and ply her channel changer. "Just the first part of *L.A. Law*," she promises, but flicks instead to an ABC news special about "American Kids – Their Diet of Danger." In their bedroom Janice is reading *Elle*, looking at the pictures, of superslim models looking stoned.

"Janice," he says. "I have something to ask you."

"What? Don't get me stirred up, I'm reading to make myself sleepy."

"Today," he says. "In that crowd going through the Edison place. Did I look as though I fit in?"

It takes her a while to shift her focus; then she sees what he wants. "Of course not, Harry. You looked much younger than the other men. You looked like one of their sons, visiting."

He decides this is as much reassurance as he dare ask for. "At least," he agrees with her, "I wasn't in a wheelchair." He reads a few pages of history, about the fight between the *Bonhomme Richard* and the *Serapis*, and how when amid the bloody explosions his chief gunner cried out "Quarter! quarter! for God's sake!" John Paul Jones *hurled a pistol at the man, felling him. But the cry had been heard by Pearson, the* Serapis' *commander, who called, "Do you ask for quarter?" Through the clash of battle, gunshot and crackle of fire the famous reply came faintly back to him: "I have not yet begun to fight!"* The vic-torious American ship was so damaged it sank the next day, and Jones took the captured *Serapis*, shorn of its mast, into Holland, *exacerbating the British resentment that already existed*. All this fury and bravery seems more wasted effort. Rabbit feels as if the human race is a vast colorful jostling bristling parade in which he is limp-ing and falling behind. He settles the book on the night table and switches off the lamp. The bar of light beneath the door transmits distant shots and shouts from some TV show, any TV show. He falls asleep with unusual speed, with scarcely a turn into his pillow. His arms, which usually get in the way, fold themselves up like pieces of blanket. His dreams include one in which he has come to a door, a door with a round top to it, and pushes at it. The glass door at McDonald's except that one you could see the hamburger head through. In his dream he knows there is a presence on the other side, a presence he dreads, hungry and still, but pushes nevertheless, and the dread increases with the pressure, so much that he awakes, his bladder aching to go to the bathroom. He can't get through the night any more. His prostate or his bladder, losing stretch like goldenrod rubber. His mistake was drinking a Schlitz while channel-surfing with Judy. Falling asleep again is not so easy, with Janice's deep breathing now and then dipping into a rasping snore just as he begins to relax and his brain to generate nonsense. The luminous bar beneath the door is gone but a kind of generalized lavender light, the light that owls and other animals of the night see to kill by, picks out the planes and big objects of the bedroom. A square bureau holds the glassy rectangle of Nelson's high-school graduation photo; a fat pale chair holds on one arm Harry's discarded linen trousers, the folds of cloth suggesting a hollow-eyed skull stretched like chewing gum. Air admitted from the balcony under the folds of the drawn curtain grazes his face. A way of going to sleep is to lie on your back and try to remember the dream you were having. Unease seizes him like a great scaly-footed parrot claw and puts him down again on his face. The next thing he knows he is hearing the mowing machines on the golf course, and the stirred-up seagulls weeping.

The lobby of the Omni Bayview, entered from under a wide maroon marquee through sliding glass doors tinted opaque like limousine windows, knocks you out, virtually blinds you with its towering space and light, its great prismatic chandelier and splashing fountain and high rear wall of plate glass flooded with the view of Deleon Bay: beach in the foreground and sea like a scintillating blue-green curtain hung from a horizon line strung between two pegs of land, rich men's islands. "Wow," Judy breathes at Harry's side. Pru and Roy, coming behind them, say nothing; but the shuffle of their sandals slows and hushes. They feel like four trespassers. The woman at the black-marble front desk is an exotic color, her skin mixed of Negro and Indian or Oriental tints and stretched tight over her cheekbones and nosebone; her eyelids have been painted a metallic green and her earlobes covered by ribbed shells of gold.

Harry is so awed he makes a mistake in uttering the magic name of admission, saying "Silberstein."

The woman blinks her amazing metallic lids, then graciously tells him, "You must mean Mr. Silvers. He is this morning's beach supervisor." With merciful disdain she directs them across the lobby, her ringed hand gesturing like a Balinese dancer's, without letting go of a slim gold pen. He leads his little party into the vast air-conditioned space, across a floor of black marble inset with strips of brass that radiate out like rays of the sun from an aluminum fountain suggesting a pipe organ, beneath a remote ceiling of hanging rectangles of gilded metal like those glittering strips farmers hang to scare away birds. A flight of downward stairs is marked TO POOL AND BEACH in solemn letters such as you see on post-office façades. After taking a wrong turn in the milky-green terrazzo corridors on the ground floor and confronting a door marked STAFF ONLY, Harry and his group find Ed Silberstein's son Gregg in a glassed-in, straw-matted area on the way to the hotel swimming pool – pools, since Harry sees there are three, fitted together like the blobs in an intelligence test, one for waders, one for divers, and a long one marked in lanes. Gregg is a curly-haired man brown as an Arab from being off and on the beach all day. In little black elastic European-style trunks and a hooded sweatshirt bearing the five-sided Omni logo, he stands less tall than his father, and his inherited sharp-chinned accountant's jaw has been softened by a mother's blood and a job of holiday facilitation. He smiles, showing teeth as white as Ed's but rounder: Ed's were so square they looked false, but Harry has never seen them slip. When Gregg speaks, his voice seems too young for his age; his curls hold bits of gray and his smile rouses creases in the sunbeaten face. He shouldn't still be horsing around on the beach.

"My father said you'd be coming. This is Mrs. Angstrom?" He means Pru, who has come instead of Janice, who after all that tramping around yesterday wanted to stay home and catch up on her errands and go to her aerobics class and bridge group and spend a little time with Nelson before he goes home. Harry is stunned that Ed's son could make this blunder but then thinks he must deal all the time with men in advanced middle age who have younger wives. And anyway Pru is no longer that young. Tall and fair-skinned like he is, she might well be his.

"Thanks for the compliment, Gregg," Harry says, pretty smoothly, considering, "but this is my daughter-in-law, Teresa." Teresa, Pru – she is like him even in having two names, an inner and an outer. "And these are my two handsome grandchildren, Judy and Roy."

Gregg tells Judy, "So you're the one who wants to be a sailor girl."

Her eyes when she lifts them to Gregg's face flood here by the pools with a skyey light that washes out their green and makes her pupils small as pencil leads. "Sort of."

Moving and speaking in a relaxed thorough way that suggests his whole day could happily be devoted to them, Ed's son leads them back into the terrazzo corridors and arranges for locker keys for them with a boy at a desk – a young black with his hair shaved into one of those muffin-tops they do now, an ugly style, with bald sides – and then leads them to the locker-room doors, and tells them how to exit directly onto the beach, where he will meet them and manage the Sunfish rentals. "How much do I owe you for all this?" Harry asks, half-expecting it will be free, arranged for by Ed in compensation for the twenty Harry dropped to him at Wednesday's golf.

But Gregg sheds a little amiability and says, "The boats are exclusively for the use of hotel guests and get included in their charges, but I think about a hundred twenty for the four of you would cover it, with the lockers and beach access and two Sunfish for an hour each."

Pru speaks up. "We don't want two. I'd be terrified."

He looks her up and down and says with a new thrust in his voice, a little friendly lean in from a guy who deals with a lot of women in this job, "No need to be terrified, Teresa. They can't sink, and lifesavers are compulsory. Worst case and you feel you have no control, just let go of the sail and we'll come out for you in the launch."

"Thanks but no thanks," Pru says, a bit perkily Harry thinks, but, then, she and this guy are about the same age. Baby boomers. Rock and roll, dope, *Leave It to Beaver*, physical fitness. And wait till they discover they both come from Ohio.

Gregg Silvers turns to him and says, "Ninety should about do it, then."

The sum seems an invitation to tip him ten, but Harry wonders if this wouldn't be insulting, since he is here as a family friend, and waits for Gregg to fetch the bill from the muffin-topped boy at the desk. When Rabbit and Roy are alone in the locker room, he tells the child, "Jesus, Roy, that just about cleaned out poor old Grandpa's wallet!"

Roy looks up at him with frightened inky eyes. "Will they put us in jail?" he asks, his voice high and precise, like wind chimes.

Harry laughs. "Where'd you get that idea?"

"Daddy hates jail."

"Well who doesn't!" Harry says, wondering if the child is quite right in the head. Roy doesn't understand you should loosen the string of bathing trunks to pull them on, and while he fumbles and struggles his little penis sticks straight out, no longer than it is thick, cute as a button mushroom. He is circumcised. Rabbit wonders what his own life would have been like if he had been circumcised. The issue comes up now and then in the newspapers. Some say the foreskin is like an eyelid; without it the constantly exposed glans becomes less sensitive, it gets thick-skinned and dull rubbing against cloth all the time. A letter he once read in a skin magazine was from a guy who got circumcised in midlife and found his sexual pleasure and responsiveness went so far down his circumcised life was hardly worth living. If Harry had been less responsive he might have been a more dependable person. Getting a hard-on you can feel the foreskin sweetly tug back, like freezing cream lifting the paper cap on the old-time milk bottles. From the numb look of his prick Roy will be a solid citizen. His grandfather reaches down a hand to lead him out to the beach.

Harry and Janice after their first year or two in Florida, when in their excitement at being here they bought a telescope for the balcony and three or four times a week would drive the two miles to the Deleon public beach for a walk and picnic supper if not a swim, gradually stopped visiting the Gulf. So it hits him now as something fresh, unforeseen, this immensity of water, of air, of a surface of flux battered into a million oscillating dents. The raw glory of it all overpowers for a moment the nagging aches and worries in his chest and releases him into self-forgetfulness. Such light-struck and level grandeur is like nothing he knew in the Pennsylvania landscape, hemmed in by woods and hills and housetops, a land dingy with centuries of use, where even the wild patches, the quarries and second-growth woodland and abandoned factories and mineshafts, had been processed by men and discarded. Here, all feels virgin, though in fact there is a history too, of Indians and conquistadores and barefoot mailmen who served the mosquito-plagued coastal settlements. On the right and left of the horizon are islands where the millionaires used to come by private railroad car for the tarpon fishing in April. Spanish and French pirates once hid among these islands. Gold is still buried in their sands. They are flat and seem very distant from where Harry and Roy stand on the beach wall. It is all so bright, so open, the world feels created anew, in synthetic elements. Sailboats, wind-surfing rigs, those motorcycles that buzz along on top of the water, plastic paddleboats, and inflated rafts dot the near water with colors gaudy as a supermarket's. A distance down the beach, in front of another hotel, someone is flying a kite – a linked pair of box kites that dip and dive and climb again in unison, trailing glittering orange ribbons. For a mile in either direction, a twinkling party of tan flesh and cloth patches is assembling itself, grainlike live bodies laid on top of the beach of sand.

Pru and Judy come out of the hotel to join them and they descend concrete steps. The hour has passed ten o'clock, and at their backs the tall hotel, shaped like an S fifteen stories high, fringed at each story with balconies like fine-toothed red combs, still has its face in shadow, though its shadow has shrunk back to the innermost of its pools. The sand is freshly raked underfoot; yesterday's footprints and plastic glasses and emptied lotion bottles have been taken away and the wooden beach chaises stacked. Today's sunbathers are arranging themselves and their equipment, their towels and mystery novels (Ruth used to read those, and what she got out of them was another mystery) and various color-coded numbers of sunscreen. Couples are greasing each other. Old smoothies already the color of leather are rubbing oil into their bald heads, the hair of their chests pure white. The smell of lotion rises to intertwine with the odor of salt air, of dead crab, of sea-weed. As he leads his group across the sand Harry feels heads lift and eyes behind sunglasses slide; he feels proud and strange to be seen with this much younger woman and two small children. His second family. Or his third or fourth. Life moves through us family after family.

At the water's slapping, hissing, frothing edge sandpipers scurry and halt, stab the foam for some morsel, and scurry on. Their feet and heads are so quick they appear mechanical. Roy cannot catch them, though they seem like toys. When Harry takes off his unlaced Nikes, the sand bites his bare feet with an unexpected chill – the tide of night still cold beneath the sunny top layer of grains. The tops of his feet show wormy blue veins, and his shins are all chalky and crackled, as if he is standing up to his knees in old age. A tremor of fright comes alive in his legs. The sea, the sun are so big: cosmic wheels he could be ground between. He is playing with fire.

Gregg is waiting for them at a hut of corrugated Fiberglas on the beach, back from the water near some palms with their roots exposed. He has taken from the hut a rudder, a centerboard, and two life jackets of black foam rubber. Rabbit doesn't like the color, the texture; he wants old-fashioned Day-Glo kapok from Thomas Edison's kapok trees. Gregg asks him, "You've done this before?"

"Sure."

But something in Harry's tone leads Gregg to be instructive: "Push the tiller away from the sail. Watch the tips of the waves for the direction of the wind. When the wind gets behind you, hold the mainsheet loose."

"O.K., sure," Harry says, having not quite listened, thinking instead, resentfully, of Ed Silberstein's bogey on the first hole yesterday and how its being enough for a win got the whole round off to a lousy start.

Gregg turns to Pru and asks, "Your little girl can swim?"

"Oh, sure," she says, picking up Harry's lazy word. "She was the champion in her swimming class at summer camp."

"*Mom*," the girl pleads. "I came in *second*."

Gregg looks down at Judy, the sun at his back so bright that the shadow on his face has a blue light of its own. "Second's pretty close to champ." Still needing to talk to Pru, Gregg says, "I wouldn't advise your little boy to go. There's an offshore breeze today, you can't feel it in the lee of the hotel here, but it takes you out there pretty fast. There's no cockpit, it's easy to slip off."

She gives Gregg Silvers her crooked wry grin and shifts her weight, as if the closeness of this man her own age makes her awkwardly aware of her near-nakedness. She is wearing a tie-dyed brown dashiki over her one-piece white suit with those high sides that expose leg up to the hipbone. The cut means you have to shave the sides off your pussy. What women go through. There's even a kind of wax job you can have done to make it permanent. But suppose bathing-suit fashions change again? Rabbit preferred that pre-Reagan look of the two-piece bikini with the lower half like a little skimpy diaper slung under the belly, like Cindy Murkett used to slosh around in. Still, this new style nicely lengthens Pru's already long legs and keeps her thickening middle in. "He's going to stay with me right on the beach," she tells Gregg Silvers, and by way of emphasis bows down, so her red hair flings forward, and pulls off her dashiki, revealing string straps and white wide shoulders mottled with pale freckles.

"How long do I have it for?" Harry, feeling ignored, asks Ed's son. Those tight little European-style bathing trunks definitely show the bump of a prick.

"One hour, sir." The "sir" just popped in absentmindedly and the boy tries to revert to friendly casualness. "No sweat if you don't bring it in on the dot. There's not much action today, a lot of people don't like taking them out in this much wind. Take number nineteen, on the end there."

As Harry moves off, he hears Gregg ask Pru, "Where're you folks from up north?"

"Pennsylvania. Actually, I'm from Akron, Ohio."

"Hey! You'll never guess where I was raised – Toledo!"

The boats are up on the dry sand in a line, along with some other big water toys – those water bikes, and squarish paddleboats. Harry pulls at the nylon painter attached to the bow and the hull is heavier than he thought; by the time he's dragged it forty feet through the sand his breathing feels shallow and that annoying binding pain has begun to flicker on the left side of his ribs. He gives the boat one more heave and sits down in the sand, near where Pru is settling herself on a beach chaise Gregg has dragged down from the stack for her. Another beachgoer has momentarily called him away. "You like those?" Rabbit pants. "Don't you like feeling the sand under your – you know, like sort of a nest?"

She says, "It gets into the bathing suit, Harry. It gets in *every*-where."

This needless emphasis, when he had got the picture, excites him, here in the bewildering brightness. He dimly remembers an old joke in high school about women making pearls. Cunts like Chesapeake oysters. That sly old Fred. He tells Judy, "Give me a second to get my breath, couldja honey? Go for a quick swim in the water so it won't be a shock when we're out on it. I'll be with you in one minute."

He should try to talk to Pru about Nelson. Something rotten there. Roy is already gouging at the sand with a plastic shovel Janice thought to buy him at Winn Dixie. Frowningly the child dumps the sand into a bucket shaped like an upside-down Garfield. Pru says, since Harry seems unable to begin, "You're awfully nice to have arranged all this. I was astonished, how much he charged."

"Well," he says, feeling slowly better as his bare legs absorb heat from the top layer of sand, "you're only a grandfather once. Or twice, in my case. You and Nelson plan any more?" This feels forward, but not in a class with the sand getting in everywhere.

"Oh no, my God," she too swiftly answers, in a trough of silence as one long low wave follows another in and breaks in a frothy cresting of glitter and a mechanical scurrying of sandpipers. "We're not ready for any more."

"You're not, huh?" he says, not sure where to take this.

She helps him, her voice in his ear as he gazes out into the Gulf. He doesn't dare turn his head to look at her bare feet, their pink toe-joints and cracked nail polish, and her long legs lifted on the chaise, exposing contrasting white pieces of spandex crotch and soft flesh underside. These new bathing suits don't do much to hold a woman's ass in. She confesses to Harry, "I don't think we're doing justice to the two we've got, with Nelson how he is."

"Yeah, how is he? He seems jumpy, and only half here."

"That's *right*," she says, too enthusiastically agreeing. That's all she says. Another wave collapses and shooshes up the sand. She has pulled back. She is waiting for him to make an inspired guess.

"He hates Toyotas," he offers.

"Oh, he'd complain if they were Jaguars," Pru says. "Nothing would satisfy him, the way he is now."

The way he is. The secret seems to be in that phrase. Was the poor kid with his white-around-the-gills look dying of something, of leukemia like that girl in *Love Story*? Of AIDS he caught somehow – how, Harry can't bear to think – hanging around that faggy Slim crowd Lyle the new accountant is part of. But it all seems distant, like those islands where pirates hid gold and rich men caught tarpon, mere thickenings of the horizon from this angle three feet above sea level. He can't focus on it, with the sun on his head. He maybe should have brought a hat, to protect his Swedish complexion. His suspicion has always been he looks foolish in a hat, his head too big already. Roy has filled the bucket and pretty carefully, considering he's only four, dumps it upside down and lifts it off. He expects to have a sand Garfield but the shape is too tricky and crumbles on one side. A bad principle, fancy shapes. Stick with simple castles and let the kids use their imaginations. Harry volunteers, speaking into the air, not quite daring to turn his head and face Pru's crotch, and those nameless bits exposed by the way her legs are up, "He was never what you'd call a terrifically happy child. I guess me and Jan are to blame for that."

"He's willing to blame you," Pru admits in her flat Ohio voice. "But I don't think you should reinforce him by blaming yourself." Her language here, as when she spoke about cholesterol the other night, seems to him disagreeably specific, like a pet's fur that is coarse and more prickly than you expect when you touch it. "I'd refuse," she says firmly, "to let a child of *mine* send me on a guilt trip."

"I don't know," Harry demurs. "We put him through some pretty wild scenes back there in the late Sixties."

"That's what the late Sixties were for everybody, wild scenes," Pru says, and goes back into that coarse semi-medical talk. "By continuing to accept the blame he's willing to assign you, you and Janice continue to infantilize him. After thirty, shouldn't we all be responsible for our own lives?"

"Beats me," he says, "I never know who was responsible for mine," and he pushes himself up from the trough his body has warmed in the sand, but not before flicking his eyes back to that strip of stretched spandex flanked by soft pieces of Pru that have never had enough sun to freckle. Little Judy has come back from swimming, her red hair soaked tight to her skull and her navy-blue bathing suit adhering to the pinhead bumps of her nipples.

"You promised a *minute*," she reminds him, water running down her face and beaded in her eyelashes like tears.

"So I did," he agrees. "Let's go Sunfishing!" He stands, and the Florida breeze catches in every corner of his skin, as if he is the kite down the beach. He feels tall under the high blue sky; the elements poured out all around him – water and sand and air and sun's fire, substances lavished in giant amounts yet still far from filling the limitless space – reawaken in him an old animal recklessness. His skin, his heart can never have enough. "Put your life jacket on," he tells his granddaughter.

"It makes me feel fat," she argues. "I don't need it, I can swim for miles, honest. At camp, way across the lake and back. When you're tired, you just turn on your back and float. It's easier in saltwater, even."

"Put it on, honey," he repeats serenely, pleased that blood of his has learned ease in an element that has always frightened him. He puts his own jacket on, and feels armored, and female, and as the kid says fat. His legs and arms have never gained much weight, only his abdomen and his face, strangely; shaving each morning, he seems to have acres of lather to remove, and catching himself sideways in a reflecting surface in glassy downtown Deleon he is astonished by this tall pale guy stuffed with kapok. "You keep an eye an us," he tells Pru, who has risen to solemnize this launching. Near-naked as she is, she helps pull the hull to the water's agitated slipslopping edge. She quiets the flapping sail, which wants

to swing the boom, while he sorts out the lines, more complicated than he remembers from the time he went Sunfishing in the
Caribbean years ago with Cindy Murkett and her black bikini, and
clips in the rudder. He lifts Judy up and on. Little Roy, when he
sees his sister about to go somewhere without him, screams and
stalks into a wave that knocks him down. Pru picks him up and
holds him on her hip. The air is so bright everything seems to be
in cutout, with that violet halo you see in movies where the
scenery is faked. Harry wades in up to his waist to walk the boat
out, then heaves himself aboard, barking his shin on a cleat, and
grabs at the line attached to the aluminum boom. What did Cindy
call it, that piece of nylon rope? The sheet. Sweet Cindy, what a
doll she once was. He steadies the rudder and pulls the sail taut.
The boat is dipping and patting the waves one by one as the
offshore breeze, in the dreamlike silence that comes within
the wind, moves the boat away from the solidity of land, of beach,
of Pru in her high-sided white suit holding screaming Roy on
her hip.

Judy is stationed on this side of the mast, poised to push the
centerboard down its slot; Harry sits awkwardly on the wet
Fiberglas with his legs bent and one hand behind him on the tiller
and the other clutching the sheet. His mind begins to assemble a
picture of directional arrows, the shining wind pressing on the
sail's straining striped height. Certain tense slants begin in his hands
and fan out to the horizon and zenith. *Like a scissors*, Cindy had
said, and a sensation of funnelled invisible power grows upon him.
"Centerboard down," he commands, a captain at last, at the mere
age of fifty-five. His scraped shin stings and his buttocks in his thin
wet bathing suit resent the pressure of bald Fiberglas. His weight
is so much greater than Judy's that the hollow hull tips upward in
front. The waves are choppier, the tugs on the sail ruder, and the
water a dirtier green than in his enhanced memory of that
Caribbean adventure at the very beginning of this decade.

Still, his companion is happy, her bright face beaded with spray.
Her thin little arms stick goosebumped out of her matte-black
rubber vest, and her whole body shivers with the immersion in
motion, the newness, the elemental difference. Rabbit looks back
toward land: Pru, the sun behind her, is a forked silhouette against

the blaze of the beach. Her figure in another minute will be impossible to distinguish from all the others tangled along the sand, the overprinted alphabet of silhouettes. Even the hotel has shrunk in the growing distance, a tall slab among many, hotels and condos for as far as he can see in either direction along this stretch of the Florida coast. The power he finds in his hands to change perspectives weighs on his chest and stomach. Seeing the little triangular sails out here when he and Janice drove the shore route or visited their bank in downtown Deleon had not prepared him for the immensity of his perspectives, any more than the sight of men on a roof or scaffold conveys the knee-grabbing terror of treading a plank at that height. "Now, Judy," he says, trying to keep any stiffness of fear from his voice, yet speaking loudly lest the dazzling amplitudes of space suck all sense from his words, "we can't keep going forever in this direction or we'll wind up in Mexico. What I'm going to do is called coming about. I say – I know it seems silly – 'Coming about, hard alee,' and you duck your head and don't slide off when the boat changes direction. Ready? Coming about, hard alee."

He is not quite decisive enough in pushing the tiller away from him, and for too many seconds, with Judy crouched in a little acrobatic ball though the boom has already passed over her head, they head lamely into the wind, in a stillness wherein the slapping of water sounds idle and he feels they are being carried backward. But then an inertia not quite squandered by his timidity swings the bow past the line of the wind and the sail stops impatiently luffing and bellies with a sulky ripple in the direction of the horizon and goes tight, and Judy stops looking worried and laughs as she feels the boat tug forward again, over the choppy, opaque waves. He pulls in sail and they move at right angles to the wind, parallel to the color-flecked shore. In their moment of arrested motion the vastness all around had transfixed them as if with arrows from every empty shining corner of air and sea, but by moving they escape and turn space to their use; the Gulf, the boat, the wind, the sun burning the exposed tips of their ears and drying the spray from the erect pale body hairs on their goosebumped arms all make together a little enclosed climate, a burrow of precise circumstance that Harry gradually adjusts to. He begins to know where the wind is coming from without squinting up at the faded telltale at the top of the mast, and to feel instinctively the planes of force his hands control, just as on a fast break after a steal or rebound of the basketball in the old days he would picture without thinking the passing pattern, this teammate to that, and the ball skidding off the backboard into the hoop on the layup. Growing more confident, he comes about again and heads toward a distant green island tipped with a pink house, a mansion probably but a squat hut from this distance, and pulls in the sail, and does not flinch when the boat heels on this new tack.

Like a good grandfather, he explains his actions to Judy as they go along, the theory and the practice, and both of them become infected by confidence, by the ease with which this toy supporting them can be made to trace an angled path back and forth, teasing the wind and the water by stealing a fraction of their glinting great magnitudes.

Judy announces, "I want to steer."

"You don't *steer* it, sweetie, like you steer a bicycle. You can't just point it where you want to go. You have to keep the wind in mind, what direction it's coming from. But yeah, O.K., scrootch your, like, backside back toward me and take hold of the tiller. Keep the boat pointed at that little island with the pink house out there. That's right. That's good. Now you're slipping off a little. Pull it a bit toward you to make it come left. That's called port. Left is port, starboard is right. Now I'm letting out the sail a little, and when I say 'Ready about,' you push the tiller toward me as hard as you can and hold it. Don't panic, it takes a second to react. Ready? Ready, Judy? O.K. Ready about, hard alee."

He helps her push through the last part of the arc, her little arm doesn't quite reach. The sail slackens and flaps. The boom swings nervously back and forth. The aluminum mast squeaks in its Fiberglas socket. A far freighter sits on the horizon like a nickel on a high tabletop. A bent-winged tern hangs motionless against the wind and cocks its head to eye them as if to ask what they are doing so far out of their element. And then the sail fills; Harry tugs it in; his hand on top of Judy's little one sets the angle of the tiller for this tack. Their two weights toward the stern lift the bow and make the Sunfish slightly wallow. The patter of waves on the hull has settled into his ears as a kind of deafness. She tacks a few more times and, seeing that's all there is to it, grows bored. Her girlish yawn is a flower of flawless teeth (the chemicals they put in toothpaste now, these kids will never know the agony he did in dental chairs) and plush arched tongue. Some man some day will use that tongue.

"You kind of lose track of time out here," Harry tells her. "But from the way the sun is it must be near noon. We should head back in. That's going to take some time, since the wind's coming out against us. We don't want your mother to get worried."

"That man said he'd send a launch out."

Harry laughs, to release the tension of the tenderness he feels toward this perfect female child, all coppery and bright and as yet unmarred. "That was just for an emergency. The only emergency we have is our noses are getting sunburned. We can sail in, it's called beating against the wind. You work as close to the wind as you can. Here, I'll pull in the sail and you try to keep us pointed toward that hotel. Not the hotel at the very far right. The one next to it, the one like a pyramid."

The merged bodies on the beach have lost to the distance their flecks of color, the tints of their bathing suits, and seem a long gray string vibrating along the Bay for miles. The water out here is an uglier color, a pale green on top of a sunken bile green, than it seems from the shore.

"Grandpa, are you cold?"

"Getting there," he admits, "now that you ask. It's chilly, this far out."

"I'll say."

"Isn't your life jacket keeping you warm?"

"It's slimy and awful. I want to take it off."

"Don't."

Time slips by, the waves idly slap, the curious tern keeps watch, but the shore doesn't seem to be drawing closer, and the spot where Roy and Pru wait seems far behind them. "Let's come about," he says, and this time, what with the child's growing boredom and his own desire to get in and conclude this adventure, he tries to trim the wind too closely. A puff comes from an unexpected direction, from the low pirate islands instead of directly offshore, and instead of the Sunfish settling at a fixed heel in a straight line at a narrow angle to the direction they have been moving in, it heels and won't stop heeling, it loses its grip on the water, on the blue air. The mast passes a certain point up under the sun and as unstoppably as if pushed by a giant malevolent hand topples sideways into the Gulf. Rabbit feels his big body together with Judy's little lithe one pitch downward feet-first into the abyss of water, his fist still gripping the line in a panic and his shin scraped again, by an edge of Fiberglas. A murderous dense cold element encloses his head in an unbreathable dark green that clamps shut his mouth and eyes and then pales and releases him to air, to sun, and to the eerie silence of halted motion.

His brain catches up to what has happened. He remembers how Cindy that time stood on the centerboard and the Sunfish came upright again, its mast hurling arcs of droplets against the sky. So there is no great problem. But something feels odd, heart-suckingly wrong. Judy. Where is she? "Judy?" he calls, his voice not his out here between horizons, nothing solid under him and waves slapping his face with a teasing malice and the hull of the Sunfish resting towering on its edge casting a narrow shade and the striped sail spread flat on the water like a many-colored scum. "*Judy!*" Now his voice belongs entirely to the hollow air, to the heights of terror; he shouts so loud he swallows water, his immersed body offering no platform for him to shout from; a bitter molten lead pours instead of breath into his throat and his heart's pumping merges with the tugs and swellings of the sea. He coughs and coughs and his eyes take on tears. She is not here. There are only the dirty-green waves, kicking water, jade where the sun shines through, layered over bile. And clouds thin and slanting in the west, forecasting a change in the weather. And the hollow mute hull of the Sunfish hulking beside him. His bladder begs him to pee and perhaps he does.

The other side. She must be there. He and the boat and sail exist in a few square yards yet enormous distances feel ranged against him. He must dive under the hull, quickly. Every second is sinking everything. The life jacket buoys him but impedes. Currents in the water push against him. He has never been a natural swimmer. Air, light, water, silence all clash inside his head in a thunderous demonstration of mercilessness. Even in this instant of perfectly dense illumination there is space for his lifelong animal distaste for putting his head underwater, and for the thought that another second of doing nothing might miraculously bring it all right; the child's smiling face will surface with saltwater sparkling in her eyelashes. But the noon sun says now or never and something holy in him screams that all can be retrieved and he opens his mouth and sucks down panicked breath through a sieve of pain in his chest and tries to burrow through a resistant opacity where he cannot see or breathe. His head is pressed upward against something hard while his hands sluggishly grope for a snagged body and find not even a protuberance where a body could snag. He tries to surface. Fiberglas presses on his back like sharkskin and then the tiller's hinged wood, dangling down dripping, scrapes his face.

"Judy!" This third time he calls her name he is burbling; gobbets of water make rainbow circles in his vision as he faces straight up into the sun; in these seconds the boat is slowly twirling and its relation to the sun, the shadow it casts on the water, is changing.

Under the sail. She must be under the sail. It seems vast in the water, a long nylon pall with its diagonal seams, its stitched numbers and sunfish silhouette. He must. His bowels burn with an acid guilt; he again forces himself under into a kind of dirty-green clay where his bubbles are jewels. Against the slither of cloth on his back he tries to tunnel forward. In this tunnel he encounters a snake, a flexible limp limb that his touch panics so it tries to strangle him and drag him down deeper. It claws his ear; his head rises into the sail and a strained white light breaks upon his eyes and there is a secret damp nylon odor but no air to breathe. His body convulsively tries to free itself from this grave; he flounders with his eyes shut; the sail's edge eventually nuzzles past his drowning face and he has dragged along Judy into the light.

Her coppery wet hair gleams an inch from his eyes; her face makes a blurred clotted impression upon him but she is writhingly alive. She keeps trying to climb on top of him and locking her arms around his head. Her body feels hot under its slippery glaze. Dark water persistently rebounds into his eyes and mouth, as if a bursting spider keeps getting between him and the sun. With his long white arm he reaches and grasps the aluminum mast; though it sinks to a steeper angle with the addition of weight, the sail and the hollow hull refuse to let it sink utterly. Harry gasps and in two jerks pulls them higher up, where the mast is out of the water. Joy that Judy lives crowds his heart, a gladness that tightens and rhythmically hurts, like a hand squeezing a ball for exercise. The space inside him has compressed, so that as he hangs there he must force down thin wedges of breath into a painful congestion. Judy keeps hanging around his neck and coughing, coughing up water and fright. The rough motion of her little body wrenches twinges out of his tender, stunned chest, where something living flutters and aches. It is as if amidst all this seawater his chest is a beaker of the same element holding an agitated squid.

Perhaps a minute has passed since their spill. After another minute, she has breath enough to attempt a smile. Her eyewhites are red from within, from the tears of her coughing. Her long little face sparkles all over, as if sprinkled with tinsel, and then a slow twirl of the Sunfish places their heads in the narrow clammy band of shadow the hull casts. To his eyes she looks in her breathless frightened pallor less like Pru than Nelson, fineboned and white around the gills, and with shadows under her eyes as if after a night of sleeplessness.

Though his pains continue underwater he can speak. "Hey," he says. "Wow. What happened, exactly?"

"I don't know, Grandpa," Judy says politely. Getting these words out sends her into another spasm of coughing. "I came up and there was this thing over me and when I tried to swim nothing happened, I couldn't get out from under."

He realizes that her fright has its limits; she thinks that even out here nothing more drastic than discomfort can befall her. She has a child's sense of immortality and he is its guardian.

"Well, it worked out," he pants. "No harm done." Besides the pain, that will not let go and is reaching up the arm that clings to the mast, there is a bottom to his breathing, and from lower down a color of nausea, of seasickness it may be, and enclosing that a feebleness, a deep need to rest. "The wind changed on us," he explains to Judy. "These things tip over too damn easy."

Now the grand strangeness of where they are, hundreds of yards from shore and hundreds of feet above sea bottom, begins to grab her. Her eyes with their perfectly spaced lashes widen and her carefully fitted thin lips begin to loosen and blur. Her voice has a quaver. "How do we get it back up?"

"Easy," he tells her. "I'll show you a trick." Did he remember how? Cindy had done it so quickly, diving right under the boat, in those glassy Caribbean waters. A line, she had to have pulled on a line. "Stay close to me but don't hang on me any more, honey. Your life vest will hold you up."

"It didn't before."

"Sure it did. You were just under the sail."

Their voices sound diminished out here in the Gulf, flying off into space without lingering in the air the way words spoken in rooms do. Treading water takes all of his breath. He mustn't black out. He must hold the sunlit day from dropping its shutter on its head. He thinks if he ever gets out of this he will lie down on a firm dry stretch of grass – he can picture it, the green blades, the thatchy gaps of rubbed earth like at the old Mt. Judge playground – and never move. Gently he lets go of the mast and with careful paddling motions, trying not to jar whatever is disturbed in his chest, takes the two nylon lines floating loose and, with an effort that by recoil action pushes his face under, tosses them over to the other side. The waves are rough enough that Judy clings to his shoulder though he asked her not to. He explains to her, "O.K. Now we're going to doggie-paddle around the boat."

"Maybe that man who liked Mom will come out in his launch."

"Maybe. But wouldn't that be embarrassing, being rescued with Roy watching?"

Judy is too worried to laugh or respond. They make their way past the tiller, the ugly wooden thing that scraped his face. The tern has left the sky but floating bits of brown seaweed, like paper mops or wigs for clowns, offer proofs of other life. The slime-stained white hull lying sideways in the water seems a corpse he can never revive. "Back off a little," he tells the clinging child. "I'm not sure how this will go."

As long as he is in the water, at least he doesn't weigh much; but when, taking hold of the line threaded through the top of the aluminum mast, he struggles to place his weight on the center-board, at first with his arms and then with his feet, he feels crushed by his own limp load of slack muscle and fat and guts. The pain in his chest gathers to such a red internal blaze that he squeezes his eyes shut to blot it out, and blindly then he feels with a suck of release the sail lift free of the water and the centerboard under him plunge toward vertical. The boat knocks him backward as it comes upright, and the loose wet sail swings its boom back and forth in a whipping tangle of line. He has no breath left and has an urge to give himself to the water, the water that hates him yet wants him.

But the child with him cheers. "Yaay! You did it! Grandpa, you O.K.?"

"I'm great. Can you get on first, honey? I'll hold the boat steady."

After several failed leaps out of the water Judy plops her belly on the curving deck, her blue-black bottom gleaming in two arcs, and scrambles to a crouching position by the mast.

"Now," he announces, "here comes the whale," and, lifting his mind clear of the striated, pulsing squeezing within his rib cage, rises up enough out of the water to seize the tipping hull with his abdomen. He grabs a cleat. The fake grain of the Fiberglas presses its fine net against his cheekbone. The hungry water still sucks at his legs and feet but he kicks it away and shakily arranges himself in his position at the tiller again. He tells Judy, "We're getting there, young lady."

"You O.K., Grandpa? You're talking kind of funny."

"Can't breathe too well. For some reason. I might throw up. Let me rest a minute. And think. We don't want to. Tip this fucker over again." The pain now is down both arms and up into his jaw. Once Rabbit told someone, a prying clergyman, *somewhere behind all this there's something that wants me to find it*. Whatever it is, it now has found *him*, and is working him over.

"Do you hurt?"

"Sure. My ear where you pulled it. My leg where I scraped it." He wants to make her smile but her starry-eyed study of him is unremittingly solemn. How strange, Rabbit thinks, his thoughts weirdly illumined by his agony, children are, shaped like us, torso and legs and ears and all, yet on a scale all their own – subcompact people made for a better but also a smaller planet. Judy looks at him uncertain of how seriously to take him, like yesterday when he ate the false peanuts.

"Stay just where you are," he tells her. "Don't rock the boat. As they say."

The tiller feels oddly large in his hands, the nylon rope un- really rough and thick. He must manage these. Untended, the boat has drifted dead into the wind. What was Cindy's phrase for that? *In irons.* He is in irons. He waggles the tiller, hard one way and gently the other, to get an angle on the wind, and timidly pulls in sail, fearing the giant hand will push them over again. Surprisingly, there are other Sunfish out in the bay, and two boys on jet skis, brutally jumping the waves, at such a distance that their yells and the slaps of impact arrive in his ears delayed. The sun has moved past noon, onto the faces of the tall hotels. The windows glint now, their comblike balconies stand out, the crowd on the beach twinkles, another kite flyer has joined the first. The sheet of water between here and shore is dented over and over by downward blows of light that throw sparks. Rabbit feels chilled in his drying skin. He feels full of a gray unrest that wants to ooze poison out through his pores. He stretches his legs straight in front of him and leans back on an elbow in an awkward approximation of lying down. Sinking into sleep would be a good idea if he weren't where he was, with this child to deliver back to the world unharmed.

He speaks rapidly, between twinges, and clearly, not wanting to repeat. "Judy. What we're going to do is as quietly as we can take two big tacks and get to shore. It may not be exactly where your mother is but we want to get to land. I feel very tired and achey and if I fall asleep you wake me up."

"Wake you up?"

"Don't look so worried. This is a fun adventure. In fact, I have a fun job for you."

"What's that?" Her voice has sharpened; she senses now that this isn't fun.

"Sing to me." When he pulls the sail tighter, it's as if he's tight- ening something within himself; pain shoots up the soft inner side of that arm to his elbow.

"Sing? I don't know any songs, Grandpa."

"Everybody knows some songs. How about 'Row, Row, Row Your Boat' to start off with?"

He closes his eyes intermittently, in obedience to the animal instinct to crawl into a cave with your pain, and her little voice above the slipslop of the waves and resistant creaking of the mast picks its wavery way through the words of the round, which he used to sing in the second grade back in the days of corduroy knickers and Margaret Schoelkopf's pigtails and high-buttoned shoes. His mind joins in, but can't spare the effort to activate his voice box, *Gently down the stream, Merrily, merrily, merrily ...* "Life is but a dream," Judy ends.

"Nice," he says. "How about 'Mary Had a Little Lamb'? Do they still teach you that at school? What the hell *do* they teach you at school these days?" Being laid so low has loosened his language, his primal need to curse and his latent political indignation. He goes on, thinking it will make him seem less alarming to his grandchild, and humorously alive, "I know we're sucking hind titty in science education, the papers keep telling us that. Thank God for the Orientals. Without these Chinese and Vietnam refugees we'd be a nation of total idiots."

Judy does know "Mary Had a Little Lamb," and "Three Blind Mice," and the verses of "Farmer in the Dell" up to the wife takes a cow, but then they both lose track. "Let's do 'Three Blind Mice' again," he orders her. "*See* how they *run*. The *mice* ran after the farmer's *wife* . . .*"

She does not take up the verse and his voice dies away. Their tack is taking them far out toward the north, toward Sarasota and Tampa and the rich men's islands where the pirates once were, but the people on the beach do look a little less like gray string, the colors of their bathing suits twinkle a bit closer, and he can make out the darting tormented flight of a volleyball. A pressure in the center of his chest has intensified and to his nausea has been added an urgent desire to take a crap. In trying to picture his real life, the life of simple comforts and modest challenges that he abandoned when his foot left the sand, he now envisions foremost the rose-colored porcelain toilet bowl in the condo, with matching padded seat, and the little stack of *Consumer Reports* and *Times* that waited on the bottom shelf of the white-painted bamboo table Janice kept her cosmetics on top of, next to the rose-tinted bathroom basin. It seems to have been a seat in paradise.

"Grandpa, I can't think of any more songs." The child's green eyes, greener than Pru's, have a watery touch of panic.

"Don't stop," he grunts, trying to keep everything in. "You're making the boat go."

"No I'm not." She manages a blurred smile. "The wind makes it go."

"In the wrong fucking direction," he says.

"Is it wrong?" she asks with the quickness of fear.

"No, I'm just kidding." It was like that sadistic squeeze he gave her hand yesterday. Must stop that stuff. When you get children growing under you, you try to rise to the occasion. "We're fine," he tells her. "Let's come about. Ready? Duck your head, honey." No more sailor talk. He yanks the tiller, the boat swings, sail sags, sun shines down through the gap of silence, hammering the water into sparks. The bow drifts across a certain imaginary line, the sail hesitantly and then decisively fills, and they tug off in another direction, south, toward the remotest glass hotel and Naples and the other set of rich men's islands. The small effort and anxiety of the maneuver wring such pain from his chest that tears have sprung into his own eyes. Yet he feels good, down deep. There is a satisfaction in his skyey enemy's having at last found him. The sense of doom hovering over him these past days has condensed into reality, as clouds condense into needed rain. There is a light-ness, a lightening, that comes along with misery: vast portions of your life are shorn off, suddenly ignorable. You become simply a piece of physical luggage to be delivered into the hands of others. Stretched out on the Fiberglas deck he is pinned flat to the floor of reality. The sensation of pressure, of unbearable fullness, with-in him now has developed a rhythm, an eccentric thrust as if a flywheel has come unconnected from its piston. Pain you can lift your head above, for a little; he minds more the breathing, the sen-sation that his access to the air has been narrowed to a slot that a fleck of mucus would clog, and worse even than the breathing, which if you can forget it seems to ease, is the involvement of his guts, the greasy gray churning and the desire to vomit and shit and yet not to, and the clammy sweating, which chills him in the wind and the sun's quick drying.

"Splish, splash, I was takin' a bath," Judy's faint voice sings, little feathers of music that fly away, "along about Saturday night ..." She has moved from nursery rhymes to television commercials, the first few lines of them until she forgets. "The good times, great taste, of McDonald's ..." "I wish I were an Oscar Mayer wiener. That is what I'd truly like to be. 'Cause if I were an Oscar Mayer wiener, everyone would be in love with me." And the one the toilet paper sings, and the "Stand by Me" imitation by those California raisins, and the "Mack the Knife" by Ray Charles as the man in the moon, and the reassurance that if you want it, we've got it, "Toy-o-ta ... Who could ask for anything more?" It is like switching channels back and forth, her little voice lifting and blowing back into his face, his eyes closed while his mind pays furtive visits in the dark to the grinding, galloping, lopsided maladjustment in his chest and then open again, to check their bearings and the tension in the sail, to test the illusion of blue sky and his fixed belief that her voice is powering the Sunfish toward the shore. "Coke is it," Judy sings, "the most refreshing taste around, Coke is it, the one that never lets you down, Coke is it, the biggest taste you ever found!"

He has to tack twice more, and by then his granddaughter has discovered within herself the treasure of songs from videos she has watched many times, of children's classics Rabbit saw when they were new, the first time in those old movie theaters with Arabian decors and plush curtains that pulled back and giant mirrors in the lobby, songs of departure, "We're off to see the Wizard, the wonderful Wizard of Oz" and "Hi-ho, hi-ho, it's off to work we go," and sad songs of something in the sky to distract us from the Depression, "Somewhere over the Rainbow," and "When You Wish upon a Star," little Jiminy Cricket out there with his top hat and furled umbrella on that moon-bathed windowsill. *That Disney, he really packed a punch.*

"Nice, Judy," Rabbit grunts. "Terrific. You were really getting into it."

"It was fun, like you said. Look, there's Mommy!"

Harry lets the sheet and tiller go. The Sunfish bobs in the breaking waves of shallow water, and Judy pulls up the centerboard and jumps off into water up to her shiny hips and pulls the boat like a barge through the last yards before the bow scrapes sand. "We tipped over and Grandpa got sick!" she shouts.

Not just Pru and Roy but Gregg Silvers have come to meet them, about a good six-iron shot up the beach from where they set out. Gregg's too-tan face gives a twitch, seeing the way Harry keeps stretched out beside the useless tiller, and seeing something Harry can't, perhaps the color of his face. How bad is he? He looks at his palms; they are mottled with yellow and blue. Swiftly Gregg takes the painter from Judy and asks Harry, "Want to stay where you are?"

Harry waits until a push of pain passes and says, "I'm getting off this fucking tub if it kills me."

But the action of standing and easing off the tipping Sunfish and wading a few feet does bad things to his slipped insides. He feels himself wade even through air, on the packed sand, against pronounced resistance. He lies down on the sand at Pru's feet, her long bare feet with chipped scarlet nails and their pink toe-joints like his mother's knuckles from doing the dishes too many times. He lies face up, looking up at her white spandex crotch. Little Roy, thinking Harry's posture playful, toddles over and stands above his grandfather's head, shedding grains of sand down into Rabbit's ears, his clenched mouth, his open eyes; his eyes squeeze shut.

The sky is a blank redness out of which Pru's factual Ohio voice falls with a concerned intonation. "We saw you go over but Gregg says it happens all the time. Then it seemed to take so long he was just about to come out in the launch."

The redness pulses with a pain spaced like ribs, stripes of pain with intervals of merciful nothingness between them. Very high up, slowly, an airplane goes over, dragging its noise behind it. "Judy got under the sail," he hears his own voice say. "Scared me." He lies there like a jellyfish washed up, bulging, tremblingly full of a desire for its lost element. Another complicated warmish thing, with fingers, is touching his wrist, feeling his pulse. First-aid training must be part of Gregg's job. To assist him in his diagnosis Harry volunteers, "Sorry to be such a crump. Out there I had this terrific desire to lie down."

"You keep lying there, Mr. Angstrom," Gregg says, sounding suddenly loud and crisp and a touch too authoritative, like his father adding up the golf scores. "We're going to get you to the hospital."

In his red blind world this news is such a relief he opens his eyes. He sees Judy standing huge and sun-haloed above him, fragments of rainbows confused with her tangled drying hair. Rabbit tries to smile comfortingly and tells her, "It must have been that birdfood I ate."

Nelson was still sleeping at eleven, but Janice was in no hurry for the confrontation. She sat out on the balcony for a while after Harry and Pru and the children went, coming back twice for things they forgot and forgetting two flippers and a bottle of sun lotion anyway, and she discovered there is a place, one step to the left of where the Norfolk pine gets in the way, from which you can see a patch, a little squarish sparkling patch between an ornamental condo turret and a Spanish-tile roof, of blue-green water, of Gulf. But of course there was no hope of seeing their sail; from this distance it would take a yacht like the one they raced off San Diego this September, the Americans outwitting with a catamaran the New Zealanders in their giant beautiful hopeless boat. Looking from their balcony always a little saddens her, reviving something buried within her, the view they had from their windows in the apartment on Wilbur Street, of all the town, Mt. Judge's slanting streets busy and innocent below. Then as now, Harry had gone off, and she was alone with Nelson.

When Nelson finally comes out in his expensive smoky-blue pajamas he is surprised and annoyed to find her here, though he does try not to show it. "I thought you'd be with the others. They sure as hell made a racket getting out of here."

"No," she tells her son, "I get enough sun and wanted to spend a little time with you before you rush back."

"That's nice," he says, and goes back into his room, and comes out a minute later wearing his bathrobe, for modesty she supposes, with his own mother. You think of all the times you changed their diapers and gave them a bath and then one day you're shut out. It's a summer-weight robe, a mauve paisley, that reminds her of what rich people used to wear in movies when she was a girl. Robes, smoking jackets, top hats and white ties, flowing white gowns if you were Ginger Rogers, up to your chin in ostrich feathers or was it white fox? Young people now don't have that to live up to, to strive toward, the rock stars just wear dirty blue jeans and even the baseball players, she has noticed looking over Harry's shoulder at the television, don't bother to shave, like the Arab terrorists. When she was a girl nobody had money but people had dreams.

She offers to make Nelson what was once his favorite breakfast, French toast. Those years on Vista Crescent before they all got into such trouble she would make a thing of its being Sunday morning with the French toast, before Nelson went off to Sunday school. He had really been such a trusting child, so easy to please, with his little cowlick in his eyebrow and his brown eyes shuttling so anxiously between her and Harry.

He says, "No thanks, Mom. Just let me get some coffee and don't hassle me with food. The thought of fried bread full of syrup makes me want to barf."

"Your appetite does seem poor lately."

"Whaddeyou want, me to get hog fat like Dad? He should lose fifty pounds, it's going to kill him."

"He's too fond of snacky things, that's where he gets the weight. The salt attracts water."

There are tarry dregs left in the Aromaster, enough to fill half a cup. Janice remembers buying that percolator at the K Mart on Route 41 when she and Harry were new down here; she had been drawn to the Krups ten-cup Brewmaster but Harry was still sold on *Consumer Reports* and said they said the Braun twelve-cup Aromaster was better. Nelson makes that face he used to make as a child with cod-liver oil and pours the eleventh-and-a-half cup down the sink. He sniffs prolongedly and picks up the *News-Press* from the counter under the see-through window. He reads aloud, "City reduces charge against football star. Lake Okeechobee's cure may be hard to swallow," but it is clear to both of them that they must talk really.

Janice says, "You sit in the living room and read the paper a minute while I make a fresh pot of coffee. Would you like the last of those Danish we bought? If you don't your father will eat it."

"No, Mom, like I said. I don't want to eat any junk."

As the water in the percolator comes to a boil, he laughs to himself in the living room. "Get this," he calls, and reads aloud, " 'The highly commended head of Cape Coral's police narcotics team will be fired because of an investigation that showed he mishandled nearly one thousand dollars' worth of cocaine he borrowed from the Sanibel Police Department. The borrowed cocaine is missing, police say, and has been replaced with a handful of baking soda in a department storage box.' " Nelson adds, as if she is too dumb to get the point, "Everybody's snorting and stealing down here, even the head of the narc squad."

"How about you?" Janice asks.

He thinks she means coffee and says "Sure" and holds out his cup without taking his eyes from the newspaper. "Says here southwestern Florida was the hottest place in the country yesterday."

Janice brings the percolator and sets it on the glass table, on a section of the newspaper she folds over to make an insulating pad. She has a superstitious fear of cracking the glass with heat, though Harry laughs at her and says you couldn't crack it with a blowtorch. Men laugh about things like this and electricity but don't always know. Bad things do happen, and then men try to pretend they didn't, or it was some other man's fault. She settles firmly on the fold-out sofa next to the wicker armchair Nelson is in, and spreads her thighs to broaden her lap the way she often saw her mother do when she was determined to be firm, and tells him, "No, I meant about you and cocaine. What *is* the story, baby?"

When he looks over at her she is reminded of that frightened sly way he looked that whole summer when he was twelve. Among the things she can never forgive herself for was the way he would come over on his bicycle to Eisenhower Avenue and stand outside Charlie's place hoping to get a glimpse of her, his mother run off with another man. He asks, "Who says there's a story?"

"Your wife says, Nelson. She says you're hooked and you're blowing a lot of money you don't have."

"That crazy lying bitch. You know how she'll say anything to make a dramatic effect. When did she fill you full of this crap?"

"Don't be so rude in your language. A body can see at a glance things aren't right. Teresa let a little out the night before last when you didn't come home till after midnight, and then yesterday we had more chances to talk, while your father was walking ahead with the children."

"Yeah, what's he trying to do, anyway, this great-big-lovable-grandpa routine he's pulling on my kids? He was never that way with *me*."

"Don't keep changing the subject. Maybe he's trying to make up with them for some of his mistakes with you. Anyway your father's not who concerns me these days. He had a hard time when we were younger giving up his freedom but he seems to be at peace now. Which is what I can't say about you. You're jumpy and rude and your mind isn't on anything that's in this room or has to do with your family. You're thinking of something else every minute and I can only think from what I read and see on television that it's drugs. Pru says it's cocaine, and probably crack now, she believes you've stayed clear of heroin, though evidently the two go together in something called speedballing."

"You need to inject that, Ma, and I'll never go near a needle. That you can count on. Jesus, you can get AIDS that way."

"Yes, well, AIDS. We all have that to worry us now." She closes her eyes and wordlessly thinks of all the misery sex has caused the world, with precious little pleasure in compensation. Nelson may have his weaknesses but her sense of him is that he has never been crazy about sex like his father – that his generation got enough of it early enough for the magic to wear off. Her poor Harry, until he began to slow down, he hopped into bed every night expecting wonders. And maybe she, too, at a time in her life, was as foolish. That time she felt she brought Charlie back from the edge of the grave with it. With sheer love. For a woman it's power, the only power they let you have until recently.

Nelson takes advantage of her silence to marshal an attack. "What if I *do* do a little toot on the weekends? It's no worse than all that sipping you do. Ever since I can remember you've had a little glass next to you in the kitchen or wherever. You know, Mom, alcohol kills, eventually. There are these scientific studies that show coke is much less harmful to the body than booze."

"Well," she says, tugging her short khaki skirt down over her thighs, "it may be less harmful but it seems to be a lot more expensive."

"That's because idiotic laws make it illegal."

"Yes, that's right – whatever bad you can say about alcohol at least it's legal. When your granddaddy Springer was young it wasn't and he never developed the taste for it, or he might not have made such a good thing out of his life for us all to enjoy." She sees his lips parting to interrupt and lifts her voice to continue, "And you're a lot like him in a lot of respects, Nelson. You have his nervous energy, you always have to be figuring at something, all the time, and I hate to see that energy of yours wasted on a self-destructive thing like this." She sees him trying to break in and concludes, "Now, you must tell me about cocaine, Nelson. You must help an old lady understand. What makes it worth it? Pru says your unpaid bills are piling way up, so it must be worth quite a lot."

Nelson in exasperation slaps his body back into the chair, so that the wicker creaks; she hears something snap. "*Mom*. I don't want to talk about my private life. I'm thirty-two years old, for Chrissake."

"Even at eighty-two you'll still be my son," she tells him.

He tells her, "You're trying to act and talk like your mother but you and I both know you're not that sharp, you're not that tough." But saying this makes him feel so guilty he looks away, toward the bright breezy Florida day beyond the balcony, with its squeaky birdsong and muffled sounds of golf, the day climbing toward noon and temperatures in the mid-eighties, the warmest spot in the entire nation. His mother keeps her eyes on his face. In the wash of light his skin looks transparent, worn thin by unhealth, by unnatural consumption. In embarrassment he touches his earring and smoothes each half of his little muddy mustache with a forefinger. "It relaxes me," he tells her at last.

Janice waits for more, and prompts, "You don't seem that relaxed." She adds, "You were a tense child, Nelson. You took everything very seriously."

He says rapidly, "How else're you supposed to take it? Like a big joke, like Dad does, as if the fucking world is nothing but a love letter to yours truly?"

"Let's try to keep talking about you, not your father. As you say, I'm a simple woman. Not sharp, not tough. I'm very ignorant about a lot of things. The simplest things about this, like how much it takes and how much it costs. I don't even know how you take it – up the nose or smoke it or what you put it in to smoke it or any of that. All I know about cocaine is what's on *Miami Vice* and the talk shows and they don't explain very much. It's just not something I ever thought would make a difference in my life."

His embarrassment increases, she sees, as when he was six and sick and she would quiz him about his bowel movements. Or once when he was fourteen and she mentioned the stains on his bedsheets. But he wants to talk, she also sees, about these details, to show off the knowledge his manhood has obtained. He sighs in surrender and closes his eyes and says, "It's hard to describe. You know that expression about drunks, 'feeling no pain'? After a hit, I feel no pain. I guess that means I feel pain the rest of the time. Everything goes from black and white to color. Everything is more intense, and more hopeful. You see the world the way it was meant to be. You feel *powerful*." This last confidence is so intimate the boy bats his eyelids, his lashes long as a girl's, and blushes.

Janice feels slightly queasy, brought this close to the something neutral and undecided in her son's sexual nature – something scared out of him – and brings her legs up on the sofa under her, the short skirt hiking up above the knees. Her legs are still firm and trim at fifty-two, her best feature as a girl and woman, her hair having always been skimpy and her breasts small and her face nondescript. She especially loves her legs here in Florida, where they turn brown and compare favorably with those of the other women, who have let themselves get out of shape or never had a shape to start with. These Jewish women tend to have piano legs, and low hips. Letting her son enjoy her ignorance, Janice asks, "How many of these snorts do you need at a time, to feel the bright colors?"

He laughs, superior. "They're called lines, Mom, if you snort them. You chop up this powder with a razor blade on a mirror usually and make them into lines about an eighth of an inch wide and an inch or two long. You inhale them into your nose with a straw or a glass tooter you can buy at these places down in Brewer near the bridge. Some of the guys use a rolled-up dollar bill; if say it's a hundred-dollar bill, that's considered cool." He smiles, remembering these crisp, glittering procedures, among friends in their condos and apartments in the high northeastern section of Brewer, backing up to Mt. Judge.

His mother asks, "Does Pru do this with you?"

His face clouds. "She used to, but then stopped when she was pregnant with Roy, and then didn't take it up again. She's become quite rigid. She says it destroys people."

"Is she right?"

"Some people. But not really. Those people would have gone under to *some*thing. Like I say, it's better for you physically than alcohol. You can do a line at work quick in the john and nobody can tell the difference, except you feel like Superman. Sell like Superman, too. When you feel irresistible, you're hard to resist." He laughs again, showing small grayish teeth like hers. His face is small like hers, as if not wanting to put too much up front where the world can damage it. Whereas Harry in his middle age has swelled, his face a moon above it all. People down here, these smart Jews, like to kid him and take advantage, like the three in that foursome.

She touches her upper lip with her tongue, not certain where to take this interview now. She knows she will not be able to pry Nelson this open soon again. He is flying back tomorrow afternoon, to make a New Year's party. She asks, "Do you do crack, too?"

He becomes more guarded. He lights a Camel and throws his head back to drink the last of the coffee. A nerve in his temple is twitching, under the gray transparent skin. "Crack's just coke that's been freebased for you – little pebbles, they call them rock. You smoke them in a kind of pipe, usually." He gestures; smoke loops around his face. "It's a nice quick lift, quicker than snorting. But then you crash quicker. You need more. You get in a run."

"You do this, then. Smoke crack."

"I've been known to. What's the diff? It's handy, it's all over the street these last couple years, it's dirt cheap, what with the competition between the gangs. Fifteen, even ten dollars a rock. They call it candy. Mom, it's no big *deal*. People your age are superstitious about drugs but it's just a way of relaxing, of getting your kicks. People since they lived in caves have had to have their kicks. Opium, beer, smack, pot – it's all been around for ages. Coke's the cleanest of them all, and the people who use it are successful by and large. It *keeps* them successful, actually. It keeps them sharp."

Her hand has come to rest on her own bare foot there on the sofa cushion. She gives her toes a squeeze, and spreads them to feel air between. "Well you see how stupid I am," she says. "I thought it was all through the slums and behind most of the crime we read about."

"The papers exaggerate. They exaggerate everything, just to sell papers. The government exaggerates, to keep our minds off what morons they are."

She bleakly nods. Daddy used to hate it, when people blamed the government. She unfolds first one leg, resting her heel on the round glass table, and then brings the other parallel, so the bare calves touch; she arches her brown, tendony insteps as if to invite admiration. Her legs still look young, and her face never did. She jackknifes her legs down and sets her feet on the rug, all business again. "Let me heat up the coffee. And wouldn't you like to split that stale Danish with me? Just to keep it out of your father's stomach?"

"You can have it all," he tells her. "Pru doesn't let me eat junk like that." Janice finds this rude. She's his mother, not Pru. As she stands in the kitchen waiting for the coffee to heat, Nelson calls in to her comfortably, finding another subject, "Here's an off-duty assistant fire chief hit a motorcycle with his blinkers and siren on – probably stoned. And they think it might rain on New Year's."

"We need it," Janice says, returning with the Aromaster and the Danish cut in half on a plate. "I like the weather warm, but this December has been unreal."

"Did you notice in the kitchen what time it was?"

"Getting toward noon, why?"

"I was thinking what a pain in the ass it is to have only one car down here. If nobody minds, when they get back, I could run some errands."

"What sort of errands would they be?"

"You know. Stuff at the drugstore. I could do with some Sominex. Roy has a rash from leaving his wet bathing suit on after swimming in all that chlorine; isn't there some ointment I could get him?"

"You wouldn't be going back to the people you were with in the fish restaurant the night before last? People who can sell you some lines, or rocks, or whatever you call them?"

"Come on, Mom, don't play detective. You can't grill me, I'm an adult. I'm sorry I told you half of what I did."

"You didn't tell me what really interests me, which is how much this habit is costing you."

"Not much, honest. Do you know, computers and cocaine are about the only items in the economy that are coming down in price? In the old days it cost a fortune, nobody but pop musicians could afford it, and now you can get a whole gram for a lousy seventy-five dollars. Of course, you don't know how much it's been cut, but you learn to get a dealer you can trust."

"Did you have any this morning? Before you came out of your bedroom to face me?"

"Hey, give me a break. I'm trying to be honest, but this is ridiculous."

"I think you did," she says, stubbornly.

He disappoints her by not denying even this. Children, why are they afraid of us? "Maybe a sniff of what was left over in the envelope, to get me started. I don't like this idea of Dad taking Judy off on a little sailboat – he can't sail for shit, and seems sort of dopey anyway these days. He seems depressed, have you noticed?"

"I can't notice everything at once. What I do notice about you, Nelson, is that you're not at all yourself. You're in what my mother used to call a state. This dealer you trust so much, do you owe him any money? How much?"

"Mom, is that any business of yours?"

He is enjoying this, she sadly perceives; he is glad to have it wormed out of him, and to place his shameful burden on her. He shows relief in just the way his voice is loosening, the way his shoulders sag in his fancy paisley bathrobe. She tells him, "Your money comes from the lot and the lot's not yours yet; it's mine, mine and your father's."

"Yeah, in a pig's eye it's his."

"How much money, Nelson?"

"There's a credit line I've developed, yeah."

"Why can't you pay your bills? You get forty-five thousand a year, plus the house."

"I know to your way of thinking that's a lot of jack, but you're thinking in pre-inflation dollars."

"You say this coke is seventy-five a gram or ten dollars a rock. How many grams or rocks can you use a day? Tell me, honey, because I want to help you."

"You do? What kind of help?"

"I can't say unless I know what kind of trouble you're in."

He hesitates, then states, "I owe maybe twelve grand."

"Oh, my." Janice feels an abyss at her feet; she had envisioned this conversation as confession and repentance and, at the end, her generous saving offer of a thousand or two. The ease with which he named a much bigger figure indicates a whole new scale of things. "How could you do it, Nelson?" she asks lamely, limply, all of Bessie Springer's righteous stiffness scared out of her.

Nelson's pale little face, sensing her shock, begins to panic, to get pink. "What's such a big deal? Twelve grand is less than a stripped Camry costs. What do you think your liquor bill runs to a year?"

"Nothing like that. Your father has never been a drinker, though back in the Murkett days he used to try."

"Those Murkett days – you know what was in them for him, doncha? Getting into Cindy Murkett's pants, that's all he cared about."

Janice stares and almost laughs. How young he is, how long ago that was, and how different from what Nelson thinks. She feels a hollowness spreading inside her. She wishes she had something to sip, a little orange-juice glass of blood-red Campari, not weakened by soda the way the women down here like to have spritzers, for luncheon or out by the pool. Her half of the cherry-filled Danish feels heavy on her stomach and now in her nervousness she can't stop picking the sugar icing off Nelson's half. His refusal to eat — his acting so superior to the mild poisons she and Harry like — is the most annoying thing about him. She tells him, stiffly, "Whatever our bill is, we pay it. We have the money and can afford it." She holds out a hand toward him and twiddles two fingers. "Could I bum one cigarette?"

"You don't smoke," he tells her.

"I don't, except when I'm around you and your wife." He shrugs and takes his pack of Camels from the table and tosses it toward her. Their complicity is complete now. The lightness of it all — the cigarette itself, the dry tingling in her nostrils as she exhales — restores matters to a scale that she can manage. She asks, "What do these men do, these dealers, when you don't pay?" She could bite her lips — she has gone over into his territory, where he is an innocent victim.

"Oh," he says, enjoying posing as casually brave, shaping the ash of his cigarette on the edge of a lovely Macoma tellin he uses as an ashtray, "it's mostly talk. They say they'll break your legs. Threaten to kidnap your kids. Maybe that's what makes me so nervous about Judy and Roy. If they threaten you often enough, they have to do something eventually. But, then, they don't like to lose a good customer. It's like the banks. You owe enough, they want to keep you in business."

Janice says, "Nelson. If I gave you the twelve thousand, would you swear off drugs for good?" She strives to make eye contact.

She expects at least an eager vow from him to cinch her gift, but the boy has the audacity, the shamelessness, to sit there and say, without giving her a glance, "I could try, but I can't honestly promise. I've tried before, to please Pru. I love coke, Mom. And it loves me. I can't explain it. It's right for me. It makes me feel *right*, in a way nothing else does. It's like the bank. You owe enough, they want to keep you in business."

She finds herself crying, without sobs, just the dry-straw ache in the throat and the wetness on her cheeks, as if a husband were calmly confessing his love for another woman. When she gets her voice together enough to speak she says, clearly enough, "Well then I'd be foolish to contribute to your ruining yourself."

He turns his head and looks her full in the face. "I'll give it up, sure. I was just thinking out loud."

"But, baby, *can* you?"

"Cinchy. I often go days without a hit. There's no withdrawal, is one of the beautiful things – no heaves, no DTs, nothing. It's just a question of making up your mind."

"But is your mind made up? I don't get the feeling it is."

"Sure it is. Like you say, I can't afford it. You and Dad own the lot, and I'm your wage slave."

"That's a way of putting it. Another way might be that we've bent over backwards to give you a responsible job, heading things up, without our interference. Your father's very bored down here. Even I'm a little bored."

Nelson takes an abrupt new tack. "Pru's no help, you know," he says.

"She isn't?"

"She thinks I'm a wimp. She always did. I was the way out of Akron and now she's out. I get none of the things a man's supposed to get from a wife."

"What are those?" Janice is truly interested; she has never heard a man spell them out.

He makes a cross evasive face. "You know – don't play naïve. Reassurance. Affection. Make the guy think he's great even if he isn't."

"I may be naïve, Nelson, but aren't there things we can only do for ourselves? Women have their own egos to keep up, they have their own problems." She hasn't been attending a weekly women's discussion group down here for nothing. She feels indignant enough, independent enough, to get up and march into the kitchen and open the cabinet doors and pull down the Campari bottle and an orange-juice glass. The aqua-enamelled clock on the stove says 12:25. The phone right beside her on the wall rings, startling her so that the bottle jumps in her hand and some of the Campari spills, watery red on the Formica counter, like thinned blood.

"Yes . . . yes . . . oh my God . . ." Nelson, sitting in the wicker chair planning his next move and wondering if twelve thou was too little to ask for, it sure as hell is less than he owes, hears his

mother's voice make each response with a tightened breathlessness, and sees by her face when she hangs up and hurries toward
him that the scale of things has changed; a new order has dawned.
His mother's Florida tan has fled, leaving her face a greenish gray.
"Nelson," she says, speaking as efficiently as a newscaster, "that was
Pru. Your father's had a heart attack. They've taken him to the
hospital. They're coming right back so I can have the car. No
point in your coming, he isn't allowed any visitors except me, and
then for only five minutes every hour. He's in intensive care."

The Deleon Community General Hospital is a modern set of
low white buildings added onto a bisque-colored core, dating
from the Thirties, with a Spanish-tile roof and curved grillework
at the windows. The complex fills two blocks on the southern side
of Tamarind Avenue, which runs parallel to Pindo Palm
Boulevard about a mile to the north. Janice spent most of yesterday here, so she knows the way into the parking garage, and which
arrows painted on the floor to follow out of the parking garage,
across a glass-enclosed second-story pedestrian bridge, which takes
them above the parking-garage ticket booths and a breadth of busy
asphalt and a hexagonal-tiled patio with arcs of oleander hedge and
of convalescents in glinting steel wheelchairs, and down a half-
flight of stairs into a lobby where street-people, multiracial but the
whites among them dyed on hands and face a deep outdoorsy
brown, doze beside the neatly tied bundles and plastic garbage bags
containing all their possessions. The lobby smells of oleander,
urine, and air freshener.

Janice, wearing a soft salmon-colored running suit with powder-blue sleeves and pants stripes, leads, and Nelson, Roy, Pru,
and Judy, all in their airplane clothes, follow, hurrying to keep up.
In just one day Janice has acquired a widow's briskness, the speed
afoot of a woman with no man to set the pace for her. Also some
remnant of old love – of old animal magnetism revived in this
thronged institutional setting not so different from the high-school
corridors where she first became aware of Rabbit Angstrom, he a
famous senior, tall and blond, and she a lowly ninth-grader, dark

and plain – pulls her toward her man, now that his animal fragility
has reawakened her awareness of his body. His, and her own.
Since his collapse she is proudly, continuously conscious of her
body's elastic health, its defiant uprightness, the stubborn miracle
of its functioning.

The children are frightened. Roy and Judy don't know what
they will see in this visit. Perhaps their grandfather has been monstrously transformed, as by a wicked witch in a fairy story, into a
toad or a steaming puddle. Or perhaps a monster is what he has
been all along, underneath the friendly kindly pose and high coaxing voice he put on for them like the wolf in grandmother's
clothes who wanted to eat Little Red Riding Hood. The sugary
antiseptic smells, the multiplicity of elevators and closed doors and
directional signs and people in white smocks and white stockings
and shoes and plastic badges, the hollow purposeful sound their
own crowd of feet makes on the linoleum floors, scrubbed and
waxed so shiny they hold moving ripples like water, widens the
ominous feeling in their childish stomachs, their suspicion of a
maze there is no escaping from, of a polished expensive trap whose
doors and valves only open one way. The world that grownups
construct for themselves seems such an extravagant creation that
malice might well be its motive. Within a hospital you feel there
is no other world. The palm trees and jet trails and drooping wires
and blue sky you can see through the windows seem part of the
panes, part of the trap.

The vaulted lobby holds two murals – at one end, happy
people of many colors work in orange groves above which the sun
seems one more round orange and, at the other, bearded Spaniards
in armor woodenly exchange obscure gifts with nearly naked
Indians, one of whom crouches with a bow and arrow behind a
spiky jungle bush. This Indian scowls with evil intent. The explorer will be killed.

A skinny strict woman at the main desk consults a computer
printout and gives them a floor number and directions to the correct elevator. This family of five crowds onto it among a man who
holds a bouquet and keeps clearing his throat, a Hispanic boy
carrying a clinking tray of vials, and a big-jawed bushy-haired
middle-aged woman pushing an ancient version of herself, only

the hair not so thick or so brightly dyed, in a wheelchair. She drags her mother out to let other people off and on and then forces the wheelchair's way back in. Judy rolls her clear green eyes heavenward in protest of how obnoxious and clumsy grownups are.

Their floor is the fourth, the topmost. Janice is struck by how much less elaborate the nurses' station is here than in the intensive cardiac-care unit. There, the uniformed women sat barricaded behind a bank of heart monitors each giving in a twitching orange line the imperfect beats from the rows of individual rooms, on three sides, with glass front walls, some doors open so you could see a dazed patient sitting up under his spaghetti of tubes, some of them closed but the curtains not drawn so you can see the two dark nostrils and triangular dying mouth of an unconscious head, and yet others with the curtains ominously drawn, to hide some desperate medical procedure in progress. She has borne two babies and escorted both of her parents into the grave so she is not a total stranger to hospitals. Here, on Floor Four, there is just a single high counter, and a few desks, and a waiting area with a hard wood settee and a coffee table holding magazines titled *Modern Health* and *Woman's Day* and *The Watchtower* and *The Monthly Redeemer*. A big black woman, with waxy tight-woven corn rows looped beneath her white cap, stops the anxious herd of Angstroms with a smile. "Only two visitors in the room at a time, please. Mr. Angstrom came out of the ICCU this morning and he's still not ready for too much *fuhnn*."

Something in her wide gleaming face and elaborately braided hair transfixes little Roy; suddenly he begins under the stress of accumulating strangeness to cry. His inky eyes widen and then squeeze shut; his rubbery lips are pulled down as if by a terrible taste. His first cry turns a number of heads in the corridor, where attendants and doctors are busy with the routines of early afternoon.

Pru takes him from Nelson's arms and presses his face into her neck. She tells her husband, "Why don't *you* take Judy in?"

Nelson's face, too, undergoes a displeased, alarmed stretching. "*I* don't want to be the first. Suppose he's delirious or something. Mom, you ought to go in first."

"For heaven's sake," she says, as if Harry's burden of exasperation with their only living child has passed to her. "I talked to

RABBIT AT REST   1193

him two hours ago over the phone and he was perfectly *normal*."
But she takes the little girl by the hand and they go down the shiny
rippled corridor looking for the room number, 326. The number
rings a faint bell with Janice. Where before? In what life?

Pru sits on the hard settee – uncushioned perhaps to discourage loiterers – and tries to murmur and joggle Roy into calm
again. In five minutes, with a sob like a hiccup, he falls asleep,
heavy and hot against her, rumpling and making feel even more
oppressive the checked suit which she put on for disembarking
into the Northern winter. The air-conditioning in here feels turned
off; the local temperature has again climbed into the eighties, ten
degrees warmer than normal this time of year. They have brought
this morning's *News-Press* as a present to Harry and while they are
waiting on the bench Nelson begins to read it. *Reagan, Bush get
subpoenas*, Pru reads over his shoulder. *Regional killings decrease in
1988. Team owner to pay for Amber's funeral.* Unlike the Brewer
Standard this one always has color on the page and today features
a green map of Great Britain with Lockerbie pinpointed and insets
of a suitcase and an exploding airplane. *Report describes sophisticated
bomb.* "Nelson," Pru says softly, so as not to wake Roy or have the
nurses hear what she wants to say. "There's been something bothering me."

"Yeah? Join the crowd."

"I don't mean you and me, for a change. Do you possibly
think –? I can't make myself say it."

"Say what?"

"Shh. Not so loud."

"Goddamn it, I'm trying to read the paper. They think they
know now exactly what kind of bomb blew up that Pan Am
flight."

"It occurred to me immediately but I kept trying to put it out
of my mind and then you fell asleep last night before we could talk."

"I was beat. That's the first good night's sleep I've had in
weeks."

"You know why, don't you? Yesterday was the first day in
weeks you've gone without cocaine."

"That had nothing to do with it. My body and blow get along
fine. I crashed because my father suddenly near-died and it's damn

depressing. I mean, if he goes, who's next in line? I'm too young not to have a father."

"You crashed because that chemical was out of your system for a change. You're under terrible neurological tension all the time and it's that drug that's doing it."

"It's my fucking whole neurological life doing it and has been doing it ever since you and I got hitched up; it's having a holier-than-thou wife with the sex drive of a frozen yogurt now that she's got all the babies she wants."

Pru's mouth when she gets angry tenses up so the upper lip stiffens in vertical wrinkles almost like a mustache. You see that she does have a faint gauzy mustache; she is getting whiskery. Her face when she's sore becomes a kind of shield pressing at him, the crêpey skin under her eyes as dead white as the parting in her hair, her whisper furious and practiced in its well-worn groove. He has heard this before: "Why should I risk my life sleeping with you, you addict, you think I want to get AIDS from your dirty needles when you're speedballing or from some cheap coke whore you screw when you're gone until two in the morning?"

Roy whimpers against her neck, and two younger nurses behind the counter in the desk area ostentatiously rustle papers as if to avoid overhearing.

"You shitty dumb bitch," Nelson says in a soft voice, lightly smiling as if what he's saying is pleasant, "I don't do needles and I don't fuck coke whores. I don't know what a coke whore is and you don't either."

"Call them what you want, just don't give me their diseases."

His voice stays low, almost caressing. "Where did you get so goddamn high and mighty, that's what I'd love to know. What makes you so fucking pure, you weren't too pure to get yourself knocked up when it suited you. And then to send Melanie back home to Brewer with me to keep putting out ass so I wouldn't run away somehow. That was really the cold-blooded thing, pimping for your own girlfriend."

Nelson finds a certain chronic comfort in his wife's fair-skinned, time-widened face, with its mustache of rage crinkles and its anger-creased triangular brow, pressing upon him, limiting his vision. It shuts out all the threatening things at the rim. She says, faltering as if she knows she is being put through a hoop, "We've been through this a million times, Nelson Angstrom, and I had no idea you'd hop into bed with Melanie, I was foolish enough to think you were in love with *me* and trying to work things out with your *parents*." This cycle of complaint is stale and hateful yet something familiar he can snuggle into. At night, when both are asleep, it is she who loops her arm, downy and long, around his sweating chest and he who curls closer to the fetal position, pressing his backside into her furry lap.

"I was," he says, plainly teasing now, "I did work them out. So what were you starting to say?"

"About what?"

"What you were going to tell me but couldn't because I fell asleep because according to you I wasn't as wired as usual." He leans his head against the bench's headrest and sighs in this new blood-clean weariness of his. Coming down makes you realize how high up you usually are. "God," he says, "it'll be good to get back to the real world. You're sort of right about yesterday, I was stuck, with Mom grabbing the car as soon as you got back. All you can deal for around Valhalla Village is Geritol."

Her voice in marital sympathy softens. "I like you like this," she confides. "Just yourself. No additives." He looks, with his tidy taut profile sealed upon his tired thoughts, his thinning temples balanced by his jutting little mustache, almost handsome. The scattered gray hairs in his rat's-tail haircut touch her, as if they are her fault.

Wearily in Pru's forgiving tone of voice he hears that she is not yet ready to let this marriage go. He has plenty of margin still. "I'm always the same," he disagrees. "I can take or leave the stuff. Yesterday, maybe you're right, out of respect for the old guy, or something. I just decided to do without. What nobody seems to understand is, it's not addictive."

"Wonderful," Pru says, the softness in her voice ebbing. "My husband the exception that proves the rule."

"Don't we have any other topic?"

"This story," she decides to begin, "of Judy's being trapped under the sail. Aren't the sails awfully small? You know what a good swimmer she is. Do you possibly think —?"

"Think what?"

"That she was just pretending, hiding from your father as a sort of game, and then it got out of hand?"

"So it just about killed him? What a thought. Poor Dad." Nelson's profile smiles; his mustache lifts closer to the underside of his small straight irritated nose. "I don't think so," he says. "She wouldn't be that cool. Think of how far out there it must have seemed to her, surrounded by sharks in her mind. She wouldn't be playing games."

"We don't know really how it was out there, or how many seconds it all took. Children's minds don't work exactly like ours, and your father's way with her is to be teasing, the way he talks to her. It's something she could have done not to be cruel but a child's idea, you know, of teasing back."

His smile now shows his small inturned teeth, which always look a little gray no matter how hard he brushes them, and flosses, and uses those handles with rubber tips once he gets into his pajamas. "I knew it was a bad idea, him taking her out there when he doesn't know shit about boats," he says. "You say he acted proud of saving her life?"

"On the beach, before the paramedics came – it seemed to take forever but they said it was only seven minutes – he seemed happy, relieved somehow even with the terrible pain and struggling for breath. He kept trying to make jokes and get us to laugh. He told me I should put new polish on my toenails."

Nelson's eyes open and he stares, not at the opposite wall where a dead benefactor's oil portrait preens, but unseeing into the past. "I had that baby sister, you know," he says, "who drowned."

"I know. How could any of us ever forget it?"

He stares some more, and says, "Maybe he was happy to have saved this one."

And indeed to Harry, as he lies on his back drugged and tied down by tubes and wires in what seems a horizonless field of white, the sight of little Judy alive and perfect in each reddish-brown hair and freckle, her long eyelashes spaced as if by a Linotype machine with two-point spaces, is a pure joy. She had tangled with the curse and survived. She is getting out of Florida, death's favorite state, alive.

His collapse twenty-six hours ago did have its blissful aspect: his sense, beginning as he lay helpless and jellyfishlike under a sky of red, of being in the hands of others, of being the blind, pained, focal point of a world of concern and expertise, at some depth was a coming back home, after a life of ill-advised journeying. Sinking, he perceived the world around him as gaseous and rising, the grave and affectionate faces of paramedics and doctors and nurses released by his emergency like a cloud of holiday balloons. His many burdens have been lifted away in this light-drenched hospital, this businesslike emporium where miracles are common if not cheap. They have relieved him of his catheter, and his only problem is a recurrent need to urinate – all this fluid they keep dripping into him – sideways into a bed pan, without pulling loose the IV tube and the wires to the heart monitor and the oxygen tubes in his nostrils.

Another small problem is fog: a football game he has been looking forward to seeing, the NFC playoff game between the Eagles and the Bears at Soldier Field in Chicago, is on the television set that comes out on a tan enamelled metal arm not two feet from his face, but the game, which began at twelve-thirty, as it goes on has become dimmer and dimmer, swallowed by an unprecedented fog blowing in off Lake Michigan. Television coverage has been reduced to the sideline cameras; people up in the stands and the announcers in their booth can see even less than Rabbit lying doped-up here in bed. "Heck of a catch by somebody," said one color commentator, Terry Bradshaw as a matter of fact, Bradshaw who in the Super Bowl at the beginning of the decade was bailed out by a circus catch by that lucky stiff Stallworth. The crowd, up high in the fog, rumbles and groans in poor sync with the television action, trying to read the game off the electronic scoreboard. The announcers – a black guy with froggy pop eyes, maybe that same guy who married Bill Cosby's television wife, and a white guy with a lumpy face – seem indignant that God could do this, mess with CBS and blot out a TV show the sponsors are paying a million dollars a minute for and millions are watching. They keep wondering aloud why the officials don't call off the game. Harry finds the fog merciful, since before it rolled in the Eagles looked poor, two perfectly thrown TD passes by Cunningham called back because of bonehead penalty plays by Anthony Toney, and then this rookie Jackson dropping a pass when he was a mile open in the end zone. The game flickering in the fog, the padded men hulking out of nothingness and then fading back again, has a peculiar beauty bearing upon Rabbit's new position at the still center of a new world, personally. The announcers keep saying they've never seen anything like it.

He has trouble at first realizing he must perform for his visitors, that it's not enough to lie here and accept the apparition of them like another channel of television. During the commercial, the one for Miller that shows the big black guy lifting the pool table so all the balls roll into the pocket supposedly, he lowers his eyes to Judy's eager face, bright and precise as watchworks free of dust and rust, and says to her, "We learned, didn't we, Judy? We learned how to come about."

"It's like a scissors," the girl says, showing with her hands. "You push toward the sail."

"Right," he says. Or is it away from? His thinking is foggy. His voice, nasal and husky, doesn't sound like his; his throat feels raw from something they did to him when he was brought into the hospital, something with oxygen, he was half out of it and then all the way out thanks to something they slipped into him in the confusion.

"Harry, what do the doctors say about you?" Janice asks. "What's going to happen?" She sits in a chair near his bed, a new kind of vinyl-cushioned wheelchair, like a revved-up version of Fred Springer's pet Barcalounger. She has that anxious skinned look to her forehead and her mouth is a dumb slot open a dark half-inch. She looks in that two-tone running suit and those bulky Adidas like a senior-league bowling champion, her face hard from too much sun, with two little knobs like welts developing over her cheekbones. The delicate skin beneath her eyebrows is getting puckery. With age we grow more ins and outs.

He tells her, "One doc told me I have an athlete's heart. Too big. Too big on the outside, that is, and too small on the inside. The muscle is too thick. Apparently the heart isn't a nice valentine like you'd think, it's a muscle. It pumps with a kind of twisting motion, like this." He shows his little audience with a twitching fist: beat, pause, beat, pause. Judy's face is transfixed by the screen of the heart monitor, which he can't see; but he supposes the effort of his small demonstration is showing up in his running cardiogram. Janice watches it too, their four eyes shiningly reflecting the electronic jiggle and their two mouths both open to make identical slots of darkness. He has never before seen any sign of heredity between them. He goes on, "They want to put some dye into my heart, by putting a long tube into some artery down at the top of my leg, so they can see exactly what's going on, but offhand they think at least one of the coronary arteries is plugged. Too many pork chops on top of all that hustle on the court when I was a kid. No problem, though. They can bypass anything, they do it every day now, as simple as plumbing with plastic pipe. They tell me it's amazing, what they've learned to do in the last ten years."

"You're going to have open-heart surgery?" Janice asks in alarm.

The fist that impersonated a heart feels cloudy and heavy; he lowers it carefully to his side on the sheet, and momentarily closes his eyes, to spare himself the sight of his worried wife. "Nothing for now. Maybe eventually. It's an option. Another option is, this catheter has a balloon in it somehow that they inflate when it's inside the plugged-up artery. It cracks the plaque. That's what they call it, plaque. I thought a plaque was what you got for winning the championship." Rabbit has to keep suppressing the impulse to laugh, at his inability to share with Janice the drug-induced peace inside his rib cage, the sense of being at last at the still center. Painkiller, blood-thinner, tranquillizer, vasodilator, and diuretic all drip into his system from above, painting the hospital world with rosy tints of benevolence and amusement. He loves the constant action, the visits to extract blood and measure blood pressure and check instruments and drips, and the parade of firm-bodied odorless young females in starchy cotton and colors of skin from every continent who tend to his helpless flesh with a sexy mix of reverence and brutal condescension, with that *trained* look on their pretty faces like actresses or geisha girls. His little white-walled room seems in his entrancement to be a stage set, crowded with unpredictable exits and entrances. Semi-private, it even has a curtain, which conceals his roommate, who was bur-bling and vomiting and groaning this morning but has fallen since into a silence that might be death. But for Harry, the play goes on, and on cue another actor enters. "Here's a doc now," he announces to Janice. "You ask him whatever you want. I'll watch the game and Judy'll watch my heart monitor. Tell me if it stops, Judy."

"Grandpa, don't joke," the dear child scolds.

The cardiologist is a big red-skinned immigrant Australian named Dr. Olman. He has a pink hooked nose, brilliant white teeth, and bleached lank hair. Years of the good life in Florida have overlaid his clipped native accent with a Southern drawl. He takes Janice's little narrow brown hand into his meaty red one and they become, in Rabbit's eyes, his cardiac parents – worried little nut-brown mother and outwardly calm and factual father. "He's been a pretty sick lad," Dr. Olman tells her, "and we've got to teach him how to take better care of himself."

"What's wrong with his heart, exactly?" Janice asks.

"The usual thing, ma'am. It's tired and stiff and full of crud. It's a typical American heart, for his age and economic status et cetera."

That strangely intense and slightly embarrassing Gallo-wine commercial, about the guy who has a blind date with a girl who turns out to be the very liquor saleswoman who advised him what bottle to take the date as a present, comes on.

"As best we can tell without cardiac catheterization," Dr. Olman is saying, "the principal narrowing is the standard one, the left anterior descending, the workhorse of the system. Luckily, he appears to have fairly well-developed collaterals, which have kept him going. You see, ma'am, whenever the heart's been starving for oxygen, it tries to develop alternative routes to get blood to the muscle. Also, from the murmur we think we hear there may be a fair bit of stenosis around the aortic valve. Not a pretty pic-ture, but by no means the worst we've ever seen."

Janice looks at her husband almost with pride. "Oh, Harry! You would mention the little aches and breathing problems, and I never took you *seri*ously. You didn't complain hard enough."

"It was *per*fect," the girl in the commercial sighingly says, at the end of their date, starry-eyed and in soft focus; you can see they will fuck, if not this date the next, and marry and live happily ever after, all by the grace of Gallo.

Dr. Olman has sized Janice up as educable and moves into a heavier sell. "Now, if his luck holds and the lesion isn't located at a bifurcation and there's not too much calcification a lot of doctors would advise you to begin modestly, with an angioplasty, and wait and see. To my own way of thinking, though, you have to offset the relative lack of trauma and expense – we can't forget expense, now can we, what with Medicare's pulling in its horns and this new chappie's promising no new taxes? – we have to offset those psychological pluses against the minus kicker, the likelihood of recurrent stenosis and having to do it all over again, the odds of which, to be honest about it, are on the shady side of fifty per cent. For my money, not to keep beating about the bush, the artery bypass is the sucker that does the job. What do you say in the States, never send a boy when you can send a man? Now, ma'am, how much do you want to know about the heart?"

"Everything," Janice says, adoring of this man willing to explain things to her, her tongue peeking through as she prepares to concentrate.

"Way to go," Dr. Olman gamely says, and makes a big fist with one hand and with the fingers of the other begins to show her how the coronary arteries lie on the heart's surface, their branches burrowing into the hardworking muscle. Harry has seen this demonstration earlier in the day and signals Judy to come closer to his bed. She is wearing the pink party dress she came down on the airplane in, and the stiff white ribbon around her braided pigtail. Yesterday's experience at sea has given her a sunburn on her nostril wings and beneath her clear green eyes, where her freckles are thinnest. She keeps staring at his heart monitor.

"What do you see?" he asks her huskily.

"It's like a little twitchy worm, that just goes and goes."

"That's life," he tells her. "That's your granddad."

Judy yields to an impulse: leaning against the bed, she tries to embrace the old man, disarraying and tugging at the tubes and wires attached to his upper body. "Oh Grandpa," she confesses, "it's all my fault!"

Her breath feels hot on his neck. He hugs her, as best he can, with the arm not pierced by the IV. "Don't be silly. What's your fault?"

"Yesterday. I scared you out there."

"You didn't scare me, sweetie. The Gulf of Mexico scared me. You weren't scared?"

Tearily she shakes her head No.

This seems another wonder to him. "Why not?" he asks.

Her smooth little face gets that tiptoe look which in a mature woman signals that she is about to lie. She says, a bit mincingly, "You were out there with me, Grandpa. And there were lots of other boats around."

He renews his trammelled hug and her slender little body is unresisting, something has gone out of it; he feels a roughness in his throat, perhaps from yesterday's gulps of saltwater. His eyes film over with the hot relief of tears. On television, men with wide shoulders and narrow hips move like gods on Olympus among the clouds. You can't even see any more who is white and who is black. Blinded though they are, the announcers keep yelling in those straining excited voices they have. A commercial shows a Subaru bumpily climbing a mountain of dead car chassis.

"Want to change the channel?" he asks Judy, and moves her hand from his bandaged wrist, where it is hurting him, to the hand control for the television set on its beige metal arm. He lies back feeling the white walls stretch all around him just like the ocean yesterday, his bed a raft. Judy flickers the TV through a wrestling match, a parade, a scare commercial with Karl Malden barking that with American Express Traveller's Checks you can't be robbed, a man and a woman in black skating in a sparkle of ice, a tongue-in-cheek horror movie about being a teenage werewolf in London, and another movie called, they learn from the station break, *The Fists of Bruce Lee*. The kung-fu violence is arresting enough to hold Judy's attention for a few minutes. Fragments of what Dr. Olman is confidentially yet, in that peppy Australian way, quite audibly telling Janice weave into the action – murderous kicks turned into slow motion by the director, graceful blurs of Oriental color. "... preliminary test ... pulmonary congestion common after a myocardial infarction ... backup of blood, leakage into the

lung tissue ... hydralazine ... inflammation of the pericardium
... Dilantin ... skin rashes, diarrhea, loss of hair ... hate to go to
a pacemaker for a man this age ..."

Bruce Lee kicks out, once, twice, thrice, and three hand-
somely costumed thugs slowly fly toward the corners of the room,
furniture shattering like fortune cookies, and suddenly Judy has
switched channels again, coming upon a commercial Harry loves,
for some skin moisturizer whose name he can never remember,
but he could never forget the look on the model's face, the way
she smiles over her naked shoulder as she slinks behind the bathroom door, and then when she comes out the satisfied wicked
purr in her expression, her wet hair turbanned in a bulky soft
towel, her breasts showing cleavage but the nipples just off the
screen, if only the screen were a little wider, if he could only slow
the action down like in a kung-fu movie, for a thirtieth of a second there might have been a nipple, and the way she relaxes into
a blue velvet sofa as if ever so profoundly satisfied, lovely eyes
closed with their greasy lids, her eyebrows slightly thick like Cindy
Murkett's, and then the part coming up where she is dressed to go
out for the evening, all moisturized still beneath her gold lamé. . . .
"No, wait, honey": he senses that Judy is about to change channels and reaches out to stop her but fails, it's back to the werewolf,
the boy's face is growing fur as he crouches in a telephone booth,
and then the ice skaters, the woman sliding backward at you
with her little skirt flipped up; and then the back of Harry's wrist
stings from the tug he gave the IV, and a flirtatious ghost of
yesterday's pain plays across his chest. The Demerol must be
wearing off. They gave him a little brown bottle of nitroglycerin on his bedside table next to the telephone and a glass
of stale water and he shakes one out shakily and puts it beneath
his tongue as they have taught him. It burns under his tongue
and then, the funny thing, a minute or two later, his asshole
tingles.

"How much junk food does he eat?" Dr. Olman is asking.

"Oh," Janice says, with enthusiasm, "he's a real addict." His
wife is, it occurs to Harry, a channel that can't be switched. The
same slightly too-high forehead, the same dumb stubborn slot of
a mouth, day after day, same time, same station. She looks up into

the doctor's big red blond face as if at an instructively beautiful sunset. The two of them make a duo, dividing him up. One takes the inside, the other the outside.

Now a turquoise Subaru is spinning along one of those steep spiky Western landscapes that the makers of automobile commercials love. A shimmery model, skinny as a rail, dimpled and square-jawed like a taller Audrey Hepburn from the *Breakfast at Tiffany's* days, steps out of the car, smiling slyly and wearing a racing driver's egg-helmet with her gown made up it seems of ropes of shimmering light. Maybe Nelson is right, Toyota is a dull company. Its commercials show people jumping into the air because they're saving a nickel. The channel jumps back to the Fiesta Bowl Parade. Youth, flowers, a giant Garfield the cat jiggling majestically along. Harry's internal climate of drugs and their afterwash seems to be undergoing a distant storm, like sunspots or those faint far hurricanes on Jupiter. Along with history, Harry has a superstitious interest in astronomy. Our Father, Who art in Heaven ...

"... tons of fat through his system," Dr. Olman is saying, "*rivers* of it, some of it *has* to stick. Marbled meats, pork sausage, liverwurst, baloney, hot dogs, peanut butter, salted nuts ..."

"He loves all that stuff, he's a terrible nibbler," Janice chimes in, anxious to please, courting, betraying her husband. "He loves nuts."

"Worst thing for him, absolutely the worst," Dr. Olman responds, his voice speeding up, losing its drawl, "*full* of fat, not to mention sodium, and cashews, macadamia nuts, they're the worst, macadamia nuts, but it's all bad, bad." In his intensity he has begun to crouch above her, as if over a slippery putt. "Anything made with hydrogenated vegetable shortenings, coconut oil, palm oil, butter, lard, egg yolk, whole milk, ice cream, cream cheese, cottage cheese, any organ meats, all these frozen TV dinners, commercial baked goods, almost anything you buy in a package, in a waxpaper bag, any of it, ma'am, is poison, bloody poison. I'll give you a list you can take home."

"You can, but my daughter-in-law is studying nutrition. She has a lot of lists already." On cue, Pru appears, hesitantly filling the doorway with her womanly-wide frame in its nappy travelling suit of three-dimensional checks. Unawares, Janice goes on buttering up Dr. Olman. "She's been saying everything you've been saying for years to Harry, but he just won't listen. He think's he's above it all, he thinks he's still a teenager."

The doctor snorts. "Even the teenagers with their super-charged metabolism aren't burning up the fats and sugars this country's food industry is pumping into them. We're having ado-lescent heart attacks all over" – his voice softens to Southerliness again – "God's green creation."

Pru steps forward, in her three dimensions. "Janice, I'm sorry," she says, still shy of using her mother-in-law's name, "I know he shouldn't have so many visitors at once but Nelson is getting fran-tic, he's afraid we're going to miss the plane."

Janice stands, so briskly the wheelchair recoils under her. She staggers but keeps her feet. "I'll leave. You say hello and bring Judy when you come. Harry, I'll drop by on my way back when I've put them on the plane. But there's an origami demonstration tonight at the Village I don't want to miss. The man has come all the way from Japan." She exits, and Judy switches off the televi-sion in the middle of an especially amusing slapstick commercial for Midas mufflers, and exits with her.

Dr. Olman shakes Pru's hand fiercely and tells her, baring his shark-white teeth, "Ma'am, teach this stubborn bastard to *eat*." He turns and punches Harry with a loosened fist on the shoulder. "For half a century, my friend," he says, "you've been pouring sludge through your gut." Then he, too, is gone.

He and Pru, suddenly alone together, feel shy. "That guy," Harry says, "keeps attacking America. If he doesn't like the food here, why doesn't he go back where he came from and eat kan-garoos?"

His tall daughter-in-law fiddles with her long red hands, twist-ing at her wedding ring, yet moves forward, to the foot of the bed. "Harry," she says. "Listen. We're *stricken* at what's happened to you."

"You and who else?" he asks, determined to be debonair – Bogie at the airport in Casablanca, Flynn at Little Big Horn, George Sanders in the collapsing temple to Dagon, Victor Mature having pushed apart the pillars.

"Nelson, obviously. I don't think he slept a wink last night, you were so much on his mind. He can't say it, but he loves you."

Harry laughs, gently, since there is this valentine inside him that might rip. "The kid and I have something going between us. Not sure love is what you'd call it." Since she hesitates in replying, looking at him with those staring mud-flecked greenish eyes that Judy's clearer paler eyes were distilled from, he goes on, "I love him all right, but maybe it's a him that's long gone. A little tiny kid, looking right up to you while you're letting him down – you never forget it."

"It's still there, under it all," Pru assures him, without saying what "it all" is. Her Sphinx-do hair is slightly wild, Harry sees in the brilliant hospital light – colorless stray filaments stand out all around her head. He feels there is a lot she wants to say but doesn't dare. He remembers how she appeared hovering above him as he lay breathless on the beach, in her white suit with its spandex crotch, anxious and womanly, her face in shadow, unlookable, at, and right beside it like a thunder-head the face of Ed Silberstein's son, his salt-stiffened black curls, his butternut skin, his prick making its bump in his tight black trunks, beside the five-sided Omni logo – a smoothie, on the make, on the rise. Hi-ho, Silvers.

"Tell me about you, Pru," Rabbit says, the words gliding out of his hoarse throat as if his being in bed and chemically relaxed has moved them to a new level of intimacy. "How's it going for *you*, with the kid? With Nelson."

People do respond, surprisingly, to the direct approach, as if we're all just waiting in our burrows to be ferreted out. She says without hesitation, "He's a wonderful father to the children. That I can say sincerely. Protective and concerned and involved. When he can focus."

"Why can't he always focus?"

Now she hesitates, unthinkingly revolving the ring on her finger.

As if all of Florida is made up of interchangeable parts, a Norfolk pine stands outside his hospital window and holds an invisible bird that makes the sound of wet wood squeaking. He heard it this morning and he hears it now. His chest seems to echo with a twinge. Just to be on the safe side he takes another nitroglycerin.

Pru blurts out, "The lot worries him, I think. Sales have been off these last years with the weaker dollar and all, and what he says are boring models, and I think he's afraid Toyota might lift the dealership."

"It would take a bomb to make them do that. We've done O.K. by Toyota over the years. When Fred Springer got that franchise Japanese products were still considered a joke."

"That was a long time ago, though. Things don't stand still," Pru says. "Nelson has trouble being patient, and to tell the truth I think it scares him to have none of the old-timers around any more, Charlie and then Manny and now Mildred, even though he fired her, and you down here half the year, and Jake gone over to Volvo-Olds over near that new mall in Oriole, and Rudy opening his own Toyota-Mazda over on 422. He feels alone, and all he has for company are these flaky types from north Brewer."

At the thought of "these flaky types" more of her hairs, glowing like electric filaments here in Florida's fluorescent light, stand out from her head in agitation. She is trying to tell him something, something is slipping, but how can a man tied up helpless in bed track it down? Rabbit has his heart to nurse. This is life and death. His drugs must be wearing off. The deadly awfulness of his situation is beginning to rise in his throat, burning like an acid regurgitation. His asshole tingles, right on schedule. He has something evil and weak inside him that might betray him at any minute into that icy blackness Bernie talked about.

Pru shrugs her wide shoulders in delayed answer to his question about how it was going. "What's a life supposed to be? They don't give you another for comparison. I love the big house, and Pennsylvania. In Akron we only ever had apartments, and the rent was always behind, and it seemed like the toilet bowl always leaked."

Rabbit tries to lift himself onto her level, out of his private apprehension of darkness, its regurgitated taste. "You're right," he says. "We ought to be grateful. But it's hard, being grateful. It seems like from the start you're put here in a kind of fix, hungry and scared, and the only way out is no good either. Hey, listen. Listen to me. You're still young. You're great-looking. Smile. Smile for me, Teresa."

Pru smiles and comes around the end of the bed and bends down to give him a kiss, not on the mouth this time like in the airport, but on the cheek, avoiding the tubes feeding oxygen into his nose. Her close presence feels huge, checked, clothy, a cloud come over him like the shadow of that hull on its side out there on the Gulf, where it was cold and hot both at once. He feels sick; the facts of his case keep wanting to rise in his throat, burning, on the verge of making him gag. "You're a sweet man, Harry."

"Yeah, sure. See you in the spring up there."

"It seems terrible, us leaving like this, but there's this party in Brewer Nelson's determined to go to tonight and changing plane reservations is impossible anyway, everything's jammed this time of year, even into Newark."

"What can you do?" he asks her. "I'll be fine. This is probably a blessing in disguise. Put some sense into my old head. Get me to lose some weight. Go for walks, eat less crap. The doc says I gotta become a new man."

"And I'll paint my toenails." Pru, standing tall again, says in a level low voice he has not exactly heard before, aimed flat at him as a man, "Don't change *too* much, Harry." She adds, "I'll send Nelson in."

"If the kid's wild to go, tell him to just go. I'll catch him later, up there."

Her mouth pinches down at one corner, her face goes slightly stiff with the impropriety of his suggestion. "He *has* to see his father," she says.

Pru exits; the white clean world around Harry widens. When everybody leaves, he will give himself the luxury of ringing for the nurse and asking for more Demerol. And see how the Eagles are doing in the fog. And close his eyes for a blessed minute.

Nelson comes in carrying little Roy in his arms, though visitors under six years old aren't supposed to be allowed. The kid wears the child like defensive armor: as long as he's carrying a kid of his own, how much can you say against him? Roy stares at Harry indignantly, as if his grandfather being in bed connected with a lot of machinery is a threatening trick. When Harry tries to beam him a smile and a wink, Roy with a snap of his head hides his face in his father's neck. Nelson too seems shocked; his eyes keep going up to the monitor, with its orange twitch of onrunning life, and then gingerly back to his father's face.

Cumbersomely keeping his grip on the leaden, staring child, Nelson steps toward the bed and sets a folded copy of the *News-Press* on the chrome-edged table already holding the water glass and the telephone and the little brown bottle of nitroglycerin. "Here's the paper when you feel like reading. There's a lot in it about that Pan Am crash you're so interested in. They think they know now exactly what kind of bomb it was – there's a kind with a barometric device that activates a timer when a certain altitude is reached."

Up, up; the air thins, the barometer registers, the timer begins to tick as the plane snugly bores through darkness and the pilot chats on the radio while the cockpit lights burn and wink around him and the passengers nod over their drinks in their slots of pastel plastic. The image, like a seed at last breaking its shell in moist soil, awakens in Harry the realization that even now as he lies here in this antiseptic white fog tangled in tubes and ties of blood and marriage he is just like the people he felt so sorry for, falling from the burst-open airplane: he too is falling, helplessly falling, toward death. The fate awaiting him behind this veil of medical attention is as absolute as that which greeted those bodies fallen smack upon the boggy Scottish earth like garbage bags full of water. *Smack, splat,* bodies bursting across the golf courses and heathery lanes of Lockerbie drenched in night. What met them was no more than what awaits him. Reality broke upon those passengers as they sat carving their airline chicken with the unwrapped silver or dozing with tubes piping Barry Manilow into their ears and that same icy black reality has broken upon him; death is not a domesticated pet of life but a beast that swallowed baby Amber and baby Becky and all those Syracuse students and returning soldiers and will swallow him, it is truly there under him, vast as a planet at night, gigantic and totally his. His death. His purely own. The burning intensifies in his sore throat and he feels all but suffocated by terror.

"Thanks," he hoarsely tells his son. "I'll read it when you go. Those damn Arabs. I'm nervous about your missing *your* plane."

"Don't be. We got tons of time still. Even Mom can't get lost on the way, can she?"

"Drive east from here to 75 and then south to Exit 21. The road feels like it's going nowhere but after three miles the airport shows up." Harry remembers his own drive along that weird highway, the lack of billboards, the palm trees skinny as paint drips, the cocoa-colored chick in the red Camaro convertible and stewardess cap who tailgated him and then didn't give him a sideways glance, her tipped-up nose and pushed-out lips, and it seems unreal, coated in a fake sunshine like enamel, like that yellow sunlight they make on TV shows from studio lights. He didn't have a worry in the world back then. He was in paradise and didn't know it. He feels his body sweating from fear, he smells his own sweat, clammy like something at the bottom of a well, and sees Nelson standing there bathed in the artificial light of the world that hasn't broken through into death yet, neat and taut in the putty-colored suit he is wearing instead of the denim jacket he wore on the flight down, but with his shirt collar still open, so he looks like an all-night gambler who took off his tie in a poker game, down here nearly a week and hardly ever saw the sun. The little smudge of his mustache annoys Harry and the kid keeps calling attention to it, sniffing and touching the underside of his nose as if he smells his father's clammy fear.

He says, "Also, Dad, I noticed the Deion Sanders case is being pushed back into the sports pages and somewhere in Section B there's an article about fighting flab that'll give you a laugh."

"Yeah, flab. I'm flabby on the inside even."

This is the cue for his son to look sincere and ask, "How're you doing anyway?" The kid's face goes a little white around the gills, as if he fears his father will really tell him. His haircut is annoying, too – short on top and too long in the back, that pathetic rat-tail. And the tiny earring.

"Pretty good, considering."

"Great. This big beefy doctor with the funny accent came out and talked to us and said that the first one is the one a lot of people don't survive and in your case now, for a while at least, it's just a matter of changing your lifestyle a little."

"That guy has a thing about potato chips and hot dogs. If God didn't want us to eat salt and fat, why did He make them taste so good?"

Nelson's eyes get dark and swarmy, the way they do whenever his father mentions God. The conversation keeps sticking, it doesn't flow, Harry keeps thinking how he is falling, the kid is like a weight on his chest. *Come on*, he says to himself, *try. You only live once.*

"Pru told me you were up all night with worry."

"Yeah, well, she exaggerates, but sort of. I don't know why I can't sleep down here. It all feels phony to me, and there's all this stuff back in Brewer I should be tending to."

"Like at the lot? Between holidays is a slow week usually. Everybody's feeling broke after Christmas."

"Well, yeah, and other stuff. I keep feeling hassled."

"That's life, Nelson. Hassle."

"I suppose."

Harry says, "I been thinking about our conversation, about Toyotas being so dull. Give 'em credit, they're trying to sex the line up. They're coming out with this Lexus luxury sedan next fall. V-8 engine even."

"Yeah, but they won't let us regular dealerships handle it. They're establishing a whole new retail network. Let 'em, it's going to flop anyway. The Japanese aren't Italians. Luxury isn't their bag."

"I forgot about that separate Lexus network. I tell ya, Nelson, I'm not quite with it. I'm in a fog."

"Join the crowd," Nelson says.

"And oh yeah – the stat sheets. I've been thinking about that. Are you having trouble moving the used? Don't get greedy. Ten per cent markup is all you should expect, it's worth shaving the profit just to keep the inventory flowing."

"O.K., Dad. If you say so. I'll check it out."

The conversation sticks again. Roy squirms in his father's grip. Harry is falling, the light is just a skin of the dark, thinner than an airplane's skin, thinner than an aluminum beer can. Grab something, anything. "She's turned out to be quite a fine woman, Pru," he volunteers to his son.

The boy looks surprised. "Yeah, she's not bad." And he volunteers, "I should try to be nicer to her."

"How?"

"Oh – you know. Clean up my act. Try to be more mature."

"You always seemed pretty mature to me. Maybe too, early on. Maybe I didn't set such a good example of maturity."

"All the more reason, then. For me, I mean."

Does Harry imagine it, or is there a stirring, a tiny dry cough-ing, behind the curtain next to him, in the bed he cannot see? His phantom roommate lives. He says, "I'm really getting anxious about you making your plane."

"Sorry about that, by the way. I feel crummy leaving. Pru and I were talking last night, if we ought to stay a few more days, but, I don't know, you make plans, you get socked in."

"Don't I know it. What could you do, staying? Your old man's fine. He's in great hands. I just have to learn to live with a not so great heart. A bum ticker. Charlie's done it for twenty years, I can do it." But then Rabbit adds, threatening to pass into the maudlin, the clingy, the elegiac, "But, then, he's a wiry little Greek and I'm a big fat Swede."

Nelson has become quite tense. He radiates a nervous desire to be elsewhere. "O.K., Dad. You're right, we'd better get moving. Give Grandpa a kiss," he tells Roy.

He leans the boy in, like shovelling off a wriggling football, to kiss his grandfather's cheek. But Roy, instead of delivering a kiss, grabs the double-barrelled baby-blue oxygen tube feeding into Harry's nose and yanks it out.

"Jesus!" Nelson says, showing emotion at last. "You all right? Did that hurt?" He whacks his son on the bottom, and sets him down on the floor.

It did hurt slightly, the sudden smarting violence of it, but Harry has to laugh. "No problem," he says. "It just sits in there, like upside-down glasses. Oxygen, I don't really need it, it's just one more perk."

Roy has gone rubber-legged with rage and collapses on the shiny floor beside the bed. He writhes and makes a scrawking breathless noise and Nelson bends down and hits him again.

"Don't hit the kid," Harry tells him, not emphatically. "He just wanted to do me a favor." As best he can with his free hand, he resettles the two pale-blue tubes one over each ear as they come from the oxygen box hung on the wall behind him and resettles the clip, with its gentle enriching whisper, on his septum. "He maybe thought it was like blowing my nose for me."

"You little shit, you could have killed your own grandfather,"

Nelson explains down at the writhing child, who has to be hauled, kicking, out from under the bed.

"Now who's exaggerating," Harry says, "I'm tougher to kill than that," and begins to believe it. Roy, white in the gills just like his dad, finds his voice and lets loose a yell and tries to throw himself out of Nelson's grasp. The rubber heels of nurses are hurrying toward them down the hall. The unseen roommate suddenly groans behind his white curtain, with a burbly, deep-pulmonary-trouble kind of groan. Roy is kicking like a landed fish and must be catching Nelson in the stomach; Harry has to chuckle, to think of the child doing that. On one grab: deft. Maybe in his four-year-old mind he thought the tubes were snakes eating at his grandfather's face; maybe he just thought they were too ugly to look at.

Full though his arms are, Nelson manages to lean in past the tangle of life-supporting connections and give Harry's cheek the quick kiss he meant Roy to bestow. A warm touch of mustache. A sea-urchin's sting. The watery monster stirring behind the bed curtain releases another burbling, wracking groan from the deeps. Alarmed nurses enter the room; their cheeks are flushed. The head nurse looms, with her waxy woven tresses, like oodles of black noodles or packets of small firecrackers.

"Oh yeah," Harry thinks to add as Nelson hurries his yelling, writhing burden away, down the hall, toward Pennsylvania. "Happy 1989!"

II. PA

SUN AND MOON, rise and fall: the well-worn wheels of nature that in Florida impinge where beach meets sea are in Pennsylvania muffled, softened, sedimented over, clothed in the profoundly accustomed. In the Penn Park quarter-acre that Janice and Harry acquired a decade ago, there is, over toward the neighboring house built of clinker bricks, a weeping cherry tree, and he likes to be back when it blossoms, around April tenth. By then, too, baseball has come north – Schmidt this year hitting two home runs in the first two games, squelching all talk that he was through – and lawns are sending up tufts of garlic. The magnolias and quince are in bloom, and the forsythia is out, its glad cool yellow calling from every yard like a sudden declaration of the secret sap that runs through everybody's lives. A red haze of budding fills the maples along the curbs and runs through the woods that still exist, here and there, ever more thinly, on the edge of developments old and new.

His first days back, Rabbit likes to drive around, freshening his memory and hurting himself with the pieces of his old self that cling to almost every corner of the Brewer area. The streets where he was a kid are still there, though the trolley cars no longer run. The iron bridges, the railroad yards rust inside the noose of bypasses that now encircles the city. The license plates still have an orange keystone in the middle, but now say *You've Got a Friend in Pennsylvania*, which he always found sappy, and sappier still those imitation plates that can be bolted on the front bumper and say *You've Got a Friend in* JESUS. The covers of telephone directories boast *The UnCommonwealth of Pennsylvania*. Behind the wheel of his car, he gravitates to Mt. Judge, the town where he was born and raised, on the opposite side of Brewer from Penn Park. In this fortresslike sandstone church with its mismatching new wing, the Mt. Judge Evangelical Lutheran, he was baptized and confirmed, in a shirt

that chafed his neck like it had been starched in lye, and here, further along Central, in front of a candy store now a photocopying
shop, he first felt himself in love, with Margaret Schoelkopf in her
pigtails and hightop shoes. His heart had felt numb and swollen
above the sidewalk squares like one of those zeppelins you used to
see in the sky, the squares of cement like city blocks far beneath
his floating childish heart. Every other house in this homely borough holds the ghost of someone he once knew who now is gone.
Empty to him as seashells in a collector's cabinet, these plain domi-
ciles with their brick-pillared porches and dim front parlors don't
change much; even the slummier row houses such as he and Janice
lived in on Wilbur Avenue when they were first married are just
the same in shape, climbing the hill like a staircase, though those
dismal old asphalt sidings the tints of bruise and dung have given
way to more festive substances imitating rough-hewn stone or
wooden clapboards, thicker on some façades than others, so there
is a little step up and down at the edges as your eye moves along
the row. Harry always forgets, what is so hard to picture in flat
Florida, the speckled busyness, the antic jammed architecture, the
distant blue hilliness forcing in the foreground the gabled houses
to climb and cling on the high sides of streets, the spiky retaining
walls and sharp slopes crowned by a barberry hedge or tulip bed,
slopes planted more and more no longer in lawn but ground cover
like ivy or juniper that you don't have to mow once a week with
those old-fashioned reel mowers. Some people would rig their
mowers with a rope on the handle so they could let it slither clattering down and then pull it back up. Rabbit smiles in his car,
remembering those wooden-handled old mowers and that long-
dead Methodist neighbor of theirs on Jackson Road Mom used to
feud with about mowing the two-foot strip of grass between the
cement walks that ran along the foundation walls of their houses.
The old Methodist couple had bought the house from the Zims
when they moved to Cleveland. Carolyn Zim had been so
pretty – like Shirley Temple only without the dimple, more of a
Deanna Durbin sultriness, on this little girl's body – that Mr. and
Mrs. fought all the time, Mom said, Mrs. being jealous. He used
to wait by his window for a glimpse in the soft evening of Carolyn
undressing for bed, across the little air space. His room: he can

almost remember the wallpaper, its extra-yellowed look above the radiator, the varnished shelf where his teddy bears sat, the bushel basket his Tinker Toy spokes and hubs and his rubber soldiers and lead airplanes lived in. There was a taste, oilclothy, or like hot windowsill paint, or the vanilla and nutmeg when Mom baked a cake, to that room he can almost taste again, but not quite, it moves into the shadows, it slips behind the silver-painted radiator with its spines imprinted with scrolling designs in blurred low relief.

Brewer, too, that torpid hive, speaks to him of himself, of his past grown awesomely deep, so that things he remembers personally, V-E day or the Sunday Truman declared war on North Korea, are history now, which most of the people in the world know about only from books. Brewer was his boyhood city, the only city he knew. It still excites him to be among its plain flowerpot-colored blocks, its brick factories and row housing and great grim churches all mixed together, everything heavy and solid and built with an outmoded decorative zeal. The all but abandoned downtown, wide Weiser Street which he can remember lit up and as crowded as a fairgrounds in Christmas season, has become a patchwork of rubble and parking lots and a few new glass-skinned buildings, stabs at renewal mostly occupied by banks and government agencies, the stores refusing to come back in from the malls on Brewer's outskirts. The old Baghdad, once one of a half-dozen first-run movie theaters along Weiser, now stands between two vacant lots, its Arab-style tiles all stripped away and its marquee, that last advertised triple-X double features, peeling and rusting and holding the letters ELP and on the line below that SAV ME – scrambled remnant of an appeal for historic restoration. The movie palaces of his boyhood, packed with sweet odors and dark velvet, murmurs and giggles and held hands, were history. HELP SAVE ME. There had been a kind of Moorish fountain in the lobby, colored lights playing on the agitated water. The music store, Chords 'n' Records, that Ollie Fosnacht used to run twenty years ago a few doors up from the Baghdad, and that then became Fidelity Audio, is still a store, called now The Light Fantastic, selling running shoes, two whole windows of them. Must be a market for them among the minorities. Mug and run.

In Rabbit's limited experience, the more improvements

they've loaded onto running shoes, the more supporting pads and power wedges and scientifically designed six-ply soles and so on, the stiffer and less comfortable they've become: as bad as shoes. And those running tights the young women wear now, so they look like spacewomen, raspberry red and electric green so tight they show every muscle right into the crack between the buttocks, what is the point of them? Display. Young animals need to display. Ollie Fosnacht's estranged wife Peggy died about eight years ago, of breast cancer that had metastasized. Rabbit reflects that she was the first woman he has slept with who has died, has actually bitten the bullet. Then realizes this is not true. There was Jill. He used to fuck Jill that crazy summer, though he could tell she didn't much like it. Too young to like it. And maybe that whore in Texas who with a curious drawling courtesy made him an unvirgin is dead now too. They don't have long lives, with the hours, the booze, the beatings.

And the drugs that most of them are into, and AIDS. But, then, who does live forever? We all take a beating. Must be the way they figure, it's sooner or later. They're just like us only more so. These guys in prison now who bite the guards to give them AIDS with their saliva. We're turning into mad dogs – the human race is one big swamp of viruses.

Back from the hollow center of Brewer, in the tight brick rows built a century ago when the great mills now abandoned or turned into factory outlet stores still smoked and vibrated, spinning textiles and casting steel, life goes on as lively as ever, though in a darker shade. He likes cruising these streets. In April at least they brim with innocent energy. Four leggy young blacks cluster about a bicycle being repaired. A Hispanic girl in the late-afternoon slant of sun steps out of her narrow slice of a house in high silk heels and a lilac-colored party dress and a diagonal purple sash and at her waist a great cloth rose: she is a flower, the moment says, and a swarm of boys has gathered, jostling, bumbling, all dressed in steel-gray windbreakers and green Army pants, a gang uniform of sorts, Harry supposes. In Brewer people still use the streets, they sit out on their steps and little porches in an expectant way you never see in Deleon. And the Pennsylvania row houses take a simple square approach to shelter, not so different from those cities of aligned

cereal boxes the teacher had you set up with cut-out doors and
crayoned-on windows in first grade; it makes Harry happy after
his winter in Florida with its condominiums interwoven with golf
courses, its tile-roofed towers of time-shared apartments, its villages that aren't villages, its thousand real-estate angles and pretti-
fications of the flimsy.

In the slate-gray two-door Celica he and Janice lock into their
garage when they take the pearl-gray Camry wagon south in the
fall, he feels safe gliding along and attracts not too many stares,
though in the tough section near the tracks, on the rounded corner step of a boarded-up tavern, a little rounded dark girl in a sweatshirt sits in the lap of a boy already barechested though the spring
air is still chilly, and alternately kisses him with a languid and determined open mouth and gazes insolently at the cars streaming by.
The half-naked boy is too stoned to stare, perhaps, but she gives
Harry a look through the Celica's side window that would wipe
him away if it could. Fuck her. Fuck him, her eyes say. She seemed
to sense what he was doing, rolling by, trying to steal a little life for
himself out of the south Brewer scene, all these lives that are young
and rising like sap where his is old and sinking.

There has been a lot of living in these tired streets. The old row
houses have been repainted, residinged, updated with aluminum
awnings and ironwork railings themselves grown old. They are
slots still being filled, with street numbers the builders set in
stained-glass fanlights above the doors. The blocks were built
solid, there would never be any renumbering. Once he lived in
one of these – number 326, the number of his hospital room
reminded him – with Ruth, and used to shop for quick necessi-
ties at that corner store there, now called ROSA'S GROCERIES (*Tienda
de Comestibles*), and stare out the window at the rose window of a
limestone church now become the PAL *Community Center /
Centro Comunidad*. The city is quicker than he remembers it, faster
on the shuffle, as the blocks flicker by, and buildings that he felt
when a boy were widely spaced now appear adjacent. The cough-
drop factory, the skyscraper courthouse, the Y where he tried to
take swimming lessons and caught pneumonia instead, coming
out into the winter streets with wet hair, are all around corners
from one another, and close to the post office with its strange long

empty lobby, busy and lighted only at one end where a grate or two is up, and to the Ben Franklin, a proud gilded downtown hotel now a Ramada Motor Inn. There his class, Mt. Judge '51, had its senior prom, he in a summer tux and Mary Ann in a lavender satin strapless gown whose crinoline petticoats gave them so much trouble in the car afterward they had to laugh, her round white thighs lost in all those rustling folds and hems, Easter eggs in a papery nest, her underpants damp from all the dancing, a spongy cotton pillow, stuffed with her moss, a powerful moist musk scent, Mary Ann the first woman whose smell he made his own, all of her his own, every crevice, every mood, before he went off to do his two years in the Army and she without a word of warning married somebody else. Maybe she sensed something about him. A loser. Though at eighteen he looked like a winner. Whenever he went out with Mary Ann, knowing she was his to harvest in the warm car, the blue family Plymouth, he felt like a winner, offhand, calm, his life set at an irresistible forward slant.

Two blocks toward the mountain from the Ben Franklin, under Eisenhower Avenue where it lifts up in a wooden-railed hump to pass over, the laborers of old hand-dug a great trench to bring the railroad tracks into the city, tracks disused now, and the cut, walled in limestone, a pit for tossing beer cans and soda bottles down into, whole garbage bags even, mattresses; Brewer was always a tough town, a railroad town, these blocks along the tracks full of tough men, bleary hoboes who'd offer to blow you for a quarter, sooty hotels where card games went on for days, bars whose front windows were cracked from the vibration of the trains going past, the mile-long trains of coal cars pulling right across Weiser, stopping all traffic, like the time he and Ruth waited for one to pass, the neon lights of a long-gone Chinese restaurant flickering in her many-colored hair.

These red-painted bricks, these imitation gray stones, have seen heartbreaking things but don't know it. A block or two toward the mountain from Ruth's old street – Summer Street it was, though they had lived there in spring, summer spelled their end – Rabbit is suddenly driving in a white tunnel, trees on both sides of the street in white blossoms, the trees young and oval in shape and blending one into the other like clouds, the sky's high blue above tingeing the topmost blossoms as it does the daytime moon. And up top where there is most light the leaves are beginning to unfold, shiny and small and heart-shaped, as he knows because he is moved enough to pull the Celica to the curb and park and get out and pull off a single leaf to study, as if it will be a clue to all this glory. Along the sidewalk in this radiant long grove shadowy people push baby carriages and stand conversing by their steps as if oblivious of the beauty suspended above them, enclosing them, already shedding a confetti of petals: they are in Heaven. He wants to ask one of them the name of these trees, and how they came to be planted here in these hard brick blocks of Brewer, luxuriant as the ficus trees that line the avenues of Naples down in Florida, but feels shy in their gaze toward him, himself a shadow in this filtered tunnel light of blossoms, a visitor, an intruder from the past, and figures they would not know anyway, or if they did know would think him too strange for asking.

But Janice knows. When he describes this experience to her, she says, "Those are these Bradford pear trees the city is planting everywhere the old elms and buttonwoods are dying off. It blossoms but doesn't bear any fruit, and is very hardy in city conditions. It doesn't mind carbon dioxide or any of that."

"Why have I never seen them before?"

"You have, Harry, I'm sure. They've been putting them in for ten years now at least. There've been articles in the paper. One of the girls over at the club's husband is on the Improvement Commission."

"I never saw anything like it. It broke me all up."

She is busy re-establishing them in the Penn Park house, cleaning away the winter's cobwebs and polishing the Koerner silver her mother left her, and she moves away from him impatiently. "You've seen, it's just you see differently now."

Since his heart attack, she means. Since nearly dying. He faintly feels with Janice now like one of the dead they used to say came back and watched over the survivors, living with them invisibly like the mice in the walls. She often doesn't seem to hear him, or take him quite seriously. She goes off across Brewer to visit Nelson and Pru and their children in Mt. Judge, or to remake acquaintance with her female buddies over at the Flying Eagle Country

Club, where the clay tennis courts are being rolled and readied and the golf course is already green and receiving play. And she is looking for a job. He thought she had been kidding after seeing *Working Girl*, but no, the women her age almost all do something now – one of her tennis buddies is a physical therapist with muscles in her arms and shoulders like you wouldn't believe, and another, Doris Eberhardt, who used to be Doris Kaufmann, has become a diamond expert and takes the bus over to New York practically every week and carries hundreds of thousands of dollars' worth of gems back and forth, and a third woman she knows works in the booming new field of de-asbestosizing homes and buildings like factories and schools. It seems there's no end of old asbestos to ferret out. Janice thinks she might go into real estate. A friend of a friend works mostly on weekends and makes over fifty thousand a year in commissions.

Harry asks her, "Why not go over and help Nelson run the lot? Something's going flooey over there."

"That's no fun, hiring myself. And you know how sensitive Nelson is at the idea of us interfering."

"Yeah – why is that?"

Janice has all the answers, now that she is back with her female crowd of know-it-alls over at the Flying Eagle. "Because he's grown up in the shadow of a dominating father."

"I'm *not* dominating. I'm a pushover, if you ask me."

"You are to him. Psychologically dominating. You're certainly a lot taller. And were a wonderful athlete."

"Were is right. A wonderful athlete whose doctors say he has to ride a golf cart and not do anything more violent than brisk walking."

"And you don't *do* it, Harry. I haven't seen you walk further than to the car and back."

"I've been doing some gardening."

"If you can call it that."

He likes to get out into their yard toward the end of the day and break off last year's dead flower stalks and bone-white old poke plants and burn them in a fire kindled on the day's newspaper, the Brewer *Standard*. The lawn needed a mowing badly when they arrived and the bulb beds should have been uncovered in March. The snowdrops and crocuses came and went while they were in Florida; the hyacinths are at their peak and the tulips up but still with pointy green heads. Rabbit feels peace at the moment of the day when the light dims and the weeping cherry glows in the dusk, its florets like small pink bachelor buttons and the whole droop-branched womanly forgiving shape of it gathering to itself a neon pallor as the shadows lengthen and dampen; the earth's revolution advances a bit more and the scraps of sunlight linger longer under the April sky with its jet trails and icy horsetails, just a few golden rags caught in the shaggy forsythia over toward the neighboring mansion built of thin yellow bricks, and the struggling hemlock, and the tallest of the rhododendrons by the palisade fence you see from the kitchen window. Janice put up a bird feeder in the hemlock a few falls ago, even though Doris Kaufmann or some other busybody told her it was cruel to birds to put up a feeder when you weren't there in the winter, a plastic sphere tilted like Saturn, and he fills it with sunflower seed when he thinks of it. Putting up bird feeders was the sort of thing her mother used to do but would never have occurred to Janice when they were younger and old Bessie was still alive. Our genes keep unfolding as long as we live. Harry tastes in his teeth a sourness that offended him on his father's breath. Poor Pop. His face yellowed like a dried apricot at the end. Bessie had the feeders all on wires and poles in her Joseph Street back yard to frustrate the squirrels. The copper beech by their old bedroom, with the nuts that would pop on their own all night, attracted the squirrels, she would say, making her lap and setting her hands on her knees as if God had cooked up squirrels just to bedevil her. Harry had liked Bessie, though she screwed him in her will. Never forgave him for that time in '59. Died of diabetes and its circulatory complications the day after Princess Di gave birth to little Prince William, the last living thing Bessie was interested in, would there be a future king of England? – that and the Hinckley trial, she thought they should hang the boy on the steps of the Capitol, right there in the sunshine, letting him off as insane was a scandal. The old lady was terrified of having her legs amputated at the end the way her own mother had. Harry can even remember Bessie's mother's name. Hannah. Hannah Koerner. Hard to believe he will ever be as dead as Hannah Koerner.

Before the April evening falls, the birds, big and little, that the
feeder attracts flutter and hop to take a drink or splash their feathers
in the blue-bottomed cement pond some earlier owner of this little
place, this snug limestone cottage tucked in among the bigger
Penn Park homes, created. The cement pool is cracked but still
holds water. Like himself, Rabbit thinks, turning toward his house
with its lit windows that seem as far away and yet as strangely close
as his parents' house used to when he was a kid playing Twenty-
one or Horse with Mim and the other children of the neighborhood out at the backboard on the garage in the alley behind their
long narrow yard on Jackson Road. Then as now, waking from
twilit daydreams, he discovered himself nearer a shining presence
than he thought, near enough for it to cast a golden shadow ahead
of his steps across the yard; then it was his future, now it is his past.

During those spring months with Ruth on Summer Street, he
used to wonder what it would be like to run to the end of the
street, straight as far as the eye could see. In the thirty years since,
he has often driven this way, to Brewer's northwestern edge and
beyond, where the highway with its motels (*Economy Lodge,
Coronet, Safe Haven*) melts into farmland and signs pointing the
way to Harrisburg and Pittsburgh begin to appear. One by one the
farms and their stone buildings, the bank barns put together with
pegs and beams and the farmhouses built square to the compass
with walls two feet thick, are going under to real-estate developments. Two miles beyond the pike to Maiden Springs, where the
Murketts used to live before they got divorced, there is a fairly
new development called Arrowdale after the old Arrowhead Farm
that was sold off by the nieces and nephews of the old spinster who
lived there so many years and had wanted to leave it to some television evangelist as a kind of salvation park, a holy-roller retreat,
but whose lawyers kept talking her out of it. Rabbit as these recent
years have gone by has watched the bulldozed land lose its raw
look and the trees and bushes grow up so it almost seems houses
have always been here. The streets curve, as they did in the
Murketts' development, but the houses are more ordinary – ranch

houses and split levels with sides of aluminum clapboards and fronts of brick varied by flagstone porchlets and unfunctional patches of masonry facing. Cement walks traverse small front yards with azaleas not quite in bloom beneath the picture windows. Bark mulch abounds, and matching porch furniture, and a tyrannical neatness absent in the older more blue-collar towns like Mt. Judge and West Brewer.

Ronnie and Thelma Harrison moved to one of these modest new houses when their three boys grew up and went off. Alex, the oldest, is an electronics engineer somewhere south of San Francisco; the middle boy, Georgie, who had had reading problems in school, is trying to be a dancer and musician in New York City; and their youngest, Ron Junior, has stayed in the county, as a part-time construction worker, though he put in two years of college at Lehigh. Thelma doesn't complain about her sons or her house, though to Harry they seem disappointing, disappointingly ordinary, for a woman of Thelma's intelligence and, in his experience of her, passion.

Thelma's disease, systemic lupus erythematosus, has cost a fortune over the years, even with the benefits from Ronnie's insurance company's health plan. And it has meant that she has not been able to go back to teaching elementary school when her boys were gone, as she had hoped. Her health has been too erratic; it has kept her at home, where Harry could usually find her. This noon when he called from a pay phone in Brewer he expected her to answer and she did. He asked if he might drive over and she said he might. She didn't sound happy to hear from him, but not distressed either: resigned, merely. He leaves the Celica out front at the curving curb, though usually over the years she opened the garage for him and closed the door electronically from within the kitchen, to hide the evidence. But now that he is as sick as if not sicker than she, he doesn't know how much they still have to conceal. The neighborhood is empty during the midday, until the buses bring the children home from school. A single whining engine is at work somewhere out of sight in Arrowdale, and the air holds a pervasive vibration and hum of traffic from the Maiden Springs Pike. Also out of sight, some birds are chirping, raucous in their nesting frenzy, though the development is skimpy on trees. A robin hops on the bit of lawn beside Thelma's cement walk, and thrashes into the air as Harry approaches. He doesn't remember robins as seeming such big fierce birds; this one looked the size of a crow. He climbs two flagstone steps and crosses a little porch; Thelma opens the front door before he can ring the bell.

She seems smaller, and her hair grayer. Her prim, rather plain face always had a sallow tinge, and this jaundice has deepened, he can observe through the makeup she uses to soften her butterfly rash, a reddening the disease has placed like a soreness across her nose and beneath her eyes. Nevertheless, her deeply known presence stirs him. They lightly kiss, when she has closed the door, a long light-blocking green shade pulled down over its central pane of bevelled glass. Her lips are cool, and faintly greasy. She stays a time within his embrace, as if expecting something more to happen, her body relaxed against his in unspeakable confession.

"You're thin," she says, drawing at last away.

"A little less fat," he tells her. "I've a long way to go before I satisfy the doctors and Janice." It seems only natural to mention Janice, though he had to make his tongue do it. Thelma knows the score, and did from the start. The whole affair was her idea, though he grew used to it over the years, and built it in. Her walk as she moves away from him into the living room seems stiff, a bit of a waddle; arthritis is part of the lupus.

"Janice," she repeats. "How *is* Wonder Woman?" Once he confided that he called Janice that and Thelma has never forgotten. Women don't forget, especially what you wish they would.

"Oh, no different. She keeps busy in Florida with all these different groups, she's kind of the baby of our condo, and a shiksa besides. You'd hardly know her, she's so on the ball. Her tennis is terrific, the people who play tell me." He is getting too enthusiastic, he realizes. "But we were happy to leave. It got *cold*. March was miserable. At least up here you expect it and have the clothes."

"You never told us about your heart attack." That "us" is a little payback for his mentioning Janice right off. You trail your spouses after you like shadows, right into bed; they becloud the sheets.

"It didn't seem worth bragging about."

"We heard about it from little Ron, who knows a boy who knows Nelson. The kiddie network. Imagine how I felt, learning about it that way. My lover nearly dies and never tells me."

"How would we, I, whoever, tell you? It's not the kind of thing they have cards for in the drugstore."

In recent years he and Janice have seen less and less of the Harrisons. Rabbit and Ron were Mt. Judge boys together and played on the high-school basketball varsities that, coached by Marty Tothero, were league champions for two out of their three years in senior high. But he has never liked Ronnie: loudmouthed, pushy, physically crude, always playing with himself in the locker room, flicking towels, giving redbellies, terrorizing the JVs. Women don't mind this kind of prick as much as Harry does. Part of Thelma's fascination for him has been that she could stand the guy, put up with his sexual tricks and remain outwardly such a prim, plain schoolteacher-type. Not really plain: with her clothes off her body is somehow better than her clothes have led you to expect. The first time they ever slept together, her breasts seemed like a girl's in *Playboy* – nipples like perfect little doorbells.

"What can I offer you?" Thelma asks. "Coffee. A beer?"

"Both are no-nos for the new me. Do you have anything like a Diet Coke or Pepsi?" He remembers Judy's little quavering voice singing *Coke is it* on that long zigzag ride into shore.

"Sure. We don't drink much any more ourselves, now that we've resigned from the Flying Eagle."

"You ever coming back?"

"I don't think so. We heard the fees went up again, as you maybe didn't notice, you're so rich, plus the assessment for repairs to the two greens close to the road that are always being vandalized. Even three years ago Ronnie figured it was costing him over eighty dollars a round, it wasn't worth it. There's a whole new younger crowd out at the Eagle now that dominates everything. They've changed the tone. It's gotten too yuppie."

"Too bad. I miss playing with old Ronnie."

"Why? You can't stand him, Harry."

"I like beating him."

Thelma nods, as if acknowledging her own contribution to Harry's beating Ronnie. But she can't help it, she loves this man, his soft pale bemusement and cool hard heart, his uncircumcised prick, his offhand style, and in her slow dying has not denied herself the pleasure of expressing this love, as much as Harry has been able to bear it. She has kept her strongest feelings contained, and the affair has enriched her transactions with God, giving her something to feel sinful about, to discuss with Him. It seems to explain her lupus, if she's an adulteress. It makes it easier on Him, if she deserves to be punished.

She goes into the kitchen for the soft drinks. Rabbit roams quietly in the living room; in preparation for his visit she has pulled not only the narrow shade on the front door but the wide one on the picture window. He pities the room – its darkness as if even weak windowlight would penetrate her skin and accelerate the destruction of her cells, its hushed funereal fussiness. Wild though she can be, with a streak of defiance as though daring to be damned, Thelma maintains a conventional local decor. Stuffed flowered chairs with broad wooden arms, plush chocolate-brown sofa with needlepointed scatter pillows and yellowing lace antimacassars, varnished little knickknack stands and taborets, a footstool on which an old watermill is depicted, symmetrical lamps whose porcelain bases show English hunting dogs in gilded ovals, an oppressively patterned muddy neo-Colonial wallpaper, and on every flat surface, fringed runners and semi-precious glass and porcelain elves and parrots and framed photographs of babies and graduating sons and small plates and kettles of hammered copper and pewter, objects to dust around but never to rearrange. This front room, but for the television set hulking in its walnut cabinet with its powdery gray-green face wearing a toupee of doilies and doodads, could have come out of Harry's adolescence, when he was gingerly paying calls on girls whose mothers came forward from the kitchen, drying their hands on their aprons, to greet him in motionless stuffed rooms such as this. The houses he has kept with Janice have had in comparison a dishevelled, gappy quality that has nevertheless given him room to breathe. This room is so finished, he feels in it he should be dead. It smells of all the insurance policies Ron sold to buy its furnishings.

"So tell me about it," Thelma says, returning with a round painted tray holding along with the two tall glasses of sparkling dark soft drink two matching small bowls of nuts. She sets the tray down on a glass-topped coffee table like an empty long picture frame.

He tells her, "For one thing, I'm not supposed to have stuff like that – salted nuts. Macadamia nuts yet! The worst thing for me, and they cost a fortune. Thel, you're wicked."

He has embarrassed her; her jaundiced skin tries to blush. Her basically thin face today looks swollen, perhaps from the cortisone she takes. "Ronnie buys them. They just happened to be around. Don't eat them if you can't, Harry. I didn't know. I don't know how to act with you, it's been so long."

"A couple won't kill me," he reassures her, and to be polite takes a few macadamia nuts into his fingers. Nuggets, they are like small lightweight nuggets with a fur of salt. He especially loves the way, when he holds one in his mouth a few seconds and then gently works it between his crowned molars, it breaks into two halves, the surface of the fissure as smooth to the tongue as glass, as baby skin. "And cashews, too," he says. "The second-worst thing for me. Dry-roasted yet."

"I seem to remember you like dry-roasted."

"There's a lot I bet you seem to remember," he says, taking a tasteless sip of his Diet Coke. First they take the cocaine out, then the caffeine, and now the sugar. He settles back with a small hand-ful of cashews; dry-roasted, they have a little acid sting to them, the tang of poison that he likes. He has taken the rocking chair, painted black with stencilled red designs and a red-and-yellow flat pillow tied in place, to sit in, and she the plush brown sofa, not sinking into it but perching on the edge, her knees together and touching the raised edge of the coffee table. They have made love on that sofa, which was not long enough to stretch out on but long enough if both parties kept their knees bent. In a way he preferred it to one of the beds, since she seemed to feel guiltier and less free with herself in a real bed, a bed her family used, and her unease would spread to him. Moving the table, he could kneel beside the sofa and have the perfect angle for kissing her cunt. On and on, deeper into her darkness where things began to shudder and respond, it got to be an end in itself. He loved it when she would clamp his face between her damp thighs like a nut in a nutcracker and come. He wondered if a man ever got his neck broken that way.

A shadow has crossed Thelma's face, a flinching as if he has consigned her to merely remembering, to the sealed and unrepeatable past like the photographs on the silent television set. But he had meant it more comfortably, settling in his rocker opposite the one person who for these last ten years has given him nothing but what he needed. Sex. Soul food.

"You too," she says, her eyes lowered to the items on the tray, which she hasn't touched, "have things to remember, I hope."

"I just was. Remembering. You seem sad," he says, accusing, for his presence should make her glad, in spite of all.

"You don't seem quite you yet. You seem – more careful."

"Jesus, you'd be too. I'll have some more macadamia nuts, if that'll please you." He eats them one by one and between bouts of chewing and feeling their furry nuggets part so smoothly in his mouth tells her about his heart attack – the boat, the Gulf, little Judy, the lying on the beach feeling like a jellyfish, the hospital, the doctors, their advice, his attempts to follow it. "They're dying to cut into me and do a bypass. But there's this less radical option they can do first and I'm supposed to see a guy up here at St. Joseph's about having it done this spring. It's called an angioplasty. There's a balloon on the end of a catheter a yard long at least they thread up into your heart from a cut they make just under your groin, the artery there. I had it done kind of in Florida but instead of a balloon it was a bunch of dyes they put in to see what my poor old ticker actually looked like. It's a funny experience: it doesn't exactly hurt but you feel very funny, demoralized like, while it's being done and terrible for days afterward. When they put the dye in, your chest goes hot like you're in an oven. Deep, it feels too deep. Like having a baby but then no baby, just a lot of computerized bad news about your coronary arteries. Still, it beats open-heart, where they saw through your sternum for starters" – he touches the center of his chest and thinks of Thelma's breasts, their nipples so perfect to suck, waiting behind her blouse, waiting for him to make his move – "and then run all your blood through a machine for hours. I mean, that machine is *you*, for the time being. It stops, you die. A guy I play golf with down there had a quadruple and a valve replacement and a pacemaker while they were at it and he says he's never been the same, it was like a truck ran over him and then backed up. His swing, too, is terrible; he's never got it back. But enough, huh? What about you? How's *your* health?"

"How do I look?" She sips the Coke but leaves all the nuts in their twin bowls for him. The pattern imitates sampler stitch, squarish flowers in blue and pink.

"Good to me," he lies. "A little pale and puffy but we all do at the end of winter."

"I'm losing it, Harry," Thelma tells him, looking up until he meets her eyes. Eyes muddier than Pru's but also what they call hazel, eyes that have seen him all over, that know him as well as a woman's can. A wife fumbles around with you in the dark; a mistress you meet in broad daylight, right on the sofa. She used to tease him about his prick wearing a bonnet, with the foreskin still on. "My kidneys are worse and the steroid dose can't go any higher. I'm so anemic I can hardly drag around the house to do the work and have to take naps every afternoon – you're right in the middle of my nap time, as a matter of fact." He makes an instinctive motion, tightening his hands on the chair arms to pull himself up, and her voice lifts toward anger. "No. Don't go. Don't you dare. For God's sake. I don't see you at all for nearly six months and then you're up here a week before you bother to call."

"Thelma, *she's* around, I can't just wander off. I was getting reacclimated. I have to take it more easy on myself now."

"You've never loved me, Harry. You just loved the fact that I loved you. I'm not complaining. It's what I deserve. You make your own punishments in life, I honest to God believe that. You get exactly what you deserve. God sees to it. Look at my hands. I used to have pretty hands. At least I thought they were pretty. Now half the fingers – *look* at them! Deformed. I couldn't even get my wedding ring off if I tried now."

He looks, leaning forward so the rocker tips under him, to examine her extended hands. The knuckles are swollen and shiny, and some of the segments with the fingernails go off at a slight angle, but he wouldn't have noticed without her calling his attention to it. "You don't want to get your wedding ring off," he tells her. "As I remember, you and Ronnie are stuck together with glue. You even eat the glue sometimes, I seem to remember your telling me."

Her hands have made Thelma angry and he is fighting back, as if she blames her hands on him. She says, "You always minded that, that I was a wife to Ronnie, along with serving you whenever it suited. But who were you to mind that, stuck fast to Janice and her money? I never tried to take you away from her, though it would have been easy at times."

"Would it?" He rocks back. "I don't know, something about that little mutt still gets to me. She won't give up. She never really figured out how the world is put together but she's still working at it. Now she's got the idea she wants to be a working girl. She's signed up at the Penn State annex over on Pine Street for those courses you have to take to get a real-estate broker's license. At Mt. Judge High I don't think she ever got over a C, even in home ec. Come to think of it, I bet she flunked home ec., the only girl in the history of the school."

Thelma grudgingly smiles; her sallow face lights up in her shadowy living room. "Good for her," she says. "If I had my health, I'd be getting out myself. This being a homemaker – they sold us a bill of goods, back there in home ec."

"How *is* Ronnie, by the way?"

"The same," she says, with a note of that languid, plaintive music the women of the county inject into their saga of their stoic days. "Not hustling so hard for the new customers now, coasting along on the old. He's out from under the children's educations, so his only financial burden is me and the doctor bills. Not that he wouldn't be willing to pay for little Ron to finish up at Lehigh if he wanted; it's been a disappointment, his becoming a kind of hippie the way he has. The funny thing was he was the cleverest of the three at school. Things just came too easy to him, I guess."

Harry has heard this before. Thelma's voice is dutiful and deliberately calm, issuing small family talk when both know that what she wants to discuss is her old issue, that flared up a minute ago, of whether he loves her or not, or why at least he doesn't need her as much as she does him. But their relationship at the very start, the Caribbean night they first slept together, was established with her in pursuit of him, and all the years since, of hidden meetings, of wise decisions to end it and thrilling abject collapses back into sex, have not disrupted the fundamental pattern of her giving and his taking, of her fearing their end more than he, and clinging, and disliking herself for clinging, and wanting to punish him for her dislike, and him shrugging and continuing to bask in the sun of her love, that rises every day whether he is there or not. He can't believe it, quite, and has to keep testing her.

"These kids," he says, taking a bluff tone as if they are making small talk in public instead of enjoying this stolen intimacy behind drawn shades in Arrowdale, "they break your heart. You ought to see Nelson when he's down there in Florida and has to live with me a little. The poor kid was jumping out of his skin."

Thelma makes an annoyed motion with her hands. "Harry, you're not actually God, it just feels that way to you. Do you really think Nelson was jumpy because of you?"

"Why else?"

She knows something. She hesitates, but cannot resist, perhaps, a bit of revenge for his taking her always for granted, for his being in Pennsylvania a week before calling. "You must know about Nelson. My boys say he's a cocaine addict. They've all used it, that generation, but Nelson they tell me is really hooked. As they say, the drug runs him, instead of him just using the drug."

Harry has rocked back as far as the rocker will take him without his shoes leaving the rug and remains in that position so long that Thelma becomes anxious, knowing that this man isn't sound inside and can have a heart attack. At last he rocks forward again and, gazing at her thoughtfully, says, "That explains a lot." He fishes in the side pocket of his tweedy gray sports coat for a small brown bottle and deftly spills a single tiny pill into his hand and puts it in his mouth, under his tongue. There is a certain habituated daintiness in the gesture. "Coke takes money, doesn't it?" he asks Thelma. "I mean, you can go through hundreds. Thousands."

She regrets her telling him, now that the satisfaction is past of shocking him, of waking him up to her existence once again. She is still at heart too much a schoolteacher; she enjoys administering a lesson. "I can't believe Janice doesn't know and hasn't discussed it with you, or that Nelson's wife hasn't come to you both."

"Pru's pretty close-mouthed," he says. "I don't see them that much. Even when we're all in the county, it's on opposite sides of Brewer. Janice is over there at her mother's old place a fair amount, but not me. She owns it, I don't."

"Harry, don't look so stunned. It's all just rumor, and really is his business, his and his family's. We all do things our parents wouldn't approve of, and they know it, and don't want to know, if you follow me. Oh, Harry, *damn* it! Now I've made you sad, when I'm dying to make you happy. Why don't you like me to make you happy? Why have you always fought it?"

"I haven't. I haven't fought it, Thel. We've had great times. It's just, we've never been exactly set up for a lot of happiness, and now —"

"Now, dear?"

"Now I know how you've been feeling all these years."

She wants for him to explain, but he can't he is suddenly afflicted by tact. She prompts, "Mortal?"

"Yeah. Close to it. I mean, things wearing thin so you sort of look right through them."

"Including me."

"Not you. Cut it out, making me jump through this same fucking hoop all the time. Why do you think I'm here?"

"To make love. To screw me. Go ahead. I mean come ahead. Why do you think I answered the door?" She has leaned forward across the table, her knees white where they press against the edge, and her face has taken on that melting crazy look women get at the decision to go with it, to fuck in spite of all, which frightens him now because it suggests a willing slide down into death.

"Wait. Thel. Let's think about this." On cue, the nitroglycerin has worked its way through and he gets that tingle. He sits back, suppressing it. "I'm supposed to avoid excitement."

She asks, amused somehow by the need to negotiate, "Have you made love with Janice?"

"Once or twice maybe. I kind of forget. You know, it's like brushing your teeth at night, you forget if you did or didn't."

She takes this in, and decides to tease him. "I made up Alex's old bed for us."

"You didn't use to like to use real beds."

"I've become very liberated," she says, smiling, extracting what pleasure she can out of his evasions.

He is tempted, picturing Thelma in bed naked, her tallowy willing body, her breasts that have nursed three boy babies and two men at least but look virginal and rosy like a baby's thumb-tips, not bumply and chewed and dark like Janice's, her buttocks glassy in texture and not finely gritty like Janice's, her pubic hair reddish and skimpy enough to see the slit through unlike Janice's opaque thick bush, and her shameless and matter-of-fact mouth, Thelma's, her frank humorous hunger, amused at being caught in the trap of lust over and over, not holding it against him all these years of off and on, in and out. But then he thinks of Ronnie – who knows where that obnoxious prick's prick has been, Rabbit can't believe he's as faithful as Thelma thinks he is, not from the way he used to carry on in the locker room, not from the way he was screwing Ruth before Harry was, and cashing in Cindy that time in the Caribbean – and of AIDS. That virus too small to imagine travelling through our fluids, even a drop or two of saliva or cunt slime, and unlocking our antibodies with its little picks, so that our insides lose their balance and we topple into pneumonia, into starvation. Love and death, they can't be pried apart any more. But he can't tell Thelma that. It would be spitting in her wide-open face.

On her own she sees he isn't up to it. She asks, "Another Coke?" He has drunk it all, he sees, and consumed without think-ing both the little bowls of fatty, sodium-soaked nuts.

"No. I ought to run. But let me sit here a little longer. Being with you is such a relief."

"Why? It seems I make claims, like all the others."

A little lightning of pain flickers across his chest, narrowing his scope of breath. Claims lie heavy around him, squeezing. Now a sexually unsatisfied mistress, another burden. But he lies, "No you don't. You've been all gravy, Thel. I know it's cost you, but you've been terrific."

"Harry, *please*. Don't sound so maudlin. You're still young. What? Fifty-five? Not even above the speed limit."

"Fifty-six two months ago. That's not old for some guys – not for a stocky little plug-ugly like Ronnie, he'll go forever. But if you're the height I am and been overweight as long, the heart gets tired of lugging it all around." He has developed, he realizes, an image of his heart as an unwilling captive inside his chest, a galley slave or one of those blinded horses that turn a mill wheel. He feels that Thelma is looking at him in a new way – clinically, with a detached appraising look far distant from the melting crazy look. He has forfeited something by not fucking her: he has lost full rank, and she is moving him out, without even knowing it. Fair enough. With her lupus, he moved her out a long while ago. If Thelma had been healthy, why wouldn't he have left Janice for her in this last decade? Instead he used all the holes she had and then hustled back into whatever model Toyota he was driving that year and back to Janice in her stubborn, stupid health. What *was* there about Janice? It must be religious, their tie, it made so little other sense.

Two ailing old friends, he and Thelma sit for half an hour, talking symptoms and children, catching up on the fate of common acquaintances – Peggy Fosnacht dead, Ollie down in New Orleans she heard, Cindy Murkett fat and unhappy working in a boutique in the new mall out near Oriole, Webb married for the fourth time to a woman in her twenties and moved from that fancy modern house in Brewer Heights with all his home carpentry to an old stone farmhouse in the south of the county, near Galilee, that he has totally renovated.

"That Webb. Anything he wants to do, he does. He really knows how to live."

"Not really. I was never as impressed with him as you and Janice were. I always thought he was a smartass know-it-all."

"You think Janice was impressed?"

Thelma is slightly flustered, and avoids his eye. "Well, there was that one night at least. She didn't complain, did she?"

"Neither did I," he says gallantly, though what he chiefly remembers is how tired he was the next morning, and how weird golf seemed, with impossible jungle and deep coral caves just off the fairway. Janice got Webb, and Ronnie sweet Cindy. Thelma told Harry that night she had loved him for years.

She nods in sarcastic acknowledgment of the compliment, and says, returning to an earlier point in their conversation, "About being mortal – I suppose it affects different people different ways, but for me there's never been a thinning out. Being alive, no matter how sick I feel, feels absolute. You're absolutely alive and when you're not you'll be absolutely something else. Do you and Janice ever go to church?"

Not too surprised, since Thelma has always been religious in her way, it goes with her conventional decor and secretive sexiness, he answers, "Rarely, actually. The churches down there have this folksy Southern thing. And most of our friends happen to be Jewish."

"Ronnie and I go every Sunday now. One of these new denominations that goes back to fundamentals. You know – we're lost, and we're saved."

"Oh yeah?" These marginal sects depress Harry. At least the moldy old denominations have some history to them.

"I believe it, sometimes," she says. "It helps the panic, when you think of all the things you'll never do that you always thought vaguely you might. Like go to Portugal, or get a master's degree."

"Well, you did some things. You did Ronnie, and me, me up brown I'd say, and you did raise three sons. You might get to Portugal yet. They say it's cheap, relatively. The only country over there I've ever wanted to go to is Tibet. I can't believe I won't make it. Or never be a test pilot, like I wanted to when I was ten. As you say, I still think I'm God."

"I didn't mean that unkindly. It's charming, Harry."

"Except maybe to Nelson."

"Even to him. He wouldn't want you any different."

"Here's a question for you, Thel. You're smart. What ever happened to the Dalai Lama?"

In her clinical appraising mood, nothing should surprise her, but Thelma laughs. "He's still around, isn't he? In fact, hasn't he been in the news a little, now that the Tibetans are rioting again? Why, Harry? Have you become a devotee of his? Is that why you don't go to church?"

He stands, not liking being teased about this. "I've always kind of identified with him. He's about my age, I like to keep track of the guy. I have a gut feeling this'll be his year." As he stands there, the rocking chair on the rebound taps his calves and his medications make him feel lightheaded. "Thanks for the nuts," he says. "There's a lot we could still say."

She stands too, stiffly fighting the plushy grip of the sofa, and with her arthritic waddle steps around the table, and places her body next to his, her face at his lapel. She looks up at him with that presumptuous solemnity of women you have fucked. She urges him, "Believe in God, darling. It helps."

He squirms, inside. "I don't *not* believe."

"That's not quite enough, I fear. Harry, darling." She likes the sound of "darling." "Before you go, let me see him at least."

"See who?"

"Him, Harry. You. With his bonnet."

Thelma kneels, there in her frilled and stagnant dim living room, and unzips his fly. He feels the clinical cool touch of her fingers and sees the gray hairs on the top of her head, radiating from her parting; his heart races in expectation of her warm mouth as in the old days.

But she just says, "Just lovely," and tucks it back, half hard, into his Jockey shorts, and rezips his fly and struggles to her feet. She is a bit breathless, as if from a task of housework. He embraces her and this time it is he who clings.

"The reason I haven't left Janice and never can now," he confesses, suddenly near tears, maudlin as she said, "is, without her, I'm shit. I'm unemployable. I'm too old. All I can be from here on in is her husband."

He expects sympathy, but perhaps his mention of Janice is one too many. Thelma goes dead, somehow, in his arms. "I don't know," she says.

"About what?"

"About your coming here again."

"Oh let me," he begs, perversely feeling at last in tune with this encounter and excited by her. "Without you, I don't have a life."

"Maybe Nature is trying to tell us something. We're too old to keep being foolish."

"Never, Thelma. Not you and me."

"You don't seem to want me."

"I want you, I just don't want Ronnie's little bugs."

She pushes at his chest to free herself. "There's nothing wrong with Ronnie. He's as safe and clean as I am."

"Yeah, well, that goes without saying, the way you two carry on. That's what I'm afraid of. I tell you, Thelma, you don't know him. He's a madman. You can't see it, because you're his loyal wife."

"Harry, I think we've reached a point where the more we say, the worse it'll get. Sex isn't what it used to be, you're right about that. We must all be more careful. *You* be careful. Keep brushing your teeth, and I'll brush mine."

It isn't until he is out on Thelma's curved walk, the door with its pulled curtain and bevelled glass shut behind him, that he catches her allusion to toothbrushing. Another slam at him and Janice. You can't say anything honest to women, they have minds like the FBI. The robin is still there, on the little lawn. Maybe it's sick, all these animals around us have their diseases too, their histories of plague. It gives Rabbit a beady eye and hops a bit away in Thelma's waxy April grass but disdains to take wing. Robin, hop. The bold yellow of dandelions has come this week to join that of daffodils and forsythia. Telltale. Flowers attracting bees as we attract each other. Our signals. Smells. If only he were back in her house he'd fuck her despite all the danger. Instead he finds safety inside his gray Celica; as he glides away the stillness of Arrowdale is broken by the return of the lumbering yellow school buses, and their release, at every corner of the curved streets, of shrilly yelling children.

THE TOYOTA TOUCH, a big blue banner says in the display windows of Springer Motors over on Route 111. *36 Months / 36,000 Miles · Limited Warranty on All New Models*, a lesser poster proclaims, and another *All-New* CRESSIDAS · *Powerful New 3.0-Liter Engine · 190 Horsepower · 4-Speed Electronically Controlled Overdrive Transmission · New Safety Shift Lock*. Nelson isn't in, to Harry's considerable relief. The day is a desultory Tuesday and the two salesmen on the floor are both young men he doesn't know, and who don't know him. Changes have been made since last

November. Nelson has had the office area repainted in brighter colors, pinks and greens like a Chinese tea-house, and has taken down the old blown-up photos of Harry in his glory days as a basketball star, with the headlines calling him "Rabbit."

"Mr. Angstrom left for lunch around one o'clock and said he might not be back this afternoon," a pudgy salesman tells him. Jake and Rudy used to have their desks out in the open along the wall, in the direction of the disco club that failed and when the Seventies went out became an appliance-rental center. One of Nelson's bright ideas was to take these desks away and line the opposite wall with cubicles, like booths in a restaurant. Maybe it creates more salesman–customer intimacy at the ticklish moment of signing the forms but the arrangement seems remote from general business operations and exposed to the noise of the service garage. In this direction, and behind toward the river and Brewer, lies the scruffy unpaved area of the lot Harry has always thought of for some reason as Paraguay, which in reality just got rid of its old dictator with the German name, Harry read in the papers recently.

"Yeah, well," he tells this fat stranger, "I'm a Mr. Angstrom too. Who is here, who knows anything?" He doesn't mean to sound rude but Thelma's revelation has upset him; he can feel his heart racing and his stomach struggling to digest the two bowls of nuts.

Another young salesman, a thinner one, comes toward them, out of a booth at the Paraguay end, and he sees it's not a man; her hair being pulled back tight from her ears and her wearing a tan trench coat to go out onto the lot to a customer fooled him. It's a female. A female car salesman. Like in that Toyota commercial, only white. He tries to control his face, so his chauvinism doesn't show.

"I'm Elvira Ollenbach, Mr. Angstrom," she says, and gives him a hard handshake that, after Thelma's pasty cold touch a half-hour ago, feels hot. "I'd know you were Nelson's dad even without the pictures he keeps on his wall. You look just like him, especially around the mouth."

Is this chick kidding him? She is a thin taut young woman, overexercised the way so many of them are now, with deep bony eyesockets and a deep no-curves voice and thin lips painted a pale luminous pink like reflecting tape and a neck so slender it makes her jaws look wide, coming to points under the lobes of her exposed white ears, which stick out. She wears gold earrings shaped like snail shells. He says to her, "I guess you've come onto the job since I was last here."

"Just since January," she says. "But before that I was three years with Datsun out on Route 819."

"How do you like it, selling cars?"

"I like it very much," Elvira Ollenbach says, and no more. She doesn't smile much, and her eyes are a little insistent.

He puts himself on the line, telling her, "You don't think of it usually as a woman's game."

She shows a little life. "I know, isn't that strange, when it's really such a natural? The women who come in don't feel so intimidated, and the men aren't so afraid to show their ignorance as they would be with another man. I love it. My dad loved cars and I guess I take after him."

"It all makes sense," he admits. "I don't know why it's been so long in coming. Women sales reps, I mean. How's business been?"

"It's been a good spring, so far. People love the Camry, and of course the Corolla plugs right along, but we've had surprisingly good luck with the luxury models, compared to what we hear from other dealers. Brewer's economy is looking up, after all these years. The dead industries have been shaken out, and the new ones, the little specialty and high-tech plants, have been coming in, and of course the factory outlets have had a fabulous reception. They're the key to the whole revival."

"Super. How about the used end of it? That been slow?"

Her deeply set eyes – shadowy, like Nelson's, but not sullen and hurt – glance up in some puzzlement. "Why no, not at all. One of the reasons Nelson had for hiring a new rep was he wanted to devote more of his own attention to the used cars, and not whole-sale so many of them out. There was a man who used to do it, with a Greek name –"

"Stavros. Charlie Stavros."

"Exactly. And ever since he retired Nelson feels the used cars have been on automatic pilot. Nelson's philosophy is that unless you cater to the lower-income young or minority buyer with a buy they can manage you've lost a potential customer for a new upscale model five or ten years down the road."

"Sounds right." She seems awfully full of Nelson, this girl. Girl, she may be thirty or more for all he can tell, everybody under forty looks like a kid to him.

The pudgy salesman, the one who's a man – a nice familiar Italian type, Brewer is still producing a few, with husky voices, hairy wrists, and with old-fashioned haircuts close above the ears – feels obliged to put his two cents in. "Nelson's really been making the used cars jump. Ads in the *Standard*, prices on the windshield knocked lower every two or three days, discounts for cash. Some people swing by every day to see what's up for grabs." He has an anxious way of standing too close and hurrying his words; his cheeks could use a shave and his breath a Cert or two. Garlic, they use it on everything.

"Discounts for cash, huh?" Harry says. "Where *is* Nelson, anyway?"

"He told us he needed to unwind," Elvira says. "He wanted to get away from the calls."

"Calls?"

"Some man keeps calling him," Elvira says. Her voice drops. "He sounds kind of foreign." Harry is getting the impression she isn't as smart as she seemed at first impression. Her insistent eyes catch a hint of this thought, for she self-protectively adds, "I probably shouldn't be saying a thing, but seeing as you're his father . . ."

"Sounds like a dissatisfied customer," Rabbit says, to help her out of it.

"Toyota doesn't get many of those," the other salesman crowds in. "Year after year, they put out the lowest-maintenance machines on the road, with a repair-free longevity that's absolutely unbelievable."

"Don't sell me, I'm sold," Harry tells him.

"I get enthusiastic. My name's Benny Leone, by the way, Mr. Angstrom. Benny for Benedict. A pleasure to see you over here. The way Nelson tells us, you've washed your hands of the car business and glad of it."

"I'm semi-retired." Do they know, he wonders, that Janice

legally owns it all? He supposes they pretty much have the picture. Most people do, in life. People know more than they let on.

Benny says, "You get all kinds of kooky calls in this business. Nelson shouldn't let it bug him."

"Nelson takes everything too seriously," Elvira adds. "I tell him, Don't let things get to you, but he can't help it. He's one of those guys so uptight he squeaks."

"He was always a very caring boy," Harry tells them. "Who else is here, besides you two? Talk about automatic pilot –"

"There's Jeremy," Benny says, "who comes in generally Wednesdays through Saturdays."

"And Lyle's here," Elvira says, and glances sideways to where a couple in bleached jeans are wandering in the glinting sea of Toyotas.

"I thought Lyle was sick," Harry says.

"He says he's in remission," Benny says, his face getting a careful look, as maybe Harry's did when he was trying not to appear a chauvinist in Elvira's eyes. She for her part has suddenly moved, in her spring trench coat, toward the bright outdoors, where the pair of potential buyers browse.

"Glad to hear it," Harry says, feeling less constrained and ceremonious talking to Benny alone. "I didn't think there was any remission from his disease."

"Not in the long run." The man's voice has gone huskier, a touch gangsterish, as if the woman's presence had constrained him too.

Harry jerks his head curtly toward the outdoors. "How's she doing really?"

Benny moves an inch even closer and confides, "She gets 'em to a certain point, then gets rigid and lets the deal slip away. Like she's afraid the rest of us will say she's too soft."

Harry nods. "Like women are always the stingiest tippers. Money spooks 'em. Still," he says, loyal to the changing times and his son's innovations, "I think it's a good idea. Like lady ministers. They have a people touch."

"Yeah," the jowly small man cautiously allows. "Gives the place a little zing. A little something different."

"Where is Lyle, did you say?" He wonders how much these

two are concealing from him, protecting Nelson. He was aware of eye signals between them as they talked. A maze of secrets, this agency he built up in his own image since 1975, when old man Springer suddenly popped, one summer day, like an overheated thermometer. A lot of hidden stress in the auto business. Chancy, yet you have a ton of steady overhead.

"He was in Nelson's office ten minutes ago."

"Doesn't he use Mildred's?" Harry explains, "Mildred Kroust was the bookkeeper for years here, when you were just a kid." In terms of Springer Motors he has become a historian. He can remember when that appliance-rental place up the road had a big sign saying D I S C O remade from a Mr. Peanut in spats and top hat brandishing his stick in neon.

But Benny seems to know all he wants to. He says, "That's a kind of conference room now. There's a couch in there if anybody needs all of a sudden to take a nap. Lyle used to, but now he works mostly at home, what with his illness."

"How long has he had it?"

Benny gets that careful look again, and says, "At least a year. That HIV virus can be inside you for five or ten before you know it." His voice goes huskier, he comes closer still. "A couple of the mechanics quit when Nelson brought him in as accountant in his condition, but you got to hand it to Nelson, he told them go ahead, quit, if they wanted to be superstitious. He spelled out how you can't get it from casual contact and told them take it or leave it."

"How'd Manny go for that?"

"Manny? Oh yeah, Mr. Manning in Service. As I understand it, that was the reason he left finally. He'd been shopping, I hear, at other agencies, but at his age it's hard to make a jump."

"You said it," Harry says. "Hey, looks like another customer out there, you better help Elvira out."

"Let 'em look, is my motto. If they're serious, they'll come in. Elvira tries too hard."

Rabbit walks across the display floor, past the performance board and the Parts window and the crash-barred door that leads into the garage, to the green doorway, set in old random-grooved Masonite now painted a dusty rose, of what used to be his office.

Elvira was right; the photographic blowups of his basketball head-lines and halftone newspaper cuts haven't been tossed out but are up on Nelson's walls, where the kid has to look at them every day. Also on the walls are the Kiwanis and Rotary plaques and a citation from the Greater Brewer Chamber of Commerce and a President's Touch Award that Toyota gave the agency a few years ago and a *Playboy* calendar, the girl for this month dressed up as a bare-assed Easter bunny, which Harry isn't so sure strikes quite the right note but at least says the whole agency hasn't gone queer.

Lyle stands up at Nelson's desk before Harry is in the room. He is very thin. He wears a thick red sweater under his gray suit. He extends a skeletal bluish hand and an unexpectedly broad smile, his teeth enormous in his shrunken face. "Hello, Mr. Angstrom. I bet you don't remember me."

But he does look dimly familiar, like somebody you played bas-ketball against forty years ago. His skull is very narrow, the crew-cut hair so evenly blond it looks dyed; the accountant's half-glasses on his nose are of thin gold wire. He is so pale, light seems to be coming through his skin. Squinting, Harry takes the offered hand in a brief shake and tries not to think of those little HIVs, intricate as tiny spaceships, slithering off onto his palm and up his wrist and arm into the sweat pores of his armpit and burrowing into his bloodstream there. He wipes his palm on the side of his jacket and hopes it looks like he's patting his pocket.

Lyle tells him, "I used to work in Fiscal Alternatives on Weiser Street when you and your wife would come and trade gold and silver."

Harry laughs, remembering. "We damn near broke our backs, lugging one load of silver dollars up the street to the fucking bank."

"You were smart," Lyle says. "You got out in time. I was impressed."

This last remark seems a touch impertinent, but Harry says amiably, "Dumb luck. That place still functioning?"

"In a *very* restricted way," Lyle says, overemphasizing, for Harry's money, the "very." It seems if you're a fag you have to exaggerate everything, to bring it all up to normal pitch. "The whole metals boom was a fad, really. They're *very* depressed now."

"It was a nifty little place. That beauty who used to do the actual buying and selling. I could never figure out how she could run the computer with those long fingernails."

"Oh, Marcia. She committed suicide."

Rabbit is stunned. She had seemed so angelic in her way. "She did? Why?"

"Oh, the usual. Personal problems," Lyle says, flicking them away with the back of his transparent hand. In Rabbit's eyes globules of blurred light move around Lyle's margins, like E.T. in the movie. "Nothing to do with the metals slump. She was just the front, the money behind it came out of Philadelphia."

As Lyle talks airily, Harry can hear his intakes of breath, a slight panting that goes with the bluish shadows at the temples, the sense of him having come from space and about to go back to space. *This guy's even worse off than I am*, Rabbit thinks, and likes him for it. He sees no signs of the Kaposi's spots, though, just a general radiant aura of a body resisting life, refusing sustenance, refusing to go along with its own system. There is a sweetish-rotten smell, like when you open the door of the unused refrigerator in a vacation place, or maybe Rabbit imagines it. Lyle suddenly, limply, sits down, as if standing has been too much effort.

Harry takes the chair across the desk, where the customers usually sit, begging for easier terms. "Lyle," Harry begins. "I'd like to inspect the books. Bank statements, receipts, payments, loans, inventory, the works."

"Why on earth why?" Lyle's eyes, as the rest of his face wastes away, stand out, more in the round than healthy people's eyes. He sits erect, one fleshless forearm for support laid in its gray sleeve parallel to the edge of Nelson's desk. Either to conserve his energy or protect the truth, he has set himself to give minimal answers.

"Oh, human curiosity. Frankly, there's something fishy about the statements I've been getting in Florida." Harry hesitates, but can't see that being specific would do any harm at this point. He still has the hope that everything can be explained away, that he can go back to not thinking about the lot. "There aren't enough used-car sales, proportionally."

"There aren't?"

"You could argue it's a variable, and with the good economy under Reagan people can afford to buy new; but in my years here there's always been a certain proportion, things average out over the course of a couple months, and that hasn't been happening in the statements since November. In fact, it's been getting weirder."

"Weirder."

"Funnier. Phonier. Whatever. When can I see the books? I'm no accountant; I want Mildred Kroust to go over them with me."

Lyle makes an effort and shifts his arm off the desk and rests both hands out of sight, on his lap. Harry is reminded by the way he moves of the ghostly slowness of the languid dead floppy bodies at Buchenwald being moved around in the post-war newsreels. Naked, loose-jointed, their laps in plain view, talk about obscene, here was something so obscene they had to show it to us so we'd believe it. Lyle tells Harry, "I keep a lot of the data at home, in my computer."

"We have a computer system here. Top of the line, an IBM. I remember our installing it."

"Mine's compatible. A little Apple that does everything."

"I bet it does. You know, frankly, just because you're sick and have to stay home a lot's no reason the Springer Motors accounts should be scattered all over Diamond County. I want them here. I want them here tomorrow."

This is the first acknowledgment either has made that Lyle is sick, that Lyle is dying. The boy stiffens, and his lips puff out a little. He smiles, that skeleton-generous grin. "I can only show the books to authorized persons," he says.

"I'm authorized. Who could be more authorized than me? I used to run the place. That's my picture all over the walls."

Lyle's eyelids, with lashes darker than his hair, lower over those bulging eyes. He blinks several times, and tries to be delicate, to keep the courtesies between them. "My understanding from Nelson is that his mother owns the company."

"Yeah, but I'm her husband. Half of what's hers is mine."

"In some circumstances, perhaps, and perhaps in some states. But not, I think, in Pennsylvania. If you *wish* to consult a lawyer —" His breathing is becoming difficult; it is almost a mercy for Harry to interrupt.

"I don't need to consult any lawyer. All I need is to have my wife call you and tell you to show me the books. Me and Mildred. I want her in on this."

"Miss Kroust, I believe, resides now in a nursing home. The Dengler Home in Penn Park."

"Good. That's five minutes from my house. I'll pick her up and come back here tomorrow. Let's set a time."

Lyle's lids lower again, and he awkwardly replaces his arm on the desktop. "When and *if* I receive your wife's authorization, and Nelson's go-ahead —"

"You're not going to get that. Nelson's the problem here, not the solution."

"I say, even *if*, I would need some days to pull all the figures together."

"Why is that? The books should be up-to-date. What's going on here with you guys?"

Surprisingly, Lyle says nothing. Perhaps the struggle for breath is too much. It is all so wearying. His hollow temples look bluer. Harry's heart is racing and his chest twingeing but he resists the impulse to pop another Nitrostat, he doesn't want to become an addict. He slumps down lower in the customer's chair, as if negotiations for now have gone as far as they can go. He tries another topic. "Tell me about it, Lyle. How does it feel?"

"What feel?"

"Being so close to, you know, the barn. The reason I ask, I had a touch of heart trouble down in Florida and still can't get used to it, how close I came. I mean, most of the time it seems unreal, I'm *me*, and all around me everything is piddling along as normal, and then suddenly at night, when I wake up needing to take a leak, or in the middle of a TV show that's sillier than hell, it hits me, and wow. The bottom falls right out. I want to crawl back into my parents but they're dead already."

Lyle's puffy lips tremble, or seem to, as he puzzles out this new turn the conversation has taken. "You come to terms with it," he says. "Everybody dies."

"But some sooner than others, huh?"

A spasm of indignation animates Lyle. "They're developing new drugs. All the time. The French. The Chinese. Trichosanthin.

TIBO derivatives. Eventually the FDA will have to let them in, even if they are a bunch of Reaganite fascist homophobes who wouldn't mind seeing us all dead. It's a question of hanging on. I have hope."

"Well, great. More power to you. But medicine can only do so much. That's what I'm learning, the hard way. You know, Lyle, it's not as though I'd never thought about death, or never had people near to me die, but I never, you could say, had the real taste of it in my mouth. I mean, it's not kidding. It wants it all." He wants that pill. He wonders if Nelson keeps a roll of Life Savers in the desk the way he himself used to. Just something to put in your mouth when you get nervous. Harry finds that every time he thinks of his death it makes him want to eat — that's why he hasn't lost more weight.

This other man's attempt to open him up has made Lyle more erect behind the desk, more hostile. He stares at Harry with those eroded-around eyes, beneath eyebrows the same metallic blond as his hair. "One good thing about it," he offers, "is you become harder to frighten. By minor things. By threats like yours, for example."

"I'm not making any threats, Lyle, I'm just trying to find out what the fuck is going on. I'm beginning to think this company is being ripped off. If I'm wrong and it's all on the up and up, you've nothing to be frightened of." Poor guy, he's biting the bullet, and less than half Harry's age. At his age, what was Harry doing? Setting type the old-fashioned way, and dreaming about ass. Ass, one way or another, does us in: membrane's too thin, those little HIVs sneak right through. Black box of nothingness, is what it felt like with Thelma. Funny appetite, for a steady diet. Being queer isn't all roses.

Lyle moves his arms around again with that brittle caution. His body has become a collection of dead sticks. "Don't make allegations, Mr. Angstrom, you wouldn't want to defend in court."

"Well, is it an allegation or a fact that you refuse to let me and an impartial accountant examine your books?"

"Mildred's not impartial. She's furious at me for replacing her. She's furious because I and my computer can do in a few hours what took her all week."

"Mildred's an honest old soul."

"Mildred's senile."

"Mildred's not the point here. The point is you're defying me to protect my son."

"I'm not defying you, Mr. Angstrom –"

"You can call me Harry."

"I'm not defying you, sir. I'm just telling you I can't accept orders from you. I have to get them from Nelson or Mrs. Angstrom."

"You'll get 'em. Sir." A smiling provocative hovering in Lyle's expression goads Harry to ask, "Do you doubt it?"

"I'll be waiting to hear," Lyle says.

"Listen. You may know about a lot of things I don't but you don't know shit about marriage. My wife will do what I tell her to. Ask her to. In a business like this we're absolutely one."

"We'll see," Lyle says. "My parents were married, as a matter of fact. I was raised in a marriage. I know a *lot* about marriage."

"Didn't do you much good."

"It showed me something to avoid," Lyle says, and smiles as broadly, as guilelessly, as when Harry came in. All teeth. Now Harry does recall him from the old days at Fiscal Alternatives – the stacks of gold and silver, and flawless cool Marcia with her long red nails. Poor beauty, did herself in. She and Monroe. Rabbit admits to himself the peculiar charm queers have, a boyish lightness, a rising above all that female muck, where life breeds.

"How's Slim?" Harry asks, rising from the chair. "Nelson used to talk a lot about Slim."

"Slim," Lyle says, too weak or rude to stand, "died. Before Christmas."

"Sorry to hear it," Harry lies. He holds out his hand over the desk to be shaken and the other man hesitates to take it, as if fearing contamination. Feverish loose-jointed bones: Rabbit gives them a squeeze and says, "Tell Nelson if you ever see him I like the new decor. Kind of a boutique look. Cute. Goes with the new sales rep. You hang loose, Lyle. Hope China comes through for you. We'll be in touch."

On the radio on the way home, he hears that Mike Schmidt, who exactly two years ago, on April 18, 1987, slugged his five

hundredth home run, against the Pittsburgh Pirates in Three
Rivers Stadium, is closing in on Richie Ashburn's total of 2,217
hits to become the hittingest Phillie ever. Rabbit remembers
Ashburn. One of the Whiz Kids who beat the Dodgers for the
pennant the fall Rabbit became a high-school senior. Curt Sim-
mons, Del Ennis, Dick Sisler in center, Andy Seminick behind the
plate. Beat the Dodgers the last game of the season, then lost to
the Yankees four straight. In 1950 Rabbit was seventeen and had
led the county B league with 817 points his junior season.
Remembering these statistics helps settle his agitated mood, stirred
up by seeing Thelma and Lyle, a mood of stirred-up unsatisfied
desire at whose fringes licks the depressing idea that nothing matters very much, we'll all soon be dead.

Janice's idea of a low-sodium diet for him is to get these frozen
dinners in plastic pouches called Low-Cal. Most of this pre-
cooked chicken and beef is full of chemicals so it doesn't go bad
on the shelf. To work it all through his system he usually has a second beer. Janice is distracted these days, full of excitement about
taking real-estate courses at the Penn State extension. "I'm not
sure I totally understand it, though the woman at the office over
on Pine Street – hasn't *that* neighborhood gone downhill, since
you and your father used to work at Verity! – she was very patient
with my questions. The classes meet three hours a week for ten
weeks, and there are two required and four electives to get this
certificate, but I don't think you need the certificate to take the
licensing exam, which for a salesperson – that's what I'd be – is
given monthly and for a broker, which maybe I'd try to be later,
only quarterly. But the gist of it is I could begin with two this April
and then take two more from July to September and if all goes
well get my license in September and start selling, strictly on a
commission basis at first, for this firm that Doris Eberhardt's new
brother-in-law is one of the partners in. She says she's told him
about me and he's interested. It's in your favor evidently to be
middle-aged, the clients assume you're experienced."

"Honey, why do you need to do this? You have the lot."

"I don't have the lot. Nelson has the lot."

"Does he? I dropped over there today and he wasn't there, just these kids he's hired. One fag, one wop, and a skirt."

"Harry. Now who's sounding prejudiced?"

He doesn't push ahead with his story, he wants to save it for when they both can focus. After dinner Janice likes to watch *Jeopardy!* even though she never knows any of the answers, and then the Phillies are playing the Mets on Channel 11. The little stone house with its fractional number on Franklin Drive draws darkling about them, just them, in the evening as the gradual Northern dusk (in Florida the sun just suddenly shuts down, and the moon takes over) seeps into the still-bare trees, quelling the birdsong, and a lemon tinge of sky in the west beyond the craggy chimneys of the big clinker-brick house deepens to an incendiary orange and then the crimson of last embers. Another few weeks, the trees will leaf in, and there won't be any sunset to see from the lozenge-pane windows of his den, when he turns his eyes aside from watching the television screen.

In the third inning, with two men on, Schmidt hits a home run, his fourth of the young season and the five hundred forty-sixth of his career. It puts the Phils ahead five to zero, and Rabbit starts switching channels, finding no basketball playoffs, only *Matlock* and *The Wonder Years*. Much as Janice irritates him when she's with him, when she isn't in the room with him, or when he can't hear her knocking around in the kitchen or upstairs above his head, he grows uneasy. He switches off the set and goes looking for her, full of his troubling news as once he was full of gold Krugerrands.

She is already in one of her nighties, upstairs, and those infuriating Florida sandals that go *flop-flop* as she walks around when he is still trying to sleep in the morning. Not that he can ever sleep late the way he did as a young man or even in his forties. He wakes around six with a little start and ever since his heart attack there is a gnawing in his stomach whose cause he can't locate until he realizes it is the terror of being trapped inside his perishing body, like being in a prison cell with a madman who might decide to kill him at any moment. She is paddling back and forth, *flop-flop*, carrying small stacks of folded cloth, laundry she has brought up the back stairs; one square stack he recognizes as folded handkerchiefs, another, less trim, as his Jockey shorts with their slowly slackening elastic waists, a third as her own underthings, which still excite him, not so much when they are on her as when empty and laundry-clean. He doesn't know how to begin. He throws his big body across the bed diagonally and lets the nubbles of its bedspread rub his face. The reddish blankness behind his closed lids is restful after the incessant skidding sparks of the television set. "Harry, is anything the matter?" Janice's voice sounds alarmed. His fragility gives him a new hold over her.

He rolls over and can't help smiling at the lumpy figure she cuts in her nightie. She looks not so different from how Judy looks in hers and not very much larger. Her scant bangs don't quite hide her high forehead, its Florida tan dulling, and her tired eyes look focused elsewhere. He begins, "There's something going wrong over at the lot. When I was over there today I asked to see the books and this fag with AIDS Nelson has put in as bookkeeper instead of Mildred told me he couldn't show them to me unless you authorized it. You're the boss, according to him."

The tip of her little tongue creeps out and presses on her upper lip. "That was silly," she says.

"I thought so, but I kept my cool. Poor guy, he's just covering up for Nelson."

"Covering up for Nelson why?"

"Well" – Harry sighs heavily, and arranges himself on the bed like an odalisque, with a hippy twist to his body – "you really want to hear this?"

"Of course." But she keeps moving around the room with her little stacks.

"I have a new theory. I think Nelson takes cocaine, and that's why he's so shifty and jumpy, and kind of paranoid."

Janice moves carefully to the bureau, *flop* and then *flop*, carrying what Harry recognizes as her salmon-colored running suit with the blue sleeves and stripes, which she never wears on the street around here, where the middle-aged are more careful about looking ridiculous. "Who told you this?" she asks.

He squirms on the bed, pulling up his legs and pushing off his suede shoes so as not to dirty the bedspread of white dotted Swiss.

"Nobody *told* me," he says. "I just put two and two together. Cocaine's everywhere and these yuppie baby boomers Nelson's age are just the ones who use it. It takes money. Lots of money, to maintain a real habit. Doesn't Pru keep complaining about all these bills they can't pay?"

Janice comes close to the bed and stands; he sees through her cotton nightie shadows of her nipples and her pubic hair. From his angle she looks strangely enormous, and in his diagonal position he undergoes one of those surges of lightheadedness as when he stands up too fast; it is not clear who is upright and who is not. Her body has kept the hard neatness it had when they were kids working at Kroll's but underneath her chin there are ugly folds that ramify into her neck. She was determined not to get fat like her mother but age catches you anyway. Janice says carefully, "Most young couples have bills they can't pay."

He sits up, to shake the lightness in his head, and because her body is there puts his arms around her hips. On second thought he reaches under her nightie and cups his hands around her solid, slightly gritty buttocks. He says, looking up past her breasts to her face, "The worst of it is, honey, I think he's been bleeding the company. I think he's been stealing and Lyle has been helping him, that's why they let Mildred go."

Her buttocks under his hands tense; he feels them squeeze together and become more spherical, with the tension of a basketball a few pounds under regulation pressure. A watery glimmer of arousal winks below his waist. Her blurred eyes look down upon him with somber concentration, the skin of her face sagging downward from the bone. He nuzzles one breast and closes his eyes again, smelling the faintly sweaty cotton, hiding from her intent downward eyes. Her voice asks, "What evidence do you have?"

This irritates him. She is dumb. "That's what I was saying. I asked to look at the accounts and bank statements today and they wouldn't let me, unless you authorized it. All you have to do is call up this Lyle."

He hears in her chest a curious stillness, and feels in her body a tension of restraint. Her nightie is transparent but she is opaque. "If you did see these figures," she asks, "would you know enough to understand them?"

He flicks her nipple with his tongue through the cotton. The glimmer below has grown to a steady glow, a swelling warmth. "Maybe not altogether," he says. "But even the monthly statements we got in Florida didn't look quite right to me. I'd take Mildred with me, and if she's too far gone — he said she's senile and over at Dengler's — I think we should hire somebody, a professional accountant in Brewer. You could call our lawyer for who he'd recommend. This may be something we have to bring the cops in on eventually." A nice April shower has started up outdoors, kindled by the slow sunset.

Her body has stiffened and jerked back an inch. "Harry! Your own son!"

"Well," he says, irritated again, "his own mother. Stealing from his own mother."

"We don't know anything for sure," Janice tells him. "It's only your theory."

"What else could Lyle have been hiding today? Now they'll have the wind up so we should start moving or they'll shred everything like Ollie North."

Now Janice is getting agitated, backing out of his arms and rubbing the back of one hand with the other, standing in the center of the carpet. He sees that the sex isn't going to happen, the first time in weeks he's really had the urge. Damn that Nelson. She says, "I think I should talk to Nelson first."

"*You* should? Why not *we*?"

"According to Lyle, I'm the only one who counts."

This hurts. "You're too soft on Nelson. He can do anything he wants with you."

"Oh, Harry, it used to be so awful, that time I ran off with Charlie! Nelson was only twelve, he'd come over on his bicycle all the way into Eisenhower Avenue and he'd stand there for an hour across the street, looking up at our windows, and a couple of times I saw him and I *hid*, I hid behind the curtain and let him just stand there until he got exhausted and rode away." Staring over Harry's head, seeing her little boy across the street, so patient and puzzled and hopeful, her dark eyes fill with tears.

"Well, hell," Rabbit says, "nobody *asked* him to go over there spying on you. *I* was taking care of him."

"With that poor crazy girl and perfectly hideous black man you were. It's just dumb luck the house didn't burn down with Nelson in it too."

"I would have got him out. If I'd been there I would have got them all out."

"You don't *know*," she says, "you don't know what you would have done. And you don't know now what the real story is, it's all just your suspicions, somebody's been poisoning your mind against Nelson. I bet it was Thelma."

"Thelma? We never see her anymore, we ought to have the Harrisons over sometime."

"*Pfaa!*" She spits this refusal, he has to admire her fury, the animal way it fluffs out her hair. "Over my dead body."

"Just a thought." This is not a good topic. He reverts: "I don't know what the real story is, but you do, huh? What has Nelson told you?"

She pinches her mouth shut so she seems to have no lips at all, like Ma Springer used to look. "Nothing really," she lies.

"Nothing *really*. Well O.K. then. You know more than I do. Good luck. It's you he's ripping off. It's your father's company he and his queer buddies are taking down the tube."

"Nelson wouldn't steal from the company."

"Honey, you don't understand the power of drugs. Read the papers. Read *People*, Richard Pryor tells all. Just the other day they pulled Yogi Berra's kid in. People who are into coke will kill their grandmother for a fix. It used to be heroin was the bottom of the barrel but crack makes heroin look mild."

"Nelson doesn't do crack. Much."

"Oh. Who says?"

She almost tells him, but gets frightened. "Nobody. I just know my own son. And from what Pru lets drop."

"Pru talks, does she? What does she say?"

"She's miserable. And the children too. Little Roy acts very odd, you must have noticed. Judy has nightmares. If it weren't for the children, Pru confessed to me, she would have left Nelson long ago."

Harry feels evaded. "Let's keep to the subject. Pru's got her problems, you've got yours. You better get your man-child out of Springer Motors fast."

"I'll talk to him, Harry. I don't want you to say a word."

"Why the fuck not? What's the fucking harm if I do?"

"You'll come on too strong. You'll drive him deeper into himself. He – he takes you too seriously."

"But not you?"

"He's sure of me. He knows I love him."

"And I don't?" His eyes water at the thought. The shower outside has already lifted, leaving a trickle in the gutters.

"You do, Harry, but there's something else too. You're another man. Men have this territorial thing. You think of the lot as yours. He thinks of it as his."

"It'll be his some day, if he's not in jail. I was looking at him down in Florida and there suddenly came into my mind the word *criminal*. Something about the shape of his head. I hate the way he's going bald. He'll look like Ronnie Harrison."

"Will you promise to let me talk to him and you do nothing?"

"You'll just let him weasel out." But in fact he has no desire to confront Nelson himself.

She knows this. She says, "No I won't, I promise." She stops rubbing the back of one hand with the fingers of the other and moves back toward him, *flop-flop*, as he sits on the bed. She rests her fingers above his ears and by the short hairs there pulls him softly toward her. "I do like the way you want to defend me," she says.

He yields to her insistent tug and rests his face on her chest again. Her nightie has a damp spot on it where he diddled her nipple with his tongue. Her nipples are chewed-looking, less perfect, realer than Thelma's. Being little, Janice's tits have kept their tilt pretty much, that perky upward thrust through those Forties angora sweaters in the high-school halls. Through the cotton her body gives off a smell, a stirred-up smoky smell. "What's in it for me?" he asks, his mouth against the wet cloth.

"Oh, a present," she says.

"When do I get it?"

"Pretty soon."

"With the mouth?"

"We'll see." She pushes his face back from her smoky warm body and with her fingers poking under his jaws makes him look up at her. "But if you say another single word about Nelson, I'll stop, and you won't get any present."

His face feels hot and his heart is racing but in a steady sweet way, contained in his rib cage the way his hard-on is contained in his pants, sweetly packed with blood; he is pleased that the Vasotec may make him lightheaded but leaves him enough blood pressure for one of these unscheduled, once in a while. "O.K., not a word," Rabbit promises, becoming efficient. "I'll quick go to the bathroom and brush my teeth and stuff and you turn off the lights. And somebody ought to take the phone off the hook. Downstairs, so we don't hear the squawking."

Strange phone calls have been coming through. Grainy voices with that rich timbre peculiar to black males ask if Nelson Angstrom is there. Harry or Janice responds that Nelson does not live here, that this is the home of his parents. "Well I ain't had no luck at the number he give me for a home number and at the place he works this here secretary always say the man is out."

"Would you like to leave a message?"

A pause. "You just tell him Julius called." Or Luther.

"Julius?"

"That's right."

"And what's it about, Julius? You want to say?"

"He'll know what it's about. You just tell him Julius called." Or Perry. Or Dave.

Or the caller would hang up without leaving a name. Or would have a thin, faintly foreign, precise way of speaking, and once wanted to speak not to Nelson but with Harry. "I am regretful to bother you, sir, but this son you have leaves me no recourse but to inform you in person."

"To inform me of what?"

"To inform you that your son has incurred serious debts and gentlemen to which I am associated, against any advice which I attempt to give them, talk of doing physical harm."

"Physical harm to Nelson?"

"Or even to certain of his near and dear. This is sorry to say and I do apologize, but these are not perhaps such gentlemen. I myself am merely the bearer of bad tidings. Do not rest the blame with me." The voice seemed to be drawing closer to the telephone mouthpiece, closer to Harry's ear, growing plaintively sincere, attempting to strike up a conspiracy, to become Harry's friend and ally. The familiar room, the den with its frost-faced TV and two silvery-pink wing chairs and bookshelves holding a smattering mostly of history books and on the upper shelves some china knickknacks (fairies under toadstools, cherubic bald monks, baby robins in a nest of porcelain straws) that used to be in Ma Springer's breakfront, all this respectable furniture changes quality, becomes murky and fluid and useless, at the insertion of this menacing plaintive voice into his ear, a voice with a heart of sorts, with an understandable human mission, an unpleasant duty to do, calling out of an extensive slippery underground: just so, the balmy blue air above the Gulf of Mexico changed for him, as if a filter had been slipped over his eyes, when the Sunfish tipped over.

Rabbit asks, treading water, "How did Nelson incur these debts?"

The voice likes getting his own words back. "He incurred them, sir, in pursuit of his satisfactions, and that is within his privileges, but he or someone on his behalf must pay. My associates have been assured that you are a very excellent father."

"Not so hot, actually. Whajou say your name was?"

"I did not say, señor. I did not give myself a name. It is the name of Angstrom that is of concern. My associates are eager to settle with anyone of that excellent name." This man, it occurred to Harry, loves the English language, as an instrument full of promise, of unexplored resources.

"My son," Harry tells him, "is an adult and his finances have nothing to do with me."

"That is your word? Your very final word?"

"It is. Listen, I live half the year in Florida and come back and –"

But the caller has hung up, leaving Harry with the sensation that the walls of his solid little limestone house are as thin as diet crackers, that the wall-to-wall carpet under his feet is soaked with water, that a pipe has burst and there is no plumber to call.

* * *

He turns to his old friend and associate Charlie Stavros, retired from being Springer Motors' Senior Sales Representative and moved from his old place on Eisenhower Avenue to a new condominium development on the far north side of the city, where the railroad had sold off an old freight yard, twenty acres of it, it's amazing what the railroads owned in their heyday. Harry isn't sure he can find the place and suggests they have lunch at Johnny Frye's downtown; Johnny Frye's Chophouse was the original name for this restaurant on Weiser Square, which became the Café Barcelona in the Seventies and then the Crêpe House later in the decade and now has changed hands again and calls itself Salad Binge, explaining in signs outside *Your Local Lo-Cal Eatery* and *Creative Soups and Organic Fresh-Food Health Dishes*, to attract the health-minded yuppies who work in the glass-skinned office building that has risen across from Kroll's, which still stands empty, its huge display windows whitewashed from the inside and its bare windowless side toward the mountain exposed in rough-mortared brick above the rubbly parking lot that extends up to the old Baghdad. ELP. SAV ME.

The downtown is mostly parking space now but the strange thing is that the space is all full. Though there is little to shop at downtown any more, except for some discount drugstores and a McCrory's five and dime that still peddles parakeet food and plastic barrettes to old people who haven't changed clothes since 1942, the number of trim youngish professionals in lightweight suits and tight linen skirts has ballooned; they work in the banks and insurance companies and state and federal agencies and there is no end of them somehow. On a sunny day they fill the woodsy park the city planners — not local, a fancy architectural firm that came in and won the competition with their design and then flew back to Atlanta — have made out of Weiser Square, where the squeaking, sparking trolley cars used to line up for passengers. They bask, these young paper-pushers, beside the abstract cement fountains, reading *The Wall Street Journal* with their coats off and neatly folded on the anodized, vandal-proof benches beside them.

The women of this race especially fascinate Harry; they wear running shoes instead of high heels but their legs are encased in sheer pantyhose and their faces adorned by big round glasses that give them a comical sexy look, as if their boobs are being echoed above in hard hornrims and coated plastic. They look like Goldie Hawns conditioned by Jane Fonda. The style these days gives them all wide mannish shoulders, and their hips have been pared and hardened by exercise bicycles and those ass-hugging pants that mold around every muscle like electric-colored paint. These women seem visitors from a slimmed-down future where sex is just another exercise and we all live in sealed cubicles and communicate through computers.

You would have thought Charlie would be dead by now. But these Mediterranean types don't even seem to get gray and paunchy. They hit a plateau around fifty that doesn't change until they drop off of it suddenly somewhere in their eighties. They use their bodies up neatly, like mopping up a dinner plate with bread. Charlie had rheumatic fever as a kid but, though carrying a heart murmur inside him and subject to angina, he hasn't ever had an episode as severe as Harry's down in the Gulf. "How the fuck do you do it, Charlie?" Rabbit asks him.

"You learn to avoid aggravation," Charlie tells him. "If anything looks to be aggravating, walk away from it. Things over at the lot had got to be aggravating, so I walked away. Christ, am I glad to be away from Toyotas! First thing I did was buy myself an old-fashioned American boat, an Olds Toronado. Soft shocks, single-finger steering, guzzles gas, I'm crazy about it. Five-liter V-8, tomato red with a white padded half-roof."

"Sounds great. You park it close by?"

"I tried and couldn't. Circled up around Spring Street twice and finally gave up and left it in a lot up past the old Baghdad and took a bus the three blocks down. So it costs a few pennies. Avoid aggravation, champ."

"I still don't understand it. Downtown Brewer's supposed to be dead and there's nowhere to park. Where are all the cars coming from?"

"They breed," Charlie explains. "These cars get pregnant as teenagers and go on welfare. They don't give a damn."

One of the things Harry has always enjoyed about Charlie is the man's feel for the big picture; the two of them used to stand by the display window over at the lot on dull mornings and rehash the day's news. Rabbit has never gotten over the idea that the news is going to mean something to him. As they seat themselves at one of the tile-topped tables that remain from the days when this was the Café Barcelona, he says, "How about Schmidt last night?" Against the Pirates in Three Rivers Stadium, the Phillies' veteran third baseman had doubled twice and surpassed Richie Ashburn's team record for total hits.

"This is still spring," Charlie tells him. "Wait till the pitchers' arms warm up. Schmidt'll wilt. He's old, not compared to you and me but in the game he's in he's old, and there's no hiding from the young pitchers over the long season."

Harry finds it salutary, to have his admiration for Schmidt checked. You can't live through these athletes, they don't know you exist. For them, only the other players exist. They go to the ballpark and there's thirty thousand there and a big bumbly roar when their names are announced and that's all of you they need. "Does it seem to you," he asks Charlie, "there's a lot of disasters lately? That Pan Am plane blowing up, and then those soccer fans in England the other day getting crushed, and now this gun exploding on the battleship for no apparent reason."

"Apparent's the key word," Charlie says. "Everything has some little tiny reason, even when we can't see it. A little spark somewhere, a little crack in the metal. Also, champ, look at the odds. How many people in the world now, five billion? With the world jammed up like it is the wonder is more of us aren't trampled to death. There's a crush on, and it's not going to get better."

Rabbit's heart dips, thinking that from Nelson's point of view he himself is a big part of the crowding. That time he screamed outside the burning house at 26 Vista Crescent, *I'll kill you*. He didn't mean it. A spark, a crack in metal. A tiny flaw. When you die you do the world a favor.

Charlie is frowning down into the menu, which is enormous, printed in photocopy in green ink on rough flecked acid-free paper. The things they can do with Xerox now. Who still uses a place like Verity Press? First letterpress went, then photo-offset. Charlie no longer wears thick squarish hornrims that set a dark bar across his eyebrows but gold aviator frames that hold his thick lavender-tinted lenses to his nose like fingers pinching a wine-glass. Charlie used to be thickset but age has whittled him so his Greek bones show – the high pinched arch to his nose, the wide slanting brow below his dark hairline. His sideburns are gray but he is shaving them shorter. Studying the menu, he chuckles. "Beefsteak Salad," he reads. "Pork Kabob Salad. What kind of salads are those?"

When the waitress comes, Charlie kids her about it. "What's with all this high-cal high-fat meat?" he asks. "You giving us a beefsteak with a little lettuce on the side?"

"The meat is shoelaced and worked in," the waitress says. She is tall and almost pretty, with her hair bleached and trained up in a fluffy Mohawk, and a row of little earrings all around the edge of one ear, and dark dusty-rosy spots rouged behind her eyes. Her tongue has some trouble in her mouth and it's cute, the earnest, deliberate way her lips move. "They found there was a call for these, you know, heartier ingredients."

So underneath everything, Rabbit thinks, it's still Johnny Frye's Chophouse. "Tell me about the Macadamia and Bacon Salad," he says.

"It's one of people's favorites," she says. "The bacon is crisp and in, like, flakes. Most of the fat has been pressed out of it. Also there's alfalfa sprouts, and some radishes and cucumber sliced real thin, and a couple kinds of lettuce, I forget the different names, and I don't know what all else, maybe some chuba – that's dried sardines."

"Sounds good," Rabbit says, before it doesn't and he has to choose again.

Charlie points out, "Nuts and bacon aren't exactly what the doctor ordered."

"You heard her, the fat's been squeezed out. Anyway a little bit can't kill you. It's more a matter of internal balance. Come on, Charlie. Loosen up."

"What's in the Seaweed Special?" Charlie asks the waitress, because both men like to hear her talk.

"Oh, hijiki of course, and wakame, and dulse and agar in with a lot of chickpeas and lentils, and leafy greens, it's wonderful if you're going macrobiotic seriously and don't mind that slightly bitter taste, you know, that seaweed tends to have."

"You've done talked me out of it, Jennifer," Charlie says, reading her name stitched onto the bodice of the lime-green jumper they wear for a uniform at Salad Binge. "I'll take the Spinach and Crab."

"For salad dressing, we have Russian, Roquefort, Italian, Creamy Italian, Poppyseed, Thousand Island, Oil and Vinegar, and Japanese."

"What's in the Japanese?" Harry asks, not just to see her lips curl and pucker around the little difficulty in her mouth, but because the Japanese interest him professionally. How do they and the Germans do it, when America's going down the tubes?

"Oh, I could ask in the kitchen if you really care, but umeboshi, I think, and tamari, of course – we don't use that commercial soy sauce – and sesame oil, and rice vinegar." Her eyes harden as she senses that these men are flirtatiously wasting her time. Feeling apologetic, they both order Creamy Italian and settle to each other.

It has been a long time, their rapport has grown rusty. Charlie does seem older, drier, when you look. The thin gold aviator frames take out of his face a lot of that masculine certainty that must have appealed to Janice twenty years ago. "Cute kid," Charlie says, arranging the silver around his plate more neatly, square to the edges of the paper placemat.

"Whatever happened to Melanie?" Rabbit asks him. Ten years ago, they had sat in this same restaurant and Melanie, a friend of Nelson's and Pru's living at the time at Ma Springer's house, had been their waitress. Then she became Charlie's girlfriend, old as he was, relatively. At least they went to Florida together. One of the things maybe that had made Florida seem attractive. But no bimbo there had offered herself to Harry. The only flickers he got were from women his own age, who looked ancient.

"She became a doctor," Charlie says. "A gastroenterologist, to be exact, in Portland, Oregon. That's where her father wound up, you'll recall."

"Just barely. He was a kind of late-blooming hippie, wasn't he?"

"He settled down with the third wife and has been a big support to Melanie. It was her mother, actually, who was flipping out, back in Mill Valley. Alcohol. Guys. Drugs."

The last word hurts Harry's stomach. "How come you know all this?"

Charlie shrugs minimally, but cannot quite suppress his little smile of pride. "We keep in touch. I was there for her when she needed a push. I told her, 'Go for it.' She still had a bit of that poor-little-me-I'm-only-a-girl thing. I gave her the boost she needed. I told her to go out there where her dad was living with his squaw and kick ass."

"Me you tell avoid aggravation, her you told to go for it."

"Different cases. Different ages. You her age, I'd tell you, 'Go for it.' I'll still tell you. As long as you avoid aggravation."

"Charlie, I have a problem."

"That's news?"

"A couple of 'em, actually. For one, I ought to do something about my heart. I just can't keep drifting along waiting for my next MI."

"You're losing me, champ."

"You know. Myocardial infarction. Heart attack. I was lucky to get away with the one I did have. The docs tell me I ought to have an open-heart, a multiple bypass."

"Go for it."

"Sure. Easy for you to say. People die having those things. I notice you never had one."

"But I did. In '87. December, you were in Florida. They replaced two valves. Aortic and mitral. When you have rheumatic fever as a kid, it's the valves that go. They don't close right. That's what gives you the heart murmur, blood running the wrong way."

Rabbit can hardly bear these images, all these details inside him, valves and slippages and crusts on the pipe. "What'd they replace them with?"

"Pig heart valves. The choice is that or a mechanical valve, a trap with a ball. With the mechanical, you click all the time. I didn't want to click if I could help it. They say it keeps you awake."

"Pig valves." Rabbit tries to hide his revulsion. "Was it

terrible? They split your chest open and ran your blood through a machine?"

"Piece of cake. You're knocked out cold. What's wrong with running your blood through a machine? What else you think you are, champ?"

A God-made one-of-a-kind with an immortal soul breathed in. A vehicle of grace. A battlefield of good and evil. An apprentice angel. All those things they tried to teach you in Sunday school, or really didn't try very hard to teach you, just let them drift in out of the pamphlets, back there in that church basement buried deeper in his mind than an air-raid shelter.

"You're just a soft machine," Charlie maintains, and lifts his squarish hands, with their white cuffs and rectangular gold links, to let Jennifer set his salad before him. He saw her coming with eyes in the back of his head. She circles the table gingerly – these men are doing something to her, she doesn't know what – and puts in front of Harry a bacon-flecked green mound bigger than a big breast. It looks rich, and more than he should eat. The tall awkward girl with her strange white rooster-comb trembling in the air still hovers, the roundnesses in her green uniform pressing on Rabbit's awareness as he sits at the square tiled table trying to frame his dilemmas.

"Is there anything more I can get you gentlemen?" Jennifer asks, her lips gently struggling to articulate. It's not a lisp she has, quite; it's like her tongue is too big. "Something to drink?"

Charlie asks her for a Perrier with lime. She says that San Pellegrino is what they have. He says it's all the same to him. Fancy water is fancy water.

Harry after an internal struggle asks what kinds of beer they have. Jennifer sighs, feeling they are putting her on, and recites, "Schlitz, Miller, Miller Lite, Bud, Bud Light, Michelob, Löwenbräu, Corona, Coors, Coors Light, and Ballantine ale on draft." All these names have an added magic from being tumbled a bit in her mouth. Not looking Charlie in the eye, Harry opts for a Mick. Jennifer nods unsmiling and goes away. If she doesn't want to excite middle-aged men, she shouldn't wear all those earrings and go so heavy on the makeup.

"Piece of cake, you were saying," he says to Charlie.

"They freeze you. You don't know a thing."

"Guy I know down in Florida, not much older than we are, had an open-heart and he says it was hell, the recuperation took forever, and furthermore he doesn't look so great even so. He swings a golf club like a cripple."

Charlie does one of his tidy small shrugs. "You got to have the basics to work with. Maybe the guy was too far gone. But you, you're in good shape. Could lose a few pounds, but you're young – what, Fifty-five?"

"Wish I was. Fifty-six last February."

"That's young, Champ. I'm getting there myself." Charlie is Janice's age.

"The way I'm going I'll be happy to hit sixty. I look at all these old crocks down in Florida, shrivelled-up mummies toddling right into their nineties in their shorts and orthopedic sneakers, perky as bejesus, and I want to ask 'em, 'What makes you so great? How did you do it?' "

"A day at a time," Charlie suggests. "One day at a time, and don't look down." Harry can tell he's getting bored with issuing reassurances, but Charlie's all he's got, now that he and Thelma are on hold. He's embarrassed to call her, now that he can't seem to deliver. He says:

"There's this other thing they can do now. An angioplasty. They cut open an artery in your groin –"

"Hey. I'm eating."

"– and poke it up all the way to your heart, would you believe. Then they pop out this balloon in the narrow place of the coronary artery and blow the damn thing up. Not with air, with salt-water somehow. It cracks the plaque. It stretches the artery back to the way it was."

"With a lot of luck it does," Charlie says. "And a year later you're back in the same boat, plugged up with macadamia nuts and beer yet."

Beer has come on the end of Jennifer's lean arm, in a frosted glass mug, golden and foam-topped and sizzling with its own excited bubbles. "If I can't have a single beer now and then, I'd just as soon be dead," Harry lies. He sips, and with a bent forefinger wipes the foam from under his nose. That gesture of

Nelson's. He wonders when she fucks how protective Jennifer has to be of that wobbly Mohawk. Some punk girls, he's read, put safety pins through their nipples.

"Coronary bypass is what you want," Charlie is telling him. "These balloons, they can only do one artery at a time. Bypass grafts, they can do four, five, six once they get in there. Whaddeyou care if they pull open your rib cage? You won't be there. You'll be way out of it, dreaming away. Actually, you don't dream. It's too deep for that. It's a big nothing, like being dead."

"I don't want it," Harry hears himself say sharply. He softens this to, "Not yet anyway." Charlie's word *pull* has upset him, made it too real, the physical exertion, pulling open these resistant bone gates so his spirit will fly out and men in pale-green masks will fish in this soupy red puddle with their hooks and clamps and bright knives. Once on television watching by mistake over Janice's shoulder one of these PBS programs on childbirth – they wouldn't put such raunchy stuff on the networks – he saw them start to cut open a woman's belly for a Caesarean. The knife in the rubber-gloved hand made a straight line and on either side yellow fat curled up and away like two strips of foam rubber. This woman's abdomen, with a baby inside, was lined in a *material*, just like foam rubber. "Down in Florida," he says, "I had a catheterization" – the word makes trouble in his mouth, as if he's become the waitress – "and it wasn't so bad, more boring than anything else. You're wide awake, and then they put like this big bowl over your chest to see what's going on inside. Where the dye is being pumped through, it's *hot*, so hot you can hardly stand it." He feels he's disappointing Charlie, being so cowardly about bypasses, and to deepen his contact with the frowning, chewing other man confides, "The worst thing of it, Charlie, is I feel half dead already. This waitress is the first girl I've wanted to fuck for months."

"Boobs," Charlie says. "Great boobs. On a skinny body. That's sexy. Like Bo Derek after her implant."

"Her hair is what gets me. Tall as she is, she adds six inches with that hairdo."

"Tall isn't bad. The tall ones don't get the play the cute little short ones do, and do more for you. Also, being skinny has its advantages, there's not all that fat to come between you and the clitoris."

This may be more male bonding than Rabbit needs. He says, "But all those earrings, don't they look painful? And is it true some punk girls —"

Charlie interrupts impatiently, "Pain is where it's at for punks. Mutilation, self-hatred, slam dancing. For these kids today, ugly is beautiful. That's their way of saying what a lousy world we're giving them. No more rain forests. Toxic waste. You know the drill."

"When I came back this spring, I went driving around the city, all the sections. Some of these Hispanics were practically screwing on the street."

"Drugs," Charlie says. "They don't know what they're doing four-fifths of the time."

"Did you see in the *Standard*, some spic truck driver from West Miami was caught over near Maiden Springs with they estimate seventy-five million dollars' worth of cocaine, five hundred kilos packed in orange crates marked 'Fragile'?"

"They can't stop dope," Charlie says, aligning his knife and fork on the edge of his empty plate, "as long as people are willing to pay a fortune for it."

"The guy was a Cuban refugee evidently, one of those we let in."

"These countries go Communist, they let us have all their crooks and crackpots." Charlie's tone is level and authoritative, but Harry feels he's losing him. It's not quite like the old days, when they had all day to kill, over in the showroom. Charlie has finished his Spinach and Crab and Rabbit has barely made a dent in his own heaping salad, he's so anxious to get advice. He gets a slippery forkful into his mouth and finds among the oily lettuce and alfalfa sprouts a whole macadamia nut, and delicately splits it with his teeth, so his tongue feels the texture of the fissure, miraculously smooth, like a young woman's body, like a marble tabletop.

When he swallows, he gets out, "That's the other thing preying on my mind. I think Nelson is into cocaine."

Charlie nods and says, "So I hear." He picks up the fork he's just aligned and reaches over with it toward Harry's big breast of bacon-garnished greenery. "Let me help you out with all that, champ."

"You've heard he's into cocaine?"

"Mm. Yeah. He's like his granddad, jumpy. He needs crutches. I never found the kid easy to deal with."

"Me *neither*," Harry says eagerly, and it comes tumbling out. "I went over there last week to have it out with him about cocaine, I'd just got wind of it, and he was off somewhere, he usually is, but this accountant he's hired, a guy dying of AIDS would you believe, was there and when I asked to look at the books just about gave me the up-yours sign and said I had to get Janice's say-so. And she, the dumb mutt, doesn't want to give it. I think she's scared of what she'll find out. Her own kid robbing her blind. The used sales are down, the monthly stat sheets have been looking fishy to me for months."

"You'd know. Doesn't sound good," Charlie agrees, reaching again with his fork. A macadamia nut – each one nowadays costs about a quarter – escapes in Harry's direction and only his quick reflexes prevent it from falling into his lap and staining with salad oil the russet slacks he took out of the cleaner's bag and put on for the first time today, the first spring day that's felt really warm. The sudden motion gives him a burning pang behind his rib cage. That evil child is still playing with matches in there.

He tries to ignore the pain and goes on, "And now we get these phone calls at funny hours, guys with funny voices asking for Nelson or even telling *me* they want money."

"They play rough," Charlie says. "Dope is big business." He reaches once more.

"Hey, leave me *some*thing. How do you stay so skinny? So what shall I do?"

"Maybe Janice should talk to Nelson."

"That's just what I told her."

"Well then."

"But the bitch won't. At least she hasn't so far that I know of."

"This is good," Charlie says, "this health stuff, but it's all like Chinese food, it doesn't fill you up."

"So what did you say your verdict was?"

"Sometimes, between a husband and wife, all the history gets in the way. Want me to sound old Jan-Jan out, see where's she's coming from?"

Harry hesitates hardly at all before saying, "Charlie, if you could, that would be super."

"Would you gentlemen like some dessert?"

Jennifer has materialized. Turning his head in surprise at the sound of her sweetly impeded voice, Harry sees, inches from his eyes, that Charlie as usual is right: great boobs, gawky and self-hating as the rest of her is. Her parents must have put a lot of protein, a lot of Cheerios and vitamin-enriched bread, into those boobs. In his fragile freighted mood they seem two more burdens on his brain. The stretched chest of her green jumper lifts as she takes in breath to say, "Today our special is a cheesecake made from low-fat goat's milk topped with delicious creamed gooseberries."

Rabbit, his eyebrows still raised by the waitress's breasts, looks over at Charlie. "Whaddeyou think?"

Charlie shrugs unhelpfully. "It's your funeral."

The phone is ringing, ringing, like thrilling cold water poured into the mossy warm crevices of his dream. He was dreaming of snuggling into something, of having found an aperture that just fit. The phone is on Janice's side; he gropes for it across her stubbornly sleeping body and, with a throat dry from mouthbreathing, croaks, "Hello?" The bedside clock seems to have only one hand until he figures out it's ten minutes after two. He expects one of those men's voices and tells himself they should take the phone off the hook downstairs whenever they go to bed. His heart's pounding seems to fill the dark room to its corners, suffocatingly.

A tremulous young woman's voice says, "Harry? It's Pru. Forgive me for waking you up, but I —" Shame, fear trip her voice into silence. She feels exposed.

"Yeah, go on," he urges softly.

"I'm desperate. Nelson has gone crazy, he's already hit me and I'm afraid he'll start in on the children!"

"Really?" he says stupidly. "Nelson wouldn't do that." But people do it, it's in the papers, all the time.

"Who on earth is it?" Janice asks irritably, yanked from her own dreams. "Tell them you have no money. Just hang up."

Pru is sobbing, on the end of the line, ". . . can't *stand* it any more . . . it's been such hell . . . for *years.*"

"Yeah, yeah," Harry says, still feeling stupid. "Here's Janice," he says, and passes the hot potato into her fumbling hand, out from under the covers. His sudden window into Pru, the hot bright unhappy heart of her, felt illicit. He switches on his bedside light, as if that will help clear this all up. The white jacket of the history book he is still trying to get through, with its clipper ship in an oval of cloud and sea, leaps up shiny under the pleated lampshade. Since he began reading the book last Christmas afternoon, the author herself has died, putting a kind of blight on the book. Yet he feels it would be bad luck never to finish it.

"Yes," Janice is saying into the phone, at wide intervals. "Yes. Did he really? Yes." She says, "We'll be right over. Stay away from him. What about going into Judy's room with her and locking yourselves in? Mother had a bolt put on the door, it must be still there."

Still Pru's voice crackles on, like an acid eating into the night's silence, the peace that had been in the room ten minutes before. Bits of his interrupted dream come back to him. A visit to some anticipated place, on a vehicle like a trolley car, yes, it had been an old-time trolley car, the tight weave of cane seats, he had forgotten how they looked, the way they smelled warmed by the sun, and the porcelain loops to hang from, the porcelain buttons to press, the dusty wire grates at the windows, the air and light coming in, on old-fashioned straw hats, the women with paper flowers in theirs, all heading somewhere gay, an amusement park, a fair, who was with him? There had been a companion, a date, on the seat beside him, but he can't come up with her face. The tunnel of love. The trolley car turned into something carrying them, him, into a cozy tunnel of love. It fit.

"Could the neighbors help?"

More crackling, more sobbing. Rabbit gives Janice the "cut" signal you see on TV – a finger across the throat – and gets out of bed. The aroma of his old body lifts toward him as he rests his bare feet on the carpet, a stale meaty cheesy scent. Their bedroom in the limestone house has pale-beige Antron broadloom; a houseful of unpatterned wall-to-wall seemed snug and modern to him

when they ordered it all, but in their ten years of living here certain spots – inside the front door, the hall outside the door down
to the cellar, the bedroom on either side of the bed – have collected dirt from shoes and sweat from feet and turned a gray no
rug shampoo could remove, a grimy big fingerprint your life has
left. Patterned carpets like people had when he was a boy – angular flowers and vines and mazes he would follow with his eyes until
he felt lost in a jungle – swallowed the dirt somehow, and then
the housewives up and down Jackson Road would beat it out of
them this time of year, on their back-yard clotheslines, making
little swirling clouds in the cool April air, disappearing into the
dust of the world. He collects clean underwear and socks from the
bureau and then is a bit stumped, what to wear to an assault.
Formal, or rough and ready? Harry's brain is skidding along like a
surfer on the pumping of his heart.

"Hi honey," Janice is saying in another tone, high-pitched and
grandmotherly. "Don't be scared. We all love you. Your daddy
loves you, yes he does, very much. Grandpa and I are coming right
over. You must let us get dressed now so we can do that. It'll take
just twenty minutes, honey. We'll hurry, yes. You be good till
then and do whatever your mother says." She hangs up and stares
at Harry from beneath her skimpy rumpled bangs. "My God," she
says. "He punched Pru in the face and smashed up everything in
the bathroom when he couldn't find some cocaine he thought he
hid in there that he wanted."

"He wants, he wants," Harry says.

"He told her we're all stealing from him."

"Ha," Harry says, meaning it's the reverse.

Janice says, "How can you laugh when it's your own son?"

Who is this woman, this little nut-hard woman, to chasten
him? Yet he feels chastened. He doesn't answer but instead says in
a measured, mature manner, "Well, it's probably good this is
coming to a head, if we all survive it. It gets it out in the open at
least."

She puts on what she never wears in the daylight up north, her
salmon running suit with the powder-blue sleeves and stripe. He
opts for a pair of pressed chinos fresh from the drawer and the
khaki shirt he puts on to do light yard chores, and his oldest

jacket, a green wide-wale corduroy with leather buttons: kind of a casual Saturday-afternoon look. Retirement has made them both more clothes-conscious than before; in Florida, the retirees play dress-up every day, as if they've become their own paper dolls.

They take the slate-gray Celica, the more Batmobilelike and steely car, on this desperate mission in the dead of the night. Along the stilled curving streets of Penn Park, the oaks are just budding but the maples are filling in, no longer red in tint but dense with translucent tender new leaves. The houses have an upstairs night light on here and there, or a back-porch light to keep cats and raccoons away from the garbage, but only the streetlamps compete with the moon. The trimmed large bushes of the groomed yards, the yews and arborvitae and rhododendrons, look alert by night, like jungle creatures come to the waterhole to drink and caught in a camera's flash. It seems strange to think that while we sleep these bushes are awake, exhaling oxygen, growing; they do not sleep. Stars do not sleep, but above the housetops and trees crowns shine in a cold arching dusty sprinkle. Why do we sleep? What do we rejoin? His dream, the way it fit him all around. At certain angles the lit asphalt feels in the corners of his eyes like snow. Penn Park becomes West Brewer and a car or two is still awake and moving on blanched deserted Penn Boulevard, an extension of Weiser with a supermarket parking lot on one side and on the other a low brick row of shops from the Thirties, little narrow stores selling buttons and bridal gowns and pastry and Zipf Chocolates and Sony TVs and hobby kits to make model airplanes with – they still manufacture and sell those in this era when all the kids are supposedly couch potatoes and all the planes are these wallowing wide-body jets with black noses like panda bears, not sleek killing machines like Zeros, Messerschmitts, Spitfires, Mustangs. Funny to think that with all that world-war effort manufacturers still had the O.K. to make those little models, keeping up morale in the kiddie set. All the shops are asleep. A flower shop shows a violet growing light, and a pet store a dimly lit aquarium. The cars parked along the curbs display a range of unearthly colors, no longer red and blue and cream but cindery lunar shades, like nothing you can see or even imagine by daylight.

Harry pops a nitroglycerin pill and tells Janice accusingly, "The doctors say I should avoid aggravation."

"It wasn't me who woke us up at two in the morning, it was your daughter-in-law."

"Yeah, because your precious son was beating up on her."

"According to *her*," Janice states. "We haven't heard Nelson's side of it."

The underside of his tongue burns. "What makes you think he has a side? What're you saying, you think she's lying? Why would she lie? Why would she call us up at two in the morning to lie?"

"She has her agenda, as people say. He was a good bet for her when she got herself pregnant but now that he's in a little trouble he's not such a good bet and if she's going to get herself another man she better move fast because her looks won't last forever."

He laughs, in applause. "You've got it all figured out." Discreetly, distantly, his asshole tingles, from the pill. "She *is* good-looking, isn't she? Still."

"To some men she would seem so. The kind that don't mind big tough women. What I never liked about her, though, was she makes Nelson look short."

"He *is* short," Harry says. "Beats me why. My parents were both tall. My whole family's always been tall."

Janice considers in silence her responsibility for Nelson's shortness.

There are any number of ways to get to Mt. Judge through Brewer but tonight, the streets all but deserted and the stoplights blinking yellow, he opts for the most direct, going straight over the Running Horse Bridge, that once he and Jill walked over in moonlight though not so late at night as this, straight up Weiser past the corner building that used to house JIMBO's *Friendly* LOUNGE until trouble with the police finally closed it and that now has been painted pastel condo colors and remodelled into a set of offices for yuppie lawyers and financial advisers, past Schoenbaum Funeral Directors with its stately building of white brick on the left and the shoeshine parlor that sells New York papers and hot roasted peanuts, the best peanuts in town, still selling them all those years since he was a kid not much older than Judy now. His idea then of the big time was to take the trolley around the mountain and come into downtown Brewer on a Saturday morning and buy a dime bag of peanuts still warm from the roaster and walk all around cracking them and letting the shells fall where they would, at his feet on the sidewalks of Weiser Square. Once an old bum grumbled at him for littering; even the bums had a civic conscience then. Now the old downtown is ghostly, hollow in lunar colors and closed to traffic at Fifth Street, where the little forest planted by the city planners from Atlanta to make a pedestrian mall looms with ghostly branches under the intense blue lights installed to discourage muggings and sex and drug transactions beneath these trees which grow taller every year and make the downtown gloomier. Rabbit turns left on Fifth, past the post office and the Ramada Inn that used to be the Ben Franklin with its grand ballroom, which always makes him think of Mary Ann and her crinolines and the fragrance between her legs, and over to Eisenhower Avenue, above number 1204 where Janice hid out with Charlie that time, and takes an obtuse-angled turn right, heading up through the Hispanic section, which used to be German working-class, across Winter, Spring, and Summer streets with the blinding lights and occasional moving shadow, spics out looking for some kind of a deal, the nights still a little cool to bring out all the street trash, to Locust Boulevard and the front of Brewer High School, a Latin-inscribed Depression monument, ambitious for the common good like something Communists would put up, the whole country close to Communism in the Thirties, people not so selfish then, built the year Harry was born, 1933, and going to outlast him it looks like. Of pale-yellow brick and granite quoins, it clings to the greening mountainside like a grand apparition.

"What do you think she meant," he asks Janice, " 'gone crazy'? How crazy can you go from cocaine?"

"Doris Kaufmann, I mean Eberhardt, has a brother-in-law whose stepson by his wife's first marriage had to go to a detox center out near the middle of the state. He got to be paranoid and thought Hitler was still alive and had agents everywhere to get just him. He was Jewish."

"Did he beat up his wife and children?"

"He didn't have a wife, I think. We don't know for sure Nelson's threatened the children."

"Pru said he did."

"Pru was very upset. It's the money I think upsets her, more than anything."

"It doesn't upset you?"

"Not as much as it seems to you and Pru. Money isn't something I worry about, Harry. Daddy always said, 'If I don't have two nickels to rub together, I'll rub two pennies.' He had faith he could always make enough, and he did, and I guess I inherited his philosophy."

"Is that the reason you keep letting Nelson get away with murder?"

Janice sighs and sounds more than ever like her mother, Bessie Koerner Springer, who lived her whole life overweight, without a lick of exercise except housework, sitting in her big house with its shades down to protect the curtains and upholstery from sunlight and sighing about the pains in her legs. "Harry, what can I do, seriously? It's not as if he's still a child, he's thirty-two."

"You could fire him from the lot, for starters."

"Yes, and shall I fire him as my son, too – tell him I'm sorry, but he hasn't worked out? He's my father's grandson, don't forget. Daddy built that lot up out of nothing and he would have wanted Nelson to run it, run it even if he runs it into the ground."

"Really?" Such a ruinous vision startles him. Having money makes people reckless. Bet a million. Junk bonds. "Couldn't you fire him provisionally, until he shapes up?"

Janice's tone has the bite of impatience, of fatigue. "All this is so easy for you to say – you're just sore since Lyle told you I was the real boss, you're trying to make me suffer for it. *You* do it, you do whatever you think should be done at the lot and tell them I said you should. I'm tired of it. I'm tired of you and Nelson fighting your old wars through me."

Streetlights flicker more swiftly on his hands as the Celica moves more rapidly through the city park, above the tennis courts and the World War II tank painted a thick green to forestall rust, repainted so often they've lost the exact military green Harry remembers. What did they call it? Olive drab. He feels under the barrage of streetlights bombarded, and Brewer seems empty of life like those bombed-out German cities after the war. "They wouldn't believe me," he tells her spitefully, "they'd still come to you. And I'm like you," he tells her more gently, "scared of what I'll stir up."

After the park there is a stoplight that says red, and a locally famous old turreted house roofed in round fishscale slate shingles, and then a shopping mall where the cineplex sign advertises SEE YOU DREAM TEAM SAY ANYTHING OUT OF CONTROL. Then they're on 422 and a territory bred into their bones, streets they crossed and recrossed in all seasons as children, Central, Jackson, Joseph, the hydrants and mailboxes of the borough of Mt. Judge like buttons fastening down their lives, their real lives, everything drained of color at this nadir of the night, the streets under the burning blue mercury lights looking rounded like bread-loaves and crusted with snow, the brick-pillared porches treacherous emplacements up behind their little flat laps of lawn and tulip bed. Number 89 Joseph, the Springers' big stucco house where when Rabbit was courting Janice in his old Nash he used to hate to come because it made his own family's semi-detached house on Jackson Road look poor, has all its lights ablaze, like a ship going down amid the silent darkened treetops and roof peaks of the town. The huge spreading copper-beech tree on the left side where Harry and Janice's bedroom used to be, a tree so dense the sun never shone in and its beech nuts popping kept Harry awake all fall, is gone, leaving that side bare, its windows exposed and on fire. Nelson had it cut down. *Dad, it was eating up the whole house. You couldn't keep paint on the woodwork on that side, it was so damp. The lawn wouldn't even grow.* Harry couldn't argue, and couldn't tell the boy that the sound of the rain in that great beech had been the most religious experience of his life. That, and hitting a pure golf shot.

They park outside, under the maples that are shedding chartreuse fuzz and sticky stuff this time of year. He always hates that about parking here. He'll get the car washed Monday.

Pru has been watching for their arrival. She pulls the door open as their feet hit the porch, as if there's an electric eye. Like Thelma the other week. Judy is with her, in some fuzzy Oshkosh B'Gosh pajamas that are too small for her. The child's feet look surprisingly long and white and bony, with the inches of exposed ankle.

"Where's Roy?" Harry asks instantly.

"Nelson's putting him in bed," Pru says, with a wry downward tug of one side of her mouth, a kind of apology.

"To bed?" Harry says. "You trust him with the kid?"

She says, "Oh yes. He's calmed down since I called. I think he shocked himself, hitting me so hard. It did him good." In the illumination of the front hall they can see the pink welt along one cheekbone, the lopsided puffiness of her upper lip, the redness around her eyes as if rubbed and rubbed with a scouring pad. She is wearing that quilted shorty morning-glory bathrobe but not as in Florida over bare legs; under it she has on a long blue nightgown. But you can see the outline of her legs through the thin cloth, like fish moving through murky water. Fake-fur-lined bedroom slippers clothe her feet, so he can't check out her toenail polish.

"Hey, is this some kind of false alarm?" Harry asks.

"When you see Nelson I don't think you'll think so," Pru tells him, and turns to the other woman. "Janice, I've had it. I want out. I've kept the lid on as long as I can and now I've *had* it!" And the eyes that have scoured their lids with tears begin to water again, and she embraces the older woman before Janice has quite straightened out from bending down to kiss and hug Judy hello.

Harry's guts give a tug: he can feel Pru's attempt to make a sweeping connection; he can feel his wife's resistance. Pru was raised a Catholic, showy, given to big gestures, and Janice a tight little Protestant. The embrace breaks up quickly.

Judy takes Harry's fingertips. When he stoops to peck her on the cheek, her hair gets in his eye. The little girl giggles and says in his ear, "Daddy thinks ants are crawling all over him."

"He's always feeling itchy," Pru says, sensing that her attempt to sweep Janice into her escape plan has failed, she must do some more selling of the situation. "That's the coke. They call it formication. His neurotransmitters are fucked up. Ask me anything, I know it all. I've been going to Narc-Anon in Brewer for a year now."

"Huh," Rabbit says, not quite liking her tough tone. "And what else do they tell you?"

She looks straight at him, her green eyes glaring with tears and shock, and manages that smile of hers, downtwisted at the corner.

Her upper lip being puffy gives it a sad strangeness tonight. "They tell you it's not your problem, the addicts can only do it themselves. But that still leaves it your problem."

"What happened here tonight, exactly?" he asks. He has to keep speaking up. He feels Janice pulling back, distancing herself irritatingly, like that time they took the kids to Jungle Gardens in the Camry.

Judy doesn't find her grandparents as much fun as usual and leaves Harry's side to go lean against her mother, pressing her carrot-colored head back against Pru's belly. Pru protectively encircles the child's throat with a downy freckled forearm. Now two pairs of greenish eyes stare, as if Harry and Janice are not the rescue squad but hostile invaders.

Pru's voice sounds tough and weary. "The usual sort of garbage. He came home after one and I asked him where he'd been and he told me none of my business and I guess I didn't take it as docilely as usual because he said if I was going to be that way he needed a hit to calm his nerves, and when the coke wasn't in the bathroom where he thought he hid it in an aspirin bottle he smashed things up and when I didn't like that he came out after me and started slugging me all over the place."

Judy says, "It woke me up. Mommy came into my room to get away and Daddy's face was all funny, like he wasn't really seeing anything."

Harry asks, "Did he have a knife or anything?"

Pru's eyebrows knit crossly at the suggestion. "Nelson would never go for a knife. He can't stand blood and never helps in the kitchen. He wouldn't know which end of a knife to use."

Judy says, "He said he was real sorry afterwards."

Pru has been smoothing Judy's long red hair back from her face and now, just the middle fingers touching her forehead and cheeks, tucks back her own. She has outgrown the Sphinx look; it hangs limp to her shoulders. "He calmed down after I called you. He said, 'You called them? I can't believe it. You called my parents?' It was like he was too stunned to be angry. He kept saying this is the end and how sorry he was for everything. He makes no sense." She grimaces and lightly pushes Judy away from her body and tightens the robe around her middle, with a shiver. For a second they all seem to have forgotten their lines. In crises there is something in our instincts which whittles, which tries to reduce the unignorable event back to the ignorable normal. "I could use a cup of coffee," Pru says.

Janice asks, "Shouldn't we go upstairs to Nelson first?"

Judy likes this idea and leads the way upstairs. Following her milky bare feet up the stair treads, Harry feels guilty that his granddaughter has to wear outgrown pajamas while all those Florida acquaintances of theirs have different-colored slacks for every day of the week and twenty sports coats hanging in cleaner's bags. The house, which he remembers from way back in the days of the Springers, when they were younger than he is now, seems rather pathetically furnished, now that he looks, in remnants from the old days, including the battered old brown Barcalounger that used to be Fred Springer's throne, along with nondescript newer stuff from Schaechner's or one of the shabby furniture places that have sprung up along the highways leading out of the city, mingled among the car lots and fast-food joints. The stairs still have the threadbare Turkish runner the Springers had tacked down forty years ago. The house has descended to Nelson and Pru in stages and they never really have taken it on as their own. You try to do something nice for kids, offer them a shortcut in life, a little padding, and it turns out to be the wrong thing, undermining them. This was no house for a young couple.

All the lights being turned on gives the house a panicky overheated air. They ascend the stairs in the order Judy, Harry, Janice, and Pru, who maybe regrets having called them by now and would rather be nursing her face and planning her next move in solitude. Nelson greets them in the hallway, carrying Roy in his arms. "Oh," he says, seeing his father, "the big cheese is here."

"Don't mouth off at me," Harry tells him. "I'd rather be home in bed."

"It wasn't my idea to call you."

"It was your idea though to go beating up your wife, and scaring the hell out of your kids, and otherwise acting like a shit." Harry fishes in the side pocket of his chinos to make sure the little vial of heart pills is there. Nelson is trying to play it cool, still wearing the black slacks and white shirt he was out on the town in, and having the kid on his arm, but his thinning hair is bristling out from his head and his eyes in the harsh hallway light are frantic, full of reflected sparks like that time outside the burning house at 26 Vista Crescent. Even in the bright light his pupils look dilated and shiny-black and there is a tremor to him, a shiver now and then as if this night nearly in May is icy cold. He looks even thinner than in Florida, with that same unpleasant sore-looking nose above the little half-ass blur of a mustache. And that earring yet.

"Who are you to go around deciding who's acting like a shit?" he asks Harry, adding, "Hi, Mom. Welcome home."

"Nelson, this just won't do."

"Let me take Roy," Pru says in a cool neutral voice, and she pushes past the elder Angstroms and without looking her husband in the face plucks the sleepy child from him. Involuntarily she grunts with the weight. The hall light, with its glass shade faceted like a candy dish, crowns her head with sheen as she passes under it, into Roy's room, which was Nelson's boyhood room in the old days, when Rabbit would lie awake hearing Melanie creep along the hall to this room from her own, the little room at the front of the house with the dress dummy. Now she's some gastroenterologist. In the harsh overhead light, Nelson's face, white around the gills, shows an electric misery and a hostile cockiness, and Janice's a dark confused something, a retreat into the shadows of her mind; her capacity for confusion has always frightened Harry. He realizes he is still in charge. Little Judy looks up at him brightly, titillated by being awake and a witness to these adult transactions. "We can't just stand here in the hall," he says. "How about the big bedroom?"

Harry and Janice's old bedroom has become Nelson and Pru's. A different bedspread – their old Pennsylvania Dutch quilt of little triangular patches has given way to a puff patterned with yellow roses, Pru does like flowered fabrics – but the same creaky bed, with the varnished knobbed headboard that never hit your back quite right when you tried to read. Different magazines on the bedside tables – *Racing Cars* and *Rolling Stone* instead of *Time* and *Consumer Reports* – but the same cherry table on Harry's old side, with its sticky drawer. Among the propped-up photographs on the bureau is one of him and Janice, misty-eyed and lightly tinted, taken on their twenty-fifth wedding anniversary in March of 1981. They look embalmed, Rabbit thinks, suspended in that tinted bubble of time. The ceiling light in this room, glass like the hall light, is also burning. He asks, "Mind if I switch that off? All these lights on, I'm getting a headache."

Nelson says sourly, "You're the big cheese. Help yourself."

Judy explains, "Mommy said to turn them all on while Daddy was chasing her. She said if it got worse I should throw a chair through a front window and yell for help and the police would hear."

With the light switched off, Rabbit can see out into the dark gulf of air where the copper beech used to be. The neighbor's house is closer than he ever thought, in his ten years of living here. Their upstairs lights are on. He can see segments of wall and furniture but no people. Maybe they were thinking of calling the police. Maybe they already have. He switches on the lamp on the cherry table, so the neighbors can look in and see that everything is under control.

"She overreacted," Nelson explains, fitfully gesturing. "I was trying to make a point and Pru wouldn't hold still. She never listens to me any more."

"Maybe you don't say enough she wants to hear," Harry tells his son. The kid in his white shirt and dark trousers looks like a magician's assistant, and keeps tapping himself on the chest and back of the neck and rubbing his arms through the white cloth as if he's about to do a trick. The boy is embarrassed and scared but keeps losing focus, Rabbit feels; there are other presences for him in the room besides the bed and furniture and his parents and daughter, a mob of ghosts which only he can see. A smell comes off him, liquor and a kind of post-electrical ozone. He is sweating; his gills are wet.

"O.K., O.K.," Nelson says. "I treated myself to a bender tonight, I admit it. It's been a helluva week at the lot. California wants to have this nationwide Toyotathon to go with a TV-commercial blitz and they expect to see a twenty-per-cent increase of new sales to go with the discounts they're offering. They let me know they haven't been liking our figures lately."

"Them and who else?" Harry says. "Did your buddy Lyle tell ya I was over there the other day?"

"Snooping around last week, yeah, he sure did. He hasn't come to work since. Thanks a bunch. You put Elvira into a snit, too, with all your sexist flirtatious stuff."

"I wasn't sexist, I wasn't flirtatious. I was just surprised to see a woman selling cars and asked her how it was going. The cunt, I was just as pleasant as I could be."

"She didn't think so."

"Well screw her, then. From my look at her she can take care of herself. What's your big huff for – you boffing her?"

"Dad, when are you going to get your mind off boffing? You're what, fifty-seven? –"

"Fifty-six."

"– and you're so damn adolescent. There's more things in the world than who's boffing who."

"Tell me about it. Tell me about how the me generation has a bender. You can't keep snorting this stuff every half-hour to keep high, your nose'd burn out. Yours looks sort of shot already. What do you do with crack? How do you take it in? It's just little crystals, isn't it? Do you need all that fancy burning stuff and tubes they show on TV? Where do you do it, then? You can't just haul all that paraphernalia into the Laid–Back or whatever they call it now, or can you?"

"Harry, please," Janice says.

Judy contributes, bright–eyed at three in the morning, "Daddy has lots of funny little pipes."

"Shut up honey, would you mind?" Nelson says. "Go find Mommy and she'll put you to bed."

Harry turns on Janice. "Let me *ask* him. Why should we all go around on tiptoe forever pretending the kid's not a hophead? Face it, Nellie, you're a mess. You're a mess and you're a menace. You need help."

Self-pity focuses the boy's features for a second. "People keep telling me I need help but *they're* no help is what I notice. A wife who doesn't give me shit, a father who's no kind of father at all and never was, a mother ..." He trails off, not daring offend his one ally.

"A mother," Harry finishes for him, "who's letting you rob her blind."

This gets to him a little, burns through the jittery buzz in his eyes. "I'm not robbing anybody," he says, numbly, as though a voice in his head told him to say it. "Everything's been worked out. Hey, I feel sick. I think I have to throw up."

Harry raises his hand in lofty blessing. "Go to it. You know where the bathroom is."

The bathroom door is to the right of the dresser with the color snapshots of the kids at various stages of growing and the tinted one of Harry and Janice looking embalmed, mistily staring at the same point in space. Looking in, Harry sees all sorts of litter on the floor. Prell, Crest, pills. Luckily most things come in plastic containers these days so there isn't much breakage. The door closes.

Janice tells him, "Harry, you're coming on too strong."

"Well, hell, nobody else is coming on at all. You expect it to go away by itself. It won't. The kid is hooked."

"Let's just not talk about the money," she begs.

"Why not? Just what is so fucking sacred about money, that everybody's scared to talk about it?"

The tip of her tongue peeks from between her worried lips. "With money you get into legal things."

Judy is still with them and has been listening: her clear young eyes with their bluish whites, her reddish-blonde eyebrows with their little cowlick, her little face pale as a clock's face and as precise pluck at Harry's anger, undermine his necessary indignation. Retching noises from behind the bathroom door now frighten her. Harry explains, "It'll make your daddy feel better. He's getting rid of poison." But the thought of Nelson being sick upsets him too, and those bands of constriction around his chest, the playful malevolent singeing deep within, reassert their threat. He fishes in his pants pocket for the precious brown vial. Thank God he remembered to bring it. He unscrews the top and shakes out a small white Nitrostat and places it, as debonairly as he used to light a cigarette, beneath his tongue.

Judy smiles upward. "Those pills fix that bad heart I gave you."

"You didn't give me my bad heart, honey, I wish you'd get that out of your mind." He is bothered by Janice's remark about money and legal things and the implication that they are getting in over their heads. ANGSTROM, SON INCARCERATED. *Joint Scam*

Sinks Family Concern. The lights in the neighbor's upstairs windows have gone off and that relieves some pressure. He could feel Ma Springer turning in her grave at the possibility that her old house has become a bother to the neighborhood. Nelson comes out of the bathroom looking shaken, wide-eyed. The poor kid has seen some terrible things in his day: Jill's body carried from the burned-out house in a rubber bag, his mother hugging the little dead body of his baby sister. You can't really blame him for anything. He has washed his face and combed his hair so his pallor has this gleam. He lets a shudder run from his head down into his body, like a dog shaking itself dry after running in a ditch.

For all his merciful thoughts Harry goes back on the attack. "Yeah," he says, even as the kid is closing the bathroom door, "and another new development over there I wasn't crazy about is this fat Italian you've hired. What are you letting the Mafia into the lot for?"

"Dad, you are incredibly prejudiced."

"I don't have prejudices, just facts. The Mafia is a fact. It's being scared out of the drug trade, too violent, and is getting into more and more legitimate businesses. It was all on *60 Minutes.*"

"Mom, get him off me."

Janice gets up her courage and says, "Nelson, your father's right. You need some help."

"I'm fine," he whines. "I need some *sleep,* is what I need. You have any idea what time it is? – it's after three. Judy, you should go back to bed."

"I'm too wired," the child says, smiling, showing her perfect oval teeth.

Harry asks her, "Where'd you learn that word?"

"I'm too jazzed," she says. "Kids at school say that."

Harry asks Nelson, "And who're these guys keep calling our house at all hours asking for money?"

"They think I owe them money," Nelson answers. "Maybe I do. It's temporary, Dad. It'll all work out. Come, Judy. I'll put you to bed."

"Not so fast," Harry says. "How much do you owe, and how're you going to pay 'em?"

"Like I said, I'll work it out. They shouldn't be calling your number, but they're crude guys. They don't understand term

financing. Go back to Florida if you don't like your phone ringing. Change your number, that's what I did."

"Nelson, when will it end?" Janice asks, tears making her voice
crack, just from looking at him. In his white shirt with his electric
movements Nelson has the frailty and doomed alertness of a cor-
nered animal. "You must get off this stuff."

"I am, Mom. I am off. Starting tonight."

"Ha," Harry says.

Nelson insists to her, "I can handle it. I'm no addict. I'm a
recreational user."

"Yeah," Harry says, "like Hitler was a recreational killer." It
must be the mustache made him think of Hitler. If the kid would
just shave it off, and chuck the earring, he maybe could feel some
compassion, and they could make a fresh start.

But, then, Harry thinks, how many fresh starts for him are left?
This room, where he spent ten years sleeping beside Janice, listening to her snore, smelling her nice little womanly sweat, her
unconscious releases of gas, making some great love sometimes,
that time with the Krugerrands, and other times disgustedly
watching her stumble in tipsy from a night downstairs sipping
sherry or Campari, this room with the copper beech outside the
window leafing in and changing the light and then losing its leaves
and giving the light back and the beech nuts popping like little
firecrackers and Ma Springer's television mumbling on and making the bedside lamp vibrate when a certain pitch was reached on
the program-ending surge of music, Ma sound asleep and never
hearing it, this room soaked in his life, how many more times will
he see it? He hadn't expected to see it tonight. Now all at once,
as happens at his age, fatigue like an inner overflowing makes him
feel soggy, dirty, distracted. Little sparks are going off and on in
the corners of his eyes. Avoid aggravation. He'd better sit down.
Janice has sat down on the bed, their old bed, and Nelson has
pulled up the padded stool patterned with yellow roses Pru must
use to perch on in her underwear when she sits putting on makeup at her dresser mirror before going out with him to the Laid-
Back or some yuppie buddies' party in northeast Brewer. How
sorry is he supposed to feel for his son when the kid has a big tall
hippy dish like that to boff?

Nelson has changed his tune. He leans toward his mother, his fingers intertwined to still their shaking, his lips tensed to bite back his nausea, his dark eyes full of an overflowing confusion like her own. He is pleadingly, disjointedly, explaining himself: ". . . the only time I feel *hu*man, like other people I guess feel all the time. But when I went after Pru that way tonight it was like a monster or something had taken over my body and I was standing outside watching and felt no connection with myself. Like it was all on television. You're right, I got to ease off. I mean, it's getting so I can't start the day without . . . a hit . . . and all day all I think about . . . That's not human either."

"You poor baby," she says. "I know. I know just what you're saying. It's lack of self-esteem. I had it for years. Remember, Harry, how I used to drink when we were young?"

Trying to pull him into it, make him a parent too. He won't have it, yet. He won't buy in. "When we were young? How about when we were middle-aged, like now even? Hey look, what's this supposed to be, a therapy session? This kid just clobbered his wife and is conning the pants off us and you're *let*ting him!"

Judy, lying diagonally on the bed behind her grandmother, and studying them all with upside-down eyes, joins in, observing, "When Grandpa gets mad his upper lip goes all stiff just like Mommy's does."

Nelson comes out of his fog of self-pity enough to say to her, "Honey, I'm not sure you should be hearing all this."

"Let me put her back to bed," Janice offers, not moving though.

Harry doesn't want to be left alone with Nelson. He says, "No, I'll do it. You two keep talking. Hash it out. I've had my say to this jailbait."

Judy laughs shrilly, her head still upside down on the bed, her reversed eyelids monstrous. "That's a funny word," her mouth says, the teeth all wrong, big on bottom and little on top. " 'Jailbait.' You mean 'jailbird.' "

"No, Judy," Harry tells her, taking her hand and trying to pull her upright. "first you're jailbait, then you're a jailbird. When you're in jail, you're a jailbird."

"Where the holy fuck is her mother?" Nelson asks the air in front of his face. "That damn Pru, she's always telling me what a jerk I am, then she's out to lunch half the time herself. Notice how broad in the beam she's getting? That's alcohol. The kids come home from school and find her sound asleep." He says this to Janice, placating her, badmouthing his wife to his mother, then suddenly turns to Harry.

"Dad," he says. "Want to split a beer?"

"You must be crazy."

"It'll help bring us down," the boy wheedles. "It'll help us to sleep."

"I'm fighting sleep; Jesus. It's not *me* who's wired or whatever you call it. Come on, Judy. Don't give Grandpa a hard time. He hurts all over." The child's hand seems damp and sticky in his, and she makes a game of his pulling her off the bed, resisting to the point that he feels a squeeze in his chest. And when he gets her upright beside the bed, she goes limp and tries to collapse onto the rug. He holds on and resists the impulse to slap her. To Janice he says sharply, "Ten more minutes. You and the kid talk. Don't let him con you. Set up some kind of plan. We got to get some order going in this crazy family."

As he pulls the bedroom door halfway shut, he hears Nelson say, "Mom, how about you? Wouldn't half a beer be good? We have Mick, and Miller's."

Judy's room, wherein Ma Springer used to doze and pretend to watch television, and from whose front windows you can see patches of Joseph Street, deserted like tundra, blanched by the streetlights, through the sticky Norway maples, is crowded with stuffed toys, teddy bears and giraffes and Garfields; but Harry feels they are all old toys, that nobody has brought this child a present for some time. Her childhood is wearing out before she is done with it. She turned nine in January and who noticed? Janice sent her a Dr. Seuss book and a flowered bathing cap from Florida. Judy crawls without hesitation or any more stalling into her bed, under a tattered red puff covered with Peanuts characters. He asks her if she doesn't need to go pee-pee first. She shakes her head and stares up at him from the pillow as if amused by how little he knows about her insides. Slant slices of streetlight enter around the window shades and he asks her if she would like him to draw the curtains. Judy says No, she doesn't like it totally dark. He asks her if the cars going by bother her and she says No, only the big trucks that shake the house sometimes and there's a law that says they shouldn't come this way but the police are too lazy to enforce it. "Or too busy," he points out, always one to defend the authorities. Strange that he should have this instinct, since in his life he hasn't been especially dutiful. Jailbait himself on a couple of occasions. But the authorities these days seem so helpless, so unarmed. He asks Judy if she wants to say a prayer. She says No thanks. She is clutching some stuffed animal that looks shapeless to him, without arms or legs. Monstrous. He asks her about it and she shows him that it is a stuffed toy dolphin, with gray back and white belly. He pats its polyester fur and tucks it back under the covers with her. Her chin rests on the white profile of Snoopy wearing his aviator glasses. Linus clutches his blanket; Pigpen has little stars of dirt around his head; Charlie Brown is on his pitcher's mound, and then is knocked head over heels by a rocketing ball. Sitting on the edge of the bed, wondering if Judy expects a bedtime story, Harry sighs so abjectly, so wearily, that both are surprised, and nervously laugh. She suddenly asks him if everything will be all right.

"How do you mean, honey?"

"With Mommy and Daddy."

"Sure. They love you and Roy, and they love each other."

"They say they don't. They fight."

"A lot of married people fight."

"My friends' parents don't."

"I bet they do, but you don't see it. They're being good because you're in the house."

"When people fight a lot, they get divorced."

"Yes, that happens. But only after a *lot* of fighting. Has your daddy ever hit your mommy before, like tonight?"

"Sometimes she hits him. She says he's wasting all our money."

Harry has no ready answer to that. "It'll work out," he says, just as Nelson has. "Things work out, usually. It doesn't always seem that way, but they usually do."

"Like you that time you fell on the sand and couldn't get up."

"Wasn't that a funny way to act? Yes, and see, here I am, as good as new. It worked out."

Her face broadens in the dark; she is smiling. Her hair is spread in dark rays across the glowing pillow. "You were so funny in the water. I teased you."

"You teased me how?"

"By hiding under the sail."

He casts his weary mind back and tells her, "You weren't teasing, honey. You were all blue and gaspy when I got you out. I saved your life. Then you saved mine."

She says nothing. The dark pits of her eyes absorb his version, his adult memory. He leans down and kisses her warm dry forehead. "Don't you worry about anything, Judy. Grandma and I will take good care of your daddy and all of you."

"I know," she says after a pause, letting go. We are each of us like our little blue planet, hung in black space, upheld by nothing but our mutual reassurances, our loving lies.

Emerging opposite to the closed door of the old sewing room, where Melanie used to sleep, Rabbit sneaks down the hall past the half-closed door to the master bedroom – he can hear Janice and Nelson talking, their voices braided into one – and to the room beyond, a back room with a view of the back yard and the little fenced garden he used to tend. This was Nelson's room in the distant days when he went to high school and wore long hair and a headband like an Indian and tried to learn the guitar that had been Jill's and spent a small fortune on his collection of rock LPs, records all obsolete now, everything is tapes, and tapes are becoming obsolete, everything will be CDs. This room is now little Roy's. Its door is ajar; with three fingertips on its cool white wood Harry pushes it open. Light enters it not as sharp slices from the proximate streetlights above Joseph Street but more mistily, from the lights of the town diffused and scattered, a yellow star-swallowing glow arising foglike from the silhouettes of maples and gables and telephone poles. By this dim light he sees Pru's long body pathetically asleep across Roy's little bed. One foot has kicked off its fake-furry slipper and sticks out bare from its nightie, so filmy it clings to the shape of her bent full-thighed leg, her short quilted robe ruched up to her waist, rumpled in folds whose valleys seem bottomless in the faint light. One long white hand of hers rests extended on the rumpled covers, the other is curled in a loose fist and fitted into the hollow between her lips and chin; the bruise on her cheekbone shows like a leech attached there and her hair, its carrot-color black in the dark, is disarrayed. Her breath moves in and out with a shallow exhausted rasp. He inhales through his nose, to smell her. Perfumy traces float in her injured aura.

As he bends over for this inspection, Rabbit is startled by the twin hard gleam of open eyes: Roy is awake. Cuddled on his bed by his mother, sung a song that has put the singer to sleep, the strange staring child reaches up through the darkness to seize the loose skin of his grandfather's looming face and to twist it, his small sharp fingernails digging in so that Harry has to fight crying out. He pulls this fierce little crab of a hand away from his cheek, disembeds it finger by finger, and with a vengeful pinch settles it back onto Roy's chest. In his animal hurt Harry has hissed aloud; seeing Pru stir as if to awake, her hand making an agitated motion toward her tangled hair, he backs rapidly from the room.

Janice and Nelson are in the bright hall looking for him. With their thinning hair and muddled scowling expressions they seem siblings. He tells them in a whisper, "Pru fell asleep on Roy's bed."

Nelson says, "That poor bitch. She'd be O.K. if she'd just get off my case."

Janice tells Harry, "Nelson says he feels much more like himself now and we should go home to bed."

Their voices seem loud, after the foglit silence of Roy's room, and he pointedly keeps his own low. "What have you two settled? I don't want this to happen again."

In Nelson's old room, Roy has begun to cry. *He* should cry; it's Harry's cheek that hurts.

"It won't, Harry," Janice says. "Nelson has promised to see a counsellor."

He looks at his son to see what this means. The boy visibly suppresses a smile of collusion, over the necessity of placating women. Harry tells Janice, "I *said*, Don't let him con ya."

Her forehead, which her bangs do not cover, creases in impatience. "Harry, it's time to go." She is, as Lyle informed him, the boss.

On the drive back, he vents his indignation. "What did he say? What about the money?" Route 422 shudders with tall trucks, transcontinental eighteen-wheelers. They make better time in the dead of the night.

Janice says, "He's running the lot and it would be too unmanning to take it from him. I can't run it and you're going into the hospital for that angio-thing. Plasty."

"Not till the week after next," he says. "We could always put it off."

"I know that's what you'd like but we just can't go on pretending you're fine. It's been nearly four months since New Year's and in Florida they said you should recover enough in three. Dr. Breit told me you're not losing weight and avoiding sodium the way you were told and you could have a recurrence of what happened on the Sunfish any time."

Dr. Breit is his cardiologist at the St. Joseph's Hospital in Brewer — a fresh-faced freckled kid with big glasses in flesh-colored plastic rims. Janice's telling him all this in her mother's matter-of-fact, determined voice carves a dreadful hollowness within him. The sloping park as they cruise through on Cityview Drive seems fragile and papery, the illuminated trees unreal. There is nothing beneath these rocks, these steep lawns and proud row houses, but atoms and nothingness, waiting for him to take his tight-fitting place among them. *Dear God, reach down. Pull my bad heart out of me.* Thelma said it helped. Janice's mind, far from prayer, is moving on, her voice decided and a bit defiant. "As for the money, Nelson did allow as there has to be some financial restructuring."

"Restructuring! That's what everybody up the creek talks about. South American countries, those Texas S and Ls. Did he really say 'restructuring'?"

"Well, it's not a word *I* would have thought to use. Though I expect when I start with my courses it'll be one of the things they teach."

"Your courses, Jesus," he says. That tank, painted the wrong green, how much longer before nobody remembered why it was there — the ration stamps, the air-raid drills, the screaming eight-column headlines every morning, God versus Satan a simple matter of the miles gained each day on the road to Aachen? "What did he say about himself and Pru?"

"He doesn't think she's found another man yet," Janice says. "So we don't think she'll really leave."

"Well, that's nice and hard-boiled of you both. But what about *her*, her own welfare? You saw her battered face tonight. How much more should she take? Face it, the kid is utterly gonzo. Do you see the way he was twitching all the time? And throwing up then? Did you hear him offer me a beer? A beer, for Chrissake, when we should have been the cops really. He's damn lucky the neighbors didn't call 'em."

"He was just trying to be hospitable. It's a great trial to him, Harry, that you're so unsympathetic."

"Unsympathetic! What's to be sympathetic with? He cheats, he snivels, he snorts or whatever, he's a lush besides, over at the lot he hires these gangsters and guys with AIDS —"

"Really, you should hear yourself. I wish I had a tape recorder."

"So do I. Tape me; I'm talking truth. So what's he going to do about the dope?" Even at this hour, going on four, a few men in sneakers and jeans are awake in the park, conferring behind trees, waiting on benches. "Did he promise to give it up?"

"He promised to see a counsellor," Janice says. "He admits he might have a problem. I think that's a good night's work. Pru has all sorts of names and agencies from these Narc-Anon meetings she's been going to."

"Names, agencies, we can't expect society to run our lives for us, to baby us from cradle to grave. That's what the Communists try to do. There comes a point when you got to take responsibility." He fingers his pants pocket to make sure the little hard cylindrical bottle is there. He won't take a pill now, but save it for when they get home. With a small glass of milk in the kitchen. And a Nutter-Butter cookie to dip into the milk. Shaped like a big peanut, a Nutter-Butter is delicious dipped into milk, first up to the peanut waist, and then the rest for a second bite.

Janice says, "I wish my parents were still alive to hear you talk about responsibility. My mother thought you were the most irresponsible person she ever met."

This hurts, slightly. He had liked Ma Springer toward the end, and thought she liked him. Hot nights out on the screened porch, pinochle games up in the Poconos. They both found Janice a bit slow.

Out of the park, he heads the slate-gray Celica down Weiser, through the heart of Brewer. The Sunflower Beer clock says 3:50, above the great deserted city heart. Something cleansing about being awake at this forsaken hour. It's a new world. A living, crouching shadow – a cat, or can it be a raccoon? – stares with eyes like circular reflectors in his headlights, sitting on the cement stairs of a dry fountain there on the edge of the little woods the city planners have created. At the intersection of Weiser and Sixth, Rabbit has to turn right. In the old days you could drive straight to the bridge. The wild kids in high school liked to drive down the trolley tracks, between the islands where passengers would board.

As his silence lengthens, Janice says placatingly, "Weren't those children dear? Harry, you don't want them to live in one of those sad one-parent households."

Rabbit has always been squeamish about things being put into him – dental drills, tongue depressors, little long knives to clean out earwax, suppositories, the doctor's finger when once a year he sizes up your prostate gland. So the idea of a catheter being inserted at the top of his right leg, and being pushed along steered with a little flexible tip like some eyeless worm you find wriggling out of an apple where you just bit, is deeply repugnant to him, though not as much so as being frozen half to death and sawed open and your blood run through some complicated machine while they sew a slippery warm piece of your leg vein to the surface of your trembling poor cowering heart.

In the hospital in Deleon they gave him some articles to try to read and even showed him a little video: the heart sits in a protective sac, the pericardium, which has to be cut open, *snipped* the video said cheerfully like it was giving a sewing lesson. It showed it happening: cold narrow scalpels attack the shapeless bloody blob as it lies there in your chest like a live thing in a hot puddle, a cauldron of tangled juicy stew, convulsing, shuddering with a periodic sob, trying to dodge the knives, undressed of the sanitary pod God or whoever never meant human hands to touch. Then when the blood has been detoured to the gleaming pumping machine just like those in those horrible old Frankenstein movies with Boris Karloff the heart stops beating. You see it happen: your heart lies there dead in its soupy puddle. You, the natural you, are technically dead. A machine is living for you while the surgeons' hands in their condomlike latex gloves fiddle and slice and knit away. Harry has trouble believing how his life is tied to all this mechanics – that the *me* that talks inside him all the time scuttles like a water-striding bug above this pond of body fluids and their slippery conduits. How could the flame of him ever have ignited out of such wet straw?

The angioplasty seemed far less deep a violation than the coronary bypass. It was scheduled for a Friday. Youngish-old Dr. Breit, with his painfully fair skin and his plastic-rimmed glasses too big for his button nose, explained the operation – the procedure, he preferred to call it – in the lulling voice of a nightclub singer who has done the same lyrics so often her mind is free to wander as she sings. The cardiologist's real preference was the bypass, Harry could tell. The angioplasty to Breit was just a sop, kid stuff, until the knives could descend. "The rate of restenosis is thirty per cent in three months' time," he warned Harry, there in his office with the framed color photos of a little pale woman who resembled him as one hamster resembles another and of little children arranged in front of their parents like a small stepladder, all with curly fair hair and squints and those tiny pink noses, "and twenty per cent of PTCA patients wind up having a CABG eventually anyway. Sorry – that's percutaneous transluminal coronary angioplasty versus coronary artery bypass graft."

"I guessed," Harry said. "Still, let's do the balloon first, and save the knives for later." A lot later, he thinks to himself.

"Fair enough," said Dr. Breit, semi-singingly, his tone clipped and grim and even-tempered and resigned. Like a golfer: you lose this match but you'll play again next week. "You think the way ninety per cent of all heart patients do. They love the idea of the

PTCA, and no heart specialist can talk them out of it. It's irrational, but so's the human species. Tell you what, Harold." No one had told him Harry was never called Harold, though that was his legal name. Rabbit let it go; it made him feel a child again. His mother used to call him Hassy. "We'll give you a treat. You can watch the whole procedure on TV. You'll be under local anesthetic, it'll help you pass the time."

"Do I have to?"

Dr. Breit seemed momentarily bothered. For so fair a man, he sweated a great deal, his upper lip always dewy. "We screen off the monitor usually, for the patients we think are too excitable or frail. There's always a slight chance of a coronary occlusion and that wouldn't be too good, to be watching it happen. But you, you're not frail. You're no nervous nelly. I've sized you up as a pretty tough-minded guy, Harold, with a fair amount of intellectual curiosity. Was I wrong?"

It was like a ten-dollar press, when you're already thirty dollars down. You can't refuse. "No," he told the young doctor. "That's me all right."

Dr. Breit actually does not perform the procedure: it needs a specialist, a burly menacing man with thick brown forearms, Dr. Raymond. But Breit is there, his face peeping like a moon – big specs glinting, upper lip dewy with nervous perspiration – over the mountainous lime-green shoulders of Dr. Raymond and the surgical caps of the nurses. The operation takes two attending nurses; this is no little "procedure"; Harry's been sandbagged. And it takes two rooms of the hospital, the room where it happens and a monitoring room with several TV screens that translate him into jerking bright lines, vital signs: the Rabbit Angstrom Show, with a fluctuating audience as the circulating nurse and Dr. Breit and some others never named to him, lime-green extras, come and watch a while and leave again. There is even, he has been casually told, a surgical team standing by just in case he needs immediate bypass surgery.

Another double-cross: they shave him, down beside his privates, without warning, where the catheter will go in. They give him a pill to make him light in the head and then when he's helpless on the operating table under all these lights they scrape away at the right half of his groin area and pubic bush; he's never had much body hair and wonders if at his age it will ever grow back. The needle that comes next feels bigger and meaner than the Novocain needle the dentist uses; its "pinch" – Dr. Raymond murmurs, "Now you'll feel a pinch" – doesn't let go as quickly. But then there's no pain, just an agony of mounting urinary pressure as the dyes build up in his system, injected repeatedly with a hot surge like his chest is being cooked in a microwave. Jesus. He closes his eyes a few times to pray but it feels like a wrong occasion, there is too much crowding in, of the actual material world. No old wispy Biblical God would dare interfere. The one religious consolation he clings to through his three-and-a-half-hour ordeal is a belief that Dr. Raymond, with his desert tan and long melancholy nose and bearish pack of fat across his shoulders, is Jewish: Harry has this gentile prejudice that Jews do everything a little better than other people, something about all those generations crouched over the Torah and watch-repair tables, they aren't as distracted as other persuasions, they don't expect to have as much fun. They stay off booze and dope and have a weakness only (if that history of Hollywood he once read can be trusted) for broads.

The doctors and their satellites murmurously crouch over Harry's sheeted, strategically exposed body, under a sharp light, in a room whose tiles are the color of Russian salad dressing, on the fourth floor of St. Joseph's Hospital, where decades ago his two children were born – Nelson, who lived, and Rebecca, who died. In those years nuns ran the place, with their black and white and cupcake frills around their pasty faces, but now nuns have blended into everybody else or else faded away. Vocations drying up, nobody wants to be selfless any more, everybody wants their fun. No more nuns, no more rabbis. No more good people, waiting to have their fun in the afterlife. The thing about the afterlife, it kept this life within bounds somehow, like the Russians. Now there's just Japan, and technology, and the profit motive, and getting all you can while you can.

Turning his head to the left, Rabbit can see, over the shoulders that crowd around his body like green cotton tummocks, the shadow of his heart on an X-ray monitor screen, a twitching pale-gray ghost dimly webbed by its chambered structure and darkened

in snaky streaks and bulbous oblongs by injections of the opacify-
ing dye. The thin wire tip of the catheter, inquisitive in obedience
to Dr. Raymond's finger on the trigger, noses forward and then
slowly eels, in little cautious jerking stabs, diagonally down into a
milky speckled passageway, a river or tentacle within him, organic
and tentative in shape where the catheter is black and positive,
hard-edged as a gun. Harry watches to see if his heart will gag and
try to disgorge the intruder. Like a finger down his throat, he
thinks, feeling a wave of nausea and yet a test pilot's detachment
from this picture on the screen, blanched and hard to read like a
section of aerial map, and these conferring voices around him.
"We're home," Dr. Breit murmurs, as if not to awaken something. "That's your LAD, your left anterior descending. The
widow-maker, they call it. By far the most common site of lesions.
See how stenotic those walls are? How thickened with plaque?
Those little agglutinated specks – that's plaque. I'd say your lumi-
nal narrowing is close to eighty-five per cent."

"Rice Krispies," Harry tries to say, but his mouth is too dry,
his voice cracks. All he wanted was to acknowledge that yes, he
sees it all, he sees his tangled shadowy self laid out like a diagram,
he sees the offending plaque, like X-rayed Rice Krispies. He nods
a little, feeling even more gingerly than when getting a haircut or
having his prostate explored. Too vigorous a nod, and his heart
might start to gag. He wonders, is this what having a baby is like,
having Dr. Raymond inside you? How do women stand it, for
nine months? Not to mention being screwed in the first place?
Can they really like it? Or queers being buggered? It's something
you never see really discussed, even on Oprah.

"Now comes the tricky part," Dr. Breit breathes, like a golf
commentator into the mike as a crucial putt is addressed. Harry
feels and then sees on the monitor his heart beat faster, twist as if
to escape, twist in that convulsive spiral motion Dr. Olman in
Florida demonstrated with his fist; the shadowy fist is angry, again
and again, seventy times a minute; the anger is his life, his soul,
mind over matter, electricity over muscle. The mechanically precise dark ghost of the catheter is the worm of death within him.
Godless technology is fucking the pulsing wet tubes we inherited
from the squid, the boneless sea-cunts. He feels again that feath-

ery touch of nausea. Can he possibly throw up? It would jar and jam the works, disrupt the concentrating green tummocks he is buried beneath. He mustn't. He must be still.

He sees, on the monitor, behind the inquisitive tip, a segment of the worm thicken and swell, pressing the pallid Rice Krispies together against the outlines of the filmy crimped river descending down his heart, and stay inflated, pressing, filling; it has been explained to him that if the LAD has not developed any collateral arteries the blood flow will cease and another heart attack begin, right on camera. You are *there*.

"Thirty seconds," Dr. Breit breathes, and Dr. Raymond deflates the balloon. "Looking good, Ray." Harry feels no pain beyond the knifelike sweet pressure in his bladder and a soreness in the far back of his throat as if from swallowing all that saltwater out on the Gulf. "Once more, Harold, and we'll call it a day."

"How're ya doing?" Dr. Raymond asks him, in one of those marbles-in-the-mouth voices muscular men sometimes have, Pennsylvanians especially.

"Still here," Harry says, in a brave voice that sounds high in his ears, as if out of a woman's throat.

The tense insufflation repeats, and so do the images on the TV screen, silent like the bumping of molecules under the microscope on a nature program, or like computer graphics in an insurance commercial, where fragments flickeringly form the logo. It seems as remote from his body as the records of his sins that angels are keeping. Were his heart to stop, it would be mere shadowplay. He sees, when the catheter's bulge subsides a second time, that the Rice Krispies have been pushed to the sides of his LAD. He feels blood flowing more freely into his heart, rich in combustible oxygen; his head in gratitude and ecstasy grows faint.

"Looking good," Dr. Breit says, sounding nervous.

"Whaddya mean?" Dr. Raymond responds – "looking *great*," like those voices on television that argue about the virtues of Miller Lite.

The nurse who that evening comes into his room (a private room, $160 more a day, but it's worth it to him; in Florida the guy in the bed next to him finally died, gurgling and moaning all day and then shitting all over himself as a last pronouncement) and takes Harry's temperature and blood pressure and brings his allotment of pills in a little paper cup has a round kind face. She is a bit overweight but it's packed on firm. She looks familiar. She has pale-blue eyes in sockets that make a dent above the cheekbones in the three-quarters view, and her upper lip has that kind of puffy look he likes, like Michelle Pfeiffer. Her hair shows under her nurse's cap as browny-red, many-colored, with even a little gray, though she is young enough to be his daughter.

She lifts the strange plastic rocket-shaped thermometer that gives its reading in red segmented numbers from his mouth and enwraps his left arm with the Velcro-fastened blood-pressure cuff. As she inflates it she asks, "How's the Toyota business?"

"Not bad. The weak dollar doesn't help. My son runs the place now, basically. How'd you know I sold Toyotas?"

"My boyfriend then and I bought a car from you about ten years ago." She lifts those bleached blue eyes mockingly. "Don't you remember?"

"It's *you*! Yes. Of course. Of course I remember. An orange Corolla." She is his daughter; or at least he imagines she is, though Ruth out of spite would never admit it to him. As the girl stands close to his bed, he reads her badge: ANNABELLE BYER; R.N. She still has her maiden name.

Annabelle frowns, and deflates the blood-pressure cuff, as tight around his arm as a policeman's grip. "Let's try that again in a minute. It shot up while we were talking."

He asks her, "How'd the Corolla work out? How'd the boyfriend work out, for that matter? What the hell was his name? Big red-eared country kid."

"Don't talk, please, until I've got my reading. I'll be quiet. Try to think of something soothing."

He thinks of Ruth's farm, the Byer place, the slope down through the orchard from the line of scrub trees he used to spy behind – the little square stone house, the yellow shells of the abandoned school buses, the dark collie that tried to herd him down there, as though he knew Harry belonged there with the others. Fritzie, that was that dog's name. Sharp teeth, black gums.

Oo boy, scary. Calm down. Think of the big sky of Texas, above the hot low barracks at Fort Larson, himself in fresh khaki, with a pass for the evening. Freedom, a soft breeze, a green sunset on the low horizon. Think of playing basketball against Oriole High, that little country gym, the backboards flush against the walls, before all the high schools merged into big colorless regionals and shopping malls began eating up the farmland. Think of sledding with Mim in her furry hood, in Mt. Judge behind the hat factory, on a winter's day so short the streetlights come on an hour before suppertime calls you home.

"That's better," the nurse says. "One forty over ninety-five. Not great, but not bad. In answer to your questions: the car lasted longer than the boyfriend. I traded in the car after eight years; it had a hundred twenty thousand miles on the speedometer. Jamie moved out about a year after we moved into town. He went back to Galilee. Brewer was too tough for him."

"And you? Is it too tough for you?"

"No, I like it. I like the action."

Action like her mother used to get? *You were a real hooer?* Dusk and May's fully arrived leafiness soften his private room; it is a quiet time on the hospital floor, after dinner and the post-work surge of visitors. Harry dares ask, "You married now? Or live with a guy?"

She smiles, her natural kindness contending a moment with surprise at his curiosity, his presumption, and then smoothing her face into calm again. The dusk seems to be gathering it closer, the pale round glimmer of her face. But her voice discloses a city dryness, a guardedness that might rise up. "No, as a matter of fact I live with my mother. She sold the farm we inherited from my father and moved in with me after Jamie moved out."

"I think I know that farm. I've passed it on the road." Harry's violated, tired heart feels weighted by so much information, as his groin had been weighted down, literally sandbagged, in the hours after the angioplasty. To think of that other world, with all its bushes and seasons and green days and brown, where this child's life had passed without him. "Does Ruth –" he begins, and ends, "What does she do? Your mother."

The girl gives him a look but then answers readily, as if the question passed some test. "She works for one of these investment companies from out of state, money markets and mutual funds and all that, that have branch offices in the new glass building down-town, across from where Kroll's used to be."

"A stenographer," Rabbit remembers. "She could take dicta-tion and type."

The girl actually laughs, in surprise at his groping command of the truth. She is beginning to be pert, to drop her nurse's manner. She has backed off a step from his bed, and her full thighs press against the crisp front of her white uniform so that even standing up she has a lap. Why is Ruth turning this girl into a spinster? She tells him, "She was hired for that but being so much older than the other women they've let her have some more responsibility. She's a kind of junior exec now. Did you know my mother, ever?"

"I'm not sure," he lies.

"You must have, in the days when she was single. She told me she knew quite a few guys before meeting up with my father." She smiles, giving him permission to have known her mother.

"I guess she did," Harry says, sad at the thought. Always he has wanted to be every woman's only man, as he was his mother's only son. "I met her once or twice."

"You should see her," Annabelle goes on pertly. "She's lost a lot of weight and dresses real snappy. I kid her, she has more boyfriends than I do."

Rabbit closes his eyes and tries to picture it, at their age. *Come on. Work.* Dressing snappy. Once a city girl, always a city girl. Her hair, that first time he saw her, rimmed with red neon like wilt.

The girl he thinks is his daughter goes on, "I'll tell her you're in here, Mr. Angstrom." Though he is trying now to withdraw, into his evening stupor, an awakening affinity between them has stirred her to a certain forwardness. "Maybe she'll remember more than you do."

Outside the sealed hospital windows, in the slowly thickening dusk, sap is rising, and the air even in here feels languid with pollen. Involuntarily Harry's eyes close again. "No," he says, "that's O.K. Don't tell her anything. I doubt if she'd remember anything." He is suddenly tired, too tired for Ruth. Even if this girl is his daughter, it's an old story, going on and on, like a radio nobody's listening to.

*　*　*

They keep him in the hospital for five nights. Janice visits him Saturday. She is very busy on the outside; the classes she has to take to be a real-estate salesman have begun to meet, "The Laws of Real Property and Conveyancing" for three hours one night, and the other, "Procedures of Mortgages and Financing," on another. Also, she has been spending a lot of daytime hours with Pru and the grandchildren, and Charlie Stavros called her up and took her out to lunch.

Rabbit protests, "The bastard, he did? I'm not even dead yet."

"Of course not, darling, and nobody expects you to be. He said it was your idea, from when *you* had lunch together. Charlie's concerned about us, is all. He thinks I shouldn't just be letting things slide but should get an outside accountant and our lawyer and look at the books over at the lot, just like you wanted."

"You believe it when Charlie tells you, but not when I do."

"Honey, you're my husband, and husbands get wives all confused. Charlie's just an old friend, and he has an outsider's impartiality. Also, he loved my father, and feels protective toward the firm."

Harry has to chuckle, though he doesn't like to laugh now or do anything that might joggle his heart, that delicate web of jumping shadow he saw on the radiograph monitor during his operation. Sometimes, when shows like *Cosby* or *Perfect Strangers* or *Golden Girls* begin to tickle him too much, he switches off the set, rather than stress his heart with a laugh. These shows are all idiotic but not as totally stupid as this new one everybody raves about, *Roseanne*, starring some fat woman whose only talent as far as he can see is talking fast without moving her mouth. "Janice," he says seriously, "I think the only person who ever loved your father was you. And maybe your mother, at the beginning. Though it's hard to picture."

"Don't be rude to the dead," she tells him, unruffled. She looks plumped up, somehow; without that steady diet of tennis and swimming Valhalla Village provides she is maybe gaining weight. They are still members up at the Flying Eagle, but haven't made it out that way as much as in past springs. They had enjoyed good friendly times up there without realizing they would end. And, with his heart, Harry doesn't quite know how much to get into golf again. Even with a cart, you can be out there on the seventh hole and keel over and by the time they bring you in, through the other foursomes, there's been no oxygen to the brain for ten minutes. Five minutes is all it takes, and you're a vegetable.

"Well, are you going to do it? Call in another accountant."

"I've done it already!" she announces, the proud secret she's been waiting for the conversation to elicit. "Charlie had called up Mildred on his own already and we went over there to this very nice nursing home right near us, she's *per*fectly sensible and competent, just a little unsteady on her legs, and we went over to the lot and this Lyle who was so mean to you wasn't there but I was able to reach him over the phone at his home number. I said we wanted to look over the accounts since October and he said the accounts were mostly in these computer disks he keeps at his house and he was too sick to see us today, so I said maybe he was too sick to be our accountant then."

"You said that?"

"Yes I did. The first thing they teach you in this class on conveyancing is never to pussy-foot around, you do somebody and a potential sale more harm by not being clear than by speaking right out, even if they might not like hearing it at first. I told him he was fired and he said you can't fire somebody with AIDS, it's discrimination, and I said he should bring in his books and disks tomorrow or a policeman would be out to get them."

"You said all that?" Her eyes are bright and her hair bushes out from her little nut of a face, getting tan again, with a touch of double chin now that she's putting on weight. Harry admires her as you admire children you have raised, whose very success pulls them away, into the world's workings, into distance and estrangement.

"Maybe not as smoothly as I'm saying it to you, but I got it all out. Ask Charlie, he was right there. I don't like what these queers have done to Nelson. They've corrupted him."

"Gay," Harry says wearily. "We call them gay now." He is still trying to keep up with America, as it changes styles and costumes and vocabulary, as it dances ahead ever young, ever younger. "And what did Lyle say then?"

"He said we shall see. He asked whether I'd consulted with Nelson about all this. I said no but I wasn't sure Nelson was fit to consult with these days. I said in my opinion he and his friends were milking Nelson for all he was worth and had turned him into a human wreck and a dope addict and Charlie wrote on a pad of paper for me to see, 'Cool it.' Elvira and Benny were out in the showroom all ears even though the office door was closed. *Oh*, but that fairy got me mad," Janice explains, "he sounded so above-it-all and bored on the phone, as if dealing with women like me was just more than his poor sensitive body and spirit could bear."

Rabbit is beginning to know how Lyle felt. "He probably was tired," he says in his defense. "That disease he has does an awful job on you. Your lungs fill up."

"Well, he should have kept his penis out of other men's bottoms then," Janice says, lowering her voice though, so the nurses and orderlies in the hall don't hear.

Bottoms. Thelma. That casket of nothingness. Probing the void. "And I don't know," Rabbit wearily pursues, "in a situation like Nelson's, who corrupts who. Maybe *I* corrupted the poor kid, twenty years ago."

"Oh Harry, don't be so hard on yourself. It's depressing to see you like this. You've changed so. What have they done to you, these doctors?"

He's glad she asked. He tells her, "They stuck a long thin thing into me and I could see it on television in my heart. Right on the screen, my own poor heart, while it was pumping to keep me alive. They shouldn't be allowed to go into your heart like that. They should just let people die."

"Darling, what a stupid way to talk. It's modern science, you should be grateful. You're going to be fine. Mim called all worried and I told her how minor it was and gave her your number here."

"Mim." Just the syllable makes him smile. His sister. The one other survivor of that house on Jackson Road, where Mom and Pop set up their friction, their heat, their comedy, their parade of days. At nineteen Mim took her bony good looks and went west, to Las Vegas. One of her gangster pals with a sentimental streak set her up with a beauty parlor when her looks began to go, and now she owns a Laundromat as well as the hairdresser's. Vegas must be a great town for Laundromats. Nobody lives there, everybody is just passing through, leaving a little bit of dirt like on the pale Antron carpets back at 14½ Franklin Drive. Harry and Janice visited Mim once, seven or eight years ago. These caves of glowing slot machines, no clocks anywhere, just a perpetual two o'clock in the morning, and you step outside and to your surprise the sun is blazing, and the sidewalks so hot a dog couldn't walk on them. What with Sinatra and Wayne Newton, he expected a lot of glitz, but in fact the gambling addicts were no classier than the types you see pulling at the one-armed bandits down in Atlantic City. Only there was a Western flavor, their voices and faces lined with little tiny cracks. Mim's face and voice had those tiny cracks too, though she had had a face-lift, to tighten up what she called her "wattles." Life is a hill that gets steeper the more you climb.

"*Harry.*" Janice has been telling him something. "What did I just say?"

"I have no idea." Irritably he adds, "Why bother to talk to me when you've got Charlie back advising you, to say the least?"

She flares a little; her lips pinch in and her face comes forward. "Advising me is all he's doing and he's doing that because you asked him to. Because he loves you."

She wouldn't have spoken this way before going to Florida and those women's groups, of "love" as something that is all over the map, like oil drips from speeding automobiles. She is trying to stir him, he dimly recognizes, back into life, into the fray. He tries to play along. "Me?"

"Yes, you, Harry Angstrom."

"Why would he, for Chrissake?"

"I have no idea," Janice says. "I've never understood what men see in each other." She tries a joke. "Maybe he's gone *gay* in his old age."

"He's never married," Harry admits. "You think he'd be interested in coming back to work for Springer Motors?"

She is gathering up her things — a black leather pocketbook packed like a bomb, the old-fashioned round kind people used to throw and not the flattened Semtex that terrorists smuggle into suit-cases in airplanes, and her real-estate textbook and photocopied sample documents stapled together, for her class tonight, and a new spring coat she's got herself, a kind of jonquil-yellow gabardine with a broad belt and wide shoulders. She looks girlish, fluffy-haired, putting it on. "I asked him," she says, "and he says absolute-ly not. He says he's into these partnerships with his cousins, rental properties in the north end of the city and over toward the old fair-grounds, and a rug-cleaning business his nephew started up with another boy and they needed backers, and Charlie says that's enough for him, he couldn't stand to go back into a salaried job and all that withholding tax and the aggravation of being expected somewhere like at the lot every day. He likes his freedom."

"We all do," sighs Rabbit. "Hey, Janice. I was thinking just the other day we ought to get the wall-to-wall carpets in our house cleaned. No fault of yours, but they're filthy, honey."

Dr. Breit comes in Sunday morning and tells him, "Harold, you're looking A-1. Ray does beautiful work. They say around the OR, 'He could tickle a tapeworm under the chin with that catheter.'" Breit looks up through his furry eyelashes for the expected laugh, doesn't get it, and perches on the edge of the bed for extra intimacy. "I've been reviewing our own films plus the stuff the jerks down at Deleon Community finally got around to sending us. Your lumen in the LAD has gone up from fifteen per cent of normal to sixty. But I can't say I'm crazy about your RCA, the right coronary artery; it shows I'd put it at about eighty-per-cent blockage, which is fine and dandy as long as the well-developed collateral is supplying the right ventricle from the cir-cumflex. But a lesion is developing at the bifurcation of the circumflex and the LAD, and a lesion at a bifurcation is tougher to treat with angioplasty. Same thing – I assume you're interested in this – if the lesion is too long, or in a hyperkinetic AV groove, or in a situation where in the middle of the procedure you might get stranded without enough collateral circulation. In those kinds of cases, it can get hairy."

His legs are a little short for sitting on the bed comfortably; he bounces his ham a little closer to Harry's legs, and Harry feels the blood inside his supine body sway. Breit smiles and his voice grows confidential, like when he was murmuring over Dr. Raymond's shoulders. "The fact is, Harold, PTCA is a pretty Mickey Mouse treatment, and what I want you to seriously consider as you lie here these few days, even though as I say this procedure appears to have produced good results for the time being, is, now that you've tested the waters, going ahead with a CABG. Not right away. We're talking four, six months down the road before we go in again. We'd bypass both the RCA and the CFX, and the LAD depending on the restenosis, and you'll be a new man, with damn close to a brand-new heart. While we're in there we might want to look at that leaky aortic valve and think about a pacemaker. Frankly, we may have had a little postoperative MI; your electro-cardiogram shows some new Q waves and there's been an eleva-tion of the CPK isoenzyme, with positive MB bands."

"You mean," Harry says, not totally snowed, "I've been hav-ing a heart attack just lying here?"

Dr. Breit shrugs daintily. All his gestures have a daintiness that goes with his milky-pink skin. His voice is a bit squeaky, piped through his blistered-looking lips. He says, "PTCA is an invasive procedure, nobody said it wasn't. A little trauma is to be expected. Your heart shows myocardial scarring from way back. All a heart attack is is some heart muscle dying. A little can die without your noticing. It happens to all of us, just as everybody over a certain age has some emphysema. It's called the aging process and there's no escaping it. Not in this life."

Harry wonders about the next life, but decides not to ask. He doubts that Breit knows more than *The National Enquirer*. "You're telling me I've come into this hospital for I don't know how many thousands of dollars for a Mickey Mouse operation?"

"Rome wasn't built in a day, Harold, and your heart isn't going to be rebuilt in a week. Angioplasty does some good, at least for a while, in about eighty per cent of the cases. But bypass is up to around ninety-nine per cent initial success. Look. It's the differ-ence between scrubbing out your toilet bowl with a long brush and actually replacing the pipes. There are places you can't reach with a brush, and deposits that have become chemically bonded. A man your age, in generally good health, shouldn't be thinking twice about it. You owe it not only to yourself but to your wife and son. And those cunning little grandchildren I've heard about."

The faster Breit talks, the more constricted Harry's chest feels. He gets out, "Let me see if I understand it. They rip veins out of your legs and sew them to your heart like jug handles?"

A frown clouds the young doctor's face. He is overrunning the allotted time for his visit, Rabbit supposes. With visible patience he licks his sore-looking lips and explains, "They take a super-ficial vein from your leg and in some cases the mammary chest artery, because arteries hold up better under arterial pressure than veins. But you don't have to worry about any of that. You're not the surgeon, it's our bailiwick. This operation is done tens of thousands of times in the United States every year – believe me, Harold, it's a piece of cake."

"You'd do it here?"

Breit's eyes behind his flesh-colored glasses are strange furry slits, with puffy pink lids. "The facilities don't exist yet in this physical plant," he admits. "You'd have to go to Philadelphia, I doubt we could slot you into Lancaster, they're booked solid for months."

"Then it can't be such a *ve*ry little deal, if you need all these facilities." Since childhood, Rabbit has had a prejudice against Philadelphia. Dirtiest city in the world: they live on poisoned water. And Lancaster is worse – Amish farmers, overwork their animals to death, inbred so much half are humpbacks and dwarfs. He saw them in the movie *Witness* being very quaint, Kelly McGillis wiping her bare tits with a sponge and everybody chip-ping in to build that barn, but it didn't fool him. "Maybe Florida would be the place," he offers Dr. Breit. Florida always seems unreal to him when he's up here and having the operation there might be the same as not having it at all.

Dr. Breit's sore-looking mouth gets stern; his upper lip has sweat on it. Why is he selling this so hard? Does he have a monthly quota, like state cops with speeding tickets? "I haven't been that impressed by our dealings with Deleon," he says. "But you think about it, Harold. If I were in your shoes, it's what I'd have done – without any hesitation. You're just toying with your life otherwise."

Yeah, Rabbit thinks when the doctor is gone from the room, *but you're not in my shoes. And what's life for but to toy with?*

Mim phones. He takes a moment to recognize her voice, it is so dry and twangy, so whisky-and-cigarette-cracked. "What are they doing to you now?" she asks. She has always taken the attitude that he is a lamb among wolves in Diamond County and he should have gotten out like she did.

"They've got me in the hospital," he tells her. He could almost cry, like a boy. "They stuck a balloon up through my leg into my heart and pumped it full of saltwater to open up an artery that was plugged up with old grease I've been eating. Then afterwards they put a sandbag on the incision down at my thigh and told me not to move my leg for six hours or I'd bleed to death. That's how hospitals are; they tell you what they're going to do is about as simple as having a haircut and then midway through they tell you you might bleed to death. And then this morning the doctor comes around and tells me it was a Mickey Mouse operation and hardly worth bothering with. He wants me to go for broke and have a multiple bypass. Mim, they split you right open like a coconut and rip veins out of your legs."

"Yeah, I know," she says. "You gonna do it?"

Rabbit says, "I suppose they'll talk me into it eventually. I mean, they've got you by the balls. You're scared, and what else is there?"

"Guys I know out here have had open-heart and swear by it. I can't see it made that much difference, they still spend all day sitting on their fat asses getting manicures and talking on the phone, but then they weren't such dynamite before either. When you get to our age, Harry, it's work to stay alive."

"Come on, Mim. You're only fifty."

"For a woman out here, that's ancient. That's cow pasture. That's hang-it-up time, if you're a woman. You don't get the stares any more, it's like you've gone invisible."

"Boy, you did use to get the stares," he says proudly. He remembers her when she was nineteen – dyed-in blonde streak, big red cinch-in belt, sexy soft sweaters, skinny arms ending in a clash of bangle bracelets, buck teeth she couldn't help revealing when she smiled, lips smeared with lipstick like she had eaten a jam sandwich, a leggy colt of a girl dying to break out of Brewer, to kick or fuck her way through the fence. She made it, too. Rabbit never could have made it out there. He was too soft. Even Florida bakes the spirit out of him. He needed to stay where they remembered him when. "So when are you coming east?" he asks Mim.

"Well, how bad are you, Harry?"

"Not that bad. I just complain a lot. All I have to do is stay away from animal fats and salt and don't get aggravated."

"Who would aggravate you?"

"The usual," he says. "Nellie's been having some problems. Hey, you'll never guess who's back on the scene squiring Janice around while I'm laid up. Your old boyfriend, Charlie Stavros."

"Chas was not what I'd ever call a boyfriend. I took him on that time to get him off your wife's back. Around here you're not a boyfriend until you at least set the girl up in a condo."

He is striving to keep her interested. People who've made it like she has, they get bored easily. "How the hell *is* Vegas?" he asks. "Is it hot there yet? How about you coming east to get away from the heat for a couple of weeks? We'll put you up in the guest room above the den and you'll get to know your great-niece and -nephew. Judy's a real little lady now. She's gonna be a looker – not like you, but a looker."

"Harry, the last time I came to Pennsylvania I nearly died from the humidity. I don't know how you people do it, day after day; it was like being wrapped in warm washcloths. It's that heavy climate is doing you in. That pollen is off the scale."

"Yeah," he weakly agrees. The phone receiver feels soggy in his hand. His own capacity to be interested isn't what it should be. He's free to wander the halls now, and you see amazing things: less than an hour ago, an amazing visitor, a young Brewer girl, she couldn't have been more than fifteen, all in black, black jacket, tight black pants, pointed black boots, and her hair dyed yellowy white and cut short and mussed every which way so her skull reminded him of a wet Easter chick, plus a little flowery cruciform tattoo pricked right beside her eye. But his heart couldn't quite rise to it, he felt he'd seen even this before, girls doing wicked things to themselves believing their youth would shine through and all would heal.

"Maybe I'll come in the fall if you can last it out," Mim tells him.

"Oh I can last," he says. "You aren't going to get rid of big brother so easy." But the connection feels strained, and he can sense Mim groping, in the little pauses, for what to say next. "Hey, Mim," he says. "Do you remember if Pop complained of chest pains?"

"He had emphysema, Harry. Because he wouldn't stop smoking. You stopped. You were smart. Me, I'm down to a pack a day. But I don't think I ever really inhaled."

"I seem to remember him complaining of feeling full in the chest. He'd sneak his hand inside his shirt and rub his chest."

"Maybe he itched. Harry, Pop died because he couldn't breathe. Mom died because of her Parkinson's. I suppose their hearts failed in the end but so does everybody's, because that's what life is, a strain on the heart."

His little sister has become so dogmatic, everything cut and dried. She's mad at something, too. Just like little Roy. "Hey," he says, not wanting to let go however, "and another thing I was wondering about. Remember how you used to always sing, 'Shoo-fly pie and apple pan dowdy?'"

"Yeah. Kind of."

"What's the line that comes after 'Makes your eyes light up, your tummy say "howdy" '?"

In the silence he can hear chatter in the background, beauty-parlor chatter, and a hair dryer whirring. "I have no fucking idea," she says finally. "Are you sure I used to sing this song?"

"Well, I was, but never mind. How's *your* life?" he asks. "Any new irons in the fire? When're we going to marry you off?"

"Harry, come off it. The only reason anybody out here'd marry an old bag like me would be as some kind of cover. Or a tax dodge, if the accountant could figure one."

"Speaking of accountants," he begins, and he might have told her all about Nelson and Lyle and Janice, and the voices on the phone, but she doesn't want to hear him; she says hurriedly, in a lowered voice, "Harry, a real special customer has just come in, even *you've* heard of her, and I got to hang up. You take care of yourself, now. You sound on the mend. Any time they get to be too much for you, you can come on out here for some sun and fun."

What sort of fun, he would have liked to ask – in the old days she was always offering to get a girl for him if he came out alone, though he never did – and he would have liked to have heard more of why she thinks he is on the mend. But Mim has hung up. She has a life to get on with. His arm hurts in its crook from holding the phone. Ever since they invaded his arteries with dyes and balloons, he has aches and pains in remote and random joints, as if his blood is no longer purely his own. Once you break the cap on a ginger-ale bottle, there is never again as much fizz.

The nurse with the round pale face – a country kind of face – comes in Monday evening and says to him, "My mother is having to drop something off for me tonight. Should I ask her to come up and see you for a second?"

"Did she say she'd be willing?" *When I think of you thinking she's your daughter it's like rubbing her all over with shit*, Ruth had said the last time they talked.

The young woman in her folded cap smiles. "I mentioned the other night, casual-like, that you were here, and I think she would be. She didn't say anything rude or anything." There is on her face a trace of a blush, a simper, a secret. If something does not soon happen to her, it will become a silly empty face. Innocence is just an early stage of stupidity.

This has not been the best day for Harry. The sounds of traffic and work resuming on the street outside reminded him of how out of it he still is. Janice didn't visit, and now her evening class has begun. All day gray clouds packed the sky, in long rolls of nimbus, and trailed black wisps above the brick chimneys, but no rain has actually fallen. The view from his window consists of several intricately notched bands of ornamental brickwork capping the third stories of narrow buildings that hold at street level a coffee shop, a dry cleaner's, an office-supplies store. The corner building is painted gray, the middle one blue, and the third, with the most ornate window framing, beige. It has slowly dawned upon the people of Brewer that you can paint over brick with any color you choose, not just brick red. People live behind the upper windows across the street, but though Harry faithfully stares he has not yet been rewarded with the sight of a woman undressing, or even of anyone coming to the window to look out. Further depressing him, he has not been able to have a bowel movement since entering St. Joseph's three days ago. The first day, he blamed the awkwardness of the bedpan and his solicitude for the nurses who would have to carry what he produced away, and the second day, the change of diet from what he usually eats – the food the hospital dieticians conjure up looks pretty good but tastes like wet cardboard and chews like chaff, so bland as to shut down his salivary glands – but on the third day, when he can wander the halls and use the bathroom behind a closed door in his room, he blames himself, his decrepitude, his drying up, the running down of his inner processes. Running out of even gas.

It is strange that this girl (hardly that, she would be only three years younger than Nelson) should offer to bring him her mother, for last night he dreamed about Ruth. As the world around him goes gray, his dreams have taken on intense color. Ruth – Ruth as she had been, the spring they lived and slept together, both of them twenty-six, she fleshy, cocky, pretty in a coarse heavy careless way – was wearing a sea-blue dress, with small white polka dots, and he was pressing his body against it, with her body inside it, and telling her how lovely a color it was on her, while the hair on her head glistened red, brown, and gold, close to his eyes. Ruth had turned her head not, he felt, in aversion from him but in natural embarrassment at the situation, for she seemed to be living with him and Janice, all together, and Janice was somewhere near them – upstairs, though the furniture around them was sunstruck floral-patterned wicker, as from their Florida condo, which has no upstairs. His embrace of Ruth felt semi-permitted, like an embrace of a legal relation, and his praise of her vivid dress was meant to urge her into his own sense of well-being, of their love being at last all right. He hid his face beside her throat, in the curtain of her many-colored hair, and knew he could fuck her forever, on and on, bottomlessly spilling himself into her solid beauty. When he awoke it was with the kind of absolute hard-on he almost never has while awake, what with the anti-hypertensive medicine and his generally gray mood. He saw while the dream still freshly clung to him in sky-blue shreds that the white polka dots were the confettilike bits of blossom that littered the sidewalk a month ago on that street of Bradford pear trees up near Summer, where he had once lived with Ruth, and that the splashy sunlight was what used to pour in on Ma Springer's iron table of ferns and African violets, in the little sun-room across the foyer from the gloomy living room. For though the furniture of the dream was Florida, the house they were all sharing had certainly been the old Springer manse.

Harry asks the round-faced nurse, "How much do you know about me and your mother?"

The blush deepens a shade. "Oh, nothing. She never lets on about the time before she settled down with my father." It now sounds rather conventional, Ruth's time as a single woman; but at the time she was beyond the pale, a lost soul scandalous to the narrow world of Mt. Judge. "I figure you were a special friend."

"Maybe not that special," Harry tells her.

He feels bad, because there is nothing much she can say to that, his lie, just stand there polite with her puffy upper lip, a nurse being patient with a patient. He is leaving her out on a limb. He loves her; love flows through him like a blind outpouring, an anesthesia. He tells his possible daughter, "Look, it's a cute idea, but if she came up it would be because you asked her to rather than she wanted to on her own, and, frankly, Annabelle" – he has never called her by her name before – "I'd just as soon she didn't see me like this. You say she's lost weight and looks snappy. I'm fat and a medical mess. Maybe she'd be too much for me."

The girl's face returns to being pale and prim. Boundaries have been restored, just as he's getting to feel paternal. "Very well," Annabelle says. "I'll tell her you've been released, if she asks."

"Might she ask? Wait. Don't get prissy. Tell me, why did you want to get us together?"

"You seem so interested in her. Your face comes to life when I mention her."

"It does? Maybe it's looking at you that does it." He dares go on, "I've been wondering, though, if you should still be living with her. Maybe you ought to get out from under her wing."

"I did, for a while. I didn't like it. Living alone is tough. Men can get nasty."

"Can we really? I'm sorry to hear it."

Her face softens into a dear smile, that curls her upper lip at the edges and buckles the plump part in the middle. "Anyway, she says just what you say. But I like it, for now. It's not like she's my mother any more, she's a roommate. Believe me, bad things can happen to women who live alone in this city. Brewer isn't New York but it isn't Penn Park, either."

Of course. She can read his address right off the chart at the foot of the bed. To her he is one of those Penn Park snobs he himself has always resented. "Brewer's a rugged town," he agrees, sinking back into his pillow. "Always was. Coal and steel. Bars and cathouses all along the railroad tracks right through the middle of the city, when I was young." He glances away, at the ornamental brickwork, the hurrying dry dark clouds. He tells his nurse, "You know best how to live your own life. Tell your mother, if she asks, that maybe we'll meet some other time." Under the pear trees, in Paradise.

Lying there these days, Harry thinks fondly of those dead bricklayers who bothered to vary their rows at the top of the three buildings across the street with such festive patterns of recess and protrusion, diagonal and upright, casting shadows in different ways at different times of the day, these men of another century up on their scaffold, talking Pennsylvania Dutch among themselves, or were Italians doing all the masonry even then? Lying here thinking of all the bricks that have been piled up and knocked down and piled up again on the snug square streets that lift toward Mt. Judge, he tries to view his life as a brick of sorts, set in place with a slap in 1933 and hardening ever since, just one life in rows and walls and blocks of lives. There is a satisfaction in such an overview, a faint far-off communal thrill, but hard to sustain over against his original and continuing impression that Brewer and all the world beyond are just frills on himself, like the lace around a plump satin valentine, himself the heart of the universe, like the Dalai Lama, who in the news lately – Tibet is still restless, after nearly forty years of Chinese rule – was reported to have offered to resign. But the offer was greeted with horror by his followers, for whom the Dalai Lama can no more resign godhood than Harry can resign selfhood.

He watches a fair amount of television. It's right there, in front of his face; its wires come out of the wall behind him, just like oxygen. He finds that facts, not fantasies, are what he wants: the old movies on cable AMC seem stiff and barky in their harshly lit black and white, and the old TV shows on NIK impossibly tinny with their laugh tracks and spray-set Fifties hairdos, and even the incessant sports (rugby from Ireland, curling from Canada) a waste of his time, stories told people with time to kill, where he has time left only for truth, the truth of DSC or Channel 12, MacNeil-Lehrer so gravely bouncing the news between New York and Washington and reptiles on *Smithsonian World* flickering their forked tongues in the desert blaze or the giant turtles of Galápagos on *World of Survival* battling for their lives or the Russians battling the Nazis in the jumpy film clips of World War II as narrated by Sir Laurence Olivier ("Twenty million dead," he intones at the end, as the frame freezes and goes into computer-blur and the marrow-chilling theme music comes up, thrilling Harry to think he was there, on the opposite side of the Northern Hemisphere, jumping on tin cans and balling up tin foil for his anti-Hitler bit, a ten-year-old participant in actual history) and *War and Peace in the Nuclear Age* and *Nature's Way* and *Portraits of Power* and *Wonders of the World* and *Wildlife Chronicles* and *Living Body* and *Planet Earth* and struggle and death and cheetahs gnawing wildebeests and tarantulas fencing with scorpions and tiny opossums scrambling for the right nipple under the nature photographer's harsh lights and weaverbirds making the most intricate damn nests just to attract one little choosy female and the incredible cleverness and variety and energy and waste of it all, a kind of crash course he is giving himself in the ways of the world. There is just no end to it, no end of information.

The nightly news has a lot of China on it – Gorbachev visiting, students protesting in Tiananmen Square, but not protesting Gorbachev, in fact they like him, all the world likes him, despite that funny mark on his head shaped like Japan. What the Chinese students seem to want is freedom, they want to be like Americans, but they look like Americans already, in blue jeans and T-shirts. Meanwhile in America itself the news is that not only President George Bush but Mrs. Bush the First Lady take showers with their dog Millie, and if that's all the Chinese want we should be able to give it to them, or something close, though it makes Harry miss Reagan slightly, at least he was dignified, and had that dream distance; the powerful thing about him as President was that you never knew how much he knew, nothing or everything, he was like God that way, you had to do a lot of it yourself. With this new one you know he knows something, but it seems a small something. Rabbit doesn't want to have to picture the President and middle-aged wife taking showers naked with their dog. Reagan and Nancy had their dignity, their computer-blur, even when their bowel polyps and breasts were being snipped off in view of billions.

Janice comes in at six on Tuesday while he is eating his last bland supper – he is being released tomorrow. She is wearing her new coat and a gray skirt and a low-cut magenta blouse almost as vivid as the polka-dot dress Ruth wore in his dream. His wife looks energized, businesslike, her salt-and-pepper hair trimmed and given body by a hairdresser who has eliminated the bangs, gelled them back into a softly bristling mass, parted low on one side. Janice reminds him of those heightened and rapid-talking women on television who give the news. She in fact is brimming with news. Her eyes seem to be wearing contact lenses of an unnatural glitter until he realizes those are tears, prepared for him during the station break.

"Oh Harry," she begins, "it's worse than we thought! Thousands and thousands!"

"Thousands of what?"

"Of dollars Nelson stole! Charlie and I and this accountant his nephew knows – Mildred says she was too old for doing an audit and anyway is too busy in the nursing home – went over there today, Charlie said I *had* to be there, he and the accountant weren't enough, and I asked to see the books, Nelson *was* there for once, and he looked at me in this heartbreaking hopeless way I'll never forget as long as I live and said, Sure, Mom, what did I want to know? He told us everything. At first, when he needed money so desperately for the, you know, the cocaine, he would just write himself a check marked 'Expenses' or 'Operating Cash,' but Mildred, she was still around then, questioned him about it and he got scared. Anyway, these little amounts, a hundred or even two at a time, weren't really enough to keep him going, so he got the idea of offering people a discount on the used cars if they paid in cash or with a check written directly out to him."

"I *told* you there weren't enough used sales on the statements," Harry says, in a triumph that feels rather flat. Ever since they poked that catheter in, there's been something drained about his emotional responses. "How many cars did he pull this stunt with?"

"Well, he doesn't really remember, but Charlie says we can reconstruct it from the records, the NV-1s and so on, it will just take time. Of course, Nelson didn't approach every customer with this sort of shady deal, he had to pick and choose, the ones that looked poor enough not to look a gift horse in the face. He was clever about it, Nelson is much more clever than you ever gave him credit for."

"I never said the kid wasn't clever."

"Oh, but Harry" – the shell of tears is refreshed, the brown eyes spill, shiny trails glitter beside her blunt little knob of a nose, a nose with no more character than a drawer pull. She tugs a paper facial tissue from the box the hospital puts on his night table – as she leans forward he glimpses the tops of her tidy breasts through the loose neck of the magenta peasant-style blouse he has never seen before, something she has bought for the real-estate course and these meetings with Charlie and her general stepping-out into the world, without him. He feels a flash of unpleasant heat, as in catheterization. His own wife's tits, surprising him like that. Janice dabbles at her face, her muddled mutt's face, and leans even farther forward, so he feels her breath on his face, smells some faint mint of a Life Saver. To hide the tobacco on her breath. Her tears shine under his eyes; her shaky voice is low so only he can hear. "– he didn't even stop with that. He was doing crack by this time and the amount of money he needed was incredible. He and Lyle worked out this scheme, here it gets very technical –"

"Wait," he tells her. The culinary aide has come in to remove his tray. She is a plump Hispanic woman with long red fingernails and a distinct mustache.

"You no eat enough," she scolds, with her shy smile of pearl-size teeth.

"Enough," he says. "For now. Very good. *Bueno*."

She has a notebook on which she writes the percentages of the food he has consumed. A third of the overcooked watery string beans, half the pale oval of tasteless veal, scarcely a leaf of the coarse green salad drowned in an orange grease, a bite of the tapioca pudding, whose wobbly texture in his mouth made him shudder. "For breakfast," she reads from her clipboard, "pieces pineapple, cream of wheat, whole-wheat toast, coffee decaf."

"I can hardly wait," he tells her.

"Eat more now," she suggests.

He holds firm. "No thanks, too cold now. My wife's here."

She reads from the chart. "Says here last day tomorrow."

"How about that?" Harry asks her. "The big wide world. I'll miss you. And all your healthy eats. Your *comestibles*."

As she removes his plastic tray, her long red fingernails scrape on its underside with a noise that puts his teeth on edge. He is reminded of that platinum-haired bimbo who used to tickle the computer keys at Fiscal Alternatives. Her fingernails were too long too. Dead, Lyle said. If there *is* an afterlife where the dead all gather, would he get a chance to deepen their acquaintance? But without money around, what would they talk about?

When the woman goes, Janice resumes. The tip of her tongue protrudes a second or two between her lips as she tries to think. "I'm not sure I understand it entirely, but you know how we keep a rolling inventory – so many trucks and vans and cars a month from Mid-Atlantic Toyota in Maryland."

"Between twenty and twenty-five a month is how it's been running," Harry tells her, to let her know he may be flat on his back but knew his business. "We haven't been able to move three hundred new units a year except that one year, '86, after Nelson first took over. The strong yen's been killing us, and Honda and Nissan taking a bigger bite. Ford Ranger put a real dent in our one-ton pickup last year."

"Harry, try to focus. The way it was explained to me is that there's this Toyota Motors Credit Corporation in California that finances our inventory direct with Mid-Atlantic and gets paid when we sell a car and adds to our credit account when we order one for the lot. What Nelson was doing, each month he'd report one or two sales fewer than there actually were and so Toyota would roll over the indebtedness on these cars while he and Lyle put the proceeds in a separate account they'd opened up in the company name, you know how banks now are always offering you all these different accounts, savings and checking with savings and capital accounts with limited checks and so on. So every month we'd owe this TMCC for one or two more cars than were actually on the lot and our debt to them kept getting bigger and our actual inventory was getting smaller; in two or three years if nothing had happened we would have had no new cars in stock at all and owed Mid-Atlantic Toyota a fortune!"

"How much do we actually owe 'em?" His mind can't quite assign weight to these facts, these phantom Toyotas, yet. He is still thinking hospital thoughts – the pineapple he's been promised for breakfast, and whether or not he has taken his digitalis for the evening.

"Nobody knows, Harry. Nelson doesn't exactly remember and Lyle says a lot of the disks he was keeping the accounts on have been accidentally erased."

"Accidentally on purpose, as they used to say," he says. "What a shit. What a pair of shits."

"I know, it's *hor*rible," Janice says, "and Lyle is horrible on the phone. He says he's dying and doesn't care *what* we do to him! He sounded kind of crazy in the head; isn't that one of the things that happens?" The weight of the facts hits her and bears her suddenly down into hysteria; the tears flow accompanied by sobs and she tries to rest her wet face on his blanketed chest, but she is too short, perched on the chair beside his high bed, and instead presses her eyes and mouth against the hard mattress edge, burbling her disbelief that he would do this to her.

"He" means Nelson; Harry is off the hook for once. In her grief her whole head is hot, even the top of her skull, like a pot come to boil. He comfortingly rubs it, through her little new hairdo, and tries not to smile. *Serve them both right*, he thinks. Springers. Her dark hair is so fine it sticks to his fingers like cobwebs. For a good five minutes he massages her warm unhappy head with his fingertips while staring at the blank television screen and thinking that he is missing the six-o'clock news, followed by national news at six-thirty. Somehow he can't believe that what Janice is trying to tell him ranks with the national news, for reality. She may be his wife but she's no Connie Chung, let alone Diane Sawyer with her wide-apart blue eyes and melting mouth and stunned look like some beautiful blonde ox. "So what's going to happen?" he asks Janice at last.

She lifts her tear-smeared face and, surprisingly, has some answers. Charlie must have been coaching her. "Well, once we find out how much we owe TMCC we'll have to settle up. We've been paying interest on the inventory so they shouldn't care too much, it's like a mortgage, only Nelson has sold the house without telling them."

"If he faked any signatures, that's forgery," Harry says, and a black dye of despair is beginning to enter his heart, as he sees what a lost cause his son is. *Human garbage*, like his own father once said of him. He asks, "What's going to happen with the kid?"

Janice blinks her wet lashes. What she has to say seems to her so momentous she withholds it a moment. Her voice has the juicy precision Ma Springer would speak with when she had made up her mind. "He's agreed to enter a rehab place. Immediately."

"Good, I guess. What made him agree?"

"I said it was either that or I'd fire him from the lot. And prosecute."

"Wow. You said that? Prosecute?"

"I did, Harry. I made myself."

"To your own son?"

"I had to. He's been sinking, and he knows it. He was grateful, really. We had it out right there on the lot, out where the

weeds are, while Charlie and the accountant stayed inside. Then
we made some phone calls, from your old office."

"Where *is* this rehab place?"

"In North Philadelphia. It's the one his counsellor recommends, if he can get Nelson in. They're all overcrowded, you
know. Society can't keep up. There are some day-treatment programs in Brewer but his counsellor says the important thing is to
get away from the entire environment the drugs are part of."

"So he really did go to a counsellor, after that blowup with
Pru."

"Yes, to everybody's surprise. And even more surprisingly,
Nelson seems to like him. Respect him. It's a black man."

Harry feels a jealous, resentful pang. His boy is being taken
over. His fatherhood hasn't been good enough. They're calling
in the professionals. "For how long is the rehab?"

"The complete program is ninety days. The first month is
detox and intensive therapy, and then he lives in a halfway house
for sixty days and gets some kind of a job, a community-service
sort of thing probably, just something to get him back out into the
normal world."

"He'll be gone all summer. Who'll run the lot?"

Janice puts her hand over his, a gesture that feels to him learned,
coached. "You will, Harry."

"Honey, I can't. I'm a sick son of a bitch."

"Charlie says your attitude is terrible. You're giving in to your
heart. He says the best thing is a positive spirit and lots of activity."

"Yeah, why doesn't he come back and run the lot if he's so
fucking active?"

"He has all these other fish to fry these days."

"Yeah, and you seem to be one of them. I'm hearing you
sizzle."

She giggles, along with the ugly tears drying on her face.
"Don't be so silly. He's just an old friend, who's been wonderful
in this crisis."

"While I've been useless, right?"

"You've been in the *hos*pital, dear. You've been being brave
in *your* way. Anyway as we all know there are things you can't do
for me, only I can do them for myself."

He is disposed to argue this, it sounds pious in a new-fashioned way he distrusts, but if he's ever going to get back into the game he must let up and avoid aggravation. He asks, "How did Nelson take your getting tough?"

"Like I said, he liked it. He's just been begging for the rest of us to take over, he knew he was way out of control. Pru is thrilled to think he's going to get help. Judy is thrilled."

"Is Roy thrilled?"

"He's too little to understand, but as you say yourself the atmosphere around that house has been poisonous."

"Did I say poisonous?"

She doesn't bother to answer. She has straightened up and is wiping her face with a licked facial tissue.

"Will I have to see the kid before he goes?"

"No, baby. He's going tomorrow morning, before we bring you home."

"Good. I just don't know as I could face him. When you think of what he's done, he's flushed the whole bunch of us, not just you and me but his kids, everybody, right down the toilet. He's sold us all out to a stupid drug."

"Well, my goodness, Harry – I've known you to act selfishly in your life."

"Yeah, but not for a little white powder."

"They can't help it. It becomes their life. Anyway, evidently they were buying drugs for Lyle, too. I mean drugs for his illness – medicines for AIDS you can't buy yet in this country and are terribly expensive, they have to be smuggled."

"It's a sad story," Rabbit says, after a pause. Inky depression circulates in his veins. He's been in the hospital too long. He's forgotten what life is like. He asks Janice, "Where are you going now, in that snappy blouse?"

She rolls her eyes upward at him, from the mirror of her purse as she fixes her face, and then her face goes wooden and stubborn, bluffing it through. "Charlie said he'd take me out to dinner. He's worried I'm going to crash, psychologically, after all this trauma. I need to process."

"Process?"

"Talk things through."

"You can talk them through with me. I'm just lying here with nothing to do, I've already missed the sports section of the news."

She makes that *mmmm* mouth women make after putting on lipstick, rolling her lips together in a complacent serious way, and tells him, "You're not impartial. You have your own agenda with Nelson, and with me for that matter."

"What's so impartial about Charlie, he wants to get into your pants again. If he hasn't already."

She pops the lipstick back into her bomb-shaped pocketbook and touches up her new hairdo with her fingers, glancing from several angles at herself in the mirror, and snaps the lid shut. She says, "That's sweet of you, Harry, to pretend to think I'm still interesting to anybody in that way, but in fact I'm not, except maybe once in a while to my own husband, I hope."

He says, embarrassed, for he knows he's been letting her down in that department lately, "Sure, but you know, for a man, it's all a matter of blood pressure, and –"

"We'll talk about it when you're home. I told Charlie I'd meet him at seven –"

"Where? The salad bar that used to be Johnny Frye's? It's only two blocks from here. You can walk."

"No, actually. There's a new Vietnamese place out near Maiden Springs he wanted to try. It's a bit of a drive and, you know me, I'll probably get lost. And then on top of everything I have fifty pages of a book on British realty law, full of all these funny old obsolete words, I have to read before class tomorrow night."

"You won't be home tomorrow night? My first night home?" He is making a complaint of it, scoring points, but he wishes she'd go and leave him alone with the television screen.

"We'll see," Janice says, rising. "I have an idea." Then she asks, "Aren't you proud of me?" She bends forward to press her hot busy face against his. "Managing everything the way I am?"

"Yeah," he lies. He preferred her incompetent. She leaves with her jonquil-yellow new coat over her arm and he thinks she is gaining weight behind, she has that broad-beamed look women of the county wear when they come into their own.

* * *

Harry watches what is left of Tom Brokaw and is settling into a seven-o'clock show on life in Antarctica when, of all people, the Harrisons come visiting. Not just Thelma – she's brought Ron along, or Ron has brought her, since she is thinner and sallower than he has ever seen her, and moves as if every step might break a bone. She smiles regretfully; her eyes apologize for the shape she's in, for Ronnie's being with her, for her being unable to stay away. "We were here in the hospital seeing my doctor," she explains, "and Ron Junior had heard you were in."

"For what they call a little procedure," he says, and gestures toward the chair Janice has pulled up to the bed and that's probably still warm from her broad beam. "Ron, there's that big padded chair over in the corner if you want to pull it over; it's on wheels."

"I'll stand," he says. "We can only stay a minute."

He is sullen, but Rabbit didn't ask the Harrisons to come visit and doesn't see why he should be bullied. "Suit yourself." He asks Thelma, "How are *you*?"

Thelma sighs elaborately. "You know doctors. They never admit they don't have an answer. I'm on home dialysis twice a week, Ronnie's a saint to put up with me. He took a course on how to cope with the machine."

"Ronnie always was a saint," Harry tells her, everybody in the room knowing that Ronnie Harrison was just about his least favorite person in the world, though he had known him from kindergarten. A dirty-mouthed plug-ugly even at the age of five, and now bald as a prick's tip, with wisps above his big droopy ears. Ronnie in high school and afterward had a certain chunkiness, but the approach of old age has pulled the chunks like taffy, leaving hollows in his face and lumps and a painful stringiness around the throat. Harry says, as if she doesn't already know, "Janice is taking courses too, to learn how to sell real estate. I guess so she has a trade in case I pop off."

Thelma's eyelids flutter, a bony hand wearing a wedding ring gestures the possibility away. The sicker she gets, the more dried-out and schoolteacherish she looks. That was one of the jokes of her being his mistress, her looking so prim and being so wild in bed, but maybe the real her was the schoolteacher and the other was put on purely for him. "Harry, you're not going to pop off," she tells him urgently, afraid for him. That strange way women have, of really caring about somebody beyond themselves. "They do wonderful things with hearts now, they stitch and mend them just like rag dolls." She manages a thin smile. "Want to see what I have?"

He thinks he knows what she has, all of it, but she unbuttons her sleeve and with that matter-of-fact baring which was her style Thelma shows him the underside of her bared arm. Two purple bruised patches on her slender wrist are connected by a translucent U of some plastic tubing taped flat against the jaundiced skin. "That's called my shunt," she says, pronouncing the last word carefully. "It connects an artery and vein and when I have the dialysis we take it off and connect me to the machine."

"Pretty," seems all he can say. He tells them about his angioplasty, but is already tired of describing it, and trying to convey the creepy business of seeing the dark shadow of the catheter like a snaky forefinger inch ever more intimately into his heart's paler, trembling shades. "My coronary artery could have occluded and I would have gone into CA. Cardiac arrest."

"But you didn't, you jerk," Ronnie says, standing erect and abandoning his shadow on the wall. "The Old Master," he says, a sardonic phrase he used to kid Harry with in their basketball-playing days. Funny, all of his life Harrison has been shadowing Harry with his ugly flesh, a reminder of everything sweaty and effortful in life Rabbit squeamishly hoped to glide over and avoid. "Nobody lays a finger on the Old Master. He makes it all look easy." Ronnie used to resent how Marty Tothero would put him, Ronnie, into the game when the bruisers on the other side were roughing Harry up, to give rough stuff back. An enforcer, they call it now.

"It was never as easy as I made it look," Rabbit tells him. He turns to Thelma, wanting to be tender, since she had braved her husband's anger by bringing him here. She had never balked at humiliating Ronnie to give Harry her gift of love, and indeed, sick as the two lovers are, her nearness does give him that socketed feeling you have with certain women, that graceful feeling you can do no wrong. "How about you, Thel? Your docs think they're licking it?"

"Oh, they never say die, but a body gets tired. You can fight only so long. The pains I can live with, and the weakness all the time, but the kidneys going is really demoralizing. It takes away your pleasure in life if you can't take such things for granted. Harry, you know that part of the Bible they used to read to us in assembly, before the Bible got outlawed, about a time for everything? A time to gather up stones, a time to cast them away? I'm beginning to think there's a time to give up."

"Thel, don't say that," Ronnie says, with an urgency of his own. He loves this woman too, also calls her Thel. It occurs to Harry that two men for a woman and vice versa is about right, just as we need two kinds of days, workdays and holidays, and day and night. Ronnie sounds angry, that she would talk of giving up, but this May evening is slowly melting him into the shadowy wall, so it is beginning to seem that Harry and Thelma are alone together, as in so many stolen afternoons, their hearts beating, the school buses braking outside on the curved street signalling that he must go, and as in that room in the Caribbean, their first time together, when they stayed awake until dawn and then fell asleep as one body as the tropical blue air between the louvers paled and the palm trees ceased their nighttime stirring. Ronnie's disembodied voice says to her angrily, "You have three boys who want to see you grow old."

Thelma smiles slyly at Harry, her face colorless and waxy in the May day fading above the fancy brickwork cornices and chimneys visible through the windows. "Why would they want to see that, Ron?" she asks mischievously, not taking her gaze from Harry's face. "They're grown men. I've done all I can do for them."

Poor Ron has no answer. Maybe he's choked up. Rabbit takes pity and says to him, "How's the insurance business going, Ron?"

"It's levelled out," his voice says gruffly. "Not bad, not good. The S and L mess hurt some companies but not ours. At least people've stopped borrowing against their policies at five per cent and investing at ten the way they were. That was killing our figures."

"One of the nice things about getting to be old geezers like us," Harry says, "is people like you stop trying to sell me insurance." Footsteps and tingling pans sound from the hall, where the lights seem bright suddenly. Night has come.

"Not necessarily," Ron is saying. "I could get you a pretty fair deal on some twenty-payment straight life, if you and Janice are interested. I know a doctor who doesn't look too close. You've survived one coronary, that's in your favor. Let me work up some figures."

Harry ignores him. To Thelma he says, "Your boys are in good shape?"

"We think so. Good enough. Alex has had an offer from a high-tech place in Virginia, outside Washington. Georgie thinks he has a spot with a musical-comedy troupe in the Catskills this summer."

"Here's something Janice just told me. She's got Nelson to sign up for a drug rehab."

"That's nice," Thelma says, so softly and sincerely here in the gloom that her voice seems to exist not in the air but already in his blood, inserted intravenously. All the afternoons when their bodies intertwined and exchanged fluids are not gone but safe inside him, his cells remembering.

"You're nice to say so," he says, and dares to grasp her cool hand, the one without the shunt, and move it up from her lap so the back of his own hand brushes a breast.

Ronnie's voice comes forward from the wall. "We gotta go, Thel."

"Ron, thanks for bringing her by."

"Anything for the Old Master. We were in the building."

"Master of nothing at this point."

Ronnie grunts. "Who's to say?" He's not all bad.

Thelma has stiffly stood and, bending by his bed, asks, right out in front of Ronnie, "Darling, can you manage a little kiss?"

He may imagine it, but Thelma's pale cool departing face, swiftly pressed against his, their lips meeting a bit askew, gives off a faint far tang of urine. When he is alone in his room again he remembers how sometimes when he kissed Thelma goodbye at her house her mouth would be flavored by the sour-milk taste of his prick, the cheesy smegma secreted beneath his foreskin. She would be still all soft and blurred by their lovemaking and unaware, and he would try to conceal his revulsion, a revulsion at his own smell on her lips. It was like, another sad thing to remember, the time when Nixon, with Watergate leaking out all around

him, during one of the oil crunches went on television to tell us
so earnestly to turn our thermostats down, for not only would it
save oil but scientific studies showed that colder houses were
healthier for us. That big scowling scared face on television, the
lips wet and fumbling. Their President, crook or not, going down
in disgrace but trying to say what needed to be said; Harry as a
loyal American did go and turn his thermostat down.

Janice wakes up early out of nervousness; it is going to be a long
and complicated day for her, of seeing Nelson off at nine and picking Harry up at noon and taking a quiz in British property law at
seven, in the Brewer extension of Penn State in a renovated disused elementary school on South Pine Street, a section she isn't
too easy about parking the car in at night. In Penn Park in mid-
May the day begins with a kiss of coolness as in Florida; the little
limestone house is cozier now that the surrounding trees are fully
leafed. She has enjoyed, enough to add to her feelings of guilt,
these days of Harry's being in the hospital and her being free to
come and go without explanation, and to get into bed as early or
late as she pleases, and to watch what television shows she wants
to. Wednesday nights, for instance, she likes *Unsolved Mysteries*,
but Harry is always sitting beside her in the study or in bed telling
her how ridiculous these so-called mysteries are and how they
always derive, if you think about it, from the testimony of people
who are either mentally unbalanced or have something to gain
financially. The older Harry gets the more cynical he is; he used
to be religious in a funny way. They couldn't put the show on
television if there weren't some truth to it and that Robert Stack
seems ever so sensible. Last night, what with being out with
Charlie at that Vietnamese place along the Maiden Springs Pike
(it was nice, but she never figured out what she was supposed to
do with those bubbly brittle rice things like warped pancakes that
were so tasteless you must be supposed to dip them in something),
she missed all but the last ten minutes of *thirtysomething* which she
likes to watch Tuesdays because it's so different from how she
was when she was thirty-something, all those demands on her,

mother wife daughter, and then being Charlie's mistress for a while and feeling so inadequate and guilty and having no female friends really except Peggy Fosnacht who went and slept with Harry anyway and now is dead, terrible to think, all rotten and parchmenty like a mummy in her casket, too hideous for the mind to grasp but it happens anyway, even to people your own age. With Harry gone, she can eat Campbell's chicken noodle soup cold out of the can if she wants, with a few Ritz crackers crushed in, and not have to worry about giving him a good balanced low-fat low-sodium meal that he complains to her is tasteless. Maybe being a widow won't be so very bad is the thought she keeps trying not to think.

Last night it rained hard for an hour, she was kept awake by its drumming on the air-conditioner, and they say showers this evening again, though the sun is making a kind of tawny fog slanting across the yard through the neighbor's tall trees to where Harry has his little vegetable garden in imitation of the one his parents had in the back yard on Jackson Road, all he grows is lettuce and carrots and kohlrabi, he does love to nibble. She sees with her coffee that Bryant and Willard are getting along better on the *Today* show after that unfortunate thing with Bryant's private memo being exposed in all the papers, really nothing's private any more, the scandalmongers never rest, always hoping for another Watergate, her father's death was brought on by Watergate she has always felt. The news is mostly about China and Gorbachev, you can never trust Communists not to gang up on you, and Panama where that evil pockmarked Noriega just won't leave, and how Pennsylvania voters yesterday turned down the tax reform that Governor Casey wanted; people thought it would mean a tax increase and if there's anything you can count on Americans to be these last ten years it's selfish.

She tries to pick an outfit suitable for seeing your son off to a drug clinic and then babysitting for Roy all morning while Pru drives Nelson into North Philadelphia, which she's very nervous about, who wouldn't be, they do terrible things now, deliberately rear-end you and then drive off with your car when you get out, there is no such thing any more as a good Philadelphia neighborhood, and for a striking-looking younger woman like Pru is it's worse. Pru hopes to be back by noon so Janice can go pick Harry

up at the hospital, by twelve-thirty at the latest the nurse on duty
warned, they don't like to give them lunch that last day and the
girls coming round to make the beds don't like having somebody
in one of them dirtying the sheets and then leaving. It makes her
stomach nervous to think of Harry and his heart, men are so fragile it turns out, though that nice young intelligent Dr. Breit
seemed delighted with what the balloon did, but Harry's image of
himself has changed, he speaks of himself almost as if he's somebody he knew a long time ago, and he seems more of a baby than
he ever did, letting her make all the decisions. She doesn't see how
she can leave him alone in their house his first night out of the
hospital, but she can't miss the quiz either, it really makes more
sense with all this coming and going and the children upset about
their father's going off to the rehab to shift her base of operations
to Mother's house and to wear the smart light wool outfit she
bought two years ago at the Wanamaker's out at the mall on the
old fairgrounds (didn't they use to get excited in school, getting
the day off and all the rides, the one where four of you were in a
kind of cylinder and the boy opposite would be above you and
then below and the sky every which way and your skirt doing
heaven knows what, the smells of sawdust and cotton candy, and
the freaks and animals and prizes for tossing little hoops at pegs that
were bigger than they looked), a navy-blue-and-white outfit with
a kicky blue pleated skirt and off-white satin jersey and blue buttonless jacket with wide shoulders that always come back from the
cleaner's with the padding askew or bent or torn loose, it's a terrible fashion as far as dry cleaning goes. The first time she posed
for Harry in that suit he said it made her look like a little policeman – the shoulders and the piping on the pockets, she supposed,
gave it the look of a uniform but it would do all day, she thinks,
from having not to break down in saying goodbye to Nelson to
taking this quiz with all the strange old terms in it, curtilage and
messuage and socage and fee simple and fee tail and feoffee
and copyhold and customary freehold and mortmain and devises
and *lex loci rei sitae*. The little old elementary-school desks have
been uprooted and taken away in favor of one-armed chairs of
combination aluminum tubing and orange plastic, but the old
blackboards are still there, gray with chalk dust rubbed in over the

years, and the high windows you have to have a pole to raise and lower, and those high floating lights like flattened moons, like big hollow flowers upside down on their thin stems. Janice loves being back in class again, trying to follow the teacher and learn new things but also aware of the other students, their breathing and their feet scraping and the silent effort of their minds. The class is women three out of four and most younger than she but not all, to her relief she is not the oldest person in the class and not the dumbest either. The years with their heartbreak and working off and on over at the lot have taught her some things; she wishes her parents were alive to see her, sitting with these twenty-five others studying to get their licenses, the city sounds and Hispanic music and customized Hispanic cars revving their engines on Pine Street beyond the tall windows, sitting there with her notebooks and pencils and yellow highlighter (they didn't have those when she went to high school); but of course if they were alive she wouldn't be doing this, she wouldn't have the mental space. They were wonderful parents but had never trusted her to manage by herself, and her marrying Harry confirmed them in their distrust. She made bad decisions.

The teacher, Mr. Lister, is a doleful tall rumpled man with jowls that make him look like a dog. He gave her a B on the last quiz and likes her, she can tell. The other students, even the younger ones, like her too, and lend her cigarettes in the bathroom break at eight-thirty and invite her to come out with them for a beer afterward at ten. She hasn't accepted yet but she might some night when things are more normal with Harry, just to show she's not stuck-up. At least she hasn't let herself go to fat like some of the women her age in the class – shocking, really, to see flesh piled up like that, and not doing anything to reduce, just carrying these hundreds of pounds back and forth and scarcely able to squeeze them into the desks. You wonder how long people can live like that. One of the few natural blessings God handed Janice was a tidy figure and that she has tried to keep, for Harry's sake as well as her own. He does seem prouder of her, the older they get. He looks at her sometimes as if she's just dropped down out of the moon.

Even with hurrying this morning, she gets caught in the slow traffic through the thick of the Brewer rush hour. All these cars, where are they going? By the side of the highway as it heads around the side of the mountain you can see erosion from last night's heavy rain – big twisted ditches of red clay washed away, weeds and all. At Joseph Street she parks and goes up the walk scared of what chaos she'll find, but Nelson is dressed in one of those putty-colored suits he has and Pru in brown slacks and a khaki-colored mannish shirt under a red cardigan sweater with the arms loosely knotted around her shoulders, an outfit to drive in. Both she and Nelson look pale and drawn; you can almost see the agitated psychic energy around their heads, like one of those manifestations Harry scoffs at on *Unsolved Mysteries*.

In the kitchen, showing Janice the special peanut-butter-and-honey sandwich she has made just the way Roy likes it (otherwise he throws everything on the floor, even the TastyKake for dessert), Pru perhaps thinks the older woman notices something wrong in her manner and explains in a hurried low voice, "Nelson had some coke hidden around the house and thought we should use it up before he goes. It was too much even for him, so I did a few lines. I honestly don't know what he sees in it – it burned and I sneezed and then couldn't fall asleep but otherwise felt nothing. *Nothing*. I said to him, 'If this is all it is I don't see any problem in giving it up,' I'd have a harder time giving up Hershey bars."

But just the fact that she is talking so much, confessing so freely, stroking the lank red hair back from her forehead with a caressing gesture of both hands, with trembling fingertips, indicates to Janice that there has been a chemical event. Her son is poisonous. Everything he touches. With all her maternal effort she's brought destruction into the world.

Nelson has stayed in the front room, sitting on the Barcalounger with Roy in his arms, murmuring to the boy and gently blowing to tickle his ear. He looks up at his mother with resentment written all over his face. He says to her, "You know why I'm doing this, don't you?"

"To save your own life," Janice tells him, lifting the child out of his lap. Roy is growing heavier by the day and she puts him down on his own legs. "Time you start making him walk," she explains to Nelson.

"Just like you're making me go to this stupid useless place,"

Nelson says. "I want that perfectly clear. I'm going because you're making me and not because I admit I have any problem."

A weight of weariness floods her, as if she is at the end and not the beginning of her day. "From what it seems you've done with the money, we all have a problem."

The boy scarcely flinches, but does for an instant lower his eyelids, with their beautiful lashes, a little long for a boy's. She has always found those lashes heartbreaking. "It's just debt," he says. "If Lyle weren't so sick now he'd have explained it to you better. We were just borrowing against future income. It would have all worked out."

Janice thinks of the quiz she must face tonight and of poor Harry with that metal worm they put into his heart and she tells her son, "Darling, you've been stealing, and not just pennies from the change jar. You're an addict. You've been out of your head. You've not been yourself for I don't know how long and that's all any of us want, for you to be yourself again."

His lips, thin like her own, tighten so as to disappear under his mustache, that seems to be growing out, getting droopier. "I'm a recreational user just like you're a social drinker. We need it. We losers need a lift."

"I'm not a loser, Nelson, and I hope you're not." She feels a tightness growing in her but she tries to keep her voice low and level like Charlie would. "We had this same conversation in Florida and you made promises then you didn't keep. Your problem is too much for me, it's too much for your wife, it's too much for your father – much too much for him."

"Dad doesn't give a damn."

"He does. Don't interrupt. And your problem is too much for you. You need to go to this place where they've developed a method, where they're experienced. Your counsellor wants you to go."

"Ike says it's all a con. He says everything's a con."

"That's just his black way of talking. He got you in, he wants you to go."

"Suppose I can't stand it?" She and Harry never sent him off to summer camp, for fear he couldn't stand it.

"You must stand it, or –"

"Yeah, or what, Mom?"

"Or else."

He tries to mock her: "Oh sure. What are you and Charlie and old Harry going to do to me, put me in jail?" It is a real question; in nervousness he loudly sniffs, and then rubs his pink nostrils.

She tries to give him a real answer, saying in the level soft voice, "We wouldn't be the ones doing it. The Toyota Company and the police would be doing it, if they were called in."

He sniffs again, in disbelief. "Why would you call them in? I'll put the money back. I was always going to put it back. You care more about the dumb lot than you care about me."

His tone is trying for a bantering lightness, but her own mood has hardened; outrage has seized her, and self-righteousness. "You stole from me, never mind that. But you stole from your grand-father. You stole from what he had built."

Nelson's guarded eyes widen; his pallor seems a prisoner's in the murky parlor light. "Granpop always wanted me to run the lot. And what about my kids? What about Judy and Roy if you carry through on all these threats?" Roy has whimpered and col-lapsed to the floor, and is leaning against her ankles, hoping to dis-tract her, hating the sounds of this conversation.

"You should have been thinking of them before now," Janice says stonily. "You've been stealing from them, too." She takes a weary pride in her stoniness; her head is numb but clear, with the product of her own womb pleading and wriggling beneath her. This numbness she feels must be the *power* her women's group in Florida talks about, the power men have always had.

Nelson tries outrage of his own. "Ah, fuck, Mom. Don't give me all this, all this 'How could you do this to your mother and father?' What about what you did to me, all that mess around when Becky died so I never had a sister, and then that time you ran away with your oily Greek and crazy Dad brought Jill and then Skeeter into the house and they tried to make me take dope when I was just a little kid?"

Janice realizes that with all her stoniness and inner hardness she has been crying, her throat feels raw and tears have been flowing stupidly down her face. She wipes at them with the back of her hand and asks shakily, "How much dope did they make you do?"

He squirms, retreats a bit. "I don't know," he says. "They let me take a puff of pot now and then. But they were doing worse stuff and didn't try to hide it from me."

She works with a balled-up Kleenex at drying her face and eyes, thinking what a messy start she is having to this day, in a costume that was supposed to see her through the roles of mother, grandmother, ministering wife, eager student, and prospective working girl. "Your childhood I guess wasn't ideal," she admits, stabbing under her eyes, feeling distracted, ready for her next role, "but then whose is? You shouldn't sit in judgment of your parents. We did the best we could while being people too."

He protests, "Being people too!"

She tells him: "You know, Nelson, when you're little you think your parents are God but now you're old enough to face the fact that they're not. Your father isn't well and I'm trying to make something of what little life I have left and we just can't focus on you and your misbehavior as much as you think we should. You're of an age now to take responsibility for your own life. It's plain to everybody who knows you that your only chance is to stick with this program in Philadelphia. We're all going to try to hold the fort here for three months but when you come back in August you'll be on your own. You won't get any favors at least from me."

He sneers. "I thought mothers were supposed to love their kids no matter what." As if to challenge her physically he pushes up out of his grandfather's Barcalounger and stands close. He is three inches taller than she.

She feels the rawness in her throat and the heat in her eyes beginning again. "If I didn't love you," she says, "I'd let you go on destroying yourself." Her store of words is exhausted; she launches herself toward the white sneering face and embraces the boy, who grudgingly, after a resistant wriggle, responds and hugs her back, patting her shoulder blade with what Harry's mother used to call "those little Springer hands." Now, *there*, Janice thinks, was a hateful mother, who never said No to her son in all her life.

Nelson is saying in her ear that he'll be fine, everything will be fine, he just got a little overextended.

Pru comes downstairs carrying two big suitcases. "I don't know how often they wear suits," she says, "but I thought they must have a lot of physical therapy so I packed all the shorts and athletic socks I could find. And blue jeans, for when they make you scrub the floors."

"Bye bye Daddy," Roy is saying down among their legs. Since Pru has her hands full, Janice hoists him up, heavy and leggy though he is getting to be, for his father's farewell kiss. The child hangs on to Nelson's ear in parting and she wonders where Roy got this idea of inflicting pain to show affection.

When his parents have gone off in the burgundy-red Celica Supra that Nelson drives, Roy leads his grandmother into the back yard where Harry's old vegetable garden with the little chicken-wire fence he could step over has been replaced with a swing-and-slide set bought five years ago for Judy and pretty well gone to rust and disuse. Already, though the summer is young, tall weeds flourish around the metal feet of it. Janice thinks she recognizes the ferny tops of carrots and kohlrabi among the plantain and dandelions, the dandelions' yellow flowers now seedy white pompons that fly apart at the swat of the broken hockey stick whose taped-up handle little Roy swings like a samurai sword. The Springers moved to this house when Janice was eight and from the back yard the big house looks naked to her without the copper beech. The sky is full of puffy scudding clouds with those purply-dark centers that can bring rain. The weatherman this morning had called for more, though not as violent as last night's showers. She takes Roy for a little walk over the sidewalk squares of Joseph Street, some of them replaced but here and there a crack she remembers still unmended and two slabs still tilted up by a sycamore root in a way that made a treacherous bump for a girl on roller skates. She tells Roy some of this, and the names of families that used to live in the houses of the neighborhood, but he gets cranky and tired within the block; children now don't seem to have the physical energy, the eagerness to explore, that she remembers, girls as well as boys, her knees always skinned and dirty, her mother always complaining about the state of her clothes. Roy's interest during their walk flickers up only when they come to a string of little soft anthills like coffee grounds between two sidewalk cracks. He kicks them open and then stamps the scurrying armies suddenly pouring out to defend the queen. Such slaughter wearies him, the ants keep coming, and she finally has to pick the lummox up and carry him back to the house, his sneakers drumming sluggishly against her belly and pleated skirt.

One of the cable channels has cartoons all morning. Gangs of outlined superheroes, who move one body part at a time and talk with just their lower lips, do battle in space with cackling villains from other galaxies. Roy falls asleep watching, one of Pru's oat-bran low-sugar cookies broken in two wet crumbling halves in his hands. This house where Janice lived so long – the potted violets, the knickknacks, the cracked brown Barcalounger Daddy loved to relax on, to wait with closed eyes for one of his headaches to subside, the dining-room table Mother used to complain was being ruined by the lazy cleaning women who like to spray on Pledge every time and ruin the finish with gummy wax build-up – deepens her guilt in regard to Nelson. His pale frightened face seems still to glow in the dark living room: she pulls up the shade, sur-prising the sleepy wasps crawling on the sill like arthritic old men. Across the street, at what used to be the Schmehlings' house, a pink dogwood has grown higher than the porch roof; its shape in bloom drifts sideways like those old photos of atomic bomb-test clouds in the days when we were still scared of the Russians. To think that she could be so cruel to Nelson just because of money. The mem-ory of her hardness with him makes her shake, chilling the some-thing soft still left in the center of her bones, giving her a little physical convulsion of self-disgust such as after you vomit.

Yet no one will share these feelings with her. Not Harry, not Pru. Pru comes back not at noon but after one o'clock. She says traffic was worse than anyone would imagine, miles of the Turnpike reduced to one lane, North Philadelphia enormous, block after block of row houses. And then the rehab place took its own sweet time about signing Nelson in; when she complained, they let her know that they turned down three for every one they admitted. Pru seems a semi-stranger, taller in stature and fiercer in expression than Janice remembered as a mother-in-law. The link between them has been removed.

"How did he seem?" Janice asks her.

"Angry but sane. Full of practical instructions about the lot he wanted me to pass on to his father. He made me write them all down. It's as if he doesn't realize he's not running the show any more."

"I feel so terrible about it all I couldn't eat any lunch. Roy fell asleep in the TV chair and I didn't know if I should wake him or not."

Pru pokes back her hair wearily. "Nelson kept the kids up too late last night, running around kissing them, wanting them to play card games. He gets manicky on the stuff, so he can't let anybody alone. Roy has his play group at one, I better quick take him."

"I'm sorry, I knew he had the play group but didn't know where it was or if Wednesday was one of the days."

"I should have told you, but who would have thought driving to Philadelphia and back would be such a big deal? In Ohio you just zip up to Cleveland and back without any trouble." She doesn't directly blame Janice for missing Roy's play group, but her triangular brow expresses irritation nevertheless.

Janice still seeks absolution from this younger woman, asking, "Do *you* think I should feel so terrible?"

Pru, whose eyes have been shuttling from detail to detail of what is, after all, as far as use and occupancy go, her house, now for a moment focuses on Janice a look of full cold clarity. "Of course not," she says. "This is the only chance Nelson has. And you're the only one who could make him do it. Thank God you did. You're doing exactly the right thing."

Yet the words are so harshly stated Janice finds herself unreassured. She licks the center of her upper lip, which feels dry. There is a little crack in the center of it that never quite heals. "But I feel so – what's the word? – mercenary. As if I care more about the company than my son."

Pru shrugs. "It's the way things are structured. You have the clout. Me, Harry, the kids – Nelson just laughs at us. To him we're negligible. He's sick, Janice. He's not your son, he's a monster con artist who used to be your son."

And this seems so harsh that Janice starts to cry; but her daughter-in-law, instead of offering to lend comfort, turns and sets about, with her air of irritated efficiency, waking up Roy and putting him in clean corduroy pants for play school.

"I'm late too. We'll be back," Janice says, feeling dismissed. She and Pru have previously agreed that, rather than risk leaving Harry alone in the Penn Park house while she does her three hours at the Penn State extension, she will bring him back here for his first night out of the hospital. As she drives into Brewer she looks forward to seeing him on his feet again, and to sharing with him her guilt over Nelson.

But he disappoints her just as Pru did. His five nights in St. Joseph's have left him self-obsessed and lackadaisical. He seems brittle and puffy, suddenly; his hair, still a dull blond color, has been combed by him in the same comb-ridged pompadour he used to wear coming out of the locker room in high school. His hair has very little gray, but his temples are higher and the skin there, in the hollow at the corner of the eyebrows, has a crinkly dryness. He is like a balloon the air just slowly goes out of: over days it wrinkles and sinks to the floor. His russet slacks and blue cotton sports coat look loose on him; the hospital diet has squeezed pounds of water out of his system. Drained of spirit as well, he seems halting and blinky the way her father became in his last five years, closing his eyes in the Barcalounger, waiting for the headache to pass. It feels wrong: in their marriage in the past Harry's vitality always towered over hers – his impulsive needs, his sense of being generally cherished, his casual ability to hurt her, his unspoken threat to leave at any moment. It feels wrong that she is picking him up in her car, when he is dressed and wet-combed like the boy that comes for you on a date. He was sitting meekly in the chair by his bed, with his old gym bag, holding medicine and dirty underwear, between his feet in their big suede Hush Puppies. She took his arm and with cautious steps he moved to the elevator, as the nurses called goodbye. One plump younger one seemed especially sad to see him go, and the Hispanic culinary aide said to Janice with flashing eyes, "Make him eat right!"

She expects Harry to be more grateful; but a man even slightly sick assumes that women will uphold him, and in this direction, men to women, the flow of gratitude is never great. In the car, his first words are insulting: "You have on your policeman's uniform."

"I need to feel presentable for my quiz tonight. I'm afraid I won't be able to concentrate. I can't stop thinking about Nelson."

He has slumped down in the passenger seat, his knees pressed against the dashboard, his head laid back against the headrest in a conceited way. "What's to think?" he asks. "Did he wriggle out of going? I *thought* he'd run."

"He didn't run at all, that was one of the things that made it so sad. He went off just the way he used to go to school. Harry, I wonder if we're doing the right thing."

Harry's eyes are closed, as if against the battering of sights to see through the car windows – Brewer, its painted brick buildings, its heavy sandstone churches, its mighty courthouse, its new little green-glass skyscraper, and the overgrown park where Weiser Square had once been and which is now the home of drug addicts and the homeless who live in cardboard boxes and keep their clothes in stolen shopping carts. "What else can we do?" he asks indolently. "What does Pru think?"

"Oh, she's for it. It gets him off her hands. I'm sure he's been a handful lately. You can see in her mind she's single already, all independent and brisk and a little rude to me, I thought."

"Don't get touchy. What does Charlie think? How was your Vietnamese dinner last night?"

"I'm not sure I understand Vietnamese food, but it was nice. Short but sweet. I even got home in time to catch the end of *thirty-something*. It was the season finale – Gary tried to protect Susannah from a magazine exposé being written by Hope, who found out that Susannah was stealing from the social-service center." All this in case he thinks she slept with Charlie, to show there wasn't time. Poor Harry, he doesn't believe you can grow beyond that.

He groans, still keeping his eyes shut. "Sounds awful. Sounds like life."

"Charlie's real proud of me," she says, "for standing up to Nelson. We had a grim little talk this morning, Nelson and me, where he said I loved the company more than him. I wonder if he isn't right, if we haven't become very materialistic since you first knew me. He seemed so little, Harry, so hurt and defiant, just the way he was the time I went off to live with Charlie. Abandoning a twelve-year-old like that, I'm the one should have been put in jail, what *was* I thinking of? It's true what he says, who am I to lecture him, to send him off to this dreary place? I was

just about the age he is now when I did it, too. So *young*, really."
She is crying again; she wonders if you can become addicted to tears
like everything else. All the darkness and fumbling and unthinkable
shames of her life feel regurgitated in this unstoppable salty outpour.
She can hardly see to drive, and laughs at her own snuffling.

Harry's head rolls loosely on the headrest, as if he is basking in
an invisible sun. The clouds are crowding out the hazy sky, their
dark hearts merging into an overcast. "You were trying something
out," Harry tells her. "You were trying to live while you were still
alive."

"But I had no *right*, you had no right either, to do the things
we did!"

"For Chrissake, don't bawl. It was the times," he says. "The
Sixties. The whole country was flipping out back then. We
weren't so bad. We got back together."

"Yes, and sometimes I wonder if that wasn't just more self-
indulgence. We haven't made each other happy, Harry."

She wants to face this with him but he smiles as if in his sleep.
"You've made me happy," he says. "I'm sorry to hear it didn't
work both ways."

"Don't," she says. "Don't just score points. I'm trying to be
serious. You know I've always loved you, or wanted to, if you'd
let me. Ever since high school, at least ever since Kroll's. That's
one of the things Charlie was telling me last night, how crazy
about you I've always been." Her face heats; his failure to respond
embarrasses her; she hurries on, turning left on Eisenhower. A gap
in the clouds makes the hood of the Camry glare; then it is dipped
deeper into cloud shadow. "It really was a pretty restaurant," she
says, "the way they've fixed it up and everything, these little
Vietnamese women so petite they made me feel like a horse. But
they spoke perfect English, with Pennsylvania accents – second
generation, can it be? Has it been that long since the war? We
should go there sometime."

"I wouldn't dream of intruding. It's your and Charlie's place."
He opens his eyes and sits up. "Hey. Where're we going? This is
the way to Mt. Judge."

She says, "Harry, now don't get mad. You know I have to go
to class and take the quiz tonight, and I'd feel too funny leaving

you alone for three hours just out of the hospital, so Pru and I worked it out that you and I would sleep in Mother's old bed, which they moved across the hall into the old sewing room when Mother's room became Judy's room. This way you'll have babysitters while I'm off."

"Why can't I go to my own fucking house? I was looking forward to it. I lived in that damn barn of your mother's for ten years and that was enough."

"Just for one night, honey. Please – otherwise I'll be sick with worry and flunk my quiz. There are all those Latin and funny old English words you're expected to know."

"My heart's fine. Better than ever. It's like a sink trap after all the hair and old toothpaste has been cleaned out. I saw the bastards do it. Nothing will happen if you leave me alone, I promise."

"That nice Dr. Breit told me before they did it there was a chance of a coronary occlusion."

"That was while they were doing it, with the catheter in. The catheter's out now. It's been out nearly a week. Come on, honey. Take me home."

"Just one night, Harry, please. It's a kindness to everybody. Pru and I thought it would distract the children from their father's not being there."

He sinks back into his seat, giving up. "What about my pajamas? What about my toothbrush?"

"They're there. I brought them over this morning. I tell you, this day. I've really had to plan. Now, after we've got you settled, I *must* study, absolutely."

"I don't want to be in the same house with Roy," he says, sulking humorously, resigned to what after all is a tiny adventure, a night back in Mt. Judge. "He'll hurt me. Down in Florida he yanked the oxygen tube right out of my nose."

Janice remembers Roy stamping on all those ants but nevertheless says, "I spent the whole morning with him and he couldn't have been sweeter."

Pru and Roy are not there. Janice leads Rabbit upstairs and suggests he lie down. Ma's old bed has been freshly made up; his off-white pajamas are folded nicely on his pillow. He sees in the murky far corner next to an old wooden-cased Singer sewing machine the dressmaker's dummy, dust-colored, eternally head-less and erect. Ma's big bed crowds the room so there are just a few inches of space on one side next to the window and on the other beside the wall with its wainscoting. The sewing room has a wainscoting of varnished beaded boards, set upright and trimmed at chest-level with a strip of molding. The door of a shallow closet in the corner is made of the same boards. When he opens it, the door bumps annoyingly on the bedpost of Ma's old bed, a bed-post turned with a flattened knob at the top like a hard, brown-painted mushroom, and the paint on it has crackled into small rectangles, like a puddle that has dried. He opens the door to hang up his blue coat, among cobwebby crammed old irons and toast-ers, coverlets folded and preserved in yellowing cellophane moth bags, and a rack of Fred Springer's dead neckties. Harry folds back his shirtsleeves and begins to feel like himself; the idea of spend-ing a day back in Mt. Judge is beginning to amuse him. "Maybe I'll take a little walk."

"Should you?" Janice asks.

"Absolutely. It's the best thing for you, that's what everybody at the hospital says. They had me walking the halls."

"I thought you might want to lie down."

"Later, maybe. You go study. Go on, this quiz of yours is mak-ing me nervous."

He leaves her at the dining-room table with her book and her photocopies and heads up Joseph Street to Potter Avenue, where the ice-plant water used to run down in the gutter. The gutter has been long dry but the cement was permanently tinged green. Rabbit walks away from the center of the borough with its dry cleaners and Turkey Hill Minit Market and Pizza Hut and Sunoco and discount stereo and new video store that used to be a shoe store and aerobics class above what had been a bakery when he was a boy. The smell of warm dough and icing out of its doors would make him drool. He walks uphill to where Potter Avenue meets Wilbur Street; here a green mailbox used to lean on a con-crete post and now the bigger boxy kind with the rounded top stands instead, painted blue. A fire hydrant painted red, white, and blue for the Bicentennial in the Seventies has been given a fresh and garish coat of the orange you see on life jackets and joggers' vests and hunters' outfits, as if a fog creeping into our way of life is making everything harder to see. He walks up Wilbur, feeling the steep slope tug at his heart. The street in its lower blocks holds pretentious large houses like the Springers', stucco and brick and slate, fortresslike, with gables and acres of roof, some of them now split up into condos reached by wooden outside stairs that look tacky. Beyond the alley where long ago there used to be a telephone pole with a backboard bolted to it, Rabbit's chest has that full feeling, his ribs like bands of pressure, and he pops a Nitrostat under his tongue and waits for the relief and the tingle, while cool cloud shadows slide rapidly across the forested edge of the mountain above him. He had hoped he would need to take fewer pills but maybe it takes time for the operation to sink in.

He continues hiking, alone on the sloping sidewalk, up into the block where he and Janice lived when they were first married. Built all at once in the Thirties, a row of frame semi-detached climbs the hill like a staircase. Like the fire hydrant, they have become brighter, painted in fanciful storybook colors, pale purple and canary yellow, aqua and orange, colors that no respectable Pennsylvania householder would have applied when Harry was young. Life was not only bigger but more solemn then. Colors were bruise and dung, in gritty sidings that rubbed off on your fingers and were tar underneath.

His own house, the seventh in the row, number 447, had tired wooden steps that have been replaced with concrete inset with irregular multicolored pieces of broken tile and covered with a central runner of green outdoor carpeting; the house door into the vestibule has been painted a high-gloss ochre on its panels and maroon on its stiles, so a bold double cross is figured forth, ornamented by a brass knocker in the shape of a fox's head. Camaros and BMWs are parked out front; glass curtains and splashy abstract prints dress the windows. This row, a kind of slum when Harry and Janice and two-year-old Nelson lived here, has been spruced up: festive yuppie money has taken it over. These apartments are fashionable, high above the town as they are. Back then, thirty years ago, from the third floor, the view across the asphalted rooftops to the peaked houses and parked cars lower down just seemed an enlargement of their discontent, their defeat, a sense of defeat the years have brought back to him, after what seemed for a while to be triumphs. There had been, being here makes him remember, those cheap sliding screens at the windows, and a rusty furnace odor in the vestibule, and a plastic clown some kid had left in the dirt under the front-porch steps, now concrete carpeted green like those traffic islands down at Valhalla Village.

This row used to end Wilbur Street; development had stopped at a gravel turnaround, and an abandoned gravel quarry made the transition to the mountain's shaggy back side. Now a double row, not quite new, of shingled condominiums, with strangely exaggerated chimneys and gables like houses in a child's storybook, occupies still higher ground. The windows and doors and trim boards of these condos are tinted in pale and playful colors. The plantings and little lawns are still tenuous; last night's downpour washed from the deforested acres of the mountain reddish mud that has drifted, hardening, all along the fresh curbs and overflowed onto the street's blue-black asphalt. We're using it all up, Harry thinks. The world.

He turns and walks downhill. On Potter Avenue he continues past Joseph and goes into a Turkey Hill Minit Market and to suppress his melancholy buys a ninety-nine-cent bag of Corn Chips. NET WT. 6¼ OZ. 177 grams. *Manufactured by Keystone Food Prod., Inc., Easton, Pa. 18042 U.S.A. Ingredients: Corn, vegetable oil (contains one or more of the following oils: peanut, cottonseed, corn, partially hydrogenated soybean), salt.* Doesn't sound so bad. KEEP ON KRUNCHIN', the crinkly pumpkin-colored bag advises him. He loves the salty ghost of Indian corn and the way each thick flake, an inch or so square, solider than a potato chip and flatter than a Frito and less burny to the tongue than a triangular red-peppered Dorito, sits edgy in his mouth and then shatters and dissolves between his teeth. There are certain things you love putting into your mouth – Nibs, Good & Plentys, dry-roasted peanuts, lima beans cooked not too soft – and the rest is more or less disagreeable mush, or meat that gives the teeth too tough a fight and if you think about it almost makes you gag. Ever since childhood, Rabbit has had mixed feelings about eating, especially the creatures that not too long ago were living just like you. Sometimes he imagines he can taste the terror of the ax in the slice of turkey or chicken and the happy snorting and wallowing in pork and the stupid monotony of a cow's life in beef, and in lamb a hint of urine like that whiff from Thelma's face in the hospital. Her dialysis now and their night in that tropical hut, bodily fluids, but there were limits to what bodies can do, and limits of involvement what with Janice and Ron and the kids and fussy living rooms all over Diamond County, and some limitation within him really, a failure or refusal to love any substance but his own. And she too, she did tend afterwards to be curiously severe with him, as though he had become disgusting now that she had eaten, his sour-milk smell tainting her satisfied mouth. His meat having been eaten by her and now she being eaten by all that microscopic chewing from within. Lupus means wolf, she had told him, one of the auto-immune diseases in which the body attacks itself, antibodies attack your own tissue, self-hatred of a sort. Thinking of Thelma, Harry feels helpless and in his helplessness hard-hearted. The Corn Chips as he walks along the pavement begin to accumulate in his gut into a knotted muchness, a little ball of acid, and yet he cannot resist putting just one more into his mouth, to feel its warped salty edges, its virgin crunchiness, on his tongue, between his teeth, among these salivating membranes. By the time he gets back to 89 Joseph behind its wall of sticky leafed-out Norway maples he has consumed the full bag, even the fragments of salt and corn small enough for an ant to carry back to his brown queen bloated in her maze beneath the sidewalk; he has wrapped himself around all 6¼ ounces of sheer poison, pure sludge in his arteries, an oily aftertaste in his throat and between his teeth. He hates himself, with a certain relish.

Janice is working at the dining-room table, making lists for herself to memorize. When she looks up, her eyes have a rubbed frowning look and her mouth is open a dark slot. He hates to see it, hates to see her struggling so hard not to be dumb. His long walk has left him so tired he goes upstairs and takes off his slacks to keep the crease and lies down on Ma Springer's bed, on top of the covers but under the Amish quilt, a patchwork quilt that releases to his nostrils a memory of how Ma smelled toward the end, with a musty far odor of fleshly corners gone unwashed.

He finds himself suddenly scared to be out of the hospital white-ness, the antisepsis, the halls of softly clattering concern focused upon him . . . sick him.

He must have fallen asleep, for when he opens his eyes the day has a different tone through the room's single window: a cooler, shadowed menace. The rain coming closer. The clouds and tree-tops merging. From the sounds downstairs, Pru and both children are home, and footsteps move about in the hall outside much as years ago he would hear Melanie and Nelson sneak back and forth at night. It is not night, it is late afternoon. The children, home from school, have been instructed to be quiet because Grandpa is sleeping; but they are unable to resist the spurts of squalling and of glee that come over them. Life is noise. Rabbit's stomach hurts, he forgets why.

After they hear him make a trip down the hall to the bathroom, they come and visit him, the poor little semi-orphans. Their four eyes, two green, two brown, feast on him from the bed's edge. Judy's face seems longer and graver than it was in Florida. She will have an Angstrom leanness, a hunted look. Her dress is lilac-colored, with white smocking. Does he imagine a touch of extra redness to her lips? Does Pru allow that? Certainly the child's hair has been given an artificial wave, a carrot-colored crimp. She asks, "Grandpa, did it hurt in the hospital?"

"Not much, Judy. It hurt my feelings, mostly, to be there at all."

"Did they fix that thing inside you?"

"Oh, yes. Don't you worry about that. My doctors says I'm better than ever."

"How come you're in bed, then?"

"Because Grandma was studying for her quiz and I didn't want to bother her."

"She says you're going to sleep over."

"Looks that way, doesn't it? A pajama party. Before you were born, Judy, Grandma and I lived here for years and years, with your great-grandmother Springer. You remember her?"

The child's eyes stare, their green intensified by the maple trees at the window. "A little bit. She had fat legs and wore thick orange stockings."

"That's right." But can Ma be no more than that in this child's memory? Do we dwindle so fast to next to nothing?

"I used to hate her stockings," Judy goes on, as if sensing his need for more and trying to meet it.

"Those were Sup-Hose," Harry explains.

"And she wore funny little round glasses she never took off. She'd let me play with the case. It snapped."

Roy, bored to hear all this about a woman he never met, begins to talk. His round face strains upward as if he's trying to swallow something rough, and his arched eyebrows pull his dark shiny eyes painfully open. "Daddy – Daddy won't –" or perhaps he said "went"; he seems unable to wrestle his thoughts into shape and begins again with the strained word "Daddy."

Impatiently Judy gives him a push; he falls against a bedpost, there in the narrow space between the mattress edge and the beaded wainscoting. "Shut up if you can't talk," she tells him. "Daddy's in a rehab place getting better."

The child has hit his head; he stares at his grandfather as if waiting to be told what to do. "Ouch," Harry says for him, and, sitting up against Ma Springer's old brown headboard, opens his arms to the child. Roy dives against his chest and lets himself bawl, about his hurt head. His hair, when Harry rubs it, is stickily fine, like Janice's yesterday, when she cried. Something about being helpless in bed, people hit you up for sympathy. They've got you where they want you.

Judy talks right through Roy's aggrieved noise. "Grandpa, want to watch one of my videos with me? I have *Dumbo* and *The Sound of Music* and *Dirty Dancing*."

"I'd love to see *Dirty Dancing* sometime, I've seen the other two, but shouldn't you be doing your homework before dinner?"

The child smiles. "That's what Daddy always says. He never wants to watch a video with me." She looks at Roy being cradled and pulls at her brother's arm. "Come on, stupid. Don't lean on Grandpa's chest, you'll hurt him."

They go away. A ghostly moment as Judy stood by the bed reminded him of Jill, another of the many dead people he knows. The numbers are growing. Life is like a game they used to play on the elementary-school playground, Fox-in-the-Morning. You all lined up on one side of the asphalt area marked out for games. One person was "it," and that one would call out "Fox in the morning," and you would all run to the other side, and "it" would grab one victim from the running throng and drag him or her into the circle painted on the asphalt, and then there would be two "it"s, and these would capture a few more on the next massed gallop from safety to safety, and these four would become eight, and soon a whole mob would be roving the center; the proportions were reversed. The last person left uncaught became "it" for the next game.

Sparse specks of rain have appeared on the panes. His eyelids feel heavy again; a fog within is rising up to swallow his brain. When you are sleepy an inner world smaller than a seed in sunlight expands and becomes irresistible, breaking the shell of consciousness. It is so strange; there must be some other way of being alive than all this eating and sleeping, this burning and freezing, this sun and moon. Day and night blend into each other but still are nothing the same.

The call to dinner comes from far away, through many thicknesses of lath and plaster and hollow air, and from its sharp tone is being repeated. He can't believe he's been asleep; no time has passed, just a thought or two took a strange elastic shape as it went around a corner. His mouth feels furry. The specks of rain on the window are still few, few enough to be counted. He recalls remembering today the window screens they had in the Wilbur Street apartment, the kind you used to buy in hardware stores before combination storms made them obsolete. They never precisely fit, leaving splinters of light through which the mosquitoes and midges could crawl, but that wasn't the something tragic about them. Tragedy lay in a certain filtered summer breath they admitted, the glint of sun along segments of the mesh, an overlooked fervor in their details – the bent screening, the sliding adjustable frame stamped with the manufacturer's name, the motionless molding of the window itself, like the bricks that all through Brewer loyally hold their pattern though the masons that laid them long ago are dead. Something tragic in matter itself, the way it keeps watch no matter how great our misery. He went back to the apartment that day after Becky died and nothing was changed. The water in the tub, the chops in the skillet. The call to dinner repeats again, closer, in Janice's sharp voice, at the foot of the stairs: "*Harry. Din*ner."

"*Com*ing, for Chrissake," he says.

Janice called but the meal was cooked by Pru; it is light, delicious, healthful. Baked sole garnished with parsley and chives and flavored with pepper and lemon, asparagus served steaming in a rectangular microwave dish, and in a big wooden bowl a salad including celery and carrot slices and dates and green grapes. The salad bowl and microwave equipment are new since Ma Springer died.

Everybody eats but nobody has much to say except Janice, who chatters on bravely about her quiz, her class, the people in it, some of them women like herself developing midlife careers and others young people that seem much the way we were in the Fifties, running scared, economically, and playing everything safe. She mentions her teacher, Mr. Lister, and Judy laughs out loud at the name, repeating it, the rhyme of it. "Don't laugh, Judy, he has such a sad face," Janice says.

Judy tells some involved story about what a boy at school did today: he accidentally spilled paint for a poster they were making all over the floor and when the teacher bawled him out took the spilled jar and shook it at her so some got on her dress. Meanwhile there is this one black boy in the class, his family has just moved to Mt. Judge from Baltimore, and he was painting his face all over with these designs that have a secret meaning, he said. Her talk is a little like her excited channel-flipping and it occurs to Harry that she is making it up or confusing her own classroom with classroom shows she has seen on television.

Pru asks Harry how he is feeling. He says fine; his breathing does feel freer since the operation – "the procedure, the doctors like to call it" – and his memory for that matter better. He wonders how soft in the head he was getting before without realizing it. Really, he says, apologizing to her for her trouble, thanking her for the good healthy meal that he has managed to get down on top of the fermenting lump of Corn Chips, saying he could perfectly well have been left alone in his own house tonight.

Janice says she knows it is probably foolish but she could never forgive herself if he took a bad turn while she was in class and how could she concentrate on liens and curtilage and *lex loci* thinking he was back in the house drowning?

The other adults at the table hold their breaths at this slip; Harry gently says, when the silence gets unbearable, "You don't mean drowning," and Janice asks, "Did I say drowning?," knowing now in her ear's recall that she did. Harry sees that she only seems to have forgotten Rebecca, that in her own mind she is always and will always be the woman who drowned her own baby. It was this time of year, late spring, they are approaching the anniversary, in June. Janice rises, flustered, blushing, shamed.

"Who wants coffee besides me?" she asks, all eyes upon her, like an actress who must come up with some line.

"And there's some butter-pecan ice cream for dessert if anybody wants," Pru says, her flat Ohio voice having fallen over the years into the local locutions, that considerate Pennsylvania way of speaking as if to make things clear in a stupefying haze. She has taken off the cardigan and folded back the cuffs of her mannish khaki shirt so that half her downy freckled forearms show, there at the kitchen table, under the faceted-glass light fixture overhead.

"My favorite flavor," Harry says, pitying his wife, wanting to help her out of the brightly lit center of the stage; even little Roy with his inky eyes is staring at Janice, sensing something strange, a curse nobody mentions.

"Harry, that's the worst possible thing for you," Janice says, grateful for this opportunity he has given her for a quarrel, a scene. "Ice cream and nuts both."

Pru says, "I got some frozen yogurt with Harry in mind. Peach and banana I think are the flavors."

"It's not the same," Harry says, clowning to keep the attention of both women. "I want butter-pecan. *With* something. How about some good old-fashioned apple strudel, with all that sort of wallpaper paste inside? Or some sticky buns? Or shoo-fly pie? *Yum*: huh, Roy?"

"Oh, Harry, you're going to kill yourself!" Janice cries, excessively, her grief centered elsewhere.

"There's something called ice milk," Pru is saying, and he feels that her heart too is elsewhere, that throughout the meal she has been maneuvering around the covered-up hole of Nelson's absence, which no one has mentioned, not even the wide-eyed children.

"Shoo-fly pie," Roy says, in an oddly deep and mannish voice, and when they explain to him that there isn't really any, that it was just a joke of Grandpa's, he feels he has made a mistake, and in his weariness at learning all day to be more independent he begins to whimper.

"Makes your eyes light up," Rabbit sings to him, "and your tummy say 'howdy.' "

Pru takes Roy upstairs while Janice serves Judy butter-pecan ice cream and stacks the dishes into the dishwasher. Harry kept his spoon and digs into Judy's dish while Janice's back is turned. He loves that second when the tongue flattens the ice cream against the roof of the mouth and the fragments of pecan emerge like stars at evening. "Oh Grandpa, you shouldn't," Judy says, looking at him with genuine fright, though her lips want to smile.

He touches his own lips with a finger and promises, "Just one spoonful," while going for another.

The child calls for help: "Grandma!"

"He's just teasing," Janice says, but asks him, "Would you like your own dish?"

This gets him up from the table. "I shouldn't have ice cream, that's the worst thing for me," he tells her, and scolds, seeing the jumble of plates she has stacked in the dishwasher, "My God, you have no system – look at all the space you're wasting!"

"You stack it, then," she says, a modern woman, and while he does, fitting the dishes closer together, in harrowlike rows, she gathers together her papers and book and purse from the dining-room table. "Damn," she says, and comes to the kitchen to tell Harry, "All my planning this morning what to wear and I forget to bring a raincoat." The rain has settled in outside, sheathing the house in a loud murmur.

"Maybe Pru could lend you one."

"It would fall off me," she says. But she goes upstairs to where Pru is putting Roy to bed and after a conversation Harry can't hear comes down in a cherry-red waterproof plastic coat, with wide lapels and a belt too long and gleaming zigzags under the light. "Do I look ridiculous?"

"Not exactly," he tells her. It excites him, this transposition: you follow the zigzagging creases up expecting to see red-haired Pru staring back and instead it's Janice's middle-aged face, framed in a splashy bandanna not hers either.

"Also, *damn*, I'm so mad at myself, I left my lucky pen on the upstairs table back home. And there's no time to drive back for it, in all this rain."

"Maybe you're taking all this too seriously," he says. "What're you trying to prove to the teacher?"

"I'm trying to prove something to my*self*," she says. "Tell Pru I've left and that I'll be back at ten-thirty, maybe eleven if we decide to go out for beers afterward. You go to bed and rest. You look tired, honey." She gives him in parting a pointed little lingering kiss, grateful for something. Glad to go. All these other male advisers she suddenly has – Charlie, Mr. Lister, the new accountant – seem an invasion as devious as that televised catheter nudging forward into his shadowy webbed heart.

The murmur around the house sounds louder after Janice's footsteps on the porch and the sound of the Camry starting up. She has a panicky way of racing the engine before she puts a car in gear, and usually jumps off like a drag-racer. Janice is wrapped in Pru's cherry raincoat, and he is the man of Pru's house.

On the set in the living room, he and Judy watch the end of ABC news on Channel 6 (that Peter Jennings: here he is telling Americans all about America and he still says "aboot" for "about," he's so Canadian) and then, with Judy punching the remote control, they skip back and forth between *Jeopardy!* and *Simon and Simon* and the seven-o'clock syndicated reruns of *Cosby* and *Cheers*. Pru drifts downstairs, having put Roy down, and into the kitchen to tidy up totally after Janice's half-ass job and then through the dining room checking that all the windows are shut against the rain and into the sun room where she picks a few dead leaves off the plants on Ma Springer's old iron table there. Finally she comes into the living room and sits on the old sofa beside him, while Judy in the Barcalounger channel-surfs. On the *Cosby Show* rerun, the Huxtables are having one of those child-rearing crises bound to dissolve like a lump of sugar in their warm good humor, their mutual lovingness: Vanessa and her friends get all excited about entering a local dance contest, with lip synching, and get instruction from an old black nightclub pianist and when the time comes to demonstrate for their parents in their living room they bump and grind with a sexuality so startling and premature that Mrs. Huxtable, Claire, in real life the terrific Phylicia Rashad, married to the frog-eyed black sports commentator, restores decency, stopping the record and sending the girls back upstairs, yet with that smile of hers, that wide white slightly lippy black woman's smile, implying that indecency is all right, in its place, its wise time, as in one of those mutually ogling Huxtable snuggles that end many a *Cosby Show*. Beside him on the sofa Pru is staring at the screen with a jewel, a tear glittering in a corner of the eye toward him. From the Barcalounger Judy snaps the channel to a shot of tropical sky and a huge mottled turtle turning its head slowly while a Godlike voiceover intones, " . . . *determined to defend its breeding grounds.*"

"Goddamn it, Judy, put it back to the Cosbys right *now*," Harry says, furious less for himself than for Pru, to whom the show seemed to be a vision of lost possibilities.

Judy, startled just like the girls on the show, does put it back, but by now it's a commercial, and she cries, as the insult sinks in, "I want Daddy back! Everybody else is mean to me!"

She starts to cry, Pru rises to comfort her, Rabbit retreats in disgrace. He circles the house, listening to the rain, marvelling that he once lived here, remembering the dead and the dead versions of the living who lived here with him, finding a half-full jar of dry-roasted cashews on a high kitchen shelf and, on the kitchen television set, a cable rerun of last night's playoff game between the Knicks and the Bulls. He hates the way Michael Jordan's pink tongue rolls around in his mouth as he goes up for a dunk. He has seen Jordan interviewed, he's an intelligent guy, why does he swing his tongue around like an imbecile? The few white players there are on the floor look pathetically naked, their pasty sweat, their fuzzy armpit hair; it seems incredible to Harry that he himself was ever out there in this naked game, though in those days

the shorts were a little longer and the tank-top armholes not quite
so big. He has finished off the jar of cashews without noticing and
suddenly the basketball – Jordan changing direction in midair not
once but twice and sinking an awkward fall-back jumper with
Ewing's giant hand square in his face – pains him with its rubbery
activity, an extreme of bodily motion his nerves but not his muscles can remember. He needs a Nitrostat from the little bottle in
the coat jacket in that shallow closet upstairs. The hauntedness of
the downstairs is getting to him. He turns off the kitchen light and
holds his breath passing Ma Springer's old breakfront in the darkened dining room, where the wallpaper crawls with the streetlight
projections of rain running down the windows.

In the upstairs hall, he hears from Ma's old room, now Judy's,
the murmur of a television set, and dares tap the door and push in.
The little girl has been put into a sleeveless nightie and, holding
her stuffed dolphin, sits propped up on two pillows while her
mother sits on the bed beside her. The TV set flickering at the foot
of the bed picks out pale patches – the whites of Judy's eyes, her
bare shoulders, the dolphin's belly, Pru's long forearms laid across
the child's flat chest. He clears his throat and says, "Hey, Judy –
sorry if I got a bit mean down there."

With a hushing impatient hand motion she indicates that her
grandfather is forgiven and ought to come in and watch with
them. In the blue unsteady light, he picks out a child's straight
chair and brings it close to the bed and lowers himself to it; he virtually squats. Raindrops glint on the panes in the light from Joseph
Street. He looks at Pru's profile for the glint of a tear but her face
is composed. Her nose comes to a sharp point, her lips are clamped
together. They are watching *Unsolved Mysteries*: pale, overweight
American faces float into the camera's range, earnestly telling of
UFOs seen over sugar-beet fields, above shopping malls, in
Navajo reservations, while their homely rooms and furniture,
exposed to the glaring lights the cameras require, have the detailed
hard weirdness of diatoms seen under a microscope. Harry is
struck by how well, really, these small-town sheriffs and trailer-
camp housewives, and even the drifters and dropouts who just
happened to be tripping out on a deserted picnic grounds when
the geniuses commanding the UFOs decided to land and sample

the terrestrial fauna, speak – a nation of performers, of smoothly talking heads, has sprung up under the lights, everybody rehearsed for their thirty seconds of nationwide attention. During the commercials, Judy skips to other channels, to Jacques Cousteau in a diving suit, to Porky Pig in his big-buttoned blue vest (odd, those old cartoon animals all going around with bare bottoms), to a stringy-haired rock singer mouthing his mike in a lathered-up agony like a female porn star approaching a blow job, to a courtroom scene where the judge's shifty eyes in a second show that he is in on a deal, a hummingbird beating its surprisingly flexible wings in slow motion, Angela Lansbury looking shocked, Greer Garson looking gently out of focus in black and white, and back to *Unsolved Mysteries*, now about an infant who disappeared from a New York hospital, making Robert Stack, in his mystical raincoat, extra quizzical. Having been rude before, Rabbit holds his tongue. He feels fragile. The flickering images bear down upon him, relentless as heartbeats. With the mystery of the vanished baby still unsolved, he rises and kisses Judy goodnight, his face gliding past the bigger one next to hers. "Love you, Grandpa," the child mechanically says, forgiving or forgetful.

"Lights are off downstairs," he mutters to Pru.

"I need to go down anyway," she says, softly, both of them fearful of breaking the spell that exists between the child and the television set.

Her face, as his face glided past it on the way to kiss another, exuded an aura, shampooey-powdery, just as the trees outside the house are yielding to the rain a leafy fresh tree-smell.

This green wet fragrance is present in his room too, the old sewing room, where the headless dress dummy stands. He changes into the clean pajamas Janice uncharacteristically had the foresight to bring. A blooming cottony weariness has overtaken him, enveloping him like the rain. In the narrow room its sound is more distinct than elsewhere, and complicated, a conversation involving the porch roof, the house gutter, the echoing downspout, the yielding leaves of the maples, the swish of a passing car. Closest to him, periodic spurts of dripping between the storm window and the wooden sash suggest some leakage into the walls and an eventual trouble of rot. Not his problem. Fewer and fewer things are.

The window is open a little for air and stray droplets prick the skin of his hands as he stands a moment looking out. Mt. Judge doesn't change much, at least here in the older section, but has dropped away beneath his life as if beneath a rising airplane. His life flowed along this shining asphalt, past these tilted lawns and brick-pillared porches, and left no trace. The town never knew him, the way he had imagined as a child it did, every pebble and milkbox and tulip bed eyelessly watching him pass; each house had been turned inward, into itself. A blurred lit window across the street displays an empty easy chair, a set of brassheaded fireplace tools, a brick mantel supporting a pair of oblivious candlesticks.

Rabbit hurries in bare feet down the hall to the bathroom and back and into bed, before it is nine o'clock. At the hospital by now the last visitors would be long gone, the flurry of bathroom-going and pill-taking that followed their departure subsided, the lights and nurses' voices in the hall turned down. There is no reading lamp in his room, just a paper-shaded overhead he resists switching on. He noticed a stack of old *Consumer's Digest*s in the closet but figures the products they evaluated will all be off the market by now. The history book Janice gave him, that he can't get through although he is more than halfway, is back in the Penn Park den. Nor is the streetlight enough to read by. It projects rhomboidal ghosts of the windowpanes, alive with a spasmodic motion as raindrops tremblingly gather and then break downward in sudden streaks. Like the origins of life in one of those educational television shows he watches: molecules collecting and collecting at random and then twitched into life by lightning. Behind his head, past the old brown headboard with its jigsaw scrolls and mushroom-topped posts, his dead mother-in-law's sewing machine waits for her little swollen foot to press its treadle into life, and her short plump fingers to poke a wetted thread through its rusted needle. About as likely that to happen as life just rising up out of molecules. A smothered concussion, distant thunder, sounds in the direction of Brewer, and the treetops stir. Harry's head is up on two pillows so the full feeling in his chest is eased. His heart is giving him no pain, just floats wounded on the sea of ebbing time. Time passes, he doesn't know how much, before the door handle turns and clicks and a slant rod of hall light stabs into the amniotic isolation of the little borrowed room.

Pru's head, with coppery highlights on the top of her hair, pokes in. "You awake?" she asks in almost a whisper. Her voice seems roughened and her face is a milky heart-shaped shadow.

"Yep," Rabbit says. "Just lying here listening to the rain. You get Judy settled?"

"*Finally*," the young woman says, and with the exasperated emphasis enters the room wholly, standing erect. She is wearing that shorty bathrobe of hers, her legs cased in a white shadow descending to her ankles. "She's very upset about Nelson, naturally."

"Naturally. Sorry I blew up at her," he says. "The last thing the poor kid needs." He pushes up on his elbows, feeling himself somehow host, his heart thundering at the strangeness, though after his days in the hospital he should be used to people seeing him in bed.

"I don't know," Pru says. "Maybe it was just what she needed. A little structure. She thinks she has a right to all the TV sets in the world. Mind if I smoke?"

"Not at all."

"I mean, I see the window's a little bit open, but if it –"

"It doesn't," he says. "I like it. Other people's smoke. Almost as good as your own. After thirty years, I still miss it. How come you haven't given it up, with all this health kick?"

"I had," Pru says. Her face in the blue-green flare of her Bic lighter – a little tube as of lipstick – looks flinty, determined, a face stripped to essentials, with a long shadow leaping across her cheek from her nose. The flame goes out. She loudly exhales. Her voice continues in the renewed shadows. "Except for maybe one or two at night to keep myself from eating. But now, this thing with Nelson – why not? What does anything matter?" Her hovering face shows one profile, then the other. "There's no place to sit in here. This is an awful room."

He smells not only her cigarette smoke but her femininity, the faint department-store sweetness that clings to women, in the lotions they use, the shampoo. "It's cozy," he says, and moves his legs so she can sit on the bed.

"I bet you were asleep," Pru says. "I'll only stay for this cigarette. I just need a little adult company." She inhales like a man, deep, so the smoke comes out thin in a double jet from her mouth and nostrils, and keeps coming for several breaths. "I hope putting the kids down with Nelson gone isn't such a nightmare every night. They need so much reas*sur*ance."

"I thought he wasn't here a lot of nights."

"This time of night he usually was. The action over at the Laid-Back doesn't begin until around ten. He'd come home from work, eat, be with the kids, and then get restless. I honestly think most nights he didn't plan to go out for a couple hits again, it just came over him and he couldn't help himself." She takes another drag. He hears her intake, like a sigh with several levels, and remembers how it was, to smoke. It was creating out of air an extension of yourself. "With the kids, he was helpful. However much of a shit he was to everybody else, he wasn't a bad father. Isn't. I shouldn't talk about him as if he's dead."

He asks her, "What time is it, anyway?"

"Quarter after nine or so."

Janice would get back at ten-thirty at the earliest. There was plenty of time to see this through. He relaxes back into his pillows. Good he had that nap this afternoon. "Is that how you see it?" he asks. "He was a shit to you?"

"Absolutely. Terrible. Out all night doing God knows what, then this snivelling and begging for forgiveness afterwards. I hated that worse than the chasing; my father was a boozer and a chaser, but then he wouldn't whine to Mom about it, he'd at least let her do the whining. This immature dependence of Nelson's was totally outside my experience."

Her cigarette tip glows. A distant concussion of thunder steps closer. Pru's presence here feels hot in Harry's mind, she is awkwardly big and all sharp angles in the sac of his consciousness. Her talk seems angular and tough, the gritty Akron toughness overlaid with a dismissive vocabulary learned from professional copers. He doesn't like hearing his son called immature. "You knew him for some time out at Kent," he points out, almost hostilely. "You knew what you were taking on."

"Harry, I *did*n't," she says, and the cigarette tip loops through an agitated arc. "I thought he'd grow, I never dreamed how enmeshed he was, with you two. He's still trying to work out what you two did to him, as if you were the only parents in the world who didn't keep wiping their kid's ass until he was thirty. I tell him: Get real, Nelson. Lousy parents are par for the course. My God. Nothing's ideal. Then he gets sore and tells me what a cold fish I am. He means sex. A thing that goes fast with coke is shame; these women that are hooked will do *any*thing. I say to him, You're not going to give me AIDS from one of your coke whores. So he goes out again. It's a vicious circle. It's been going on for years."

"How many years, would you say?"

When she shrugs her shoulders, Ma's old bed shakes. "More than you'd think. That crowd around Slim was always doing pot and uppers – gays don't give a damn, they have all this money only for themselves. Maybe two years ago Nelson became a big enough user on his own to need to steal. At first he just stole from us, money that should have gone into the house and stuff, and then he started stealing from you – the company. I hope you send him to jail, I really do." She has been cupping her hand beneath the cigarette, to catch the ash, and now she looks around for an ash-tray and sees none and finally flips the butt toward the window, where it sparks against the screen and sizzles out on the wet sill. Her voice is hoarsening and finding a certain swing, a welling up. "I have no use for him any more. I'm scared to fuck him, I'm scared to be legally associated with him. I've wasted my life. You don't know what it's like. You're a man, you're free, you can do what you want in life, until you're sixty at least you're a buyer. A woman's a seller. She has to be. And she better not haggle too long. I'm thirty-three. I've had my shot, Harry. I wasted it on Nelson. I had my little hand of cards and played them and now I'm folded, I'm through. My husband hates me and I hate him and we don't even have any money to split up! I'm scared – *so* scared. And my kids are scared, too. I'm trash and they're trash and they know it."

"Hey, hey," he has to say. "Come on. Nobody's trash." But even as he says it he knows this is an old-fashioned idea he would have trouble defending. We're all trash, really. Without God to lift us up and make us into angels we're all trash.

Her sobbing is shaking the bed so badly that in his delicate post-op state he feels queasy. To quiet her big body he reaches out and pulls her toward him. As if expecting his touch, she huddles tightly, though a blanket and a sheet are between them, and continues sobbing in a bitter, lower register, her breath hot on his chest, where a pajama button has come undone. His chest. They want to carve it up. "At least you're healthy," he tells her. "Me, all they need to do is nail down the coffin lid. I can't run, I can't fuck, I can't eat anything I like, I know damn well they're going to talk me into a bypass. *You're* scared? You're still young. You've got lots of cards still. Think of how scared I feel."

In his arms Pru says in a voice gone calm again, "People have bypass operations all the time now."

"Yeah, easy for you to say. Like me telling you people are married to shits all the time. Or you telling me people have their kids turn out to be dope-addict embezzlers all the time."

A small laugh. A flash of light outside and, after some seconds, thunder. Both listen. She asks, "Does Janice say you can't fuck?"

"We don't talk about it. We just don't do it much lately. There's been too much else going on."

"What did your doctor say?"

"I forget. My cardiologist's about Nelson's age, we were all too shy to go into it."

Pru sniffs and says, "I hate my life." She seems to him to be unnaturally still, like a rabbit in oncoming headlights.

He lets the hand of the arm around her broad back move up across the bumps of the quilted robe and enter the silken cave at the nape of her neck, to toy with the warm hair there. "I know the feeling," he says, content to toy, aware through the length of his body of a cottony sleepiness waiting to claim him.

She tells him, "You were one of the things I liked about Nelson. Maybe I thought Nelson would grow into somebody like you."

"Maybe he did. You don't get to see what a bastard I can be."

"I can imagine," she says. "But people provoke you."

He goes on, "I see a lot of myself in the kid." The nape of her neck tingles under his fingers, the soft hairs rising to his electricity. "I'm glad you're letting your hair grow long," he says.

"It gets too long." Her hand has come to rest on his bare chest, where the button is unbuttoned. He pictures her hands with their pink-knuckled vulnerable raw look. She is left-handed, he remembers. The oddity of this excites him further. Not waiting too long to think about it, he with his free hand lifts hers from his chest and places it lower, where an erection has surprisingly sprouted from his half-shaved groin. His gesture has the pre-sexual quality of one child sharing with another an interesting discovery – a stone that moves, or a remarkably thick-bodied butterfly. The eyes widen in the dim face inches from his on the pillow. Tiny points of light are caught in her lashes. He lets his face drift, on the tide of blood risen within him, across those inches to set their mouths together, carefully testing for the angle, while her fingers caress him in a rhythm slower than that of his thudding heart. As the space narrows to nothing he is watchful of his heart, his accomplice in sin. Their kiss tastes to him of the fish she so nicely prepared, its lemon and chives, and of asparagus.

Rain whips at the screen. The leak onto the windowsill accelerates its tapping. A brilliant close flash shocks the air everywhere and less than a second later a heart-stopping crack and splintering of thunder crushes the house from above. As if in overflow of this natural heedlessness, Pru says "*Shit*," jumps from the bed, slams shut the window, pulls down the shade, tears open her bathrobe and sheds it, and, reaching down, pulls her nightie up over her head. Her tall pale wide-hipped nakedness in the dimmed room is lovely much as those pear trees in blossom along that block in Brewer last month were lovely, all his it had seemed, a piece of Paradise blundered upon, incredible.

III. MI

BY MID-JUNE the weeds have taken over: burdock and chicory stand three feet tall along the stony dry shoulders of Route 111, and the struggling little yew hedge meant to dress up the base of the Springer Motors display window has crabgrass and purslane spreading through the rotting bark mulch, which hasn't been renewed for a couple of years. It's one of the things Harry keeps making a mental note to do: call the landscaping service and renew the mulch and replace the dead yews, about a third of them, they look like hell, like missing teeth. Across the four-lane highway, its traffic thicker and faster than ever though the state still holds to the fifty-five-mile-an-hour speed limit, the takeout restaurant called the Chuck Wagon has been replaced by a Pizza Hut, one of the six or so around Brewer now. What do people see in it? All those gummy wedges of dough and cheese, that when you try to eat them pull long strings out in front of your face. But, on Saturdays when in the weekend mood Benny runs over and brings back an order for whoever wants it, Harry allows himself a pepperoni with peppers and onions but no anchovies, please. Like little snails stuck in the mud.

Today is not Saturday, it is Monday, the day after Father's Day. Nobody sent Harry a card. He and Janice have visited Nelson twice, for family therapy at this gloomy big rehab center in North Philly, full of banisters and bulletin boards and a damp mimeograph smell that reminds him of the basement Sunday school he went to, and both times it was like a quarrel around the kitchen table only with a referee, a lean pale colored woman with fancy spectacles and one of these sweet churchgoing smiles Harry associates with the better type of Philadelphia black. They go over the old stuff – the baby's death, the mess in the Sixties with Janice moving out and Jill and Skeeter moving in, the crazy way Nelson got himself married to this Kent State secretary an inch taller and a year older than he, a Catholic furthermore, and the kind of crazy way the young couple moved into the old Springer house and the older couple moved out and in fact lives half the year in Florida, all so the kid can run wild with the car agency; Harry explains how from his point of view Nelson's been spoiled rotten by his mother because of her guilt complex and that's why the kid feels entitled to live in never-never land with all these fags and druggies and let his wife and children go around in rags. When he talks, the mocha-colored therapist's smile gets even more pious and patient and then she turns to one of the others, Nelson or Janice or Pru, and asks them how they feel about what they've just heard, as if what he's saying isn't a description of facts but a set of noises to be rolled into some general mishmash. All this "talking through" and "processing" therapists like to do cheapens the world's facts; it reduces decisions that were the best people could do at the time to dream moves, to reflexes that have been "processed" in a million previous cases like so much shredded wheat. He feels anticipated and discounted in advance, whatever he says, and increasingly aggravated, and winds up telling Janice and Pru to go next time without him.

Benny comes over to where Harry stands at the window looking out and asks, "Whajja do for Father's Day?"

Harry is pleased to have an answer. "Nelson's wife brought our grandchildren over in the afternoon and I did a cookout for everybody on the outdoor grill." It sounds ideally American but had its shaky underside. Their grill, for one thing, is a metal sphere that *Consumer Reports* said years ago was a classic but that Harry never has quite the patience for, you must wait until the briquettes are gray and ashy, but he's afraid of waiting too long, so there was a lot of staring at the raw hamburger patties not cooking, with Janice annoying him by offering to cook them in the kitchen, since the children were being eaten alive by mosquitoes. For another, the grandchildren brought him cute grandfather's cards, all right, both by this new artist Gary Larson that everybody else thinks is so funny, but this uniformity – they were even signed by the same red pen, Judy's with quite a girlish flourish to the "y" and Roy's a bunch of aimless but intense pre-literate stabs – suggested a lack of planning, a quick stop at the drugstore on the way over from the Flying Eagle. Pru and the kids arrived with their hair wet from the pool. She brought a bowl of salad she had made at home.

"Sounds terrific," Benny says, in his husky small voice.

"Yeah," Harry agrees, explaining, as if his image of Pru with her wet long hair holding this big wooden bowl of lettuce and sliced radishes on her hip was visible to them both, "we've arranged a temporary membership for Nelson's wife over at the country club, and they'd been swimming over there most of the day."

"Nice," Benny says. "She seems a nice gal, Teresa. Never came over here to the lot much, but I hate to see a family like that having a hard time."

"They're managing," Harry says, and changes the subject. "D'jou watch any of the Open?" Somebody really should go out and pick up all the wrappers that blow over from the Pizza Hut and get caught in the struggling little yew hedge. But he doesn't like to bend over, and doesn't quite feel he can order Benny to do it.

"Naa, I can't get turned on by games," the pudgy young sales representative says, more aggressively than the question requires. "Even baseball, a game or two, I'm bored. You know, what's in it for me? So what?, if you follow me."

There used to be a stately old maple tree across Route 111 that the Pizza Hut cut down to expand its red-roofed facility. The roof is shaped like a hat, with two slants. He ought to be grateful, Harry thinks, to have a lively business along this struggling little strip. "Well," he tells Benny, not wanting to argue, "with the Phils in last place you aren't missing much. The worst record in baseball, and now they've traded away two of their old all-stars. Bedrosian and Samuel. There's no such thing as loyalty any more."

Benny continues to explain himself, unnecessarily. "Me, I'd rather do something my*self* on a nice Sunday, not sit there like a couch potato, you know what I mean? Get outdoors with my little girl at the neighbor's pool, or go take the family for a walk up the mountain, if it's not too hot, you know."

These people who keep saying "you know": as if if they don't keep nailing your attention to their words it'll drift off. "That's the way I used to be," Harry tells him, relaxing as the disturbing image of Pru holding the great bowl on her hip recedes, and feeling philosophical and pleasurably melancholic the way he usually does gazing out this big window. Above his head the big blue paper banner spelling ᴀᴍᴀяᴀᴛᴏʏᴏᴛ with the sun shining through it is beginning to come unstuck from the glass. "Always doing some sport as a kid, and up until recently out on the golf course, flogging the stupid ball."

"You could still do that," Benny says, with that Italian huskiness, faintly breathless. "In fact, I bet your doc advises it. That's what mine advises, exercise. You know, for my weight."

"I probably should do something," Harry agrees, "to keep the circulation going. But, I don't know, golf suddenly seemed stupid. I realized I'd never get any better at it, at this point. And the guys I had my old foursome with have pretty well moved away. It's all these blond beefy yuppie types up at the club, and they all ride carts. They're in such a fucking hurry to get back to making money they ride around in carts, wearing the grass off the course. I used to like to walk and carry. You'd strengthen your legs. That's where the power of a golf swing is, believe it or not. In the legs. I was mostly arms. I knew the right thing to do, I could see it in the other guys and the pros on TV, but I couldn't make myself do it."

The length and inward quality of this speech make Benny uneasy. "You ought to be getting some exercise," he says. "Especially with your history."

Rabbit doesn't know if he means his recent medical history, or his ancient history of high-school athletics. The framed blowups of his old basketball photos have come out of Nelson's office and back onto the walls, rose-colored though they are, above the performance board. That was something he did carry through on, unlike the rotting bark mulch. ANGSTROM HITS FOR 42. "When Schmidt quit, that got to me," he tells Benny, even though the guy keeps saying he is no sports nut. Maybe he enjoys bullying him with it, boring him. He wonders how much Benny was in on Nelson's shenanigans, but didn't have the heart or energy to fire him when he came back to run the lot. Get through the day, and the cars sell themselves. Especially the Camry and Corolla. Who could ask for anything more?

"All he had to do," he explains to Benny, "to earn another half million was stay on the roster until August fifteenth. And he began the season like a ball of fire, two home runs the first two games, coming off that rotator-cuff surgery. But, like Schmidt himself said, it got to the point where he'd tell his body to do something and it wouldn't do it. He knew what he had to do and couldn't do it, and he faced the fact and you got to give him credit. In this day and age, he put honor over money."

"Eight errors," Elvira Ollenbach calls in her deep voice from over in her booth, on the wall toward Paraguay, where she has been filling out the bill of sale and NV-1 for an ivory Corolla LE she sold yesterday to one of these broads that come in and ask to deal with her. They have jobs, money, even the young ones that used to be home making babies. If you look, more and more, you see women driving the buses, the delivery trucks. It's getting as bad as Russia; next thing we'll have women coalminers. Maybe we already do. The only difference between the two old super-powers is they sell their trees to Japan in different directions. "An error each in the last two games against the Giants," Elvira inexorably recites. "And hitting .203, just two hits his last forty-one at bats." Her head is full, between her pretty little jug ears, with figures. Her father was a sports addict, she has explained, and to communicate with him she followed all this stuff and now can't break the habit.

"Yeah," Rabbit says, he feels weakly, taking some steps toward her desk. "But still, it took a lot of style. Just a week ago, did you see, there was this interview in some Philadelphia paper where he said how great he felt and he was only in a slump like any over-eager kid? Then he was man enough to change his mind. When all he had to do was hang around to collect a million and a half total. I like the way he went out," Rabbit says, "quick, and on his own nickel."

Elvira, not looking up from her paperwork, her pendulous gold earrings bobbing as she writes, says, "They would have cut him by August, the way he was going. He spared himself the humiliation."

"Exactly," Harry says, still weakly, torn between a desire to strike an alliance with this female and an itch to conquer her, to

put her in her place. Not that she and Benny have been difficult
to deal with. Docile, rather, as if anxious that they not be swept
out of the lot along with Lyle and Nelson. It was easiest for Harry
to accept them as innocents and not rock the agency worse than
it was being rocked. Both of them have connections in Brewer
and move Toyotas, and if the conversations during idle time –
"down" time, young people called it now – weren't as satisfying,
as clarifying, as those he used to have with Charlie Stavros, perhaps the times were less easy to clarify. Reagan left everybody in
a daze, and now the Communists were acting confused too.
"How about those elections in Poland?" he says. "Voting the
Party out – who ever would have thought we'd live to see the
day? And Gorby telling all the world the contractors who put up
those sand castles in Armenia were crooks? And in China, what's
amazing isn't the crackdown but that the kids were allowed to run
the show for a month and nobody knew what to do about it! It's
like nobody's in charge of the other side any more. I miss it," he
says. "The cold war. It gave you a reason to get up in the morning."

He says these things to be provocative, to get a rise out of
Benny or Elvira, but his words drift away like the speech of old
people on the porches when he was a boy. Not for the first time
since returning to the lot does he feel he is not really there, but is
a ghost being humored. His words are just noises. In Nelson's old
office, and the office next to it where Mildred used to be, the
accountant Janice has hired on Charlie's advice is going through
the books, a task so extensive he has brought a full-time assistant.
These two youngish men, who dress in gray suits of which they
hang up the jackets when arriving, putting them on again when
they depart, feel like the real management of the firm.

"Elvira," he says, always enjoying pronouncing her name, "did
you see this morning in the paper where four men were charged
with a felony for chaining themselves to a car in front of an abortion clinic? And with contributing to the delinquency of a minor
since they had a seventeen-year-old boy along?" He knows where
she stands: pro-choice. All these independent bimbos are. He takes
a kind of pro-life tilt to gall her but his heart isn't really in it and
she knows it. She leaves her desk and comes striding toward him,

thrillingly thin, holding the completed NV-1s, her wide-jawed little head balanced with its pulled-back shiny-brown hair on her slender neck, her dangling big gold earrings shaped like Brazil nuts. He retreats a step and the three of them stand together at the window, Harry between them and a head taller.

"Wouldn't you *know*," she says, "it would be all men. Why do they *care* so much? Why are they so passionate about what some women they don't even know do with their bodies?"

"They think it's murder," Harry says. "They think the fetus is a little separate person from the morning after on."

His way of putting it feeds into her snort of disgust. "*Tccha*, they don't know what they think," she says. "If men could get knocked up this wouldn't even be a debate. Would it, Benny?"

She is bringing him in to dilute whatever Harry is trying to do to her with this provocative topic. Benny says carefully, huskily, "My church says abortion is a sin."

"And you believe them, until you want to do it, right? Tell us about you and Maria – you use birth control? Seventy per cent of young married Catholics do, you know that?"

A strange aspect of his encounter with Pru, Harry remembers, had been the condom she had produced, out of the pocket of her shorty bathrobe. Either she always kept one there or had foreseen fucking him before coming into the room. He wasn't used to them, not since the Army, but went along with it without a protest, it was her show. The thing had been a squeeze, he had been afraid he couldn't keep up his own pressure against it, and his pubic hair, where he had some left after the angioplasty, the way they shaved him, got caught at the base in the unrolling, a little practical fussing there, she helped in the dim light, it maybe had made him slower to come, not a bad thing, as she came twice, under him once and then astraddle, rain whipping at the window behind the drawn shade, her hips so big and broad in his hands he didn't feel fat himself, her tits atwitter as she jiggled in pursuit of the second orgasm, he near to fainting with worry over joggling his defective heart. A certain matter-of-fact shamelessness about Pru reduced a bit the poetry of his first sight of her naked and pale like that street of blossoming trees. She did it all but was blunt about it and faintly wooden, as if the dressmaker's dummy in the dark behind him had grown limbs and a head with swinging car-rot-colored hair. To keep his prick up he kept telling himself, *This is the first time I've ever fucked a left-handed woman.*

Benny is blushing. He's not used to talking this way with a woman. "Maybe so," he admits. "If it's not a mortal sin, you don't have to confess it unless you want to."

"That saves the priest a lot of embarrassment," Elvira tells him. "Suppose no matter what you two use Maria kept getting knocked up, what would you do? You don't want that precious little girl of yours to feel crowded, you can give her the best the way things are. What's more important, quality of life for the family you already have, or a little knot of protein the size of a termite?"

Benny has a kind of squeaking girlish voice that excitement can bring out. "Lay *off*, Ellie. Don't make me think about it. You're offending my religion. I wouldn't mind a couple more kids, what the hell. I'm young."

Harry tries to help him out. "Who's to say what's the quality of life?" he asks Elvira. "Maybe the extra kid is the one that's going to invent the phonograph."

"Not out of the ghetto he isn't. He's the kid that mugs you for crack money sixteen years later."

"You don't have to get racist about it," Harry says, having been mugged in a sense by a white kid, his own son.

"It's the opposite of racist, it's realistic," Elvira tells him. "It's the poor black teenage mother whose right to abortion these crazy fundamentalist jerks are trying to take away."

"Yeah," he responds, "it's the poor black teenage mother who wants to have the baby, because she never had a doll to play with and she loves the idea of sticking the taxpayer with another wel-fare bill. Up yours, Whitey – that's what the birth statistics are saying."

"Now who's sounding racist?"

"Realistic, you mean."

Relaxed in the aftermath of love, and grateful to be still alive, he had asked Pru how queer she thought Nelson was, with all this palling around with Lyle and Slim. Her breath, in the watery light from the window, was made visible by fine jets of inhaled cigarette smoke as she thoughtfully answered, only a little taken aback by the question, "No, Nelson likes girls. He's a mamma's boy but he takes after you that way. They just look bigger to him than to you." Coming into the room less than an hour later, Janice had sniffed the cigarette smoke but he had pretended to be too sleepy to discuss it. Pru took the second butt away with the condom but the first one, drowned over on the windowsill, was by next morning so saturated and flattened it could have been there for ages, a historical relic of Nelson and Melanie. Rabbit sighs and says, "You're right, Elvira. People should have a choice. Even if they make bad ones." From the room he was in with Pru his mind moves to the one he had shared with Ruth, one flight up on Summer Street, and the last time he saw it: she told him she was pregnant and called him Mr. Death and he begged her to have the baby. *Have it, have it you say: how? Will you marry me?* She mocked him, but pleaded too, and in the end, yes, to be realistic, probably did have the abortion. *If you can't work it out, I'm dead to you; I'm dead to you and this baby of yours is dead too.* That nurse with the round face and sweet disposition in St. Joseph's had nothing to do with him, just like Ruth told him the last time he saw her, in her farmhouse ten years ago. He had had one daughter and she died; God didn't trust him with another. He says aloud, "Schmidt did what Rose is too dumb to: quit, when you've had it. Take your medicine, don't prolong the agony with all these lawyers."

Benny and Elvira look at him, alarmed by how his mind has wandered. But he enjoys his sensation, of internal roaming. When he first came to the lot as Chief Sales Rep, after Fred Springer had died, he was afraid he couldn't fill the space. But now as an older man, with his head so full of memories, he fills it without even trying.

Through the plate glass he sees a couple in their thirties, maybe early forties, everybody looks young to him now, out on the lot among the cars, stooping to peek into the interiors and at the factory sticker on the windows. The woman is plump and white and in a halter top showing her lardy arms, and the man darker, much darker — Hispanics come in all these shades — and skinny, in a grape-colored tank top cut off at the midriff. Their ducking heads move cautiously, as if afraid of an Indian ambush out in the prairie of glittering car roofs, a pioneer couple in their way, at least in this part of the world where the races don't much mix.

Benny asks Elvira, "You want 'em, or do I?"

She says, "You do. If the woman needs a little extra, bring her in and I'll chat her up. But don't aim it all at her, just because she's white. They're both going to be miffed if you snub the man."

"Whaddeya think I am, a bigot?" Benny says mock-comically, but his demeanor is sad and determined as he walks out of the air-conditioning into the June humidity and heat.

"You shouldn't ride him about his religion," Harry tells Elvira.

"I don't. I just think that damn Pope he's got ought to be put in jail for what he does to women."

Peggy Fosnacht, Rabbit remembers, before she had a breast cut off and then upped and died, had been wild with anger toward the Pope. Anger is what gives you cancer, he has read somewhere. If you've been around long enough, he reflects, you've heard it all, the news and the commentary both, churned like the garbage in a Disposall that doesn't drain, the media every night trying to whip you up into a frenzy so you'll run out and buy all the depressing stuff they advertise, laxatives and denture adhesive cream, Fixodent and Sominex and Tylenol and hemorrhoid medicine and mouthwash against morning mouth. Why does the evening news assume the people who watch it are in such decrepit plugged-up shape? It's enough to make you switch the channel. The commercials revolt him, all that friendly jawing among these folksy cracker-barrel types about rectal itching and burning, and the one of the young/old beautiful woman in soft focus stretching so luxuriously in her white bathrobe because she's just taken a shit and all those people in the Ex-Lax ad saying "Good morning" one after the other so you can't help picturing the world filling up with our smiling American excrement, we'll have to pay poor third-world countries to dump it pretty soon, like toxic waste. "Why pick on the Pope?" Harry asks. "Bush is just as bad, anti-choice."

"Yes, but he'll change when the women start voting Republicans out. There's no way to vote the Pope out."

"Do you ever get the feeling," he asks her, "now that Bush is in, that we're kind of on the sidelines, that we're sort of like a big Canada, and what we do doesn't much matter to anybody else?

Maybe that's the way it ought to be. It's a kind of relief, I guess, not to be the big cheese."

Elvira has decided to be amused. She fiddles with one of her Brazil-nut earrings and looks up at him slantwise. "You matter to everybody, Harry, if that's what you're hinting at."

This is the most daughterly thing she has ever said to him. He feels himself blush. "I wasn't thinking of me, I was thinking of the country. You know who I blame? The old Ayatollah, for calling us the Great Satan. It's like he put the evil eye on us and we shrank. Seriously. He really stuck it to us, somehow."

"Don't live in a dream world, Harry. We still need you down here."

She goes out to the lot, where a quartet of female teenagers have showed up, all in jackets of stone-washed denim. Who knows, even teenagers these days have money enough for a Toyota. Maybe it's an all-girl rock band, shopping for a van to tour in. Harry wanders in to the office where the visiting accountants are nesting, day after day, in piles of paper. The one in charge has a rubbery tired face with dark rings under his eyes, and the assistant seems to be a kind of moron, a simpleton at speaking anyway, with not enough back to his head. As if to make up for any deficiency he always wears a clean white shirt with a tight necktie, pinned to his chest with a tieclip.

"Ah," the one in charge says, "just the guy we need. Does the name Angus Barfield mean anything to you?" The rings under his eyes are so deep and deeply bruised they go all the way around his sockets; he looks like a raccoon. Though his face shows a lot of wear, his hair is black as shoe polish, and lies as flat on his head as if painted in place. These accountants have to be tidy, all those numbers they write down, thousands and millions, and never a five that could be confused with a three or a seven with a one. As he cocks a ringed eye at Harry waiting for an answer, his rubbery mouth slides around in a restless wise-guy motion.

"No," Harry says, "and yet, wait. There's a faint bell. Barfield."

"A good guy for you to know," the accountant says, with a sly grimace and twist of his lips. "From December to April, he was buying a Toyota a month." He checks a paper under his shirt-sleeved forearm. He has very long black hairs on his wrists. "A

Corolla four-door, a Tercel five-speed hatchback, a Camry wagon, a deluxe two-passenger 4-Runner, and in April he really went fancy and took on a Supra Turbo with a sport roof, to the tune of twenty-five seven. Totals up to just under seventy-five K. All in the same name and the same address on Willow Street."

"Where's Willow?"

"That's one of the side streets up above Locust, you know. The area's gotten kind of trendy."

"Locust," Harry repeats, struggling to recall. He has heard the odd name "Angus" before, from Nelson's lips. Going off to a party in north Brewer.

"Single white male. Excellent credit ratings. Not much of a haggler, paid list price every time. The only trouble with him as a customer," the accountant says, "is according to city records he's been dead for six months. Died before Christmas." He purses his lips into a little bunch under one nostril and lifts his eyebrows so high his nostrils dilate in sympathy.

"I got it," Harry says, with a jarring pounce of his heart. "That's Slim. Angus Barfield was the real name of a guy everybody called Slim. He was a, a gay I guess, about my son's age. Had a good job in downtown Brewer – administered one of those HUD job-training programs for high-school dropouts. He was a trained psychologist, I think Nelson once told me."

The moronic assistant, who has been listening with the staring effort of a head that can only hold one thing at a time, giggles: the humor of insanity spills over onto psychologists. The other twists up the lower part of his face in a new way, as if demonstrating knots. "Bank loan officers love government employees," he says. "They're sure and steady, see?"

Since the man seems to expect it, Harry nods, and the accountant dramatically slaps the tidy chaos of papers spread out on the desk. "December to April, Brewer Trust extended five car loans to this Angus Barfield, made over to Springer Motors."

"How could they, to the same guy? Common sense –"

"Since computers, my friend, common sense has gone out the window. It's joined your Aunt Matilda's ostrich-feather hat. The auto-loan department of a bank is just tiddledywinks; the computer checked his credit and liked it and the loan was approved.

The checks were cashed but never showed up in the company credits. We think your pal Lyle opened a dummy somewhere." The man stabs a stack of bank statements with a finger; it has black hairs between the knuckles and bends back so far Rabbit winces and looks away. This rubbery guy is one of those born teachers Rabbit has instinctively avoided all his life. "Let me put it like this. A computer is like a Frenchman. It seems real smart until you know the language. Once you know the language, you realize it's dumb as hell. Quick, sure. But quick ain't the same as smart."

"But," Harry gropes to say, "but for Lyle and Nelson, Lyle especially, to use poor Slim's name in a scam like this when he had just died, when he was just about buried – would they have actually been so hard-hearted?"

The accountant slumps a little under the weight of such naïveté. "These were hungry boys. The dead have no feelings, that I've heard about. The guy's credit hadn't been pulled from the computer, and between these loans from Brewer Trust and the diddled inventory with Mid-Atlantic Toyota, some two hundred grand was skimmed from this operation, that we can verify so far. That's a lot of Toll House cookies."

The assistant giggles again. Rabbit, hearing the sum, goes cold with the premonition that this debt will swallow him. Here amid all these papers arrayed on the desk where he himself used to work, keeping a roll of Life Savers in the lefthand middle drawer, a fatal hole is being hatched. He taps his jacket pocket for the reassuring lump of the Nitrostat bottle. He'll take one as soon as he gets away. The night he and Pru fucked, both of them weary and half crazy with their fates, the old bed creaking beneath them had seemed another kind of nest, an interwoven residue of family fortunes, Ma Springer's musty old-lady scent released from the mattress by this sudden bouncing where for years she had slept alone, an essence of old mothballed blankets stored in attic cedar chests among plush-bound family albums and broken cane-seated rockers and veiled hats in round hat-boxes, an essence arising not only from the abused bed but from the old sewing apparatus stored here and Fred's forgotten neckties in the closet and the dust balls beneath the venerable four-poster. All those family traces descended to this, this coupling by thunder and lightning. It was now as if it had never been. He and Pru are severely polite with each other, and Janice, ever more the working girl, has ceased to create many occasions when the households mingle. The Father's Day cook-out was an exception, and the children were tired and cranky and bug-bitten by the time the grilled hamburgers were finally ready to be consumed.

Harry laughs, as idiotically as the assistant accountant. "Poor Slim," he says, trying to harmonize with the head accountant's slanginess. "Some pal Lyle turned out to be, buying him all those wheels he didn't need."

On July Fourth, for Judy's sake, he marches in a Mt. Judge parade. Her Girl Scout troop is in it and the troop leader's husband, Clarence Eifert, is on the organizing committee. They needed a man tall enough to be Uncle Sam and Judy told Mrs. Eifert that her grandfather was wonderfully tall. Actually, six three isn't tall by today's standards, you'd be a dwarf in the NBA at that height, but several members of the committee, a generation older than Mr. Eifert, remembered Rabbit Angstrom from his high-school glory days and became enthusiastic, even though Harry lives now in Penn Park on the other side of Brewer. He was a Mt. Judge boy and something of a hero once. He has become more corpulent than our national symbol should be but he has the right fair skin and pale blue eyes and a good soldierly bearing. He served during Korea. He did his bit.

The bell-bottom trousers with their broad red stripes have to be left unbuttoned at the stomach, but since they are held up by tricolor suspenders, and a pale-blue vest patterned in stars comes down over the belt area, it doesn't much matter. Harry and Janice fuss a good deal at the costume in the week before the Fourth. They actually go buy a formal shirt with French cuffs and a wing collar to go with the floppy red cravat, and decide that somehow his suede Hush Puppies go better with the red-striped trousers, look more like boots, than the formal black shoes he keeps for weddings and funerals. The swallowtail coat, of a wool darker blue than the vest, with three unbuttonable brass buttons on both sides, fits well enough, but the fuzzy flared top hat with its hatband of big silver stars perches on his high head unsteadily, a touch tight with the white nylon wig, so it feels like it might totter and fall off.

Janice bites the tip of her tongue thoughtfully. "Do you need the wig? Your hair's so pale anyway."

"But it's cut too short for Uncle Sam. I would have let it grow out if I'd known."

"Well," she says, "why wouldn't Uncle Sam have a modern haircut? He's not dead, is he?"

He tests the hat without the wig and says, "It does feel better, actually."

"And frankly, Harry, the wig on you is somehow alarming. It makes you look like a very big red-faced woman."

"Look, I'm doing this for our granddaughter, there's no need to get insulting."

"It's not insulting, it's interesting. I never saw your female side before. I bet you would have made a nicer woman than either your mother or Mim. They should have been men, both of them."

Mom was mean to Janice from the moment he first brought her home from Kroll's, and Mim once stole Charlie Stavros from her, or so Janice interpreted it. "I'm getting hot and itchy in this outfit," Harry says. "Let's try the goatee."

The goatee in place, Janice says, "Oh, *yes*. It slims your face right down. I wonder why you never grew a beard." There is this subtle past tense that keeps creeping into her remarks about him. "Mr. Lister is growing a beard now, and it makes him look a lot less doleful. He has these sagging jowls."

"I don't want to hear about that creep." He adds, "When I talk, the stickum doesn't feel like enough."

"It must be, it's gone through a lot of other parades."

"That's its problem, you dope. Is there any way to renew the stickum?"

"Just don't move your chin too much. I could call up Doris Eberhardt; when she was married to Kaufmann they were big into amateur theatricals."

"Don't get that pushy bitch on my case. Maybe somebody at the parade will have some spare stickum."

But the mustering of the parade is a confused and scattered business, held on the grounds of the old Mt. Judge High School, now the junior high school and slated to be torn down because of the asbestos in it everywhere and the insurance rates on the wooden floors. When Harry went there, they all just breathed the asbestos and took their chances on the floors catching fire. There are marching bands and antique cars and 4-H floats and veterans in their old uniforms all milling around on the asphalt of the parking lot and the brown grass of the baseball outfield, with the only organizing principle provided by men and women in green T-shirts stencilled MT. JUDGE INDEPENDENCE DAY COMMITTEE and those plastic truck-driver caps with a bill in front and a panel of mesh at the back. Looking to be told where to go, Rabbit wanders in this area where long ago he had roamed with wet-combed duck-tailed hair and a corduroy shirt tight across his back, the sleeves folded back and, out of basketball season, a cigarette pack squaring the shirt pocket. He expects to come across his old girlfriend, Mary Ann, as she had been then, in saddle shoes and white socks and a short pleated cheerleader's skirt, her calves straight and smooth and round-muscled between the skirt and the socks, and her face, with the dimple in one cheek and the touch of acne on her forehead, springing into joyful recognition at the sight of him. Instead, strange people with puzzled Eighties faces keep asking directions, because he is dressed as Uncle Sam and should know. He has to keep telling them he doesn't know anything.

The old high school, built in the Twenties of orange brick, had a tall windowless wall at the back, across from a board-and-tarpaper equipment shed long since torn down, and this black and gravelly area has profound associations for him, a power in its mute bricks and secluding space, for it was here after school and until twilight called you home that the more questing and footloose of the town's children tended to gather, girls as well as boys, hanging out, shooting baskets at the hoop attached to the blank brickwork (flat on the wall like those in the gym in Oriole), necking against the torn-tarpaper boards of the equipment shed, talking (the girls held by the boys' braced arms as in a row of soft cages), teasing, passing secrets, feeling their way, avoiding going home, so that the gritty leftover space here behind the school was charged with a solemn excitement, the questing energy of adolescents. Now in this area, repaved and cleaned up, the shed and backboards gone, Rabbit comes upon Judy's Girl Scout troop, some of them in uniform and some posed in costume on a flatbed truck, a float illustrating Liberty, the tallest and prettiest girl in a white bedsheet and spiked crown holding a big bronze book and gilded torch, and others grouped around her cardboard pedestal with their faces painted red and brown and black and yellow to represent the races of mankind, the faces painted because there aren't any Indian or Negro or Asian little girls in Mt. Judge, at least any that have joined the Girl Scouts.

Judy is one of those in badged and braided khaki uniform around the truck, and she is so amazed to see her grandfather in his towering costume that she takes his hand, as if to tie him to the earth, to reality. He has difficulty bending his head to see her, for fear that his top hat might fall off. As if addressing the distant back-stop of the baseball diamond, he asks her, "How does the goatee look? The little beard, Judy."

"Fine, Grandpa. You scared me at first. I didn't know who you were."

"It feels to me like it might fall off any second."

"It doesn't look that way. I love the big stripy pants. Doesn't the vest squeeze your tummy?"

"That's the least of my problems. Judy, listen. Think you could do me a favor? It just occurred to me, they make a Scotch tape now that's sticky on both sides. If I gave you a couple dollars think you could run over to the little store across Central and get me some?" Always, under names and managements that shift with the years, there has been a store across from the school to sell its students bubble gum and candy and cap-guns and caps and tablets and cigarettes and skin magazines and whatever else young people thought they had to have. With difficulty, keeping his head stiffly upright, he digs through the layers of his costume to his wallet in a pouchy side pocket of the striped pants and, holding it up to his face, digs out two one-dollar bills. Just in case, he adds another. Things these days always cost more than he expects.

"Suppose it's not open because of the holiday!"

"It'll be open. It was always open."

"Suppose the parade starts; I got to be on the truck!"

"No it won't, the parade can't start without me. Come on, Judy. Think of all I've done for you. Think of how I saved you on the boat that time. Who got me into this damn parade in the first place? *You* did!"

He doesn't dare look down, lest his hat come off, but he can hear from her voice she is near tears. Her hair makes a reddish blur in the bottom of his vision. "O.K., I'll try, but . . ."

"Remember," he says, and as his chin stiffens in admonishment he feels his goatee loosen, "sticky on *both* sides. Scotch makes it. Run, honey!" His heart is racing; he gropes through his clothes to make sure he remembered to bring the little bottle of nitroglycerin. He finds its life-giving nugget deep in the pouchy pocket. When he brings his fingers to his face, to tamp down the goatee, he sees they are trembling. If his goatee doesn't stick, he won't be Uncle Sam, and the entire parade will flounder; it will jam up here on the school grounds forever. He walks around with little steps, ignoring everybody, trying to quiet his heart. This is aggravating.

When Judy at last comes back, panting, she tells him, "They were *dumb*. They mostly sell only food now. Junky things like Cheez Doodles. The only Scotch tape they have is sticky on one side only. I got some anyway. Was that O.K.?"

Drum rolls sound on the parking lot, scattered at first, a few kids impatiently clowning around, and then in unison, gathering mass, an implacable momentum. The motors of antique cars and trucks bearing floats are starting up, filling the holiday air with blue exhaust. "O.K.," Harry says, unable to look down at his granddaughter lest his hat fall off, pocketing the tape and the change from three dollars, pressed upon him from below. Estranged from his costumed body, he feels on stilts, his feet impossibly small.

"I'm sorry, Grandpa. I did the best I could." Judy's little light voice, out of sight beneath him, wobbles and crackles with tears, like water sloshing in sun.

"You did great," he tells her.

A frantic stocky woman in a green committee T-shirt and truck-driver hat comes and hustles him away, to the head of the parade, past floats and drum-and-bugle corps, Model A Fords and civic leaders in neckties and a white limousine. A Mt. Judge patrol car with its blue light twirling and its siren silent will be the spear-head, then Harry at a distance. As if he doesn't know the route: as a child he used to participate in parades, in the crowd of town kids riding bicycles with red, white, and blue crêpe paper threaded through the spokes. Down Central to Market a block short of 422, through the heart of the little slanting diagonal downtown, then left and uphill along Potter Avenue, through blocks of brick semi-detached houses up on their terraced lawns behind the retaining walls, then downhill past Kegerise Alley as they used to call it, Kegerise Street it is now, with its small former hosiery factories and machine shops renamed Lynnex and Data Development and Business Logistical Systems, up to Jackson, the high end, a block from his old house, and on down to Joseph and past the big Baptist church, and sharp right on Myrtle past the post office and the gaunt old Oddfellows' Hall to end at the reviewing stand set up in front of the Borough Hall, in the little park that was full in the Sixties of kids smoking pot and playing guitars but now on a nor-mal day holds just a few old retired persons and homeless drifters with million-dollar tans. The green-chested woman, along with a marshal with a big cardboard badge, a squinty stooped jeweller called Himmelreich – Rabbit was in school a few grades behind his father, whom everybody said was Jewish – makes sure he delays enough to let a distance build between him and the lead car, so Uncle Sam doesn't look too associated with the police. Imme-diately next in the parade is the white limousine carrying the Mt. Judge burgess and what borough councilmen aren't off in the Poconos or at the Jersey Shore. From further behind come the sounds of the drum-and-bugle corps and some bagpipers hired from Chester County and the scratchy pop tunes playing on the floats to help illustrate Liberty and the Spirit of 1776 and ONE WORLD/UN MUNDO and Head, Heart, Hands, and Health, and at the tail end a local rock singer doing ecstatic imitations of Presley and Orbison and Lennon while a megawatt electric fan loudly blows on all the amplifying equipment stacked on his flatbed truck. But up front, at the head of the parade, it is oddly silent, hushed. What a precarious weird feeling it is for Harry at last to put his suede-booted feet on the yellow double line of the town's main street and start walking! He feels giddy, ridiculous, enormous. Behind him there is the white limousine purring along in low gear, so he cannot stop walking, and far ahead, so far ahead it twinkles out of sight around corners and bends in the route, the police car; but immediately ahead there is nothing but the eerie emptiness of normally busy Central Street under a dazed July sky blue above the telephone wires. He is the traffic, his solitary upright body. The stilled street has its lunar details, its pockmarks, its scars, its ancient metal lids. The tremor in his heart and hands becomes an exalted sacrificial feeling as he takes those few steps into the asphalt void, rimmed at this end of the route with only a few spectators, a few bare bodies in shorts and sneakers and tinted shirts along the curb.

They call to him. They wave ironically, calling "Yaaaay" at the idea of Uncle Sam, this walking flag, this incorrigible taxer and frisky international mischief-maker. He has nothing to do but wave back, carefully nodding so as not to spill his hat or shake loose his goatee. The crowd as it thickens calls out more and more his name, "Harry," or "Rabbit" – "Hey, Rabbit! Hey, hotshot!" They remember him. He hasn't heard his old nickname so often in many years; nobody in Florida uses it, and his grandchildren would be puzzled to hear it. But suddenly from these curbstones there it is again, alive, affectionate. This crowd seems a strung-out recycled version of the crowd that used to jam the old auditorium-gym Tuesday and Friday nights, basketball nights, in the dead of the winter, making their own summer heat with their bodies, so that out on the floor sweat kept burning your eyes and trickling down from under your hair, behind your ears, down your neck to the hollow between your collar bones. Now the sweat builds under his wool swallowtail coat, on his back and his belly, which indeed is squeezed as Judy said, and under his hat even without the wig; thank God Janice got him out of that, she isn't always a dumb mutt.

His sweat, as with increasing ease and eagerness he waves at the crowd that clusters at the corners and in the shade of the Norway maples and on the sandstone retaining walls and terraced lawns up into the cool shadow of the porches, loosens his goatee, undermines the adhesive. He feels one side of it softly separate from his chin and without breaking stride – Uncle Sam has a bent-kneed, cranky stride not quite Harry's loping own – he digs out the Scotch tape from the pouchy pocket and tears off an inch, with the tab of red plaid paper. It wants to stick to his fingers; after several increasingly angry flicks it flutters away onto the street. Then he pulls off another piece, which he presses onto his own face and the detaching edge of synthetic white beard; the tape holds, though it must make a rectangular gleam on his face. The spectators who see him improvise this repair cheer. He takes to doffing his tall heavy hat, with a cautious bow to either side, and this stirs more applause and friendly salutation.

The crowd he sees from behind his wave, his smile, his adhesive gleam amazes him. The people of Mt. Judge are dressed for summer, with a bareness that since Harry's childhood has crept up from children into the old. White-haired women sit in their aluminum lawn chairs down by the curb dressed like fat babies in checks and frills, their shapeless veined legs cheerfully protruding. Middle-aged men have squeezed their keglike thighs into bicycle shorts meant for boys. Young mothers have come from their back-yard aboveground swimming pools in bikinis and high-sided slips of spandex that leave half their asses and boobs exposed. On their cocked hips they hold heat-flushed babies in nothing but diapers and rubber pants. There seem so many young – babies, tots, a bubbling up of generation on generation since the town brought him forth. Then it was full of the old: as he walked to school of a morning, severe and scolding women would come out of their houses shaking brooms and wearing thick dark stockings and housedresses with buttons all down the front. Now a cheerful innocent froth of flesh lines Jackson Road. Bare knees are bunched like grapes, and barrels of naked brown shoulders hulk in the dappled curbside shade. There are American flags on gilded sticks, and balloons, balloons in all colors, even metallic balloons shaped like hearts and pillows, held in hands and tied to bushes, to the handles of strollers containing yet more babies. A spirit of indulgence, a conspiring to be amused, surrounds and upholds his parade as he leads it down the stunning emptiness at the center of the familiar slanting streets.

Harry puts some Scotch tape on the other side of his goatee and out of the same pocket fishes his pill vial and pops a Nitrostat. The uphill section of the route tested him, and now turning downhill jars his heels and knees. When he draws too close to the cop car up ahead, carbon monoxide washes into his lungs. Mingled music from behind pushes him on: the gaps of "American Patrol" are filled with strains of "Yesterday." He concentrates on the painted yellow line, besmirched here and there by skid marks, dotted for stretches where passing is permitted but mostly double like the inflexible old trolley tracks, long buried or torn up for scrap. Cameras click at him. Voices call his several names. They know him, but he sees no face he knows, not one, not even Pru's wry red-haired heart-shape or Roy's black-eyed stare or Janice's brown little stubborn nut of a face. They said they would be at the corner of Joseph and Myrtle, but here near the Borough Hall the crowd is thickest, the summer-cooked bodies four and five deep, and his loved ones have been swallowed up.

The whole town he knew has been swallowed up, by the decades, but another has taken its place, younger, more naked, less fearful, better. And it still loves him, as it did when he would score forty-two points for them in a single home game. He is a legend, a walking cloud. Inside him a droplet of explosive has opened his veins like flower petals uncurling in the sun. His eyes are burning with sweat or something allergic, his head aches under the pressure cooker of the tall top hat. The greenhouse effect, he thinks. The hole in the ozone. When the ice in Antarctica goes, we'll all be drowned. Scanning the human melt for the glint of a familiar face, Harry sees instead a beer can being brazenly passed back and forth, the flash of a myopic child's earnest spectacles, a silver hoop earring in the lobe of a Hispanic-looking girl. Along the march he noticed a few black faces in the crowd, as cheerful and upholding as the rest, and some Orientals – an adopted Vietnamese orphan, a chunky Filipino wife. From far back in the still-unwinding parade the bagpipers keen a Highland killing song and the rock impersonator whimpers ". . . imagine all the *peo*ple" and, closer to the front, on a scratchy tape through crackling speakers, Kate Smith belts out, dead as she is, dragged into the grave by sheer gangrenous weight, "God Bless America" – ". . . to the *o*ceans, white with *foam*." Harry's eyes burn and the impression giddily – as if he has been lifted up to survey all human history – grows upon him, making his heart thump worse and worse, that all in all this is the happiest fucking country the world has ever seen.

It was the sort of foolish revelation he might have once shared with Thelma, in the soft-speaking unembarrassment that follows making love. Thelma was suddenly dead. Dead of kidney failure, thrombocytopenia, and endocarditis, toward the end of July, as the cool dawn of another hot blue-gray day broke on the ornamental roof-level brickwork opposite St. Joseph's Hospital in Brewer. Poor Thelma, her body had just been plain worn out by her long struggle. Ronnie tried to keep her at home to the end, but that last week she was too much to handle. Hallucinations, raving, sarcastic anger. Quite a lot of anger, at Ron of all people, who had been so devoted a husband, after being such a scapegrace in his young unmarried days. She was only fifty-five – a year younger than Harry, two years older than Janice. She died the same week the DC-10 bringing people from Denver to Philadelphia by way of Chicago crashed in Sioux City, Iowa, trying to land at two hundred miles an hour, running on no controls but the thrust of the two remaining engines, cartwheeling on the runway, breaking up in a giant fireball, and yet well over a hundred surviving, some of them dangling upside down from the seat belts in a section of fuselage, some of them walking away and getting lost in the cornfields next to the runway. It seemed to Rabbit the first piece of news that summer that wasn't a twentieth anniversary of something – of Woodstock, the Manson murders, Chappaquidick, the moon landing. The TV news has been full of resurrected footage.

The funeral service is in a sort of no-brand-name church about a mile beyond Arrowdale. Looking for it, Harry and Janice got lost and wound up at the mall in Maiden Springs, where a six-theater cineplex advertised on its crammed display board HONEY I SHRUNK BATMAN GHOSTBUST II KARATE KID III DEAD POETS GREAT BALLS. The lazy girl in the booth didn't know where the church might be, nor did the pimply usher inside, in the big empty scarlet lobby smelling of buttered popcorn and melting M&Ms.

Harry was angry with himself: all those times he sneaked out to Arrowdale to visit Thelma, now he can't find her goddamn church. When finally, hot, embarrassed, and furious at each other's incompetence, the Angstroms arrive, the church is just a plain raw building, a warehouse with windows and a stump of an anodized aluminum steeple, set in a treeless acre of red soil sown skimpily with grass and crisscrossed by car ruts. Inside, the walls are cinder-block, and the light through the tall clear windows bald and merciless. Folding chairs do instead of pews, and childish felt banners hang from the metal beams overhead, showing crosses, trumpets, crowns of thorns mixed in with Biblical verse numbers – Mark 15:32, Rev. 1:10, John 19:2. The minister wears a brown suit and necktie and shirt with an ordinary collar, and looks rather mussed, and breathless, like the plump young manager of an appliance store who sometimes has to help out in handling the heavy cartons. His voice is amplified by a tiny stalk of a microphone almost invisible at the oak lectern. He talks of Thelma as a model housewife, mother, churchgoer, sufferer. The description describes no one, it is like a dress with no one in it. The minister senses this, for he goes on to mention her "special" sense of humor, her particular way of regarding things which enabled her to bear herself so courageously throughout her long struggle with her physical affliction. During a pastoral visit to Thelma in her last tragic week in the hospital, the minister had ventured to speculate with her on the eternal mystery of why the Lord visits afflictions upon some and not upon others, and cures some and lets many remain uncured. Even in the divine Gospel, let us remind ourselves, this is so, for what of the many lepers and souls possessed who did *not* happen to be placed in Jesus' path, or were *not* aggressive enough to press themselves forward in the vast crowds that flocked to Him on the Plain and on the Mount, at Capernaum and at Galilee? And what was Thelma's reply? She said, there in that hospital bed of pain and suffering, that she guessed she deserved it as much as the next. This woman was truly humble, truly uncomplaining. On an earlier, less stressful occasion, the minister recalls with a quickening of his voice that indicates an anecdote is coming, he was visiting her in her immaculate home, and she had explained her physical affliction to him as a

minor misunderstanding, as a matter of some tiny wires in her system being crossed. Then she had suggested, with that gentle
humorous expression that all of us here who loved her remember
– and yet in all grievous seriousness as well – that perhaps God was
responsible only for what we ourselves could experience and see,
and not responsible for anything at the microscopic level.

He looks up, uncertain of the effect this reminiscence has
made, and the little congregation of mourners, perhaps hearing
Thelma's voice in the odd remark and thus enabled to conjure up
the something schoolteacherish and sardonic and strict in her living manner, or perhaps sensing the minister's need to be rescued
from the spectre of unjustifiable suffering, politely titters. With
relief, the brown-suited man, like a talk-show host wrapping up,
rolls on to the rote assurances, the psalm about green pastures, the
verses from Ecclesiastes about a time for everything, the hymn that
says now the day is over.

Harry sits there beside snuffly Janice in her policeman's outfit
thinking of the wanton naked Thelma he knew, how little she had
to do with the woman the minister described; but maybe the minister's Thelma was as real as Harry's. Women are actresses, tuning
their part to each little audience. Her part with him was to adore
him, to place her body at his service as if disposing of it. Her body
was ill and sallow and held death within it like a silky black box.
There was a faint insult, a kind of dismissal, in her attitude of helpless captivity to the awkward need to love. He could not love her
as she did him, there was a satisfying self-punishment in his relative distraction, an irony she relished. Yet however often he left
her she never wanted him to leave. The glazed ghost of her leans
up against him when he stands for the blessing, stands close to his
chest with sour-milk breath silently begging him not to go. Janice
snuffles again but Harry keeps his own grief for Thelma tight
against his heart, knowing Janice doesn't want to see it.

Outside, in the embarrassing sunlight, Webb Murkett, his face
smilingly creased more deeply than ever, a cigarette still dangling
from his long upper lip like a camel's, goes from group to group
introducing his new wife, a shy girl in her twenties, younger than
Nelson, younger than Annabelle, a fluffy small blonde dressed in
dark ruffles and shaped like a seal, like a teenaged swimming

champ, with no pronounced indentations. Webb does like them zaftig. Harry feels sorry for her, dragged up to this religious warehouse to bury the wife of an old golf partner of her husband's. Cindy, Webb's last wife, whom Harry adored not so many years ago, is also here, alone, looking dumpy and irritated and unsteady on black heels skimpy as sandals, as she takes a pose on the thickly grassed ruts of red earth that do for a church parking lot. While Janice sticks with Webb and his bride, Harry gallantly goes over to Cindy standing there like a lump, squinting in the hot hazed sun.

"Hi," he says, wondering how she could let herself go so badly. She has taken on the standard Diamond County female build – bosom like a shelf and ass like you're carrying your own bench around with you. Her dear little precise-featured face, in the old days enigmatic in its boyish pertness, with its snub nose and wide-apart eyes, is framed by fat and underlined by chins; she has no neck, like those Russian dolls that nest one inside the other. Her hair that used to be cut short has been teased and permed into that big-headed look young women favor now. It adds to her bulk.

"Harry. How are you?" Her voice has a funereal caution and she extends a soft hand, wide as a bear's paw, for him to shake; he takes it in his but also under cover of the sad occasion bends down and plants a kiss on her damp and ample cheek. Her look of irritated lumpiness slightly eases. "Isn't it awful about Thel?" she asks.

"Yeah," he agrees. "But it was coming a long time. She saw it coming." He figures it's all right to suggest he knew the dead woman's mind; Cindy was there in the Caribbean the night they swapped. He had wanted Cindy and wound up with Thelma. Now both are beyond desiring.

"You know, don't you?" Cindy says. "I mean, you sense when the time is near if you're sick like that. You sense everything." Rabbit remembers a little cross in the hollow of her throat you could see when she wore a bathing suit, and how, like a lot of people of her generation, she was into spookiness – astrology, premonitions – though not as bad as Buddy Inglefinger's girl-friend Valerie, a real old-style hippie, six feet tall and dripping beads.

"Maybe women more than men," he says to Cindy tactfully. He lurches a bit deeper into frankness. "I've had some physical problems lately and they give me the feeling I've walked through my entire life in a daze."

This is too deep for her, too confessional. There was always in his relations with Cindy a wall, just behind her bright butter-scotch-brown eyes, a barrier where the signals stopped. *Silly Cindy*, Thelma called her.

"Somebody told me," he tells her, "you're with a boutique over in that new mall near Oriole."

"I'm thinking of quitting, actually. Whatever I earn is taken off Webb's alimony so why should I bother? You can see how welfare mothers get that way."

"Well," he says, "a job gets you out in the world. Meet people." *Meet a guy, get married again*, is his unspoken thought. But who would want to hitch up with such a slab of beef? She'd sink any Sunfish you'd try to sail with her now.

"I'm thinking of maybe becoming a physical therapist. Another girl at the boutique is learning to do holistic massage."

"Sounds nice," Harry says. "Which holes?"

This is crude enough that she dares begin, "You and Thelma —" But she stops and looks at the ground.

"Yeah?" That old barrier keeps him from encouraging her. She is not the audience for which he wants to play the part of Thelma's bereft lover.

"You'll miss her, I know," Cindy says weakly.

He feigns innocence. "Frankly, Janice and I haven't been seeing that much of the Harrisons lately — Ronnie's resigned from the club, too much money he says, and I've hardly had a chance this summer to get over there myself. It's not the same, the old gang is gone. A lot of young twerps. They hit the ball a mile and win all the weekend sweeps. My daughter-in-law uses the pool, with the kids."

"I hear you're back at the lot."

"Yeah," he says, in case she knows anyway, "Nelson screwed up. I'm just holding the fort."

He wonders if he is saying too much, but she is looking past him. "I must go, Harry. I can't stand another second of watching Webb cavort with that simpering ridiculous baby doll of his. He's over sixty!"

The lucky stiff. He made it to sixty. In the little silence that her indignant remark imposes on the air, an airplane goes over, dragging its high dull roar behind it. With a smile not fully friendly he tells her, "You've all kept him young." A woman you've endured such a gnawing of desire for, you can't help bearing a little grudge against, when the ache is gone.

A number of people are making their escapes and Harry thinks he should go over and say a word to Ronnie. His old nemesis is standing in a loose group with his three sons and their women. Alex, the computer whiz, has a close haircut and a nerdy near-sighted look. Georgie has a would-be actor's long pampered hair and the coat and tie he put on for his mother's funeral look like a costume. Ron Junior has the pleasantest face — Thelma's smile — and the muscle and tan of an outdoor worker. Shaking their hands, Harry startles them by knowing their names. When you're sexually involved with a woman, some of the magic spills down into her children, that she also spread her legs for.

"How's Nelson doing?" Ron Junior asks him, from the look on his face not trying to be nasty. It must have been this boy, around Brewer as he is, who told Thelma about Nelson's habit.

Harry answers him man to man. "Good, Ron. He went through the detox treatment for a month and now he's living with about twenty other, what do they say, substance abusers, at what they call a 'concept house,' a halfway house in North Philly. He's got a volunteer job working with inner-city kids at a playground."

"That's great, Mr. Angstrom. Nelson's a great guy, basically."

"I don't go visit him any more, I couldn't stand this family therapy they try to give you, but his mother and Pru swear he loves it, working with these tough black kids."

Georgie, the prettiest boy and Thelma's favorite, has been overhearing and volunteers, "The only trouble with Nelson, he's too sensitive. He lets things get to him. In show business you learn to let it slide off your back. You know, fuck 'em. Otherwise you'd kill yourself." He pats the back of his hairdo.

Alex, the oldest, adds in his nerdy prim way, "Well I tell you, the drugs out in California were getting to *me*, that's why I was happy when this job in Fairfax came through. I mean, *every*body does it. All weekend they do it, on the beaches, on the thruways;

*ev*erybody's stoned. How can you raise a family? Or save any money?"

Her boys are men now, with flecks of gray hair and little wise wrinkles around their mouths, with wives and small children, Thelma's grandchildren, looking to their fathers for shelter in the weedy tangle of the world. Her boys look more mature in Harry's eyes than Ronnie, in whom he must always see the obnoxious brat from Wenrich Alley, and the loud-mouthed locker-room showoff of high-school days. People he once loved slide from him but Ronnie is always there, like the smelly underside of his own body, like the Jockey underpants that get dirty every day.

Ronnie is playing the grieving widower to a T; he looks like he's been through a washer, his eyelashes poking white from his tear-reddened lids, his kinky brass-colored hair reduced to gray wisps above his droopy ears. Rabbit tries to overcome his old aversion, their old rivalry, by giving the other man's hand an expressive squeeze and saying, "Really sorry."

But the old hostile devil lights up in Harrison's face, once meaty and now drawn and hollowed-out and stringy. With a glance at his sons and a small over-there jab of his head, he takes Harry's arm in a grip purposely too hard and leads him out of earshot, a few steps away on the rutted dried mud. He says to him, in the hurried confidential voice of men together in an athletic huddle, "You think I don't know you were banging Thel for years?"

"I – I've never much thought about what you know or don't know, Ronnie."

"You son of a bitch. That night we swapped down in the islands was just the beginning, wasn't it? You kept seeing her up here."

"Ron, I thought you said you knew. You should have asked Thelma if you were curious."

"I didn't want to hassle her. She was fighting to live and I loved her. Toward the end, we talked about it."

"So you *did* hassle her?"

"She wanted to clear the slate. You son of a bitch. The Old Master. You're the coldest most selfish bastard I ever met."

"Why? What makes me so bad? Maybe she wanted me. Maybe the favors were mutual." Over Ronnie's shoulder, Harry sees mourners waiting to say goodbye, hesitant, conscious of the heat of this hurried conversation. Harrison has become pink in the face and perhaps Rabbit has too. He says, "Ronnie, people are watching. This isn't the time."

"There won't be another time. I don't ever want to see you again as long as I live. You disgust me."

"Yeah, and you disgust me. You always have, Ron. You got a prick where your head ought to be. Who can blame her, if Thel gave herself a little vacation from eating your shit now and then?"

Ronnie's face is quite pink and his eyes are watering; he has never let go of Harry's forearm, as if this hold is his last warm contact with his dead wife. His voice lowers into a new intensity; Harry has to bend his head to hear. "I don't give a fuck you banged her, what kills me is you did it without giving a shit. She was crazy for you and you just lapped it up. You narcissistic cocksucker. She wasted herself on you. She went against everything she wanted to believe in and you didn't even appreciate it, you didn't love her and she knew it, she told me herself. She told me in the hospital asking my forgiveness." Ronnie takes breath to go on, but tears block his throat.

Rabbit's own throat aches, thinking of Thelma and Ronnie at the last, her betraying her lover when her body had no more love left in it. "Ronnie," he whispers. "I *did* appreciate her. I did. She was a fantastic lay."

"You cocksucker" is all Ronnie can get out, repetitively, and then they both turn to face the mourners waiting to pay their respects and climb into their cars and salvage what is left of this hot hazy Saturday, with lawns to mow and gardens to weed all across Diamond County. Janice and Webb are among those staring. They must guess what the conversation has been about; in fact, most of those here must guess, even the three sons. Though he had always been discreet on his visits to Arrowdale, hiding his Toyota in her garage and never getting caught in bed with her by a sick child returning early from school or a repairman letting himself in an unlocked door, these things have a way of getting out into the air. Like a tire, it needs only a pinhole of a leak. People sense it. Word has got around, or it will now. Well, fuck 'em, like

Georgie said. Fuck 'em all, including Webb's child bride, who from the shape of her might be pregnant. That Webb, what a character.

A nice thing happens. Ronnie and Harry, Harrison and Angstrom, with a precision as if practiced, execute a crisscross. They smile, despite their pink eyelids and raw throats, at the little watching crowd and neatly cross paths as they move toward their kin, Harry toward Janice in her navy-blue suit with white trim and wide shoulders, and Ronnie back to his sons and the center of his sad occasion. Once teammates, always teammates. Rabbit, remembering how Ronnie once screwed Ruth a whole weekend in Atlantic City and then bragged to him about it, can't feel sorry for him at all.

I Love What You Do for Me, Toyota. That is the new paper banner the company has sent down to hang in the big display window. At times, standing at the window, when a cloud dense with moisture darkens the atmosphere or an occluding truck pulls up past the yew hedge for some business at the service doors, Harry catches a sudden reflection of himself and is startled by how big he is, by how much space he is taking up on the planet. Stepping out on the empty roadway as Uncle Sam last month he had felt so eerily tall, as if his head were a giant balloon floating above the marching music. Though his inner sense of himself is of an innocuous passive spirit, a steady small voice, that doesn't want to do any harm, get trapped anywhere, or ever die, there is this other self seen from outside, a six-foot-three ex-athlete weighing two-thirty at the least, an apparition wearing a sleek gray summer suit shining all over as if waxed and a big head whose fluffy shadowy hair was trimmed at Shear Joy Hair Styling (unisex, fifteen bucks minimum) to rest exactly on the ears, a fearsome bulk with eyes that see and hands that grab and teeth that bite, a body eating enough at one meal to feed three Ethiopians for a day, a shameless consumer of gasoline, electricity, newspapers, hydrocarbons, carbohydrates. A boss, in a shiny suit. His recent heart troubles have become, like his painfully and expensively crowned back teeth, part of his respectability's full-blown equipage.

Harry needs a good self-image today, for the lot is going to be visited at eleven by a representative of the Toyota Corporation, a Mr. Natsume Shimada, hitherto manifested only as a careful signature, each letter individually formed, on creamy stiff stationery from the American Toyota Motor Sales headquarters in Torrance, California. Word of the financial irregularities anatomized by the two accountants Janice hired under Charlie's direction has filtered upward, higher and higher, as letters from Mid-Atlantic Toyota in Glen Burnie, Maryland, were succeeded by mail from the Toyota Motor Credit Corporation's offices in Baltimore and then by courteous but implacable communications from Torrance itself, signed with what seems an old-fashioned stub-tipped fountain pen by Mr. Shimada, in sky-blue ink.

"Nervous?" Elvira asks, sidling up beside him in a slim seersucker suit. For the hot weather she had her hair cut short behind, exposing sexy dark down at the back of her neck. Did Nelson used to boff her? If Pru wasn't putting out, he had to boff somebody. Unless coke whores were enough, or the kid was secretly gay. Insofar as he can bear to contemplate his son's sex life, Elvira seems a little too classy, too neuter to go along with it. But maybe Harry is underestimating the amount of energy in the world: he tends to do that, now that his own is sagging.

"Not too," he answers. "How do I look?"

"Very imposing. I like the new suit."

"It's kind of a gray metallic. They developed the fabric while doing the moon shots."

Benny is doing a dance of door-opening and hood-popping out on the lot with a couple so young they keep looking at each other for confirmation, both talking at once and then falling silent simultaneously, paralyzed by their wish not to be tricked out of a single dollar. August sales are on and Toyota is offering thousand-dollar rebates. In the old days you sold only at their list price, no haggling, take it or leave it, a quality product. Their old purity has been corrupted by American methods. Toyota has stooped to the scramble. "You know," he tells Elvira, "in all the years the lot has been selling these cars I don't recall it ever being visited by an actual Japanese. I thought they all stayed over there in Toyota City enjoying the tea ceremony."

"And the geisha girls," Elvira says slyly. "Like Mr. Uno."

Harry smiles at the topical allusion. This girl – woman – keeps up. "Yeah, he wasn't Numero Uno very long, was he?"

Her earrings today are like temple bells, little curved lids of dull silver wired together in trembling oblongs the size of butterfly cocoons. They shiver with a touch of indignation when she tells him, "It's really Nelson and Lyle should be facing Mr. Shimada."

He shrugs. "What can you do? The lawyer got Lyle on the phone finally and the guy just laughed at him. Said he was taking oxygen just to get out of bed and go to the toilet and could die any time. Furthermore he said the disease had spread to his brain and he had no idea what the lawyer was talking about. And he'd had to sell his computer and didn't keep any of the disks. In other words he told the lawyer to – to go jump in the lake." Suppressing "fuck himself" like that was maybe a way of courting Elvira, he doesn't know. Late in the game as it is, you keep trying. He likes her being so thin – she makes Pru and even Janice look thick – and there is something cool and quiet about her he finds comforting, like a television screen when you can't hear the words, just see the flicker. "I had to laugh," he says, of Lyle's last communications. "Dying has its advantages."

She asks at his side, "Won't Nelson be home in a week or so?"

"That's the schedule," Harry says. "Summer flies by, doesn't it? You notice it in the evening now. It's still warm but gets dark earlier and earlier. It's a thing you forget from year to year, that late-summer darkness. The cicadas. That smell of baked-out lawns. Except this summer's been so damn rainy – in my little garden, God, the weeds won't stop growing, and the lettuce and broccoli are so leggy they're falling over. And the pea vines have spread like Virginia creeper, up over the fence and into the neighbor's yard."

"At least it hasn't been so terribly hot like it was the summer before," Elvira says, "when everybody kept talking about the greenhouse effect. Maybe there is no greenhouse effect."

"Oh, there is," Rabbit tells her, with a conviction he didn't know he had. Across Route 111, above the red hat-shaped roof of the Pizza Hut, a flock of starlings, already migrating south, speckle the telephone wires like a bar of musical notation. "I won't live to see it," he says, "but you will, and my grandchildren. New York, Philly, their docks will be underwater, once Antarctica starts melting. All of the Jersey Shore." Ronnie Harrison and Ruth: what a shit, that guy.

"How is he doing, have you heard much? Nelson."

"He's dropped us a couple of cards of the Liberty Bell. He sounded cheerful. In a way, the kid's been always looking for more structure than we could ever give him, and I guess a rehab program is big on structure. He talks to Pru on the phone, but they don't encourage too much outside contact at this point."

"What does Pru think about everything?" Does Harry imagine it, an edge of heightened interest here, as if the sound on the TV set clicked back in?

"Hard to know what Pru thinks," he says. "I have the impression she was about ready to pack it in, the marriage, before he sent himself off. She and Janice and the kids have been up at the Poconos."

"That makes it lonely for you," Elvira Ollenbach says.

Could this be a feeler? Is he supposed to have her come on over? Have a couple daiquiris in the den, stroke the dark nape of her neck, see if her pussy matches up, up in that slanty spare bedroom where all the old *Playboys* were stashed in the closet when they moved in – the thought of that wiry young female body seeking to slake its appetites on his affects him like the thought of an avalanche. It would make a wreck of his routine. "At my age I don't mind it," he says. "I can watch the TV shows I want. *National Geographic*, *Disney*, *World of Nature*. When Janice is there she makes us watch all these family situation shows with everybody clowning around in the living room. This *Roseanne*, I asked her what the hell she sees in it, she told me, 'I like her. She's fat and messy and mean, like most of the women in America.' I watch less and less. I try to have just one beer and go to bed early."

The young woman silently offers to move away, back to her cubicle in the direction of Paraguay. But he likes her near him, and abruptly asks, "You know who I'm sick of hearing about?"

"Who?"

"Pete Rose. 'Djou read in the *Standard* the other day how he's been in hot water before, in 1980 when he and a lot of the other Phils were caught taking amphetamines and the club traded away Randy Leach, the only player who admitted to it, and the rest of 'em just brazened it through?"

"I glanced at it. It was a Brewer doctor supplying the prescriptions."

"That's right, our own little burg. So that's why he thinks he can bluff it through now. Nobody else has to pay for what they do, everybody else gets away with everything. Ollie North, drug dealers, what with the jails being full and everybody such a bleeding heart anyway. Break the law, burn the flag, who the fuck cares?"

"Don't get yourself upset, Harry," she says, in her maternal, retreating mode. "The world is full of cheaters."

"Yeah, we should know."

She makes no response at all, having turned her back. Maybe she had been balling Nelson after all.

"I always thought he was an ugly ballplayer, anyway," he feels compelled to say, concerning Rose. "If you have to do it all with hustle and grit, you shouldn't be out there."

Out there, in the dog-days outdoors whose muggy alternation of light and shadow flickeringly gives him back his own ominous reflection, Harry notices that the refurbished yew hedge – he had a lawn service replace the dead bushes and renew the bark mulch – has collected a number of waxpaper pizza wrappers and Styrofoam coffee cups that have blown in from Route 111. He can't have their Japanese visitor see a mess like that. He goes outside, and the hot polluted air, bouncing off the asphalt, takes his breath away. The left side of his ribs gives a squeeze. He puts a Nitrostat to melt beneath his tongue before he begins to stoop. The more wastepaper he gathers, the more it seems there is – candy wrappers, cigarette-pack cellophane, advertising fliers and whole pages of newspaper wrinkled by rain and browned by the sun, big soft-drink cups with the plastic lid still on and the straw still in and the dirty water from melted ice still sloshing around. There is no end of crud in the world. He should have brought out a garbage bag, he has both hands full and can feel his face getting

red as he tries to hold yet one more piece of crumpled sticky cardboard in his fanned fingers. A limousine cracklingly pulls into the
lot while Harry is still picking up the trash, and he has to run inside
to cram it all into the wastebasket in his office. Puffing, his heart
thudding, his metallic-gray suit coat pulling at the buttons, he
rushes back across the showroom to greet Mr. Shimada at the
entrance, shaking his hand with a hand unwashed of street grit,
dried sugar, and still-sticky pizza topping.

Mr. Shimada is an impeccable compact man of about five six,
carrying an amazingly thin oxblood-red briefcase and wearing a
smoke-blue suit with an almost invisible pinstripe, tailored to display a dapper breadth of his gold-linked French cuffs and high
white collar, on a shirt with a pale-blue body. He looks dense, like
a beanbag filled to the corners with buckshot, and in good physical trim, though stocky, with a burnish of California tan on his
not unfriendly face. "Is very nice meeting you," he says. "Area
most nice." He speaks English easily, but with enough of an accent
to cost Harry a second's response time answering him.

"Well, not around here exactly," he answers, instantly thinking that this is tactless, for why would Toyota want to locate its
franchise in an ugly area? "I mean, the farm country is what we're
famous for, barns with hex signs and all that." He wonders if he
should explain "hex sign" and decides it's not worth it. "Would
you like to look around the facility? At the setup?" In case "facility" didn't register. Talking to foreigners really makes you think
about the language.

Mr. Shimada slowly, stiffly turns his head and shoulders together, one way and then the other, to take in the showroom. "I
see," he smiles. "Also in Torrance I study many photos and froor
pran. Oh! Rovely rady!"

Elvira has left her desk and sashays toward their visitor, sucking in her cheeks to make herself look more glamorous. "Miss
Olshima, I mean Mr. Shimada" – Harry had been practicing the
name, telling himself it was like Ramada with shit at the beginning, only to botch it in the crunch – "this is Miss Ollenbach, one
of our best sales reps. Representatives."

Mr. Shimada first gives her an instinctive little hands-at-the-
sides bow. When they shake hands, it's like both of them are

trying to knock each other out with their smiles, they hold them so long. "Is good idea, to have both sexes serring," he says to Harry. "More and more common thing."

"I don't know why it took us all so long to think of it," Harry admits.

"Good idea take time," the other man says, curbing his smile a little, letting an admonitory sternness tug downward his rather full yet flat lips. Harry remembers from his boyhood in World War II how very cruel the Japanese were to their prisoners on Bataan. The first thing you heard about them, after Pearl Harbor, was that they were ridiculously small, manning tiny submarines and planes called Zeros, and then, as those early Pacific defeats rolled in, that they were fanatic in the service of their Emperor, robot-monkeys that had to be torched out of their caves with flame-throwers. What a long way we've come since then. Harry feels one of his surges of benevolence, of approval of a world that isn't asking for it. Mr. Shimada seems to be asking Elvira if she prays.

"Play tennis, you mean?" she asks back. "Yes, as a matter of fact. Whenever I can. How did you know?"

His flat face breaks into twinkling creases and, quick as a monkey, he taps her wrist, where a band of relative pallor shows on her sunbrowned skin. "Sweatband," he says, proudly.

"That's clever," Elvira says. "You must play, too, in California. Everybody does."

"All free time. Revel five, hoping revel four."

"That's fabulous," she comes back, but a sideways upward glance at Harry asks how much longer she has to be a geisha girl.

"Good fetch, no backhand," Mr. Shimada tells her, demonstrating.

"Turn your *back* to the net, and take the racket back *low*," Elvira tells him, also demonstrating. "Hit the ball out *front*, don't let it *play you*."

"Talk just as pro," Mr. Shimada tells her, beaming.

No doubt about it, Elvira is impressive. You can see how rangy and quick she would be on the court. Harry is beginning to relax. When the phantom tennis lesson is over, he takes their guest on a quick tour through the office space and through the shelved tunnel of the parts department, where Roddy, the Assistant Parts

Manager, a viciously pretty youth with long lank hair he keeps flicking back from his face, his face and hands filmed with gray grease, gives them a dirty white-eyed look. Harry doesn't introduce them, for fear of besmirching Mr. Shimada with a touch of grease. He leads him to the brass-barred door of the rackety, cavernous garage, where Manny, the Service Manager Harry had inherited from Fred Springer fifteen years ago, has been replaced by Arnold, a plump young man with an advanced degree from voke school, where he was taught to wear washable coveralls that give him the figure of a Kewpie doll, or a snowman. Mr. Shimada hesitates at the verge of the echoing garage – men's curses cut through the hammering of metal on metal – and takes a step backward, asking, "Emproyee moraru good?"

This must be "morale." Harry thinks of the mechanics, their insatiable gripes and constant coffee breaks and demands for ever more costly fringe benefits, and their frequent hungover absences on Monday and suspiciously early departures on Friday, and says, "Very good. They clear twenty-two dollars an hour, with bonuses and benefits. The first job I ever took, when I was fifteen, I got thirty-five cents an hour."

Mr. Shimada is not interested. "Brack emproyees, are any? I see none."

"Yeah, well. We'd like to hire more, but it's hard to find qualified ones. We had a man a couple years ago, had good hands and got along with everybody, but we had to let him go finally because he kept showing up late or not showing up at all. When we called him on it, he said he was on Afro-American time." Harry is ashamed to tell him what the man's nickname had been – Blackie. At least we don't still sell Black Sambo dolls with nigger lips like they do in Tokyo, he saw on *60 Minutes* this summer.

"Toyota strive to be fair-practices emproyer," says Mr. Shimada. "Wants to be good citizen of your pruraristic society. In prant in Georgetown, Kentucky, many bracks work. Not just assembry line, executive positions."

"We'll work on it," Rabbit promises him. "This is a kind of conservative area, but it's coming along."

"Very pretty area."

"Right."

Back in the showroom, Harry feels obliged to explain, "My son picked these colors for the walls and woodwork. My son Nelson. I would have gone for something a little less, uh, choice, but he's been the effective manager here, while I've been spending half the year in Florida. My wife loves the sun down there. She plays tennis, by the way. Loves the game."

Mr. Shimada beams. His lips seem flattened as if by pressing up against glass, and his eyeglasses, their squarish gold rims, seem set exceptionally tight against his eyes. "We know Nelson Angstrom," he says. He has trouble with the many consonants of the last name, making it "Ank-a-stom." "A most famous man at Toyota company."

A constriction in Harry's chest and a watery looseness below his belt tell him that they have arrived, after many courtesies, at the point of the visit. "Want to come into my office and sit?"

"With preasure."

"Anything one of the girls could get you? Coffee? Tea? Not like your tea, of course. Just a bag of Lipton's —"

"Is fine without." Rather unceremoniously, he enters Harry's office and sits on the vinyl customer's chair, with padded chrome arms, facing the desk. He sets his wonderfully thin briefcase on his lap and lightly folds his hands upon it, showing two dazzling breadths of white cuff. He waits for Harry to seat himself behind the desk and then begins what seems to be a prepared speech. "Arways," he says, "we in Japan admire America. As boy during Occupation, rooked way up to big GI soldiers, their happy easy-go ways. Enemy soldiers, but not bad men. Powerful men. Our Emperor's advisers have red him down unfortunate ways, so General MacArthur, he seemed to us as Emperor had been, distant and first-rate. We worked hard to do what he suggest — rebuild burned cities, learn democratic ways. Japanese very humble at first in regard to America. You know Toyota story. At first, very modest, then bigger, we produce a better product for the rittle man's money, yes? You ask for it, we got it, yes?"

"Good slogan," Harry tells him. "I like it better than some of the recent ones've been coming down."

But Mr. Shimada does not expect to be even slightly interrupted. His burnished, manicured hands firmly flatten on the thin oxblood briefcase and he inclines his upper body forward to make his voice clear. "Nevertheress, these years of postwar, Japanese, man and woman, have great respect for United States. Rike big brother. But in recent times big brother act rike rittle brother, always cry and comprain. Want many favors in trade, saying Japanese unfair competition. Why unfair? Make something, cheaper even with duty and transportation costs, people rike, people buy. American way in old times. But in new times America make nothing, just do mergers, do acquisitions, rower taxes, raise national debt. Nothing comes out, all goes in – foreign goods, foreign capital. America take everything, give nothing. Rike big brack hole."

Mr. Shimada is proud of this up-to-date analogy and of his unanswerable command of English. He smiles to himself and opens, with a double snap as startling as a gunshot, his briefcase. From it he takes a single sheet of stiff creamy paper, sparsely decorated with typed figures. "According to figures here, between November '88 and May '89 Springer Motors fail to report sale of nine Toyota vehicles totarring one hundred thirty-seven thousand four hundred at factory price. This sum accumurating interest come to as of this date one hundred forty-five thousand eight hundred." With one of his reflexive, half-suppressed bows, he hands the paper across the desk.

Harry covers it with his big hand and says, "Yeah, well, but it's accountants *we* hired reported all this to you. It's not as if Springer Motors as a company is trying to cheat anybody. It's a screwy – an unusual – situation that developed and that's being corrected. My son had a drug problem and hired a bad egg as chief accountant and together they ripped us all off. The Brewer Trust, too, in another scam – they had a dead mutual friend buying cars, would you believe it? But listen: my wife and I – technically she's the owner here – we have every intention of paying Mid-Atlantic Toyota back every penny we owe. And I'd like to see, sometime, how you're computing that interest."

Mr. Shimada leans back a bit and makes his briefest speech. "How soon?"

Harry takes a plunge. "End of August." Three weeks away. They might have to take out a bank loan, and Brewer Trust is already on their case. Well, let Janice's accountants work it out if they're so smart.

Mr. Shimada blinks, behind those lenses embedded in his flat face, and seems to nod in concord. "End of August. Interest computed at twelve per cent monthly compounded as in standard TMCC loan." He snaps shut his briefcase and balances it on its edge beside his chair. He gazes obliquely at the framed photographs on Harry's desk: Janice, when she still had bangs, in a spangly long dress three or four years ago, about to go off to the Valhalla Village New Year's Eve party, a flashlit color print Fern Drechsel took with a Nikkomat Bernie had just given her for a Hanukkah present and that came out surprisingly well, Janice's face in anticipation of the party looking younger than her years, a bit overexposed and out of focus and starry-eyed; Nelson's high-school graduation picture, in a blazer and necktie but his hair down to his shoulders, long as a girl's; and, left over from Nelson's tenure at this desk, a framed black-and-white posed school photo of Harry in his basketball uniform, holding the ball above his shining right shoulder as if to get off a shot, his hair crewcut, his eyes sleepy, his tank top stencilled MJ.

Mr. Shimada's less upright posture in the chair indicates a new, less formal level of discourse. "Young people now most interesting," he decides to say. "Not scared of starving as through most human history. Not scared of atom bomb as until recently. But scared of something – not happy. In Japan, too. Brue jeans, rock music not make happiness enough. In former times, in Japan, very simple things make men happy. Moonright on fish pond at certain moment. Cricket singing in bamboo grove. Very small things bring very great feering. Japan a rittle ireand country, must make do with very near nothing. Not rike endless China, not rike U.S. No oiru wells, no great spaces. We have only our people, their disciprine. Riving now five years in Carifornia, it disappoints me, the rack of disciprine in people of America. Many good qualities, of course. Good tennis, good hearts. Roads of fun. I have many most dear American friends. Always they aporogize to me for Japanese internment camps in Frankrin Roosevelt days. Always I say to them, surprised, 'Was war!' In war, people need disciprine. Not just in war. Peace a kind of war also. We fight now not

Americans and British but Nissan, Honda, Ford. Toyota agency must be a prace of disciprine, a prace of order."

Harry feels he must interrupt, he doesn't like the trend of this monologue. "We think this agency is. Sales have been up eight per cent this summer, bucking the national trend. I'm always saying to people, 'Toyota's been good to us, and we've been good to Toyota.'"

"No more, sorry," Mr. Shimada says simply, and resumes: "In United States, is fascinating for me, struggle between order and freedom. Everybody mention freedom, all papers terevision anchor people everybody. Much rove and talk of freedom. Skateboarders want freedom to use beach boardwalks and knock down poor old people. Brack men with radios want freedom to self-express with super-jumbo noise. Men want freedom to have guns and shoot others on freeways in random sport. In Carifornia, dog shit much surprise me. Everywhere, dog shit, dogs must have important freedom to shit everywhere. Dog freedom more important than crean grass and cement pavement. In U.S., Toyota company hope to make ireands of order in ocean of freedom. Hope to strike proper barance between needs of outer world and needs of inner being, between what in Japan we call *giri* and *ninjō*." He leans forward and, with a flash of wide white cuff, taps the page of figures on Harry's desk. "Too much disorder. Too much dog shit. Pay by end of August, no prosecution for criminal activities. But no more Toyota franchise at Singer Motors."

"Springer," Harry says automatically. "Listen," he pleads. "No one feels worse about my son's falling apart than I do."

Now it is Mr. Shimada who interrupts; his own speech, with whatever beautiful shadows in Japanese it was forming in his mind, has whipped him up. "Not just son," he says. "Who is father and mother of such son? Where are they? In Frorida, enjoying sunshine and tennis, while young boy prays games with autos. Nelson Ank-a-stom too much a boy still to be managing Toyota agency. He roses face for Toyota company." This statement tugs his flat lips far down, in a pop-eyed scowl.

Hopelessly Harry argues, "You want the sales staff young, to attract the young customers. Nelson'll be thirty-three in a couple months." He thinks it would be a waste of breath, and maybe

offensive, to explain to Mr. Shimada that at that same age Jesus
Christ was old enough to be crucified and redeem mankind. He
makes a final plea: "You'll lose all the good will. For thirty years
the people of Brewer have known where to come to buy Toyotas.
Out here right on Route One One One."

"No more," Mr. Shimada states. "Too much dog shit, Mr.
Ank-strom." His third try and he almost has it. You got to hand
it to them. "Toyota does not enjoy bad games prayed with its
ploduct." He picks up his slim briefcase and stands. "You keep
invoice. Many more papers to arrive. Most preasant if regretful
visit, and good talk on topics of general interest. Perhaps you
would be kind to discuss with rimo driver best way to find Route
Four Two Two. Mr. Krauss has agency there."

"You're going to see Rudy? He used to work here. I taught
him all he knows."

Mr. Shimada has stiffened, in that faintly striped smoky-blue
suit. "Good teacher not always good parent."

"If Rudy's going to be the only Toyota in town, he ought to
get rid of Mazda. That Wankel engine never really worked out.
Too much like a squirrel cage."

Harry feels lightheaded, now that the ax has fallen. Anticipation
is the worst; letting go has its pleasant side. "Good luck with
Lexus, by the way," he says. "People don't think luxury when
they think Toyota, but things can change."

"Things change," says Mr. Shimada. "Is world's sad secret."
Out in the showroom, he asks, "Rovely rady?" Elvira with her
clicking brisk walk traverses the showroom floor, her earrings
doing a dance along the points of her jaw. Their visitor asks,
"Could prease have business card, in case of future reference?"
She digs one out of her suit pocket, and Mr. Shimada accepts it,
studies it seriously, bows with his hands at his side, and then,
to strike a jocular American note, imitates a tennis backhand.

"You've got it," she tells him. "Take it back *low*."

He bows again and, turning to Harry, beams so broadly his eye-
glass frames are lifted by the creasing of his face. "Good ruck with
many probrems. Perhaps before too rate should buy Rexus at
dealer price." This is, it would seem, a little Japanese joke.

Harry gives the manicured hand a gritty squeeze. "Don't think

I can afford even a Corolla now," he says and, in a reflex of good will really, manages a little bow of his own. He accompanies his visitor outdoors to the limousine, whose black driver is leaning against the fender eating a slice of pizza, and a cloud pulls back from the sun; a colorless merciless dog-day brilliance makes Harry wince; all joking falls away and he abruptly feels fragile and ill with loss. He cannot imagine the lot without the tall blue TOYOTA sign, the glinting still lake of well-made cars in slightly bitter Oriental colors. Poor Janice, she'll be knocked for a loop. She'll feel she's let her father down.

But she doesn't react too strongly; she is more interested these days in her real-estate courses. Janice has completed one pair of ten-week courses and is into another. She has long phone conversations with her classmates about the next quiz or the fascinating personality of their teacher, Mr. Lister with his exciting new beard. "I'm sure Nelson has some plan," she says. "And if he doesn't, we'll all sit down and negotiate one."

"Negotiate! Two hundred thousand disappearing dollars! And you don't have Toyotas to sell any more."

"Were they really so great, Harry? Nelson hated them. Why can't we get an American franchise – isn't Detroit making a big comeback?"

"Not so big they can afford Nelson Angstrom."

She pretends he's joking, saying, "Aren't you awful?" Then she looks at his face, is startled and saddened by what she sees there, and crosses their kitchen to reach up and touch his face. "Harry," she says. "You *are* taking it hard. Don't. Daddy used to say, 'For every up there's a down, and for every down there's an up.' Nelson will be home in a week and we can't do a thing really until then." Outside the kitchen window screen, where moths keep bumping, the early-August evening has that blended tint peculiar to the season, of light being withdrawn while summer's warmth remains. As the days grow shorter, a dryness of dead grass and chirring insects has crept in even through this summer of heavy rains, of more thunderstorms and flash floods in Diamond County than Harry can ever remember. Out in their yard, he notices now a few brown leaves shed by the weeping cherry, and the flower stalks of the violet hosta dying back. In his mood of isolation and lassitude he is drawing closer to the earth, the familiar mother with his infancy still in her skirts, in the shadows beneath the bushes.

"Shit," he says, a word charged for him with magic since the night three months ago when Pru used it to announce her despairing decision to sleep with him, once. "What kind of plans can Nelson have? He'll be lucky to stay out of jail."

"You can't go to jail for stealing from your own family. He had a medical problem, he was sick the same way you were sick only it was addiction instead of angina. You're both getting better."

He hears in the things she says, more and more, other voices, opinions and a wisdom gathered away from him. "Who have you been talking to?" he says. "You sound like that know-it-all Doris Kaufmann."

"Eberhardt. I haven't talked to Doris for weeks and weeks. But some of the women taking the real-estate program, we go out afterwards to this little place on Pine Street that's not too rough, at least until later, and one of them, Francie Alvarez, says you got to think of any addiction as a medical condition just like they caught the flu, or otherwise you'd go crazy, blaming the addicts around you as if they can help it."

"So what makes you think Nelson's cure will take? Just because it cost us six grand, that doesn't mean a thing to the kid. He just went in to let things blow over. You told me yourself he told you once he loves coke more than anything in the world. More than you, more than me, more than his own kids."

"Well, sometimes in life you have to give up things you love."

Charlie. Is that who she's thinking of, to make her voice sound so sincere, so sadly wise and wisely firm? Her eyes for this moment in dying August light have a darkness that invites him in, to share a wisdom her woman's life has taught her. Her fingers touch his cheek again, a touch like a fly that when you're trying to fall asleep keeps settling on your face, the ticklish thin skin here and there. It's annoying; he tries to shake her off with a snap of his head. She pulls her hand back but still stares so solemnly. "It's you I worry about, more than Nelson. Is the angina coming back? The breathlessness?"

"A twinge now and then," he admits. "Nothing a pill doesn't fix. It's just something I'm going to have to live with."

"I wonder if you shouldn't have had the bypass."

"The balloon was bad enough. Sometimes I feel like they left it inside me."

"Harry, at least you should do more exercise. You go from the lot to the TV in the den to bed. You never play golf any more."

"Well, it's no fun with the old gang gone. The kids out there at the Flying Eagle don't want an old man in their foursome. In Florida I'll pick it up again."

"That's something else we ought to talk about. What's the point of my getting the salesperson's license if we go right down to Florida for six months? I can never build up any local presence."

"Local presence, you've got lots of it. You're Fred Springer's daughter and Harry Angstrom's wife. And now you're a famous coke addict's mother."

"I mean professionally. It's a phrase Mr. Lister uses. It means the people know you're always there, not off in Florida like some person who doesn't take her job seriously."

"So," he says. "Florida was good enough to stash me in when I was manager at Springer Motors, to get me out of Nelson's way, but now you think you're a working girl we can just forget it, Florida."

"Well," Janice allows, "I *was* thinking, one possibility, to help with the company's debts, might be to sell the condo."

"*Sell* it? Over my dead body," he says, not so much meaning it as enjoying the sound of his voice, indignant like one of those perpetually outraged fathers on a TV sitcom, or like silver-haired Steve Martin in the movie *Parenthood*, which they saw the other night because one of Janice's real-estate buddies thought it was so funny. "My blood's got too thin to go through a Northern winter."

In response Janice looks as if she is about to cry, her dark-brown eyes warm and glassy-looking just like little Roy's before he lets loose with one of his howls. "Harry, don't confuse me," she begs. "I can't even take the license exam until October, I can't believe you'd immediately make me go down to Florida where the license is no good just so you can play golf with some people older and worse than you. Who beat you anyway, and take twenty dollars every time."

"Well what am *I* supposed to do around here while you run around showing off? The lot's finished, *kaput*, or whatever the Japanese word is, *finito*, and even if it's not, if the kid's half-way straightened out you'll want him back there and he can't stand me around, we crowd each other, we get on each other's nerves."

"Maybe you won't now. Maybe Nelson will just have to put up with you and you with him."

Harry humbly tells her, "I'd be willing." Father and son, together against the world, rebuilding the lot up from scratch: the vision excites him, for the moment. Shooting the bull with Benny and Elvira while Nelson skitters around out there in the lake of rooftops, selling used cars like hotcakes. Springer Motors back to what it used to be before Fred got the Toyota franchise. So they owe a few hundred thousand – the government owes trillions and nobody cares.

She sees hope in his face and touches his cheek a third time. At night now, Harry, having to arise at least once and sometimes, if there's been more than one beer with television, twice, has learned to touch his way across the bedroom in the pitch dark, touching the glass top of the bedside table and then with an outreached arm after a few blind steps the slick varnished edge of the high bureau and from there to the knob of the bathroom door. Each touch, it occurs to him every night, leaves a little deposit of sweat and oil from the skin of his fingertips; eventually it will darken the varnished bureau edge as the hems of his golf-pants pockets have been rendered grimy by his reaching in and out for tees and ball markers, round after round, over the years; and that accumulated deposit of his groping touch, he sometimes thinks when the safety of the bathroom and its luminescent light switch has been attained, will still be there, a shadow on the varnish, a microscopic cloud of his body oils, when he is gone.

"Don't push me, honey," Janice says, in a rare tone of direct appeal that makes his hard old heart accelerate with revived husbandly feeling. "This horrible thing with Nelson really has been a stress, though I may not always show it. I'm his mother, I'm humiliated, I don't know what's going to happen, exactly. Everything's in flux."

His chest feels full; his left ribs cage a twinge. His vision of working side by side with Nelson has fled, a pipe dream. He tries to make Janice, so frighteningly, unusually somber and frontal, smile with a tired joke. "I'm too old for flux," he tells her.

Nelson is scheduled to return from rehab the same day that the second U.S. Congressman in two weeks, a white Republican this time, is killed in a plane crash. One in Ethiopia, one in Louisiana; one a former Black Panther, and this one a former sheriff. You don't think of being a politician as being such a hazardous profession; but it makes you fly. Pru drives to get her husband at the halfway house in North Philadelphia while Janice babysits. Soon after they arrive, Janice comes home to Penn Park. "I thought they should be alone with each other, the four of them," she explains to Harry.

"How did he seem?"

She thoughtfully touches her upper lip with the tip of her tongue. "He seemed . . . serious. Very focused and calm. Not at all jittery like he was. I don't know how much Pru told him about Toyota withdrawing the franchise and the hundred forty-five thousand you promised we'd pay so soon. I didn't want to fling it at him right off the bat."

"What *did* you say, then?"

"I said he looked wonderful – he looks a little heavy, actually – and told him you and I were very proud of him for sticking it out."

"Huh. Did he ask about me? My health?"

"Not exactly, Harry – but he knows we'd have said something if anything more was wrong with you. He seemed mostly inter-ested in the children. It was really very touching – he took them both off with him into the room where Mother used to have all the plants, what we called the sun parlor, and apologized for hav-ing been a bad father to them and explained about the drugs and how he had been to a place where they taught him how to never take drugs again."

"Did he apologize to you for having been a bad son? To Pru for being a crappy husband?"

"I have no idea what he and Pru said to each other – they had hours in the car together, the traffic around Philadelphia is getting worse and worse, what with all the work on the Expressway. All the roads and bridges are falling apart at once."

"He didn't ask about me at all?"

"He did, of course he did, honey. You and I are supposed to go over there for dinner tomorrow night."

"Oh. So I can admire the drugless wonder. Great."

"You mustn't talk like that. He needs all of our support. Returning to your milieu is the hardest part of recovery."

"Milieu, huh? So that's what we are."

"That's what they call it. He's going to have to stay away from that druggy young people's crowd that meets at the Laid-Back. So his immediate family must work very hard to fill in the gap."

"Oh my God, don't sound so fucking goody-goody," he says. Resentment churns within him. He resents Nelson's getting all this attention for being a prodigal son. He resents Janice's learning new words and pushing outward into new fields, away from him. He resents the fact that the world is so full of debt and nobody has to *pay* – not Mexico or Brazil, not the sleazy S and L banks, not Nelson. Rabbit never had much use for old-fashioned ethics but their dissolution eats at him.

The night and the next day pass, in bed and at the lot. He tells Benny and Elvira that Nelson is back and he looked fat to his mother but didn't announce any plans. Elvira has received a call from Rudy Krauss asking if she wanted to come over to Route 422 and sell for him. A Mr. Shimada spoke very highly of her. Also she hears that Jake is leaving the Volvo-Olds in Oriole and heading up a Lexus agency toward Pottstown. For now though she would rather hang loose here and see what Nelson has in mind. Benny's been asking around at other agencies and isn't too worried. "What happens happens, you know what I mean? As long as I got my health and my family – those are my priorities." Harry has asked them not to tell anyone in Service yet about Mr. Shimada's surprise attack. He feels increasingly detached; as he walks the plastic-tiled display floor, his head seems to float above it as dizzily high as his top-hatted head above the pitted, striped asphalt that day of the parade. He is growing. He drives home, catches the beginning of Brokaw on 10 (he may have a kind of hare lip, but at least he doesn't say "aboot") before Janice insists he get back in the Celica with her and drive across Brewer to Mt. Judge for the zillionth time in his life.

Nelson has shaved his mustache and taken off his earring. His face has a playground tan and he does look plump. His upper lip, exposed again, seems long and puffy and bulging outward, like Ma Springer's used to. That's who it turns out he resembles; she had a tight stuffed-skin sausage look that Harry can see now develop- ing in Nelson. The boy moves with a certain old-lady stiffness, as if the rehab has squeezed the drugs and the jitters out of him but also his natural nervous quickness. For the first time, he seems to his father middle-aged, and his thinning hair and patches of exposed scalp part of him and not just a condition that will heal. He reminds Harry of a minister, a slightly sleek and portly repre- sentative of some no-name sect like that lamebrain who buried Thelma. A certain acquired formality extends to his clothes: though the evening is seasonably humid and warm, he wears a striped necktie with a white shirt, making Harry feel falsely youth- ful in his soft-collared polo shirt with the Flying Eagle emblem.

Nelson met his parents at the door and after embracing his mother attempted to do the same with his father, awkwardly wrapping both arms around the much taller man and pulling him down to rub scratchy cheeks. Harry was taken by surprise and not pleased: the embrace felt showy and queer and forced, the kind of thing these TV evangelists tell you to do to one another, before they run off screen and get their secretaries to lay them. He and Nelson have hardly touched since the boy's age hit double digits. Some kind of reconciliation or amends was no doubt intended but to Harry it felt like a rite his son has learned elsewhere and that has nothing to do with being an Angstrom.

Pru in her turn seems bewildered by suddenly having a minis- ter for a husband; when Harry bends down expecting the soft warm push of her lips on his, he gets instead her dry cheek, averted with a fearful quickness. He is hurt but can't believe he has done any- thing wrong. Since their episode that wild and windy night, the silence from her side has indicated a wish to pretend it never hap- pened, and with his silence he has indicated that he is willing. He hasn't the strength any more, the excess vitality, for an affair – its danger, its demand performances, the secrecy added like a filigree to your normal life, your gnawing preoccupation with it and with the constant threat of its being discovered and ended. He can't bear to think of Nelson's knowing, whereas Ronnie's knowing he didn't much mind. He even enjoyed it, like a sharp elbow given under the basket. Thelma and he had been two of a kind, each able to gauge the risks and benefits, able to construct together a stolen space in which they could feel free for an hour, free of everything but each other. Within your own generation – the same songs, the same wars, the same attitudes toward those wars, the same rules and radio shows in the air – you can gauge the possibilities and impossibilities. With a person of another generation, you are treading water, playing with fire. So he doesn't like to feel even this small alteration in Pru's temperature, this coolness like a rebuke.

The children eat with them, Judy and Harry on one side of the Springers' mahogany dining-room table, set as if for a holiday, Janice and Roy on the other, Pru and Nelson at the heads. Nelson offers grace; he makes them all hold hands and shut their eyes and after they're ready to scream with embarrassment pronounces the words, "Peace. Health. Sanity. Love."

"Amen," says Pru, sounding scared.

Judy can't stop staring up at Harry, to see what he makes of it. "Nice," he tells his son. "That something you learned at the detox place?"

"Not detox, Dad, rehab."

"Whatever it was, it was full of religion?"

"You got to admit you're powerless and dependent on a higher power, that's the first principle of AA and NA."

"As I remember it, you didn't use to go much for any higher-power stuff."

"I didn't, and still don't, in the form that orthodox religion presents it in. All you have to believe in is a power greater than ourselves – God as we understand Him."

Everything sounds so definite and pat, Harry has to fight the temptation to argue. "No, great," he says. "Anything that gets you through the night, as Sinatra says." Mim had quoted that to him once. In this Springer house tonight Harry feels a huge and regretful distance from Mim and Mom and Pop and all that sunken God-fearing Jackson Road Thirties-Forties world.

"You used to believe a lot of that stuff," Nelson tells him.

"I did. I do," Rabbit says, annoying the kid, he knows, with his amiability. But he has to add, "Hallelujah. When they stuck that catheter into my heart, I saw the light."

Nelson announces, "They tell you at the center that there'll be people who mock you for going straight, but they don't say one of them will be your own father."

"I'm not mocking anything. Jesus. Have all the peace and love and sanity you want. I'm all for it. We're all all for it. Right, Roy?"

The little boy stares angrily at being suddenly singled out. His loose wet lower lip begins to tremble; he turns his face toward his mother's side. Pru tells Harry, in a soft directed voice in which he does sense a certain mist of acknowledgment, of rain splashing at a screened window, "Roy's been very upset, readjusting to Nelson's coming back."

"I know how he feels," Harry says. "We'd all gotten used to his not being around."

Nelson looks toward Janice in protest and appeal and she says, "Nelson, tell us about the counselling work you did," in the fake tone of one who has already heard about it.

As Nelson speaks, he sits with a curious tranquillized stillness; Harry is used to the kid, from little on up, being full of nervous elusive twitches, that yet had something friendly and hopeful about them. "Mostly," he says, "you just listen, and let them work it out through their own verbalization. You don't have to say much, just show you're willing to wait, and listen. The most hardened street kids eventually open up. Once in a while you have to remind them you've been there yourself, so their war stories don't impress you. A lot have been dealers, and when they start bragging how much money they made all you have to do is ask, 'Where is it now?' They don't have it," Nelson tells the listening table, his own staring children. "They blew it."

"Speaking of blowing it —" Harry begins.

Nelson overrides him with his steady-voiced sermon. "You try to get them to see themselves that they are addicts, that they weren't outsmarting anybody. The realization has to come from them, from within, it's not something they can accept imposed on them by you. Your job is to listen; it's your silence, mostly, that leads them past their own internal traps. You start talking, they start resisting. It takes patience, and faith. Faith that the process will work. And it does. It invariably does. It's thrilling to see it happen, again and again. People want to be helped. They know things are wrong."

Harry still wants to speak but Janice intercedes by telling him, loudly for their audience at the table, "One of Nelson's ideas about the lot is to make it a treatment center. Brewer doesn't have anything like the facilities it needs to cope with the problem. The drug problem."

"That's the absolutely dumbest idea I've ever heard," Harry says promptly. "Where's the money in it? You're dealing with people who have *no* money, they've blown it all for drugs."

Nelson is goaded into sounding a bit more like his old self. He whines, "There's *grant* money, Dad. Federal money. State. Even do-nothing Bush admits we got to do *some*thing."

"You've got twenty employees you've fucked up over there at the lot, and most of 'em have families. What happens to the mechanics in Service? What about your sales reps − poor little Elvira?"

"They can get other jobs. It's not the end of the world. People don't stick with jobs the way your scared generation did."

"Yeah, scared − with your generation on the loose we got reason to be scared. How would you ever turn that cement-block shed over there into a hospital?"

"It wouldn't be a hospital −"

"You're already one hundred fifty thousand in the hole to Toyota Inc. and two weeks to pay it off in. Not to mention the seventy-five grand you owe Brewer Trust."

"Those purchases in Slim's name, the cars never left the lot, so there's really no −"

"Not to mention the used you sold for cash you put in your own pocket."

"Harry," Janice says, gesturing toward their audience of listening children. "This isn't the place."

"There *is* no place where I can get a handle on what this lousy kid has done! Over two hundred thousand fucking shekels −

where's it going to come from?" Sparks of pain flicker beneath the muscles of his chest, he feels a dizziness in which the faces at the table float as in a sickening soup. Bad sensations have been worsening lately; it's been over three months since that angioplasty opened his LAD. Dr. Breit warned that restenosis often sets in after three months.

Janice is saying, "But he's learned so much, Harry. He's so much wiser. It's as if we sent him to graduate school with the money."

"School, all this school! What's so great about school all of a sudden? School's just another rip-off. All it teaches you is how to rip off dopes that haven't been to school yet!"

"I don't want to go back to school," Judy pipes up. "Everybody there is stuck-up. Everybody says the fourth grade is *hard*."

"I don't mean *your* school, honey." Rabbit can hardly breathe; his chest feels full of bits of Styrofoam that won't dissolve. He must get himself unaggravated.

From the head of the table Nelson radiates calm and solidity. "Dad, I was an addict. I admit it," he says. "I was doing crack, and a run of that gets to be expensive. You're afraid to crash, and need a fresh hit every twenty minutes. If you go all night, you can run through thousands. But that money I stole didn't all go to my habit. Lyle needed big money for some experimental stuff the FDA jerks are sitting on and has to be smuggled in from Europe and Mexico."

"Lyle," Harry says with satisfaction. "How is the old computer whiz?"

"He seems to be holding his own for the time being."

"He'll outlive me," Harry says, as a joke, but the real possibility of it stabs him like an icicle. "So Springer Motors," he goes on, trying to get a handle on it, "went up in coke and pills for a queer." How queer, he wonders, staring at his middle-aged, fattened-up, rehabilitated son, is the kid? Pru's answer to that had never quite satisfied him. If Nelson wasn't queer, how come she let Harry ball her? A lot of pent-up hunger there, her coming twice like that.

Nelson tells him, in that aggravating tranquillized nothing-can-touch-me tone, "You get too excited, Dad, about what really isn't, in this day and age, an awful lot of money. You have this Depression thing about the dollar. There's nothing holy about the dollar, it's just a unit of measurement."

"Oh. Thanks for explaining that. What a relief."

"As to Toyota, it's no big loss. The company's been stale for years, in my opinion. Look at their TV ads for the Lexus compared with Nissan's for the Infiniti: there's no comparison. Infiniti's are fan*tas*tic, there's no car in them, just birds and trees, they're selling a *con*cept. Toyota's selling another load of tin. Don't be so fixated about Toyota. Springer Motors is still there," Nelson states. "The company still has assets. Mom and I are working it out, how to deploy them."

"Good luck," Harry says, rolling up his napkin and reinserting it in its ring, a child's ring of some clear substance filled with tiny needles of varied color. "In our thirty-three years of marriage your mother hasn't been able to deploy the ingredients of a decent meal on the table, but maybe she'll learn. Maybe Mr. Lister'll teach her how to deploy. Pru, that was a lovely meal. Excuse the conversation. You really have a way with fish. Loved those little spicy like peas on top." As he shakes out a Nitrostat from the small bottle he carries everywhere, he sees his hands trembling in a new way – not just a tremor, but jumping, as if with thoughts all their own, that they aren't sharing with him.

"Capers," Pru says softly.

"Harry, Nelson is coming back to the lot tomorrow," Janice says.

"Great. That's another relief."

"I wanted to say, Dad, thanks for filling in. The summer stat sheets look pretty good, considering."

"Con*sid*ering? We pulled off a miracle over there. That Elvira is dynamite. As I guess you know. This Jap that gave us the ax wants to hire her for Rudy over on 422. The inventory is being shifted to his lot." He turns to Janice and says, "I can't believe you're putting this loser back in charge."

Janice says, in the calm tone everybody at the table is acquiring, as if to humor a madman, "He's not a loser. He's your son and he's a new person. We can't deny him a chance."

In a voice more wifely than Janice's, Pru adds, "He really has changed, Harry."

"A day at a time," Nelson recites, "with the help of a higher power. Once you accept that help, Dad, it's amazing how nothing gets you down. All these years, I think I've been seriously depressed; everything seemed too much. Now I just put it all in God's hands, roll over, and go to sleep. You have to keep up the program, of course. There're local meetings, and I drive down to Philly once a week to see my therapist and check on some of my old kids. I love counselling." He turns to his mother and smiles. "I love it, and it loves me."

Harry asks him, "These druggy kids you deal with, they all black?"

"Not all. After a while you don't even see that any more. White or black, they have the same basic problem. Low self-esteem."

Such knowingness, such induced calm and steadiness and virtue: it makes Rabbit feel claustrophobic. He turns to his grand-daughter, looking for an opening, a glint, a ray of undoctored light. He asks her, "What do you make of all this, Judy?"

The child's face wears a glaze of perfection – perfect straight teeth, perfectly spaced lashes, narrow gleams in her green eyes and along the strands of her hair. Nature is trying to come up with another winner. "I like having Daddy back," she says, "and not so crazy. He's more responsible." Again, he feels that words are being recited, learned at a rehearsal he wasn't invited to attend. But how can he wish anything for this child but the father she needs?

Out on the curb, he asks Janice to drive the Celica, though it means adjusting the seat and the mirrors. Heading back around the mountain, he asks her, "You really don't want me back at the lot?" He looks down at his hands. Their jumping has subsided but is still fascinating.

"I think for now, Harry. Let's give Nelson the space. He's try-ing so hard."

"He's full of AA bullshit."

"It's not bullshit if you need it to live a normal life."

"He doesn't look like himself."

"He will as you get used to him."

"He reminds me of your mother. She was always laying down the law."

"Everybody knows he looks just like you. Only not as tall, and he has my eyes."

The park, its shadowy walks, its decrepit tennis courts, its memorial tank that will never fire another shot. You can't see these things so clearly when you're driving. They go by like museum exhibits whose labels have all peeled off. He tries to climb out of his trapped and angry mood. "Sorry if I sounded ugly at dinner, in front of the grandchildren."

"We were prepared for much worse," she says serenely.

"I didn't mean to bring up the money or any of that stuff at all. But somebody has to. You're in real trouble."

"I know," Janice says, letting the streetlights of upper Weiser wash over her – her stubborn blunt-nosed profile, her little hands tight on the steering wheel, the diamond-and-sapphire ring she inherited from her mother. "But you have to have faith. You've taught me that."

"I have?" He is pleasantly surprised, to think that in thirty-three years he has taught her anything. "Faith in what?"

"In us. In life," she says. "Another reason I think you should stay away from the lot now, you've been looking tired. Have you been losing weight?"

"A couple pounds. Isn't that good? Isn't that what the hell I'm supposed to be doing?"

"It depends on how you do it," Janice says, so annoyingly full of new information, new presumption. She reaches over and gives his inner upper thigh, right where they inserted the catheter and he could have bled to death, a squeeze. "We'll be fine," she lies.

Now August, muggy and oppressive in its middle weeks, is bringing summer to a sparkling distillation, a final clarity. The fairways at the Flying Eagle, usually burnt-out and as hard as the cart-paths this time of year, with all the rain they've had are still green, but for the rough of reddish-brown buckgrass, and an occasional spindly maple sapling beginning to show yellow. It's the young trees that turn first – more tender, more attuned. More fearful.

Ronnie Harrison still swings like a blacksmith: short back-swing, ugly truncated follow-through, sometimes a grunt in the middle. No longer needed at the lot, needing a partner if he was going to take up golf again, Rabbit remembered Thelma's saying how they had had to resign from the club because of her medical bills. Over the phone, Ronnie had seemed surprised – Harry had surprised himself, dialling the familiar digits trained into his fingers by the dead affair – but had accepted, surprisingly. They were making peace, perhaps, over Thelma's body. Or reviving a friend-ship – not a friendship, an involvement – that had existed since they were little boys in knickers and hightop sneakers scampering through the pebbly alleys of Mt. Judge. When Harry thinks back through all those years, to Ronnie's pugnacious thick-lipped dull-eyed face as it loomed on the elementary-school playground, to Ronnie crowingly playing with his big pale cucumber of a prick (circumcised, and sort of flat on its upper side) in the locker room, and then to Ronnie on the rise and on the make in his bachelor years around Brewer, one of the guys it turned out who had gone with Ruth before Rabbit did, Ronnie in those years full of smart-ass talk and dirty stories, a slimy operator, and then to Ronnie mar-ried to Thelma and working for Schuylkill Mutual, a kind of a sad sack really, plugging along doggedly, delivering his pitch, talking about "your loved ones" and when you're "out of the picture," slowly becoming the wanly smiling bald man in the photo on Thelma's dresser whom Harry could feel looking up his ass, so once to Thelma's amusement he got out of bed and put the photo flat on the bureau top, so afterwards she always turned it away before he arrived of an afternoon, and then to Ronnie as a wid-ower, with the face of a bleached prune, pulled-looking wrinkles down from his eyes, an old guy's thin skin showing pink at the cheekbones, Harry feels that Ronnie has always been with him, a presence he couldn't avoid, an aspect of himself he didn't want to face but now does. That clublike cock, those slimy jokes, the blue eyes looking up his ass, what the hell, we're all just human, bod-ies with brains at one end and the rest just plumbing.

Their first round, playing as a twosome, they have a good enough time so that they schedule another, and then a third. Ronnie has his old clients but he's no longer out there generating new business among the young husbands, he can take an afternoon off with a little notice. Their games are rusty and erratic, and the match usually comes down to the last hole or two. Will Harry's fine big free swing deliver the ball into the fairway or into the woods? Will Ronnie look up and skull an easy chip across the green into the sand trap, or will he keep his head down, his hands ahead, and get the ball close, to save a par? The two men don't talk much, lest the bad blood between them surface; the sight of the other messing up is so hilariously welcome as to suggest affection. They never mention Thelma.

On the seventeenth, a long par-four with a creek about one hundred ninety yards out, Ronnie plays up short with a four-iron. "That's a chickenshit way to play it," Harry tells him, and goes with a driver. Concentrating on keeping his flying right elbow close to his body, he catches the ball sweet, clearing the creek by thirty yards. Ronnie, compensating, tries too hard on his next shot: needing to take a three-wood, he roundhouses a big banana ball into the pine woods on the Mt. Pemaquid side of the fairway. Thus relieved of pressure, Rabbit thinks *Easy does it* on his six-iron and clicks off a beauty that falls into the heart of the green as if straight down a drainpipe. His par leaves him one up, so he can't lose, and only has to tie to win. Expansively he says to Ronnie as they ride the cart to the eighteenth tee, "How about that Voyager Two? To my mind that's more of an achievement than putting a man on the moon. In the *Standard* yesterday I was reading where some scientist says it's like sinking a putt from New York to Los Angeles."

Ronnie grunts, sunk in a losing golfer's self-loathing.

"Clouds on Neptune," Rabbit says, "and volcanos on Triton. What do you think it means?"

One of his Jewish partners down in Florida might have come up with some angle on the facts, but up here in Dutch country Ronnie gives him a dull suspicious look. "Why would it mean anything? Your honor."

Rabbit feels rubbed the wrong way. You try to be nice to this guy and he snubs you. He is an ugly prick and always was. You offer him the outer solar system to think about and he brushes it aside. He crushes it in his coarse brain. Harry feels a fine excessiveness in that spindly machine's feeble but true transmissions across millions of miles, a grace of sorts that chimes with the excessive beauty of this crystalline late-summer day. He needs to praise. Ronnie must know some such need, or he and Thelma wouldn't have attended that warehouse of a no-name church. "Those three rings nobody ever saw before," Harry insists, "just like drawn with a pencil," echoing Bernie Drechsel's awe at the thinness of flamingo legs.

But Ronnie has moved off, over by the ball washer, pretending not to hear. He has a bum knee from an old football injury and begins to limp toward the end of a round. He takes a series of vicious practice swings, anxious to begin the hole and avenge his previous poor showing. Disappointed, distracted by thoughts of brave Voyager, Rabbit lets his right elbow float at the top of the backswing and cuts weakly across the ball, slicing it, on a curve as uncanny as if plotted by computer, into the bunker in the buck-grass to the right of the fairway. The eighteenth is a par-five that flirts with the creek coming back but should be an easy par; in his golfing prime he more than once birdied it. Yet he has to come out of the bunker sideways with a wedge and then hits his three-iron – not his best club but he needs the distance – fat, trying too hard just like Ronnie on the last hole, and winds up in the creek, his yellow Pinnacle finally found under a patch of watercress. The drop consumes another stroke and he's so anxious to nail his nine-iron right to the pin he pulls it, so he lies five on the deep fringe to the left of the green. Ronnie has been poking along, hitting ugly low shots with his blacksmith's swing but staying out of trouble, on in four; so Rabbit's only hope is to chip in. It's a grassy lie and he fluffs it, like the worst kind of moronic golfing coward he forgets to hit down and through, and the ball moves maybe two feet, onto the froghair short of the green in six, and Ronnie has a sure two putts for a six and a crappy, crappy win. If there's one thing Harry hates, it's losing to a bogey. He picks up his Pinnacle and with a sweeping heave throws the ball into the pine woods. Something in his chest didn't like the big motion but it is bliss of sorts to see the tormenting orb disappear in a distant swish and thud. The match ends tied.

"So, no blood," Ronnie says, having rolled his twelve-footer to within a gimme.

"Good match," Harry grunts, deciding against shaking hands. The shame of his collapse clings to him. Who says the universe isn't soaked in disgrace?

As they transfer balls and tees and sweaty gloves to the pocket of their bags, Ronnie, now that it's his turn to feel expansive, volunteers, "Didja see last night on Peter Jennings, the last thing, they showed the photographs of the rings and the moon moving away and then a composite they had made of the various shots of Neptune projected onto a ball and twirled, so the whole planet was there, like a toy? Incredible," Ronnie admits, "what they can do with computer graphics."

The image faintly sickens Harry, of Voyager taking those last shots of Neptune and then sailing off into the void, forever. How can you believe how much void there is?

The golf bags in the rack here by the pro shop throw long shafts of shadow. These days are drawing in. Harry is thirsty, and looks forward to a beer on the club patio, at one of the outdoor tables, under a big green-and-white umbrella, beside the swimming pool with its cannonballing kids and budding bimbos, while the red sun sinks behind the high horizon of Mt. Pemaquid. Before they head up for the beers, the two men look directly at each other, by mistake. On an unfortunate impulse, Rabbit asks, "Do you miss her?"

Ronnie gives him an angled squint. His eyelids look sore under his white eyelashes. "Do you?"

Ambushed, Rabbit can barely pretend he does. He used Thelma, and then she was used up. "Sure," he says.

Ronnie clears his ropy throat and checks that the zipper on his bag is up and then shoulders the bag to take to his car. "Sure you do," he says. "Try to sound sincere. You never gave a fuck. No. Excuse me. A fuck is exactly what you gave."

Harry hangs between impossible alternatives – to tell him how much he enjoyed going to bed with Thelma (Ronnie's smiling photo watching) or to claim that he didn't. He answers merely, "Thelma was a lovely woman."

"For me," Ronnie tells him, dropping his pugnacious manner and putting on his long widower's face, "it's like the bottom of the world has dropped out. Without Thel, I'm just going through the motions." His voice gets all froggy, disgustingly. When Harry invites him up on the patio for the beers, he says, "No, I better be getting back. Ron Junior and his newest significant other are having me over for dinner." When Harry tries to set a date for the next game, he says, "Thanks, old bunny, but you're the member here. You're the one with the rich wife. You know the Flying Eagle rules – you can't keep having the same guest. Anyway, Labor Day's coming. I better start getting back on the ball, or Schuylkill'll think I'm the one who died."

He drives his slate-gray Celica home to Penn Park. Janice's Camry is not in the driveway and he thinks the phone ringing inside might be her. She's almost never here any more – off at her classes, or over in Mt. Judge babysitting, or at the lot consulting with Nelson, or in Brewer with her lawyer and those accountants Charlie told her to hire. He works the key in the lock – maddening, the scratchy way the key doesn't fit in the lock instantly, it reminds him of something from way back, something unpleasant that hollows his stomach, but what? – and shoves the door open with his shoulder and reaches the hall phone just as it's giving what he knows will be its dying ring. "Hello." He can hardly get the word out.

"Dad? What's the matter?"

"Nothing. Why?"

"You sound so winded."

"I just came in. I thought you were your mother."

"Mom's *been* here. I'm still at the lot, she suggested I call you. I've got this great idea."

"I've heard it. You want to open a drug treatment center."

"Maybe some day down the road. But for now I think we should work on the lot as what it is. It looks great, by the way, with all those little Toyotas in those funny colors of theirs gone. People are still coming in to buy used, they think we must be having a bargain sale, and a couple of companies are interested in the location – Hyundai for instance has this big new place over past Hayesville but the location is up behind a cloverleaf and nobody can figure out how to get to it, there's too much landscaping, they'd love to have a spot right on 111 – but what I'm calling about was this idea I got last night, I ran it past Mom, she said to talk to you."

"O.K., O.K., you're good to include me," Harry says.

"Last night I was out on the river, you know over where they have all these little river cottages with colored lights and porches and steps going down into the water?"

"I don't know, actually, I've never been there, but go on."

"Well, Pru and I were over there last night with Jason and Pam, you may have heard me mention them."

"Vaguely." All these pauses for confirmation, they are wearing Harry down. Why can't the kid just spit it out? Is his father such an ogre?

"Anyway this guy they know has one of these cottages, it was neat, the colored lights and music on the radios and up and down the river all these boats, people water skiing and all —"

"Sounds terrific. I hope Jason and Pam don't belong to that old Lyle-Slim crowd."

"They knew 'em, but they're *straight*, Dad. They're even thinking of having a baby."

"If you're going to keep coke licked, you got to stay away from the old coke crowd."

"Like I said, they're real straight arrow. One of their best friends is Ron Harrison, Jr., the carpenter."

What is that supposed to mean? Does Nelson know about him and Thelma? "O.K., O.K.," Harry says.

"So we were sitting there on the porch and this fantastic thing goes by — a motorcycle on the water. They have different names for them — wet bikes, surf jets, jet skis —"

"Yeah, I've seen 'em in Florida, out on the ocean. They look unsafe."

"Dad, this was the best I ever saw — it went like a rocket. Just *buzzed* along. Jason said it's called a Yamaha Waverunner and it operates on a new principle, I don't know, it compresses water somehow and then shoots it out the back, and he said the only guy who sells 'em, a dinky little back-yard shop up toward Shoe-makersville, can't keep 'em in stock, and anyway he's not that interested, he's a retired farmer who just does it as a hobby. So I called Yamaha's sales office in New York this morning and talked to a guy. It wouldn't be just Waverunners we'd sell, of course, we'd carry the motorcycles, and their snowmobiles and trailers, and they make generators a lot of small companies use and these three- and four-wheelers, ATVs, that farmers have now to get around their places, a lot more efficient than electric golf carts –"

"Nelson. Wait. Don't talk so fast. What about Manny and the boys over in Service?"

"It isn't Manny any more, Dad. It's Arnold."

"I meant to say Arnold. The guy who looks like a pig in pajamas mincing around. I know who Arnold is. I don't care who he is, he or she for that matter, who heads the fucking service division, they're used to *cars*, big things with four wheels that run on gasoline instead of compressed water."

"They can adjust. People can adjust, if you're under a certain age. Anyway, Mom and I have already trimmed Service. We let go three mechanics, and are running some ads for inspection packages. We want to pep up the used end, for a while it'll be only used just like Grandpa Springer started out, he used to tell me how he kept the Toyotas out in back out of sight, people had this distrust of Japanese products. In a way it's better already, the people without much to spend aren't scared off by the new car showroom and the yen exchange rate and all. So –?"

"So?"

"What do you think of the Yamaha idea?"

"O.K., now remember. You asked. And I appreciate your asking. I'm touched by that, I realize you don't have to ask me anything, you and your mother have the lot locked up. But in answer to your question, I think it's the dumbest thing I've ever heard. Jet skis are a fad. Next year it'll be jet roller skates. The profit on a toy like a motorcycle or a snowmobile is maybe a tenth that on a solid family car – can you sell ten times as many? Don't forget, there's a Depression coming."

"Who says?"

"*I* say; *eve*rybody says! Everybody says Bush is just like Hoover. You're too young to remember Hoover."

"That was an inflated stock market. The market if anything is undersold now. Why would we have a Depression?"

"Because we don't have any *dis*cipline! We're drowning in debt! We don't even own our own country any more! My image of this is you were sitting there on the porch of that shack with all these colored lights stoned on something or other and this thing buzzes by and you think, 'Wow! Salvation!' You're almost thirty-three and you're still into toys and fads. You came back from that detox place stuffed full of good intentions and now you're getting rocks in the brain again."

There is a pause. The old Nelson would have combatted him with some childish defensive whining. But the voice on the other end of the line at last says, with a touch of the ministerial gravity and automated calm Rabbit had noticed at dinner the other week, "What you don't realize about a consumer society, Dad, is it's all fads in a way. People don't buy things because they *need* 'em. You actually need very little. You buy something because it's be*yond* what you need, it's something that will en*hance* your life, not just keep it plugging along."

"It sounds to me like you did too much mystic meditation at that detox place."

"You say detox just to bug me. It was a treatment center, and then a halfway house for rehab. The detox part of it just takes a couple days. It's getting the relational poison out of your system that takes longer."

"Is that what I am to you? Relational poison?" Being snubbed by Ronnie Harrison won't stop rankling, underneath this conversation. Just because you boffed a man's dead wife, he shouldn't get bitter about it. He's known Ronnie all his life.

Again, Nelson is silent. Then: "Maybe, but not only. I keep trying to love you, but you don't really want it. You're afraid of it, it would tie you down. You've been scared all your life of being tied down."

Rabbit cannot speak; he is letting a Nitrostat dissolve under his tongue. It burns like a little pellet of red candy, and induces a floating dilated feeling that adds inches to his sensation of height. The kid will make him cry if he thinks about it. He says, "Let's cut the psychology and get down to earth. What the hell do you and your mother intend to do about that hundred fifty thousand dollars Toyota has to have by the end of the month or else it will prosecute?"

"Oh," the boy says airily, "didn't Mom tell you? That's been settled. They've been paid. We took out a loan."

"A loan? Who would trust you?"

"Brewer Trust. A second mortgage on the lot property, it's worth at least half a million. A hundred forty-five, and they consolidated it with the seventy-five for Slim's five cars, which will be coming back to us pretty much as a credit on the rolling inventory we were maintaining with Mid-Atlantic Motors. As soon as they took our inventory over to Rudy's lot, don't forget, they started owing *us*."

"And you're somehow going to pay back Brewer Trust selling water scooters?"

"You don't have to pay a loan back, they don't *want* you to pay it back; they just want you to keep up the installments. Meanwhile, the value of the dollar goes down and you get to tax-deduct all the interest. We were underfinanced, in fact, before."

"Thank God you're back in the saddle. How does your mother like the Yamaha connection?"

"She likes it. She's not like you; she's open, and willing to be creative. Dad, there's something I think we should try to process sometime. Why do you resent it so, me and Mom getting out into the world and trying to learn new things?"

"I don't resent it. I respect it."

"You hate it. You act jealous and envious. I say this in love, Dad. You feel stuck, and you want everybody to be stuck with you."

He tries giving back the kid a little of his own medicine, some therapeutic silence. His Nitrostat rings that little bell in the seat of his pants, and his dilated blood vessels lift weight from the world around him, making it seem delicate and distant, like Neptune's rings. "It wasn't me," he says at last, "who ran Springer Motors into the ground. But do what you want. You're the Springer, not me."

He can hear a voice in the background, a female voice, and then that seashell sound of a telephone mouthpiece with a hand placed over it. When Nelson's voice returns, it has changed tint, as if dipped in something, by what has passed between him and Elvira. Love juices have flowed. Maybe the kid is normal after all. "Elvira has something she wants to ask you. What do you think of the Pete Rose settlement?"

"Tell her I think it was the best both sides could do. And I think he should get into the Hall of Fame anyway, on the strength of his numbers. But tell her Schmidt is my idea of a classy ballplayer. Tell her I miss her."

Hanging up, Harry pictures the showroom, the late-afternoon light on the dust on the display windows, tall to the sky now with all the banners down, and the fun going on, amazingly, without him.

The thready lawn behind their little limestone house at 14½ Franklin Drive has the dry kiss of autumn on it: brown patches and the first few fallen leaves, cast off by the weeping cherry, his neighbor's black walnut, the sweet cherry that leans close to the house so he can watch the squirrels scrabble along its branches, and the willow above the empty cement fish pond with the blue-painted bottom and rim of real seashells. These trees still seem green and growing but their brown leaves are accumulating in the grass. Even the hemlock toward the neighboring house of thin yellow bricks, and the rhododendrons along the palisade fence separating the Angstroms' yard from the property of the big mock-Tudor house of clinker bricks, and the shaggy Austrian pines whose cast-off needles clutter the cement pond, though all ever-green, are tinged by summer's end, dusty and sweetly dried-out like the smell that used to come from the old cedar hope chest where Mom kept spare blankets and their good embroidered linen tablecloth for Thanksgiving and Christmas and the two old crazy quilts she had inherited from the Renningers. It was family legend that these quilts were fabulously valuable but when, in some family crunch when Harry was in his early teens, they tried to sell them, the best offer they could get was sixty dollars apiece. After much talk around the porcelain kitchen table, they took the offer, and now authentic old quilts like that bring thousands if in good condition. When he thinks about those old days and the amounts of money they considered important it's as if they were being cheated, getting by on slave wages, eating bread that cost eleven cents a loaf. They were living in a financial dungeon, back there on Jackson Road, and the fact that everybody else was in it too only makes it sadder. Just thinking about those old days lately depresses him; it makes him face life's constant depreciation. Lying awake at night, afraid he will never fall asleep or will fall asleep forever, he feels a stifling uselessness in things, a kind of atomic decay whereby the precious glowing present turns, with each tick of the clock, into the leaden slag of history.

The forsythia and beauty bush both have been getting out of hand during this wet summer and Harry, on this cloudy cool Thursday before the Labor Day weekend, has been trying to prune them back into shape for the winter. With the forsythia, you take out the oldest stem from the base, making the bush younger and thinner and more girlish suddenly, and then cut back the most flagrant skyward shoots and the down-drooping branches on their way to reroot in among the day lilies. It doesn't do to be tender-hearted; the harder you cut back now, the more crammed with glad yellow blossoms the stubby branches become in the spring. The beauty bush poses a tougher challenge, an even tighter tangle. Any attempt to follow the tallest stems down to their origin gets lost in the net of interwoven branchlets, and the bottom thicket of small trunks is so dense as to repel a clipper or pruning saw; there is not a knife's-width of space. The bush in this season of neglect has grown so tall he really should go to the garage for the aluminum stepladder. But Rabbit is reluctant to face the garage's grimy tumble of cast-aside tires and stiff hoses and broken flowerpots and rusted tools inherited from the previous owners, who failed to clean out the garage the same way they left a stack of *Playboy*s in an upstairs closet. In ten years he and Janice have added their own stuff to the garage, so that gradually there wasn't space for one car let alone two in it; it has become a cave of deferred decisions and sentimentally cherished junk so packed that if he tries to extract the ladder several old paint cans and a lawn sprinkler bereft of its washers will come clattering down. So he stretches and reaches into the beauty bush until his chest begins to ache, with the sensation of an inflexible patch stitched to the inner side of his skin. His nitroglycerin pills got left in the sweat-rimmed pocket of his plaid golf slacks last night when he went to bed early, alone, having fed himself a beer and some Corn Chips after that match with Ronnie ended so sourly.

To placate the pain, he switches to weeding the day lilies and the violet hosta. Wherever a gap permits light to activate the sandy soil, chickweed and crabgrass grow, and purslane with its hollow red stems covers the earth in busy round-leaved zigzags. Weeds too have their styles, their own personalities that talk back to the gardener in the daze of the task. Chickweed is a good weed, soft on the hands unlike thistles and burdock, and pulls easily; it knows when the jig is up and comes willingly, where wild cucumber keeps breaking off at one of its many joints, and grass and red sorrel and poison ivy spread underground, like creeping diseases that cannot be cured. Weeds don't know they're weeds. Safe next to the trunk of the weeping cherry a stalk of blue lettuce has grown eight feet tall, taller than he. Those days he spent ages ago being Mrs. Smith's gardener among her rhododendrons, the one time he ever felt rooted in a job. *Fine strong young man*, she had called him at the end, gripping him with her claws.

A block and a half away, the traffic on Penn Boulevard murmurs and hisses, its purr marred by the occasional sudden heave and grind of a great truck shifting gears, or by an angry horn, or the wop-wop-wopping bleat of an ambulance rushing some poor devil to the hospital. You see them now and then, driving down a side street, these scenes: some withered old lady being carried in a stretcher down her porch stairs in a slow-motion sled ride, her hair unpinned, her mouth without its dentures, her eyes staring skyward as if to disown her body; or some red-faced goner being loaded into the double metal doors while his abandoned mate in her bathrobe snivels on the curb and the paramedics close around his body like white vultures feeding. Rabbit has noticed a certain frozen peacefulness in such terminal street tableaux. A certain dignity in the doomed one, his or her moment come round at last; a finality that isolates the ensemble like a spotlit crèche. You would think people would take it worse than they do. They don't scream, they don't accuse God. We curl into ourselves, he supposes. We become numb bundles of used-up nerves. Earthworms on the hook.

From far across the river, a siren wails in the heart of Brewer. Above, in a sky gathering its fishscales for a rainy tomorrow, a small airplane rasps as it coasts into the airport beyond the old fairgrounds. What Harry instantly loved about this house was its hiddenness: not so far from all this traffic, it is yet not easy to find, on its macadamized dead end, tucked with its fractional number among the more conspicuous homes of the Penn Park rich. He always resented these snobs and now is safe among them. Pulling into his dead-end driveway, working out back in his garden, watching TV in his den with its wavery lozenge-paned windows, Rabbit feels safe as in a burrow, where the hungry forces at loose in the world would never think to find him.

Janice pulls in in the pearl-gray Camry wagon. She is fresh from the afternoon class at the Penn State extension on Pine Street: "Real Estate Mathematics – Fundamentals and Applications." In a student outfit of sandals and wheat-colored sundress, with a looseknit white cardigan thrown over her shoulders, her forehead free of those Mamie Eisenhower bangs, she looks snappy, and brushed glossy, and younger than her age. Everything she wears these days has shoulders; even her cardigan has shoulders. She walks to him over what seems a great distance in the little quarter-acre yard, their property expanded by what has become a mutual strangeness. Unusually, she presents her face to be kissed. Her nose feels cold, like a healthy puppy's. "How was class?" he dutifully asks.

"Poor Mr. Lister seems so sad and preoccupied lately," she says. "His beard has come in all full of gray. We think his wife is leaving him. She came to class once and acted very snooty, we all thought."

"You all are getting to be a mean crowd. Aren't these classes about over? Labor Day's coming."

"Poor Harry, do you feel I've deserted you this summer? What are you going to do with all this mess you've pruned away? The beauty bush looks absolutely ravaged."

He admits, "I was getting tired and making bad decisions. That's why I stopped."

"Good thing," she says. "There wouldn't have been anything left but stumps. We'd have to call it the ugliness bush."

"Listen, you, I don't see you out here helping. Ever."

"The outdoors is your responsibility, the indoors is mine – isn't that how we do it?"

"I don't know how *we* do anything any more, you're never here. In answer to your question, I'd planned to stack what I cut over behind the fish pond to dry out and then burn it next spring when we're back from Florida."

"You're planning ahead right into 1990; I'm impressed. That year is still very unreal to me. Won't the yard look ugly all winter then, though?"

"It won't look ugly, it'll look natural, and we won't be here to see it anyway."

Her tongue touches the upper lip of her mouth, which has opened in thought. But she says nothing, just "I guess we won't, if we do things as normal."

"If ?"

She doesn't seem to hear, gazing at the fence-high heap of pruned branches.

He says, "If you're so in charge of the indoors, what are we having for dinner?"

"Damn," she says. "I meant to stop by at the farm stand there at the end of the bridge and pick up some sweet corn, but then I had so much else on my mind I sailed right by. I thought we'd have the corn with what's left of Tuesday's meatloaf and those dinner rolls in the breadbox before they get moldy. There was a wonderful tip in the *Standard* about how to freshen stale bread in the microwave, I forget what exactly, something to do with water. There must be a frozen veg in the freezer part we can have instead of sweet corn."

"Or else we could sprinkle salt and sugar on ice cubes," he says. "One thing I know's in the fridge is ice cubes."

"Harry, it's been on my *mind* to go shopping, but the IGA is so far out of the way and the prices at the Turkey Hill are ridiculous, and the convenience store over on Penn Boulevard has those surly kids behind the counter who I think punch extra figures into the cash register."

"You're a shrewd shopper, all right," Harry tells her. The mackerel sky is forming a solid gray shelf in the southwest; they move together toward the house, away from the shadow of coming dark.

Janice says, "So." Saying "so" is something she's picked up recently, from her fellow-students or her teachers, as the word for beginning to strike a deal. "You haven't asked me how I did on my last quiz. We got them back."

"How did you do?"

"Beautifully, really. Mr. Lister gave me a B minus but said it would have been a B plus if I could organize my thoughts better and clean up my spelling. I know it's 'i' before 'e' sometimes and the other way around some other times, but *when?*"

He loves her when she talks to him like this, as if he has all the answers. He leans the long-handled clippers in the garage against the wall behind a dented metal trash can and hangs the pruning saw on its nail. Shadowy in her sundress, she moves ahead of him up the back stairs and the kitchen light comes on. Inside the kitchen, she rummages, with that baffled frowning expression of hers, biting her tongue tip, in the refrigerator for edible fragments. He goes and touches her waist in the wheat-colored dress, lightly cups her buttocks as she bends over looking. Tenderly, he complains, "You didn't come home until late last night."

"You were asleep, poor thing. I didn't want to risk waking you so I slept in the guest room."

"Yeah, I get so groggy, suddenly. I keep wanting to finish that book on the American Revolution but it knocks me out every time."

"I shouldn't have given it to you for Christmas. I thought you'd enjoy it."

"I did. I do. Yesterday was a hard day. First Ronnie tied me on the last hole when I had the bastard all but beaten, and then he snubbed my invitation to play again. And then Nelson called all jazzed up with some crazy scheme about water scooters and Yamaha."

"I'm sure Ronnie has his reasons," Janice says. "I'm surprised he played with you at all. How do you feel about Brussels sprouts?"

"I don't mind them."

"To me, they always taste spoiled; but they're all we have. I *promise* to get to the IGA tomorrow and stock up for the long weekend."

"We going to have Nelson and his tribe over?"

"I thought we might all meet at the club. We've hardly used it this summer."

"He sounded hyper on the phone – do you think he's back on the stuff already?"

"Harry, Nelson is *very* straight now. That place really has given him religion. But I agree, Yamaha isn't the answer. We must raise some capital and put ourselves on a solvent basis before we start courting another franchise. I've been talking to some of the other women getting their licenses –"

"You discuss our personal financial problems?"

"Not ours as such, just as a case study. It's all purely hypo-thetical. In real-estate class we always have a lot of case studies. And they all thought it was gro*tesque* to be carrying a mortgage amounting to over twenty-five hundred a month on the lot when we have so much other property."

Rabbit doesn't like the trend here. He points out, "But this place is already mortgaged. What do we pay? Seven hundred a month."

"I *know* that, silly. Don't forget, this is my business now." She has stripped the Brussels sprouts of their waxpaper box and put them in the plastic safe dish and put it in the microwave and punches out the time – three blips, a peep, and then a rising hum. "We bought this place ten years ago," she tells him, "for seventy-eight thousand and put fifteen down and have about ten or fifteen more in equity by now, it doesn't accumulate very fast in the first half of payback, there's a geometric curve they tell you about, so let's say there's still fifty outstanding; in any case, housing prices have gone way up in this area since 1980, it's been flattening out but hasn't started to go *down* yet, though it might this winter, you'd begin by asking two twenty, two thirty let's say, with the Penn Park location, and the seclusion, the fact that it has real lime-stone walls and not just facing, it has what they call historic value; we certainly wouldn't settle for less than two hundred, which minus the fifty would give us one fifty, which would wipe out two-thirds of what we owe Brewer Trust!"

Rabbit has rarely heard this long an utterance from Janice, and it takes him a few seconds to understand what she has been say-ing. "You'd sell this place?"

"Well, Harry, it *is* very extravagant to keep it just for the sum-mer essentially, especially when there's all that extra room over at Mother's."

"I love this place," he tells her. "It's the only place I've ever

lived where I felt at home, at least since Jackson Road. This place
has class. It's us."

"Honey, I've loved it too, but we must be practical, that's what
you've always been telling me. We don't need to own four properties, plus the lot."

"Why not sell the condo, then?"

"I thought of that, but we'd be lucky to get out of it what we
paid for it. In Florida, places are like cars – people like them brand
new. The new malls and everything are to the east."

"What about the Poconos place?"

"There's not enough money there either. It's an unheated
shack. We need two hundred thousand, honey."

"*We* didn't roll up that debt to Toyota – Nelson did it, Nelson
and his faggy boyfriends."

"Well, you can say that, but *he* can't pay it back, and he was
acting as part of the company."

"What about the lot? Why can't you sell the lot? That much
frontage on Route 111 is worth a fortune; it's the real downtown,
now that people are scared to go into the old downtown because
of the spics."

A look of pain crosses Janice's face, rippling her exposed forehead; for once, he realizes, he is thinking slower than she is.
"Never," she says curtly. "The lot is our number-one asset. We
need it as a base for Nelson's future, Nelson's and your grandchildren's. That's what Daddy would want. I remember when he
bought it after the war, it had been a country gas station, with a
cornfield next to it, that had closed during the war when there
were no cars, and he took Mother and me down to look at it, and
I found this dump out back, out in that brambly part you call
Paraguay, all these old auto parts and green and brown soda bottles that I thought were so valuable, it was like I had discovered
buried treasure I thought, and I got my school dress all dirty so
that Mother would have been mad if Daddy hadn't laughed and
told her it looked like I had a taste for the car business. Springer
Motors won't sell out as long as I'm alive and well, Harry.
Anyway," she goes on, trying to strike a lighter note, "I don't
know anything about industrial real estate. The beauty of selling
this place is I can do it myself and get the salesperson's half of the

broker's commission. I can't believe we can't get two for it; half of six per cent of two hundred thousand is six thousand dollars – all mine!"

He is still playing catch-up. "You'd sell it – I mean, you personally?"

"Of course, you big lunk, for a real-estate broker. It would be my entrée, as they call it. How could Pearson and Schrack, for instance, or Sunflower Realty, not take me on as a rep if I could bring in a listing like that right off the bat?"

"Wait a minute. We'd live in Florida most of the time –"

"*Some* of the time, honey. I don't know how much I could get away at first, I need to establish myself. Isn't Florida, honestly, a little boring? So flat, and everybody we know so old."

"And the rest of the time we'd live in Ma's old house? Where would Nelson and Pru go?"

"They'd be *there*, obviously. Harry, you seem a little slow. Have you been taking too many pills? Just the way we and Nelson used to live with Mother and Daddy. That wasn't so bad, was it? In fact, it was nice. Nelson and Pru would have built-in baby-sitters, and I wouldn't have to do all this housekeeping by myself."

"What housekeeping?"

"You don't notice it, men never do, but there's an awful lot of simple drudgery to keeping two separate establishments going. You know how you always worry about one place being robbed while we're in the other. This way, we'd have one room at Mother's, I mean Nelson's – I'm sure they'd give us our old room back – and we'd never have to worry!"

Those bands of constriction, with their edges pricked out in pain, have materialized across Harry's chest. His words come out with difficulty. "How do Nelson and Pru feel about us moving in?"

"I haven't asked yet. I thought I might this evening, after I ran it by you. I really don't see how they can say no; it's my house, legally. So: what do you think?" Her eyes, which he is used to as murky and careful, often blurred by sherry or Campari, shine at the thought of her first sale.

He isn't sure. There was a time, when he was younger, when the thought of any change, even a disaster, gladdened his heart with the possibility of a shake-up, of his world made new. But at present he is aware mostly of a fluttering, binding physical resistance within him to the idea of being uprooted. "I hate it, offhand," he tells her. "I don't want to go back to living as somebody's tenant. We did that for ten years and finally got out of it. People don't live all bunched up, all the generations, any more."

"But they *do*, honey – that's one of the trends in living, now that homes have become so expensive and the world so crowded."

"Suppose they have more children."

"They won't."

"How do you know?"

"I just do. Pru and I have discussed it."

"Does Pru ever feel crowded, I wonder, by her mother-in-law?"

"I wouldn't know why. We both want the same thing – a happy and healthy Nelson."

Rabbit shrugs. Let her stew in her own juice, the cocky little mutt. Going off to school and thinking she's learned everybody's business. "You go over after supper and see how they like your crazy plan. I'm dead set against it, if my vote counts. Sell off the lot and tell the kid to get an honest job, is my advice."

Janice stops watching the microwave tick down its numbers and comes close to him, unexpectedly, touching his face again with that ghostly searching gesture, tucking her body against his to remind him sexually of her smallness, her smallness fitting his bigness, when they first met and still now. He smells her brushed-back salt-and-pepper hair and sees the blood-tinged whites of her dark eyes. "Of course your vote counts, it counts more than anybody's, honey." When did Janice start calling him honey? When they moved to Florida and got in with those Southerners and Jews. The Jewish couples down there had this at-rest quality, matched like pairs of old shoes, the men accepting their life as the only one they were going to get, and pleased enough. It must be a great religion, Rabbit thinks, once you get past the circumcision.

He and Janice let the house issue rest as a silent sore spot between them while they eat. He helps her clear and they add their plates to those already stacked in the dishwasher, waiting to be run through. With just the two of them, and Janice out of the house so much, it takes days for a sufficient load to build up on the racks. She telephones Nelson to see if they're going to be in and puts her white cardigan back on and gets back into the Camry and drives off to Mt. Judge. Wonder Woman. Rabbit catches the tail end of Jennings, a bunch of twitchy old black-and-white clips about World War II beginning with the invasion of Poland fifty years ago tomorrow, tanks versus cavalry, Hitler shrieking, Chamberlain looking worried; then he goes out into the dusk and the mosquitoes to stack the already wilting brush more neatly in the corner behind the cement pond with its fading blue bottom and widening crack. He gets back into the house in time for the last ten minutes of *Wheel of Fortune*. That Vanna! Can she strut! Can she clap her hands when the wheel turns! Can she turn those big letters around! She makes you proud to be a two-legged mammal.

By the end of the *Cosby* summer rerun, one of those with too much Theo in it, Harry is feeling sleepy, depressed by the idea of Janice selling the house but soothed by the thought that she'll never do it. She's too scatterbrained, she and the kid will just drift along deeper and deeper into debt like the rest of the world; the bank will play ball as long as the lot has value. The Phillies are out in San Diego and in sixth place anyway. He turns the TV sound way down and by the comforting shudder of the silenced imagery stretches out his feet on the Turkish hassock they brought from Ma Springer's house when they moved and slumps down deeper into the silvery-pink wing chair he and Janice bought at Schaechner's ten years ago. His shoulders ache from all that pruning. He thinks of his history book but it's upstairs by the bed. There is a soft ticking at the lozenge-pane windows: rain, as on that evening at the beginning of summer, when he'd just come out of the hospital, the narrow room with the headless sewing dummy, another world, a dream world. The phone wakes him when it rings. He looks at the thermostat clock as he goes to the hall phone. 9:20. Janice has been over there a long time. He hopes it isn't one of those coke dealers that still now and then call, about money they are owed or a new shipment of fresh "material" that has come in. You wonder how these dealers get so rich, they seem so disorganized and hit-or-miss. He was having a dream in the wing chair, some intense struggle already fading and unintelligible, with an unseen antagonist, but in a vivid domed space, like an old-time railroad terminal only the ceiling was lower and paler, a chapel of some kind, a tight space that clings to his mind, making his hand look ancient and strange – the back swollen and bumpy, the fingers withered – as it reaches for the receiver on the wall.

"Harry." He has never heard Janice's voice sound like this, so stony, so dead.

"Hi. Where are you? I was getting afraid you'd had an accident."

"Harry, I –" Something grabs her throat and will not let her speak.

"Yeah?"

Now she is speaking through tears, staggering over gulps, suppressed sobs, lumps in her throat. "I described my idea to Nelson and Pru, and we all agreed we shouldn't rush into it, we should discuss it thoroughly, he seemed more receptive than she, maybe because he understands the financial problems –"

"Yeah, yeah. Hey, it doesn't sound so bad so far. She's used to considering the house as hers, no woman likes to share a kitchen."

"After she'd put the children to bed, she came down with this look on her face and said there was something then that Nelson and I should know, if we were all going to live together."

"Yeah?" His own voice is still casual but he is no longer sleepy; he can see what is coming like a tiny dot in the distance that becomes a rocket ship in a space movie.

Janice's voice firms up, goes dead and level and lower, as if others might be listening outside the door. She would be in their old bedroom, sitting on the edge of the bed, Judy asleep beyond one wall and Roy behind the wall opposite. "She said you and she slept together that night you stayed here your first night out of the hospital."

The spaceship is upon him, with all its rivets and blinking lights. "She said that?"

"Yes she did. She said she doesn't know how it happened, except there'd always been this little attraction between you two and that night everything seemed so desperate."

A little attraction. He supposes that was fair, though tough. It had felt like more than that from his side. It had felt like he was seeing himself reflected, mirrored in a rangy young long-haired left-handed woman.

"Well? Is she telling the truth?"

"Well, honey, what can I say, I guess in a way –"

A big sob: he can picture Janice's face exactly, twisted and helpless and ugly, old age collapsing in upon her.

"– but at the time," Rabbit goes on, "it seemed sort of natural, and we haven't done anything since, not even said a word. We've been pretending it didn't happen."

"Oh, Harry. How *could* you? Your own daughter-in-law. Nelson's *wife*."

He feels she is beginning to work from a script, saying standard things, and into the vault of his shocked and shamed consciousness there is admitted a whiff of boredom.

"This is the worst thing you've ever done, ever, ever," Janice tells him. "The absolute worst. That time you ran away, and then Peggy, my *best* friend, and that poor hippie girl, and Thelma – don't think for one moment I didn't know about Thelma – but now you've done something truly unforgivable."

"Really?" The word comes out with an unintended hopeful lilt.

"I will never forgive you. Never," Janice says, returning to a dead-level tone.

"Don't *say* that," he begs. "It was just a crazy moment that didn't hurt anybody. Whajou put me and her in the same house at night for? Whajou think I was, dead already?"

"I *had* to go to class, there was a *quiz*, I wouldn't have gone ordinarily, I felt so *guilty*. That's a laugh. *I* felt guilty. I see now why they have gun laws. If I had a gun, I'd shoot you. I'd shoot you both."

"What else did Pru say?" Answering, he figures, will bring her down a bit from this height of murderous rage.

Janice answers, "She didn't say much of anything. Just the flat facts and then folded her hands in her lap and kept giving me and Nelson that defiant stare of hers. She didn't seem repentant, just tough, and obviously not wanting me to come live in the house. That's why she told."

He feels himself being drawn into alignment with Janice, against the others, with a couple's shared vision, squinting this way at Pru. He feels relieved, beginning already to be forgiven, and faintly disappointed.

"She is tough," he agrees, soothingly. "Pru. Whaddeya expect, from an Akron steamfitter's daughter?" He decides against telling Janice, now at least, how in making their love Pru had come twice, and he had faintly felt used, expertly.

His reprieve is only just beginning. It will take weeks and months and years of whittling at it. With her new business sense Janice won't give anything away cheap. "We want you over here, Harry," she says.

"Me? Why? It's late," he says. "I'm bushed from all those bushes."

"Don't think you're out of this and can be cute. This is a hideous thing. None of us will ever be the same."

"We never are," he dares say.

"Think of how Nelson feels."

This hurts. He hadn't wanted to think about it.

She tells him, "Nelson is being very calm and using all that good psychological work they did at the treatment center. He says this will need a lot of processing and we must begin right now. If we don't start right in we'll all harden in our positions."

Rabbit tries to conspire again, to elicit another wifely description. "Yeah – how *did* the kid take it?"

But she only says, "I think he's in shock. He himself said he hasn't begun to get in touch with his real feelings."

Harry says, "He can't be on too high a horse after all the stunts he's been pulling all these years. Coke whores all over Brewer, and if you ask me that Elvira over at the lot is more than just a token skirt. When she's around he sounds like he's been given a shot of joy juice."

But Janice doesn't relent. "You have hurt Nelson incredibly much," she says. "Anything he does from now on you can't blame him. I mean, Harry, what you've done is the kind of perverted thing that makes the newspapers. It was *mon*strous."

"Honey –"

"Quit it with the 'honey.'"

"What's this 'perverted'? We aren't at all blood-related. It was just like a normal one-night stand. She was hard-up and I was at death's door. It was her way of playing nurse."

More sobbing, he never knows what will trigger it. "Harry, you can't make jokes."

"Those weren't jokes." But he feels chastised, dry-mouthed, spanked.

"You get right over here and help undo some of the damage you've done for once in your life." And she hangs up, having sounded comically like her mother in the juicy way she pronounced "for once."

A life knows few revelations; these must be followed when they come. Rabbit sees clearly what to do. His acts take on a decisive haste. He goes upstairs and packs. The brown canvas suit bag. The big yellow rigid Tourister with the dent in one corner where an airline handler slung it. Jockey shorts, T-shirts, socks, polo shirts in their pastel tints, dress shirts in their plastic envelopes, golf slacks, Bermuda shorts. A few ties though he has never liked ties. All his clothes are summer clothes these days; the wool suits and sweaters wait in mothproof bags for fall days, October into November, that will not come this year, for him. He takes four lightweight sports coats and two suits, one a putty-colored and the other the shiny gray like armor. In case there's a wedding or a funeral. A raincoat, a couple of sweaters. A pair of black laced shoes tucks into two pockets of his folding suit bag and blue-and-white Nikes into the sides of the suitcase. He should start jogging again. His toothbrush and shaving stuff. His pills, buckets of them. What else? Oh yes. He grabs *The First Salute* from his bedside table and tucks it in, he'll finish it if it kills him. He leaves a light burning in the upstairs hall to discourage burglars, and the carriage lamp beside the front door numbered 14½. He loads the car in two trips, feeling the weight of the suitcases in his chest. He looks around the bare hall. He goes into the den, his feet silent on the Antron wall-to-wall carpeting, and looks out the lozenge panes at the glowing night-time silhouette of the weeping cherry.

He plumps the pillow and straightens the arm guards on the wing chair he fell asleep in, not long ago but on the far side of a gulf. The he who fell asleep was somebody else, a pathetic somebody. At the front door again, he feels a night breeze on his face, hears the muffled rush of traffic over on Penn Boulevard. He sets the latch and softly slams the door. Janice has her key. He thinks of her over there in the Springers' big stucco house that always reminded him of an abandoned enormous ice-cream stand. Forgive me.

Rabbit gets into the Celica. *Take a Ride in the Great Indoors:* one of the new slogans they'd been trying to push. You can have too many slogans, they begin to cancel out. The engine starts up; reverse gear carries him smoothly backwards. *I Love When You Set Me Free, Toyota.* The digital clock says 10:07. Traffic on Penn Boulevard is starting to thin, the diners and gas stations are beginning to darken. He turns right at the blinking red light and then right again at the Brewer bypass along the Running Horse River. The road lifts above the trees at a point near the elephant-gray gas tanks and the bypassed old city shows a certain grandeur. Its twenty-story courthouse built in the beginning of the Depression is still the tallest building, the concrete eagles with flared wings at each corner lit by spotlights, and the sweeping shadow of Mt. Judge, crowned by the star-spatter of the Pinnacle Hotel, hangs behind everything like an unmoving tidal wave. The streetlamps show Brewer's brick tint like matches cupped in ruddy hands. Then, quite quickly, the city and all it holds are snatched from view. Groves of weed trees half-hide the empty factories along the river, and one might be anywhere in the United States on a four-lane divided highway.

He and Janice have done this Southward drive so often he knows the options: he can get off at 222 and proceed directly but pokily toward Lancaster through a string of stoplight-ridden Brewer suburbs, or he can stay on 422 a few miles to 176 and head directly south and then cut west to Lancaster and York. The first time he tried this trip, thirty years ago last spring come to think of it, he made the mistake of heading south too soon, toward Wilmington and a vision of barefoot du Pont women. But the East slants west, and the trick is to bear west until 83, which didn't exist in those days, and then drive south right into the maw of that two-headed monster, Baltimore-Washington. *Monstrous*, she said. Well, in a way, you could say, being alive is monstrous. Those crazy molecules. All by themselves? Never.

He turns on the radio, searching among the jabber of rock music and talk shows for the sweet old tunes, the tunes he grew up on. It used to be easier to search with the old dial you twisted, instead of these jumpy digitized scan buttons: you could feel your way. The scan comes suddenly upon the silky voices of Dinah Shore and Buddy Clark entwined in the duet of "Baby, It's Cold Outside." Thrilling, it turns his spine to ice water, when, after all that melodious banter it's hard to understand every word of, they halt, and harmonize on the chorus line. *Coooold, out, side.* Then this same station of oldies, fading under the underpasses, crackling when the road curves too close to power lines, offers up a hit he's totally forgotten, how could he have? – the high-school dances, the dolled-up couples shuffling to the languid waltz beat, the paper streamers drooping from the basketball nets, the rusty heater warmth of the dash-lit interior of Pop's Plymouth, the living warm furtive scent, like the flavor of a food so strong you must choke it down at first, rising from between Mary Ann's thighs. *Vaya con Dios, my darling.* The damp triangle of underpants, the garter belts girls wore then. The dewy smooth freshness of their bodies, all of them, sweatily wheeling beneath the crêpe paper, the colored lights. *Vaya con Dios, my love.* Oh my. It hurts. The emotion packed into these phrases buried in some d.j.'s dusty racks of 78s like the cotton wadding in bullets, like those seeds that come to life after a thousand years in some pyramid. Though the stars recycle themselves and remake all the heavy atoms Creation needs, Harry will never be that person again, that boy with that girl, his fingertips grazing the soft insides of her thighs, a few atoms rubbing off, a few molecules.

Then, "Mule Train," by Frankie Laine, not one of the great Laines but great enough, and "It's Magic," by Doris Day. Those pauses back then: *It's ma-   gic.* They knew how to hurt you, back then when there were two eight-team baseball leagues and you could remember all the players. People then were not exactly softer, they were harder in fact, but they were easier to hurt, though in fewer places.

He has to leave 176 for 23 through Amish country, it's the one really local stretch of road, but there shouldn't be any buggies out this late to slow him down. Rabbit wants to see once more a place in Morgantown, a hardware store with two pumps outside, where a thickset farmer in two shirts and hairy nostrils had advised him to know where he was going before he went there. Well, now he does. He has learned the road and figured out the destination. But what had been a country hardware store was now a slick little real-estate office. Where the gas pumps had been, fresh black asphalt showed under the moonlight the stark yellow stripes of diagonal parking spaces.

No, it isn't moonlight, he sees; it is the sulfurous illumination that afflicts busy paved places all night. Though the hour is near eleven, a traffic of giant trucks heaves and snorts and groans through the sleepy stone town; the realtor's big window is full of Polaroid snapshots of property for sale, and Route 23, once a narrow road on the ridge between two farm valleys as dark at night as manure, now blazes with the signs that are everywhere. PIZZA HUT. BURGER KING. Rent a Movie. Turkey Hill MINIT MARKET. Quilt World. Shady Maple SMORGASBORD. Village Herb Shop. Country Knives. Real estate makes him think of Janice and his heart dips at the picture of her waiting with Nelson and Pru for him to show up over at the Springers' and panicking by now, probably imagining he's had a car accident, and coming back with her key to the deserted house, all fluttery and hot-breathed the way she gets. Maybe he should have left a note like she did him that time. *Harry dear – I must go off a few days to think.* But she said never forgive him, *shoot you both*, she upped the stakes, let her stew in her own juice, thinks she's so smart suddenly, going back to school. Nelson the same way. Damned if they're going to get him sitting in on some family-therapy session run by his own son whose big redheaded wife he's boffed. Only really good thing he's done all year, as he looks back on it. Damned if he'll face the kid, give him the satisfaction, all white in the gills from this new grievance. Rabbit doesn't want to get counselled.

The eleven-o'clock news comes on the radio. Jim Bakker, on trial in Charlotte, North Carolina, on twenty-four counts of fraud in connection with his scandal-ridden PTL television ministry, collapsed today in court and is being held for up to sixty days for psychiatric evaluation at the Federal Correctional Institute. Dr. Basil Jackson, a psychiatrist who has been treating Bakker for nine months, said that the once-charismatic evangelist has been hallu-cinating: leaving the courtroom Wednesday after former PTL executive Steve Nelson collapsed on the witness stand, Bakker saw the people outside as animals intent upon attacking and injuring him. Bakker's wife, Tammy, said from her luxurious home in Orlando, Florida, that Bakker over the phone had seemed to be experiencing a terrible emotional trauma and that she prayed with him and they agreed that they would trust in the Lord. In Los Angeles, Jessica Hahn, the former PTL secretary whose sexual encounter with Bakker in 1980 led to his downfall, told reporters, quote, I'm not a doctor but I do know about Jim Bakker. I believe Jim Bakker is a master manipulator. I think this is a sympathy stunt just like it is every time Tammy gets on TV and starts crying and saying how abused they are, end quote. In Washington, the Energy Department is searching for mysteriously missing amounts of tritium, the heavy-hydrogen isotope necessary to the making of hydrogen bombs. Also in Washington, *Science* magazine reports that the new bomb detector, called a TNA for thermal neutron analysis, installed today at JFK Airport in New York City, is set to detect two point five pounds of plastic explosives and would not have detected the bomb, thought to contain only one pound of Semtex explosive, which brought down Pan Am Flight 103 over Lockerbie, Scotland. In Toronto, movie superstar Marlon Brando told reporters that he has made his last movie. "It's horrible," he said of the motion picture, entitled *The Freshman*. "It's going to be a flop, but after this, I'm retiring. You can't imagine how happy I am." In Bonn, West Germany, Chancellor Helmut Kohl telephoned the new Polish Prime Minister, Tadeusz Mazowiecki, in a plea for better relations between their two countries. It was fifty years ago tomorrow, indeed almost right to this minute when allowances are made for time zones, that Germany under Adolf Hitler invaded Poland, precipitating World War II, in which an estimated fifty million persons were to perish. Like, *wow!* In sports, the Phillies are losing in San Diego and Pittsburgh is idle. As to the weather, it could be better, and it could be worse. *Mezzo, mezzo.* I didn't say messy, but look out for thunder-showers, you Lancaster County night owls. Oh yes, Brando also called his new and terminal movie a "stinker." No sweat, for a fellow who began his career in a torn undershirt.

Rabbit smiles in the whispering, onrushing cave of the car; this guy must think nobody is listening, gagging it up like this. Lonely in those radio studios, surrounded by paper coffee cups and perforated acoustic tiles. Hard to know the effect you're making. Hard to believe God is always listening, never gets bored. The dashboard lights of the Celica glow beneath his line of vision like the lights of a city about to be bombed.

The superhighway crosses the Susquehanna and at York catches 83. As Harry drives south, the station fades behind him, toward the end of Louis Prima's "Just a Gigolo," that fantastic chorus where the chorus keeps chanting "Just a gigolo" in a kind of affectionate mockery of that wheezy wonderful voice: it makes your scalp prickle with joy. Rabbit fumbles with the scan button but can't find another oldies station, just talk shows, drunks calling in, the host sounding punchy himself, his mouth running on automatic pilot, abortion, nuclear waste, unemployment among young black males, CIA complicity in the AIDS epidemic, Boesky, Milken, Bush and North, Noriega, *you can't tell me that* – Rabbit switches the radio off, hating the sound of the human voice. Vermin. We are noisy vermin, crowding even the air. Better the murmur of the tires, the green road signs looming in the lights and parabolically enlarging and then whisked out of sight like magicians' handkerchieves. It's getting close to midnight, but before he stops he wants to be out of the state. Even that botched time ages ago he got as far as West Virginia. To get out of Pennsylvania you have to climb a nameless mountain, beyond Hungerford. Signs and lights diminish. The lonely highway climbs. High lakes gleam under what is, now, in a gap between clouds, true moonlight. He descends into Maryland. There is a different feeling: groomed center strips, advertisements for Park and Ride for commuters. Civilization. Out of the sticks. His eyelids feel sandy, his heart fluttery and sated. He pulls off 83 into a Best Western well north of Baltimore, pleased to think that nobody in the world, nobody but the stocky indifferent

Asian-American desk clerk, knows his location. Where oh where is the missing tritium?

He likes motel rooms – the long clammy slot of hired space, the two double beds, the television set with its invitation to buy an R-rated movie, the shag carpet, the framed prints of big birds, the sanitized towels, the hush of anonymity, the closeted echo of old sex. He sleeps well, as if he has slipped off his body with its troubles and left it lying on the other double bed. In his dream he is back at the lot, with a young woman who seems to be in charge. She wears a white cap and dangly earrings but when he leans close and tries to explain himself to her, to convey his indispensable use-fulness to the enterprise, contrary to what she may have heard from Janice, she makes a wry mouth and her face melts under his eyes in a kind of visual scream.

For breakfast, he succumbs to the temptation and has two fried eggs, though the yolks are terrible for your arteries, with bacon on the side. Rabbit likes the very American moment of packing up his car in sleepy unspeaking companionship with the other motel guests, elderly couples, cranky families, as they drift from the breakfast room across the parking lot with its long milky morning shadows. On the road again, with the radio again. The same news as the night before, amplified by the final baseball scores (Phils lost, five to one) and the news from Asia, where it is already afternoon for the busy Japanese currency speculators, the restive Chinese students, the doll-like Filipino hookers, the unhappily victorious Vietnamese, the up-and-coming although riotous Koreans, the tottering Burmese socialists, the warring Cambodian factions including the mindless Khmer Rouge minions of the most atro-cious national leader since Hitler and Stalin, the infamous Pol Pot. Like, wow! Wake up, songbirds! The d.j., not last night's but just as crazy and alone with himself, plays some rockabilly song Rabbit likes, about getting down, "make a little love, get down tonight." It occurs to Harry he didn't even jerk off last night, though motel rooms usually excite him. Boy, is he showing his age.

As Baltimore nears, the condominiums multiply, thicken, entire hills and valleys loaded with them, pastel gingerbread stair-cases containing invisible people. 83 ends seamlessly at 695 and with all the commuters in their neckties he drones around the

Beltway, jostling for his space in the world as if he still deserves it. Then he takes up 95, which will be his home all the way to Florida. There are two ways around Washington, he and Janice have tried them both, the boringly expert travellers down in the condo like the Silbersteins say 495 passing to the north and west is actually quicker, but he likes the little glimpse of the monuments you get by staying east on 95 and crossing the Potomac on a broad bridge into Alexandria. The frozen far heart, ice-cream white, of the grand old republic.

After all that megalopolis, Virginia feels bucolically vacant. The fields look bigger than those in Pennsylvania, the hills gentler and more open, with meadows and horses, a gracious mist in the air, once in a while a pillared manse on a pale-green rise like something embroidered on a sampler by a slaveowner's spinster daughter. A military tinge: Fort Belvoir Engineer Proving Ground, Quantico Marine Corps Base. Harry thinks of his Army time and it comes back as a lyric tan, a translucent shimmer of aligned faceless men, the curious peace of having no decisions to make, of being told entirely what to do. War is a relief in many ways. Without the Cold War, what's the point of being an American? Still, we held them off. We creamed those oafs. Hitler, Stalin, and now Gorby. History will remember that, if not thank us. There is very little thanks in history. Dog eat dog. It becomes hard now to find stations on the radio that are not country music or religion. "Pray for difficult marriages," one preacher says, his grainy molasses-brown voice digging so deep into himself you can picture his shut eyes, the sweat on his temples, "pray for Christian husbands under stress, for Christian wives worried about their men; pray for all hostages, for prisoners in prison, for victims of the ghetto, for all those with AIDS." Rabbit switches the station and resolves to call home when he stops for lunch.

How many rivers there are! After the Potomac, the Accotink, the Pohick, the Occoquan, the Rappahannock, the Pamunkey, the Ni, the Po, the Matta, the South Anna. The bridges thus marked are mere moments of the highway. Unseen towns are named: Massaponax, Ladysmith, Cedar Forks. North of Richmond, shacks in a thickening scatter mark the beginning of the true South, of rural blacks. Harry pulls into a Howard

Johnson's on the Richmond outskirts. His ears ring, the ankle of his accelerator foot aches, his neck is stiff, the heat has gone up several notches since the motel parking lot this morning. Inside the air-conditioned restaurant, salesmen with briefcases are at all the pay phones. He eats too much lunch, consuming the last French fry that came with his tasteless hamburger, mopping up salt with it in his fingers like his grandson Roy does, and then ordering apple pie to see if it's any different in Virginia. It's sweeter and gluier; it lacks that cinnamon they sprinkle on in Pennsylvania. A phone is available after he pays the check and with three dollars' worth of quarters ready he dials not the gray limestone house on Franklin Drive but the house where he used to live, the Springer house in Mt. Judge.

A little girl answers. The operator breaks in and Rabbit inserts three minutes' worth of quarters. He says, "Hi, Judy. It's Grandpa."

"Hi, Grandpa," she says, very calmly. Perhaps nothing of last night's revelation has filtered down to her yet. Or perhaps children this young are so innocent of what adulthood involves that nothing surprises them.

"How's it going?" he asks.

"O.K."

"You looking forward to school starting next week?"

"Kind of. Summer gets kind of boring."

"How's Roy? Is he bored by summer too?"

"He's so stupid he doesn't know what boring is. He's been put down for his nap now but is still bawling. Mommy's flipping out." Since Harry seems stuck for a response, she volunteers, "Daddy's not here, he's over at the lot."

"That's O.K., I'd just as soon talk to your mommy actually. Could you get her for me? Judy," he impulsively adds, before the child can leave the phone.

"Yeah?"

"You study hard, now. Don't you worry about those kids who think they're so much. You're a very lovely girl and everything will come to you if you wait. Don't force it. Don't force growing up. Everything will be fine."

This is too much to try to cram into her. She is only nine. Ten more years before she can go west like Mim and break out. "I know," Judy says, with a sigh, and perhaps she does. After a rattle of the receiver on wood and voices in the background and footsteps hastily enlarging, Pru arrives at the telephone, breathless.

"Harry!"

"Hi there, Teresa. How's it going?" This seductive nonchalant tone, all wrong, but it just came out.

"Not so good," she says. "Where on earth are you?"

"Far away, where everybody wants me. Hey. Whajou tell for?"

"Oh Harry, I *had* to." She starts to cry. "I *could*n't let Nelson not know, he's trying to be so straight. It's pathetic. He's been confessing all this dreadful stuff to me, I can't tell you or anybody the half of it, and at night we pray together, pray aloud kneeling by the bed, he's just so desperate to lick the drugs and be a decent father and husband, just be *nor*mal."

"He is, huh? Well, great. Still, you didn't need to turn us in, it only happened once, and there wasn't any follow-up, in fact I thought you'd totally forgotten about it."

"How could you think I'd forgotten? You must think I'm a real slut."

"Well, no, but, you know, you've been having a lot on your mind. For me, it was almost like I'd dreamed it." He means this as a compliment.

But Pru's voice hardens. "Well, it meant a little more to me than *that*." Women: you never know which side they want to dance on. "It was a terrible betrayal of my husband," she pronounces solemnly.

"Well," Rabbit says, "he hasn't been all that great a husband, as far as I can see. Hey, is Judy listening to all this?"

"I'm on the upstairs phone. I asked her to hang up downstairs."

"And did she? *Judy!*" Harry shouts. "I *see* you there!"

There is a fumbling soft rattle and a new clarity in the connection. Pru says, "Shit."

Rabbit reassures her. "I forget exactly what we said but I doubt if she understood much."

"She understands more than she lets on. Girls do."

"Well, anyway," he says. "Did he confess to affairs with men as well as women? Nelson."

"I can't possibly answer that question," she says, in a flat dry voice forever closed to him. Another woman's voice, warmer, courteous, faintly lazy, probably black, breaks in, saying, "Sir, yore three minutes are u-up. Please deposit a dollar ten saints if you wish continuation."

"Maybe I'm done," he says, to both women.

Pru shouts, over their imperilled connection, "Harry, where are you?"

"On the road!" he shouts back. He still has a little stack of change in front of him and inserts four quarters and a dime. As they gong away, he sings a snatch of a song he just heard on the radio, Willie Nelson's signature: "On the road again . . ."

This makes Pru sob; it's as bad as talking to Janice. "Oh *don't*," she cries. "Don't *tease* us all, we can't help it we're all tied down back here."

Pity touches him, with the memory of her beauty naked like blossoms that night in the narrow musty room as the rain intensi-fied. She is stuck back there, she is saying, with the living. "I'm tied down too," he tells her. "I'm tied to my carcass."

"What shall I tell Janice?"

"Tell her I'm on the way to the condo. Tell her she can come join me whenever she wants. I just didn't like the squeeze you all put on me last night. I get claustrophobic in my old age."

"I *never* should have slept with you, it's just at the time . . ."

"It was," he says. "It was a great idea at the time. Tell me – how'd you think I did, looking back on it? For an old guy."

She hesitates, then says, "That's it, that's the trouble. I don't see you as an old guy, Harry. I never did."

O.K., he has won this from her. This woman-to-man voice. Who could ask for anything more? Let her go. He says, "Don't you fret, Pru. You're a great dish. Tell Nelson to loosen up. Just because he got over crack he doesn't have to turn into Billy Graham." Or Jim Bakker. Harry hangs up, and the telephone startles him by returning, with a pang and clatter, the dime and four quarters. That operator with the Southern voice must have been listening and taken a shine to him.

As the afternoon wears on toward Fayetteville, North Caro-lina, where there is a Comfort Inn he and Janice have stayed at in

years past, he hears an amazing thing on the car radio. They inter-
rupt a string of Forties swing classics to announce that Bartlett
Giamatti, Commissioner of Baseball and former president of Yale
University, died of a heart attack on the island of Martha's
Vineyard, Massachusetts, late this afternoon. *Pete Rose strikes back*,
Rabbit thinks. Professor Giamatti, who was only fifty-one years
of age, retired after lunch in his summer home in Edgartown, and
at three o'clock was found by his wife and son in full cardiac arrest.
Only fifty-one, Rabbit thinks. Police took Giamatti to the Martha's
Vineyard Hospital where he was worked upon for an hour and a
half; the emergency team several times succeeded in restoring the
electric mechanism of the heartbeat, but Giamatti was at last pronounced dead. That little electric twitch: without it we're so
much rotting meat. One of the first things he ought to do in
Florida is make an appointment with Dr. Morris, to keep himself
out of the hands of that hawk-faced Australian, Dr. Olman. *Dying
to sink his knife into me*. Giamatti had been an English instructor at
Yale, the news says, and became the youngest president in the history of the university, and in eleven years reversed that institution's
trend into red ink and academic mediocrity. As president of the
National League, he had aroused some players' ire by tampering
with the strike zone and the balk rule. As commissioner, his brief
tenure was dominated by the painful Rose affair, whose settlement
a week ago left Giamatti in an apparently strong position. He
was a heavy man and a heavy smoker. *At least I'm no smoker*. And
now, a tune our listeners never get tired of requesting, "In the
Mood."

Fayetteville used to be a hot town, with all the soldiers from
Fort Bragg, Rabbit remembers from a segment of *60 Minutes* he
once watched. The downtown had some blocks of triple-X
movies and sleazy hotels the city fathers finally in despair tore
down entirely and made into a park. After a dinner of deep-fried
shrimp, with onion rings and white bread fried on one side, a
Southern delicacy he guesses, at the Comfort Inn – one of those
restaurants with a salad bar big as a little cafeteria, so you wonder
as you sit there waiting for the waitress if you're missing the boat
– Harry cruises in the slate-gray Celica, his private Batmobile,
toward the center of wicked Fayetteville. He can find for a hot

spot only a shadowy broad street of blacks loitering in doorways here and there, waiting for some message, some event from beyond. No hookers in hotpants or spandex exercise tights, just a big red-bearded white man in studded black leather who keeps revving his motorcycle, twisting the throttle and producing a tremendous noise. The blacks don't blink. They keep waiting. Even at evening the shadowy air is hot, they move through it languidly like sick fish, their hands flapping at the wrists in that angled black way.

Back in his long room with its watery scent of cement from underneath the rug, with walls painted altogether yellow, moldings and pipes and air-conditioning vents and light-switch plates rollered and sprayed yellow, Rabbit thinks of adding $5.50 to his bill to watch something called *Horny Housewives* but instead watches, free, bits of *Perfect Strangers* (it makes him uneasy, two guys living together, even if one of them is a comical Russian) and pre-season football between the Seahawks and 49ers. The trouble with these softcore porn movies on hotel circuits, in case some four-year-old with lawyers for parents happens to hit the right buttons they show tits and ass and even some pubic hair but no real cunt and no pricks, no pricks hard or soft at all. It's very frustrating. It turns out pricks are what we care about, you have to see them. Maybe we're all queer, and all his life he's been in love with Ronnie Harrison. Nice, today, the way Pru burst out with that *Shit* again and then *Don't tease*. That level woman-to-man voice, as if he had his arms about her, her voice relaxing into their basic relation, cock to cunt, doing Nelson in. In bed at last in the dark he jerks off, picturing himself with a pair of coffee-colored hookers from old Fayetteville, to show himself he's still alive.

The morning radio news is dull. Giamatti's death, warmed over. Baseball mourns. Economy shows moderate growth. Bombardments in Beirut between Christians and Muslims worse than ever. Ex-HUD aide says files were shredded. Supreme Court ruling against organized prayer before football games is rousing indignation all over the Southland. In Montgomery, Mayor Emory Folmar marched to the fifty-yard line and led a prayer there. His remarks over the public-address system linked football and prayer as American tradition. In Sylacauga, Alabama, local

ministers rose in the bleachers and led the crowd of three thousand in the Lord's Prayer. In Pensacola, Florida, preachers equipped
with bullhorns led spectactors in prayer. *Fanatics*, Rabbit tells
himself. Southerners are as scary as the Amish.

From here on down to the Florida line Route 95 is like a long
green tunnel between tall pines. Little shacks peek through. A sign
offers *Pecan Rolls 3 for $1.00.* Bigger signs in Hispanic colors, orange
and yellow on black, lime green, splashy and loud, miles and miles
of them, begin to advertise something called South of the Border.
Bear Up a Leetle Longer. You Never Sausage a Place! With a big
basketball curving right off the billboard, *Have a Ball.* When you
finally get there, after all these miles of pine tunnel, it's a junky
amusement park just across the South Carolina border: a village of
souvenir shops, a kind of a space needle wearing a sombrero. Tacos,
tacky. South Carolina is a wild state. The first to secede. The pines
get taller, with a tragic feeling. FIREWORKS are offered everywhere
for sale. The land gets hillier. Trucks loaded with great tree trunks
rumble unstoppably by on the downslope and labor to nearly a
standstill on the up. Rabbit is nervously aware now of his
Pennsylvania plates being Northern. Swerve out of line a bit and
they'll throw him in the Pee Dee River. The Lynches River. The
Pocatoligo River. Animals on this highway are hit so hard they don't
squash, they explode, impossible to know what they were. Possums.
Porcupines. Some dear old Southern lady's darling pet pussycat.
Reduced to fur stains amid the crescent fragments of exploded truck
tires. Just think, he lay down for lunch and that was it.

Janice must have got the message from Pru, she may be already
at the condo waiting, flying down from Philly and renting a car at
the airport, better enjoy his freedom while he has it. He has come
upon a black gospel station, an elastic fat voice shouting, "He'll be
there, but you got to call him names." Endlessly repeated, with
unexpected rhythmic variations. "Roll that stone away, do you
know the story?" A commercial interrupts at last and, would you
believe, it's for Toyotas. Those Japs don't miss a trick, you have to
hand it to them. Selling right in the slave quarters. *Your pruraristic society.* Harry's neck hurts from holding his head in one position so long.
He's beginning to feel bloated on radio, on travel. God's country.
He could have made it smaller and still made the same point.

He'll be there. Funny, about Harry and religion. When God hadn't a friend in the world, back there in the Sixties, he couldn't let go of Him, and now when the preachers are all praying through bullhorns he can't get it up for Him. He is like a friend you've had so long you've forgotten what you liked about Him. You'd think after that heart scare, but in a way the closer you get the less you think about it, like you're in His hand already. Like you're out on the court instead of on the bench swallowing down butterflies and trying to remember the plays.

Perry Como comes on and sings "Because." Rabbit's scalp prickles at the end, the skin of his eyes stings. *Because – you – are – miiiine!* Como the best, probably: Crosby had something sly-Irish about him, clowning around with Lamour and Hope, and Sinatra – if there's one way in which Rabbit Angstrom has been out of step with mankind, it's Sinatra. He doesn't like his singing. He didn't like it when bobbysoxers were jumping out of their underpants for this skinny hollow-cheeked guy up on the stage at the Paramount, and he didn't like it when he mellowed into this Las Vegas fat cat making all these moony albums you're supposed to screw to all across the nation: oceans of jism. White with foam. His singing has always sounded flat to Rabbit, like he's grinding it out. Now, to Mim, Sinatra is a god, but that's more a matter of lifestyle, turning night into day and pally with gangsters and Presidents and that square gangster way of carrying your shoulders (Charlie Stavros has it) and Chairman of the Board and Sammy Davis, Jr., and Dean Martin before they dried out finally, if in fact they did, both men have terrible health problems he read somewhere, in one of those ridiculous scandal sheets Janice brings home from the Minit Market. Sometimes Harry envies Mim the glamorous dangerous life he guesses she's lived, he's glad for her, she always had that edge, wanting speed even if it killed her, even if it flipped her off the handlebars of his old Elgin. But the fast lane too gets to be a rut. He doesn't regret the life he led, though Brewer isn't *New York New York* or *Chicago my kind of town* the way Sinatra grinds it out. What he enjoyed most, it turns out in retrospect, and he didn't know it at the time, was standing around in the showroom, behind the dusty big window with the banners, bouncing on the balls of his feet to keep up his leg muscles, waiting for a customer, shooting the bull with Charlie or whoever, earning his paycheck, filling his slot in the big picture, doing his bit, getting a little recognition. That's all we want from each other, recognition. Your assigned place in the rat race. In the Army, too, you had it: your number, your bunk, your assigned duties, your place in line, your pass for Saturday night, four beers and fuck a whore in a ranch house. *Honey, you didn't pay to be no two-timer.* There's more to being a human being than having your own way. Fact is, it has come to Rabbit this late in life, you don't have a way apart from what other people tell you. Your mother first, and poor Pop, then the Lutheran minister, that tough old heinie Fritz Kruppenbach, you had to respect him though, he said what he believed, and then all those schoolteachers, Marty Tothero and the rest, trying to give you an angle to work from, and now all these talk-show hosts. Your life derives, and has to give. Maybe if your mother was in the fast lane like Annabelle's you are naturally leery of the opposite sex. We haven't set these kids terrific examples.

The pine trees have gaps now. Marshy stretches open the sky up, there are cabins on stilts, trees with shaggy balls on them, colored wash hanging on lines. Homely hand-lettered signs. *Dad's Real Southern Cookin'*. Bi-Lo. A long bridge over Lake Marion, this enormous body of water in the middle of nowhere. Highways branch off to the capital, Columbia, where he's never been, though he and Janice did once detour over to Charleston and back on Route 17. Another time, they diverted to Savannah and spent the night in a made-over plantation house with high domed ceilings and louvers on the windows. They did do some fun things, he and Jan. The thing about a wife, though, and he supposes a husband for that matter, is that almost anybody would do, inside broad limits. Yet you're supposed to adore them till death do you part. Till the end of time. Ashepoo River. Wasn't that a comic strip, years ago?

He gets off the highway at a vast rest stop, an oasis in this wilderness – gas pumps, a restaurant, a little department store selling groceries, beer, fireworks, suntan lotion. At the counter a couple of young black men, glittery black in the heat, arms bare up to the shoulder, a mean little Malcolm X goatee on one of them. They have a menace down here, their color shouts, they are a *race*, they are everywhere. But the elderly white waitress has no trouble with these two black boys. The three chat and smile in the same dragged accent, making a little breeze with their mouths. Nice to see it. For this, the Civil War.

To test if he can still use his own voice, Rabbit asks the fat white man one empty stool away from him at the counter, a man who has made for himself at the salad bar a mountain of lettuce and red beets and coleslaw and cottage cheese and kidney beans and chickpeas, "About how many more hours is it to the Florida line?" He lets his Pennsylvania accent drag a little extra, hoping to pass.

"Four," the man answers with a smile. "I just came from there. Where you headin' for in Florida?"

"Way the other end. Deleon. My wife and I have a condo there, I'm driving down alone, she'll be following later."

The man keeps smiling, smiling and chewing. "I know Deleon. Nice old town."

Rabbit has never noticed much that is old about it. "From our balcony we used to have a look at the sea but they built it up."

"Lot of building on the Gulf side now, the Atlantic side pretty well full. Began my day in Sarasota."

"Really? That's a long way to come."

"That's why I'm makin' such a pig of myself. Hadn't eaten more than a candy bar since five o'clock this morning. After a while you got to stop, you begin to see things."

"What sort of things?"

"This stretch I just came over, lot of patchy ground fog, it gets to you. Just coffee gets to your stomach." This man has a truly nice way of smiling and chewing and talking all at once. His mouth is wide but lipless, like a Muppet's. He has set his truck driver's cap, with a bill and a mesh panel in the back, beside his plate; his good head of gray hair, slightly wavy like a rich man's, is permanently dented by the edge of the cap.

"You drivin' one of those big trucks? I don't know how you guys do it. How far you goin'?"

All the salad on the plate has vanished and the smile has broadened. "Boston."

"Boston! All that way?" Rabbit has never been to Boston, to him it is the end of the world, tucked up in under Maine. People living that far north are as fantastic to him as Eskimos.

"Today, tomorrow, whatever you call it, I expect to have this rig in Boston Sunday afternoon, twenty-four hours from now."

"But when do you sleep?"

"Oh, you pull over and get an hour here, an hour there."

"That's amazing."

"Been doin' it for fifteen years. I had retired, but came back to it. Couldn't stand it around the house. Nothin' on TV that was any good. How about you?"

"Me?" On the lam. A bad LAD. He realizes what the question means, and answers, "Retired, I guess."

"More power to ya, fella. I couldn't take it," the truck driver says. "Retirement taxed my brain." The elderly waitress so friendly with the two young blacks brings the hungry man an oval platter heavy with fried steak soaking in a pink mix of oil and blood, and three vegetables in little round side dishes, and a separate plate of golden-brown corn pone.

Harry somewhat reluctantly – he has made a friend – pushes away from the counter. "Well, more power to *you*," he says.

And now this fat pale miracle man, who will be in Boston faster than a speeding bullet, who like Thomas Alva Edison only needs a catnap now and then, has his wide Muppet mouth too full to speak, and merely smiles and nods, and loses a snaky droplet of steak juice down the far side of his egg-shaped little chin. No-body's perfect. We're only human. Look at Jim Bakker. Look at Bart Giamatti.

In his Celica Harry crosses the Tuglifinny River. The Salke-hatchie. The Little Combahee. The Coosawatchie. The Turtle. Kickapoo, he thinks – not Ashepoo. Kickapoo Joy Juice in *Li'l Abner*. Between spates of black music that has that peculiar exciting new sound of boards being slapped on the floor, he hears commercials for the Upchurch Music Company ("an instrument that brings musical pleasure to generations to come") and a deodorizer called Tiny Cat. Why would a deodorizer be called Tiny Cat? He crosses the Savannah and leaves South Carolina and its fireworks at last. Because he is punchy from miles of miles, he turns off at the city exit and drives into the downtown and parks by a grand old courthouse and buys a hot pastrami sandwich at a little sandwich joint on the main street there. He sits eating it, trying not to have any of the juice spill out of the waxpaper and spot his pants, like that sickening driblet from the mouth of the guy back at the lunch place hours ago. This piece of Savannah, a block from the river, seems a set of outdoor rooms, walled in by row houses with high steps and curtains of dusty trees; a huge heat still rests on the day though the shadows are deepening, thickening on the soft old façades, sadder and rosier than those in Brewer. A group of pigeons gathers around his bench, curious to see if he will spare any of the bun or Bar-B-Q potato chips. A young bum with long yellow hair like George Custer and that brown face you get from being homeless gives him a glittering wild eye from a bench behind a tree, in the next room as it were. A tall obelisk rises in commemoration of something, no doubt the glorious dead. Little chattering brown birds heave in and out of the trees as they try to decide whether the day is over. He better push on. He neatly packages his wastepaper and milk carton in the bag the sandwich came in and leaves it in a public trash basket, his gift to Savannah, the trace he will leave, like the cloud of finger-moisture on the edge of the bureau back home. The pigeons chuff and chortle off in indignant disappointment. The bum has silently come up behind him and asks him in no particular accent, the limp snarl of the drugged, if he has a cigarette. "Nope," Rabbit tells him. "Haven't smoked in thirty years." He remembers the moment when on a sudden resolve he canned a half-pack of Philip Morris, the nice old tobacco-brown pack, in somebody's open barrel in an alley in Mt. Judge. Left that trace too.

Rabbit moves toward his car with a racing heart, as the bum follows and mumbles behind him about spare change. He fiddles with the key and gets in and slams the door. The Celica, thank God, isn't too overheated after all its miles to start promptly; George Custer, locked outside, blinks and turns, pretending not to notice. Harry drives cautiously through the outdoor rooms, around the tall monument, and gets lost on the way out of Savannah. He is caught in endless black neighborhoods, gently collapsing houses built of wood clapboard that last saw fresh paint in the days of Martin Luther King. They talk about assassination conspiracies but that was one that Harry could believe in. He can believe in it but he can't remember the name of the man they put in jail for it. A three-name name. Escaped once, but they caught him. James Earl something. So much for history. Panicking, he stops at a grocery store, the kind with a troughed wooden floor with shiny-headed nails that used to be in Mt. Judge when he was a boy, except that everybody in here is black; a lanky man the color of a dried bean pod, much amused, tells him how to get back to the superhighway, gesturing with long hands that flap loosely on his wrists.

Back on 95, Rabbit pushes through Georgia. As darkness comes on, it begins to rain, and with his old eyes, that can't sort out the lights too well at night any more, the rain is oppressive. He even turns off the radio, he feels so battered by pellets of experience. His body from being in one position so long feels as if somebody's been pounding it with sandbags. He better pull in. He finds a Ramada Inn beyond Brunswick. He eats a fried-catfish special that doesn't sit too well on top of the pastrami, especially the candied yams and the pecan pie; but why be in Georgia if you can't have pecan pie? The walk back to his room past the other motel doors, on cement sheltered by the continuous balcony overhead, is quietly blissful. In out of the rain. Sense enough. They can't catch me. But his snug moment of happiness reminds him of all those exposed unhappy loved ones back in Diamond County. Guilt gouges at his heart like a thumb in a semi-sensitive eye.

Halfway through *The Golden Girls*, it seems suddenly tedious, all that elderly sexiness, and the tough-mouthed old grandmother, people ought to know when to give up. He watches instead on the educational channel a *Living Planet* segment about life at the polar extremes. He's seen it before, but it's still surprising, how David Attenborough turns over those rocks in this most desolate place in Antarctica and there are lichens underneath, and all through the sunless abysmal winter these male penguins shuffling around in continuous blizzards with eggs on the tops of their webbed feet. Life, it's incredible, it's wearing the world out. A ten-o'clock news on the same channel tells the same old stuff he's been hearing on the radio all day. Poor Giamatti. A female baby panda born in the National Zoo in Washington. Reagan thought AIDS was as mild as measles until Rock Hudson died, reveals his former physician Brigadier General John Hutton. Another tattletale: Navy Commander David R. Wilson claims in this month's *U.S. Naval Institute Proceedings* magazine that the U.S.S. *Vincennes* was known among other ships in the Persian Gulf for her aggressive and imprudent actions for at least a month before the *Vincennes* gunned down an Iranian civil airliner containing over two hundred seventy men, women, and children. Poor devils, Iranians or not. Little children, women in shawls, end over end, hitting the dark hard water. New head of Japan in Washington, provisional government in Panama, mobs of East Germans in Hungary waiting to cross the border into the free world. Poor devils, they don't know the free world is wearing out.

Rabbit makes himself ready for bed, sleeping in the day's underwear, and tries to think about where he is, and who. This is the last night when he is nowhere. Tomorrow, life will find him again. Janice on the phone, the Golds next door. He feels less light than he thought he would, escaping Brewer. You are still you. The U.S. is still the U.S., held together by credit cards and Indian names. Harry becomes dead weight on the twin bed. Lost in the net of thread-lines on the map, he sleeps as in his mother's womb, another temporary haven.

Morning. The rain is just a memory of puddles on the sunstruck asphalt. Sunday. He goes for the French toast and link sausages, figuring tomorrow morning he'll be back to stale oat bran. Janice never cleans out the cupboards when they leave. Efficient, in a way, if you don't mind feeding ants and roaches. He keeps tasting maple syrup and eggs he didn't quite like. French toast is never as good as what Mom would cook up before sending him off to Sunday school: the flat baked golden triangles of bread, the syrup from the can shaped and painted like a log cabin, its spout the chimney. Putting his suitcase in the trunk, he is struck, not for the first time, by how the Celica's taillights are tipped, giving it, from the back, a slant-eyed look.

Within an hour he crosses the St. Marys River and a highway sign says WELCOME TO FLORIDA and the radio commercials are for Blue Cross, denture fixatives, pulmonary clinics. The roadside becomes sandy and the traffic thickens, takes on glitter. Jacksonville suddenly looms, an Oz of blue-green skyscrapers, a city of dreams at the end of the pine-tree tunnel, gleaming glass boxes heaped around the tallest, the Baptist Hospital. You rise up onto bridges over the St. Johns River far below, and Jacksonville shines from a number of angles like a jewel being turned in your hand, and you pay a toll, and must stay alert not to wind up heading toward Green Cove Springs or Tallahassee. Route 95 is now just one among many superhighways. The cars get wide and fat, the trucks carry rolls of fresh sod instead of skinned pine trunks. All around him, floating like misplaced boats, are big white campers and vans, Winnebagos and Starcrafts, Pathfinders and Dolphins, homes on wheels, the husband at the helm, his elbow out the window, the wife at home behind him, making the bed. From all of the states these caravans come to Florida, wearing even Colorado's green mountain profile and Maine's gesturing red lobster. He notices a new kind of Florida license plate, a kind of misty tricolor memorial to the Challenger, among the many still with the green Florida-shaped stain in the middle like something spilled on a necktie. And wasn't that the disgrace of the decade, sending that poor New Hampshire schoolteacher and that frizzy-haired Jewish girl, not to mention the men, one of them black and another Oriental, all like some Hollywood cross-section of America, up to be blown into bits on television a minute later? Now the probers think they were probably conscious, falling toward the water, conscious for two or three minutes. Harry descends deeper into Florida, glad to be back among the palms and white roofs and tropical thinness, the clouds blue on gray on white on blue, as if the great skymaker is working here with lighter materials.

You take 95 parallel to the East Coast to 4, and then skim diagonally over through all that Disney World that poor little Judy wanted to go to, next time they come they must schedule it in. Where some of the self-appointed travel experts at the condo (he always did think Ed Silberstein a know-it-all, even before his son tried to put the make on Pru) advise staying on 4 all the way to 75 and saving in minutes what you lose in miles, or at least taking 17 to Port Charlotte, he likes to move south on 27, right through the hot flat belly of the state, through Haines City and Lake Wales, into the emptiness west of the Seminole reservation and Lake Okeechobee, and then over to Deleon on Route 80.

In Florida, there is no trouble finding Golden Oldies stations on the car radio. We're all oldies down here. The music of your life, some of the announcers like to call it, and it keeps tumbling in, Patti Page begging "Never let me gooooo, I love you soooooo," and then doing so perkily that Latin-American bit with "Aye yi yi" and the caballeros, and finishing "I've waited all my life, to give you all my love, my heart belongs to you," and then Tony Bennett or one of those other mooing Italians with "Be My Love," speaking of all my love, and then Gogi Grant and "The Wayward Wind," he hasn't thought of Gogi Grant for ages, it's a rare song that doesn't light up some of his memory cells, while the landscape outside the car windows beyond the whoosh of the air-conditioner gets more and more honkytonk – *Flea World*, *Active Adult Living* and car after car goes by with an orange Garfield stuck to the back window with paws that are suction cups. "Why you ramble, no one knows," Nat "King" Cole singing "Rambling Rose," ending so gently, "Why I want you, no one knows," you can just about see that wise slow smile, and then "Tzena, Tzena," he hasn't heard that for years either, the music doesn't come ethnic any more, and "Oh, My Papa," speaking of ethnic, and Kay Starr really getting her back into "Wheel of Fortune," all those hiccups, hard-driving, "Pu*leazzze* let it be now," and "A-Tisket, A-Tasket," that really goes back, he was walking to grade school then with Lottie Bingaman, in love with Margaret Schoelkopf, and Presley's "Love Me Tender," knock him all you want, before he got fat and druggy and spooked in the end he had a real voice, a beautiful voice, not like foghorn Sinatra, and then Ray Charles, now there's another real voice, "I Can't Stop Loving You," "dreaming of yesterdayssss," the way it trails off like that, that funny blind man's waggle of the head, and Connie Francis, "Where the Boys Are," a voice to freeze your scalp all right, but whose life *are* these songs? That was beach-party era, he was all married and separated and reconciled and working at Verity Press by then, no more parties for him. Ronnie Harrison and Ruth fucking all weekend at the Jersey Shore: that still rankles.

The station fades out and in trying to find another he passes through a broadcast church service, evangelical, a man shouting "Jesus knows! Jesus looks into your heart! Jesus sees the death in your heart!" and Harry passes on, coming upon, too late for all of the sobbing, Johnny Ray's "Cry," "If your *sweet*heart sends a *let*ter of good*bye*," that was around the time he had to go into the Army and part from Mary Ann, he didn't know it would be for good, they argued about Johnny Ray, Rabbit insisting the guy had to be a fruit to sing that way, and then down in Texas he realized the song was for him, his sweetheart sent a letter. Next number, Dean Martin comes on loafing through "That's Amore": by now Harry had come back and taken up with Janice, the quiet girl behind the nuts counter at Kroll's, her little tight body, the challenge of her puzzled dark eyes, he remembers because he would joke, "That's a*more*," after they would fuck in the room Linda Hammacher would let them use, with its view of the dove-gray gas tanks by the river. "Only the Lonely," the late Roy Orbison warbles. "There goes my baby, there goes my heart," in that amazing voice that goes higher and higher till you think it must break like crystal, as in a way it did; Rabbit supposed his being dead is what makes this one a Golden Oldie.

The songs roll on, broken every half-hour by summaries of the news. A bombing in Colombia has injured eighty-four, the Colombian woes are increased by a drop in coffee prices, President Bush's upcoming speech on the nation's drug problems rouses Washington speculation, can he do a Reagan? Also in Washington, officials are still hopeful that the newborn baby panda, fighting for its life in an incubator, will survive. Locally, manatees continue active in the Caloosahatchee Basin, and the Dolphins were beaten yesterday in Miami by the Philadelphia Eagles, twenty to ten. Rabbit likes hearing this score, but the old songs, all that syrup about love, love, the sweetness, the cuteness, the doggies in the window and Mommy kissing Santa Claus and the naughty lady of Shady Lane, the background strings and pizzicato bridges and rising brass crescendos meant to thrill the pants off you, wear him down: he resents being made to realize, this late, that the songs of his life were as moronic as the rock the brainless kids now feed on, or the Sixties and Seventies stuff that Nelson gobbled up

– all of it designed for empty heads and overheated hormones, an ocean white with foam, and listening to it now is like trying to eat a double banana split the way he used to. It's all *disposable*, cooked up to turn a quick profit. They lead us down the garden path, the music manufacturers, then turn around and lead the next generation down with a slightly different flavor of glop.

Rabbit feels betrayed. He was reared in a world where war was not strange but change was: the world stood still so you could grow up in it. He knows when the bottom fell out. When they closed down Kroll's, Kroll's that had stood in the center of Brewer all those years, bigger than a church, older than the courthouse, right at the head of Weiser Square there, with every Christmas those otherworldly displays of circling trains and nodding dolls and twinkling stars in the corner windows as if God Himself put them there to light up this darkest time of the year. As a little kid he couldn't tell what God did from what people did; it all came from above somehow. He can remember standing as a child in the cold with his mother gazing into this world of tinselled toys as real as any other, the air biting at his cheeks, the sound of the Salvation Army bells begging, the smell of the hot soft pretzels sold on Weiser Square those years, the feeling around him of adult hurrying – bundled-up bodies pushing into Kroll's where you could buy the best of everything from drapes to beds, toys to pots, china to silver. When he worked there back in Shipping you saw the turnover, the hiring and firing, the discontinued lines, the abrupt changes of fashion, the panicky gamble of all this merchandising, but still he believed in the place as a whole, its power, its good faith. So when the system just upped one summer and decided to close Kroll's down, just because shoppers had stopped coming in because the downtown had become frightening to white people, Rabbit realized the world was not solid and benign, it was a shabby set of temporary arrangements rigged up for the time being, all for the sake of the money. You just passed through, and they milked you for what you were worth, mostly when you were young and gullible. If Kroll's could go, the courthouse could go, the banks could go. When the money stopped, they could close down God Himself.

For miles in the vicinity of Disney World and beyond, lesser amusement and theme parks hold out their cups for the tourist overflow. Waxworks. Wet 'n' Wild, a water slide. Sea World. Circus World, not the one that's redux down in Sarasota. What a dumb word, as dumb as faux, you see it everywhere suddenly, faux fur, faux jewelry. *False* is what they mean. A museum of old dolls and toys. Old, old, they sell things as antiques now that aren't even as old as he is, another racket. On Route 27, going due south, you enter slightly rolling dry pale farm country, bleached by heat, with pale cattle in wide parched fields and orange groves with their dark dense irrigated green, and giant tanks holding water, shaped like giant mushrooms, like spaceships come from beyond. At the side of the road little wobbly hand-painted signs offer BOILED PEANUTS, tiny Mexican girls manning the stands, and there is, in faint echo of the giant theme parks to the north, a touching dusty amusement park, spindly structures put together for a minute's giddy sensation, idle, waiting for the evening's little customers.

The sun is high now and the morning's tattered gray clouds have melted away and the heat is serious, crushing, frightening when he steps out of the Celica at a Texaco to use the facilities because there is no escape from it, like snow at the South Pole, it even drifts into the men's room, as humid a heat as in the Pennsylvania summer but more searing, more wrathful. The road is wide but has lights and roads coming from the bleached farmland; the small cities drift by, Lake Wales, Frostproof, Avon Park, Sebring, and he wonders about the lives led there, away from the coasts, away from the condos and the fishing charters, by people who wake up and go to work just like those in Brewer, only everything flattened by the sun: how did they get here, so near the edge of the world, on this sand spit that a little rise in sea level because of Antarctica melting because of carbon dioxide in the atmosphere would wash away? A column of thick smoke appears on his left, toward the Seminole reservation, thick and poisonous, a disaster, an atomic bomb, war has been declared while he's been drowning in musical memories; he expects to run into a forest fire, but nothing happens, the column of smoke slowly recedes on his left, he'll never know what it was. A dump most likely. Harry's whole body feels cramped because of long sitting and he takes a

Nitrostat because of the cute little rush it gives you, the inner loosening, the tickle.

The land gets less and less settled and more scraggy. The towns take on funny names like Lake Placid and Venus and Old Venus and Palmdale; just beyond Palmdale, after you cross the Fisheating Creek, at Harrisburg no less, the state capital up there but a nothing down here, you bear right on 29, a narrow road so straight and flat you can see for miles, trucks coming at you through a shimmer that cuts off their wheels, rednecks in pickups pushing in the rearview mirror to pass, hardly any signs, a feeling all around of swamp, so remote from civilization the radio station fades, its last song of your life before it finally fades is somebody called Connie Boswell, way before Rabbit's time, singing "Say It Isn't So" with a rueful little lisp, quietly as if she's just talking it to you, "You've found somebody newww," the band behind her soft and tinny like those that used to play in hotel lobbies with lots of potted palms, a Twenties feeling, they lived hard, no worry about smoking and drinking and cholesterol, just do it, "Ssay it isn't sso," he could almost cry, she sounds so sincere, so truly wounded. What *is* Janice's game, anyway? He'll find out soon enough.

You think 29 will never end, between its ditches of swamp water, its stiff gray vegetation, but it finally comes into 80, at La Belle, streaming west just south of the Caloosahatchee, and then you're almost home, there are signs to the Southwest Florida Regional Airport and planes roaring low overhead, he could shoot them down through his windshield if he were the *Vincennes*. For nostalgia's sake, to get back into it, the Florida thing, he pushes on past Interstate 75 to Route 41. Starvin' Marvin. Universal Prosthetics. Superteller. STARLITE MOTEL. That time he and Janice wound up in a motel like they were an illicit couple when in fact they'd been married for thirteen years. Unlucky number but they survived it. Thirty-three years married this year. Thirty-four since they first fucked. Back in Kroll's he never realized she'd come into money eventually. She just seemed a pathetic little mutt behind the nuts counter, "Jan" stitched to her brown smock, something insecure and sexy about her, a secure independent woman like Elvira probably isn't so much into sex, Jan was, she was amazed when he went down on her like he used to for Mary

Ann in the car, only now on a bed. Mom didn't take to Jan; standing in the kitchen with soapy hands she would say Fred Springer was a con artist with his used cars. Now Springer Motors is *kaput*, *finito*. Down the tubes just like Kroll's. Nothing is sacred.

Harry comes to his turning off 41. The plumes of pampas grass, the flowering shrubs along the curving streets look different this time of year, more florid. He has never been down here at this time of year before. It seems emptier, fewer cars in the driveways, more curtains drawn, the sidewalks looking less walked-on than ever, the traffic thinner even though this is rush hour, with that late-afternoon pall in the air, like tarnish on silver. He doesn't see a single squashed armadillo on Pindo Palm Boulevard. The guard at the security gate of Valhalla Village, a lean bespectacled black Harry hasn't seen before, doesn't know him, but finds his name on the list of tenants and waves him through without a smile, all efficiency, probably college-educated, over-qualified.

The code on the inner entrance door of Building B doesn't work. So many numbers in his life, he may be getting it wrong. But after the third time it fails to click him in, he figures it's not him, the code has been changed. And so, limping from a stiffness in his right leg from pushing on the accelerator for over three days, Harry has to hobble over across the carpeted traffic island and the asphalt, in the dazing heat, through the rush of half-forgotten tropical aromas, hibiscus, bougainvillea, dry palm thatch, crunchy broad-bladed St. Augustine grass, to the management office in Building C to get it, the new code.

They say they sent the notice to his summer address up north; he tells them, "My wife must have torn it up or lost it or something." His voice talking to people again sounds odd and croaky, coming from several feet outside himself, like the to-one-side echo or chorus that sometimes startles you on the car stereo system. He feels awkward and vulnerable out of the car: a sea snail without its shell. On his way by, he looks into Club Nineteen and is surprised to see nobody at the tables, inside or out, though a couple of foursomes are waiting on the first tee, in the lengthening shadows. You don't play, he guesses, in the middle of the day this time of year.

The elevator has a different color inspection card in the slip-in frame, the peach-colored corridor smells of a different air freshener, with a faint nostalgic tang of lemonade. The door of 413 opens easily, his two keys scratch into their wiggly slots and turn, there are no cobwebs to brush against his face, no big brown hairy spiders scuttling away on the carpet. He imagines all sorts of spooky things lately. The condo is like it always was, as absolutely still as a reconstruction of itself – the see-through shelves, the birds and flowers Janice made of small white shells, the big green glass egg that used to sit in Ma Springer's living room, the blond square sofa, the fake-bamboo desk, the green-gray dead television screen. Nobody bothered to disturb or rob the place: kind of a snub. He carries his two bags into the bedroom and opens the sliding door onto the balcony. The sound of his footsteps makes deep dents in the silence of the place. An electric charge of reproach hangs in the stagnant air. The condo hadn't expected him, he is early. Having arrived at it after such a distance makes everything appear magnified, like the pitted head of a pin under a microscope. The whole apartment – its furniture, its aqua cabinets and Formica countertop, its angles of fitted door frame and baseboard – seems to Rabbit a tight structure carefully hammered together to hold a brimming amount of fear.

A white telephone sits waiting to ring. He picks it up. There is no buzz. God on the line. Disconnected for the season. Today is Sunday, tomorrow is Labor Day. The old familiar riddle: how do you telephone the phone company without a telephone?

But the phone, once it is connected, still doesn't ring. The days go by empty. The Golds next door are back in Framingham. Bernie and Fern Drechsel are up north bouncing between their two daughters' houses, one in Westchester County and the other still in Queens, and their son's lovely home in Princeton and a cottage he has in Manahawkin. The Silbersteins have a place in North Carolina they go to from April to November. Once when Harry asked Ed why they didn't go back to Toledo, Ed looked at him with that smartass squint and asked, "You ever been to Toledo?" The Valhalla dining room is spooky – empty tables and an echoing click of silver on china and Bingo only once a week. The golf course has noisy foursomes on it early in the morning, waking Harry up with the moon still bright in the sky – younger men, local Deleon business types who buy cut-rate off-season memberships – and then the fairways from ten to about four bake in the mid-nineties heat, deserted but for the stray dog cutting diagonally across or the cats scratching in the sand traps. When Harry one morning gets up his nerve for a round by himself, planning to take a cart, he discovers the pro shop has lost his golf shoes. The kid at the counter – the pro and assistant pro are both still up north at country clubs that don't close down until late October – says he's sure they're somewhere, it's just that this time of year there's a different system.

The only other person in the fourth-floor corridor who seems to be here is the crazy woman in 402, Mrs. Zabritski, a widow with wild white hair, pinned up by two old tortoise-shell combs that just add to the confusion. The Golds have told him she survived one of the concentration camps when a girl. She looks at Harry as if he's crazy too, to be here.

He explains to her one day, since they meet at the elevator and she looks at him funny, "I had this sudden impulse to come down early this year. My wife's just starting up in the real-estate business and I got bored hanging around the house."

Mrs. Zabritski's little neckless head is screwed around at an angle on her shoulder, as if she's bracing an invisible telephone against her ear. She stares up at him furiously, her lips baring her long false teeth in a taut oval that reminds him of that Batman logo you saw everywhere this summer. Her eyes have veiny reds to them, stuck hot and round in their skeletal sockets, that wasting-away look Lyle had. "It's hell," the tiny old lady seems to pronounce, her lips moving stiffly, trying to keep her teeth in.

"It's what? What is?"

"This weather," she says. "Your wife –" She halts, her lips working.

"My wife what?" Rabbit tries to curb his tendency to shout, since hearing doesn't seem to be one of her problems, regardless of that pained way her head is cocked.

"Is a cute little thing," she finishes, but looks angry saying it. Her hair sticks up in wisps as if it was moussed and abandoned.

"She'll be down soon," he almost shouts, embarrassed as much by his secrets, his hopeful lies, as by her dwarfish warped craziness. This is the kind of woman he's ended up with, after Mary Ann and then Janice and Ruth's silky-sack heaviness and Peggy Fosnacht's splayed eyes and Jill's adolescent breasts and stoned compliance and Thelma with her black casket and Pru glowing dimly in the dark like a tough street in blossom, not to mention that tired whore in Texas with the gritty sugar in her voice and that other paid lay in his life, a girl he once in a great while remembers, at a Verity Press outing in the Brewer Polish-American Club, she was skinny and had a cold and kept her bra and sweater on, there in this room off to the side, where she was waiting on a mattress like a kind of prisoner, young, her belly and thighs sweaty from the cold she had but pure and pale, a few baby-blue veins where the skin molded around the pelvic bones, her pussy an old-fashioned natural dark ferny triangle, flourishing, not shaved at the sides to suit a bathing suit the way you see in the skin magazines. You paid the guy who stood outside the door, ten dollars for ten minutes, he hadn't shaved very recently, Rabbit assumed he was her brother, or maybe her father. He assumed the girl was Polish because of the name of the club, she might have been eighteen, Mrs. Zabritski would have been that age after getting out of the concentration camp, smooth-skinned, lithe, a young survivor. What time does to people; her face is broken into furrows that crisscross each other like a checkerboard of skin.

"She should wait," Mrs. Zabritski says.

"I'll tell her you said so," he says loudly, fighting the magnetism sucking at him out of the unspoken fact that she is a woman and he is a man and both are alone and crazy, a few doors apart in this corridor like a long peach-colored chute glinting with silver lines in the embossed wallpaper. All his life seems to have been a journey into the bodies of women, why should his journey end now? Say she was eighteen when the war ended, he was twelve, she is only six years older. Sixty-two. Not so bad, can still work up some juice. Beu Gold is older, and sexy.

He tries to watch TV but it makes him restless. The last of the summer reruns are mixed in with previews of new shows that don't look that much different: families, laugh tracks, zany drop-ins, those three-sided living-room sets with the stairs coming down in the background like in *Cosby*, and front doors on the right through which the comical good-natured grandparents appear, bearing presents and presenting problems. The door is on the right in *Cosby* and on the left in *Roseanne*. That fat husband's going to have his cardiovascular problems too. TV families and your own are hard to tell apart, except yours isn't interrupted every six minutes by commercials and theirs don't get bogged down into nothingness, a state where nothing happens, no skit, no zany visitors, no outburst on the laugh track, nothing at all but boredom and a lost feeling, especially when you get up in the morning and the moon is still shining and men are making noisy bets on the first tee.

At first he thinks Janice has tried so hard to reach him those four days before the phone got connected on Thursday that she's lost faith in their old number. Then he begins to accept her silence as a definite statement. *I'll never forgive you.* O.K., he'll be damned if he'll call her. Dumb mutt. Rich bitch. Working girl yet. Thinks she's so fucking hot running everybody's lives with those accountants and lawyers Charlie put her on to, he's known her so drunk she couldn't get herself to the bathroom to pee. The few times Harry has weakened, impulsively, usually around four or five when he can't stand the sound of the golf games beginning up again and it's still hours to dinner, the telephone in the little limestone house in Penn Park rings and rings without an answer. He hangs up in a way relieved. Nothingness has a purity. Like running. He showed her he still had some kick in his legs and now she's showing him she can still be stubborn. Her silence frightens him. He fights off images of some accident she might have, slipping in the bathtub or driving the Camry off the road, having had too much to drink over at Nelson's or at some Vietnamese restaurant with Charlie, without him knowing. Police frogmen finding her drowned in the back seat like that girl from Wilkes-Barre twenty years ago. But no, he'd be notified, if anything were to happen, somebody would call him, Nelson or Charlie or Benny at the lot, if there still is a lot. Each day down here, events in

Pennsylvania seem more remote. His whole life seems, as he rotates through the empty condo rooms, each with its view across the parallel fairways to a wilderness of Spanish-tile roofs, to have been unreal, or no realer than the lives on TV shows, and now it's too late to make it real, to be serious, to reach down into the earth's iron core and fetch up a real life for himself.

The local air down here this time of year is full of violence, as if the natives are on good behavior during the winter season. Hurricane alarms (*Gabrielle packs punch*), head-on car crashes, masked holdups at Publix. The day after Labor Day, lightning kills a young football player leaving the field after practice; the story says Florida has more deaths by lightning than any other state. In Cape Coral, a Hispanic police officer is charged with beating his cocker spaniel to death with a crowbar. Sea turtles are dying by the thousands in shrimp nets. A killer called Petit whose own mother says he looks like Charles Manson is pronounced mentally fit to stand trial. That Deion Sanders is still making the front page of the Fort Myers *News-Press*: one day he knocks in four runs and a homer playing baseball for the Yankees, the next he signs for millions to play football for the Atlanta Falcons, and the very next he's being sued by the auxiliary cop he hit last Christmas at that shopping mall, and on Sunday he bobbles a punt return for the Falcons but runs it back for a touchdown anyway, the only man in human history to hit a home run and score a touchdown in pro ball the same week.

Deion has right stuff

Enjoy it while he can. He calls himself Prime Time and is always on the TV news wearing sunglasses and gold chains. Rabbit watches that big kid Becker beat Lendl in the U.S. Tennis Open final and gets depressed, Lendl seemed old and tired and stringy, though he's only twenty-eight.

He talks to nobody, except for Mrs. Zabritski when she catches him in the hall, and the teenage Florida-cracker salesclerks when he buys his food and razor blades and toilet paper, and the people who feel obliged to make chitchat, the other retirees, in the Valhalla dining room; they always ask about Janice so it gets to be embarrassing and he more and more just heats up something frozen and stays in the condo, ransacking the cable channels for something worthy to kill time with. In his solitude, his heart becomes his companion. He listens to it, tries to decipher its messages. It has different rhythms at different times of the day, a *thorrumph thorrumph* sluggish slightly underwater beat in the morning, and toward evening, when the organism gets tired and excited at once, a more skittish thudding, with the accent on the first beat and grace notes added, little trips and pauses now and then. It twinges when he gets up out of bed and then again when he lies down and whenever he thinks too hard about his situation, having set himself adrift like this. He could have gone over that night and faced the music but how much music is a man supposed to face? So he and Pru did fuck, once. What are we put here in the first place for? These women complain about men seeing nothing but tits and ass when they look at them but what are we supposed to see? We've been programmed to tits and ass. Except guys like Slim and Lyle, the tits got left out of their program. One thing he knows is if he had to give parts of his life back the last thing he'd give back is the fucking, even that sniffly girl in the Polish-American Club, she hardly said two words, and wiped her nose with a handkerchief while he was on top of her, but nevertheless she showed him something, a flourishing bush, and took him in, where it mattered. A lot of this other stuff you're supposed to be grateful for isn't where it matters. When he gets up from the deep wicker chair indignantly – he can't stand *Cheers* now that Shelley Long is gone, that guy with the Cro-Magnon brow he never did like – and goes into the kitchen to refill his bowl of Keystone Corn Chips, which not all of the stores down here carry but you can get over at the Winn Dixie on Pindo Palm Boulevard, Harry's heart confides to him a dainty little gallop, the kind of lacy riff the old swing drummers used to do, hitting the rims as well as the skins and ending with a tingling pop off the high hat, the music of his life. When this happens he gets an excited, hurried, full feeling in his chest. It doesn't hurt, it's just there, muffled inside that mess inside himself he doesn't like to think about, just like he never cared for rare roast beef, as it used to come on the take-out subs from the Chuck Wagon across Route 111 before it became the

Pizza Hut. Any sudden motion now, he feels a surge of circulation, a tilt of surprise in the head that makes one leg feel shorter than the other for a second. And the pains, maybe he imagines it, but the contractions of the bands across his ribs, the feeling of something having been sewn there from the inside, seems to cut deeper, more burningly, as though the thread the patch was sewn with is growing thicker, and red hot. When he turns off the light at night, he doesn't like feeling his head sink back onto a single pillow, his head seems sunk in a hole then, it's not that he can't breathe exactly, he just feels more comfortable, less *full*, if he has his head up on the two pillows and lies facing the ceiling. He can turn on his side but his old way of sleeping, flat on his stomach with his feet pointing down over the edge, has become impossible; there is a nest of purple slithering half-dead thoughts he cannot bear to put his face in. There is a whole host of goblins, it turns out, that Janice's warm little tightly knit body, even snoring and farting as it sometimes did, protected him from. In her absence he sleeps with his heart, listening to it race and skip when his rest is disturbed, when kids who have climbed the fence yell on the empty moonlit golf course, when a siren bleats somewhere in downtown Deleon, when a big jet from the north heads in especially low to the Southwest Florida Regional Airport, churning the air. He awakes in lavender light and then lets his heart's slowing beat drag him back under.

His dreams are delicious, like forbidden candy – intensely colored overpopulated rearrangements of old situations stored in his brain cells, rooms like the little living room at 26 Vista Crescent, with the fireplace they never used and the lamp with the driftwood base, or the old kitchen at 303 Jackson, with the wooden ice box and the gas stove with its nipples of blue flame and the porcelain table with the worn spots, skewed and new and crowded with people at the wrong ages, Mim with lots of green eye makeup at the age Mom was when they were kids, or Nelson as a tiny child sliding out from under a car in the greasy service section of Springer Motors, looking woebegone and sickly with his smudged face, or Marty Tothero and Ruth and even that nitwit Margaret Kosko, he hasn't thought of her name for thirty years, but there she was in his brain cells, just as clear with her underfed city pallor as she was that night in the booth of the Chinese restaurant, Ruth next to him and Margaret next to Mr. Tothero whose head looks lopsided and gray like that of a dying rhinoceros, the four of them eating now in the Valhalla dining room with its garbled bas-relief of Vikings and sumptuous salad bar where the dishes underneath the plastic sneeze guard are bright and various as jewels, arranged in rainbow order like the crayons in the Crayola boxes that were always among his birthday presents in February, a little stadium of waxy-smelling pointed heads there in the bright February window-light, filtered through icicles and the stunned sense of being a year older. Harry wakes from these dreams reluctantly, as if their miniaturized visions are a substance essential to his nutrition, or a whirring finely fitted machine he needs to reinsert himself into, like poor Thelma and her dialysis machine. He awakes always on his stomach, and only as his head clears and re-creates present time, establishing the felt-gray parallel lines he sees as the dawn behind the curved slats of Venetian blinds and the insistent pressure on his face as the cool Gulf breeze coming in where he left the sliding door ajar, does his solitude begin to gnaw again, and his heart to talk to him. At times it seems a tiny creature, a baby, pleading inside him for attention, for rescue, and at others a sinister intruder, a traitor muttering in code, an alien parasite nothing will expel. The pains, when they come, seem hostile and deliberate, the knives of a strengthening enemy.

He makes an appointment with Dr. Morris. He is able to get one surprisingly soon, the day after next. These doctors are scrambling down here, a glut of them, too many miners at the gold rush, the geriatric immigrants still hanging up north this time of year. The office is in one of those low stucco clinics along Route 41. Soothing music plays constantly in the waiting room, entwining with the surf-sound of traffic outside. The doctor has aged since the last appointment. He is bent-over and shuffly, with arthritic knuckles. His shrivelled jaw looks not quite clean-shaven; his nostrils are packed with black hair. His son, young Tom, pink and sleek in his mid-forties, gives Harry a freckled fat hand in the hall, and is wearing his white clinical smock over kelly-green golf slacks. He is established in an adjacent office, primed to take over the full practice. But for now the old doctor clings to his own patients. Harry tries to describe his complex sensations. Dr. Morris, with an impatient jerk of his arthritic hand, waves him toward the examination room. He has him strip to his Jockey undershorts, weighs him, tut-tuts. He seats him on the examination table and listens to his chest through his stethoscope, and taps his naked back with a soothing, knobby touch, and solemnly, silently takes Harry's hands in his. He studies the fingernails, turns them over, studies the palms, grunts. Close up, he gives off an old man's sad leathery, moldy smell.

"Well," Harry asks, "what do you think?"

"How much do you exercise?"

"Not much. Not since I got down here. I do a little gardening up north. Golf – but I've kind of run out of partners."

Dr. Morris ponders him through rimless glasses. His eyes, once a sharp blue, have that colorless sucked look to the irises. His eyebrows are messy tangled tufts of white and reddish-brown, his forehead and cheeks are flecked with small blotches and bumps. His projecting eyebrows lift, like turrets taking aim. "You should walk."

"Walk?"

"Briskly. Several miles a day. What sorts of food are you eating?"

"Oh – stuff you can heat up. TV-dinner kind of thing. My wife is still up north but she doesn't cook that much even when she's here. Now, my daughter-in-law –"

"You ever eat any of this salty junk that comes in bags?"

"Well – once in a great while."

"You should watch your sodium intake. Snack on fresh vegetables if you want to snack. Read the labels. Stay away from salt and animal fats. I think we've been through all this, when you were in the hospital" – he lifts his forearm and checks his record – "nine months ago."

"Yeah, I did for a while, I still do, it's just that day to day, it's easier –"

"To poison yourself. Don't. Don't be lazy about it. And you should lose forty pounds. Without the salt in your diet you'd lose ten in retained water in two weeks. I'll give you a diet list, if you've lost the one I gave you before. You may get dressed."

The doctor has grown smaller, or his desk has grown bigger, since Harry's last visit here. He sits down, dressed, at the desk and begins, "The pains —"

"The pains will moderate with better conditioning. Your heart doesn't like what you're feeding it. Have you been under any special stress lately?"

"Not really. Just the normal flack. A couple family problems, but they seem to be clearing up."

The doctor is writing on his prescription pad. "I want you to have blood tests and an EKG at the Community General. Then I want to consult with Dr. Olman. Depending on how the results look, it may be time for another catheterization."

"Oh Jesus. Not that again."

The messy eyebrows go up again, the prim dry lips pinch in. Not a clever generous Jewish mouth. A crabby Scots economy in the way he thinks and talks, on the verge of impatience, having seen so many hopelessly deteriorating patients in his life. "What didn't you like? Were the hot flashes painful?"

"It just felt funny," Harry tells him, "having that damn thing inside me. It's the *idea* of it."

"Well, do you prefer the idea of a life-threatening restenosis of your coronary artery? It's been, let's see, nearly six months since you had the angioplasty at" — he reads his records, with difficulty — "St. Joseph's Hospital in Brewer, Pennsylvania."

"They made me *watch*," Harry tells him. "I could see my own damn heart on TV, full of like Rice Krispies."

A tiny Scots smile, dry as a thistle. "Was that so bad?"

"It was" — he searches for the word — "insulting." In fact when you think about it his whole life from here on in is apt to be insulting. Pacemakers, crutches, wheelchairs. Impotence. Once in the Valhalla locker room a very old tall guy — somebody's guest, he never saw him again — came out of the shower and his muscles were so shrivelled his thighs from the back blended right up into his buttocks so his asshole seemed to flow down into the entire long space between his legs. His ass had lost its cheeks and Harry couldn't stop staring at the fleshly chasm.

Dr. Morris is making, in a deliberate, tremulous hand, notes to add to his folder. Without looking up, he says, "There are a number of investigative instruments now that don't involve a catheter. Scans using IV technetium 99 can identify acutely damaged heart muscle. Then there is echocardiography. We won't rush into anything. Let's see what you can do on your own, with a healthier regimen."

"Great."

"I want to see you in four weeks. Here are slips for the blood tests and EKG, and prescriptions for a diuretic and a relaxant for you at night. Don't forget the diet lists. Walk. Not violently, but vigorously, two or three miles a day."

"O.K.," Rabbit says, beginning to rise from his chair, feeling as light as a boy called into the principal's office and dismissed with a light reprimand.

But Dr. Morris fixes him with those sucked-out old blue eyes and says, "Do you have any sort of a job? According to my last information here, you were in charge of a car agency."

"That's gone. My son's taken over and my wife wants me to stay out of the kid's way. The agency was founded by her father. They'll probably wind up having to sell it off."

"Any hobbies?"

"Well, I read a lot of history. I'm a kind of a buff, you could say."

"You need more than that. A man needs an occupation. He needs something to do. The best thing for a body is a healthy interest in life. Get interested in something outside yourself, and your heart will stop talking to you."

The smell of good advice always makes Rabbit want to run the other way. He resumes rising from the chair and takes Dr. Morris' many slips of paper out into the towering heat. The few other people out on the parking lot seem tinted smoke rising from their shadows, barely existing. The radio in the Celica is full of voices yammering about Deion Sanders, about Koch losing the New York Democratic primary to a black, about the SAT scores dropping in Lee County, about President Bush's televised appeal to America's schoolchildren yesterday. "The man's not *doing* anything!" one caller howls.

Well, Rabbit thinks, doing nothing works for Bush, why not for him? On the car seat next to him Dr. Morris' prescriptions and

medical slips and Xeroxed diet sheets lift and scatter in the breeze
from the car air-conditioning. On another station he hears that
the Phillies beat the Mets last night, two to one. Dickie Thon
homered with one out in the ninth, dropping the pre-season pennant favorites five and a half games behind the once-lowly
Chicago Cubs. Harry tries to care but has trouble. Ever since
Schmidt retired. Get interested is the advice, but in truth you are
interested in less and less. It's Nature's way.

But he does begin to walk. He even drives to the Palmetto
Palm Mall and buys a pair of walking Nikes, with a bubble of
special hi-tech air to cushion each heel. He sets out between nine
and ten in the morning, after eating breakfast and digesting the
News-Press, and then again between four and five, returning to a
nap and then dinner and then television and a page or two of his
book and a sound sleep, thanks to the walking. He explores
Deleon. First, he walks the curving streets of low stucco houses
within a mile of Valhalla Village, with unfenced front yards of tall-
ish tough grass half-hiding bits of dried palm frond, a Florida texture in that, a cozy sere Florida scent. Encountering a UPS man
delivering or a barking small dog – a flat-faced Pekinese with its
silky long hair done up in ribbons – is like finding life on Mars.
Then, growing ever fonder of his Nikes (that bubble in the heel,
he thought at first it was just a gimmick but maybe it does add
bounce), he makes his way to the downtown and the river, where
the town first began, as a fort in the Seminole wars and a shipping
point for cattle and cotton.

He discovers, some blocks back from the beachfront and the
green glass hotels, old neighborhoods where shadowy big spicy
gentle trees, live oaks and gums and an occasional banyan widening out on its crutches, overhang wooden houses once painted
white but flaking down to gray bareness, with louvered windows
and roofs of corrugated tin. Music rises from within these houses,
scratchy radio music, and voices raised in argument or jabbery
jubilation, bright fragments of overheard life. The sidewalks are
unpaved, small paths such as cats make have been worn diagonally
between the trees, in and out of private property, the parched grass
growing in patches, packed dirt littered with pods and nuts. It
reminds Harry of those neighborhoods he blundered into trying

to get out of Savannah, but also of the town of his childhood, Mt. Judge in the days of Depression and distant war, when people still sat on their front porches, and there were vacant lots and odd-shaped cornfields, and men back from work in the factories would water their lawns in the evenings, and people not long off the farm kept chickens in back-yard pens, and peddled the eggs for odd pennies. Chickens clucking and pecking and suddenly squawking: he hasn't heard that sound for forty years, and hasn't until now realized what he's been missing. For chicken coops tucked here and there dot this sleepy neighborhood he has discovered.

In the daytime here, under the heavy late-summer sun, there are few people moving, just women getting in and out of cars with pre-school children. The slams of their car doors carry a long way down the dusty straight streets, under the live oaks. At some corners there are grocery stores that also sell beer and wine in the permissive Southern way, and pastel-painted bars with the door open on a dark interior, and video rental places with horror and kung-fu tapes displayed in the window, the boxes' colors being bleached by the sun. One day he passes an old-fashioned variety store, in a clapboarded one-story building, displaying all sorts of innocent things – erector sets, model airplane kits, Chinese-checker boards and marbles – that he hadn't known were still being sold. He almost goes in but doesn't dare. He is too white.

Toward late afternoon, when he takes his second walk of the day, the neighborhood begins to breathe, a quickness takes hold, men and boys return to it, and Rabbit walks more briskly, proclaiming with his stride that he is out for the exercise, just passing through, not spying. These blocks are black, and there are miles of them, a vast stagnant economic marsh left over from Deleon's Southern past, supplying the hotels and condos with labor, with waiters and security guards and chambermaids. To Harry, whose Deleon has been a glitzy community of elderly refugees, these blocks feel like a vast secret, and as the shadows lengthen under the trees, and the chickens cease their day-long clucking, his senses widen to grasp the secret better, as when in whispering knickers he would move through Mt. Judge unseen, no taller than a privet hedge, trying to grasp the unspeakable adult meaning of the lit windows, of the kitchen noises filtering across the yards mysterious and damp as jungles. An unseen child would cry, a dog would bark, and he would tingle with the excitement of simply being himself, at this point of time and space, with worlds to know and forever to live, Harold C. Angstrom, called Hassy in those lost days never to be relived. He prolongs his walks, feeling stronger, more comfortable in this strange city where he is at last beginning to exist as more than a visitor; but as darkness approaches, and the music from the glowing slatted windows intensifies, he begins to feel conspicuous, his whiteness begins to glimmer, and he heads back to the car, which he has taken to parking in a lot or at a meter downtown, as base for his widening explorations.

Coming back one day around six-thirty, just in time for a shower and a look at the news while his TV dinner heats in the oven, he is startled by the telephone's ringing. He has ceased to listen for it as intensely as in that first lonely week. When it does ring, it has been one of those recordings ("Hello there, this is Sandra") selling health insurance or a no-frills burial plan or reduced-fee investment services, going through all the numbers by computer, you wonder how it pays, Harry always hangs up and can't imagine who would listen and sign up for this stuff. But this time the caller is Nelson, his son.

"Dad?"

"Yes," he says, gathering up his disused voice, trying to imagine what you can say to a son whose wife you've boffed. "Nellie," he says, "how the hell is everybody?"

The distant voice is gingerly, shy, also not sure what is appropriate. "We're fine, pretty much."

"You're staying clean?" He didn't mean to take the offensive so sharply; the other voice, fragile in its distance, is stunned into silence for a moment.

"You mean the drugs. Sure. I don't even think about coke, except at NA meetings. Like they say, you give your life over to a higher power. You ought to try it, Dad."

"I'm working on it. Listen, no kidding, I am. I'm proud of you, Nelson. Keep taking it a day at a time, that's all anybody can do."

Again, the boy seems momentarily stuck. Maybe this came over as too preachy. Who is he to preach? Shit, he was just trying to share, like you're supposed to. Harry holds his tongue.

"There's been so much going on around here," Nelson tells him, "I really haven't thought about myself that much. A lot of my problem, I think, was idleness. Hanging around the lot all day waiting for some action, for the customers to show up, really preys on your self-confidence. I mean, you have no control. It was degrading."

"I did it, for fifteen years I did it, every day."

"Yeah, but you have a different sort of temperament. You're more happy-go-lucky."

"Stupid, you mean."

"Hey Dad, I didn't call up to quarrel. This isn't exactly fun for me, I've been putting it off. But I got some things to say."

"O.K., say 'em." *This isn't working out.* He doesn't want to be this way, he is putting his anger at Janice onto the kid. Her silence has hurt him. He can't stop, adding, "You've sure taken your time saying anything, I've been down here all by myself for two weeks. I saw old Dr. Morris and he thinks I'm so far gone I should stop eating."

"Well," Nelson says back, "if you were so crazy to talk you could have come over that night instead of getting in the car and disappearing. We weren't going to kill you, we just wanted to talk it through, to understand what had happened, really, in terms of family dynamics. Pru's as good as admitted it was a way of getting in touch with her own father."

"With Blubberlips Lubell? Tell her thanks a lot." But he is not displeased to hear Nelson taking a firmer tone with him. You're not a man in this world until you've got on top of your father. In his own case, it was easier, the system had beaten Pop so far down already. "Coming over there that night felt like a set-up," he explains to Nelson.

"Well, Mom didn't think any of us should try to get in touch if that's the kind of cowardly trick you were going to pull. She wasn't too happy you telephoned Pru instead of her, either."

"I kept trying our number but she's never home."

"Well, whatever. She wanted me to let you know a couple things. One, she has an offer on the house, not as much as she'd hoped for, one eighty-five, but the market's pretty flat right now and she thinks we should take it. It would reduce the debt to Brewer Trust to the point where we could manage it."

"Let me get this straight. This is the Penn Park house you're talking about? The little gray stone house I've always loved?"

"What other house could you think? We can't sell the Mt. Judge house – where would we all live?"

"Tell me, Nelson, I'm just curious. How does it feel to have smoked up your parents' house in crack?"

The boy begins to sound more like himself. He whines, "I keep *tell*ing you, I was never that much into crack. The crack just came into it toward the end, it was so much more convenient than free-basing. I'm *sor*ry, Jesus. I went to rehab, I took the vows, I'm trying to make amends like they say. Who are you to still be on my case?"

Who indeed? "O.K.," Rabbit says. "Sorry to mention it. What else did your mother tell you to tell me?"

"Hyundai *is* interested in the lot, the location is just what they want and don't have. They'd enlarge the building out toward the back like I always wanted to do." *Goodbye, Paraguay*, Rabbit thinks. "They'd keep the service people on, with a little retraining, and some of the sales force, Elvira might go over to Rudy's on 422. Hyundai's made her a counteroffer. But they don't want *me*. No way. Word gets around, I guess, among these Oriental companies."

"I guess," Harry says. Too much *ninjō*, not enough *giri*. "I'm sorry."

"Don't be sorry, Dad. It frees me up. I'm thinking of becoming a social worker."

"A *so*cial worker!"

"Sure, why not? Help other people instead of myself for a change. It's a two-year course at the Penn State extension, I could still get in for this October."

"Sure, why not, come to think of it," Rabbit agrees. He is beginning to dislike himself, for being so agreeable, for wanting to worm back into everybody's good graces.

"Me and the lawyers all think if it goes through we should lease to Hyundai rather than sell; if we sell the house in Penn Park we wouldn't need any more capital and should keep the lot as an investment, Mom says it's going to be worth *millions* by the year 2000."

"Wow," Harry says unenthusiastically. "You and your mom are quite a team. Anything else to hit me with?"

"Well, this maybe isn't any of your business, but Pru thought it was. We're trying to get pregnant."

"We?"

"We want to have a third child. All this has made us realize how much we've been neglecting our marriage and how much really we have invested in making it *work*. Not only for Judy and Roy, but for our*selves*. We love each other, Dad."

Maybe this is supposed to make him feel jealous, and there is a pang, just under the right ventricle. But Rabbit's basic emotion is relief, at being excused from having to keep any kind of candle burning at Pru's shrine. Good luck to her, her and her sweet slum hunger. "Great," he tells the boy. He can't resist adding, "Though I'm not so sure social workers make enough to support three kids." And, getting mad, feeling squeezed, he goes on, "And tell your mother I'm not so sure I want to sign our house away. It's not like the lot, we're co-owners, and she needs my signature on the sales agreement. If we split up, my signature ought to be worth quite a bit, tell her."

"Split up?" The boy sounds frightened. "Who's saying anything about splitting up?"

"Well," Harry says, "we seem split up now. At least I don't see her down here, unless she's under the bed. But don't you worry about it, Nelson. You've been through this before and I felt lousy about it. You get on with your own life. It sounds like you're doing fine. I'm proud of you. Or did I say that?"

"But everything kind of depends on selling the Penn Park house."

"Tell her I'll think about it. Tell Judy and Roy I'll give 'em a call one of these days."

"But, Dad –"

"Nelson, I got this low-cal frozen dinner in the oven and the buzzer went off five minutes ago. Tell your mother to call me sometime if she wants to talk about it. Must run. Terrific to talk to you. Really." He hangs up.

He has been buying low-cal frozen meals, raw vegetables like cabbage and carrots, and no more sodium-laden munchies. He has lost three pounds on the bathroom scale, if he weighs himself naked and right in the morning after taking a crap. At night, to keep himself away from the TV and the breadbox in the kitchen drawer and the beer in the refrigerator, he gets into bed and reads the book Janice gave him for last Christmas. Its author has joined Roy Orbison and Bart Giamatti in that beyond where some celebrities like Elvis and Marilyn expand like balloons and become gods but where most shrivel and shrink into yellowing obituaries not much bigger than Harry's will be in the Brewer *Standard*. In the *News-Press* he doesn't expect to get an inch. He read in her obituary that the author had been a niece of Roosevelt's Secretary of the Treasury Henry Morgenthau, Jr. Harry remembers Morgenthau: the pointy-nosed guy who kept urging him and his schoolmates to buy war stamps with their pennies. It's a small world, and a long life in a way.

He has reached the exciting part of the book, where, after years of frustration and starvation and lousy support from his fellow would-be Americans, Washington has hopes of joining up with a French fleet sailing from the Caribbean to trap Cornwallis and his army at York in the Chesapeake Bay. It seems impossible that it will work. The logistics of it need perfect timing, and the communications take weeks, ships to land and back. Anyway, what's in it for France? *Instead of an aggressive ally, they were tied to a dependent client, unable to establish a strong government and requiring transfusions of men-at-arms and money to keep its war effort alive. The war, like all wars, was proving more expensive for the Bourbons than planned.* What was in it for the soldiers? *The American troops, for too long orphans of the battle, unkempt, underfed and unpaid while Congress rode in carriages and dined at well-laid tables, would not march without pay.* What was in it for Washington? He couldn't even have known he'd get his face on the dollar bill. But he hangs in there, patching, begging, scrambling, his only assets the fatheadedness of the British commanders, all gouty noblemen wishing they were home in their castles, and the fact that, just like in Vietnam, the natives weren't basically friendly. Washington gets his troops across the Hudson while Clinton cowers defensively in New York. De Grasse gets his fleet heading north because Admiral Rodney cautiously chooses the defense of Barbados over pursuit. But, still, the odds of the troops and the ships arriving at the Chesapeake at the same time and Cornwallis remaining a sitting duck in Yorktown are preposterous. All that transport, all those men trudging and horses galloping along the New World's sandy, woodsy roads, winding through forests, past lonely clearings, among bears and wolves and chipmunks and Indians and passenger pigeons, it makes Harry sleepy to think about. The tangle of it all, the trouble. He reads ten pages a night; his is a slow march.

He does not always gravitate in his health walks to the black section of Deleon; he discovers and explores posh streets he never dreamed were there, long roads parallel to the beach, giving the passerby glimpses of backs of houses that front on the ocean, wooden back stairs and sundecks, three-car garages at the end of driveways surfaced in crushed seashells, plantings of hibiscus and jacaranda, splashing sounds coming from a fenced-in swimming pool, the purr of air-conditioners lost amid the retreating and advancing shush of the surf. *Posh, shoosh.* Some people have it made; not for them a condo where they steal your view of the Gulf from the balcony. No matter how hard you climb, there are always the rich above you, who got there without effort. Lucky stiffs, holding you down, making you discontent so you buy more of the crap advertised on television.

Occasional breaks in the developed oceanfront property permit a look at the Gulf, its striped sails and scooting jet skis, its parachutes being pulled by powerboats, its far gray stationary freighters. Bicyclers in bathing suits pass him with a *whirr*; a beefy young mailman in blue-gray shorts and socks to match pushes along one of these pouches on rubber wheels they have now, like baby strollers. We're getting soft. A nation of couch potatoes. The man who brought the mail to Jackson Road, he forgets his name, an iron-haired man with a handsome unhappy face, Mom said his wife had left him, used to carry this scuffed leather pouch, leaning to one side against its pull especially on Fridays when the magazines came to the houses, *Life* and the *Post*. Mr. Abendroth. That was his name. Left by his wife: Harry as a boy used to try to imagine what could have been so terribly wrong with him, to earn such a disgrace in life.

His Nikes with the bubbles of air in the heels take him along crushed-shell sidewalks, so white they hurt his eyes when the sun is high. And he walks through an area of marinas cut into coral shell, neat straight streets of water sliced out, full of powerboats tied up obedient and empty, their rub rails tapping the sliced coral, their curved sides seeming to tremble and twitch in the sunlight reflected in bobbling stripes off the calm water as it lightly kicks and laps. *Tap. Lap.* No Trespassing signs abound, but not so much for him, a respectable-looking white man past middle age. Each boat ties up as much money as a house used to cost and a number of them no doubt are involved in cocaine smuggling, put-putting out in the dead of the night when the moon is down, crime and the sea have always mixed, pirates ever since there have been ships, law ends with the land, man is nothing out there, a few bubbles as he goes down under the mindless waves: that must be why Harry has always been afraid of it, the water. He loves freedom but a grassy field is his idea of enough. People down here are crazy about boats but not him. Give him terra firma. Away from the water he walks miles of plain neighborhoods, glorified cabins put up after the war for people without much capital who yet wanted a piece of the sun Washington won for them or else were born here, this strange thin vacation-land their natural home, their houses shedding paint like a sunbather's clothes, surrounded not by barberry and yew bushes but spiky cactuses fattening in the baking heat, America too hot and dry really for European civilization to take deep root.

But it is the widespread black section that draws him back, he doesn't quite know why, whether because he is exerting his national right to go where he pleases or because this ignored part of Deleon is in some way familiar, he's been there before, before his life got too soft. On the Monday after a pretty good weekend for blacks – a black Miss America got elected, and Randall Cunningham brought the Eagles back from being down to the Redskins twenty to nothing – Rabbit ventures several blocks farther than he has dared walk before and comes upon, beyond an abandoned high school built about when Brewer High was, an ochre-brick edifice with tall gridded windows and a piece of Latin in cement over the main entrance, a recreation field – a wide tan emptiness under the sun, with a baseball diamond and backstop at the far end, a pair of soccer goals set up in the outfield, and, nearer the street, two pitted clay tennis courts with wire nets slack and bent from repeated assaults and, also of pale tamped earth, a basketball court. A backboard and netless hoop lifted up on pipe legs preside at either end. A small pack of black boys are scrimmaging around one basket. Legs, shouts. Puffs of dust rise from their striving, stop-and-starting feet. Some benches have been placed in an unmowed strip of seedy blanched weeds next to the cement sidewalk. The benches are backless so you can sit facing the street or facing the field. Rabbit seats himself on the end of one, facing neither way, so he can watch the basketball while seeming to be doing something else, just resting a second on his way through, not looking at anything, minding his own business.

The kids, six of them, in shorts and tank tops, vary in heights and degrees of looseness, but all have that unhurried look he likes to see, missing shots or making them, passing back out and then crossing over in a screen, dribbling as if to drive in and then stopping dead to pass off in a droll behind-the-back toss, imitating the fancy stuff they see on television, all together making a weave, nobody trying too hard, it's a long life, a long afternoon. Their busy legs are up to their knees in a steady haze of pink dust lifting from the clay, their calves dulled but for where sweat makes dark rivulets, their sneakers solidly coated a rosy earth color. There is a breeze here, stirred up by the empty space stretching to the baseball backstop. Rabbit's watch says four o'clock, school is over, but the brick high school has been abandoned, the real action is elsewhere, at some modern low glassy high school you take a bus to, out on the bulldozed edges of the city. Rabbit is happy to think that the world isn't yet too crowded to have a few of these underused pockets left. Grass, he observes, has crept onto the dirt court, in the middle, where the pounding, pivoting feet rarely come. Shallow semicircular troughs have been worn around the baskets at either end.

Though he is sitting some distance away – a good firm chip shot, or a feathered wedge – the players eye him. They're doing this for themselves, not as a show for some fat old honky walking around where he shouldn't be. Where's his car? Feeling heat from their sidelong glances, not wanting so delicate a relation to turn awkward, Harry sighs ostentatiously and heaves himself up from the bench and walks away the way he came, taking note of the street signs so he can find this peaceful place again. If he comes every day he'll blend in. Blacks don't have this racist thing whites do, about keeping their neighborhoods pure. They can't be too angry these days, with their third Miss America just elected. The funny thing about the final judges' panel, it held two celebrities he feels he knows, has taken into himself, *loves*, actually: Phylicia Rashad, who for his money is the real star of *The Cosby Show*, with those legs and that nice loose smile, and Mike Schmidt, who had the grace to pack it in when he could no longer produce. So there is life after death of a sort. Schmidt judges. Skeeter lives. And the weekend before last, a young black girl beat Chrissie Evert in the last U.S. Open match she'll ever play. She packed it in too. There comes a time.

Now the *News-Press* wears daily banner headlines tracking Hurricane Hugo – *Deadly Hugo roars into islands*, *Hugo rips into Puerto Rico*. Tuesday, he walks in the expensive beachfront areas and scans the sky for hurricane signs, for clouds God's finger might write, and reads none. In the hall that evening, happening to be standing with him at the elevators, Mrs. Zabritski turns those veiny protuberant eyes up at him out of her skeletal face and pronounces, "Terrible thing."

"What is?"

"The thing coming," she says, her white hair looking already wind-tossed, lifted out from her skull in all directions.

"Oh, it'll never get here," Harry reassures her. "It's all this media hype. You know, hype, phony hullabaloo. They have to make news out of something, every night."

"Yeah?" Mrs. Zabritski says, coyly. The way her neck twists into her hunched shoulders gives her head a flirtatious tilt she may not mean. But then again she may. Didn't he hear on some TV show that even in the Nazi death camps there were romances? This windowless corridor, with its peach-and-silver wallpaper, is an eerie cryptlike space he is always anxious to get out of. The big vase on the marble half-moon table, with green glaze running into golden, could be holding someone's ashes. Still the elevator refuses to arrive. His female companion clears her throat and volunteers, "Wednesday buffet tomorrow. I like extra much the buffet."

"Me too," he tells her. "Except I can't choose and then I wind up taking too much and then eating it all." What is she suggesting, that they go together? That they have a date? He's stopped telling her that Janice is coming down.

"Do you do the kosher?"

"I don't know. Those scallops wrapped in bacon, are they kosher?"

She stares at him as if he were the crazy one, stares so hard her eyeballs seem in danger of snapping the bloody threads that hold them fast in their sockets. Then she must have decided he was joking, for a careful stiff smile slowly spreads across the lower half of her face, crisscrossed by wrinkles like a quilt sewn of tiny squares of skin. He thinks of that little sniffly slut in the Polish-American Club, her silken skin below the waist, below the sweater, and feels bitter toward Janice, for leaving him at his age at the mercy of women. He eats at his table alone but is so disturbed by Mrs. Zabritski's making a pass at him that he takes two Nitrostats to quell his heart.

After dinner, in bed, on September 1, 1781, the French troops make a dazzling impression upon the citizens of Philadelphia. *Ecstatic applause greeted the dazzling spectacle of the French as they passed in review in their bright white uniforms and white plumes. Wearing colored lapels and collars of pink, green, violet or blue identifying their regiments, they were the most brilliantly appointed soldiers in Europe.* Joseph Reed, the President of the State of Pennsylvania, entertained the French officers at a ceremonial dinner *of which the main feature was an immense ninety-pound turtle with soup served in its shell.* Talk about cholesterol. Didn't seem to bother them, but, then, how old did those poor devils get to be? Not fifty-six, most of them. The troops are scared to march south for fear of malaria. Rochambeau has talked Washington out of attacking New York, and at this point seems to be the brains of the Revolution. He wants to rendezvous with De Grasse at the head of the Chesapeake. De Grasse has evaded Hood by sailing the back-alley route between the Bahamas and Cuba. It will never work.

Hugo heading for U.S., the *News-Press* headline says next morning. For breakfast now, Harry has switched from Frosted Flakes to Nabisco Shredded Wheat 'n' Bran, though he forgets exactly why, something about fiber and the bowels. He does hope he never reaches the point where he has to think all the time about shitting. Ma Springer, toward the end, got to talking about her bowel movements like they were family heirlooms, each one precious. On the evening news half the commercials are for laxatives and the other half for hemorrhoid medicine, as if only assholes watch the news. That walking corpse in the locker room. After breakfast Harry walks along Pindo Palm Boulevard and brings back a bag of groceries from Winn Dixie, passing up the Keystone Corn Chips and going heavy on the low-cal frozen dinners. The day's predicted showers come at noon but seem over by three and in a kind of trance Rabbit drives into downtown Deleon, parks at a two-hour meter, and walks the mile to the playing field he discovered Monday. Today two sets of boys are on the dirt court, each using one basket. One set is energetically playing a two-on-two, but the other consists of three boys at a desultory game of what he used to call Horse. You take a shot, and if it goes in the next guy has to make the same shot, and if he misses he's an H, or an H-O, and when he's a HORSE he's out. Rabbit takes the bench within a chip shot of this group and frankly watches – after all, is it a free country or not?

The three are in their early teens at best, and don't know what to make of this sudden uninvited audience. One of these old ofays after some crack or a black boy's dick? Their languid motions stiffen, they jostle shoulders and pass each other sliding silent messages that make one another giggle. One of them perhaps deliberately lets a pass flip off his hands and bounce Harry's way. He leans off his bench end and stops it left-handed, not his best hand but it remembers. It remembers exactly. That taut pebbled roundness, the smooth seams between, the little circlet for taking the air valve. A big pebbled ball that wants to fly. He flips it back, a bit awkwardly, sitting, but still with a little zing to show he's handled one before. Somewhat satisfied, the trio resume Horse, trying skyhooks, under-the-basket layups, fall-back jumpers, crazy improvised underhanded or sidearm shots that now and then go in, by accident or miracle. One such wild toss rockets off the rim and comes Rabbit's way. This time he stands up with the ball and advances with it toward the boys. He feels himself big, a big shape with the sun behind him. His shadow falls across the face of the nearest boy, who wears an unravelling wool cap of many colors. Another boy has the number 8 on his tank top. "What's the game?" Harry asks them. "You call it Horse?"

"We call it Three," the wool cap answers reluctantly. "Three misses, you out." He reaches for the ball but Rabbit lifts it out of his reach.

"Lemme take a shot, could I?"

The boys' eyes consult, they figure this is the way to get the ball back. "Go 'head," Wool Cap says.

Harry is out on an angle to the left maybe twenty feet and as his knees dip and his right arm goes up he feels the heaviness of the years, all those blankets of time, since he did this last. A bank shot. He has the spot on the backboard in his sights, but the ball doesn't quite have the length and, instead of glancing off and in, jams between the wood and hoop and kicks back into the hands of Number 8.

"Hey man," the third one, the one who looks most Hispanic and most sullen, taunts him, "you're history!"

"I'm rusty," Rabbit admits. "The air down here is different than I'm used to."

"You want to see somebody sink that shot?" Number 8, the tallest, asks him. He stands where Harry stood, and opens his mouth and lets his pink tongue dangle the way Michael Jordan does. He gently paws the air above his forehead so the ball flies from his long loose brown hand. But he misses also, hitting the rim on the right. This breaks some of the ice. Rabbit holds still, waiting to see what they will do with him.

The boy in the hat of concentric circles, a Black Muslim hat, Harry imagines, takes the rebound and now says, "Let me sink that mother," and indeed it does go in, though the boy kind of flings it and, unlike Number 8, will never be a Michael Jordan.

Now or never. Harry asks, "Hey, how about letting me play one game of, whaddeya call it, Three? One quick game and I'll go. I'm just out walking for exercise."

The sullen Hispanic-looking boy says to the others, "Why you lettin' this man butt in? This ain't for my blood," and goes off and sits on the bench. But the other two, figuring perhaps that one white man is the tip of the iceberg and the quickest way around trouble is through it, oblige the interloper and let him play. He goes a quick two misses down – a floating double-pump Number 8 pulls off over the stretched hands of an imaginary crowd of defenders, and a left-handed pop the wool hat establishes and Number 8 matches – but then Rabbit finds a ghost of his old touch and begins to dominate. Take a breath of oxygen, keep your eye on the front of the rim, and it gets easy. The distance between your hands and the hoop gets smaller and smaller. You and it, ten feet off the ground, above it all. He even shows them a stunt he perfected in the gravel alleys of Mt. Judge, the two-handed backwards set, the basket sighted upside, the head bent way back.

Seen upside down, how blue and stony-gray the cloudy sky appears – an abyss, a swallowing, upheaving kind of earth! He sinks the backwards set shot and all three of them laugh. These kids never take two-handed set shots, it's not black style, and by doing nothing else from five steps out Rabbit might have cleaned up. But, since they were good sports to let him in, he lets himself get sloppy-silly on a few one-handers, and Number 8 gains back control.

"Here you see a Kareem sky-hook," the boy says, and does sink a hook from about six feet out, on the right.

"When *I* was a kid," Rabbit tells them, "a guy called Bob Pettit, played for St. Louis, used to specialize in those." Almost on purpose, he misses. "That gives me three. I'm out. Thanks for the game, gentlemen."

They murmur wordlessly, like bees, at this farewell. To the boy sitting on the bench out of protest, he says, "All yours, amigo." Bending down to pick up the furled golf umbrella he brought along in case it rained again, Harry smiles to see that his walking Nikes are coated with a pink-tan dust just like these black boys' sneakers.

He walks back to his car at the meter feeling lightened, purged like those people on the Milk of Magnesia commercials who drift around in fuzzy focus in their bathrobes ecstatic at having become "regular." His bit of basketball has left him feeling cocky. He stops at a Joy Food Store on the way back to Valhalla Village and buys a big bag of onion-flavored potato chips and a frozen lasagna to heat up in the oven instead of going down to the buffet and risking running into Mrs. Zabritski. He's beginning to think he owes her something, for keeping him company on the floor, for being another lonely refugee.

In the condo, the phone is silent. The evening news is all Hugo and looting in St. Croix and St. Thomas in the wake of the devastation and a catastrophic health-plan repeal in Washington that gets big play down here because of all the elderly and a report on that French airliner that disappeared on the way from Chad to Paris. The wreckage has been found, scattered over a large area of the Sahara desert. From the wide distribution of the debris it would appear to have been a bomb. *Just like that plane over Lockerbie,* Rabbit thinks. His cockiness ebbs. Every plane had a bomb ticking away in its belly. We can explode any second.

The rooms and furniture of the condo in these days he's been living here alone have taken on the tension and menace of a living person who is choosing to remain motionless. At night he can feel the rooms breathe and think. They are thinking about him. The blank TV, the blond sofa, the birds made of small white shells, the taut bedspread in the room where Nelson and Pru stayed last New Year's, the aqua kitchen cabinets that seemed too intense once they were painted and still do, the phone that refuses to ring all have a certain power, the ability to outlast him. He is flesh, they are inanimate things. The well-sealed hollow space that greeted his arrival seventeen days ago now does brim with fear, with a nervous expectancy that the babble of the TV, the headlines in the paper, the ticking warmth of the oven and the minutes ticking down on the timer panel, even the soft scuffle and rustle of his body's own movements hold at bay for their duration; but when these small commotions are over the silence comes back, the presence of absence, the unanswerable question that surrounds his rustling upright stalk of warm blood. The lasagna is gluey and like napalm on the tongue but he eats it all, a portion for two, while flipping channels between Jennings and Brokaw looking for the best clips of hurricane damage and wind, wild wet wind screaming through rooms just like this one, knocking out entire glass sliding doors and skimming them around like pie plates. Everything flies loose, the world is crashing, nothing in life can be nailed down. Terrific.

He suddenly needs, as suddenly as the need to urinate comes upon a man taking diuretics, to talk to his grandchildren. He is a grandfather, they can't deny him that. He has to look up Nelson's number in the address book on the fake-bamboo desk, it was changed last winter, he's forgotten it already, your mind at Harry's age lets all sorts of things slip. He finds the book, kept in Janice's half-formed schoolgirl hand, in a variety of slants. He dials, having to hang up once when he thinks he might have dialled an 8 for a 9. Pru answers. Her voice is casual, light, tough. He almost hangs up again.

"Hi," he says. "It's me."

"Harry, you really shouldn't be –"

"I'm not. I don't want to talk to you. I want to talk to my grandchildren. Isn't it about time for Roy's birthday?"

"Next month."

"Just think. He'll be four."

"He *is* four. He'll be five."

"Time for kindergarten," Harry says. "Incredible. I understand you and little Nellie are working on a third. Terrific."

"Well, we're just seeing what happens."

"No more condoms, huh? What about him and AIDS?"

"Harry, please. This is none of your business. But he was tested, if you must know, and is HIV-negative."

"Terrific. One more thing off my mind. The kid's straight, and the kid's clean. Pru, I think I'm going crazy down here. My dreams – they're like cut-up comic strips."

He can picture her smiling wryly at this, her mouth tugging down on one side, her free hand pushing back from her forehead with two fingers stray strands of carrot-colored hair. Sexy; but what has it got her? A would-be social worker for a husband, living space in another woman's house, and a future of drudging and watching her looks fade away in the mirror. Her voice in his ear is like a periscope glimpse, blurred by salt spray, of the upper world. She is up there, he is down here.

Her tone is changing, sinking toward friendliness. Once you've fucked them, their voices ever hold these warm grainy traces. "Harry, what are you doing down there for amusement?"

"Oh, I walk around a lot, getting to know the town. Nice old town, Deleon. Tell Janice if you ever see her that there's a rich Jewish widow giving me the eye."

"She's right here for dinner, actually. We're celebrating because she sold a house. Not *your* house, she can't sell that until you agree, but a house for the real-estate company, for Pearson and Schrack. She's showing houses for them weekends, till she gets her license."

"That's fantastic! Put her on and I'll congratulate her."

Pru hesitates. "I'll have to ask her if she wants to talk to you."

His stomach feels hollow suddenly, scared. "You don't have to do that. I called to talk to the kids, honest."

"I'll put Judy on, she's right at my elbow, all excited about the *hur*ricane. You take care of yourself, Harry."

"Sure. You know me. Careful."

"I know you," she says. "A crazy man." She sounded Dutch, the cozy settled way she said that. She's assimilating. One more middle-aged Brewer broad.

There is a clatter and whispering and now Judy has the phone and cries, "Oh Grandpa, we're all so worried about you and the *hur*ricane!"

He says, "Who's all so worried? Not my Judy. Not after she brought me in on that crippled Sunfish. The TV says Hugo is going to hit the Carolinas. That's six hundred miles away. It was sunny here today, mostly. I played a little basketball with some kids not much older than you."

"It rained here. All day."

"And you're having Grandma to dinner tonight," he tells her.

Judy says, "She says she doesn't want to talk to you. What did you do to make her so mad?"

"Oh, I don't know. Maybe I channel-surfed too much. Hey, Judy, know what? On the way down I drove right by Disney World, and I promised myself that the next time you're here we'll all go."

"You don't have to. A lot of the kids at school have been, and they say it gets boring."

"How's school going?"

"I like the teachers and all but I can't stand the other kids. They're all assholes."

"Don't say that. Such language. What's the matter, do they ignore you?"

"I wish they would. They tease me about my freckles. They call me Carrottop." Her little voice breaks.

"Well, then. They like you. They think you're terrific. Just don't wear too much lipstick until you're fifteen. Remember what I told you last time we talked?"

"You said don't force it."

"Right. Don't force it. Let nature do its work. Do what your mommy and daddy tell you. They love you very much."

She wearily sighs, "I know."

"You're the light of their lives. You ever hear that expression before, 'the light of their lives'?"

"No."

"Well then, you've learned something. Now go do your thing, honey. Could you put Roy on?"

"He's too dumb to talk."

"No he's not. Put him on. Tell him his grandpa wants to give him some words of wisdom."

The phone clatters down and in the background there is a kind of shredded wheat of family noises — he thinks he even hears Janice's voice, sounding decisive the way Ma Springer's used to. Footsteps approach through the living room he knows so well — the Barcalounger, the picture windows with the drawn curtains, the piecrust-edged knickknack table, though the green glass egg, with the teardrop of emptiness inside, that used to sit on it is now on the shelves here, a few feet from his eyes. Pru's voice says, "Janice says she doesn't want to talk to you, Harry, but here's Roy."

"Hi, Roy," Harry says.

Silence. God on the line again.

"How's it going up there? I hear it rained all day."

More silence.

"Are you being a good boy?"

Silence, but with a touch of breathing in it.

"You know," Harry says, "it may not feel like much to you right now, but these are important years."

"Hi, Grandpa," the child's voice at last pronounces.

"Hi," Harry has to respond, though it puts him back to the beginning. "I miss you down here," he says.

Silence.

"A little birdie comes to the balcony every morning and asks, 'Where's Roy? Where's Roy?'"

Silence, which is what this lie deserves. But then the child comes out with the other thing he's perhaps been coached to say: "I love you, Grandpa."

"Well, I love *you*, Roy. Happy Birthday, by the way, for next month. Five years old! Think of it."

"Happy Birthday," the child's voice repeats, in that oddly deep, manlike way it sometimes has.

Harry finds himself waiting for more but then realizes there is no more. "O.K.," he says, "I guess that does it, Roy. I've loved talking with you. Give everybody my love. Hang up now. You can hang up."

Silence, and then a clumsy soft clatter, and the buzz of a dead line. Strange, Rabbit thinks, hanging up his own receiver, that he had to make the child do it first. Chicken in a suicide pact.

Alone, he is terrified by the prospect of an entire evening in these rooms. It is seven-thirty, plenty of time to still make the buffet, though his mouth feels tender from all that hot lasagna and the bagful of onion potato chips, full of sharp edges and salt. He will just go down and pick a few low-cal items off the buffet table. Talking to his family has exhilarated him; he feels them all safely behind him. Without showering, he puts on a shirt, coat, and tie. Mrs. Zabritski isn't at the elevator. In the half-empty Mead Hall, under the berserk gaze of the Viking warriors in the big ceramic mural, he helps himself generously to, among other items, the scallops wrapped in bacon. The mix of textures, of crisp curved bacon and rubbery yielding scallops, in his sensitive mouth feels so delicious his appetite becomes bottomless. He goes back for more, and more creamed asparagus and potato pancakes, then suddenly is so full his heart feels squeezed. He takes a Nitrostat and skips dessert and coffee, even decaf. Carefully he treads back across the alien texture of that Florida grass and the carpeted traffic island beneath the warm dome of stars, really a deep basin we are looking down into, he saw that this afternoon when he did the upside-down set shot, we are stuck fast to the Earth like flies on a ceiling. He feels stuffed and dizzy. The air is thick, the Milky Way just barely shows, like the faint line of fair hair up the middle of some women's bellies.

He gets back into the condo in time for the last fifteen minutes of *Growing Pains*, the only show on TV where every member of the family is repulsive, if you count Roseanne's good-old-boy husband as not repulsive. Then he flips back and forth between *Unsolved Mysteries* on Channel 20 and an old Abbott and Costello on 36 that must have been funnier when it came out, the same year he graduated from high school. Costello's yips seem mechanical and aggravating, and Abbott looks old, and cruel when he slaps his fat buddy. People yelled and snapped at one another like animals then. Maybe the Sixties did some good after all. Among the commercials that keep interrupting is that Nissan Infiniti one of crickets and lily ponds, no car at all, just pure snob Nature. The Lexus commercials he's seen are almost as vague – an idyllic road shiny with rain. They're both skirting the issue: can the Japanese establish a luxury image? Or will people with thirty-five thousand to burn prefer to buy European? Thank God, Harry no longer has to care. Jake down toward Pottstown has to care, but not Harry.

He brushes his teeth, taking care to floss and rinse with Peridex. Without Janice here he is becoming staid in his habits, another old-fogey bachelor fussing with his plumbing and nostril hairs. Nostril hairs: he never wants to look like Dr. Morris. His double dinner burns in his stomach but when he sits on the toilet nothing comes out. Phillips' Milk of Magnesia, he should get some. Another of their commercials has a black man talking about MOM and that was unfortunate, his color made the shit too real. In bed, on the march to Yorktown, the allied armies come upon British atrocities around Williamsburg. De Grasse's Swedish aide Karl Gustaf Tornquist, a latter-day Viking, noted in his journal, *On a beautiful estate a pregnant woman was found murdered in her bed through several bayonet stabs; the barbarians had opened both of her breasts and written above the bed canopy: "Thou shalt never give birth to a rebel." In another room, was just as horrible a sight – five cut-off heads arranged on a cupboard in place of plaster-cast-figures which lay broken to pieces on the floor. Dumb animals were no less spared. The pastures were in many places covered with dead horses, oxen, and cows.* Harry tries to fall asleep through a screen of agitation bred by these images. He has always thought of the Revolution as a kind of gentlemen's war, without any of that Vietnam stuff. He begins to have those slippery half-visions, waking dreams that only upon reflection make no sense. He sees a woman's round stomach, with smooth seams and a shining central fuzz, split open and yield yards and yards of red string, like the inside of a baseball. Then he is lying beside a body, a small man dressed all in black, a body limp and without muscle, a ventriloquist's dummy, wearing sunglasses. He awakes in the dark, too early for the sound of lawnmowers, for the cheep of the dull brown bird in the Norfolk pine, for the chatter of the young businessmen's dawn foursomes. He makes his way to the bathroom amid motionless glossy shapes and slants of dim light – the blue oven-timer numerals, the yellowish guard lights on the golf-course fence. He urinates sitting down, like a woman, and returns to bed. Always he sleeps on his old side of the bed, as if Janice is still on her side. He dreams now of the portal with the round top, but this time it pushes open easily, on noiseless unresistant hinges, upon a bustling brightness within. It is somehow Ma Springer's downstairs, only you step down into it, a kind of basement, brighter than her house ever was, with a many-colored carnival gaudiness, like something in Latin America, like the cruise-ship commercial they keep playing in the middle of the news, and full of welcoming people he hardly knows, or can barely remember: Mrs. Zabritski as a slender young girl, though still with that inviting inquisitive crick in her neck, and wearing a racily short fringed skirt like they wore in the Sixties, and Marty Tothero carrying a mailman's pouch that matches his lopsided face, and Mom and Pop in their prime, looking tall and rangy in their Sunday best, bringing a baby girl home from the hospital wrapped in a pink blanket, just its tiny tipped-up nose and a single tiny closed-eyelid eye showing, and a tall soberly staring dark-eyed man with lacquered black hair like an old ad for Kreml, who gives him a manly handshake, while Janice at his side whispers to him that this of course is Roy, Roy all grown up, and as tall as he. Awaking, Rabbit can still feel the pressure on his hand, and a smile of greeting dying on his face.

Hugo aims at SE coast. USAir jet crashes in N.Y. river. Bomb probably caused crash of French DC-10. Lee slows boaters in manatee territory. Harry feeds himself oat bran and digests the *News-Press. Chaos reigned on St. Croix, as police and National Guardsmen joined machete-armed mobs on a post-Hugo looting spree. Tourists pleaded with reporters landing on the island to get them off.* What fucking crybabies. It occurs to him that his dream might relate to all this Caribbean news, the pre-weekend party they have at resort hotels, to welcome the new arrivals and jolly everybody into a melting pot. He steps out onto his narrow balcony to seize the day. The paper said today would be sunny despite Hugo and so it is. The distant blue-green sky-scrapers hurl back blobs of light from the morning sun at his back. The Gulf cannot be seen but he can smell it out there. He tries to remember who all was at the party but can't; dream people don't stick to the ribs. The plane in New York skidded off the end of the runway and two people were killed. Just two. One hundred seventy-one died in the Sahara. A caller in London gave all the credit to Allah. Harry doesn't mind that one as much as the Lockerbie Pan Am bomb. Like everything else on the news, you get bored, disasters get to seem a gimmick, like all those TV time-outs in football.

While other, younger men shout and kid on the golf course behind the curtained sliding doors, Harry makes the bed and sweeps the kitchen floor, and adds his orange-juice glass and cereal bowl to the orderly array in the dishwasher waiting to add up to a load's worth. Not quite there yet. When Janice shows up at last he wants the state of the place to give her an object lesson in housekeeping.

At ten, he goes out for his morning walk. He looks at the north-east sky, toward the hurricane that is snubbing Florida, and is struck by the clouds, how intricate they are, tattered, gray on white on blue, with tilted sheets of fishscales and rows of long clouds shaggy underneath but rounded on top as if by action of swiftly running water, like the rhythmic ribs of sand the tide leaves. A glassy wind blows through the sunlight. There is something in the air that makes it slightly difficult to breathe. Lack of ozone? Or too much ozone? It may be his imagination, but the sky seems clean of air-planes. Usually you can see them layered in their slow circling slants, coming in to land at the Southwest Florida Regional Airport. The planes have been chased from the sky. Under the sun a kind of highway of haze in bars recedes to the northeast horizon like the reflections the moon stacks up in a calm ocean.

On an impulse he decides to take the Celica and drive down-town and park at a meter near the First Federal Bank and walk toward the black section. This afternoon, he thinks, he might feel like trying to get in some holes of golf. The pro shop called up a few days ago and said they found his shoes.

At the recreation field beyond the empty ochre high school, a lone tall boy in denim cutoffs is shooting baskets by himself. His tank top is an electric turquoise stencilled with a snarling tiger head – orange-and-white-striped fur, yellow eyes, the tongue and end of the nose an unreal violet. On this boy, though, the outfit has a certain propriety, the dignity of a chosen uniform. Older than the kids yesterday, eighteen at least, he is a deliberate performer, making good serious economical moves, dribbling in, studying the ground, staring at the hoop, sizing up the shot with two hands on the ball, letting go with the left hand underneath only at the last while shooting. He wears ankle-high black sneakers and no socks; his haircut is one of those muffin-shapes on the top of the skull, with a series of X's along the sides and back where the shaved part begins. Sitting on the bench, the opposite end from a small red knapsack the boy has evidently left there, Rabbit watches him a good while, while the sun shines and the glassy wind blows and passing clouds dip the dirt field and the surrounding frame houses in shadow. The houses have the colors of sun-faded wash and seem remote and silent. You don't see people going in and out.

To vary his attitude Harry sometimes tips his white face back as if to sunbathe, coating his vision in red, letting photons burn through his translucent eyelids. One time when he opens his eyes the boy is standing close, darker than a cloud. There is something matte about his blackness, and his high cheekbones and the thinness of his lips hint at Indian blood.

"You want sumpin'?" His voice is light, level, unsmiling. It seems to come out of the tiger's snarling violet mouth.

"No, nothing," Rabbit says. "My sitting here bother you?"

"You after no Scotty?" With the hand not holding the basketball against his hip he makes the smallest, most delicate little motion of cracking a whip. Rabbit darts his eyes at the knapsack and brings them back to the tiger's mouth.

"No, thanks," he says. "Never touch it. How about a little one-on-one, though? Since you seem to be out here alone."

"I *heard* some cheesecake come here yesterday was foolin' around."

"Just foolin', that's what I do. I'm retired."

"How come you come out here to do your foolin'? Lot of foolin'-around places over there in your end of Deleon." He pronounces it the local way, *Dealya-in*.

"It's pretty boring over there," Harry tells him. "I like it here, where there isn't so much glitz. D'ya mind?"

The boy, taken a bit off balance, thinks for an answer, and Rabbit's hands dart out and rest on the basketball, a more worn one than the boys yesterday had, and not leather-colored but scuffed red, white, and blue. Its rough-smooth surface feels warm. "Come on," he begs, growling the "on." "Gimme the ball."

Tiger's expression doesn't change, but the ball comes loose. With it, Harry strides onto the packed dirt. He feels precariously tall, as when this summer he stepped out alone onto the macadam street. He put on Bermuda shorts this morning, in case he got to play. Dust and reflected sun caress his bare calves, his chalky old man's calves that never had much hair and now have almost none – actually none, where socks have rubbed for over fifty years.

He goes for a jumper from pretty far out and it lucks in. He and Tiger take shots alternately, careful not to touch and bouncing their passes to each other. "You played once," the tall boy says.

"Long time ago. High school. Never got to college. Different style then than you guys have now. But if you feel like practicing your moves one-on-one, I'm game. Play to twenty-one. Honor system – call fouls on yourself."

There seems a leaden sadness in Tiger's stare, but he nods, and takes the ball bounced to him. He walks with a cocky slump – shoulders down, butt out – out to the half-court line scratched in the dirt with the heels of sneakers. From the back, the kid is all bones and tendons, polished by sweat but not too much, the sloped shoulders matte beneath the turquoise straps.

"Wait," Harry says. "I better take a pill first. Don't mind me."

The Nitrostat burns under his tongue, and by the time Tiger has come in and has his layup blocked, and Rabbit has dribbled out and missed a twenty-footer, the pill's little kick has reached his other end. He feels loose and deeply free at first. Tiger has some good herky-jerky moves, and can get a step on the heavier older man whenever he wants, but he wastes a lot of shots. The stop-and-pop style doesn't give you quite the time to get in harmony with the target, and there isn't enough height to Tiger's arc. The ball comes off his hands flat and turns the hoop's circle into a slot. And he is giving Harry an inch or two in height; Rabbit lifts a few close-in jumpers over the boy's fingertips – soft, high, in, just like that, air balls only right through the netless hoop, a scabby orange circle bent awry by too many show offs practicing slam-dunks and hanging on imitating Darryl Dawkins – and Tiger begins to press tighter, inviting a turn around the corner and a break for the basket if Harry can find the surge. Tiger's elbows and sharp knees rattle off his body and he has to laugh at the old sensation, the jostle and press. He is aware of his belly being slung up and down by the action and of a watery weariness entering into his knees, but adrenaline and nostalgia overrule. Tiger begins to exploit his opponent's slowness more cruelly, more knifingly, slipping and slashing by, and Rabbit kicks himself up a notch, feeling his breath come harder, through a narrower passage. Still, the sun feels good, springing sweat from his pores like calling so many seeds into life. The nature of this exertion is to mix him with earth and sky: earth, the packed pink-tan glaring dust printed over and over with the fanned bars of his Nikes and the cagelike grid of Tiger's black sneakers, stamped earth in the rim of his vision as he dribbles; and sky, wide white sky when he looks up to follow his shot or the other's. The clouds have gathered in an agitated silvery arena around the blinding sun, a blue bullring. Rabbit accidentally in one twist of upward effort stares straight into the sun and can't for a minute brush away its blinking red moon of an afterimage. His chest feels full, his head dizzy; his pulse rustles in his ears, the soaked space between his shoulder blades holds a jagged pain. Tiger retrieves his own rebound and holds the ball against his hip in his graceful way and gives Harry a deliberate stare. His skin is like a grinding stone of fine black grits. His ears are small and flat to his head and his hair above the row of X's is kinked as tight as nature can make it; sun glints from every circular particle.

"Hey man, you all right?"

"I'm. Fine."

"You puffin' pretty bad."

"You wait. Till you're my age."

"How about coolin' it? No big deal."

This is gracious, Rabbit sees, through the sweat in his eyebrows and the pounding of his blood. He feels as if his tree of veins and arteries is covered with big pink blossoms. No big deal. No big deal you're too out of shape for this. No big deal you aren't good even for a little one-on-one. His sweat is starting to cake on his legs, with the dust. He's afraid he's going to lose the rhythm, the dance, the whatever it is, the momentum, the grace. He asks, "Aren't you. Having fun?" He is enjoying scaring Tiger with his big red face, his heaving cheesecake bulk, his berserk icy blue eyes.

Tiger says, "Sure, man. Medium fun." At last he smiles. Wonderful even teeth, in lavender gums. Even the ghetto kids get orthodontia now.

"Let's keep our bargain. Play to twenty-one. Like we said. Eighteen up, right?"

"Right." Neither player has called a foul.

"Go. Your ball, Tiger." The pain in Harry's back is spreading, like clumsy wings. The young black man whips around him for a quick under-the-basket layup. Harry takes the ball out and stops short a step inside the half-court line and, unguarded, lets fly an old-fashioned two-handed set shot. He knows as it leaves his hands it will drop; a groove in the shape of the day guides it down.

"Man," Tiger says admiringly, "that is pure horseshit," and he tries to imitate it with a long one-hander that rockets straight back off the rim, its arc is too low. Rabbit grabs the rebound but then can't move with it, his body weighs a ton, his feet have lost their connection to his head. Tiger knifes in between him and the basket, leans right in his face with a violet snarl, then eases back a little, so Rabbit feels a gap, a moment's slackness in the other in which to turn the corner; he takes one slam of a dribble, carrying his foe on his side like a bumping sack of coal, and leaps up for the peeper. The hoop fills his circle of vision, it descends to kiss his lips, he can't miss.

Up he goes, way up toward the torn clouds. His torso is ripped by a terrific pain, elbow to elbow. He bursts from within; he feels something immense persistently fumble at him, and falls unconscious to the dirt. Tiger catches the ball on its fall through the basket and feels a body bump against him as if in purposeful foul. Then he sees the big old white man, looking choked and kind of sleepy in the face, collapse soundlessly, like a rag doll being dropped. Tiger stands amazed above the fallen body – the plaid Bermuda shorts, the brand-new walking Nikes, the blue golf shirt with a logo of intertwined V's. Adhesive dust of fine clay clings to one cheek of the unconscious flushed face like a shadow, like half of a clown's mask of paint. Shocked numb, the boy repeats, "Pure horseshit."

The impulse to run ripples through him, draining his head of practical thoughts. He doesn't want to get mixed up with nobody. From the end of the bench he retrieves the knapsack, the kind very small Boy Scouts might use on a one-night camping trip, and, holding it and the basketball close to his chest, walks deliberately away. In the middle of the block, he begins to run, under the high excited sky. An airplane goes over, lowering on a slow diagonal.

Seen from above, his limbs splayed and bent, Harry is as alone on the court as the sun in the sky, in its arena of clouds. Time passes. Then the social net twitches; someone who in the houses bordering the lonely recreation field has been watching through a curtained window calls 911. Minutes later, several of the elderly poor battened down against danger in their partitioned little rooms, with only television for a friend, mistake the approaching sirens for a hurricane alert, and believe that the storm has veered back from South Carolina toward them.

"The infarction looks to be transmural," Dr. Olman tells Janice, and clarifies: "Right through the gosh-darn wall." He tries to show her with the skin and flesh of his fist the difference between this and a sub-endocardial infarction that you can live with. "Ma'am, the whole left ventricle is *shot*," he says. "My guess is there was a complete restenosis since this April's procedure up north." His big face, with its sunburnt hook nose and jutting Australian jaw, assaults and confuses Janice in her sleeplessness and grief. All this activity of the doctor's hands, as if he's trying to turn

Harry inside out for her, now that it's too late. "Too late for a bypass now," Dr. Olman almost snorts, and with an effort tames his voice into its acquired Southern softness. "Even if by a miracle, ma'am, he were to pull through this present trauma, where you and I have healthy flexible muscle he'd just have a wad of scar tissue. You can replace arteries and valves but there's no substitute yet for live heart muscle." He exudes controlled anger, like a golfer who has missed three short putts in a row. He is so young, Janice groggily thinks, he blames people for dying. He thinks they do it to make his job more difficult.

After last evening's visit from the Penn Park police (how young they seemed, too, how scared to be bringing their ugly news; the Deleon hospital had called them finally because neither the number of the condo phone nor the number they got for his driver's-license address from Information would answer, she had been out showing a young couple some properties, one a split-level in Brewer Heights and the other an old sandstone farmhouse over toward Oriole; the police came into her driveway the minute she got home, their twirling blue light licking the limestone walls so all the neighbors must have wondered) and then telephoning to reach Mim, who wasn't answering her phone either, and to get seats for herself and Nelson on some kind of night flight to Florida, with Eastern still mostly out on strike and everything going in or out of Atlanta cancelled or delayed because of the hurricane, and then the drive to South Philly and the airport, the miles of Schuylkill Expressway under repair, and among all the confusing barrels with reflective tape Nelson's taking a turn that wound them up in the dead middle of the city right there by Independence Hall – it seemed to happen in a minute – and then the hours of waiting with nothing to do but soothe Nelson and read newspapers people had abandoned on the plastic chairs and remember Harry all the ways he was from the day she first saw him in the high-school corridors and at the basketball games, out there on the court so glorious and blond, like a boy made of marble, and then the empty condo, so tidy except for the stacks of old newspapers he would never throw out and the junk-food crumbs in the wicker easy chair, but no traces of another woman in the bedroom, just that book she got him for last Christmas with the sailing ship on the jacket, and Nelson right beside her overreacting to everything so she almost wished he had let her come alone – after a while the mother in you dies just like heart muscle she supposes – and a few hours of ragged sleep that ended too early when the boys began to mow the greens and the men began to play, with Nelson actually complaining at breakfast that there weren't any Frosted Flakes, just these bran cereals that taste like horse chow, after all this Janice felt much like her husband did emerging from his long drive on Labor Day weekend, as if her body had been pounded all over with sandbags. In the hall, the newspaper was delivered to the door on this as on every other day:

Hugo clobbers
South Carolina

Dr. Morris, the old one, Harry's doctor, must have heard she is in the hospital; he comes into the waiting room of the intensive cardiac care unit looking himself not so well, spotty and whiskery, in an unpressed brown suit. He takes her hand and looks her right in the eye through his rimless glasses and tells her, "Sometimes it's time," which is fine for him, being near eighty, or at least over seventy-five. "He came in to me some days ago and I didn't like what I heard in his chest. But with an impairment like his a person can live two weeks or twenty years, there's no telling. It can be a matter of attitude. He seemed to have become a wee bit morbid. We agreed he needed something to do, he was too young for retirement."

Tears are in Janice's eyes constantly ever since the blue police lights appeared but this remark and the old man's wise and kind manner freshen them. Dr. Morris paid closer attention to Harry toward the end than she did. In a way since those glimpses of him shining on the basketball court she had slowly ceased to see him, he had become invisible. "Did he mention me?" she asks, wondering if Harry had revealed that they were estranged.

The old doctor's sharp Scots gaze pierces her for a second. "Very fondly," he tells her.

At this hour in the morning, a little after nine o'clock, with dirty breakfast trays still being wheeled along the halls, there is no one else in the ICCU waiting room, and Nelson in his own agitation keeps wandering off, to telephone Pru, to go to the bathroom, to get a cup of coffee and some Frosted Flakes at a cafeteria he's discovered in another wing. The waiting room is tiny, with one window looking toward the parking lot, damp at the edges from the lawn sprinklers last night, and a low table of mostly religious magazines, and a hard black settee and chairs and floor lamps of bent pipes and plastic shades, they don't want you to get too comfortable, they really want the patient all to themselves. While she's in this limbo alone Janice thinks she should pray for Harry's recovery, a miracle, but when she closes her eyes to do it she encounters a blank dead wall. From what Dr. Olman said he would never be alive the way he was and as Dr. Morris said, sometimes it's time. He had come to bloom early and by the time she got to know him at Kroll's he was already drifting downhill, though things did look up when the money from the lot began to be theirs. With him gone, she can sell the Penn Park house. *Dear God, dear God*, she prays. *Do what You think best.*

A young black nurse appears at the open door and says so softly, yet with a beautiful half-smile, "He's conscious now," and leads her into the intensive-care unit, which she remembers from last December – the central circular desk like an airport control tower, full of TV sets showing in jumping orange lines each patient's heartbeat, and on three sides the rows of individual narrow bedrooms with glass front walls. When she sees her Harry lying in one of them as white as his sheets with all these tubes and wires going in and out of him, lying behind the wall of glass, an emotion so strong she fears for a second she might vomit hits her from behind, a crashing wave of sorrow and terrified awareness of utter loss like nothing ever in her life except the time she accidentally drowned her own dear baby. She had never meant never to forgive him, she had been intending one of these days to call, but the days slipped by; holding her silence had become a kind of addiction. How could she have hardened her heart so against this man who for better or worse had placed his life beside hers at the altar? It hadn't been Harry really, it had been Pru, what man could resist, she and Pru and Nelson had analyzed it to the point of exhaustion. She was satisfied it wouldn't happen again and she had a life to get on with. Now this. Just when. He called her stupid, it was true she was slower than he was, and slower to come into her own, but he was beginning to respect her, it was hard for him to respect any woman, his mother had done that to him, the hateful woman. Though all four of their parents were alive when they courted at Kroll's she and Harry were orphans really, he more than she even. He saw something in her that would hold him fast for a while. She wants him back, back from this element he is sinking in, she wants it so much she might vomit, his desertions and Pru and Thelma and all whatever else are washed away by the grandeur of his lying there so helpless, so irretrievable.

The nurse slides the door open. Above his baby-blue nose tubes for oxygen his blue eyes are open but he doesn't seem to hear. He sees her, sees his wife here, little and dark-complected and stubborn in her forehead and mouth, blubbering like a waterfall and talking about forgiveness. "I forgive you," she keeps saying while he can't remember for what. He lies there floating in a wonderful element, a bed of happy unfeeling that points of pain now and then poke through. He listens to Janice blubber and marvels at how small she grows, sitting in that padded wheelchair they give you, small like something in a crystal snowball, but finer, fine like a spiderweb, every crease in her face and rumpled gray saleswoman's suit. She forgives him, and he thanks her, or thinks that he thanks her. He believes she takes his hand. His consciousness comes and goes, and he marvels that in its gaps the world is being tended to, just as it was in the centuries before he was born. There is a terrible deep dryness in his throat, but he knows the sensation will pass, the doctors will do something about it. Janice seems one of those bright figures in his dream, the party they were having. He thinks of telling her about Tiger and *I won* but the impulse passes. He is nicely tired. He closes his eyes. The red cave he thought had only a front entrance and exit turns out to have a back door as well.

His wife's familiar and beloved figure has been replaced by that of Nelson, who is also unhappy. "You didn't *talk* to her, Dad," the kid complains. "She said you stared at her but didn't talk."

O.K., he thinks, *what else am I doing wrong?* He feels sorry about what he did to the kid but he's doing him a favor now, though Nelson doesn't seem to know it.

"Can't you say anything? Talk to me, Dad!" the kid is yelling, or trying not to yell, his face white in the gills with the strain of it, and some unaskable question tweaking the hairs of one eyebrow, so they grow up against the grain. He wants to put the kid out of his misery. *Nelson*, he wants to say, *you have a sister.*

But does he say it? His son's anxious straining expression hasn't changed. What he next says, though, shows he may have understood the word "sister." "We phoned Aunt Mim, Dad, and she'll get here as soon as she can. She has to change planes in Kansas City!"

From his expression and the pitch of his voice, the boy is shouting into a fierce wind blowing from his father's direction. "Don't *die*, Dad, *don't*!" he cries, then sits back with that question still on his face, and his dark wet eyes shining like stars of a sort. Harry shouldn't leave the question hanging like that, the boy depends on him.

"Well, Nelson," he says, "all I can tell you is, it isn't so bad." Rabbit thinks he should maybe say more, the kid looks wildly expectant, but enough. Maybe. Enough.

ACKNOWLEDGMENTS

Portions of these novels appeared in *The Atlantic*, *Esquire*, and *Playboy*.

Grateful acknowledgment is made to the following for permission to reprint previously published material:

Alfred A. Knopf, Inc.: Excerpt from 'A Rabbit as King of the Ghosts' by Wallace Stevens. From *The Collected Poems of Wallace Stevens*. Copyright 1942 by Wallace Stevens, copyright renewed 1970 by Holly Stevens. Used by permission.

Rightsong Music, Inc.: Excerpts from 'Hot Stuff' by Pete Bellotte, Harold Faltermeyer, and Keith Forsey. Copyright © 1979 by Rick's Music, Inc., and Revelation Music/Ed. Intro. Published in the USA by Rightsong Music, Inc. Excerpt from 'One Night in a Lifetime' by Pete Bellotte and Harold Faltermeyer. Copyright © 1979 by Rick's Music, Inc., and Revelation Music/Ed. Intro. Published in the USA by Rightsong Music, Inc. Excerpt from 'Can't Get to Sleep at Night' by Bob Conti and Bruce Sudano. Copyright © 1979 by Rick's Music, Inc., Earborn Music, and Purple Cow Music. Administered by Rightsong Music, Inc., throughout the world. International Copyright Secured. All Rights Reserved. Used by permission.

Beachaven Music Corp. and Jarest Music Co: Excerpt from 'Vaya con Dios' by Larry Russell, Buddy Pepper, and Inez James. Copyright © Beachaven Music Corp. and Jarest Music Co. Reprinted by permission.

CPP/Belwin, Inc. and International Music Publications: Excerpt from 'We're Off to See the Wizard' by H. Arlen and E. Y. Harburg. Copyright 1938 (Renewed 1966) by Metro-Goldwyn-Mayer, Inc., Culver City, California. Copyright 1939 (Renewed 1967) by Metro-Goldwyn-Mayer, Inc. Rights assigned to EMI Catalogue Partnership. All rights throughout the world controlled and administered by EMI Feist Catalog, Inc. International copyright secured. All rights reserved. Made in USA. Excerpt from 'All My Love' by P. Durand, M. Parish, and H. Contet. Copyright 1948, 1950 by Mills Music, Inc. (Copyright renewed), c/o Filmtrax Copyright Holdings, Inc. Used by permission. All rights reserved. Excerpt from 'Splish, Splash' by Murray Kaufman and Bobby Darin. Copyright © 1958 (Renewed 1986) by Unart Music Corp. Rights assigned to EMI Catalogue Partnership. All rights controlled and administered by EMI Unart Catalog, Inc. All rights reserved. International copyright secured.

1519